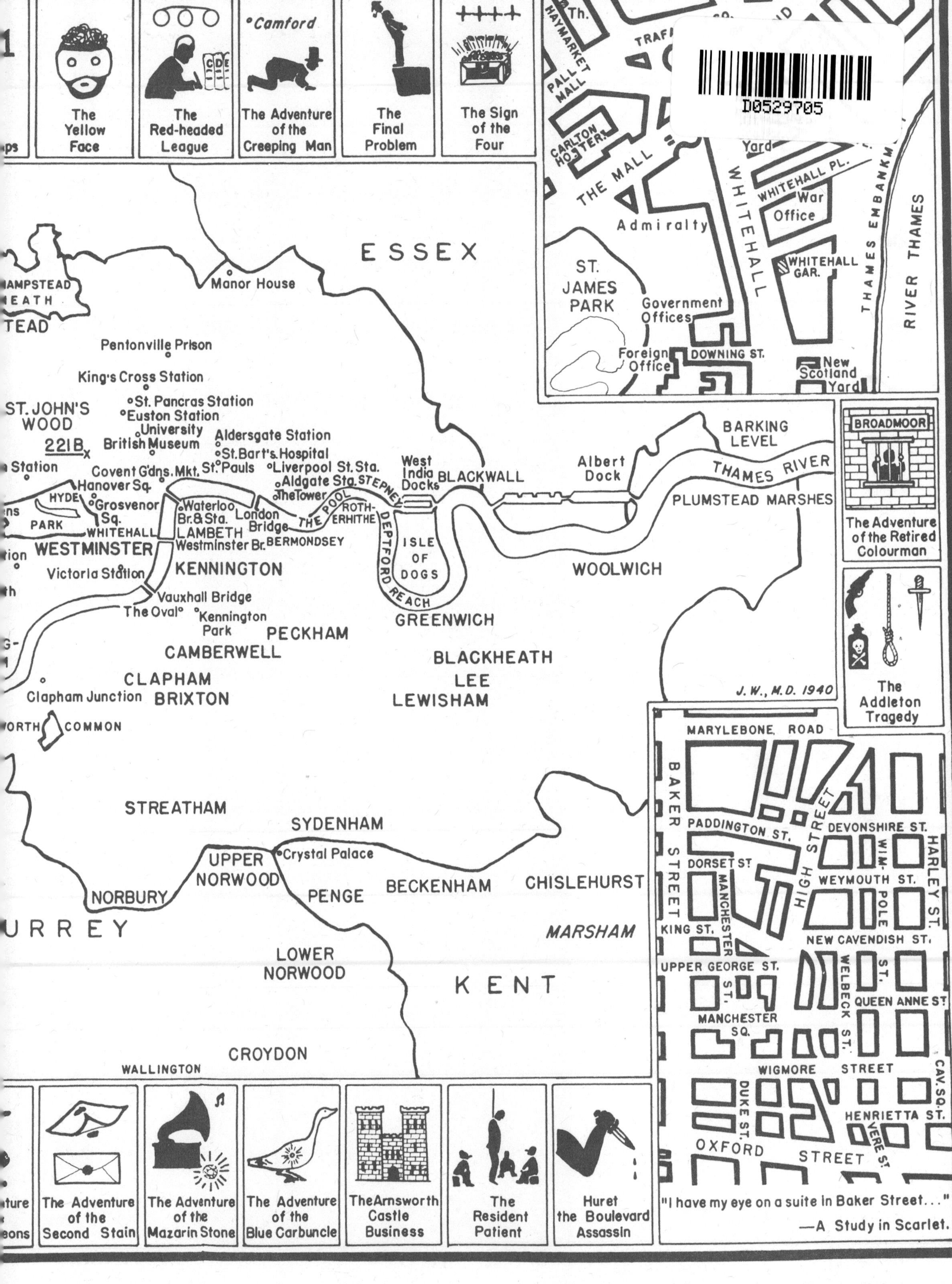

The Yellow Face
The Red-headed League
Camford
The Adventure of the Creeping Man
The Final Problem
The Sign of the Four
D0529705
TRAFA
HAYMARKET
PALL MALL
CARLTON HOUSE TER.
THE MALL
Yard
WHITEHALL PL.
WHITEHALL
War Office
Admiralty
THAMES EMBANKMENT
RIVER THAMES
WHITEHALL GAR.
ST. JAMES PARK
Government Offices
Foreign Office
DOWNING ST.
New Scotland Yard
ESSEX
HAMPSTEAD HEATH
Manor House
Pentonville Prison
King's Cross Station
ST. JOHN'S WOOD
St. Pancras Station
Euston Station
University
221B
British Museum
Aldersgate Station
St. Bart's Hospital
Covent G'dns. Mkt.
St. Pauls
Liverpool St. Sta.
West India Docks
BLACKWALL
Albert Dock
BARKING LEVEL
THAMES RIVER
BROADMOOR
The Adventure of the Retired Colourman
Hanover Sq.
Aldgate Sta.
STEPNEY
The Tower
HYDE PARK
Grosvenor Sq.
Waterloo
Br. & Sta.
London Bridge
THE POOL
ROTHERHITHE
PLUMSTEAD MARSHES
WHITEHALL
LAMBETH
WESTMINSTER
Westminster Br.
BERMONDSEY
DEPTFORD REACH
ISLE OF DOGS
Victoria Station
KENNINGTON
WOOLWICH
Vauxhall Bridge
The Oval
Kennington Park
PECKHAM
GREENWICH
CAMBERWELL
BLACKHEATH
LEE
LEWISHAM
CLAPHAM
Clapham Junction
BRIXTON
J. W., M.D. 1940
The Addleton Tragedy
COMMON
MARYLEBONE ROAD
BAKER STREET
STREATHAM
SYDENHAM
PADDINGTON ST.
HIGH STREET
DEVONSHIRE ST.
UPPER NORWOOD
Crystal Palace
DORSET ST.
WIMPOLE
HARLEY ST.
WEYMOUTH ST.
NORBURY
PENGE
BECKENHAM
CHISLEHURST
MANCHESTER ST.
KING ST.
MARSHAM
NEW CAVENDISH ST.
URREY
LOWER NORWOOD
KENT
UPPER GEORGE ST.
WELBECK ST.
QUEEN ANNE ST.
MANCHESTER SQ.
CROYDON
WALLINGTON
WIGMORE STREET
CAV. SQ.
DUKE ST.
HENRIETTA ST.
VERE ST.
OXFORD STREET
The Adventure of the Second Stain
The Adventure of the Mazarin Stone
The Adventure of the Blue Carbuncle
The Arnsworth Castle Business
The Resident Patient
Huret the Boulevard Assassin
"I have my eye on a suite in Baker Street . . ."
—A Study in Scarlet.

Also By William S. Baring-Gould

The Lure of the Limerick

Sherlock Holmes of Baker Street

With Ceil Baring-Gould

The Annotated Mother Goose

The ANNOTATED Sherlock Holmes

VOLUME II

THE FOUR NOVELS AND THE FIFTY-SIX SHORT STORIES COMPLETE

BY SIR ARTHUR CONAN DOYLE

Edited, with an Introduction, Notes, and Bibliography by

WILLIAM S. BARING-GOULD

Illustrated with Maps, Diagrams, Coats-of-Arms, Photographs, and Drawings by Charles Doyle, Howard K. Elcock, D. H. Friston, A. Gilbert, James Grieg, George Hutchinson, William H. Hyde, Charles Raymond Macauley, Sidney Paget, Frederic Dorr Steele, Arthur Twidle, Frank Wiles, and Numerous Others

Clarkson N. Potter, Inc./Publisher **NEW YORK**

DISTRIBUTED BY CROWN PUBLISHERS, INC.

Text of the Sherlock Holmes stories printed by permission of the Sir Arthur Conan Doyle Estate, and by arrangement with John Murray (Publishers) Ltd, of London, and Doubleday & Company, Inc., New York.

Photographs by G. F. Allen reproduced by permission.

Map of Meiringen. Copyright Brügger S.A., Ltd., Meiringen. Reproduced by permission of Brügger S.A., Ltd., Meiringen.

Photographs from *In the Footsteps of Sherlock Holmes* by Michael Harrison. Copyright © 1960, by Michael Harrison. Reproduced by permission of Michael Harrison.

Illustration on page 342, by Joseph Camana, reproduced by permission from *Cases of Sherlock Holmes,* Everyreader Series adaptation by William Kottmeyer, copyright © 1947, by McGraw-Hill, Inc. Based on original stories by Sir Arthur Conan Doyle.

Photograph by Reece Winston reproduced by permission.

Inquiries should be addressed to
Clarkson N. Potter, Inc., One Park Avenue
New York, N.Y. 10016

LIBRARY OF CONGRESS CATALOG CARD NUMBER: 67-22406

ISBN: 0-517-502917

PRINTED IN THE UNITED STATES OF AMERICA

DESIGNED BY SALLY STEIN

SECOND EDITION

30 29 28 27 26 25 24 23 22 21

V. FROM DR. WATSON'S RETURN TO BAKER STREET TO HIS MARRIAGE TO MARY MORSTAN

[late December, 1887, or early January, 1888, to *circa* May 1, 1889]

Continued from Vol. I

36

THE HOUND OF THE BASKERVILLES

[*Tuesday, September 25, to Saturday, October 20, 1888*]

I ◆ MR SHERLOCK HOLMES

Mr Sherlock Holmes, who was usually very late in the mornings, save upon those not infrequent occasions when he stayed **1**
up all night, was seated at the breakfast-table. I stood upon
the hearth-rug and picked up the stick which our visitor had
left behind him the night before. It was a fine, thick piece of **2**
wood, bulbous-headed, of the sort which is known as a 'Penang
lawyer.' Just under the head was a broad silver band, nearly **3**
an inch across. 'To James Mortimer, M.R.C.S., from his **4**
friends of the C.C.H.,' was engraved upon it, with the date
'1884.' It was just such a stick as the old-fashioned family prac- **5**
titioner used to carry—dignified, solid, and reassuring.

'Well, Watson, what do you make of it?'

Holmes was sitting with his back to me, and I had given him no sign of my occupation.

'How did you know what I was doing? I believe you have eyes in the back of your head.'

'I have, at least, a well-polished, silver-plated coffee-pot in front of me,' said he. 'But, tell me, Watson, what do you make of our visitor's stick? Since we have been so unfortunate as to miss him and have no notion of his errand, this accidental souvenir becomes of importance. Let me hear you reconstruct the man by an examination of it.'

'I think,' said I, following so far as I could the methods of my companion, 'that Dr Mortimer is a successful elderly medical man, well-esteemed, since those who know him give him this mark of their appreciation.'

'Good!' said Holmes. 'Excellent!'

'I think also that the probability is in favour of his being a country practitioner who does a great deal of his visiting on foot.'

'Why so?'

'Because this stick, though originally a very handsome one, has been so knocked about that I can hardly imagine a town practitioner carrying it. The thick iron ferrule is worn down, so it is evident that he has done a great amount of walking with it.'

1 *who was usually very late in the mornings.* "Triumphant indeed must have been an occasion when Watson finished [breakfast] before Holmes," Mr. Vincent Starrett wrote in "The Singular Adventures of Martha Hudson"; "one such is recorded in the opening lines of *The Hound of the Baskervilles*. Sherlock Holmes, as we behold him, is still seated at the breakfast table, while Watson stands upon the hearth-rug, examining the handsome stick left by Dr. James Mortimer the night before. Obviously he has already finished, and in the warm glow of comfortable satiety he dares to venture some pregnant observations of his own."

2 *our visitor had left behind him the night before.* "It is curious," the late Gavin Brend observed in *My Dear Holmes*, "how frequently Holmes' clients . . . took insufficient care of their property. The result was always highly satisfactory, for Holmes invariably made a reconstruction of the missing client from the missing article."

3 *a 'Penang lawyer.'* A walking stick with a knobbed head, made from the stem of a small palm (*Licuala acutifida*) that grows in Penang, an island in the straits of Malacca.

4 *M.R.C.S.* Member of the Royal College of Surgeons.

5 *'1884.'* A date later corroborated by Watson's *Medical Directory*.

'Perfectly sound!' said Holmes.

'And then again, there is the "friends of the C.C.H." I should guess that to be the Something Hunt, the local hunt to whose members he has possibly given some surgical assistance, and which has made him a small presentation in return.'

'Really, Watson, you excel yourself,' said Holmes, pushing back his chair and lighting a cigarette. 'I am bound to say that
6 in all the accounts which you have been so good as to give of my own small achievements you have habitually underrated your own abilities. It may be that you are not yourself luminous, but you are a conductor of light. Some people without possessing genius have a remarkable power of stimulating
7 it. I confess, my dear fellow, that I am very much in your debt.'

He had never said as much before, and I must admit that his words gave me keen pleasure, for I had often been piqued by his indifference to my admiration and to the attempts which I had made to give publicity to his methods. I was proud, too, to think that I had so far mastered his system as to apply it in a way which earned his approval. He now took the stick from my hands and examined it for a few minutes with his naked eyes. Then, with an expression of interest, he laid down his cigarette, and, carrying the cane to the window, he looked over it again with a convex lens.

'Interesting, though elementary,' said he, as he returned to his favourite corner of the settee. 'There are certainly one or two indications upon the stick. It gives us the basis for several deductions.'

'Has anything escaped me?' I asked, with some self-importance. 'I trust that there is nothing of consequence which I have overlooked?'

'I am afraid, my dear Watson, that most of your conclusions were erroneous. When I said that you stimulated me I meant, to be frank, that in noting your fallacies I was occasionally guided towards the truth. Not that you are entirely wrong in this instance. The man is certainly a country practitioner. And he walks a good deal.'

'Then I was right.'

'To that extent.'

. . . HE LOOKED OVER IT AGAIN WITH A CONVEX LENS.

Illustration by Sidney Paget for the *Strand Magazine*, August, 1901.

6 *in all the accounts which you have been so good as to give.* It has been said that the case must be after the Return (1894) because Holmes here speaks of "all the accounts" Watson has been "so good as to give of my own small achievements," and Watson later speaks of "the attempts which I had made to give publicity to [Holmes'] methods." The case is certainly after December, 1887, when *A Study in Scarlet* was published, because Stapleton, as we shall see, knew Watson as Holmes' biographer ("The records of your detective have reached us here, and you could not celebrate him without being known yourself"). But Watson began to *chronicle* Holmes' adventures as early as May, 1887 ("A Scandal in Bohemia"). More than a year later it would be quite proper for Holmes to speak of "all the accounts." And Watson, spurred by the appearance in print of *A Study in Scarlet*, would undoubtedly be making attempts to have other of his chronicles published.

7 *a remarkable power of stimulating it.* "Such double-edged testimony to Watson's assistance is only too typical," Mr. T. S. Blakeney wrote in *Sherlock Holmes: Fact or Fiction?*: "a long array of caustic comments on his friend's honest but scarcely brilliant qualities could be culled from Holmes' conversations. Indeed, the very last recorded for us, late at night on the second of August—'the most terrible August in the history of the world'—closed on just such a backhanded compliment. 'Good old Watson! You are the one fixed point in a changing age' ["His Last Bow"]. It was a securely-founded friendship which survived this withering frankness of expression."

'But that was all.'

'No, no, my dear Watson, not all—by no means all. I would suggest, for example, that a presentation to a doctor is more likely to come from a hospital than from a hunt, and that when the initials "C.C." are placed before that hospital the words "Charing Cross" very naturally suggest themselves.'

'You may be right.'

'The probability lies in that direction. And if we take this as a working hypothesis we have a fresh basis from which to start our construction of this unknown visitor.'

'Well, then, supposing that "C.C.H." does stand for "Charing Cross Hospital," what further inferences may we draw?' **8**

'Do none suggest themselves? You know my methods. Apply them!'

'I can only think of the obvious conclusion that the man has practised in town before going to the country.'

'I think that we might venture a little farther than this. Look at it in this light. On what occasion would it be most probable that such a presentation would be made? When would his friends unite to give him a pledge of their good will? Obviously at the moment when Dr Mortimer withdrew from the service of the hospital in order to start in practice for himself. We know there has been a presentation. We believe there has been a change from a town hospital to a country practice. Is it, then, stretching our inference too far to say that the presentation was on the occasion of the change?'

'It certainly seems probable.'

'Now, you will observe that he could not have been on the *staff* of the hospital, since only a man well-established in a London practice could hold such a position, and such a one would not drift into the country. What was he, then? If he was in the hospital and yet not on the staff, he could only have been a house-surgeon or a house-physician—little more than a senior student. And he left five years ago—the date is on
the stick. So your grave, middle-aged family practitioner van- **9**
ishes into thin air, my dear Watson, and there emerges a
young fellow under thirty, amiable, unambitious, absent- **10**
minded, and the possessor of a favourite dog, which I should describe roughly as being larger than a terrier and smaller than a mastiff.'

I laughed incredulously as Sherlock Holmes leaned back in his settee and blew little wavering rings of smoke up to the ceiling.

'As to the latter part, I have no means of checking you,' said I, 'but at least it is not difficult to find out a few particulars about the man's age and professional career.'

From my small medical shelf I took down the Medical Directory and turned up the name. There were several Mortimers, but only one who could be our visitor. I read his record aloud.

> Mortimer, James, M.R.C.S., 1882, Grimpen, Dartmoor, Devon. House-surgeon, from 1882 to 1884, at Charing Cross Hospital. Winner of the Jackson Prize for Comparative Pathology, with essay entitled 'Is Disease a Reversion?' Corresponding member of the Swedish Pathological Society. Author of 'Some Freaks of Atavism' (*Lancet*, 1882), 'Do We Progress?' (*Journal of Psychology*, March, 1883). Medical Officer for the parishes of Grimpen, Thorsley, and High Barrow.

'No mention of that local hunt, Watson,' said Holmes, with

8 *"Charing Cross Hospital."* This great hospital was founded in 1818, but the building which knew Dr. Mortimer was begun in 1829. "It has a pleasing reassuring frontage, in straight-forward Regency," Mr. William H. Gill wrote in "Some Notable Sherlockian Buildings."

9 *five years ago—the date is on the stick.* The earliest date so far assigned to this case is 1886 (Bell, followed by Heldenbrand and Randall); the latest is 1900 (Zeisler, followed by Folsom and Pattrick). Messrs. Blakeney, Frisbie, Hoff, Knox, Morley, Petersen, Sidgwick, and Smith all chose 1889; Howard and Welch picked 1894; Schonberg 1896; Christ 1897; and Brend and Jones both opted for 1899.

Watson appears to date the adventure quite definitely in 1889. We believe, however, that 1889 is impossible: Watson in 1889 was married and practicing medicine; here there is not a hint that he has either a wife or a consulting room. On the contrary, he is living in Baker Street, and when ordered off to Devonshire for an indefinite stay, he makes no reference to wife, patients, or an accommodating neighbor-doctor. Holmes, we feel, may not have meant *exactly* five years ago; after all, he was speaking informally, in a demonstration to Watson alone, and could have said "five years" if 1884 were somewhat less or somewhat more than five years ago. But he certainly meant closer to five than to four or six years; the case can hardly have taken place *before* July, 1888, or *after* June, 1890. As we shall shortly see, the case took place in late September and the first three weeks of October; the approximate date of the adventure is therefore September–October, 1888, or 1889, and there are, as we have said, good reasons for eliminating 1889.

10 *a young fellow under thirty.* If the date on the stick and in the *Medical Directory* is accepted, this is additional evidence that *The Hound of the Baskervilles* took place within a few years of 1884.

a mischievous smile, 'but a country doctor, as you very astutely observed. I think that I am fairly justified in my inferences. As to the adjectives, I said, if I remember right, amiable, unambitious, and absent-minded. It is my experience that it is only an amiable man in this world who receives testimonials, only an unambitious one who abandons a London career for the country and only an absent-minded one who leaves his stick and not his visiting-card after waiting an hour in your room.'

'And the dog?'

'Has been in the habit of carrying this stick behind his master. Being a heavy stick the dog has held it tightly by the middle, and the marks of his teeth are very plainly visible. The dog's jaw, as shown in the space between these marks, is too broad in my opinion for a terrier and not broad enough for a mastiff. It may have been—yes, by Jove, it *is* a curly-haired spaniel.'

He had risen and paced the room as he spoke. Now he halted in the recess of the window. There was such a ring of conviction in his voice that I glanced up in surprise.

'My dear fellow, how can you possibly be so sure of that?'

'For the very simple reason that I see the dog himself on our very doorstep, and there is the ring of its owner. Don't move, I beg you, Watson. He is a professional brother of yours, and your presence may be of assistance to me. Now is the dramatic moment of fate, Watson, when you hear a step upon the stair which is walking into your life, and you know not whether for good or ill. What does Dr James Mortimer, the man of science, ask of Sherlock Holmes, the specialist in crime? Come in!'

The appearance of our visitor was a surprise to me since I had expected a typical country practitioner. He was a very tall, thin man, with a long nose like a beak, which shot out between two keen, grey eyes, set closely together and sparkling brightly from behind a pair of gold-rimmed glasses. He was clad in a professional but rather slovenly fashion, for his frock-coat was dingy and his trousers frayed. Though young, his long back was already bowed, and he walked with a forward thrust of his head and a general air of peering benevolence. As he entered his eyes fell upon the stick in Holmes's hand, and he ran towards it with an exclamation of joy.

. . . HIS EYES FELL UPON THE STICK IN HOLMES' HAND . . .

Illustration by Sidney Paget for the *Strand Magazine*, August, 1901.

'I am so very glad,' said he. 'I was not sure whether I had
left it here or in the Shipping Office. I would not lose that **11**
stick for the world.'

'A presentation, I see,' said Holmes.

'Yes, sir.'

'From Charing Cross Hospital?'

'From one or two friends there on the occasion of my marriage.'

'Dear, dear, that's bad!' said Holmes, shaking his head.

Dr Mortimer blinked through his glasses in mild astonishment.

'Why was it bad?'

'Only that you have disarranged our little deductions. Your marriage, you say?'

'Yes, sir. I married, and so left the hospital, and with it all hopes of a consulting practice. It was necessary to make a home of my own.'

'Come, come, we are not so far wrong after all,' said Holmes. 'And now, Dr James Mortimer——'

'Mister, sir, Mister—a humble M.R.C.S.'

'And a man of precise mind, evidently.'

'A dabbler in science, Mr Holmes, a picker-up of shells on the shores of the great unknown ocean. I presume that it is Mr Sherlock Holmes whom I am addressing and not——'

'No, this is my friend Dr Watson.'

'Glad to meet you, sir. I have heard your name mentioned
in connection with that of your friend. You interest me
very much, Mr Holmes. I had hardly expected so dolicho-
cephalic a skull or such well-marked supra-orbital development. Would you have any objection to my running my finger **12**
along your parietal fissure? A cast of your skull, sir, until the **13**
original is available, would be an ornament to any anthropological museum. It is not my intention to be fulsome, but I
confess that I covet your skull.' **14**

Sherlock Holmes waved our strange visitor into a chair.

'You are an enthusiast in your line of thought, I perceive, sir, as I am in mine,' said he. 'I observe from your forefinger that you make your own cigarettes. Have no hesitation in lighting one.'

The man drew out paper and tobacco and twirled the one up in the other with surprising dexterity. He had long, quivering fingers as agile and restless as the antennæ of an insect.

Holmes was silent, but his little darting glances showed me the interest which he took in our curious companion.

'I presume, sir,' said he at last, 'that it was not merely for the purpose of examining my skull that you have done me the honour to call here last night and again today?'

'No, sir, no; though I am happy to have had the opportunity of doing that as well. I came to you, Mr Holmes, because I recognize that I am myself an unpractical man, and because I am suddenly confronted with a most serious and extraordinary problem. Recognizing, as I do, that you are the second highest expert in Europe——'

'Indeed, sir! May I inquire who has the honour to be the first?' asked Holmes, with some asperity.

'To the man of precisely scientific mind the work of Monsieur Bertillon must always appeal strongly.' **15**

'Then had you not better consult him?'

'I said, sir, to the precisely scientific mind. But as a practical

11 *the Shipping Office.* The first of many indications that the first day of the case was certainly not a Monday, since Dr. Mortimer could not have gone to the Shipping Office on a Sunday.

12 *supra-orbital development.* Dr. Mortimer is saying that he had not expected Holmes to have so long a skull or so much of his skull above the orbit of the eye.

13 *parietal fissure?* The parietal, or intraparietal fissure, is that in the upper portion of the convex surface of the parietal lobe of the brain.

14 *I confess that I covet your skull.* In "Dr. Mortimer Before the Bar," Mr. Benjamin Clark has suggested that Dr. James Mortimer, from the start of *The Hound of the Baskervilles*, was up to no good.

Mr. Jerry Neal Williamson has carried this one step further ("Dr. Mortimer-Moriarty") by alleging that "Dr. James Mortimer" was, in reality, Colonel James *Moriarty*, brother to the Napoleon of Crime, Professor James Moriarty.

15 *Monsieur Bertillon.* Alphonse Bertillon, 1853–1914, French anthropologist and the inventor of the system bearing his name. Under this system, records on anthropometric measurements and personal characteristics, such as the color of the eyes, the thumblines, fingerprints, scars, deformities, and the like (sometimes, also, photographs) are used as a means of identification, especially as applied to criminals. The measurements and characteristics are recorded on cards and classified according to the length of the head. The system was inaugurated in the United States in 1887; it was introduced in print in Bertillon's great work *Les Signalements Anthropométriques* (Paris, 1886). Though Holmes on this occasion was piqued, he later ("The Adventure of the Naval Treaty") "expressed his enthusiastic admiration of the French savant." To attempt to date either *The Hound of the Baskervilles* or "The Adventure of the Naval Treaty" by these remarks is, however, somewhat perilous, for Bertillon instituted his scientific classification as early as 1884, and Holmes and Mortimer, as men of precisely scientific minds, might both have known of him long before the publication of his theories.

man of affairs it is acknowledged that you stand alone. I trust, sir, that I have not inadvertently——'

'Just a little,' said Holmes. 'I think, Dr Mortimer, you would do wisely if without more ado you would kindly tell me plainly what the exact nature of the problem is in which you demand my assistance.'

2 ◆ THE CURSE OF THE BASKERVILLES

'I have in my pocket a manuscript,' said Dr James Mortimer.

'I observed it as you entered the room,' said Holmes.

'It is an old manuscript.'

'Early eighteenth century, unless it is a forgery.'

'How can you say that, sir?'

'You have presented an inch or two of it to my examination all the time that you have been talking. It would be a poor expert who could not give the date of a document within a decade or so. You may possibly have read my little mono-
16 graph upon the subject. I put that at 1730.'

'The exact date is 1742.' Dr Mortimer drew it from his breast-pocket. 'This family paper was committed to my care by Sir Charles Baskerville, whose sudden and tragic death some three months ago created so much excitement in Devonshire. I may say that I was his personal friend as well as his medical attendant. He was a strong-minded man, sir, shrewd, practical, and as unimaginative as I am myself. Yet he took this document very seriously, and his mind was prepared for just such an end as did eventually overtake him.'

Holmes stretched out his hand for the manuscript, and flattened it upon his knee.

'You will observe, Watson, the alternative use of the long *s*
17 and the short. It is one of several indications which enabled me to fix the date.'

I looked over his shoulder at the yellow paper and the faded script. At the head was written: 'Baskerville Hall,' and below, in large scrawling figures: '1742.'

'It appears to be a statement of some sort.'

'Yes, it is a statement of a certain legend which runs in the Baskerville family.'

'But I understand that it is something more modern and practical upon which you wish to consult me?'

'Most modern. A most practical, pressing matter, which must be decided within twenty-four hours. But the manuscript is short and is intimately connected with the affair. With your permission I will read it to you.'

Holmes leaned back in his chair, placed his finger-tips together, and closed his eyes, with an air of resignation. Dr Mortimer turned the manuscript to the light, and read in a high, crackling voice the following curious, old-world narrative:

> 'Of the origin of the Hound of the Baskervilles there have been many statements, yet as I come in a direct line from Hugo Baskerville, and as I had the story from my father, who also had it from his, I have set it down with all belief that it occurred

16 *my little monograph upon the subject.* "From the fact that Holmes assumed Dr. James Mortimer may have read this paper, one deduces that it probably saw publication in some journal which enjoyed a wide circulation among men who followed the scientific professions," Mr. Walter Klinefelter wrote in "The Writings of Sherlock Holmes."

17 *the alternative use of the long* s *and the short.* If the thought was that the long *s* was used strictly in alternation or by chance, this was not so, as Mr. Arthur Godfrey pointed out in an issue of the *Baker Street Journal.* The long *s* was never used as the initial letter of a word if the capital S was used, nor was it used at the end of a word. It occurred only in the *body* of a word, and it was there used properly exclusively, except when it was doubled, and then the second *s* was a short one.

'IT APPEARS TO BE A STATEMENT OF SOME SORT.'

This reproduction of the Legend of the Baskervilles was the work of the late Owen F. Frisbie, of the Five Orange Pips of Westchester County, as a presentation to his friend Mr. Benjamin Clark, also of the Five Orange Pips. It now hangs on the wall of the barroom of the Sherlock Holmes Tavern in London.

even as is here set forth. And I would have you believe, my sons, that the same Justice which punishes sin may also most graciously forgive it, and that no ban is so heavy but that by prayer and repentance it may be removed. Learn then from this story not to fear the fruits of the past, but rather to be circumspect in the future, that those foul passions whereby our family has suffered so grievously may not again be loosed to our undoing.

'Know then that in the time of the Great Rebellion (the
history of which by the learned Lord Clarendon I most earnestly **18**
commend to your attention) this Manor of Baskerville was held by Hugo of that name, nor can it be gainsaid that he was a most wild, profane, and godless man. This, in truth, his neighbours might have pardoned, seeing that saints have never flourished in those parts, but there was in him a certain wanton and cruel humour which made his name a by-word through the West. It chanced that this Hugo came to love (if, indeed, so dark a passion may be known under so bright a name) the daughter of a yeoman who held lands near the Baskerville estate. But the young maiden, being discreet and of good repute, would ever avoid him, for she feared his evil name. So it came to pass that one Michaelmas this Hugo, with five or six of his idle and wicked companions, stole down upon the farm and carried off the maiden, her father and brothers being from home, as he well knew. When they had brought her to the Hall the maiden was placed in an upper chamber, while Hugo and his friends sat down to a long carouse as was their nightly custom. Now, the poor lass upstairs was like to have her wits turned at the singing and shouting and terrible oaths which came up to her from below, for they say that the words used by Hugo Baskerville, when he was in wine, were such as might blast the man who said them. At last in the stress of her fear she did that which might have daunted the bravest or most active man, for by the aid of the growth of ivy which covered (and still covers) the south wall, she came down from under the eaves, and so homeward across the moor, there being three leagues betwixt the Hall and her father's farm.

'It chanced that some little time later Hugo left his guests to carry food and drink—with other worse things, perchance—to his captive, and so found the cage empty and the bird escaped. Then, as it would seem, he became as one that hath a devil, for rushing down the stairs into the dining-hall, he sprang upon the great table, flagons and trenchers flying before him, and he cried aloud before all the company that he would that very night render his body and soul to the Powers of Evil if he might but overtake the wench. And while the revellers stood aghast at the fury of the man, one more wicked or, it may be, more drunken than the rest, cried out that they should put the hounds upon her. Whereat Hugo ran from the house, crying to his grooms that they should saddle his mare and unkennel the pack, and giving the hounds a kerchief of the maid's, he swung them to the line, and so off full cry in the moonlight over the moor.

'Now, for some space the revellers stood agape, unable to understand all that had been done in such haste. But anon their bemused wits awoke to the nature of the deed which was like to be done upon the moorlands. Everything was now in an uproar, some calling for their pistols, some for their horses, and some for another flask of wine. But at length some sense came back to their crazed minds, and the whole of them, thirteen in number, took horse and started in pursuit. The moon shone clear above them, and they rode swiftly abreast, taking that course which the maid must needs have taken if she were to reach her own home.

'They had gone a mile or two when they passed one of the night shepherds upon the moorlands, and they cried to him to

18 *Lord Clarendon.* Edward Hyde, Earl of Clarendon, 1608–1674, English Royalist statesman, historian, Premier and Lord Chancellor; impeached and retired to France. The book referred to is his *History of the Great Rebellion*, 1702.

know if he had seen the hunt. And the man, as the story goes, was so crazed with fear that he could scarce speak, but at last he said that he had indeed seen the unhappy maiden, with the hounds upon her track. "But I have seen more than that," said he, "for Hugo Baskerville passed me upon his black mare, and there ran mute behind him such a hound of hell as God forbid should ever be at my heels."

'So the drunken squires cursed the shepherd and rode onwards. But soon their skins turned cold, for there came a sound of galloping across the moor, and the black mare, dabbled with white froth, went past with trailing bridle and empty saddle. Then the revellers rode close together, for a great fear was on them, but they still followed over the moor, though each, had he been alone, would have been right glad to have turned his horse's head. Riding slowly in this fashion, they came at last upon the hounds. These, though known for their valour and their breed, were whimpering in a cluster at the head of a deep dip or goyal, as we call it, upon the moor, some slinking away and some, with starting hackles and staring eyes, gazing down the narrow valley before them.

'The company had come to a halt, more sober men, as you may guess, than when they started. The most of them would by no means advance, but three of them, the boldest, or, it may be, the most drunken, rode forward down the goyal. Now it opened into a broad space in which stood two of those great stones, still to be seen there, which were set by certain forgotten peoples in the days of old. The moon was shining bright upon the clearing, and there in the centre lay the unhappy maid where she had fallen, dead of fear and of fatigue. But it was not the sight of her body, nor yet was it that of the body of Hugo Baskerville lying near her, which raised the hair upon the heads of these three dare-devil roysterers, but it was that, standing over Hugo, and plucking at his throat, there stood a foul thing, a great, black beast, shaped like a hound, yet larger than any hound that ever mortal eye has rested upon. And even as they looked the thing tore the throat out of Hugo Baskerville, on which, as it turned its blazing eyes and dripping jaws upon them, the three shrieked with fear and rode for dear life, still screaming, across the moor. One, it is said, died that very night of what he had seen, and the other twain were but broken men for the rest of their days.

'Such is the tale, my sons, of the coming of the hound which is said to have plagued the family so sorely ever since. If I have set it down it is because that which is clearly known hath less terror than that which is but hinted at and guessed. Nor can it be denied that many of the family have been unhappy in their deaths, which have been sudden, bloody, and mysterious. Yet may we shelter ourselves in the infinite goodness of Providence, which would not for ever punish the innocent beyond that third or fourth generation which is threatened in Holy Writ. To that Providence, my sons, I hereby commend you, and I counsel you by way of caution to forbear from crossing the moor in those
19 dark hours when the powers of evil are exalted.

'[This from Hugo Baskerville to his sons Rodger and John, with instructions that they say nothing thereof to their sister Elizabeth.]'

When Dr Mortimer had finished reading this singular narrative he pushed his spectacles up on his forehead and stared across at Mr Sherlock Holmes. The latter yawned and tossed the end of his cigarette into the fire.

'Well?' said he.

'Do you not find it interesting?'

'To a collector of fairy-tales.'

Dr Mortimer drew a folded newspaper out of his pocket.

'Now, Mr Holmes, we will give you something a little more

'". . . SUCH A HOUND OF HELL AS GOD FORBID SHOULD EVER BE AT MY HEELS."'

Illustration by Sidney Paget for the *Strand Magazine*, August, 1901.

19 *when the powers of evil are exalted.* As Mr. Bliss Austin has demonstrated in his monograph, "Dartmoor Revisited, or Discoveries in Devonshire," the "West-Country legend" Conan Doyle used as his point of departure for the legend of the Baskervilles would seem to have been that of Sir Richard Cabell, Lord of the Manor of Brooke, in the parish of Buckfastleigh. He was a gentleman of evil repute and on the night of his death, black hounds breathing fire and smoke raced over Dartmoor and howled around his manor house. According to the Reverend Sabine Baring-Gould, in his *Methuen's Little Guide to Devon,* Sir Richard's death took place in 1677. A pagoda-like building called the Sepulchre was erected over his grave to prevent his coming back to trouble the neighborhood again. It is still said that he will gnaw your finger if you venture to insert it in the keyhole of the locked door.

recent. This is the *Devon County Chronicle* of June 14th of this year. It is a short account of the facts elicited at the death of Sir Charles Baskerville which occurred a few days before that date.' **20**

My friend leaned a little forward and his expression became intent. Our visitor readjusted his glasses and began:

'The recent sudden death of Sir Charles Baskerville, whose name has been mentioned as the probable Liberal candidate for Mid-Devon at the next election, has cast a gloom over the county. Though Sir Charles had resided at Baskerville Hall for a comparatively short period his amiability of character and extreme generosity had won the affection and respect of all who had been brought into contact with him. In these days of *nouveaux riches* **21**
it is refreshing to find a case where the scion of an old county family which has fallen upon evil days is able to make his own fortune and to bring it back with him to restore the fallen grandeur of his line. Sir Charles, as is well known, made large sums of money in South African speculation. More wise than those who go on until the wheel turns against them, he realized his gains and returned to England with them. It is only two years since he took up his residence at Baskerville Hall, and it is common talk how large were those schemes of reconstruction and improvement which have been interrupted by his death. Being himself childless, it was his openly-expressed desire that the whole countryside should, within his own lifetime, profit by his good fortune, and many will have personal reasons for bewailing his untimely end. His generous donations to local and county charities have been frequently chronicled in these columns.

'The circumstances connected with the death of Sir Charles cannot be said to have been entirely cleared up by the inquest, but at least enough has been done to dispose of those rumours to which local superstition has given rise. There is no reason whatever to suspect foul play, or to imagine that death could be from any but natural causes. Sir Charles was a widower, and a man who may be said to have been in some ways of an eccentric habit of mind. In spite of his considerable wealth he was simple in his personal tastes, and his indoor servants at Baskerville Hall consisted of a married couple named Barrymore, the husband acting as butler and the wife as housekeeper. Their evidence, corroborated by that of several friends, tends to show that Sir Charles's health has for some time been impaired, and points especially to some affection of the heart, manifesting itself in changes of colour, breathlessness, and acute attacks of nervous depression. Dr James Mortimer, the friend and medical attendant of the deceased, has given evidence to the same effect.

'The facts of the case are simple. Sir Charles Baskerville was in the habit every night before going to bed of walking down the famous Yew Alley of Baskerville Hall. The evidence of the Barrymores shows that this had been his custom. On the 4th of June Sir Charles had declared his intention of starting next day for London, and had ordered Barrymore to prepare his luggage. That night he went out as usual for his nocturnal walk, in the course of which he was in the habit of smoking a cigar. He never returned. At twelve o'clock Barrymore, finding the hall door still open, became alarmed and, lighting a lantern, went in search of his master. The day had been wet, and Sir Charles's footmarks were easily traced down the Alley. Half-way down this walk there is a gate which leads out on to the moor. There were indications that Sir Charles had stood for some little time here. He then proceeded down the Alley, and it was at the far end of it that his body was discovered. One fact which has not been explained is the statement of Barrymore that his master's footprints altered their character from the time that he passed the moor-gate, and that he appeared from thence onwards to

20 *a few days before that date.* We are shortly told that Sir Charles died "on the 4th of June." Since this was "some three months" before Dr. Mortimer's visit to Holmes, it would seem that the visit took place in the month of September. (In the original *Strand Magazine* version of the story, however, and in a number of subsequent book editions, the *Devon County Chronicle* of *May 14th* is referred to, and Sir Charles is said to have died "on the 4th of May.")

21 nouveaux riches. French: those who have recently become rich; parvenus.

have been walking upon his toes. One Murphy, a gipsy horse-dealer, was on the moor at no great distance at the time, but he appears by his own confession to have been the worse for drink. He declares that he heard cries, but is unable to state from what direction they came. No signs of violence were to be discovered upon Sir Charles's person and though the doctor's evidence pointed to an almost incredible facial distortion—so great that Dr Mortimer refused at first to believe that it was indeed his friend and patient who lay before him—it was explained that
22 that is a symptom which is not unusual in cases of dyspnœa and death from cardiac exhaustion. This explanation was borne out by the post-mortem examination, which showed long-standing organic disease, and the coroner's jury returned a verdict in accordance with the medical evidence. It is well that this is so, for it is obviously of the utmost importance that Sir Charles's heir should settle at the Hall, and continue the good work which has been so sadly interrupted. Had the prosaic finding of the coroner not finally put an end to the romantic stories which have been whispered in connection with the affair, it might have been difficult to find a tenant for Baskerville Hall. It is understood that the next-of-kin is Mr Henry Baskerville, if he be still alive, the son of Sir Charles Baskerville's younger brother. The young man, when last heard of, was in America, and inquiries are being instituted with a view to informing him of his good fortune.'

Dr Mortimer refolded his paper and replaced it in his pocket.

'Those are the public facts, Mr Holmes, in connection with the death of Sir Charles Baskerville.'

'I must thank you,' said Sherlock Holmes, 'for calling my attention to a case which certainly presents some features of interest. I had observed some newspaper comment at the time, but I was exceedingly preoccupied by that little affair of the
23 Vatican cameos, and in my anxiety to oblige the Pope I lost touch with several interesting English cases. This article, you say, contains all the public facts?'

'It does.'

'Then let me have the private ones.' He leaned back, put his finger-tips together, and assumed his most impassive and judicial expression.

'In doing so,' said Dr Mortimer, who had begun to show signs of some strong emotion, 'I am telling that which I have not confided to anyone. My motive for withholding it from the coroner's inquiry is that a man of science shrinks from placing himself in the public position of seeming to indorse a popular superstition. I had the further motive that Baskerville Hall, as the paper says, would certainly remain untenanted if anything were done to increase its already rather grim reputation. For both these reasons I thought that I was justified in telling rather less than I knew, since no practical good could result from it, but with you there is no reason why I should not be perfectly frank.

'The moor is very sparsely inhabited, and those who live near each other are thrown very much together. For this reason I saw a good deal of Sir Charles Baskerville. With the exception of Mr Frankland, of Lafter Hall, and Mr Stapleton, the naturalist, there are no other men of education within many miles. Sir Charles was a retiring man, but the chance of his illness brought us together, and a community of interests in science kept us so. He had brought back much scientific information from South Africa, and many a charming evening we have spent together discussing the comparative anatomy

22 *dyspnœa.* Labored breathing due to inadequate action of the heart and a consequent want of aeration of the blood.

23 *the Pope.* It was Pope Leo XIII, 1810–1903, whom Holmes obliged by solving the affair of the Vatican cameos. Holmes was later to investigate the sudden death of Cardinal Tosca at the express desire of this same Pope ("The Adventure of Black Peter").

of the Bushman and the Hottentot.

'Within the last few months it became increasingly plain to me that Sir Charles's nervous system was strained to breaking point. He had taken this legend which I have read you exceedingly to heart—so much so that, although he would walk in his own grounds, nothing would induce him to go out upon the moor at night. Incredible as it may appear to you, Mr Holmes, he was honestly convinced that a dreadful fate overhung his family, and certainly the records which he was able to give of his ancestors were not encouraging. The idea of some ghastly presence constantly haunted him, and on more than one occasion he has asked me whether I had on my medical journeys at night ever seen any strange creature or heard the baying of a hound. The latter question he put to me several times, and always with a voice which vibrated with excitement.

'I can well remember driving up to his house in the evening, some three weeks before the fatal event. He chanced to be at
his hall door. I had descended from my gig and was standing **24**
in front of him, when I saw his eyes fix themselves over my shoulder, and stare past me with an expression of the most dreadful horror. I whisked round and had just time to catch a glimpse of something which I took to be a large black calf passing at the head of the drive. So excited and alarmed was he that I was compelled to go down to the spot where the animal had been and look around for it. It was gone, however, and the incident appeared to make the worst impression upon his mind. I stayed with him all the evening and it was on that occasion, to explain the emotion which he had shown, that he confided to my keeping that narrative which I read to you when first I came. I mention this small episode because it assumes some importance in view of the tragedy which followed, but I was convinced at the time that the matter was entirely trivial and that his excitement had no justification.

'It was at my advice that Sir Charles was about to go to London. His heart was, I knew, affected, and the constant anxiety in which he lived, however chimerical the cause of it might be, was evidently having a serious effect upon his health. I thought that a few months among the distractions of town would send him back a new man. Mr Stapleton, a mutual friend, who was much concerned at his state of health, was of the same opinion. At the last instant came this terrible catastrophe.

'On the night of Sir Charles's death Barrymore the butler, who made the discovery, sent Perkins the groom on horseback to me, and as I was sitting up late I was able to reach Baskerville Hall within an hour of the event. I checked and corroborated all the facts which were mentioned at the inquest. I followed the footsteps down the Yew Alley, I saw the spot at the moor-gate where he seemed to have waited, I remarked the change in the shape of the prints after that point, I noted that there were no other footsteps save those of Barrymore on the soft gravel, and finally I carefully examined the body, which had not been touched until my arrival. Sir Charles lay on his face, his arms out, his fingers dug into the ground, and his features convulsed with some strong emotion to such an extent that I could hardly have sworn to his identity. There was certainly no physical injury of any kind. But one false statement was made by Barrymore at the

24 *gig*. A light one-horse two-wheeled carriage.

inquest. He said that there were no traces upon the ground round the body. He did not observe any. But I did—some little distance off, but fresh and clear.'

'Footprints?'

'Footprints.'

'A man's or a woman's?'

Dr Mortimer looked strangely at us for an instant, and his voice sank almost to a whisper as he answered:

25 'Mr Holmes, they were the footprints of a gigantic hound!'

3 THE PROBLEM

I confess that at these words a shudder passed through me. There was a thrill in the doctor's voice which showed that he was himself deeply moved by that which he told us. Holmes leaned forward in his excitement, and his eyes had the hard, dry glitter which shot from them when he was keenly interested.

'You saw this?'

'As clearly as I see you.'

'And you said nothing?'

'What was the use?'

'How was it that no one else saw it?'

'The marks were some twenty yards from the body, and no one gave them a thought. I don't suppose I should have done so had I not known this legend.'

'There are many sheep-dogs on the moor?'

'No doubt, but this was no sheep-dog.'

'You say it was large?'

'Enormous.'

'But it had not approached the body?'

'No.'

'What sort of night was it?'

'Damp and raw.'

'But not actually raining?'

'No.'

'What is the alley like?'

'There are two lines of old yew hedge, twelve feet high and impenetrable. The walk in the centre is about eight feet across.'

'Is there anything between the hedges and the walk?'

'Yes, there is a strip of grass about six feet broad on either side.'

'I understand that the yew hedge is penetrated at one point by a gate?'

'Yes, the wicket-gate which leads on to the moor.'

'Is there any other opening?'

'None.'

'So that to reach the Yew Alley one either has to come down it from the house or else to enter it by the moor-gate?'

'There is an exit through a summer-house at the far end.'

25 *the footprints of a gigantic hound!'* "As any naturalist will assure you, it is not possible to identify the breed of a dog by his footprints," Professor Remsen Ten Eyck Schenck objected. "As Gertrude Stein might put it, when it comes to pawprints 'a dog is a dog is a dog.' One can eliminate some possibilities, of course, on the basis of size, and might even in some cases adduce further information as to whether the dog were smooth-coated or long-haired, since an excessively shaggy dog will have enough hair around his paws to blur the outlines of his tracks perceptibly. But to decide just like that whether a given set of prints were made by a Great Dane, a hound, a Newfoundland, a St. Bernard, or just plain dog? Never!"

To this Mr. Robert Clyne responded: "Technically [Professor Schenck] may be right—but he has not taken into consideration the psychological impact of the legend. Mortimer was acting quite normally in assuming that the dog was a hound."

'Had Sir Charles reached this?'

'No; he lay about fifty yards from it.'

'Now, tell me, Dr Mortimer—and this is important—the marks which you saw were on the path and not on the grass?'

'No marks could show on the grass.'

'Were they on the same side of the path as the moor-gate?'

'Yes; they were on the edge of the path on the same side as the moor-gate.'

'You interest me exceedingly. Another point. Was the wicket-gate closed?'

'Closed and padlocked.'

'How high was it?'

'About four feet high.'

'Then anyone could have got over it?'

'Yes.'

'And what marks did you see by the wicket-gate?'

'None in particular.'

'Good Heaven! Did no one examine?'

'Yes, I examined myself.'

'And found nothing?'

'It was all very confused. Sir Charles had evidently stood there for five or ten minutes.'

'How do you know that?'

'Because the ash had twice dropped from his cigar.'

'Excellent! This is a colleague, Watson, after our own heart. But the marks?'

'He had left his own marks all over that small patch of gravel. I could discern no others.'

Sherlock Holmes struck his hand against his knee with an impatient gesture.

'If I had only been there!' he cried. 'It is evidently a case of extraordinary interest, and one which presented immense opportunities to the scientific expert. That gravel page upon which I might have read so much has been long ere this smudged by the rain and defaced by the clogs of curious peasants. Oh, Dr Mortimer, Dr Mortimer, to think that you should not have called me in! You have indeed much to answer for.'

'I could not call you in, Mr Holmes, without disclosing these facts to the world and I have already given my reasons for not wishing to do so. Besides, besides——'

'Why do you hesitate?'

'There is a realm in which the most acute and most experienced of detectives is helpless.'

'You mean that the thing is supernatural?'

'I did not positively say so.'

'No, but you evidently think it.'

'Since the tragedy, Mr Holmes, there have come to my ears several incidents which are hard to reconcile with the settled order of Nature.'

'For example?'

'I find that before the terrible event occurred several people had seen a creature upon the moor which corresponds with this Baskerville demon, and which could not possibly be any animal known to science. They all agreed that it was a huge creature, luminous, ghastly and spectral. I have cross-examined these men, one of them a hard-headed countryman, one a farrier, and one a moorland farmer, who all tell the **26**

'YOU HAVE INDEED MUCH TO ANSWER FOR.'

Illustration by Sidney Paget for the *Strand Magazine*, September, 1901.

26 *a farrier.* One who shoes horses; a blacksmith.

same story of this dreadful apparition, exactly corresponding to the hell-hound of the legend. I assure you that there is a reign of terror in the district, and that it is a hardy man who will cross the moor at night.'

'And you, a trained man of science, believe it to be supernatural?'

'I do not know what to believe.'

Holmes shrugged his shoulders. 'I have hitherto confined my investigations to this world,' said he. 'In a modest way I have combated evil, but to take on the Father of Evil himself would, perhaps, be too ambitious a task. Yet you must admit that the footmark is material.'

'The original hound was material enough to tug a man's throat out, and yet he was diabolical as well.'

'I see that you have quite gone over to the supernaturalists. But now, Dr Mortimer, tell me this. If you hold these views, why have you come to consult me at all? You tell me in the same breath that it is useless to investigate Sir Charles's death, and that you desire me to do it.'

'I did not say that I desired you to do it.'

'Then how can I assist you?'

'By advising me as to what I should do with Sir Henry Baskerville, who arrives at Waterloo Station'—Dr Mortimer looked at his watch—'in exactly one hour and a quarter.'

'He being the heir?'

'Yes. On the death of Sir Charles we inquired for this young gentleman, and found that he had been farming in Canada. From the accounts which have reached us he is an excellent fellow in every way. I speak now not as a medical man but as a trustee and executor of Sir Charles's will.'

'There is no other claimant, I presume?'

'None. The only other kinsman whom we have been able to trace was Rodger Baskerville, the youngest of three brothers of whom poor Sir Charles was the elder. The second brother, who died young, is the father of this lad Henry. The third, Rodger, was the black sheep of the family. He came of the old masterful Baskerville strain, and was the very image, they tell me, of the family picture of old Hugo. He made England too hot to hold him, fled to Central America, and died there in 1876 of yellow fever. Henry is the last of the Baskervilles. In one hour and five minutes I meet him at Waterloo Station. I have had a wire that he arrived at Southampton this morning. Now, Mr Holmes, what would you advise me to do with him?'

'Why should he not go to the home of his fathers?'

'It seems natural, does it not? And yet, consider that every Baskerville who goes there meets with an evil fate. I feel sure that if Sir Charles could have spoken with me before his death he would have warned me against bringing this, the last of the old race, and the heir to great wealth, to that deadly place. And yet it cannot be denied that the prosperity of the whole poor, bleak countryside depends upon his presence. All the good work which has been done by Sir Charles will crash to the ground if there is no tenant of the Hall. I fear lest I should be swayed too much by my own obvious interest in the matter, and that is why I bring the case before you and ask for your advice.'

Holmes considered for a little time. 'Put into plain words, the matter is this,' said he. 'In your opinion there is a diabolical agency which makes Dartmoor an unsafe abode for a Baskerville—that is your opinion?'

'At least I might go the length of saying that there is some evidence that this may be so.'

'Exactly. But surely, if your supernatural theory be correct, it could work the young man evil in London as easily as in Devonshire. A devil with merely local powers like a parish vestry would be too inconceivable a thing.'

'You put the matter more flippantly, Mr Holmes, than you would probably do if you were brought into personal contact with these things. Your advice, then, as I understand it, is that the young man will be as safe in Devonshire as in London. He comes in fifty minutes. What would you recommend?'

'I recommend, sir, that you take a cab, call off your spaniel, who is scratching at my front door, and proceed to Waterloo to meet Sir Henry Baskerville.'

'And then?'

'And then you will say nothing to him at all until I have made up my mind about the matter.'

'How long will it take you to make up your mind?'

'Twenty-four hours. At ten o'clock tomorrow, Dr Mortimer, I will be much obliged to you if you will call upon me here, and it will be of help to me in my plans for the future if you will bring Sir Henry Baskerville with you.'

'I will do so, Mr Holmes.'

He scribbled the appointment on his shirt-cuff and hurried off in his strange, peering, absent-minded fashion. Holmes stopped him at the head of the stair.

'Only one more question, Dr Mortimer. You say that before Sir Charles Baskerville's death several people saw this apparition upon the moor?'

'Three people did.'

'Did any see it after?'

'I have not heard of any.'

'Thank you. Good morning.'

Holmes returned to his seat with that quiet look of inward satisfaction which meant that he had a congenial task before him.

'Going out, Watson?'

'Unless I can help you.'

'No, my dear fellow, it is at the hour of action that I turn to you for aid. But this is splendid, really unique from some points of view. When you pass Bradley's would you ask him to send up a pound of the strongest shag tobacco? Thank you. It would be as well if you could make it convenient not to return before evening. Then I should be very glad to compare impressions as to this most interesting problem which has been submitted to us this morning.'

I knew that seclusion and solitude were very necessary for my friend in those hours of intense mental concentration during which he weighed every particle of evidence, constructed alternative theories, balanced one against the other, and made up his mind as to which points were essential and which immaterial. I therefore spent the day at my club, and did not return to Baker Street until evening. It was nearly nine o'clock when I found myself in the sitting-room once more.

My first impression as I opened the door was that a fire had broken out, for the room was so filled with smoke that the

HE SCRIBBLED THE APPOINTMENT ON HIS SHIRT-CUFF . . .

Illustration by Sidney Paget for the *Strand Magazine*, September, 1901.

27 *a showery and miry day*. As we shall shortly see, the day was a Tuesday—in our view, Tuesday, September 25, 1888. On that day, according to the London *Times*, "Rain has fallen in the south and southeast. No bright sunshine has been registered at Westminster today."

28 *Stamford's*. This is clearly an error on Watson's part, for in the eighties, as today, London's leading map seller, and the sole agent for Ordnance and geological survey maps of England and Wales was Edward *Stanford* of 26 Cockspur Street, Charing Cross, now at 12 Long Acre.

29 *the hamlet of Grimpen*. No map of Dartmoor —not even a "very-large"-scale map—will show us Grimpen. If we look closely, however, we will have little difficulty in picking out a hamlet called *Widecombe-in-the-Moor*, which we suggest was "Grimpen." Widecombe was once famous for Widecombe Fair, celebrated in the English ballad of that title:

Tom Pearse, Tom Pearse, lend me your grey mare.
All along, down along, out along lee.
For I want to go to Widecombe Fair
Wi' Bill Brewer, Jan Stewer, Peter Gurney, Peter Davy,
Dan'l Whiddon, Harry Hawk,
Old Uncle Tom Cobleigh and all.

30 *Here is Lafter Hall*. No Lafter Hall appears on our map, but there is a *Laughter* Tor, and it seems fair to assume that Laughter ("Lafter") Hall stood somewhere in its vicinity.

31 *High Tor*. Again, there is no "High Tor" on our map; Holmes perhaps referred to *Higher Tor* or to *Higher White Tor*, both shown.

32 *Foulmire*. This must, we think, be Watsonese for *Fox Tor Mire*, of which the Reverend Sabine Baring-Gould wrote in his *Book of Dartmoor*, first published in 1900 by Methuen & Co., Ltd., of London: it "once bore a very bad name. The only convict who really got away from Princetown [Prison] and was not recaptured was last seen making a bee-line for Fox Tor Mire."

33 *fourteen miles away*. Closer to *four* than to "fourteen"—to remain on the moor.

light of the lamp upon the table was blurred by it. As I entered, however, my fears were set at rest, for it was the acrid fumes of strong, coarse tobacco, which took me by the throat and set me coughing. Through the haze I had a vague vision of Holmes in his dressing-gown coiled up in an arm-chair with his black clay pipe between his lips. Several rolls of paper lay around him.

'Caught cold, Watson?' said he.

'No, it's this poisonous atmosphere.'

'I suppose it *is* pretty thick, now that you mention it.'

'Thick! It is intolerable.'

'Open the window, then! You have been at your club all day, I perceive.'

'My dear Holmes!'

'Am I right?'

'Certainly, but how——?'

He laughed at my bewildered expression.

'There is a delightful freshness about you, Watson, which
makes it a pleasure to exercise any small powers which I
possess at your expense. A gentleman goes forth on a showery
27 and miry day. He returns immaculate in the evening with the
gloss still on his hat and his boots. He has been a fixture, therefore, all day. He is not a man with intimate friends. Where, then, could he have been? Is it not obvious?'

'Well, it is rather obvious.'

'The world is full of obvious things which nobody by any chance ever observes. Where do you think that I have been?'

'A fixture also.'

'On the contrary, I have been to Devonshire.'

'In spirit?'

'Exactly. My body has remained in this arm-chair; and has,
I regret to observe, consumed in my absence two large pots
of coffee and an incredible amount of tobacco. After you left
28 I sent down to Stamford's for the Ordnance map of this por-
tion of the moor, and my spirit has hovered over it all day. I flatter myself that I could find my way about.'

'A large-scale map, I presume?'

'Very large.' He unrolled one section and held it over his knee. 'Here you have the particular district which concerns us. That is Baskerville Hall in the middle.'

'With a wood round it?'

'Exactly. I fancy the Yew Alley, though not marked under
that name, must stretch along this line, with the moor, as you
perceive, upon the right of it. This small clump of buildings
29 here is the hamlet of Grimpen, where our friend Dr Mortimer
has his headquarters. Within a radius of five miles there are,
as you see, only a very few scattered dwellings. Here is Lafter
30 Hall, which was mentioned in the narrative. There is a house
indicated here which may be the residence of the naturalist
—Stapleton, if I remember right, was his name. Here are two
31-32 moorland farm-houses, High Tor and Foulmire. Then four-
33 teen miles away the great convict prison of Princetown. Be-
tween and around these scattered points extends the desolate, lifeless moor. This, then, is the stage upon which tragedy has been played, and upon which we may help to play it again.'

'It must be a wild place.'

'Yes, the setting is a worthy one. If the devil did desire to have a hand in the affairs of men——'

'Then you are yourself inclining to the supernatural explanation.'

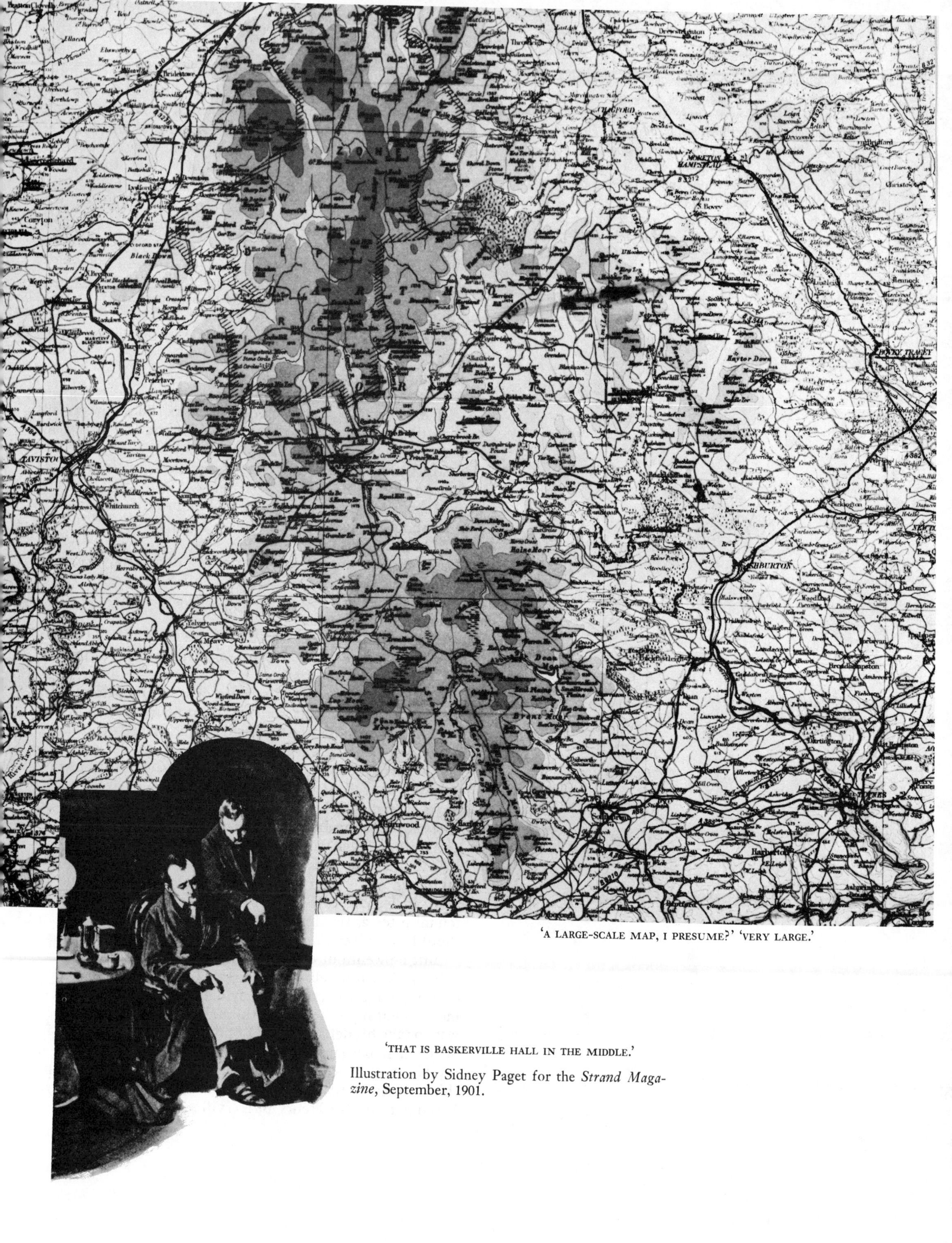

'A LARGE-SCALE MAP, I PRESUME?' 'VERY LARGE.'

'THAT IS BASKERVILLE HALL IN THE MIDDLE.'

Illustration by Sidney Paget for the *Strand Magazine*, September, 1901.

'The devil's agents may be of flesh and blood, may they not? There are two questions waiting for us at the outset. The one is whether any crime has been committed at all; the second is, what is the crime and how was it committed? Of course, if Dr Mortimer's surmise should be correct, and we are dealing with forces outside the ordinary laws of Nature, there is an end of our investigation. But we are bound to exhaust all other hypotheses before falling back upon this one. I think we'll shut that window again, if you don't mind. It is a singular thing, but I find that a concentrated atmosphere helps a
34 concentration of thought. I have not pushed it to the length of getting into a box to think, but that is the logical outcome of my convictions. Have you turned the case over in your mind?'

'Yes, I have thought a good deal of it in the course of the day.'

'What do you make of it?'

'It is very bewildering.'

'It has certainly a character of its own. There are points of distinction about it. That change in the footprints, for example. What do you make of that?'

'Mortimer said that the man had walked on tiptoe down that portion of the alley.'

'He only repeated what some fool had said at the inquest. Why should a man walk on tiptoe down the alley?'

'What then?'

'He was running, Watson—running desperately, running for his life, running until he burst his heart and fell dead upon his face.'

'Running from what?'

'There lies our problem. There are indications that the man was crazed with fear before ever he began to run.'

'How can you say that?'

'I am presuming that the cause of his fears came to him across the moor. If that were so, and it seems most probable, only a man who had lost his wits would have run *from* the house instead of towards it. If the gipsy's evidence may be taken as true, he ran with cries for help in the direction where help was least likely to be. Then again, whom was he waiting for that night, and why was he waiting for him in the Yew Alley rather than in his own house?'

'You think that he was waiting for someone?'

'The man was elderly and infirm. We can understand his taking an evening stroll, but the ground was damp and the night inclement. Is it natural that he should stand for five or ten minutes, as Dr Mortimer, with more practical sense than I should have given him credit for, deduced from the cigar ash?'

'But he went out every evening.'

'I think it unlikely that he waited at the moor-gate every evening. On the contrary, the evidence is that he avoided the moor. That night he waited there. It was the night before he was to take his departure for London. The thing takes shape, Watson. It becomes coherent. Might I ask you to hand me my violin, and we will postpone all further thought upon this business until we have had the advantage of meeting Dr Mortimer and Sir Henry Baskerville in the morning.'

34 *a concentrated atmosphere helps a concentration of thought.* "If it is true that the English people enjoy a 'frowst' more than others," Mr. T. S. Blakeney wrote in *Sherlock Holmes: Fact or Fiction?*, "Holmes was, on unimpeachable testimony, English of the English. Watson awoke at The Cedars to find the room 'full of dense tobacco haze' ('The Man with the Twisted Lip'), and in *The Hound of the Baskervilles* found Holmes rejoicing in an atmosphere \so intolerable that he thought a fire had broken out."

4 SIR HENRY BASKERVILLE

Our breakfast-table was cleared early, and Holmes waited in his dressing-gown for the promised interview. Our clients were punctual to their appointment, for the clock had just struck ten when Dr Mortimer was shown up, followed by the young baronet. The latter was a small, alert, dark-eyed man about thirty years of age, very sturdily built, with thick black eyebrows, and a strong, pugnacious face. He wore a ruddy-tinted tweed suit, and had the weather-beaten appearance of one who has spent most of his time in the open air, and yet there was something in his steady eye and the quiet assurance of his bearing which indicated the gentleman.

'This is Sir Henry Baskerville,' said Dr Mortimer.

'Why, yes,' said he, 'and the strange thing is, Mr Sherlock Holmes, that if my friend here had not proposed coming round to you this morning I should have come on my own. I understand that you think out little puzzles, and I've had one this morning which wants more thinking out than I am able to give to it.'

'Pray take a seat, Sir Henry. Do I understand you to say that you have yourself had some remarkable experience since you arrived in London?'

'Nothing of much importance, Mr Holmes. Only a joke, as like as not. It was this letter, if you can call it a letter, which reached me this morning.'

He laid an envelope upon the table, and we all bent over it. It was of common quality, greyish in colour. The address, 'Sir Henry Baskerville, Northumberland Hotel,' was printed in rough characters; the post-mark 'Charing Cross,' and the date of posting the preceding evening.

'Who knew that you were going to the Northumberland Hotel?' asked Holmes, glancing keenly across at our visitor.

'No one could have known. We only decided after I met Dr Mortimer.'

'But Dr Mortimer was, no doubt, already stopping there?'

'No, I had been staying with a friend,' said the doctor. 'There was no possible indication that we intended to go to this hotel.'

'Hum! Someone seems to be very deeply interested in your movements.' Out of the envelope he took a half-sheet of foolscap paper folded into four. This he opened and spread flat upon the table. Across the middle of it a single sentence had been formed by the expedient of pasting printed words upon it. It ran: 'As you value your life or your reason keep away from the moor.' The word 'moor' only was printed in ink.

'Now,' said Sir Henry Baskerville, 'perhaps you will tell me, Mr Holmes, what in thunder is the meaning of that, and who is it that takes so much interest in my affairs?'

'What do you make of it, Dr Mortimer? You must allow that there is nothing supernatural about this, at any rate?'

'No, sir, but it might very well come from someone who was convinced that the business is supernatural.'

'What business?' asked Sir Henry, sharply. 'It seems to me that all you gentlemen know a great deal more than I do about my own affairs.'

'You shall share our knowledge before you leave this room,

'THIS IS SIR HENRY BASKERVILLE . . .'

Portrait by Sidney Paget for the *Strand Magazine*, September, 1901.

Sir Henry. I promise you that,' said Sherlock Holmes. 'We will confine ourselves for the present, with your permission, to this very interesting document, which must have been put together and posted yesterday evening. Have you yesterday's *Times*, Watson?'

'It is here in the corner.'

'Might I trouble you for it—the inside page, please, with the leading articles?' He glanced swiftly over it, running his
eyes up and down the columns. 'Capital article this on Free
35 Trade. Permit me to give you an extract from it. "You may
be cajoled into imagining that your own special trade or your own industry will be encouraged by a protective tariff, but it stands to reason that such legislation must in the long run keep away wealth from the country, diminish the value of our imports, and lower the general conditions of life in this island." What do you think of that, Watson?' cried Holmes, in high glee, rubbing his hands together with satisfaction. 'Don't you think that is an admirable sentiment?'

Dr Mortimer looked at Holmes with an air of professional interest, and Sir Henry Baskerville turned a pair of puzzled dark eyes upon me.

'I don't know much about the tariff and things of that kind,' said he; 'but it seems to me we've got a bit off the trail so far as that note is concerned.'

'On the contrary, I think we are particularly hot upon the trail, Sir Henry. Watson here knows more about my methods than you do, but I fear that even he has not quite grasped the significance of this sentence.'

'No, I confess that I see no connection.'

'And yet, my dear Watson, there is so very close a connection that the one is extracted out of the other. "You," "your," "your," "life," "reason," "value," "keep away," "from the." Don't you see now whence these words have been taken?'

'By thunder, you're right! Well, if that isn't smart!' cried Sir Henry.

'If any possible doubt remained it is settled by the fact that "keep away" and "from the" are cut out in one piece.'

'Well, now—so it is!'

'Really, Mr Holmes, this exceeds anything which I could have imagined,' said Dr Mortimer, gazing at my friend in amazement. 'I could understand anyone saying that the words were from a newspaper; but that you should name which, and add that it came from the leading article, is really one of the most remarkable things which I have ever known. How did you do it?'

'I presume, doctor, that you could tell the skull of a negro from that of an Esquimaux?'

'Most certainly.'

'But how?'

'Because that is my special hobby. The differences are obvious. The supra-orbital crest, the facial angle, the maxillary curve, the——'

'But this is my special hobby, and the differences are equally obvious. There is as much difference to my eyes between the leaded bourgeois type of a *Times* article and the slovenly print of an evening halfpenny paper as there could be between your negro and your Esquimaux. The detection of
types is one of the most elementary branches of knowledge
36 to the special expert in crime, though I confess that once

HE GLANCED SWIFTLY OVER IT, RUNNING HIS EYES UP AND DOWN THE COLUMNS.

Illustration by Sidney Paget for the *Strand Magazine*, September, 1901.

35 *'Capital article this on Free Trade.* The late Gavin Brend, in *My Dear Holmes*, expressed his opinion that an article on Free Trade would not have appeared in the *Times* until 1902 or 1903, but we do not feel that this can be allowed to stand; surely, since the days of Pitt, Free Trade has been a topic of discussion in England. It must be admitted, however, that the late Dr. Ernest Bloomfield Zeisler carefully examined the London *Times* for the last Tuesday in September for every year from 1884 to 1889 and 1894 to 1899 without finding the article in question.

36 *the special expert in crime.* "There is . . . little doubt," Miss Madeleine B. Stern wrote in "Sherlock Holmes: Rare Book Collector," "that specimens of Granjon's civilite, the Estienne, the Bodoni, Fourneir Le Jeune, the great Enschede type specimen book with its exotic fonts, had all . . . found their way to Holmes' library . . ."

From *The Times*, Aug. 18th, 1890

LONDON, MONDAY, AUGUST 18, 1890.

THE SESSION.

The reproach of barrenness has been levelled at many recent Sessions, but in hardly any recorded case has it been as completely justified as in the present year. Party men may endlessly debate the question whether the larger share of responsibility for this disappointing result was due to the obstructive tactics of the Opposition or to the mismanagement of business by the Government, but an impartial judgment will not find much difficulty in assigning its proper weight to each of these influences.

'. . . THE LEADED BOURGEOIS TYPE OF A TIMES ARTICLE . . .'

As Holmes remarked, a *Times* article is entirely distinctive. It is set in small Bourgeois, 9 pt., 2 pt. leaded, and is Miller and Richards "modern face."

From *The Leeds Mercury*, Sept. 6th, 1890

The fatal accident to a lady at Starbeck by falling out of a railway carriage compartment owing to the door not having been fastened is, it should be understood, a form of accident entirely preventable if the method of shutting carriage-doors in use on one of the Scotch railways were adopted. On the Caledonian Railway, a compartment door only requires to be drawn inwards in order to shut itself. The lock has a double mechanism. Slamming the door to is practically an effectual closing of the door, and the turning of the door handle by hand, although an additional security, is not positively necessary, unless there is something defective in the lock. In this way a door cannot be open when it appears to be closed. Rights of patent, and refusal to allow other railways to make use of this ingenious method of fastening, probably explain why it is not in use on all other railways. If this be the explanation, it is regrettable, in the interests of public safety.

'. . . I CONFESS THAT ONCE WHEN I WAS VERY YOUNG I CONFUSED THE LEEDS MERCURY WITH THE WESTERN MORNING NEWS.'

The type used in the *Leeds Mercury* (now the *Yorkshire Post*) (*above*) at this period was Minion 7 pt., 1½ pt. leaded. That in the *Western Morning News* (*below*) was Old Style, Non-pareil (6 pt., 1½ pt. leaded).

when I was very young I confused the *Leeds Mercury* with the *Western Morning News*. But a *Times* leader is entirely distinctive, and these words could have been taken from nothing else. As it was done yesterday the strong probability was that we should find the words in yesterday's issue.'

'So far as I can follow you, then, Mr Holmes,' said Sir Henry Baskerville, 'someone cut out this message with a scissors——'

'Nail-scissors,' said Holmes. 'You can see that it was a very short-bladed scissors, since the cutter had to take two snips over "keep away." '

'That is so. Someone, then, cut out the message with a pair of short-bladed scissors, pasted it with paste——'

'Gum,' said Holmes.

'With gum on to the paper. But I want to know why the word "moor" should have been written?'

'Because he could not find it in print. The other words were all simple, and might be found in any issue, but "moor" would be less common.'

'Why, of course, that would explain it. Have you read anything else in this message, Mr Holmes?'

'There are one or two indications, and yet the utmost pains have been taken to remove all clues. The address, you observe, is printed in rough characters. But *The Times* is a paper which is seldom found in any hands but those of the highly educated. We may take it, therefore, that the letter was composed by an educated man who wished to pose as an uneducated one, and his effort to conceal his own writing suggests that that writing might be known, or come to be known by you. Again, you will observe, that the words are not gummed on in an accurate line, but that some are much

From *The Western Morning News*, 28th October, 1890

THE HAMPSTEAD MURDER.

PRISONER BEFORE THE MAGISTRATE.

EVIDENCE OF THE HUSBAND.

Mrs. Pearcy, who is charged with the murder of Mrs. Hogg, at Hampstead, was removed from Kentish Town to Marylebone Police Court at a quarter to eight yesterday morning. Since her arrest she has been very calm, making no reference to the crime, except remarking when charged:—"I know nothing about it." Her appearance would indicate her as being inferior in class to the deceased woman, but she certainly does not betray that vicious character which the police allege her to be endowed with. Her indifference, whether assumed or not, gave way during Sunday night, when she wept freely. When escorted from the cell to the prison van, which had been backed into the station-yard to avoid the assembled crowd, her eyes were blood-shot, and she looked dejected. The van was provided with additional officers, but as it passed through the crowd no feeling was expressed.

At the Marylebone Police Court yesterday Mary Eleanor Pearcy, 24, married, was brought up by Detective-Inspector Banister, of the S Division, before Mr. Cooke, charged with the murder of Phœbe Hogg, at 2, Priory-street, on the 24th inst. She was further charged on suspicion with killing and slaying Phœbe Hanslope Hogg, aged 18 months. Mr. Freake Palmer, solicitor, defended.

Frank Samuel Hogg, of 141, Prince of Wales's-road, a furniture remover, said the deceased, Phœbe Hogg, was his wife. (The witness wept bitterly.) The child, Phœbe Hanslope Hogg, was his daughter. She was 18 months old. He last saw them on Friday morning, about nine o'clock. The witness then left to go to his work, and returned home at ten o'clock at night. He then found that his wife was not at home. His wife was 31 years of age last May. He went to the house of the prisoner, who had been friendly with his wife, to know if she had seen her. The prisoner's house was about six minutes' walk from his house. The prisoner was not at home, and he did not see her that night. He had not seen or spoken to her since the Wednesday before. To his knowledge there had not been any quarrel between his wife and the prisoner. He carried a latch-key of the prisoner's door, and had been in the habit of visiting her. He did not think his wife knew that he went there.

higher than others. "Life," for example, is quite out of its proper place. That may point to carelessness or it may point to agitation and hurry upon the part of the cutter. On the whole I incline to the latter view, since the matter was evidently important, and it is unlikely that the composer of such a letter would be careless. If he were in a hurry it opens up the interesting question why he should be in a hurry, since any letter posted up to early morning would reach Sir Henry before he would leave his hotel. Did the composer fear an interruption—and from whom?'

'We are coming now rather into the region of guess-work,' said Dr Mortimer.

'Say, rather, into the region where we balance probabilities and choose the most likely. It is the scientific use of the imagination, but we have always some material basis on which to start our speculations. Now, you would call it a guess, no doubt, but I am almost certain that this address has been written in an hotel.'

'How in the world can you say that?'

'If you examine it carefully you will see that both the pen and the ink have given the writer trouble. The pen has spluttered twice in a single word, and has run dry three times in a short address, showing that there was very little ink in the bottle. Now, a private pen or ink-bottle is seldom allowed to be in such a state, and the combination of the two must be quite rare. But you know the hotel ink and the hotel pen, where it is rare to get anything else. Yes, I have very little hesitation in saying that could we examine the wastepaper baskets of the hotels round Charing Cross until we found the remains of the mutilated *Times* leader we could lay our hands straight upon the person who sent this singular message. Halloa! Halloa! What's this?'

... HOLDING IT ONLY AN INCH OR TWO FROM HIS EYES.

Illustration by Sidney Paget for the *Strand Magazine*, September, 1901.

He was carefully examining the foolscap, upon which the words were pasted, holding it only an inch or two from his eyes.

'Well?'

'Nothing,' said he, throwing it down. 'It is a blank half-sheet of paper, without even a watermark upon it. I think we have drawn as much as we can from this curious letter; and now, Sir Henry, has anything else of interest happened to you since you have been in London?'

'Why, no, Mr Holmes. I think not.'

'You have not observed anyone follow or watch you?'

'I seem to have walked right into the thick of a dime novel,' said our visitor. 'Why in thunder should anyone follow or watch me?'

'We are coming to that. You have nothing else to report to us before we go into this matter?'

'Well, it depends upon what you think worth reporting.'

'I think anything out of the ordinary routine of life well worth reporting.'

Sir Henry smiled. 'I don't know much of British life yet, for I have spent nearly all my time in the States and in Canada. But I hope that to lose one of your boots is not part of the ordinary routine of life over here.'

'You have lost one of your boots?'

'My dear sir,' cried Dr Mortimer, 'it is only mislaid. You will find it when you return to the hotel. What is the use of troubling Mr Holmes with trifles of this kind?'

'Well, he asked me for anything outside the ordinary routine.'

'Exactly,' said Holmes, 'however foolish the incident may seem. You have lost one of your boots, you say?'

'Well, mislaid it, anyhow. I put them both outside my door last night, and there was only one in the morning. I could get no sense out of the chap who cleans them. The worst of it is that I only bought the pair last night in the Strand, and I have never had them on.'

'If you have never worn them, why did you put them out to be cleaned?'

'They were tan boots, and had never been varnished. That was why I put them out.'

'Then I understand that on your arrival in London yesterday you went out at once and bought a pair of boots?'

'I did a good deal of shopping. Dr Mortimer here went round with me. You see, if I am to be squire down there I must dress the part, and it may be that I have got a little careless in my ways out West. Among other things I bought these brown boots—gave six dollars for them—and had one stolen before ever I had them on my feet.'

'It seems a singularly useless thing to steal,' said Sherlock Holmes. 'I confess that I share Dr Mortimer's belief that it will not be long before the missing boot is found.'

'And now, gentlemen,' said the baronet, with decision, 'it seems to me that I have spoken quite enough about the little that I know. It is time that you kept your promise, and gave me a full account of what we are all driving at.'

'Your request is a very reasonable one,' Holmes answered. 'Dr Mortimer, I think you could not do better than to tell your story as you told it to us.'

Thus encouraged, our scientific friend drew his papers from his pocket, and presented the whole case as he had done upon the morning before. Sir Henry Baskerville listened with the deepest attention, and with an occasional exclamation of surprise.

'Well, I seem to have come into an inheritance with a vengeance,' said he, when the long narrative was finished. 'Of course, I've heard of the hound ever since I was in the nursery. It's the pet story of the family, though I never thought of taking it seriously before. But as to my uncle's death—well, it all seems boiling up in my head, and I can't get it clear yet. You don't seem quite to have made up your mind whether it's a case for a policeman or a clergyman.'

'Precisely.'

'And now there's this affair of the letter to me at the hotel. I suppose that fits into its place.'

'It seems to show that someone knows more than we do about what goes on upon the moor,' said Dr Mortimer.

'And also,' said Holmes, 'that someone is not ill-disposed towards you, since they warn you of danger.'

'Or it may be that they wish for their own purposes to scare me away.'

'Well, of course, that is possible also. I am very much indebted to you, Dr Mortimer, for introducing me to a problem which presents several interesting alternatives. But the practical point which we now have to decide, Sir Henry, is whether it is or is not advisable for you to go to Baskerville Hall.'

'Why should I not go?'

'. . . I ONLY BOUGHT THE PAIR LAST NIGHT IN THE STRAND . . .'

G. H. Harris' bootshop in the Strand, at which Sir Henry Baskerville bought a pair of brown boots in 1888. The business, founded in 1865 by George Harris (who with his brother stands outside), has since been transferred to Savoy Buildings; The Bun Shop, though rebuilt, still survives. The photograph is from Michael Harrison's *In the Footsteps of Sherlock Holmes*.

'There seems to be danger.'

'Do you mean danger from this family fiend or do you mean danger from human beings?'

'Well, that is what we have to find out.'

'Whichever it is, my answer is fixed. There is no devil in hell, Mr Holmes, and there is no man upon earth who can prevent me from going to the home of my own people, and you may take that to be my final answer.' His dark brows knitted and his face flushed to a dusky red as he spoke. It was evident that the fiery temper of the Baskervilles was not extinct in this their last representative. 'Meanwhile,' said he, 'I have hardly had time to think over all that you have told me. It's a big thing for a man to have to understand and to decide at one sitting. I should like to have a quiet hour by myself to make up my mind. Now, look here, Mr Holmes, it's half-past eleven now, and I am going back right away to my hotel. Suppose you and your friend, Dr Watson, come round and lunch with us at two? I'll be able to tell you more clearly then how this thing strikes me.'

'Is that convenient to you, Watson?'

'Perfectly.'

'Then you may expect us. Shall I have a cab called?'

'I'd prefer to walk, for this affair has flurried me rather.'

'I'll join you in a walk, with pleasure,' said his companion.

'Then we meet again at two o'clock. Au revoir, and good morning!'

We heard the steps of our visitors descend the stair and the bang of the front door. In an instant Holmes had changed from the languid dreamer to the man of action.

'Your hat and boots, Watson, quick! Not a moment to lose!' He rushed into his room in his dressing-gown, and was back again in a few seconds in a frock-coat. We hurried together down the stairs and into the street. Dr Mortimer and Baskerville were still visible about two hundred yards ahead of us in the direction of Oxford Street.

'Shall I run on and stop them?'

'Not for the world, my dear Watson. I am perfectly satisfied with your company, if you will tolerate mine. Our friends
37 are wise, for it is certainly a very fine morning for a walk.'

He quickened his pace until we had decreased the distance which divided us by about half. Then, still keeping a hundred yards behind, we followed into Oxford Street and so down Regent Street. Once our friends stopped and stared into a shop window, upon which Holmes did the same. An instant afterwards he gave a little cry of satisfaction, and, following the direction of his eager eyes, I saw that a hansom cab with a man inside which had halted on the other side of the street was now walking slowly onwards again.

'There's our man, Watson! Come along! We'll have a good look at him, if we can do no more.'

At that instant I was aware of a bushy black beard and a pair of piercing eyes turned upon us through the side window of the cab. Instantly the trap-door at the top flew up, something was screamed to the driver, and the cab flew madly off down Regent Street. Holmes looked eagerly round for another, but no empty one was in sight. Then he dashed in wild pursuit amid the stream of the traffic, but the start was too great, and already the cab was out of sight.

'There now!' said Holmes, bitterly, as he emerged pant-

37 *a very fine morning.* If this was the morning of Wednesday, September 26, 1888, as we believe, it was "a very fine morning." Said the *Times:* "In London the sheltered thermometer did not fall below 49 deg. . . . The rain noticed on Tuesday has ceased."

'THERE'S OUR MAN, WATSON! COME ALONG!'

Sidney Paget's famous "Regent Street" picture as he drew it for the *Strand Magazine*, September, 1901. In both the *Strand* and the Newnes book edition, however, the picture was printed *in reverse*, and many later editions have done the same thing.

ing and white with vexation from the tide of vehicles. 'Was ever such bad luck and such bad management, too? Watson, Watson, if you are an honest man you will record this also and set it against my successes!'

'Who was the man?'

'I have not an idea.'

'A spy?'

'Well, it was evident from what we have heard that Baskerville has been very closely shadowed by someone since he has been in town. How else could it be known so quickly that it was the Northumberland Hotel which he had chosen? If they had followed him the first day, I argued that they would follow him also the second. You may have observed that I twice strolled over to the window while Dr Mortimer was reading his legend.'

'Yes, I remember.'

'I was looking out for loiterers in the street, but I saw none. We are dealing with a clever man, Watson. This matter cuts very deep, and though I have not finally made up my mind whether it is a benevolent or a malevolent agency which is in touch with us, I am conscious always of power and design. When our friends left I at once followed them in the hopes of marking down their invisible attendant. So wily was he that he had not trusted himself upon foot, but he had availed himself of a cab, so that he could loiter behind or dash past them and so escape their notice. His method had the additional advantage that if they were to take a cab he was all ready to follow them. It has, however, one obvious disadvantage.'

'It puts him in the power of the cabman.'

'Exactly.'

'What a pity we did not get the number!'

'My dear Watson, clumsy as I have been, you surely do not seriously imagine that I neglected to get the number? 2704 is our man. But that is no use to us for the moment.'

'I fail to see how you could have done more.'

'On observing the cab I should have instantly turned and walked in the other direction. I should then at my leisure have hired a second cab, and followed the first at a respectful distance, or, better still, have driven to the Northumberland Hotel and waited there. When our unknown had followed Baskerville home we should have had the opportunity of playing his own game upon himself, and seeing where he made for. As it is, by an indiscreet eagerness, which was taken advantage of with extraordinary quickness and energy by our opponent, we have betrayed ourselves and lost our man.'

We had been sauntering slowly down Regent Street during this conversation, and Dr Mortimer, with his companion, had long vanished in front of us.

'There is no object in our following them,' said Holmes. 'The shadow has departed and will not return. We must see what further cards we have in our hands, and play them with decision. Could you swear to that man's face within the cab?'

'I could swear only to the beard.'

'And so could I—from which I gather that in all probability it was a false one. A clever man upon so delicate an errand has no use for a beard save to conceal his features. Come in here, Watson!'

He turned into one of the district messenger offices, where he was warmly greeted by the manager.

'Ah, Wilson, I see you have not forgotten the little case in which I had the good fortune to help you?'

'No, sir, indeed I have not. You saved my good name, and perhaps my life.'

'My dear fellow, you exaggerate. I have some recollection, Wilson, that you had among your boys a lad named Cartwright, who showed some ability during the investigation.'

'Yes, sir, he is still with us.'

'Could you ring him up? Thank you! And I should be glad to have change of this five-pound note.'

A lad of fourteen, with a bright, keen face, had obeyed the summons of the manager. He stood now gazing with great reverence at the famous detective.

'Let me have the Hotel Directory,' said Holmes. 'Thank you! Now, Cartwright, there are the names of twenty-three hotels here, all in the immediate neighbourhood of Charing Cross. Do you see?'

'Yes, sir.'

'You will visit each of these in turn.'

'Yes, sir.'

'You will begin in each case by giving the outside porter one shilling. Here are twenty-three shillings.'

'Yes, sir.'

'You will tell him that you want to see the waste paper of yesterday. You will say that an important telegram has miscarried, and that you are looking for it. You understand?'

'Yes, sir.'

'But what you are really looking for is the centre page of *The Times* with some holes cut in it with scissors. Here is a copy of *The Times*. It is this page. You could easily recognize it, could you not?'

'Yes, sir.'

'In each case the outside porter will send for the hall porter, to whom also you will give a shilling. Here are twenty-three shillings. You will then learn in possibly twenty cases out of the twenty-three that the waste of the day before has been burned or removed. In the three other cases you will be shown a heap of paper, and you will look for this page of *The Times* among it. The odds are enormously against your finding it. There are ten shillings over in case of emergencies. Let me have a report by wire at Baker Street before evening. And now, Watson, it only remains for us to find out by wire the identity of the cabman, No. 2704, and then we will drop into
38 one of the Bond Street picture-galleries and fill in the time until we are due at the hotel.'

'NOW, CARTWRIGHT, THERE ARE THE NAMES OF TWENTY-THREE HOTELS HERE . . .'

Illustration by Sidney Paget for the *Strand Magazine*, September, 1901.

38 *Bond Street.* "Bond Street was built in 1686 by Sir Thomas Bond of Peckham, Comptroller of the Household to Henrietta Maria, as Queen Mother, who was created a baronet by Charles II, and bought part of the Clarendon estate from the Duke of Albemarle. The author of *Tristram Shandy*, Laurence Sterne, died at 'the Silk Bag Shop,' No. 41, March 18, 1768, without a friend near him."—Augustus J. C. Hare, *Walks in London*, Vol. II.

It is possible that one of the picture galleries Holmes and Watson visited was the Grosvenor Gallery at No. 134. Opened May, 1877, by Sir Coutts Lindsay, it had a doorway by Palladio, brought from the Church of St. Lucia at Venice, inserted in what Hare called "an inartistic front of mountebank architecture."

5 THREE BROKEN THREADS

Sherlock Holmes had, in a very remarkable degree, the power of detaching his mind at will. For two hours the strange business in which we had been involved appeared to be forgotten, and he was entirely absorbed in the pictures of the

. . . WE FOUND OURSELVES AT THE NORTHUMBERLAND HOTEL.

At No. 11, Northumberland Street. It is pleasant to record that the building now houses the Sherlock Holmes Tavern. The photograph is from *Sherlock Holmes: A Biography*, by William S. Baring-Gould.

modern Belgian masters. He would talk of nothing but art, of which he had the crudest ideas, from our leaving the gallery until we found ourselves at the Northumberland Hotel.

'Sir Henry Baskerville is upstairs expecting you,' said the clerk. 'He asked me to show you up at once when you came.'

'Have you any objection to my looking at your register?' said Holmes.

'Not in the least.'

The book showed that two names had been added after that of Baskerville. One was Theophilus Johnson and family,
of Newcastle; the other Mrs Oldmore and maid, of High **39**
Lodge, Alton. **40**

'Surely that must be the same Johnson whom I used to know,' said Holmes, to the porter. 'A lawyer, is he not, grey-headed, and walks with a limp?'

'No, sir, this is Mr Johnson the coal-owner, a very active gentleman, not older than yourself.'

'Surely you are mistaken about his trade?'

'No, sir; he has used this hotel for many years, and he is very well known to us.'

'Ah, that settles it. Mrs Oldmore, too; I seem to remember the name. Excuse my curiosity, but often in calling upon one friend one finds another.'

'She is an invalid lady, sir. Her husband was once Mayor
of Gloucester. She always comes to us when she is in town.' **41**

'Thank you; I am afraid I cannot claim her acquaintance. We have established a most important fact by these questions, Watson,' he continued, in a low voice, as we went upstairs together. 'We know now that the people who are so interested in our friend have not settled down in his own hotel. That means that while they are, as we have seen, very anxious to watch him, they are equally anxious that he should not see them. Now, this is a most suggestive fact.'

'What does it suggest?'

'It suggests—halloa, my dear fellow, what on earth is the matter?'

As we came round the top of the stairs we had run up against Sir Henry Baskerville himself. His face was flushed with anger, and he held an old and dusty boot in one of his hands. So furious was he that he was hardly articulate, and

39 *Newcastle.* The county seat of Northumberland, on the River Tyne. Its great coal-shipping industry gave rise to the popular expression "as useless as carrying coals to Newcastle."

40 *Alton.* A market town in Hampshire.

41 *Gloucester.* The county seat of Gloucestershire, an industrial city on the Severn.

when he did speak it was in a much broader and more Western dialect than any which we had heard from him in the morning.

'Seems to me they are playing me for a sucker in this hotel,' he cried. 'They'll find they've started in to monkey with the wrong man unless they are careful. By thunder, if that chap can't find my missing boot there will be trouble. I can take a joke with the best, Mr Holmes, but they've got a bit over the mark this time.'

'Still looking for your boot?'

'Yes, sir, and mean to find it.'

'But surely, you said that it was a new brown boot?'

'So it was, sir. And now it's an old black one.'

'What! you don't mean to say——?'

'That's just what I do mean to say. I only had three pairs in the world—the new brown, the old black, and the patent leathers, which I am wearing. Last night they took one of my brown ones, and today they have sneaked one of the black. Well, have you got it? Speak out, man, and don't stand staring!'

An agitated German waiter had appeared upon the scene.

'No, sir; I have made inquiry all over the hotel, but I can hear no word of it.'

'Well, either that boot comes back before sundown, or I'll see the manager and tell him that I go right straight out of this hotel.'

'It shall be found, sir—I promise you that if you will have a little patience it will be found.'

'Mind it is, for it's the last thing of mine that I'll lose in this den of thieves. Well, well, Mr Holmes, you'll excuse my troubling you about such a trifle——'

'I think it's well worth troubling about.'

'Why, you look very serious over it.'

'How do you explain it?'

'I just don't attempt to explain it. It seems the very maddest, queerest thing that ever happened to me.'

'The queerest, perhaps,' said Holmes, thoughtfully.

'What do you make of it yourself?'

'Well, I don't profess to understand it yet. This case of yours is very complex, Sir Henry. When taken in conjunction with your uncle's death I am not sure that of all the five hun-
42 dred cases of capital importance which I have handled there is one which cuts so deep. But we hold several threads in our hands, and the odds are that one or other of them guides us to the truth. We may waste time in following the wrong one, but sooner or later, we must come upon the right.'

We had a pleasant luncheon in which little was said of the business which had brought us together. It was in the private sitting-room to which we afterwards repaired that Holmes asked Baskerville what were his intentions.

'To go to Baskerville Hall.'

'And when?'

'At the end of the week.'

'On the whole,' said Holmes, 'I think that your decision is a wise one. I have ample evidence that you are being dogged in London, and amid the millions of this great city it is difficult to discover who these people are or what their object can be. If their intentions are evil they might do you a mischief, and we should be powerless to prevent it. You did not know, Dr Mortimer, that you were followed this morning from my house?'

42 *the five hundred cases of capital importance which I have handled.* In "The Adventure of the Speckled Band," which Watson may have chronicled as late as 1891, he tells us that he has been glancing over his notes "of the seventy odd cases in which I have during the last eight years studied the methods of my friend Sherlock Holmes." Holmes himself in 1891 speaks of "over a thousand cases" ("The Final Problem"). It is therefore apparent that there were many cases in which Watson had no opportunity to share. If *The Hound of the Baskervilles* took place before 1891, as many commentators believe, it is also apparent that at least half of Holmes' "thousand cases" were "of capital importance."

Dr Mortimer started violently. 'Followed! By whom?'
'That, unfortunately, is what I cannot tell you. Have you among your neighbours or acquaintances on Dartmoor any man with a black, full beard?'

'No—or, let me see—why, yes. Barrymore, Sir Charles's butler, is a man with a full, black beard.'

'Ha! Where is Barrymore?'

'He is in charge of the Hall.'

'We had best ascertain if he is really there, or if by any possibility he might be in London.'

'How can you do that?'

'Give me a telegraph form. "Is all ready for Sir Henry?" That will do. Address to Mr Barrymore, Baskerville Hall. Which is the nearest telegraph-office? Grimpen. Very good, we will send a second wire to the postmaster, Grimpen: "Telegram to Mr Barrymore, to be delivered into his own hand. If absent, please return wire to Sir Henry Baskerville, Northumberland Hotel." That should let us know before evening whether Barrymore is at his post in Devonshire or not.'

'That's so,' said Baskerville. 'By the way, Dr Mortimer, who is this Barrymore, anyhow?'

'He is the son of the old caretaker, who is dead. They have looked after the Hall for four generations now. So far as I know, he and his wife are as respectable a couple as any in the county.'

'At the same time,' said Baskerville, 'it's clear enough that so long as there are none of the family at the Hall these people have a mighty fine home and nothing to do.'

'That is true.'

'Did Barrymore profit at all by Sir Charles's will?' asked Holmes.

'He and his wife had five hundred pounds each.'

'Ha! Did they know that they would receive this?'

'Yes; Sir Charles was very fond of talking about the provisions of his will.'

'That is very interesting.'

'I hope,' said Dr Mortimer, 'that you do not look with suspicious eyes upon everyone who received a legacy from Sir Charles, for I also had a thousand pounds left to me.'

'Indeed! And anyone else?'

'There were many insignificant sums to individuals and a large number of public charities. The residue all went to Sir Henry.'

'And how much was the residue?'

'Seven hundred and forty thousand pounds.' **43**

Holmes raised his eyebrows in surprise. 'I had no idea that so gigantic a sum was involved,' said he.

'Sir Charles had the reputation of being rich, but we did not know how very rich he was until we came to examine his securities. The total value of the estate was close on to a million.'

'Dear me! It is a stake for which a man might well play a desperate game. And one more question, Dr Mortimer. Supposing that anything happened to our young friend here—you will forgive the unpleasant hypothesis!—who would inherit the estate?'

'Since Rodger Baskerville, Sir Charles's younger brother, died unmarried, the estate would descend to the Desmonds, who are distant cousins. James Desmond is an elderly clergyman in Westmorland.' **44**

'. . . IT'S CLEAR ENOUGH THAT SO LONG AS THERE ARE NONE OF THE FAMILY AT THE HALL THESE PEOPLE HAVE A MIGHTY FINE HOME AND NOTHING TO DO.'

A scene from the 20th Century-Fox Film production of *The Hound of the Baskervilles:* Lionel Atwill as Dr. Mortimer, Basil Rathbone as Sherlock Holmes, Nigel Bruce as Dr. Watson. Sir Henry Baskerville was played by Richard Greene, best known today for his Robin Hood on the television screen.

43 *'Seven hundred and forty thousand pounds.'* After the five hundred pounds ($2,500) each to Mr. and Mrs. Barrymore and the thousand pounds ($5,000) to Dr. Mortimer, the estate amounted to some $3,700,000 in U. S. currency at the time.

44 *Westmorland.* A largely mountainous county in the north of England, the most sparsely populated county in England. Dairy farming and cattle raising are the chief occupations.

'Thank you. These details are all of great interest. Have you met Mr James Desmond?'

'Yes; he once came down to visit Sir Charles. He is a man of venerable appearance and of saintly life. I remember that he refused to accept any settlement from Sir Charles, though he pressed it upon him.'

'And this man of simple tastes would be the heir to Sir Charles's thousands?'

'He would be the heir to the estate, because that is entailed. He would also be the heir to the money unless it were willed otherwise by the present owner, who can, of course, do what he likes with it.'

'And have you made your will, Sir Henry?'

'No, Mr Holmes, I have not. I've had no time, for it was only yesterday that I learned how matters stood. But in any case I feel that the money should go with the title and estate. That was my poor uncle's idea. How is the owner going to restore the glories of the Baskervilles if he has not money enough to keep up the property? House, land, and dollars must go together.'

'Quite so. Well, Sir Henry, I am of one mind with you as to the advisability of your going down to Devonshire without delay. There is only one provision which I must make. You certainly must not go alone.'

'Dr Mortimer returns with me.'

'But Dr Mortimer has his practice to attend to, and his house is miles away from yours. With all the good will in the world, he may be unable to help you. No, Sir Henry, you must take with you someone, a trusty man, who will be always by your side.'

'Is it possible that you could come yourself, Mr Holmes?'

'If matters came to a crisis I should endeavour to be present in person; but you can understand that, with my extensive consulting practice and with the constant appeals which reach me from many quarters, it is impossible for me to be absent from London for an indefinite time. At the present instant one of the most revered names in England is being
45 besmirched by a blackmailer, and only I can stop a disastrous scandal. You will see how impossible it is for me to go to Dartmoor.'

'Whom would you recommend, then?'

Holmes laid his hand upon my arm.

'If my friend would undertake it there is no man who is better worth having at your side when you are in a tight place. No one can say so more confidently than I.'

The proposition took me completely by surprise, but before I had time to answer Baskerville seized me by the hand and wrung it heartily.

'Well, now, that is real kind of you, Dr Watson,' said he. 'You see how it is with me, and you know just as much about the matter as I do. If you will come down to Baskerville Hall and see me through I'll never forget it.'

The promise of adventure had always a fascination for me, and I was complimented by the words of Holmes and by the eagerness with which the baronet hailed me as a companion.

'I will come with pleasure,' said I. 'I do not know how I could employ my time better.'

'And you will report very carefully to me,' said Holmes. 'When a crisis comes, as it will do, I will direct how you shall act. I suppose that by Saturday all might be ready?'

45 *one of the most revered names in England is being besmirched by a blackmailer.* As we have seen, it has been suggested that this "most revered name" was that of Albert Edward, Prince of Wales. For a pastiche of this adventure, see "The Adventure of the Two Women," by Adrian M. Conan Doyle in *The Exploits of Sherlock Holmes.*

'Would that suit Dr Watson?'

'Perfectly.'

'Then on Saturday, unless you hear to the contrary, we shall meet at the 10.30 train from Paddington.' **46**

We had risen to depart when Baskerville gave a cry of triumph, and diving into one of the corners of the room he drew a brown boot from under a cabinet.

'My missing boot!' he cried.

'May all our difficulties vanish as easily!' said Sherlock Holmes.

'But it is a very singular thing,' Dr Mortimer remarked. 'I searched this room carefully before lunch.'

'And so did I,' said Baskerville. 'Every inch of it.'

'There was certainly no boot in it then.'

'In that case the waiter must have placed it there while we were lunching.'

The German was sent for, but professed to know nothing of the matter, nor could any inquiry clear it up. Another item had been added to that constant and apparently purposeless series of small mysteries which had succeeded each other so rapidly. Setting aside the whole grim story of Sir Charles's death, we had a line of inexplicable incidents all within the limits of two days, which included the receipt of the printed letter, the black-bearded spy in the hansom, the loss of the new brown boot, the loss of the old black boot, and now the return of the new brown boot. Holmes sat in silence in the cab as we drove back to Baker Street, and I knew from his drawn brows and keen face that his mind, like my own, was busy in endeavouring to frame some scheme into which all these strange and apparently disconnected episodes could be fitted. All afternoon and late into the evening he sat lost in tobacco and thought.

Just before dinner two telegrams were handed in. The first ran:

> Have just heard that Barrymore is at the Hall.—BASKERVILLE.

The second:

> Visited twenty-three hotels as directed, but sorry to report unable to trace cut sheet of *Times*.—CARTWRIGHT.

'There go two of my threads, Watson. There is nothing more stimulating than a case where everything goes against you. We must cast round for another scent.'

'We have still the cabman who drove the spy.'

'Exactly. I have wired to get his name and address from the Official Registry. I should not be surprised if this were an answer to my question.'

The ring at the bell proved to be something even more satisfactory than an answer, however, for the door opened and a rough-looking fellow entered who was evidently the man himself.

'I got a message from the head office that a gent at this address had been inquiring for 2704,' said he. 'I've driven my cab this seven years and never a word of complaint. I came here straight from the Yard to ask you to your face what you had against me.'

'I have nothing in the world against you, my good man,' said Holmes. 'On the contrary, I have half a sovereign for you if you will give me a clear answer to my questions.'

'Well, I've had a good day and no mistake,' said the cab-

46 *the 10.30 train from Paddington.'* The terminus of the Great Western Railway, now British Railways (Western Region). Its office buildings, partly destroyed in the blitz, are 580 feet long, and the platforms under the curved roof are 700 feet long. The roofing consists of three spans, each 50 feet in width. The center span is 54 feet high, and the side divisions 46 feet. Despite its age, Paddington still invites favorable comparison with more modern railway termini. There was a 10:30 Paddington to Plymouth train in Holmes' and Watson's day, but it seems to have run only on Sundays. On Saturdays, the best train left at 12:45 P.M.

man, with a grin. 'What was it you wanted to ask, sir?'

'First of all your name and address, in case I want you again.'

47 'John Clayton, 3, Turpey Street, the Borough. My cab is out of Shipley's Yard, near Waterloo Station.'

Sherlock Holmes made a note of it.

'Now, Clayton, tell me all about the fare who came and watched this house at ten o'clock this morning and afterwards followed the two gentlemen down Regent Street.'

The man looked surprised and a little embarrassed.

'Why, there's no good my telling you things, for you seem to know as much as I do already,' said he. 'The truth is that the gentleman told me that he was a detective, and that I was to say nothing about him to anyone.'

'My good fellow, this is a very serious business, and you may find yourself in a pretty bad position if you try to hide anything from me. You say that your fare told you that he was a detective?'

'Yes, he did.'

'When did he say this?'

'When he left me.'

'Did he say anything more?'

'He mentioned his name.'

Holmes cast a swift glance of triumph at me.

'Oh, he mentioned his name, did he? That was imprudent. What was the name that he mentioned?'

'His name,' said the cabman, 'was Mr Sherlock Holmes.'

Never have I seen my friend more completely taken aback than by the cabman's reply. For an instant he sat in silent amazement. Then he burst into a hearty laugh:

'A touch, Watson—an undeniable touch!' said he. 'I feel a foil as quick and supple as my own. He got home upon me very prettily that time. So his name was Sherlock Holmes, was it?'

'Yes, sir, that was the gentleman's name.'

'Excellent! Tell me where you picked him up, and all that occurred.'

'He hailed me at half-past nine in Trafalgar Square. He
48 said that he was a detective, and he offered me two guineas if I would do exactly what he wanted all day and ask no questions. I was glad enough to agree. First we drove down to the Northumberland Hotel, and waited there until two gentlemen came out and took a cab from the rank. We followed their cab until it pulled up somewhere near here.'

'This very door,' said Holmes.

'Well, I couldn't be sure of that, but I dare say my fare knew all about it. We pulled up half-way down the street and waited an hour and a half. Then the two gentlemen passed us, walking, and we followed down Baker Street and along——'

'I know,' said Holmes.

'Until we got three-quarters down Regent Street. Then my gentleman threw up the trap, and he cried that I should drive right away to Waterloo Station as hard as I could go. I whipped up the mare, and we were there under the ten minutes. Then he paid up his two guineas, like a good one, and away he went into the station. Only just as he was leaving he turned round and said: "It might interest you to know that you have been driving Mr Sherlock Holmes." That's how I came to know the name.'

47 *the Borough.* Clayton presumably means the borough of Marylebone, in which Baker Street is located. With its long straight streets and fine vistas, Marylebone has been called a "princely parish" (Thomas H. Shepherd, *London in the Nineteenth Century*, published in 1829).

48 *two guineas.* About $10.50 U.S.

'I see. And you saw no more of him?'

'Not after he went into the station.'

'And how would you describe Mr Sherlock Holmes?'

The cabman scratched his head. 'Well, he wasn't altogether such an easy gentleman to describe. I'd put him at forty years of age, and he was of a middle height, two or three inches
shorter than you, sir. He was dressed like a toff, and he had **49**
a black beard, cut square at the end, and a pale face. I don't know as I could say more than that.'

'Colour of his eyes?'

'No, I can't say that.'

'Nothing more that you can remember?'

'No, sir; nothing.'

'Well, then, here is your half-sovereign. There's another one waiting for you if you can bring any more information. Good night!'

'Good night, sir, and thank you!'

John Clayton departed chuckling, and Holmes turned to me with a shrug of the shoulders and a rueful smile.

'Snap goes our third thread, and we end where we began,' said he. 'The cunning rascal! He knew our number, knew that Sir Henry Baskerville had consulted me, spotted who I was in Regent Street, conjectured that I had got the number of the cab and would lay my hands on the driver, and so sent back this audacious message. I tell you, Watson, this time we have got a foeman who is worthy of our steel. I've been checkmated in London. I can only wish you better luck in Devon- **50**
shire. But I'm not easy in my mind about it.'

'About what?'

'About sending you. It's an ugly business, Watson, an ugly, dangerous business, and the more I see of it the less I like it. Yes, my dear fellow, you may laugh, but I give you my word that I shall be very glad to have you back safe and sound in Baker Street once more.'

49 *a toff*. In old American slang, a dude; one who is stylishly dressed or who has a smart appearance.

50 *I've been checkmated in London.* In "The Adventure of the Retired Colourman," Holmes notes that Josiah Amberley excelled at chess—and comments, "One mark, Watson, of a scheming mind." While most Sherlockian students hold that Holmes was not himself a player, his talk is studded with terms that relate to the game. "I must plan some fresh opening move, for this gambit won't work," he says in "The Adventure of the Illustrious Client." "Check number one," he tells Watson on another occasion ("The Adventure of the Priory School") and "It is a provoking check," he says on another (*The Sign of the Four*). Most impressive of all is "The Adventure of the Blanched Soldier," which we are told *Holmes wrote himself*. Here he has Mr. Dodd say to Colonel Emsworth: "He looked up at last with the expression of one who has seen his adversary make a dangerous move at chess, and had decided how to meet it." We know that Simpson's-in-the-Strand was one of Holmes' favorite restaurants ("The Adventure of the Dying Detective," "The Adventure of the Illustrious Client") and it is worth noting here that Simpson's, in Holmes' and Watson's day, was not only a restaurant but also a chess divan, a principal gathering place in London for chessplayers, amateur and professional. It seems difficult to believe that Holmes did not indulge in an occasional game there.

6 ◆ BASKERVILLE HALL

Sir Henry Baskerville and Dr Mortimer were ready upon the
appointed day, and we started as arranged for Devonshire. **51**
Mr Sherlock Holmes drove with me to the station, and gave me his last parting injunction and advice.

'I will not bias your mind by suggesting theories or suspicions, Watson,' said he; 'I wish you simply to report facts in the fullest possible manner to me, and you can leave me to do the theorizing.'

'What sort of facts?' I asked.

'Anything which may seem to have a bearing, however indirect, upon the case, and especially the relations between young Baskerville and his neighbours, or any fresh particulars concerning the death of Sir Charles. I have made some inquiries myself in the last few days, but the results have, I fear,

51 *the appointed day*. Saturday, September 29, 1888, by our reckoning.

been negative. One thing only appears to be certain, and that is that Mr James Desmond, who is the next heir, is an elderly gentleman of a very amiable disposition, so that this persecution does not arise from him. I really think that we may eliminate him entirely from our calculations. There remain the people who will actually surround Sir Henry Baskerville upon the moor.'

'Would it not be well in the first place to get rid of this Barrymore couple?'

'By no means. You could not make a greater mistake. If they are innocent it would be a cruel injustice, and if they are guilty we should be giving up all chance of bringing it home to them. No, no, we will preserve them upon our list of suspects. Then there is a groom at the Hall, if I remember right. There are two moorland farmers. There is our friend Dr Mortimer, whom I believe to be entirely honest, and there is his wife, of whom we know nothing. There is this naturalist Stapleton, and there is his sister, who is said to be a young lady of attractions. There is Mr Frankland, of Lafter Hall, who is also an unknown factor, and there are one or two other neighbours. These are the folk who must be your very special study.'

'I will do my best.'

'You have arms, I suppose?'

'Yes, I thought it as well to take them.'

'Most certainly. Keep your revolver near you night and day, and never relax your precautions.'

Our friends had already secured a first-class carriage, and were waiting for us upon the platform.

'No, we have no news of any kind,' said Dr Mortimer, in answer to my friend's questions. 'I can swear to one thing, and that is that we have not been shadowed during the last
52 two days. We have never gone out without keeping a sharp watch, and no one could have escaped our notice.'

'You have always kept together, I presume?'

'Except yesterday afternoon. I usually give up one day to pure amusement when I come to town, so I spent it at the
53 Museum of the College of Surgeons.'

'And I went to look at the folk in the park,' said Baskerville. 'But we had no trouble of any kind.'

'It was imprudent, all the same,' said Holmes, shaking his head and looking very grave. 'I beg, Sir Henry, that you will not go about alone. Some great misfortune will befall you if you do. Did you get your other boot?'

'No, sir, it is gone for ever.'

'Indeed. That is very interesting. Well, good-bye,' he added, as the train began to glide down the platform. 'Bear in mind, Sir Henry, one of the phrases in that queer old legend which Dr Mortimer has read to us, and avoid the moor in those hours of darkness when the powers of evil are exalted.'

I looked back at the platform when we had left it far behind, and saw the tall, austere figure of Holmes standing motionless and gazing after us.

The journey was a swift and pleasant one, and I spent it in making the more intimate acquaintance of my two companions, and in playing with Dr Mortimer's spaniel. In a very few hours the brown earth had become ruddy, the brick had changed to granite, and red cows grazed in well-hedged fields where the lush grasses and more luxuriant vegetation spoke

52 *we have not been shadowed during the last two days.* As the late Dr. Ernest Bloomfield Zeisler wrote: "Sir Henry says he will leave at the end of the week; the Master instructs him to leave on Saturday, evidently the next following Saturday after the first day [of the adventure]. On the second day Sir Henry and Dr. Mortimer were shadowed. On the Saturday of departure the Master says he has made some inquiries 'in the last few days,' and Dr. Mortimer says they have 'not been shadowed during the last two days.' Since on Saturday morning they had not been shadowed the preceding two days but had been shadowed on the second day, it follows that the second day was Wednesday and the first day Tuesday.

53 *the Museum of the College of Surgeons.'* On the south side of Lincoln's Inn Fields, built in 1835. The Museum, which stood to the right of the College itself, was founded by John Hunter and "was intended to illustrate, as far as possible, the whole subject of life, by preparations of the bodies in which its phenomena are represented." One of the exhibits that might have attracted Dr. Mortimer was the skeleton of the elephant Chunee, brought to England in 1810; it stood 12 feet 4 inches high.

of a richer, if a damper climate. Young Baskerville stared eagerly out of the window, and cried aloud with delight as he recognized the familiar features of the Devon scenery.

'I've been over a good part of the world since I left it, Dr Watson,' said he; 'but I have never seen a place to compare with it.'

'I never saw a Devonshire man who did not swear by his county,' I remarked.

'It depends upon the breed of men quite as much as on the county,' said Dr Mortimer. 'A glance at our friend here reveals the rounded head of the Celt, which carries inside it the Celtic enthusiasm and power of attachment. Poor Sir Charles's head was of a very rare type, half Gaelic, half Ivernian in its characteristics. But you were very young when you last saw Baskerville Hall, were you not?'

'I was a boy in my teens at the time of my father's death, and had never seen the Hall, for he lived in a little cottage on the south coast. Thence I went straight to a friend in America I tell you it is all as new to me as it is to Dr Watson, and I'm as keen as possible to see the moor.'

'Are you? Then your wish is easily granted, for there is your first sight of the moor,' said Dr. Mortimer, pointing out of the carriage window.

Over the green squares of the fields and the low curve of a wood there rose in the distance a grey, melancholy hill, with a strange jagged summit, dim and vague in the distance, like some fantastic landscape in a dream. Baskerville sat for a long time, his eyes fixed upon it, and I read upon his eager face how much it meant to him, this first sight of that strange spot where the men of his blood had held sway so long and left their mark so deep. There he sat, with his tweed suit and his American accent, in the corner of a prosaic railway-carriage, and yet as I looked at his dark and expressive face I felt more than ever how true a descendant he was of that long line of high-blooded, fiery, and masterful men. There were pride, valour and strength in his thick brows, his sensitive nostrils, and his large hazel eyes. If on that forbidding moor a difficult and dangerous quest should lie before us, this was at least a comrade for whom one might venture to take a risk with the certainty that he would bravely share it.

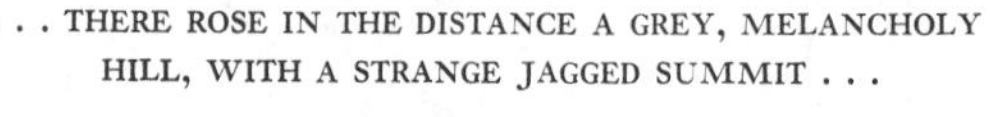
. . . THERE ROSE IN THE DISTANCE A GREY, MELANCHOLY HILL, WITH A STRANGE JAGGED SUMMIT . . .

The "grey, melancholy hill" was, we think, what many hold to be the most impressive of all the Dartmoor hills—Brent Tor, shown left in a painting by E. A. Tozer from the Reverend Sabine Baring-Gould's *A Book of Dartmoor*. But Watson is slightly deceived by the distance when he writes of its "strange and jagged summit": what he saw crowning Brent Tor was the tower of its church, St. Michael of the Rock, shown close up in the photograph below.

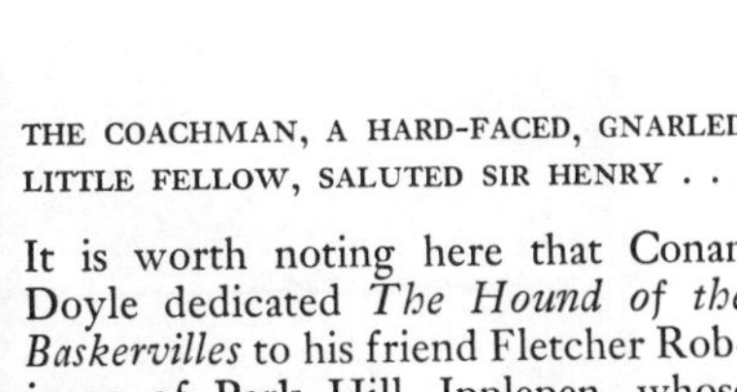

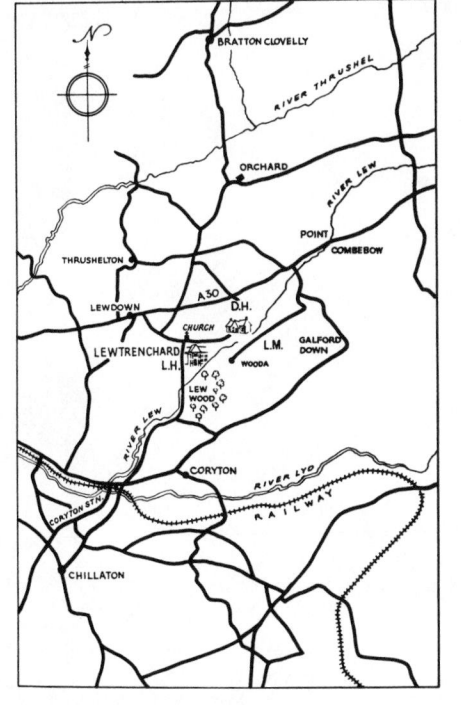

THE TRAIN PULLED UP AT A SMALL WAYSIDE STATION . . .

In his admirable article, "Always on Sunday, Watson!", Mr. William H. Gill has suggested that the station was either Brent or Ivy Bridge, both of which lie to the south of the moor (see our "very-large"-scale map of Dartmoor). Your editor would like to propose a third possibility: that Watson and his party continued along the line to Coryton Station (no longer in use, even as a "halt-on-demand"). Coryton Station, shown on the detail map above, lies on the north and west of the moor just ten miles as the crow flies from Princetown Prison.

The train pulled up at a small wayside station, and we all descended. Outside, beyond the low, white fence, a wagonette
54 with a pair of cobs was waiting. Our coming was evidently a great event, for station-master and porters clustered round us to carry out our luggage. It was a sweet, simple country spot, but I was surprised to observe that by the gate there stood two soldierly men in dark uniforms, who leaned upon their short rifles and glanced keenly at us as we passed. The coachman, a hard-faced, gnarled little fellow, saluted Sir Henry Baskerville, and in a few minutes we were flying swiftly down the broad white road. Rolling pasture lands curved upwards on either side of us, and old gabled houses peeped out from amid the thick green foliage, but behind the peaceful and sunlit countryside there rose ever, dark against the evening sky, the long, gloomy curve of the moor, broken by the jagged and sinister hills.

The wagonette swung round into a side road, and we curved upwards through deep lanes worn by centuries of wheels, high banks on either side, heavy with dripping moss and fleshy hart's-tongue ferns. Bronzing bracken and mottled bramble gleamed in the light of the sinking sun. Still steadily rising, we passed over a narrow granite bridge, and skirted a noisy stream, which gushed swiftly down, foaming and roaring amid the grey boulders. Both road and stream wound up through a valley dense with scrub oak and fir. At every turning Baskerville gave an exclamation of delight, looking eagerly about him and asking countless questions. To his eyes all seemed beautiful, but to me a tinge of melancholy lay upon the countryside, which bore so clearly the mark of the waning year. Yellow leaves carpeted the lanes and fluttered down upon us as we passed. The rattle of our wheels died away as we drove through drifts of rotting vegetation—sad gifts, as it seemed to me, for Nature to throw before the carriage of the returning heir of the Baskervilles.

'Halloa!' cried Dr Mortimer, 'what is this?'

A steep curve of heath-clad land, an outlying spur of the moor, lay in front of us. On the summit, hard and clear like an equestrian statue upon its pedestal, was a mounted soldier, dark and stern, his rifle poised ready over his forearm. He was watching the road along which we travelled.

'What is this, Perkins?' asked Dr Mortimer.

Our driver half turned in his seat.

55 'There's a convict escaped from Princetown, sir. He's been
56 out three days now, and the warders watch every road and every station, but they've had no sight of him yet. The farmers about here don't like it, sir, and that's a fact.'

THE COACHMAN, A HARD-FACED, GNARLED LITTLE FELLOW, SALUTED SIR HENRY . . .

It is worth noting here that Conan Doyle dedicated *The Hound of the Baskervilles* to his friend Fletcher Robinson of Park Hill, Ipplepen, whose *coachman*, Harry M. Baskerville, shown left, provided the name used in the adventure.

54 *a wagonette with a pair of cobs.* A wagonette was a four-wheeled carriage, open, or made with a removable cover, furnished with a seat or bench at each side facing inward and with one or two seats or benches arranged laterally in front. The "cobs" which drew it were short-legged, strong horses, usually reserved for heavy carriage work.

55 *'There's a convict escaped from Princetown, sir.* No very unusual occurrence; even today, hardly a month passes when there is not an alarm out for an escaped prisoner on the moor.

56 *He's been out three days now.* The convict must therefore have escaped on the preceding Wednesday night or early on the Thursday morning.

'Well, I understand that they get five pounds if they can give information.'

'Yes, sir, but the chance of five pounds is but a poor thing compared to the chance of having your throat cut. You see, it isn't like any ordinary convict. This is a man that would stick at nothing.'

'Who is he, then?'

'It is Selden, the Notting Hill murderer.'

I remembered the case well, for it was one in which Holmes had taken an interest on account of the peculiar ferocity of the crime and the wanton brutality which had marked all the actions of the assassin. The commutation of his death sentence had been due to some doubts as to his complete sanity, so atrocious was his conduct. Our wagonette had topped a rise and in front of us rose the huge expanse of the moor, mottled with gnarled and craggy cairns and tors. A cold wind swept down from it and set us shivering. Somewhere there, on that desolate plain, was lurking this fiendish man, hiding in a burrow like a wild beast, his heart full of malignancy against the whole race which had cast him out. It needed but this to complete the grim suggestiveness of the barren waste, the chilling wind, and the darkling sky. Even Baskerville fell silent and pulled his overcoat more closely around him.

'BASKERVILLE HALL,' SAID HE.

Illustration by Sidney Paget for the *Strand Magazine*, October, 1901.

We had left the fertile country behind and beneath us. We looked back on it now, the slanting rays of a low sun turning the streams to threads of gold and glowing on the red earth new turned by the plough and the broad tangle of the woodlands. The road in front of us grew bleaker and wilder over huge russet and olive slopes, sprinkled with giant boulders. Now and then we passed a moorland cottage, walled and roofed with stone, with no creeper to break its harsh outline. Suddenly we looked down into a cup-like depression, patched with stunted oaks and firs which had been twisted and bent by the fury of years of storm. Two high, narrow towers rose over the trees. The driver pointed with his whip.

'Baskerville Hall,' said he.

Its master had risen, and was staring with flushed cheeks and shining eyes. A few minutes later we had reached the lodge gates, a maze of fantastic tracery in wrought iron, with weather-bitten pillars on either side, blotched with lichens, and surmounted by the boars' heads of the Baskervilles. The lodge was a ruin of black granite and bared ribs of rafters, but facing it was a new building, half constructed, the first-fruit of Sir Charles's South African gold.

Through the gateway we passed into the avenue, where the wheels were again hushed amid the leaves, and the old trees shot their branches in a sombre tunnel over our heads. Baskerville shuddered as he looked up the long, dark drive to where the house glimmered like a ghost at the farther end.

'Was it here?' he asked, in a low voice.

'No, no, the Yew Alley is on the other side.'

The young heir glanced round with a gloomy face.

'It's no wonder my uncle felt as if trouble were coming on him in such a place as this,' said he. 'It's enough to scare any man. I'll have a row of electric lamps up here inside of six months, and you won't know it again with a thousand-candle power Swan and Edison right here in front of the hall door.' **57**

57 *Swan and Edison.* Sir Joseph Wilson Swan, 1828–1914, an English inventor in photography and electricity, widely known for the incandescent lamp bearing his name, and Thomas Alva Edison, 1847–1913, one of the world's greatest inventors and the holder of more than a thousand important patents; he invented the incandescent lamp in 1879. Since the Swan and Edison lamps are of two different varieties, it must be presumed that Sir Henry actually said "Swan *or* Edison."

. . . AND THE HOUSE LAY BEFORE US.

A rather thorough investigation of the halls and houses in the vicinity of Coryton Station has unhappily, to date, revealed none that might be described as having "twin towers, ancient, crenellated, and pierced with many loopholes . . ."

Until a more fitting candidate presents itself, then, let us consider the claims of Lew House (or Hall), at Lew Trenchard, near Lew Down, Devon, shown above.

It has, to begin with, "lodge gates" which are "a maze of fantastic tracery in wrought iron, with weather-bitten pillars on either side, blotched with lichens . . ." It has, in addition, an avenue opening into a broad expanse of turf, and the house itself is "a heavy block of a building from which a porch" projects. "The whole front" is "draped in ivy, with a patch clipped bare here and there where a window or a coat-of-arms" breaks "through the dark veil." It also has "heavy mullioned windows," "high chimneys" and a "steep, high-angled roof."

Note now on our detail map (*see* p. 38) that between Lew House and the moor itself is a small stand of trees called Lew Wood. *Lew* Wood, we submit, is what Watson chose to call the *Yew* Alley.

Lew House has a notable collection of paintings, including both a Kneller and a Reynolds (*see* Notes 92 and 93); some of these hang in the Long Gallery (*shown below*), which looks out over Lew Wood and on to the moor—an ideal spot for the early-morning signaling of a butler named Barrymore.

Our identification of Lew House as "Baskerville Hall" is perhaps strengthened by the fact that the coat-of-arms of the family which has owned Lew House for many generations is charged—not with *boars'* heads—but with *bears'* heads proper, muzzled and ringed or.

On the basis of the boars' heads alone, Dr. Julian Wolff has identified "Baskerville Hall" as Mount Edgcumbe in Devonshire, the family seat of the Edgcumbes, whose coat-of-arms is blazoned: Gules, on a bend erminois, between two cottises or, three boars' heads couped, argent. It is also interesting to note that the Manor House, North Bovey, was used for Baskerville Hall in Gainsborough Pictures' 1932 motion-picture version of *The Hound of the Baskervilles.*

The avenue opened into a broad expanse of turf, and the house lay before us. In the fading light I could see that the centre was a heavy block of building from which a porch projected. The whole front was draped in ivy, with a patch clipped bare here and there where a window or a coat-of-arms broke through the dark veil. From this central block rose the twin towers, ancient, crenellated, and pierced with many loopholes. To right and left of the turrets were more modern wings of black granite. A dull light shone through heavy mullioned windows, and from the high chimneys which rose from the steep, high-angled roof there sprang a single black column of smoke.

'Welcome, Sir Henry! Welcome to Baskerville Hall!'

A tall man had stepped from the shadow of the porch to open the door of the wagonette. The figure of a woman was silhouetted against the yellow light of the hall. She came out and helped the man to hand down our bags.

'You don't mind my driving straight home, Sir Henry?' said Dr Mortimer. 'My wife is expecting me.'

'Surely you will stay and have some dinner?'

'No, I must go. I shall probably find some work awaiting me. I would stay to show you over the house, but Barrymore will be a better guide than I. Good-bye, and never hesitate night or day to send for me if I can be of service.'

The wheels died away down the drive while Sir Henry and I turned into the hall, and the door clanged heavily behind us. It was a fine apartment in which we found ourselves, large, lofty, and heavily raftered with huge balks of age-blackened oak. In the great old-fashioned fireplace behind the high iron dogs a log-fire crackled and snapped. Sir Henry and I held out our hands to it, for we were numb from our long drive. Then we gazed round us at the high, thin window of old stained glass, the oak panelling, the stags' heads, the coats-of-arms upon the walls, all dim and sombre in the subdued light of the central lamp.

'It's just as I imagined it,' said Sir Henry. 'Is it not the very picture of an old family home? To think that this should be the same hall in which for five hundred years my people have lived! It strikes me solemn to think of it.'

I saw his dark face lit up with a boyish enthusiasm as he gazed about him. The light beat upon him where he stood, but long shadows trailed down the walls and hung like a black canopy above him. Barrymore had returned from taking our luggage to our rooms. He stood in front of us now with the subdued manner of a well-trained servant. He was a remarkable-looking man, tall, handsome, with a square black beard and pale distinguished features.

'Would you wish dinner to be served at once, sir?'

'Is it ready?'

'In a very few minutes, sir. You will find hot water in your rooms. My wife and I will be happy, Sir Henry, to stay with you until you have made your fresh arrangements, but you will understand that under the new conditions this house will require a considerable staff.'

'What new conditions?'

'I only meant, sir, that Sir Charles led a very retired life, and we were able to look after his wants. You would, naturally, wish to have more company, and so you will need changes in your household.'

"WELCOME, SIR HENRY! WELCOME TO BASKERVILLE HALL!"

Illustration by Sidney Paget for the *Strand Magazine*, October, 1901.

'Do you mean that your wife and you wish to leave?'

'Only when it is quite convenient to you, sir.'

'But your family have been with us for several generations, have they not? I should be sorry to begin my life here by breaking an old family connection.'

I seemed to discern some signs of emotion upon the butler's white face.

'I feel that also, sir, and so does my wife. But to tell the truth, sir, we were both very much attached to Sir Charles, and his death gave us a shock and made these surroundings very painful to us. I fear that we shall never again be easy in our minds at Baskerville Hall.'

'But what do you intend to do?'

'I have no doubt, sir, that we shall succeed in establishing ourselves in some business. Sir Charles's generosity has given us the means to do so. And now, sir, perhaps I had best show you to your rooms.'

A square balustraded gallery ran round the top of the old hall, approached by a double stair. From this central point two long corridors extended the whole length of the building, from which all the bedrooms opened. My own was in the same wing as Baskerville's and almost next door to it. These rooms appeared to be much more modern than the central part of the house, and the bright paper and numerous candles did something to remove the sombre impression which our arrival had left upon my mind.

... THE DINING-ROOM WHICH OPENED OUT OF THE HALL WAS A PLACE OF SHADOW AND GLOOM.

Illustration by Sidney Paget for the *Strand Magazine*, October, 1901.

But the dining-room which opened out of the hall was a place of shadow and gloom. It was a long chamber with a step separating the daïs where the family sat from the lower portion reserved for their dependants. At one end a minstrels' gallery overlooked it. Black beams shot across above our heads, with a smoke-darkened ceiling beyond them. With rows of flaring torches to light it up, and the colour and rude hilarity of an old-time banquet, it might have softened; but now, when two black-clothed gentlemen sat in the little circle of light thrown by a shaded lamp, one's voice became hushed and one's spirit subdued. A dim line of ancestors, in every variety of dress, from the Elizabethan knight to the buck of the Regency, stared down upon us and daunted us by their silent company. We talked little, and I for one was glad when the meal was over and we were able to retire into the modern billiard-room and smoke a cigarette.

'My word, it isn't a very cheerful place,' said Sir Henry. 'I suppose one can tone down to it, but I feel a bit out of the picture at present. I don't wonder that my uncle got a little jumpy if he lived all alone in such a house as this. However, if it suits you, we will retire early tonight, and perhaps things may seem more cheerful in the morning.'

I drew aside my curtains before I went to bed and looked
out from my window. It opened upon the grassy space which
lay in front of the hall door. Beyond, two copses of trees
58 moaned and swung in a rising wind. A half moon broke
through the rifts of racing clouds. In its cold light I saw beyond the trees a broken fringe of rocks and the long, low curve of the melancholy moor. I closed the curtain, feeling that my last impression was in keeping with the rest.

And yet it was not quite the last. I found myself weary and yet wakeful, tossing restlessly from side to side, seeking for the sleep which would not come. Far away a chiming clock

58 *A half moon.* Watson is quite correct: the moon on the night of Saturday, September 29, 1888, was just one day past the half. But Watson must have retired rather later than he recalled doing: the half-moon did not rise until 11:22 that night.

struck out the quarters of the hours, but otherwise a deathly silence lay upon the old house. And then suddenly, in the very dead of the night, there came a sound to my ears, clear, resonant, and unmistakable. It was the sob of a woman, the muffled, strangling gasp of one who is torn by an uncontrollable sorrow. I sat up in bed and listened intently. The noise could not have been far away, and was certainly in the house. For half an hour I waited with every nerve on the alert, but there came no other sound save the chiming clock and the rustle of the ivy on the wall.

7 THE STAPLETONS OF MERRIPIT HOUSE

The fresh beauty of the following morning did something to **59**
efface from our minds the grim and grey impression which had been left upon both of us by our first experience of Baskerville Hall. As Sir Henry and I sat at breakfast the sunlight flooded in through the high mullioned windows, throwing watery patches of colour from the coats-of-arms which covered them. The dark panelling glowed like bronze in the golden rays, and it was hard to realize that this was indeed the chamber which had struck such a gloom into our souls upon the evening before.

'I guess it is ourselves and not the house that we have to blame!' said the baronet. 'We were tired with our journey and chilled by our drive, so we took a grey view of the place. Now we are fresh and well, so it is all cheerful once more.'

'And yet it was not entirely a question of imagination,' I answered. 'Did you, for example, happen to hear someone, a woman I think, sobbing in the night?'

'That is curious, for I did when I was half asleep fancy that I heard something of the sort. I waited quite a time, but there was no more of it, so I concluded that it was all a dream.'

'I heard it distinctly, and I am sure that it was really the sob of a woman.'

'We must ask about this right away.'

He rang the bell and asked Barrymore whether he could account for our experience. It seemed to me that the pallid features of the butler turned a shade paler still as he listened to his master's question.

'There are only two women in the house, Sir Henry,' he answered. 'One is the scullery-maid, who sleeps in the other wing. The other is my wife, and I can answer for it that the sound could not have come from her.'

And yet he lied as he said it, for it chanced that after breakfast I met Mrs Barrymore in the long corridor with the sun full upon her face. She was a large, impassive, heavy-featured woman with a stern, set expression of mouth. But her tell-tale eyes were red and glanced at me from between swollen lids. It was she, then, who wept in the night, and if she did so her husband must know it. Yet he had taken the obvious risk of discovery in declaring that it was not so. Why had he done

59 *The fresh beauty of the following morning.* Watson later tells us that the day (Sunday, September 30, 1888) was "sunlit" but "windy." The London *Times* reported that the weather on that day was "fine and bright at our southern, south-western and central stations." The wind "blew strongly on some parts of our coasts."

. . . LEADING ME AT LAST TO A SMALL GREY HAMLET . . .

This is Widecombe-in-the-Moor, which your editor believes to have been Dr. Watson's "Grimpen."

this? And why did she weep so bitterly? Already round this pale-faced, handsome, black-bearded man there was gathering an atmosphere of mystery and of gloom. It was he who had been the first to discover the body of Sir Charles, and we had only his word for all the circumstances which led up to the old man's death. Was it possible that it was Barrymore, after all, whom we had seen in the cab in Regent Street? The beard might well have been the same. The cabman had described a somewhat shorter man, but such an impression might easily have been erroneous. How could I settle the point for ever? Obviously the first thing to do was to see the Grimpen postmaster, and find whether the test telegram had really been placed in Barrymore's own hands. Be the answer what it might, I should at least have something to report to Sherlock Holmes.

Sir Henry had numerous papers to examine after breakfast, so that the time was propitious for my excursion. It was a pleasant walk of four miles along the edge of the moor, leading me at last to a small grey hamlet, in which two larger buildings, which proved to be the inn and the house of Dr Mortimer, stood high above the rest. The postmaster, who
60 was also the village grocer, had a clear recollection of the telegram.

'Certainly, sir,' said he, 'I had the telegram delivered to Mr Barrymore exactly as directed.'

'Who delivered it?'

'My boy here. James, you delivered that telegram to Mr Barrymore at the Hall last week, did you not?'

'Yes, father, I delivered it.'

'Into his own hands?' I asked.

'Well, he was up in the loft at the time, so that I could not put it into his own hands, but I gave it into Mrs Barrymore's hands, and she promised to deliver it at once.'

'Did you see Mr Barrymore?'

'No, sir; I tell you he was in the loft.'

'If you didn't see him, how do you know he was in the loft?'

'Well, surely his own wife ought to know where he is,' said the postmaster, testily. 'Didn't he get the telegram? If there is any mistake it is for Mr Barrymore himself to complain.'

It seemed hopeless to pursue the inquiry any farther, but it was clear that in spite of Holmes's ruse we had no proof that Barrymore had not been in London all the time. Suppose that it were so—suppose that the same man had been the last who had seen Sir Charles alive, and the first to dog the new heir when he returned to England. What then? Was he the agent of others, or had he some sinister design of his own? What interest could he have in persecuting the Baskerville family? I thought of the strange warning clipped out of the leading article of *The Times*. Was that his work, or was it possibly the doing of someone who was bent upon counteracting his schemes? The only conceivable motive was that which had been suggested by Sir Henry, that if the family could be scared away a comfortable and permanent home would be secured for the Barrymores. But surely such an explanation as that would be quite inadequate to account for the deep and subtle scheming which seemed to be weaving an invisible net round
61 the young baronet. Holmes himself had said that no more complex case had come to him in all the long series of his sensational investigations. I prayed, as I walked back along

60 *The postmaster, who was also the village grocer.* Watson must have called upon the postmaster at his home rather than at his shop, since the day was a Sunday.

61 *the young baronet.* A baronet is a kind of hereditary knight, a title invented by King James I to pay for the settlement of Ulster. There are today about 1,500 of them.

the grey, lonely road, that my friend might soon be freed from his preoccupations and able to come down to take this heavy burden of responsibility from my shoulders.

Suddenly my thoughts were interrupted by the sound of running feet behind me and by a voice which called me by name. I turned, expecting to see Dr Mortimer, but to my surprise it was a stranger who was pursuing me. He was a small, slim, clean-shaven, prim-faced man, flaxen-haired and lean-jawed, between thirty and forty years of age, dressed in a grey suit and wearing a straw hat. A tin box for botanical specimens hung over his shoulder, and he carried a green butterfly-net in one of his hands.

'You will, I am sure, excuse my presumption, Dr Watson,' said he, as he came panting up to where I stood. 'Here on the moor we are homely folk, and do not wait for formal introductions. You may possibly have heard my name from our
mutual friend, Mortimer. I am Stapleton, of Merripit House.' **62**

'Your net and box would have told me as much,' said I, 'for I knew that Mr Stapleton was a naturalist. But how did you know me?'

'I have been calling on Mortimer, and he pointed you out to me from the window of his surgery as you passed. As our road lay the same way, I thought that I would overtake you and introduce myself. I trust that Sir Henry is none the worse for his journey?'

'He is very well, thank you.'

'We were all rather afraid that after the sad death of Sir Charles the new baronet might refuse to live here. It is asking much of a wealthy man to come down and bury himself in a place of this kind, but I need not tell you that it means a very great deal to the countryside. Sir Henry has, I suppose, no superstitious fears in the matter?'

'I do not think that it is likely.'

'Of course you know the legend of the fiend dog which haunts the family?'

'I have heard it.'

'It is extraordinary how credulous the peasants are about here! Any number of them are ready to swear that they have seen such a creature upon the moor.' He spoke with a smile, but I seemed to read in his eyes that he took the matter more seriously. 'The story took a great hold upon the imagination of Sir Charles, and I have no doubt that it led to his tragic end.'

'But how?'

'His nerves were so worked up that the appearance of any dog might have had a fatal effect upon his diseased heart. I fancy that he really did see something of the kind upon that last night in the Yew Alley. I feared that some disaster might occur, for I was very fond of the old man, and I knew that his heart was weak.'

'How did you know that?'

'My friend Mortimer told me.'

'You think, then, that some dog pursued Sir Charles, and that he died of fright in consequence?'

'Have you any better explanation?'

'I have not come to any conclusion.'

'Has Mr Sherlock Holmes?'

The words took away my breath for an instant, but a glance at the placid face and steadfast eyes of my companion showed

62 *Merripit House.*' A glance at our "very-large"-scale map will show Merripit, in the heart of the moor.

that no surprise was intended.

'It is useless for us to pretend that we do not know you, Dr Watson,' said he. 'The records of your detective have
63 reached us here, and you could not celebrate him without being known yourself. When Mortimer told me your name he could not deny your identity. If you are here, then it follows that Mr Sherlock Holmes is interesting himself in the matter, and I am naturally curious to know what view he may take.'

'I am afraid that I cannot answer that question.'

'May I ask if he is going to honour us with a visit himself?'

'He cannot leave town at present. He has other cases which engage his attention.'

'What a pity! He might throw some light on that which is so dark to us. But as to your own researches, if there is any possible way in which I can be of service to you, I trust that you will command me. If I had any indication of the nature of your suspicions, or how you propose to investigate the case, I might perhaps even now give you some aid or advice.'

'I assure you that I am simply here upon a visit to my friend Sir Henry, and that I need no help of any kind.'

'Excellent!' said Stapleton. 'You are perfectly right to be wary and discreet. I am justly reproved for what I feel was an unjustifiable intrusion, and I promise you that I will not mention the matter again.'

We had come to a point where a narrow grassy path struck off from the road and wound away across the moor. A steep, boulder-sprinkled hill lay upon the right which had in bygone days been cut into a granite quarry. The face which was turned towards us formed a dark cliff, with ferns and brambles growing in its niches. From over a distant rise there floated a grey plume of smoke.

'A moderate walk along this moor-path brings us to Merripit House,' said he. 'Perhaps you will spare an hour that I may have the pleasure of introducing you to my sister.'

My first thought was that I should be by Sir Henry's side. But then I remembered the pile of papers and bills with which his study table was littered. It was certain that I could not help him with those. And Holmes had expressly said that I should study the neighbours upon the moor. I accepted Stapleton's invitation, and we turned together down the path.

'It is a wonderful place, the moor,' said he, looking round over the undulating downs, long green rollers, with crests of jagged granite foaming up into fantastic surges. 'You never tire of the moor. You cannot think the wonderful secrets which it contains. It is so vast, and so barren, and so mysterious.'

'You know it well, then?'

'I have only been here two years. The residents would call me a new-comer. We came shortly after Sir Charles settled. But my tastes led me to explore every part of the country round, and I should think that there are few men who know it better than I do.'

'Is it so hard to know?'

'Very hard. You see, for example, this great plain to the north here, with the queer hills breaking out of it. Do you observe anything remarkable about that?'

'It would be a rare place for a gallop.'

63 *'The records of your detective have reached us here.* It would seem, as we have noted, that the adventure can have taken place no earlier than 1888, by reason of Stapleton's clear reference to Watson's published writings. But this view has been challenged by Mr. Peter A. Ruber, who writes ("On a Defense of H. W. Bell"): ". . . Stapleton does not refer to having read Watson's chronicles. Holmes' famous career would hardly have escaped the notice of the newspapers, no matter how many times he gave credit to Lestrade or Gregson and the rest of the minions of Scotland Yard. During these years Holmes surely would have been without problems had it not been for the . . . publicity that spread his fame world-wide."

'You would naturally think so, and the thought has cost folk their lives before now. You notice those bright green spots scattered thickly over it?'

'Yes, they seem more fertile than the rest.'

Stapleton laughed. 'That is the great Grimpen Mire,' said he. 'A false step yonder means death to man or beast. Only yesterday I saw one of the moor ponies wander into it. He never came out. I saw his head for quite a long time craning out of the bog-hole, but it sucked him down at last. Even in dry seasons it is a danger to cross it, but after these autumn rains it is an awful place. And yet I can find my way to the very heart of it and return alive. By George, there is another of those miserable ponies!'

Something brown was rolling and tossing among the green sedges. Then a long, agonized, writhing neck shot upwards and a dreadful cry echoed over the moor. It turned me cold with horror, but my companion's nerves seemed to be stronger than mine.

'It's gone!' said he. 'The Mire has him. Two in two days, and many more, perhaps, for they get in the way of going there in the dry weather, and never know the difference until the Mire has them in its clutch. It's a bad place, the great Grimpen Mire.'

'And you say you can penetrate it?'

'Yes, there are one or two paths which a very active man can take. I have found them out.'

'But why should you wish to go into so horrible a place?'

'Well, you see the hills beyond? They are really islands cut off on all sides by the impassable Mire, which has crawled round them in the course of years. That is where the rare plants and the butterflies are, if you have the wit to reach them.'

'I shall try my luck some day.'

He looked at me with a surprised face. 'For God's sake put such an idea out of your mind,' said he. 'Your blood would be upon my head. I assure you that there would not be the least chance of your coming back alive. It is only by remembering certain complex landmarks that I am able to do it.'

'Halloa!' I cried. 'What is that?'

A long, low moan, indescribably sad, swept over the moor. It filled the whole air, and yet it was impossible to say whence it same. From a dull murmur it swelled into a deep roar and then sank back into a melancholy, throbbing murmur once again. Stapleton looked at me with a curious expression in his face.

'Queer place, the moor!' said he.

'But what is it?'

'The peasants say it is the Hound of the Baskervilles calling for its prey. I've heard it once or twice before, but never quite so loud.'

I looked round, with a chill of fear in my heart, at the huge swelling plain, mottled with the green patches of rushes. Nothing stirred over the vast expanse save a pair of ravens, which croaked loudly from a tor behind us.

'You are an educated man. You don't believe such nonsense as that?' said I. 'What do you think is the cause of so strange a sound?'

'Bogs make queer noises sometimes. It's the mud settling, or the water rising, or something.'

'THAT IS THE GREAT GRIMPEN MIRE,' SAID HE.

As is well known, Watson's "Great Grimpen Mire" is *Grimspound Bog*, three miles to the north and west of Widecombe-in-the-Moor, shown above in a photograph by C. E. Robinson from the Reverend Sabine Baring-Gould's *A Book of Dartmoor*. The trifling change of name here is a nice example of Watson's Victorian primness, for as Mr. Michael Harrison has reminded us (in *In the Footsteps of Sherlock Holmes*) the word "bog" is British schoolboy slang for "latrine."

'No, no, that was a living voice.'

'Well, perhaps it was. Did you ever hear a bittern booming?'

'No, I never did.'

'It's a very rare bird—practically extinct—in England now, but all things are possible upon the moor. Yes, I should not be surprised to learn that what we have heard is the cry of
64 the last of the bitterns.'

'It's the weirdest, strangest thing that ever I heard in my life.'

'Yes, it's rather an uncanny place altogether. Look at the hillside yonder. What do you make of those?'

The whole steep slope was covered with grey circular rings of stone, a score of them at least.

'What are they? Sheep-pens?'

'No, they are the homes of our worthy ancestors. Prehistoric
65 man lived thickly on the moor, and as no one in particular has lived there since, we find all his little arrangements exactly as he left them. These are his wigwams with the roofs off. You can even see his hearth and his couch if you have the curiosity to go inside.'

'But it is quite a town. When was it inhabited?'

'Neolithic man—no date.'

'What did he do?'

'He grazed his cattle on these slopes, and he learned to dig for tin when the bronze sword began to supersede the stone axe. Look at the great trench in the opposite hill. That is his mark. Yes, you will find some very singular points about the moor, Dr Watson. Oh, excuse me an instant. It is surely
66 Cyclopides.'

A small fly or moth had fluttered across our path, and in an instant Stapleton was rushing with extraordinary energy and speed in pursuit of it. To my dismay the creature flew straight for the great Mire, but my acquaintance never paused for an instant, bounding from tuft to tuft behind it, his green net waving in the air. His grey clothes and jerky, zigzag, irregular progress made him not unlike some huge moth himself. I was standing watching his pursuit with a mixture of admiration for his extraordinary activity and fear lest he should lose his footing in the treacherous Mire, when I heard the sound of steps, and, turning round, found a woman near me upon the path. She had come from the direction in which the plume of smoke indicated the position of Merripit House, but the dip of the moor had hid her until she was quite close.

I could not doubt that this was the Miss Stapleton of whom I had been told, since ladies of any sort must be few upon the moor, and I remembered that I had heard someone describe her as being a beauty. The woman who approached me was certainly that, and of a most uncommon type. There could not have been a greater contrast between brother and sister, for Stapleton was neutral-tinted, with light hair and grey eyes, while she was darker than any brunette whom I have seen in England—slim, elegant and tall. She had a proud, finely cut face, so regular that it might have seemed impassive were it not for the sensitive mouth and the beautiful dark, eager eyes. With her perfect figure and elegant dress she was, indeed, a strange apparition upon a lonely moorland path. Her eyes were on her brother as I turned, and then she quickened her pace towards me. I had raised

64 *the last of the bitterns.'* "Stapleton ascribes the sound to a bittern—after having ascertained that Dr. Watson was not familiar with the bittern (*Botaurus stellaris*), as indeed he was not," Miss Lisa McGaw wrote in "Some Trifling Notes on Sherlock Holmes and Ornithology." "The bittern is a bird of the marsh, not the moor, and though all things are possible on the moor, the chance of a bittern booming in an alien locale at that precise moment is almost as negligible as was the bittern population in England at that time. Formerly abundant in Norfolk and Lincolnshire, the bittern nearly became extinct."

65 *Prehistoric man lived thickly on the moor.* This is quite true. Near Hound Tor, for example, not far from Grimspound, there is almost a metropolis of Neolithic huts which may be visited to this day.

66 *It is surely Cyclopides.'* Cyclopides, as the editors of the Catalogue of the Sherlock Holmes Exhibition have shown, is no longer valid as a generic name; it was created in 1819 by Hübner for five species, only one of which is British. This is the butterfly now known as the Chequered Skipper. "However, [Stapleton's] statement 'He is very rare' is, for Dartmoor, a considerable understatement; for it would have been the first and only record for that part of England. . . . It is nevertheless likely that the butterfly in question was one of the group (*Hesperiidae*) known as the Skippers. They all have a distinctive darting and rapid flight, and Watson's 'a small fly or moth' is very suggestive, since this group of butterflies is primitive and approaches the moths in a number of respects." Two Skippers which are known in Devon, but not on the moor, are the Lulworth Skipper and the Silver-spotted Skipper; of the remaining Skippers (the Dingy Skipper, the Grizzled Skipper, the Small Skipper and the Large Skipper), all are known on the moor, but none of them are "very rare" and it would be very seldom indeed that any of them would be found so late in the year.

my hat, and was about to make some explanatory remark, when her own words turned all my thoughts into a new channel.

'Go back!' she said. 'Go straight back to London, instantly.'

I could only stare at her in stupid surprise. Her eyes blazed at me, and she tapped the ground impatiently with her foot.

'Why should I go back?' I asked.

'I cannot explain.' She spoke in a low, eager voice, with a curious lisp in her utterance. 'But for God's sake do what I ask you. Go back, and never set foot upon the moor again.'

'But I have only just come.'

'Man, man!' she cried. 'Can you not tell when a warning is for your own good? Go back to London! Start tonight! Get away from this place at all costs! Hush, my brother is coming! Not a word of what I have said. Would you mind getting that
orchid for me among the mare's-tails yonder? We are very **67**
rich in orchids on the moor, though, of course, you are rather late to see the beauties of the place.'

Stapleton had abandoned the chase, and came back to us breathing hard and flushed with his exertions.

'Halloa, Beryl!' said he, and it seemed to me that the tone of his greeting was not altogether a cordial one.

'Well, Jack, you are very hot.'

'Yes, I was chasing a Cyclopides. He is very rare, and seldom found in the late autumn. What a pity that I should have missed him!'

He spoke unconcernedly, but his small light eyes glanced incessantly from the girl to me.

'You have introduced yourselves, I can see.'

'Yes. I was telling Sir Henry that it was rather late for him to see the true beauties of the moor.'

'Why, who do you think this is?'

'I imagine that it must be Sir Henry Baskerville.'

'No, no,' said I. 'Only a humble commoner, but his friend. My name is Dr Watson.'

A flush of vexation passed over her expressive face.

'We have been talking at cross purposes,' said she.

'Why, you had not very much time for talk,' her brother remarked, with the same questioning eyes.

'I talked as if Dr Watson were a resident instead of being merely a visitor,' said she. 'It cannot much matter to him whether it is early or late for the orchids. But you will come on, will you not, and see Merripit House?'

A short walk brought us to it, a bleak moorland house, once the farm of some grazier in the old prosperous days, but now put into repair and turned into a modern dwelling. An orchard surrounded it, but the trees, as is usual upon the moor, were stunted and nipped, and the effect of the whole place was mean and melancholy. We were admitted by a strange, wizened, rusty-coated old manservant, who seemed in keeping with the house. Inside, however, there were large rooms furnished with an elegance in which I seemed to recognize the taste of the lady. As I looked from their windows at the interminable granite-flecked moor rolling unbroken to the farthest horizon I could not but marvel at what could have brought this highly educated man and this beautiful woman to live in such a place.

'Queer spot to choose, is it not?' said he, as if in answer to my thought. 'And yet we manage to make ourselves fairly

67 *that orchid.* What was the orchid? The first difficulty is the lateness of the season, a time of year when few if any orchids would be in flower. The second difficulty is Miss Stapleton's statement that the orchid grew among mare's-tails (*Hippuris vulgaris L.*), which appear to be unknown on Dartmoor. It is probable that the plant referred to by Miss Stapleton was not the mare's-tail but the marsh horsetail (*Equisetum palustre*). Taking these difficulties into consideration, the editors of the Catalogue of the Sherlock Holmes Exhibition cast their vote for *Spiranthes spiralis* (*L.*) *Koch* (Ladies' tresses); it grows on Dartmoor, flowers from September to October, but would *not* be a plant of wet places that would be growing among either mare's-tail or horsetail. On the other hand, Mr. R. F. May, taking into consideration the same difficulties in his essay "*The Hound of the Baskervilles:* A Botanical Enquiry," felt that the orchid might well have been the Marsh Spotted Orchid (*Dacrylorchis maculata* subspecies *ericetorum*). "This orchid grows in damp acid peaty soil and in spongy marshes and is widely established in suitable places all over Britain. This plant has been seen in flower occasionally as late as the second half of September . . ."

68 *mechanical and uninteresting.* ". . . the . . . statement is nonsensical," Mr. Frederick Bryan-Brown wrote in "Sherlockian Schools and Schoolmasters," "as how, if he really felt it a privilege to mould the young minds, could he find the work mechanical and uninteresting? Frustrating? Yes. Exasperating? Often. Infuriating? Sometimes, but never mechanical and uninteresting."

happy, do we not, Beryl?'

'Quite happy,' said she, but there was no ring of conviction in her words.

'I had a school,' said Stapleton. 'It was in the North country. The work to a man of my temperament was mechani-
68 cal and uninteresting, but the privilege of living with youth, of helping to mould those young minds and of impressing them with one's own character and ideals, was very dear to me. However, the fates were against us. A serious epidemic broke out in the school, and three of the boys died. It never recovered from the blow, and much of my capital was irretrievably swallowed up. And yet, if it were not for the loss of the charming companionship of the boys, I could rejoice over my own misfortune, for, with my strong tastes for botany and zoology, I find an unlimited field of work here, and my sister is as devoted to Nature as I am. All this, Dr Watson, has been brought upon your head by your expression as you surveyed the moor out of our window.'

'It certainly did cross my mind that it might be a little dull —less for you, perhaps, than for your sister.'

'No, no, I am never dull,' said she, quickly.

'We have books, we have our studies, and we have interesting neighbours. Dr Mortimer is a most learned man in his own line. Poor Sir Charles was also an admirable companion. We knew him well, and miss him more than I can tell. Do you think that I should intrude if I were to call this afternoon and make the acquaintance of Sir Henry?'

'I am sure that he would be delighted.'

'Then perhaps you would mention that I propose to do so. We may in our humble way do something to make things more easy for him until he becomes accustomed to his new surroundings. Will you come upstairs, Dr Watson, and inspect my collection of Lepidoptera? I think it is the most complete one in the south-west of England. By the time that you have looked through them lunch will be almost ready.'

But I was eager to get back to my charge. The melancholy of the moor, the death of the unfortunate pony, the weird sound which had been associated with the grim legend of the Baskervilles—all these things tinged my thoughts with sadness. Then on the top of these more or less vague impressions there had come the definite and distinct warning of Miss Stapleton, delivered with such intense earnestness that I could not doubt that some grave and deep reason lay behind it. I resisted all pressure to stay for lunch, and I set off at once upon my return journey, taking the grass-grown path by which we had come.

It seems, however, that there must have been some short cut for those who knew it, for before I had reached the road I was astounded to see Miss Stapleton sitting upon a rock by the side of the track. Her face was beautifully flushed with her exertions, and she held her hand to her side.

'I have run all the way in order to cut you off, Dr Watson,' said she. 'I had not even time to put on my hat. I must not stop, or my brother may miss me. I wanted to say to you how sorry I am about the stupid mistake I made in thinking that you were Sir Henry. Please forget the words I said, which have no application whatever to you.'

'But I can't forget them, Miss Stapleton,' said I. 'I am Sir Henry's friend, and his welfare is a very close concern of mine.

Tell me why it was that you were so eager that Sir Henry should return to London.'

'A woman's whim, Dr Watson. When you know me better you will understand that I cannot always give reasons for what I say or do.'

'No, no. I remember the thrill in your voice. I remember the look in your eyes. Please, please, be frank with me, Miss Stapleton, for ever since I have been here I have been conscious of shadows all round me. Life has become like that great Grimpen Mire, with little green patches everywhere into which one may sink and with no guide to point the track. Tell me, then, what it was that you meant, and I will promise to convey your warning to Sir Henry.'

An expression of irresolution passed for an instant over her face, but her eyes had hardened again when she answered me.

'You make too much of it, Dr Watson,' said she. 'My brother and I were very much shocked by the death of Sir Charles. We knew him very intimately, for his favourite walk was over the moor to our house. He was deeply impressed with the curse which hung over his family, and when this tragedy came I naturally felt that there must be some grounds for the fears he had expressed. I was distressed, therefore, when another member of the family came down to live here, and I felt that he should be warned of the danger which he will run. That was all which I intended to convey.'

'But what is the danger?'

'You know the story of the hound?'

'I do not believe in such nonsense.'

'But I do. If you have any influence with Sir Henry, take him away from a place which has always been fatal to his family. The world is wide. Why should he wish to live at the place of danger?'

'Because it *is* the place of danger. That is Sir Henry's nature. I fear that unless you can give me some more definite information than this it would be impossible to get him to move.'

'I cannot say anything definite, for I do not know anything definite.'

'I would ask you one more question, Miss Stapleton. If you meant no more than this when you first spoke to me, why should you not wish your brother to overhear what you said? There is nothing to which he, or anyone else, could object.'

'My brother is very anxious to have the Hall inhabited, for he thinks that it is for the good of the poor folk upon the moor. He would be very angry if he knew that I had said anything which might induce Sir Henry to go away. But I have done my duty now, and I will say no more. I must get back, or he will miss me and suspect that I have seen you. Good-bye!'

She turned, and had disappeared in a few minutes among the scattered boulders, while I, with my soul full of vague fears, pursued my way to Baskerville Hall.

'YOU KNOW THE STORY OF THE HOUND?'

Illustration by Sidney Paget for the *Strand Magazine*, November, 1901.

8 FIRST REPORT OF DR WATSON

From this point onwards I will follow the course of events by transcribing my own letters to Mr Sherlock Holmes which
69 lie before me on the table. One page is missing, but otherwise they are exactly as written, and show my feelings and suspicions of the moment more accurately than my memory, clear as it is upon these tragic events, can possibly do.

70 BASKERVILLE HALL, *Oct. 13th.*

My dear Holmes,

My previous letters and telegrams have kept you pretty well up-to-date as to all that has occurred in this most God-forsaken corner of the world. The longer one stays here the more does the spirit of the moor sink into one's soul, its vastness, and also its grim charm. When you are once out upon its bosom you have left all traces of modern England behind you, but on the other hand you are conscious everywhere of the homes and the work of the prehistoric people. On all sides of you as you walk are the houses of these forgotten folk, with their graves and the huge monoliths which are supposed to have marked their temples. As you look at their grey stone huts against the scarred hillsides you leave your own age behind you, and if you were to see a skin-clad, hairy man crawl out from the low door, fitting a flint-tipped arrow on to the string of his bow, you would feel that his presence there was more natural than your own. The strange thing is that they should have lived so thickly on what must always have been most unfruitful soil. I am no antiquarian, but I could imagine that they were some unwarlike and harried race who were forced to accept that which none other would occupy.

All this, however, is foreign to the mission on which you sent me, and will probably be very uninteresting to your severely practical mind. I can still remember your complete indifference as to whether the sun moved round the earth or the earth round the sun. Let me, therefore, return to the facts concerning Sir Henry Baskerville.

If you have not had any report within the last few days it is because up till today there was nothing of importance to relate. Then a very surprising circumstance occurred, which I shall tell you in due course. But, first of all, I must keep you in touch with some of the other factors in the situation.

One of these, concerning which I have said little, is the escaped convict upon the moor. There is strong reason now to believe that he has got right away, which is a considerable relief to the lonely householders of this district. A fortnight
71 has passed since his flight, during which he has not been seen and nothing has been heard of him. It is surely inconceivable that he could have held out upon the moor during all that time. Of course, so far as his concealment goes there is no difficulty at all. Any one of these stone huts would give him a hiding-place. But there is nothing to eat unless he were to catch and slaughter one of the moor sheep. We think, therefore, that he has gone, and the outlying farmers sleep the better in consequence.

We are four able-bodied men in this household, so that we could take good care of ourselves, but I confess that I have

69 *One page is missing.* Why should a page be missing? Holmes was not careless with Watson's correspondence, we may be sure. The statement is particularly curious because the two letters, as reproduced, seem to be complete.

70 Oct. *13*th. A Saturday in our year, 1888.

71 *A fortnight has passed since his flight.* Since Selden escaped on the night of Wednesday, September 26th, or the morning of Thursday, September 27th, a fortnight had *not* passed since his flight. But Watson undoubtedly means that a fortnight had passed since he, Watson, *heard* on Saturday, September 29th, that Selden had escaped.

had uneasy moments when I have thought of the Stapletons. They live miles from any help. There are one maid, an old manservant, the sister and the brother, the latter not a very strong man. They would be helpless in the hands of a desperate fellow like this Notting Hill criminal, if he could once effect an entrance. Both Sir Henry and I were concerned at their situation, and it was suggested that Perkins the groom should go over to sleep there, but Stapleton would not hear of it.

The fact is that our friend the baronet begins to display a considerable interest in our fair neighbour. It is not to be wondered at, for time hangs heavily in this lonely spot to an active man like him, and she is a very fascinating and beautiful woman. There is something tropical and exotic about her which forms a singular contrast to her cool and unemotional brother. Yet he also gives the idea of hidden fires. He has certainly a very marked influence over her, for I have seen her continually glance at him as she talked as if seeking approbation for what she said. I trust that he is kind to her. There is a dry glitter in his eyes, and a firm set of his thin lips, which go with a positive and possibly a harsh nature. You would find him an interesting study.

He came over to call upon Baskerville on that first day, and the very next morning he took us both to show us the spot where the legend of the wicked Hugo is supposed to have had its origin. It was an excursion of some miles across the moor to a place which is so dismal that it might have suggested the story. We found a short valley between rugged tors which led to an open, grassy space flecked over with the white cotton grass. In the middle of it rose two great stones, worn and sharpened at the upper end, until they looked like the huge, corroding fangs of some monstrous beast. In every way it corresponded with the scene of the old tragedy. Sir Henry was much interested, and asked Stapleton more than once whether he did really believe in the possibility of the interference of the supernatural in the affairs of men. He spoke lightly, but it was evident that he was very much in earnest. Stapleton was guarded in his replies, but it was easy to see that he said less than he might, and that he would not express his whole opinion out of consideration for the feelings of the baronet. He told us of similar cases, where families had suffered from some evil influence, and he left us with the impression that he shared the popular view upon the matter.

On our way back we stayed for lunch at Merripit House, and it was there that Sir Henry made the acquaintance of Miss Stapleton. From the first moment that he saw her he appeared to be strongly attracted by her, and I am much mistaken if the feeling was not mutual. He referred to her again and again on our walk home, and since then hardly a day has passed that we have not seen something of the brother and sister. They dine here tonight, and there is some talk of our going to them next week. One would imagine that such a **72** match would be very welcome to Stapleton, and yet I have more than once caught a look of the strongest disapprobation in his face when Sir Henry has been paying some attention to his sister. He is much attached to her, no doubt, and would lead a lonely life without her, but it would seem the height of selfishness, if he were to stand in the way of her making

. . . THE SPOT WHERE THE LEGEND OF THE WICKED HUGO IS SUPPOSED TO HAVE HAD ITS ORIGIN.

Hound Tor, as seen in a painting by E. A. Tozer, from the Reverend Sabine Baring-Gould's *A Book of Dartmoor*. In fact, there are *two* Hound Tors on the moor—not to mention a *Greathound* Tor.

72 *there is some talk of our going to them next week.* Watson later writes: "We are to dine at Merripit House next Friday" and his letters to Holmes and his diary datings make clear that this was Friday, the 19th. Between 1881 (when Holmes and Watson met) and 1901 (when *The Hound of the Baskervilles* was first published) there are only four years in which October 19th fell on a Friday: 1883 (too early), 1888, 1894, and 1900 (too late). Our choice therefore lies between 1888 and 1894, and your editor submits that the evidence is heavily in favor of 1888.

so brilliant a marriage. Yet I am certain that he does not wish their intimacy to ripen into love, and I have several times observed that he has taken pains to prevent them from being
73 *tête-à-tête*. By the way, your instructions to me never to allow Sir Henry to go out alone will become very much more onerous if a love-affair were to be added to our other difficulties. My popularity would soon suffer if I were to carry out your orders to the letter.

74 The other day—Thursday, to be more exact—Dr Mortimer lunched with us. He has been excavating a barrow at Long Down, and has got a prehistoric skull which fills him with great joy. Never was there such a single-minded enthusiast as he! The Stapletons came in afterwards, and the good doctor took us all to the Yew Alley, at Sir Henry's request, to show us exactly how everything occurred upon that fatal night. It is a long, dismal walk, the Yew Alley, between two high walls of clipped hedge, with a narrow band of grass upon either side. At the far end is an old, tumble-down summer-house. Half-way down is the moor-gate where the old gentleman left his cigar-ash. It is a white wooden gate with a latch. Beyond it lies the wide moor. I remembered your theory of the affair and tried to picture all that had occurred. As the old man stood there he saw something coming across the moor, something which terrified him so that he lost his wits, and ran and ran until he died of sheer horror and exhaustion. There was the long, gloomy tunnel down which he fled. And from what? A sheep-dog of the moor? Or a spectral hound, black, silent, and monstrous? Was there a human agency in the matter? Did the pale, watchful Barrymore know more than he cared to say? It was all dim and vague, but always there is the dark shadow of crime behind it.

One other neighbour I have met since I wrote last. This is Mr Frankland, of Lafter Hall, who lives some four miles to the south of us. He is an elderly man, red-faced, white-haired, and choleric. His passion is for the British law, and he has spent a large fortune in litigation. He fights for the mere pleasure of fighting, and is equally ready to take up either side of a question, so that it is no wonder that he has found it a costly amusement. Sometimes he will shut up a right of way and defy the parish to make him open it. At others he will with his own hands tear down some other man's gate and declare that a path has existed there from time immemorial, defying the owner to prosecute him for trespass. He is learned in old manorial and communal rights, and he applies his knowledge sometimes in favour of the villagers
75 of Fernworthy and sometimes against them, so that he is periodically either carried in triumph down the village street or else burned in effigy, according to his latest exploit. He is said to have about seven law-suits upon his hands at present, which will probably swallow up the remainder of his fortune, and so draw his sting and leave him harmless for the future. Apart from the law he seems a kindly, good-natured person, and I only mention him because you were particular that I should send some description of the people who surround us. He is curiously employed at present, for, being an amateur astronomer, he has an excellent telescope, with which he lies upon the roof of his own house and sweeps the moor all day in the hope of catching a glimpse of the escaped convict. If he would confine his energies to this all would be well, but

73 tête-à-tête. French: in private talk; face to face.

74 *Thursday, to be more exact*. Watson refers to Thursday, October 11th.

75 *the villagers of Fernworthy*. There is no *village* of Fernworthy on the map of Dartmoor, but there was, and is, a substantial *farming district* of that very name only three miles from Lew House.

there are rumours that he intends to prosecute Dr Mortimer for opening a grave without the consent of the next-of-kin, because he dug up the neolithic skull in the barrow on Long Down. He helps to keep our lives from being monotonous, and gives a little comic relief where it is badly needed.

And now, having brought you up-to-date in the escaped convict, the Stapletons, Dr Mortimer, and Frankland, of Lafter Hall, let me end on that which is most important, and tell you more about the Barrymores, and especially about the surprising development of last night.

First of all about the test telegram, which you sent from London in order to make sure that Barrymore was really here. I have already explained that the testimony of the postmaster shows that the test was worthless and that we have no proof one way or the other. I told Sir Henry how the matter stood, and he at once, in his downright fashion, had Barrymore up and asked him whether he had received the telegram himself. Barrymore said that he had.

'Did the boy deliver it into your own hands?' asked Sir Henry.

Barrymore looked surprised, and considered for a little time.

'No,' said he, 'I was in the box-room at the time, and my wife brought it up to me.'

'Did you answer it yourself?'

'No; I told my wife what to answer, and she went down to write it.'

In the evening he recurred to the subject of his own accord.

'I could not quite understand the object of your questions this morning, Sir Henry,' said he. 'I trust that they do not mean that I have done anything to forfeit your confidence?'

Sir Henry had to assure him that it was not so and pacify him by giving him a considerable part of his old wardrobe, the London outfit having now all arrived.

Mrs Barrymore is of interest to me. She is a heavy, solid person, very limited, intensely respectable, and inclined to be puritanical. You could hardly conceive a less emotional subject. Yet I have told you how, on the first night here, I heard her sobbing bitterly, and since then I have more than once observed traces of tears upon her face. Some deep sorrow gnaws ever at her heart. Sometimes I wonder if she has a guilty memory which haunts her, and sometimes I suspect Barrymore of being a domestic tyrant. I have always felt that there was something singular and questionable in this man's character, but the adventure of last night brings all my suspicions to a head.

And yet it may seem a small matter in itself. You are aware that I am not a very sound sleeper, and since I have been on guard in this house my slumbers have been lighter than ever. Last night, about two in the morning, I was aroused by a stealthy step passing my room. I rose, opened my door, and peeped out. A long black shadow was trailing down the corridor. It was thrown by a man who walked softly down the passage with a candle held in his hand. He was in shirt and trousers, with no covering to his feet. I could merely see the outline, but his height told me that it was Barrymore. He walked very slowly and circumspectly, and there was something indescribably guilty and furtive in his whole appearance.

I have told you that the corridor is broken by the balcony which runs round the hall, but that it is resumed upon the farther side. I waited until he had passed out of sight, and then I followed him. When I came round the balcony he had reached the end of the farther corridor, and I could see from the glimmer of light through an open door that he had entered one of the rooms. Now, all these rooms are unfurnished and unoccupied, so that his expedition became more mysterious than ever. The light shone steadily, as if he were standing motionless. I crept down the passage as noiselessly as I could and peeped round the corner of the door.

Barrymore was crouching at the window with the candle held against the glass. His profile was half turned towards me, and his face seemed to be rigid with expectation as he stared out into the blackness of the moor. For some minutes he stood watching intently. Then he gave a deep groan, and with an impatient gesture he put out the light. Instantly, I made my way back to my room, and very shortly came the stealthy steps passing once more upon their return journey. Long afterwards when I had fallen into a light sleep I heard a key turn somewhere in a lock, but I could not tell whence the sound came. What it all means I cannot guess, but there is some secret business going on in this house of gloom which sooner or later we shall get to the bottom of. I do not trouble you with my theories, for you asked me to furnish you only with facts. I have had a long talk with Sir Henry this morning, and we have made a plan of campaign founded upon my observations of last night. I will not speak about it just now, but it should make my next report interesting reading.

. . . HE STARED OUT INTO THE BLACKNESS OF THE MOOR.

Illustration by Sidney Paget for the *Strand Magazine*, November, 1901. Watson in speaking of the darkness of the night is again quite correct: the moon set at 10:40 P.M. on that Friday night, so it *would* have been very dark at two on the Saturday morning.

9 ◆ SECOND REPORT OF DR WATSON

The Light upon the Moor

76 BASKERVILLE HALL, *Oct. 15th.*

My dear Holmes,

If I was compelled to leave you without much news during the early days of my mission you must acknowledge that I am making up for lost time, and that events are now crowding thick and fast upon us. In my last report I ended upon my top note with Barrymore at the window, and now I have quite a budget already which will, unless I am much mistaken, considerably surprise you. Things have taken a turn which I could not have anticipated. In some ways they have within the last forty-eight hours become much clearer and in some ways they have become more complicated. But I will tell you all, and you shall judge for yourself.

Before breakfast on the morning following my adventure I went down the corridor and examined the room in which Barrymore had been on the night before. The western window through which he had stared so intently has, I noticed, one peculiarity above all other windows in the house—it

76 Oct. *15*th. A Monday in our year, 1888.

commands the nearest outlook on to the moor. There is an opening between two trees which enables one from this point of view to look right down upon it, while from all the other windows it is only a distant glimpse which can be obtained. It follows, therefore, that Barrymore, since only this window would serve his purpose, must have been looking out for something or somebody upon the moor. The night was very dark, so that I can hardly imagine how he could have hoped to see anyone. It had struck me that it was possible that some love intrigue was on foot. That would have accounted for his stealthy movements and also for the uneasiness of his wife. The man is a striking-looking fellow, very well equipped to steal the heart of a country girl, so that this theory seemed to have something to support it. That opening of the door which I had heard after I had returned to my room might mean that he had gone out to keep some clandestine appointment. So I reasoned with myself in the morning, and I tell you the direction of my suspicions, however much the result may have shown that they were unfounded.

But whatever the true explanation of Barrymore's movements might be, I felt that the responsibility of keeping them to myself until I could explain them was more than I could bear. I had an interview with the baronet in his study after breakfast, and I told him all that I had seen. He was less surprised than I had expected.

'I knew that Barrymore walked about nights, and I had a mind to speak to him about it,' said he. 'Two or three times I have heard his steps in the passage, coming and going, just about the hour you name.'

'Perhaps, then, he pays a visit every night to that particular window,' I suggested.

'Perhaps he does. If so, we should be able to shadow him, and see what it is that he is after. I wonder what your friend Holmes would do if he were here?'

'I believe that he would do exactly what you now suggest,' said I. 'He would follow Barrymore and see what he did.'

'Then we shall do it together.'

'But surely he would hear us.'

'The man is rather deaf, and in any case we must take our chance of that. We'll sit up in my room tonight, and wait until he passes.' Sir Henry rubbed his hands with pleasure, and it was evident that he hailed the adventure as a relief to his somewhat quiet life upon the moor.

The baronet has been in communication with the architect who prepared the plans for Sir Charles, and with a contractor from London, so that we may expect great changes to begin here soon. There have been decorators and furnishers up
from Plymouth, and it is evident that our friend has large **77**
ideas, and means to spare no pains or expense to restore the grandeur of his family. When the house is renovated and refurnished, all that he will need will be a wife to make it complete. Between ourselves, there are pretty clear signs that this will not be wanting if the lady is willing, for I have seldom seen a man more infatuated with a woman than he is with our beautiful neighbour, Miss Stapleton. And yet the course of true love does not run quite as smoothly as one would under the circumstances expect. Today, for example, its surface was broken by a very unexpected ripple, which has caused our friend considerable perplexity and annoyance.

77 *Plymouth*. The nearest town of any great size to "Baskerville Hall." Plymouth was the rendezvous of the anti-Armada fleet; Drake, Hawkins, and Raleigh set out from Plymouth; and it was the last English port touched by the *Mayflower* on her voyage to the New World.

SIR HENRY PUT HIS HAND UPON MY SHOULDER . . .

Illustration by Sidney Paget for the *Strand Magazine*, December, 1901.

After the conversation which I have quoted about Barrymore, Sir Henry put on his hat and prepared to go out. As a matter of course, I did the same.

'What, are *you* coming, Watson?' he asked, looking at me in a curious way.

'That depends on whether you are going on the moor,' said I.

'Yes, I am.'

'Well, you know what my instructions are. I am sorry to intrude, but you heard how earnestly Holmes insisted that I should not leave you, and especially that you should not go alone upon the moor.'

Sir Henry put his hand upon my shoulder, with a pleasant smile.

'My dear fellow,' said he, 'Holmes, with all his wisdom, did not foresee some things which have happened since I have been on the moor. You understand me? I am sure that you are the last man in the world who would wish to be a spoil-sport. I must go out alone.'

It put me in a most awkward position. I was at a loss what to say or what to do, and before I had made up my mind he picked up his cane and was gone.

But when I came to think the matter over my conscience reproached me bitterly for having on any pretext allowed him to go out of my sight. I imagined what my feelings would be if I had to return to you and to confess that some misfortune had occurred through my disregard for your instructions. I assure you my cheeks flushed at the very thought. It might not even now be too late to overtake him, so I set off at once in the direction of Merripit House.

I hurried along the road at the top of my speed without seeing anything of Sir Henry, until I came to the point where the moor-path branches off. There, fearing that perhaps I had come in the wrong direction, after all, I mounted a hill from which I could command a view—the same hill which is cut into the dark quarry. Thence I saw him at once. He was on the moor-path, about a quarter of a mile off, and a lady was by his side who could only be Miss Stapleton. It was clear that there was already an understanding between them and that they had met by appointment. They were walking slowly along in deep conversation, and I saw her making quick little movements of her hands as if she were very earnest in what she was saying, while he listened intently, and once or twice shook his head in strong dissent. I stood among the rocks watching them, very much puzzled as to what I should do next. To follow them and break into their intimate conversation seemed to be an outrage, and yet my clear duty was never for an instant to let him out of my sight. To act the spy upon a friend was a hateful task. Still, I could see no better course than to observe him from the hill, and to clear my conscience by confessing to him afterwards what I had done. It is true that if any sudden danger had threatened him I was too far away to be of use, and yet I am sure that you will agree with me that the position was very difficult, and that there was nothing more which I could do.

Our friend, Sir Henry, and the lady had halted on the path, and were standing deeply absorbed in their conversation, when I was suddenly aware that I was not the only witness of their interview. A wisp of green floating in the air caught my eye, and another glance showed me that it was carried on a stick by a man who was moving among the broken ground. It was Stapleton with his butterfly-net. He was very much closer to the pair than I was, and he appeared to be moving in their direction. At this instant Sir Henry suddenly drew Miss Stapleton to his side. His arm was round her, but it seemed to me that she was straining away from him with her face averted. He stooped his head to hers, and she raised one hand as if in protest. Next moment I saw them spring apart and turn hurriedly round. Stapleton was the cause of the interruption. He was running wildly towards them, his absurd net dangling behind him. He gesticulated and almost danced with excitement in front of the lovers. What the scene meant I could not imagine, but it seemed to me that Stapleton was abusing Sir Henry, who offered explanations, which became more angry as the other refused to accept them. The lady stood by in haughty silence. Finally Stapleton turned upon his heel and beckoned in a peremptory way to his sister, who, after an irresolute glance at Sir Henry, walked off by the side of her brother. The naturalist's angry gestures showed that the lady was included in his displeasure. The baronet stood for a minute looking after them, and then he walked slowly back the way that he had come, his head hanging, the very picture of dejection.

. . . SIR HENRY SUDDENLY DREW MISS STAPLETON TO HIS SIDE.

Illustration by Sidney Paget for the *Strand Magazine*, December, 1901.

What all this meant I could not imagine, but I was deeply ashamed to have witnessed so intimate a scene without my friend's knowledge. I ran down the hill, therefore, and met the baronet at the bottom. His face was flushed with anger and his brows were wrinkled, like one who is at his wits' ends what to do.

'Halloa, Watson! Where have you dropped from?' said he. 'You don't mean to say that you came after me in spite of all?'

I explained everything to him: how I had found it impossible to remain behind, how I had followed him and how I had witnessed all that had occurred. For an instant his eyes blazed at me, but my frankness disarmed his anger, and he broke at last into a rather rueful laugh.

'You would have thought the middle of that prairie a fairly safe place for a man to be private,' said he, 'but, by thunder, the whole countryside seems to have been out to see me do my wooing—and a mighty poor wooing at that! Where had you engaged a seat?'

'I was on that hill.'

'Quite in the back row, eh? But her brother was well up to the front. Did you see him come out on us?'

'Yes, I did.'

'Did he ever strike you as being crazy—this brother of hers?'

'I can't say that he ever did.'

'I dare say not. I always thought him sane enough until today, but you can take it from me that either he or I ought to be in a strait-jacket. What's the matter with me, anyhow? You've lived near me for some weeks, Watson. Tell me straight, now! Is there anything that would prevent me from making a good husband to a woman that I loved?'

'I should say not.'

'He can't object to my worldly position, so it must be myself that he has this down on. What has he against me? I never hurt man or woman in my life that I know of. And yet he would not so much as let me touch the tips of her fingers.'

'Did he say so?'

'That, and a deal more. I tell you, Watson, I've only known her these few weeks, but from the first I just felt that she was made for me, and she, too—she was happy when she was with me, and that I'll swear. There's a light in a woman's eyes that speaks louder than words. But he has never let us get together, and it was only today for the first time that I saw a chance of having a few words with her alone. She was glad to meet me, but when she did it was not love that she would talk about, and she wouldn't have let me talk about it either if she could have stopped it. She kept coming back to it that this was a place of danger, and that she would never be happy until I had left it. I told her that since I had seen her I was in no hurry to leave it, and that if she really wanted me to go, the only way to work it was for her to arrange to go with me. With that I offered in as many words to marry her, but before she could answer down came this brother of hers, running at us with a face on him like a madman. He was just white with rage, and those light eyes of his were blazing with fury. What was I doing with the lady? How dared I offer her attentions which were distasteful to her? Did I think that because I was a baronet I could do what I liked? If he had not been her brother I should have known better how to answer him. As it was I told him that my feelings towards his sister were such as I was not ashamed of, and that I hoped that she might honour me by becoming my wife. That seemed to make the matter no better, so then I lost my temper, too, and I answered him rather more hotly than I should, perhaps, considering that she was standing by. So it ended by his going off with her, as you saw, and here am I as badly puzzled a man as any in this country. Just tell me what it all means, Watson, and I'll owe you more than ever I can hope to pay.'

I tried one or two explanations, but, indeed, I was completely puzzled myself. Our friend's title, his fortune, his age, his character, and his appearance are all in his favour, and I know nothing against him, unless it be this dark fate which runs in his family. That his advances should be rejected so brusquely without any reference to the lady's own wishes, and that the lady should accept the situation without protest, is very amazing. However, our conjectures were set at rest by a visit from Stapleton himself that very afternoon. He had come to offer apologies for his rudeness of the morning, and after a long private interview with Sir Henry in his study the upshot of their conversation was that the breach is quite healed, and that we are to dine at Merripit House next Friday as a sign of it.

'I don't say now that he isn't a crazy man,' said Sir Henry; 'I can't forget the look in his eyes when he ran at me this morning, but I must allow that no man could make a more handsome apology than he has done.'

'Did he give any explanation of his conduct?'

'His sister is everything in his life, he says. That is natural enough, and I am glad that he should understand her value. They have always been together, and according to his account he has been a very lonely man with only her as a companion, so that the thought of losing her was really terrible to him. He had not understood, he said, that I was becoming attached to her, but when he saw with his own eyes that it was really so, and that she might be taken away from him, it gave him such a shock that for a time he was not responsible for what he said or did. He was very sorry for all that had passed, and he recognized how foolish and how selfish it was that he should imagine that he could hold a beautiful woman like his sister to himself for her whole life. If she had to leave him he had rather it was to a neighbour like myself than to anyone else. But in any case it was a blow to him, and it would take him some time before he could prepare himself to meet it. He would withdraw all opposition upon his part if I would promise for three months to let the matter rest, and to be content with cultivating the lady's friendship during that time without claiming her love. This I promised, and so the matter rests.'

So there is one of our small mysteries cleared up. It is something to have touched bottom anywhere in this bog in which we are floundering. We know now why Stapleton looked with disfavour upon his sister's suitor—even when that suitor was so eligible a one as Sir Henry. And now I pass on to another thread which I have extricated out of the tangled skein, the mystery of the sobs in the night, of the tear-stained face of Mrs Barrymore, of the secret journey of the butler to the western lattice-window. Congratulate me, my dear Holmes, and tell me that I have not disappointed you as an agent—that you do not regret the confidence which you showed in me when you sent me down. All these things have by one night's work been thoroughly cleared.

I have said 'by one night's work,' but, in truth, it was by
two nights' work, for on the first we drew entirely blank. I **78**
sat up with Sir Henry in his room until nearly three o'clock in the morning, but no sound of any sort did we hear except the chiming clock upon the stairs. It was a most melancholy vigil, and ended by each of us falling asleep in our chairs. Fortunately we were not discouraged, and we determined to try again. The next night we lowered the lamp and sat smoking cigarettes, without making the least sound. It was incredible how slowly the hours crawled by, and yet we were helped through it by the same sort of patient interest which the hunter must feel as he watches the trap into which he hopes the game may wander. One struck, and two, and we had almost for the second time given it up in despair, when in an instant we both sat bolt upright in our chairs, with all our weary senses keenly on the alert once more. We had heard the creak of a step in the passage.

Very stealthily we heard it pass along until it died away in the distance. Then the baronet gently opened his door, and we set out in pursuit. Already our man had gone round the gallery, and the corridor was all in darkness. Softly we stole along until we had come into the other wing. We were just in time to catch a glimpse of the tall, black-bearded figure, his shoulders rounded, as he tiptoed down the passage. Then he passed through the same door as before, and the light of the candle framed it in the darkness and shot one single yellow beam across the gloom of the corridor. We shuffled cautiously towards it, trying every plank before we dared to put our whole weight upon it. We had taken the precaution of leaving our boots behind us, but, even so, the old boards snapped and creaked beneath our tread. Sometimes it seemed impossible that he should fail to hear our approach. However, the man is fortunately rather deaf, and he was entirely

78 *by two nights' work.* That is, the night of Saturday to Sunday, October 13th to 14th, and the night of Sunday to Monday, October 14th to 15th.

'WHAT ARE YOU DOING HERE, BARRYMORE?'

Illustration by Sidney Paget for the *Strand Magazine*, December, 1901.

preoccupied in that which he was doing. When at last we reached the door and peeped through we found him crouching at the window, candle in hand, his white, intent face pressed against the pane, exactly as I had seen him two nights before.

We had arranged no plan of campaign, but the baronet is a man to whom the most direct way is always the most natural. He walked into the room, and as he did so Barrymore sprang up from the window with a sharp hiss of his breath, and stood, livid and trembling, before us. His dark eyes, glaring out of the white mask of his face, were full of horror and astonishment as he gazed from Sir Henry to me.

'What are you doing here, Barrymore?'

'Nothing, sir.' His agitation was so great that he could hardly speak, and the shadows sprang up and down from the shaking of his candle. 'It was the window, sir. I go round at night to see that they are fastened.'

'On the second floor?'

'Yes, sir, all the windows.'

'Look here, Barrymore,' said Sir Henry, sternly, 'we have made up our minds to have the truth out of you, so it will save you trouble to tell it sooner rather than later. Come now! No lies! What were you doing at that window?'

The fellow looked at us in a helpless way, and he wrung his hands together like one who is in the last extremity of doubt and misery.

'I was doing no harm, sir. I was holding a candle to the window.'

'And why were you holding a candle to the window?'

'Don't ask me, Sir Henry—don't ask me! I give you my word, sir, that it is not my secret, and that I cannot tell it. If it concerned no one but myself I would not try to keep it from you.'

A sudden idea occurred to me, and I took the candle from the window-sill, where the butler had placed it.

'He must have been holding it as a signal,' said I. 'Let us see if there is any answer'

I held it as he had done, and stared out into the darkness of the night. Vaguely I could discern the black bank of the trees and the lighter expanse of the moor, for the moon was behind the clouds. And then I gave a cry of exultation, for a tiny pin-point of yellow light had suddenly transfixed the dark veil, and glowed steadily in the centre of the black square framed by the window.

'There it is!' I cried.

'No, no, sir, it is nothing—nothing at all,' the butler broke in; 'I assure you, sir——'

'Move your light across the window, Watson!' cried the baronet. 'See, the other moves also! Now, you rascal, do you deny that it is a signal? Come, speak up! Who is your confederate out yonder, and what is this conspiracy that is going on?'

The man's face became openly defiant. 'It is my business, and not yours. I will not tell.'

'Then you leave my employment right away.'

'Very good, sir. If I must, I must.'

'And you go in disgrace. By thunder, you may well be ashamed of yourself. Your family has lived with mine for over a hundred years under this roof, and here I find you deep in some dark plot against me.'

'No, no, sir; no, not against you!'

It was a woman's voice, and Mrs Barrymore, paler and more horror-struck than her husband, was standing at the door. Her bulky figure in a shawl and skirt might have been comic were it not for the intensity of feeling upon her face.

'We have to go, Eliza. This is the end of it. You can pack our things,' said the butler.

'Oh, John, John, have I brought you to this? It is my doing, Sir Henry—all mine. He has done nothing except for my sake, and because I asked him.'

'Speak out, then! What does it mean?'

'My unhappy brother is starving on the moor. We cannot let him perish at our very gates. The light is a signal to him that food is ready for him, and his light out yonder is to show the spot to which to bring it.'

'Then your brother is——'

'The escaped convict, sir—Selden, the criminal.'

'That's the truth, sir,' said Barrymore. 'I said that it was not my secret, and that I could not tell it to you. But now you have heard it, and you will see that if there was a plot it was not against you.'

This, then, was the explanation of the stealthy expeditions at night and the light at the window. Sir Henry and I both stared at the woman in amazement. Was it possible that this stolidly respectable person was of the same blood as one of the most notorious criminals in the country?

'Yes, sir, my name was Selden, and he is my younger brother. We humoured him too much when he was a lad, and gave him his own way in everything, until he came to think that the world was made for his pleasure, and that he could do what he liked in it. Then, as he grew older, he met wicked companions, and the devil entered into him, until he broke my mother's heart and dragged our name in the dirt. From crime to crime he sank lower and lower, until it is only the mercy of God which has snatched him from the scaffold; but to me, sir, he was always the little curly-headed boy that I had nursed and played with, as an elder sister would. That was why he broke prison, sir. He knew that I was here, and that we could not refuse to help him. When he dragged himself here one night, weary and starving, with the warders hard at his heels, what could we do? We took him in and fed him and cared for him. Then you returned, sir, and my brother thought he would be safer on the moor than anywhere else until the hue and cry was over, so he lay in hiding there. But every second night we made sure if he was still there by putting a light in the window, and if there was an answer my husband took out some bread and meat to him. Every day we hoped that he was gone, but as long as he was there we could not desert him. That is the whole truth, as I am an honest Christian woman, and you will see that if there is blame in the matter it does not lie with my husband, but with me, for whose sake he has done all that he has.'

The woman's words came with an intense earnestness which carried conviction with them.

'Is this true, Barrymore?'

'Yes, Sir Henry. Every word of it.'

'Well, I cannot blame you for standing by your own wife. Forget what I have said. Go to your room, you two, and we shall talk further about this matter in the morning.'

When they were gone we looked out of the window again. Sir Henry had flung it open, and the cold night wind beat in

'THE ESCAPED CONVICT, SIR—SELDEN, THE CRIMINAL.'

Illustration by Sidney Paget for the *Strand Magazine*, December, 1901.

upon our faces. Far away in the black distance there still glowed that one tiny point of yellow light.

'I wonder he dares,' said Sir Henry.

'It may be so placed as to be only visible from here.'

'Very likely. How far do you think it is?'

'Out by the Cleft Tor, I think.'

'Not more than a mile or two off.'

'Hardly that.'

'Well, it cannot be far if Barrymore had to carry out the food to it. And he is waiting, this villain, beside that candle. By thunder, Watson, I am going out to take that man!'

The same thought had crossed my own mind. It was not as if the Barrymores had taken us into their confidence. Their secret had been forced from them. The man was a danger to the community, an unmitigated scoundrel for whom there was neither pity nor excuse. We were only doing our duty in taking this chance of putting him back where he could do no harm. With his brutal and violent nature, others would have to pay the price if we held our hands. Any night, for example, our neighbours, the Stapletons, might be attacked by him, and it may have been the thought of this which made Sir Henry so keen upon the adventure.

'I will come,' said I.

'Then get your revolver and put on your boots. The sooner we start the better, as the fellow may put out his light and be off.'

In five minutes we were outside the door, starting upon our expedition. We hurried through the dark shrubbery, amid the dull moaning of the autumn wind and the rustle of the falling leaves. The night-air was heavy with the smell of damp and decay. Now and again the moon peeped out for an
79 instant, but clouds were driving over the face of the sky, and
80 just as we came out on the moor a thin rain began to fall. The
light still burned steadily in front.

'Are you armed?' I asked.

'I have a hunting-crop.'

'We must close in on him rapidly, for he is said to be a desperate fellow. We shall take him by surprise and have him at our mercy before he can resist.'

'I say, Watson,' said the baronet, 'what would Holmes say to this? How about that hour of darkness in which the power of evil is exalted?'

As if in answer to his words there rose suddenly out of the vast gloom of the moor that strange cry which I had already heard upon the borders of the great Grimpen Mire. It came with the wind through the silence of the night, a long, deep mutter, then a rising howl, and then the sad moan in which it died away. Again and again it sounded, the whole air throbbing with it, strident, wild, and menacing. The baronet caught my sleeve, and his face glimmered white through the darkness.

'Good heavens, what's that, Watson?'

'I don't know. It's a sound they have on the moor. I heard it once before.'

It died away, and an absolute silence closed in upon us. We stood straining our ears, but nothing came.

'Watson,' said the baronet, 'it was the cry of a hound.'

My blood ran cold in my veins, for there was a break in his voice which told of the sudden horror which had seized him.

'OUT BY THE CLEFT TOR, I THINK.'

The Cleft Tor can only be the famous *Cleft Rock;* it is not shown on our map, but it stands just above Holne Chase, which is shown; Cleft Rock is a tourist attraction today as surely as it was in 1888. Our photograph, by J. Amery, Esq., is from *A Book of Dartmoor* by the Reverend Sabine Baring-Gould.

79 *Now and again the moon peeped out for an instant.* Not for just an instant, surely, for Watson shortly hereafter sees the man on the moor "for a long time in the moonlight." According to Watson, "the moon was low upon the right"; later, Holmes says: "I was so imprudent as to allow the moon to rise behind me." There was a moon (three-quarters full) at this time, but it was rising in the afternoon, not in the early morning. Holmes must have said "shine" rather than "rise."

80 *a thin rain began to fall.* "Foggy or misty in the south and south-east of England," said the *Times* of London.

'What do they call this sound?' he asked.

'Who?'

'The folk on the countryside.'

'Oh, they are ignorant people. Why should you mind what they call it?'

'Tell me, Watson. What do they say of it?'

I hesitated, but could not escape the question.

'They say it is the cry of the Hound of the Baskervilles.'

He groaned, and was silent for a few moments.

'A hound it was,' he said at last, 'but it seemed to come from miles away over yonder, I think.'

'It was hard to say whence it came.'

'It rose and fell with the wind. Isn't that the direction of the great Grimpen Mire?'

'Yes, it is.'

'Well, it was up there. Come now, Watson, didn't you think yourself that it was the cry of a hound? I am not a child. You need not fear to speak the truth.'

'Stapleton was with me when I heard it last. He said that it might be the calling of a strange bird.'

'No, no, it was a hound. My God, can there be some truth in all these stories? Is it possible that I am really in danger from so dark a cause? You don't believe it, do you, Watson?'

'No, no.'

'And yet it was one thing to laugh about it in London, and it is another to stand out here in the darkness of the moor and to hear such a cry as that. And my uncle! There was the footprint of the hound beside him as he lay. It all fits together. I don't think that I am a coward, Watson, but that sound seemed to freeze my very blood. Feel my hand!'

It was as cold as a block of marble.

'You'll be all right tomorrow.'

'I don't think I'll get that cry out of my head. What do you advise that we do now?'

'Shall we turn back?'

'No, by thunder; we have come out to get our man, and we will do it. We are after the convict and a hell-hound, as likely as not, after us. Come on. We'll see it through if all the fiends of the pit were loose upon the moor.'

We stumbled slowly along in the darkness, with the black loom of the craggy hills around us, and the yellow speck of light burning steadily in front. There is nothing so deceptive as the distance of a light upon a pitch-dark night, and sometimes the glimmer seemed to be far away upon the horizon and sometimes it might have been within a few yards of us. But at last we could see whence it came, and then we knew that we were indeed very close. A guttering candle was stuck in a crevice of the rocks which flanked it on each side so as to keep the wind from it, and also to prevent it from being visible, save in the direction of Baskerville Hall. A boulder of granite concealed our approach, and crouching behind it we gazed over it at the signal light. It was strange to see this single candle burning there in the middle of the moor, with no sign of life near it—just the one straight, yellow flame and the gleam of the rock on each side of it.

'What shall we do now?' whispered Sir Henry.

'Wait here. He must be near his light. Let us see if we can get a glimpse of him.'

The words were hardly out of my mouth when we both saw him. Over the rocks, in the crevice of which the candle burned, there was thrust out an evil, yellow face, a terrible animal face, all seamed and scored with vile passions. Foul with mire, with a bristling beard, and hung with matted hair, it might well have belonged to one of those old savages who dwelt in the burrows on the hillsides. The light beneath him was reflected in his small, cunning eyes, which peered fiercely to right and left through the darkness, like a crafty and savage animal who has heard the steps of the hunters.

OVER THE ROCKS, IN THE CREVICE OF WHICH THE CANDLE BURNED, THERE WAS THRUST OUT AN EVIL, YELLOW FACE . . .

Illustration by Sidney Paget for the *Strand Magazine*, December, 1901.

Something had evidently aroused his suspicions. It may have been that Barrymore had some private signal which we had neglected to give, or the fellow may have had some other reason for thinking that all was not well, but I could read his fears upon his wicked face. Any instant he might dash out the light and vanish in the darkness. I sprang forward, therefore, and Sir Henry did the same. At the same moment the convict screamed out a curse at us and hurled a rock which splintered up against the boulder which had sheltered us. I caught one glimpse of his short, squat, strongly-built figure as he sprang to his feet and turned to run. At the same moment by a lucky chance the moon broke through the clouds. We rushed over the brow of the hill, and there was our man running with great speed down the other side, springing over the stones in his way with the activity of a mountain goat. A lucky long shot of my revolver might have crippled him, but I had brought it only to defend myself if attacked, and not to shoot an unarmed man who was running away.

We were both fair runners and in good condition, but we soon found that we had no chance of overtaking him. We saw him for a long time in the moonlight until he was only a small speck moving swiftly among the boulders upon the side of a distant hill. We ran and ran until we were completely blown, but the space between us grew ever wider. Finally we stopped and sat panting on two rocks, while we watched him disappearing in the distance.

And it was at this moment that there occurred a most strange and unexpected thing. We had risen from our rocks and were turning to go home, having abandoned the hopeless chase. The moon was low upon the right, and the jagged pinnacle of a granite tor stood up against the lower curve of its silver disc. There, outlined as black as an ebony statue on that shining background, I saw the figure of a man upon the tor. Do not think that it was a delusion, Holmes. I assure you that I have never in my life seen anything more clearly. As far as I could judge, the figure was that of a tall, thin man. He stood with his legs a little separated, his arms folded, his head bowed, as if he were brooding over that enormous wilderness of peat and granite which lay before him. He might have been the very spirit of that terrible place. It was not the convict. This man was far from the place where the latter had disappeared. Besides, he was a much taller man. With a cry of surprise I pointed him out to the baronet, but in the instant during which I had turned to grasp his arm the man was gone. There was the sharp pinnacle of granite still cutting the lower edge of the moon, but its peak bore no trace of that silent and motionless figure.

I wished to go in that direction and to search the tor, but it was some distance away. The baronet's nerves were still quivering from that cry, which recalled the dark story of his family, and he was not in the mood for fresh adventures. He had not seen this lonely man upon the tor, and could not feel the thrill which his strange presence and his commanding attitude had given to me. 'A warder, no doubt,' said he. 'The moor has been thick with them since this fellow escaped.' Well, perhaps his explanation may be the right one, but I should like to have some further proof of it. Today we mean to communicate to the Princetown people where they should look for their missing man, but it is hard lines that we have not actually had the triumph of bringing him back as our own prisoner. Such are the adventures of last night, and you must acknowledge, my dear Holmes, that I have done you very well in the matter of a report. Much of what I tell you is no doubt quite irrelevant, but still I feel that it is best that I should let you have all the facts and leave you to select for yourself those which will be of most service to you in helping you to your conclusions. We are certainly making some progress. So far as the Barrymores go, we have found the motive of their actions, and that has cleared up the situation very much. But the moor with its mysteries and its strange inhabitants remains as inscrutable as ever. Perhaps in my next I may be able to throw some light upon this also. Best of all would it be if you could come down to us. In any case you will hear from me again in the course of the next few days.

THERE, OUTLINED AS BLACK AS AN EBONY STATUE ON THAT SHINING BACKGROUND, I SAW THE FIGURE OF A MAN UPON THE TOR.

Illustration by Sidney Paget for the *Strand Magazine*, December, 1901.

10 ◆ EXTRACT FROM THE DIARY OF DR WATSON

So far I have been able to quote from the reports which I have forwarded during these early days to Sherlock Holmes. Now, however, I have arrived at a point in my narrative where I am compelled to abandon this method and to trust once more to my recollections, aided by the diary which I kept at the time. A few extracts from the latter will carry me on to those scenes which are indelibly fixed in every detail upon my memory. I proceed, then, from the morning which followed our abortive chase of the convict and our other strange experiences upon the moor.

October 16th.—A dull and foggy day, with a drizzle of rain. **81-82**
The house is banked in with rolling clouds, which rise now and then to show the dreary curves of the moor, with thin, silver veins upon the sides of the hills, and the distant boulders gleaming where the light strikes upon their wet faces. It is melancholy outside and in. The baronet is in a black reaction after the excitements of the night. I am conscious myself of a weight at my heart and a feeling of impending danger—ever-present danger, which is the more terrible because I am unable to define it.

And have I not cause for such a feeling? Consider the long

81 October *16*th. Tuesday, October 16th, 1888, in our view. But there is a discrepancy here: Watson has told us that he will proceed "from the morning which followed our abortive chase of the convict and our other strange experiences on the moor," and this would have been the morning of Monday, October 15th. It seems clear that after the exhausting night on the moor and the composition of a lengthy letter to Holmes, Watson slept away most of Monday the 15th. Writing in his diary on Tuesday, October 16th, it would therefore seem to him that the abortive chase took place only the night before.

82 *A dull and foggy day, with a drizzle of rain.* Again, Watson was quite correct. The *Times* of London wrote of this day: "Dull, unsettled weather has set in at many of our . . . stations. In the central and south-eastern parts of England . . . a good deal of fog or mist has prevailed locally."

sequence of incidents which have all pointed to some sinister influence which is at work around us. There is the death of the last occupant of the Hall, fulfilling so exactly the conditions of the family legend, and there are the repeated reports from peasants of the appearance of a strange creature upon the moor. Twice I have with my own ears heard the sound which resembled the distant baying of a hound. It is incredible, impossible, that it should really be outside the ordinary laws of Nature. A spectral hound which leaves material footmarks and fills the air with its howling is surely not to be thought of. Stapleton may fall in with such a superstition, and Mortimer also; but if I have one quality upon earth it is common sense, and nothing will persuade me to believe in such a thing. To do so would be to descend to the level of these poor peasants who are not content with a mere fiend-dog, but must needs describe him with hell-fire shooting from his mouth and eyes. Holmes would not listen to such fancies, and I am his agent. But facts are facts, and I have twice heard this crying upon the moor. Suppose that there were really some huge hound loose upon it; that would go far to explain everything. But where could such a hound lie concealed, where did it get its food, where did it come from, how was it that no one saw it by day? It must be confessed that the natural explanation offers almost as many difficulties as the other. And always, apart from the hound, there was the fact of the human agency in London, the man in the cab, and the letter which warned Sir Henry against the moor. This at least was real, but it might have been the work of a protecting friend as easily as an enemy. Where was that friend or enemy now? Had he remained in London, or had he followed us down here? Could he—could he be the stranger whom I had seen upon the tor?

It is true that I have had only the one glance at him, and yet there are some things to which I am ready to swear. He is no one whom I have seen down here, and I have now met all the neighbours. The figure was far taller than that of Stapleton, far thinner than that of Frankland. Barrymore it might possibly have been, but we had left him behind us, and I am certain that he could not have followed us. A stranger, then, is still dogging us, just as a stranger had dogged us in London. We have never shaken him off. If I could lay my hands upon that man, then at last we might find ourselves at the end of all our difficulties. To this one purpose I must now devote all my energies.

My first impulse was to tell Sir Henry all my plans. My second and wisest one is to play my own game and speak as little as possible to anyone. He is silent and distrait. His nerves have been strangely shaken by that sound upon the moor. I will say nothing to add to his anxieties, but I will take my own steps to attain my own end.

We had a small scene this morning after breakfast. Barrymore asked leave to speak with Sir Henry, and they were closeted in his study some little time. Sitting in the billiard-room, I more than once heard the sound of voices raised, and I had a pretty good idea what the point was which was under discussion. After a time the baronet opened his door and called for me.

'Barrymore considers that he has a grievance,' he said. 'He thinks that it was unfair on our part to hunt his brother-in-law down when he, of his own free will, had told us the secret.'

The butler was standing, very pale but very collected, before us.

'I may have spoken too warmly, sir,' said he, 'and if I have I am sure that I beg your pardon. At the same time, I was very much surprised when I heard you two gentlemen come back this morning and learned that you had been chasing Selden. The poor fellow has enough to fight against without my putting more upon his track.'

'If you had told us of your own free will it would have been a different thing,' said the baronet. 'You only told us, or rather your wife only told us, when it was forced from you and you could not help yourself.'

'I didn't think you would have taken advantage of it, Sir Henry—indeed I didn't.'

'The man is a public danger. There are lonely houses scattered over the moor, and he is a fellow who would stick at nothing. You only want to get a glimpse of his face to see that. Look at Mr Stapleton's house, for example, with no one but himself to defend it. There's no safety for anyone until he is under lock and key.'

'He'll break into no house, sir. I give you my solemn word upon that. And he will never trouble anyone in this country again. I assure you, Sir Henry, that in a very few days the necessary arrangements will have been made and he will be on his way to South America. For God's sake, sir, I beg of you not to let the police know that he is still on the moor. They have given up the chase there, and he can lie quiet until the ship is ready for him. You can't tell on him without getting my wife and me into trouble. I beg you, sir, to say nothing to the police.'

'What do you say, Watson?'

I shrugged my shoulders. 'If he were safely out of the country it would relieve the taxpayer of a burden.'

'But how about the chance of his holding someone up before he goes?'

'He would not do anything so mad, sir. We have provided him with all that he can want. To commit a crime would be to show where he was hiding.'

'That is true,' said Sir Henry. 'Well, Barrymore——'

'God bless you, sir, and thank you from my heart! It would have killed my poor wife had he been taken again.'

'I guess we are aiding and abetting a felony, Watson? But, after what we have heard, I don't feel as if I could give the man up, so there is an end of it. All right, Barrymore, you can go.'

With a few broken words of gratitude the man turned, but he hesitated and then came back.

'You've been so kind to us, sir, that I should like to do the best I can for you in return. I know something, Sir Henry, and perhaps I should have said it before, but it was long after the inquest that I found it out. I've never breathed a word about it yet to mortal man. It's about poor Sir Charles's death.'

The baronet and I were both upon our feet.

'Do you know how he died?'

'No, sir, I don't know that.'

'What, then?'

'I know why he was at the gate at that hour. It was to meet

a woman.'

'To meet a woman! He?'

'Yes, sir.'

'And the woman's name?'

'I can't give you the name, sir, but I can give you the initials. Her initials were L.L.'

'How do you know this, Barrymore?'

'Well, Sir Henry, your uncle had a letter that morning. He
had usually a great many letters, for he was a public man and
well known for his kind heart, so that everyone who was in
trouble was glad to turn to him. But that morning, as it
chanced, there was only this one letter, so I took the more
83 notice of it. It was from Coombe Tracey, and it was addressed
in a woman's hand.'

'Well?'

'Well, sir, I thought no more of the matter, and never would have done had it not been for my wife. Only a few weeks ago she was cleaning out Sir Charles's study—it had never been touched since his death—and she found the ashes of a burned letter in the back of the grate. The greater part of it was charred to pieces, but one little slip, the end of a page, hung together, and the writing could still be read, though it was grey on a black ground. It seemed to us to be a postscript at the end of the letter, and it said: "Please, please, as you are a gentleman, burn this letter, and be at the gate by ten o'clock." Beneath it were signed the initials L.L.'

'Have you got that slip?'

'No, sir, it crumbled all to bits after we moved it.'

'Had Sir Charles received any other letters in the same writing?'

'Well, sir, I took no particular notice of his letters. I should not have noticed this one only it happened to come alone.'

'And you have no idea who L.L. is?'

'No, sir. No more than you have. But I expect if we could lay our hands upon that lady we should know more about Sir Charles's death.'

'I cannot understand, Barrymore, how you came to conceal this important information.'

'Well, sir, it was immediately after that our own trouble came to us. And then again, sir, we were both of us very fond of Sir Charles, as we well might be considering all that he has done for us. To rake this up couldn't help our poor master, and it's well to go carefully when there's a lady in the case. Even the best of us——'

'You thought it might injure his reputation?'

'Well, sir, I thought no good could come of it. But now you have been kind to us, and I feel as if it would be treating you unfairly not to tell you all that I know about the matter.'

'Very good, Barrymore; you can go.'

When the butler had left us, Sir Henry turned to me. 'Well, Watson, what do you think of this new light?'

'It seems to leave the darkness rather blacker than before.'

'So I think. But if we can only trace L.L. it should clear up the whole business. We have gained that much. We know that there is someone who has the facts if we can only find her. What do you think we should do?'

'Let Holmes know all about it at once. It will give him the clue for which he has been seeking. I am much mistaken if it does not bring him down.'

83 *Coombe Tracey.* A fair-sized town on the railroad is required, for it is at Coombe Tracey that Lestrade later springs from a first-class carriage of the London express to shake hands with Holmes and Watson. We find such a town—*Bovey* Tracey—on the east of the moor, and it seems unnecessary to look further for the original of Watson's "Coombe Tracey," an ingenious combination of Widecombe and Bovey Tracey.

I went at once to my room and drew up my report of the morning's conversation for Holmes. It was evident to me that he had been very busy of late, for the notes which I had from Baker Street were few and short, with no comments upon the information which I had supplied, and hardly any reference to my mission. No doubt his blackmailing case is absorbing all his faculties. And yet this new factor must surely arrest his attention and renew his interest. I wish that he were here.

October 17th.—All day today the rain poured down, rust- 84
ling on the ivy and dripping from the eaves. I thought of the convict out upon the bleak, cold, shelterless moor. Poor fellow! Whatever his crimes, he has suffered something to atone for them. And then I thought of that other one—the face in the cab, the figure against the moon. Was he also out in that deluge—the unseen watcher, the man of darkness? In the evening I put on my waterproof and I walked far upon the sodden moor, full of dark imaginings, the rain beating upon my face and the wind whistling about my ears. God help those who wander into the Great Mire now, for even the firm uplands are becoming a morass. I found the Black Tor upon which I had seen the solitary watcher, and from its craggy summit I looked out myself across the melancholy downs. Rain squalls drifted across their russet face, and the heavy, slate-coloured clouds hung low over the landscape, trailing in grey wreaths down the sides of the fantastic hills. In the distant hollow on the left, half hidden by the mist, the two thin towers of Baskerville Hall rose above the trees. They were the only signs of human life which I could see, save only those prehistoric huts which lay thickly upon the slopes of the hills. Nowhere was there any trace of that lonely man whom I had seen on the same spot two nights before.

As I walked back I was overtaken by Dr Mortimer driving in his dog-cart over a rough moorland track, which led from the outlying farm-house of Foulmire. He has been very attentive to us, and hardly a day has passed that he has not called at the Hall to see how we were getting on. He insisted upon my climbing into his dog-cart and he gave me a lift homewards. I found him much troubled over the disappearance of his little spaniel. It had wandered on to the moor and had never come back. I gave him such consolation as I might, but I thought of the pony on the Grimpen Mire, and I do not fancy that he will see his little dog again.

'By the way, Mortimer,' said I, as we jolted along the rough road, 'I suppose there are few people living within driving distance of this whom you do not know?'

'Hardly any, I think.'

'Can you, then, tell me the name of any woman whose initials are L.L.?'

He thought for a few minutes. 'No,' said he. 'There are a few gipsies and labouring folk for whom I can't answer, but among the farmers or gentry there is no one whose initials are those. Wait a bit, though,' he added, after a pause. 'There is Laura Lyons—her initials are L.L.—but she lives in Coombe Tracey.'

'Who is she?' I asked.

'She is Frankland's daughter.'

'What? Old Frankland the crank?'

'Exactly. She married an artist named Lyons, who came sketching on the moor. He proved to be a blackguard and

I FOUND THE BLACK TOR UPON WHICH I HAD SEEN THE SOLITARY WATCHER . . .

The Black Tor, shown here in a drawing by A. B. Collier for the Reverend Sabine Baring-Gould's *A Book of Dartmoor*, exists to this day, and has on it a logan stone that can be rocked by means of a natural handle.

84 *All day today the rain poured down.* Although the *Times* did not report specifically on the weather at its southern stations in its remarks for Wednesday, October 17th, it noted "rain at Sumburgh Head," "thick local fogs" and "no bright sunshine at Westminster."

deserted her. The fault, from what I hear, may not have been entirely on one side. Her father refused to have anything to do with her, because she had married without his consent, and perhaps for one or two other reasons as well. So, between the old sinner and the young one the girl has had a pretty bad time.'

'How does she live?'

'I fancy old Frankland allows her a pittance, but it cannot be more, for his own affairs are considerably involved. Whatever she may have deserved, one could not allow her to go hopelessly to the bad. Her story got about, and several of the people here did something to enable her to earn an honest living. Stapleton did for one, and Sir Charles for another. I gave a trifle myself. It was to set her up in a typewriting business.'

He wanted to know the object of my inquiries, but I managed to satisfy his curiosity without telling him too much, for there is no reason why we should take anyone into our confidence. Tomorrow morning I shall find my way to Coombe Tracey, and if I can see this Mrs Laura Lyons, of equivocal reputation, a long step will have been made towards clearing one incident in this chain of mysteries. I am certainly developing the wisdom of the serpent, for when Mortimer pressed his questions to an inconvenient extent I asked him casually to what type Franklin's skull belonged, and so heard nothing but craniology for the rest of our drive. I have not lived for years with Sherlock Holmes for nothing.

I have only one other incident to record upon this tempestuous and melancholy day. This was my conversation with Barrymore just now, which gives me one more strong card which I can play in due time.

'YOU KNOW THAT THERE IS ANOTHER MAN, THEN?'

Illustration by Sidney Paget for the *Strand Magazine*, January, 1902.

Mortimer had stayed to dinner, and he and the baronet played écarté afterwards. The butler brought me my coffee into the library, and I took the chance to ask him a few questions.

'Well,' said I, 'has this precious relation of yours departed, or is he still lurking out yonder?'

'I don't know, sir. I hope to Heaven that he has gone, for he has brought nothing but trouble here! I've not heard of him since I left out food for him last, and that was three days ago.'

'Did you see him then?'

'No, sir; but the food was gone when next I went that way.'

'Then he was certainly there?'

'So you would think, sir, unless it was the other man who took it.'

I sat with my coffee-cup half-way to my lips, and stared at Barrymore.

'You know that there is another man, then?'

'Yes, sir; there is another man upon the moor.'

'Have you seen him?'

'No, sir.'

'How do you know of him, then?'

'Selden told me of him, sir, a week ago or more. He's in hiding, too, but he's not a convict, so far as I can make out. I don't like it, Dr Watson—I tell you straight, sir, that I don't like it.' He spoke with a sudden passion of earnestness.

'Now, listen to me, Barrymore! I have no interest in this matter but that of your master. I have come here with no object except to help him. Tell me, frankly, what it is that you don't like.'

Barrymore hesitated for a moment, as if he regretted his outburst, or found it difficult to express his own feelings in words.

'It's all these goings-on, sir,' he cried, at last, waving his hand towards the rain-lashed window which faced the moor. 'There's foul play somewhere, and there's black villainy brewing, to that I'll swear! Very glad I should be, sir, to see Sir Henry on his way back to London again!'

'But what is it that alarms you?'

'Look at Sir Charles's death! That was bad enough, for all that the coroner said. Look at the noises on the moor at night. There's not a man would cross it after sundown if he was paid for it. Look at this stranger hiding out yonder, and watching and waiting! What's he waiting for? What does it mean? It means no good to anyone of the name of Baskerville, and very glad I shall be to be quit of it all on the day that Sir Henry's new servants are ready to take over the Hall.'

'But about this stranger,' said I. 'Can you tell me anything about him? What did Selden say? Did he find out where he hid, or what he was doing?'

'He saw him once or twice, but he is a deep one, and gives nothing away. At first he thought that he was the police, but soon he found that he had some lay of his own. A kind of gentleman he was, as far as he could see, but what he was doing he could not make out.'

'And where did he say that he lived?'

'Among the old houses on the hillside—the stone huts where the old folk used to live.'

'But how about his food?'

'Selden found out that he has got a lad who works for him and brings him all he needs. I dare say he goes to Coombe Tracey for what he wants.'

'Very good, Barrymore. We may talk further of this some other time.'

When the butler had gone I walked over to the black window, and I looked through a blurred pane at the driving clouds and at the tossing outline of the wind-swept trees. It is a wild night indoors, and what must it be in a stone hut upon the moor? What passion of hatred can it be which leads a man to lurk in such a place at such a time? And what deep and earnest purpose can he have which calls for such a trial? There, in that hut upon the moor, seems to lie the very centre of that problem which has vexed me so sorely. I swear that another day shall not have passed before I have done all that man can do to reach the heart of the mystery.

11 ◆ THE MAN ON THE TOR

The extract from my private diary which forms the last chapter has brought my narrative up to the 18th of October, a time when these strange events began to move swiftly towards their terrible conclusion. The incidents of the next few days are indelibly graven upon my recollection, and I can tell them without reference to the notes made at the time. I start, then, from the day which succeeded that upon which I had established two facts of great importance, the one that Mrs Laura Lyons of Coombe Tracey had written to Sir Charles Baskerville and made an appointment with him at the very place and hour that he met his death, the other that the lurking man upon the moor was to be found among the stone huts upon the hillside. With these two facts in my possession I felt that either my intelligence or my courage must be deficient if I could not throw some further light upon these dark places.

I had no opportunity to tell the baronet what I had learned about Mrs Lyons upon the evening before, for Dr Mortimer remained with him at cards until it was very late. At breakfast, however, I informed him about my discovery, and asked him whether he would care to accompany me to Coombe Tracey. At first he was very eager to come, but on second thoughts it seemed to both of us that if I went alone the results might be better. The more formal we made the visit the less information we might obtain. I left Sir Henry behind, therefore, not without some prickings of conscience, and drove off upon my new quest.

When I reached Coombe Tracey I told Perkins to put up the horses, and I made inquiries for the lady whom I had come to interrogate. I had no difficulty in finding her rooms, which were central and well appointed. A maid showed me in without ceremony, and as I entered the sitting-room a lady who was sitting before a Remington typewriter, sprang up with a pleasant smile of welcome. Her face fell, however, when she saw that I was a stranger, and she sat down again and asked me the object of my visit.

The first impression left by Mrs Lyons was one of extreme beauty. Her eyes and hair were of the same rich hazel colour, and her cheeks, though considerably freckled, were flushed with the exquisite bloom of the brunette, the dainty pink which lurks at the heart of the sulphur rose. Admiration was, I repeat, the first impression. But the second was criticism. There was something subtly wrong with the face, some coarseness of expression, some hardness, perhaps, of eye, some looseness of lip which marred its perfect beauty. But these, of course, are afterthoughts. At the moment I was simply conscious that I was in the presence of a very handsome woman, and that she was asking me the reasons for my visit. I had not quite understood until that instant how delicate my mission was.

'I have the pleasure,' said I, 'of knowing your father.'

It was a clumsy introduction, and the lady made me feel it.

'There is nothing in common between my father and me,' she said. 'I owe him nothing, and his friends are not mine. If it were not for the late Sir Charles Baskerville and some other kind hearts I might have starved for all that my father cared.'

'It was about the late Sir Charles Baskerville that I have come here to see you.'

The freckles started out on the lady's face.

'What can I tell you about him?' she asked, and her fingers played nervously over the stops of her typewriter.

'You knew him, did you not?'

'I have already said that I owe a great deal to his kindness. If I am able to support myself it is largely due to the interest which he took in my unhappy situation.'

'Did you correspond with him?'

The lady looked quickly up, with an angry gleam in her hazel eyes.

'What is the object of these questions?' she asked, sharply.

'The object is to avoid a public scandal. It is better that I should ask them here than that the matter should pass outside our control.'

She was silent and her face was very pale. At last she looked up with something reckless and defiant in her manner.

'Well, I'll answer,' she said. 'What are your questions?'

'Did you correspond with Sir Charles?'

'I certainly wrote to him once or twice to acknowledge his delicacy and his generosity.'

'Have you the dates of those letters?'

'No.'

'Have you ever met him?'

'Yes, once or twice, when he came into Coombe Tracey. He was a very retiring man, and he preferred to do good by stealth.'

'But if you saw him so seldom and wrote so seldom, how did he know enough about your affairs to be able to help you, as you say that he has done?'

She met my difficulty with the utmost readiness.

'There were several gentlemen who knew my sad history and united to help me. One was Mr Stapleton, a neighbour and intimate friend of Sir Charles. He was exceedingly kind, and it was through him that Sir Charles learned about my affairs.'

I knew already that Sir Charles Baskerville had made Stapleton his almoner upon several occasions, so the lady's statement bore the impress of truth upon it.

'Did you ever write to Sir Charles asking him to meet you?' I continued.

Mrs Lyons flushed with anger again.

'Really, sir, this is a very extraordinary question.'

'I am sorry, madam, but I must repeat it.'

'Then I answer—certainly not.'

'Not on the very day of Sir Charles's death?'

The flush had faded in an instant, and a deathly face was before me. Her dry lips could not speak the 'No' which I saw rather than heard.

'Surely your memory deceives you,' said I. 'I could even quote a passage of your letter. It ran, "Please, please, as you are a gentleman, burn this letter, and be at the gate by ten o'clock."'

I thought that she had fainted, but she recovered herself by a supreme effort.

'Is there no such thing as a gentleman?' she gasped.

'You do Sir Charles an injustice. He *did* burn the letter. But sometimes a letter may be legible even when burned. You acknowledge now that you wrote it?'

'Yes, I did write it,' she cried, pouring out her soul in a torrent of words. 'I did write it. Why should I deny it? I have no reason to be ashamed of it. I wished him to help me. I believed that if I had an interview I could gain his help, so I asked him to meet me.'

'But why at such an hour?'

'Because I had only just learned that he was going to London next day and might be away for months. There were reasons why I could not get there earlier.'

'But why a rendezvous in the garden instead of a visit to the house?'

'Do you think a woman could go alone at that hour to a bachelor's house?'

'Well, what happened when you did get there?'

'I never went.'

'Mrs Lyons!'

'No, I swear it to you on all I hold sacred. I never went. Something intervened to prevent my going.'

'What was that?'

'That is a private matter. I cannot tell it.'

'You acknowledge, then, that you made an appointment with Sir Charles at the very hour and place at which he met his death, but you deny that you kept the appointment?'

'That is the truth.'

Again and again I cross-questioned her, but I could never get past that point.

'Mrs Lyons,' said I, as I rose from this long and inconclusive interview, 'you are taking a very great responsibility and putting yourself in a very false position by not making an absolutely clean breast of all that you know. If I have to call in the aid of the police you will find how seriously you are compromised. If your position is innocent, why did you in the first instance deny having written to Sir Charles upon that date?'

'Because I feared that some false conclusion might be drawn from it, and that I might find myself involved in a scandal.'

'And why were you so pressing that Sir Charles should destroy your letter?'

'If you have read the letter you will know.'

'I did not say that I had read all the letter.'

'You quoted some of it.'

'I quoted the postscript. The letter had, as I said, been burned, and it was not all legible. I ask you once again why it was that you were so pressing that Sir Charles should destroy this letter which he received on the day of his death.'

'The matter is a very private one.'

'The more reason why you should avoid a public investigation.'

'I will tell you, then. If you have heard anything of my unhappy history you will know that I made a rash marriage and had reason to regret it.'

'I have heard so much.'

'My life has been one incessant persecution from a husband whom I abhor. The law is upon his side, and every day I am faced by the possibility that he may force me to live with him. At the time that I wrote this letter to Sir Charles I had learned that there was a prospect of my regaining my freedom if certain expenses could be met. It meant everything to me—peace of mind, happiness, self-respect—everything. I knew Sir Charles's generosity, and I thought that if he heard the story from my own lips he would help me.'

'Then how is it that you did not go?'

'Because I received help in the interval from another source.'

'Why, then, did you not write to Sir Charles and explain this?'

'So I should have done had I not seen his death in the paper next morning.' **85**

The woman's story hung coherently together, and all my questions were unable to shake it. I could only check it by finding if she had, indeed, instituted divorce proceedings against her husband at or about the time of the tragedy.

It was unlikely that she would dare to say that she had not been to Baskerville Hall if she really had been, for a trap would be necessary to take her there, and could not have returned to Coombe Tracey until the early hours of the morning. Such an excursion could not be kept secret. The probability was, therefore, that she was telling the truth, or, at least, a part of the truth. I came away baffled and disheartened. Once again I had reached that dead wall which seemed to be built across every path by which I tried to get at the object of my mission. And yet the more I thought of the lady's face and of her manner the more I felt that something was being held back from me. Why should she turn so pale? Why should she fight against every admission until it was forced from her? Why should she have been so reticent at the time of the tragedy? Surely the explanation of all this could not be as innocent as she would have me believe. For the moment I could proceed no farther in that direction, but must turn back to that other clue which was to be sought for among the stone huts upon the moor.

And that was a most vague direction. I realized it as I drove back and noted how hill after hill showed traces of the ancient people. Barrymore's only indication had been that the stranger lived in one of these abandoned huts, and many hundreds of them are scattered throughout the length and breadth of the moor. But I had my own experience for a guide, since it had shown me the man himself standing upon the summit of the Black Tor. That, then, should be the centre of my search. From there I should explore every hut upon the moor until I lighted upon the right one. If this man were inside it I should find out from his own lips, at the point of my revolver if necessary, who he was and why he had dogged us so long. He might slip away from us in the crowd of Regent Street but it would puzzle him to do so upon the lonely moor. On the other hand, if I should find the hut, and its tenant should not be within it, I must remain there, however long the vigil, until he returned. Holmes had missed him in London. It would indeed be a triumph for me if I could run him to earth where my master had failed.

Luck had been against us again and again in this inquiry, but now at last it came to my aid. And the messenger of good fortune was none other than Mr Frankland, who was standing, grey-whiskered and red-faced, outside the gate of his garden, which opened on to the high road along which I travelled.

'Good day, Dr Watson,' cried he, with unwonted good humour, 'you must really give your horses a rest, and come in to have a glass of wine and to congratulate me.'

My feelings towards him were far from being friendly after what I had heard of his treatment of his daughter, but I was anxious to send Perkins and the wagonette home, and the opportunity was a good one. I alighted and sent a message to Sir Henry that I should walk over in time for dinner. Then

85 *had I not seen his death in the paper next morning.* This was quick work, as Sir Charles was not discovered until midnight.

I followed Frankland into his dining-room.

'It is a great day for me, sir—one of the red-letter days of my life,' he cried, with many chuckles. 'I have brought off a double event. I mean to teach them in these parts that law is law, and that there is a man here who does not fear to invoke it. I have established a right of way through the centre of old Middleton's park, slap across it, sir, within a hundred yards of his own front door. What do you think of that? We'll teach these magnates that they cannot ride rough-shod over the rights of the commoners, confound them! And I've closed the wood where the Fernworthy folk used to picnic. These infernal people seem to think that there are no rights of property, and that they can swarm where they like with their papers and their bottles. Both cases decided, Dr Watson, and both in my favour. I haven't had such a day since I had Sir John Morland for trespass, because he shot in his own warren.'

'How on earth did you do that?'

'Look it up in the books, sir. It will repay reading—Frankland *v.* Morland Court of Queen's Bench. It cost me £200, but I got my verdict.'

'Did it do you any good?'

'None, sir, none. I am proud to say that I had no interest in the matter. I act entirely from a sense of public duty. I have no doubt, for example, that the Fernworthy people will burn me in effigy tonight. I told the police last time they did it that they should stop these disgraceful exhibitions. The county constabulary is in a scandalous state, sir, and it has not afforded me the protection to which I am entitled. The case of Frankland *v.* Regina will bring the matter before the attention of the public. I told them that they would have occasion to regret their treatment of me, and already my words have come true.'

'How so?' I asked.

The old man put on a very knowing expression.

'Because I could tell them what they are dying to know; but nothing would induce me to help the rascals in any way.'

I had been casting round for some excuse by which I could get away from his gossip, but now I began to wish to hear more of it. I had seen enough of the contrary nature of the old sinner to understand that any strong sign of interest would be the surest way to stop his confidences.

'Some poaching case, no doubt?' said I, with an indifferent manner.

'Ha, ha, my boy, a very much more important matter than that! What about the convict on the moor?'

I started. 'You don't mean that you know where he is?' said I.

'I may not know exactly where he is, but I am quite sure that I could help the police to lay their hands on him. Has it never struck you that the way to catch that man was to find out where he got his food, and so trace it to him?'

He certainly seemed to be getting uncomfortably near the truth. 'No doubt,' said I; 'but how do you know that he is anywhere upon the moor?'

'I know it because I have seen with my own eyes the messenger who takes him his food.'

My heart sank for Barrymore. It was a serious thing to be in the power of this spiteful old busybody. But his next remark took a weight from my mind.

'You'll be surprised to hear that his food is taken to him

by a child. I see him every day through my telescope upon the roof. He passes along the same path at the same hour, and to whom should he be going except to the convict?'

Here was luck indeed! And yet I suppressed all appearance of interest. A child! Barrymore had said that our unknown was supplied by a boy. It was on his track, and not upon the convict's, that Frankland had stumbled. If I could get his knowledge it might save me a long and weary hunt. But incredulity and indifference were evidently my strongest cards.

'I should say that it was much more likely that it was the son of one of the moorland shepherds taking out his father's dinner.'

The least appearance of opposition struck fire out of the old autocrat. His eyes looked malignantly at me, and his grey whiskers bristled like those of any angry cat.

'Indeed, sir!' said he, pointing out over the wide-stretching moor. 'Do you see that Black Tor over yonder? Well, do you see the low hill beyond with the thorn-bush upon it? It is the stoniest part of the whole moor. Is that a place where a shepherd would be likely to take his station? Your suggestion, sir, is a most absurd one.'

I meekly answered that I had spoken without knowing all the facts. My submission pleased him and led him to further confidences.

'You may be sure, sir, that I have very good grounds before I come to an opinion. I have seen the boy again and again with his bundle. Every day, and sometimes twice a day, I have been able—but wait a moment, Dr Watson. Do my eyes deceive me, or is there at the present moment something moving upon that hillside?'

It was several miles off, but I could distinctly see a small dark dot against the dull green and grey.

'Come, sir, come!' cried Frankland, rushing upstairs. 'You will see with your own eyes and judge for yourself.'

The telescope, a formidable instrument mounted upon a tripod, stood upon the flat leads of the house. Frankland clapped his eye to it and gave a cry of satisfaction.

'Quick, Dr Watson, quick, before he passes over the hill!'

There he was, sure enough, a small urchin with a little bundle upon his shoulder, toiling slowly up the hill. When he reached the crest I saw the ragged, uncouth figure outlined for an instant against the cold blue sky. He looked round him, with a furtive and stealthy air, as one who dreads pursuit. Then he vanished over the hill.

'Well! Am I right?'

'Certainly, there is a boy who seems to have some secret errand.'

'And what the errand is even a county constable could guess. But not one word shall they have from me, and I bind you to secrecy also, Dr Watson. Not a word! You understand?'

'Just as you wish.'

'They have treated me shamefully—shamefully. When the facts come out in Frankland *v.* Regina I venture to think that a thrill of indignation will run through the country. Nothing would induce me to help the police in any way. For all they cared it might have been me, instead of my effigy, which these rascals burned at the stake. Surely you are not going! You will help me to empty the decanter in honour of this great occasion!'

But I resisted all his solicitations and succeeded in dissuading him from his announced intention of walking home with me. I kept the road as long as his eye was on me, and then I struck off across the moor and made for the stony hill over which the boy had disappeared. Everything was working in my favour, and I swore that it should not be through lack of energy or perseverance that I should miss the chance which Fortune had thrown in my way.

The sun was already sinking when I reached the summit of the hill, and the long slopes beneath me were all golden-green on one side and grey shadow on the other. A haze lay low upon the farthest skyline, out of which jutted the fantastic shapes of Belliver and Vixen Tor. Over the wide expanse there was no sound and no movement. One great grey bird, a gull or curlew, soared aloft in the blue heaven. He and I seemed to be the only living things between the huge arch of the sky and the desert beneath it. The barren scene, the sense of loneliness, and the mystery and urgency of my task all struck a chill into my heart. The boy was nowhere to be seen. But down beneath me, in a cleft of the hills, there was a circle of the old stone huts, and in the middle of them there was one which retained sufficient roof to act as a screen against the weather. My heart leaped within me as I saw it. This must be the burrow where the stranger lurked. At last my foot was on the threshold of his hiding-place—his secret was within my grasp.

. . . THE FANTASTIC SHAPES OF BELLIVER AND VIXEN TOR.

Both of these are actual tors, and Watson has made no attempt to disguise their names, beyond changing BELLEVER to BELLIVER. Both will be found on our map, and Vixen Tor is shown above in a photograph by J. Shortridge for the Reverend Sabine Baring-Gould's *A Book of Dartmoor*. Both Belliver (Bellever) and Vixen Tor do have "fantastic shapes," and Watson might well have added that, viewed from one point, Vixen Tor and the Sphinx of Egypt bear a marked resemblance.

As I approached the hut, walking as warily as Stapleton would do when with poised net he drew near the settled butterfly, I satisfied myself that the place had indeed been used as a habitation. A vague pathway among the boulders led to the dilapidated opening which served as a door. All was silent within. The unknown might be lurking there, or he might be prowling on the moor. My nerves tingled with the sense of adventure. Throwing aside my cigarette, I closed my hand upon the butt of my revolver, and, walking swiftly up to the door, I looked in. The place was empty.

But there were ample signs that I had not come upon a false scent. This was certainly where the man lived. Some blankets rolled in a waterproof lay upon that very stone slab upon which neolithic man had once slumbered. The ashes of a fire were heaped in a rude grate. Beside it lay some cooking utensils and a bucket half-full of water. A litter of empty tins showed that the place had been occupied for some time, and I saw, as my eyes became accustomed to the chequered light,

THIS MUST BE THE BURROW WHERE THE STRANGER LURKED.

Reliable local authority assures us that this photograph by Stuart Black, F.R.P.S. (from *Sherlock Holmes: A Biography*, by William S. Baring-Gould) shows the veritable hut which housed for a time "The Man on the Tor."

a pannikin and a half-full bottle of spirits standing in the corner. In the middle of the hut a flat stone served the purpose of a table, and upon this stood a small cloth bundle—the same, no doubt, which I had seen through the telescope upon the shoulder of the boy. It contained a loaf of bread, a tinned tongue, and two tins of preserved peaches. As I set it down again, after having examined it, my heart leaped to see that beneath it there lay a sheet of paper with writing upon it. I raised it, and this was what I read, roughly scrawled in pencil:

'Dr Watson has gone to Coombe Tracey.'

For a minute I stood there with the paper in my hands thinking out the meaning of this curt message. It was I, then, and not Sir Henry, who was being dogged by this secret man. He had not followed me himself, but he had set an agent—the boy, perhaps—upon my track, and this was his report. Possibly I had taken no step since I had been upon the moor which had not been observed and repeated. Always there was this feeling of an unseen force, a fine net drawn round us with infinite skill and delicacy, holding us so lightly that it was only at some supreme moment that one realized that one was indeed entangled in its meshes.

If there was one report there might be others, so I looked round the hut in search of them. There was no trace, however, of anything of the kind, nor could I discover any sign which might indicate the character or intentions of the man who lived in this singular place, save that he must be of Spartan habits, and cared little for the comforts of life. When I thought of the heavy rains and looked at the gaping roof I understood how strong and immutable must be the purpose which had kept him in that inhospitable abode. Was he our malignant enemy, or was he by chance our guardian angel? I swore that I would not leave the hut until I knew.

Outside the sun was sinking low and the west was blazing with scarlet and gold. Its reflection was shot back in ruddy patches by the distant pools which lay amid the great Grimpen Mire. There were the two towers of Baskerville Hall, and there a distant blur of smoke which marked the village of Grimpen. Between the two, behind the hill, was the house of the Stapletons. All was sweet and mellow and peaceful in the golden evening light, and yet as I looked at them my soul shared none of the peace of Nature, but quivered at the vagueness and the terror of that interview which every instant was bringing nearer. With tingling nerves, but a fixed purpose, I sat in the dark recess of the hut and waited with sombre patience for the coming of its tenant.

And then at last I heard him. Far away came the sharp clink of a boot striking upon a stone. Then another and yet another, coming nearer and nearer. I shrank back into the darkest corner, and cocked the pistol in my pocket, determined not to discover myself until I had an opportunity of seeing something of the stranger. There was a long pause, which showed that he had stopped. Then once more the footsteps approached and a shadow fell across the opening of the hut.

'It is a lovely evening, my dear Watson,' said a well-known **86**
voice. 'I really think that you will be more comfortable out side than in.'

. . . A SHADOW FELL ACROSS THE OPENING OF THE HUT.

Illustration by Sidney Paget for the *Strand Magazine*, January, 1902.

86 *'It is a lovely evening.* And Watson has previously told us that "All was sweet and mellow and peaceful in the golden evening light." Said the *Times* of London of this day: "The thick fogs which have lately prevailed over England have entirely disappeared. . . . Weather . . . was fine at most of the English and Continental stations."

For a moment or two I sat breathless, hardly able to believe my ears. Then my senses and my voice came back to me, while a crushing weight of responsibility seemed in an instant to be lifted from my soul. That cold, incisive, ironical voice could belong to but one man in all the world.

'Holmes!' I cried—'Holmes!'

'Come out,' said he, 'and please be careful with the revolver.'

I stooped under the rude lintel, and there he sat upon a stone outside, his grey eyes dancing with amusement as they fell upon my astonished features. He was thin and worn, but clear and alert, his keen face bronzed by the sun and rough-
87 ened by the wind. In his tweed suit and cloth cap he looked like any other tourist upon the moor, and he had contrived, with that cat-like love of personal cleanliness which was one of his characteristics, that his chin should be as smooth and
88 his linen as perfect as if he were in Baker Street.

'I never was more glad to see anyone in my life,' said I, as I wrung him by the hand.

'Or more astonished, eh?'

'Well, I must confess to it.'

'The surprise was not all on one side, I assure you. I had no idea that you had found my occasional retreat, still less that you were inside it, until I was within twenty paces of the door.'

'My footprint, I presume?'

'No, Watson; I fear that I could not undertake to recognize your footprint amid all the footprints of the world. If you seriously desire to deceive me you must change your tobacconist; for when I see the stub of a cigarette marked Bradley,
89 Oxford Street, I know that my friend Watson is in the neighbourhood. You will see it there beside the path. You threw it down, no doubt, at that supreme moment when you charged into the empty hut.'

'Exactly.'

'I thought as much—and knowing your admirable tenacity, I was convinced that you were sitting in ambush, a weapon within reach, waiting for the tenant to return. So you actually thought that I was the criminal?'

'I did not know who you were, but I was determined to find out.'

'Excellent, Watson! And how did you localize me? You saw me, perhaps, on the night of the convict hunt, when I was so imprudent as to allow the moon to rise behind me?'

'Yes, I saw you then.'

'And have, no doubt, searched all the huts until you came to this one?'

'No, your boy had been observed, and that gave me a guide where to look.'

'The old gentleman with the telescope, no doubt. I could not make it out when first I saw the light flashing upon the lens.' He rose and peeped into the hut, 'Ha, I see that Cartwright has brought up some supplies. What's this paper? So you have been to Coombe Tracey, have you?'

'Yes.'

'To see Mrs Laura Lyons?'

. . . THERE HE SAT UPON A STONE OUTSIDE . . .

Illustration by Sidney Paget for the *Strand Magazine*, February, 1902.

87 *cloth cap.* "In sixty adventures," the late Professor Jay Finley Christ wrote in "The Pipe and the Cap," "the fore-and-aft, or deerstalker, is noted only *three* times, and it never is called by either of these names. In 'The Boscombe Valley Mystery' . . . it is 'his close-fitting cloth cap'; in 'Silver Blaze' . . . it is 'an ear-flapped travelling cap,' and in *The Hound of the Baskervilles* . . . it says 'in his tweed suit and cloth cap, he looked like any other tourist.' Sidney Paget drew all of these *as* deer-stalkers, and in the same period (1891–1901) the *Strand Magazine* offered at least nine other illustrations of such caps. Some of the latter were done for stories by A. Conan Doyle ('The Club-Footed Grocer,' 1898), some by Paget for non-Doyle stories, some by other artists for other authors . . ."

To this the artist's daughter, Miss Winifred Paget, has added: "As a young man my father lived in the country, and it was during this time that he wore that surely now most famous of all hats—the deerstalker—and the fact that he liked it and found it comfortable inspired him to depict Holmes wearing it on so many occasions."

'Exactly.'

'Well done! Our researches have evidently been running on parallel lines, and when we unite our results I expect we shall have a fairly full knowledge of the case.'

'Well, I am glad from my heart that you are here, for indeed the responsibility and the mystery were both becoming too much for my nerves. But how in the name of wonder did you come here, and what have you been doing? I thought that you were in Baker Street working out that case of blackmailing.'

'That was what I wished you to think.'

'Then you use me, and yet do not trust me!' I cried, with some bitterness. 'I think that I have deserved better at your hands, Holmes.'

'My dear fellow, you have been invaluable to me in this as in many other cases, and I beg that you will forgive me if I have seemed to play a trick upon you. In truth, it was partly for your own sake that I did it, and it was my appreciation of the danger which you ran which led me to come down and examine the matter for myself. Had I been with Sir Henry and you it is evident that my point of view would have been the same as yours, and my presence would have warned our very formidable opponents to be on their guard. As it is, I have been able to get about as I could not possibly have done had I been living at the Hall, and I remain an unknown factor in the business, ready to throw in all my weight at a critical moment.'

'But why keep me in the dark?'

'For you to know could not have helped us, and might possibly have led to my discovery. You would have wished to tell me something, or in your kindness you would have brought me out some comfort or other, and so an unnecessary risk would be run. I brought Cartwright down with me—you remember the little chap at the Express office—and he has seen after my simple wants: a loaf of bread and a clean collar. What does man want more? He has given me an extra pair of eyes upon a very active pair of feet, and both have been invaluable.'

'Then my reports have all been wasted!' My voice trembled as I recalled the pains and the pride with which I had composed them.

Holmes took a bundle of papers from his pocket.

'Here are your reports, my dear fellow, and very well thumbed, I assure you. I made excellent arrangements, and they are only delayed one day upon their way. I must compliment you exceedingly upon the zeal and the intelligence which you have shown over an extraordinarily difficult case.'

I was still rather raw over the deception which had been practised upon me, but the warmth of Holmes's praise drove my anger from my mind. I felt also in my heart that he was right in what he said, and that it was really best for our purpose that I should not have known that he was upon the moor.

'That's better,' said he, seeing the shadow rise from my face. 'And now tell me the result of your visit to Mrs Laura Lyons—it was not difficult for me to guess that it was to see her that you had gone, for I am already aware that she is the one person in Coombe Tracey who might be of service to us in the matter. In fact, if you had not gone today it is exceedingly probable that I should have gone tomorrow.'

The sun had set and dusk was settling over the moor. The air had turned chill, and we withdrew into the hut for

88 *as perfect as if he were in Baker Street.* "This spruce appearance sounds so unlike the Holmes we know that one cannot help wondering if there was any feminine reason for it," Dr. Richard Asher wrote in "Holmes and the Fair Sex." "After all there was at Coombe Tracey, a few miles away, the redoubtable Mrs. Laura Lyons. . . . Or could it possibly have been Mrs. Barrymore, the butler's wife at Baskerville Hall?"

89 *Bradley, Oxford Street.* "In actual fact," Mr. J. C. Wimbush wrote in "Watson's Tobacconist," "there has always been a dearth of tobacconists in Oxford Street itself, that is, between Marble Arch and Oxford Circus. There is one, however, which was quite definitely . . . in existence . . . till 1890. It occupied what is now the southeast corner of the [D. H. Evans store], and its name is R. H. Hoar & Co., Ltd. . . . now situated at No. 6, Prince's Street, which runs north from Oxford Street just west of the Circus."

warmth. There, sitting together in the twilight, I told Holmes of my conversation with the lady. So interested was he that I had to repeat some of it twice before he was satisfied.

'This is most important,' said he, when I had concluded. 'It fills up a gap which I had been unable to bridge in this most complex affair. You are aware, perhaps, that a close intimacy exists between this lady and the man Stapleton?'

'I did not know of a close intimacy.'

'There can be no doubt about the matter. They meet, they write, there is a complete understanding between them. Now, this puts a very powerful weapon into our hands. If I could only use it to detach his wife——'

'His wife?'

'I am giving you some information now, in return for all that you have given me. The lady who has passed here as Miss Stapleton is in reality his wife.'

'Good heavens, Holmes! Are you sure of what you say? How could he have permitted Sir Henry to fall in love with her?'

'Sir Henry's falling in love could do no harm to anyone except Sir Henry. He took particular care that Sir Henry did not *make* love to her, as you have yourself observed. I repeat that the lady is his wife and not his sister.'

'But why this elaborate deception?'

'Because he foresaw that she would be very much more useful to him in the character of a free woman.'

All my unspoken instincts, my vague suspicions, suddenly took shape and centred upon the naturalist. In that impassive, colourless man, with his straw hat and his butterfly-net, I seemed to see something terrible—a creature of infinite patience and craft, with a smiling face and a murderous heart.

'It is he, then, who is our enemy—it is he who dogged us in London?'

'So I read the riddle.'

'And the warning—it must have come from her!'

'Exactly.'

The shape of some monstrous villainy, half seen, half guessed, loomed through the darkness which had girt me so long.

'But are you sure of this, Holmes? How do you know that the woman is his wife?'

'Because he so far forgot himself as to tell you a true piece of autobiography upon the occasion when he first met you, and I dare say he has many a time regretted it since. He *was* once a schoolmaster in the North of England. Now, there is no one more easy to trace than a schoolmaster. There are scholastic agencies by which one may identify any man who has been in the profession. A little investigation showed me that a school had come to grief under atrocious circumstances, and that the man who had owned it—the name was different—had disappeared with his wife. The descriptions agreed. When I learned that the missing man was devoted to entomology the identification was complete.'

The darkness was rising, but much was still hidden by the shadows.

'If this woman is in truth his wife, where does Mrs Laura Lyons come in?' I asked.

'That is one of the points upon which your own researches have shed a light. Your interview with the lady has cleared the situation very much. I did not know about a projected divorce between herself and her husband. In that case, regarding Stapleton as an unmarried man, she counted no doubt upon becoming his wife.'

'And when she is undeceived?'

'Why, then we may find the lady of service. It must be our first duty to see her—both of us—tomorrow. Don't you think, Watson, that you are away from your charge rather long? Your place should be at Baskerville Hall.'

The last red streaks had faded away in the west and night had settled upon the moor. A few faint stars were gleaming in a violet sky.

'One last question, Holmes,' I said, as I rose. 'Surely there is no need of secrecy between you and me. What is the meaning of it all? What is he after?'

Holmes's voice sank as he answered—'It is murder, Watson—refined, cold-blooded, deliberate murder. Do not ask me for particulars. My nets are closing upon him, even as his are upon Sir Henry, and with your help he is already almost at my mercy. There is but one danger which can threaten us. It is that he should strike before we are ready to do so. Another day—two at the most—and I have my case complete, but until then guard your charge as closely as ever a fond mother watched her ailing child. Your mission today has justified itself, and yet I could almost wish that you had not left his side—Hark!'

A terrible scream—a prolonged yell of horror and anguish burst out of the silence of the moor. That frightful cry turned the blood to ice in my veins.

'Oh, my God!' I gasped. 'What is it? What does it mean?'

Holmes had sprung to his feet, and I saw his dark, athletic outline at the door of the hut, his shoulders stooping, his head thrust forward, his face peering into the darkness.

'Hush!' he whispered. 'Hush!'

The cry had been loud on account of its vehemence, but it had pealed out from somewhere far off on the shadowy plain. Now it burst upon our ears, nearer, louder, more urgent than before.

'Where is it?' Holmes whispered; and I knew from the thrill of his voice that he, the man of iron, was shaken to the soul. 'Where is it, Watson?'

'There, I think.' I pointed into the darkness.

'No, there!'

Again the agonized cry swept through the silent night, louder and much nearer than ever. And a new sound mingled with it, a deep, muttered rumble, musical and yet menacing, rising and falling like the low, constant murmur of the sea.

'The hound!' cried Holmes. 'Come, Watson, come! Great heavens, if we are too late!'

He had started running swiftly over the moor, and I had followed at his heels. But now from somewhere among the broken ground immediately in front of us there came one last despairing yell, and then a dull, heavy thud. We halted and listened. Not another sound broke the heavy silence of the windless night.

I saw Holmes put his hand to his forehead, like a man distracted. He stamped his feet upon the ground.

'He has beaten us, Watson. We are too late.'

'No, no, surely not!'

'Fool that I was to hold my hand. And you, Watson, see what comes of abandoning your charge! But, by Heaven, if the worst has happened, we'll avenge him!'

Blindly we ran through the gloom, blundering against boulders, forcing our way through gorse bushes, panting up hills and rushing down slopes, heading always in the direction whence those dreadful sounds had come. At every rise Holmes looked eagerly round him, but the shadows were thick upon the moor and nothing moved upon its dreary face.

'Can you see anything?'

'Nothing.'

'But, hark, what is that?'

A low moan had fallen upon our ears. There it was again upon our left! On that side a ridge of rocks ended in a sheer cliff, which overlooked a stone-strewn slope. On its jagged face was spread-eagled some dark, irregular object. As we ran towards it the vague outline hardened into a definite shape. It was a prostrate man face downwards upon the ground, the head doubled under him at a horrible angle, the shoulders rounded and the body hunched together as if in the act of throwing a somersault. So grotesque was the attitude that I could not for the instant realize that that moan had been the passing of his soul. Not a whisper, not a rustle, rose now from the dark figure over which we stooped. Holmes laid his hand upon him, and held it up again, with an exclamation of horror. The gleam of the match which he struck shone upon his clotted fingers and upon the ghastly pool which widened slowly from the crushed skull of the victim. And it shone upon something else which turned our hearts sick and faint within us—the body of Sir Henry Baskerville!

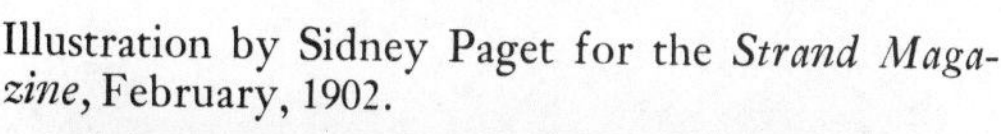

IT WAS A PROSTRATE MAN FACE DOWNWARDS UPON THE GROUND . . .

Illustration by Sidney Paget for the *Strand Magazine*, February, 1902.

There was no chance of either of us forgetting that peculiar ruddy tweed suit—the very one which he had worn on the first morning that we had seen him in Baker Street. We caught the one clear glimpse of it, and then the match flickered and went out, even as the hope had gone out of our souls. Holmes groaned, and his face glimmered white through the darkness.

'The brute! the brute!' I cried, with clenched hands. 'Oh, Holmes, I shall never forgive myself for having left him to his fate.'

'I am more to blame than you, Watson. In order to have my case well rounded and complete, I have thrown away the life of my client. It is the greatest blow which has befallen me in my career. But how could I know—how *could* I know—that he would risk his life alone upon the moor in the face of all my warnings?'

'That we should have heard his screams—my God, those screams!—and yet have been unable to save him! Where is this brute of a hound which drove him to his death? It may be lurking among these rocks at this instant. And Stapleton, where is he? He shall answer for this deed.'

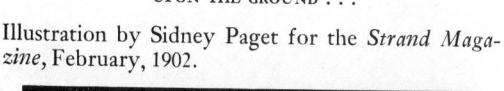

'He shall. I will see to that. Uncle and nephew have been murdered—the one frightened to death by the very sight of a beast, which he thought to be supernatural, the other driven to his end in his wild flight to escape from it. But now we have to prove the connection between the man and the beast. Save from what we heard, we cannot even swear to the existence of the latter, since Sir Henry has evidently died from the fall. But, by heavens, cunning as he is, the fellow shall be in my power before another day is past!'

We stood with bitter hearts on either side of the mangled
body, overwhelmed by this sudden and irrevocable disaster
which had brought all our long and weary labours to so
piteous an end. Then, as the moon rose, we climbed to the **90**
top of the rocks over which our poor friend had fallen, and
from the summit we gazed out over the shadowy moor, half
silver and half gloom. Far away, miles off, in the direction of
Grimpen, a single steady, yellow light was shining. It could
only come from the lonely abode of the Stapletons. With a
bitter curse I shook my fist at it as I gazed.

'Why should we not seize him at once?'

'Our case is not complete. The fellow is wary and cunning to the last degree. It is not what we know, but what we can prove. If we make one false move the villain may escape us yet.'

'What can we do?'

'There will be plenty for us to do tomorrow. Tonight we can only perform the last offices to our poor friend.'

Together we made our way down the precipitous slope and approached the body, black and clear against the silvered stones. The agony of those contorted limbs struck me with a spasm of pain and blurred my eyes with tears.

'We must send for help, Holmes! We cannot carry him all the way to the Hall. Good heavens, are you mad?'

He had uttered a cry and bent over the body. Now he was dancing and laughing and wringing my hand. Could this be my stern, self-contained friend? These were hidden fires, indeed!

'A beard! A beard! The man has a beard!'

'A beard?'

'It is not the baronet—it is—why, it is my neighbour, the convict!'

With feverish haste we had turned the body over, and that dripping beard was pointing up to the cold, clear moon. There could be no doubt about the beetling forehead, the sunken animal eyes. It was, indeed, the same face which had glared upon me in the light of the candle from over the rock—the face of Selden, the criminal.

Then in an instant it was all clear to me. I remembered how the baronet had told me that he had handed his old wardrobe to Barrymore. Barrymore had passed it on in order to help Selden in his escape. Boots, shirt, cap—it was all Sir Henry's. The tragedy was still black enough, but this man had at least deserved death by the laws of his country. I told Holmes how the matter stood, my heart bubbling over with thankfulness and joy.

'Then the clothes have been the poor fellow's death,' said he. 'It is clear enough that the hound has been laid on from some article of Sir Henry's—the boot which was abstracted in the hotel, in all probability—and so ran this man down. There is one very singular thing, however: How came Selden, in the darkness, to know that the hound was on his trail?'

'He heard him.'

'To hear a hound upon the moor would not work a hard man like this convict into such a paroxysm of terror that he would risk recapture by screaming wildly for help. By his cries he must have run a long way after he knew the animal was on his track. How did he know?'

'A greater mystery to me is why this hound, presuming that

90 *Then, as the moon rose*. But the moon did not rise about nine o'clock on the evening of Thursday, October 18, 1888, as Watson tells us it did: it rose at 5:05 P.M. on that date.

IT WAS . . . THE FACE OF SELDEN, THE CRIMINAL.

Illustration by Sidney Paget for the *Strand Magazine*, February, 1902.

'WHO—WHO'S THIS?' HE STAMMERED.

Illustration by Sidney Paget for the *Strand Magazine*, February, 1902.

all our conjectures are correct——'

'I presume nothing.'

'Well, then, why this hound should be loose tonight. I suppose that it does not always run loose upon the moor. Stapleton would not let it go unless he had reason to think that Sir Henry would be there.'

'My difficulty is the more formidable of the two, for I think that we shall very shortly get an explanation of yours, while mine may remain for ever a mystery. The question now is, what shall we do with this poor wretch's body? We cannot leave it here to the foxes and the ravens.'

'I suggest that we put it in one of the huts until we can communicate with the police.'

'Exactly. I have no doubt that you and I could carry it so far. Halloa, Watson, what's this? It's the man himself, by all that's wonderful and audacious! Not a word to show your suspicions—not a word, or my plans crumble to the ground.'

A figure was approaching us over the moor, and I saw the dull red glow of a cigar. The moon shone upon him, and I could distinguish the dapper shape and jaunty walk of the naturalist. He stopped when he saw us, and then came on again.

'Why, Dr Watson, that's not you, is it? You are the last man that I should have expected to see out on the moor at this time of night. But, dear me, what's this? Somebody hurt? Not —don't tell me that it is our friend Sir Henry!'

He hurried past me and stooped over the dead man. I heard a sharp intake of his breath and the cigar fell from his fingers.

'Who—who's this?' he stammered.

'It is Selden, the man who escaped from Princetown.'

Stapleton turned a ghastly face upon us, but by a supreme effort he had overcome his amazement and his disappointment. He looked sharply from Holmes to me.

'Dear me! What a very shocking affair! How did he die?'

'He appears to have broken his neck by falling over these rocks. My friend and I were strolling on the moor when we heard a cry.'

'I heard a cry also. That was what brought me out. I was uneasy about Sir Henry.'

'Why about Sir Henry in particular?' I could not help asking.

'Because I had suggested that he should come over. When he did not come I was surprised, and I naturally became alarmed for his safety when I heard cries upon the moor. By the way'—his eyes darted again from my face to Holmes's—'did you hear anything else besides a cry?'

'No,' said Holmes; 'did you?'

'No.'

'What do you mean, then?'

'Oh, you know the stories that the peasants tell about a phantom hound, and so on. It is said to be heard at night upon the moor. I was wondering if there were any evidence of such a sound tonight.'

'We heard nothing of the kind,' said I.

'And what is your theory of this poor fellow's death?'

'I have no doubt that anxiety and exposure have driven him off his head. He has rushed about the moor in a crazy state and eventually fallen over here and broken his neck.

'That seems the most reasonable theory,' said Stapleton,

and he gave a sigh which I took to indicate his relief. 'What do you think about it, Mr Sherlock Holmes?'

My friend bowed his compliments.

'You are quick at identification,' said he.

'We have been expecting you in these parts since Dr Watson came down. You are in time to see a tragedy.'

'Yes, indeed. I have no doubt that my friend's explanation will cover the facts. I will take an unpleasant remembrance back to London with me tomorrow.'

'Oh, you return tomorrow?'

'That is my intention.'

'I hope your visit has cast some light upon those occurrences which have puzzled us?'

Holmes shrugged his shoulders. 'One cannot always have the success for which one hopes. An investigator needs facts, and not legends or rumours. It has not been a satisfactory case.'

My friend spoke in his frankest and most unconcerned manner. Stapleton still looked hard at him. Then he turned to me.

'I would suggest carrying this poor fellow to my house, but it would give my sister such a fright that I do not feel justified in doing it. I think that if we put something over his face he will be safe until morning.'

And so it was arranged. Resisting Stapleton's offer of hospitality, Holmes and I set off to Baskerville Hall, leaving the naturalist to return alone. Looking back we saw the figure moving slowly away over the broad moor, and behind him that one black smudge on the silvered slope which showed where the man was lying who had come so horribly to his end.

'We're at close grips at last,' said Holmes, as we walked together across the moor. 'What a nerve the fellow has! How he pulled himself together in the face of what must have been a paralysing shock when he found that the wrong man had fallen a victim to his plot. I told you in London, Watson, and I tell you now again, that we have never had a foeman more worthy of our steel.'

'I am sorry that he has seen you.'

'And so was I at first. But there was no getting out of it.'

'What effect do you think it will have upon his plans, now that he knows you are here?'

'It may cause him to be more cautious, or it may drive him to desperate measures at once. Like most clever criminals, he may be too confident in his own cleverness and imagine that he has completely deceived us.'

'Why should we not arrest him at once?'

'My dear Watson, you were born to be a man of action. Your instinct is always to do something energetic. But supposing, for argument's sake, that we had him arrested tonight, what on earth the better off should we be for that? We could prove nothing against him. There's the devilish cunning of it! If he were acting through a human agent we could get some evidence, but if we were to drag this great dog to the light of day it would not help us in putting a rope round the neck of its master.'

'Surely we have a case.'

'Not a shadow of one—only surmise and conjecture. We should be laughed out of court if we came with such a story and such evidence.'

91 *Sufficient for tomorrow is the evil thereof.* Holmes again quotes Scripture: "Sufficient unto the day is the evil thereof," Matthew, 10:16.

'There is Sir Charles's death.'

'Found dead without a mark upon him. You and I know that he died of sheer fright, and we know also what frightened him; but how are we to get twelve stolid jurymen to know it? What signs are there of a hound? Where are the marks of its fangs. Of course, we know that a hound does not bite a dead body, and that Sir Charles was dead before ever the brute overtook him. But we have to *prove* all this, and we are not in a position to do it.'

'Well, then, tonight?'

'We are not much better off tonight. Again, there was no direct connection between the hound and the man's death. We never saw the hound. We heard it; but we could not prove that it was running upon this man's trail. There is a complete absence of motive. No, my dear fellow; we must reconcile ourselves to the fact that we have no case at present, and that it is worth our while to run any risk in order to establish one.'

'And how do you propose to do so?'

'I have great hopes of what Mrs Laura Lyons may do for
us when the position of affairs is made clear to her. And I
have my own plan as well. Sufficient for tomorrow is the evil
91 thereof; but I hope before the day is past to have the upper
hand at last.'

I could draw nothing further from him, and he walked, lost in thought, as far as the Baskerville gates.

'Are you coming up?'

'Yes; I see no reason for further concealment. But one last word, Watson. Say nothing of the hound to Sir Henry. Let him think that Selden's death was as Stapleton would have us believe. He will have a better nerve for the ordeal which he will have to undergo tomorrow, when he is engaged, if I remember your report aright, to dine with these people.'

'And so am I.'

'Then you must excuse yourself, and he must go alone. That will be easily arranged. And now, if we are too late for dinner, I think that we are both ready for our suppers.'

13 ◆ FIXING THE NETS

Sir Henry was more pleased than surprised to see Sherlock Holmes, for he had for some days been expecting that recent events would bring him down from London. He did raise his eyebrows, however, when he found that my friend had neither any luggage nor any explanations for its absence. Between us we soon supplied his wants, and then over a belated supper we explained to the baronet as much of our experience as it seemed desirable that he should know. But first I had the unpleasant duty of breaking the news of Selden's death to Barrymore and his wife. To him it may have been an unmitigated relief, but she wept bitterly in her apron. To all the world he was the man of violence, half animal and half demon; but to her he always remained the little wilful boy of her own girlhood, the child who had clung to her hand. Evil indeed is the man who has not one woman to mourn him.

'I've been moping in the house all day since Watson went off in the morning,' said the baronet. 'I guess I should have some credit, for I have kept my promise. If I hadn't sworn not to go about alone I might have had a more lively evening, for I had a message from Stapleton asking me over there.'

'I have no doubt that you would have had a more lively evening,' said Holmes, dryly. 'By the way, I don't suppose you appreciate that we have been mourning over you as having broken your neck?'

Sir Henry opened his eyes. 'How was that?'

'This poor wretch was dressed in your clothes. I fear your servant who gave them to him may get into trouble with the police.'

'That is unlikely. There was no mark on any of them, so far as I know.'

'That's lucky for him—in fact, it's lucky for all of you, since you are all on the wrong side of the law in this matter. I am not sure that as a conscientious detective my first duty is not to arrest the whole household. Watson's reports are most incriminating documents.'

'But how about the case?' asked the baronet. 'Have you made anything out of the tangle? I don't know that Watson and I are much the wiser since we came down.'

'I think that I shall be in a position to make the situation rather more clear to you before long. It has been an exceedingly difficult and most complicated business. There are several points upon which we still want light—but it is coming, all the same.'

'We've had one experience, as Watson has no doubt told you. We heard the hound on the moor, so I can swear that it is not all empty superstition. I had something to do with dogs when I was out West, and I know one when I hear one. If you can muzzle that one and put him on a chain I'll be ready to swear you are the greatest detective of all time.'

'I think I will muzzle him and chain him all right if you will give me your help.'

'Whatever you tell me to do I will do.'

'Very good; and I will ask you also to do it blindly, without always asking the reason.'

'Just as you like.'

'If you will do this I think the chances are that our little problem will soon be solved. I have no doubt——'

He stopped suddenly and stared fixedly up over my head into the air. The lamp beat upon his face, and so intent was it and so still that it might have been that of a clear-cut classical statue, a personification of alertness and expectation.

'What is it?' we both cried.

I could see as he looked down that he was repressing some internal emotion. His features were still composed, but his eyes shone with amused exultation.

'Excuse the admiration of a connoisseur,' said he, as he waved his hand towards the line of portraits which covered the opposite wall. 'Watson won't allow that I know anything of art, but that is mere jealousy, because our views upon the subject differ. Now, these are a really very fine series of portraits.'

'Well, I'm glad to hear you say so,' said Sir Henry, glancing

HE STOPPED SUDDENLY AND STARED FIXEDLY UP OVER MY HEAD INTO THE AIR.

Illustration by Sidney Paget for the *Strand Magazine*, March, 1902.

92 *Kneller*. Sir Godfrey Kneller, 1646–1723. He succeeded Lely as court painter to Charles II, and many of his portraits hang at Hampton Court.

93 *Reynolds*. Sir Joshua Reynolds, 1723–1792. He and his assistants painted some 2,000 portraits and historical paintings, notable for their richness of color; in design he surpassed his rivals Gainsborough and Romney.

94 *Rodney*. George Brydges Rodney, first Baron Rodney, 1719–1792, British admiral. His defeat (1782) of a French fleet under De Grasse in the West Indies led to better peace terms with the French after the American Revolution.

95 *Pitt*. William Pitt, 1759–1806, Prime Minister (1783–1801) under George III.

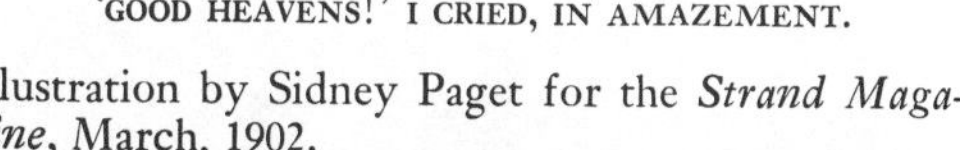

'GOOD HEAVENS!' I CRIED, IN AMAZEMENT.

Illustration by Sidney Paget for the *Strand Magazine*, March, 1902.

with some surprise at my friend. 'I don't pretend to know much about these things, and I'd be a better judge of a horse or a steer than of a picture. I didn't know that you found time for such things.'

'I know what is good when I see it, and I see it now. That's
92 a Kneller, I'll swear, that lady in the blue silk over yonder,
93 and the stout gentleman with the wig ought to be a Reynolds.
They are all family portraits, I presume?'

'Every one.'

'Do you know the names?'

'Barrymore has been coaching me in them, and I think I can say my lessons fairly well.'

'Who is the gentleman with the telescope?'

'That is Rear-Admiral Baskerville, who served under Rod-
94 ney in the West Indies. The man with the blue coat and the
roll of paper is Sir William Baskerville, who was Chairman
95 of Committees of the House of Commons under Pitt.'

'And this Cavalier opposite to me—the one with the black velvet and the lace?'

'Ah, you have a right to know about him. That is the cause of all the mischief, the wicked Hugo, who started the Hound of the Baskervilles. We're not likely to forget him.'

96 I gazed with interest and some surprise upon the portrait.

'Dear me!' said Holmes, 'he seems a quiet, meek-mannered man enough, but I dare say that there was a lurking devil in his eyes. I had pictured him as a more robust and ruffianly person.'

'There's no doubt about the authenticity, for the name and the date, 1647, are on the back of the canvas.'

Holmes said little more, but the picture of the old roysterer seemed to have a fascination for him, and his eyes were continually fixed upon it during supper. It was not until later, when Sir Henry had gone to his room, that I was able to follow the trend of his thoughts. He led me back into the banqueting-hall, his bedroom candle in his hand, and he held it up against the time-stained portrait on the wall.

'Do you see anything there?'

I looked at the broad plumed hat, the curling love-locks, the white lace collar, and the straight, severe face which was framed between them. It was not a brutal countenance, but it was prim, hard and stern, with a firm-set, thin-lipped mouth, and a coldly intolerant eye.

'Is it like anyone you know?'

'There is something of Sir Henry about the jaw.'

'Just a suggestion, perhaps. But wait an instant!'

He stood upon a chair, and holding up the light in his left hand, he curved his right arm over the broad hat, and round the long ringlets.

'Good heavens!' I cried, in amazement.

The face of Stapleton had sprung out of the canvas.

'Ha, you see it now. My eyes have been trained to examine faces and not their trimmings. It is the first quality of a criminal investigator that he should see through a disguise.'

'But this is marvellous. It might be his portrait.'

97 'Yes, it is an interesting instance of a throw-back, which appears to be both physical and spiritual. A study of family portraits is enough to convert a man to the doctrine of re-incarnation. The fellow is a Baskerville—that is evident.'

'With designs upon the succession.'

'Exactly. This chance of the picture has supplied us with one of our most obvious missing links. We have him, Watson, we have him, and I dare swear that before tomorrow night he will be fluttering in our net as helpless as one of his own butterflies. A pin, a cork, and a card, and we add him to the Baker Street collection!'

He burst into one of his rare fits of laughter as he turned away from the picture. I have not heard him laugh often, and it has always boded ill to somebody.

I was up betimes in the morning, but Holmes was afoot earlier still, for I saw him as I dressed coming up the drive.

'Yes, we should have a full day today,' he remarked, and he rubbed his hands with the joy of action. 'The nets are all in place, and the drag is about to begin. We'll know before the day is out whether we have caught our big, lean-jawed pike, or whether he has got through the meshes.'

'Have you been on the moor already?'

'I have sent a report from Grimpen to Princetown as to the death of Selden. I think I can promise that none of you will be troubled in the matter. And I have also communicated with my faithful Cartwright, who would certainly have pined away at the door of my hut as a dog does at his master's grave if I had not set his mind at rest about my safety.'

'What is the next move?'

'To see Sir Henry. Ah, here he is!'

'Good morning, Holmes,' said the baronet. 'You look like a general who is planning a battle with his chief of the staff.'

'That is the exact situation. Watson was asking for orders.'

'And so do I.'

'Very good. You are engaged, as I understand, to dine with our friends the Stapletons tonight.'

'I hope that you will come also. They are very hospitable people, and I am sure that they would be very glad to see you.'

'I fear that Watson and I must go to London.'

'To London?'

'Yes, I think that we should be more useful there at the present juncture.'

The baronet's face perceptibly lengthened. 'I hoped that you were going to see me through this business. The Hall and the moor are not very pleasant places when one is alone.'

'My dear fellow, you must trust me implicitly and do exactly what I tell you. You can tell your friends that we should have been happy to have come with you, but that urgent business required us to be in town. We hope very soon to return to Devonshire. Will you remember to give them that message?'

'If you insist upon it.'

'There is no alternative, I assure you.'

I saw by the baronet's clouded brow that he was deeply hurt by what he regarded as our desertion.

'When do you desire to go?' he asked, coldly.

'Immediately after breakfast. We will drive into Coombe Tracey, but Watson will leave his things as a pledge that he will come back to you. Watson, you will send a note to Stapleton to tell him that you regret that you cannot come.'

'I have a good mind to go to London with you,' said the baronet. 'Why should I stay here alone?'

'Because it is your post of duty. Because you gave me your

96 *I gazed with interest and some surprise upon the portrait.* "It is not known for certain who painted the portrait of Hugo Baskerville," Lord Donegall wrote in "Who Painted Hugo Baskerville?" "It is, however, fairly safe to deduce that, as the family portraits at Baskerville Hall included a Reynolds and a Kneller, it was the tradition of the Baskerville family to be painted by the best-known artist of the time. There is therefore little doubt that the portrait of Hugo Baskerville, painted in the 1640's, while he was serving the cause of Charles I, is the work of Franz Hals, the famous Dutch artist, one of whose best known works is the *Laughing Cavalier.*"

97 *a throw-back.* But now a problem arises. What about Dr. Mortimer? "If he knew enough about atavism to write a book on the subject, he must have been well-versed in it indeed," Mr. Charles M. Pickard wrote in "The Reticence of Doctor Mortimer." "Then too, he had been in the Hall many times, visiting Sir Charles, and he had seen the portrait often. Surely he must have noticed the resemblance between Stapleton and Hugo. Besides, he tells Holmes that he has heard that Rodger Baskerville is the image of Hugo. Why, then, didn't he put two and two together and reason that 1) Stapleton was really a Baskerville; 2) that he was most likely Rodger's son; and 3) none of the trouble had arisen until Stapleton moved in. If he deduced the first two points, he must have come to the conclusion that Stapleton was up to no good."

word that you would do as you were told, and I tell you to stay.'

'All right, then, I'll stay.'

'One more direction! I wish you to drive to Merripit House. Send back your trap, however, and let them know that you intend to walk home.'

'To walk across the moor?'

'Yes.'

'But that is the very thing which you have so often cautioned me not to do.'

'This time you may do it with safety. If I had not every confidence in your nerve and courage I would not suggest it, but it is essential that you should do it.'

'Then I will do it.'

'And as you value your life, do not go across the moor in any direction save along the straight path which leads from Merripit House to the Grimpen Road, and is your natural way home.'

'I will do just what you say.'

'Very good. I should be glad to get away as soon after breakfast as possible, so as to reach London in the afternoon.'

I was much astounded by this programme, though I remembered that Holmes had said to Stapleton on the night before that his visit would terminate next day. It had not crossed my mind, however, that he would wish me to go with him, nor could I understand how we could both be absent at a moment which he himself declared to be critical. There was nothing for it, however, but implicit obedience; so we bade good-bye to our rueful friend, and a couple of hours afterwards we were at the station of Coombe Tracey and had dispatched the trap upon its return journey. A small boy was waiting upon the platform.

'Any orders, sir?'

'You will take this train to town, Cartwright. The moment you arrive you will send a wire to Sir Henry Baskerville, in my name, to say that if he finds the pocket-book which I have dropped he is to send it by registered post to Baker Street.'

'Yes, sir.'

'And ask at the station office if there is a message for me.'

The boy returned with a telegram, which Holmes handed to me. It ran—

'Wire received. Coming down with unsigned warrant. Arrive five-forty.—Lestrade.'

'That is in answer to mine of this morning. He is the best of the professionals, I think, and we may need his assistance. Now, Watson, I think that we cannot employ our time better than by calling upon your acquaintance, Mrs Laura Lyons.'

His plan of campaign was beginning to be evident. He would use the baronet in order to convince the Stapletons that we were really gone, while we should actually return at the instant when we were likely to be needed. That telegram from London, if mentioned by Sir Henry to the Stapletons, must remove the last suspicions from their minds. Already I seemed to see our nets drawing closer round that lean-jawed pike.

Mrs Laura Lyons was in her office, and Sherlock Holmes opened his interview with a frankness and directness which considerably amazed her.

'I am investigating the circumstances which attended the

death of the late Sir Charles Baskerville,' said he. 'My friend here, Dr Watson, has informed me of what you have communicated, and also of what you have withheld in connection with that matter.'

'What have I withheld?' she asked defiantly.

'You have confessed that you asked Sir Charles to be at the gate at ten o'clock. We know that that was the place and hour of his death. You have withheld what the connection is between these events.'

'There is no connection.'

'In that case the coincidence must indeed be an extraordinary one. But I think that we shall succeed in establishing a connection after all. I wish to be perfectly frank with you, Mrs Lyons. We regard this case as one of murder, and the evidence may implicate not only your friend, Mr Stapleton, but his wife as well.'

The lady sprang from her chair. 'His wife!' she cried.

'The fact is no longer a secret. The person who has passed for his sister is really his wife.'

Mrs Lyons had resumed her seat. Her hands were grasping the arms of her chair, and I saw that the pink nails had turned white with the pressure of her grip.

'His wife!' she said again. 'His wife! He was not a married man.'

Sherlock Holmes shrugged his shoulders.

'Prove it to me! Prove it to me! And if you can do so——!' The fierce flash of her eyes said more than any words.

'I have come prepared to do so,' said Holmes, drawing
several papers from his pocket. 'Here is a photograph of the
couple taken in York four years ago. It is indorsed "Mr and 98
Mrs Vandeleur," but you will have no difficulty in recognizing him, and her also, if you know her by sight. Here are three written descriptions by trustworthy witnesses of Mr and Mrs Vandeleur, who at that time kept St Oliver's private school. Read them, and see if you can doubt the identity of these people.'

She glanced at them, and then looked up at us with the set, rigid face of a desperate woman.

'Mr Holmes,' she said, 'this man had offered me marriage on condition that I could get a divorce from my husband. He has lied to me, the villain, in every conceivable way. Not one word of truth has he ever told me. And why—why? I imagined that all was for my own sake. But now I see that I was never anything but a tool in his hands. Why should I preserve faith with him who never kept any with me? Why should I try to shield him from the consequences of his own wicked acts? Ask me what you like, and there is nothing which I shall hold back. One thing I swear to you, and that is, that when I wrote the letter I never dreamed of any harm to the old gentleman, who had been my kindest friend.'

'I entirely believe you, madam,' said Sherlock Holmes. 'The recital of these events must be very painful to you, and perhaps it will make it easier if I tell you what occurred, and you can check me if I make any material mistake. The sending of this letter was suggested to you by Stapleton?'

'He dictated it.'

'I presume that the reason he gave was that you would receive help from Sir Charles for the legal expenses connected with your divorce?'

THE LADY SPRANG FROM HER CHAIR.

Illustration by Sidney Paget for the *Strand Magazine*, March, 1902.

98 *York.* The great ecclesiastical and educational center of the North of England, second only to Canterbury in the Church of England.

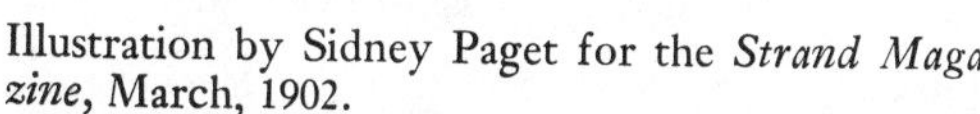

WE ALL THREE SHOOK HANDS . . .

Illustration by Sidney Paget for the *Strand Magazine*, March, 1902.

'Exactly.'

'And then after you had sent the letter he dissuaded you from keeping the appointment?'

'He told me that it would hurt his self-respect that any other man should find the money for such an object, and that though he was a poor man himself he would devote his last penny to removing the obstacles which divided us.'

'He appears to be a very consistent character. And then you heard nothing until you read the reports of the death in the paper?'

'No.'

'And he made you swear to say nothing about your appointment with Sir Charles?'

'He did. He said that the death was a very mysterious one, and that I should certainly be suspected if the facts came out. He frightened me into remaining silent.'

'Quite so. But you had your suspicions?'

She hesitated and looked down. 'I knew him,' she said. 'But if he had kept faith with me I should always have done so with him.'

'I think that on the whole you have had a fortunate escape,' said Sherlock Holmes. 'You have had him in your power and he knew it, and yet you are alive. You have been walking for some months very near to the edge of a precipice. We must wish you good morning now, Mrs Lyons, and it is probable that you will very shortly hear from us again.'

'Our case becomes rounded off, and difficulty after difficulty thins away in front of us,' said Holmes, as we stood waiting for the arrival of the express from town. 'I shall soon be in the position of being able to put into a single connected narrative one of the most singular and sensational crimes of modern times. Students of criminology will remember the analogous incidents in Grodno, in Little Russia, in the year '66, and of course there are the Anderson murders in North Carolina, but this case possesses some features which are entirely its own. Even now we have no clear case against this very wily man. But I shall be very much surprised if it is not clear enough before we go to bed this night.'

The London express came roaring into the station, and a small, wiry bulldog of a man had sprung from a first-class carriage. We all three shook hands, and I saw at once from the reverential way in which Lestrade gazed at my companion that he had learned a good deal since the days when they had first worked together. I could well remember the scorn which the theories of the reasoner used then to excite in the practical man.

'Anything good?' he asked.

'The biggest thing for years,' said Holmes. 'We have two hours before we need think of starting. I think we might employ it in getting some dinner, and then, Lestrade, we will take the London fog out of your throat by giving you a breath of the pure night-air of Dartmoor. Never been there? Ah, well, I don't suppose you will forget your first visit.'

14 • THE HOUND OF THE BASKERVILLES

One of Sherlock Holmes's defects—if, indeed, one may call it a defect—was that he was exceedingly loth to communicate his full plans to any other person until the instant of their fulfilment. Partly it came no doubt from his own masterful nature, which loved to dominate and surprise those who were around him. Partly also from his professional caution, which urged him never to take any chances. The result, however, was very trying for those who were acting as his agents and assistants. I had often suffered under it, but never more so than during that long drive in the darkness. The great ordeal was in front of us; at last we were about to make our final effort, and yet Holmes had said nothing, and I could only surmise what his course of action would be. My nerves thrilled with anticipation when at last the cold wind upon our faces and the dark, void spaces on either side of the narrow road told me that we were back upon the moor once again. Every stride of the horses and every turn of the wheels was taking us nearer to our supreme adventure.

Our conversation was hampered by the presence of the driver of the hired wagonette, so that we were forced to talk of trivial matters when our nerves were tense with emotion and anticipation. It was a relief to me, after that unnatural restraint, when we at last passed Frankland's house and knew that we were drawing near to the Hall and to the scene of action. We did not drive up to the door, but got down near the gate of the avenue. The wagonette was paid off and ordered to return to Coombe Tracey forthwith, while we started to walk to Merripit House.

'Are you armed, Lestrade?'

The little detective smiled. 'As long as I have my trousers, I have a hip-pocket, and as long as I have my hip-pocket I have something in it.'

'Good! My friend and I are also ready for emergencies.'

'You're mighty close about this affair, Mr Holmes. What's the game now?'

'A waiting game.'

'My word, it does not seem a very cheerful place,' said the detective, with a shiver, glancing round him at the gloomy slopes of the hill and at the huge lake of fog which lay over the Grimpen Mire. 'I see the lights of a house ahead of us.'

'That is Merripit House and the end of our journey. I must request you to walk on tiptoe and not to talk above a whisper.'

We moved cautiously along the track as if we were bound for the house, but Holmes halted us when we were about two hundred yards from it.

'This will do,' said he. 'These rocks upon the right make an admirable screen.'

'We are to wait here?'

'Yes, we shall make our little ambush here. Get into this hollow, Lestrade. You have been inside the house, have you not, Watson? Can you tell the position of the rooms? What are those latticed windows at this end?'

'I think they are the kitchen windows.'

'And the one beyond, which shines so brightly?'

'That is certainly the dining-room.'

'The blinds are up. You know the lie of the land best. Creep forward quietly and see what they are doing—but for Heaven's sake don't let them know that they are watched!'

I tiptoed down the path and stooped behind the low wall which surrounded the stunted orchard. Creeping in its shadow, I reached a point whence I could look straight through the uncurtained window.

There were only two men in the room, Sir Henry and Stapleton. They sat with their profiles towards me on either side of the round table. Both of them were smoking cigars, and coffee and wine were in front of them. Stapleton was talking with animation, but the baronet looked pale and distrait. Perhaps the thought of that lonely walk across the ill-omened moor was weighing heavily upon his mind.

As I watched them Stapleton rose and left the room, while Sir Henry filled his glass again and leaned back in his chair, puffing at his cigar. I heard the creak of a door and the crisp sound of boots upon gravel. The steps passed along the path on the other side of the wall under which I crouched. Looking over, I saw the naturalist pause at the door of an out-house in the corner of the orchard. A key turned in a lock, and as he passed in there was a curious scuffling noise from within. He was only a minute or so inside, and then I heard the key turn once more, and he passed me and re-entered the house. I saw him rejoin his guest and I crept quietly back to where my companions were waiting to tell them what I had seen.

'You say, Watson, that the lady is not there?' Holmes asked, when I had finished my report.

'No.'

'Where can she be, then, since there is no light in any other room except the kitchen?'

'I cannot think where she is.'

I have said that over the great Grimpen Mire there hung a dense, white fog. It was drifting slowly in our direction, and banked itself up like a wall on that side of us, low, but thick and well defined. The moon shone on it, and it looked like a great shimmering icefield, with the heads of the distant tors as rocks borne upon its surface. Holmes's face was turned towards it, and he muttered impatiently as he watched its sluggish drift.

'It's moving towards us, Watson.'

'Is that serious?'

'Very serious, indeed—the one thing upon earth which could have disarranged my plans. He can't be very long now. It is already ten o'clock. Our success and even his life may depend upon his coming out before the fog is over the path.'

99 The night was clear and fine above us. The stars shone
100 cold and bright, while a half-moon bathed the whole scene in a soft, uncertain light. Before us lay the dark bulk of the house, its serrated roof and bristling chimneys hard outlined against the silver-spangled sky. Broad bars of golden light from the lower windows stretched across the orchard and the moor. One of them was suddenly shut off. The servants had left the kitchen. There only remained the lamp in the dining-room where the two men, the murderous host and the unconscious guest, still chatted over their cigars.

Every minute that white woolly plain which covered one-half of the moor was drifting closer and closer to the house. Already the first thin wisps of it were curling across the golden

. . . I REACHED A POINT WHENCE I COULD LOOK STRAIGHT THROUGH THE UNCURTAINED WINDOW.

Illustration by Sidney Paget for the *Strand Magazine*, March, 1902.

99 *The night was clear and fine above us.* "Fair weather at all but our extreme western and northern stations," the London *Times* reported of the weather on Friday, October 19, 1888. "Fine weather is . . . likely to continue in most districts, with fog in many parts of England."

100 *a half-moon bathed the whole scene.* The moon may well have bathed the whole scene after ten o'clock (Holmes: "It is already ten o'clock"); it rose at 5:23 P.M., set at 5:37 A.M., but it was *not* a half-moon—it was full on that very day.

square of the lighted window. The farther wall of the orchard was already invisible, and the trees were standing out of a swirl of white vapour. As we watched it the fog-wreaths came crawling round both corners of the house and rolled slowly into one dense bank, on which the upper floor and the roof floated like a strange ship upon a shadowy sea. Holmes struck his hand passionately upon the rock in front of us, and stamped his feet in his impatience.

'If he isn't out in a quarter of an hour the path will be covered. In half an hour we won't be able to see our hands in front of us.'

'Shall we move farther back upon higher ground?'

'Yes, I think it would be as well.'

So as the fog-bank flowed onwards we fell back before it until we were half a mile from the house, and still that dense white sea, with the moon silvering its upper edge, swept slowly and inexorably on.

'We are going too far,' said Holmes. 'We dare not take the chance of his being overtaken before he can reach us. At all costs we must hold our ground where we are.' He dropped on his knees and clapped his ear to the ground. 'Thank heaven, I think that I hear him coming.'

A sound of quick steps broke the silence of the moor. Crouching among the stones, we stared intently at the silver-tipped bank in front of us. The steps grew louder, and through the fog, as through a curtain, there stepped the man whom we were awaiting. He looked round him in surprise as he emerged into the clear, starlit night. Then he came swiftly along the path, passed close to where we lay, and went on up the long slope behind us. As he walked he glanced continually over either shoulder, like a man who is ill at ease.

'Hist' cried Holmes, and I heard the sharp click of a cocking pistol. 'Look out! It's coming!'

HE LOOKED ROUND HIM IN SURPRISE AS HE EMERGED INTO THE CLEAR, STARLIT NIGHT.

Illustration by Sidney Paget for the *Strand Magazine*, March, 1902.

101 *threw himself face downwards upon the ground.* "Picayune and piddling derogators sneer at Lestrade who threw himself upon the ground in terror after beholding the horrendous hound—but sprang to his feet, immediately thereafter, and ran to the aid of Sir Henry Baskerville," Mr. Elliot Kimball wrote in "Watson's Neurosis." "At basis, courage has nothing in common with a positive manifestation, like the flow of gastric juice, or the twitch of a muscle fiber; it is, essentially, a subjective revelation of a NEGATION: the *repression* of a biological common denominator called FEAR. Confronted with the hideous unknown, Lestrade succumbed, momentarily, to dread (an entirely human reaction)—but rose above that devastating paralysis—and such behavior is *admirable* in the courageous little man. He who is too stupid to know fear is senseless, not brave; the man who knows fear, and finds it within him to subdue that fear is courageous, and deserves commendation for the feat."

There was a thin, crisp, continuous patter from somewhere in the heart of that crawling bank. The cloud was within fifty yards of where we lay, and we glared at it, all three, uncertain what horror was about to break from the heart of it. I was at Holmes's elbow, and I glanced for an instant at his face. It was pale and exultant, his eyes shining brightly in the moonlight. But suddenly they started forward in a rigid, fixed stare, and his lips parted in amazement. At the same instant Lestrade gave a yell of terror and threw himself face downwards
101 upon the ground. I sprang to my feet, my inert hand grasping my pistol, my mind paralysed by the dreadful shape which had sprung out upon us from the shadows of the fog. A hound it was, an enormous coal-black hound, but not such a hound as mortal eyes have ever seen. Fire burst from its open mouth, its eyes glowed with a smouldering glare, its muzzle and hackles and dewlap were outlined in flickering flame. Never in the delirious dream of a disordered brain could anything more savage, more appalling, more hellish, be conceived than that dark form and savage face which broke upon us out of the wall of fog.

With long bounds the huge black creature was leaping down the track, following hard upon the footsteps of our friend. So paralysed were we by the apparition that we allowed him to pass before we had recovered our nerve. Then Holmes and I both fired together, and the creature gave a hideous howl, which showed that one at least had hit him. He did not pause, however, but bounded onwards. Far away on the path we saw Sir Henry looking back, his face white in the moonlight, his hands raised in horror, glaring helplessly at the frightful thing which was hunting him down.

But that cry of pain from the hound had blown all our fears to the winds. If he was vulnerable he was mortal, and if we could wound him we could kill him. Never have I seen a man run as Holmes ran that night. I am reckoned fleet of foot, but he outpaced me as much as I outpaced the little professional. In front of us as we flew up the track we heard

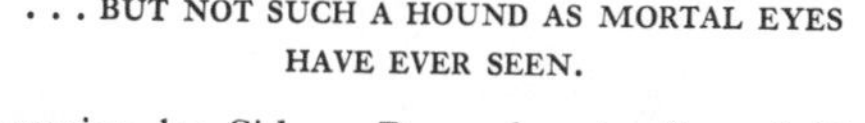
. . . BUT NOT SUCH A HOUND AS MORTAL EYES HAVE EVER SEEN.

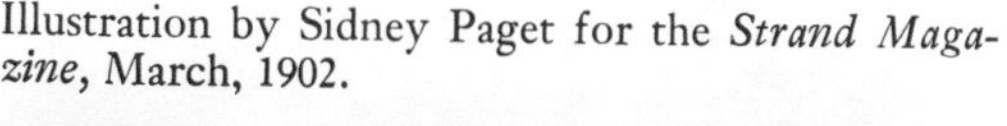
Illustration by Sidney Paget for the *Strand Magazine*, March, 1902.

NEVER HAVE I SEEN A MAN RUN AS HOLMES RAN THAT NIGHT.

Miss Jane Jackson's diorama of the pursuit on the moor as displayed at Madame Tussaud's Wax Museum on the Marylebone Road, London. Dr. Edward J. Van Liere has written ("Sherlock Holmes and Doctor Watson, Perennial Athletes") that "Watson's statement . . . bespeaks high praise of Holmes as an exceptionally fast man. Watson, as a college student, had doubtless seen first-class track men perform, but nevertheless he distinctly implies that Holmes as a runner was in a class by himself."

scream after scream from Sir Henry and the deep roar of the hound. I was in time to see the beast spring upon its victim, hurl him to the ground and worry at his throat. But the next instant Holmes had emptied five barrels of his revolver into the creature's flank. With a last howl of agony and a vicious snap in the air it rolled upon its back, four feet pawing furiously, and then fell limp upon its side. I stooped, panting, and pressed my pistol to the dreadful, shimmering head, but it was useless to press the trigger. The giant hound was dead.

Sir Henry lay insensible where he had fallen. We tore away his collar, and Holmes breathed a prayer of gratitude when we saw that there was no sign of a wound and that the rescue had been in time. Already our friend's eyelids shivered and he made a feeble effort to move. Lestrade thrust his brandy-flask between the baronet's teeth, and two frightened eyes were looking up at us.

'My God!' he whispered. 'What was it? What, in Heaven's name, was it?'

'It's dead, whatever it is,' said Holmes. 'We've laid the family ghost once and for ever.'

In mere size and strength it was a terrible creature which was lying stretched before us. It was not a pure bloodhound and it was not a pure mastiff; but it appeared to be a combination of the two—gaunt, savage, and as large as a small **102**
lioness. Even now, in the stillness of death, the huge jaws seemed to be dripping with a bluish flame, and the small, deep-set, cruel eyes were ringed with fire. I placed my hand upon the glowing muzzle, and as I held them up my own fingers smouldered and gleamed in the darkness.

'Phosphorus,' I said.

'A cunning preparation of it,' said Holmes, sniffing at the dead animal. 'There is no smell which might have interfered with his power of scent. We owe you a deep apology, Sir Henry, for having exposed you to this fright. I was prepared for a hound, but not for such a creature as this. And the fog gave us little time to receive him.'

102 *it appeared to be a combination of the two.* "From its gigantic size I would hazard that there was more likely some Great Dane or Scottish Wolfhound mixture involved," Mr. Stuart Palmer wrote in "Notes on Certain Evidences of Caniphobia in Mr. Sherlock Holmes and His Associates."

And the late Owen Frisbie commented ("On the Origin of the Hound of the Baskervilles"): "Dr. Watson's statement that the Hound appeared to be a combination of bloodhound and mastiff does not hold up. . . . We conclude that we must look to the staghound for size and drive, and to the bloodhound for ability and will to take the line of a human."

. . . HOLMES HAD EMPTIED FIVE BARRELS OF HIS REVOLVER INTO THE CREATURE'S FLANK.

Illustration by Sidney Paget for the *Strand Magazine*, April, 1902. The flank, as Mr. Robert Keith Leavitt has commented in "Annie Oakley in Baker Street," is "A far from surely lethal portion of the beast, and one from which any reflected bullet, or any passing clear through the body, might have hit Sir Henry Baskerville with grievous or even fatal results." And surely Watson should have written "five *chambers*" rather than "five barrels" of Holmes' revolver?

'PHOSPHORUS,' I SAID.

Illustration by Sidney Paget for the *Strand Magazine*, April, 1902. But phosphorus is "a very deadly poison to dog and man," as Mr. Stuart Palmer pointed out in "Notes of Certain Evidences of Caniphobia in Mr. Sherlock Holmes and His Associates." Mr. D. A. Redmond has suggested ("Some Chemical Problems in the Canon") that the substance was not phosophorus but barium sulphide.

'You have saved my life.'

'Having first endangered it. Are you strong enough to stand?'

'Give me another mouthful of that brandy, and I shall be ready for anything. So! Now, if you will help me up. What do you propose to do?'

'To leave you here. You are not fit for further adventures tonight. If you will wait, one or other of us will go back with you to the Hall.'

He tried to stagger to his feet; but he was still ghastly pale and trembling in every limb. We helped him to a rock, where he sat shivering with his face buried in his hands.

'We must leave you now,' said Holmes. 'The rest of our work must be done, and every moment is of importance. We have our case, and now we only want our man.'

'It's a thousand to one against our finding him at the house,' he continued, as we retraced our steps swiftly down the path. 'Those shots must have told him that the game was up.'

'We were some distance off, and this fog may have deadened them.'

'He followed the hound to call him off—of that you may be certain. No, no, he's gone by this time! But we'll search the house and make sure.'

The front door was open, so we rushed in and hurried from room to room, to the amazement of a doddering old man-servant, who met us in the passage. There was no light save in the dining-room, but Holmes caught up the lamp, and left no corner of the house unexplored. No sign could we see of the man whom we were chasing. On the upper floor, however, one of the bedroom doors was locked.

'There's someone in here!' cried Lestrade. 'I can hear a movement. Open this door!'

A faint moaning and rustling came from within. Holmes struck the door just over the lock with the flat of his foot, and it flew open. Pistol in hand, we all three rushed into the room.

But there was no sign within it of that desperate and defiant villain whom we expected to see. Instead we were faced by an object so strange and so unexpected that we stood for a moment staring at it in amazement.

The room had been fashioned into a small museum, and the walls were lined by a number of glass-topped cases full of that collection of butterflies and moths the formation of which had been the relaxation of this complex and dangerous man. In the centre of this room there was an upright beam, which had been placed at some period as a support for the old worm-eaten balk of timber which spanned the roof. To this post a figure was tied, so swathed and muffled in the sheets which had been used to secure it that one could not for the moment tell whether it was that of a man or a woman. One towel passed round the throat, and was secured at the back of the pillar. Another covered the lower part of the face and over it two dark eyes—eyes full of grief and shame and a dreadful questioning—stared back at us. In a minute we had torn off the gag, unswathed the bonds, and Mrs Stapleton sank upon the floor in front of us. As her beautiful head fell upon her chest I saw the clear red weal of a whip-lash across her neck.

'The brute!' cried Holmes. 'Here, Lestrade, your brandy-bottle! Put her in the chair! She has fainted from ill-usage and exhaustion.'

She opened her eyes again. 'Is he safe?' she asked. 'Has he escaped?'

'He cannot escape us, madam.'

'No, no, I did not mean my husband. Sir Henry? Is he safe?'

'Yes.'

'And the hound?'

'It is dead.'

She gave a long sigh of satisfaction. 'Thank God! Thank God! Oh, this villain! See how he has treated me!' She shot her arms out from her sleeves, and we saw with horror that they were all mottled with bruises. 'But this is nothing—nothing! It is my mind and soul that he has tortured and defiled. I could endure it all, ill-usage, solitude, a life of deception, everything, as long as I could still cling to the hope that I had his love, but now I know that in this also I have been his dupe and his tool.' She broke into passionate sobbing as she spoke.

'You bear him no good-will, madam,' said Holmes. 'Tell us, then, where we shall find him. If you have ever aided him in evil, help us now and so atone.'

'There is but one place where he can have fled,' she answered. 'There is an old tin mine on an island in the heart of the Mire. It was there that he kept his hound, and there also he had made preparations so that he might have a refuge. That is where he would fly.'

The fog-bank lay like white wool against the window. Holmes held the lamp towards it.

'See,' said he. 'No one could find his way into the Grimpen Mire tonight.'

She laughed and clapped her hands. Her eyes and teeth gleamed with fierce merriment.

'He may find his way in, but never out,' she cried. 'How can he see the guiding wands tonight? We planted them together, he and I, to mark the pathway through the Mire. Oh, if I could only have plucked them out today! Then indeed you would have had him at your mercy.'

It was evident to us that all pursuit was in vain until the fog had lifted. Meanwhile we left Lestrade in possession of the house, while Holmes and I went back with the baronet to Baskerville Hall. The story of the Stapletons could no longer be withheld from him, but he took the blow bravely when he learned the truth about the woman whom he had loved. But the shock of the night's adventures had shattered his nerves, and before morning he lay delirious in a high fever, under the care of Dr Mortimer. The two of them were destined to travel together round the world before Sir Henry had become once more the hale, hearty man that he had been before he became master of that ill-omened estate.

And now I come rapidly to the conclusion of this singular narrative, in which I have tried to make the reader share those dark fears and vague surmises which clouded our lives so long, and ended in so tragic a manner. On the morning after the death of the hound the fog had lifted and we were guided by Mrs Stapleton to the point where they had found a pathway through the bog. It helped us to realize the horror of this

'THE BRUTE!' CRIED HOLMES. 'HERE, LESTRADE, YOUR BRANDY-BOTTLE!'

Illustration by Sidney Paget for the *Strand Magazine*, April, 1902.

HE HELD AN OLD BLACK BOOT IN THE AIR.

Illustration by Sidney Paget for the *Strand Magazine*, April, 1902.

. . . A STAPLE AND CHAIN, WITH A QUANTITY OF GNAWED BONES, SHOWED WHERE THE ANIMAL HAD BEEN CONFINED.

Illustration by Sidney Paget for the *Strand Magazine*, April, 1902.

woman's life when we saw the eagerness and joy with which she laid us on her husband's track. We left her standing upon the thin peninsula of firm, peaty soil which tapered out into the widespread bog. From the end of it a small wand planted here and there showed where the path zigzagged from tuft to tuft of rushes among those green-scummed pits and foul quagmires which barred the way to the stranger. Rank reeds and lush, slimy water-plants sent an odour of decay and a heavy miasmatic vapour into our faces, while a false step plunged us more than once thigh-deep into the dark, quivering mire, which shook for yards in soft undulations around our feet. Its tenacious grip plucked at our heels as we walked, and when we sank into it it was as if some malignant hand was tugging us down into those obscene depths, so grim and purposeful was the clutch in which it held us. Once only we saw a trace that someone had passed that perilous way before us. From amid a tuft of cotton-grass which bore it up out of the slime some dark thing was projecting. Holmes sank to his waist as he stepped from the path to seize it, and had we not been there to drag him out he could never have set his foot upon firm land again. He held an old black boot in the air. 'Meyers, Toronto,' was printed on the leather inside.

'It is worth a mud bath,' said he. 'It is our friend Sir Henry's missing boot.'

'Thrown there by Stapleton in his flight.'

'Exactly. He retained it in his hand after using it to set the hound upon his track. He fled when he knew the game was up, still clutching it. And he hurled it away at this point of his flight. We know at least that he came so far in safety.'

But more than that we were never destined to know, though there was much which we might surmise. There was no chance of finding footsteps in the mire, for the rising mud oozed swiftly in upon them, but as we at last reached firmer ground beyond the morass we all looked eagerly for them. But no slightest sign of them ever met our eyes. If the earth told a true story, then Stapleton never reached that island of refuge towards which he struggled through the fog upon that last night. Somewhere in the heart of the great Grimpen Mire, down in the foul slime of the huge morass which had sucked him in, this cold and cruel-hearted man is for ever buried.

Many traces we found of him in the bog-girt island where
he had hid his savage ally. A huge driving-wheel and a shaft
half-filled with rubbish showed the position of an abandoned
mine. Beside it were the crumbling remains of the cottages
103 of the miners, driven away, no doubt, by the foul reek of the
surrounding swamp. In one of these a staple and chain, with
a quantity of gnawed bones, showed where the animal had
been confined. A skeleton with a tangle of brown hair adher-
ing to it lay among the *débris*.

104 'A dog!' said Holmes. 'By Jove, a curly-haired spaniel. Poor Mortimer will never see his pet again. Well, I do not know that this place contains any secret which we have not already fathomed. He could hide his hound, but he could not hush its voice, and hence came those cries which even in daylight were not pleasant to hear. On an emergency he could keep the hound in the out-house at Merripit, but it was always a risk, and it was only on the supreme day, which he regarded as the end of all his efforts, that he dared do it. This paste in the tin is no doubt the luminous mixture with which the

creature was daubed. It was suggested, of course, by the story of the family hell-hound, and by the desire to frighten old Sir Charles to death. No wonder the poor devil of a convict ran and screamed, even as our friend did, and as we ourselves might have done, when he saw such a creature bounding through the darkness of the moor upon his track. It was a cunning device, for, apart from the chance of driving your victim to his death, what peasant would venture to inquire too closely into such a creature should he get sight of it, as many have done, upon the moor! I said it in London, Watson, and I say it again now, that never yet have we helped to hunt down a more dangerous man than he who is lying yonder'—he swept his long arm towards the huge mottled expanse of green-splotched bog which stretched away until it merged into the russet slopes of the moor.

15 ◆ A RETROSPECTION

It was the end of November, and Holmes and I sat, upon a raw and foggy night, on either side of a blazing fire in our sitting-room in Baker Street. Since the tragic upshot of our visit to Devonshire he had been engaged in two affairs of the utmost importance, in the first of which he had exposed the
atrocious conduct of Colonel Upwood in connection with the **105**
famous card scandal of the Nonpareil Club, while in the **106**
second he had defended the unfortunate Mme Montpensier **107**
from the charge of murder which hung over her in connection with the death of her step-daughter, Mlle Carère, the young lady who, as it will be remembered, was found six months later alive and married in New York. My friend was in excellent spirits over the success which had attended a succession of difficult and important cases, so that I was able to induce him to discuss the details of the Baskerville mystery. I had waited patiently for the opportunity, for I was aware that he would never permit cases to overlap, and that his clear and logical mind would not be drawn from its present work to dwell upon memories of the past. Sir Henry and Dr Mortimer were, however, in London, on their way to that long voyage which had been recommended for the restoration of his shattered nerves. They had called upon us that very afternoon, so that it was natural that the subject should come up for discussion.

'The whole course of events,' said Holmes, 'from the point of view of the man who called himself Stapleton, was simple and direct, although to us, who had no means in the beginning of knowing the motives of his actions and could only learn part of the facts, it all appeared exceedingly complex. I have had the advantage of two conversations with Mrs

103 *Beside it were the crumbling remains of the cottages of the miners.* It is pleasant to report that the Vitifer tin mines and the picturesquely named Golden Door Mine all do lie on a direct line between Grimpen-Grimspound and Merripit, the tiny village where Stapleton lived at Merripit House in the heart of the moor (see our "very-large"-scale map).

104 *'By Jove, a curly-haired spaniel.* "Sheer brilliance," Mr. Stuart Palmer commented in "Notes on Certain Evidences of Caniphobia in Mr. Sherlock Holmes and His Associates," "since the skeletal remains of a spaniel differ slightly if at all from any other small dog."

And Mr. Benjamin Clark wrote of this discovery ("Dr. Mortimer Before the Bar"): Watson "makes it clear that access to the island where the hound was chained was possible only to those who knew of and followed Stapleton's markers. That an animal could stray to the island, in such a miasmatic atmosphere, leaping from tuft to tuft, his power of scent useless, since 'rising mud oozed swiftly' over footsteps, is frankly incredible. It would be even more incredible to assume that if the hound was loose on the day of the spaniel's disappearance he had killed the small dog and carried him back to his lair as he was led thither by Stapleton. For it is obvious that the hound alone could not find his way through the bog without perishing like the moorland ponies. Moreover, meat, in those days, was not so hard to come by as to suggest that Stapleton would undertake the highly hazardous step of kidnaping a neighbor's dog to feed his brute. With all such impossible solutions removed, we are left with one which, improbable though it may appear at first, not only provides the only possible answer to explain the presence of the spaniel's remains on the island but opens the way to explaining certain otherwise baffling points in what Holmes told Lestrade was 'the biggest thing for years.' *The only way in the least degree likely that* the spaniel could have penetrated the bog was, of course, in the company of his master, Dr. James Mortimer. If this contention is valid, it necessarily follows that Dr. Mortimer must have been in league with Stapleton; for even if the doctor had come on the path to the island by chance he would, if he were an honest man, have immediately publicized his discovery of the hound."

105 *Colonel Upwood.* Dr. Julian Wolff, in his *Practical Handbook of Sherlockian Heraldry*, has identified Colonel Upwood with Sir William Gordon Cumming, at one time a lieutenant-colonel in the Scots Guards. In 1891 Sir William (according to the Literary Supplement of the London *Times*, February 28, 1948, and April 24, 1948) was accused of cheating at cards and the Prince of Wales himself was subpoenaed as a witness. Largely because of the Prince's evidence, Sir William lost the case. The Baccarat Case, as it was known, "aroused great interest and many people were convinced of Sir William's innocence."

Stapleton, and the case has now been so entirely cleared up that I am not aware that there is anything which has remained a secret to us. You will find a few notes upon the matter under the heading B in my indexed list of cases.'

'Perhaps you would kindly give me a sketch of the course of events from memory.'

'Certainly, though I cannot guarantee that I carry all the facts in my mind. Intense mental concentration has a curious way of blotting out what has passed. The barrister who has his case at his fingers' end, and is able to argue with an expert upon his own subjects, finds that a week or two of the courts will drive it all out of his head once more. So each of my cases displaces the last, and Mlle Carère has blurred my recollection of Baskerville Hall. Tomorrow some other little problem may be submitted to my notice, which will in turn dispossess the fair French lady and the infamous Upwood. So far as the case of the Hound goes, however, I will give you the course of events as nearly as I can, and you will suggest anything which I may have forgotten.

'My inquiries show beyond all question that the family portrait did not lie, and that this fellow was indeed a Baskerville. He was a son of that Rodger Baskerville, the younger brother of Sir Charles, who fled with a sinister reputation to South America, where he was said to have died unmarried. He did, as a matter of fact, marry, and had one child, this fellow, whose real name is the same as his father. He married Beryl Garçia, one of the beauties of Costa Rica, and, having purloined a considerable sum of public money, he changed his name to Vandeleur and fled to England, where he estab-
108 lished a school in the east of Yorkshire. His reason for attempting this special line of business was that he had struck up an acquaintance with a consumptive tutor upon the voyage home, and that he had used this man's ability to make the undertaking a success. Fraser, the tutor, died, however, and the school which had begun well, sank from disrepute into infamy. The Vandeleurs found it convenient to change their

'PERHAPS YOU WOULD KINDLY GIVE ME A SKETCH OF THE COURSE OF EVENTS FROM MEMORY.'

Illustration by Sidney Paget for the *Strand Magazine*, April, 1902.

106 *the Nonpareil Club.* In "Who Was Cecil Forrester?", Mr. Robert Keith Leavitt has noted that "Nonpareil is the English name for a type [size], corresponding to our six-point. Obviously the Nonpareil Club was a discreet, footnote kind of club composed of journalists." For a pastiche of this adventure by Adrian M. Conan Doyle, see "The Adventure of the Abbas Ruby" in *The Exploits of Sherlock Holmes.*

107 *the unfortunate Mme Montpensier.* For a pastiche of this adventure, by Adrian M. Conan Doyle and John Dickson Carr, see "The Adventure of the Black Baronet" in *The Exploits of Sherlock Holmes.*

108 *Yorkshire.* This largest of the English counties borders on the North Sea and extends almost to the Irish Sea. Besides having been, most probably, the county of Holmes' birth, it has many other literary associations: with Caedmon, Laurence Sterne, and the Brontë sisters.

name to Stapleton, and he brought the remains of his fortune, his schemes for the future, and his taste for entomology to the south of England. I learn at the British Museum that he was a recognized authority upon the subject, and that the name of Vandeleur has been permanently attached to a certain moth which he had, in his Yorkshire days, been the first to describe.

'We now come to that portion of his life which has proved to be of such intense interest to us. The fellow had evidently made inquiry, and found that only two lives intervened between him and a valuable estate. When he went to Devonshire his plans were, I believe, exceedingly hazy, but that he meant mischief from the first is evident from the way in which he took his wife with him in the character of his sister. The idea of using her as a decoy was clearly already in his mind, though he may not have been certain how the details of his plot were to be arranged. He meant in the end to have the estate, and he was ready to use any tool or run any risk for that end. His first act was to establish himself as near to his ancestral home as he could, and his second was to cultivate a friendship with Sir Charles Baskerville and with the neighbours.

'The baronet himself told him about the family hound, and so prepared the way for his own death. Stapleton, as I will continue to call him, knew that the old man's heart was weak, and that a shock would kill him. So much he had learned from Dr Mortimer. He had heard also that Sir Charles was superstitious, and had taken this grim legend very seriously. His ingenious mind instantly suggested a way by which the baronet could be done to death, and yet it would be hardly possible to bring home the guilt to the real murderer.

'Having conceived the idea, he proceeded to carry it out with considerable finesse. An ordinary schemer would have been content to work with a savage hound. The use of artificial means to make the creature diabolical was a flash of genius upon his part. The dog he bought in London from Ross and Mangles, the dealers in Fulham Road. It was the strongest and most savage in their possession. He brought it down by the North Devon line, and walked a great distance over the moor, so as to get it home without exciting any remarks. He had already on his insect hunts learned to penetrate the Grimpen Mire, and so had found a safe hiding-place for the creature. Here he kennelled it and waited his chance.

'But it was some time coming. The old gentleman could not be decoyed outside of his grounds at night. Several times Stapleton lurked about with his hound, but without avail. It was during these fruitless quests that he, or rather his ally, was seen by peasants, and that the legend of the demon dog received a new confirmation. He had hoped that his wife might lure Sir Charles to his ruin, but here she proved unexpectedly independent. She would not endeavour to entangle the old gentleman in a sentimental attachment which might deliver him over to his enemy. Threats and even, I am sorry to say, blows failed to move her. She would have nothing to do with it, and for a time Stapleton was at a deadlock.

'He found a way out of his difficulties through the chance that Sir Charles, who had conceived a friendship for him, made him the minister of his charity in the case of this unfortunate woman, Mrs Laura Lyons. By representing himself as a single man, he acquired complete influence over her, and he gave her to understand that in the event of her obtaining a divorce from her husband he would marry her. His plans were suddenly brought to a head by his knowledge that Sir Charles was about to leave the Hall on the advice of Dr Mortimer, with whose opinion he himself pretended to coincide. He must act at once, or his victim might get beyond his power. He therefore put pressure upon Mrs Lyons to write this letter, imploring the old man to give her an interview on the evening before his departure for London. He then, by a specious argument, prevented her from going, and so had the chance for which he had waited.

'Driving back in the evening from Coombe Tracey, he was in time to get his hound, to treat it with his infernal paint, and to bring the beast round to the gate at which he had reason to expect that he would find the old gentleman waiting. The dog, incited by its master, sprang over the wicket-gate and pursued the unfortunate baronet, who fled screaming down the Yew Alley. In that gloomy tunnel it must indeed have been a dreadful sight to seee that huge black creature, with its flaming jaws and blazing eyes, bounding after its victim. He fell dead at the end of the alley from heart disease and terror. The hound had kept upon the grassy border while the baronet had run down the path, so that no track but the man's was visible. On seeing him lying still the creature had probably approached to sniff at him, but, finding him dead, had turned away again. It was then that it left the print which was actually observed by Dr Mortimer. The hound was called off and hurried away to its lair in the Grimpen Mire, and a mystery was left which puzzled the authorities, alarmed the countryside, and finally brought the case within the scope of our observation.

'So much for the death of Sir Charles Baskerville. You perceive the devilish cunning of it, for really it would be almost impossible to make a case against the real murderer. His only accomplice was one who could never give him away, and the grotesque, inconceivable nature of the device only served to make it more effective. Both of the women concerned in the case, Mrs Stapleton and Mrs Laura Lyons, were left with a strong suspicion against Stapleton. Mrs Stapleton knew that he had designs upon the old man, and also of the existence of the hound. Mrs Lyons knew neither of these things, but had been impressed by the death occurring at the time of an uncancelled appointment which was only known to him. However, both of them were under his influence, and he had nothing to fear from them. The first half of his task was successfully accomplished, but the more difficult still remained.

'It is possible that Stapleton did not know of the existence of an heir in Canada. In any case he would very soon learn it from his friend Dr Mortimer, and he was told by the latter all details about the arrival of Henry Baskerville. Stapleton's first idea was that this young stranger from Canada might possibly be done to death in London without coming down to Devonshire at all. He distrusted his wife ever since she had refused to help him in laying a trap for the old man, and he dared not leave her long out of his sight for fear he should lose his influence over her. It was for this reason that he took
her to London with him. They lodged, I find, at the Mex-
109 borough Private Hotel, in Craven Street, which was actually
one of those called upon by my agent in search of evidence.

109 *Craven Street.* In Craven Street, leading from the Victoria Embankment to the Strand, there are several small hotels and restaurants which cater almost exclusively to short-term visitors to the metropolis.

Here he kept his wife imprisoned in her room while he, disguised in a beard, followed Dr Mortimer to Baker Street, and afterwards to the station and to the Northumberland Hotel. His wife had some inkling of his plans; but she had such a fear of her husband—a fear founded upon brutal ill-treatment—that she dare not write to warn the man whom she knew to be in danger. If the letter should fall into Stapleton's hands her own life would not be safe. Eventually, as we know, she adopted the expedient of cutting out the words which would form the message, and addressing the letter in a disguised hand. It reached the baronet, and gave him the first warning of his danger.

'It was very essential for Stapleton to get some article of Sir Henry's attire, so that, in case he was driven to use the dog, he might always have the means of setting him upon his track. With characteristic promptness and audacity he set about this at once, and we cannot doubt that the boots or chambermaid of the hotel was well bribed to help him in his design. By **110**
chance, however, the first boot which was procured for him was a new one, and, therefore, useless for his purpose. He then had it returned and obtained another—a most instructive incident, since it proved conclusively to my mind that we were dealing with a real hound, as no other supposition could explain this anxiety to obtain an old boot and this indifference to a new one. The more *outré* and grotesque an incident is the more carefully it deserves to be examined, and the very point which appears to complicate a case is, when duly considered and scientifically handled, the one which is most likely to elucidate it.

'Then we had the visit from our friends next morning, shadowed always by Stapleton in the cab. From his knowledge **111**
of our rooms and of my appearance, as well as from his general conduct, I am inclined to think that Stapleton's career of crime has been by no means limited to this single Baskerville affair. It is suggestive that during the last three years there have been four considerable burglaries in the West country, for none of which was any criminal ever arrested. The last of these, at Folkestone Court, in May, was remarkable for the cold-blooded pistolling of the page, who surprised the masked and solitary burglar. I cannot doubt that Stapleton recruited his waning resources in this fashion, and that for years he has been a desperate and dangerous man.

'We had an example of his readiness of resource that morning when he got away from us so successfully, and also of his audacity in sending back my own name to me through the cabman. From that moment he understood that I had taken over the case in London, and that therefore there was no chance for him there. He returned to Dartmoor and awaited the arrival of the baronet.'

'One moment!' said I. 'You have, no doubt, described the sequence of events correctly, but there is one point which you have left unexplained. What became of the hound when its master was in London?'

'I have given some attention to this matter, and it is undoubtedly of importance. There can be no question that Stapleton had a confidant, though it is unlikely that he ever placed himself in his power by sharing all his plans with him. There was an old manservant at Merripit House, whose name was Anthony. His connection with the Stapletons can be

110 *well bribed to help him in his design.* Mr. Benjamin S. Clark, pursuing his theory that Dr. James Mortimer was Stapleton's accomplice, wrote ("Dr. Mortimer Before the Bar"): "Now of course it is obvious that Mortimer stole the boot. The alternative explanation that one of the hotel employees had been bribed by Stapleton cannot bear the light of close scrutiny. In the first place, the risk to Stapleton, even disguised, was so great as to make it out of proportion to the gaining of a few days (for, as a visitor to Baskerville Hall, he could surely accomplish the same purpose more easily). Also, with no preliminaries (Stapleton had only just arrived in London) to walk into a strange hotel and find a bribable 'boots' to run the major risk of losing his job for a bribe that could not be suspiciously large, was a feat that could hardly be given better odds than a thousand to one."

111 *shadowed always by Stapleton in the cab.* "The simple question as to why Stapleton (taking the Holmesian explanation at face value) was following the two has apparently never been seriously examined," Mr. Clark continued. "We know that the entomologist had located Sir Henry's hotel (one boot had already been stolen) and he had spotted the visit to 221B Baker Street. Why, then, should he be running the risk of shadowing his victim *back* to his hotel? It will be recalled that Dr. Mortimer and Sir Henry were strolling along casually, looking in shop windows, and it was a fair guess that the hotel was then or later their destination, since Stapleton *knew* that they hadn't checked out. It goes beyond the bounds of credibility that Stapleton was following them in the fear that Holmes had advised the consulting of Scotland Yard. (If such had been the case Sir Henry and the doctor wouldn't have been walking.) No! Stapleton waited outside Holmes' office against the possibility that a diversion might be necessary, as indeed it was, since Holmes had just been told of the disappearance of the boot and was obviously suspicious. On leaving Baker Street, Dr. Mortimer presumably signaled to his confederate in the cab that (as anticipated) he was in need of some move to distract the detective, because—and this cannot be repeated too often—Mortimer had at all costs to be kept free from any taint of suspicion. Stapleton's dash in the cab was successful in accomplishing this purpose. Thenceforward he occupied all of Holmes' attention, and Dr. Mortimer, in the popular phrase, was 'as safe as a church.'"

traced for several years, as far back as the schoolmastering days, so that he must have been aware that his master and mistress were really husband and wife. This man has disappeared and has escaped from the country. It is suggestive that Anthony is not a common name in England, while Antonio is so in all Spanish or Spanish-American countries. The man, like Mrs Stapleton herself, spoke good English, but with a curious lisping accent. I have myself seen this old man cross the Grimpen Mire by the path which Stapleton had marked out. It is very probable, therefore, that in the absence of his master it was he who cared for the hound, though he may never have known the purpose for which the beast was used.

'The Stapletons then went down to Devonshire, whither they were soon followed by Sir Henry and you. One word now as to how I stood myself at that time. It may possibly recur to your memory that when I examined the paper upon which the printed words were fastened I made a close inspection for the watermark. In doing so I held it within a few inches of my eyes, and was conscious of a faint smell of the scent known as white jessamine. There are seventy-five perfumes, which it is very necessary that a criminal expert should be
112 able to distinguish from each other, and cases have more than once within my own experience depended upon their prompt recognition. The scent suggested the presence of a lady, and already my thoughts began to turn towards the Stapletons. Thus I had made certain of the hound, and had guessed at the criminal before ever we went to the West country.

'It was my game to watch Stapleton. It was evident, however, that I could not do this if I were with you, since he would be keenly on his guard. I deceived everybody, therefore, yourself included, and I came down secretly when I was supposed to be in London. My hardships were not so great as you imagine, though such trifling details must never interfere with the investigation of a case. I stayed for the most part at Coombe Tracey, and only used the hut upon the moor when it was necessary to be near the scene of action. Cartwright had come down with me, and in his disguise as a country boy he was of great assistance to me. I was dependent upon him for food and clean linen. When I was watching Stapleton, Cartwright was frequently watching you, so that I was able to keep my hand upon all the strings.

'I have already told you that your reports reached me rapidly, being forwarded instantly from Baker Street to Coombe Tracey. They were of great service to me, and especially that one incidentally truthful piece of biography of Stapleton's. I was able to establish the identity of the man and the woman, and knew at last exactly how I stood. The case had been considerably complicated through the incident of the escaped convict and the relations between him and the Barrymores. This also you cleared up in a very effective way, though I had already come to the same conclusions from my own observations.

'By the time that you discovered me upon the moor I had a complete knowledge of the whole business, but I had not a case which could go to a jury. Even Stapleton's attempt upon Sir Henry that night, which ended in the death of the unfortunate convict did not help us much in proving murder against our man. There seemed to be no alternative but to

112 *that a criminal expert should be able to distinguish.* The late Christopher Morley thought it probable that Holmes may even have written a monograph Upon the Distinction Between the Various Perfumes: A Monograph on Natural and Synthetic Fragrances with Analyses of the 75 Primary Scents and a Memorandum by J. H. W. on the Types of Women Likely to Favour the Several Modes of Allure.

catch him red-handed, and to do so we had to use Sir Henry, alone and apparently unprotected, as a bait. We did so, and at the cost of a severe shock to our client we succeeded in completing our case and driving Stapleton to his destruction. That Sir Henry should have been exposed to this is, I must confess, a reproach to my management of the case, but we had no means of foreseeing the terrible and paralysing spectacle which the beast presented, nor could we predict the fog which enabled him to burst upon us at such short notice. We succeeded in our object at a cost which both the specialist and Dr Mortimer assure me will be a temporary one. A long journey may enable our friend to recover not only from his shattered nerves but also from his wounded feelings. His love for the lady was deep and sincere, and to him the saddest part of all this black business was that he should have been deceived by her.

'It only remains to indicate the part which she had played throughout. There can be no doubt that Stapleton exercised an influence over her which may have been love or may have been fear, or very possibly both, since they are by no means incompatible emotions. It was, at least, absolutely effective. At his command she consented to pass as his sister, though he found the limits of his power over her when he endeavoured to make her the direct accessory to murder. She was ready to warn Sir Henry so far as she could without implicating her husband, and again and again she tried to do so. Stapleton himself seems to have been capable of jealousy, and when he saw the baronet paying court to the lady, even though it was part of his own plan, still he could not help interrupting with a passionate outburst which revealed the fiery soul which his self-contained manner so cleverly concealed. By encouraging the intimacy he made it certain that Sir Henry would frequently come to Merripit House, and that he would sooner or later get the opportunity which he desired. On the day of the crisis, however, his wife turned suddenly against him. She had learned something of the death of the convict, and she knew that the hound was being kept in the out-house on the evening that Sir Henry was coming to dinner. She taxed her husband with his intended crime, and a furious scene followed, in which he showed her for the first time that she had a rival in his love. Her fidelity turned in an instant to bitter hatred, and he saw that she would betray him. He tied her up, therefore, that she might have no chance of warning Sir Henry, and he hoped, no doubt, that when the whole countryside put down the baronet's death to the curse of his family, as they certainly would do, he could win his wife back to accept an accomplished fact, and to keep silent upon what she knew. In this I fancy that in any case he made a miscalculation, and that, if we had not been there, his doom would none the less have been sealed. A woman of Spanish blood does not condone such an injury so lightly. And now, my dear Watson, without referring to my notes, I cannot give you a more detailed account of this curious case. I do not know that anything essential has been left unexplained.'

'He could not hope to frighten Sir Henry to death, as he had done the old uncle, with his bogy hound.'

'The beast was savage and half-starved. If its appearance did not frighten its victim to death, at least it would paralyse the resistance which might be offered.'

'No doubt. There only remains one difficulty. If Stapleton came into the succession, how could he explain the fact that he, the heir, had been living unannounced under another name so close to the property? How could he claim it without causing suspicion and inquiry?'

113 'It is a formidable difficulty, and I fear that you ask too much when you expect me to solve it. The past and the present are within the field of my inquiry, but what a man may do in the future is a hard question to answer. Mrs Stapleton has heard her husband discuss the problem on several occasions. There were three possible courses. He might claim the property from South America, establish his identity before the British authorities there, and so obtain the fortune without ever coming to England at all; or he might adopt an elaborate disguise during the short time that he need be in London; or, again, he might furnish an accomplice with the proofs and papers, putting him in as heir, and retaining a claim upon some proportion of his income. We cannot doubt, from what we know of him, that he would have found some way out of the difficulty. And now, my dear Watson, we have had some weeks of severe work, and for one evening, I think, we may turn our thoughts into more pleasant channels. I have a box for *Les Huguenots*. Have you
114 heard the De Reszkes? Might I trouble you then to be ready in half an hour, and we can stop at Marcini's for a little dinner on the way?'

'MIGHT I TROUBLE YOU THEN TO BE READY IN HALF AN HOUR . . .'

Illustration by Sidney Paget for the *Strand Magazine*, April, 1902.

113 *'It is a formidable difficulty.* "Based on Holmes' interpretation of the case, the difficulty was not only formidable but well-nigh insuperable," Mr. Benjamin S. Clark wrote in "Dr. Mortimer Before the Bar." "The detective suggested that there were three possible courses Stapleton might pursue, two of which we can safely dismiss as ridiculous: namely, that Stapleton would appear in London in an 'elaborate disguise,' or furnish an accomplice with proofs and papers as an heir and retain a claim on part of the income. The third course proposed was that Stapleton claim the property from South America, establish his identity before the British authorities there, and so obtain the fortune without ever coming to England at all. The rather considerable 'rub' here, which seems to have been overlooked, is that not too many years earlier, after marrying the Costa Rican beauty, Beryl Garcia (presumably under the name of Baskerville, which as a claimant he would have to resume), Stapleton 'purloined a considerable sum of public money,' and, changing his name to Vandeleur, fled to England. However, if we meet this difficulty by shifting the locale to, say Australia, such a course of action, while it had infinitely more merit than the other two, was still not without serious risks. . . . But assume that, instead of the claim to the estate originating with Stapleton, a trusted friend of the family—lately executor of Sir Charles Baskerville's will—sees to it that documents or letters are found which indicate the possible existence of a hitherto unknown heir. Of course this friend will inform the court of his discovery, at the same time furnishing a clue to the whereabouts of the lucky individual . . ."

114 *the De Reszkes?* Jean de Reszke (1850–1925), Polish operatic tenor and teacher, was known for both lyric and Wagnerian roles. He was the leading tenor of the Metropolitan Opera, New York, from 1891 to 1901. His brother Edouard de Reszke (1855–1917) was a leading bass at the Metropolitan from 1891 to 1903.

According to Mr. Harold Schonberg, the music critic of *The New York Times*, "the only time the De Reszkes . . . ever sang together in *Les Huguenots* was at the Metropolitan Opera House, and the performance in question took place on November 25, 1896." On the other hand, Mr. Anthony Boucher, in correspondence with Dr. Charles Goodman, has stated that the De Reszkes sang the opera together 21 times from 1891 to 1901 at the Metropolitan alone, not counting touring engagement in London and elsewhere.

Elsewhere ("The Records of Baker Street") Mr. Boucher has asked: "Were the De Reszkes [Holmes'] real reason for wishing to hear *Les Huguenots?* How charmingly convincing a contralto may be in such roles [as the page Urbain] the modern audience may judge from the performances of Hertha Glaz; how brilliantly difficult is the music of Urbain's great entrance air, *Nobles seigneurs!* may be perceived from Victor's recent reissue of Louise Homer's 1905 recording

(Victor Heritage Series 15-1011). Irene Adler's spectacular entrance as Urbain must have been unforgettable; and it is more than understandable that a man might haunt later performances of *Les Huguenots,* half in vain hopes of finding a new portrayal to eclipse her memory, half to nurse the pleasant pain of recollection."

Auctorial and Bibliographical Note: In the March of 1901, Conan Doyle and his friend Fletcher Robinson (who later wrote *The Chronicles of Addington Peace;* London: Harper, 1905) were on a golfing holiday at the Royal Links Hotel at Cromer in Norfolk. "One raw Sunday afternoon when a wind rushed off the North Sea," while lounging in the comfort of their private sitting room, Robinson began telling legends of Dartmoor, one of which concerned a spectral hound. By the end of the month, Conan Doyle was at work on the story, which, at first, he had no intention of making an adventure of Sherlock Holmes. Then he thought to himself, "Why should I invent a character when I had him already in the form of Holmes?" It has been said that the novel is the only tale of Sherlock Holmes, long or short, in which the story dominates Holmes rather than Holmes dominating the story; in any case, critics are generally agreed that it is by far the best of the four Holmes novels, and many consider it Holmes' (and Watson's) finest hour. (The readers of the *Observer* placed *The Hound of the Baskervilles* second on their list of the favorite Holmes novels and short stories.) Conan Doyle had suggested that Robinson collaborate with him on the novel; although Robinson refused the offer, Conan Doyle acknowledged his debt by dedicating the novel to him. The dedication is curious in that three versions of it exist. The first is a footnote in the *Strand:*

> This story owes its inception to my friend, Mr. Fletcher Robinson, who has helped me both in the general plot and in the local details.
> —A. C. D.

In the first book edition, published by George Newnes, Ltd., London, in 1902, the dedication reads:

> My dear Robinson:
> It was to your account of a West-Country legend that this tale owes its inception. For this and for your help in detail all thanks
> Yours most truly,
> A. Conan Doyle
>
> Hindhead
> Haslemere

So it appears in all subsequent English, as opposed to the American, editions. But when, in the same year, 1902, McClure Phillips of New York published the first American edition, the dedication was slightly changed. It read:

> My dear Robinson:
> It was your account of a west country legend which first suggested the idea of this little tale to my mind.
> For this, and for the help which you have given me in its evolution, all thanks.
> Yours most truly,
> A. Conan Doyle

The apparent confusion here was at last clarified by Sir Arthur himself. In his Preface to *The Complete Sherlock Holmes,* he wrote:

> Then came the *Hound of the Baskervilles.* It arose from a remark by that fine fellow whose premature death was a loss to the world, Fletcher Robinson, that there was a spectral dog near his home on Dartmoor. That remark was the inception of the book, but I should add that the plot and every word of the actual narrative was my own.

When the complete manuscript of the novel was sent to McClure, Phillips in New York, they in turn handed the sheets, after they had served their purposes, to the American News Company for advertising purposes. Single sheets were sent to booksellers all over the country, where many of them were framed and used for window displays. Over the years, Mr. Lew D. Feldman of the House of El Dieff was able to obtain a number of these sheets for collectors. The only complete chapter known to have survived is XI ("The Man on the Tor"). It consists of 16 pages, folio. Auctioned in New York City on March 18, 1946, it brought $115. It is presently owned by the New York Public Library.

37

THE ADVENTURE OF THE COPPER BEECHES

[Friday, April 5, to Saturday, April 20, 1889]

"TO the man who loves art for its own sake," remarked Sherlock Holmes, tossing aside the
1 advertisement sheet of the *Daily Telegraph*, "it is frequently in its least important and lowliest manifestations that the keenest pleasure is to be derived. It is pleasant to me to observe, Watson, that you have so far
2 grasped this truth that in these little records of our cases which you have been good enough to draw up, and, I am bound to say, occasionally to embellish, you have given
3 prominence not so much to the many *causes célèbres* and sensational trials in which I have figured, but rather to those incidents which may have been trivial in themselves, but which have given room for those faculties of deduction and of logical synthesis which I have made my special province."

"And yet," said I, smiling, "I cannot quite hold myself absolved from the charge of sensationalism which has been urged against my records."

"You have erred, perhaps," he observed, taking up a glowing cinder with the tongs, and lighting with it the long cherrywood pipe which was wont to replace his clay when he was in a disputatious rather than a meditative mood—"you have erred, perhaps, in attempting to put colour and life into each of your statements, instead of confining yourself to the task of placing upon record that severe reasoning from cause to effect which is really the only notable feature about the thing."

"It seems to me that I have done you full justice in the matter," I remarked with some coldness, for I was repelled by the egotism which I had more than once observed to
4 be a strong factor in my friend's singular character.

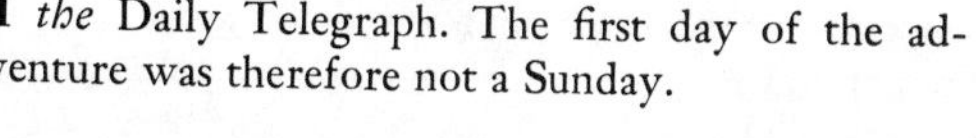

1 *the* Daily Telegraph. The first day of the adventure was therefore not a Sunday.

2 *these little records of our cases.* Holmes later asks, "What do the public . . . care about the finer shades of analysis and deduction" displayed in them. This must mean that the case took place after December, 1887, when *A Study in Scarlet* was published in *Beeton's Christmas Annual.* Since the case, as we shall see, could not have taken place later than the spring of 1890, and Watson's second published case, *The Sign of the Four*, did not reach the public until the November of that year, Holmes must also have been thinking of Watsonian chronicles still in manuscript.

3 causes célèbres, French: celebrated cases.

4 *my friend's singular character.* "Watson was a keen student of human nature, however obtuse he may have pictured himself to be—for strategic reasons—in his stories," Mr. Robert Winthrop Adams wrote in "John H. Watson, M.D., Characterologist." "He well knew that, as Epictetus remarked, 'What a man sayeth of thee concerneth him that sayeth it more than it concerneth thee.' So he shrugged off Holmes' criticism with a mild disclaimer and kept right on putting 'colour and life' into his statements. In his very next [published] story ["Silver Blaze"] he polishes up the report of an almost routine investigation until it shines as one of the very best short stories in the Saga. What luck for us that Watson, with characteristic British obstinacy, refused to let the gleaming light of his story-telling genius be hidden under the bushel of his friend's dominant intellectuality!"

"YOU HAVE ERRED, PERHAPS," HE OBSERVED, TAKING UP A GLOWING CINDER WITH THE TONGS . . .

Illustration by Sidney Paget for the *Strand Magazine*, June, 1892.

" No, it is not selfishness or conceit," said he, answering, as was his wont, my thoughts rather than my words.
" If I claim full justice for my art, it is because it is an
impersonal thing—a thing beyond myself. Crime is common. Logic is rare. Therefore it is upon the logic rather
than upon the crime that you should dwell. You have
degraded what should have been a course of lectures into a
series of tales." **5**

It was a cold morning of the early spring, and we sat **6**
after breakfast on either side of a cheery fire in the old
room in Baker Street. A thick fog rolled down between **7**
the lines of dun-coloured houses, and the opposing windows loomed like dark, shapeless blurs, through the heavy
yellow wreaths. Our gas was lit, and shone on the white
cloth, and glimmer of china and metal, for the table had
not been cleared yet. Sherlock Holmes had been silent
all the morning, dipping continuously into the advertisement columns of a succession of papers, until at last, having apparently given up his search, he had emerged in no
very sweet temper to lecture me upon my literary short-
comings.

" At the same time," he remarked, after a pause, during
which he had sat puffing at his long pipe and gazing down
into the fire, " you can hardly be open to a charge of
sensationalism, for out of these cases which you have been
so kind as to interest yourself in, a fair proportion do not
treat of crime, in its legal sense, at all. The small matter
in which I endeavoured to help the King of Bohemia, the
singular experience of Miss Mary Sutherland, the problem
connected with the man with the twisted lip, and the incident of the noble bachelor, were all matters which are outside the pale of the law. But in avoiding the sensational, I **8**
fear that you may have bordered on the trivial."

" The end may have been so," I answered, " but the
methods I hold to have been novel and of interest."

" Pshaw, my dear fellow, what do the public, the great
unobservant public, who could hardly tell a weaver by his
tooth or a compositor by his left thumb, care about the **9-10**
finer shades of analysis and deduction ! But, indeed, if
you are trivial, I cannot blame you, for the days of the
great cases are past. Man, or at least criminal man, has
lost all enterprise and originality. As to my own little
practice, it seems to be degenerating into an agency for
recovering lost lead pencils and giving advice to young
ladies from boarding-schools. I think that I have touched
bottom at last, however. This note I had this morning **11**
marks my zero point, I fancy. Read it ! " He tossed a
crumpled letter across to me.

It was dated from Montague Place upon the preceding **12**
evening, and ran thus :

" DEAR MR. HOLMES,—I am very anxious to consult
you as to whether I should or should not accept a situation
which has been offered to me as governess. I shall call at
half-past ten to-morrow, if I do not inconvenience you.—
Yours faithfully,

" VIOLET HUNTER." **13**

" Do you know the young lady ? " I asked.

" Not I."

" It is half-past ten now."

5 *a series of tales.*" Although Holmes allegedly did not approve of Watson's methods, he was sometimes pleased to fill out the record. In "The Adventure of the Norwood Builder," he says: "Well, well, I daresay that a couple of rabbits would account for both the blood and for the charred ashes. If you ever write an account, Watson, you can make rabbits serve your turn." And when Holmes applied himself to the task of writing up one of his adventures ("The Blanched Soldier") with no help from his Boswell, even he had to admit that "having taken my pen in my hand, I do begin to realize that the matter must be presented in such a way as may interest the reader."

6 *It was a cold morning of the early spring.* In your editor's view, it was *Friday, April 5, 1889*, a day on which the temperature fell to a low of 37.8°. Said the London *Times:* "Temperature . . . falling decidedly over England. . . . A very cold night is likely to occur over England tonight." Virtually all other commentators except Christ and Walter, who date the adventure 1891, believe that it took place in the spring of 1890.

7 *the old room in Baker Street.* All chronologists except your editor would seem to agree that Watson was married at the time of this adventure. This presents them with a difficulty, since Watson is here completely silent about a wife or professional duties and appears to be living in Baker Street, not for a few days only, but for the entire fortnight covered by the adventure. In our view, the adventure was the last shared by the doctor and the detective before Watson's marriage to Mary Morstan *circa* May 1, 1889.

8 *all matters which are outside the pale of the law.* "Leaving aside the question of whether Neville St. Clair had not been obtaining money under false pretences, there is as clear a case of bigamy in the incident of 'The Noble Bachelor' as one could wish for," Mr. S. T. L. Harbottle wrote in "Sherlock Holmes and the Law."

9 *a weaver by his tooth.* "Probably the best description [of a weaver's tooth] is given by Burket in *Oral Medicine*, Lippincott, Philadelphia, 1946, on page 573," Professor Remsen Ten Eyck Schenck wrote in "The Effect of Trades Upon the Body." " 'Tailors and seamstresses who are in the habit of cutting their thread with their teeth may show a characteristic tooth defect which consists of sharp V-shaped notches in the middle of the incisal edge of the incisors. The notching is most prominent in the upper incisors. When it is no longer possible to cut the thread because of loss of tooth structure, then the teeth on the opposite side are utilized.' "

10 *a compositor by his left thumb.* "A compositor's left thumb is often characterized by the formation of a callus on the tip, often with abrasion of the skin lower down, across the 'ball' of

" Yes, and I have no doubt that is her ring."

" It may turn out to be of more interest than you think.
14 You remember that the affair of the blue carbuncle, which appeared to be a mere whim at first, developed into a serious investigation. It may be so in this case also."

" Well, let us hope so ! But our doubts will very soon be solved, for here, unless I am much mistaken, is the person in question."

As he spoke the door opened, and a young lady entered the room. She was plainly but neatly dressed, with a bright, quick face, freckled like a plover's egg, and with the brisk manner of a woman who has had her own way to make in the world.

" You will excuse my troubling you, I am sure," said she, as my companion rose to greet her ; " but I have had a very strange experience, and as I have no parents or relations of any sort from whom I could ask advice, I thought that perhaps you would be kind enough to tell me what I should do."

" Pray take a seat, Miss Hunter. I shall be happy to do anything that I can to serve you."

I could see that Holmes was favourably impressed by the manner and speech of his new client. He looked her over in his searching fashion, and then composed himself with his lids drooping and his finger-tips together to listen to her story.

" I have been a governess for five years," said she, " in the family of Colonel Spence Munro, but two months ago the Colonel received an appointment at Halifax, in Nova Scotia, and took his children over to America with him, so that I found myself without a situation. I advertised and I answered advertisements, but without success. At last the little money which I had saved began to run short, and I was at my wits' end as to what I should do.

" There is a well-known agency for governesses in the West End called Westaway's, and there I used to call about once a week in order to see whether anything had turned up which might suit me. Westaway was the name of the founder of the business, but it is really managed by Miss Stoper. She sits in her own little office, and the ladies who are seeking employment wait in an ante-room, and are then shown in one by one, when she consults her ledgers, and sees whether she has anything which would suit them.

" Well, when I called last week I was shown into the little office as usual, but I found that Miss Stoper was not alone. A prodigiously stout man with a very smiling face, and a great heavy chin which rolled down in fold upon fold over his throat, sat at her elbow with a pair of glasses on his nose, looking very earnestly at the ladies who entered. As I came in he gave quite a jump in his chair, and turned quickly to Miss Stoper :

" ' That will do,' said he ; ' I could not ask for anything better. Capital ! Capital ! ' He seemed quite enthusiastic and rubbed his hands together in the most genial fashion. He was such a comfortable-looking man that it was quite a pleasure to look at him.

" ' You are looking for a situation, miss ? ' he asked.

" ' Yes, sir.'

the digit," Professor Schenck continued. "In setting type, the 'stick' is held in the left hand and the type placed in it with the right. As each piece of type is dropped into the stick, the left thumb slides it into position against the last addition, and then holds the accumulated mass snugly in a corner."

11 *This note I had this morning.* Additional evidence that the opening day of the case was not a Sunday.

12 *Montague Place.* Not to be confused with Montague *Street,* where Holmes had rooms when he opened his practice in London. Montague Place runs at right angles to Montague Street, but like it, is a street which borders the British Museum.

13 "VIOLET. Holmes' hobby of collecting Violets has been noted by many commentators, many of whom suppose that women so named had some special importance to him. Miss Esther Longfellow, in "The Distaff Side of Baker Street" found the supposition "absurd when we face the probability that every tenth woman in England was, and still is, called Violet."

14 *the affair of the blue carbuncle.* Chronologically minded readers will of course have noted that this case must follow "A Scandal in Bohemia," "A Case of Identity," "The Man with the Twisted Lip," "The Adventure of the Noble Bachelor," and, now, "The Adventure of the Blue Carbuncle."

" 'THAT WILL DO,' SAID HE; 'I COULD NOT ASK FOR ANYTHING BETTER. CAPITAL! CAPITAL!' "

Illustration by Sidney Paget for the *Strand Magazine,* June, 1892.

" 'As governess ?'

" 'Yes, sir.'

" 'And what salary do you ask ?'

" 'I had four pounds a month in my last place with Colonel Spence Munro.'

" 'Oh, tut, tut ! sweating—rank sweating !' he cried, throwing his fat hands out into the air like a man who is in a boiling passion. 'How could anyone offer so pitiful a sum to a lady with such attractions and accomplishments ?'

" 'My accomplishments, sir, may be less than you imagine,' said I. 'A little French, a little German, music
and drawing——' 15

" 'Tut, tut !' he cried. This is all quite beside the question. The point is, have you or have you not the bearing and deportment of a lady ? There it is in a nutshell. If you have not, you are not fitted for the rearing of a child who may some day play a considerable part in the history of the country. But if you have, why, then how could any gentleman ask you to condescend to accept anything under the three figures ? Your salary with me, madam, would commence at a hundred pounds a year.'

" You may imagine, Mr. Holmes, that to me, destitute as I was, such an offer seemed almost too good to be true. The gentleman, however, seeing perhaps the look of incredulity upon my face, opened a pocket-book and took
out a note. 16

" 'It is also my custom,' said he, smiling in the most pleasant fashion until his eyes were just two shining slits, amid the white creases of his face, 'to advance to my young ladies half their salary beforehand, so that they may meet any little expenses of their journey and their wardrobe.'

" It seemed to me that I had never met so fascinating and so thoughtful a man. As I was already in debt to my tradesmen, the advance was a great convenience, and yet there was something unnatural about the whole transaction which made me wish to know a little more before I quite committed myself.

" 'May I ask where you live, sir ?' said I.

" 'Hampshire. Charming rural place. The Copper Beeches, five miles on the far side of Winchester. It is the most lovely country, my dear young lady, and the dearest old country house.'

" 'And my duties, sir ? I should be glad to know what they would be.'

" 'One child—one dear little romper just six years old. Oh, if you could see him killing cockroaches with a slipper ! Smack ! smack ! smack ! Three gone before you could wink !' He leaned back in his chair and laughed his eyes into his head again.

" I was a little startled at the nature of the child's amusement, but the father's laughter made me think that perhaps he was joking.

" 'My sole duties, then,' I asked, 'are to take charge of a single child ?'

" 'No, no, not the sole, not the sole, my dear young lady,' he cried. 'Your duty would be, as I am sure your good sense would suggest, to obey any little commands which my wife might give, provided always that they were such commands as a lady might with propriety obey.

15 *'A little French, a little German, music and drawing* ——' "We may be sure [that Violet Hunter] knew of [Holmes'] French ancestry, of his knowledge of German, of his love for music, and that art was in his blood," Mr. Isaac S. George wrote in "Violet the Hunter." "She simply parades for Holmes' benefit the talents she feels he would appreciate in a woman as a companion; but she is careful not to overdo it. . . . She uses Rucastle's words to emphasize her qualities as a potential wife and mother."

16 *took out a note.* What note? Not a £50 note, surely: it would be unheard of to advance a full half year's salary. "Furthermore," the late A. Carson Simpson wrote in *Numismatics in the Canon*, Part II, "we know that he was thinking in terms of the more usual *quarterly* salary payments, rather than annual, for his second offer was of '£30 a quarter, or £120 a year.' On the basis of his original offer, her quarterly pay would have been £25 and half of that is £12-10-0; there were no single notes for either of these amounts, nor any combination of notes for the latter figure." Weighing the probabilities, Mr. Simpson voted for a £10 note, an approximation of £12-10-0.

" 'OH, IF YOU COULD SEE HIM KILLING COCKROACHES WITH A SLIPPER! SMACK! SMACK! SMACK!' "

Illustration by G. da Fonseca from *Premières Aventures de Sherlock Holmes;* Paris: Librarie Félix Juvier, n.d.

You see no difficulty, heh ? '

" ' I should be happy to make myself useful.'

" ' Quite so. In dress now, for example ! We are faddy people, you know—faddy, but kind-hearted. If you were asked to wear any dress which we might give you, you would not object to our little whim. Heh ? '

" ' No,' said I, considerably astonished at his words.

" ' Or to sit here, or sit there, that would not be offensive, to you ? '

" ' Oh, no.'

" ' Or to cut your hair quite short before you come to us ? '

" I could hardly believe my ears. As you may observe, Mr. Holmes, my hair is somewhat luxuriant, and of a rather peculiar tint of chestnut. It has been considered
17 artistic. I could not dream of sacrificing it in this offhand fashion.

" ' I am afraid that that is quite impossible,' said I. He had been watching me eagerly out of his small eyes, and I could see a shadow pass over his face as I spoke.

" ' I am afraid that it is quite essential,' said he. ' It is a little fancy of my wife's, and ladies' fancies, you know, madam, ladies' fancies must be consulted. And so you won't cut your hair ? '

" ' No, sir, I really could not,' I answered firmly.

" ' Ah, very well ; then that quite settles the matter. It is a pity, because in other respects you would really have done very nicely. In that case, Miss Stoper, I had best inspect a few more of your young ladies.'

" The manageress had sat all this while busy with her papers without a word to either of us, but she glanced at me now with so much annoyance upon her face that I could not help suspecting that she had lost a handsome commission through my refusal.

' Do you desire your name to be kept upon the books ? ' she asked.

" ' If you please, Miss Stoper.'

" ' Well, really, it seems rather useless, since you refuse the most excellent offers in this fashion,' said she sharply. ' You can hardly expect us to exert ourselves to find another such opening for you. Good day to you, Miss Hunter.' She struck a gong upon the table, and I was shown out by the page.

" Well, Mr. Holmes, when I got back to my lodgings and found little enough in the cupboard, and two or three bills upon the table, I began to ask myself whether I had not done a very foolish thing. After all, if these people had strange fads, and expected obedience on the most extraordinary matters, they were at least ready to pay for their eccentricity. Very few governesses in England are getting a hundred a year. Besides, what use was my hair to me ? Many people are improved by wearing it short, and perhaps I should be among the number. Next day I was inclined to think that I had made a mistake, and by the day after I was sure of it. I had almost overcome my pride, so far as to go back to the agency and inquire whether the place was still open, when I received this letter from the gentleman himself. I have it here, and I will read it to you :

17 *It has been considered artistic.* Dr. Richard Asher is another commentator who believes that Miss Hunter had designs on Holmes. In "Holmes and the Fair Sex" he writes: "Throwing modesty to the winds, [Violet Hunter] pointed out her charms to [Holmes] in a singularly brazen fashion. . . . No doubt she wished to draw Holmes' attention to her best feature and keep his eyes off her face which Watson records was 'freckled like a plover's egg.' "

"The Copper Beeches, near Winchester.

"Dear Miss Hunter,—Miss Stoper has very kindly given me your address, and I write from here to ask you whether you have reconsidered your decision. My wife is very anxious that you should come, for she has been much attracted by my description of you. We are willing to give thirty pounds a quarter, or £120 a year, so as to recompense you for any little inconvenience which our fads may cause you. They are not very exacting after all. My wife is fond of a particular shade of electric blue, and would like you to wear such a dress indoors in the morning. You need not, however, go to the expense of purchasing one, as we have one belonging to my dear daughter Alice (now in Philadelphia) which would, I should think, fit you very well. Then, as to sitting here or there, or amusing yourself in any manner indicated, that need cause you no inconvenience. As regards your hair, it is no doubt a pity, especially as I could not help remarking its beauty during our short interview, but I am afraid that I must remain firm upon this point, and I only hope that the increased salary may recompense you for the loss. Your duties, as far as the child is concerned, are very light. Now do try to come, and I shall meet you with the dog-cart at Winchester. Let me know your train.—Yours faithfully,

"Jephro Rucastle.

"That is the letter which I have just received, Mr.
Holmes, and my mind is made up that I will accept it. I **18**
thought, however, that before taking the final step, I should like to submit the whole matter to your consideration."

"Well, Miss Hunter, if your mind is made up, that settles the question," said Holmes, smiling.

"But you would not advise me to refuse?"

"I confess that it is not the situation which I should
like to see a sister of mine apply for." **19**

"What is the meaning of it all, Mr. Holmes?"

"Ah, I have no data. I cannot tell. Perhaps you have yourself formed some opinion?"

"Well, there seems to me to be only one possible solution. Mr. Rucastle seemed to be a very kind, good-natured man. Is it not possible that his wife is a lunatic, that he desires to keep the matter quiet for fear she should be taken to an asylum, and that he humours her fancies in every way in order to prevent an outbreak."

"That is a possible solution—in fact, as matters stand, it is the most probable one. But in any case it does not seem to be a nice household for a young lady."

"But the money, Mr. Holmes, the money!"

"Well, yes, of course, the pay is good—too good. That is what makes me uneasy. Why should they give you £120 a year, when they could have their pick for £40? There must be some strong reason behind."

"I thought that if I told you the circumstances you would understand afterwards if I wanted your help. I should feel so much stronger if I felt that you were at the back of me."

18 *my mind is made up that I will accept it.* "It is just here that the lady gives herself away completely," Mr. Isaac S. George wrote in "Violet the Hunter." "As soon as she finishes reading the letter, without *asking or waiting* for advice; in fact before Holmes *has a chance to open his mouth*, she says flatly: "My mind is made up that I will accept it.' . . . Of *all* people, she consults a private detective for advice about accepting a position *after she has decided to take it.*"

19 *which I should like to see a sister of mine apply for.*" Commentators have taken this statement to mean that Holmes had a sister or sisters as well as a brother (or brothers): "May we venture on a very long shot and surmise, as Mr. Morley has also done, that Sherlock's remark . . . points to Holmes' sisters who, in the collapse of the family fortune, were perhaps forced to the genteel drudgery of governessing?" Messrs. J. H. and Humfrey Michell wrote in "Sherlock Holmes the Chemist."

Indeed, Mr. H. B. Williams has surmised that Violet Hunter was Holmes' (half) sister. "If the father of Mycroft and Sherlock had passed away and the mother had remarried a cousin, let us say (as was often the custom in those days) [Violet Hunter might well have been Holmes' half-sister]" ("Half-Sister; Half Mystery").

Mr. Robert Schutz is in full agreement with this view, as he states in "Half-Sister; No Mystery": "There is no direct evidence to contradict the assumption that Holmes' mother married a Mr. Hunter after the death of Sherlock's father, and gave birth to a daughter named Violet, twelve years after the birth of Sherlock."

HOLMES SHOOK HIS HEAD GRAVELY.

Illustration by Sidney Paget for the *Strand Magazine*, June, 1892.

" Oh, you may carry that feeling away with you. I assure you that your little problem promises to be the most interesting which has come my way for some months. There is something distinctly novel about some of the features. If you should find yourself in doubt or in danger——"

" Danger ! What danger do you foresee ? "

Holmes shook his head gravely. " It would cease to be a danger if we could define it," said he. " But at any time, day or night, a telegram would bring me down to your help."

" That is enough." She rose briskly from her chair with the anxiety all swept from her face. " I shall go down to Hampshire quite easy in my mind now. I shall write to Mr. Rucastle at once, sacrifice my poor hair to-night, and start for Winchester to-morrow." With a few grateful words to Holmes she bade us both good night, and bustled off upon her way.

" At least," said I, as we heard her quick, firm step descending the stairs, " she seems to be a young lady who is very well able to take care of herself."

" And she would need to be," said Holmes gravely ; " I am much mistaken if we do not hear from her before many days are past."

It was not very long before my friend's prediction was
20 fulfilled. A fortnight went by, during which I frequently
found my thoughts turning in her direction, and wondering what strange side-alley of human experience this lonely woman had strayed into. The unusual salary, the curious conditions, the light duties, all pointed to something abnormal, though whether a fad or a plot, or whether the man were a philanthropist or a villain, it was quite beyond my powers to determine. As to Holmes, I observed that he sat frequently for half an hour on end, with knitted brows and an abstracted air, but he swept the matter away with a wave of his hand when I mentioned it. " Data ! data ! data ! " he cried impatiently. " I can't make bricks
21 without clay." And yet he would always wind up by
muttering that no sister of his should ever have accepted such a situation.

The telegram which we eventually received came late
22 one night, just as I was thinking of turning in, and Holmes
was settling down to one of those all-night researches which he frequently indulged in, when I would leave him stooping over a retort and a test-tube at night, and find him in the same position when I came down to breakfast in the morning. He opened the yellow envelope, and then, glancing at the message, threw it across to me.

" Just look up the trains in Bradshaw," said he, and turned back to his chemical studies.

The summons was a brief and urgent one.

" Please be at the Black Swan Hotel at Winchester at
23 midday to-morrow," it said. " Do come ! I am at my
wits' end.

" HUNTER."

" Will you come with me ? " asked Holmes, glancing up.

20 *A fortnight went by.* Watson would seem, if he was speaking quite literally, to be saying that he is writing as of the fifteenth "case day."

21 *"I can't make bricks without clay."* In the adventure of "The Crooked Man" Holmes admits that his Biblical knowledge is a little rusty. But here he is probably not misquoting Exodus, 5:7: "Ye shall no more give the people straw to make bricks." Bricks *are* made from clay; Holmes was merely stating a fact.

22 *late one night.* The night of the fifteenth day —or perhaps a day or two later?

23 *"Do come!* "And the phrase 'Do come!'," Mr. Isaac S. George wrote in "Violet the Hunter" "—is that a message from a person in trouble to a consulting detective? from a patient to a doctor? from a lawyer to a client or from one businessman to another? It most certainly is *not*. It is a cordial social message; a sugary, sentimental message often used by hospitable hostesses, ardent swains and romantically-inclined — yes, even designing — women."

24 *my analysis of the acetones.* "Acetone is a single chemical substance, not a category," Professor Remsen Ten Eyck Schenck wrote in "Baker Street Fables." "The term analysis could not meaningfully be employed here, either, since it implies the identification of the ingredients of a mixture. The statement is thus nonsensical from two standpoints."

To this Mr. Leon S. Holstein replied (" '7. Knowledge of Chemistry—Profound' "): "It is true that

" I should wish to."

" Just look it up, then."

" There is a train at half-past nine," said I, glancing over my Bradshaw. " It is due at Winchester at 11.30."

" That will do very nicely. Then perhaps I had better
postpone my analysis of the acetones, as we may need to be **24**
at our best in the morning."

By eleven o'clock the next day we were well upon our **25**
way to the old English capital. Holmes had been buried
in the morning papers all the way down, but after we had **26**
passed the Hampshire border he threw them down, and
began to admire the scenery. It was an ideal spring day, **27**
a light blue sky, flecked with little fleecy white clouds drifting across from west to east. The sun was shining very brightly, and yet there was an exhilarating nip in the air, which set an edge to a man's energy. All over the
country-side, away to the rolling hills around Aldershot, **28**
the little red and grey roofs of the farm-steadings peeped out from amidst the light green of the new foliage.

" Are they not fresh and beautiful ? " I cried, with all the enthusiasm of a man fresh from the fogs of Baker Street.

But Holmes shook his head gravely.

" Do you know, Watson," said he, " that it is one of the curses of a mind with a turn like mine that I must look at everything with reference to my own special subject. You look at these scattered houses, and you are impressed by their beauty. I look at them, and the only thought which comes to me is a feeling of their isolation, and of the impunity with which crime may be committed there."

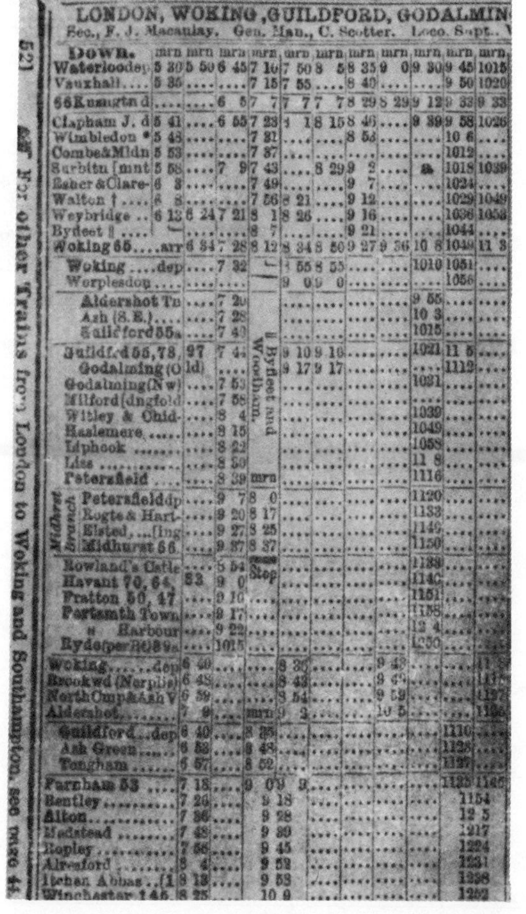

LONDON, WOKING, GUILDFORD, GODALMIN[G]
Sec., F. J. Macaulay. Gen. Man., C. Scotter. Loco. Supt.

521 For other Trains from London to Woking and Southampton, see page 4[illegible]

"IT IS DUE AT WINCHESTER AT 11.30."

The relevant page in *Bradshaw's Guide.* "Naturally," Lord Dongegall once noted, "Watson does not record what Holmes said to him when they found themselves on a 9:30 A.M. train by which they could not reach Winchester until 52 minutes after they were supposed to meet Miss Hunter at the Black Swan. On the other hand, Watson may have had a second look at Bradshaw's, in time to get an un-breakfasted, infuriated Holmes on the 7:50, ariving at Winchester at 10:09 A.M. Had this been the case, however, Miss Hunter would hardly have been 'waiting for us.' "

acetone is acetone and is not a categorical designation; but the adverse critics should know that there is a series of products usually designated as the *ketone* or *acetone oils,* and in common parlance these are often referred to as *acetones.* It was the analysis of these materials that Violet Hunter's telegram caused to be put aside for more pressing matters."

And Mr. D. A. Redmond has suggested ("Some Chemical Problems in the Canon") that Holmes said, not "acetones" but "acetone bodies": "The adrenalin content of the blood, we know, rises suddenly during severe stresses of emotions, or intense muscular activity. The acetone or ketone bodies indicate this as well as certain metabolic conditions. For this reason the Master may have been investigating the *acetone bodies* in blood—we know his intense interest in blood [A *Study in Scarlet*]."

25 *the next day.* The sixteenth case day, at the earliest.

26 *the morning papers.* If this was indeed the sixteenth case day, as it appears to have been, it could not have been a Sunday, and the first day of the adventure was therefore not a Saturday.

27 *an ideal spring day.* In our view, the day was Saturday, April 20, 1889. *Whitaker's Almanack* tells us that no rain fell on that day and that there was a southwest wind. Since the *Times* of London of course published no Sunday edition, there was no report on the weather of the 20th in that paper, but the *Times* reported that the preceding day —Friday the 19th—was a day on which "conditions have been fair and genial, and temperature has risen."

" Good heavens ! " I cried. " Who would associate crime with these dear old homesteads ? "

" They always fill me with a certain horror. It is my belief, Watson, founded upon my experience, that the lowest and vilest alleys in London do not present a more dreadful record of sin than does the smiling and beautiful country-side."

" You horrify me ! "

" But the reason is very obvious. The pressure of public opinion can do in the town what the law cannot accomplish. There is no lane so vile that the scream of a tortured child, or the thud of a drunkard's blow, does not beget sympathy and indignation among the neighbours, and then the whole machinery of justice is ever so close that a word of complaint can set it going, and there is but a step between the crime and the dock. But look at these lonely houses, each in its own fields, filled for the most part with poor ignorant folk who know little of the law. Think of the deeds of hellish cruelty, the hidden wickedness which may go on, year in, year out, in such places, and
29 none the wiser. Had this lady who appeals to us for help gone to live in Winchester, I should never have had a fear for her. It is the five miles of country which makes the danger. Still, it is clear that she is not personally threatened."

" No. If she can come to Winchester to meet us she can get away."

" Quite so. She has her freedom."

" What *can* be the matter, then ? Can you suggest no explanation ? "

" I have devised seven separate explanations, each of
30 which would cover the facts as far as we know them. But which of these is correct can only be determined by the fresh information which we shall no doubt find waiting for us. Well, there is the tower of the Cathedral, and we shall soon learn all that Miss Hunter has to tell."

31 The " Black Swan " is an inn of repute in the High Street, at no distance from the station, and there we found the young lady waiting for us. She had engaged a sitting-room, and our lunch awaited us upon the table.

" I am so delighted that you have come," she said earnestly, " it is so kind of you both ; but indeed I do not know what I should do. Your advice will be altogether invaluable to me."

" Pray tell us what has happened to you."

" I will do so, and I must be quick, for I have promised Mr. Rucastle to be back before three. I got his leave to come into town this morning, though he little knew for what purpose."

" Let us have everything in its due order." Holmes thrust his long thin legs out towards the fire, and composed himself to listen.

" In the first place, I may say that I have met, on the whole, with no actual ill-treatment from Mr. and Mrs. Rucastle. It is only fair to them to say that. But I cannot understand them, and I am not easy in my mind about them."

" What can you not understand ? "

" Their reasons for their conduct. But you shall have

28 *Aldershot.* Aldershot, to be visited by Holmes and Watson in the adventure of "The Crooked Man," is a military depot of long standing. "It lies to the west of the main road connecting Farnborough in the north with Farnham in the south," Mr. Michael Harrison wrote in *In the Footsteps of Sherlock Holmes,* "and is enclosed within a fairly regular rectangle formed by the main road, on the east, the Basingstroke Canal on the north, and the curving Blackwater River on the west and south. . . . Severely utilitarian in design, no less than in function, Aldershot was built and developed as a great camp; such town as there was existed merely to supply the needs of the barracks . . ."

29 *and none the wiser.* "Holmes' reaction was decidedly unEnglish," Professor Clarke Olney commented in "The Literacy of Sherlock Holmes"; "French, perhaps, even, one is tempted to say, Russian."

30 *the facts as far as we know them.* Compare Holmes' remark to Watson in "The Adventure of the Missing Three-Quarter": "I had seven different schemes for getting a glimpse of that telegram."

31 *an inn of repute. Baedeker's Guide to Britain* (1897 edition) does in fact recommend the Black Swan as a good place to stay when visiting historic Winchester.

it all just as it occurred. When I came down Mr. Rucastle met me here, and drove me in his dog-cart to Copper Beeches. It is, as he said, beautifully situated, but it is not beautiful in itself, for it is a large square block of a house, whitewashed, but all stained and streaked with damp and bad weather. There are grounds round it, woods on three sides, and on the fourth a field which slopes down to the Southampton high-road, which curves past about a hundred yards from the front door. This ground in front belongs to the house, but the woods all round are part of Lord Southerton's preserves. A clump of copper beeches immediately in front of the hall door has given its name to the place.

" I was driven over by my employer, who was as amiable as ever, and was introduced by him that evening to his wife and the child. There was no truth, Mr. Holmes, in the conjecture which seemed to us to be probable in your rooms at Baker Street. Mrs. Rucastle is not mad. I found her to be a silent, pale-faced woman, much younger than her husband, not more than thirty, I should think, while he can hardly be less than forty-five. From their conversation I have gathered that they have been married about seven years, that he was a widower, and that his only child by the first wife was the daughter who has gone to Philadelphia. Mr. Rucastle told me in private that the reason why she had left them was that she had an unreasoning aversion to her stepmother. As the daughter could not have been less than twenty, I can quite imagine that her position must have been uncomfortable with her father's young wife.

" Mrs. Rucastle seemed to me to be colourless in mind as well as in feature. She impressed me neither favourably nor the reverse. She was a nonentity. It was easy to see that she was passionately devoted both to her husband and to her little son. Her light grey eyes wandered continually from one to the other, noting every little want and forestalling it if possible. He was kind to her also in his bluff boisterous fashion, and on the whole they seemed to be a happy couple. And yet she had some secret sorrow, this woman. She would often be lost in deep thought, with the saddest look upon her face. More than once I have surprised her in tears. I have thought sometimes that it was the disposition of her child which weighed upon her mind, for I have never met so utterly spoilt and so ill-natured a little creature. He is small for his age, with a head which is quite disproportionately large. His whole life appears to be spent in an alternation between savage fits of passion and gloomy intervals of sulking. Giving pain to any creature weaker than himself seems to be his one idea of amusement, and he shows quite remarkable talent in planning the capture of mice, little birds, and insects. But I would rather not talk about the creature, Mr. Holmes, and, indeed, he has little to do with my story."

" I am glad of all details," remarked my friend, " whether they seem to you to be relevant or not."

" I shall try not to miss anything of importance. The one unpleasant thing about the house, which struck me at once, was the appearance and conduct of the servants.

"I AM SO DELIGHTED THAT YOU HAVE COME," SHE SAID EARNESTLY . . .

Illustration by Sidney Paget for the *Strand Magazine*, June, 1892.

“I READ FOR ABOUT TEN MINUTES . . .”

Illustration by Sidney Paget for the *Strand Magazine*, June, 1892.

There are only two, a man and his wife. Toller, for that's his name, is a rough, uncouth man, with grizzled hair and whiskers, and a perpetual smell of drink. Twice since I have been with them he has been quite drunk, and yet Mr. Rucastle seemed to take no notice of it. His wife is a very tall and strong woman with a sour face, as silent as Mrs. Rucastle, and much less amiable. They are a most unpleasant couple, but fortunately I spend most of my time in the nursery and my own room, which are next to each other in one corner of the building.

" For two days after my arrival at the Copper Beeches my life was very quiet ; on the third, Mrs. Rucastle came down just after breakfast and whispered something to her husband.

" ' Oh yes,' said he, turning to me, ' we are very much obliged to you, Miss Hunter, for falling in with our whims so far as to cut your hair. I assure you that it has not detracted in the tiniest iota from your appearance. We shall now see how the electric blue dress will become you. You will find it laid out upon the bed in your room and if you would be so good as to put it on we should both be extremely obliged.'

" The dress which I found waiting for me was of a peculiar shade of blue. It was of excellent material, a sort of beige, but it bore unmistakable signs of having been worn before. It could not have been a better fit if I had been measured for it. Both Mr. and Mrs. Rucastle expressed a delight at the look of it which seemed quite exaggerated in its vehemence. They were waiting for me in the drawing-room, which is a very large room, stretching along the entire front of the house, with three long windows reaching down to the floor. A chair had been placed close to the central window, with its back turned towards it. In this I was asked to sit, and then Mr. Rucastle, walking up and down on the other side of the room, began to tell me a series of the funniest stories that I have ever listened to. You cannot imagine how comical he was, and I laughed until I was quite weary. Mrs. Rucastle, however, who has evidently no sense of humour, never so much as smiled, but sat with her hands in her lap, and a sad, anxious look upon her face. After an hour or so, Mr. Rucastle suddenly remarked that it was time to commence the duties of the day, and that I might change my dress, and go to little Edward in the nursery.

" Two days later this same performance was gone through under exactly similar circumstances. Again I changed my dress, again I sat in the window, and again I laughed very heartily at the funny stories of which my employer had an immense repertoire, and which he told inimitably. Then he handed me a yellow-backed novel, and, moving my chair a little sideways, that my own shadow might not fall upon the page, he begged me to read aloud to him. I read for about ten minutes, beginning in the heart of a chapter, and then suddenly, in the middle of a sentence, he ordered me to cease and change my dress.

" You can easily imagine, Mr. Holmes, how curious I became as to what the meaning of this extraordinary performance could possibly be. They were always very careful, I observed, to turn my face away from the window, so that I became consumed with the desire to see what was going on behind my back. At first it seemed to be impossible, but I soon devised a means. My hand mirror had been broken, so a happy thought seized me, and I concealed a little of the glass in my handkerchief. On the next occasion, in the midst of my laughter, I put my handkerchief up to my eyes, and was able with a little management to see all that there was behind me. I confess that I was disappointed. There was nothing.

" At least, that was my first impression. At the second glance, however, I perceived that there was a man standing in the Southampton road, a small bearded man in a grey suit, who seemed to be looking in my direction. The road is an important highway, and there are usually people there. This man, however, was leaning against the railings which bordered our field, and was looking earnestly. I lowered my handkerchief, and glanced at Mrs. Rucastle to find her eyes fixed upon me with a most searching gaze. She said nothing, but I am convinced that she had divined that I had a mirror in my hand, and had seen what was behind me. She rose at once.

" ' Jephro,' said she, ' there is an impertinent fellow upon the road there who stares up at Miss Hunter.'

" ' No friend of yours, Miss Hunter ? ' he asked.

" ' No ; I know no one in these parts.'

" ' Dear me ! How very impertinent ! Kindly turn round, and motion him to go away.'

" ' Surely it would be better to take no notice ? '

" ' No, no, we should have him loitering here always. Kindly turn round, and wave him away like that.'

" I did as I was told, and at the same instant Mrs. Rucastle drew down the blind. That was a week ago, and from that time I have not sat again in the window, nor have I worn the blue dress, nor seen the man in the road."

" Pray continue," said Holmes. " Your narrative promises to be a most interesting one."

" You will find it rather disconnected, I fear, and there may prove to be little relation between the different incidents of which I speak. On the very first day that I was at Copper Beeches, Mr. Rucastle took me to a small outhouse which stands near the kitchen door. As we approached it I heard the sharp rattling of a chain, and the sound as of a large animal moving about.

" ' Look in here ! ' said Mr. Rucastle, showing me a slit between two planks. ' Is he not a beauty ? '

" I looked through, and was conscious of two glowing eyes, and of a vague figure huddled up in the darkness.

" ' Don't be frightened,' said my employer, laughing at
the start which I had given. ' It's only Carlo, my mastiff. **32**
I call him mine, but really old Toller, my groom, is the only man who can do anything with him. We feed him once a day, and not too much then, so that he is always as keen as mustard. Toller lets him loose every night, and God help the trespasser whom he lays his fangs upon. For goodness' sake don't you ever on any pretext set your foot over the threshold at night, for it is as much as your life is worth.'

" The warning was no idle one, for two nights later I **33**
happened to look out of my bedroom window about two o'clock in the morning. It was a beautiful moonlight

32 *Carlo.* Evidently a popular name for a dog in the Holmes-Watson era: the spaniel in "The Adventure of the Sussex Vampire" was also named Carlo.

33 *two nights later.* Miss Hunter was to go to the Copper Beeches on the day after her visit to Holmes at 221B; "For two days" after this her life was very quiet; "on the third" day she caught her glimpse of the small bearded man in the grey suit; and "two nights later" would bring us to the fifth day.

34 night, and the lawn in front of the house was silvered over and almost as bright as day. I was standing wrapt in the peaceful beauty of the scene, when I was aware that something was moving under the shadow of the copper beeches. As it emerged into the moonshine I saw what it was. It was a giant dog, as large as a calf, tawny-tinted, with hanging jowl, black muzzle, and huge projecting bones. It walked slowly across the lawn and vanished into the shadow upon the other side. That dreadful silent sentinel sent a chill to my heart, which I do not think that any burglar could have done.

" And now I have a very strange experience to tell you. I had, as you know, cut off my hair in London, and I had placed it in a great coil at the bottom of my trunk. One evening, after the child was in bed, I began to amuse myself by examining the furniture of my room, and by rearranging my own little things. There was an old chest of drawers in the room, the two upper ones empty and open, the lower one locked. I had filled the two first with my linen, and as I had still much to pack away, I was naturally annoyed at not having the use of the third drawer. It struck me that it might have been fastened by a mere oversight, so I took out my bunch of keys and tried to open it. The very first key fitted to perfection, and I drew the drawer open. There was only one thing in it, but I am sure that you would never guess what it was. It was my coil of hair.

" I took it up and examined it. It was of the same peculiar tint, and the same thickness. But then the impossibility of the thing obtruded itself upon me. How *could* my hair have been locked in the drawer ? With trembling hands I undid my trunk, turned out the contents, and drew from the bottom my own hair. I laid the two tresses together, and I assure you they were identical. Was it not extraordinary ? Puzzle as I would, I could make nothing at all of what it meant. I returned the strange hair to the drawer, and I said nothing of the matter to the Rucastles, as I felt that I had put myself in the wrong by opening a drawer which they had locked.

" I am naturally observant as you may have remarked,
35 Mr. Holmes, and I soon had a pretty good plan of the whole house in my head. There was one wing, however, which appeared not to be inhabited at all. A door which faced that which led into the quarters of the Tollers opened into this suite, but it was invariably locked. One day, however, as I ascended the stair, I met Mr. Rucastle coming out through this door, his keys in his hand, and a look on his face which made him a very different person to the round jovial man to whom I was accustomed. His cheeks were red, his brow was all crinkled with anger, and the veins stood out at his temples with passion. He locked the door, and hurried past me without a word or a look.

" This aroused my curiosity ; so when I went out for a walk in the grounds with my charge, I strolled round to the side from which I could see the windows of this part of the house. There were four of them in a row, three of which were simply dirty, while the fourth was shuttered up. They were evidently all deserted. As I strolled up and down, glancing at them occasionally, Mr. Rucastle came out to me, looking as merry and jovial as ever.

34 *It was a beautiful moonlight night.* Tuesday, April 9, 1889—the day we believe this to have been —was a day on which the moon was one day past the half; it set at 2:37 in the morning, so that it would have been shining brightly about 2:00 A.M., as Miss Hunter said.

35 "*I am naturally observant, as you may have remarked, Mr. Holmes.* Another attempt of Violet's to ingratiate herself with Sherlock?

"I TOOK IT UP AND EXAMINED IT."

Illustration by Sidney Paget for the *Strand Magazine*, June, 1892.

" 'Ah!' said he, 'you must not think me rude if I passed you without a word, my dear young lady. I was preoccupied with business matters.'

" I assured him that I was not offended. 'By the way,' said I, 'you seem to have quite a suite of spare rooms up there, and one of them has the shutters up.'

" 'Photography is one of my hobbies,' said he. 'I have made my dark-room up there. But, dear me! what an observant young lady we have come upon. Who would have believed it? Who would have ever believed it?" He spoke in a jesting tone, but there was no jest in his eyes as he looked at me. I read suspicion there, and annoyance, but no jest.

" Well, Mr. Holmes, from the moment that I understood that there was something about that suite of rooms which I was not to know, I was all on fire to go over them. It was not mere curiosity, though I have my share of that. It was more a feeling of duty—a feeling that some good might come from my penetrating to this place. They talk of woman's instinct; perhaps it was woman's instinct which gave me that feeling. At any rate, it was there; and I was keenly on the look-out for any chance to pass the forbidden door.

" It was only yesterday that the chance came. I may tell you that, besides Mr. Rucastle, both Toller and his wife find something to do in these deserted rooms, and I once saw him carrying a large black linen bag with him through the door. Recently he has been drinking hard, and yesterday evening he was very drunk; and, when I came upstairs, there was the key in the door. I have no doubt at all that he had left it there. Mr. and Mrs. Rucastle were both downstairs, and the child was with them, so that I had an admirable opportunity. I turned the key gently in the lock, opened the door, and slipped through.

" There was a little passage in front of me, unpapered and uncarpeted, which turned at a right angle at the farther end. Round this corner were three doors in a line, the first and third of which were open. They each led into an empty room, dusty and cheerless, with two windows in the one, and one in the other, so thick with dirt that the evening light glimmered dimly through them. The centre door was closed, and across the outside of it had been fastened one of the broad bars of an iron bed, padlocked at one end to a ring in the wall, and fastened at the other with stout cord. The door itself was locked as well, and the key was not there. This barricaded door corresponded clearly with the shuttered window outside, and yet I could see by the glimmer from beneath it that the room was not in darkness. Evidently there was a skylight which let in light from above. As I stood in the passage gazing at this sinister door, and wondering what secret it might veil, I suddenly heard the sound of steps within the room, and saw a shadow pass backwards and forwards against the little slit of dim light which shone out from under the door. A mad, unreasoning terror rose up in me at the sight, Mr. Holmes. My overstrung nerves failed me suddenly, and I turned and ran—ran as though some dreadful hand were behind me, clutching at the skirt of my dress. I rushed down the passage, through the door, and straight into the arms of Mr. Rucastle, who was waiting outside.

" 'So,' said he, smiling, 'it was you, then. I thought it must be when I saw the door open.'

" 'Oh, I am so frightened!' I panted.

" 'My dear young lady! my dear young lady!'—you cannot think how caressing and soothing his manner was—'and what has frightened you, my dear young lady?'

" But his voice was just a little too coaxing. He overdid it. I was keenly on my guard against him.

" 'I was foolish enough to go into the empty wing,' I answered. 'But it is so lonely and eerie in this dim light that I was frightened and ran out again. Oh, it is so dreadfully still in there!'

" 'Only that?' said he, looking at me keenly.

" 'Why, what do you think?' I asked.

" 'Why do you think that I lock this door?'

" 'I am sure that I do not know.'

" 'It is to keep people out who have no business there. Do you see?' He was still smiling in the most amiable manner.

" 'I am sure if I had known——'

" 'Well, then, you know now. And if you ever put your foot over that threshold again——' here in an instant the smile hardened into a grin of rage, and he glared down at me with the face of a demon, 'I'll throw you to the mastiff.'

" 'OH, I AM SO FRIGHTENED!' I PANTED."

Illustration by Sidney Paget for the *Strand Magazine*, June, 1892.

" I was so terrified that I do not know what I did. I suppose that I must have rushed past him into my room. I remember nothing until I found myself lying on my bed trembling all over. Then I thought of you, Mr. Holmes. I could not live there longer without some advice. I was frightened of the house, of the man, of the woman, of the servants, even of the child. They were all horrible to me. If I could only bring you down all would be well. Of course I might have fled from the house, but my curiosity was almost as strong as my fears. My mind was soon made up. I would send you a wire. I put on my hat and cloak, went down to the office, which is about half a mile from the house, and then returned, feeling very much easier. A horrible doubt came into my mind as I approached the door lest the dog might be loose, but I remembered that Toller had drunk himself into a state of insensibility that evening, and I knew that he was the only one in the household who had any influence with the savage creature, or who would venture to set him free. I slipped in in safety, and lay awake half the night in my joy at the thought of seeing you. I had no difficulty in getting leave to come into Winchester this morning, but I must be back before three o'clock, for Mr. and Mrs. Rucastle are going on a visit, and will be away all the evening, so that I must look after the child. Now I have told you all my adventures, Mr. Holmes, and I should be very glad if you could tell me what it all means, and, above all, what I should do."

Holmes and I had listened spellbound to this extraordinary story. My friend rose now, and paced up and down the room, his hands in his pockets, and an expression of the most profound gravity upon his face.

" Is Toller still drunk?" he asked.

" Yes. I heard his wife tell Mrs. Rucastle that she could do nothing with him."

" That is well. And the Rucastles go out to-night ? "

" Yes."

" Is there a cellar with a good strong lock ? "

" Yes, the wine cellar."

" You seem to me to have acted all through this matter like a brave and sensible girl, Miss Hunter. Do you think that you could perform one more feat ? I should not ask it of you if I did not think you a quite exceptional woman."

" I will try. What is it ? "

" We shall be at the Copper Beeches by seven o'clock, my friend and I. The Rucastles will be gone by that time, and Toller will, we hope, be incapable. There only remains Mrs. Toller, who might give the alarm. If you could send her into the cellar, on some errand, and then turn the key upon her, you would facilitate matters immensely."

" I will do it."

" Excellent ! We shall then look thoroughly into the affair. Of course there is only one feasible explanation. You have been brought there to personate someone, and the real person is imprisoned in this chamber. That is obvious. As to who this prisoner is, I have no doubt that it is the daughter, Miss Alice Rucastle, if I remember right, who was said to have gone to America. You were chosen, doubtless, as resembling her in height, figure, and the colour of your hair. Hers had been cut off, very possibly in some illness through which she has passed, and so, of course, yours had to be sacrificed also. By a curious chance you came upon her tresses. The man in the road was, undoubtedly, some friend of hers—possibly her fiancé—and no doubt as you wore the girl's dress, and were so like her, he was convinced from your laughter, whenever he saw you, and afterwards from your gesture, that Miss Rucastle was perfectly happy, and that she no longer desired his attentions. The dog is let loose at night to prevent him from endeavouring to communicate with her. So much is fairly clear. The most serious point in the case is the disposition of the child."

" What on earth has that to do with it ? " I ejaculated.

" My dear Watson, you as a medical man are continually gaining light as to the tendencies of a child by the study of the parents. Don't you see that the converse is equally valid. I have frequently gained my first real insight into the character of parents by studying their children. This child's disposition is abnormally cruel, merely for cruelty's sake, and whether he derives this from his smiling father, as I should suspect, or from his mother, it bodes evil for the poor girl who is in their power."

" I am sure that you are right, Mr. Holmes," cried our client. " A thousand things come back to me which make me certain that you have hit it. Oh, let us lose not an instant in bringing help to this poor creature."

" We must be circumspect, for we are dealing with a very cunning man. We can do nothing until seven o'clock. At that hour we shall be with you, and it will not be long before we solve the mystery."

We were as good as our word, for it was just seven when

we reached the Copper Beeches, having put up our trap at a wayside public-house. The group of trees, with their dark leaves shining like burnished metal in the light of the
36-37 setting sun, were sufficient to mark the house even had Miss Hunter not been standing smiling on the door-step.

" Have you managed it ? " asked Holmes.

A loud thudding noise came from somewhere downstairs. " That is Mrs. Toller in the cellar," said she. " Her husband lies snoring on the kitchen rug. Here are his keys, which are the duplicates of Mr. Rucastle's."

" You have done well indeed ! " cried Holmes, with enthusiasm. " Now lead the way, and we shall soon see the end of this black business."

We passed up the stair, unlocked the door, followed on down a passage, and found ourselves in front of the barricade which Miss Hunter had described. Holmes cut the cord and removed the transverse bar. Then he tried the various keys in the lock, but without success. No sound came from within, and at the silence Holmes' face clouded over.

" I trust that we are not too late," said he. " I think, Miss Hunter, that we had better go in without you. Now, Watson, put your shoulder to it, and we shall see whether we cannot make our way in."

It was an old rickety door and gave at once before our united strength. Together we rushed into the room. It was empty. There was no furniture save a little pallet bed, a small table, and a basketful of linen. The skylight above was open, and the prisoner gone.

" There has been some villainy here," said Holmes ; " this beauty has guessed Miss Hunter's intentions, and has carried his victim off."

" But how ? "

" Through the skylight. We shall soon see how he managed it." He swung himself up on to the roof. " Ah, yes," he cried, " here's the end of a long light ladder against the eaves. That is how he did it."

" But it is impossible," said Miss Hunter, " the ladder was not there when the Rucastles went away."

" He has come back and done it. I tell you that he is a clever and dangerous man. I should not be very much surprised if this were he whose step I hear now upon the stair. I think, Watson, that it would be as well for you to have your pistol ready."

The words were hardly out of his mouth before a man appeared at the door of the room, a very fat and burly man, with a heavy stick in his hand. Miss Hunter screamed and shrunk against the wall at the sight of him, but Sherlock Holmes sprang forward and confronted him.

" You villain," said he, " where's your daughter ? "

The fat man cast his eyes round, and then up at the open skylight.

" It is for me to ask you that," he shrieked, " you thieves ! Spies and thieves ! I have caught you, have I ? You are in my power. I'll serve you ! " He turned and clattered down the stairs as hard as he could go.

" He's gone for the dog ! " cried Miss Hunter.

" I have my revolver," said I.

" Better close the front door," cried Holmes, and we all

36 *in the light of the setting sun.* Saturday, April 20, 1889, was a day on which sunset was at 7:02 P.M.

37 *were sufficient to mark the house.* "You must have seen the house (it's still standing)," Mr. Gordon Sewell wrote in "Holmes and Watson in the South Country," "one of those square, stuccoed, late Georgian villas between Otterbourne and Chandler's Ford."

"YOU VILLAIN," SAID HE, "WHERE'S YOUR DAUGHTER?"

Illustration by Sidney Paget for the *Strand Magazine*, June, 1892.

rushed down the stairs together. We had hardly reached the hall when we heard the baying of a hound, and then a **38** scream of agony, with a horrible worrying sound which it was dreadful to listen to. An elderly man with a red face and shaking limbs came staggering out at a side-door.

" My God ! " he cried. " Someone has loosed the dog. It's not been fed for two days. Quick, quick, or it'll be too late ! "

Holmes and I rushed out, and round the angle of the house, with Toller hurrying behind us. There was the huge famished brute, its black muzzle buried in Rucastle's throat, while he writhed and screamed upon the ground. Running up, I blew its brains out, and it fell over with its keen white teeth still meeting in the great creases of his neck. With much labour we separated them, and carried him, living but horribly mangled, into the house. We laid him upon the drawing-room sofa, and having despatched the sobered Toller to bear the news to his wife, I did what I could to relieve his pain. We were all assembled round him when the door opened, and a tall, gaunt woman entered the room.

" Mrs. Toller ! " cried Miss Hunter.

" Yes, miss. Mr. Rucastle let me out when he came back before he went up to you. Ah, miss, it is a pity you didn't let me know what you were planning, for I would have told you that your pains were wasted."

" Ha ! " said Holmes, looking keenly at her. " It is clear that Mrs. Toller knows more about this matter than anyone else."

" Yes, sir, I do, and I am ready enough to tell what I know."

" Then pray sit down, and let us hear it, for there are several points on which I must confess that I am still in the dark."

" I will soon make it clear to you," said she ; " and I'd have done so before now if I could ha' got out from the cellar. If there's police-court business over this, you'll remember that I was the one that stood your friend, and that I was Miss Alice's friend too.

" She was never happy at home, Miss Alice wasn't, from the time that her father married again. She was slighted like, and had no say in anything ; but it never really became bad for her until after she met Mr. Fowler at a friend's house. As well as I could learn, Miss Alice had rights of her own by will, but she was so quiet and patient, she was, that she never said a word about them, but just left everything in Mr. Rucastle's hands. He knew he was safe with her ; but when there was a chance of a husband coming forward, who would ask for all that the law could give him, then her father thought it time to put a stop on it. He wanted her to sign a paper so that whether she married or not, he could use her money. When she wouldn't do it, he kept on worrying her until she got brain fever, and for six weeks was at death's door. Then she got better at last, all worn to a shadow, and with her beautiful hair cut off ; but that didn't make no change in her young man, and he stuck to her as true as man could be."

" Ah," said Holmes, " I think that what you have been good enough to tell us makes the matter fairly clear, and that I can deduce all that remains. Mr. Rucastle, then, I

38 *the baying of a hound.* But Carlo, we know, was a mastiff, and "a mastiff might give a roar or a growl, but could not conceivably 'bay,' and furthermore, the hound belongs to an entirely different group of dogs, the largest of which are the Irish wolfhound and the Scottish deerhound, which both exceed the mastiff in height, but not in substance"—Mrs. Eleanor S. Cole, "Holmes, Watson and the K-9's."

RUNNING UP, I BLEW ITS BRAINS OUT . . .

Illustration by Sidney Paget for the *Strand Magazine*, June, 1892. Watson's statement here is perhaps another indication that he, not Holmes, was the better shot with a handgun. Holmes needed five shots to finish off the Hound of the Baskervilles, but Watson apparently needed only one shot to blow out the brains of the unpleasant mastiff Carlo.

presume, took to this system of imprisonment ? "

" Yes, sir."

" And brought Miss Hunter down from London in order to get rid of the disagreeable persistence of Mr. Fowler."

" That was it, sir."

" But Mr. Fowler, being a persevering man, as a good seaman should be, blockaded the house, and, having met you, succeeded by certain arguments, metallic or otherwise, in convincing you that your interests were the same as his."

" Mr. Fowler was a very kind-spoken, free-handed gentleman," said Mrs. Toller serenely.

" And in this way he managed that your good man should have no want of drink, and that a ladder should be ready at the moment when your master had gone out."

" You have it, sir, just as it happened."

" I am sure we owe you an apology, Mrs. Toller," said Holmes, " for you have certainly cleared up everything which puzzled us. And here comes the country surgeon and Mrs. Rucastle, so I think, Watson, that we had best escort Miss Hunter back to Winchester, as it seems to me
39 that our *locus standi* now is rather a questionable one."

And thus was solved the mystery of the sinister house with the copper beeches in front of the door. Mr. Rucastle survived, but was always a broken man, kept alive solely through the care of his devoted wife. They still live with their old servants, who probably know so much of Rucastle's past life that he finds it difficult to part from them. Mr. Fowler and Miss Rucastle were married, by special licence, in Southampton the day after their flight, and he is now the holder of a Government appointment in the Island of Mauritius. As to Miss Violet Hunter, my friend Holmes, rather to my disappointment, manifested no fur-
40 ther interest in her when once she had ceased to be the
centre of one of his problems, and she is now the head of a
41 private school at Walsall, where I believe that she has met
with considerable success.

39 locus standi. Latin: rightful position; a legal term and another indication of Holmes' knowledge of the law.

40 *manifested no further interest in her.* ". . . how delightful, the Doctor thought naively, if he and Holmes should both marry governesses—and alumnae of the same agency, for undoubtedly Mary, too, had been a client of Westaway's," the late Christopher Morley commented ("Dr. Watson's Secret").

41 *Walsall.* A town in Staffordshire.

Auctorial Note: It was Conan Doyle's mother, as we have seen—the Ma'am—who prevented, for a time, the "death" of Sherlock Holmes. Conan Doyle, ready at this time to rid himself of his creation "forever," would have done so had his mother not sent him an idea for a Holmes story that should concern a girl with "beautiful golden hair: who kidnapped and her hair shorn should be made to impersonate some other girl for a villainous purpose"; the golden-haired girl became the less spectacular chestnut-haired Violet Hunter of "The Adventure of the Copper Beeches"—and Holmes, for the time being, lived on.

VI. FROM DR. WATSON'S SECOND MARRIAGE TO THE DISAPPEARANCE OF SHERLOCK HOLMES

[Wednesday, May 1, 1889, to Monday, May 4, 1891]

"Miss Morstan has done me the honour to accept me as a husband in prospective."

He gave a most dismal groan.

"I feared as much," said he.

—*The Sign of the Four*

38

THE BOSCOMBE VALLEY MYSTERY

[Saturday, June 8, to Sunday, June 9, 1889]

1 WE were seated at breakfast one morning, my wife and I, when the maid brought in a telegram. It was from Sherlock Holmes, and ran in this way:

" Have you a couple of days to spare ? Have just been wired for from the West of England in connection with Boscombe Valley tragedy. Shall be glad if you will come with me. Air and scenery perfect. Leave Paddington by the 11.15."

" What do you say, dear ? " said my wife, looking across at me. " Will you go ? "

" I really don't know what to say. I have a fairly
2 long list at present."
3 " Oh, Anstruther would do your work for you. You have been looking a little pale lately. I think that the change would do you good, and you are always so interested in Mr. Sherlock Holmes' cases."

" I should be ungrateful if I were not, seeing what I
gained through one of them," I answered. " But if I
4 am to go I must pack at once, for I have only half an hour."

My experience of camp life in Afghanistan had at least had the effect of making me a prompt and ready traveller. My wants were few and simple, so that in less than the time stated I was in a cab with my valise, rattling away to Paddington Station. Sherlock Holmes was pacing up and down the platform, his tall, gaunt figure made even gaunter and taller by his long grey travelling-cloak and close-fitting cloth cap.

" It is really very good of you to come, Watson," said he. " It makes a considerable difference to me, having someone with me on whom I can thoroughly rely. Local aid is always either worthless or else biased. If you will keep the two corner seats I shall get the tickets."

We had the carriage to ourselves save for an immense
5 litter of papers which Holmes had brought with him. Among these he rummaged and read, with intervals of note-taking and of meditation, until we were past Reading. Then he suddenly rolled them all into a gigantic ball, and tossed them up on to the rack.

1 *my wife.* While all chronologists are agreed that this wife was Mary Morstan, few are agreed on when Watson married her. For 1887: Bell and Brend (November); Morley (probably February or March). For 1888: Blakeney and Folsom (November). For 1889: Baring-Gould (*circa* May 1st); Christ (late February or early March); Zeisler (January). In your editor's view John and Mary were married some seven and a half months after their meeting at the time of *The Sign of the Four.* Both would have felt it proper that well over a year should elapse between the doctor's first and second marriage. Contributing to the delay were Watson's financial condition (he had to raise the price of a practice) and Mary's mental and physical condition—Holmes' "I trust Mrs. Watson has entirely recovered from all the little excitements connected with our adventure of The Sign of the Four" ("The Stockbroker's Clerk") indicates that her health would not permit a marriage soon after the climax of that case. Mr. S. C. Roberts has written (*Doctor Watson*) that the ceremony probably took place very quietly at St. Mark's or St. Hilda's, Camberwell. He adds that it is at least doubtful that Holmes could be induced to be best man, "since Watson would hardly be likely to omit a record of so personal a tribute . . ." But Mr. T. S. Blakeney (*Sherlock Holmes: Fact or Fiction?*) comments that since "Watson never even records his wedding, he could hardly mention what part in it Holmes may have played."

2 *I have a fairly long list at present.*" We note that *this* practice, unlike the practice of 1887, which "was never very absorbing" ("The Red-Headed League"), was a busy one.

3 *Anstruther.* In "The Stockbroker's Clerk," Watson says to Holmes: "I do my neighbor's [practice] when he goes. He is always ready to work off the debt."

" Have you heard anything of the case ? " he asked.

" Not a word. I have not seen a paper for some days." **6**

" The London press has not had very full accounts. I have just been looking through all the recent papers in order to master the particulars. It seems, from what I gather, to be one of those simple cases which are so extremely difficult."

" That sounds a little paradoxical."

" But it is profoundly true. Singularity is almost invariably a clue. The more featureless and commonplace a crime is, the more difficult is it to bring it home. In this case, however, they have established a very serious case against the son of the murdered man."

" It is a murder, then ? "

" Well, it is conjectured to be so. I shall take nothing for granted until I have the opportunity of looking personally into it. I will explain the state of things to you, as far as I have been able to understand it, in a very few words.

" Boscombe Valley is a country district not very far
from Ross, in Herefordshire. The largest landed pro- **7**
prietor in that part is a Mr. John Turner, who made his money in Australia, and returned some years ago to the old country. One of the farms which he held, that of Hatherley, was let to Mr. Charles McCarthy, who was also an ex-Australian. The men had known each other in the Colonies, so that it was not unnatural that when they came to settle down they should do so as near each other as possible. Turner was apparently the richer man, so McCarthy became his tenant, but still remained, it seems, upon terms of perfect equality, as they were frequently together. McCarthy had one son, a lad of eighteen, and Turner had an only daughter of the same age, but neither of them had wives living. They appear to have avoided the society of the neighbouring English families, and to have led retired lives, though both the McCarthys were fond of sport, and were frequently seen at the race meetings of the neighbourhood. McCarthy kept two servants—a man and a girl. Turner had a considerable household, some half-dozen at the least. That is as much as I have been able to gather about the families. Now for the facts.

" On June 3—that is, on Monday last—McCarthy left **8**
his house at Hatherley about three in the afternoon, and walked down to the Boscombe Pool, which is a small lake formed by the spreading out of the stream which runs down the Boscombe Valley. He had been out with his serving-man in the morning at Ross, and he had told the man that he must hurry, as he had an appointment of importance to keep at three. From that appointment he never came back alive.

" From Hatherley Farm-house to the Boscombe Pool is a quarter of a mile, and two people saw him as he passed over this ground. One was an old woman, whose name is not mentioned, and the other was William Crowder, a gamekeeper in the employ of Mr. Turner. Both these witnesses depose that Mr. McCarthy was walking alone. The gamekeeper adds that within a few minutes of his seeing Mr. McCarthy pass he had seen his son, Mr. James McCarthy, going the same way with a gun under

WE HAD THE CARRIAGE TO OURSELVES . . .

Illustration by Sidney Paget for the *Strand Magazine*, October, 1891.

4 *I have only half an hour.*" Why was Watson, the busy medico, breakfasting at so late an hour as 10:45 A.M.?

5 *save for an immense litter of papers.* The day of the train ride *could* have been a Sunday and the papers those of the week before, but the presumption here is that Holmes and Watson traveled to Boscombe Valley on a weekday.

6 *I have not seen a paper for some days.*" A further indication that Watson's practice at this time was an exceedingly busy one.

7 *Ross, in Herefordshire.* In fact, Boscombe is on the northern border of Somerset.

8 "*On June 3—that is, on Monday last.* In all the Canonical years before October, 1891, when "The Boscombe Valley Mystery" was published in the *Strand Magazine*, June 3rd fell on a Monday only once—in 1889. With Bigelow, Morley, Pattrick, and Zeisler dissenting—all of these vote for 1890—all other chronologists accept 1889 as the year of the adventure.

his arm. To the best of his belief, the father was actually in sight at the time, and the son was following him. He thought no more of the matter until he heard in the evening of the tragedy that had occurred.

" The two McCarthys were seen after the time when William Crowder, the gamekeeper, lost sight of them. The Boscombe Pool is thickly wooded round, with just a fringe of grass and of reeds round the edge. A girl of
9 fourteen, Patience Moran, who is the daughter of the lodgekeeper of the Boscombe Valley Estate, was in one of the woods picking flowers. She states that while she was there she saw, at the border of the wood and close by the lake, Mr. McCarthy and his son, and that they appeared to be having a violent quarrel. She heard Mr. McCarthy the elder using very strong language to his son, and she saw the latter raise up his hand as if to strike his father. She was so frightened by their violence that she ran away, and told her mother when she reached home that she had left the two McCarthys quarrelling near Boscombe Pool, and that she was afraid that they were going to fight. She had hardly said the words when young Mr. McCarthy came running up to the lodge to say that he had found his father dead in the wood, and to ask for the help of the lodge-keeper. He was much excited, without either his gun or his hat, and his right hand and sleeve were observed to be stained with fresh blood. On following him they found the dead body of his father stretched out upon the grass beside the Pool. The head had been beaten in by repeated blows of some heavy and blunt weapon. The injuries were such as might very well have been inflicted by the butt-end of his son's gun, which was found lying on the grass within a few paces of the body. Under these circumstances the young man was instantly arrested, and a verdict of ' Wilful Murder ' having been returned at the inquest on Tuesday, he was on Wednesday brought before the
10 magistrates at Ross, who have referred the case to the next assizes. Those are the main facts of the case as they came out before the coroner and at the police-court."

" I could hardly imagine a more damning case," I remarked. " If ever circumstantial evidence pointed to a criminal it does so here."

" Circumstantial evidence is a very tricky thing," answered Holmes thoughtfully ; " it may seem to point very straight to one thing, but if you shift your own point of view a little, you may find it pointing in an equally uncompromising manner to something entirely different. It must be confessed, however, that the case looks exceedingly grave against the young man, and it is very possible that he is indeed the culprit. There are several people in the neighbourhood, however, and among them Miss Turner, the daughter of the neighbouring landowner, who believe in his innocence, and who have retained
11 Lestrade, whom you may remember in connection with the Study in Scarlet, to work out the case in his interest. Lestrade, being rather puzzled, has referred the case to me, and hence it is that two middle-aged gentlemen are flying westward at fifty miles an hour, instead of quietly digesting their breakfasts at home."

"ON FOLLOWING HIM THEY FOUND THE DEAD BODY OF HIS FATHER . . ."

Illustration by Sidney Paget for the *Strand Magazine*, October, 1891.

9 *A girl of fourteen, Patience Moran.* As noted in "The Red-Headed League," Magistrate S. Tupper Bigelow has identified Patience Moran as a niece of Colonel Sebastian Moran and also as the "girl of fourteen" who did a bit of cooking for Jabez Wilson and kept his place clean. This of course assumes that "The Red-Headed League" and "The Boscombe Valley Mystery" both took place within one year's time.

" I am afraid," said I, " that the facts are so obvious that you will find little credit to be gained out of this case."

" There is nothing more deceptive than an obvious fact," he answered, laughing. " Besides, we may chance to hit upon some other obvious facts which may have been by no means obvious to Mr. Lestrade. You know me too well to think that I am boasting when I say that I shall either confirm or destroy his theory by means which he is quite incapable of employing, or even of understanding. To take the first example to hand, I very clearly perceive that in your bedroom the window is upon the right-hand side, and yet I question whether Mr. Lestrade would have noted even so self-evident a thing as that."

" How on earth—— ! "

" My dear fellow, I know you well. I know the military neatness which characterizes you. You shave every
morning, and in this season you shave by the sunlight,
but since your shaving is less and less complete as we get
farther back on the left side, until it becomes positively
slovenly as we get round the angle of the jaw, it is surely
very clear that that side is less well illuminated than the
other. I could not imagine a man of your habits looking 12
at himself in an equal light, and being satisfied with such
a result. I only quote this as a trivial example of observation and inference. Therein lies my *métier*, and it is 13
just possible that it may be of some service in the investigation which lies before us. There are one or two minor
points which were brought out in the inquest, and which
are worth considering."

" What are they ? "

" It appears that his arrest did not take place at once, but after the return to Hatherley Farm. On the inspector of constabulary informing him that he was a prisoner, he remarked that he was not surprised to hear it, and that it was no more than his deserts. This observation of his had the natural effect of removing any traces of doubt which might have remained in the minds of the coroner's jury."

" It was a confession," I ejaculated.

" No, for it was followed by a protestation of innocence."

" Coming on the top of such a damning series of events, it was at least a most suspicious remark."

" On the contrary," said Holmes, " it is the brightest rift which I can at present see in the clouds. However innocent he might be, he could not be such an absolute imbecile as not to see that the circumstances were very black against him. Had he appeared surprised at his own arrest, or feigned indignation at it, I should have looked upon it as highly suspicious, because such surprise or anger would not be natural under the circumstances, and yet might appear to be the best policy to a scheming man. His frank acceptance of the situation marks him as either an innocent man, or else as a man of considerable self-restraint and firmness. As to his remark about his deserts, it was also not unnatural if you consider that he stood by the dead body of his father, and that there is no doubt that he had that very day so far forgotten his filial

10 *he was on Wednesday brought before the magistrates.* Had Holmes made this statement on Thursday, June 6th, he would surely have said that McCarthy was brought before the magistrates "yesterday." The case began, then, on Friday, June 7th; Saturday, June 8th; or Sunday, June 9th. Had it begun on Monday, June 10th, Holmes would probably have said earlier that Monday, June 3rd, was "a week ago today" rather than "Monday last," although this day is not impossible.

11 *retained Lestrade.* "Some have pounced on the word 'retained' as used by Holmes to conclude that Lestrade had gone into private practice for a period, but that judgment is not necessarily warranted, for it was not uncommon for Scotland Yarders to aid the provincial police, and Holmes' use of the word was purely conversational," Mr. L. S. Holstein wrote in "Inspector G. Lestrade."

12 *that side is less well illuminated than the other.* "Was not the calculator, to be able to draw this inference, required to impart a factor into the equation which may not have represented the fact, namely, that it was his friend's custom to face north when pursuing this routine, so that the light would strike on the right cheek?" Mr. J. B. Mackenzie asked in "Sherlock Holmes' Plots and Strategy."

13 métier. French: trade; profession.

duty as to bandy words with him, and even, according to the little girl whose evidence is so important, to raise his hand as if to strike him. The self-reproach and contrition which are displayed in his remark appear to me to be the signs of a healthy mind, rather than of a guilty one."

I shook my head. "Many men have been hanged on far slighter evidence," I remarked.

"So they have. And many men have been wrongfully hanged."

"What is the young man's own account of the matter?"

"It is, I am afraid, not very encouraging to his supporters, though there are one or two points in it which are suggestive. You will find it here, and may read it for yourself."

He picked out from his bundle a copy of the local Herefordshire paper, and having turned down the sheet, he pointed out the paragraph in which the unfortunate young man had given his own statement of what had occurred. I settled myself down in the corner of the carriage, and read it very carefully. It ran in this way:

"Mr. James McCarthy, the only son of the deceased, was then called, and gave evidence as follows: 'I had
14 been away from home for three days at Bristol, and had only just returned upon the morning of last Monday, the 3rd. My father was absent from home at the time of my arrival, and I was informed by the maid that he had driven over to Ross with John Cobb, the groom. Shortly after my return I heard the wheels of his trap in the yard, and, looking out of my window, I saw him get out and walk rapidly out of the yard, though I was not aware in which direction he was going. I then took my gun, and strolled out in the direction of the Boscombe Pool, with the intention of visiting the rabbit warren which is upon the other side. On my way I saw William Crowder, the gamekeeper, as he has stated in his evidence; but he is mistaken in thinking that I was following my father. I had no idea that he was in front of me. When about a hundred yards from the Pool I heard a cry of "Cooee!" which was a usual signal between my father and myself. I then hurried forward, and found him standing by the Pool. He appeared to be much surprised at seeing me, and asked me rather roughly what I was doing there. A conversation ensued, which led to high words, and almost to blows, for my father was a man of a very violent temper. Seeing that his passion was becoming ungovernable, I left him, and returned towards Hatherley Farm. I had not gone more than one hundred and fifty yards, however, when I heard a hideous outcry behind me, which caused me to run back again. I found my father expiring on the ground, with his head terribly injured. I dropped my gun, and held him in my arms, but he almost instantly expired. I knelt beside him for some minutes, and then made my way to Mr. Turner's lodge-keeper, his house being the nearest, to ask for assistance. I saw no one near my father when I returned, and I have no idea how he came by his injuries. He was not a popular man, being somewhat cold and forbidding in his manners; but he had, as far as I know, no active enemies. I know nothing further of the matter."

14 *Bristol.* In Gloucestershire, on the Avon near the mouth of the Severn—a major world port as well as an industrial center.

"I DROPPED MY GUN, AND HELD HIM IN MY ARM . . ."

Illustration by Sidney Paget for the *Strand Magazine*, October, 1891.

" The Coroner : Did your father make any statement to you before he died ?

" Witness : He mumbled a few words, but I could only catch some allusion to a rat.

" The Coroner : What did you understand by that ?

" Witness : It conveyed no meaning to me. I thought that he was delirious.

" The Coroner : What was the point upon which you and your father had this final quarrel ?

" Witness : I should prefer not to answer.

" The Coroner : I am afraid that I must press it.

" Witness : It is really impossible for me to tell you. I can assure you that it has nothing to do with the sad tragedy which followed.

" The Coroner : That is for the Court to decide. I need not point out to you that your refusal to answer will prejudice your case considerably in any future proceedings which may arise.

" Witness : I must still refuse.

" The Coroner : I understand that the cry of ' Cooee ' was a common signal between you and your father ?

" Witness : It was.

" The Coroner : How was it, then, that he uttered it before he saw you, and before he even knew that you had returned from Bristol ?

" Witness (with considerable confusion) : I do not know.

" A Juryman : Did you see nothing which aroused your suspicions when you returned on hearing the cry, and found your father fatally injured ?

" Witness : Nothing definite.

" The Coroner : What do you mean ?

" Witness : I was so disturbed and excited as I rushed out into the open, that I could think of nothing except my father. Yet I have a vague impression that as I ran forward something lay upon the ground to the left of me. It seemed to me to be something grey in colour, a coat of some sort, or a plaid perhaps. When I rose from my father I looked round for it, but it was gone.

" ' Do you mean that it disappeared before you went for help ? '

" ' Yes, it was gone.'

" ' You cannot say what it was ? '

" ' No, I had a feeling something was there.'

" ' How far from the body ? '

" ' A dozen yards or so.'

" ' And how far from the edge of the wood ?

" ' About the same.'

" ' Then if it was removed it was while you were within a dozen yards of it ? '

" ' Yes, but with my back towards it.'

" This concluded the examination of the witness."

" I see," said I, as I glanced down the column, " that the coroner in his concluding remarks was rather severe upon young McCarthy. He calls attention, and with reason, to the discrepancy about his father having signalled to him before seeing him, also to his refusal to give details of his conversation with his father, and his singular account of his father's dying words. They are all, as he remarks, very much against the son."

Holmes laughed softly to himself, and stretched himself out upon the cushioned seat. " Both you and the coroner have been at some pains," said he, " to single out the very strongest points in the young man's favour. Don't you see that you alternately give him credit for having too much imagination and too little ? Too little, if he could not invent a cause of quarrel which would give him the sympathy of the jury ; too much, if he evolved from his own inner consciousness anything so *outré* as a dying reference to a rat, and the incident of the vanishing cloth. No, sir, I shall approach this case from the point of view that what this young man says is true, and we shall see
whither that hypothesis will lead us. And now here is
15 my pocket Petrarch, and not another word shall I say of
this case until we are on the scene of action. We lunch
16 at Swindon, and I see that we shall be there in twenty
minutes."

It was nearly four o'clock when we at last, after passing
through the beautiful Stroud Valley and over the broad
17 gleaming Severn, found ourselves at the pretty little
country town of Ross. A lean, ferret-like man, furtive and sly-looking, was waiting for us upon the platform. In spite of the light brown dust-coat and leather leggings which he wore in deference to his rustic surroundings, I had no difficulty in recognizing Lestrade, of Scotland Yard. With him we drove to the " Hereford Arms," where a room had already been engaged for us.

" I have ordered a carriage," said Lestrade, as we sat over a cup of tea. " I knew your energetic nature, and that you would not be happy until you had been on the scene of the crime."

" It was very nice and complimentary of you," Holmes answered. " It is entirely a question of barometric pressure."

Lestrade looked startled. " I do not quite follow," he said.

" How is the glass ? Twenty-nine, I see. No wind,
18 and not a cloud in the sky. I have a caseful of cigarettes
here which need smoking, and the sofa is very much superior to the usual country hotel abomination. I do not think that it is probable that I shall use the carriage to-night."

Lestrade laughed indulgently. " You have, no doubt, already formed your conclusions from the newspapers," he said. " The case is as plain as a pikestaff, and the more one goes into it the plainer it becomes. Still, of course, one can't refuse a lady, and such a very positive one, too. She had heard of you, and would have your opinion, though I repeatedly told her that there was nothing which you could do which I had not already done. Why, bless my soul ! here is her carriage at the door."

He had hardly spoken before there rushed into the room one of the most lovely young women that I have ever seen in my life. Her violet eyes shining, her lips parted, a pink flush upon her cheeks, all thought of her natural reserve lost in her overpowering excitement and concern.

" Oh, Mr. Sherlock Holmes ! " she cried, glancing from one to the other of us, and finally, with a woman's quick intuition, fastening upon my companion, " I am

15 *my pocket Petrarch.* Petrarch, or Francesco Petrarca, 1304–1374, Italian poet, surpassed in Italian literature only by Dante.

"While it may excite some wonder that Holmes should have carried with him so delightful a little rarity, there can be no question that the volume to which he referred was any other than the charming *Il Petrarca* printed in italic letter at Lyons in 1550, ruled in red, and adorned with the delicate heart-shaped woodcut medallion showing portraits of Petrarch and Laura by Bernard Salomon," Miss Madeleine B. Stern wrote in "Sherlock Holmes: Rare Book Collector."

But Mr. S. F. Blake, in "Sherlock Holmes and the Italian Cipher," wrote that he hesitated to accept Miss Stern's confident selection "in view of the fact that in the *Catalogue of Printed Books in the British Museum* some 40 columns are devoted to listing their editions of Petrarch's works in Italian and other languages from 1468 or 1470 on. . . . Aside from the lack of any indication in the text pointing to this edition rather than to dozens of others, is it likely that any true bibliophile would carry in his pocket so rare an item as a 339-year-old volume of so noted a writer as Petrarch? Surely, if he indeed possessed this item, he would have left it safe at home with his other bibliographical treasures . . . , and contented himself on a railway journey with one of the more modern and less irreplaceable issues. At least 19 different 12mo, 16mo, or 32mo editions in Italian were published in the nineteenth century (up to 1886), but my own guess is that Holmes carried the Bohn 1859 edition in English."

Mr. H. B. Williams ("Then Falls Thy Shadow") points to the fact that in the sonnets of Petrarch are to be found the portrayal of perfect love which can never be consummated, and suggests that Holmes made Petrarch his pocket companion because the sonnets "mirrored a torture forever burning within the core of his [own] being"—his love "for a woman who never could be possessed," Irene Adler.

16 *We lunch at Swindon.* They *had* to lunch at Swindon; according to *Express Trains, English and Foreign,* by E. Foxwell and T. C. Farrar, London: Smith, Elder & Co., 1889: "Inclusive speed of trains on the Great Western is lessened by the obligation to pause ten minutes at Swindon, an obligation from which the refreshment proprietors will not free the company until the year 1940." In fact, however, the restriction was withdrawn in 1895.

17 *the broad gleaming Severn.* The river Severn runs through Western England and North Wales to the Bristol Channel, a distance of 210 miles; it is remarkable for having a bore that rises at times to nine feet.

18 *No wind, and not a cloud in the sky.* Later Holmes says: "It is of importance that it should

so glad that you have come. I have driven down to tell you so. I know that James didn't do it. I know it, and I want you to start upon your work knowing it, too. Never let yourself doubt upon that point. We have known each other since we were little children, and I know his faults as no one else does ; but he is too tender-hearted to hurt a fly. Such a charge is absurd to anyone who really knows him."

" I hope we may clear him, Miss Turner," said Sherlock Holmes. " You may rely upon my doing all that I can."

" But you have read the evidence. You have formed some conclusion ? Do you not see some loophole, some flaw ? Do you not yourself think that he is innocent ? "

" I think that it is very probable."

" There now ! " she cried, throwing back her head and looking defiantly at Lestrade. " You hear ! He gives me hope."

Lestrade shrugged his shoulders. " I am afraid that my colleague has been a little quick in forming his conclusions," he said.

" But he is right. Oh ! I know that he is right. James never did it. And about his quarrel with his father, I am sure that the reason why he would not speak about it to the coroner was because I was concerned in it."

" In what way ? " asked Holmes.

" It is no time for me to hide anything. James and his father had many disagreements about me. Mr. McCarthy was very anxious that there should be a marriage between us. James and I have always loved each other as brother and sister, but of course he is young and has seen very little of life yet, and—and—well, he naturally did not wish to do anything like that yet. So there were quarrels, and this, I am sure, was one of them."

" And your father ? " asked Holmes. " Was he in favour of such a union ? "

" No, he was averse to it also. No one but Mr. McCarthy was in favour of it." A quick blush passed over her fresh young face as Holmes shot one of his keen, questioning glances at her.

" Thank you for this information," said he. " May I see your father if I call to-morrow ? "

" I am afraid the doctor won't allow it."

" The doctor ? "

" Yes, have you not heard ? Poor father has never been strong for years back, but this has broken him down completely. He has taken to his bed, and Dr. Willows says that he is a wreck, and that his nervous system is shattered. Mr. McCarthy was the only man alive who
had known dad in the old days in Victoria." 19

" Ha ! In Victoria ! That is important."

" Yes, at the mines."

" Quite so ; at the gold mines, where, as I understand, Mr. Turner made his money."

" Yes, certainly."

" Thank you, Miss Turner. You have been of material assistance to me."

" You will tell me if you have any news to-morrow. No doubt you will go to the prison to see James. Oh,

not rain before we go over the ground," and Watson adds: "There was no rain as Holmes had foretold." And Watson tells us that the morning of the second—and closing—day of the case "broke bright and cloudless." In *Whitaker's Almanack* we read that 0.08 inches of rain fell on Friday, June 7, 1889, and that 1.37 inches fell on Monday, June 10, 1889. There was *no* rain, however, on either Saturday, June 8, 1889, or Sunday, June 9, 1889. On the Saturday, the barometer read 29.716 (on the Sunday, 29.489) and there was virtually *no wind* on the Saturday (the pressure was only 0.5 pounds). *Saturday, June 8, and Sunday, June 9, 1889,* fit Holmes' and Watson's descriptions exactly.

19 *Victoria.* The most densely populated and smallest state (except Tasmania) in Australia.

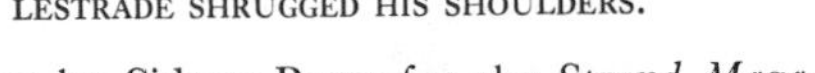

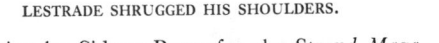

LESTRADE SHRUGGED HIS SHOULDERS.

Illustration by Sidney Paget for the *Strand Magazine*, October, 1891.

20 *Hereford.* Municipal borough on the Wye, birthplace of Nell Gwyn and David Garrick.

21 *yellow-backed novel.* A popular, cheap novel —so called from the former practice, especially in England, of binding such books in yellow board or paper covers.

if you do, Mr. Holmes, do tell him that I know him to be innocent."

" I will, Miss Turner."

" I must go home now, for dad is very ill, and he misses me so if I leave him. Good-bye, and God help you in your undertaking." She hurried from the room as impulsively as she had entered, and we heard the wheels of her carriage rattle off down the street.

" I am ashamed of you, Holmes," said Lestrade with dignity, after a few minutes' silence. " Why should you raise up hopes which you are bound to disappoint ? I am not over-tender of heart, but I call it cruel."

" I think that I see my way to clearing James McCarthy," said Holmes. " Have you an order to see him in prison ? "

" Yes, but only for you and me."

" Then I shall reconsider my resolution about going
20 out. We have still time to take a train to Hereford and see him to-night ? "

" Ample."

" Then let us do so. Watson, I fear that you will find it very slow, but I shall only be away a couple of hours."

I walked down to the station with them, and then wandered through the streets of the little town, finally returning to the hotel, where I lay upon the sofa and tried to
21 interest myself in a yellow-backed novel. The puny plot of the story was so thin, however, when compared to the deep mystery through which we were groping, and I found my attention wander so constantly from the fiction to the fact, that I at last flung it across the room, and gave myself up entirely to a consideration of the events of the day. Supposing that this unhappy young man's story was absolutely true, then what hellish thing, what absolutely unforeseen and extraordinary calamity, could have occurred between the time when he parted from his father and the moment when, drawn back by his screams, he rushed into the glade ? It was something terrible and deadly. What could it be ? Might not the nature of the injuries reveal something to my medical instincts ? I rang the bell, and called for the weekly county paper, which contained a verbatim account of the inquest. In the surgeon's deposition it was stated that the posterior third of the left parietal bone and the left half of the occipital bone had been shattered by a heavy blow from a blunt weapon. I marked the spot upon my own head. Clearly such a blow must have been struck from behind. That was to some extent in favour of the accused, as when seen quarrelling he was face to face with his father. Still, it did not go for very much, for the older man might have turned his back before the blow fell. Still, it might be worth while to call Holmes' attention to it. Then there was the peculiar dying reference to a rat. What could that mean ? It could not be delirium. A man dying from a sudden blow does not commonly become delirious. No, it was more likely to be an attempt to explain how he met his fate. But what could it indicate ? I cudgelled my brains to find some possible explanation. And then the incident of the grey cloth, seen by young McCarthy.

. . . WHERE I LAY UPON THE SOFA AND TRIED TO INTEREST MYSELF IN A YELLOW-BACKED NOVEL.

Illustration by Sidney Paget for the *Strand Magazine*, October, 1891.

If that were true, the murderer must have dropped some part of his dress, presumably his overcoat, in his flight, and must have had the hardihood to return and carry it away at the instant when the son was kneeling with his back turned not a dozen paces off. What a tissue of mysteries and improbabilities the whole thing was ! I did not wonder at Lestrade's opinion, and yet I had so much faith in Sherlock Holmes' insight that I could not lose hope as long as every fresh fact seemed to strengthen his conviction of young McCarthy's innocence.

It was late before Sherlock Holmes returned. He came back alone, for Lestrade was staying in lodgings in the town.

" The glass still keeps very high," he remarked, as he **22**
sat down. " It is of importance that it should not rain before we are able to go over the ground. On the other hand, a man should be at his very best and keenest for such nice work as that, and I did not wish to do it when fagged by a long journey. I have seen young McCarthy."

" And what did you learn from him ? "

" Nothing."

" Could he throw no light ? "

" None at all. I was inclined to think at one time that he knew who had done it, and was screening him or her, but I am convinced now that he is as puzzled as everyone else. He is not a very quick-witted youth, though comely to look at, and, I should think, sound at heart."

" I cannot admire his taste," I remarked, " if it is indeed a fact that he was averse to a marriage with so charming a young lady as this Miss Turner."

" Ah, thereby hangs a rather painful tale. This fellow is madly, insanely in love with her, but some two years ago, when he was only a lad, and before he really knew her, for she had been away five years at a boarding-school, what does the idiot do but get into the clutches of a barmaid in Bristol, and marry her at a registry office ! No one knows a word of the matter, but you can imagine how maddening it must be to him to be upbraided for not doing what he would give his very eyes to do, but what he knows to be absolutely impossible. It was sheer frenzy of this sort which made him throw his hands up into the air when his father, at their last interview, was goading him on to propose to Miss Turner. On the other hand, he had no means of supporting himself, and his father, who was by all accounts a very hard man, would have thrown him over utterly had he known the truth. It was with his barmaid wife that he had spent the last three days in Bristol, and his father did not know where he was. Mark that point. It is of importance. Good has come out of evil, however, for the barmaid, finding from the papers that he is in serious trouble, and likely to be hanged, has thrown him over utterly, and has written to him to say that she has a husband already in the Bermuda Dockyard, so that there is really no tie between them. I think that that bit of news has consoled young McCarthy for all that he has suffered."

" But if he is innocent, who has done it ? "

" Ah ! who ? I would call your attention very particularly to two points. One is that the murdered man had

22 "*The glass still keeps very high.*" But 29 inches, Holmes' previous reading, "is a *low* barometer reading for London and Southern England—not 'very high' as Holmes appears to have supposed. The June normal is about 30 inches. Perhaps the great man's instrument was an aneroid out of proper adjustment."—Mr. E. L. Hawke of the Royal Meteorological Society, London, in a letter to your editor, July 31, 1955.

an appointment with someone at the Pool, and that the someone could not have been his son, for his son was away, and he did not know when he would return. The second is that the murdered man was heard to cry 'Cooee!' before he knew that his son had returned. Those are the crucial points upon which the case depends.
23 And now let us talk about George Meredith, if you please, and we shall leave minor points until to-morrow."

There was no rain, as Holmes had foretold, and the morning broke bright and cloudless. At nine o'clock Lestrade called for us with the carriage, and we set off for Hatherley Farm and the Boscombe Pool.

"There is serious news this morning," Lestrade observed. "It is said that Mr. Turner, of the Hall, is so ill that his life is despaired of."

"An elderly man, I presume?" said Holmes.

"About sixty; but his constitution has been shattered by his life abroad, and he has been in failing health for some time. This business has had a very bad effect upon him. He was an old friend of McCarthy's, and, I may add, a great benefactor to him, for I have learned that he gave him Hatherley Farm rent free."

"Indeed! That is interesting," said Holmes.

"Oh, yes! In a hundred other ways he has helped him. Everybody about here speaks of his kindness to him."

"Really! Does it not strike you as a little singular that this McCarthy, who appears to have had little of his own, and to have been under such obligations to Turner, should still talk of marrying his son to Turner's daughter, who is, presumably, heiress to the estate, and that in such a very cocksure manner, as if it was merely a case of a proposal and all else would follow? It is the more strange since we know that Turner himself was averse to the idea. The daughter told us as much. Do you not deduce something from that?"

"We have got to the deductions and the inferences," said Lestrade, winking at me. "I find it hard enough to tackle facts, Holmes, without flying away after theories and fancies."

"You are right," said Holmes demurely; "you do find it very hard to tackle the facts."

"Anyhow, I have grasped one fact which you seem to find it difficult to get hold of," replied Lestrade with some warmth.

"And that is?"

"That McCarthy, senior, met his death from McCarthy, junior, and that all theories to the contrary are the merest moonshine."

"Well, moonshine is a brighter thing than fog," said Holmes, laughing. "But I am very much mistaken if this is not Hatherley Farm upon the left."

"Yes, that is it." It was a widespread, comfortable-looking building, two-storied, slate-roofed, with great yellow blotches of lichen upon the grey walls. The drawn blinds and the smokeless chimneys, however, gave it a stricken look, as though the weight of this horror still lay heavy upon it. We called at the door, when the maid, at Holmes' request, showed us the boots which her master

23 *George Meredith.* English novelist and poet, 1828–1909, whose writings are notable for their psychological insight and close inspection of the relationship between the individual and social events (we know that Conan Doyle, like Holmes, was attracted by Meredith: he remarked in *Through the Magic Door* that "his beloved *Richard Feveral* . . . lurks in yonder corner. What a great book it is, how wise and how witty!").

"May we not infer that Meredith's *Ordeal of Richard Feveral,* in the three-volume 1859 first edition . . . [was] among the choice items in the Holmes treasure-room?" Miss Madeleine B. Stern wrote in "Sherlock Holmes: Rare Book Collector."

And Mr. H. B. Williams ("Then Falls Thy Shadow") saw here "one more proof of the strong hold that the memory of Irene Adler had upon Holmes. As before, it is just a few words and here we must bow to the innate delicacy of John Watson, a delicacy which forbade him to set down the full conversation on this particular occasion. It is remarkable how this woman was able to break through the Master's iron guard and direct a portion of his conversational proclivities. . . . Irene Adler and George Meredith, what possible connection can they have? Yet one does not have too far to go into the life of Meredith before the key of Holmes' interest is found. George Meredith is also one of that suffering brotherhood who loves one who belongs to another, and thus, is forever lost. . . . Meredith and Janet Ross. The Master never did anything but what was buttressed by sound causes. Thus, in his desire to talk about George Meredith he found surcease from the strain of trying to keep *The* Woman locked within his breast."

wore at the time of his death, and also a pair of the son's, though not the pair which he had then had. Having measured these very carefully from seven or eight different points, Holmes desired to be led to the courtyard, from which we all followed the winding track which led to Boscombe Pool.

Sherlock Holmes was transformed when he was hot upon such a scent as this. Men who had only known the quiet thinker and logician of Baker Street would have failed to recognize him. His face flushed and darkened. His brows were drawn into two hard, black lines, while his eyes shone out from beneath them with a steely glitter. His face was bent downwards, his shoulders bowed, his lips compressed, and the veins stood out like whip-cord in his long, sinewy neck. His nostrils seemed to dilate with a purely animal lust for the chase, and his mind was so absolutely concentrated upon the matter before him, that a question or remark fell unheeded upon his ears, or at the most only provoked a quick, impatient snarl in reply. Swiftly and silently he made his way along the track which ran through the meadows, and so by way of the woods to the Boscombe Pool. It was damp, marshy ground, as is all that district, and there were marks of many feet, both upon the path and amid the short grass which bounded it on either side. Sometimes Holmes would hurry on, sometimes stop dead, and once he made quite a little *détour* into the meadow. Lestrade and I walked behind him, the detective indifferent and contemptuous, while I watched my friend with the interest which sprang from the conviction that every one of his actions was directed towards a definite end.

The Boscombe Pool, which is a little reed-girt sheet of water some fifty yards across, is situated at the boundary between the Hatherley Farm and the private park of the wealthy Mr. Turner. Above the woods which lined it upon the farther side we could see the red jutting pinnacles which marked the site of the rich landowner's dwelling. On the Hatherley side of the Pool the woods grew very thick, and there was a narrow belt of sodden grass twenty paces across between the edge of the trees and the reeds which lined the lake. Lestrade showed us the exact spot at which the body had been found, and indeed, so moist was the ground, that I could plainly see the traces which had been left by the fall of the stricken man. To Holmes, as I could see by his eager face and peering eyes, very many other things were to be read upon the trampled grass. He ran round, like a dog who is picking up a scent, and then turned upon my companion.

" What did you go into the Pool for ? " he asked.

" I fished about with a rake. I thought there might be some weapon or other trace. But how on earth—— ? "

" Oh, tut, tut ! I have no time. That left foot of yours with its inward twist is all over the place. A mole could trace it, and there it vanishes among the reeds. Oh, how simple it would all have been had I been here before they came like a herd of buffalo, and wallowed all over it. Here is where the party with the lodge-keeper came, and they have covered all tracks for six or eight feet round the body. But here are three separate tracks of the

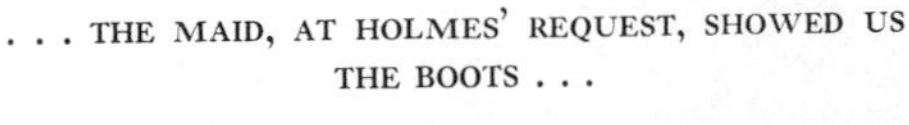

. . . THE MAID, AT HOLMES' REQUEST, SHOWED US THE BOOTS . . .

Illustration by Sidney Paget for the *Strand Magazine,* October, 1891.

FOR A LONG TIME HE REMAINED THERE . . .

Illustration by Sidney Paget for the *Strand Magazine*, October, 1891.

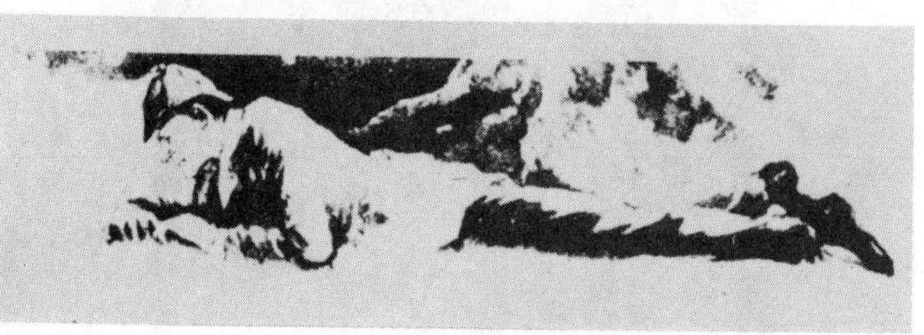

same feet." He drew out a lens, and lay down upon his waterproof to have a better view, talking all the time rather to himself than to us. "These are young McCarthy's feet. Twice he was walking, and once he ran swiftly so that the soles are deeply marked, and the heels hardly visible. That bears out his story. He ran when he saw his father on the ground. Then here are the father's feet as he paced up and down. What is this, then? It is the butt end of the gun as the son stood listening. And this? Ha, ha! What have we here? Tip-toes, tip-toes! Square, too, quite unusual boots! They come, they go, they come again—of course that was for the cloak. Now where did they come from?" He ran up and down, sometimes losing, sometimes finding the track, until we were well within the edge of the wood and under the shadow of a great beech, the largest tree in the neighbourhood. Holmes traced his way to the farther side of this, and lay down once more upon his face with a little cry of satisfaction. For a long time he remained there, turning over the leaves and dried sticks, gathering up what seemed to me to be dust into an envelope, and examining with his lens not only the ground, but even the bark of the tree as far as he could reach. A jagged stone was lying among the moss, and this also he carefully examined and retained. Then he followed a pathway through the wood until he came to the high-road, where all traces were lost.

"It has been a case of considerable interest," he remarked, returning to his natural manner. "I fancy that this grey house on the right must be the lodge. I think that I will go in and have a word with Moran, and perhaps write a little note. Having done that, we may drive back to our luncheon. You may walk to the cab, and I shall be with you presently."

It was about ten minutes before we regained our cab, and drove back into Ross, Holmes still carrying with him the stone which he had picked up in the wood.

"This may interest you, Lestrade," he remarked, holding it out. "The murder was done with it."

"I see no marks."

"There are none."

"How do you know, then?"

"The grass was growing under it. It had only lain there a few days. There was no sign of a place whence it had been taken. It corresponds with the injuries. There is no sign of any other weapon."

"And the murderer?"

"Is a tall man, left-handed, limps with the right leg, wears thick-soled shooting-boots and a grey cloak, smokes Indian cigars, uses a cigar-holder, and carries a blunt penknife in his pocket. There are several other indications, but these may be enough to aid us in our search."

Lestrade laughed. "I am afraid that I am still a sceptic," he said. "Theories are all very well, but we have to deal with a hard-headed British jury."

24 "*Nous verrons*," answered Holmes calmly. "You work your own method, and I shall work mine. I shall

24 "Nous verrons." French: "We shall see."

be busy this afternoon, and shall probably return to London by the evening train."

" And leave your case unfinished ? "

" No, finished."

" But the mystery ? "

" It is solved."

" Who was the criminal, then ? "

" The gentleman I describe."

" But who is he ? "

" Surely it would not be difficult to find out. This is not such a populous neighbourhood."

Lestrade shrugged his shoulders. " I am a practical man," he said, " and I really cannot undertake to go about the country looking for a left-handed gentleman with a game leg. I should become the laughing-stock of Scotland Yard."

" All right," said Holmes quietly. " I have given you the chance. Here are your lodgings. Good-bye. I shall drop you a line before I leave."

Having left Lestrade at his rooms we drove to our hotel, where we found lunch upon the table. Holmes was silent and buried in thought, with a pained expression upon his face, as one who finds himself in a perplexing position.

" Look here, Watson," he said, when the cloth was cleared ; " just sit down in this chair and let me preach to you for a little. I don't quite know what to do, and I should value your advice. Light a cigar, and let me expound."

" Pray do so."

" Well, now, in considering this case there are two points about young McCarthy's narrative which struck us both instantly, although they impressed me in his favour and you against him. One was the fact that his father should, according to his account, cry ' Cooee ! ' before seeing him. The other was his singular dying reference to a rat. He mumbled several words, you understand, but that was all that caught the son's ear. Now from this double point our research must commence, and we will begin it by presuming that what the lad says is absolutely true."

" What of this ' Cooee ! ' then ? "

" Well, obviously it could not have been meant for the son. The son, as far as he knew, was in Bristol. It was mere chance that he was within earshot. The ' Cooee ! ' was meant to attract the attention of whoever it was that he had the appointment with. But ' Cooee ' is a distinctly Australian cry, and one which is used between Australians. There is a strong presumption that the person whom McCarthy expected him to meet at Boscombe Pool was someone who had been in Australia."

" What of the rat, then ? "

Sherlock Holmes took a folded paper from his pocket and flattened it out on the table. " This is a map of the Colony of Victoria," he said. " I wired to Bristol for it last night." He put his hand over part of the map. " What do you read ? " he asked.

" ARAT," I read.

"And now?" He raised his hand.

"BALLARAT."

"Quite so. That was the word the man uttered, and of which his son only caught the last two syllables. He was trying to utter the name of his murderer. So-and-so of Ballarat."

25 "It is wonderful!" I exclaimed.

"It is obvious. And now, you see, I had narrowed the field down considerably. The possession of a grey garment was a third point which, granting the son's statement to be correct, was a certainty. We have come now out of mere vagueness to the definite conception of an Australian from Ballarat with a grey cloak."

"Certainly."

"And one who was at home in the district, for the Pool can only be approached by the farm or by the estate, where strangers could hardly wander."

"Quite so."

"Then comes our expedition of to-day. By an examination of the ground I gained the trifling details which I gave to that imbecile Lestrade, as to the personality of the criminal."

"But how did you gain them?"

"You know my method. It is founded upon the observance of trifles."

"His height I know that you might roughly judge from the length of his stride. His boots, too, might be told from their traces."

"Yes, they were peculiar boots."

"But his lameness?"

"The impression of his right foot was always less distinct than his left. He put less weight upon it. Why? Because he limped—he was lame."

"But his left-handedness?"

"You were yourself struck by the nature of the injury as recorded by the surgeon at the inquest. The blow was struck from immediately behind, and yet was upon the left side. Now, how can that be unless it were by a left-handed man? He had stood behind that tree during the interview between the father and son. He had even smoked there. I found the ash of a cigar, which my special knowledge of tobacco ashes enabled me to pronounce as an Indian cigar. I have, as you know, devoted some attention to this, and written a little monograph on the ashes of 140 different varieties of pipe, cigar, and cigarette tobacco. Having found the ash, I then looked round and discovered the stump among the moss where he had tossed it. It was an Indian cigar, of the variety which are rolled in Rotterdam."

"And the cigar-holder?"

"I could see that the end had not been in his mouth. Therefore he used a holder. The tip had been cut off, not bitten off, but the cut was not a clean one, so I deduced a blunt penknife."

"Holmes," I said, "you have drawn a net round this man from which he cannot escape, and you have saved an innocent human life as truly as if you had cut the cord which was hanging him. I see the direction in which all this points. The culprit is——"

"Mr. John Turner," cried the hotel waiter, opening

25 *"It is wonderful!" I exclaimed.* But it might be pointed out that there are many other towns in Australia—Ararat, for example—to which "ARAT" would equally apply.

"HE HAD STOOD BEHIND THAT TREE . . ."

Illustration by Sidney Paget for the *Strand Magazine*, October, 1891.

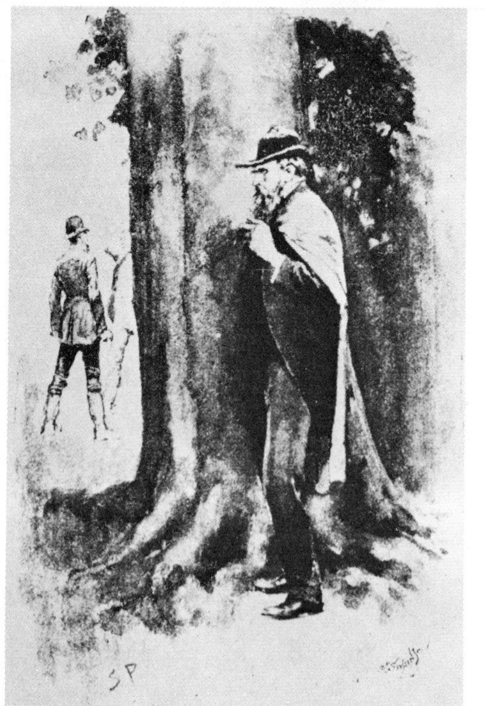

the door of our sitting-room, and ushering in a visitor.

The man who entered was a strange and impressive figure. His slow, limping step and bowed shoulders gave the appearance of decrepitude, and yet his hard, deep-lined, craggy features, and his enormous limbs showed that he was possessed of unusual strength of body and of character. His tangled beard, grizzled hair, and outstanding, drooping eyebrows combined to give an air of dignity and power to his appearance, but his face was of an ashen white, while his lips and the corners of his nostrils were tinged with a shade of blue. It was clear to me at a glance that he was in the grip of some deadly and chronic disease.

" Pray sit down on the sofa," said Holmes gently. " You had my note ? "

" Yes, the lodge-keeper brought it up. You said that you wished to see me here to avoid scandal."

" I thought people would talk if I went to the Hall."

" And why did you wish to see me ? " He looked across at my companion with despair in his weary eyes, as though his question were already answered.

" Yes," said Holmes, answering the look rather than the words. " It is so. I know all about McCarthy."

The old man sank his face in his hands. " God help me ! " he cried. " But I would not have let the young man come to harm. I give you my word that I would have spoken out if it went against him at the Assizes."

" I am glad to hear you say so," said Holmes gravely.

" I would have spoken now had it not been for my dear girl. It would break her heart—it will break her heart when she hears that I am arrested."

" It may not come to that," said Holmes.

" What ! "

" I am no official agent. I understand that it was your daughter who required my presence here, and I am acting in her interests. Young McCarthy must be got off, however."

" I am a dying man," said old Turner. " I have had diabetes for years. My doctor says it is a question whether I shall live a month. Yet I would rather die under my own roof than in a gaol."

Holmes rose and sat down at the table with his pen in his hand and a bundle of paper before him. " Just tell us the truth," he said. " I shall jot down the facts. You will sign it, and Watson here can witness it. Then I could produce your confession at the last extremity to save young McCarthy. I promise you that I shall not use it unless it is absolutely needed."

" It's as well," said the old man ; " it's a question whether I shall live to the Assizes, so it matters little to me, but I should wish to spare Alice the shock. And now I will make the thing clear to you ; it has been a long time in the acting, but will not take me long to tell.

" You didn't know this dead man, McCarthy. He was a devil incarnate. I tell you that. God keep you out of the clutches of such a man as he. His grip has been upon me these twenty years, and he has blasted my life. I'll tell you first how I came to be in his power.

" It was in the early 'sixties at the diggings. I was a young chap then, hot-blooded and reckless, ready to turn

"MR. JOHN TURNER," CRIED THE HOTEL WAITER . . .

Illustration by Sidney Paget for the *Strand Magazine*, October, 1891.

my hand to anything ; I got among bad companions, took to drink, had no luck with my claim, took to the bush, and, in a word, became what you would call over here a highway robber. There were six of us, and we had a wild, free life of it, sticking up a station from time to time, or stopping the wagons on the road to the diggings. Black Jack of Ballarat was the name I went under, and our party is still remembered in the colony as the Ballarat Gang.

" One day a gold convoy came down from Ballarat to Melbourne, and we lay in wait for it and attacked it. There were six troopers and six of us, so it was a close thing, but we emptied four of their saddles at the first volley. Three of our boys were killed, however, before we got the swag. I put my pistol to the head of the wagon-driver, who was this very man McCarthy. I wish to the Lord that I had shot him then, but I spared him, though I saw his wicked little eyes fixed on my face, as though to remember every feature. We got away with the gold, became wealthy men, and made our way over
26 to England without being suspected. There I parted from my old pals, and determined to settle down to a quiet and respectable life. I bought this estate, which chanced to be in the market, and I set myself to do a little good with my money, to make up for the way in which I had earned it. I married, too, and though my wife died young, she left me my dear little Alice. Even when she was just a baby her wee hand seemed to lead me down the right path as nothing else had ever done. In a word, I turned over a new leaf, and did my best to make up for the past. All was going well when McCarthy laid his grip upon me.

" I had gone up to town about an investment, and I met him in Regent Street with hardly a coat to his back or a boot to his foot.

" ' Here we are, Jack,' says he, touching me on the arm ; ' we'll be as good as a family to you. There's two of us, me and my son, and you can have the keeping of us. If you don't—it's a fine, law-abiding country is England, and there's always a policeman within hail.'

" Well, down they came to the West Country, there was no shaking them off, and there they have lived rent free on my best land ever since. There was no rest for me, no peace, no forgetfulness ; turn where I would, there was his cunning, grinning face at my elbow. It grew worse as Alice grew up, for he soon saw I was more afraid of her knowing my past than of the police. Whatever he wanted he must have, and whatever it was I gave him without question, land, money, houses, until at last he asked for a thing which I could not give. He asked for Alice.

" His son, you see, had grown up, and so had my girl, and as I was known to be in weak health, it seemed a fine stroke to him that his lad should step into the whole property. But there I was firm. I would not have his cursed stock mixed with mine ; not that I had any dislike to the lad, but his blood was in him, and that was enough. I stood firm. McCarthy threatened. I braved him to

26 *and made our way over to England.* In "Some Diggings Down Under," Mrs. Jennifer Chorley has written: "Black Jack's account of the gold robbery appears to be a condensed version of two famous bushranging exploits: 1) of 1853 (the McIvor Gold Robbery); and 2) of 1862 (the Eugowra Escort Robbery). The second raid was on the way to Sydney but both raids featured fights between six troopers and six bushrangers. In one, the driver was wounded and, in the other, killed. In both raids the bushrangers escaped, and though some were later caught and executed, some were never captured and the gold was never recovered. The raids, which included ambushes, seem to bear the mark of the same gang and a few weeks after Eugowra '*a man named Turner* was arrested at Yass.' No doubt he later escaped as his name is not among those executed later. All the bushrangers used a multitude of aliases."

do his worst. We were to meet at the Pool midway between our houses to talk it over.

"When I went down there I found him talking with his son, so I smoked a cigar, and waited behind a tree until he should be alone. But as I listened to his talk all that was black and bitter in me seemed to come uppermost. He was urging his son to marry my daughter with as little regard for what she might think as if she were a slut from off the streets. It drove me mad to think that I and all that I held most dear should be in the power of such a man as this. Could I not snap the bond? I was already a dying and a desperate man. Though clear of mind and fairly strong of limb, I knew that my own fate was sealed. But my memory and my girl! Both could be saved, if I could but silence that foul tongue. I did it, Mr. Holmes. I would do it again. Deeply as I have sinned, I have led a life of martyrdom to atone for it. But that my girl should be entangled in the same meshes which held me was more than I could suffer. I struck him down with no more compunction than if he had been some foul and venomous beast. His cry brought back his son; but I had gained the cover of the wood, though I was forced to go back to fetch the cloak which I had dropped in my flight. That is the true story, gentlemen, of all that occurred."

"Well, it is not for me to judge you," said Holmes, as the old man signed the statement which had been drawn out. "I pray that we may never be exposed to such a temptation."

"I pray not, sir. And what do you intend to do?"

"In view of your health, nothing. You are yourself **27**
aware that you will soon have to answer for your deed at a higher court than the Assizes. I will keep your confession, and, if McCarthy is condemned, I shall be forced to use it. If not, it shall never be seen by mortal eye; and your secret, whether you be alive or dead, shall be safe with us."

"Farewell! then," said the old man solemnly. "Your own death-beds, when they come, will be the easier for the thought of the peace which you have given to mine." Tottering and shaking in all his giant frame, he stumbled slowly from the room.

"FAREWELL! THEN," SAID THE OLD MAN SOLEMNLY.

Illustration by Sidney Paget for the *Strand Magazine*, October, 1891.

27 *"In view of your health, nothing.* Mr. John Ball, Jr. ("Early Days in Baker Street") sees in this case another "revelation of Holmes' high official position" in the British government. "Consider this carefully: the crime was murder. Lestrade was on the case, and Lestrade was far from a fool. In a rural area, where prominent individuals are well known, Holmes supplied Lestrade with a detailed and unmistakable description of the murderer. A tall left-handed cripple would be easy for even Lestrade to find—and Lestrade, in fact, actually reported to Holmes the condition of this man's health. Yet Holmes in his own person pardoned the murderer, and Lestrade quietly dropped the case and did not make an arrest. It is inconceivable that a Scotland Yard inspector would let a known murderer off scot free unless he was under direct orders to do so."

" God help us ! " said Holmes, after a long silence. " Why does Fate play such tricks with poor helpless worms ? I never hear of such a case as this that I do not think of Baxter's words, and say : ' There, but for the
28 grace of God, goes Sherlock Holmes.' "

James McCarthy was acquitted at the Assizes, on the strength of a number of objections which had been drawn
29 out by Holmes, and submitted to the defending counsel. Old Turner lived for seven months after our interview, but he is now dead ; and there is every prospect that the son and daughter may come to live happily together, in ignorance of the black cloud which rests upon their past.

28 *'There, but for the grace of God, goes Sherlock Holmes.'* " A paraphrase of the words uttered by John Bradford, 1510–1555, whenever he saw a criminal go by; wrongly credited by Holmes to the great English divine Richard Baxter, 1615–1691.

29 *submitted to the defending counsel.* "Since when," Mr. Albert P. Blaustein asked in "Sherlock Holmes As a Lawyer," "do laymen prepare objections for proceedings in a court of law? Have we convinced the skeptic [that Holmes was a lawyer]?"

Bibliographical Note: According to Professor David A. Randall, "The Boscombe Valley Mystery" was first published in book form in an unauthorized collection of Conan Doyle's short stories titled *The Doings of Raffles Haw*, New York: Lovell, Coryell & Co., August, 1892, as "Number Five in the Belmore Series."

39

THE STOCKBROKER'S CLERK

[Saturday, June 15, 1889]

SHORTLY after my marriage I had bought a con- 1
nection in the Paddington district. Old Mr. 2
Farquhar, from whom I purchased it, had at one
time an excellent general practice, but his age, and an
affliction of the nature of St. Vitus' dance from which he
suffered, had very much thinned it. The public, not
unnaturally, goes upon the principle that he who would
heal others must himself be whole, and looks askance at
the curative powers of the man whose own case is beyond
the reach of his drugs. Thus, as my predecessor weakened his practice declined, until when I purchased it
from him it had sunk from twelve hundred to little more
than three hundred a year. I had confidence, however, 3
in my own youth and energy, and was convinced that in a 4
very few years the concern would be as flourishing as ever.

For three months after taking over the practice I was
kept very closely at work, and saw little of my friend
Sherlock Holmes, for I was too busy to visit Baker Street,
and he seldom went anywhere himself save upon professional business. I was surprised, therefore, when one
morning in June, as I sat reading the *British Medical* 5
Journal after breakfast, I heard a ring at the bell followed 6
by the high, somewhat strident, tones of my old companion's voice.

" Ah, my dear Watson," said he, striding into the room, " I am very delighted to see you. I trust that Mrs. Watson has entirely recovered from all the little excitements connected with our adventure of the ' Sign of Four ' ? "

" Thank you, we are both very well," said I, shaking him warmly by the hand.

" And I hope also," he continued, sitting down in the rocking-chair, " that the cares of medical practice have not entirely obliterated the interest which you used to take in our little deductive problems."

" On the contrary," I answered ; " it was only last night that I was looking over my old notes and classifying some of our past results."

" I trust that you don't consider your collection closed ? "

" Not at all. I should wish nothing better than to have some more of such experiences."

" To-day, for example ? "

" Yes ; to-day, if you like."

" And as far off as Birmingham ? "

1 *Shortly after my marriage.* This is certainly Watson's marriage to Mary Morstan, for Holmes later says: "I trust that Mrs. Watson has entirely recovered from all the little excitements connected with our adventure of the 'Sign of the Four.'" The year in which chronologists place this adventure consequently depends upon the date they assign to Watson's marriage to Mary. The ranks are fairly evenly divided between 1888 (Andrew, Bell, Brend, Harrison, Heldenbrand, Hoff, Knox, Morley, and Roberts) and 1889 (Baring-Gould, Blakeney, Christ, Folsom, Pattrick, Petersen, Smith, and Zeisler).

2 *the Paddington district.* In "The Adventure of the Engineer's Thumb," Watson tells us that his consulting room at this time was "no very great distance from Paddington Station." "Watson [like Holmes] seems to have been attracted by the quiet appeal of Georgian architecture for he appears to have practiced from houses of this period wherever he lived," Mr. William H. Gill wrote in "Some Notable Sherlockian Buildings." "His references to Paddington Station seem to show that he lived on the very last Estate to be laid out in London in a gracious manner. The superb Paddington Estate, bounded by the Edgware Road, the Grand Union Canal, Hyde Park and the Westbourne Brook, contained some of the prettiest houses in the fast-spreading metropolis, and there is no doubt that Watson lived in the neighbourhood of Norfolk Square. These tall, stucco-fronted professional-class houses would have suited a rising young medical practitioner, and had none of the flamboyance of the later period. The Paddington Estate was laid out by George Gutch in 1838 and coincided with the arrival of the Great Western Railway, the favourite line of Holmes and Watson."

"It is impossible to say in which of Paddington's many streets Watson lived," Mr. Michael Harrison wrote (*In the Footsteps of Sherlock Holmes*); "he could have lived in Eastbourne Terrace, which runs alongside the west wall of Paddington Station, and connects Praed Street with Bishop's Bridge Road. It was a respectable street in his day —though its degeneration into a 'red lamp' street was inevitable—but it was noisy. It is far more

"HA! NOTHING COULD BE BETTER!" SAID HOLMES . . .

Illustration by Sidney Paget for the *Strand Magazine*, March, 1893.

likely that Watson lived across Praed Street, in Spring Street or London Street or even in Norfolk Square, which is separated from Praed Street only by a block of houses. He would thus be near enough to the Station to be known to the staff, while sufficiently removed from the traffic of Praed Street to enjoy a certain amount of quiet. His rent would have been (for a three-storeyed house in, say, Spring Street) about £60 [$300] per annum; a four-storeyed house in nearby Norfolk Square would have been about £80 [$400]; both figures exclusive of rates."

3 *from twelve hundred to little more than three hundred a year.* From $6,000 to little more than $1,500.

4 *my own youth and energy.* "Youth is, after all, a somewhat elastic term," the late Dr. Samuel R. Meaker wrote in "Watson Medicus," "but we would put Watson at a ripe 37 at this time. As to energy, he admitted frankly at his first meeting with Holmes that he was extremely lazy, and there is no evidence to show that he later reformed in this respect, except for brief periods."

5 *one morning in June.* It was a Saturday morning, as we learn later. Watson's statement that he "saw little" of Holmes for three months after taking over the practice has been interpreted by some commentators to mean that he bought the practice some three months *before* the adventure of "The Stockbroker's Clerk"—in March, let us say, and that he married Mary Morstan shortly before this, perhaps in January or February. But this is not necessarily the case: Watson says he saw "little," not "nothing," of Holmes during the first three months of his practice. In our view, Watson purchased his Paddington practice "shortly" after his marriage to Mary *circa* May 1, 1889.

7 " Certainly, if you wish it."

" And the practice ? "

" I do my neighbour's when he goes. He is always ready to work off the debt."

" Ha ! Nothing could be better ! " said Holmes, leaning back in his chair and looking keenly at me from under his half-closed lids. " I perceive that you have been unwell lately. Summer colds are always a little trying."

" I was confined to the house by a severe chill for three days last week. I thought, however, that I had cast off every trace of it."

" So you have. You look remarkably robust."

" How, then, did you know of it ? "

" My dear fellow, you know my methods."

" You deduced it, then ? "

" Certainly."

" And from what ? "

" From your slippers."

I glanced down at the new patent leathers which I was wearing. " How on earth—— ? " I began, but Holmes answered my question before it was asked.

" Your slippers are new," he said. " You could not have had them more than a few weeks. The soles which you are at this moment presenting to me are slightly scorched. For a moment I thought they might have got wet and been burned in the drying. But near the instep there is a small circular wafer of paper with the shopman's hieroglyphics upon it. Damp would of course have removed this. You had then been sitting with your feet outstretched to the fire, which a man would hardly do
8 even in so wet a June as this if he were in his full health."

Like all Holmes' reasoning, the thing seemed simplicity itself when it was once explained. He read the thought upon my features, and his smile had a tinge of bitterness.

" I am afraid that I rather give myself away when I explain," said he. " Results without causes are much more impressive. You are ready to come to Birmingham, then ? "

" Certainly. What is the case ? "

" You shall hear it all in the train. My client is outside in a four-wheeler. Can you come at once ? "

" In an instant." I scribbled a note to my neighbour, rushed upstairs to explain the matter to my wife, and joined Holmes upon the doorstep.

" Your neighbour is a doctor ? " said he, nodding at the brass plate.

" Yes. He bought a practice, as I did."

" An old-established one ? "

" Just the same as mine. Both have been ever since the houses were built."

" Ah, then you got hold of the better of the two."

" I think I did. But how do you know ? "

" By the steps, my boy. Yours are worn three inches deeper than his. But this gentleman in the cab is my client, Mr. Hall Pycroft. Allow me to introduce you to him. Whip your horse up, cabby, for we have only just time to catch our train."

The man whom I found myself facing was a well-built,

fresh-complexioned young fellow with a frank, honest face and a slight, crisp, yellow moustache. He wore a very shiny top-hat and a neat suit of sober black, which made him look what he was—a smart young City man, of the class who have been labelled Cockneys, but who give us our crack Volunteer regiments, and who turn out more fine athletes and sportsmen than any body of men in these islands. His round, ruddy face was naturally full of cheeriness, but the corners of his mouth seemed to me to be pulled down in a half-comical distress. It was not, however, until we were all in a first-class carriage and well started upon our journey to Birmingham, that I was able to learn what the trouble was which had driven him to Sherlock Holmes.

" We have a clear run here of seventy minutes," Holmes remarked. " I want you, Mr. Hall Pycroft, to tell my friend your very interesting experience exactly as you have told it to me, or with more detail if possible. It will be of use to me to hear the succession of events again. It is a case, Watson, which may prove to have something in it, or may prove to have nothing, but which at least presents those unusual and *outré* features which are as dear to you as they are to me. Now, Mr. Pycroft, I shall not interrupt you again."

Our young companion looked at me with a twinkle in his eye.

" The worst of the story is," said he, " that I show myself up as such a confounded fool. Of course, it may
work out all right, and I don't see that I could have done
otherwise ; but if I have lost my crib and get nothing in 9
exchange, I shall feel what a soft Johnny I have been.
I'm not very good at telling a story, Dr. Watson, but it
is like this with me.

**" I used to have a billet at Coxon & Woodhouse, of
Drapers' Gardens, but they were let in early in the spring 10
through the Venezuelan loan, as no doubt you remember,
and came a nasty cropper. I had been with them five
years, and old Coxon gave me a ripping good testimonial
when the smash came ; but, of course, we clerks were all
turned adrift, the twenty-seven of us. I tried here and
tried there, but there were lots of other chaps on the
same lay as myself, and it was a perfect frost for a long
time. I had been taking three pounds a week at
Coxon's, and I had saved about seventy of them, but
I soon worked my way through that and out at the other
end. I was fairly at the end of my tether at last, and
could hardly find the stamps to answer the advertisements or the envelopes to stick them to. I had worn out
my boots padding up office stairs, and I seemed just as
far from getting a billet as ever.**

**" At last I saw a vacancy at Mawson & Williams', the
great stockbroking firm in Lombard Street. I dare say
E.C. is not much in your line, but I can tell you that this 11
is about the richest house in London. The advertisement was to be answered by letter only. I sent in my
testimonial and application, but without the least hope
of getting it. Back came an answer by return saying that
if I would appear next Monday I might take over my
new duties at once, provided that my appearance was**

6 *as I sat reading the* British Medical Journal. Mr. S. C. Roberts has suggested ("A Note on the Watson Problem") that "it seems fair to deduce that the date was not later than 10 June" since "monthly Journals are normally read soon after their arrival at the beginning of the month."

7 *"Certainly, if you wish it."* "Watson jumped at the chance to go to Birmingham with Holmes," the late Christopher Morley wrote in "Dr. Watson's Secret." "He thought he might be able to persuade Sherlock to run out to Walsall (only eight miles away) to see Miss Hunter at the school where she was headmistress."

8 *so wet a June as this.* Baring-Gould, Christ, and Zeisler are agreed that the day was *Saturday, June 15, 1889.* As Dr. Zeisler wrote: "from the London *Times* we learn that there was some rain on the 1st and the 3rd, the 6th was a most foul day with immense rains all day, the 7th was hardly less wet than the 6th, there was rain all day long on the 10th, and there was rain on the 12th, 14th, and 15th. In the London *Times* for June 11, 1889, on page 3, we find that 'For more than three days there has not been one gleam of sunshine in London; the rainfall has amounted to more than half the average for the whole month.' . . . Whereas the 1st and the 8th were too early in the month to speak of a 'wet June,' this would have been entirely applicable on June 15th. Inasmuch as there was no rain at all after the 16th it is not likely that the Master would have called it a wet month on either the 22nd or the 29th . . ."

In our view, Watson must have caught his chill on the Monday afternoon following his return from Boscombe Valley, that is, on the 10th of June. No doubt, having been away from his practice for two days, he was out all day in the all-day rain. We believe that Watson was confined to his house on the Tuesday, Wednesday, and Thursday, the 11th to the 13th, recovering in time to join Holmes in the adventure of "The Stockbroker's Clerk" on Saturday, June 15th.

9 *lost my crib.* Cockney slang for "lost my job."

10 *Drapers' Gardens.* One of the many courts and narrow streets, leading nowhere in particular, which throng the home of the Stock Exchange brokers and their clerks—that quarter of the City which is enclosed by Moorgate on the west, London Wall on the north, Old Broad Street on the east, and Throgmorton Street on the south.

11 *E.C.* Eastern Central, the designation of the Post Office district in which most of the great London stockbrokering enterprises are to be found.

"... THE GREAT STOCKBROKING FIRM IN LOMBARD STREET."

Lombard Street is "The street of bankers, which derived its name from the Italian merchants who frequented it before the reign of Edward II," Augustus J. C. Hare wrote in *Walks in London*, Vol. I. "Jane Shore, the beloved of Edward IV, was the wife of a goldsmith in this street; Guy, the founder of Guy's Hospital, was a bookseller here; and here, where his father was a linen-draper, the poet Pope was born in 1688 amongst the merchants and money-makers." Our photograph, by G. F. Allen, is from the *Second County Life Picture Book of London;* London: Country Life, 1953.

satisfactory. No one knows how these things are worked. Some people say the manager just plunges his hand into the heap and takes the first that comes. Anyhow, it was my innings that time, and I don't ever wish to feel better
12 pleased. The screw was a pound a week rise, and the duties just about the same as at Coxon's.

" And now I come to the queer part of the business. I was in diggings out Hampstead way—17 Potter's Terrace, was the address. Well, I was sitting doing a smoke that very evening after I had been promised the appointment, when up came my landlady with a card which had 'Arthur Pinner, financial agent,' printed upon it. I had never heard the name before, and could not imagine what he wanted with me, but of course I asked her to show him up. In he walked—a middle-sized, dark-haired, dark-eyed, black-bearded man, with a touch of the sheeny about his nose. He had a brisk kind of way with him and spoke sharply, like a man that knew the value of time.

" ' Mr. Hall Pycroft, I believe ? ' said he.

" ' Yes, sir,' I answered, and pushed a chair towards him.

" ' Lately engaged at Coxon & Woodhouse's ? '

" ' Yes, sir.'

" ' And now on the staff of Mawson's ? '

" ' Quite so.'

" ' Well,' said he. ' The fact is that I have heard some really extraordinary stories about your financial ability. You remember Parker who used to be Coxon's manager ?

" 'MR. HALL PYCROFT, I BELIEVE?' SAID HE."

Illustration by William H. Hyde for *Harper's Weekly*, March 11, 1893. Sidney Paget illustrated the same scene for the *Strand Magazine*, March, 1893.

12 *The screw.* Cockney slang for "the salary."

He can never say enough about it.'

" Of course I was pleased to hear this. I had always been pretty smart in the office, but I had never dreamed that I was talked about in the City in this fashion.

" ' You have a good memory ? ' said he.

" ' Pretty fair,' I answered, modestly.

" ' Have you kept in touch with the market while you have been out of work ? ' he asked.

" ' Yes ; I read the Stock Exchange List every morning.'

" ' Now, that shows real application ! ' he cried. ' That is the way to prosper ! You won't mind my testing you, will you ? Let me see ! How are Ayrshires ? '

" ' One hundred and five, to one hundred and five and a quarter.' **13**

" ' And New Zealand Consolidated ? '

" ' A hundred and four.'

" ' And British Broken Hills ? '

" ' Seven to seven and six.'

" ' Wonderful ! ' he cried, with his hands up. ' This **14** quite fits in with all that I had heard. My boy, my boy, you are very much too good to be a clerk at Mawson's ! '

" This outburst rather astonished me, as you can think. ' Well,' said I, ' other people don't think quite so much of me as you seem to do, Mr. Pinner. I had a hard enough fight to get this berth, and I am very glad to have it.'

" ' Pooh, man, you should soar above it. You are not in your true sphere. Now I'll tell you how it stands with me. What I have to offer is little enough when measured by your ability, but when compared with Mawson's it is light to dark. Let me see ! When do you go to Mawson's ? '

" ' On Monday.'

" ' Ha ! ha ! I think I would risk a little sporting flutter that you don't go there at all.'

" ' Not go to Mawson's ? '

" ' No, sir. By that day you will be business manager of the Franco-Midland Hardware Company, Limited, with one hundred and thirty-four branches in the towns and villages of France, not counting one in Brussels and one in San Remo.'

" This took my breath away. ' I never heard of it,' said I.

" ' Very likely not. It has been kept very quiet, for the capital was all privately subscribed, and it is too good a thing to let the public into. My brother, Harry Pinner, is promoter, and joins the board after allotment as managing director. He knew that I was in the swim down here, and he asked me to pick up a good man cheap—a young, pushing man with plenty of snap about him. Parker spoke of you, and that brought me here to-night. We can only offer you a beggarly five hundred to start with——'

" ' Five hundred a year ! ' I shouted.

" ' Only that at the beginning, but you are to have an overriding commission of 1 per cent on all business done by your agents, and you may take my word for it that this will come to more than your salary.'

" ' But I know nothing about hardware.'

13 " '*One hundred and five, to one hundred and five and a quarter.*' In some American editions of the Canon, the bid and asked prices are given as "One hundred and six and a quarter to one hun-hundred and five and seven-eights." Since bid and asked prices are given in that order, these figures incorrectly suggest that the bid was higher than the asking price.

14 " '*Wonderful!' he cried, with his hands up.* Writing in "Doctor Watson—Punter or Speculator?", Mr. R. M. McLaren has noted that "British Broken Hill was a mining company in Australia which was finally absorbed into North Broken Hill. New Zealand Consolidated went into liquidation in 1900. The third stock mentioned was 'Ayrshires.' . . . It is unlikely that this referred to an Ayr County Council loan since there would be no daily fluctuation in the price of such a stock. It is almost certain that this was a Stock Exchange nickname now forgotten. During their lifetime the stocks of the London, Midland and Scottish and the London and North Eastern Railway Companies were always referred to as 'Brum' and 'Berwick.' It is probable that, in a similar way at the time, the stocks of the former Glasgow and South Western Railway were known as 'Ayrshires.' "

" ' Tut, my boy, you know about figures.'

" My head buzzed, and I could hardly sit still in the chair. But suddenly a little chill of doubt came over me.

" ' I must be frank with you,' said I. ' Mawson only gives me two hundred, but Mawson is safe. Now, really, I know so little about your company that——'

" ' Ah, smart, smart ! ' he cried, in a kind of ecstasy of delight. ' You are the very man for us ! You are not to be talked over, and quite right too. Now here's a note for a hundred pounds ; and if you think that we can do business you may just slip it into your pocket as an advance upon your salary.'

" ' That is very handsome,' said I. ' When shall I take over my new duties ? '

" ' Be in Birmingham to-morrow at one,' said he. ' I have a note in my pocket here which you will take to my brother. You will find him at 126B Corporation Street, where the temporary offices of the company are situated. Of course he must confirm your engagement, but between ourselves it will be all right.'

" ' Really, I hardly know how to express my gratitude, Mr. Pinner,' said I.

" ' Not at all, my boy. You have only got your deserts. There are one or two small things—mere formalities—which I must arrange with you. You have a bit of paper beside you there. Kindly write upon it, " I am perfectly willing to act as business manager to the Franco-Midland Hardware Company, Limited, at a minimum salary of £500." '

" I did as he asked, and he put the paper in his pocket.

" ' There is one other detail,' said he. ' What do you intend to do about Mawson's ? '

" I had forgotten all about Mawson's in my joy.

" ' I'll write and resign,' said I.

" ' Precisely what I don't want you to do. I had a row over you with Mawson's manager. I had gone up to ask him about you, and he was very offensive—accused me of coaxing you away from the service of the firm, and that sort of thing. At last I fairly lost my temper. " If you want good men you should pay them a good price," said I. " He would rather have our small price than your big one," said he. " I'll lay you a fiver," said I, " that when he has my offer you will never so much as hear from him again." " Done ! " said he. " We picked him out of the gutter, and he won't leave us so easily." Those were his very words.'

" ' The impudent scoundrel ! ' I cried. ' I've never so much as seen him in my life. Why should I consider him in any way ? I shall certainly not write if you would rather that I didn't.'

" ' Good ! That's a promise ! ' said he, rising from his chair. ' Well, I am delighted to have got so good a man for my brother. Here is your advance of a hundred pounds, and here is the letter. Make a note of the address, 126B Corporation Street, and remember that one o'clock to-morrow is your appointment. Good night, and may you have all the fortune that you deserve.'

" That's just about all that passed between us as near as I can remember it. You can imagine, Dr. Watson, how pleased I was at such an extraordinary piece of good fortune. I sat up half the night hugging myself over it, and next day I was off to Birmingham in a train that would take me in plenty of time for my appointment. I took my things to an hotel in New Street, and then I made my way to the address which had been given me.

" It was a quarter of an hour before my time, but I
thought that would make no difference. 126B was a
passage between two large shops which led to a winding **15**
stone stair, from which there were many flats, let as
offices to companies or professional men. The names of
the occupants were painted up at the bottom on the wall,
but there was no such name as the Franco-Midland Hardware Company, Limited. I stood for a few minutes with
my heart in my boots, wondering whether the whole
thing was an elaborate hoax or not, when up came a man
and addressed me. He was very like the chap that I had
seen the night before, the same figure and voice, but he
was clean shaven and his hair was lighter.

" ' Are you Mr. Hall Pycroft ? ' he asked.

" ' Yes,' said I.

" ' Ah ! I was expecting you, but you are a trifle before your time. I had a note from my brother this morning, in which he sang your praises very loudly.'

" ' I was just looking for the offices when you came.'

" ' We have not got our name up yet, for we only secured these temporary premises last week. Come up with me and we will talk the matter over.'

" I followed him to the top of a very lofty stair, and there right under the slates were a couple of empty and dusty little rooms, uncarpeted and uncurtained, into which he led me. I had thought of a great office with shining tables and rows of clerks such as I was used to, and I dare say I stared rather straight at the two deal chairs and one little table, which, with a ledger and a waste-paper basket, made up the whole furniture.

" ' Don't be disheartened, Mr. Pycroft,' said my new acquaintance, seeing the length of my face. ' Rome was not built in a day, and we have lots of money at our backs, though we don't cut much dash yet in offices. Pray sit down and let me have your letter.'

" I gave it to him, and he read it over very carefully.

" ' You seem to have made a vast impression upon my brother Arthur,' said he, ' and I know that he is a pretty shrewd judge. He swears by London, you know, and I by Birmingham, but this time I shall follow his advice. Pray consider yourself definitely engaged.'

" ' What are my duties ? ' I asked.

" ' You will eventually manage the great depôt in Paris, which will pour a flood of English crockery into the shops of one hundred and thirty-four agents in France. The purchase will be completed in a week, and meanwhile you will remain in Birmingham and make yourself useful.'

" ' How ? '

" For answer he took a big red book out of a drawer. ' This is a directory of Paris,' said he, ' with the trades after the names of the people. I want you to take it home with you, and to mark off all the hardware sellers with their addresses. It would be of the greatest use to me to have them.'

15 *126B was a passage between two large shops.* In "Browsings in Birmingham," Mr. Anthony G. Cooper has written that he investigated "126B Corporation Street" in the summer of 1959 and found that address to be part of a building called "Kings Hall," built in 1888.

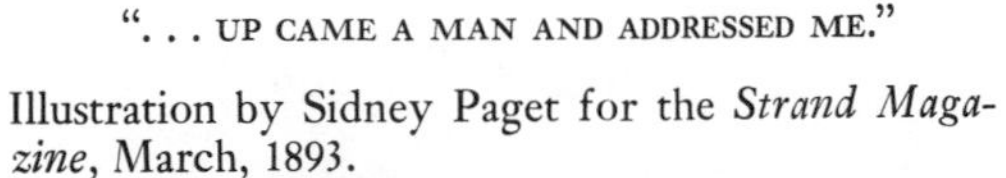

". . . UP CAME A MAN AND ADDRESSED ME."

Illustration by Sidney Paget for the *Strand Magazine*, March, 1893.

16 *Friday—that is, yesterday.* Establishing the day of the adventure as a Saturday.

" 'Surely, there are classified lists?' I suggested.

" 'Not reliable ones. Their system is different to ours. Stick at it and let me have the lists by Monday, at twelve. Good day, Mr. Pycroft; if you continue to show zeal and intelligence, you will find the company a good master.'

" I went back to the hotel with the big book under my arm, and with very conflicting feelings in my breast. On the one hand I was definitely engaged, and had a hundred pounds in my pocket. On the other, the look of the offices, the absence of name on the wall, and other of the points which would strike a business man, had left a bad impression as to the position of my employers. However, come what might, I had my money, so I settled down to my task. All Sunday I was kept hard at work, and yet by Monday I had only got as far as H. I went round to my employer, found him in the same dismantled kind of room, and was told to keep at it until Wednesday, and then come again. On Wednesday it was still unfinished, so I hammered away until Friday—that is, yester-
16 day. Then I brought it round to Mr. Harry Pinner.

" 'Thank you very much,' said he. 'I fear that I underrated the difficulty of the task. This list will be of very material assistance to me.'

" 'It took some time,' said I.

" 'And now,' said he, 'I want you to make a list of the furniture shops, for they all sell crockery.'

" 'Very good.'

" 'And you can come up to-morrow evening at seven, and let me know how you are getting on. Don't overwork yourself. A couple of hours at Day's Music-Hall in the evening would do you no harm after your labours.' He laughed as he spoke, and I saw with a thrill that his second tooth upon the left-hand side had been very badly stuffed with gold."

Sherlock Holmes rubbed his hands with delight, and I stared in astonishment at our client.

" You may well look surprised, Dr. Watson, but it is this way," said he. " When I was speaking to the other chap in London at the time that he laughed at my not going to Mawson's, I happened to notice that his tooth was stuffed in this very identical fashion. The glint of the gold in each case caught my eye, you see. When I put that with the voice and figure being the same, and only those things altered which might be changed by a razor or a wig, I could not doubt that it was the same man. Of course, you expect two brothers to be alike, but not that they should have the same tooth stuffed in the same way. He bowed me out and I found myself in the street, hardly knowing whether I was on my head or my heels. Back I went to my hotel, put my head in a basin of cold water, and tried to think it out. Why had he sent me from London to Birmingham; why had he got there before me; and why had he written a letter from himself to himself? It was altogether too much for me, and I could make no sense of it. And then suddenly it struck me that what was dark to me might be very light to Mr. Sherlock Holmes. I had just time to get up to town by the night train, to see him this morning, and to bring you both back with me to Birmingham."

There was a pause after the stockbroker's clerk had concluded his surprising experience. Then Sherlock Holmes cocked his eye at me, leaning back on the cushions with a pleased and yet critical face, like a connoisseur who had just taken his first sip of a comet vintage.

" Rather fine, Watson, is it not ? " said he. " There are points in it which please me. I think you will agree with me that an interview with Mr. Arthur Harry Pinner in the temporary offices of the Franco-Midland Hardware Company, Limited, would be a rather interesting experience for both of us."

" But how can we do it ? " I asked.

" Oh, easily enough," said Hall Pycroft, cheerily. " You are two friends of mine who are in want of a billet, and what could be more natural than that I should bring you both round to the managing director ? "

" Quite so ! Of course ! " said Holmes. " I should like to have a look at the gentleman and see if I can make anything of his little game. What qualities have you, my friend, which would make your services so valuable ? or is it possible that——" He began biting his nails and staring blankly out of the window, and we hardly drew another word from him until we were in New Street.

At seven o'clock that evening we were walking, the three of us, down Corporation Street to the company's offices.

" It is of no use our being at all before our time," said our client. " He only comes there to see me apparently, for the place is deserted up to the very hour he names."

" That is suggestive," remarked Holmes.

" By Jove, I told you so ! " cried the clerk. " That's he walking ahead of us there."

He pointed to a smallish, blond, well-dressed man, who was bustling along the other side of the road. As we watched him he looked across at a boy who was bawling out the latest edition of the evening paper, and, running over among the cabs and 'buses, he bought one from him. Then clutching it in his hand he vanished through a doorway.

" There he goes ! " cried Hall Pycroft. " Those are the company's offices into which he has gone. Come with me and I'll fix it up as easily as possible."

Following his lead we ascended five stories, until we found ourselves outside a half-opened door, at which our client tapped. A voice within bade us " Come in," and we entered a bare, unfurnished room, such as Hall Pycroft had described. At the single table sat the man whom we had seen in the street, with his evening paper spread out in front of him, and as he looked up at us it seemed to me that I had never looked upon a face which bore such marks of grief, and of something beyond grief—of a horror such as comes to few men in a lifetime. His brow glistened with perspiration, his cheeks were of the dull dead white of a fish's belly, and his eyes were wild and staring. He looked at his clerk as though he failed to recognize him, and I could see, by the astonishment

. . . I HAD NEVER LOOKED UPON A FACE WHICH BORE SUCH MARKS OF GRIEF . . .

Illustration by William H. Hyde for *Harper's Weekly*, March 11, 1893. Sidney Paget illustrated the same scene for the *Strand Magazine*, March, 1893.

depicted upon our conductor's face, that this was by no means the usual appearance of his employer.

" You look ill, Mr. Pinner," he exclaimed.

" Yes, I am not very well," answered the other, making obvious efforts to pull himself together, and licking his dry lips before he spoke. " Who are these gentlemen whom you have brought with you ? "

17 " One is Mr. Harris, of Bermondsey, and the other is Mr. Price, of this town," said our clerk, glibly. " They are friends of mine, and gentlemen of experience, but they have been out of a place for some little time, and they hoped that perhaps you might find an opening for them in the company's employment."

" Very possibly ! Very possibly ! " cried Mr. Pinner, with a ghastly smile. " Yes, I have no doubt that we shall be able to do something for you. What is your particular line, Mr. Harris ? "

" I am an accountant," said Holmes.

" Ah, yes, we shall want something of the sort. And you, Mr. Price ? "

" A clerk," said I.

" I have every hope that the company may accommodate you. I will let you know about it as soon as we come to any conclusion. And now I beg that you will go. For God's sake, leave me to myself ! "

These last words were shot out of him, as though the constraint which he was evidently setting upon himself had suddenly and utterly burst asunder. Holmes and I glanced at each other, and Hall Pycroft took a step towards the table.

" You forget, Mr. Pinner, that I am here by appointment to receive some directions from you," said he.

" Certainly, Mr. Pycroft, certainly," the other answered in a calmer tone. " You may wait here a moment, and there is no reason why your friends should not wait with you. I will be entirely at your service in three minutes, if I might trespass upon your patience so far." He rose with a very courteous air, and bowing to us he passed out through a door at the farther end of the room, which he closed behind him.

" What now ? " whispered Holmes. " Is he giving us the slip ? "

" Impossible," answered Pycroft.

" Why so ? "

" That door leads into an inner room."

" There is no exit ? "

" None."

" Is it furnished ? "

" It was empty yesterday."

" Then what on earth can he be doing ? There is something which I don't understand in this matter. If ever a man was three parts mad with terror, that man's name is Pinner. What can have put the shivers on him ? "

" He suspects that we are detectives," I suggested.

" That's it," said Pycroft.

Holmes shook his head. " He did not turn pale. He *was* pale when we entered the room," said he. " It is just possible that——"

His words were interrupted by a sharp rat-tat from the direction of the inner door.

17 *Bermondsey*. A metropolitan borough on the right bank of the Thames below London Bridge. The name means "the island of Beormund" (a Saxon personal name) and indicates the formerly marshy character of the place. In Bermondsey is Rotherhithe, the scene of some of Holmes' investigations in "The Adventure of the Dying Detective."

" What the deuce is he knocking at his own door for ? " cried the clerk.

Again and much louder came the rat-tat-tat. We all gazed expectantly at the closed door. Glancing at Holmes I saw his face turn rigid, and he leaned forward in intense excitement. Then suddenly came a low gurgling, gargling sound and a brisk drumming upon woodwork. Holmes sprang frantically across the room and pushed at the door. It was fastened on the inner side. Following his example, we threw ourselves upon it with all our weight. One hinge snapped, then the other, and down came the door with a crash. Rushing over it, we found ourselves in the inner room.

It was empty.

But it was only for a moment that we were at fault. At one corner, the corner nearest the room which we had left, there was a second door. Holmes sprang to it and pulled it open. A coat and waistcoat were lying on the floor, and from a hook behind the door, with his own braces round his neck, was hanging the managing director of the Franco-Midland Hardware Company. His knees were drawn up, his head hung at a dreadful angle to his body, and the clatter of his heels against the door made the noise which had broken in upon our conversation. In an instant I had caught him round the waist and held him up, while Holmes and Pycroft untied the elastic bands which had disappeared between the livid creases of skin. Then we carried him into the other room, where he lay with a slate-coloured face, puffing his purple lips in and out with every breath—a dreadful wreck of all that he had been but five minutes before.

" What do you think of him, Watson ? " asked Holmes.

I stooped over him and examined him. His pulse was feeble and intermittent, but his breathing grew longer, and there was a little shivering of his eyelids which showed a thin white slit of ball beneath.

" It has been touch and go with him," said I, " but he'll live now. Just open that window and hand me the water carafe." I undid his collar, poured the cold water over his face, and raised and sank his arms until he drew a long natural breath.

" It's only a question of time now," said I, as I turned away from him.

Holmes stood by the table with his hands deep in his trousers pockets and his chin upon his breast.

" I suppose we ought to call the police in now," said he ; " and yet I confess that I like to give them a complete case when they come."

" It's a blessed mystery to me," cried Pycroft, scratching his head. " Whatever they wanted to bring me all the way up here for, and then——"

" Pooh ! All that is clear enough," said Holmes impatiently. " It is this last sudden move."

" You understand the rest, then ? "

" I think that is fairly obvious. What do you say, Watson ? "

I shrugged my shoulders.

" I must confess that I am out of my depths," said I.

" Oh, surely, if you consider the events at first they can

RUSHING OVER IT, WE FOUND OURSELVES IN THE INNER ROOM.

Illustration by Sidney Paget for the *Strand Magazine*, March, 1893.

HALL PYCROFT SHOOK HIS CLENCHED HANDS IN THE AIR.

Illustration by Sidney Paget for the *Strand Magazine*, March, 1893.

only point to one conclusion."

" What do you make of them ? "

" Well, the whole thing hinges upon two points. The first is the making of Pycroft write a declaration by which he entered the service of this preposterous company. Do you not see how very suggestive that is ? "

" I am afraid I miss the point."

" Well, why did they want him to do it ? Not as a business matter, for these arrangements are usually verbal, and there was no earthly business reason why this should be an exception. Don't you see, my young friend, that they were very anxious to obtain a specimen of your handwriting, and had no other way of doing it ? "

" And why ? "

" Quite so. Why ? When we answer that, we have made some progress with our little problem. Why ? There can be only one adequate reason. Someone wanted to learn to imitate your writing, and had to procure a specimen of it first. And now if we pass on to the second point, we find that each throws light upon the other. That point is the request made by Pinner that you should not resign your place, but should leave the manager of this important business in the full expectation that a Mr. Hall Pycroft, whom he had never seen, was about to enter the office upon the Monday morning."

" My God ! " cried our client, " what a blind beetle I have been ! "

" Now you see the point about the handwriting. Suppose that someone turned up in your place who wrote a completely different hand from that in which you had applied for the vacancy, of course the game would have been up. But in the interval the rogue learnt to imitate you, and his position was therefore secure, as I presume that nobody in the office had ever set eyes upon you ? "

" Not a soul," groaned Hall Pycroft.

" Very good. Of course, it was of the utmost importance to prevent you from thinking better of it, and also to keep you from coming into contact with anyone who might tell you that your double was at work in Mawson's office. Therefore they gave you a handsome advance on your salary, and ran you off to the Midlands, where they gave you enough work to do to prevent your going to London, where you might have burst their little game up. That is all plain enough."

" But why should this man pretend to be his own brother ? "

" Well, that is pretty clear also. There are evidently only two of them in it. The other is personating you at the office. This one acted as your engager, and then found that he could not find you an employer without admitting a third person into his plot. That he was most unwilling to do. He changed his appearance as far as he could, and trusted that the likeness, which you could not fail to observe, would be put down to a family resemblance. But for the happy chance of the gold stuffing your suspicions would probably have never been aroused."

Hall Pycroft shook his clenched hands in the air.

"Good Lord!" he cried. "While I have been fooled in this way, what has this other Hall Pycroft been doing at Mawson's? What should we do, Mr. Holmes? Tell me what to do!"

"We must wire to Mawson's."

"They shut at twelve on Saturdays."

"Never mind; there may be some door-keeper or attendant——"

"Ah, yes; they keep a permanent guard there on account of the value of the securities that they hold. I remember hearing it talked of in the City."

"Very good, we shall wire to him, and see if all is well, and if a clerk of your name is working there. That is clear enough, but what is not so clear is why at sight of us one of the rogues should instantly walk out of the room and hang himself."

"The paper!" croaked a voice behind us. The man was sitting up, blanched and ghastly, with returning reason in his eyes, and hands which rubbed nervously at the broad red band which still encircled his throat.

"The paper! Of course!" yelled Holmes, in a paroxysm of excitement. "Idiot that I was! I thought so much of our visit that the paper never entered my head for an instant. To be sure, the secret must lie there." He flattened it out on the table, and a cry of triumph burst from his lips.

"Look at this, Watson!" he cried. "It is a London
paper, an early edition of the *Evening Standard*. Here **18**
is what we want. Look at the headlines—'Crime in the City. Murder at Mawson & Williams'. Gigantic Attempted Robbery; Capture of the Criminal.' Here, Watson, we are all equally anxious to hear it, so kindly read it aloud to us."

It appeared from its position in the paper to have been the one event of importance in town, and the account of it ran in this way:

"A desperate attempt at robbery, culminating in the death of one man and the capture of the criminal, occurred this afternoon in the City. For some time back Mawson & Williams, the famous financial house, have been the guardians of securities which amount in the aggregate to a sum of considerably over a million sterling. So conscious was the manager of the responsibility which devolved upon him in consequence of the great interests at stake, that safes of the very latest construction have been employed, and an armed watchman has been left day and night in the building. It appears that last week a new clerk, named Hall Pycroft, was engaged by the firm. This person appears to have been none other than Beddington, the famous forger and cracksman, who, with his brother, has only recently emerged from a five years' spell of penal servitude. By some means, which are not yet clear, he succeeded in winning, under a false name, this official position in the office, which he utilized in order to obtain mouldings of various locks and a thorough knowledge of the position of the strong-room and the safes.

"It is customary at Mawson's for the clerks to leave at
midday on Saturday. Sergeant Tuson, of the City Police, **19**

18 *an early edition of the* Evening Standard. "If everything went well it would have been just possible to get a few quire of that [issue of the *Evening Standard*] to Birmingham by 7 P.M.," Mr. John Hyslop wrote in "Sherlock Holmes and the Press." "But it would have been by no means an early edition. It would have been the very latest. And the Birmingham *Evening Despatch*, with a much fuller story, ought to have reached the fish and chip shops by the time that London paper arrived." Mr. Hyslop also pointed out that the headline, "Capture of the criminal," "is a gross breach of journalistic ethics: . . . the man is found guilty by the newspaper before he has even appeared before a magistrate."

19 *Sergeant Tuson.* Mr. Michael Harrison has suggested (*In the Footsteps of Sherlock Holmes*) that the name "Tuson may be an echo of Watson's impecunious days; it is the name of a well-known firm of pawnbrokers with branches in London and the provinces."

was somewhat surprised therefore to see a gentleman with a carpet bag come down the steps at twenty minutes past one. His suspicions being aroused, the sergeant followed the man, and with the aid of Constable Pollock succeeded, after a most desperate resistance, in arresting him. It was at once clear that a daring and gigantic robbery had been committed. Nearly a hundred thousand pounds' worth of American railway bonds, with a large amount of scrip in other mines and companies, were discovered in the bag. On examining the premises the body of the unfortunate watchman was found doubled up and thrust into the largest of the safes, where it would not have been discovered until Monday morning had it not been for the prompt action of Sergeant Tuson. The man's skull had been shattered by a blow from a poker, delivered from behind. There could be no doubt that Beddington had obtained entrance by pretending that he had left something behind him, and having murdered the watchman, rapidly rifled the large safe, and then made off with his booty. His brother, who usually works with him, has not appeared in this job, as far as can at present be ascertained, although the police are making energetic inquiries as to his whereabouts."

"Well, we may save the police some little trouble in that direction," said Holmes, glancing at the haggard figure huddled up by the window. "Human nature is a strange mixture, Watson. You see that even a villain and a murderer can inspire such affection that his brother turns to suicide when he learns that his neck is forfeited. However, we have no choice as to our action. The doctor and I will remain on guard, Mr. Pycroft, if you will have the kindness to step out for the police."

"WELL, WE MAY SAVE THE POLICE SOME LITTLE TROUBLE IN THAT DIRECTION," SAID HOLMES . . .

Illustration by Sidney Paget for the *Strand Magazine*, March, 1893.

40

THE NAVAL TREATY

[Tuesday, July 30, to Thursday, August 1, 1889]

THE July which immediately succeeded my marriage was made memorable by three cases of 1
interest in which I had the privilege of being
associated with Sherlock Holmes, and of studying his
methods. I find them recorded in my notes under the
headings of "The Adventure of the Second Stain," 2
"The Adventure of the Naval Treaty," and "The
Adventure of the Tired Captain." The first of these, 3
however, deals with interests of such importance, and
implicates so many of the first families in the kingdom,
that for many years it will be impossible to make it
public. No case, however, in which Holmes was ever
engaged has illustrated the value of his analytical methods
so clearly or has impressed those who were associated with
him so deeply. I still retain an almost verbatim report
of the interview in which he demonstrated the true facts
of the case to Monsieur Dubuque, of the Paris police, and
Fritz von Waldbaum, the well-known specialist of Dantzig, both of whom had wasted their energies upon what
proved to be side-issues. The new century will have
come, however, before the story can be safely told.
Meanwhile, I pass on to the second upon my list, which
promised also, at one time, to be of national importance,
and was marked by several incidents which give it a
quite unique character.

During my school-days I had been intimately associated
with a lad named Percy Phelps, who was of much the
same age as myself, though he was two classes ahead of
me. He was a very brilliant boy, and carried away every
prize which the school had to offer, finishing his exploits
by winning a scholarship, which sent him on to continue
his triumphant career at Cambridge. He was, I remember, extremely well connected and even when we were all
little boys together, we knew that his mother's brother was
Lord Holdhurst, the great Conservative politician. This 4
gaudy relationship did him little good at school; on the
contrary, it seemed rather a piquant thing to us to chevy
him about the playground and hit him over the shins with
a wicket. But it was another thing when he came out 5
into the world. I heard vaguely that his abilities and the

1 *The July which immediately succeeded my marriage.* Watson's marriage to Mary Morstan, in the opinion of all chronologists. His "immediately" is taken by some as an indication that the marriage was in the spring of the year, rather than the preceding winter. The year, however, is again a matter of controversy, with supporters for 1887, 1888, and 1889.

2 *"The Adventure of the Second Stain."* Watson shortly tells us that in *this* "Adventure of the Second Stain" he retained in his notes "an almost verbatim report of the interview in which [Holmes] demonstrated the true facts of the case to Monsieur Dubuque, of the Paris police, and Fritz von Waldbaum, the well-known specialist of Dantzig, both of whom had wasted their energies in what proved to be side-issues." Now, this incident certainly did not take place in "The Adventure of the Second Stain" as recorded by Watson for the *Strand Magazine* (December, 1904) and *Collier's Weekly* (January 28, 1905). A number of distinguished commentators nevertheless maintain that the two adventures were one and the same. Mr. Anatole Chujoy, for example, in "The Only Second Stain," has written that "When Watson finally received permission from Holmes to relate 'The Adventure of the Second Stain,' he wrote it out in full, as he had promised his readers in 'The Adventure of the Naval Treaty.' He then showed the manuscript to Holmes, perhaps to check on some obscure detail. Reading the story, Holmes realized that some of the dramatis personae, or perhaps their progeny, were still alive and could be recognized. To avoid hurting them unnecessarily, after so many years or, perhaps, fearing libel action against Watson, Holmes cut the story short at the climactic moment of the return of the dangerous letter to the despatch-box and left out entirely the spy-hunt that followed it. Watson, of course, had not expected that Holmes would censor 'The Second Stain': he had never done so before. Hence the apparent discrepancy between the reference to the story in 'The Naval Treaty' and the story itself."

The late Gavin Brend, on the other hand, argued in *My Dear Holmes* that Watson's references in "The Yellow Face" and "The Adventure of the Naval Treaty" were part of a code. He noted that both were published in 1893, a year in which Holmes was believed dead by all but his brother Mycroft. To give Sherlock certain information, Mycroft Holmes drafted paragraphs which he asked Watson to incorporate in his accounts of the two cases. Sherlock, reading Watson's accounts, would then know that when the phrase "the second stain" appeared, the matter just preceding or following it was not to be taken literally.

These are ingenious explanations, indeed, but commentators who hold that the recorded adventure and "The Adventure of the Second Stain" referred to in "The Adventure of the Naval Treaty" are the same must still explain why the recorded adventure took place in the autumn, not in July, and in an autumn in which Watson was unmarried and living in Baker Street during the entire period of the adventure. Further, even Watson could hardly have forgotten that he had dated the "Second Stain" of "The Naval Treaty" quite precisely (for Watson); had that adventure and the published adventure been one and the same, it would have been pointless for him to go to such pains to conceal the date of the published adventure ("It was, then, in a year, and even in a decade, that shall be nameless . . .").

In our view, then, Watson retained notes of *three* adventures which he associated in one way or another with a "second strain": 1) the recorded adventure; 2) the "failure" mentioned in "The Yellow Face"; and 3) the adventure which took place in the July immediately following his marriage to Mary Morstan.

3 "*The Adventure of the Tired Captain.*" Mr. Alan Wilson has written a pastiche stemming from this reference of the doctor's which will be found in the *Sherlock Holmes Journal*, Vol. IV, No. 1, Winter, 1958, pp. 8–11, and Vol. IV, No. 2, Spring, 1959, pp. 48–51.

But Mr. Rolfe Boswell has held that Watson himself chronicled "The Adventure of the Tired Captain" as "The Adventure of the Missing Three-Quarter": "After all, Cyril Overton, 'the skipper of the Rugger team of Cambridge 'Varsity,' . . . *was* a captain. . . . That he was tired followed from Watson's description . . . 'haggard with anxiety.' "

4 *Lord Holdhurst, the great Conservative politician.* Mr. O. F. Grazebrook, in his *Studies in Sherlock Holmes, II: Politics and Premiers*, has identified Lord Holdhurst with Lord Salisbury, who was Prime Minister in 1888. But this ignores Watson's later comment: "The Cabinet Minister and *future* Prime Minister."

influence which he commanded had won him a good position at the Foreign Office, and then he passed completely out of my mind until the following letter recalled his existence :

6 " BRIARBRAE, WOKING.

" MY DEAR WATSON,—I have no doubt that you can remember ' Tadpole ' Phelps, who was in the fifth form when you were in the third. It is possible even that you may have heard that, through my uncle's influence, I obtained a good appointment at the Foreign Office, and that I was in a situation of trust and honour until a horrible misfortune came suddenly to blast my career.

" There is no use writing the details of that dreadful event. In the event of your acceding to my request, it is probable that I shall have to narrate them to you. I
7 have only just recovered from nine weeks of brain fever, and am still exceedingly weak. Do you think that you could bring your friend, Mr. Holmes, down to see me ? I should like to have his opinion of the case, though the authorities assure me that nothing more can be done. Do try to bring him down, and as soon as possible. Every minute seems an hour while I live in this horrible suspense. Assure him that, if I have not asked his advice sooner, it was not because I did not appreciate his talents, but because I have been off my head ever since the blow fell. Now I am clear again, though I dare not think of it too much for fear of a relapse. I am still so weak that I have to write, as you see, by dictating. Do try and bring him.

" Your old schoolfellow,
" PERCY PHELPS."

. . . WON HIM A GOOD POSITION AT THE FOREIGN OFFICE . . .

The Foreign Office, where Percy Phelps had a good position, as seen from St. James's Park. With the Home Office and the Colonial Office, it is housed in a fine quadrangle of buildings enclosed by Whitehall, Downing Street, St. James's Park, and King Charles Street. These were erected between 1868 and 1873 from the designs of Sir Gilbert Scott, in the Italian style, at a cost of £500,000.

There was something that touched me as I read this letter, something pitiable in the reiterated appeals to bring Holmes. So moved was I that, even if it had been a difficult matter, I should have tried it ; but, of course, I knew well that Holmes loved his art so, that he was ever as ready to bring his aid as his client could be to receive it. My wife agreed with me that not a moment should be lost in laying the matter before him, and so, within an hour of breakfast-time, I found myself back once more in the old rooms in Baker Street.

Holmes was seated at his side-table clad in his dressing-gown and working hard over a chemical investigation. A large curved retort was boiling furiously in the bluish flame of a Bunsen burner, and the distilled drops were condensing into a two-litre measure. My friend hardly glanced up as I entered, and I, seeing that his investigation must be of importance, seated myself in an arm-chair and waited. He dipped into this bottle or that, drawing out a few drops of each with his glass pipette, and finally brought a test-tube containing a solution over to the table. In his right hand he had a slip of litmus-paper.

" You come at a crisis, Watson," said he. " If this paper remains blue, all is well. If it turns red, it means a man's life." He dipped it into the test-tube, and it flushed at once into a dull, dirty crimson. " Hum ! I thought as much ! " he cried. " I shall be at your service in one instant, Watson. You will find tobacco in the Persian slipper." He turned to his desk and scribbled off several telegrams, which were handed over to the page-boy. Then he threw himself down in the chair opposite, and drew up his knees until his fingers clasped round his long, thin shins.

" A very commonplace little murder," said he. " You've got something better, I fancy. You are the stormy petrel of crime, Watson. What is it ? "

I handed him the letter, which he read with the most concentrated attention.

" It does not tell us very much, does it ? " he remarked, as he handed it back to me.

" Hardly anything."

" And yet the writing is of interest."

" But the writing is not his own."

" Precisely. It is a woman's."

" A man's surely ! " I cried.

" No, a woman's ; and a woman of rare character. You see, at the commencement of an investigation, it is something to know that your client is in close contact with someone who for good or evil has an exceptional nature. My interest is already awakened in the case. If you are ready, we will start at once for Woking and see this diplomatist who is in such evil case, and the lady to whom he dictates his letters."

We were fortunate enough to catch an early train at Waterloo, and in a little under an hour we found ourselves among the fir-woods and the heather of Woking. Briarbrae proved to be a large detached house standing in extensive grounds, within a few minutes' walk of the station. On sending in our cards we were shown into an elegantly appointed drawing-room, where we were joined in a few minutes by a rather stout man, who received us with much

5 *a wicket.* Watson in this sentence is guilty of two "colonialisms," pointing to his boyhood in Australia: "playground," to a youngster reared in England would be "playing field," and "wicket" would be "stump."

6 Woking. Woking lies twelve miles northeast of Aldershot and due north of Guildford, in Surrey.

7 *nine weeks of brain fever.* Joseph Harrison later says that his sister Annie had nursed Phelps "these two months back." Phelps says the treaty was stolen "Nearly ten weeks ago—to be more accurate, on the 23rd of May . . ." "Here I have lain, Mr. Holmes, over nine weeks, unconscious, and raving with brain fever. . . . It is only during the last three days that my memory has quite returned." Forbes says that "The clerk, Gorot, has been shadowed all these nine weeks . . ." Holmes says, on the first day of the case, that "nearly ten weeks have elapsed . . ." Phelps later spoke of his "ten long weeks of agony." Percy Phelps' letter to Watson could not have been delivered until Saturday, July 27th, at the very earliest. But the first day of the case was not a Saturday: Holmes called on Lord Holdhurst at the Foreign Office late in the afternoon, which would not have been open late in the afternoon on a Saturday. Much less would it have been open on a Sunday; nor could Phelps' letter have been delivered on a Sunday; nor could Holmes have advertised in the evening papers. Thus the case must have opened on one of the three days Monday, July 29th; Tuesday, July 30th; or Wednesday, July 31st.

HOLMES WAS . . . WORKING HARD OVER A CHEMICAL INVESTIGATION.

Illustration by Sidney Paget for the *Strand Magazine*, October, 1893.

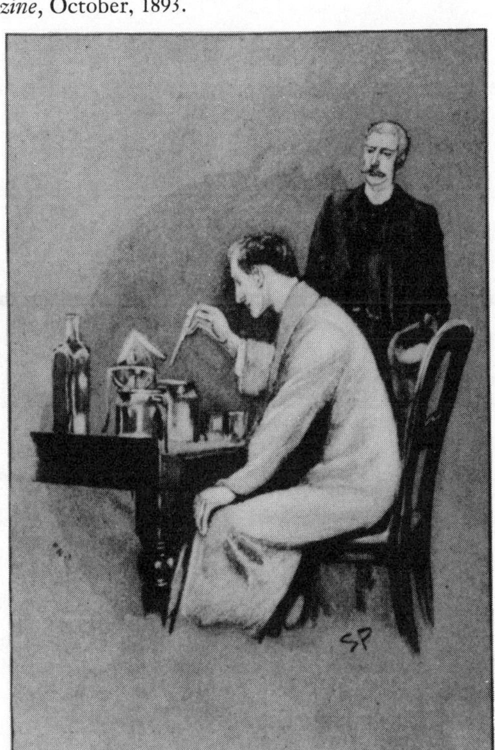

BRIARBRAE PROVED TO BE A LARGE DETACHED HOUSE STANDING IN EXTENSIVE GROUNDS . . .

"It is tempting to identify 'Briarbrae' with an existing 'large detached house, standing in extensive grounds, within a few minutes' walk of the station'—Woodham Hall, which lies just off the crossroads at Horsell Common," Mr. Michael Harrison wrote in *In the Footsteps of Sherlock Holmes.* But most commentators now consider 'Briarbrae' to have been Inchcape House (*shown above*), previously "Heatherside," Woking, now destroyed. "To enter the gate of Inchcape and Little Inchcape is to re-enter the enchanted world of 1887," Mrs. Jennifer Chorley wrote in "'Briarbrae' Revisited." "There stands the coach-house whose long-suffering horses awaited the summons to bear Holmes and Watson to the station (the journey on foot takes all of three minutes!) There, the 'side-entrance for tradespeople,' and, far off, one hears the church clock striking the quarters. . . . The 'extensive grounds' are still quite large although part of the gardens are now the site of a Presbyterian Church, and the huge clumps of rhododendrons (some 15–20 feet tall) and fir trees and a large conservatory evoke the Victorian era perfectly. The house is dated 1828 but its solid red dignity seems typically Victorian in spirit."

A YOUNG MAN, VERY PALE AND WORN, WAS LYING UPON A SOFA NEAR THE OPEN WINDOW . . .

Illustration by William H. Hyde for *Harper's Weekly*, October 14, 1893.

hospitality. His age may have been nearer forty than thirty, but his cheeks were so ruddy and his eyes so merry, that he still conveyed the impression of a plump and mischievous boy.

"I am so glad that you have come," said he, shaking our hands with effusion. "Percy has been inquiring for you all the morning. Ah, poor old chap, he clings to any straw. His father and mother asked me to see you, for the mere mention of the subject is very painful to them."

"We have had no details yet," observed Holmes. "I perceive that you are not yourself a member of the family."

Our acquaintance looked surprised, and then glancing down he began to laugh.

"Of course you saw the 'J. H.' monogram on my locket," said he. "For a moment I thought you had done something clever. Joseph Harrison is my name, and as Percy is to marry my sister Annie, I shall at least be a relation by marriage. You will find my sister in his room, for she has nursed him hand-and-foot these two months back. Perhaps we had better go in at once, for I know how impatient he is."

The chamber into which we were shown was on the same floor as the drawing-room. It was furnished partly as a sitting- and partly as a bedroom, with flowers arranged daintily in every nook and corner. A young man, very pale and worn, was lying upon a sofa near the open window, through which came the rich scent of the garden and the balmy summer air. A woman was sitting beside him, and rose as we entered.

"Shall I leave, Percy?" she asked.

He clutched her hand to detain her. "How are you, Watson?" said he, cordially. "I should never have known you under that moustache, and I daresay you would not be prepared to swear to me. This, I presume, is your celebrated friend, Mr. Sherlock Holmes?"

I introduced him in a few words, and we both sat down. The stout young man had left us, but his sister still remained, with her hand in that of the invalid. She was a striking-looking woman, a little short and thick for symmetry, but with a beautiful olive complexion, large, dark Italian eyes, and a wealth of deep black hair. Her rich tints made the white face of her companion the more worn and haggard by the contrast.

"I won't waste your time," said he, raising himself upon the sofa. "I'll plunge into the matter without further preamble. I was a happy and successful man, Mr. Holmes, and on the eve of being married, when a sudden and dreadful misfortune wrecked all my prospects in life.

"I was, as Watson may have told you, in the Foreign Office, and through the influence of my uncle, Lord Holdhurst, I rose rapidly to a responsible position. When my uncle became Foreign Minister in this Administration he gave me several missions of trust, and as I always brought them to a successful conclusion, he came at last to have the utmost confidence in my ability and tact.

"Nearly ten weeks ago—to be more accurate, on the 23rd of May—he called me into his private room and, after complimenting me upon the good work which I had done, informed me that he had a new commission of trust for me to execute.

" ' This,' said he, taking a grey roll of paper from his
bureau, ' is the original of that secret treaty between
England and Italy, of which, I regret to say, some rumours 8
have already got into the public Press. It is of enormous importance that nothing further should leak out. The French or Russian Embassies would pay an immense sum to learn the contents of these papers. They should not leave my bureau were it not that it is absolutely necessary to have them copied. You have a desk in your office ? '

" ' Yes, sir.'

" ' Then take the treaty and lock it up there. I shall
give directions that you may remain behind when the
others go, so that you may copy it at your leisure, without 9
fear of being overlooked. When you have finished, re-lock both the original and the draft in the desk, and hand them over to me personally to-morrow morning.'

"I WON'T WASTE YOUR TIME," SAID HE . . .

Illustration by Sidney Paget for the *Strand Magazine*, October, 1893.

" 'THEN TAKE THE TREATY AND LOCK IT UP THERE.' "

Illustration by Sidney Paget for the *Strand Magazine*, October, 1893.

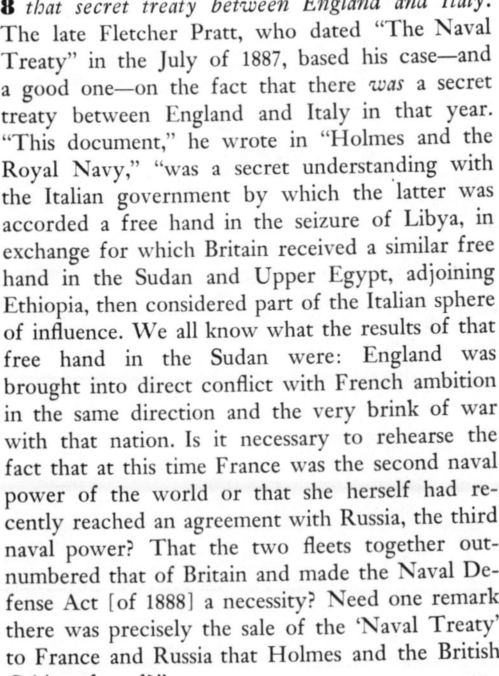

8 *that secret treaty between England and Italy.* The late Fletcher Pratt, who dated "The Naval Treaty" in the July of 1887, based his case—and a good one—on the fact that there *was* a secret treaty between England and Italy in that year. "This document," he wrote in "Holmes and the Royal Navy," "was a secret understanding with the Italian government by which the latter was accorded a free hand in the seizure of Libya, in exchange for which Britain received a similar free hand in the Sudan and Upper Egypt, adjoining Ethiopia, then considered part of the Italian sphere of influence. We all know what the results of that free hand in the Sudan were: England was brought into direct conflict with French ambition in the same direction and the very brink of war with that nation. Is it necessary to rehearse the fact that at this time France was the second naval power of the world or that she herself had recently reached an agreement with Russia, the third naval power? That the two fleets together outnumbered that of Britain and made the Naval Defense Act [of 1888] a necessity? Need one remark there was precisely the sale of the 'Naval Treaty' to France and Russia that Holmes and the British Cabinet feared?"

9 *so that you may copy it at your leisure.* In an unpublished paper, "We Ask the Questions!", Mr. Thomas L. Stix has asked why should not the British Foreign Office have had duplicating machines. "True, the photostatic process had not been invented, but the railroad duplicator was in general use in 1880. It was not a cumbersome machine. It was moderately priced and it was used to insure accuracy and speed, certainly better by far than a hand-made copy by a sleepy subordinate. The French tissue copy was also available, but took more time. . . ."

10 *the Triple Alliance.* The secret Dual Alliance of Germany and Austria-Hungary, formed in 1879, was joined in 1882 by Italy and thus became the Triple Alliance.

" I took the papers and——"

" Excuse me an instant," said Holmes ; " were you alone during this conversation ? "

" Absolutely."

" In a large room ? "

" Thirty feet each way."

" In the centre ? "

" Yes, about it."

" And speaking low ? "

" My uncle's voice is always remarkably low. I hardly spoke at all."

" Thank you," said Holmes, shutting his eyes ; " pray go on."

" I did exactly what he had indicated, and waited until the other clerks had departed. One of them in my room, Charles Gorot, had some arrears of work to make up, so I left him there and went out to dine. When I returned he was gone. I was anxious to hurry my work, for I knew that Joseph, the Mr. Harrison whom you saw just now, was in town, and that he would travel down to Woking by the eleven o'clock train, and I wanted if possible to catch it.

" When I came to examine the treaty I saw at once that it was of such importance that my uncle had been guilty of no exaggeration in what he had said. Without going into details, I may say that it defined the position
10 of Great Britain towards the Triple Alliance, and foreshadowed the policy which this country would pursue in the event of the French fleet gaining a complete ascendency over that of Italy in the Mediterranean. The questions treated in it were purely naval. At the end were the signatures of the high dignitaries who had signed it. I glanced my eyes over it, and then settled down to my task of copying.

" It was a long document, written in the French language, and containing twenty-six separate articles. I copied as quickly as I could, but at nine o'clock I had only done nine articles, and it seemed hopeless for me to attempt to catch my train. I was feeling drowsy and stupid, partly from my dinner and also from the effects of a long day's work. A cup of coffee would clear my brain. A commissionaire remains all night in a little lodge at the foot of the stairs, and is in the habit of making coffee at his spirit-lamp for any of the officials who may be working overtime. I rang the bell, therefore, to summon him.

" To my surprise, it was a woman who answered the summons, a large, coarse-faced, elderly woman, in an apron. She explained that she was the commissionaire's wife, who did the charing, and I gave her the order for the coffee.

" I wrote two more articles, and then, feeling more drowsy than ever, I rose and walked up and down the room to stretch my legs. My coffee had not yet come, and I wondered what the cause of the delay could be. Opening the door, I started down the corridor to find out. There was a straight passage dimly lit which led from the room in which I had been working, and was the only exit from it. It ended in a curving staircase, with the commissionaire's lodge in the passage at the bottom. Halfway down this staircase is a small landing, with another passage running into it at right angles. The second one leads, by means of a second small stair, to a side-door used by servants, and also as a short cut by clerks when coming from Charles Street.

" Here is a rough chart of the place."

" Thank you. I think that I quite follow you," said Sherlock Holmes.

" It is of the utmost importance that you should notice this point. I went down the stairs and into the hall, where I found the commissionaire fast asleep in his box, with the kettle boiling furiously upon the spirit-lamp, for the water was spurting over the floor. I had put out my hand and was about to shake the man, who was still sleeping soundly, when a bell over his head rang loudly, and he woke with a start.

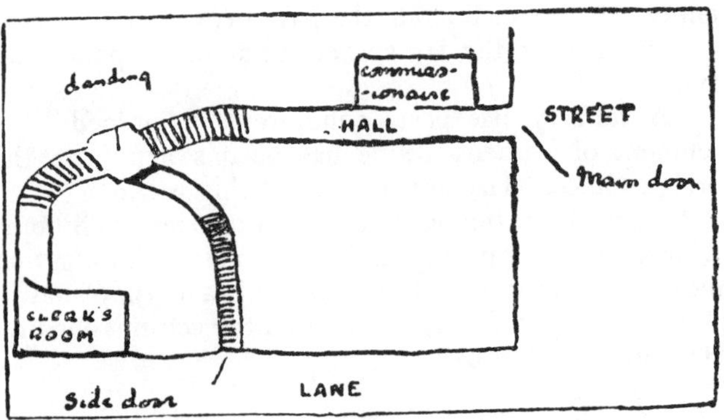

" HERE IS A ROUGH CHART OF THE PLACE."

" ' Mr. Phelps, sir ! ' said he, looking at me in bewilderment.

" ' I came down to see if my coffee was ready.'

" ' I was boiling the kettle when I fell asleep, sir.' He looked at me and then up at the still quivering bell, with an ever-growing astonishment upon his face.

" ' If you was here, sir, then who rang the bell ? ' he asked.

" ' The bell ! ' I said. ' What bell is it ? '

" ' It's the bell of the room you were working in.'

" A cold hand seemed to close round my heart. Someone, then, was in that room where my precious treaty lay upon the table. I ran frantically up the stairs and along the passage. There was no one in the corridor, Mr. Holmes. There was no one in the room. All was exactly as I left it, save only that the papers committed to my care had been taken from the desk on which they lay. The copy was there and the original was gone."

Holmes sat up in his chair and rubbed his hands. I could see that the problem was entirely to his heart. " Pray, what did you do then ? " he murmured.

" I recognized in an instant that the thief must have come up the stairs from the side-door. Of course I must have met him if he had come the other way."

" You were satisfied that he could not have been concealed in the room all the time, or in the corridor which you have just described as dimly lighted ? "

" It is absolutely impossible. A rat could not conceal

". . . I FOUND THE COMMISSIONAIRE FAST ASLEEP IN HIS BOX . . ."

Illustration by Sidney Paget for the *Strand Magazine*, October, 1893.

". . . THE PAPERS COMMITTED TO MY CARE HAD BEEN TAKEN FROM THE DESK . . ."

Illustration by William H. Hyde for *Harper's Weekly*, October 14, 1893.

himself either in the room or the corridor. There is no cover at all."

"Thank you. Pray proceed."

"The commissionaire, seeing by my pale face that something was to be feared, had followed me upstairs. Now we both rushed along the corridor and down the steep steps which led to Charles Street. The door at the bottom was closed but unlocked. We flung it open and rushed out. I can distinctly remember that as we did so there came three chimes from a neighbouring church. It was a quarter to ten."

11 "That is of enormous importance," said Holmes, making a note upon his shirt cuff.

"The night was very dark, and a thin, warm rain was
12 falling. There was no one in Charles Street, but a great traffic was going on, as usual, in Whitehall, at the extremity. We rushed along the pavement, bareheaded as we were, and at the far corner we found a policeman standing.

"'A robbery has been committed,' I gasped. 'A document of immense value has been stolen from the Foreign Office. Has anyone passed this way?'

"'I have been standing here for a quarter of an hour, sir,' said he; 'only one person has passed during that time—a woman, tall and elderly, with a Paisley shawl.'

"'Ah, that is only my wife,' cried the commissionaire. Has no one else passed?'

"'No one.'

"'Then it must be the other way that the thief took,' cried the fellow, tugging at my sleeve.

"But I was not satisfied, and the attempts which he made to draw me away increased my suspicions.

"'Which way did the woman go?' I cried.

"'I don't know, sir. I noticed her pass, but I had no special reason for watching her. She seemed to be in a hurry.'

"'How long ago was it?'

"'Oh, not very many minutes.'

"'Within the last five?'

"'Well, it could not be more than five.'

"'You're only wasting your time, sir, and every minute now is of importance,' cried the commissionaire. 'Take my word for it that my old woman has nothing to do with it, and come down to the other end of the street. Well, if you won't, I will,' and with that he rushed off in the other direction.

"But I was after him in an instant and caught him by the sleeve.

"'Where do you live?' said I.

"'No. 16 Ivy Lane, Brixton,' he answered; 'but don't let yourself be drawn away upon a false scent, Mr. Phelps. Come to the other end of the street, and let us see if we can hear of anything.'

"Nothing was to be lost by following his advice. With the policeman we both hurried down, but only to find the street full of traffic, many people coming and going, but all only too eager to get to a place of safety upon so wet a night. There was no lounger who could tell us who had passed.

11 *"That is of enormous importance," said Holmes.* "What is of importance here," Mr. Michael Harrison wrote (*In the Footsteps of Sherlock Holmes*), "is that the nearest church to Charles Street, Whitehall, is St. Margaret's Westminster, adjoining Westminster Abbey. Both St. Margaret's and the Abbey's clock chime; but only a few yards away from the two is Big Ben, whose chime drowns all lesser chimes for a good half-mile around. It is extraordinary not only that Phelps should have mentioned the chiming of 'a neighbourhood church' when Big Ben was practically overhead, but that Holmes should not have remarked upon this."

12 *"The night was very dark, and a thin, warm rain was falling.* "'The July which immediately succeeded my marriage' was in 1889," the late Professor Jay Finley Christ wrote (*An Irregular Chronology*) "and the treaty was stolen on the rainy evening of May 23rd. The latter was a Tuesday, and a .19 inch rain fell on that date."

" Then we returned to the office, and searched the stairs and the passage without result. The corridor which led to the room was laid down with a kind of creamy linoleum, which shows an impression very easily. We examined it very carefully, but found no outline of any footmark."

" Had it been raining all the evening ? "

" Since about seven."

" How is it, then, that the woman who came into the room about nine left no traces with her muddy boots ? "

" I am glad you raise the point. It occurred to me at the time. The charwomen are in the habit of taking off their boots at the commissionaire's office, and putting on list slippers." 13

" That is very clear. There were no marks, then, though the night was a wet one ? The chain of events is certainly one of extraordinary interest. What did you do next ? "

" We examined the room also. There was no possibility of a secret door, and the windows are quite thirty feet from the ground. Both of them were fastened on the inside. The carpet prevents any possibility of a trap-door, and the ceiling is of the ordinary whitewashed kind. I will pledge my life that whoever stole my papers could only have come through the door."

" How about the fireplace ? "

" They use none. There is a stove. The bell-rope hangs from the wire just to the right of my desk. Whoever rang it must have come right up to the desk to do it. But why should any criminal wish to ring the bell ? It is a most insoluble mystery."

" Certainly the incident was unusual. What were your next steps ? You examined the room, I presume, to see if the intruder had left any traces—any cigar-end, or dropped glove, or hairpin, or other trifle ? "

" There was nothing of the sort."

" No smell ? "

" Well, we never thought of that."

" Ah, a scent of tobacco would have been worth a great deal to us in such an investigation."

" I never smoke myself, so I think I should have observed it if there had been any smell of tobacco. There was absolutely no clue of any kind. The only tangible fact was that the commissionaire's wife—Mrs. Tangey was the name—had hurried out of the place. He could give no explanation save that it was about the time when the woman always went home. The policeman and I agreed that our best plan would be to seize the woman before she could get rid of the papers, presuming that she had them.

" The alarm had reached Scotland Yard by this time, and Mr. Forbes, the detective, came round at once and took up the case with a great deal of energy. We hired a hansom, and in half an hour we were at the address which had been given to us. A young woman opened the door, who proved to be Mrs. Tangey's eldest daughter. Her mother had not come back yet, and we were shown into the front room to wait.

" About ten minutes later a knock came at the door, and here we made the one serious mistake for which I

13 *list slippers.*" Slippers made of list, a kind of textile.

blame myself. Instead of opening the door ourselves we allowed the girl to do so. We heard her say, 'Mother, there are two men in the house waiting to see you,' and an instant afterwards we heard the patter of feet rushing down the passage. Forbes flung open the door, and we both ran into the back room or kitchen, but the woman had got there before us. She stared at us with defiant eyes, and then suddenly recognizing me, an expression of absolute astonishment came over her face.

" 'Why, if it isn't Mr. Phelps, of the office ! ' she cried.

" 'Come, come, who did you think we were when you ran away from us ? ' asked my companion.

14 " 'I thought you were the brokers,' said she. 'We've had some trouble with a tradesman.'

" 'That's not quite good enough,' answered Forbes. 'We have reason to believe that you have taken a paper of importance from the Foreign Office, and that you ran in here to dispose of it. You must come back with us to Scotland Yard to be searched.'

" It was in vain that she protested and resisted. A four-wheeler was brought, and we all three drove back in it. We had first made an examination of the kitchen, and especially of the kitchen fire, to see whether she might have made away with the papers during the instant that she was alone. There were no signs, however, of any ashes or scraps. When we reached Scotland Yard she was handed over at once to the female searcher. I waited in an agony of suspense until she came back with her report. There were no signs of the papers.

" Then, for the first time, the horror of my situation came in its full force upon me. Hitherto I had been acting, and action had numbed thought. I had been so confident of regaining the treaty at once that I had not dared to think of what would be the consequence if I failed to do so. But now there was nothing more to be done, and I had leisure to realize my position. It was horrible ! Watson there would tell you that I was a nervous, sensitive boy at school. It is my nature. I thought of my uncle and of his colleagues in the Cabinet, of the shame which I had brought upon him, upon myself, upon everyone connected with me. What though I was the victim of an extraordinary accident ? No allowance is made for accidents where diplomatic interests are at stake. I was ruined ; shamefully, hopelessly ruined. I don't know what I did. I fancy I must have made a scene. I have a dim recollection of a group of officials who crowded round me endeavouring to soothe me. One of them drove down with me to Waterloo and saw me into the Woking train. I believe that he would have come all the way had it not been that Dr. Ferrier, who lives near me, was going down by that very train. The doctor most kindly took charge of me, and it was well he did so, for I had a fit in the station, and before we reached home I was practically a raving maniac.

" You can imagine the state of things here when they were roused from their beds by the doctor's ringing, and found me in this condition. Poor Annie here and my mother were broken-hearted. Dr. Ferrier had just heard enough from the detective at the station to be able to

14 *the brokers.*' Persons licensed to appraise and sell furniture distrained for nonpayment of rent; bailiffs.

" 'WHY, IF IT ISN'T MR. PHELPS, OF THE OFFICE!" SHE CRIED.

Illustration by Sidney Paget for the *Strand Magazine*, October, 1893.

give an idea of what had happened, and his story did not mend matters. It was evident to all that I was in for a long illness, so Joseph was bundled out of this cheery bedroom, and it was turned into a sick-room for me. Here I have lain, Mr. Holmes, for over nine weeks, unconscious, and raving with brain fever. If it had not been for Miss Harrison here and for the doctor's care I should not be speaking to you now. She has nursed me by day, and a hired nurse has looked after me by night, for in my mad fits I was capable of anything. Slowly my reason has cleared, but it is only during the last three days that my memory has quite returned. Sometimes I wish that it never had. The first thing I did was to wire to Mr. Forbes, who had the case in hand. He came out and assured me that, though everything has been done, no trace of a clue has been discovered. The commissionaire and his wife have been examined in every way without any light being thrown upon the matter. The suspicions of the police then rested upon young Gorot, who, as you may remember, stayed overtime in the office that night. His remaining behind and his French name were really the only two points which could suggest suspicion ; but as a matter of fact, I did not begin work
until he had gone, and his people are of Huguenot extrac- **15**
tion, but as English in sympathy and tradition as you and I are. Nothing was found to implicate him in any way, and there the matter dropped. I turn to you, Mr. Holmes, as absolutely my last hope. If you fail me, then my honour as well as my position are for ever forfeited."

The invalid sank back upon his cushions, tired out by this long recital, while his nurse poured him out a glass of some stimulating medicine. Holmes sat silently with his head thrown back and his eyes closed in an attitude which might seem listless to a stranger, but which I knew betokened the most intense absorption.

" Your statement has been so explicit," said he at last, " that you have really left me very few questions to ask. There is one of the very utmost importance, however. Did you tell anyone that you had this special task to perform ? "

" No one."

" Not Miss Harrison here, for example ? "

" No. I had not been back to Woking between getting the order and executing the commission."

" And none of your people had by chance been to see you ? "

" None."

" Did any of them know their way about in the office ? "

" Oh, yes ; all of them had been shown over it."

" Still, of course, if you said nothing to anyone about the treaty, these inquiries are irrelevant."

" I said nothing."

" Do you know anything of the commissionaire ? "

" Nothing, except that he is an old soldier."

" What regiment ? "

" Oh, I have heard—Coldstream Guards." **16**

" Thank you. I have no doubt I can get details from Forbes. The authorities are excellent at amassing facts,

15 *Huguenot.* The Huguenots are the Calvinist Protestants of France. When the Edict of Nantes, which gave them complete toleration, was revoked in 1685, countless Huguenots fled to England (and to Holland, Germany, Switzerland, and America) where they contributed substantially to civic and industrial life.

16 *Coldstream Guards.*" "Watson, anxious to establish the good character of his man, assigns him to one of the most famous regiments in the whole British army," Mrs. Crighton Sellars wrote in "Dr. Watson and the British Army." "The Coldstreams ('Coalies'), now of the Household Brigade, were the fighting regiment of General Monk, which marched with him into London on February 2, 1660, to end the sway of the Roundheads and herald the return of the Monarchy."

though they do not always use them to advantage. What a lovely thing a rose is ! "

He walked past the couch to the open window, and held up the drooping stalk of a moss rose, looking down at the dainty blend of crimson and green. It was a new phase of his character to me, for I had never before seen him show any keen interest in natural objects.

" There is nothing in which deduction is so necessary as in religion," said he, leaning with his back against the shutters. " It can be built up as an exact science by the reasoner. Our highest assurance of the goodness of Providence seems to me to rest in the flowers. All other things, our powers, our desires, our food, are really necessary for our existence in the first instance. But this rose is an extra. Its smell and its colour are an embellishment of life, not a condition of it. It is only goodness which
17 gives extras, and so I say again that we have much to
18 hope from the flowers."

Percy Phelps and his nurse looked at Holmes during this demonstration with surprise and a good deal of disappointment written upon their faces. He had fallen into a reverie, with the moss rose between his fingers. It had lasted some minutes before the young lady broke in upon it.

" Do you see any prospect of solving this mystery, Mr. Holmes ? " she asked, with a touch of asperity in her voice.

" Oh, the mystery ! " he answered, coming back with a start to the realities of life. " Well, it would be absurd to deny that the case is a very abstruse and complicated one ; but I can promise you that I will look into the matter and let you know any points which may strike me."

" Do you see any clue ? "

" You have furnished me with seven, but of course I must test them before I can pronounce upon their value."

" You suspect someone ? "

" I suspect myself——"

" What ? "

" Of coming to conclusions too rapidly."

" Then go to London and test your conclusions."

" Your advice is very excellent, Miss Harrison," said Holmes, rising. " I think, Watson, we cannot do better. Do not allow yourself to indulge in false hopes, Mr. Phelps. The affair is a very tangled one."

" I shall be in a fever until I see you again," cried the diplomatist.

" Well, I'll come out by the same train to-morrow, though it's more than likely that my report will be a negative one."

" God bless you for promising to come," cried our client. " It gives me fresh life to know that something is being done. By the way, I have had a letter from Lord Holdhurst."

" Ha ! What did he say ? "

" He was cold, but not harsh. I dare say my severe illness prevented him from being that. He repeated that the matter was of the utmost importance, and added that no steps would be taken about my future—by which he means, of course, my dismissal—until my health was restored and I had an opportunity of repairing my misfortune."

17 *It is only goodness which gives extras.* Holmes "ignores the elementary fact, for students of natural history, that colour and scent are not 'extras' in blossoms," Mr. Vernon Rendall wrote in "The Limitations of Sherlock Holmes." "They are designed to attract the insects which fertilize them and so help produce the seed. Alone among great men, Ruskin adopted a similar standpoint when he noticed flowers—he was too pure to think of seed."

18 *we have much to hope from the flowers."* This is the only passage in the long Saga in which Holmes speaks forthrightly of religion. Compare Matthew 6:28, 29: "Consider the lilies of the field, how they grow; they toil not, neither do they spin. And yet I say unto you, That even Solomon in all his glory was not arrayed like one of these."

"WHAT A LOVELY THING A ROSE IS!"

Illustration by Sidney Paget for the *Strand Magazine*, October, 1893.

"Well, that was reasonable and considerate," said Holmes. "Come, Watson, for we have a good day's work before us in town."

Mr. Joseph Harrison drove us down to the station, and we were soon whirling up in a Portsmouth train. Holmes was sunk in profound thought, and hardly opened his mouth until we had passed Clapham Junction.

"It's a very cheering thing to come into London by any of these lines which run high and allow you to look down upon the houses like this."

I thought he was joking, for the view was sordid enough, but he soon explained himself.

"Look at those big, isolated clumps of buildings rising up above the slates, like brick islands in a lead-coloured sea."

"The Board schools."

"Lighthouses, my boy! Beacons of the future! Capsules, with hundreds of bright little seeds in each, out of which will spring the wiser, better England of
the future. I suppose that man Phelps does not drink?" **19**

"I should not think so."

"Nor should I. But we are bound to take every possibility into account. The poor devil has certainly got himself into very deep water, and it's a question whether we shall ever be able to get him ashore. What did you think of Miss Harrison?"

"A girl of strong character."

"Yes, but she is a good sort, or I am mistaken. She and
her brother are the only children of an ironmaster somewhere up Northumberland way. Phelps got engaged to **20**
her when travelling last winter, and she came down to be introduced to his people, with her brother as escort. Then came the smash, and she stayed on to nurse her lover, while brother Joseph, finding himself pretty snug, stayed on too. I've been making a few independent inquiries,
you see. But to-day must be a day of inquiries." **21**

"My practice——" I began.

"Oh, if you find your own cases more interesting than mine——" said Holmes, with some asperity.

"I was going to say that my practice could get along very well for a day or two, since it is the slackest time in the year."

"Excellent," said he, recovering his good humour. "Then we'll look into this matter together. I think that we should begin by seeing Forbes. He can probably tell us all the details we want, until we know from what side the case is to be approached."

"You said you had a clue."

"Well, we have several, but we can only test their value by further inquiry. The most difficult crime to track is the one which is purposeless. Now, this is not
purposeless. Who is it that profits by it? There is the **22**
French Ambassador, there is the Russian, there is whoever might sell it to either of these, and there is Lord Holdhurst."

"Lord Holdhurst!"

"Well, it is just conceivable that a statesman might find himself in a position where he was not sorry to have such a document accidentally destroyed."

19 *the wiser, better England of the future.* "It would be difficult to find a more concise expression of the confident aspirations of late Victorian Liberalism," Mr. S. C. Roberts wrote in "The Personality of Sherlock Holmes." "Fundamentally, there can be no doubt that Holmes believed in democracy and progress."

20 *Northumberland.* A border county in the north of England—one with a rugged coastline, high moorlands, and fertile valleys in the interior.

21 *I've been making a few independent inquiries, you see.* But, as Mr. Guy Warrack rightly asked ("Passed to You, Admiralty Intelligence"), "from whom and, above all, *when?*"

22 *Who is it that profits by it?* "For many centuries," Mr. Morris Rosenblum wrote in "Some Latin Byways in the Canon," "the Latin original of that query ["*Cui bono?*"] has been a pitfall for those who had little Latin and those who had not a little. [They constantly translated it in the sense of 'What good is it?" "To what end does it serve?" —but its real meaning is "Who gains by it?" "To whom is it an advantage?"] . . . Holmes applied the phrase correctly, not only because of his thorough comprehension of ancient and medieval Latin, but also because of his encyclopedic knowledge of crime. He had met the phrase in the works of Cicero, especially in the oration *Pro Roscio Amerino*, a defense plea in a murder case of a type dear to the Holmesian heart."

. . . THE VIEW WAS SORDID ENOUGH . . .

Illustration by Sidney Paget for the *Strand Magazine*, October, 1893.

"I'VE HEARD OF YOUR METHODS BEFORE NOW, MR. HOLMES," SAID HE TARTLY.

Illustration by Sidney Paget for the *Strand Magazine*, October, 1893.

" Not a statesman with the honourable record of Lord Holdhurst."

" It is a possibility, and we cannot afford to disregard it. We shall see the noble lord to-day, and find out if he can tell us anything. Meanwhile, I have already set inquiries upon foot."

" Already ? "

" Yes, I sent wires from Woking station to every evening paper in London. This advertisement will appear in each of them."

He handed over a sheet torn from the notebook. On it was scribbled in pencil :

" £10 Reward.—The number of the cab which dropped a fare at or about the door of the Foreign Office in Charles Street, at a quarter to ten in the evening of May 23rd. Apply 221B Baker Street."

" You are confident that the thief came in a cab ? "

" If not, there is no harm done. But if Mr. Phelps is correct in stating that there is no hiding-place either in the room or the corridors, then the person must have come from outside. If he came from outside on so wet a night, and yet left no trace of damp upon the linoleum, which was examined within a few minutes of his passing, then it is exceedingly probable that he came in a cab. Yes, I think that we may safely deduce a cab."

" It sounds plausible."

" That is one of the clues of which I spoke. It may lead us to something. And then, of course, there is the bell—which is the most distinctive feature of the case. Why should the bell ring ? Was it the thief that did it out of bravado ? Or was it someone who was with the thief who did it in order to prevent the crime ? Or was it an accident ? Or was it—— ? " He sank back into the state of intense and silent thought from which he had emerged, but it seemed to me, accustomed as I was to his every mood, that some new possibility had dawned suddenly upon him.

It was twenty-past three when we reached our terminus, and after a hasty luncheon at the buffet we pushed on at once to Scotland Yard. Holmes had already wired to Forbes, and we found him waiting to receive us : a small, foxy man, with a sharp but by no means amiable expression. He was decidedly frigid in his manner to us, especially when he heard the errand upon which we had come.

" I've heard of your methods before now, Mr. Holmes," said he, tartly. " You are ready enough to use all the information that the police can lay at your disposal, and then you try to finish the case yourself and bring discredit upon them."

" On the contrary," said Holmes ; " out of my last fifty-three cases my name has only appeared in four, and the police have had all the credit in forty-nine. I don't blame you for not knowing this ; for you are young and inexperienced ; but if you wished to get on in your new duties you will work with me, and not against me."

" I'd be very glad of a hint or two," said the detective, changing his manner. " I've certainly had no credit from the case so far."

" What steps have you taken ? "

" Tangey, the commissionaire, has been shadowed. He left the Guards with a good character, and we can find nothing against him. His wife is a bad lot, though. I fancy she knows more about this than appears."

" Have you shadowed her ? "

" We have set one of our women on to her. Mrs. Tangey drinks, and our woman has been with her twice when she was well on, but she could get nothing out of her."

" I understand that they have had brokers in the house ? "

" Yes, but they were paid off."

" Where did the money come from ? "

" That was all right. His pension was due ; they have not shown any sign of being in funds."

" What explanation did she give of having answered the bell when Mr. Phelps rang for the coffee ? "

" She said that her husband was very tired and she wished to relieve him."

" Well, certainly that would agree with his being found, a little later, asleep in his chair. There is nothing against them, then, but the woman's character. Did you ask her why she hurried away that night ? Her haste attracted the attention of the police-constable."

" She was later than usual, and wanted to get home."

" Did you point out to her that you and Mr. Phelps, who started at least twenty minutes after her, got there before her ? "

" She explains that by the difference between a 'bus and a hansom."

" Did she make it clear why, on reaching her house, she ran into the back kitchen ? "

" Because she had the money there with which to pay off the brokers."

" She has at least an answer for everything. Did you ask her whether in leaving she met anyone or saw anyone loitering about Charles Street ? "

" She saw no one but the constable."

" Well, you seem to have cross-examined her pretty thoroughly. What else have you done ? "

" The clerk, Gorot, has been shadowed all these nine weeks, but without result. We can show nothing against him."

" Anything else ? "

" Well, we have nothing else to go upon—no evidence of any kind."

" Have you formed any theory about how that bell rang ? "

" Well, I must confess that it beats me. It was a cool hand, whoever it was, to go and give the alarm like that."

" Yes, it was a queer thing to do. Many thanks to you for what you have told me. If I can put the man into your hands you shall hear from me. Come along, Watson ! "

" Where are we going to now ? " I asked, as we left the office.

" We are now going to interview Lord Holdhurst, the Cabinet Minister and future Premier of England."

We were fortunate in finding that Lord Holdhurst was
23 still in his chambers at Downing Street, and on Holmes sending in his card we were instantly shown up. The statesman received us with that old-fashioned courtesy for which he is remarkable, and seated us on the two luxurious easy chairs on either side of the fireplace. Standing on the rug between us, with his slight, tall figure, his sharp-featured, thoughtful face, and his curling hair prematurely tinged with grey, he seemed to represent that not too common type, a nobleman who is in truth noble.

" Your name is very familiar to me, Mr. Holmes," said he, smiling. " And, of course, I cannot pretend to be ignorant of the object of your visit. There has only been one occurrence in these offices which could call for your attention. In whose interest are you acting, may I ask ? "

" In that of Mr. Percy Phelps," answered Holmes.

" Ah, my unfortunate nephew ! You can understand that our kinship makes it the more impossible for me to screen him in any way. I fear that the incident must have a very prejudicial effect upon his career."

" But if the document is found ? "

" Ah, that, of course, would be different."

" I had one or two questions which I wished to ask you, Lord Holdhurst."

" I shall be happy to give you any information in my power."

" Was it in this room that you gave your instructions as to the copying of the document ? "

" It was."

" Then you could hardly have been overheard ? "

" It is out of the question."

" Did you ever mention to anyone that it was your intention to give out the treaty to be copied ? "

" Never."

" You are certain of that ? "

" Absolutely."

" Well, since you never said so, and Mr. Phelps never said so, and nobody else knew anything of the matter, then the thief's presence in the room was purely accidental. He saw his chance and he took it."

The statesman smiled. " You take me out of my province there," said he.

Holmes considered for a moment. " There is another very important point which I wish to discuss with you," said he. " You feared, as I understand, that very grave results might follow from the details of this treaty becoming known ? "

A shadow passed over the expressive face of the statesman. " Very grave results, indeed."

" And have they occurred ? "

" Not yet."

" If the treaty had reached, let us say, the French or Russian Foreign Office, you would expect to hear of it ? "

" I should," said Lord Holdhurst, with a wry face.

" Since nearly ten weeks have elapsed, then, and nothing has been heard, it is not unfair to suppose that for some reason the treaty has not reached them ? "

23 *Downing Street.* "There is a fascination in the air of this little cul-de-sac," Theodore Hook wrote; "an hour's inhalation of its atmosphere affects some men with giddiness, others with blindness, and very frequently with the most obvious boastfulness." Named for Sir George Downing, Secretary of State in 1668, Downing Street is today known the world over for No. 10, the official residence of the British Prime Minister.

STANDING ON THE RUG BETWEEN US, . . . HE SEEMED TO REPRESENT THAT NOT TOO COMMON TYPE, A NOBLEMAN WHO IS IN TRUTH NOBLE.

Illustration by William H. Hyde for *Harper's Weekly*, October 21, 1893. Sidney Paget illustrated the same scene for the *Strand Magazine*, November, 1893.

Lord Holdhurst shrugged his shoulders.

"We can hardly suppose, Mr. Holmes, that the thief took the treaty in order to frame it and hang it up."

"Perhaps he is waiting for a better price."

"If he waits a little longer he will get no price at all. The treaty will cease to be a secret in a few months."

"That is most important," said Holmes. "Of course it is a possible supposition that the thief has had a sudden illness——"

"An attack of brain fever, for example?" asked the statesman, flashing a swift glance at him.

"I did not say so," said Holmes, imperturbably. "And now, Lord Holdhurst, we have already taken up too much of your valuable time, and we shall wish you good day."

"Every success to your investigation, be the criminal who it may," answered the nobleman, as he bowed us out at the door.

"He's a fine fellow," said Holmes, as we came out into Whitehall. "But he has a struggle to keep up his position. He is far from rich, and has many calls. You noticed, of course, that his boots had been re-soled? Now, Watson, I won't detain you from your legitimate work any longer. I shall do nothing more to-day, unless I have an answer to my cab advertisement. But I should be extremely obliged to you if you would come down with me to Woking to-morrow, by the same train which we took to-day."

I met him accordingly next morning, and we travelled down to Woking together. He had had no answer to his advertisement, he said, and no fresh light had been thrown upon the case. He had, when he so willed it, the utter immobility of countenance of a Red Indian, and I could not gather from his appearance whether he was satisfied or not with the position of the case. His conversation, I remember, was about the Bertillon system of measurements, and he expressed his enthusiastic admiration of the French savant.

We found our client still under the charge of his devoted nurse, but looking considerably better than before. He rose from the sofa and greeted us without difficulty when we entered.

"Any news?" he asked, eagerly.

"My report, as I expected, is a negative one," said Holmes. "I have seen Forbes, and I have seen your uncle, and I have set one or two trains of inquiry upon foot which may lead to something."

"You have not lost heart, then?"

"By no means."

"God bless you for saying that!" cried Miss Harrison. "If we keep our courage and our patience, the truth must come out."

"We have more to tell you than you have for us," said Phelps, re-seating himself upon the couch.

"I hoped you might have something."

"Yes, we have had an adventure during the night, and one which might have proved to be a serious one." His expression grew very grave as he spoke, and a look of something akin to fear sprang up in his eyes. "Do you

"ANY NEWS?" HE ASKED, EAGERLY.

Illustration by Sidney Paget for the *Strand Magazine*, November, 1893.

know," said he, "that I begin to believe that I am the unconscious centre of some monstrous conspiracy, and that my life is aimed at as well as my honour?"

"Ah!" cried Holmes.

"It sounds incredible, for I have not, as far as I know, an enemy in the world. Yet from last night's experience I can come to no other conclusion."

"Pray let me hear it."

"You must know that last night was the very first night that I have ever slept without a nurse in the room. I was so much better that I thought I could dispense with one. I had a night-light burning, however. Well, about two in the morning I had sunk into a light sleep, when I was suddenly aroused by a slight noise. It was like the sound which a mouse makes when it is gnawing a plank, and I lay listening to it for some time under the impression that it must come from that cause. Then it grew louder, and suddenly there came from the window a sharp metallic snick. I sat up in amazement. There could be no doubt what the sounds were now. The faint ones had been caused by someone forcing an instrument through the slit between the sashes, and the second by the catch being pressed back.

"There was a pause then for about ten minutes, as if the person were waiting to see whether the noise had awoken me. Then I heard a gentle creaking as the window was very slowly opened. I could stand it no longer, for my nerves are not what they used to be. I sprang out of bed and flung open the shutters. A man was crouching at the window. I could see little of him, for he was gone like a flash. He was wrapped in some sort of cloak, which came across the lower part of his face. One thing only I am sure of, and that is that he had some weapon in his hand. It looked to me like a long knife. I distinctly saw the gleam of it as he turned to run."

"This is most interesting," said Holmes. "Pray, what did you do then?"

"I should have followed him through the open window if I had been stronger. As it was, I rang the bell and roused the house. It took me some little time, for the bell rings in the kitchen, and the servants all sleep upstairs. I shouted, however, and that brought Joseph down, and he roused the others. Joseph and the groom found marks on the flower-bed outside the window, but the weather has been so dry lately that they found it hopeless to follow the trail across the grass. There's a place, however, on the wooden fence which skirts the road which shows signs, they tell me, as if someone had got over and had snapped the top of the rail in doing so. I have said nothing to the local police yet, for I thought I had best have your opinion first."

This tale of our client's appeared to have an extraordinary effect upon Sherlock Holmes. He rose from his chair and paced about the room in uncontrollable excitement.

"Misfortunes never come singly," said Phelps, smiling, though it was evident that his adventure had somewhat shaken him.

"You have certainly had your share," said Holmes.

" Do you think you could walk round the house with me ? "

" Oh, yes, I should like a little sunshine. Joseph will **24**
come too."

" And I also," said Miss Harrison.

" I am afraid not," said Holmes, shaking his head. " I think I must ask you to remain sitting exactly where you are."

The young lady resumed her seat with an air of displeasure. Her brother, however, had joined us, and we set off all four together. We passed round the lawn to the outside of the young diplomatist's window. There were, as he had said, marks upon the flower-bed, but they were hopelessly blurred and vague. Holmes stooped over them for an instant, and then rose, shrugging his shoulders.

" I don't think anyone could make much of this," said he. " Let us go round the house and see why this particular room was chosen by the burglar. I should have thought those larger windows of the drawing-room and dining-room would have had more attractions for him."

" They are more visible from the road," suggested Mr. Joseph Harrison.

" Ah, yes, of course. There is a door here which he might have attempted. What is it for ? "

" It is the side-entrance for tradespeople. Of course, it is locked at night."

" Have you ever had an alarm like this before ? "

" Never," said our client.

" Do you keep plate in the house, or anything to attract burglars ? "

" Nothing of value."

Holmes strolled round the house with his hands in his pockets, and a negligent air which was unusual with him.

" By the way," said he to Joseph Harrison, " you found some place, I understand, where the fellow scaled the fence. Let us have a look at that."

The young man led us to a spot where the top of one of the wooden rails had been cracked. A small fragment of the wood was hanging down. Holmes pulled it off and examined it critically.

" Do you think that was done last night ? It looks rather old, does it not ? "

" Well, possibly so."

" There are no marks of anyone jumping down upon the other side. No, I fancy we shall get no help here. Let us go back to the bedroom and talk the matter over."

Percy Phelps was walking very slowly, leaning upon the arm of his future brother-in-law. Holmes walked swiftly across the lawn, and we were at the open window of the bedroom long before the others came up.

" Miss Harrison," said Holmes, speaking with the utmost intensity of manner, " you must stay where you are all day. Let nothing prevent you from staying where you are all day. It is of most vital importance."

" Certainly, if you wish it, Mr. Holmes," said the girl, in astonishment.

24 *I should like a little sunshine.* Joseph Harrison later said to his sister, "Why do you sit moping here, Annie? Come out into the sunshine!" The sun shone for only 3.1 hours on Tuesday, July 30th. On Wednesday, July 31st, on the other hand, the sun shone for 12.7 hours; this must be the second day. Your editor holds that the case began on *Tuesday, July 30th,* and ended on *Thursday, August 1, 1889.*

HOLMES PULLED IT OFF AND EXAMINED IT CRITICALLY.

Illustration by Sidney Paget for the *Strand Magazine*, November, 1893.

25 *the spare bedroom.* Watson's former bedroom, since he was no longer living at 221B Baker Street.

" When you go to bed lock the door of this room on the outside and keep the key. Promise to do this."

" But Percy ? "

" He will come to London with us."

" And I am to remain here ? "

" It is for his sake. You can serve him ! Quick ! Promise ! "

She gave a nod of assent just as the other two came up.

" Why do you sit moping there, Annie ? " cried her brother. " Come out into the sunshine ! "

" No, thank you, Joseph. I have a slight headache, and this room is deliciously cool and soothing."

" What do you propose now, Mr. Holmes ? " asked our client.

" Well, in investigating this minor affair we must not lose sight of our main inquiry. It would be a very great help to me if you could come up to London with us."

" At once ? "

" Well, as soon as you conveniently can. Say in an hour."

" I feel quite strong enough, if I can really be of any help."

" The greatest possible."

" Perhaps you would like me to stay there to-night."

" I was just going to propose it."

" Then if my friend of the night comes to revisit me, he will find the bird flown. We are all in your hands, Mr. Holmes, and you must tell us exactly what you would like done. Perhaps you would prefer that Joseph came with us, so as to look after me ? "

" Oh, no ; my friend Watson is a medical man, you know, and he'll look after you. We'll have our lunch here, if you will permit us, and then we shall all three set off for town together."

It was arranged as he suggested, though Miss Harrison excused herself from leaving the bedroom, in accordance with Holmes' suggestion. What the object of my friend's manœuvres was I could not conceive, unless it were to keep the lady away from Phelps, who, rejoiced by his returning health and by the prospect of action, lunched with us in the dining-room. Holmes had a still more startling surprise for us, however, for after accompanying us down to the station and seeing us into our carriage, he calmly announced that he had no intention of leaving Woking.

" There are one or two small points which I should desire to clear up before I go," said he. " Your absence, Mr. Phelps, will in some ways rather assist me. Watson, when you reach London you would oblige me by driving at once to Baker Street with our friend here, and remaining with him until I see you again. It is fortunate that you are old schoolfellows, as you must have much to talk
25 over. Mr. Phelps can have the spare bedroom to-night, and I shall be with you in time for breakfast, for there is a train which will take me into Waterloo at eight."

" But how about our investigation in London ? " asked Phelps, ruefully.

" We can do that to-morrow. I think that just at present I can be of more immediate use here."

" You might tell them at Briarbrae that I hope to be back to-morrow night," cried Phelps, as we began to move from the platform.

" I hardly expect to go back to Briarbrae," answered Holmes, and waved his hand to us cheerily as we shot out from the station.

Phelps and I talked it over on our journey, but neither of us could devise a satisfactory reason for this new development.

" I suppose he wants to find out some clue as to the burglary last night, if a burglar it was. For myself, I don't believe it was an ordinary thief."

" What is your idea, then ? "

" Upon my word, you may put it down to my weak nerves or not, but I believe there is some deep political intrigue going on around me, and that, for some reason that passes my understanding, my life is aimed at by the conspirators. It sounds high-flown and absurd, but consider the facts ! Why should a thief try to break in at a bedroom window, where there could be no hope of any plunder, and why should he come with a long knife in his hand ? "

" You are sure it was not a housebreaker's jemmy ? "

" Oh, no ; it was a knife. I saw the flash of the blade quite distinctly."

" But why on earth should you be pursued with such animosity ? "

" Ah ! that is the question."

" Well, if Holmes takes the same view, that would account for his action, would it not ? Presuming that your theory is correct, if he can lay his hands upon the man who threatened you last night, he will have gone a long way towards finding who took the naval treaty. It is absurd to suppose that you have two enemies, one of whom robs you while the other threatens your life."

" But Mr. Holmes said that he was not going to Briarbrae."

" I have known him for some time," said I, " but I never knew him do anything yet without a very good reason," and with that our conversation drifted off into other topics.

But it was a weary day for me. Phelps was still weak after his long illness, and his misfortunes made him querulous and nervous. In vain I endeavoured to interest him in Afghanistan, in India, in social questions, in anything which might take his mind out of the groove. He would always come back to his lost treaty ; wondering, guessing, speculating, as to what Holmes was doing, what steps Lord Holdhurst was taking, what news we should have in the morning. As the evening wore on his excitement became quite painful.

" You have implicit faith in Holmes ? " he asked.

" I have seen him do some remarkable things."

" But he never brought light into anything quite so dark as this ? "

" Oh, yes ; I have known him solve questions which presented fewer clues than yours."

" But not where such large interests are at stake ? "

" I don't know that. To my certain knowledge he has

"I HARDLY EXPECT TO GO BACK TO BRIARBRAE," ANSWERED HOLMES . . .

Illustration by Sidney Paget for the *Strand Magazine*, November, 1893.

26 *three of the reigning Houses of Europe.* Watson presumably refers to Bohemia, Holland, and Scandinavia.

26 acted on behalf of three of the reigning Houses of Europe in very vital matters."

" But you know him well, Watson. He is such an inscrutable fellow, that I never quite know what to make of him. Do you think he is hopeful ? Do you think he expects to make a success of it ? "

" He has said nothing."

" That is a bad sign."

" On the contrary, I have noticed that when he is off the trail he generally says so. It is when he is on a scent, and is not quite absolutely sure yet that it is the right one, that he is most taciturn. Now, my dear fellow, we can't help matters by making ourselves nervous about them, so let me implore you to go to bed, and so be fresh for whatever may await us to-morrow."

I was able at last to persuade my companion to take my advice, though I knew from his excited manner that there was not much hope of sleep for him. Indeed, his mood was infectious, for I lay tossing half the night myself, brooding over this strange problem, and inventing a hundred theories, each of which was more impossible than the last. Why had Holmes remained at Woking ? Why had he asked Miss Harrison to stay in the sick-room all day ? Why had he been so careful not to inform the people at Briarbrae that he intended to remain near them ? I cudgelled my brains until I fell asleep in the endeavour to find some explanation which would cover all these facts.

It was seven o'clock when I awoke, and I set off at once for Phelps' room, to find him haggard and spent after a sleepless night. His first question was whether Holmes had arrived yet.

" He'll be here when he promised," said I, " and not an instant sooner or later."

And my words were true, for shortly after eight a hansom dashed up to the door and our friend got out of it. Standing in the window, we saw that his left hand was swathed in a bandage and that his face was very grim and pale. He entered the house, but it was some little time before he came upstairs.

" He looks like a beaten man," cried Phelps.

I was forced to confess that he was right. " After all," said I, " the clue of the matter lies probably here in town."

Phelps gave a groan.

" I don't know how it is," said he, " but I had hoped for so much from his return. But surely his hand was not tied up like that yesterday ? What can be the matter ? "

" You are not wounded, Holmes ? " I asked, as my friend entered the room.

" Tut, it is only a scratch through my own clumsiness," he answered, nodding his good morning to us. " This case of yours, Mr. Phelps, is certainly one of the darkest which I have ever investigated."

" I feared that you would find it beyond you."

" It has been a most remarkable experience."

" That bandage tells of adventures," said I. " Won't you tell us what has happened ? "

" After breakfast, my dear Watson. Remember that I have breathed thirty miles of Surrey air this morning. I suppose there has been no answer to my cabman advertisement ? Well, well, we cannot expect to score every time."

The table was all laid, and, just as I was about to ring, Mrs. Hudson entered with the tea and coffee. A few minutes later she brought in the covers, and we all drew up to the table, Holmes ravenous, I curious, and Phelps in the gloomiest state of depression.

" Mrs. Hudson has risen to the occasion," said Holmes, uncovering a dish of curried chicken. " Her cuisine is a little limited, but she has as good an idea of breakfast as a Scotchwoman. What have you there, Watson ? "

" Ham and eggs," I answered.

" Good ! What are you going to take, Mr. Phelps : curried fowl, eggs, or will you help yourself ? "

" Thank you, I can eat nothing," said Phelps.

" Oh, come ! Try the dish before you."

" Thank you, I would really rather not."

" Well, then," said Holmes, with a mischievous twinkle, " I suppose that you have no objection to helping me ? "

Phelps raised the cover, and as he did so he uttered a scream, and sat there staring with a face as white as the plate upon which he looked. Across the centre of it was lying a little cylinder of blue-grey paper. He caught it up, devoured it with his eyes, and then danced madly about the room, pressing it to his bosom and shrieking out in his delight. Then he fell back into an arm-chair, so limp and exhausted with his own emotions that we had to pour brandy down his throat to keep him from fainting.

" There ! there ! " said Holmes, soothingly, patting him upon the shoulder. " It was too bad to spring it on you like this ; but Watson here will tell you that I never can resist a touch of the dramatic."

Phelps seized his hand and kissed it. " God bless you ! " he cried ; " you have saved my honour."

" Well, my own was at stake, you know," said Holmes. " I assure you, it is just as hateful to me to fail in a case as it can be to you to blunder over a commission."

Phelps thrust away the precious document into the innermost pocket of his coat.

" I have not the heart to interrupt your breakfast any further, and yet I am dying to know how you got it and where it was."

Sherlock Holmes swallowed a cup of coffee and turned his attention to the ham and eggs. Then he rose, lit his pipe, and settled himself down into his chair.

" I'll tell you what I did first, and how I came to do it afterwards," said he. " After leaving you at the station I went for a charming walk through some admirable Surrey
scenery to a pretty little village called Ripley, where I 27
had my tea at an inn, and took the precaution of filling 28
my flask and of putting a paper of sandwiches in my pocket. There I remained until evening, when I set off for Woking again and found myself in the high-road outside Briarbrae just after sunset.

" Well, I waited until the road was clear—it is never a

PHELPS RAISED THE COVER . . .

Illustration by William H. Hyde for *Harper's Weekly*, October 21, 1893. Sidney Paget illustrated the same scene for the *Strand Magazine*, November, 1893.

27 *a pretty little village called Ripley.* Ripley is some four miles from Woking by the road which winds its fantastically irregular course across the River Wey and Send Common.

28 *an inn.* "I can see no possible objection to identifying 'an inn' with the famous Talbot Inn, an old, red-brick, white-porched coaching house, which, in Holmes' day, was dozing through the 'recession' between the passing of the stagecoach and the coming of the cycle and motorcycle," Mr. Michael Harrison wrote (*In the Footsteps of Sherlock Holmes*).

"... MR. JOSEPH HARRISON STEPPED OUT INTO THE MOONLIGHT."

Illustration by Sidney Paget for the *Strand Magazine*, November, 1893. Professor Christ and Dr. Zeisler both noted that Watson must have mistaken a "twilight" by Holmes for "moonlight," since the moon was *not* shining at two o'clock in the morning on any of the possible days.

very frequented one at any time, I fancy—and then I clambered over the fence into the grounds."

"Surely the gate was open?" ejaculated Phelps.

"Yes; but I have a peculiar taste in these matters. I chose the place where the three fir trees stand, and behind their screen I got over without the least chance of anyone in the house being able to see me. I crouched down among the bushes on the other side, and crawled from one to the other—witness the disreputable state of my trouser knees—until I had reached the clump of rhododendrons just opposite to your bedroom window. There I squatted down and awaited developments.

"The blind was not down in your room, and I could see Miss Harrison sitting there reading by the table. It was a quarter past ten when she closed her book, fastened the shutters, and retired. I heard her shut the door, and felt quite sure that she had turned the key in the lock."

"The key?" ejaculated Phelps.

"Yes, I had given Miss Harrison instructions to lock the door on the outside and take the key with her when she went to bed. She carried out every one of my injunctions to the letter, and certainly without her co-operation you would not have that paper in your coat pocket. She departed then, the lights went out, and I was left squatting in the rhododendron bush.

"The night was fine, but still it was a very weary vigil. Of course, it has the sort of excitement about it that the sportsman feels when he lies beside the watercourse and waits for the big game. It was very long, though—almost as long, Watson, as when you and I waited in that deadly room when we looked into the little problem of the 'Speckled Band.' There was a church clock down at Woking which struck the quarters, and I thought more than once that it had stopped. At last, however, about two in the morning, I suddenly heard the gentle sound of a bolt being pushed back, and the creaking of a key. A moment later the servants' door was opened and Mr. Joseph Harrison stepped out into the moonlight."

"Joseph!" ejaculated Phelps.

"He was bare-headed, but he had a black cloak thrown over his shoulder, so that he could conceal his face in an instant if there were any alarm. He walked on tiptoe under the shadow of the wall, and when he reached the window, he worked a long-bladed knife through the sash and pushed back the catch. Then he flung open the window and, putting his knife through the crack in the shutters, he thrust the bar up and swung them open.

"From where I lay I had a perfect view of the inside of the room and of every one of his movements. He lit the two candles which stand upon the mantelpiece, and then he proceeded to turn back the corner of the carpet in the neighbourhood of the door. Presently he stooped and picked out a square piece of board, such as is usually left to enable plumbers to get at the joints of the gas pipes. This one covered, as a matter of fact, the T-joint which gives off the pipe which supplies the kitchen underneath. Out of this hiding-place he drew that little cylinder of paper, pushed down the board, rearranged the carpet, blew out the candles, and walked straight into my arms as I stood waiting for him outside the window.

" Well, he has rather more viciousness than I gave him credit for, has Master Joseph. He flew at me with his
knife, and I had to grass him twice, and got a cut over **29**
the knuckles, before I had the upper hand of him. He looked ' murder ' out of the only eye he could see with when we had finished, but he listened to reason and gave up the papers. Having got them I let my man go, but I wired full particulars to Forbes this morning. If he is quick enough to catch his bird, well and good ! But if, as I shrewdly suspect, he finds the nest empty before he gets there, why, all the better for the Government. I fancy that Lord Holdhurst, for one, and Mr. Percy Phelps, for another would very much rather that the affair never got so far as a police-court."

" My God ! " gasped our client. " Do you tell me that during these long ten weeks of agony, the stolen papers were within the very room with me all the time ? "

" So it was."

" And Joseph ! Joseph a villain and a thief ! "

" Hum ! I am afraid Joseph's character is a rather deeper and more dangerous one than one might judge from his appearance. From what I have heard from him this morning, I gather that he has lost heavily in dabbling with stocks, and that he is ready to do anything on earth to better his fortunes. Being an absolutely selfish man, when a chance presented itself he did not allow either his sister's happiness or your reputation to hold his hand."

Percy Phelps sank back in his chair. " My head whirls," said he ; " your words have dazed me."

" The principal difficulty in your case," remarked Holmes, in his didactic fashion, " lay in the fact of there being too much evidence. What was vital was overlaid and hidden by what was irrelevant. Of all the facts which were presented to us, we had to pick just those which we deemed to be essential, and then piece them together in their order, so as to reconstruct this very remarkable chain of events. I had already begun to suspect Joseph, from the fact that you had intended to travel home with him that night, and that therefore it was a likely enough thing that he should call for you—knowing the Foreign Office well—upon his way. When I heard that someone had been so anxious to get into the bedroom, in which no one but Joseph could have concealed anything—you told us in your narrative how you had turned Joseph out when you arrived with the doctor—my suspicions all changed to certainties, especially as the attempt was made on the first night upon which the nurse was absent, showing that the intruder was well acquainted with the ways of the house."

" How blind I have been ! "

" The facts of the case, as far as I have worked them out, are these : This Joseph Harrison entered the office through the Charles Street door, and knowing his way he walked straight into your room the instant after you left it. Finding no one there he promptly rang the bell, and at the instant that he did so his eyes caught the paper

29 *I had to grass him twice*. "Grass" in some of the American texts sometimes appears as "grasp." To "grass" is an old sporting term meaning to knock or bring down. "But to knock a man down twice may seem excessively rough treatment, even if he is armed with a long-bladed knife," Mr. James Edward Holroyd wrote. "I suggest that one has to go back to the earlier part of the story for the explanation. When Holmes and Watson first arrive at Briarbrae, Woking, they are greeted by this same J. H. with 'Percy has been enquiring for you all morning. Ah, poor chap, he clings to any straw.' Holmes would not like that. I think he remembered it and gave the prospective brother-in-law an extra one for luck when he got him alone!"

upon the table. A glance showed him that chance had put in his way a State document of immense value, and in a flash he had thrust it into his pocket and was gone. A few minutes elapsed, as you remember, before the sleepy commissionaire drew your attention to the bell, and those were just enough to give the thief time to make his escape.

" He made his way to Woking by the first train, and, having examined his booty and assured himself that it really was of immense value, he concealed it in what he thought was a very safe place, with the intention of taking it out again in a day or two, and carrying it to the French Embassy, or wherever he thought that a long price was to be had. Then came your sudden return. He, without a moment's warning, was bundled out of his room, and from that time onwards there were always at least two of you there to prevent him from regaining his treasure. The situation to him must have been a maddening one. But at last he thought he saw his chance. He tried to steal in, but was baffled by your wakefulness. You may remember that you did not take your usual draught that night."

" I remember."

" I fancy that he had taken steps to make that draught efficacious, and that he quite relied upon your being unconscious. Of course, I understood that he would repeat the attempt whenever it could be done with safety. Your leaving the room gave him the chance he wanted. I kept Miss Harrison in it all day, so that he might not anticipate us. Then, having given him the idea that the coast was clear, I kept guard as I have described. I already knew that the papers were probably in the room, but I had no desire to rip up all the planking and skirting in search of them. I let him take them, therefore, from the hiding-place, and so saved myself an infinity of trouble. Is there any other point which I can make clear ? "

" Why did he try the window on the first occasion," I asked, " when he might have entered by the door ? "

" In reaching the door he would have to pass seven bedrooms. On the other hand, he could get out on to the lawn with ease. Anything else ? "

" You do not think," asked Phelps, " that he had any murderous intention ? The knife was only meant as a tool."

" It may be so," answered Holmes, shrugging his shoulders. " I can only say for certain that Mr. Joseph Harrison is a gentleman to whose mercy I should be extremely unwilling to trust."

"IS THERE ANY OTHER POINT WHICH I CAN MAKE CLEAR?"

Illustration by Sidney Paget for the *Strand Magazine*, November, 1893.

THE CARDBOARD BOX

[Saturday, August 31, to Monday, September 2, 1889]

IN choosing a few typical cases which illustrate the remarkable mental qualities of my friend, Sherlock Holmes, I have endeavoured, so far as possible, to select those which presented the minimum of sensationalism, while offering a fair field for his talents. It is, however, unfortunately, impossible entirely to separate the sensational from the criminal, and a chronicler is left in the dilemma that he must either sacrifice details which are essential to his statement, and so give a false impression of the problem, or he must use matter which chance, and not choice, has provided him with. With this short preface I shall turn to my notes of what proved to be a strange, though a peculiarly terrible, chain of events.

It was a blazing hot day in August. Baker Street was **1**
like an oven, and the glare of the sunlight upon the yellow brickwork of the house across the road was painful to the eye. It was hard to believe that these were the same walls which loomed so gloomily through the fogs of winter. Our blinds were half-drawn, and Holmes lay curled upon the sofa, reading and re-reading a letter which he had received by the morning post. For myself, my term of service in India had trained me to stand heat better than cold, and a thermometer at 90 was no hardship. But the morning paper was uninteresting. Parliament had
risen. Everybody was out of town, and I yearned for **2**
the glades of the New Forest or the shingle of Southsea. **3-4**
A depleted bank account had caused me to postpone my
holiday, and as to my companion, neither the country nor **5**
the sea presented the slightest attraction to him. He loved to lie in the very centre of five millions of people, with his filaments stretching out and running through them, responsive to every little rumour or suspicion of unsolved crime.
Appreciation of nature found no place among his many gifts, **6**
and his only change was when he turned his mind from the evil-doer of the town to track down his brother of the country.

Finding that Holmes was too absorbed for conversation I had tossed aside the barren paper and, leaning back in my chair, I fell into a brown study. Suddenly my companion's voice broke in upon my thoughts.

1 *It was a blazing hot day in August.* The day, as we shall see, was a Saturday. The year must be 1889 or 1890: Holmes later mentions the case of *The Sign of the Four,* which we know took place in September, 1888; Watson's account of the adventure of "The Cardboard Box" was published in January, 1893; in the Augusts of 1891 and 1892 Holmes was believed to be dead by all except his brother Mycroft.

2 *Parliament had risen.* Such a report would appear in the morning paper on the day after the event. In the year under consideration, Parliament must therefore have risen on a Friday. In 1890, Parliament rose on August 18th, a Wednesday. In addition, there was no day in August, 1890, after the 18th when the temperature was higher than 69.6°. In 1889, on the other hand, Parliament rose on August 30th, a Friday. On the next day, the Saturday, the temperature hit 81.1°, making it an exceedingly hot day for England. We hold that the adventure began on *Saturday, August 31, 1889;* it closed two days later on *Monday, September 2, 1889.*

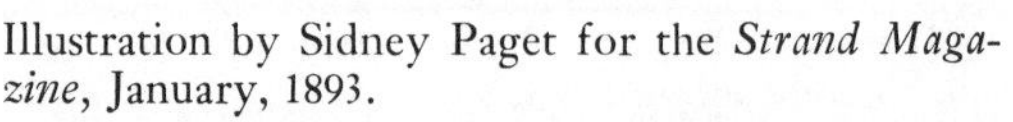
. . . I FELL INTO A BROWN STUDY.

Illustration by Sidney Paget for the *Strand Magazine,* January, 1893.

3 *the New Forest.* The 145 miles of the New Forest stretch from Southampton Water to the Wiltshire border. The New Forest was enclosed by that lover of the chase, William the Conqueror, and in it William Rufus, the inept son of a gifted father, was killed, perhaps accidentally, perhaps by design, by the arrow shot by William Tyrrell. There are few deer left today, and little other game in the Forest, which is Crown property, but it is still a sanctuary for birds, many of them rare in England, and its trees, birds, and quiet solitude make it a beauty spot of a kind hardly to be found anywhere else in England.

4 *the shingle of Southsea.* The beach at Southsea, the suburb of Portsmouth where, curiously enough, Dr. Arthur Conan Doyle early practiced medicine.

5 *A depleted bank account had caused me to postpone my holiday.* Watson in the August of 1889 was both married and in practice. Why, then, do we find him in this adventure living in Baker Street with Holmes? We believe the answer is clear when one properly interprets this statement. August, 1889, was less than a year after the excitements of *The Sign of the Four.* No doubt Mary Morstan Watson had not yet completely recovered from them. In such a heat wave as London was experiencing, Watson undoubtedly hoped that they might flee the metropolis together. When finances made this impossible, he gallantly gave up his own holiday and sent Mary off alone. To ease his loneliness, he moved for about a fortnight into Baker Street, bringing a few books and pictures with him. Mary—and Watson—returned to their own home shortly before September 7, 1889.

6 *Appreciation of nature found no place among his many gifts.* But this we cannot allow: see Holmes' comments on the beauty of the morning in *The Sign of the Four.* Read his little sermon on the rose in "The Naval Treaty." Our picture of Donnithorpe and the Norfolk countryside in "The *Gloria Scott*" comes only from Holmes, as does our picture of Hurlstone and West Surrey in "The Musgrave Ritual." "Of late I have been tempted to look into the problems of nature . . ." Holmes says in "The Final Problem." "Let us walk in these beautiful woods, Watson, and give a few hours to the birds and flowers," he says in "The Adventure of Black Peter." And in "The Adventure of the Lion's Mane," he writes: "On the morning of which I speak the wind had abated, and all nature was newly washed and fresh. It was impossible to work upon so delightful a day, and I strolled out before breakfast to enjoy the exquisite air."

7 *you expressed incredulity.*" Holmes can hardly be referring here to the conversation recorded by Watson in *A Study in Scarlet.* We note, too, that Holmes apparently has changed his views: Dupin, "a very inferior fellow," has become "a close

"You are right, Watson," said he. "It does seem a most preposterous way of settling a dispute."

"Most preposterous!" I exclaimed, and then suddenly realizing how he had echoed the inmost thought of my soul, I sat up in my chair and stared at him in blank amazement.

"What is this, Holmes?" I cried. "This is beyond anything which I could have imagined."

He laughed heartily at my perplexity.

"You remember," said he, "that some little time ago when I read you the passage in one of Poe's sketches in which a close reasoner follows the unspoken thoughts of his companion, you were inclined to treat the matter as a mere *tour-de-force* of the author. On my remarking that I was constantly in the habit of doing the same thing you
7 expressed incredulity."

"Oh, no!"

"Perhaps not with your tongue, my dear Watson, but certainly with your eyebrows. So when I saw you throw down your paper and enter upon a train of thought, I was very happy to have the opportunity of reading it off, and eventually of breaking into it, as a proof that I had been
8 *en rapport* with you."

But I was still far from satisfied. "In the example which you read to me," said I, "the reasoner drew his conclusions from the actions of the man whom he observed. If I remember right, he stumbled over a heap of stones, looked up at the stars, and so on. But I have been seated quietly in my chair, and what clues can I have given you?"

"You do yourself an injustice. The features are given to man as the means by which he shall express his emotions, and yours are faithful servants."

"Do you mean to say that you read my train of thoughts from my features?"

"Your features, and especially your eyes. Perhaps you cannot yourself recall how your reverie commenced?"

"No, I cannot."

"Then I will tell you. After throwing down your paper, which was the action which drew my attention to you, you sat for half a minute with a vacant expression. Then your eyes fixed themselves upon your newly framed
9 picture of General Gordon, and I saw by the alteration in
your face that a train of thought had been started. But it
did not lead very far. Your eyes flashed across to the
10 unframed portrait of Henry Ward Beecher which stands
upon the top of your books. Then you glanced up at the wall, and of course your meaning was obvious. You were thinking that if the portrait were framed, it would just cover that bare space and correspond with Gordon's picture over there."

"You have followed me wonderfully!" I exclaimed.

"So far I could hardly have gone astray. But now your thoughts went back to Beecher, and you looked hard across as if you were studying the character in his features. Then your eyes ceased to pucker, but you continued to look across, and your face was thoughtful. You were recalling the incidents of Beecher's career. I was well aware that you could not do this without thinking of the mission which he undertook on behalf of the North at the

time of the Civil War, for I remember your expressing your passionate indignation at the way in which he was received by the more turbulent of our people. You felt **11**
so strongly about it, that I knew you could not think of Beecher without thinking of that also. When a moment later I saw your eyes wander away from the picture, I suspected that your mind had now turned to the Civil War, and when I observed that your lips set, your eyes sparkled, and your hands clenched, I was positive that you were indeed thinking of the gallantry which was shown by both sides in that desperate struggle. But then, again, your face grew sadder ; you shook your head. You were dwelling upon the sadness and horror and useless waste of life. Your hand stole towards your own old wound and a smile quivered on your lips, which showed me that the ridiculous side of this method of settling international questions had forced itself upon your mind. At this point I agreed with you that it was preposterous, and was glad to find that all my deductions had been correct."

" Absolutely ! " said I. " And now that you have explained it, I confess that I am as amazed as before."

" It was very superficial, my dear Watson, I assure you. I should not have intruded it upon your attention had you not shown some incredulity the other day. But I have in my hands here a little problem which may prove to be more difficult of solution than my small essay in thought-reading. Have you observed in the paper a short paragraph referring to the remarkable contents of a packet sent through the post to Miss Cushing, of Cross Street, Croydon ? " **12**

" No, I saw nothing."

" Ah ! then you must have overlooked it. Just toss it over to me. Here it is, under the financial column. Perhaps you would be good enough to read it aloud."

I picked up the paper which he had thrown back to me, and read the paragraph indicated. It was headed, " A Gruesome Packet."

" Miss Susan Cushing, living at Cross Street, Croydon, has been made the victim of what must be regarded as a peculiarly revolting practical joke, unless some more sinister meaning should prove to be attached to the incident. At two o'clock yesterday afternoon a small packet, wrapped in brown paper, was handed in by the postman. A cardboard box was inside, which was filled with coarse salt. On emptying this, Miss Cushing was horrified to find two human ears, apparently quite freshly severed. The box had been sent by parcel post from Belfast upon the morning before. There is no indication as to the sender, and the matter is the more mysterious as Miss Cushing, who is a maiden lady of fifty, has led a most retired life, and has so few acquaintances or correspondents that it is a rare event for her to receive anything through the post. Some years ago, however, when she resided at Penge, she let apart- **13**
ments in her house to three young medical students, whom she was obliged to get rid of on account of their noisy and irregular habits. The police are of opinion that this outrage may have been perpetrated upon Miss Cushing by these youths, who owed her a grudge, and who hoped to frighten her by sending her these relics of the dissecting-rooms. Some probability is lent to the theory by the fact that one of these students came from the North of Ireland, and, to the best of Miss Cushing's belief, from Belfast. In the meantime, the matter is being actively investigated, Mr. Lestrade, one of the very smartest of our detective officers, being in charge of the case."

reasoner." "It may therefore be assumed," Miss Madeleine B. Stern wrote in "Sherlock Holmes: Rare Book Collector," "that . . . probably between 1881 and [the time of "The Cardboard Box"], Holmes acquired a copy of the New York, Wiley and Putnam, 1845, edition of Poe's *Tales*, including both 'The Murders in the Rue Morgue,' which contained the passage in question [*see below*], and 'The Mystery of Marie Rogêt.' "

8 en rapport. French: harmony of relation; accordance; correspondence; agreement; sympathetic relation.

9 *General Gordon.* General Charles George Gordon ("Chinese Gordon"), 1833–1885, British soldier and administrator, Commander of the Chinese army that suppressed the Taiping Rebellion, Governor of the Egyptian Sudan, 1877–1880. Trying to crush the power of the Mahdi, he was killed at the siege of Khartoum. Popular indignation at his death helped to cause the fall of the Gladstone government in 1885.

10 *Henry Ward Beecher.* For Watson's possible interest or interests in Henry Ward Beecher, see Chapter 9, "Good Old Watson!"

11 *the more turbulent of our people.* "*Punch*'s reactions to the Beecher visit are worth looking at," Mr. Whitfield J. Bell, Jr., wrote in "Holmes and History"; "a brief account will be found in Carl Sandburg's *Lincoln: The War Years*, II, 515–7."

12 *Croydon?"* A suburb of London in Surrey, important since Holmes' and Watson's day for its airport, used by the military during World War II.

13 *Penge.* A district centering around the Sydenham-Crystal Palace Hill.

"So much for the *Daily Chronicle*," said Holmes, as I finished reading. "Now for our friend Lestrade. I had a note from him this morning, in which he says: 'I think that this case is very much in your line. We have every hope of clearing the matter up, but we find a little difficulty in getting anything to work upon. We have, of course, wired to the Belfast post office, but a large number of parcels were handed in upon that day, and they have no means of identifying this particular one, or of remembering the sender. The box is a half-pound box of honeydew
14 tobacco, and does not help us in any way. The medical-student theory still appears to me to be the most feasible, but if you should have a few hours to spare, I should be very happy to see you out here. I shall be either at the house or in the police-station all day.' What say you, Watson? Can you rise superior to the heat, and run down to Croydon with me on the off chance of a case for your annals?"

"I was longing for something to do."

"You shall have it then. Ring for our boots, and tell them to order a cab. I'll be back in a moment, when I have changed my dressing-gown and filled my cigar-case."

A shower of rain fell while we were in the train, and the heat was far less oppressive in Croydon than in town. Holmes had sent on a wire, so that Lestrade, as wiry, as dapper, and as ferret-like as ever, was waiting for us at the station. A walk of five minutes took us to Cross
15 Street, where Miss Cushing resided.

It was a very long street of two-story brick houses, neat and prim, with whitened stone steps and little groups of aproned women gossiping at the doors. Half-way down, Lestrade stopped and tapped at a door, which was opened by a small servant girl. Miss Cushing was sitting in the front room, into which we were ushered. She was a placid-faced woman, with large, gentle eyes, and grizzled hair curving down over her temples on each side. A worked antimacassar lay upon her lap and a basket of coloured silks stood upon a stool beside her.

"They are in the outhouse, those dreadful things," said she, as Lestrade entered. "I wish that you would take them away altogether."

"So I shall, Miss Cushing. I only kept them here until my friend, Mr. Holmes, should have seen them in your presence."

"Why in my presence, sir?"

"In case he wished to ask any questions."

"What is the use of asking me questions, when I tell you I know nothing whatever about it?"

"Quite so, madam," said Holmes, in his soothing way. "I have no doubt that you have been annoyed more than enough already over this business."

"Indeed, I have, sir. I am a quiet woman and live a retired life. It is something new for me to see my name in the papers and to find the police in my house. I won't have those things in here, Mr. Lestrade. If you wish to see them you must go to the outhouse."

It was a small shed in the narrow garden which ran behind the house. Lestrade went in and brought out a yellow cardboard box, with a piece of brown paper and

14 *honeydew tobacco.* A kind of smoking tobacco sweetened with molasses.

15 *Cross Street.* "The nearness of 'Cross Street'—it is, in reality, Cross *Road*—to the station . . . shows that the station in question was that known as 'East Croydon,' whose entrance is on George Street, Croydon's main thoroughfare," Mr. Michael Harrison wrote (*In the Footsteps of Sherlock Holmes*). "Coming out of East Croydon Station into George Street, the three men would have turned left, walked for a few yards along George Street, then turned left again, into Cherry Orchard Street, off which Cross Road branches. Watson's memory is a little at fault in describing Cross Road as a 'very long street'—it is, in fact, an exceedingly short one, but Watson's memory may be confusing Cross Road with St. James's Road, into which Cross Road leads, and which is, in truth, a very long road."

"WHAT IS THE USE OF ASKING ME QUESTIONS, WHEN I TELL YOU I KNOW NOTHING WHATEVER ABOUT IT?"

Illustration by Sidney Paget for the *Strand Magazine*, January, 1893.

some string. There was a bench at the end of the path, and we all sat down while Holmes examined, one by one, the articles which Lestrade had handed to him.

" The string is exceedingly interesting," he remarked, holding it up to the light and sniffing at it. " What do you make of this string, Lestrade ? "

" It has been tarred."

" Precisely. It is a piece of tarred twine. You have also, no doubt, remarked that Miss Cushing has cut the cord with a scissors, as can be seen by the double fray on each side. This is of importance."

" I cannot see the importance," said Lestrade.

" The importance lies in the fact that the knot is left intact, and that this knot is of a peculiar character."

" It is very neatly tied. I had already made a note to that effect," said Lestrade, complacently.

" So much for the string, then," said Holmes, smiling ; " now for the box wrapper. Brown paper, with a distinct smell of coffee. What, did not observe it ? I think there can be no doubt of it. Address printed in rather straggling characters : ' Miss S. Cushing, Cross Street, Croydon.' Done with a broad-pointed pen, probably a J, and with very inferior ink. The word Croydon has been originally spelt with an *i*, which has been changed to *y*. The parcel was directed then by a man—the printing is distinctly masculine—of limited education and unacquainted with the town of Croydon. So far, so good ! The box is a yellow, half-pound honeydew box, with nothing distinctive save two thumb marks at the left bottom corner. It is filled with rough salt of the quality used for preserving hides and other of the coarser commercial purposes. And embedded in it are these very singular enclosures."

He took out the two ears as he spoke, and laying a board across his knee, he examined them minutely, while Lestrade and I, bending forward on each side of him, glanced alternately at these dreadful relics and at the thoughtful, eager face of our companion. Finally he returned them to the box once more, and sat for a while in deep meditation.

" You have observed, of course," said he at last, " that the ears are not a pair."

" Yes, I have noticed that. But if this were the practical joke of some students from the dissecting-rooms, it would be as easy for them to send two odd ears as a pair."

" Precisely. But this is not a practical joke."

" You are sure of it ? "

" The presumption is strongly against it. Bodies in the dissecting-rooms are injected with preservative fluid. These ears bear no signs of this. They are fresh too. They have been cut off with a blunt instrument, which would hardly happen if a student had done it. Again, carbolic or rectified spirits would be the preservatives which would suggest themselves to the medical mind, certainly not rough salt. I repeat that there is no practical joke here, but that we are investigating a serious crime."

A vague thrill ran through me as I listened to my companion's words and saw the stern gravity which had

. . . LAYING A BOARD ACROSS HIS KNEE, HE EXAMINED THEM MINUTELY . . .

Illustration by Sidney Paget for the *Strand Magazine*, January, 1893.

hardened his features. This brutal preliminary seemed to shadow forth some strange and inexplicable horror in the background. Lestrade, however, shook his head like a man who is only half convinced.

" There are objections to the joke theory, no doubt," said he ; " but there are much stronger reasons against the other. We know that this woman has led a most quiet and respectable life at Penge and here for the last twenty years. She has hardly been away from her home for a day during that time. Why on earth, then, should any criminal send her the proofs of his guilt, especially as, unless she is a most consummate actress, she understands quite as little of the matter as we do ? "

" That is the problem which we have to solve," Holmes answered, " and for my part I shall set about it by presuming that my reasoning is correct, and that a double murder has been committed. One of these ears is a woman's, small, finely formed, and pierced for an ear-ring. The other is a man's, sun-burned, discoloured, and also pierced for an ear-ring. These two people are presumably dead, or we should have heard their story before now. To-day is Friday. The packet was posted on Thursday morning. The tragedy, then, occurred on Wednesday or Tuesday, or
16 earlier. If the two people were murdered, who but their murderer would have sent this sign of his work to Miss Cushing ? We may take it that the sender of the packet is the man whom we want. But he must have some strong reason for sending Miss Cushing this packet. What reason then ? It must have been to tell her that the deed was done ; or to pain her, perhaps. But in that case she knows who it is. Does she know ? I doubt it. If she knew, why should she call the police in ? She might have buried the ears, and no one would have been the wiser. That is what she would have done if she had wished to shield the criminal. But if she does not wish to shield him she would give his name. There is a tangle here which needs straightening out." He had been talking in a high, quick voice, staring blankly up over the garden fence, but now he sprang briskly to his feet and walked towards the house.

" I have a few questions to ask Miss Cushing," said he.

" In that case I may leave you here," said Lestrade, " for I have another small business on hand. I think that I have nothing further to learn from Miss Cushing. You will find me at the police-station."

" We shall look in on our way to the train," answered Holmes. A moment later he and I were back in the front room, where the impassive lady was still quietly working away at her antimacassar. She put it down on her lap as we entered, and looked at us with her frank, searching blue eyes.

" I am convinced, sir," she said, " that this matter is a mistake, and that the parcel was never meant for me at all. I have said this several times to the gentleman from Scotland Yard, but he simply laughs at me. I have not an enemy in the world, as far as I know, so why should anyone play me such a trick ? "

" I am coming to be of the same opinion, Miss Cushing,"

16 *or earlier.* The *Daily Chronicle* of "today" reported that "at two o'clock yesterday afternoon a small packet . . . was handed in [at Croydon] by the postman. The box had been sent by parcel post from Belfast the morning before." "Two days" after the day on which the case opened, Holmes received "a bulky envelope" from Lestrade. A packet posted in Belfast in the morning could not possibly reach Croydon the same day; the newspaper must therefore have been correct in saying that it was posted one day and received the next. Holmes, having read the newspaper, should therefore have said either: "Today is Friday. The packet was posted on Wednesday morning. The tragedy, then, occurred on Tuesday or Monday, or earlier"; or, "Today is Saturday. The packet was posted on Thursday morning. The tragedy, then, occurred on Wednesday, or Tuesday, or earlier." We believe that the second alternative is the correct one, for two reasons: 1) If the case opened on a Friday, the bulky envelope received from Lestrade two days later must have arrived on a Sunday. If the case opened on a Saturday, on the other hand, it must have arrived on a Monday. It is far more likely that Lestrade used the regular post in the usual way than that he went to the expense of hiring a special messenger, as he would have had to do if the envelope were delivered on a Sunday. 2) In the first alternative, we would have to believe that Watson misquoted Holmes not once but thrice; in the second alternative, however, we need only change the "Friday" to "Saturday" to make the statement make sense. We hold that the murders were on Wednesday, that the packet was posted on Thursday and received on Friday, and that the case began on a Saturday and closed on the Monday two days later.

said Holmes, taking a seat beside her. "I think that it is more than probable . . ." He paused, and I was surprised, on glancing round, to see that he was staring with singular intentness at the lady's profile. Surprise and satisfaction were both for an instant to be read upon his eager face, though when she glanced round to find out the cause of his silence he had become as demure as ever. I stared hard myself at her flat, grizzled hair, her trim cap, her little gilt ear-rings, her placid features; but I could see nothing which could account for my companion's evident excitement.

"There were one or two questions——"

"Oh, I am weary of questions!" cried Miss Cushing, impatiently.

"You have two sisters, I believe."

"How could you know that?"

"I observed the very instant that I entered the room that you have a portrait group of three ladies upon the mantelpiece, one of whom is undoubtedly yourself, while the others are so exceedingly like you that there could be no doubt of the relationship."

"Yes, you are quite right. Those are my sisters, Sarah and Mary."

"And here at my elbow is another portrait, taken at Liverpool, of your younger sister, in the company of a man who appears to be a steward by his uniform. I observe that she was unmarried at the time."

"You are very quick at observing."

"That is my trade."

"Well, you are quite right. But she was married to Mr. Browner a few days afterwards. He was on the South American line when that was taken, but he was so fond of her that he couldn't abide to leave her for so long, and he got into the Liverpool and London boats."

"Ah, the *Conqueror*, perhaps?"

"No, the *May Day*, when last I heard. Jim came down **17**
here to see me once. That was before he broke the pledge; but afterwards he would always take drink when he was ashore, and a little drink would send him stark, staring mad. Ah! it was a bad day that ever he took a glass in his hand again. First he dropped me, then he quarrelled with Sarah, and now that Mary has stopped writing we don't know how things are going with them."

It was evident that Miss Cushing had come upon a subject on which she felt very deeply. Like most people who lead a lonely life, she was shy at first, but ended by becoming extremely communicative. She told us many details about her brother-in-law the steward, and then wandering off on to the subject of her former lodgers, the medical students, she gave us a long account of their delinquencies, with their names and those of their hospitals. Holmes listened attentively to everything, throwing in a question from time to time.

"About your second sister, Sarah," said he. "I wonder, since you are both maiden ladies, that you do not keep house together."

"Ah! you don't know Sarah's temper, or you would wonder no more. I tried it when I came to Croydon, and we kept on until about two months ago, when we had to

17 "*No, the* May Day. The *Conqueror* and the *May Day*, real ships, were located by Mr. Richard W. Clarke ("On the Nomenclature of Watson's Ships") "in the Liverpool registry under ownership of the Liverpool, Dublin and London Steam Packet Co."

part. I don't want to say a word against my own sister, but she was always meddlesome and hard to please, was Sarah."

"You say that she quarrelled with your Liverpool relations."

"Yes, and they were the best of friends at one time. Why, she went up there to live in order to be near them. And now she has no word hard enough for Jim Browner. The last six months that she was here she would speak of nothing but his drinking and his ways. He had caught her meddling, I suspect, and given her a bit of his mind, and that was the start of it."

"Thank you, Miss Cushing," said Holmes, rising and bowing. "Your sister Sarah lives, I think you said, at
18 New Street, Wallington? Good-bye, and I am very sorry that you should have been troubled over a case with which, as you say, you have nothing whatever to do."

There was a cab passing as we came out, and Holmes hailed it.

"How far to Wallington?" he asked.

"Only about a mile, sir."

"Very good. Jump in, Watson. We must strike while the iron is hot. Simple as the case is, there have been one or two very instructive details in connection with it. Just pull up at a telegraph office as you pass, cabby."

Holmes sent off a short wire, and for the rest of the drive lay back in the cab with his hat tilted over his nose to keep the sun from his face. Our driver pulled up at a house which was not unlike the one which we had just quitted. My companion ordered him to wait, and had his hand upon the knocker, when the door opened and a grave young gentleman in black, with a very shiny hat, appeared on the step.

"Is Miss Cushing at home?" asked Holmes.

"Miss Sarah Cushing is extremely ill," said he. "She has been suffering since yesterday from brain symptoms of great severity. As her medical adviser, I cannot possibly take the responsibility of allowing anyone to see her. I should recommend you to call again in ten days." He drew on his gloves, closed the door, and marched off down the street.

"Well, if we can't, we can't," said Holmes, cheerfully.

"Perhaps she could not, or would not have told you much."

"I did not wish her to tell me anything. I only wanted to look at her. However, I think that I have got all that I want. Drive us to some decent hotel, cabby, where we may have some lunch, and afterwards we shall drop down upon friend Lestrade at the police-station."

We had a pleasant little meal together, during which Holmes would talk about nothing but violins, narrating with great exultation how he had purchased his own Stradivarius, which was worth at least five hundred guineas, at a Jew broker's in Tottenham Court Road for
19 fifty-five shillings. This led him to Paganini, and we sat for an hour over a bottle of claret while he told me anecdote after anecdote of that extraordinary man. The afternoon was far advanced and the hot glare had softened into a mellow glow before we found ourselves at the police-

18 *New Street, Wallington?* Wallington is a residential district close to which many Roman remains have been found. With Beddington and Carshalton, it extends for a distance of about two and a half miles along the main road between Croydon and Sutton. "Where 'New Street' was, I cannot say," Mr. Michael Harrison wrote (*In the Footsteps of Sherlock Holmes*). "In Wallington there are Newminster Road, Newstead Walk and Newhouse Walk; but these are all streets of recent buildings."

19 *fifty-five shillings.* Holmes paid about $13.75 for a violin which was worth at least $2,500. Mr. Michael Harrison has remarked (*In the Footsteps of Sherlock Holmes*) that only an expert would have spotted that the violin was a Stradivarius, since "Antonio Stradivari put his small label right within the body of the instrument . . ."

"HOW FAR TO WALLINGTON?" HE SAID.

Illustration by Sidney Paget for the *Strand Magazine*, January, 1893.

station. Lestrade was waiting for us at the door.

"A telegram for you, Mr. Holmes," said he.

"Ha! It is the answer!" He tore it open, glanced his eyes over it, and crumpled it into his pocket. "That's all right," said he.

"Have you found out anything?"

"I have found out everything!"

"What!" Lestrade stared at him in amazement. "You are joking."

"I was never more serious in my life. A shocking crime has been committed, and I think I have now laid bare every detail of it."

"And the criminal?"

Holmes scribbled a few words upon the back of one of his visiting-cards and threw it over to Lestrade.

"That is the name," he said. "You cannot effect an arrest until to-morrow night at the earliest. I should prefer that you do not mention my name at all in connection with the case, as I choose to be only associated with those crimes which present some difficulty in their solution. Come on, Watson." We strode off together to the station, leaving Lestrade still staring with a delighted face at the card which Holmes had thrown him.

"The case," said Sherlock Holmes, as we chatted over our cigars that night in our rooms at Baker Street, "is one where, as in the investigations which you have chronicled under the names of the 'Study in Scarlet' and of the
'Sign of Four,' we have been compelled to reason back- 20
ward from effects to causes. I have written to Lestrade asking him to supply us with the details which are now wanting, and which he will only get after he has secured his man. That he may be safely trusted to do, for although he is absolutely devoid of reason, he is as tenacious as a bulldog when he once understands what he has to do, and indeed, it is just this tenacity which has brought him to the top at Scotland Yard."

"Your case is not complete, then?" I asked.

"It is fairly complete in essentials. We know who the author of the revolting business is, although one of the victims still escapes us. Of course, you have formed your own conclusions."

"I presume that this Jim Browner, the steward of a Liverpool boat, is the man whom you suspect?"

"Oh! it is more than a suspicion."

"And yet I cannot see anything save very vague indications."

"On the contrary, to my mind nothing could be more clear. Let me run over the principal steps. We approached the case, you remember, with an absolutely blank mind, which is always an advantage. We had formed no theories. We were simply there to observe and to draw inferences from our observations. What did we see first? A very placid and respectable lady, who seemed quite innocent of any secret, and a portrait which showed me that she had two younger sisters. It instantly flashed across my mind that the box might have been meant for one of these. I set the idea aside as one which could be disproved or confirmed at our leisure. Then we

. . . HE TOLD ME ANECDOTE AFTER ANECDOTE OF THAT EXTRAORDINARY MAN.

A portrait of Niccolo Paganini attributed to Holmes' great uncle, Horace Vernet. Paganini, 1782–1840, "was lionized on reaching Paris," Mr. James C. Iraldi wrote in "That Extraordinary Man." "He moved in the highest circles, was invited everywhere, met everyone worth meeting—including Horace Vernet, the famous artist, for whom he sat for a portrait. Would it be so inconceivable as to imagine that, in the course of those sittings, Paganini met—and loved—Vernet's sister—the same lady who was destined to become—the grandmother of Sherlock Holmes?"

20 *the 'Sign of Four.' The Sign of the Four* was not to be *published* until November, 1890, but Holmes had quite obviously read Watson's *manuscript* of the adventure by this time.

went to the garden, as you remember, and we saw the very singular contents of the little yellow box.

" The string was of the quality which is used by sailmakers aboard ship, and at once a whiff of the sea was perceptible in our investigation. When I observed that the knot was one which is popular with sailors, that the parcel had been posted at a port, and that the male ear was pierced for an ear-ring which is so much more common among sailors than landsmen, I was quite certain that all the actors in the tragedy were to be found among our seafaring classes.

" When I came to examine the address of the packet I observed that it was to Miss S. Cushing. Now, the oldest sister would, of course, be Miss Cushing, and although her initial was ' S ' it might belong to one of the others as well. In that case we should have to commence our investigation from a fresh basis altogether. I therefore went into the house with the intention of clearing up this point. I was about to assure Miss Cushing that I was convinced that a mistake had been made, when you may remember that I came suddenly to a stop. The fact was that I had just seen something which filled me with surprise, and at the same time narrowed the field of our inquiry immensely.

" As a medical man, you are aware, Watson, that there is no part of the body which varies so much as the human ear. Each ear is as a rule quite distinctive, and differs from all other ones. In last year's *Anthropological Journal* you will find two short monographs from my pen upon
21 the subject. I had, therefore, examined the ears in the box with the eyes of an expert, and had carefully noted their anatomical peculiarities. Imagine my surprise then, when, on looking at Miss Cushing, I perceived that her ear corresponded exactly with the female ear which I had just inspected. The matter was entirely beyond coincidence.
22 There was the same shortening of the pinna, the same broad curve of the upper lobe, the same convolution of the inner cartilage. In all essentials it was the same ear.

" Of course, I at once saw the enormous importance of the observation. It was evident that the victim was a blood relation, and probably a very close one. I began to talk to her about her family, and you remember that she at once gave us some exceedingly valuable details.

" In the first place, her sister's name was Sarah, and her address had, until recently, been the same, so that it was quite obvious how the mistake had occurred, and for whom the packet was meant. Then we heard of this steward, married to the third sister, and learned that he had at one time been so intimate with Miss Sarah that she had actually gone up to Liverpool to be near the Browners, but a quarrel had afterwards divided them. This quarrel had put a stop to all communications for some months, so that if Browner had occasion to address a packet to Miss Sarah, he would undoubtedly have done so to her old address.

" And now the matter had begun to straighten itself out wonderfully. We had learned of the existence of this steward, an impulsive man, of strong passions—you remember that he threw up what must have been a very superior berth, in order to be nearer to his wife—subject,

21 *two short monographs from my pen upon the subject.* The "*Anthropological Journal*" is a carelessness on the part of Dr. Watson, as the late Earle F. Walbridge pointed out in "Jabez Wilson Reports"; Holmes referred to the *Journal of Anthropology*, later the *Journal of the Royal Anthropological Society*.

"It is interesting to note," the late Christopher Morley wrote in "Was Sherlock Holmes an American?", "that when Holmes spoke . . . of having written two monographs on Ears . . . the alert editor of the *Strand* at once took the hint. A few months later, in October and November, 1893, the *Strand* printed 'A Chapter on Ears,' with photos of the ears of famous people—including an ear of Dr. Oliver Wendell Holmes. Surely, from so retiring a philosopher, then eighty-four years old, this intimate permission could not have been had without the privileged intervention of Sherlock."

"There is no question," Miss Madeleine B. Stern added in "Sherlock Holmes: Rare Book Collector," "that for his aural researches [Holmes] obtained a copy of Falloppio's *Observationes anatomicae* (Venice, 1561), a work containing the first scientific account of the structure of the ear."

22 *the pinna.* The projecting portion of the exterior ear.

"... THIS STEWARD, AN IMPULSIVE MAN, OF STRONG PASSIONS ..."

Portrait of Jim Browner by Sidney Paget for the *Strand Magazine*, January, 1893.

too, to occasional fits of hard drinking. We had reason to believe that his wife had been murdered, and that a man—presumably a seafaring man—had been murdered at the same time. Jealousy, of course, at once suggests itself as the motive for the crime. And why should these proofs of the deed be sent to Miss Sarah Cushing? Probably because during her residence in Liverpool she had some hand in bringing about the events which led to the tragedy. You will observe that this line of boats calls at Belfast, Dublin, and Waterford; so that, presuming that Browner had committed the deed, and had embarked at once upon his steamer, the *May Day*, Belfast would be the first place at which he could post his terrible packet.

"A second solution was at this stage obviously possible, and although I thought it exceedingly unlikely, I was determined to elucidate it before going further. An unsuccessful lover might have killed Mr. and Mrs. Browner, and the male ear might have belonged to the husband. There were many grave objections to this theory, but it was conceivable. I therefore sent off a telegram to my friend Algar, of the Liverpool Force, and asked him to find out if Mrs. Browner were at home, and if Browner had departed in the *May Day*. Then we went on to Wallington to visit Miss Sarah.

"I was curious, in the first place, to see how far the family ear had been reproduced in her. Then, of course, she might give us very important information, but I was not sanguine that she would. She must have heard of the business the day before, since all Croydon was ringing with it, and she alone could have understood for whom the packet was meant. If she had been willing to help justice she would probably have communicated with the police already. However, it was clearly our duty to see her, so we went. We found that the news of the arrival of the packet—for her illness dated from that time—had such an effect upon her as to bring on brain fever. It was clearer than ever that she understood its full significance, but equally clear that we should have to wait some time for any assistance from her.

"However, we were really independent of her help. Our answers were waiting for us at the police-station, where I had directed Algar to send them. Nothing could be more conclusive. Mrs. Browner's house had been closed for more than three days, and the neighbours were of opinion that she had gone south to see her relatives. It had been ascertained at the shipping offices that Browner had left aboard of the *May Day*, and I calculate that she is due in the Thames to-morrow night. When he arrives he will be met by the obtuse but resolute Lestrade, and I have no doubt that we shall have all our details filled in."

Sherlock Holmes was not disappointed in his expectations. Two days later he received a bulky envelope, which contained a short note from the detective, and a typewritten document, which covered several pages of foolscap.

"Lestrade has got him all right," said Holmes, glancing up at me. "Perhaps it would interest you to hear what he says."

"My dear Mr. Holmes,—

"In accordance with the scheme which we had formed in order to test our theories"—"the 'we' is rather fine, Watson, is it not?"—"I went down to the Albert Dock yesterday at 6 p.m., and boarded the s.s. *May Day*, belonging to the Liverpool, Dublin, and London Steam Packet Company. On inquiry, I found that there was a steward on board of the name of James Browner and that he had acted during the voyage in such an extraordinary manner that the captain had been compelled to relieve him of his duties. On descending to his berth, I found him seated upon a chest with his head sunk upon his hands, rocking himself to and fro. He is a big, powerful chap, clean-shaven, and very swarthy—something like Aldridge, who helped us in the bogus laundry affair. He jumped up when he heard my business, and I had my whistle to my lips to call a couple of river police, who were round the corner, but he seemed to have no heart in him, and he held out his hands quietly enough for the darbies. We brought him along to the cells, and his box as well, for we thought there might be something incriminating; but, bar a big sharp knife, such as most sailors have, we got nothing for our trouble. However, we find that we shall want no more evidence, for on being brought before the inspector at the station, he asked leave to make a statement, which was, of course, taken down, just as he made it, by our shorthand man. We had three copies typewritten, one of which I enclose. The affair proves, as I always thought it would, to be an extremely simple one, but I am obliged to you for assisting me in my investigation. With kind regards, yours very truly,

"G. Lestrade."

Hum! The investigation really was a very simple one," remarked Holmes; "but I don't think it struck him in that light when he first called us in. However, let us see what Jim Browner has to say for himself. This is his statement, as made before Inspector Montgomery at the
23 Shadwell Police Station, and it has the advantage of being verbatim."

"Have I anything to say? Yes, I have a deal to say. I have to make a clean breast of it all. You can hang me, or you can leave me alone. I don't care a plug which you do. I tell you I've not shut an eye in sleep since I did it, and I don't believe I ever will again until I get past all waking. Sometimes it's his face, but most generally it's hers. I'm never without one or the other before me. He looks frowning and black-like, but she has a kind o' surprise upon her face. Aye, the white lamb, she might well be surprised when she read death on a face that had seldom looked anything but love upon her before.

"But it was Sarah's fault, and may the curse of a broken man put a blight on her and set the blood rotting in her veins! It's not that I want to clear myself. I know that I went back to drink, like the beast that I was. But she would have forgiven me; she would have stuck as close to me as a rope to a block if that woman had never darkened our door. For Sarah Cushing loved me—that's the root of the business—she loved me, until all her love turned to

23 *Shadwell.* One of the poorest and most densely populated districts in East London.

"... HE HELD OUT HIS HANDS QUIETLY ENOUGH FOR THE DARBIES."

Illustration by Sidney Paget for the *Strand Magazine*, January, 1893.

poisonous hate when she knew that I thought more of my wife's foot-mark in the mud than I did of her whole body and soul.

" There were three sisters altogether. The old one was just a good woman, the second was a devil, and the third was an angel. Sarah was thirty-three, and Mary was twenty-nine when I married. We were just as happy as the day was long when we set up house together, and in all Liverpool there was no better woman than my Mary. And then we asked Sarah up for a week, and the week grew into a month, and one thing led to another, until she was just one of ourselves.

" I was blue ribbon at that time, and we were putting a **24**
little money by, and all was as bright as a new dollar. My God, whoever would have thought that it could have come to this ? Whoever would have dreamed it ?

" I used to be home for the week-ends very often, and sometimes if the ship were held back for cargo I would have a whole week at a time, and in this way I saw a deal of my sister-in-law, Sarah. She was a fine tall woman, black and quick and fierce, with a proud way of carrying her head, and a glint from her eye like a spark from a flint. But when little Mary was there I had never a thought of her, and that I swear as I hope for God's mercy.

" It had seemed to me sometimes that she liked to be alone with me, or to coax me out for a walk with her, but I had never thought anything of that. But one evening my eyes were opened. I had come up from the ship and found my wife out, but Sarah at home. ' Where's Mary ? ' I asked. ' Oh, she has gone to pay some accounts.' I was impatient and paced up and down the room. ' Can't you be happy for five minutes without Mary, Jim ? ' says she. ' It's a bad compliment to me that you can't be contented with my society for so short a time.' ' That's all right, my lass,' said I, putting out my hand towards her in a kindly way, but she had it in both hers in an instant, and they burned as if they were in a fever. I looked into her eyes and I read it all there. There was no need for her to speak, nor for me either. I frowned and drew my hand away. Then she stood by my side in silence for a bit, and then put up her hand and patted me on the shoulder. ' Steady, old Jim ! ' said she ; and with a kind o' mocking laugh, she ran out of the room.

" Well, from that time Sarah hated me with her whole heart and soul, and she is a woman who can hate too. I was a fool to let her go on biding with us—a besotted fool —but I never said a word to Mary, for I knew it would grieve her. Things went on much as before, but after a time I began to find that there was a bit of a change in Mary herself. She had always been so trusting and so innocent, but now she became queer and suspicious, wanting to know where I had been and what I had been doing, and whom my letters were from, and what I had in my pockets, and a thousand such follies. Day by day she grew queerer and more irritable, and we had causeless rows about nothing. I was fairly puzzled by it all. Sarah avoided me now, but she and Mary were just inseparable. I can see now how she was plotting and scheming and poisoning my wife's mind against me, but I was such a blind beetle

24 *blue ribbon.* On the wagon; not drinking; from a small strip of blue ribbon worn as a distinctive badge by an organization of teetotallers called the Blue Ribbon Army, founded in 1878.

" 'THAT'S ALL RIGHT, MY LASS,' SAID I . . ."

Illustration by Sidney Paget for the *Strand Magazine*, January, 1893.

that I could not understand it at the time. Then I broke my blue ribbon and began to drink again, but I think I should not have done it if Mary had been the same as ever. She had some reason to be disgusted with me now, and the gap between us began to be wider and wider. And then this Alec Fairbairn chipped in, and things became a thousand times blacker.

" It was to see Sarah that he came to my house first, but soon it was to see us, for he was a man with winning ways, and he made friends wherever he went. He was a dashing, swaggering chap, smart and curled, who had seen half the world, and could talk of what he had seen. He was good company, I won't deny it, and he had wonderful polite ways with him for a sailor man, so that I think there must have been a time when he knew more of the poop than the forecastle. For a month he was in and out of my house, and never once did it cross my mind that harm might come of his soft, tricky ways. And then at last something made me suspect, and from that day my peace was gone for ever.

" It was only a little thing too. I had come into the parlour unexpected, and as I walked in at the door I saw a light of welcome on my wife's face. But as she saw who it was it faded again, and she turned away with a look of disappointment. That was enough for me. There was no one but Alec Fairbairn whose step she could have mistaken for mine. If I could have seen him then I should have killed him, for I have always been like a madman when my temper gets loose. Mary saw the devil's light in my eyes, and she ran forward with her hands on my sleeve. ' Don't, Jim, don't ! ' says she. ' Where's Sarah ? ' I asked. ' In the kitchen,' says she. ' Sarah,' says I, as I went in, ' this man Fairbairn is never to darken my door again.' ' Why not ? ' says she. ' Because I order it.' ' Oh ! ' says she, ' if my friends are not good enough for this house then I am not good enough for it either.' ' You can do what you like,' says I, ' but if Fairbairn shows his face here again, I'll send you one of his ears for a keepsake.' She was frightened by my face, I think, for she never answered a word, and the same evening she left my house.

" Well, I don't know now whether it was pure devilry on the part of this woman, or whether she thought that she could turn me against my wife by encouraging her to misbehave. Anyway, she took a house just two streets off, and let lodgings to sailors. Fairbairn used to stay there, and Mary would go round to have tea with her sister and him. How often she went I don't know, but I followed her one day, and as I broke in at the door, Fairbairn got away over the back garden wall, like the cowardly skunk that he was. I swore to my wife that I would kill her if I found her in his company again, and I led her back with me, sobbing and trembling, and as white as a piece of paper. There was no trace of love between us any longer. I could see that she hated me and feared me, and when the thought of it drove me to drink then she despised me as well.

" Well, Sarah found that she could not make a living in Liverpool, so she went back, as I understand, to live with her sister in Croydon, and things jogged on much the same as ever at home. And then came this last week and all the misery and ruin.

" It was in this way. We had gone on the *May Day* for a round voyage of seven days, but a hogshead got loose and started one of our plates, so that we had to put back into port for twelve hours. I left the ship and came home, thinking what a surprise it would be for my wife, and hoping that maybe she would be glad to see me so soon. The thought was in my head as I turned into my own street, and at that moment a cab passed me, and there she was, sitting by the side of Fairbairn, the two chatting and laughing, with never a thought for me as I stood watching them from the footpath.

" I tell you, and I give you my word for it, that from that moment I was not my own master, and it is all like a dim dream when I look back on it. I had been drinking hard of late, and the two things together fairly turned my brain. There's something throbbing in my head now, like a docker's hammer, but that morning I seemed to have all Niagara whizzing and buzzing in my ears.

" Well, I took to my heels, and I ran after the cab. I had a heavy oak stick in my hand, and I tell you I saw red from the first ; but as I ran I got cunning, too, and hung back a little to see them without being seen. They pulled up soon at the railway station. There was a good crowd round the booking-office, so I got quite close to them
without being seen. They took tickets for New Brighton. **25**
So did I, but I got in three carriages behind them. When we reached it they walked along the Parade, and I was never more than a hundred yards from them. At last I saw them hire a boat and start for a row, for it was a very hot day, and they thought no doubt that it would be cooler on the water.

" It was just as if they had been given into my hands. There was a bit of a haze, and you could not see more than a few hundred yards. I hired a boat for myself, and I pulled after them. I could see the blurr of their craft, but they were going nearly as fast as I, and they must have been a long mile from the shore before I caught them up. The haze was like a curtain all round us, and there were we three in the middle of it. My God, shall I ever forget their faces when they saw who was in the boat that was closing in upon them ? She screamed out. He swore like a madman, and jabbed at me with an oar, for he must have seen death in my eyes. I got past it and got one in with my stick, that crushed his head like an egg. I would have spared her, perhaps, for all my madness, but she threw her arms round him, crying out to him, and calling him ' Alec.' I struck again, and she lay stretched beside him. I was like a wild beast then that had tasted blood. If Sarah had been there, by the Lord, she should have joined them. I pulled out my knife, and—well, there ! I've said enough. It gave me a kind of savage joy when I thought how Sarah would feel when she had such signs as these of what her meddling had brought about. Then I tied the bodies into the boat, stove a plank, and stood by until they had sunk. I knew very well that the owner would think that they had lost their bearings in the haze, and had drifted off out to sea. I cleaned myself up, got

25 *New Brighton.* A watering place in Cheshire.

"I . . . GOT ONE IN WITH MY STICK, THAT CRUSHED HIS HEAD LIKE AN EGG."

Illustration by Sidney Paget for the *Strand Magazine*, January, 1893.

back to land, and joined my ship without a soul having a suspicion of what had passed. That night I made up the packet for Sarah Cushing, and next day I sent it from Belfast.

" There you have the whole truth of it. You can hang me, or do what you like with me, but you cannot punish me as I have been punished already. I cannot shut my eyes but I see those two faces staring at me—staring at me as they stared when my boat broke through the haze. I killed them quick, but they are killing me slow ; and if I have another night of it I shall be either mad or dead before morning. You won't put me alone into a cell, sir ? For pity's sake don't, and may you be treated in your day of agony as you treat me now."

" What is the meaning of it, Watson ? " said Holmes, solemnly, as he laid down the paper. " What object is served by this circle of misery and violence and fear ? It must tend to some end, or else our universe is ruled by chance, which is unthinkable. But what end ? There is the great standing perennial problem to which human reason is as far from an answer as ever."

A CHAPTER ON EARS.

and also as a reservoir of sound before it passes into the drum of the ear. The smaller the concha, therefore, the more sensitive the

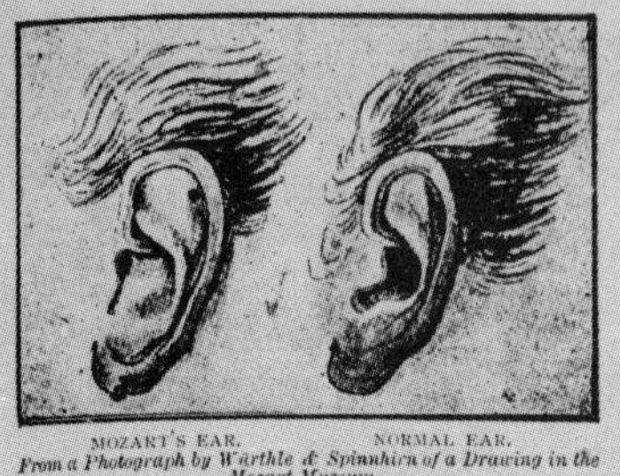

MOZART'S EAR. NORMAL EAR.
From a Photograph by Wärthle & Spinnhirn of a Drawing in the Mozart Museum.

organ to sound, as there is less medium to receive the current and distribute it.

The size of an ear is generally believed by many well-intentioned persons to be in inverse proportion to the size of the brain or amount of intellectual faculties. We see no reason to differ from this theory. The only eulogy of large ears most people have come across is that of Queen Titania, who praised the "fair, *large* ears" of Bottom, the weaver.

If the reader will accurately contemplate the ears of celebrities which appear in conjunction with these articles, they will become the possessors of some very curious facts. One of these facts is that to be gr... it is above all thin... to have an abridged h... man or woman ...

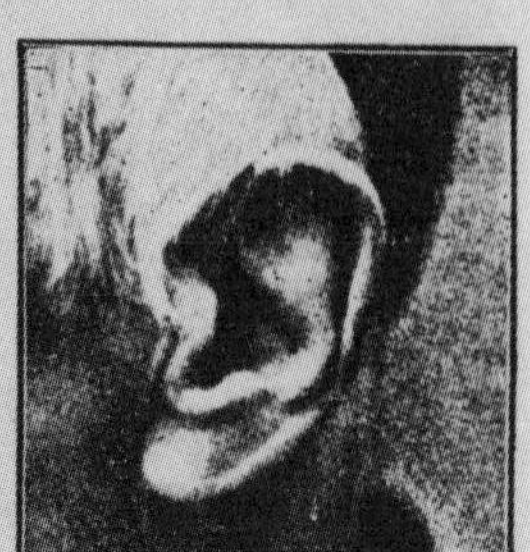

CARDINAL NEWMAN'S EAR.

cates. It is true that to inculcate this theory into the minds of youth might be, if not pernicious, at least undesirable. Knowing themselves to be equipped with the ægis of an abridged helix, children might possibly be tempted to neglect their studies in waiting for the flood which should drift them in the wake of Gladstone, and a score of his compeers.

CHARLES DICKENS'S EAR.

But if a thin helix is a boon, a prominent anti-helix is just the reverse. Anyone who has, therefore, hitherto prided himself or herself upon a prominent anti-helix, or even exhibited it to his or her friends with some complacency, should make haste to bring about an alteration—not in their ears, for that might be embarrassing—but in their views. The police bureaus of the world teem

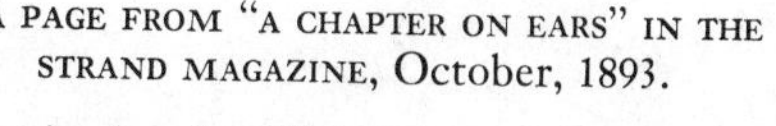

A PAGE FROM "A CHAPTER ON EARS" IN THE STRAND MAGAZINE, October, 1893.

The inspiration for Holmes' monograph on ears—or the monograph itself?

42

THE ADVENTURE OF THE ENGINEER'S THUMB

[*Saturday, September 7, to Sunday, September 8, 1889*]

OF all the problems which have been submitted to my friend Mr. Sherlock Holmes for solution during the years of our intimacy, there were only two which I was the means of introducing to his notice, that of Mr. Hatherley's thumb and that of Colonel Warburton's madness. Of these the latter may have 1 afforded a finer field for an acute and original observer, but the other was so strange in its inception and so dramatic in its details, that it may be the more worthy of being placed upon record, even if it gave my friend fewer openings for those deductive methods of reasoning by which he achieved such remarkable results. The story has, I believe, been told more than once in the newspapers, but, like all such narratives, its effect is much less striking when set forth *en bloc* in a single half-column of print than when the facts slowly evolve before your own eyes and the mystery clears gradually away as each new discovery furnishes a step which leads on to the complete truth. At the time the circumstances made a deep impression upon me, and the lapse of two years has hardly served to weaken the effect.

It was in the summer of '89, not long after my marriage, that the events occurred which I am now about to summarize. I had returned to civil practice, and had finally abandoned Holmes in his Baker Street rooms, although I continually visited him, and occasionally even persuaded him to forgo his Bohemian habits so far as to come and visit us. My practice had steadily increased, and as I happened to live at no very great distance from Paddington Station, I got a few patients from among the officials. One of these whom I had cured of a painful and lingering disease, was never weary of advertising my virtues, and of endeavouring to send me on every sufferer over whom he might have any influence.

One morning, at a little before seven o'clock, I was awakened by the maid tapping at the door, to announce that two men had come from Paddington, and were waiting in the consulting-room. I dressed hurriedly, for I knew by experience that railway cases were seldom trivial, and hastened downstairs. As I descended, my old ally, the guard, came out of the room, and closed the door tightly behind him.

1 *Colonel Warburton's madness.* A pastiche of this adventure by Rolfe Boswell appeared in the *Baker Street Journal*, Vol. XII, No. 2, New Series, June, 1962, pp. 85–98; another, by the late Norman W. Ward, appeared in *The Best of the Pips*, pp. 59–73; a third, titled "The Adventure of the Sealed Room," by Adrian M. Conan Doyle and John Dickson Carr, appeared in *The Exploits of Sherlock Holmes.*

" I've got him here," he whispered, jerking his thumb over his shoulder ; " he's all right."

" What is it, then ? " I asked, for his manner suggested that it was some strange creature which he had caged up in my room.

" It's a new patient," he whispered. " I thought I'd bring him round myself ; then he couldn't slip away. There he is, all safe and sound. I must go now, Doctor, I have my dooties, just the same as you." And off he went, this trusty tout, without even giving me time to thank him.

I entered my consulting-room, and found a gentleman seated by the table. He was quietly dressed in a suit of heather tweed, with a soft cloth cap, which he had laid down upon my books. Round one of his hands he had a handkerchief wrapped, which was mottled all over with bloodstains. He was young, not more than five-and-twenty, I should say, with a strong masculine face ; but he was exceedingly pale, and gave me the impression of a man who was suffering from some strong agitation, which it took all his strength of mind to control.

" I am sorry to knock you up so early, Doctor," said he. " But I have had a very serious accident during the night. I came in by train this morning, and on inquiring at Paddington as to where I might find a doctor a worthy fellow very kindly escorted me here. I gave the maid a card, but I see that she has left it upon the side table."

I took it up and glanced at it. " Mr. Victor Hatherley,
2 hydraulic engineer, 16A Victoria Street (3rd floor)." That was the name, style, and abode of my morning visitor. " I regret that I have kept you waiting," said I, sitting down in my library chair. " You are fresh from a night journey, I understand, which is in itself a monotonous occupation."

" Oh, my night could not be called monotonous," said he, and laughed. He laughed very heartily, with a high ringing note, leaning back in his chair, and shaking his sides. All my medical instincts rose up against that laugh.

" Stop it ! " I cried. " Pull yourself together ! " and I poured out some water from a carafe.

It was useless, however. He was off in one of those hysterical outbursts which come upon a strong nature when some great crisis is over and gone. Presently he came to himself once more, very weary and blushing hotly.

" I have been making a fool of myself," he gasped.

" Not at all. Drink this ! " I dashed some brandy into the water, and the colour began to come back to his
3 bloodless cheeks.

" That's better ! " said he. " And now, Doctor, perhaps you would kindly attend to my thumb, or rather to the place where my thumb used to be."

He unwound the handkerchief and held out his hand. It gave even my hardened nerves a shudder to look at it. There were four protruding fingers and a horrid red spongy surface where the thumb should have been. It had been hacked or torn right out from the roots.

" Good heavens ! " I cried, " this is a terrible injury. It must have bled considerably."

2 *Victoria Street.* Victoria Street, opening into Broad Sanctuary and Parliament Square, was commenced in 1845 and was seven years in course of construction, being opened to the public on August 6, 1851. When first opened it was one of the sights of London. It opened up a magnificent new vista of Westminster Abbey and the new Houses of Parliament.

3 *the colour began to come back to his bloodless cheeks.* "In the patient's already excitable condition a hot drink rather than alcoholic stimulant might seem more appropriate," Miss Helen Simpson commented in "Medical Career and Capabilities of Dr. J. H. Watson."

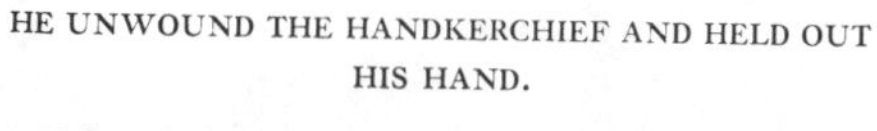

HE UNWOUND THE HANDKERCHIEF AND HELD OUT HIS HAND.

Illustration by Sidney Paget for the *Strand Magazine*, March, 1892.

" Yes, it did. I fainted when it was done ; and I think that I must have been senseless for a long time. When I came to, I found that it was still bleeding, so I tied one end of my handkerchief very tightly round the wrist, and braced it up with a twig."

" Excellent ! You should have been a surgeon."

" It is a question of hydraulics, you see, and came within my own province."

" This has been done," said I, examining the wound, by a very heavy and sharp instrument."

" A thing like a cleaver," said he.

" An accident, I presume ? "

" By no means."

" What, a murderous attack ! "

" Very murderous indeed."

" You horrify me."

I sponged the wound, cleaned it, dressed it ; and, finally, covered it over with cotton wadding and carbolized bandages. He lay back without wincing, though he bit his lip from time to time.

" How is that ? " I asked, when I had finished.

" Capital ! Between your brandy and your bandage, I feel a new man. I was very weak, but I have had a good deal to go through."

" Perhaps you had not better speak of the matter. It is evidently trying to your nerves."

" Oh, no ; not now. I shall have to tell my tale to the police ; but, between ourselves, if it were not for the convincing evidence of this wound of mine, I should be surprised if they believed my statement, for it is a very extraordinary one, and I have not much in the way of proof with which to back it up. And, even if they believe me, the clues which I can give them are so vague that it is a question whether justice will be done."

" Ha ! " cried I, " if it is anything in the nature of a problem which you desire to see solved, I should strongly recommend you to come to my friend Mr. Sherlock Holmes before you go to the official police."

" Oh, I have heard of that fellow," answered my visitor, " and I should be very glad if he would take the matter up, though of course I must use the official police as well. Would you give me an introduction to him ? "

" I'll do better. I'll take you round to him myself."

" I should be immensely obliged to you."

" We'll call a cab and go together. We shall just be in time to have a little breakfast with him. Do you feel equal to it ? "

" Yes. I shall not feel easy until I have told my story."

" Then my servant will call a cab, and I shall be with you in an instant." I rushed upstairs, explained the matter shortly to my wife, and in five minutes was inside a hansom, driving with my new acquaintance to Baker Street.

Sherlock Holmes was, as I expected, lounging about
his sitting-room in his dressing-gown, reading the agony
column of *The Times*, and smoking his before-breakfast 4
pipe, which was composed of all the plugs and dottles
left from his smokes of the day before, all carefully dried
and collected on the corner of the mantelpiece. He

4 *reading the agony column of* The Times. The day was therefore not a Sunday. Nor was it a Monday: Colonel Lysander Stark called on Mr. Hatherley "yesterday . . . just as I was leaving the office."

. . . HE SETTLED OUR NEW ACQUAINTANCE UPON THE SOFA . . .

Illustration by Sidney Paget for the *Strand Magazine*, March, 1892.

. . . A MAN RATHER OVER THE MIDDLE SIZE BUT OF AN EXCEEDING THINNESS.

Portrait of Colonel Lysander Stark by Sidney Paget for the *Strand Magazine*, March, 1892.

received us in his quietly genial fashion, ordered fresh rashers and eggs, and joined us in a hearty meal. When it was concluded he settled our new acquaintance upon the sofa, placed a pillow beneath his head, and laid a glass of brandy and water within his reach.

" It is easy to see that your experience has been no common one, Mr. Hatherley," said he. " Pray lie down there and make yourself absolutely at home. Tell us what you can, but stop when you are tired, and keep up your strength with a little stimulant."

" Thank you," said my patient, " but I have felt another man since the doctor bandaged me, and I think that your breakfast has completed the cure. I shall take up as little of your valuable time as possible, so I shall start at once upon my peculiar experiences."

Holmes sat in his big arm-chair, with the weary, heavy-lidded expression which veiled his keen and eager nature, while I sat opposite to him, and we listened in silence to the strange story which our visitor detailed to us.

" You must know," said he, " that I am an orphan and a bachelor, residing alone in lodgings in London. By profession I am a hydraulic engineer, and have had considerable experience of my work during the seven years that I was apprenticed to Venner & Matheson, the well-known firm of Greenwich. Two years ago, having served my time, and having also come into a fair sum of money through my poor father's death, I determined to start in business for myself, and took professional chambers in Victoria Street.

" I suppose that everyone finds his first independent
start in business a dreary experience. To me it has been
exceptionally so. During two years I have had three
consultations and one small job, and that is absolutely
all that my profession has brought me. My gross takings
amount to twenty-seven pounds ten. Every day, from **5**
nine in the morning until four in the afternoon, I waited
in my little den, until at last my heart began to sink, and I
came to believe that I should never have any practice at all.

" Yesterday, however, just as I was thinking of
leaving the office, my clerk entered to say there was a
gentleman waiting who wished to see me upon business.
He brought up a card, too, with the name of ' Colonel
Lysander Stark ' engraved upon it. Close at his heels **6**
came the Colonel himself, a man rather over the middle
size but of an exceeding thinness. I do not think that I
have ever seen so thin a man. His whole face sharpened
away into nose and chin, and the skin of his cheeks was
drawn quite tense over his outstanding bones. Yet this
emaciation seemed to be his natural habit, and due to no
disease, for his eye was bright, his step brisk, and his bearing assured. He was plainly but neatly dressed, and his
age, I should judge, would be nearer forty than thirty.

" ' Mr. Hatherley ? ' said he, with something of a German accent. ' You have been recommended to me, Mr. Hatherley, as being a man who is not only proficient in his profession, but is also discreet and capable of preserving a secret.'

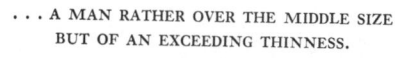

" I bowed, feeling as flattered as any young man would at such an address. ' May I ask who it was who gave me so good a character ? ' I asked.

" ' Well, perhaps it is better that I should not tell you just at this moment. I have it from the same source that you are both an orphan and a bachelor, and are residing alone in London.'

" ' That is quite correct,' I answered, ' but you will excuse me if I say that I cannot see how all this bears upon my professional qualifications. I understood that it was on a professional matter that you wished to speak to me ? '

" ' Undoubtedly so. But you will find that all I say is really to the point. I have a professional commission for you, but absolute secrecy is quite essential—*absolute* secrecy, you understand, and of course we may expect that more from a man who is alone than from one who lives in the bosom of his family.'

" ' If I promise to keep a secret,' said I, ' you may absolutely depend upon my doing so.'

" He looked very hard at me as I spoke, and it seemed to me that I had never seen so suspicious and questioning an eye.

" ' You do promise, then ? ' said he at last.

" ' Yes, I promise.'

" ' Absolute and complete silence, before, during, and after ? No reference to the matter at all, either in word or writing ? '

" ' I have already given you my word.'

" ' Very good.' He suddenly sprang up, and darting like lightning across the room he flung open the door. The passage outside was empty.

" ' That's all right,' said he, coming back. ' I know that clerks are sometimes curious as to their masters' affairs. Now we can talk in safety.' He drew up his chair very close to mine, and began to stare at me again with the same questioning and thoughtful look.

" A feeling of repulsion and of something akin to fear had begun to rise within me at the strange antics of this fleshless man. Even my dread of losing a client could not restrain me from showing my impatience.

" ' I beg that you will state your business, sir,' said I ; my time is of value.' Heaven forgive me for that last sentence, but the words came to my lips.

" ' How would fifty guineas for a night's work suit 7
you ? ' he asked.

" ' Most admirably.'

" ' I say a night's work, but an hour's would be nearer the mark. I simply want your opinion about a hydraulic stamping machine which has got out of gear. If you show us what is wrong we shall soon set it right ourselves. What do you think of such a commission as that ? '

" ' The work appears to be light, and the pay munificent.'

" ' Precisely so. We shall want you to come to-night by the last train.'

" ' Where to ? '

" ' To Eyford, in Berkshire. It is a little place near the 8
borders of Oxfordshire, and within seven miles of Reading. There is a train from Paddington which would bring you in there at about eleven fifteen.'

5 *twenty-seven pounds ten.* About $137.50 U.S. at the time.

6 *'Colonel Lysander Stark.'* This name was "almost certainly derived from Leander Starr Jameson who was such a notable, and at times notorious, figure in South African affairs during the nineties," Mr. Bliss Austin wrote in *A Baker Street Christmas Stocking* (1955). "Jameson was a native of Edinburgh and was educated for the medical profession at University College Hospital in London (M.D. 1877 or one year before Watson received his degree). Whether he was acquainted with either Dr. Watson or Dr. Conan Doyle is not clear. In 1878 he went to Kimberley where he came to know Cecil Rhodes. In 1891, Dr. Jim, as he was then called, was made Administrator of Rhodesia —and in November of that same year, Watson's report which first carried a variation of Jameson's name was submitted to the Editor of the *Strand*. One may well ask whether this was coincidence or osmosis; also, whether any significance attaches to the fact that Lysander was a highly questionable character. Later, in 1895, Dr. Jim became an international celebrity by leading an abortive raid into the Transvaal. But the other [Canonical] variation of his name [Lysander Starr in "The Adventure of the Three Garridebs"] did not appear in the *Strand* until 1925, some eight years after his death. In this case one suspects the further workings of osmosis. In any event, there seems ample grounds for Irregular speculation on this whole matter."

7 *fifty guineas.* About $262.50 U.S. at the time.

8 *Eyford, in Berkshire.* Research has so far failed to uncover an Eyford in Berkshire. There is one in Gloucestershire, but it is not on the railway.

9 *fuller's earth.* A sedimentary clay which has the property of absorbing basic colors. It is chiefly used in clarifying petroleum and refining edible oils.

" ' Very good.'

" ' I shall come down in a carriage to meet you.'

" ' There is a drive, then ? '

" ' Yes, our little place is quite out in the country. It is a good seven miles from Eyford station.'

" ' Then we can hardly get there before midnight. I suppose there would be no chance of a train back. I should be compelled to stop the night.'

" ' Yes, we could easily give you a shakedown.'

" ' That is very awkward. Could I not come at some more convenient hour ? '

" ' We have judged it best that you should come late. It is to recompense you for any inconvenience that we are paying you, a young and unknown man, a fee which would buy an opinion from the very heads of your profession. Still, of course, if you would like to draw out of the business, there is plenty of time to do so.'

" I thought of the fifty guineas, and of how very useful they would be to me. Not at all,' said I ; ' I shall be very happy to accommodate myself to your wishes. I should like, however, to understand a little more clearly what it is that you wish me to do.'

" ' Quite so. It is very natural that the pledge of secrecy which we have exacted from you should have aroused your curiosity. I have no wish to commit you to anything without your having it all laid before you. I suppose that we are absolutely safe from eavesdroppers ? '

" ' Entirely.'

" ' Then the matter stands thus. You are probably
9 aware that fuller's earth is a valuable product, and that it
is only found in one or two places in England ? '

" ' I have heard so.'

" ' Some little time ago I bought a small place—a very small place—within ten miles of Reading. I was fortunate enough to discover that there was a deposit of fuller's earth in one of my fields. On examining it, however, I found that this deposit was a comparatively small one, and that it formed a link between two very much larger ones upon the right and the left—both of them, however, in the grounds of my neighbours. These good people were absolutely ignorant that their land contained that which was quite as valuable as a gold mine. Naturally, it was to my interest to buy their land before they discovered its true value ; but, unfortunately, I had no capital by which I could do this. I took a few of my friends into the secret, however, and they suggested that we should quietly and secretly work our own little deposit, and that in this way we should earn the money which would enable us to buy the neighbouring fields. This we have now been doing for some time, and in order to help us in our operations we erected a hydraulic press. This press, as I have already explained, has got out of order, and we wish your advice upon the subject. We guard our secret very jealously, however, and if it once became known that we had hydraulic engineers coming to our little house, it would soon rouse inquiry, and then, if the facts came out, it would be good-bye to any chance of getting these fields and carrying out our plans. That is why I have made you promise me that you will not tell a human being that you are going to Eyford to-night. I hope that I make it all plain ? '

" ' I quite follow you,' said I. ' The only point which I could not quite understand, was what use you could make of a hydraulic press in excavating fuller's earth, which, as I understand, is dug out like gravel from a pit.'

" ' Ah ! ' said he carelessly, ' we have our own process. We compress the earth into bricks, so as to remove them without revealing what they are. But that is a mere detail. I have taken you fully into my confidence now, Mr. Hatherley, and I have shown you how I trust you.' He rose as he spoke. ' I shall expect you, then, at Eyford, at 11.15.'

" ' I shall certainly be there.'

" ' And not a word to a soul.' He looked at me with a last long, questioning gaze, and then, pressing my hand in a cold, dank grasp, he hurried from the room.

" Well, when I came to think it all over in cool blood I was very much astonished, as you may both think, at this sudden commission which had been entrusted to me. On the one hand, of course, I was glad, for the fee was at least tenfold what I should have asked had I set a price upon my own services, and it was possible that this order might lead to other ones. On the other hand, the face and manner of my patron had made an unpleasant impression upon me, and I could not think that his explanation of the fuller's earth was sufficient to explain the necessity for my coming at midnight, and his extreme anxiety lest I should tell anyone of my errand. However, I threw all my fears to the winds, ate a hearty supper, drove to Paddington, and started off, having obeyed to the letter the injunction as to holding my tongue.

" At Reading I had to change not only my carriage but my station. However, I was in time for the last train to Eyford, and I reached the little dim-lit station after eleven o'clock. I was the only passenger who got out there, and there was no one upon the platform save a single sleepy porter with a lantern. As I passed out through the wicket-gate, however, I found my acquaintance of the morning waiting in the shadow upon the other side. Without a word he grasped my arm and hurried me into a carriage, the door of which was standing open. He drew up the windows on either side, tapped on the woodwork, and away we went as hard as the horse could go."

" One horse ? " interjected Holmes.

" Yes, only one."

" Did you observe the colour ? "

" Yes, I saw it by the sidelights when I was stepping into the carriage. It was a chestnut."

" Tired-looking or fresh ? "

" Oh, fresh and glossy."

" Thank you. I am sorry to have interrupted you. Pray continue your most interesting statement."

" Away we went then, and we drove for at least an hour. Colonel Lysander Stark had said that it was only seven miles, but I should think, from the rate that we seemed to go, and the time that we took, that it must have been nearer twelve. He sat at my side in silence all the time, and I was aware, more than once when I glanced in his direction, that he was looking at me with great intensity. The country roads seemed to be not very good in that part of the world, for we lurched and jolted terribly. I tried to look out of the windows to see something

" 'AND NOT A WORD TO A SOUL.' "

Illustration by Sidney Paget for the *Strand Magazine*, March, 1892.

of where we were, but they were made of frosted glass, and I could make out nothing save an occasional blurr of a passing light. Now and then I hazarded some remark to break the monotony of the journey, but the Colonel answered only in monosyllables, and the conversation soon flagged. At last, however, the bumping of the road was exchanged for the crisp smoothness of a gravel drive and the carriage came to a stand. Colonel Lysander Stark sprang out, and, as I followed after him, pulled me swiftly into a porch which gaped in front of us. We stepped, as it were, right out of the carriage and into the hall, so that I failed to catch the most fleeting glance of the front of the house. The instant that I had crossed the threshold the door slammed heavily behind us, and I heard faintly the rattle of the wheels as the carriage drove away.

" It was pitch dark inside the house, and the Colonel fumbled about looking for matches, and muttering under his breath. Suddenly a door opened at the other end of the passage, and a long, golden bar of light shot out in our direction. It grew broader, and a woman appeared with a lamp in her hand, which she held above her head, pushing her face forward and peering at us. I could see that she was pretty, and from the gloss with which the light shone upon her dark dress I knew that it was a rich material. She spoke a few words in a foreign tongue in a tone as though asking a question, and when my companion answered in a gruff monosyllable she gave such a start that the lamp nearly fell from her hand. Colonel Stark went up to her, whispered something in her ear, and then, pushing her back into the room from whence she had come, he walked towards me again with the lamp in his hand.

" ' Perhaps you will have the kindness to wait in this room for a few minutes,' said he, throwing open another door. It was a quiet little plainly furnished room, with a round table in the centre, on which several German books were scattered. Colonel Stark laid down the lamp on the top of a harmonium beside the door. ' I shall not keep you waiting an instant,' said he, and vanished into the darkness.

" I glanced at the books upon the table, and in spite of my ignorance of German, I could see that two of them were treatises on science, the others being volumes of poetry. Then I walked across to the window, hoping that I might catch some glimpse of the country-side, but an oak shutter, heavily barred, was folded across it. It was a wonderfully silent house. There was an old clock ticking loudly somewhere in the passage, but otherwise everything was deadly still. A vague feeling of uneasiness began to steal over me. Who were these German people, and what were they doing, living in this strange, out-of-the-way place ? And where was the place ? I was ten miles or so from Eyford, that was all I knew, but whether north, south, east, or west, I had no idea. For that matter, Reading, and possibly other large towns, were within that radius, so the place might not be so secluded after all. Yet it was quite certain from the absolute stillness that we were in the country. I paced up and down the room humming a tune under my breath to keep up my spirits, and feeling that I was thoroughly earning my fifty-guinea fee.

" Suddenly, without any preliminary sound in the midst of the utter stillness, the door of my room swung slowly open. The woman was standing in the aperture, the darkness of the hall behind her, the yellow light from my lamp beating upon her eager and beautiful face. I could see at a glance that she was sick with fear, and the sight sent a chill to my own heart. She held up one shaking finger to warn me to be silent, and she shot a few whispered words of broken English at me, her eyes glancing back, like those of a frightened horse, into the gloom behind her.

" ' I would go,' said she, trying hard, as it seemed to me, to speak calmly ; ' I would go. I should not stay here. There is no good for you to do.'

" ' But, madam,' said I, ' I have not yet done what I came for. I cannot possibly leave until I have seen the machine.'

" ' It is not worth your while to wait,' she went on. ' You can pass through the door ; no one hinders.' And then, seeing that I smiled and shook my head, she suddenly threw aside her constraint, and made a step forward, with her hands wrung together. ' For the love of Heaven ! ' she whispered, ' get away from here before it is too late ! '

" But I am somewhat headstrong by nature, and the more ready to engage in an affair when there is some obstacle in the way. I thought of my fifty-guinea fee, of my wearisome journey, and of the unpleasant night which seemed to be before me. Was it all to go for nothing ? Why should I slink away without having carried out my commission, and without the payment which was my due ? This woman might, for all I knew, be a monomaniac. With a stout bearing, therefore, though her manner had shaken me more than I cared to confess, I still shook my head, and declared my intention of remaining where I was. She was about to renew her entreaties when a door slammed overhead, and the sound of several footsteps were heard upon the stairs. She listened for an instant, threw up her hands with a despairing gesture, and vanished as suddenly and noiselessly as she had come.

" The new-comers were Colonel Lysander Stark, and a short thick man with a chinchilla beard growing out of the creases of his double chin, who was introduced to me as Mr. Ferguson.

" ' This is my secretary and manager,' said the Colonel. ' By the way, I was under the impression that I left this door shut just now. I fear that you have felt the draught.'

" ' On the contrary,' said I, ' I opened the door myself, because I felt the room to be a little close.'

" He shot one of his suspicious glances at me. ' Perhaps we had better proceed to business, then,' said he. ' Mr. Ferguson and I will take you up to see the machine.'

" ' I had better put my hat on, I suppose.'

" ' Oh no, it is in the house.' **10**

" ' What, do you dig fuller's earth in the house ? '

" ' No, no. This is only where we compress it. But never mind that ! All we wish you to do is to examine

" 'FOR THE LOVE OF HEAVEN!' SHE WHISPERED, 'GET AWAY FROM HERE BEFORE IT IS TOO LATE!' "

Illustration by Sidney Paget for the *Strand Magazine*, March, 1892.

10 " '*Oh no, it is in the house.*' Later events made it impossible for Mr. Hatherley to recover his headgear, so a puzzler is "the source of the tweed cap which Mr. Hatherley placed on Watson's books when he came to have his wound dressed," Mr. Bliss Austin wrote in "Thumbing His Way to Fame." ". . . since, the habits of British shopkeepers being what they are, it is most unlikely that he was able to replace it in the neighborhood of Paddington at a little after 6 in the morning, one can only conclude that Elise must have recovered it for him; though why she was so solicitous over a cap when his wound was left unattended, it is not easy to understand."

the machine and to let us know what is wrong with it.'

" We went upstairs together, the Colonel first with the lamp, the fat manager and I behind him. It was a labyrinth of an old house, with corridors, passages, narrow winding staircases, and little low doors, the thresholds of which were hollowed out by the generations who had crossed them. There were no carpets, and no signs of any furniture above the ground floor, while the plaster was peeling off the walls, and the damp was breaking through in green, unhealthy blotches. I tried to put on as unconcerned an air as possible, but I had not forgotten the warnings of the lady, even though I disregarded them, and I kept a keen eye upon my two companions. Ferguson appeared to be a morose and silent man, but I could see from the little that he said that he was at least a fellow-countryman.

" Colonel Lysander Stark stopped at last before a low door, which he unlocked. Within was a small square room, in which the three of us could hardly get at one time. Ferguson remained outside, and the Colonel ushered me in.

" ' We are now,' said he, ' actually within the hydraulic press, and it would be a particularly unpleasant thing for us if anyone were to turn it on. The ceiling of this small chamber is really the end of the descending piston, and it comes down with the force of many tons upon this metal floor. There are small lateral columns of water outside which receive the force, and which transmit and multiply it in the manner which is familiar to you. The machine goes readily enough, but there is some stiffness in the working of it and it has lost a little of its force. Perhaps you will have the goodness to look it over, and to show us how we can set it right.'

" I took the lamp from him, and I examined the
11 machine very thoroughly. It was indeed a gigantic one, and capable of exercising enormous pressure. When I passed outside, however, and pressed down the levers which controlled it, I knew at once by the whishing sound that there was a slight leakage, which allowed a regurgitation of water through one of the side-cylinders. An examination showed that one of the india-rubber bands which was round the head of a driving-rod had shrunk so as not quite to fill the socket along which it worked. This was clearly the cause of the loss of power, and I pointed it out to my companions, who followed my remarks very carefully, and asked several practical questions as to how they should proceed to set it right. When I had made it clear to them, I returned to the main chamber of the machine, and took a good look at it to satisfy my own curiosity. It was obvious at a glance that the story of the fuller's earth was the merest fabrication, for it would be absurd to suppose that so powerful an engine could be designed for so inadequate a purpose. The walls were of wood, but the floor consisted of a large iron trough, and when I came to examine it I could see a crust of metallic deposit all over it. I had stooped and was scraping at this to see exactly what it was, when I heard a muttered exclamation in German, and saw the cadaverous face of the Colonel looking down at me.

11 *it was indeed a gigantic one.* "Without going into technicalities it appears to have been of the duplex type invented by Sir Charles Davy in 1886—it was therefore quite new . . ." Mr. Ian McNeil wrote in "An Engineer's Thoughts on 'The Engineer's Thumb.' "

" 'What are you doing there?' he asked.

" I felt angry at having been tricked by so elaborate a story as that which he had told me. 'I was admiring your fuller's earth,' said I; 'I think that I should be better able to advise you as to your machine if I knew what the exact purpose was for which it was used.'

" The instant that I uttered the words I regretted the rashness of my speech. His face set hard, and a baleful light sprang up in his grey eyes.

" 'Very well,' said he, 'you shall know all about the machine.' He took a step backward, slammed the little door, and turned the key in the lock. I rushed towards it and pulled at the handle, but it was quite secure, and did not give in the least to my kicks and shoves. 'Hallo!' I yelled. 'Hallo! Colonel! Let me out!'

" And then suddenly in the silence I heard a sound which sent my heart into my mouth. It was the clank of the levers, and the swish of the leaking cylinder. He had set the engine at work. The lamp still stood upon the floor where I had placed it when examining the trough. By its light I saw that the black ceiling was coming down upon me, slowly, jerkily, but, as none knew better than myself, with a force which must within a minute grind me to a shapeless pulp. I threw myself, screaming, against the door, and dragged with my nails at the lock. I implored the Colonel to let me out, but the remorseless clanking of the levers drowned my cries. The ceiling was only a foot or two above my head, and with my hand upraised I could feel its hard rough surface. Then it flashed through my mind that the pain of my death would depend very much upon the position in which I met it. If I lay on my face the weight would come upon my spine, and I shuddered to think of that dreadful snap. Easier the other way, perhaps, and yet had I the nerve to lie and look up at that deadly black shadow wavering down upon me? Already I was unable to stand erect, when my eye caught something which brought a gush of hope back to my heart.

" I have said that though floor and ceiling were of iron, the walls were of wood. As I gave a last hurried glance around, I saw a thin line of yellow light between two of the boards, which broadened and broadened as a small panel was pushed backwards. For an instant I could hardly believe that here was indeed a door which led away from death. The next I threw myself through, and lay half fainting upon the other side. The panel had closed again behind me, but the crash of the lamp, and a few moments afterwards the clang of the two slabs of metal, told me how narrow had been my escape.

" I was recalled to myself by a frantic plucking at my wrist, and I found myself lying upon the stone floor of a narrow corridor, while a woman bent over me and tugged at me with her left hand, while she held a candle in her right. It was the same good friend whose warning I had so foolishly rejected.

" 'Come! Come!' she cried breathlessly. 'They will be here in a moment. They will see that you are not there. Oh, do not waste the so precious time, but come!'

" This time, at least, I did not scorn her advice. I

I RUSHED TOWARDS IT AND PULLED AT THE HANDLE . . .

Illustration by Sidney Paget for the *Strand Magazine*, March, 1892.

12 "*'Fritz! Fritz!' she cried in English.* "Was she also of German descent, and what was her relationship to the Colonel?" Mr. Richard W. Clarke asked in "Certain Ladies of Baker Street." "She called him 'Fritz' . . . [but] was she his wife, his mistress, his sister?"

13 *my thumb had been cut off.* Was it indeed so? A man hanging as Hatherley was "could have had no more than two points of each finger above the edge of the sill, and his thumbs would have been some two or three inches below the edge on the outside of the sill," the late Professor Jay Finley Christ wrote in "Thumbs Up: Thumbs Down." "A strike from the cleaver could not have touched the thumbs unless it reached out so far that the heel of the implement was entirely beyond the edge of the sill; and even then it could not have cut off a thumb, because there was nothing below to serve as a chopping block. Moreover, even though Watson said that the blade had been sharp, he also said it appeared that the thumb 'had been hacked or torn right out from its roots,' which would have been highly unlikely under the circumstances. A sharp blade makes a clean cut!"

To this, Mr. Stanley MacKenzie responded ("The Engineer's Thumb"): "The explanation would appear to be contained in this part of Hatherley's statement: '. . . hanging with my

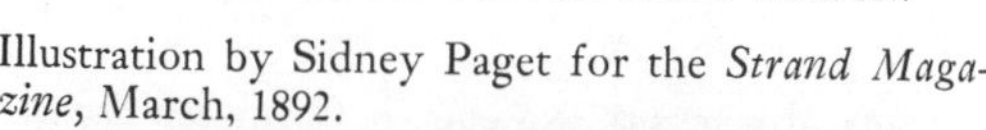

HE . . . CUT AT ME WITH HIS HEAVY WEAPON.

Illustration by Sidney Paget for the *Strand Magazine,* March, 1892.

staggered to my feet, and ran with her along the corridor and down a winding stair. The latter led to another broad passage, and, just as we reached it we heard the sound of running feet and the shouting of two voices—one answering the other—from the floor on which we were, and from the one beneath. My guide stopped, and looked about her like one who is at her wits' end. Then she threw open a door which led into a bedroom, through the window of which the moon was shining brightly.

" 'It is your only chance,' said she. 'It is high, but it may be that you can jump it.'

" As she spoke a light sprang into view at the further end of the passage, and I saw the lean figure of Colonel Lysander Stark rushing forward with a lantern in one hand, and a weapon like a butcher's cleaver in the other. I rushed across the bedroom, flung open the window, and looked out. How quiet and sweet and wholesome the garden looked in the moonlight, and it could not be more than thirty feet down. I clambered out upon the sill, but I hesitated to jump, until I should have heard what passed between my saviour and the ruffian who pursued me. If she were ill-used, then at any risk I was determined to go back to her assistance. The thought had hardly flashed through my mind before he was at the door, pushing his way past her; but she threw her arms round him, and tried to hold him back.

12 " 'Fritz! Fritz!' she cried in English, 'remember your promise after the last time. You said it should not be again. He will be silent! Oh, he will be silent!'

" 'You are mad, Elise!' he shouted, struggling to break away from her. 'You will be the ruin of us. He has seen too much. Let me pass, I say!' He dashed her to one side, and, rushing to the window, cut at me with his heavy weapon. I had let myself go, and was hanging with my fingers in the window slot and my hands across the sill, when his blow fell. I was conscious of a dull pain, my grip loosened, and I fell into the garden below.

" I was shaken, but not hurt by the fall; so I picked
myself up, and rushed off among the bushes as hard as I
could run, for I understood that I was far from being out
of danger yet. Suddenly, however, as I ran, a deadly
dizziness and sickness came over me. I glanced down at
my hand, which was throbbing painfully, and then, for
13 the first time, saw that my thumb had been cut off, and
that the blood was pouring from my wound. I endeavoured to tie my handkerchief round it, but there came a
sudden buzzing in my ears, and next moment I fell in a
dead faint among the rose-bushes.

" How long I remained unconscious I cannot tell. It
must have been a very long time, for the moon had sunk
14 and a bright morning was breaking when I came to myself.
My clothes were all sodden with dew, and my coat-sleeve
was drenched with blood from my wounded thumb. The
smarting of it recalled in an instant all the particulars of
my night's adventure, and I sprang to my feet with the
feeling that I might hardly yet be safe from my pursuers.
But, to my astonishment, when I came to look round me
neither house nor garden were to be seen. I had been
lying in an angle of the hedge close by the highroad, and

just a little lower down was a long building, which proved, upon my approaching it, to be the very station at which I had arrived upon the previous night. Were it not for the ugly wound upon my hand, all that had passed during those dreadful hours might have been an evil dream.

" Half dazed, I went into the station, and asked about the morning train There would be one to Reading in less than an hour. The same porter was on duty, I found, as had been there when I arrived. I inquired from him whether he had ever heard of Colonel Lysander Stark. The name was strange to him. Had he observed a carriage the night before waiting for me ? No, he had not. Was there a police station anywhere near ? There was one about three miles off.

" It was too far for me to go, weak and ill as I was. I determined to wait until I got back to town before telling my story to the police. It was a little past six when I arrived, so I went first to have my wound dressed, and then the doctor was kind enough to bring me along here. I put the case into your hands, and shall do exactly what you advise."

We both sat in silence for some little time after listening to this extraordinary narrative. Then Sherlock Holmes pulled down from the shelf one of the ponderous commonplace books in which he placed his cuttings.

" Here is an advertisement which will interest you," said he. " It appeared in all the papers about a year ago. Listen to this :—' Lost on the 9th inst., Mr. Jeremiah Hayling, aged 26, a hydraulic engineer. Left his lodgings at ten o'clock at night, and has not been heard of since. Was dressed in,' etc. etc. Ha ! That represents the last time that the Colonel needed to have his machine overhauled, I fancy."

" Good heavens ! " cried my patient. " Then that explains what the girl said."

" Undoubtedly. It is quite clear that the Colonel was a cool and desperate man, who was absolutely determined that nothing should stand in the way of his little game, like those out-and-out pirates who will leave no survivor from a captured ship. Well, every moment now is precious, so, if you feel equal to it, we shall go down to Scotland Yard at once as a preliminary to starting for Eyford.

Some three hours or so afterwards we were all in the train together, bound from Reading to the little Berkshire village. There were Sherlock Holmes, the hydraulic engineer, Inspector Bradstreet of Scotland Yard, a plain-clothes man, and myself. Bradstreet had spread an ordnance map of the country out upon the seat, and was busy with his compasses drawing a circle with Eyford for its centre.

" There you are," said he. " That circle is drawn at a radius of ten miles from the village. The place we want must be somewhere near that line. You said ten miles, I think, sir ? "

" It was an hour's good drive."

" And you think that they brought you back all that way when you were unconscious ? "

" They must have done so. I have a confused memory, too, of having been lifted and conveyed somewhere."

fingers in the window *slot and my hands across the sill*, when his blow fell.' The *underlining* are mine. I imagine the 'slot' to have been a recess, flush with the sill into which the bottom of the window dropped. If the sill was, say, 5″ or more wide, and one's fingers were in the slot, the palm of the hand and thumb would be flat on top of the sill. The thumb would quite naturally, stick out sideways and be in a convenient position for amputation."

Those who hold that the thumb was indeed chopped off are still faced with a problem: which thumb? As Mr. Bliss Austin wrote ("Thumbing His Way to Fame"): "Dr. Julian Wolff, in the embellishments to his excellent map of London, shows the right thumb removed, yet I incline to the belief that it was his left thumb, though the evidence is far from conclusive. Assuming that Hatherley was right-handed, which is statistically probable, he could hardly have been so dextrous in tying tourniquets or eating hearty breakfasts had his right hand been injured. I have also discussed this matter with a noted experimental psychologist whose interest I have succeeded in arousing to the extent of undertaking some tests. His preliminary results, admittedly tentative, indicate that: 'a person in the state defined as stark madness, wielding a cleaver in his own right hand again the hands of an opponent placed opposite him on a window sill, will, approximately 99.44 times out of one hundred, attack the hand opposite his right, that is, the opponent's left hand.' "

14 *the moon had sunk and a bright morning was breaking*. By working forward and backward from the facts given us, we may determine that the moon on this night was shining brightly between 1:30 and 2:00 A.M., but that it had set no later than 3:30 A.M., and that daybreak was no later than that hour. In all the summer of 1889 there were two days and two days only which met these requirements: Saturday, September 7th, and Sunday, September 8th. Since the first day of the adventure was not a Sunday, it follows that Mr. Hatherley's adventure must have taken place on the night of Friday–Saturday, September 6–7, 1889; his visit to Holmes and Holmes' part in the action was on *Saturday–Sunday, September 7–8, 1889.*

" What I cannot understand," said I, " is why they should have spared you when they found you lying fainting in the garden. Perhaps the villain was softened by the woman's entreaties."

" I hardly think that likely. I never saw a more inexorable face in my life."

" Oh, we shall soon clear up all that," said Bradstreet. " Well, I have drawn my circle, and I only wish I knew at what point upon it the folk that we are in search of are to be found."

" I think I could lay my finger on it," said Holmes quietly.

" Really, now ! " cried the inspector, " you have formed your opinion ! Come now, we shall see who agrees with you. I say it is south, for the country is more deserted there."

" And I say east," said my patient.

" I am for west," remarked the plain-clothes man. " There are several quiet little villages up there."

" And I am for north," said I ; " because there are no hills there, and our friend says that he did not notice the carriage go up any."

" Come," said the inspector, laughing ; " it's a very pretty diversity of opinion. We have boxed the compass among us. Who do you give your casting vote to ? "

" You are all wrong."

" But we can't *all* be."

" Oh, yes, you can. This is my point," he placed his finger on the centre of the circle. " This is where we shall find them."

" But the twelve-mile drive ? " gasped Hatherley.

" Six out and six back. Nothing simpler. You say yourself that the horse was fresh and glossy when you got in. How could it be that, if it had gone twelve miles over heavy roads ? "

" Indeed it is a likely ruse enough," observed Bradstreet thoughtfully. " Of course there can be no doubt as to the nature of this gang."

" None at all," said Holmes. " They are coiners on a large scale, and have used the machine to form the
15 amalgam which has taken the place of silver."

" We have known for some time that a clever gang was at work," said the inspector. " They have been turning out half-crowns by the thousand. We even traced them as far as Reading, but could get no further ; for they had covered their traces in a way that showed that they were very old hands. But now, thanks to this lucky chance, I think that we have got them right enough."

But the inspector was mistaken, for those criminals were not destined to fall into the hands of justice. As we rolled in Eyford station we saw a gigantic column of smoke which streamed up from behind a small clump of trees in the neighbourhood, and hung like an immense ostrich feather over the landscape.

" A house on fire ? " asked Bradstreet, as the train steamed off again on its way.

" Yes, sir," said the stationmaster.

" When did it break out ? "

15 *the amalgam which has taken the place of silver.*" It is to be doubted that Watson has correctly quoted Holmes, the chemist, in this sentence. "Had amalgamation really been carried out on a large scale," Mr. Bliss Austin wrote in "Thumbing His Way to Fame," "there should have been a considerable quantity of mercury about [since mercury is a necessary ingredient in any amalgam], yet the Canon states specifically that the firemen found only 'large masses of nickel and tin . . .' . . . Nor could the material used to make the spurious coins have been an amalgam of nickel or tin, because the former does not amalgamate with mercury at all, and the latter does so to such a limited extent that it would have been of little use for this purpose."

"A HOUSE ON FIRE?" ASKED BRADSTREET . . .

Illustration by Sidney Paget for the *Strand Magazine,* March, 1892.

" I hear that it was during the night, sir, but it has got worse, and the whole place is in a blaze."

" Whose house is it ? "

" Dr. Becher's."

" Tell me," broke in the engineer, " is Dr. Becher a German, very thin, with a long sharp nose ? "

The stationmaster laughed heartily. " No, sir, Dr. Becher is an Englishman, and there isn't a man in the parish who has a better lined waistcoat. But he has a gentleman staying with him, a patient as I understand, who is a foreigner, and he looks as if a little good Berkshire beef would do him no harm."

The stationmaster had not finished his speech before we were all hastening in the direction of the fire. The road topped a low hill, and there was a great widespread whitewashed building in front of us, spouting fire at every
chink and window, while in the garden in front three fire- **16**
engines were vainly striving to keep the flames under.

" That's it ! " cried Hatherley, in intense excitement. " There is the gravel drive, and there are the rose-bushes where I lay. That second window is the one that I jumped from."

" Well, at least," said Holmes, " you have had your revenge upon them. There can be no question that it was your oil lamp which, when it was crushed in the press,
set fire to the wooden walls, though no doubt they were **17**
too excited in the chase after you to observe it at the time. Now keep your eyes open in this crowd for your friends of last night, though I very much fear that they are a good hundred miles off by now."

And Holmes' fears came to be realized, for from that day to this no word has ever been heard either of the beautiful woman, the sinister German, or the morose Englishman. Early that morning a peasant had met a cart, containing several people and some very bulky boxes, driving rapidly in the direction of Reading, but there all traces of the fugitives disappeared, and even Holmes' ingenuity failed to discover the least clue to their whereabouts.

The firemen had been much perturbed at the strange arrangements which they found within, and still more so by discovering a newly-severed human thumb upon a window-sill of the second floor. About sunset, however, their efforts were at last successful, and they subdued the flames, but not before the roof had fallen in, and the whole place reduced to such absolute ruin that, save some twisted cylinders and iron piping, not a trace remained of the machinery which had cost our unfortunate acquaintance so dearly. Large masses of nickel and of tin were discovered stored in an outhouse, but no coins were to be found, which may have explained the presence of those bulky boxes which have been already referred to.

How our hydraulic engineer had been conveyed from the garden to the spot where he recovered his senses might have remained for ever a mystery were it not for the soft mould, which told us a very plain tale. He had evidently been carried down by two persons, one of whom had remarkably small feet, and the other unusually large ones.

16 *spouting fire at every chink and window.* "... the fire . . . was noteworthy as an illustration of the fire-resistant quality of British buildings, and because it explains, in part, at least, much that happened during the great fire-blitzes to which this part of England was subjected more than fifty years later," Mr. Bliss Austin wrote in "Thumbing His Way to Fame." "The blaze started about 1:30 A.M. [and] . . . burned until sunset, which would have been about 8 P.M. What house in this country would have burned so blithely for twenty hours? As an example of slow-motion combustion it is exceeded only by the celebrated bush which burned but was not consumed."

17 *set fire to the wooden walls.* "Could igniting by any chance follow under the circumstances?" Mr. J. B. MacKenzie asked in "Sherlock Holmes' Plots and Strategy." "And, even if such were possible, would not the flame have been too momentary to allow of its extension to the walls? Where, too, would a draught sufficient to keep it alive come from?"

On the whole, it was most probable that the silent Englishman, being less bold or less murderous than his companion, had assisted the woman to bear the unconscious man out of the way of danger.

"Well," said our engineer ruefully, as we took our seats to return to London, "it has been a pretty business for me! I have lost my thumb, and I have lost a fifty-guinea fee, and what have I gained?"

18 "Experience," said Holmes, laughing. "Indirectly it may be of value, you know; you have only to put it into words to gain the reputation of being excellent company for the remainder of your existence."

18 *"Experience," said Holmes, laughing.* The late Professor Jay Finley Christ was convinced that Hatherley was "a fraud who foiled Watson" (but not Holmes). ". . . one of my correspondents," he wrote in "Thumbs Up: Thumbs Down," "has suggested that this bird was in reality Mr. Jeremiah Hayling, an engineer who had disappeared a year earlier; that he had caught his hand in the press which he had been operating; that the fire (started in some manner unknown to us) offered him a chance to escape; and that he concocted the yarn about the cleaver to avoid explaining where he (Jeremiah) had been for a year. This is rather pleasing. It explains what puzzled Watson: why they 'spared you . . . fainting in the garden'; it tells us that the glib and wholly wrong description of Becher was a diversion, and that the finding of the thumb was evidence either of a plant or a Watsonian invention. As things were, a severed thumb (if there were any such) could neither drop upon the sill nor (likely) remain upon it; and it is rather hard to believe that the firemen found anything at all on a second-storey window, thirty feet above the ground, in the midst of a scene of 'absolute destruction.'"

"THANK YOU. I'LL FILL A VACANT PEG, THEN."

Illustration by Sidney Paget for the *Strand Magazine*, July, 1893.

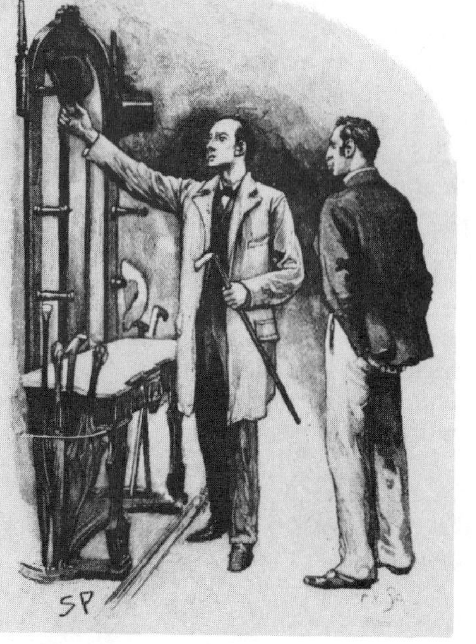

43

THE CROOKED MAN

[*Wednesday, September 11, to Thursday, September 12, 1889*]

ONE summer night, a few months after my marriage, I was seated by my own hearth smoking 1
a last pipe and nodding over a novel, for my
day's work had been an exhausting one. My wife had 2
already gone upstairs, and the sound of the locking of
the hall door some time before told me that the servants 3
had also retired. I had risen from my seat and was knocking out the ashes of my pipe, when I suddenly heard the clang of the bell.

I looked at the clock. It was a quarter to twelve. This could not be a visitor at so late an hour. A patient, evidently, and possibly an all-night sitting. With a wry face I went out into the hall and opened the door. To my astonishment, it was Sherlock Holmes who stood upon my step.

" Ah, Watson," said he, " I hoped that I might not be too late to catch you."

" My dear fellow, pray come in."

" You look surprised, and no wonder! Relieved, too, I fancy! Hum! you still smoke the Arcadia mixture of your bachelor days, then! There's no mistaking that fluffy ash upon your coat. It's easy to tell that you've been accustomed to wear a uniform, Watson; you'll never pass as a pure-bred civilian as long as you keep that
habit of carrying your handkerchief in your sleeve. 4
Could you put me up to-night?"

" With pleasure."

" You told me that you had bachelor quarters for one, and I see that you have no gentleman visitor at present. Your hat-stand proclaims as much."

" I shall be delighted if you will stay."

" Thank you. I'll fill a vacant peg, then. Sorry to see that you've had the British workman in the house. He's a token of evil. Not the drains, I hope?"

" No, the gas."

" Ah! He has left two nail marks from his boot upon your linoleum just where the light strikes it. No, thank you, I had some supper at Waterloo, but I'll smoke a pipe with you with pleasure."

I handed him my pouch, and he seated himself opposite to me, and smoked for some time in silence. I was well aware that nothing but business of importance could have

1 *a few months after my marriage.* Marriage I or Marriage II? Watson's "a few months" must mean at least three but not more than six. Reckoning from the approximate date of the first marriage would place the case in the period February–April, 1887, which is not "summer" in either the popular or the astronomical sense. Reckoning from the approximate date of the second marriage, on the other hand, would place the case in the period August–October, 1889, a period containing a month and three weeks of "summer" in the astronomical sense.

2 *had been an exhausting one.* Holmes later deduces that Watson is "professionally rather busy just now." There must have been busy periods even during the unsuccessful practice of Marriage I, but this is at least an indication that the case did indeed take place during the successful practice of Marriage II.

3 *the servants.* Further evidence of Watson's success: in the impecunious days of his first private practice, he could afford one servant only. "Watson's mention of 'the servants' seems, I feel, to imply that there were more than the bare minimum of two," Mr. Michael Harrison wrote (*In the Footsteps of Sherlock Holmes*). "What was the staff of Watson's house? Cook, housemaid and 'tweeney,' in all probability, for Watson did not keep his own carriage. . . . The total paid out in wages might have been as small as £52 [$260] per annum—or a pound a week [but] the probability is that the cook received £30 [$150] a year, the house-parlourmaid between £18 [$90] and £20 [$100], and the 'tweeney' anything from £10 [$50] to £15 [$75]."

4 *carrying your handkerchief in your sleeve.* A habit dating from Watson's army days, since the uniform tunic has no pocket for carrying a handkerchief.

brought him to me at such an hour, so I waited patiently until he should come round to it.

" I see that you are professionally rather busy just now," said he, glancing very keenly across at me.

" Yes, I've had a busy day," I answered. " It may seem very foolish in your eyes," I added, " but really I don't know how you deduced it."

Holmes chuckled to himself.

" I have the advantage of knowing your habits, my dear Watson," said he. " When your round is a short one you walk, and when it is a long one you use a hansom. As I perceive that your boots, although used, are by no means dirty, I cannot doubt that you are at present busy enough to justify the hansom."

" Excellent ! " I cried.

" Elementary," said he. " It is one of those instances where the reasoner can produce an effect which seems remarkable to his neighbour, because the latter has missed the one little point which is the basis of the deduction. The same may be said, my dear fellow, for the effect of some of these little sketches of yours, which is entirely meretricious, depending as it does upon your retaining in your own hands some factors in the problem which are never imparted to the reader. Now, at present I am in
5 the position of these same readers, for I hold in this hand several threads of one of the strangest cases which ever perplexed a man's brain, and yet I lack the one or two which are needful to complete my theory. But I'll have them, Watson, I'll have them ! " His eyes kindled and a slight flush sprang into his thin cheeks. For an instant the veil had lifted upon his keen, intense nature, but for an instant only. When I glanced again his face had resumed that Red Indian composure which had made so many regard him as a machine rather than a man.

" The problem presents features of interest," said he ; " I may even say very exceptional features of interest. I have already looked into the matter, and have come, as I think, within sight of my solution. If you could accompany me in that last step, you might be of considerable service to me."

" I should be delighted."

" Could you go as far as Aldershot to-morrow ? "

6 " I have no doubt Jackson would take my practice."

" Very good. I want to start by the 11.10 from Water-
7 loo."

" That would give me time."

" Then, if you are not too sleepy, I will give you a sketch of what has happened and of what remains to be done."

" I was sleepy before you came. I am quite wakeful now."

" I will compress the story as far as may be done without omitting anything vital to the case. It is conceivable that you may even have read some account of the matter. It is the supposed murder of Colonel Barclay, of the Royal
8 Mallows, at Aldershot, which I am investigating."

" I have heard nothing of it."

" It has not excited much attention yet, except locally. The facts are only two days old. Briefly they are these :

" The Royal Mallows is, as you know, one of the

5 *the position of these same readers.* Holmes certainly implies that Watson by this time had readers, indicating that the case took place after the publication of *A Study in Scarlet* in December, 1887. But Holmes must also be alluding to some of the chronicles *written* by Watson as early as May, 1887 ("A Scandal in Bohemia").

6 *Jackson.* But the accommodating neighbor-doctor of Marriage II was named Anstruther ("The Boscombe Valley Mystery"). While this speaks for Marriage I, it cannot be allowed to outweigh the considerably stronger evidence that the adventure of "The Crooked Man" took place during the period of Marriage II. Perhaps the neighbor-doctor's full name was Jackson Anstruther.

7 *the 11.10 from Waterloo.*" There was no 11:10 from Waterloo to Aldershot, but Holmes and Watson could have taken an 11:50.

8 *the Royal Mallows.* In American editions *the Royal Munsters*, and this is a real regiment. Holmes later speaks of "The first battalion of the Royal Mallows (which is the old 117th) . . ." This is very odd, as Mr. D. Hinrich noted in "The Royal Mallows, 1854–1888." "None could have known better than Watson, an old Army man, that the highest number borne by a line regiment of the British Army before the Cardwell reforms was that of the 109th (later the second battalion, The Prince of Wales Leinster Regiment). . . . I submit . . . that . . . the first battalion, the Royal Mallows (the old 117th) is but a *nom de guerre* for the second battalion, the Royal Irish Fusiliers (the 89th Foot)."

If, on the other hand, we accept the evidence of the American editions that "the Royal Mallows" are the Royal Munsters, we must note, with Mrs. Crighton Sellars ("Dr. Watson and the British Army") that "The Royal Munster Fusliers, at the time that Watson wrote of them, consisted of the 101st and 104th Regiments, both old regiments of the East India Company, raised by Clive. . . . Most [Royal Munster Fusiliers] were Irish, and it bears the Shamrock in addition to the Royal Tiger of Bengal, but it was not an Irish regiment in any sense. . . . I find no record of its having been in the Crimea, and it did not leave India until it came to England in 1871. . . . Aside from its Mutiny service, there seems to be nothing in the regimental history that corresponds with Watson's facts."

most famous Irish regiments in the British Army. It did wonders both in the Crimea and the Mutiny, and has since that time distinguished itself upon every possible occasion. It was commanded up to Monday night by James Barclay, a gallant veteran, who started as a full private, was raised to commissioned rank for his bravery at the time of the Mutiny, and so lived to command the regiment in which he had once carried a musket.

" Colonel Barclay had married at the time when he was a sergeant, and his wife, whose maiden name was Miss Nancy Devoy, was the daughter of a former colour-sergeant in the same corps. There was, therefore, as can be imagined, some little social friction when the young couple (for they were still young) found themselves in their new surroundings. They appear, however, to have quickly adapted themselves, and Mrs. Barclay has always, I understand, been as popular with the ladies of the regiment as her husband was with his brother officers. I may add that she was a woman of great beauty, and that even now, when she has been married for upwards of thirty years, she is still of a striking appearance. 9

" Colonel Barclay's family life appears to have been a uniformly happy one. Major Murphy, to whom I owe most of my facts, assures me that he has never heard of any misunderstanding between the pair. On the whole, he thinks that Barclay's devotion to his wife was greater than his wife's to Barclay. He was acutely uneasy if he were absent from her for a day. She, on the other hand, though devoted and faithful, was less obtrusively affectionate. But they were regarded in the regiment as the very model of a middle-aged couple. There was absolutely nothing in their mutual relations to prepare people for the tragedy which was to follow.

" Colonel Barclay himself seems to have had some singular traits in his character. He was a dashing, jovial old soldier in his usual mood, but there were occasions on which he seemed to show himself capable of considerable violence and vindictiveness. This side of his nature, however, appears never to have been turned towards his wife. Another fact which had struck Major Murphy, and three out of five of the other officers with whom I conversed, was the singular sort of depression which came upon him at times. As the Major expressed it, the smile had often been struck from his mouth, as if by some invisible hand, when he has been joining in the gaieties and chaff of the mess table. For days on end, when the mood was on him, he had been sunk in the deepest gloom. This and a certain tinge of superstition were the only unusual traits in his character which his brother officers had observed. The latter peculiarity took the form of a dislike to being left alone, especially after dark. This puerile feature in a nature which was conspicuously manly had often given rise to comment and conjecture.

" The first battalion of the Royal Mallows (which is the old 117th) has been stationed at Aldershot for some years. The married officers live out of barracks, and the Colonel has during all this time occupied a villa called Lachine, about half a mile from the North Camp. The house stands in its own grounds, but the west side of it

9 *upwards of thirty years.* As Mr. T. S. Blakeney wrote in *Sherlock Holmes: Fact or Fiction?*: "The garrison at Bhurtee was relieved by Neill's column [*see below*], and his column we know from history was operating from May to September, 1857. . . . Barclay may have married in 1857, but more likely in '58, when things had quieted down in India. Holmes says that at the time of his death Barclay had been married for 'upwards of thirty years,' and this is checked by Mrs. Barclay's remark to Wild, that he was thought to have been dead 'this thirty years.' Add over thirty years to 1858, and we may fairly reach 1889 . . ."

10 is not more than thirty yards from the high-road. A coachman and two maids form the staff of servants. These, with their master and mistress, were the sole occupants of Lachine, for the Barclays had no children, nor was it usual for them to have resident visitors.

" Now for the events at Lachine between nine and ten on the evening of last Monday.

" Mrs. Barclay was, it appears, a member of the Roman Catholic Church, and had interested herself very much in the establishment of the Guild of St. George, which was formed in connection with the Watt Street Chapel for the purpose of supplying the poor with cast-off clothing. A meeting of the Guild had been held that evening at eight, and Mrs. Barclay had hurried over her dinner in order to be present at it. When leaving the house, she was heard by the coachman to make some commonplace remark to her husband, and to assure him that she would be back before long. She then called for Miss Morrison, a young lady who lives in the next villa, and the two went off together to their meeting. It lasted forty minutes, and at a quarter-past nine Mrs. Barclay returned home, having left Miss Morrison at her door as she passed.

" There is a room which is used as a morning-room at Lachine. This faces the road, and opens by a large glass folding door on to the lawn. The lawn is thirty yards across, and is only divided from the highway by a low wall with an iron rail above it. It was into this room that Mrs. Barclay went upon her return. The blinds were not down, for the room was seldom used in the evening, but Mrs. Barclay herself lit the lamp and then rang the bell, asking Jane Stewart, the housemaid, to bring her a cup of tea, which was quite contrary to her usual habits. The Colonel had been sitting in the dining-room, but hearing that his wife had returned, he joined her in the morning-room. The coachman saw him cross the hall, and enter it. He was never seen again alive.

" The tea which had been ordered was brought up at the end of ten minutes, but the maid, as she approached the door, was surprised to hear the voices of her master and mistress in furious altercation. She knocked without receiving any answer, and even turned the handle, but only to find that the door was locked upon the inside. Naturally enough, she ran down to tell the cook, and the two women with the coachman came up into the hall and listened to the dispute which was still raging. They all agree that only two voices were to be heard, those of Barclay and his wife. Barclay's remarks were subdued and abrupt, so that none of them were audible to the listeners. The lady's, on the other hand, were most bitter, and when she raised her voice, could be plainly heard. ' You coward ! ' she repeated over and over again. ' What can be done now ? Give me back my life. I will never so much as breathe the same air as you again ! You coward ! You coward ! ' Those were scraps of her conversation, ending in a sudden dreadful cry in the man's voice, with a crash, and a piercing scream from the woman. Convinced that some tragedy had occurred, the coachman rushed to the door and strove to force it, while scream after scream issued from within. He was unable, how-

10 *not more than thirty yards from the high-road.* "Colonel Barclay, then, lived to the east of Aldershot proper, beyond the Stanhope and the Wellington Lines, and most probably between the railway and the Blackwater River, in a district now known as 'North Town,' " Mr. Michael Harrison wrote (*In the Footsteps of Sherlock Holmes*).

. . . THE TWO WOMEN WITH THE COACHMAN CAME UP INTO THE HALL AND LISTENED TO THE DISPUTE . . .

Illustration by William H. Hyde for *Harper's Weekly*, July 8, 1893.

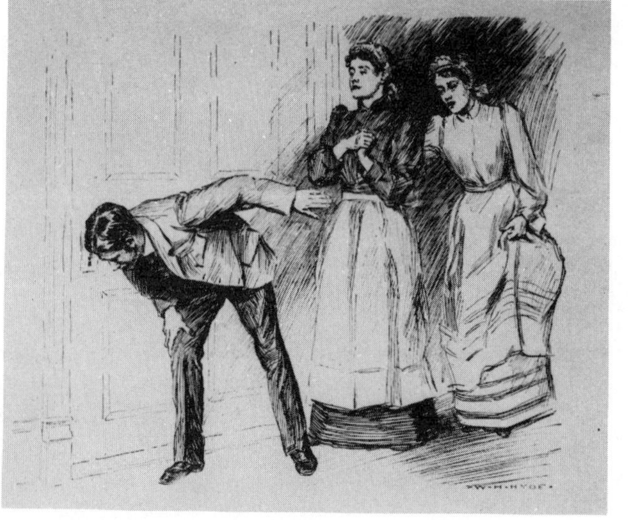

ever, to make his way in, and the maids were too distracted with fear to be of any assistance to him. A sudden thought struck him, however, and he ran through the hall door and round to the lawn, upon which the long French windows opened. One side of the window was open, which I understand was quite usual in the summertime, and he passed without difficulty into the room. His mistress had ceased to scream, and was stretched insensible upon a couch, while with his feet tilted over the side of an arm-chair, and his head upon the ground near the corner of the fender, was lying the unfortunate soldier, stone dead, in a pool of his own blood.

"Naturally the coachman's first thought, on finding that he could do nothing for his master, was to open the door. But here an unexpected and singular difficulty presented itself. The key was not on the inner side of the door, nor could he find it anywhere in the room. He went out again, therefore, through the window, and having obtained the help of a policeman and of a medical man, he returned. The lady, against whom naturally the strongest suspicion rested, was removed to her room, still in a state of insensibility. The Colonel's body was then placed upon the sofa, and a careful examination made of the scene of the tragedy.

"The injury from which the unfortunate veteran was suffering was found to be a ragged cut, some two inches long, at the back part of his head, which had evidently been caused by a violent blow from a blunt weapon. Nor was it difficult to guess what that weapon may have been. Upon the floor, close to the body, was lying a singular club of hard carved wood with a bone handle. The Colonel possessed a varied collection of weapons brought from the different countries in which he had fought, and it is conjectured by the police that this club was among his trophies. The servants deny having seen it before, but among the numerous curiosities in the house it is possible that it may have been overlooked. Nothing else of importance was discovered in the room by the police, save the inexplicable fact that neither upon Mrs. Barclay's person, nor upon that of the victim, nor in any part of the room was the missing key to be found. The door had eventually to be opened by a locksmith from Aldershot.

"That was the state of things, Watson, when upon the Tuesday morning I, at the request of Major Murphy, went down to Aldershot to supplement the efforts of the police. I think you will acknowledge that the problem was already one of interest, but my observations soon made me realize that it was in truth much more extraordinary than would at first sight appear.

"Before examining the room I cross-questioned the servants, but only succeeded in eliciting the facts which I have already stated. One other detail of interest was remembered by Jane Stewart, the housemaid. You will remember that on hearing the sound of the quarrel she descended and returned with the other servants. On that first occasion, when she was alone, she says that the voices of her master and mistress were sunk so low that she could hear hardly anything, and judged by their tones,

. . . THE COACHMAN RUSHED TO THE DOOR . . .

Illustration by Sidney Paget for the *Strand Magazine*, July, 1893.

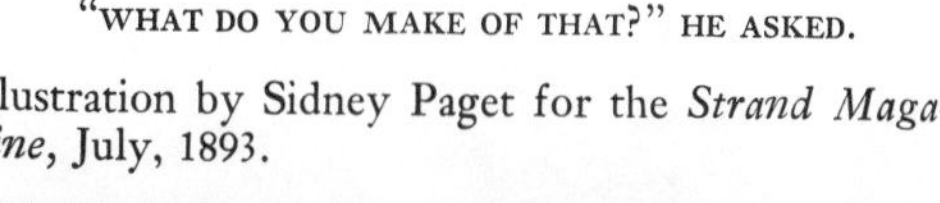

"WHAT DO YOU MAKE OF THAT?" HE ASKED.

Illustration by Sidney Paget for the *Strand Magazine*, July, 1893.

rather than their words, that they had fallen out. On my pressing her, however, she remembered that she heard the word ' David ' uttered twice by the lady. The point is of the utmost importance as guiding us towards the reason of the sudden quarrel. The Colonel's name, you remember, was James.

" There was one thing in the case which had made the deepest impression both upon the servants and the police. This was the contortion of the Colonel's face. It had set, according to their account, into the most dreadful expression of fear and horror which a human countenance is capable of assuming. More than one person fainted at the mere sight of him, so terrible was the effect. It was quite certain that he had foreseen his fate, and that it had caused him the utmost horror. This, of course, fitted in well enough with the police theory, if the Colonel could have seen his wife making a murderous attack upon him. Nor was the fact of the wound being on the back of his head a fatal objection to this, as he might have turned to avoid the blow. No information could be got from the lady herself, who was temporarily insane from an acute attack of brain fever.

" From the police I learned that Miss Morrison, who, you remember, went out that evening with Mrs. Barclay, denied having any knowledge of what it was which had caused the ill-humour in which her companion had returned.

" Having gathered these facts, Watson, I smoked several pipes over them, trying to separate those which were crucial from others which were merely incidental. There could be no question that the most distinctive and suggestive point in the case was the singular disappearance of the door-key. A most careful search had failed to discover it in the room. Therefore, it must have been taken from it. But neither the Colonel nor the Colonel's wife could have taken it. That was perfectly clear. Therefore a third person must have entered the room. And that third person could only have come in through the window. It seemed to me that a careful examination of the room and the lawn might possibly reveal some traces of this mysterious individual. You know my methods, Watson. There was not one of them which I did not apply to the inquiry. And it ended by my discovering traces, but very different ones from those which I had expected. There had been a man in the room, and he had crossed the lawn coming from the road. I was able to obtain five very clear impressions of his footmarks—one on the roadway itself, at the point where he had climbed the low wall, two on the lawn, and two very faint ones upon the stained boards near the window where he had entered. He had apparently rushed across the lawn, for his toe-marks were much deeper than his heels. But it was not the man who surprised me. It was his companion."

" His companion ! "

Holmes pulled a large sheet of tissue paper out of his pocket and carefully unfolded it upon his knee.

" What do you make of that ? " he asked.

The paper was covered with tracings of the footmarks

of some small animal. It had five well-marked footpads, an indication of long nails, and the whole print might be nearly as large as a dessert-spoon.

" It's a dog," said I.

" Did ever you hear of a dog running up a curtain ? I found distinct traces that this creature had done so."

" A monkey, then ? "

" But it is not the print of a monkey."

" What can it be, then ? "

" Neither dog, nor cat, nor monkey, nor any creature that we are familiar with. I have tried to reconstruct it from the measurements. Here are four prints where the beast has been standing motionless. You see that it is no less than fifteen inches from forefoot to hind. Add to that the length of neck and head, and you get a creature not much less than two feet long—probably more if there is any tail. But now observe this other measurement. The animal has been moving, and we have the length of its stride. In each case it is only about three inches. You have an indication, you see, of a long body with very short legs attached to it. It has not been considerate enough to leave any of its hair behind it. But its general shape must be what I have indicated, and it can run up a curtain and is carnivorous."

" How do you deduce that ? "

" Because it ran up the curtain. A canary's cage was hanging in the window, and its aim seems to have been to get at the bird."

" Then what was the beast ? "

" Ah, if I could give it a name it might go a long way towards solving the case. On the whole it was probably some creature of the weasel or stoat tribe—and yet it is larger than any of these that I have seen."

" But what had it to do with the crime ? "

" That also is still obscure. But we have learned a good deal, you perceive. We know that a man stood in the road looking at the quarrel between the Barclays—the blinds were up and the room lighted. We know also that he ran across the lawn, entered the room, accompanied by a strange animal, and that he either struck the Colonel, or, as is equally possible, that the Colonel fell down from sheer fright at the sight of him, and cut his head on the corner of the fender. Finally, we have the curious fact that the intruder carried away the key with him when he left."

" Your discoveries seem to have left the business more obscure than it was before," said I.

" Quite so. They undoubtedly showed that the affair was much deeper than was at first conjectured. I thought the matter over, and I came to the conclusion that I must approach the case from another aspect. But really, Watson, I am keeping you up, and I might just as well tell you all this on our way to Aldershot to-morrow."

" Thank you, you've gone rather too far to stop."

" It was quite certain that when Mrs. Barclay left the house at half-past seven she was on good terms with her husband. She was never, as I think I have said, ostentatiously affectionate, but she was heard by the coachman chatting with the Colonel in a friendly fashion. Now, it was equally certain that immediately on her return she had gone to the room in which she was least likely to see her husband, had flown to tea, as an agitated woman will, and, finally, on his coming in to her, had broken into violent recriminations. Therefore, something had occurred between seven-thirty and nine o'clock which had completely altered her feelings towards him. But Miss Morrison had been with her during the whole of that hour and a half. It was absolutely certain, therefore, in spite of her denial, that she must know something of the matter.

" My first conjecture was that possibly there had been some passages between this young woman and the old soldier, which the former had now confessed to the wife. That would account for the angry return and also for the girl's denial that anything had occurred. Nor would it be entirely incompatible with most of the words overheard. But there was the reference to David, and there was the known affection of the Colonel for his wife to weigh against it, to say nothing of the tragic intrusion of this other man, which might, of course, be entirely disconnected with what had gone before. It was not easy to pick one's steps, but on the whole I was inclined to dismiss the idea that there had been anything between the Colonel and Miss Morrison, but more than ever convinced that the young lady held the clue as to what it was which had turned Mrs. Barclay to hatred of her husband. I took the obvious course, therefore, of calling upon Miss Morrison, of explaining to her that I was perfectly certain that she held the facts in her possession, and of assuring her that her friend, Mrs. Barclay, might find herself in the dock upon a capital charge unless the matter were cleared up.

"MY GOD, IT'S NANCY!"

Illustration by Sidney Paget for the *Strand Magazine*, July, 1893.

" Miss Morrison is a little, ethereal slip of a girl, with timid eyes and blonde hair, but I found her by no means wanting in shrewdness and common sense. She sat thinking for some time after I had spoken, and then turning to me with a brisk air of resolution, she broke into a remarkable statement, which I will condense for your benefit.

" ' I promised my friend that I would say nothing of the matter, and a promise is a promise,' said she. ' But if I can really help her when so serious a charge is made against her, and when her own mouth, poor darling, is closed by illness, then I think I am absolved from my promise. I will tell you exactly what happened on Monday evening.

" ' We were returning from the Watt Street Mission, about a quarter to nine o'clock. On our way we had to pass through Hudson Street, which is a very quiet thoroughfare. There is only one lamp in it upon the left-hand side, and as we approached this lamp I saw a man coming towards us with his back very bent, and something like a box slung over one of his shoulders. He appeared to be deformed, for he carried his head low, and walked with his knees bent. We were passing him when he raised his face to look at us in the circle of light thrown by the lamp, and as he did so he stopped and screamed out in a dreadful voice, " My God, it's Nancy ! " Mrs.

Barclay turned as white as death, and would have fallen down had the dreadful-looking creature not caught hold of her. I was going to call for the police, but she, to my surprise, spoke quite civilly to the fellow.

" ' " I thought you had been dead this thirty years, Henry," said she, in a shaking voice.

" ' " So I have,' said he, and it was awful to hear the tones that he said it in. He had a very dark, fearsome face, and a gleam in his eyes that comes back to me in my dreams. His hair and whiskers were shot with grey, and his face was all crinkled and puckered like a withered apple.

" ' " Just walk on a little way, dear," said Mrs. Barclay. " I want to have a word with this man. There is nothing to be afraid of." She tried to speak boldly, but she was still deadly pale, and could hardly get her words out for the trembling of her lips.

" ' I did as she asked me, and they talked together for a few minutes. Then she came down the street with her eyes blazing, and I saw the crippled wretch standing by the lamp-post and shaking his clenched fists in the air, as if he were mad with rage. She never said a word until we were at the door here, when she took me by the hand and begged me to tell no one what had happened. " It is an old acquaintance of mine who has come down in the world," said she. When I promised her that I would say nothing she kissed me, and I have never seen her since. I have told you now the whole truth, and if I withheld it from the police it is because I did not realize then the danger in which my dear friend stood. I know that it can only be to her advantage that everything should be known.'

" There was her statement, Watson, and to me, as you can imagine, it was like a light on a dark night. Everything which had been disconnected before began at once to assume its true place, and I had a shadowy presentiment of the whole sequence of events. My next step obviously was to find the man who had produced such a remarkable impression upon Mrs. Barclay. If he were still in Aldershot it should not be a very difficult matter. There are not such a very great number of civilians, and a deformed man was sure to have attracted attention. I spent a day in the search, and by evening—this very evening, Watson—I had run him down. The man's 11
name is Henry Wood, and he lives in lodgings in the same street in which the ladies met him. He has only been five days in the place. In the character of a registration agent I had a most interesting gossip with his landlady. The man is by trade a conjurer and performer, going round the canteens, after nightfall, and giving a little entertainment at each. He carries some creature about with him in his box, about which the landlady seemed to be in considerable trepidation, for she had never seen an animal like it. He uses it in some of his tricks, according to her account. So much the woman was able to tell me, and also that it was a wonder the man lived, seeing how twisted he was, and that he spoke in a strange tongue sometimes, and that for the last two nights she had heard him groaning and weeping in his bedroom. He was all right as far as money went, but in his deposit he had

11 *this very evening, Watson.* Holmes says: "The facts are only two days old." He tells us that the Royal Mallows "was commanded up to Monday night by James Barclay." He says: "Now for the events at Lachine between nine and ten on the evening of last Monday." He says: "Upon the Tuesday morning I . . . went down to Aldershot . . ." He "spent a day" (the Wednesday) in the search for the crooked man, and "by evening—this very evening, Watson—I had run him down." The case, then, began on a Wednesday; it ended the following day, Thursday.

. . . HE HAD GIVEN HER WHAT LOOKED LIKE A BAD FLORIN.

"This 2/ piece," the late A. Carson Simpson wrote in *Numismatics in the Canon*, Part I, "bears an ancient name, that of the Florentine florino, which was at first a small silver coin, corresponding roughly to the penny; later it was a much more valuable gold coin. First coined in gold in 1252, it continued, with only minor changes in design, until the Florentine Republic became a Medici duchy in 1532. It circulated all over the Continent, enjoying a higher reputation there than the English silver penny. This being the case, it is not surprising that, when Edward III issued his first gold currency in 1344, its basic unit was a florin (worth exactly two of the Florentine ones) of a beautiful Gothic design inspired, perhaps, by some of the contemporary gold coins of Philippe VI de Valois. Like the earlier gold penny of Henry III, this florin contained more gold than its face value justified, and it lasted only a few months, to be replaced by the noble, later in the same year. The name was not revived until Victoria's time, when it became a silver coin. This denomination was the result of agitation for a decimal coinage, led by Sir John Bowring, the famous diplomat, Orientalist, poet and translator. Being worth 2/—, it is, of course, one-tenth of a pound sterling, and the first two types of the coin bore legends so stating. Although it is still coined, decimalization proceeded no further (except for the short-lived double-florin) probably because the traditional British system of currency, quite aside from considerations of prestige, is of such great international importance that it would be dangerous to change it." The illustration shows the florin of 1889, called the "Godless florin," because of the omission of the conventional DEI GRATIA.

given her what looked like a bad florin. She showed it to me, Watson, and it was an Indian rupee.

" So now, my dear fellow, you see exactly how we stand and why it is I want you. It is perfectly plain that after the ladies parted from this man he followed them at a distance, that he saw the quarrel between husband and wife through the window, that he rushed in, and that the creature which he carried in his box got loose. That is all very certain. But he is the only person in this world who can tell us exactly what happened in that room."

" And you intend to ask him ? "

" Most certainly—but in the presence of a witness."

" And I am the witness ? "

" If you will be so good. If he can clear the matter up, well and good. If he refuses, we have no alternative but to apply for a warrant."

" But how do you know he will be there when we return ? "

" You may be sure that I took some precautions. I have one of my Baker Street boys mounting guard over him who would stick to him like a burr, go where he might. We shall find him in Hudson Street to-morrow, Watson ; and meanwhile I should be the criminal myself if I kept you out of bed any longer."

It was midday when we found ourselves at the scene of the tragedy, and, under my companion's guidance, we made our way at once to Hudson Street. In spite of his capacity for concealing his emotions I could easily see that Holmes was in a state of suppressed excitement, while I was myself tingling with that half-sporting, half-intellectual pleasure which I invariably experienced when I associated myself with him in his investigations.

" This is the street," said he, as he turned into a short thoroughfare lined with plain two-storied brick houses—" Ah ! here is Simpson to report."

" He's in all right, Mr. Holmes," cried a small street Arab, running up to us.

" Good, Simpson ! " said Holmes, patting him on the head. " Come along, Watson. This is the house." He sent in his card with a message that he had come on important business, and a moment later we were face to face with the man whom we had come to see. In spite of
12 the warm weather he was crouching over a fire, and the little room was like an oven. The man sat all twisted and huddled in his chair in a way which gave an indescribable impression of deformity, but the face which he turned towards us, though worn and swarthy, must at some time have been remarkable for its beauty. He looked suspiciously at us now out of yellow-shot bilious eyes, and, without speaking or rising, he waved towards two chairs.

" Mr. Henry Wood, late of India, I believe ? " said Holmes, affably. " I've come over this little matter of Colonel Barclay's death."

" What should I know about that ? "

" That's what I wanted to ascertain. You know, I suppose, that unless the matter is cleared up, Mrs. Barclay, who is an old friend of yours, will in all probability be tried for murder ? "

12 *in spite of the warm weather.* We know that the case took place on a Wednesday and Thursday in the period of approximately August 1–September 22, 1889. The possible dates are: 1) July 31–August 1; 2) August 7–8; 3) August 14–15; 4) August 21–22; 5) August 28–29; 6) September 4–5; 7) September 11–12; 8) September 18–19. We know that Mrs. Watson was on holiday and Watson was living with Holmes in Baker Street at the time of "The Cardboard Box," which we have shown to have taken place in the period Saturday, August 31–Monday, September 2, 1889; by Saturday, September 7 ("The Engineer's Thumb") Mary and Watson himself had returned to their home in Paddington. It is extremely unlikely that Mary was on holiday for less than a fortnight; we can therefore eliminate August 21–22 and August 28–29 from our considerations. There are two clues to the proper period: 1) The Thursday on which Holmes concluded the case was a warm day; 2) the weather during the entire period Monday—Thursday inclusive appears to have been clear. Of the six remaining periods there was *one and one only* during which there was *no rain whatsoever:* Monday, September 9–Thursday, September 12. We hold that Holmes visited Watson on the evening of *Wednesday, September 11,* and solved the case the next day, *Thursday, September 12, 1889.* On that day the temperature rose to a high of 77.2°, so it was indeed "warm weather."

. . . HE WAS CROUCHING OVER A FIRE, AND THE LITTLE ROOM WAS LIKE AN OVEN.

Illustration by William H. Hyde for *Harper's Weekly,* July 8, 1893.

The man gave a violent start.

" I don't know who you are," he cried, " nor how you come to know what you do know, but will you swear that this is true that you tell me ? "

" Why, they are only waiting for her to come to her senses to arrest her."

" My God ! Are you in the police yourself ? "

" No."

" What business is it of yours, then ? "

" It's every man's business to see justice done."

" You can take my word that she is innocent."

" Then you are guilty ? "

" No, I am not."

" Who killed Colonel James Barclay, then ? "

" It was a just Providence that killed him. But mind you this, that if I had knocked his brains out, as it was in my heart to do, he would have had no more than his due from my hands. If his own guilty conscience had not struck him down, it is likely enough that I might have had his blood upon my soul. You want me to tell the story ? Well, I don't know why I shouldn't, for there's no cause for me to be ashamed of it.

" It was in this way, sir. You see me now with my back like a camel and my ribs all awry, but there was a time when Corporal Henry Wood was the smartest man in the 117th Foot. We were in India then, in cantonments, at a place we'll call Bhurtee. Barclay, who died the other day, was sergeant in the same company as myself, and the belle of the regiment—aye, and the finest girl that ever had the breath of life between her lips—was Nancy Devoy, the daughter of the colour-sergeant. There were two men who loved her, and one whom she loved ; and you'll smile when you look at this poor thing huddled before the fire, and hear me say that it was for my good looks that she loved me.

" Well, though I had her heart her father was set upon her marrying Barclay. I was a harum-scarum, reckless lad, and he had had an education, and was already marked for the sword-belt. But the girl held true to me, and it seemed that I would have had her, when the Mutiny broke out, and all Hell was loose in the country.

" We were shut up in Bhurtee, the regiment of us, with half a battery of artillery, a company of Sikhs, and a lot of civilians and women-folk. There were ten thousand rebels round us, and they were as keen as a set of terriers round a rat cage. About the second week of it our water gave out, and it was a question whether we could communicate with General Neill's column, which was moving up- **13**
country. It was our only chance, for we could not hope to fight our way out with all the women and children, so I volunteered to go out and warn General Neill of our danger. My offer was accepted, and I talked it over with Sergeant Barclay, who was supposed to know the ground better than any other man, and who drew up a route by which I might get through the rebel lines. At ten o'clock the same night I started off upon my journey. There were a thousand lives to save, but it was of only one that I was thinking when I dropped over the wall that night.

" My way ran down a dried-up water-course, which we

"MR. HENRY WOOD, LATE OF INDIA, I BELIEVE?" SAID HOLMES, AFFABLY.

Illustration by Sidney Paget for the *Strand Magazine*, July, 1893.

13 *General Neill's column.* General James George Smith Neill, 1810–1857.

"... I WALKED RIGHT INTO SIX OF THEM ..."

Illustration by Sidney Paget for the *Strand Magazine*, March, 1893.

hoped would screen me from the enemy's sentries, but as I crept round the corner of it I walked right into six of them, who were crouching down in the dark, waiting for me. In an instant I was stunned with a blow, and bound hand and foot. But the real blow was to my heart and not to my head, for as I came to and listened to as much as I could understand of their talk, I heard enough to tell me that my comrade, the very man who had arranged the way I was to take, had betrayed me by means of a native servant into the hands of the enemy.

"Well, there's no need for me to dwell on that part of it. You know now what James Barclay was capable of. Bhurtee was relieved by Neill next day, but the rebels took me away with them in their retreat, and it was many a long year before I ever saw a white face again. I was tortured, and tried to get away, and was captured and tortured again. You can see for yourselves the state in which I was left. Some of them that fled into Nepaul took me with them, and then afterwards I was up past Darjeeling. The hill-folk up there murdered the rebels who had me, and I became their slave for a time until I escaped, but instead of going south I had to go north, until I found myself among the Afghans. There I wandered about for many a year, and at last came back to the Punjab, where I lived mostly among the natives, and picked up a living by the conjuring tricks that I had learned. What use was it for me, a wretched cripple, to go back to England, or to make myself known to my old comrades? Even my wish for revenge would not make me do that. I had rather that Nancy and my old pals should think of Harry Wood as having died with a straight back, than see him living and crawling with a stick like a chimpanzee. They never doubted that I was dead, and I meant that they never should. I heard that Barclay had married Nancy, and that he was rapidly rising in the regiment, but even that did not make me speak.

"But when one gets old, one has a longing for home. For years I've been dreaming of the bright green fields and the hedges of England. At last I determined to see them before I died. I saved enough to bring me across, and then I came here where the soldiers are, for I know their ways, and how to amuse them, and so earn enough to keep me."

"Your narrative is most interesting," said Sherlock Holmes. "I have already heard of your meeting with Mrs. Barclay and your mutual recognition. You then, as I understand, followed her home and saw through the window an altercation between her husband and her, in which she doubtless cast his conduct to you in his teeth. Your own feelings overcame you, and you ran across the lawn and broke in upon them."

"I did, sir, and at the sight of me he looked as I have never seen a man look before, and over he went with his head on the fender. But he was dead before he fell. I read death on his face as plain as I can read that text over the fire. The bare sight of me was like a bullet through his guilty heart."

"And then?"

" Then Nancy fainted, and I caught up the key of the door from her hand, intending to unlock it and get help. But as I was doing it it seemed to me better to leave it alone and get away, for the thing might look black against me, and anyway my secret would be out if I were taken. In my haste I thrust the key into my pocket, and dropped my stick while I was chasing Teddy, who had run up the curtain. When I got him into his box, from which he had slipped, I was off as fast as I could run."

" Who's Teddy ? " asked Holmes.

The man leaned over and pulled up the front of a kind of hutch in the corner. In an instant out there slipped a beautiful reddish-brown creature, thin, and lithe, with the legs of a stoat, a long thin nose, and a pair of the finest red eyes that ever I saw in an animal's head.

" It's a mongoose ! " I cried.

" Well, some call them that, and some call them ichneumon," said the man. " Snake-catcher is what I call them, and Teddy is amazing quick on cobras. I have one here without the fangs, and Teddy catches it every night to please the folk in the canteen. Any other point, sir ? "

" Well, we may have to apply to you again if Mrs. Barclay should prove to be in serious trouble."

" In that case, of course, I'd come forward."

" But if not, there is no object of raking up this scandal against a dead man, foully as he has acted. You have, at least, the satisfaction of knowing that for thirty years of his life his conscience bitterly reproached him for his wicked deed. Ah, there goes Major Murphy on the other side of the street. Good-bye, Wood ; I want to learn if anything has happened since yesterday."

We were in time to overtake the Major before he reached the corner.

" Ah, Holmes," he said, " I suppose you have heard that all this fuss has come to nothing ? "

" What, then ? "

" The inquest is just over. The medical evidence showed conclusively that death was due to apoplexy. You see, it was quite a simple case after all."

" Oh, remarkably superficial," said Holmes, smiling. " Come, Watson, I don't think we shall be wanted in Aldershot any more."

" There's one thing," said I, as we walked down to the station ; " if the husband's name was James, and the other was Henry, what was this talk about David ? "

" That one word, my dear Watson, should have told me the whole story had I been the ideal reasoner which you are so fond of depicting. It was evidently a term of reproach."

" Of reproach ? "

" Yes, David strayed a little now and then, you know, and on one occasion in the same direction as Sergeant James Barclay. You remember the small affair of Uriah and Bathsheba ? My Biblical knowledge is a trifle rusty, I fear, but you will find the story in the first or second of Samuel." **14**

"... SOME CALL THEM ICHNEUMON ..."

The illustration is from Bewick's *A General History of Quadrupeds*, 1807.

"YOU SEE, IT WAS QUITE A SIMPLE CASE AFTER ALL."

Illustration by Sidney Paget for the *Strand Magazine*, July, 1893.

14 *the first or second of Samuel.*" Watson would have found the story in the "second of Samuel," 11–13. In recent years some Sherlockians have speculated that Holmes by faith may have been a Roman Catholic. This view has been contested by the Reverend Henry Folsom. "If Holmes were a Roman," he says, "he would have referred here to "the first or second of *Kings*.' "

44

THE ADVENTURE OF WISTERIA LODGE

[Monday, March 24, to Saturday, March 29, 1890]

I—The Singular Experience of Mr. John Scott Eccles

I FIND it recorded in my notebook that it was a bleak
and windy day towards the end of March in the year
1 1892. Holmes had received a telegram whilst we sat
at our lunch, and he had scribbled a reply. He made no
remark, but the matter remained in his thoughts, for he
stood in front of the fire afterwards with a thoughtful face,
smoking his pipe, and casting an occasional glance at the
message. Suddenly he turned upon me with a mischievous twinkle in his eyes.

"I suppose, Watson, we must look upon you as a man
of letters," said he. "How do you define the word
'grotesque'?"

"Strange—remarkable," I suggested.

He shook his head at my definition.

"There is surely something more than that," said he;
"some underlying suggestion of the tragic and the terrible.
If you cast your mind back to some of those narratives
2 with which you have afflicted a long-suffering public, you
will recognize how often the grotesque has deepened into
the criminal. Think of that little affair of the red-headed
men. That was grotesque enough in the outset, and yet
it ended in a desperate attempt at robbery. Or, again,
3 there was that most grotesque affair of the five orange pips,
which led straight to a murderous conspiracy. The word
puts me on the alert."

"Have you it there?" I asked.

He read the telegram aloud.

"Have just had most incredible and grotesque experience. May I consult you?—Scott Eccles, Post Office,
4 Charing Cross."

"Man or woman?" I asked.

"Oh, man, of course. No woman would ever send a
reply-paid telegram. She would have come."

"Will you see him?"

"My dear Watson, you know how bored I have been
5 since we locked up Colonel Carruthers. My mind is like
a racing engine, tearing itself to pieces because it is not
6 connected up with the work for which it was built. Life
is commonplace, the papers are sterile; audacity and
romance seem to have passed for ever from the criminal

1 *a bleak and windy day towards the end of March in the year 1892.* We hope to show that "The Adventure of Wisteria Lodge" took place *Monday, March 24 to Saturday, March 29, 1890.* The Monday was indeed "a bleak and windy day"—"bleak" (a minimum temperature of 36.1°, against a fifty-year average of 42°) "with a fine rain" (0.27 inch)—and "windy" (a south wind, with a pressure of 2.5 pounds to the inch). The month was certainly March: "It is late in March," Mr. Scott Eccles tells us later; that night it was "a cold, dark March evening"; five days later, Watson speaks of "the shadows of the March evening." But Watson's "1892" is certainly a typographical error: Holmes in 1892 was thought to be dead and was in fact thousands of miles removed from Baker Street, traveling in Tibet (see "The Adventure of the Empty House").

2 *those narratives with which you have afflicted a long-suffering public.* The case must be after February, 1890, the month in which *The Sign of the Four* was published.

3 *the five orange pips.* But the fact that the affair of "The Red-Headed League" and that of "The Five Orange Pips" were fresh in Holmes' mind is perhaps an indication that "The Adventure of Wisteria Lodge" should be dated within a few years at most of 1887.

4 *Post Office, Charing Cross."* The day-and-night post office in Charing Cross was one of the oldest of the London post offices; in Holmes' and Watson's day, it was tucked away on the ground floor of Morley's Hotel, but had its entrance on the south side of the Strand.

5 *Colonel Carruthers.* Not to be confused with the Mr. Robert Carruthers of "The Adventure of the Solitary Cyclist."

6 *not connected up with the work for which it was built.* Compare: "To let the brain work without sufficient material is like racing an engine. It racks itself to pieces." ("The Adventure of the

world. Can you ask me, then, whether I am ready to look into any new problem, however trivial it may prove? But here, unless I am mistaken, is our client."

A measured step was heard upon the stairs, and a moment later a stout, tall, grey-whiskered and solemnly respectable person was ushered into the room. His life history was written in his heavy features and pompous manner. From his spats to his gold-rimmed spectacles he was a Conservative, a Churchman, a good citizen, orthodox and conventional to the last degree. But some **7** amazing experience had disturbed his native composure and left its traces in his bristling hair, his flushed, angry cheeks, and his flurried, excited manner. He plunged instantly into his business.

"I have had a most singular and unpleasant experience, Mr. Holmes," said he. "Never in my life have I been placed in such a situation. It is most improper—most outrageous. I must insist upon some explanation." He swelled and puffed in his anger.

"Pray sit down, Mr. Scott Eccles," said Holmes, in a soothing voice. "May I ask, in the first place, why you came to me at all?"

"Well, sir, it did not appear to be a matter which concerned the police, and yet, when you have heard the facts, you must admit that I could not leave it where it was. Private detectives are a class with whom I have absolutely no sympathy, but none the less, having heard your name ——"

"Quite so. But, in the second place, why did you not come at once?"

"What do you mean?"

Holmes glanced at his watch.

"It is a quarter past two," he said. "Your telegram was dispatched about one. But no one can glance at your toilet and attire without seeing that your disturbance dates from the moment of your waking."

Our client smoothed down his unbrushed hair and felt his unshaven chin.

"You are right, Mr. Holmes. I never gave a thought to my toilet. I was only too glad to get out of such a house. But I have been running round making inquiries before I came to you. I went to the house agents, you know, and they said that Mr. Garcia's rent was paid up all right and that everything was in order at Wisteria Lodge."

"Come, come, sir," said Holmes, laughing. "You are like my friend Dr. Watson, who has a bad habit of telling his stories wrong end foremost. Please arrange your thoughts and let me know, in their due sequence, exactly what those events are which have sent you out unbrushed and unkempt, with dress-boots and waistcoat buttoned awry, in search of advice and assistance."

Our client looked down with a rueful face at his own unconventional appearance.

"I'm sure it must look very bad, Mr. Holmes, and I am not aware that in my whole life such a thing has ever happened before. But I will tell you the whole queer business, and when I have done so you will admit, I am sure, that there has been enough to excuse me."

But his narrative was nipped in the bud. There was a

Devil's Foot"). Mr. T. S. Blakeney feels that these remarks explain Holmes' occasional lapses into drug-taking.

7 *orthodox and conventional to the last degree.* ". . . from one glance at Scott Eccles, [Watson] gives us a string of accurate inferences worthy of Holmes himself," Mr. Nathan L. Bengis wrote in "Take a Bow, Dr. Watson."

"BUT I HAVE BEEN RUNNING AROUND AND MAKING INQUIRIES BEFORE I CAME TO YOU."

Illustration by Arthur Twidle for the *Strand Magazine*, September, 1908. ". . . the untimely death of Paget in 1908 made it necessary for other artists to assume the work of illustrating the *Strand*'s continuing series of Sherlock Holmes stories—at once an enviable and an unenviable assignment," the late James Montgomery wrote in *A Study in Pictures*. "The first illustrator to attempt this was Arthur Twidle. . . . He was selected by the *Strand* to draw ten pictures for . . . 'The Adventure of Wisteria Lodge' . . . They are splendid pictures, even though they lack a little of Paget's elusive charm, and indeed they give us considerably more detail in background than most of Paget's work. Holmes is perhaps a little taller, but possesses the same spare figure, receding temples and finely chiseled features. Watson is even more typically British than before, if such were possible. The other characters, and the settings in which all of them are placed, harmonize agreeably with the atmosphere of the times."

bustle outside, and Mrs. Hudson opened the door to usher in two robust and official-looking individuals, one of whom
8 was well known to us as Inspector Gregson of Scotland Yard, an energetic, gallant, and, within his limitations, a capable officer. He shook hands with Holmes, and introduced his comrade as Inspector Baynes of the Surrey Constabulary.

" We are hunting together, Mr. Holmes, and our trail lay in this direction." He turned his bulldog eyes upon our visitor. " Are you Mr. John Scott Eccles, of Popham House, Lee ? "

" I am."

" We have been following you about all the morning."

9 " You traced him through the telegram, no doubt," said Holmes.

" Exactly, Mr. Holmes. We picked up the scent at Charing Cross Post Office and came on here."

" But why do you follow me ? What do you want ? "

" We wish a statement, Mr. Scott Eccles, as to the events which led up to the death last night of Mr. Aloysius
10 Garcia, of Wisteria Lodge, near Esher."

Our client had sat up with staring eyes and every tinge of colour struck from his astonished face.

" Dead ? Did you say he was dead ? "

" Yes, sir, he is dead."

" But how ? An accident ? "

" Murder, if ever there was one upon earth."

" Good God ! This is awful ! You don't mean—you don't mean that I am suspected ? "

" A letter of yours was found in the dead man's pocket, and we know by it that you had planned to pass last night at his house."

" So I did."

" Oh, you did, did you ? "

Out came the official notebook.

" Wait a bit, Gregson," said Sherlock Holmes. " All you desire is a plain statement, is it not ? "

" And it is my duty to warn Mr. Scott Eccles that it may be used against him."

" Mr. Eccles was going to tell us about it when you entered the room. I think, Watson, a brandy and soda would do him no harm. Now, sir, I suggest that you take no notice of this addition to your audience, and that you proceed with your narrative exactly as you would have done had you never been interrupted."

Our visitor had gulped off the brandy and the colour had returned to his face. With a dubious glance at the inspector's notebook, he plunged at once into his extraordinary statement.

" I am a bachelor," said he, " and, being of a sociable turn, I cultivate a large number of friends. Among these are the family of a retired brewer called Melville, living at Albemarle Mansion, Kensington. It was at his table that I met some weeks ago a young fellow named Garcia. He was, I understood, of Spanish descent and connected in some way with the Embassy. He spoke perfect English, was pleasing in his manners, and as good-looking a man as ever I saw in my life.

" In some way we struck up quite a friendship, this

8 *Inspector Gregson of Scotland Yard.* This, too, is at least an indication that "The Adventure of Wisteria Lodge" is to be dated earlier rather than later, as Gregson seldom appears in the later adventures.

9 *"You traced him through the telegram, no doubt."* Scott Eccles "was traced to Baker Street through the telegram, although in what way he was traced does not appear," Colonel E. Ennalls Berl commented in "Sherlock Holmes and the Telephone." "It will be recalled that Eccles, immediately upon his arrival from Esher, went to the Spanish Embassy, and from there to Mr. Melville's house, and thence to the Charing Cross Post Office. He could have gone to any other post office to send the wire. Whatever the system might have been for tracing Eccles through a telegram, it would seem that Gregson and Baynes had to know enough to look for him or his telegram at Charing Cross Post Office."

10 *Esher.* A village in Surrey.

OUR CLIENT HAD SAT UP WITH STARING EYES . . .

Illustration by Frederic Dorr Steele for *Collier's Magazine*, August 15, 1908. Arthur Twidle illustrated the same scene for the *Strand Magazine*, September, 1908.

young fellow and I. He seemed to take a fancy to me from the first, and within two days of our meeting he came to see me at Lee. One thing led to another, and it ended in his inviting me out to spend a few days at his house, Wisteria Lodge, between Esher and Oxshott. Yesterday 11
evening I went to Esher to fulfil this engagement.

"He had described his household to me before I went there. He lived with a faithful servant, a countryman of his own, who looked after all his needs. This fellow could speak English and did his housekeeping for him. Then there was a wonderful cook, he said, a half-breed whom he had picked up in his travels, who could serve an excellent dinner. I remember that he remarked what a queer household it was to find in the heart of Surrey, and that I agreed with him, though it has proved a good deal queerer than I thought.

"I drove to the place—about two miles on the south side of Esher. The house was a fair-sized one, standing back from the road, with a curving drive which was banked with high evergreen shrubs. It was an old, tumble-down building in a crazy state of disrepair. When the trap pulled up on the grass-grown drive in front of the blotched and weather-stained door, I had doubts as to my wisdom in visiting a man whom I knew so slightly. He opened the door himself, however, and greeted me with a great show of cordiality. I was handed over to the man-servant, a melancholy, swarthy individual, who led the way, my bag in his hand, to my bedroom. The whole place was depressing. Our dinner was *tête-à-tête*, and though my host did his best to be entertaining, his thoughts seemed to continually wander, and he talked so vaguely and wildly that I could hardly understand him. He continually drummed his fingers on the table, gnawed his nails, and gave other signs of nervous impatience. The dinner itself was neither well served nor well cooked, and the gloomy presence of the taciturn servant did not help to enliven us. I can assure you that many times in the course of the evening I wished that I could invent some excuse which would take me back to Lee.

"One thing comes back to my memory which may have a bearing upon the business that you two gentlemen are investigating. I thought nothing of it at the time. Near the end of dinner a note was handed in by the servant. I noticed that after my host had read it he seemed even more distrait and strange than before. He gave up all pretence at conversation and sat, smoking endless cigarettes, lost in his own thoughts, but he made no remark as to the contents. About eleven I was glad to go to bed. Some time later Garcia looked in at my door—the room was dark at the time—and asked me if I had rung. I said that I had not. He apologized for having disturbed me so late, saying that it was nearly one o'clock. I dropped off after this and slept soundly all night.

"And now I come to the amazing part of my tale. When I woke it was broad daylight. I glanced at my watch, and the time was nearly nine. I had particularly asked to be called at eight, so I was very much astonished at this forgetfulness. I sprang up and rang for the servant. There was no response. I rang again and again,

11 *Oxshott.* A town in Surrey.

with the same result. Then I came to the conclusion that the bell was out of order. I huddled on my clothes and hurried downstairs in an exceedingly bad temper to order some hot water. You can imagine my surprise when I found that there was no one there. I shouted in the hall. There was no answer. Then I ran from room to room. All were deserted. My host had shown me which was his bedroom the night before, so I knocked at the door. No reply. I turned the handle and walked in. The room was empty, and the bed had never been slept in. He had gone with the rest. The foreign host, the foreign footman, the foreign cook, all had vanished in the night! That was the end of my visit to Wisteria Lodge."

Sherlock Holmes was rubbing his hands and chuckling as he added this bizarre incident to his collection of strange episodes.

"Your experience is, so far as I know, perfectly unique," said he. "May I ask, sir, what you did then?"

"I was furious. My first idea was that I had been the victim of some absurd practical joke. I packed my things, banged the hall door behind me, and set off for Esher, with my bag in my hand. I called at Allan Brothers', the chief land agents in the village, and found that it was from this firm that the villa had been rented. It struck me that the whole proceeding could hardly be for the purpose of making a fool of me, and that the main object must be to get out of the rent. It is late in March, so quarter-day is
12 at hand. But this theory would not work. The agent was obliged to me for my warning, but told me that the rent had been paid in advance. Then I made my way to town and called at the Spanish Embassy. The man was unknown there. After this I went to see Melville, at whose house I had first met Garcia, but I found that he really knew rather less about him than I did. Finally, when I got your reply to my wire I came out to you, since I understand that you are a person who gives advice in difficult cases. But now, Mr. Inspector, I gather, from what you said when you entered the room, that you can carry the story on, and that some tragedy has occurred. I can assure you that every word I have said is the truth, and that, outside of what I have told you, I know absolutely nothing about the fate of this man. My only desire is to help the law in every possible way."

"I am sure of it, Mr. Scott Eccles—I am sure of it," said Inspector Gregson, in a very amiable tone. "I am bound to say that everything which you have said agrees very closely with the facts as they have come to our notice. For example, there was that note which arrived during dinner. Did you chance to observe what became of it?"

"Yes, I did. Garcia rolled it up and threw it into the fire."

"What do you say to that, Mr. Baynes?"

The country detective was a stout, puffy, red man, whose face was only redeemed from grossness by two extraordinarily bright eyes, almost hidden behind the heavy creases of cheek and brow. With a slow smile he drew a folded and discoloured scrap of paper from his pocket.

"It was a dog-grate, Mr. Holmes, and he over-pitched it. I picked this out unburned from the back of it."

12 *quarter-day is at hand.* Quarter days in England and Scotland mark a traditional division of the year: they are regarded as "beginning a quarter of the year when quarterly payments, as rent, become due, and various civic and business functions are carried out, such as election, payment of taxes, hiring of help, etc." English literature, especially in essays, fiction, and poetry, abounds in allusions to these days, which in England are Christmas, Lent, Midsummer (June 24th), and Michaelmas (September 29th):

> And when the tenants come to pay their quarter's rent,
> They bring some fowl at Midsummer, a dish of fish in Lent,
> At Christmas a capon, at Michaelmas a goose,
> And somewhat else at New-Year's tide, for fear their lease fly loose.

"IT WAS A DOG-GRATE, MR. HOLMES, AND HE OVER-PITCHED IT."

Illustration by Arthur Twidle for the *Strand Magazine,* September, 1908. A dog-grate is a detached fire grate standing on supports called dogs.

Holmes smiled his appreciation.

" You must have examined the house very carefully to find a single pellet of paper."

" I did, Mr. Holmes. It's my way. Shall I read it, Mr. Gregson ? "

The Londoner nodded.

" The note is written upon ordinary cream-laid paper without watermark. It is a quarter-sheet. The paper is cut off in two snips with a short-bladed scissors. It has been folded over three times and sealed with purple wax, put on hurriedly and pressed down with some flat, oval object. It is addressed to Mr. Garcia, Wisteria Lodge. It says : ' Our own colours, green and white. Green **13**
open, white shut. Main stair, first corridor, seventh right, green baize. God speed. D.' It is a woman's writing, done with a sharp-pointed pen, but the address is either done with another pen or by someone else. It is thicker and bolder, as you see."

" A very remarkable note," said Holmes, glancing it over. " I must compliment you, Mr. Baynes, upon your attention to detail in your examination of it. A few trifling points might perhaps be added. The oval seal is undoubtedly a plain sleeve-link—what else is of such a shape ? The scissors were bent nail-scissors. Short as the two snips are, you can distinctly see the same slight curve in each."

The country detective chuckled.

" I thought I had squeezed all the juice out of it, but I see there was a little over," he said. " I'm bound to say that I make nothing of the note except that there was something on hand, and that a woman, as usual, was at the bottom of it."

Mr. Scott Eccles had fidgeted in his seat during this conversation.

" I am glad you found the note, since it corroborates my story," said he. " But I beg to point out that I have not yet heard what has happened to Mr. Garcia, nor what has become of his household."

" As to Garcia," said Gregson, " that is easily answered. He was found dead this morning upon Oxshott Common, nearly a mile from his home. His head had been smashed **14**
to pulp by heavy blows of a sand-bag or some such instrument, which had crushed rather than wounded. It is a lonely corner, and there is no house within a quarter of a mile of the spot. He had apparently been struck down first from behind, but his assailant had gone on beating him long after he was dead. It was a most furious assault. There are no footsteps nor any clue to the criminals."

" Robbed ? "

" No, there was no attempt at robbery."

" This is very painful—very painful and terrible," said Mr. Scott Eccles, in a querulous voice ; " but it is really uncommonly hard upon me. I had nothing to do with my host going off upon a nocturnal excursion and meeting so sad an end. How do I come to be mixed up with the case ? "

" Very simply, sir," Inspector Baynes answered. " The only document found in the pocket of the deceased was a letter from you saying that you would be with him on the night of his death. It was the envelope of this letter which

13 *'Our own colours, green and white.* "Green and white . . . are obviously false since they do not suit any Latin American country," Dr. Julian Wolff wrote in his *Practical Handbook of Sherlockian Heraldry*. "However, green and yellow are the colours of Brazil, and this fact furnishes a point of departure for further investigation. . . ."

14 *nearly a mile from his home.* There is Esher Common and Oxshott Heath, and Watson here seems to have combined the two. "Wisteria Lodge," it appears, lay between them, but somewhat nearer Esher than to Oxshott.

gave us the dead man's name and address. It was after nine this morning when we reached his house and found neither you nor anyone else inside it. I wired to Mr. Gregson to run you down in London while I examined Wisteria Lodge. Then I came into town, joined Mr. Gregson, and here we are."

"I think now," said Gregson, rising, "we had best put this matter into an official shape. You will come round with us to the station, Mr. Scott Eccles, and let us have your statement in writing."

"Certainly, I will come at once. But I retain your services, Mr. Holmes. I desire you to spare no expense and no pains to get at the truth."

My friend turned to the country inspector.

"I suppose that you have no objection to my collaborating with you, Mr. Baynes?"

"Highly honoured, sir, I am sure."

"You appear to have been very prompt and businesslike in all that you have done. Was there any clue, may I ask, as to the exact hour that the man met his death?"

"He had been there since one o'clock. There was rain about that time, and his death had certainly been before the rain."

"But that is perfectly impossible, Mr. Baynes," cried our client. "His voice is unmistakable. I could swear to it that it was he who addressed me in my bedroom at that very hour."

"Remarkable, but by no means impossible," said Holmes, smiling.

"You have a clue?" asked Gregson.

"On the face of it the case is not a very complex one, though it certainly presents some novel and interesting features. A further knowledge of facts is necessary before I would venture to give a final and definite opinion. By the way, Mr. Baynes, did you find anything remarkable besides this note in your examination of the house?"

The detective looked at my friend in a singular way.

"There were," said he, "one or two *very* remarkable things. Perhaps when I have finished at the police-station you would care to come out and give me your opinion of them."

"I am entirely at your service," said Sherlock Holmes, ringing the bell. "You will show these gentlemen out, Mrs. Hudson, and kindly send the boy with this telegram. He is to pay a five-shilling reply."

We sat for some time in silence after our visitors had left. Holmes smoked hard, with his brows drawn down over his keen eyes, and his head thrust forward in the eager way characteristic of the man.

"Well, Watson," he asked, turning suddenly upon me, "what do you make of it?"

"I can make nothing of this mystification of Scott Eccles."

"But the crime?"

"Well, taken with the disappearance of the man's companions, I should say that they were in some way concerned in the murder and had fled from justice."

"That is certainly a possible point of view. On the face of it you must admit, however, that it is very strange that his two servants should have been in a conspiracy

"HE IS TO PAY A FIVE-SHILLING REPLY."

Although the crown, worth five shillings, is nowhere mentioned in the Canon, it is probable that the boy paid for the reply telegram with this coin (shown here is the Victorian "Gothic" crown.) The crown, the late A. Carson Simpson wrote in *Numismatics in the Canon*, Part I, "began as a goldpiece. Its original ancestor was the half rose-noble (or half ryal) of Edward IV's light coinage of 1464, which, however, was of short duration. It was first struck under its present name by Henry VIII as the 'crown of the double rose' in his second (Wolsey) coinage of 1526. Discontinued under Bloody Mary and William & Mary (when the angelet, or half-angel, was valued at 5/—), it was restored to the coinage by Elizabeth I and continued under the name of 'Britain crown' by James I and Charles I; it was last struck in gold under the Commonwealth. Meanwhile, Edward VI had established the *silver* crown, which has been struck by all subsequent rulers except Mary I, William & Mary and William IV. In recent times, its large size and weights have made it become unpopular, as happened also the U.S. silver dollar. It still circulated, however, in the period in which we are interested, which brings us through 1902; after that year, it was not struck again for a quarter of a century."

against him and should have attacked him on the one night when he had a guest. They had him alone at their mercy every other night in the week."

"Then why did they fly?"

"Quite so. Why did they fly? There is a big fact. Another big fact is the remarkable experience of our client, Scott Eccles. Now, my dear Watson, is it beyond the limits of human ingenuity to furnish an explanation which would cover both these big facts? If it were one which would also admit of the mysterious note with its very curious phraseology, why, then it would be worth accepting as a temporary hypothesis. If the fresh facts which come to our knowledge all fit themselves into the scheme, then our hypothesis may gradually become a solution."

"But what is our hypothesis?"

Holmes leaned back in his chair with half-closed eyes.

"You must admit, my dear Watson, that the idea of a joke is impossible. There were grave events afoot, as the sequel showed, and the coaxing of Scott Eccles to Wisteria Lodge had some connection with them."

"But what possible connection?"

"Let us take it link by link. There is, on the face of it, something unnatural about this strange and sudden friendship between the young Spaniard and Scott Eccles. It was the former who forced the pace. He called upon Eccles at the other end of London on the very day after he first met him, and he kept in close touch with him until he got him down to Esher. Now, what did he want with Eccles? What could Eccles supply? I see no charm in the man. He is not particularly intelligent—not a man likely to be congenial to a quick-witted Latin. Why, then, was he picked out from all the other people whom Garcia met as particularly suited to his purpose? Has he any one outstanding quality? I say that he has. He is the very type of conventional British respectability, and the very man as a witness to impress another Briton. You saw yourself how neither of the inspectors dreamed of questioning his statement, extraordinary as it was."

"But what was he to witness?"

"Nothing, as things turned out, but everything had they gone another way. That is how I read the matter."

"I see, he might have proved an alibi."

"Exactly, my dear Watson; he might have proved an alibi. We will suppose, for argument's sake, that the household of Wisteria Lodge are confederates in some design. The attempt, whatever it may be, is to come off, we will say, before one o'clock. By some juggling of the clocks it is quite possible that they may have got Scott Eccles to bed earlier than he thought, but in any case it is likely that when Garcia went out of his way to tell him that it was one it was really not more than twelve. If Garcia could do whatever he had to do and be back by the hour mentioned he had evidently a powerful reply to any accusation. Here was this irreproachable Englishman ready to swear in any court of law that the accused was in his house all the time. It was an insurance against the worst."

"Yes, yes, I see that. But how about the disappearance of the others?"

"I have not all my facts yet, but I do not think there

HE TOSSED IT ACROSS WITH A LAUGH.

Illustration by Arthur Twidle for the *Strand Magazine*, September, 1908.

are any insuperable difficulties. Still, it is an error to argue in front of your data. You find yourself insensibly twisting them round to fit your theories."

" And the message ? "

" How did it run ? ' Our own colours, green and white.' Sounds like racing. ' Green open, white shut.' That is clearly a signal. ' Main stair, first corridor, seventh right, green baize.' This is an assignation. We may find a jealous husband at the bottom of it all. It was clearly a dangerous quest. She would not have said ' God speed ' had it not been so. ' D '—that should be a guide."

" The man was a Spaniard. I suggest that ' D ' stands for Dolores, a common female name in Spain."

" Good, Watson, very good—but quite inadmissible. A Spaniard would write to a Spaniard in Spanish. The writer of this note is certainly English. Well, we can only possess our souls in patience, until this excellent inspector comes back for us. Meanwhile we can thank our lucky fate which has rescued us for a few short hours from the insufferable fatigues of idleness."

An answer had arrived to Holmes' telegram before our Surrey officer had returned. Holmes read it, and was about to place it in his notebook when he caught a glimpse of my expectant face. He tossed it across with a laugh.

" We are moving in exalted circles," said he.

The telegram was a list of names and addresses : " Lord Harringby, The Dingle ; Sir George Folliott, Oxshott Towers ; Mr. Hynes Hynes, J.P., Purdey Place ; Mr. James Baker Williams, Forton Old Hall ; Mr. Henderson,
15 High Gable ; Rev. Joshua Stone, Nether Walsling."

" This is a very obvious way of limiting our field of operations," said Holmes. " No doubt Baynes, with his methodical mind, has already adopted some similar plan."

" I don't quite understand."

" Well, my dear fellow, we have already arrived at the conclusion that the message received by Garcia at dinner was an appointment or an assignation. Now, if the obvious reading of it is correct, and in order to keep this tryst one has to ascend a main stair and seek the seventh door in a corridor, it is perfectly clear that the house is a very large one. It is equally certain that this house cannot be more than a mile or two from Oxshott, since Garcia was walking in that direction, and hoped, according to my reading of the facts, to be back in Wisteria Lodge in time to avail himself of an alibi, which would only be valid up to one o'clock. As the number of large houses close to Oxshott must be limited, I adopted the obvious method of sending to the agents mentioned by Scott Eccles and obtaining a list of them. Here they are in this telegram, and the other end of our tangled skein must lie among them."

It was nearly six o'clock before we found ourselves in the pretty Surrey village of Esher, with Inspector Baynes as our companion.

Holmes and I had taken things for the night, and found
16 comfortable quarters at the Bull. Finally we set out in the company of the detective on our visit to Wisteria Lodge. It was a cold, dark March evening, with a sharp wind and

15 *Rev. Joshua Stone, Nether Walsling.*" "What is a parson doing in a 'large house' that is not his vicarage or rectory?" the Reverend Otis R. Rice asked in "Clergymen in the Canon." "You may say that the Reverend Mister Stone (or the Reverend Father Stone, if he had high church proclivities as is strongly to be suspected) had married a woman of large means and had graciously accepted the house at her hands or her family's. There is a remote possibility that he himself might have inhertied the property upon the death of an older childless brother or brothers. But so rarely does this happen to a member of the clergy that one may justly be skeptical. Whatever the circumstances it is scarcely edifying to learn that one who preaches or should preach the virtues of simplicity and unostentation is himself living in a 'large house' classed by the local agents with those inhabited by a Lord, a Knight, a Justice of the Peace and two men of wealth . . ."

16 *the Bull.* The only fair-sized hotel in Esher is the *Bear.*

a fine rain beating upon our faces, a fit setting for the wild common over which our road passed and the tragic goal to which it led us.

II—The Tiger of San Pedro

A cold and melancholy walk of a couple of miles brought us to a high wooden gate, which opened into a gloomy avenue of chestnuts. The curved and shadowed drive led us to a low, dark house, pitch-black against a slate-coloured sky. From the front window upon the left of the door there peeped a glimmer of a feeble light.

" There's a constable in possession," said Baynes. " I'll knock at the window." He stepped across the grass plot and tapped with his hand on the pane. Through the fogged glass I dimly saw a man spring up from a chair beside the fire, and heard a sharp cry from within the room. An instant later a white-faced, hard-breathing policeman had opened the door, the candle wavering in his trembling hand.

" What's the matter, Walters ? " asked Baynes, sharply.

The man mopped his forehead with his handkerchief and gave a long sigh of relief.

" I am glad you have come, sir. It has been a long evening and I don't think my nerve is as good as it was."

" Your nerve, Walters ? I should not have thought you had a nerve in your body."

" Well, sir, it's this lonely, silent house and the queer thing in the kitchen. Then when you tapped at the window I thought it had come again."

" That what had come again ? "

" The devil, sir, for all I know. It was at the window."

" What was at the window, and when ? "

" It was just about two hours ago. The light was just fading. I was sitting reading in the chair. I don't know what made me look up, but there was a face looking in at me through the lower pane. Lord, sir, what a face it was ! I'll see it in my dreams."

" Tut, tut, Walters ! This is not talk for a police-constable."

" I know, sir, I know ; but it shook me, sir, and there's no use to deny it. It wasn't black, sir, nor was it white, nor any colour that I know, but a kind of queer shade like clay with a splash of milk in it. Then there was the size of it—it was twice yours, sir. And the look of it—the great staring goggle eyes, and the line of white teeth like a hungry beast. I tell you, sir, I couldn't move a finger, nor get my breath, till it whisked away and was gone. Out I ran and through the shrubbery, but thank God there was no one there."

" If I didn't know you were a good man, Walters, I should put a black mark against you for this. If it were the devil himself a constable on duty should never thank

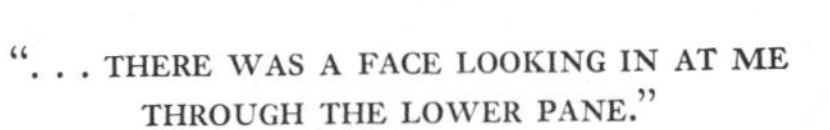

". . . THERE WAS A FACE LOOKING IN AT ME THROUGH THE LOWER PANE."

Illustration by Arthur Twidle for the *Strand Magazine*, October, 1908.

God that he could not lay his hands upon him. I suppose the whole thing is not a vision and a touch of nerves ? "

" That, at least, is very easily settled," said Holmes, lighting his little pocket lantern. " Yes," he reported, after a short examination of the grass bed, " a number twelve shoe, I should say. If he was all on the same scale as his foot he must certainly have been a giant."

" What became of him ? "

" He seems to have broken through the shrubbery and made for the road."

" Well," said the inspector, with a grave and thoughtful face, " whoever he may have been, and whatever he may have wanted, he's gone for the present, and we have more immediate things to attend to. Now, Mr. Holmes, with your permission, I will show you round the house."

The various bedrooms and sitting-rooms had yielded nothing to a careful search. Apparently the tenants had brought little or nothing with them, and all the furniture down to the smallest details had been taken over with the house. A good deal of clothing with the stamp of Marx & Co., High Holborn, had been left behind. Telegraphic inquiries had been already made which showed that Marx knew nothing of his customer save that he was a good payer. Odds and ends, some pipes, a few novels, two of them in Spanish, an old-fashioned pinfire revolver, and a guitar were amongst the personal property.

" Nothing in all this," said Baynes, stalking, candle in hand, from room to room. " But now, Mr. Holmes, I invite your attention to the kitchen."

It was a gloomy, high-ceilinged room at the back of the house, with a straw litter in one corner, which served apparently as a bed for the cook. The table was piled with half-eaten dishes and dirty plates, the debris of last night's dinner.

" Look at this," said Baynes. " What do you make of it ? "

He held up his candle before an extraordinary object which stood at the back of the dresser. It was so wrinkled

HE HELD UP HIS CANDLE BEFORE AN EXTRAORDINARY OBJECT . . .

Illustration by Frederic Dorr Steele for *Collier's Magazine*, August 15, 1908. Arthur Twidle illustrated the same scene for the *Strand Magazine*, October, 1908.

and shrunken and withered that it was difficult to say what it might have been. One could but say that it was black and leathery and that it bore some resemblance to a dwarfish human figure. At first, as I examined it, I thought that it was a mummified negro baby, and then it seemed a very twisted and ancient monkey. Finally I was left in doubt as to whether it was animal or human. A double band of white shells was strung round the centre of it.

"Very interesting—very interesting indeed!" said Holmes peering at this sinister relic. "Anything more?"

In silence Baynes led the way to the sink and held forward his candle. The limbs and body of some large white bird, torn savagely to pieces with the feathers still on, were littered all over it. Holmes pointed to the wattles on the severed head.

"A white cock," said he; "most interesting! It is really a very curious case."

But Mr. Baynes had kept his most sinister exhibit to the last. From under the sink he drew a zinc pail which contained a quantity of blood. Then from the table he took a platter heaped with small pieces of charred bone.

"Something has been killed and something has been burned. We raked all these out of the fire. We had a doctor in this morning. He says that they are not human."

Holmes smiled and rubbed his hands.

"I must congratulate you, inspector, on handling so distinctive and instructive a case. Your powers, if I may say so without offence, seem superior to your opportunities."

Inspector Baynes' small eyes twinkled with pleasure.

"You're right, Mr. Holmes. We stagnate in the provinces. A case of this sort gives a man a chance, and I hope that I shall take it. What do you make of these bones?"

"A lamb, I should say, or a kid."

"And the white cock?"

"Curious, Mr. Baynes, very curious. I should say almost unique."

"Yes, sir, there must have been some very strange people with some very strange ways in this house. One of them is dead. Did his companions follow him and kill him? If they did we should have them, for every port is watched. But my own views are different. Yes, sir, my own views are very different."

"You have a theory, then?"

"And I'll work it myself, Mr. Holmes. It's only due to my own credit to do so. Your name is made, but I have still to make mine. I should be glad to be able to say afterwards that I had solved it without your help."

Holmes laughed good-humouredly.

"Well, well, inspector," said he. "Do you follow your path and I will follow mine. My results are always very much at your service if you care to apply to me for them. I think that I have seen all that I wish in this house, and that my time may be more profitably employed elsewhere. *Au revoir* and good luck!"

I could tell by numerous subtle signs, which might have been lost upon anyone but myself, that Holmes was on a hot scent. As impassive as ever to the casual observer,

FROM UNDER THE SINK HE DREW A ZINC PAIL . . .

Illustration by Arthur Twidle for the *Strand Magazine*, October, 1908.

there were none the less a subdued eagerness and suggestion of tension in his brightened eyes and brisker manner which assured me that the game was afoot. After his habit he said nothing, and after mine I asked no questions. Sufficient for me to share the sport and lend my humble help to the capture without distracting that intent brain with needless interruption. All would come round to me in due time.

I waited, therefore—but, to my ever-deepening dis-
17 appointment I waited in vain. Day succeeded day, and my friend took no step forward. One morning he spent in town, and I learned from a casual reference that he had visited the British Museum. Save for this one excursion, he spent his days in long, and often solitary walks, or in chatting with a number of village gossips whose acquaintance he had cultivated.

" I'm sure, Watson, a week in the country will be invaluable to you," he remarked. " It is very pleasant to see the first green shoots upon the hedges and the catkins on the hazels once again. With a spud, a tin box, and an elementary book on botany, there are instructive days to be spent." He prowled about with this equipment him-
18 self, but it was a poor show of plants which he would bring back of an evening.

Occasionally in our rambles we came across Inspector Baynes. His fat, red face wreathed itself in smiles and his small eyes glittered as he greeted my companion. He said little about the case, but from that little we gathered that he also was not dissatisfied at the course of events. I must admit, however, that I was somewhat surprised when, some five days after the crime, I opened my morning paper to find in large letters :

" THE OXSHOTT MYSTERY
A SOLUTION
ARREST OF SUPPOSED ASSASSIN."

Holmes sprang in his chair as if he had been stung when I read the head-lines.

" By Jove ! " he cried. You don't mean that Baynes has got him ? "

" Apparently," said I, as I read the following report :

" Great excitement was caused in Esher and the neighbouring district when it was learned late last night that an arrest had been effected in connection with the Oxshott murder. It will be remembered that Mr. Garcia, of Wisteria Lodge, was found dead on Oxshott Common, his body showing signs of extreme violence, and that on the same night his servant and his cook fled, which appeared to show their participation in the crime. It was suggested, but never proved, that the deceased gentleman may have had valuables in the house, and that their abstraction was the motive of the crime. Every effort was made by Inspector Baynes, who has the case in hand, to ascertain the hiding-place of the fugitives, and he had good reason to believe that they had not gone far, but were lurking in some retreat which had been already prepared. It was certain from the first, however, that they would eventually be detected, as the cook, from the evidence of one or two tradespeople who have caught a glimpse of him through the window, was a man of most remarkable appearance—being a huge and hideous mulatto, with yellowish features of a pronounced negroid type. This man has been seen since the crime, for he was detected

17 *Day succeeded day.* A curious feature of this adventure is Watson's complete silence about his wife. We find him living at Baker Street once more, and not for a few days only: the case occupies almost a week. Neither does he mention his professional duties. His reticence about Mrs. Watson is not confined to this tale alone: in the story which follows, "Silver Blaze," and later, in "The Adventure of the Beryl Coronet," she is never once referred to. "Mr. S. C. Roberts has suggested that at about this period Mrs. Watson's health had begun to fail," the late H. W. Bell wrote in *Sherlock Holmes and Dr. Watson: The Chronology of Their Adventures.* "It may well be that her illness, which resulted fatally some three years later, had just been diagnosed, and that she had gone away to a sanatorium. What more natural, then, that Watson, in his loneliness and sorrow, should have returned for a while to Baker Street, leaving his patients, not for the first time, in the care of his neighbour, until he had recovered some measure of self-control."

18 *He prowled about with this equipment himself.* "It may be remarked that the only occasion Holmes ever noticed flowers was when he spoke of the beauty of a rose at the time of 'The Adventure of the Naval Treaty,'" Mr. Humfrey Michell wrote in "The Sartorial Sherlock Holmes," "and, as we well know, that remark was not prompted by a love of nature. Can we really believe that he would deceive a child when he prowled about with a spud, a tin box and an elementary book on botany during his singularly inept investigation of ["The Adventure of Wisteria Lodge"]? Assuredly that strange story should be classed among the Apocrypha."

and pursued by Constable Walters on the same evening, when he had the audacity to revisit Wisteria Lodge. Inspector Baynes, considering that such a visit must have some purpose in view, and was likely, therefore, to be repeated, abandoned the house, but left an ambuscade in the shrubbery. The man walked into the trap, and was captured last night after a struggle in which Constable Downing was badly bitten by the savage. We understand that when the prisoner is brought before the magistrates a remand will be applied for by the police, and **19**
that great developments are hoped from his capture."

" Really we must see Baynes at once," cried Holmes, picking up his hat. " We will just catch him before he starts." We hurried down the village street and found, as we had expected, that the inspector was just leaving his lodgings.

" You've seen the paper, Mr. Holmes ? " he asked, holding one out to us.

" Yes, Baynes, I've seen it. Pray don't think it a liberty if I give you a word of friendly warning."

" Of warning, Mr. Holmes ? "

" I have looked into this case with some care, and I am not convinced that you are on the right lines. I don't want you to commit yourself too far, unless you are sure."

" You're very kind, Mr. Holmes."

" I assure you I speak for your good."

It seemed to me that something like a wink quivered for an instant over one of Mr. Baynes' tiny eyes.

" We agreed to work on our own lines, Mr. Holmes. That's what I am doing."

" Oh, very good," said Holmes. " Don't blame me."

" No, sir ; I believe you mean well by me. But we all have our own systems, Mr. Holmes. You have yours, and maybe I have mine."

" Let us say no more about it."

" You're welcome always to my news. This fellow is a perfect savage, as strong as a cart-horse and as fierce as the devil. He chewed Downing's thumb nearly off before they could master him. He hardly speaks a word of English, and we can get nothing out of him but grunts."

" And you think you have evidence that he murdered his late master ? "

" I didn't say so, Mr. Holmes ; I didn't say so. We all have our little ways. You try yours and I will try mine. That's the agreement."

Holmes shrugged his shoulders as we walked away together. " I can't make the man out. He seems to be riding for a fall. Well, as he says, we must each try our own way and see what comes of it. But there's something in Inspector Baynes which I can't quite understand."

" Just sit down in that chair, Watson," said Sherlock Holmes, when we had returned to our apartment at the Bull. " I want to put you in touch with the situation, as I may need your help to-night. Let me show you the evolution of this case, so far as I have been able to follow it. Simple as it has been in its leading features, it has none the less presented surprising difficulties in the way of an arrest. There are gaps in that direction which we have still to fill.

" We will go back to the note which was handed in to Garcia upon the evening of his death. We may put aside

19 *a remand.* A judicial order for recommittal.

"THE MAN WALKED INTO THE TRAP . . ."

Illustration by Arthur Twidle for the *Strand Magazine*, October, 1908.

this idea of Baynes' that Garcia's servants were concerned in the matter. The proof of this lies in the fact that it was *he* who had arranged for the presence of Scott Eccles, which could only have been done for the purpose of an alibi. It was Garcia, then, who had an enterprise, and apparently a criminal enterprise, in hand that night, in the course of which he met his death. I say criminal because only a man with a criminal enterprise desires to establish an alibi. Who, then, is most likely to have taken his life ? Surely the person against whom the criminal enterprise was directed. So far it seems to me that we are on safe ground.

" We can now see a reason for the disappearance of Garcia's household. They were *all* confederates in the same unknown crime. If it came off then Garcia returned, any possible suspicion would be warded off by the Englishman's evidence, and all would be well. But the attempt was a dangerous one, and if Garcia did *not* return by a certain hour it was probable that his own life had been sacrificed. It had been arranged, therefore, that in such a case his two subordinates were to make for some prearranged spot, where they could escape investigation and be in a position afterwards to renew their attempt. That would fully explain the facts, would it not ? "

The whole inexplicable tangle seemed to straighten out before me. I wondered, as I always did, how it had not been obvious to me before.

" But why should one servant return ? "

" We can imagine that, in the confusion of flight, something precious, something which he could not bear to part with, had been left behind. That would explain his persistence, would it not ? "

" Well, what is the next step ? "

" The next step is the note received by Garcia at the dinner. It indicates a confederate at the other end. Now, where was the other end ? I have already shown you that it could only lie in some large house, and that the number of large houses is limited. My first days in this village were devoted to a series of walks, in which in the intervals of my botanical researches I made a reconnaissance of all the large houses and an examination of the family history of the occupants. One house, and only one, riveted my attention. It is the famous old Jacobean grange of High Gable, one mile on the farther side of Oxshott, and less than half a mile from the scene of the tragedy. The other mansions belonged to prosaic and respectable people who live far aloof from romance. But Mr. Henderson, of High Gable, was by all accounts a curious man, to whom curious adventures might befall. I concentrated my attention, therefore, upon him and his household.

" A singular set of people, Watson—the man himself the most singular of them all. I managed to see him on a plausible pretext, but I seemed to read in his dark, deep-set, brooding eyes that he was perfectly aware of my true business. He is a man of fifty, strong, active, with iron-grey hair, great bunched black eyebrows, the step of a deer, and the air of an emperor—a fierce, masterful man, with a red-hot spirit behind his parchment face. He is either a foreigner or has lived long in the Tropics, for he is yellow and sapless, but tough as whipcord. His friend and secretary, Mr. Lucas, is undoubtedly a foreigner, chocolate brown, wily, suave and cat-like with a poisonous gentleness of speech. You see, Watson, we have come already upon two sets of foreigners—one at Wisteria Lodge and one at High Gable—so our gaps are beginning to close.

" These two men, close and confidential friends, are the centre of the household ; but there is one other person, who for our immediate purpose may be even more important. Henderson has two children—girls of eleven and thirteen. Their governess is a Miss Burnet, an Englishwoman of forty or thereabouts. There is also one confidential man-servant. This little group forms the real family, for they travel about together, and Henderson is a great traveller, always on the move. It is only within the last few weeks that he has returned, after a year's absence, to High Gable. I may add that he is enormously rich, and whatever his whims may be he can very easily satisfy them. For the rest, his house is full of butlers, footmen, maid-servants, and the usual overfed, underworked staff of a large English country-house.

" So much I learned partly from village gossip and partly from my own observation. There are no better instruments than discharged servants with a grievance, and I was lucky enough to find one. I call it luck, but it would not have come my way had I not been looking out for it. As Baynes remarks, we all have our systems. It was my system which enabled me to find John Warner, late gardener of High Gable, sacked in a moment of temper by his imperious employer. He in turn had friends among the indoor servants, who unite in their fear and dislike of their master. So I had my key to the secrets of the establishment.

" Curious people, Watson ! I don't pretend to understand it all yet, but very curious people anyway. It's a double-winged house, and the servants live on one side, the family on the other. There's no link between the two save for Henderson's own servant, who serves the family's meals. Everything is carried to a certain door, which forms the one connection. Governess and children hardly go out at all, except into the garden. Henderson never by any chance walks alone. His dark secretary is like his shadow. The gossip among the servants is that their master is terribly afraid of something. ' Sold his soul to the devil in exchange for money,' says Warner, ' and expects his creditor to come up and claim his own.' Where they came from, or who they are, nobody has an idea. They are very violent. Twice Henderson has lashed at folk with his dog-whip, and only his long purse and heavy compensation have kept him out of the courts.

" Well, now, Watson, let us judge the situation by this new information. We may take it that the letter came out of this strange household, and was an invitation to Garcia to carry out some attempt which had already been planned. Who wrote the note ? It was someone within the citadel, and it was a woman. Who then, but Miss Burnet, the governess ? All our reasoning seems to point that way. At any rate, we may take it as a hypothesis, and see what consequences it would entail. I may add that Miss

Burnet's age and character make it certain that my first idea that there might be a love interest in our story is out of the question.

"If she wrote the note she was presumably the friend and confederate of Garcia. What, then, might she be expected to do if she heard of his death ? If he met it in some nefarious enterprise her lips might be sealed. Still, in her heart she must retain bitterness and hatred against those who had killed him, and would presumably help so far as she could to have revenge upon them. Could we see her, then, and try to use her ? That was my first thought. But now we come to a sinister fact. Miss Burnet has not been seen by any human eye since the night of the murder. From that evening she has utterly vanished. Is she alive ? Has she perhaps met her end on the same night as the friend whom she had summoned ? Or is she merely a prisoner ? There is the point which we still have to decide.

"You will appreciate the difficulty of the situation, Watson. There is nothing upon which we can apply for a warrant. Our whole scheme might seem fantastic if laid before a magistrate. The woman's disappearance counts for nothing, since in that extraordinary household any member of it might be invisible for a week. And yet she may at the present moment be in danger of her life. All I can do is to watch the house and leave my agent, Warner, on guard at the gates. We can't let such a situation continue. If the law can do nothing we must take the risk ourselves."

"What do you suggest ?"

"I know which is her room. It is accessible from the top of an outhouse. My suggestion is that you and I go to-night and see if we can strike at the very heart of the mystery."

It was not, I must confess, a very alluring prospect. The old house with its atmosphere of murder, the singular and formidable inhabitants, the unknown dangers of the approach, and the fact that we were putting ourselves legally in a false position, all combined to damp my ardour. But there was something in the ice-cold reasoning of Holmes which made it impossible to shrink from any adventure which he might recommend. One knew that thus, and only thus, could a solution be found. I clasped his hand in silence, and the die was cast.

But it was not destined that our investigation should have so adventurous an ending. It was about five o'clock, and the shadows of the March evening were beginning to fall, when an excited rustic rushed into our room.

"They've gone, Mr. Holmes. They went by the last train. The lady broke away, and I've got her in a cab downstairs."

"Excellent, Warner !" cried Holmes, springing to his feet. "Watson, the gaps are closing rapidly."

In the cab was a woman, half-collapsed from nervous exhaustion. She bore upon her aquiline and emaciated face the traces of some recent tragedy. Her head hung listlessly upon her breast, but as she raised it and turned her dull eyes upon us, I saw that her pupils were dark dots in the centre of the broad grey iris. She was drugged with opium.

" I watched at the gate, same as you advised, Mr. Holmes," said our emissary, the discharged gardener. " When the carriage came out I followed it to the station. She was like one walking in her sleep ; but when they tried to get her into the train she came to life and struggled. They pushed her into the carriage. She fought her way out again. I took her part, got her into a cab, and here we are. I shan't forget the face at the carriage window as I led her away. I'd have a short life if he had his way—the black-eyed, scowling, yellow devil."

We carried her upstairs, laid her on the sofa, and a couple ofcups of the strongest coffee soon cleared her brain from the mists of the drug. Baynes had been summoned by Holmes, and the situation rapidly explained to him.

" Why, sir, you've got me the very evidence I want," said the inspector, warmly, shaking my friend by the hand. " I was on the same scent as you from the first."

" What ! You were after Henderson ? "

" Why, Mr. Holmes, when you were crawling in the shrubbery at High Gable I was up one of the trees in the plantation and saw you down below. It was just who would get his evidence first."

" Then why did you arrest the mulatto ? "

Baynes chuckled.

" I was sure Henderson, as he calls himself, felt that he was suspected, and that he would lie low and make no move so long as he thought he was in any danger. I arrested the wrong man to make him believe that our eyes were off him. I knew he would be likely to clear off then and give us a chance of getting at Miss Burnet."

Holmes laid his hand upon the inspector's shoulder.

" You will rise high in your profession. You have instinct and intuition," said he.

Baynes flushed with pleasure.

" I've had a plain-clothes man waiting at the station all the week. Wherever the High Gable folk go he will keep them in sight. But he must have been hard put to it when Miss Burnet broke away. However, your man picked her up, and it all ends well. We can't arrest without her evidence, that is clear, so the sooner we get a statement the better."

" Every minute she gets stronger," said Holmes, glancing at the governess. " But tell me, Baynes, who is this man Henderson ? "

" Henderson," the inspector answered, " is Don Murillo, once called the Tiger of San Pedro."

The Tiger of San Pedro ! The whole history of the man came back to me in a flash. He had made his name as the most lewd and bloodthirsty tyrant that had ever governed any country with a pretence to civilization. Strong, fearless, and energetic, he had sufficient virtue to enable him to impose his odious vices upon a cowering people for ten or twelve years. His name was a terror through all Central America. At the end of that time there was a universal rising against him. But he was as cunning as he was cruel, and at the first whisper of coming trouble he had secretly conveyed his treasures aboard a ship which was manned by devoted adherents. It was an empty palace which was stormed by the insurgents next day. The Dictator, his two children, his secretary, and

"SHE FOUGHT HER WAY OUT AGAIN."

Illustration by Arthur Twidle for the *Strand Magazine*, October, 1908.

his wealth had all escaped them. From that moment he had vanished from the world, and his identity had been a frequent subject for comment in the European Press.

20 " Yes, sir ; Don Murillo, the Tiger of San Pedro," said Baynes. " If you look it up you will find that the San Pedro colours are green and white, same as in the note, Mr. Holmes. Henderson he called himself, but I traced him back, Paris and Rome and Madrid to Barcelona, where his ship came in in '86. They've been looking for him all the time for their revenge, but it is only now that they have begun to find him out."

21 " They discovered him a year ago," said Miss Burnet, who had sat up and was now intently following the conversation. " Once already his life has been attempted ; but some evil spirit shielded him. Now, again, it is the noble, chivalrous Garcia who has fallen, while the monster goes safe. But another will come, and yet another, until some day justice will be done ; that is as certain as the rise of to-morrow's sun." Her thin hands clenched, and her worn face blanched with the passion of her hatred.

" But how come you into this matter, Miss Burnet ? " asked Holmes. " How can an English lady join in such a murderous affair ? "

" I join in it because there is no other way in the world by which justice can be gained. What does the law of England care for the rivers of blood shed years ago in San Pedro, or for the ship-load of treasure which this man has stolen ? To you they are like crimes committed in some other planet. But *we* know. We have learned the truth in sorrow and in suffering. To us there is no fiend in hell like Juan Murillo, and no peace in life while his victims still cry for vengeance."

" No doubt," said Holmes, " he was as you say. I have heard that he was atrocious. But how are you affected ? "

" I will tell you it all. This villain's policy was to murder, on one pretext or another, every man who showed such promise that he might in time come to be a dangerous rival. My husband—yes, my real name is Signora Victor Durando—was the San Pedro Minister in London. He met me and married me there. A nobler man never lived upon earth. Unhappily, Murillo heard of his excellence, recalled him on some pretext, and had him shot. With a premonition of his fate he had refused to take me with him. His estates were confiscated, and I was left with a pittance and a broken heart.

" Then came the downfall of the tyrant. He escaped as you have just described. But the many whose lives he had ruined, whose nearest and dearest had suffered torture and death at his hands, would not let the matter rest. They banded themselves into a society which should never be dissolved until the work was done. It was my part after we had discovered in the transformed Henderson the fallen despot, to attach myself to his household and keep the others in touch with his movements. This I was able to do by securing the position of governess in his family. He little knew that the woman who faced him at every meal was the woman whose husband he had hurried at an hour's notice into eternity. I smiled on him, did my duty to his children, and bided my time. An attempt was made

20 *"Yes, sir; Don Murillo, the Tiger of San Pedro."* "The Emperor of Brazil was deposed in 1889 and spent the rest of his life in Europe, where he died [December 5, 1891]," Dr. Julian Wolff wrote in his *Practical Handbook of Sherlockian Heraldry*. "It is all so absurdly simple now. Don Murillo, the Tiger of San Pedro, was actually Dom Pedro II, the last Emperor of Brazil! One explanation has to be made, since Dom Pedro never was a tyrant. It must be remembered that Holmes and Watson received their information from a member of the opposition, Signora Victor Durando [*see below*]. Anyone who has read the opposition's opinions of our best and wisest men will easily understand."

21 *"They discovered him a year ago."* Don Murillo's ship had docked in Barcelona in 1886. His enemies had "been looking for him all the time for revenge, but it is only now that they have begun to find him out." "They discovered him a year ago." From this statement, the year cannot be earlier than 1887, and is probably several years after that.

"HE AND HIS MASTER DRAGGED ME TO MY ROOM . . ."

Illustration by Arthur Twidle for the *Strand Magazine*, October, 1908. Frederic Dorr Steele illustrated much the same scene for *Collier's Magazine*, August 15, 1908.

in Paris, and failed. We zigzagged swiftly here and there over Europe, to throw off the pursuers, and finally returned to this house, which he had taken upon his first arrival in England.

" But here also the ministers of justice were waiting. Knowing that he would return there, Garcia, who is the son of the former highest dignitary in San Pedro, was waiting with two trusty companions of humble station, all three fired with the same reasons for revenge. He could do little during the day, for Murillo took every precaution, and never went out save with his satellite Lucas, or Lopez as he was known in the days of his greatness. At night, however, he slept alone, and the avenger might find him. On a certain evening, which had been prearranged, I sent my friend final instructions, for the man was for ever on the alert, and continually changed his room. I was to see that the doors were open and the signal of a green or white light in a window which faced the drive was to give notice if all was safe, or if the attempt had better be postponed.

" But everything went wrong with us. In some way I had excited the suspicion of Lopez, the secretary. He crept up behind me, and sprang upon me just as I had finished the note. He and his master dragged me to my room, and held judgment upon me as a convicted traitress. Then and there they would have plunged their knives into me, could they have seen how to escape the consequence of the deed. Finally, after much debate, they concluded that my murder was too dangerous. But they determined to get rid for ever of Garcia. They had gagged me, and Murillo twisted my arm round until I gave him the address. I swear that he might have twisted it off had I understood what it would mean to Garcia. Lopez addressed the note which I had written, sealed it with his sleeve-link, and sent it by the hand of the servant, José. How they murdered him I do not know, save that it was Murillo's hand who struck him down, for Lopez had remained to guard me. I believe he must have waited among the gorse bushes through which the path winds and struck him down as he passed. At first they were of a mind to let him enter the house and to kill him as a detected burglar ; but they argued that if they were mixed up in an inquiry their own identity would at once be publicly disclosed and they would be open to further attacks. With the death of Garcia the pursuit might cease, since such a death might frighten others from the task.

" All would now have been well for them had it not been for my knowledge of what they had done. I have no doubt that there were times when my life hung in the balance. I was confined to my room, terrorized by the most horrible threats, cruelly ill-used to break my spirit—see this stab on my shoulder and the bruises from end to end of my arms—and a gag was thrust into my mouth on the one occasion when I tried to call from the window. For five days this cruel imprisonment continued, with hardly enough food to hold body and soul together. This afternoon a good lunch was brought me, but the moment **22** after I took it I knew that I had been drugged. In a sort of dream I remember being half-led, half-carried to the carriage ; in the same state I was conveyed to the train.

22 *This afternoon a good lunch was brought me.* The first day of the case was not a Sunday: Mr. Scott Eccles "went to the house agents" before he called on Holmes. Nor was it a Tuesday: the crime took place shortly before one o'clock of the day on which Mr. Eccles called on Holmes; "five days after the crime," Watson "opened my morning paper." Watson's "five days" is corroborated by Holmes himself: the mulatto tried to recover his fetish, without success, on the night of the first day; "He waited three days longer, and then his piety or his superstitition drove him to try once more"; the mulatto's second attempt to recover his fetish was therefore on the fifth day of the story; he was taken on that occasion by Baynes, and Watson read an account of the capture in the morning newspaper of the sixth day—"five days after the [day of the] crime," as he tells us. The first day of the case and the sixth day of the case must fall within the same week, for Baynes says: "I've had a plain-clothes man at the station all week." Since the first day of the case was not Sunday or Tuesday, it must therefore have been Monday. More, Mr. Eccles said on the first day: "Quarter-day [March 25th] is at hand." The Monday on which the case began must therefore fall on March 24th or a very few days earlier.

We have seen (Note 2) that March, 1890, is the earliest possible date for "The Adventure of Wisteria Lodge." The latest possible date is the summer of 1895, for Watson tells us that one of the cases which enlivened the months between Holmes' Return (April 1894) and "The Adventure of the Norwood Builder" (August, 1895) was that of "the papers of ex-President Murillo." This case cannot *be* "The Adventure of Wisteria Lodge," which had nothing to do with "papers," a word stressed by Watson. Watson's statement must rather refer to a case arising from papers discovered after the murder of the Tiger of San Pedro, an event that took place at the Hotel Escurial in Madrid "some six months" after Holmes concluded his part in "The Adventure of Wisteria Lodge."

The month cannot be March, 1891, for in that month, as we shall see, Holmes and Watson shared no case. It cannot be March, 1892, or March, 1893, years of the Great Hiatus. Nor can it be March, 1894—Holmes did not return to England until April of that year. March, 1895, is also ruled out: Holmes, as we shall see, spent "some weeks"—from mid-March till after the first week in April—in a University town, studying English charters ("The Adventure of the Three Students"). The month must therefore have been *March, 1890,* and the Monday *the 24th.*

Only then, when the wheels were almost moving did I suddenly realize that my liberty lay in my own hands. I sprang out, they tried to drag me back, and had it not been for the help of this good man, who led me to the cab, I should never have broken away. Now, thank God, I am beyond their power for ever."

We had all listened intently to this remarkable statement. It was Holmes who broke the silence.

" Our difficulties are not over," he remarked, shaking his head. " Our police work ends, but our legal work
23 begins."

" Exactly," said I. " A plausible lawyer could make it out as an act of self-defence. There may be a hundred crimes in the background, but it is only on this one that they can be tried."

" Come, come," said Baynes, cheerily ; " I think better of the law than that. Self-defence is one thing. To entice a man in cold blood with the object of murdering him is another, whatever danger you may fear from him. No, no ; we shall all be justified when we see the tenants
24 of High Gable at the next Guildford Assizes."

It is a matter of history, however, that a little time was still to elapse before the Tiger of San Pedro should meet with his deserts. Wily and bold, he and his companion threw their pursuer off their track by entering a lodging-house in Edmonton Street and leaving by the back-gate into Curzon Square. From that day they were seen no more in England. Some six months afterwards the Marquess of Montalva and Signor Rulli, his secretary, were both murdered in their rooms at the Hotel Escurial at Madrid. The crime was ascribed to Nihilism, and the murderers were never arrested. Inspector Baynes visited us at Baker Street with a printed description of the dark face of the secretary, and of the masterful features, the magnetic black eyes, and the tufted brows of his master. We could not doubt that justice, if belated, had come at last.

" A chaotic case, my dear Watson," said Holmes, over an evening pipe. " It will not be possible for you to present it in that compact form which is dear to your heart. It covers two continents, concerns two groups of mysterious persons, and is further complicated by the highly respectable presence of our friend Scott Eccles, whose inclusion shows me that the deceased Garcia had a scheming mind and a well-developed instinct of self-preservation. It is remarkable only for the fact that amid a perfect jungle of possibilities we, with our worthy collaborator the inspector, have kept our close hold on the essentials and so been guided along the crooked and winding path. Is there any point which is not quite clear to you ? "

" The object of the mulatto cook's return ? "

" I think that the strange creature in the kitchen may account for it. The man was a primitive savage from the backwoods of San Pedro, and this was his fetish. When his companion and he had fled to some prearranged retreat —already occupied, no doubt, by a confederate—the companion had persuaded him to leave so compromising an article of furniture. But the mulatto's heart was with it,

23 *our legal work begins.*" Perhaps another indication that Holmes was, in fact, a lawyer as well as a private investigator.

24 *Guildford.* A town in Surrey identified with the Astolat of Arthurian legend; the grave of Lewis Carroll is in Guildford.

"A CHAOTIC CASE, MY DEAR WATSON," SAID HOLMES, OVER AN EVENING PIPE.

Cover illustration by Frederic Dorr Steele for *Collier's Magazine*, August 15, 1908.

and he was driven back to it next day, when, on reconnoitring through the window, he found policeman Walters in possession. He waited three days longer, and then his piety or his superstition drove him to try once more. Inspector Baynes, who, with his usual astuteness, had minimized the incident before me, had really recognized its importance, and had left a trap into which the creature walked. Any other point, Watson ? "

" The torn bird, the pail of blood, the charred bones, all the mystery of that weird kitchen ? "

Holmes smiled as he turned up an entry in his notebook.

" I spent a morning in the British Museum reading up that and other points. Here is a quotation from Eckermann's *Voodooism and the Negroid Religions* : **25**

> " The true Voodoo-worshipper attempts nothing of importance without certain sacrifices which are intended to propitiate his unclean gods. In extreme cases these rites take the form of human sacrifices followed by cannibalism. The more usual victims are a white cock, which is plucked in pieces alive, or a black goat, whose throat is cut and body burned.

" So you see our savage friend was very orthodox in his ritual. It is grotesque, Watson," Holmes added, as he slowly fastened his notebook ; " but, as I have had occasion to remark, there is but one step from the grotesque to the horrible." **26**

". . . SACRIFICES WHICH ARE INTENDED TO PROPITIATE HIS UNCLEAN GODS."

Illustration by Arthur Twidle for the *Strand* magazine, October, 1908.

25 *Eckermann's* Voodooism and the Negroid Religions. "This is a most intriguing title about which one would like to know more," Mr. Bliss Austin wrote in *A Baker Street Christmas Stocking* for 1955. "But, in spite of some considerable effort, I have never been able to find it, or even a reference to it, in any library in this country. . . . As a last resort, I decided to try the place where Holmes had seen it, or at least implied he had seen it. So last summer, during a visit to London, I followed his example by spending a morning in the British Museum. The results were completely negative. Eckermann on Voodooism is unknown there. Which leaves me with this question: Does anyone have any clew to the existence of this work, or are we to conclude that Holmes was once again pulling Watson's leg?"

26 *but one step from the grotesque to the horrible.*" Holmes paraphrases Napoleon's saying: "There is but one step from the sublime to the ridiculous."

Bibliographical Note: "The Adventure of Wisteria Lodge" appeared as a title for this story only when book and omnibus editions were published: in *Collier's Magazine* for August 15, 1908, the whole story was entitled "The Singular Experience of Mr. J. Scott Eccles," and in England the *Strand* for September, 1908, called the first instalment "The Singular Experience of Mr. John Scott Eccles" and the second instalment, in October, "The Tiger of San Pedro."

SHERLOCK HOLMES OF BAKER STREET

A painting in oils by Roy Hunt of the Council of Four, Denver, a Scion Society of the Baker Street Irregulars.

45

SILVER BLAZE

[Thursday, September 25, and Tuesday, September 30, 1890]

"I AM afraid, Watson, that I shall have to go," said Holmes, as we sat down together to our breakfast one morning.

"Go! Where to?"

"To Dartmoor—to King's Pyland." 1

I was not surprised. Indeed, my only wonder was that he had not already been mixed up in this extraordinary case, which was the one topic of conversation through the length and breadth of England. For a whole day my companion had rambled about the room with his chin upon his chest and his brows knitted, charging and re-charging his pipe with the strongest black tobacco, and absolutely deaf to any of my questions or remarks. Fresh editions of every paper had been sent up by our newsagent only to be glanced over and tossed down into a corner. Yet, silent as he was, I knew perfectly well what it was over which he was brooding. There was but one problem before the public which could challenge his powers of analysis, and that was the singular
disappearance of the favourite for the Wessex Cup, and 2
the tragic murder of its trainer. When, therefore, he suddenly announced his intention of setting out for the scene of the drama, it was only what I had both expected and hoped for.

"I should be most happy to go down with you if I should not be in the way," said I.

"My dear Watson, you would confer a great favour upon me by coming. And I think that your time will not be mis-spent, for there are points about this case which promise to make it an absolutely unique one. We have, I think, just time to catch our train at Paddington, and I will go further into the matter upon our journey. You would oblige me by bringing with you your very excellent field-glass."

And so it happened that an hour or so later I found
myself in the corner of a first-class carriage, flying along, 3
en route for Exeter, while Sherlock Holmes, with his

1 *to King's Pyland.*" Mr. Michael Harrison, in *In the Footsteps of Sherlock Holmes,* has identified "King's Pyland" with Princetown, Devonshire.

2 *the Wessex Cup.* Watson later speaks of the same race as the Wessex *Plate.* He was not necessarily incorrect here, however: some dictionaries define *plate* as "a gold or silver cup or the like awarded as a prize in horse racing."

3 *flying along,* en route *for Exeter.* It would appear that Holmes and Watson did not travel on either of the crack trains from Paddington to Exeter, the Flying Dutchman or the Zulu, "since the Zulu left Paddington at 3:00 P.M., and the Dutchman departed at 11:45 A.M., half an hour after they were on their way," Mr. D. Marcus Hook wrote in "More on the Railway Journeys." "Yet it is difficult to believe that Holmes would have chosen to board a slower train at 11:15, even if there was one. . . . It seems reasonable to suppose, then, that they travelled on the Flying Dutchman . . . probably behind one of the 'Iron Duke' class of locomotives with eight-foot driving wheels. Perhaps it was the *Prometheus?* The only other alternative is that of the 'special.' But Holmes says across the breakfast table 'We have, I think, just time to catch our train at Paddington.' In that case they would hardly have left in a 'special' half an hour before the scheduled departure."

4 *fifty-three and a half miles an hour.*" Some have doubted that the train could be traveling at such a speed, but Mr. Hook has pointed out that the speed "was not only possible, but necessary. Both the Flying Dutchman and the Zulu were allowed 87 minutes for the run from Paddington to Swindown. . . . This gives a start-to-stop average speed of 53¼ m.p.h., and it is obvious that top running speed, to maintain this average, would have to be made well above the 53½ m.p.h. mark."

Mr. A. D. Galbraith, in "The Real Moriarty" has found this statement "completely inconsistent with Holmes' character. Again and again Holmes has been depicted as a man of precise mind, as a cold, pure reasoner. Then he must have meant that his calculation of the speed was in error by not more than a quarter of a mile an hour; that is, fifty-three and a half miles an hour was the nearest half mile an hour to the correct speed. But he timed the train with an ordinary watch, and over a fairly short interval—Watson's phrase is 'glancing at his watch,' and the speed could not be expected to be uniform for more than two minutes. He had to determine, from the second-hand of his watch, the time from the instant of passage of one telegraph post to that of another, probably a mile or more from it, and to count the posts between. Anyone who has tried this knows that an error of one second in the time is almost incredibly small; two seconds is good. An error of one second in a time interval of two minutes means an error of almost half a mile an hour, at this speed. Then the man of precise mind, even if confident of almost superhuman accuracy in his measurement of the time, would say 'between fifty-three and fifty-four miles an hour,' and a more reasonbale statement would be 'between fifty-two- and fifty-five.' Is Holmes trying to impress Watson, or is Watson trying to impress his readers?"

HOLMES . . . GAVE ME A SKETCH OF THE EVENTS . . .

Illustration by Sidney Paget for the *Strand Magazine,* December, 1892.

sharp, eager face framed in his ear-flapped travelling-cap, dipped rapidly into the bundle of fresh papers which he had procured at Paddington. We had left Reading far behind us before he thrust the last of them under the seat, and offered me his cigar-case.

" We are going well," said he, looking out of the window, and glancing at his watch. " Our rate at present is
4 fifty-three and a half miles an hour."

" I have not observed the quarter-mile posts," said I.

" Nor have I. But the telegraph posts upon this line are sixty yards apart, and the calculation is a simple one. I presume that you have already looked into this matter of the murder of John Straker and the disappearance of Silver Blaze ? "

" I have seen what the *Telegraph* and the *Chronicle* have to say."

" It is one of those cases where the art of the reasoner should be used rather for the sifting of details than for the acquiring of fresh evidence. The tragedy has been so uncommon, so complete, and of such personal importance to so many people that we are suffering from a plethora of surmise, conjecture, and hypothesis. The difficulty is to detach the framework of fact—of absolute, undeniable fact—from the embellishments of theorists and reporters. Then, having established ourselves upon this sound basis, it is our duty to see what inferences may be drawn, and which are the special points upon which the whole mystery turns. On Tuesday evening I received telegrams, both from Colonel Ross, the owner of the horse, and from Inspector Gregory, who is looking after the case, inviting my co-operation."

" Tuesday evening ! " I exclaimed. " And this is
5 Thursday morning. Why did you not go down yesterday ? "

" Because I made a blunder, my dear Watson—which is, I am afraid, a more common occurrence than anyone
6 would think who only knew me through your memoirs. The fact is that I could not believe it possible that the most remarkable horse in England could long remain concealed, especially in so sparsely inhabited a place as the north of Dartmoor. From hour to hour yesterday I expected to hear that he had been found, and that his abductor was the murderer of John Straker. When, however, another morning had come and I found that, beyond the arrest of young Fitzroy Simpson, nothing had been done, I felt that it was time for me to take action. Yet in some ways I feel that yesterday has not been wasted."

" You have formed a theory then ? "

" At least I have a grip of the essential facts of the case. I shall enumerate them to you, for nothing clears up a case so much as stating it to another person, and I can hardly expect your co-operation if I do not show you the position from which we start."

I lay back against the cushions, puffing at my cigar, while Holmes, leaning forward, with his long thin forefinger checking off the points upon the palm of his left hand, gave me a sketch of the events which had led to our journey.

"... AND THE CALCULATION IS A SIMPLE ONE."

The late Professor Jay Finley Christ, in "Sherlock Pulls a Fast One," analyzed the problem and concluded that the calculation was *not* a simple one; Mr. Guy Warrack, in *Sherlock Holmes and Music*, also maintained that to arrive at this result Holmes would have been obliged to work out in his head an arithmetical sum of overwhelming complexity, and that it would have been impossible with a pocket watch to time the passage of the telegraph poles to the necessary tenth of a second. But Mr. S. C. Roberts, in "The Music of Baker Street," a review of Mr. Warrack's book, responded: "Mr. Warrack, if we may so express it, is making telegraph-poles out of fountain-pens. What happened, surely, was something like this: About half a minute before he addressed Watson, Holmes had looked at the second hand of his watch and then counted fifteen telegraph poles (he had, of course, *seen* the quarter-mile posts, but had not *observed* them, since they were not to be the basis of his calculation.) This would give him a distance of nine hundred yards, a fraction over half-a-mile. If a second glance at his watch had shown him that thirty seconds had passed, he would have known at once that the train was traveling at a good sixty miles an hour. Actually he noted that the train had taken approximately thirty-four seconds to cover the nine hundred yards; or, in other words, it was rather more than ten per cent (i.e., 6½ from sixty). The calculation, as he said, was a simple one; what made it simple was his knowledge, which of course Watson did not share, that the telegraph poles were sixty yards apart. Mr. Warrack's talk of 'sheer bluff' is manifestly irrelevant."

Mr. George W. Welch, in "The 'Silver Blaze' Formula," devised not one but two formulas said to be simple:

> First Method:—Allow two seconds for every yard, and add another second for every 22 yards of the known interval. Then the number of objects passed in this time is the speed in miles an hour. Proof:—Let x = the speed in miles per hour, y = the interval between adjacent objects. 1 m.p.h. = 1,760 yards in 3,600 seconds = 1 yard in $\frac{3,600}{1,760}$ (= $\frac{45}{22}$ or 2.1/22 secs. = y yards in 2.1/22 y seconds x m.p.h. = xy yards in 2.1/22y seconds. Example:—Telegraph poles are set 60 yards apart. 60 × 2 = 120; 60 ÷ 22 = 3 (approx.); 120 + 3 = 123. Then, if after 123 seconds the observer is half-way between the 53rd and 54th poles, the speed is 53½ miles an hour.
>
> Second Method:—When time or space will not permit the first method to be used, allow one second for every yard of the known interval, and multiply by 2.1/22 the number of objects passed in this time. The product is the speed in miles an hour. Example:—Telegraph poles are set 60 yards apart. After 60 seconds the observer is about 10 yards beyond the 26th pole. 26.1/6 × 2 = 52.1/3; 26.1/6 divided by 22 = 1.1/6 (approx.); 52.1/3 = 1.1/6 = 53½. Therefore the speed is 53½ miles an hour. The advantage of the first method is that the time to be used can be worked out in advance, leaving the observer nothing to do but count the objects against the second hand of his watch.

"Now," Dr. Julian Wolff wrote in "The Dynamics of the Binomial Theorem," "let us examine the problem in the light of pure reason. First of all, the speed in feet per second is easily found by determining the number of seconds taken to travel a known number of feet. Thus the speed when traveling 10 intervals between telegraph poles (1800 feet, since Holmes said that the posts were 60 yards apart) in T seconds is $\frac{1800}{T}$ feet per second. Multiplying this by 3600 gives the speed in feet per hour, and dividing the answer by 5280 gives the speed in miles per hour. Thus:

$$\text{miles per hour} = \frac{\frac{1800}{T} \times 3600}{5280} = \frac{1227.27}{T}$$

In other words, all that has to be done to determine the speed of the train in miles per hour is to divide 1227.27 (1227 is close enough for all ordinary purposes, such as puzzling Watson, for instance) by the number of seconds required to travel 1800 feet. And for those who do not care to perform even that calculation—and it is a simple one—a graph has been appended" (*see below.*)

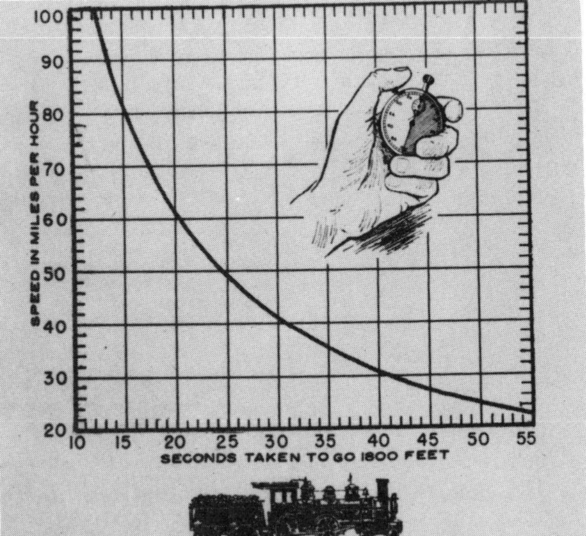

" Silver Blaze," said he, " is from the Isonomy stock, and holds as brilliant a record as his famous ancestor. He is now in his fifth year, and has brought in turn each of the prizes of the turf to Colonel Ross, his fortunate owner. Up to the time of the catastrophe he was first favourite for the Wessex Cup, the betting being three to one on. He has always, however, been a prime favourite with the racing public, and has never yet disappointed them, so that even at short odds enormous sums of money have been laid upon him. It is obvious, therefore, that there were many people who had the strongest interest in preventing Silver Blaze from being there at the fall of the flag next Tuesday.

" This fact was, of course, appreciated at King's Pyland, where the Colonel's training stable is situated. Every precaution was taken to guard the favourite. The trainer, John Straker, is a retired jockey, who rode in Colonel Ross's colours before he became too heavy for the weighing-chair. He has served the Colonel for five years as jockey, and for seven as trainer, and has always shown himself to be a zealous and honest servant. Under him were three lads, for the establishment was a small one, containing only four horses in all. One of these lads sat up each night in the stable, while the others slept in the loft. All three bore excellent characters. John Straker, who is a married man, lived in a small villa about two hundred yards from the stables. He has no children, keeps one maid-servant, and is comfortably off. The country round is very lonely, but about half a mile to the north there is a small cluster of villas which have
7 been built by a Tavistock contractor for the use of invalids and others who may wish to enjoy the pure Dartmoor air. Tavistock itself lies two miles to the west, while across the moor, also about two miles distant, is the larger
8 training establishment of Capleton, which belongs to Lord Backwater, and is managed by Silas Brown. In every

5 "*And this is Thursday morning.* Holmes tells us that he received telegrams inviting him to investigate the death of John Straker and the disappearance of Silver Blaze "on Tuesday evening." "From hour to hour yesterday [Wednesday] I expected to hear that he had been found. When, however, another morning [Thursday] had come . . ." This corroborates Watson's "And this is Thursday morning." The day, as we shall see, was a genial one: there is no mention of any rain and "the reds had all faded into greys" after the setting of the sun, indicating clear, bright weather.

6 *your memoirs.* The case must therefore be placed after the publication of *A Study in Scarlet* in December, 1887.

7 *Tavistock.* Largest of the moor towns in Devonshire.

8 *Capleton. Mapleton* in some American editions. Professor Christ thought they might have been the Falmouth House Stables of Mr. John Blundell Maple, Member of Parliament for Camberwell.

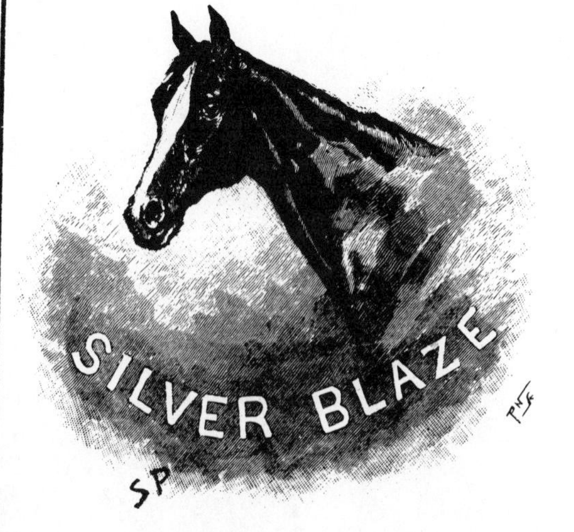

"SILVER BLAZE," SAID HE, IS FROM THE ISONOMY STOCK . . ."

Portrait of Silver Blaze by Sidney Paget for the *Strand Magazine*, December, 1892. "Isonomy" is misprinted "Somomy" in most American texts, which is unfortunate, because Isonomy was a real horse, and a remarkable one. He won the Cambridgeshire at Newmarket in 1878, the Manchester Plate and the Ascot Gold Cup in 1879, and the Ascot Gold Cup again in 1880. Isonomy first went to stud in 1881, and "Silver Blaze" was "in his fifth year": Silver Blaze could be said to be "in his fifth year" after his fourth birthday—but even if he were the first of Isonomy's many progeny, he could not have reached his fourth birthday until 1886; the case certainly took place *no* earlier than that year.

The late Professor Jay Finley Christ, in a notable speculation ("Silver Blaze: An Identification As of 1893 A.D."), has shown that "Down to the year 1892, when 'Silver Blaze' was published, there was one really outstanding horse of the Isonomy line. That horse was by some trick of fate called *Common*, but was far from acting

other direction the moor is a complete wilderness, inhabited only by a few roaming gipsies. Such was the general situation last Monday night, when the catastrophe occurred.

" On that evening the horses had been exercised and watered as usual, and the stables were locked up at nine o'clock. Two of the lads walked up to the trainer's house, where they had supper in the kitchen, while the third, Ned Hunter, remained on guard. At a few minutes after nine the maid, Edith Baxter, carried down to the stables his supper, which consisted of a dish of curried mutton.

". . . THE MAID . . . CARRIED DOWN TO THE STABLES HIS SUPPER . . ."

Illustration by William H. Hyde for *Harper's Weekly*, February 25, 1893.

the part, as he turned out to be one of the truly great sons of Isonomy. . . . Sired by Isonomy and out of Thistle, Common was foaled in 1888. In '91, as a three-year-old, he was practically the horse of the year. Coming to the Two Thousand Guinea Stake as an 'outsider,' with no two-year-old performance to herald his greatness, Common won the Two Thousand 'very easily indeed' in April. In the Derby 'he again won easily'; and the St. James Place Stakes at Ascot he won 'in a canter.' . . . He completed the year (and his racing career) with the winning of the St. Leger at Doncaster in September of 1891, where the odds on him were 5 to 4. . . ."

Horses called Silvio and St. Blaise were both Derby winners, as the late Gavin Brend pointed out in "From the Horse's Mouth," Silvio in 1877, St. Blaise in 1883, but neither of these horses were of the Isonomy stock. "If we confine our attention to Isonomy's progeny the most hopeful claimant from the standpoint of phonetics would seem to be Seabreeze who won the Oaks and St. Leger in 1888 but who, I regret to say, was not a colt but a filly."

She took no liquid, as there was a water-tap in the stables, and it was the rule that the lad on duty should drink nothing else. The maid carried a lantern with her, as
9 it was very dark, and the path ran across the open moor.

" Edith Baxter was within thirty yards of the stables when a man appeared out of the darkness and called to her to stop. As he stepped into the circle of yellow light thrown by the lantern she saw that he was a person of gentlemanly bearing, dressed in a grey suit of tweed with a cloth cap. He wore gaiters, and carried a heavy stick with a knob to it. She was most impressed, however, by the extreme pallor of his face and by the nervousness of his manner. His age, she thought, would be rather over thirty than under it.

" ' Can you tell me where I am ? ' he asked. ' I had almost made up my mind to sleep on the moor when I saw the light of your lantern.'

" ' You are close to the King's Pyland training stables,' she said.

" ' Oh, indeed ! What a stroke of luck ! ' he cried. ' I understand that a stable boy sleeps there alone every night. Perhaps that is his supper which you are carrying to him. Now I am sure that you would not be too proud to earn the price of a new dress, would you ? ' He took a piece of white paper folded up out of his waistcoat pocket. ' See that the boy has this to-night, and you shall have the prettiest frock that money can buy.'

" She was frightened by the earnestness of his manner, and ran past him to the window through which she was accustomed to hand the meals. It was already open, and Hunter was seated at the small table inside. She had begun to tell him of what had happened, when the stranger came up again.

" ' Good evening,' said he, looking through the window, ' I wanted to have a word with you.' The girl has sworn that as he spoke she noticed the corner of the little paper packet protruding from his closed hand.

" ' What business have you here ? ' asked the lad.

" ' It's business that may put something into your pocket,' said the other. ' You've two horses in for the Wessex Cup—Silver Blaze and Bayard. Let me have the straight tip, and you won't be a loser. Is it a fact that at the weights Bayard could give the other a hundred yards in five furlongs, and that the stable have put their money on him ? '

" ' So you're one of those damned touts,' cried the lad. ' I'll show you how we serve them in King's Pyland.' He sprang up and rushed across the stable to unloose the dog. The girl fled away to the house, but as she ran she looked back, and saw that the stranger was leaning through the window. A minute later, however, when Hunter rushed out with the hound he was gone, and though the lad ran all round the buildings he failed to find any trace of him."

" One moment ! " I asked. " Did the stable boy, when he ran out with the dog, leave the door unlocked behind him ? "

" Excellent, Watson ; excellent ! " murmured my companion. " The importance of the point struck me so forcibly, that I sent a special wire to Dartmoor yesterday

"... A MAN APPEARED OUT OF THE DARKNESS ..."

Illustration by Sidney Paget for the *Strand Magazine*, December, 1892.

9 *as it was very dark.* Most chronologists have followed Mr. Bell's inference from this that the season was early autumn. An exception was the late Dr. Ernest Bloomfield Zeisler, who held that the darkness must have been due to clouds, presaging the storm during the night, since "it was obviously not dark at well past nine" on the day Holmes and Watson visited Tavistock ("Some Observations Upon 'Silver Blaze' ").

to clear the matter up. The boy locked the door before he left it. The window, I may add, was not large enough for a man to get through.

" Hunter waited until his fellow-grooms had returned, when he sent a message up to the trainer and told him what had occurred. Straker was excited at hearing the account, although he does not seem to have quite realized its true significance. It left him, however, vaguely uneasy, and Mrs. Straker, waking at one in the morning, found that he was dressing. In reply to her inquiries, he said that he could not sleep on account of his anxiety about the horses, and that he intended to walk down to the stables to see that all was well. She begged him to remain at home, as she could hear the rain pattering against the windows, but in spite of her entreaties he pulled on his large mackintosh and left the house.

" Mrs. Straker awoke at seven in the morning, to find that her husband had not yet returned. She dressed herself hastily, called the maid, and set off for the stables. The door was open ; inside, huddled together upon a chair, Hunter was sunk in a state of absolute stupor, the favourite's stall was empty, and there were no signs of his trainer.

" The two lads who slept in the chaff-cutting loft above the harness-room were quickly roused. They had heard nothing during the night, for they are both sound sleepers. Hunter was obviously under the influence of some powerful drug ; and, as no sense could be got out of him, he was left to sleep it off while the two lads and the two women ran out in search of the absentees. They still had hopes that the trainer had for some reason taken out the horse for early exercise, but on ascending the knoll near the house, from which all the neighbouring moors were visible, they not only could see no signs of the favourite, but they perceived something which warned them that they were in the presence of a tragedy.

" About a quarter of a mile from the stables, John Straker's overcoat was flapping from a furze bush. Immediately beyond there was a bowl-shaped depression in the moor, and at the bottom of this was found the dead body of the unfortunate trainer. His head had been shattered by a savage blow from some heavy weapon, and he was wounded in the thigh, where there was a long, clean cut, inflicted evidently by some very sharp instrument. It was clear, however, that Straker had defended himself vigorously against his assailants, for in his right hand he held a small knife, which was clotted with blood up to the handle, while in his left he grasped a red and black silk cravat, which was recognized by the maid as having been worn on the preceding evening by the stranger who had visited the stables.

" Hunter, on recovering from his stupor, was also quite positive as to the ownership of the cravat. He was equally certain that the same stranger had, while standing at the window, drugged his curried mutton, and so deprived the stables of their watchman.

" As to the missing horse, there were abundant proofs in the mud which lay at the bottom of the fatal hollow, that he had been there at the time of the struggle. But

"HIS HEAD HAD BEEN SHATTERED BY A SAVAGE BLOW FROM SOME HEAVY WEAPON . . ."

Illustration by Sidney Paget for the *Strand Magazine*, December, 1892. William H. Hyde illustrated the same scene for *Harper's Weekly*, February 25, 1893.

from that morning he has disappeared ; and although a large reward has been offered, and all the gipsies of Dartmoor are on the alert, no news has come of him. Finally an analysis has shown that the remains of his supper, left by the stable lad, contain an appreciable quantity of powdered opium, while the people of the house partook of the same dish on the same night without any ill effect.

" Those are the main facts of the case stripped of all surmise and stated as baldly as possible. I shall now recapitulate what the police have done in the matter.

" Inspector Gregory, to whom the case has been committed, is an extremely competent officer. Were he but gifted with imagination he might rise to great heights in his profession. On his arrival he promptly found and arrested the man upon whom suspicion naturally rested. There was little difficulty in finding him, for he was thoroughly well known in the neighbourhood. His name, it appears, was Fitzroy Simpson. He was a man of excellent birth and education, who had squandered a fortune upon the turf, and who lived now by doing a little quiet and genteel bookmaking in the sporting clubs of London. An examination of his betting-book shows that bets to the amount of five thousand pounds had been registered by him against the favourite.

" On being arrested he volunteered the statement that he had come down to Dartmoor in the hope of getting some information about the King's Pyland horses, and also about Desborough, the second favourite, which was in charge of Silas Brown, at the Capleton stables. He did not attempt to deny that he had acted as described upon the evening before, but declared that he had no sinister designs, and had simply wished to obtain first-hand information. When confronted with the cravat he turned very pale, and was utterly unable to account for its presence in the hand of the murdered man. His wet clothing showed that he had been out in the storm of the night before, and his stick, which was a Penang lawyer, weighted with lead, was just such a weapon as might, by repeated blows, have inflicted the terrible injuries to which the trainer had succumbed.

" On the other hand, there was no wound upon his person, while the state of Straker's knife would show that one, at least, of his assailants must bear his mark upon him. There you have it all in a nutshell, Watson, and if you can give me any light I shall be infinitely obliged to you."

I had listened with the greatest interest to the statement which Holmes, with characteristic clearness, had laid before me. Though most of the facts were familiar to me, I had not sufficiently appreciated their relative importance, nor their connection with each other.

" Is it not possible," I suggested, " that the incised wound upon Straker may have been caused by his own knife in the convulsive struggles which follow any brain injury ? "

" It is more than possible ; it is probable," said Holmes. " In that case, one of the main points in favour of the accused disappears."

" And yet," said I, " even now I fail to understand what the theory of the police can be."

" I am afraid that whatever theory we state has very grave objections to it," returned my companion. " The police imagine, I take it, that this Fitzroy Simpson, having drugged the lad, and having in some way obtained a duplicate key, opened the stable door, and took out the horse, with the intention, apparently, of kidnapping him altogether. His bridle is missing, so that Simpson must have put it on. Then, having left the door open behind him, he was leading the horse away over the moor, when he was either met or overtaken by the trainer. A row naturally ensued, Simpson beat out the trainer's brains with his heavy stick without receiving any injury from the small knife which Straker used in self-defence, and then the thief either led the horse on to some secret hiding-place, or else it may have bolted during the struggle, and be now wandering out on the moors. That is the case as it appears to the police, and improbable as it is, all other explanations are more improbable still. However, I shall very quickly test the matter when I am once upon the spot, and until then I really cannot see how we can get much further than our present position."

It was evening before we reached the little town of Tavistock, which lies, like the boss of a shield, in the middle of the huge circle of Dartmoor. Two gentlemen were awaiting us at the station ; the one a tall fair man with lion-like hair and beard, and curiously penetrating light blue eyes, the other a small alert person, very neat and dapper, in a frock-coat and gaiters, with trim little side-whiskers and an eye-glass. The latter was Colonel Ross, the well-known sportsman, the other Inspector Gregory, a man who was rapidly making his name in the English detective service.

" I am delighted that you have come down, Mr. Holmes," said the Colonel. " The Inspector here has done all that could possibly be suggested ; but I wish to leave no stone unturned in trying to avenge poor Straker, and in recovering my horse."

" Have there been any fresh developments ? " asked Holmes.

" I am sorry to say that we have made very little progress," said the Inspector. " We have an open carriage outside, and as you would no doubt like to see the
place before the light fails, we might talk it over as we **10**
drive."

A minute later we were all seated in a comfortable landau and were rattling through the quaint old Devonshire town. Inspector Gregory was full of his case, and poured out a stream of remarks, while Holmes threw in an occasional question or interjection. Colonel Ross leaned back with his arms folded and his hat tilted over his eyes, while I listened with interest to the dialogue of the two detectives. Gregory was formulating his theory, which was almost exactly what Holmes had foretold in the train.

" The net is drawn pretty close round Fitzroy Simpson," he remarked, " and I believe myself that he is our man. At the same time, I recognize that the evidence is purely circumstantial, and that some new development may upset it."

" How about Straker's knife ? "

"I AM DELIGHTED THAT YOU HAVE COME DOWN, MR. HOLMES," SAID THE COLONEL.

Illustration by Sidney Paget for the *Strand Magazine*, December, 1892.

10 *before the light fails.* It is not possible to reckon the time of sunset too accurately from the data given, but it is noteworthy that Holmes and Watson "completed a long agenda before dark," in the late Gavin Brend's phrase, although they arrived at Tavistock at "evening." We are no doubt safe in saying that sunset could not have been much before 5:30 P.M. This would indicate that the time of the year was late September.

11 *He has lodged twice at Tavistock in the summer.* Simpson may not have lodged there twice in the *same* summer, but since he was "well known" in Tavistock, the implication is strong that he had lodged there at least once in a summer just past; another indication that the season of the year is autumn.

" We have quite come to the conclusion that he wounded himself in his fall."

" My friend Dr. Watson made that suggestion to me as we came down. If so, it would tell against this man Simpson."

" Undoubtedly. He has neither a knife nor any sign of a wound. The evidence against him is certainly very strong. He had a great interest in the disappearance of the favourite, he lies under the suspicion of having poisoned the stable boy, he was undoubtedly out in the storm, he was armed with a heavy stick, and his cravat was found in the dead man's hand. I really think we have enough to go before a jury."

Holmes shook his head. " A clever counsel would tear it all to rags," said he. " Why should he take the horse out of the stable ? If he wished to injure it, why could he not do it there ? Has a duplicate key been found in his possession ? What chemist sold him the powdered opium ? Above all, where could he, a stranger to the district, hide a horse, and such a horse as this ? What is his own explanation as to the paper which he wished the maid to give to the stable boy ? "

" He says that it was a ten-pound note. One was found in his purse. But your other difficulties are not so formidable as they seem. He is not a stranger to the dis-
11 trict. He has twice lodged at Tavistock in the summer. The opium was probably brought from London. The key, having served its purpose, would be hurled away. The horse may lie at the bottom of one of the pits or old mines upon the moor."

" What does he say about the cravat ? "

" He acknowledges that it is his, and declares that he had lost it. But a new element has been introduced into the case which may account for his leading the horse from the stable."

Holmes pricked up his ears.

" We have found traces which show that a party of gipsies encamped on Monday night within a mile of the spot where the murder took place. On Tuesday they were gone. Now, presuming that there was some understanding between Simpson and these gipsies, might he not have been leading the horse to them when he was overtaken, and may they not have him now ? "

" It is certainly possible."

" The moor is being scoured for these gipsies. I have also examined every stable and outhouse in Tavistock, and for a radius of ten miles."

" There is another training stable quite close, I understand ? "

" Yes, and that is a factor which we must certainly not neglect. As Desborough, their horse, was second in the betting, they had an interest in the disappearance of the favourite. Silas Brown, the trainer, is known to have had large bets upon the event, and he was no friend to poor Straker. We have, however, examined the stables, and there is nothing to connect him with the affair."

" And nothing to connect this man Simpson with the interests of the Capleton stable ? "

" Nothing at all."

Holmes leaned back in the carriage and the conversation ceased. A few minutes later our driver pulled up at a neat little red-brick villa with overhanging eaves, which stood by the road. Some distance off, across a paddock, lay a long grey-tiled outbuilding. In every other direction the low curves of the moor, bronze-coloured from the
fading ferns, stretched away to the skyline, broken only **12**
by the steeples of Tavistock, and by a cluster of houses away to the westward, which marked the Capleton stables. We all sprang out with the exception of Holmes, who continued to lean back with his eyes fixed upon the sky in front of him, entirely absorbed in his own thoughts. It was only when I touched his arm that he roused himself with a violent start and stepped out of the carriage.

" Excuse me," said he, turning to Colonel Ross, who had looked at him in some surprise. " I was day-dreaming." There was a gleam in his eyes and a suppressed excitement in his manner which convinced me, used as I was to his ways, that his hand was upon a clue, though I could not imagine where he had found it.

" Perhaps you would prefer at once to go on to the scene of the crime, Mr. Holmes ? " said Gregory.

" I think that I should prefer to stay here a little and go into one or two questions of detail. Straker was brought back here, I presume ? "

" Yes, he lies upstairs. The inquest **is** to-morrow."

" He has been in your service some years, Colonel Ross ? "

" I have always found him an excellent servant."

" I presume that you made an inventory of what he had in his pockets at the time of his death, Inspector ? "

" I have the things themselves in the sitting-room, if you would care to see them."

" I should be very glad."

We all filed into the front room, and sat round the central table, while the Inspector unlocked a square tin box and laid a small heap of things before us. There was
a box of vestas, two inches of tallow candle, an A.D.P. **13**
briar-root pipe, a pouch of sealskin with half an ounce of **14**
long-cut cavendish, a silver watch with a gold chain, five **15**
sovereigns in gold, an aluminium pencil-case, a few papers, and an ivory-handled knife with a very delicate
inflexible blade marked Weiss & Co., London. **16**

" This is a very singular knife," said Holmes, lifting it up and examining it minutely. " I presume, as I see blood-stains upon it, that it is the one which was found in the dead man's grasp. Watson, this knife is surely in your line."

" It is what we call a cataract knife," said I.

" I thought so. A very delicate blade devised for very delicate work. A strange thing for a man to carry with him upon a rough expedition, especially as it would not shut in his pocket."

" The tip was guarded by a disc of cork which we found beside his body," said the Inspector. " His wife tells us that the knife had lain for some days upon the dressing-

12 *bronze-coloured from the fading ferns.* Watson speaks later of "the faded ferns and brambles" which caught the evening light. Ferns on Dartmoor do not fade until the latter part of September or the first part of October—still another indication, to most chronologists, that this is an autumnal case. However, the late Dr. Ernest Bloomfield Zeisler wrote ("Some Observations Upon 'Silver Blaze' "): "First the ferns were 'fading'; several hours later they were 'faded.' This would be impossible unless these terms were descriptions of the *appearance* of the ferns in the evening light. Even green ferns would appear bronze-coloured and fading late in the day when the sun was low; and even green ferns would, several hours later, shortly before sunset, appear faded."

13 *vestas.* A vesta is a friction match, so named from the Roman goddess of the hearth and fire.

14 *an A.D.P. briar-root pipe.* "What is an A.D.P. pipe?" we asked Lord Donegall, editor of the *Sherlock Holmes Journal.* And Lord Donegall kindly replied (October 5, 1964): ". . . I went to Dunhill's and asked the oldest inhabitant, who has served me for 40 years . . . if he knew what an 'A.D.P.' pipe was. 'Indeed, yes, M'Lord,' said the Sage of Jermyn Street. 'In the old days A.D.P. stood for Alfred Dunhill Pipe!' . . . However, I have made further researches. During the courses of these, I discovered that there is a small factory outside Ancona, Italy, which specialises in roots for pipes from the *small* briar; as opposed to the Algerian *large* briar. Furthermore, that in the old days, . . . the late lamented Mr. Alfred D. bought his entire supply of briar roots from the Ancona factory. So, I now discount the too-easy glib answer of the Sage in favour of my own theory: I contend that A.D.P. meant 'Ancona Della Piccola.' The *sous-entendu* following 'Piccola' would, of course, be 'Pipa di Radice di Scopa.' "

15 *cavendish.* A kind of smoking tobacco softened and pressed into solid cakes; so called from the name of the maker.

16 *Weiss & Co., London.* "There is a London firm by this name which specializes in instruments used in eye surgery," the late Dr. Roland Hammond wrote in "The Attempted Mayhem of 'Silver Blaze.' "

table, and that he had picked it up as he left the room. It was a poor weapon, but perhaps the best that he could lay his hand on at the moment."

"Very possible. How about these papers ?"

"Three of them are receipted hay-dealers' accounts. One of them is a letter of instructions from Colonel Ross. This other is a milliner's account for thirty-seven pounds fifteen, made out by Madame Lesurier, of Bond Street, to William Darbyshire. Mrs. Straker tells us that Darbyshire was a friend of her husband's, and that occasionally his letters were addressed here."

"Madame Darbyshire had somewhat expensive tastes," remarked Holmes, glancing down the account. "Twenty-
17 two guineas is rather heavy for a single costume. However, there appears to be nothing more to learn, and we may now go down to the scene of the crime."

As we emerged from the sitting-room a woman who had been waiting in the passage took a step forward and laid her hand upon the Inspector's sleeve. Her face was haggard, and thin, and eager ; stamped with the print of a recent horror.

"Have you got them ? Have you found them ?" she panted.

"No, Mrs. Straker ; but Mr. Holmes, here, has come from London to help us, and we shall do all that is possible."

"Surely I met you in Plymouth, at a garden-party, some little time ago, Mrs. Straker," said Holmes.

"No, sir ; you are mistaken."

"Dear me ; why, I could have sworn to it. You wore a costume of dove-coloured silk with ostrich feather trimming."

"I never had such a dress, sir," answered the lady.

"Ah ; that quite settles it," said Holmes ; and, with an apology, he followed the Inspector outside. A short walk across the moor took us to the hollow in which the body had been found. At the brink of it was the furze bush upon which the coat had been hung.

"There was no wind that night, I understand," said Holmes.

"None ; but very heavy rain."

"In that case the overcoat was not blown against the furze bushes, but placed there."

"Yes, it was laid across the bush."

"You fill me with interest. I perceive that the ground has been trampled up a good deal. No doubt many feet have been there since Monday night."

"A piece of matting has been laid here at the side, and we have all stood upon that."

"Excellent."

"In this bag I have one of the boots which Straker wore, one of Fitzroy Simpson's shoes, and a cast horseshoe of Silver Blaze."

"My dear Inspector, you surpass yourself !"

Holmes took the bag, and descending into the hollow he pushed the matting into a more central position. Then stretching himself upon his face and leaning his chin upon his hands he made a careful study of the trampled mud in front of him.

"Halloa !" said he, suddenly, "what's this ?"

17 "*Twenty-two guineas.* About $115.50 U.S. at the time.

"HAVE YOU GOT THEM? HAVE YOU FOUND THEM?" SHE PANTED.

Illustration by Sidney Paget for the *Strand Magazine*, December, 1892.

It was a wax vesta, half burned, which was so coated with mud that it looked at first like a little chip of wood.

" I cannot think how I came to overlook it," said the Inspector, with an expression of annoyance.

" It was invisible, buried in the mud. I only saw it because I was looking for it."

" What ! You expected to find it ? "

" I thought it not unlikely." He took the boots from the bag and compared the impressions of each of them with marks upon the ground. Then he clambered up to the rim of the hollow and crawled about among the ferns and bushes.

" I am afraid that there are no more tracks," said the Inspector. " I have examined the ground very carefully for a hundred yards in each direction."

" Indeed ! " said Holmes, rising, " I should not have the impertinence to do it again after what you say. But I should like to take a little walk over the moors before it grows dark, that I may know my ground to-morrow, and I think that I shall put this horseshoe into my pocket for luck."

Colonel Ross, who had shown some signs of impatience at my companion's quiet and systematic method of work, glanced at his watch.

" I wish you would come back with me, Inspector," said he. " There are several points on which I should like your advice, and especially as to whether we do not owe it to the public to remove our horse's name from the entries for the Cup."

" Certainly not," cried Holmes, with decision ; " I should let the name stand."

The Colonel bowed. " I am very glad to have had your opinion, sir," said he. " You will find us at poor Straker's house when you have finished your walk, and we can drive together into Tavistock."

He turned back with the Inspector, while Holmes and I walked slowly across the moor. The sun was beginning to sink behind the stables of Capleton, and the long sloping plain in front of us was tinged with gold, deepening into rich, ruddy brown where the faded ferns and brambles caught the evening light. But the glories of the landscape were all wasted upon my companion, who was sunk in the deepest thought.

" It's this way, Watson," he said, at last. " We may leave the question of who killed John Straker for the instant, and confine ourselves to finding out what has become of the horse. Now, supposing that he broke away during or after the tragedy, where could he have gone to ? The horse is a very gregarious creature. If left to himself, his instincts would have been either to return to King's Pyland or go over to Capleton. Why should he run wild upon the moor ? He would surely have been seen by now. And why should gipsies kidnap him ? These people always clear out when they hear of trouble, for they do not wish to be pestered by the police. They could not hope to sell such a horse. They would run a great risk and gain nothing by taking him. Surely that is clear."

" Where is he, then ? "

" I have already said that he must have gone to King's

Pyland or to Capleton. He is not at King's Pyland, therefore he is at Capleton. Let us take that as a working hypothesis, and see what it leads us to. This part of the moor, as the Inspector remarked, is very hard and dry. But it falls away towards Capleton, and you can see from here that there is a long hollow over yonder, which must have been very wet on Monday night. If our supposition is correct, then the horse must have crossed that, and there is the point where we should look for his tracks."

We had been walking briskly during this conversation, and a few more minutes brought us to the hollow in question. At Holmes' request I walked down the bank to the right, and he to the left, but I had not taken fifty paces before I heard him give a shout, and saw him waving his hand to me. The track of a horse was plainly outlined in the soft earth in front of him, and the shoe which he took from his pocket exactly fitted the impression.

" See the value of imagination," said Holmes. " It is the one quality which Gregory lacks. We imagined what might have happened, acted upon the supposition, and find ourselves justified. Let us proceed."

We crossed the marshy bottom and passed over a quarter of a mile of dry, hard turf. Again the ground sloped and again we came on the tracks. Then we lost them for half a mile, but only to pick them up once more quite close to Capleton. It was Holmes who saw them first, and he stood pointing with a look of triumph upon his face. A man's track was visible beside the horse's.

" The horse was alone before," I cried.

" Quite so. It was alone before. Halloa ! what is this ?"

The double track turned sharp off and took the direction of King's Pyland. Holmes whistled, and we both followed along after it. His eyes were on the trail, but I happened to look a little to one side, and saw to my surprise the same tracks coming back again in the opposite direction.

" One for you, Watson," said Holmes, when I pointed it out ; " you have saved us a long walk which would have brought us back on our own traces. Let us follow the return track."

We had not to go far. It ended at the paving of asphalt which led up to the gates of the Capleton stables. As we approached a groom ran out from them.

" We don't want any loiterers about here," said he.

" I only wished to ask a question," said Holmes, with his finger and thumb in his waistcoat pocket. " Should I be too early to see your master, Mr. Silas Brown, if I were to call at five o'clock to-morrow morning ? "

" Bless you, sir, if anyone is about he will be, for he is always the first stirring. But here he is, sir, to answer your questions for himself. No, sir, no ; it's as much as my place is worth to let him see me touch your money. Afterwards, if you like."

As Sherlock Holmes replaced the half-crown which he had drawn from his pocket, a fierce-looking elderly man strode out from the gate with a hunting-crop swinging in his hand.

" What's this, Dawson ? " he cried. " No gossiping ! Go about your business ! And you—what the devil do you want here ? "

"Ten minutes' talk with you, my good sir," said Holmes, in the sweetest of voices.

"I've no time to talk to every gadabout. We want no strangers here. Be off, or you may find a dog at your heels."

Holmes leaned forward and whispered something in the trainer's ear. He started violently and flushed to the temples.

"It's a lie!" he shouted. "An infernal lie!"

"Very good! Shall we argue about it here in public, or talk it over in your parlour?"

"Oh, come in if you wish to."

Holmes smiled. "I shall not keep you more than a few minutes, Watson," he said. "Now, Mr. Brown, I am quite at your disposal."

It was quite twenty minutes, and the reds had all faded into greys before Holmes and the trainer reappeared. Never have I seen such a change as had been brought about in Silas Brown in that short time. His face was ashy pale, beads of perspiration shone upon his brow, and his hands shook until the hunting-crop wagged like a branch in the wind. His bullying, overbearing manner was all gone too, and he cringed along at my companion's side like a dog with its master.

"Your instructions will be done. It shall be done," said he.

"There must be no mistake," said Holmes, looking round at him. The other winced as he read the menace in his eyes.

"Oh, no, there shall be no mistake. It shall be there. Should I change it first or not?"

Holmes thought a little and then burst out laughing. "No, don't," said he. "I shall write to you about it. No tricks now or——"

"Oh, you can trust me, you can trust me!"

"You must see to it on the day as if it were your own."

"You can rely upon me."

"Yes, I think I can. Well, you shall hear from me to-morrow." He turned upon his heel, disregarding the trembling hand which the other held out to him, and we set off for King's Pyland.

"A more perfect compound of the bully, coward and sneak than Master Silas Brown I have seldom met with," remarked Holmes, as we trudged along together.

"He has the horse, then?"

"He tried to bluster out of it, but I described to him so exactly what his actions had been upon that morning, that he is convinced that I was watching him. Of course, you observed the peculiarly square toes in the impressions, and that his own boots exactly corresponded to them. Again, of course, no subordinate would have dared to have done such a thing. I described to him how when, according to his custom, he was the first down, he perceived
a strange horse wandering over the moor; how he went **18**
out to it, and his astonishment at recognizing from the white forehead which has given the favourite its name that chance had put in his power the only horse which could beat the one upon which he had put his money. Then I described how his first impulse had been to lead him

"BE OFF, OR YOU SHALL FIND A DOG AT YOUR HEELS."

Illustration by Sidney Paget for the *Strand Magazine*, December, 1892.

18 *he perceived a strange horse wandering over the moor.* Holmes asked if he would find Silas Brown up and about if he called at Capleton at five o'clock in the morning, and was told by the stable boy that Brown was always "the first stirring." On the Tuesday morning, Brown had risen as early as usual, presumably, and had been able to perceive a strange horse on the moor. We can be sure that day must have broken between three and four in the morning on that occasion. All clues to the season, then, point to a journey to Devonshire in the last week of September and a race that must have been run *circa* October 1st, certainly within the first ten days of October.

back to King's Pyland, and how the devil had shown him how he could hide the horse until the race was over, and how he had led it back and concealed it at Capleton. When I told him every detail he gave it up, and thought only of saving his own skin."

" But his stables had been searched."

" Oh, an old horse-faker like him has many a dodge."

" But are you not afraid to leave the horse in his power now, since he has every interest in injuring it ? "

" My dear fellow, he will guard it as the apple of his eye. He knows that his only hope of mercy is to produce it safe."

" Colonel Ross did not impress me as a man who would be likely to show much mercy in any case."

" The matter does not rest with Colonel Ross. I follow my own methods, and tell as much or as little as I choose. That is the advantage of being unofficial. I don't know whether you observed it, Watson, but the Colonel's manner has been just a trifle cavalier to me. I am inclined now to have a little amusement at his expense. Say nothing to him about the horse."

" Certainly not, without your permission."

" And, of course, this is all quite a minor case compared with the question of who killed John Straker."

" And you will devote yourself to that ? "

" On the contrary, we both go back to London by the night train."

I was thunderstruck by my friend's words. We had only been a few hours in Devonshire, and that he should give up an investigation which he had begun so brilliantly was quite incomprehensible to me. Not a word more could I draw from him until we were back at the trainer's house. The Colonel and the Inspector were awaiting us in the parlour.

" My friend and I return to town by the midnight express," said Holmes. " We have had a charming little breath of your beautiful Dartmoor air."

The Inspector opened his eyes, and the Colonel's lips curled in a sneer.

" So you despair of arresting the murderer of poor Straker," said he.

Holmes shrugged his shoulders. " There are certainly grave difficulties in the way," said he. " I have every hope, however, that your horse will start upon Tuesday, and I beg that you will have your jockey in readiness. Might I ask for a photograph of Mr. John Straker ? "

The Inspector took one from an envelope in his pocket and handed it to him.

" My dear Gregory, you anticipate all my wants. If I might ask you to wait here for an instant, I have a question which I should like to put to the maid."

" I must say that I am rather disappointed in our London consultant," said Colonel Ross, bluntly, as my friend left the room. " I do not see that we are any further than when he came."

" At least, you have his assurance that your horse will run," said I.

19 *"That was the curious incident."* This is perhaps the most famous example of what the late Monsignor Ronald Knox felicitously termed the *Sherlockismus.*

20 *Four days later.* Since the race was on Tuesday, Watson is presumably counting from the Friday morning on which he and Holmes returned to London from Devonshire.

21 *Winchester.* We have seen that the adventure must have taken place in the autumn of a year later than 1887 (when *A Study in Scarlet* was published in *Beeton's Christmas Annual*) and before 1891 (in the April of which year Holmes was presumed dead). The possible years are therefore 1888, 1889, and 1890. Turning to the *Almanack,* we find six possible dates for the race: 1) Tuesday, October 2, 1888; 2) Tuesday, October 9, 1888; 3) Tuesday, October 1, 1889; 4) Tuesday, October 8, 1889; 5) Tuesday, September 30, 1890; and 6) Tuesday, October 7, 1890. We can at once eliminate the two dates in 1888 and the October 1st of 1889; *no* race meetings were

" Yes, I have his assurance," said the Colonel, with a shrug of his shoulders. " I should prefer to have the horse."

I was about to make some reply in defence of my friend, when he entered the room again.

" Now, gentlemen," said he, " I am quite ready for Tavistock."

As we stepped into the carriage one of the stable lads held the door open for us. A sudden idea seemed to occur to Holmes, for he leaned forward and touched the lad upon the sleeve.

" You have a few sheep in the paddock," he said. " Who attends to them ? "

" I do, sir."

" Have you noticed anything amiss with them of late ? "

" Well, sir, not of much account ; but three of them have gone lame, sir."

I could see that Holmes was extremely pleased, for he chuckled and rubbed his hands together.

" A long shot, Watson ; a very long shot ! " said he, pinching my arm. " Gregory, let me recommend to your attention this singular epidemic among the sheep. Drive on, coachman ! "

Colonel Ross still wore an expression which showed the poor opinion which he had formed of my companion's ability, but I saw by the Inspector's face that his attention had been keenly aroused.

" You consider that to be important ? " he asked.

" Exceedingly so."

" Is there any other point to which you would wish to draw my attention ? "

" To the curious incident of the dog in the night-time."

" The dog did nothing in the night-time."

" That was the curious incident," remarked Sherlock **19**
Holmes.

Four days later Holmes and I were again in the train **20**
bound for Winchester, to see the race for the Wessex Cup. **21**
Colonel Ross met us, by appointment, outside the station, and we drove in his drag to the course beyond the town. His face was grave and his manner was cold in the extreme.

" I have seen nothing of my horse," said he.

" I suppose that you would know him when you saw him ? " asked Holmes.

The Colonel was very angry. " I have been on the turf for twenty years, and never was asked such a question as that before," said he. " A child would know Silver Blaze with his white forehead and his mottled off foreleg."

" How is the betting ? "

" Well, that is the curious part of it. You could have got fifteen to one yesterday, but the price has become shorter and shorter, until you can hardly get three to one now."

" Hum ! " said Holmes. " Somebody knows something, that is clear ! "

I COULD SEE THAT HOLMES WAS EXTREMELY PLEASED . . .

Illustration by Sidney Paget for the *Strand Magazine*, December, 1892.

held in Britain on those days. We must eliminate the October 8th of 1889 and the October 7th of 1890 because of the weather: in 1889, according to the London *Times*, there was "rain in almost all parts of the kingdom" on Thursday, October 3rd (which would have been the day of the journey to Devonshire); in 1890 there was no rain on either the 29th or the 30th of September (which would have been the night of Straker's murder and the disappearance of Silver Blaze). Only Tuesday, September 30, 1890, remains as the day of the race, but it is fitting that we check the corresponding dates for the murder and the journey to Devonshire with the weather columns of the *Times*. The night of the murder would have been the night of Monday, September 22nd to Tuesday, September 23rd. Said the *Times*' weather report for the Tuesday evening: "In the course of the past 24 hours the weather has been in a very . . . unsettled condition. . . . Thunder showers have been prevalent, especially in the south and south-east, and in many localities the rainfall has been large. The wind has . . . remained light in force." The day of the journey to Devonshire would have been Thursday, September 25th—a day on which the "weather was fine and bright in the east and south of England." We therefore hold that the adventure took place on *Thursday, September 25, and Tuesday, September 30, 1890*. It is true that the race meeting of September 30, 1890, was *not* at Winchester (indeed, Dr. Zeisler demonstrated that "in all the years between 1881 and 1903 there is no horse race scheduled at Winchester except on" July 17, 1888), but this need not worry us: as we shall see, Watson at this time was hardly a "Handy Guide to the Turf." He could have been as confused as to the *place* of the race as he was on other racing matters.

22 *drag.* A private stagecoach, with seats inside and on top.

23 (*purple cap, black sleeves*). "We are given what purports to be a copy of the race card," the late Gavin Brend wrote in *My Dear Holmes*, "but it in fact appears to have been compiled after the event, and from memory, by someone who was not accustomed to studying racing colours. Of the six starters only two, Silver Blaze and The Negro, appear to be sufficiently and adequately equipped. Pugilist has a pink cap and blue and black jacket. This might get by Messrs. Weatherby and Sons, who are responsible for the registration of racing colours, but we think it very doubtful. 'Blue and black jacket' is not sufficient. It should be 'blue and black stripes,' or 'blue and black hoops,' or 'blue and black quarters,' or possibly 'blue, black sleeves.' Iris seems to be short a cap, for his description is merely 'yellow and black stripes.' Desborough, 'yellow cap and sleeves,' appears to be even more exiguously clad, and Rasper, 'purple cap, black sleeves' is in the same precarious situation. Surely a racing man, accustomed to studying the colours on his race card, would realize that something else is required to connect the two sleeves?" We may add here that *no* races are reserved for four- and five-year-old horses, that any proper race card would state the age, weight, pedigree and trainer of each horse entered, as well as the time of the race.

24 *Fifteen to five against Desborough!* "There are a few examples of unreduced fractions sanctioned by long usage in racing odds, such as '6 to 4,' '100 to 8,' and '100 to 6,' but *not* we submit '15 to 5.' This we cannot accept in any circumstances whatsoever," Mr. Brend wrote.

25 *I stand to win a little on this next race.* On the *next race*—or on the race *just run?* Was Holmes in fact about to collect his winnings on Silver Blaze? "All facts point to the conclusion that Holmes with the connivance of Mr. Silas Brown, and probably with that of Lord Backwater, whose horse, Desborough, ran in the same race . . . deliberately framed the Wessex Plate," Mr. Robert Keith Leavitt wrote in "Nummi in Arca or The Fiscal Holmes."

". . . Leavitt's suggestion that Backwater's horse was pulled has the cogency almost of demonstrable fact," the late Elmer Davis seconded in his Introduction to *The Return of Sherlock Holmes.*

"Brown was to keep Silver Blaze in hiding as long as possible while Holmes, dashing down to London by the night train [on the Thursday preceding the race] was to place bets at as long odds as he could possibly get on Silver Blaze," Mr. Charles B. Stephens wrote in "Silas Brown, or, Who Shot Desborough's Bolt?" "To make doubly certain of the success of the coup, Brown was to instruct Desborough's jockey to run just the sort of race that Watson [later recorded] without

22 As the drag drew up in the enclosure near the grand-stand, I glanced at the card to see the entries. It ran :

Wessex Plate. 50 sovs. each, h ft, with 1,000 sovs. added, for four- and five-year olds. Second £300. Third £200. New course (one mile and five furlongs).

1. Mr. Heath Newton's The Negro (red cap, cinnamon jacket).
2. Colonel Wardlaw's Pugilist (pink cap, blue and black jacket).
3. Lord Backwater's Desborough (yellow cap and sleeves).
4. Colonel Ross's Silver Blaze (black cap, red jacket).
5. Duke of Balmoral's Iris (yellow and black stripes).

23 6. Lord Singleford's Rasper (purple cap, black sleeves).

" We scratched our other one and put all hopes on your word," said the Colonel. " Why, what is that ? Silver Blaze favourite ? "

" Five to four against Silver Blaze ! " roared the ring. " Five to four against Silver Blaze ! Fifteen to five
24 against Desborough ! Five to four on the field ! "

" There are the numbers up," I cried. " They are all six there."

" All six there ! Then my horse is running," cried the Colonel, in great agitation. " But I don't see him. My colours have not passed."

" Only five have passed. This must be he."

As I spoke a powerful bay horse swept out from the weighing enclosure and cantered past us, bearing on its back the well-known black and red of the Colonel.

" That's not my horse," cried the owner. " That beast has not a white hair upon its body. What is this that you have done, Mr. Holmes ? "

" Well, well, let us see how he gets on," said my friend, imperturbably. For a few minutes he gazed through my field-glass. " Capital ! An excellent start ! " he cried suddenly. " There they are, coming round the curve ! "

From our drag we had a superb view as they came up the straight. The six horses were so close together that a carpet could have covered them, but half-way up the yellow of the Capleton stable showed to the front. Before they reached us, however, Desborough's bolt was shot, and the Colonel's horse, coming away with a rush, passed the post a good six lengths before its rival, the Duke of Balmoral's Iris making a bad third.

" It's my race anyhow," gasped the Colonel, passing his hand over his eyes. " I confess that I can make neither head nor tail of it. Don't you think that you have kept up your mystery long enough, Mr. Holmes ? "

" Certainly, Colonel. You shall know everything. Let us all go round and have a look at the horse together. Here he is," he continued, as we made our way into the weighing enclosure where only owners and their friends find admittance. " You have only to wash his face and his leg in spirits of wine and you will find that he is the same old Silver Blaze as ever."

" You take my breath away ! "

" I found him in the hands of a faker, and took the liberty of running him just as he was sent over."

" My dear sir, you have done wonders. The horse looks very fit and well. It never went better in its life. I owe you a thousand apologies for having doubted your ability. You have done me a great service by recovering my horse. You would do me a greater still if you could lay your hands on the murderer of John Straker."

"I have done so," said Holmes, quietly.

The Colonel and I stared at him in amazement. "You have got him! Where is he, then?"

"He is here."

"Here! Where?"

"In my company at the present moment."

The Colonel flushed angrily. "I quite recognize that I am under obligations to you, Mr. Holmes," said he, "but I must regard what you have just said as either a very bad joke or an insult."

Sherlock Holmes laughed. "I assure you that I have not associated you with the crime, Colonel," said he; "the real murderer is standing immediately behind you!"

He stepped past and laid his hand upon the glossy neck of the thoroughbred.

"The horse!" cried both the Colonel and myself.

"Yes, the horse. And it may lessen his guilt if I say that it was done in self-defence, and that John Straker was a man who was entirely unworthy of your confidence. But there goes the bell; and as I stand to win a little on
this next race, I shall defer a more lengthy explanation 25
until a more fitting time."

We had the corner of a Pullman car to ourselves that 26
evening as we whirled back to London, and I fancy that the journey was a short one to Colonel Ross as well as to myself, as we listened to our companion's narrative of the events which had occurred at the Dartmoor training stables upon that Monday night, and the means by which he had unravelled them.

"I confess," said he, "that any theories which I had formed from the newspaper reports were entirely erroneous. And yet there were indications there, had they not been overlaid by other details which concealed their true import. I went to Devonshire with the conviction that Fitzroy Simpson was the true culprit, although, of course, I saw that the evidence against him was by no means complete.

"It was while I was in the carriage, just as we reached the trainer's house, that the immense significance of the curried mutton occurred to me. You may remember that I was distrait, and remained sitting after you had all alighted. I was marvelling in my own mind how I could possibly have overlooked so obvious a clue."

"I confess," said the Colonel, "that even now I cannot see how it helps us."

"It was the first link in my chain of reasoning. Powdered opium is by no means tasteless. The flavour is not disagreeable, but it is perceptible. Were it mixed with any ordinary dish, the eater would undoubtedly detect it, and would probably eat no more. A curry was exactly the medium which would disguise this taste. By no possible supposition could this stranger, Fitzroy Simpson, have caused curry to be served in the trainer's family that night, and it is surely too monstrous a coincidence to suppose that he happened to come along with powdered opium upon the very night when a dish happened to be

HE STEPPED PAST AND LAID HIS HAND UPON THE GLOSSY NECK OF THE THOROUGHBRED.

Illustration by Sidney Paget for the *Strand Magazine*, December, 1892.

grasping its significance. . . . The evidence seems all too clear that it was Holmes, himself, who master-minded the manipulation of the betting odds to his own advantage, in derogation of his obligations to the man who had employed him for the investigation."

This same unhappy view is held by the famous sports columnist of the New York *Herald Tribune*, Mr. Red Smith; as is evident from a reading of his essay "The Nefarious Holmes" in *Views of Sport:* "Whenever Holmes' activities impinged upon the field of sports, he exhibited an ethical blind spot of shocking dimensions and it is common knowledge that he was the architect of an extraordinary piece of skullduggery in connection with a horse race." The essay further states that in 1891 Holmes said that his earnings from recent cases had left him free to live as he wished ("The Final Problem"); yet Holmes in "The Adventure of the Priory School" (1901) had to confess, "I am a poor man," and although Holmes received princely fees for his services he was practically always broke—"obviously because the bookies took everything he didn't have to lay out for happy dust." Mr. Smith then goes on to charge that: "It has been established that Mr. Sherlock Holmes was a horse player of degenerate principles who thought nothing of fixing a race, and when you bear in mind his first-hand knowledge of the use and effect of cocaine, he probably had his syringe

served which would disguise the flavour. That is unthinkable. Therefore Simpson becomes eliminated from the case, and our attention centres upon Straker and his wife, the only two people who could have chosen curried mutton for supper that night. The opium was added after the dish was set aside for the stable boy, for the others had the same for supper with no ill effects. Which of them, then, had access to that dish without the maid seeing them ?

" Before deciding that question I had grasped the significance of the silence of the dog, for one true inference invariably suggests others. The Simpson incident had shown me that a dog was kept in the stables, and yet, though someone had been in and had fetched out a horse, he had not barked enough to arouse the two lads in the loft. Obviously the midnight visitor was someone whom the dog knew well.

" I was already convinced, or almost convinced, that John Straker went down to the stables in the dead of the night and took out Silver Blaze. For what purpose ? For a dishonest one, obviously, or why should he drug his own stable boy ? And yet I was at a loss to know why. There have been cases before now where trainers have made sure of great sums of money by laying against their own horses, through agents, and then prevented them from winning by fraud. Sometimes it is a pulling jockey. Sometimes it is some surer and subtler means. What was it here ? I hoped that the contents of his pockets might help me to form a conclusion.

" And they did so. You cannot have forgotten the singular knife which was found in the dead man's hand, a knife which certainly no sane man would choose for a weapon. It was, as Dr. Watson told us, a form of knife which is used for the most delicate operations known in surgery. And it was to be used for a delicate operation that night. You must know, with your wide experience of turf matters, Colonel Ross, that it is possible to make a slight nick upon the tendons of a horse's ham, and to do it subcutaneously so as to leave absolutely no
27 trace. A horse so treated would develop a slight lameness which would be put down to a strain in exercise or a touch of rheumatism, but never to foul play."

" Villain ! Scoundrel ! " cried the Colonel.

" We have here the explanation of why John Straker wished to take the horse out on to the moor. So spirited a creature would have certainly roused the soundest of sleepers when it felt the prick of the knife. It was absolutely necessary to do it in the open air."

" I have been blind ! " cried the Colonel. " Of course, that was why he needed the candle, and struck the match."

" Undoubtedly. But in examining his belongings, I was fortunate enough to discover, not only the method of the crime, but even its motives. As a man of the world, Colonel, you know that men do not carry other people's bills about in their pockets. We have most of us quite enough to do to settle our own. I at once concluded that

in the veins of more than one thoroughbred."

Needless to say, this underhanded attack on Holmes in the public prints has met with spirited rebuttals, notably from Mr. Edward T. Buxton ("He Solved the Case and Won the Race"): Holmes "knew that at a word from him Silas Brown would have received a stiff jailing as well as being barred from his livelihood for the rest of his days, and that the 'bully and sneak' was well aware of it. Holmes also knew, however, that in spite of other faults the trainer for Lord Backwater's great Mapleton racing stables had to be thoroughly competent in his profession. With such a man under his thumb Holmes had the one man available who could train Silver Blaze to win the Wessex Cup. He had to, or go to jail. But it was also clear that . . . Colonel Ross would never have agreed to any such common-sense procedure, so Holmes very probably kept him in the dark . . ." There is still, of course, no reason why Holmes, under these circumstances, might not have placed a little something on Silver Blaze's nose. We are again in "deep waters."

26 *a Pullman car.* Some critics have doubted that Holmes and Watson and Colonel Ross would return to London from Winchester in "a Pullman car," but "this would be correct enough, as the L.S.W.R. (London & South Western Railway) did use Pullman cars on its Bournemouth service," as Mr. Edgar S. Rosenberger pointed out in "The Railway Journeys of Sherlock Holmes."

27 *so as to leave absolutely no trace.* The researches of the late Dr. Roland Hammond, reported in "The Attempted Mayhem of 'Silver Blaze,'" convinced him that "such an injury could not be inflicted to the tendons of a horse's ham with the instrument called for in the specifications."

Straker was leading a double life, and keeping a second establishment. The nature of the bill showed that there was a lady in the case, and one who had expensive tastes. Liberal as you are with your servants, one hardly expects that they can buy twenty-guinea walking dresses for their women. I questioned Mrs. Straker as to the dress without her knowing it, and having satisfied myself that it had never reached her, I made a note of the milliner's address, and felt that by calling there with Straker's photograph, I could easily dispose of the mythical Darbyshire.

" From that time on all was plain. Straker had led out the horse to a hollow where his light would be invisible. Simpson, in his flight, had dropped his cravat, and Straker had picked it up with some idea, perhaps, that he might use it in securing the horse's leg. Once in the hollow he had got behind the horse, and had struck a light, but the creature, frightened at the sudden glare, and with the strange instinct of animals feeling that some mischief was intended, had lashed out, and the steel shoe had struck Straker full on the forehead. He had already, in spite of the rain, taken off his overcoat in order to do his delicate task, and so, as he fell, his knife gashed his thigh. Do I make it clear ? "

" Wonderful ! " cried the Colonel. " Wonderful ! You might have been there."

" My final shot was, I confess, a very long one. It struck me that so astute a man as Straker would not undertake this delicate tendon-nicking without a little practice. What could he practise on ? My eyes fell upon the sheep, and I asked a question which, rather to my surprise, showed that my surmise was correct."

" You have made it perfectly clear, Mr. Holmes."

" When I returned to London I called upon the milliner, who at once recognized Straker as an excellent customer, of the name of Darbyshire, who had a very dashing wife with a strong partiality for expensive dresses. I have no doubt that this woman had plunged him over head and ears in debt, and so led him into this miserable plot."

" You have explained all but one thing," cried the Colonel. " Where was the horse ? "

" Ah, it bolted and was cared for by one of your neighbours. We must have an amnesty in that direction, I think. This is Clapham Junction, if I am not mistaken,
and we shall be in Victoria in less than ten minutes. If **28**
you care to smoke a cigar in our rooms, Colonel, I shall be happy to give you any other details which might interest you."

28 *Victoria.* But Holmes, traveling from Winchester, would be riding the London & South Western Railway, later the western division of the Southern Railway, and his London terminus would be, not Victoria, but Waterloo Station (nor would a train from Winchester to London pass through Clapham Junction). Is this perhaps another indication that Watson was wrong when he said that the race was at Winchester?

Auctorial Note: In his autobiography, *Memories and Adventures*, Sir Arthur Conan Doyle wrote:

> Sometimes I have got upon dangerous ground where I have taken risks through my own want of knowledge of the correct atmosphere. I have, for example, never been a racing man, and yet I ventured to write "Silver Blaze" in which the mystery depends upon the laws of training and racing. The story is all right, and Holmes may have been at the top of his form, but my ignorance cries aloud to heaven. I read an excellent and very damaging criticism of the story in some sporting paper, written clearly by a man who *did* know, in which he explained the exact penalties which would come upon everyone concerned if they had acted as I described. Half would have been in jail, and the other half warned off the turf forever. However, I have never been nervous about details, and one must be masterful sometimes.

Although Conan Doyle omitted "Silver Blaze" from his "best" list (as did the readers of the *Observer*), it is clear that he thought highly of the story; indeed, he wagered his wife a shilling that she could not guess the name of the murderer. And critics generally have written that "Silver Blaze" gave Sherlock Holmes one of his finest hours. "In our estimation," Ellery Queen wrote in his anthology, *Sporting Blood*, " 'Silver Blaze' belongs prominently to any list of the five leading Sherlockian short stories. It represents the great Holmes at his incisive, dynamic best; despite its author's biographical apology, it reveals no obvious turf errors—at least, to the lay reader; and we could find no finer yarn to head our parade of The Great Sports Detective Stories."

46

THE ADVENTURE OF THE BERYL CORONET

[Friday, December 19, to Saturday, December 20, 1890]

"HOLMES," said I, as I stood one morning in our bow-window looking down the street, " here is a madman coming along. It seems rather sad that his relatives should allow him to come out alone."

My friend rose lazily from his arm-chair, and stood with his hands in the pockets of his dressing-gown, looking over my shoulder. It was a bright, crisp February morning, and the snow of the day before still lay deep upon the
1 ground, shimmering brightly in the wintry sun. Down the centre of Baker Street it had been ploughed into a brown crumbly band by the traffic, but at either side and on the heaped-up edges of the footpaths it still lay as white as when it fell. The grey pavement had been cleaned and scraped, but was still dangerously slippery, so that there were fewer passengers than usual. Indeed, from the direction of the Metropolitan station no one was coming save the single gentleman whose eccentric conduct had drawn my attention.

He was a man of about fifty, tall, portly, and imposing, with a massive, strongly marked face and a commanding figure. He was dressed in a sombre yet rich style, in black frock-coat, shining hat, neat brown gaiters, and well-cut pearl-grey trousers. Yet his actions were in absurd contrast to the dignity of his dress and features, for he was running hard, with occasional little springs, such as a weary man gives who is little accustomed to set any tax upon his legs. As he ran he jerked his hands up and down, waggled his head, and writhed his face into the most extraordinary contortions.

" What on earth can be the matter with him ? " I asked.

" He is looking up at the numbers of the houses."

" I believe that he is coming here," said Holmes, rubbing his hands.

" Here ? "

" Yes ; I rather think he is coming to consult me professionally. I think that I recognize the symptoms. Ha ! did I not tell you ? " As he spoke, the man, puffing and blowing, rushed at our door, and pulled at our bell until the whole house resounded with the clanging.

A few moments later he was in our room, still puffing, still gesticulating, but with so fixed a look of grief and despair in his eyes that our smiles were turned in an instant to

1 *the snow of the day before still lay deep upon the ground.* The adventure, as we shall see, opened on a Friday, as Watson says and infers it did, in the opinion of most chronologists, but Watson's "February" is demonstrably wrong: in all the possible years (the farther limit is set by the fact that Watson's account of the adventure appeared in the May, 1892, issue of the *Strand Magazine*) there appear to have been only two Februarys in which there was a substantial fall of snow. The first was in February, 1881, (six inches on the 20th–21st, four inches on the 23rd). But in February, 1881, Watson had yet to share a case with Holmes and professed to know nothing of his companion's unusual occupation. The second substantial fall of snow was in February, 1886. But this was on the 28th, a Sunday, an impossible day in view of other statements in Watson's account of the adventure. Can we find a Thursday in a month other than February in the years under consideration on which there was a heavy fall of snow in London? We can, thanks to Mr. E. L. Hawke of the Royal Meteorological Society. In a letter to your editor dated November 29, 1954, Mr. Hawke wrote:

> A fairly careful search through the London weather archives of 1881–1890 has brought to light only two Thursday snowfalls of appreciable amount:
>
> a. March 17, 1887. A light daytime fall, not exceeding half an inch in depth. But there was already snow left from a heavy storm two days earlier; this had covered the ground five or six inches deep in N. W. London. Sharp frost during the night of the 17th–18th. Over six hours' sunshine on the Friday (18th). Moon near last quarter.
>
> b. December 18, 1890. A substantial and general fall throughout London. Average depth three to four inches. Hard frost at night. No sunshine on the Friday (19th). Moon near first quarter.

The information we have received from the adventure of "The Reigate Squires" (in March,

horror and pity. For a while he could not get his words out, but swayed his body and plucked at his hair like one who has been driven to the extreme limits of his reason. Then, suddenly springing to his feet, he beat his head against the wall with such force that we both rushed upon him, and tore him away to the centre of the room. Sherlock Holmes pushed him down into the easy chair, and, sitting beside him, patted his hand, and chatted with him in the easy, soothing tones which he knew so well how to employ.

"You have come to me to tell me your story, have you not?" said he. "You are fatigued with your haste. Pray wait until you have recovered yourself, and then I shall be most happy to look into any little problem which you may submit to me."

The man sat for a minute or more with a heaving chest, fighting against his emotion. Then he passed his handkerchief over his brow, set his lips tight, and turned his face towards us.

"No doubt you think me mad?" said he.

"I see that you have had some great trouble," responded Holmes.

"God knows I have!—a trouble which is enough to unseat my reason, so sudden and so terrible is it. Public disgrace I might have faced, although I am a man whose character has never yet borne a stain. Private affliction also is the lot of every man; but the two coming together, and in so frightful a form, have been enough to shake my very soul. Besides, it is not I alone. The very noblest in the land may suffer, unless some way be found out of this horrible affair."

"Pray compose yourself, sir," said Holmes, "and let me have a clear account of who you are, and what it is that has befallen you."

"My name," answered our visitor, "is probably familiar to your ears. I am Alexander Holder, of the banking firm of Holder & Stevenson, of Threadneedle Street."

1887, Holmes was on the Continent, bringing to a successful conclusion the taxing affair of the Netherland-Sumatra Company) makes 1887 quite impossible. The case began, then, on *Friday, December 19, 1890;* it ended the next day, *Saturday, December 20, 1890.*

"THE MAN SAT FOR A MINUTE WITH A HEAVING CHEST, FIGHTING AGAINST HIS EMOTION. THEN HE PASSED HIS HANDKERCHIEF OVER HIS BROW..."

Illustration by Sidney Paget for the *Strand Magazine*, May, 1892.

The name was indeed well known to us, as belonging to the senior partner in the second largest private banking concern in the City of London. What could have happened, then, to bring one of the foremost citizens of London to this most pitiable pass? We waited, all curiosity, until with another effort he braced himself to tell his story.

" I feel that time is of value," said he, " that is why I
2 hastened here when the police inspector suggested that I should secure your co-operation. I came to Baker Street by the Underground, and hurried from there on foot, for the cabs go slowly through this snow. That is why I was so out of breath, for I am a man who takes very little exercise. I feel better now, and I will put the facts before you as shortly and yet as clearly as I can.

" It is, of course, well known to you, that in a successful banking business as much depends upon our being able to find remunerative investments for our funds, as upon our increasing our connection and the number of our depositors. One of our most lucrative means of laying out money is in the shape of loans, where the security is unimpeachable. We have done a good deal in this direction during the last few years, and there are many noble families to whom we have advanced large sums upon the security of their pictures, libraries, or plate.

" Yesterday morning I was seated in my office at the Bank, when a card was brought in to me by one of the clerks. I started when I saw the name, for it was that of none other than—well, perhaps even to you I had better say no more than that it was a name which is a household word all over the earth—one of the highest, noblest, most
3 exalted names in England. I was overwhelmed by the honour, and attempted, when he entered, to say so, but he plunged at once into business with the air of a man who wishes to hurry quickly through a disagreeable task.

" ' Mr. Holder,' said he, ' I have been informed that you are in the habit of advancing money.'

" ' The firm do so when the security is good,' I answered.

" ' It is absolutely essential to me,' said he, ' that I should have fifty thousand pounds at once. I could of course borrow so trifling a sum ten times over from my friends, but I much prefer to make it a matter of business, and to carry out that business myself. In my position you can readily understand that it is unwise to place oneself under obligations.'

" ' For how long, may I ask, do you want this sum?' I asked.

" ' Next Monday I have a large sum due to me, and I shall then most certainly repay what you advance, with whatever interest you think it right to charge. But it is very essential to me that the money should be paid at once.'

" ' I should be happy to advance it without further parley from my own private purse,' said I, ' were it not that the strain would be rather more than it could bear. If, on the other hand, I am to do it in the name of the firm, then in justice to my partner I must insist that, even in your case, every business-like precaution should be taken.'

" ' I should much prefer to have it so,' said he, raising up a square, black morocco case which he had laid beside his chair. ' You have doubtless heard of the Beryl coronet?'

THE NAME WAS INDEED WELL KNOWN TO US . . .

Dr. Julian Wolff has conjectured (*Practical Handbook of Sherlockian Heraldry*) that "This great banker, whose name was indeed well known to Holmes, may have been one of the Glyns. It is difficult to conceive of so precious a possession as the Beryl Coronet being entrusted to any other banker. This great family has gained many honours in banking and public life. Anyone bearing one of the highest, noblest, and most exalted names in England could hardly deal with any other in a matter so important and so confidential. Robson's has the arms: 'ar. an eagle displ. with two heads sa. guttee d'or.' "

2 *the police inspector.* Gregson or Lestrade or another?

3 *one of the highest, noblest, most exalted names in England.* The late Edgar W. Smith's identification of this illustrious client as His Royal Highness, Albert Edward, Prince of Wales ("A Scandal in Identity") was supported by the late A. Carson Simpson in his essay, "Whose Was It? Conjectures on a Coronet," which demonstrates that H.R.H. was also the Duke of Rothesay, the oldest duchy in Scotland, and therefore the legitimate wearer of a duke's coronet which was, at the same time, "a national possession" and one that the Prince could easily get his hands on.

" ' One of the most precious public possessions of the Empire,' said I.

" ' Precisely.' He opened the case, and there, embedded in soft, flesh-coloured velvet, lay the magnificent piece of jewellery which he had named. ' There are thirty-nine enormous beryls,' said he, ' and the price of the gold chasing is incalculable. The lowest estimate would put the worth of the coronet at double the sum which I have asked. I am prepared to leave it with you as my security.'

" I took the precious case into my hands and looked in some perplexity from it to my illustrious client.

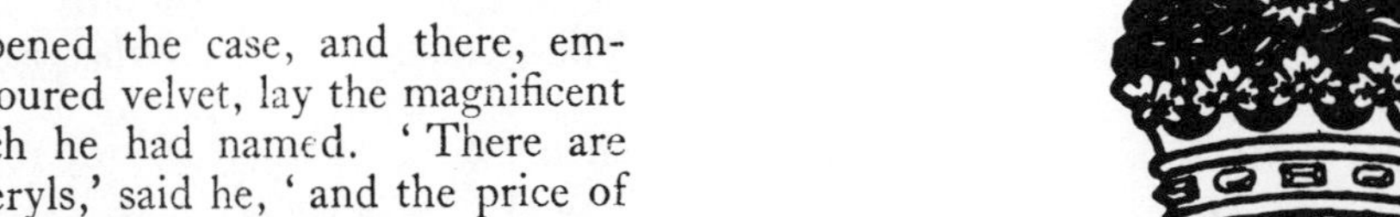

"THERE . . . LAY THE MAGNIFICENT PIECE OF JEWELLERY . . ."

The coronet worn by a duke on state and official occasions, when he must appear in public so distinguished, and clad in his robes, is decorated on the circlet with engraving, and bears on the upper edge eight strawberry leaves. The cap, which is the same for all nobility, is of crimson velvet, turned up (or guarded) ermine. The coronet of a duke should not be confused with the ducal coronet so often blazoned in heraldic achievements. This is represented quite differently: first, the cap is absent; second, the circlet is generally plain, though it may be jewelled; and finally only three strawberry leaves decorate the upper edge; it is used in place of a wreath of the colors between helmet and crest, and for crowning or gorging animals.

"I TOOK THE PRECIOUS CASE INTO MY HANDS . . ."

Illustration by Sidney Paget for the *Strand Magazine*, May, 1892.

" ' You doubt its value ? ' he asked.

" ' Not at all. I only doubt——'

" ' The propriety of my leaving it. You may set your mind at rest about that. I should not dream of doing so were it not absolutely certain that I should be able in four
days to reclaim it. It is a pure matter of form. Is the **4**
security sufficient ? '

" ' Ample.'

" ' You understand, Mr. Holder, that I am giving you a strong proof of the confidence which I have in you, founded upon all that I have heard of you. I rely upon you not only to be discreet and to refrain from all gossip upon the matter, but, above all, to preserve this coronet with every possible precaution, because I need not say that a great public scandal would be caused if any harm were to befall it. Any injury to it would be almost as serious as its complete loss, for there are no beryls in the world to match these, and it would be impossible to replace them. I leave it with you, however, with every confidence, and I shall call for it in person on Monday morning.'

" Seeing that my client was anxious to leave, I said no more ; but, calling for my cashier, I ordered him to pay over fifty thousand-pound notes. When I was alone once more, however, with the precious case lying upon the table

4 *in four days.* Watson has quoted Holder as saying: "Yesterday morning I was seated in my office at the Bank." The illustrious client who came to him on that day said he would have a large sum due him "next Monday" and so "should be able in four days" to reclaim the coronet. "Yesterday" was therefore a Thursday and Holmes' part in the case began on a Friday.

in front of me, I could not but think with some misgivings of the immense responsibility which it entailed upon me. There could be no doubt that, as it was a national possession, a horrible scandal would ensue if any misfortune should occur to it. I already regretted having ever consented to take charge of it. However, it was too late to alter the matter now, so I locked it up in my private safe, and turned once more to my work.

" When evening came, I felt that it would be an imprudence to leave so precious a thing in the office behind me. Bankers' safes had been forced before now, and why should not mine be ? If so, how terrible would be the position in which I should find myself ! I determined, therefore, that for the next few days I would always carry the case backwards and forwards with me, so that it might never be really out of my reach. With this intention, I called a cab, and drove out to my house at Streatham, carrying the jewel with me. I did not breathe freely until I had taken it upstairs, and locked it in the bureau of my dressing-room.

" And now a word as to my household, Mr. Holmes, for I wish you to thoroughly understand the situation. My groom and my page sleep out of the house, and may be set aside altogether. I have three maid-servants who have been with me a number of years, and whose absolute reliability is quite above suspicion. Another, Lucy Parr, the second waiting-maid, has only been in my service a few months. She came with an excellent character, however, and has always given me satisfaction. She is a very pretty girl, and has attracted admirers who have occasionally hung about the place. That is the only drawback which we have found to her, but we believe her to be a thoroughly good girl in every way.

" So much for the servants. My family itself is so small that it will not take me long to describe it. I am a widower, and have an only son, Arthur. He has been a disappointment to me, Mr. Holmes, a grievous disappointment. I have no doubt that I am myself to blame. People tell me that I have spoiled him. Very likely I have. When my dear wife died I felt that he was all I had to love. I could not bear to see the smile fade even for a moment from his face. I have never denied him a wish. Perhaps it would have been better for both of us had I been sterner, but I meant it for the best.

" It was naturally my intention that he should succeed me in my business, but he was not of a business turn. He was wild, wayward, and, to speak the truth, I could not trust him in the handling of large sums of money. When he was young he became a member of an aristocratic club, and there, having charming manners, he was soon the intimate of a number of men with long purses and expensive habits. He learned to play heavily at cards and to squander money on the turf, until he had again and again to come to me and implore me to give him an advance upon his allowance, that he might settle his debts of honour. He tried more than once to break away from the dangerous company which he was keeping, but each time the influence of his friend Sir George Burnwell was enough to draw him back again.

" And, indeed, I could not wonder that such a man as Sir George Burnwell should gain an influence over him, for he has frequently brought him to my house, and I have found myself that I could hardly resist the fascination of his manner. He is older than Arthur, a man of the world to his finger-tips, one who has been everywhere, seen everything, a brilliant talker, and a man of great personal beauty. Yet when I think of him in cold blood, far away from the glamour of his presence, I am convinced from his cynical speech, and the look which I have caught in his eyes, that he is one who should be deeply distrusted. So I think, and so, too, thinks my little Mary, who has a woman's quick insight into character.

" And now there is only she to be described. She is my niece ; but when my brother died five years ago and left her alone in the world I adopted her, and have looked upon her ever since as my daughter. She is a sunbeam in my house—sweet, loving, beautiful, a wonderful manager and housekeeper, yet as tender and quiet and gentle as a woman could be. She is my right hand. I do not know what I could do without her. In only one matter has she ever gone against my wishes. Twice my boy has asked her to marry him, for he loves her devotedly, but each time she has refused him. I think that if anyone could have drawn him into the right path it would have been she, and that his marriage might have changed his whole life ; but now, alas ! it is too late—for ever too late !

" Now, Mr. Holmes, you know the people who live under my roof, and I shall continue with my miserable story.

" When we were taking coffee in the drawing-room that night, after dinner, I told Arthur and Mary my experience, and of the precious treasure which we had under our roof, suppressing only the name of my client. Lucy Parr, who had brought in the coffee, had, I am sure, left the room ; but I cannot swear that the door was closed. Mary and Arthur were much interested, and wished to see the famous coronet, but I thought it better not to disturb it.

" ' Where have you put it ? " asked Arthur.

" ' In my own bureau.'

" ' Well, I hope to goodness the house won't be burgled during the night,' said he.

" ' It is locked up,' I answered.

" ' Oh, any old key will fit that bureau. When I was a youngster I have opened it myself with the key of the box-room cupboard.'

" He often had a wild way of talking, so that I thought little of what he said. He followed me to my room, however, that night with a very grave face.

" ' Look here, dad,' said he, with his eyes cast down. ' Can you let me have two hundred pounds ? '

" ' No, I cannot ! ' I answered sharply. ' I have been far too generous with you in money matters.'

" ' You have been very kind,' said he ; ' but I must have this money, or else I can never show my face inside the club again.'

" ' And a very good thing, too ! ' I cried.

" ' Yes, but you would not have me leave it a dishonoured man,' said he. ' I could not bear the disgrace. I must raise the money in some way, and if you will not let me have it, then I must try other means.'

" 'OH, ANY OLD KEY WILL FIT THAT BUREAU.' "

Illustration by Sidney Paget for the *Strand Magazine*, May, 1892. "Surely a very strange sort of banker, whose idea of safe-custody for one of the most precious of public possessions was to put it away in a bureau that could be opened by 'any old key,' after telling his family where it was," Mr. T. S. Blakeney commented in "Thoughts on 'The Sign of the Four.' " "If this was the best he could do, what must the strong rooms at Holder & Stevenson's have been like. John Clay [of "The Red-Headed League"] missed the chance of a lifetime when he went burrowing into the vaults of the City & Suburban Bank, when he could, apparently, have just walked into Holder & Stevenson and helped himself."

" I was very angry, for this was the third demand dur-
5 ing the month. ' You shall not have a farthing from me,'
I cried, on which he bowed and left the room without another word.

" When he was gone I unlocked my bureau, made sure that my treasure was safe, and locked it again. Then I started to go round the house to see that all was secure—a duty which I usually leave to Mary, but which I thought it well to perform myself that night. As I came down the stairs I saw Mary herself at the side-window of the hall, which she closed and fastened as I approached.

" ' Tell me, dad,' said she, looking, I thought, a little disturbed, ' did you give Lucy, the maid, leave to go out to-night ? '

" ' Certainly not.'

" ' She came in just now by the back door. I have no doubt that she has only been to the side-gate to see someone, but I think that it is hardly safe, and should be stopped.'

" ' You must speak to her in the morning, or I will, if you prefer it. Are you sure that everything is fastened ? '

" ' Quite sure, dad.'

" ' Then, good night.' I kissed her, and went to my bedroom, where I was soon asleep.

" I am endeavouring to tell you everything, Mr. Holmes, which may have any bearing upon the case, but I beg that you will question me upon any point which I do not make clear."

" On the contrary, your statement is singularly lucid."

" I come to a part of my story now in which I should wish to be particularly so. I am not a very heavy sleeper, and the anxiety in my mind tended, no doubt, to make me even less so than usual. About two in the morning, then, I was awakened by some sound in the house. It had ceased ere I was wide awake, but it had left an impression behind it as though a window had gently closed somewhere. I lay listening with all my ears. Suddenly, to my horror, there was a distinct sound of footsteps moving softly in the next room. I slipped out of bed, all palpitating with fear, and peeped round the corner of my dressing-room door.

" ' Arthur ! ' I screamed, ' you villain ! you thief ! How dare you touch that coronet ? '

" The gas was half up, as I had left it, and my unhappy boy, dressed only in his shirt and trousers, was standing beside the light, holding the coronet in his hands. He appeared to be wrenching at it, or bending it with all his strength. At my cry he dropped it from his grasp, and turned as pale as death. I snatched it up and examined it. One of the gold corners, with three of the beryls in it, was missing.

" ' You blackguard ! ' I shouted, beside myself with rage. ' You have destroyed it ! You have dishonoured me for ever ! Where are the jewels you have stolen ? '

" ' Stolen ! ' he cried.

" ' Yes, you thief ! ' I roared, shaking him by the shoulder.

" ' There are none missing. There cannot be any missing,' said he.

" ' There are three missing. And you know where they

5 *the third demand during the month.* Perhaps an indication that "The Adventure of the Beryl Coronet" took place later rather than earlier in the month under consideration.

" 'YOU SHALL NOT HAVE A FARTHING FROM ME . . .' "

Shown is the 1841 Victoria farthing. "The farthing (fourthing or quarter-penny)," the late A. Carson Simpson wrote in *Numismatics in the Canon:* Part I, "was originally made from the silver penny, as a home-workshop project, in the same way as the halfpenny; it required only an additional cut along the other arm of the voided cross. This type was also replaced by a circular silver farthing, one year earlier than the halfpenny." This is the only Canonical reference to the farthing.

are. Must I call you a liar as well as a thief? Did I not see you trying to tear off another piece?'

"'You have called me names enough,' said he; 'I will not stand it any longer. I shall not say another word about this business since you have chosen to insult me. I will leave your house in the morning, and make my own way in the world.'

"'You shall leave it in the hands of the police!' I cried, half mad with grief and rage. 'I shall have this matter probed to the bottom.'

"'You shall learn nothing from me,' said he, with a passion such as I should not have thought was in his nature. 'If you choose to call the police, let them find what they can.'

"By this time the whole house was astir, for I had raised my voice in my anger. Mary was the first to rush into my room, and at the sight of the coronet and of Arthur's face, she read the whole story, and, with a scream, fell down senseless on the ground. I sent the housemaid for the police, and put the investigation into their hands at once. When the inspector and a constable entered the house, Arthur, who had stood sullenly with his arms folded, asked me whether it was my intention to charge him with theft. I answered that it had ceased to be a private matter, but had become a public one, since the ruined coronet was national property. I was determined that the law should have its way in everything.

"'At least,' said he, 'you will not have me arrested at once. It would be to your advantage as well as mine if I might leave the house for five minutes.'

"'That you may get away, or perhaps that you may conceal what you have stolen,' said I. And then realizing the dreadful position in which I was placed, I implored him to remember that not only my honour, but that of one who was far greater than I, was at stake; and that he threatened to raise a scandal which would convulse the nation. He might avert it all if he would but tell me what he had done with the three missing stones.

"'You may as well face the matter,' said I; 'you have been caught in the act, and no confession could make your guilt more heinous. If you but make such reparation as is in your power, by telling us where the beryls are, all shall be forgiven and forgotten.'

"'Keep your forgiveness for those who ask for it,' he answered, turning away from me with a sneer. I saw that he was too hardened for any words of mine to influence him. There was but one way for it. I called in the inspector, and gave him into custody. A search was made at once, not only of his person, but of his room, and of every portion of the house where he could possibly have concealed the gems; but no trace of them could be found, nor would the wretched boy open his mouth for all our persuasions and our threats. This morning he was removed to a cell, and I, after going through all the police formalities, have hurried round to you, to implore you to use your skill in unravelling the matter. The police have openly confessed that they can at present make nothing of it. You may go to any expense which you think necessary. I have already offered a reward of a thousand pounds. My

"AT MY CRY HE DROPPED IT FROM HIS GRASP . . ."

Illustration by Sidney Paget for the *Strand Magazine*, May, 1892.

God, what shall I do! I have lost my honour, my gems, and my son in one night. Oh, what shall I do!"

He put a hand on either side of his head, and rocked himself to and fro, droning to himself like a child whose grief has got beyond words.

Sherlock Holmes sat silent for some few minutes, with his brows knitted and his eyes fixed upon the fire.

"Do you receive much company?" he asked.

"None, save my partner with his family, and an occasional friend of Arthur's. Sir George Burnwell has been several times lately. No one else, I think."

"Do you go out much in society?"

"Arthur does. Mary and I stay at home. We neither of us care for it."

"That is unusual in a young girl."

"She is of a quiet nature. Besides, she is not so very young. She is four-and-twenty."

"This matter, from what you say, seems to have been a shock to her also."

"Terrible! She is even more affected than I."

"You have neither of you any doubt as to your son's guilt?"

"How can we have, when I saw him with my own eyes with the coronet in his hands?"

"I hardly consider that a conclusive proof. Was the remainder of the coronet at all injured?"

"Yes, it was twisted."

"Do you not think, then, that he might have been trying to straighten it?"

"God bless you! You are doing what you can for him and for me. But it is too heavy a task. What was he doing there at all? If his purpose were innocent, why did he not say so?"

"Precisely. And if he were guilty, why did he not invent a lie? His silence appears to me to cut both ways. There are several singular points about the case. What did the police think of the noise which awoke you from your sleep?"

"They considered that it might be caused by Arthur's closing his bedroom door."

"A likely story! As if a man bent on felony would slam the door so as to awake a household. What did they say, then, of the disappearance of these gems?"

"They are still sounding the planking and probing the furniture in the hope of finding them."

"Have they thought of looking outside the house?"

"Yes, they have shown extraordinary energy. The whole garden has already been minutely examined."

"Now, my dear sir," said Holmes, "is it not obvious to you now that this matter really strikes very much deeper than either you or the police were at first inclined to think? It appeared to you to be a simple case; to me it seems exceedingly complex. Consider what is involved by your theory. You suppose that your son came down from his bed, went, at great risk, to your dressing-room, opened your bureau, took out your coronet, broke off by main force a small portion of it, went off to some other place, concealed three gems out of the thirty-nine, with such skill that nobody can find them, and then returned with the other thirty-six into the room in which he exposed himself to the greatest danger of being discovered. I ask you now, is such a theory tenable ? "

" But what other is there ? " cried the banker with a gesture of despair. " If his motives were innocent, why does he not explain them ? "

" It is our task to find that out," replied Holmes, " so now, if you please, Mr. Holder, we will set off for Streatham together and devote an hour to glancing a little more closely into details."

My friend insisted upon my accompanying them in their expedition, which I was eager enough to do, for my curiosity and sympathy were deeply stirred by the story to which we had listened. I confess that the guilt of the banker's son appeared to me to be as obvious as it did to his unhappy father, but still I had such faith in Holmes' judgment that I felt that there must be some grounds for hope as long as he was dissatisfied with the accepted explanation. He hardly spoke a word the whole way out to the southern suburb, but sat with his chin upon his breast, and his hat drawn over his eyes, sunk in the deepest thought. Our client appeared to have taken fresh heart at the little glimpse of hope which had been presented to him, and he even broke into a desultory chat with me over his business affairs. A short railway journey, and a shorter walk, brought us to Fairbank, the modest residence of the great financier.

Fairbank was a good-sized square house of white stone, standing back a little from the road. A double carriage sweep, with a snow-clad lawn, stretched down in front to the two large iron gates which closed the entrance. On the right side was a small wooden thicket which led into a narrow path between two neat hedges stretching from the road to the kitchen door, and forming the tradesmen's entrance. On the left ran a lane which led to the stables, and was not itself within the grounds at all, being a public, though little used, thoroughfare. Holmes left us standing at the door, and walked slowly all round the house, across the front, down the tradesmen's path, and so round by the garden behind into the stable lane. So long was he that Mr. Holder and I went into the dining-room, and waited by the fire until he should return. We were sitting there in silence when the door opened, and a young lady came in. She was rather above the middle height, slim, with dark hair and eyes, which seemed the darker against the absolute pallor of her skin. I do not think that I have ever seen such deadly paleness in a woman's face. Her lips, too, were bloodless, but her eyes were flushed with crying. As she swept silently into the room she impressed me with a greater sense of her grief than the banker had done in the morning, and it was the more striking in her as she was evidently a woman of strong character, with immense capacity for self-restraint. Disregarding my presence, she went straight to her uncle, and passed her hand over his head with a sweet womanly caress.

" You have given orders that Arthur should be liberated, have you not, dad ? " she asked.

" No, no, my girl, the matter must be probed to the bottom."

DISREGARDING MY PRESENCE, SHE WENT STRAIGHT TO HER UNCLE . . .

Illustration by Sidney Paget for the *Strand Magazine,* May, 1892.

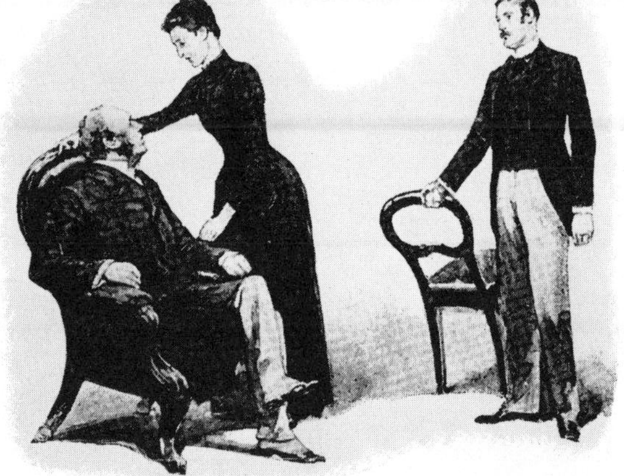

" But I am so sure that he is innocent. You know what women's instincts are. I know that he has done no harm, and that you will be sorry for having acted so harshly."

" Why is he silent, then, if he is innocent ? "

" Who knows ? Perhaps because he was so angry that you should suspect him."

" How could I help suspecting him, when I actually saw him with the coronet in his hand ? "

" Oh, but he had only picked it up to look at it. Oh, do, do take my word for it that he is innocent. Let the matter drop, and say no more. It is so dreadful to think of our dear Arthur in prison ! "

" I shall never let it drop until the gems are found—never, Mary ! Your affection for Arthur blinds you as to the awful consequences to me. Far from hushing the thing up, I have brought a gentleman down from London to inquire more deeply into it."

" This gentleman ? " she asked, facing round to me.

" No, his friend. He wished us to leave him alone. He is round in the stable lane now."

" The stable lane ? " She raised her dark eyebrows. " What can he hope to find there ? Ah, this, I suppose, is he. I trust, sir, that you will succeed in proving, what I feel sure is the truth, that my cousin Arthur is innocent of this crime."

" I fully share your opinion, and, I trust with you, that we may prove it," returned Holmes, going back to the mat to knock the snow from his shoes. " I believe I have the honour of addressing Miss Mary Holder. Might I ask you a question or two ? "

" Pray do, sir, if it may help to clear this horrible affair up."

" You heard nothing yourself last night ? "

" Nothing, until my uncle here began to speak loudly. I heard that, and I came down."

" You shut up the windows and doors the night before. Did you fasten all the windows ? "

" Yes."

" Were they all fastened this morning ? "

" Yes."

" You have a maid who has a sweetheart ? I think that you remarked to your uncle last night that she had been out to see him ? "

" Yes, and she was the girl who waited in the drawing-room, and who may have heard uncle's remarks about the coronet."

" I see. You infer that she may have gone out to tell her sweetheart, and that the two may have planned the robbery."

" But what is the good of all these vague theories," cried the banker impatiently, " when I have told you that I saw Arthur with the coronet in his hands ? "

" Wait a little, Mr. Holder. We must come back to that. About this girl, Miss Holder. You saw her return by the kitchen door, I presume ? "

" Yes ; when I went to see if the door was fastened for the night I met her slipping in. I saw the man, too, in the gloom."

" Do you know him ? "

" Oh, yes ; he is the greengrocer who brings our vegetables round. His name is Francis Prosper."

" He stood," said Holmes, " to the left of the door—that is to say, farther up the path than is necessary to reach the door ? "

" Yes, he did."

" And he is a man with a wooden leg ? "

Something like fear sprang up in the young lady's expressive black eyes. " Why, you are like a magician," said she. " How do you know that ? " She smiled, but there was no answering smile in Holmes' thin, eager face.

" I should be very glad now to go upstairs," said he. " I shall probably wish to go over the outside of the house again. Perhaps I had better take a look at the lower windows before I go up."

He walked swiftly round from one to the other, pausing only at the large one which looked from the hall on to the stable lane. This he opened, and made a very careful examination of the sill with his powerful magnifying lens. " Now we shall go upstairs," said he, at last.

The banker's dressing-room was a plainly furnished little chamber with a grey carpet, a large bureau, and a long mirror. Holmes went to the bureau first, and looked hard at the lock.

" Which key was used to open it ? " he asked.

" That which my son himself indicated—that of the cupboard of the lumber-room."

" Have you it here ? "

" That is it on the dressing-table."

Sherlock Holmes took it up and opened the bureau.

" It is a noiseless lock," said he. " It is no wonder that it did not wake you. This case, I presume, contains the coronet. We must have a look at it." He opened the case, and, taking out the diadem, he laid it upon the table. It was a magnificent specimen of the jeweller's art, and the thirty-six stones were the finest that I have ever seen. At one side of the coronet was a crooked cracked edge, where a corner holding three gems had been torn away.

" Now, Mr. Holder," said Holmes ; " here is the corner which corresponds to that which has been so unfortunately lost. Might I beg that you will break it off."

The banker recoiled in horror. " I should not dream of trying," said he.

" Then I will." Holmes suddenly bent his strength upon it, but without result. " I feel it give a little," said he ; " but, though I am exceptionally strong in the fingers, it would take me all my time to break it. An ordinary man could not do it. Now, what do you think would happen if I did break it, Mr. Holder ? There would be a noise like a pistol shot. Do you tell me that all this happened within a few yards of your bed, and that you heard nothing of it ? "

" I do not know what to think. It is all dark to me."

" But perhaps it may grow lighter as we go. What do you think, Miss Holder ? "

" I confess that I still share my uncle's perplexity."

" Your son had no shoes or slippers on when you saw him ? "

SOMETHING LIKE FEAR SPRANG UP IN THE YOUNG LADY'S EXPRESSIVE BLACK EYES.

Illustration by Sidney Paget for the *Strand Magazine*, May, 1892.

HE . . . WAS DOWN AGAIN IN A FEW MINUTES DRESSED AS A COMMON LOAFER.

Illustration by Sidney Paget for the *Strand Magazine*, May, 1892.

" He had nothing on save only his trousers and shirt."

" Thank you. We have certainly been favoured with extraordinary luck during this inquiry, and it will be entirely our own fault if we do not succeed in clearing the matter up. With your permission, Mr. Holder, I shall now continue my investigations outside."

He went alone, at his own request, for he explained that any unnecessary footmarks might make his task more difficult. For an hour or more he was at work, returning at last with his feet heavy with snow and his features as inscrutable as ever.

" I think that I have seen now all that there is to see, Mr. Holder," said he ; " I can serve you best by returning to my rooms."

" But the gems, Mr. Holmes. Where are they ? "

" I cannot tell."

The banker wrung his hands. " I shall never see them again ! " he cried. " And my son ? You give me hopes ? "

" My opinion is in no way altered."

" Then for God's sake what was this dark business which was acted in my house last night ? "

" If you can call upon me at my Baker Street rooms to-morrow morning between nine and ten I shall be happy to do what I can to make it clearer. I understand that you give me *carte blanche* to act for you, provided only that I get back the gems, and that you place no limit on the sum I may draw."

" I would give my fortune to have them back."

" Very good. I shall look into the matter between this and then. Good-bye ; it is just possible that I may have to come over here again before evening."

It was obvious to me that my companion's mind was now made up about the case, although what his conclusions were was more than I could even dimly imagine. Several times during our homeward journey I endeavoured to sound him upon that point, but he always glided away to some other topic, until at last I gave it over in despair. It was not yet three when we found ourselves in our room once more. He hurried to his chamber, and was down again in a few minutes dressed as a common loafer. With his collar turned up, his shiny seedy coat, his red cravat, and his worn boots, he was a perfect sample of the class.

" I think that this should do," said he, glancing into the glass above the fireplace. " I only wish that you could come with me, Watson, but I fear that it won't do. I may be on the trail in this matter, or I may be following a will-o'-the-wisp, but I shall soon know which it is. I hope that I may be back in a few hours." He cut a slice of beef from the joint upon the sideboard, sandwiched it between two rounds of bread, and, thrusting this rude meal into his pocket, he started off upon his expedition.

I had just finished my tea when he returned, evidently in excellent spirits, swinging an old elastic-sided boot in his hand. He chucked it down into a corner and helped himself to a cup of tea.

" I only looked in as I passed," said he. " I am going right on."

" Where to ? "

" Oh, to the other side of the West End. It may be some time before I get back. Don't wait up for me in case I should be late."

" How are you getting on ? "

" Oh, so-so. Nothing to complain of. I have been out to Streatham since I saw you last, but I did not call at the house. It is a very sweet little problem, and I would not have missed it for a good deal. However, I must not sit gossiping here, but must get these disreputable clothes off and return to my highly respectable self."

I could see by his manner that he had stronger reasons for satisfaction than his words alone would imply. His eyes twinkled, and there was even a touch of colour upon his sallow cheeks. He hastened upstairs, and a few minutes later I heard the slam of the hall door, which told me that he was off once more upon his congenial hunt.

I waited until midnight, but there was no sign of his return, so I retired to my room. It was no uncommon thing for him to be away for days and nights on end when he was hot upon a scent, so that his lateness caused me no surprise. I do not know at what hour he came in, but when I came down to breakfast in the morning, there he was with a cup of coffee in one hand and the paper in the other, as fresh and trim as possible.

" You will excuse my beginning without you, Watson," said he ; " but you remember that our client has rather an early appointment this morning."

" Why, it is after nine now," I answered. " I should not be surprised if that were he. I thought I heard a ring."

It was, indeed, our friend the financier. I was shocked by the change which had come over him, for his face, which was naturally of a broad and massive mould, was now pinched and fallen in, while his hair seemed to be at least a shade whiter. He entered with a weariness and lethargy which was even more painful than his violence of the morning before, and he dropped heavily into the armchair which I pushed forward for him.

" I do not know what I have done to be so severely tried," said he. " Only two days ago I was a happy and prosperous man, without a care in the world. Now I am left to a lonely and dishonoured age. One sorrow comes close upon the heels of another. My niece Mary has deserted me."

" Deserted you ? "

" Yes. Her bed this morning had not been slept in, her room was empty, and a note lay for me upon the hall table. I had said to her last night, in sorrow and not in anger, that if she had married my boy all might have been well with him. Perhaps it was thoughtless of me to say so. It is to that remark that she refers in this note : ' My dearest Uncle—I feel that I have brought this trouble upon you, and that if I had acted differently this terrible misfortune might never have occurred. I cannot, with this thought in my mind, ever again be happy under your roof, and I feel that I must leave you for ever. Do not worry about my future, for that is provided for ; and, above all, do not search for me, for it will be fruitless labour, and an ill service to me. In life or in death, I am ever your loving—MARY.' What could she mean by that note, Mr. Holmes? Do you think it points to suicide?"

"No, no, nothing of the kind. It is perhaps the best possible solution. I trust, Mr. Holder, that you are nearing the end of your troubles."

"Ha! You say so! You have heard something, Mr. Holmes; you have learned something! Where are the gems?"

"You would not think a thousand pounds apiece an excessive sum for them?"

"I would pay ten."

"That would be unnecessary. Three thousand will cover the matter. And there is a little reward, I fancy. Have you your cheque-book? Here is a pen. Better make it out for four thousand pounds."

With a dazed face the banker made out the required cheque. Holmes walked over to his desk, took out a little triangular piece of gold with three gems in it, and threw it down upon the table.

With a shriek of joy our client clutched it up.

"You have it!" he gasped. "I am saved! I am saved!"

The reaction of joy was as passionate as his grief had been, and he hugged his recovered gems to his bosom.

"There is one other thing you owe, Mr. Holder," said Sherlock Holmes, rather sternly.

"Owe!" He caught up a pen. "Name the sum, and I will pay it."

"No, the debt is not to me. You owe a very humble apology to that noble lad, your son, who has carried himself in this matter as I should be proud to see my own son
6 do, should I ever chance to have one."

"Then it was not Arthur who took them?"

"I told you yesterday, and I repeat to-day, that it was not."

"You are sure of it! Then let us hurry to him at once, to let him know that the truth is known."

"He knows it already. When I had cleared it all up I had an interview with him, and finding that he would not tell me the story, I told it to him, on which he had to confess that I was right, and to add the very few details which were not yet quite clear to me. Your news of this morning, however, may open his lips."

"For Heaven's sake tell me, then, what is this extraordinary mystery!"

"I will do so, and I will show you the steps by which I reached it. And let me say to you, first, what it is hardest for me to say and for you to hear. There has been an understanding between Sir George Burnwell and your niece, Mary. They have now fled together."

"My Mary? Impossible!"

"It is, unfortunately, more than possible; it is certain. Neither you nor your son knew the true character of this man when you admitted him into your family circle. He is one of the most dangerous men in England—a ruined gambler, an absolutely desperate villain; a man without

6 *as I should be proud to see my own son do.* Like Holmes' remark in "The Adventure of the Copper Beeches" ("I confess that it is not the situation which I should like to see a sister of mine apply for") this statement has furnished commentators with considerable grounds for speculation.

Mr. Rex Stout has suggested ("Watson Was a Woman") that Lord Peter Death Bredon Wimsey was a son of the Master Detective; Dr. John D. Clark ("Some Notes Relating to a Preliminary Investigation Into the Paternity of Nero Wolfe") and your editor (*Sherlock Holmes of Baker Street*) have supported the theory that a better case can be made for someone considerably closer to Mr. Stout than Lord Peter; Mr. Marion Prince has put in a claim ("Sherlock and Son") for Inspector Stanley Hopkins; the late A. Carson Simpson advanced the interesting theory ("I'm Off for Philadelphia in the Morning") that Joseph Rouletabille, the young reporter-detective hero of seven novels by Gaston Leroux, 1868–1927, distinguished French journalist and author, was a son of Sherlock; and Mr. Manly Wade Wellman's candidate for the honor ("The Great Man's Great Son") is Bertie Wooster's bulging-browed valet, Jeeves.

"The End of Sherlock Holmes," an unusual pastiche signed A.E.P., would have us believe that Holmes married Miss Alice Falkland (of William Gillette's play, *Sherlock Holmes*) *circa* 1903–1905 and by her had a son. Mr. Ellery Queen, commenting on this in his *Misadventures of Sherlock Holmes*, there added: "Other instances dealing with the scion of Sherlock Holmes include John Kendrick Bangs' Raffles Holmes, who was the 'son' of Sherlock and the 'grandson' of Raffles . . . ; and Sherlock Holmes, Jr., the hero of a color-comic series that appeared in the Sunday supplements of many American newspapers between 1911 and 1914, drawn by no less a person than Sidney Smith, the creator of the famous 'Gumps.' There is also Frederic Arnold Kummer's and Basil Mitchell's Shirley Holmes, daughter of Sherlock, assisted by Joan Watson, daughter of Dr. Watson . . ."

heart or conscience. Your niece knew nothing of such 7
men. When he breathed his vows to her, as he had done to a hundred before her, she flattered herself that she alone had touched his heart. The devil knows best what he said, but at last she became his tool, and was in the habit of seeing him nearly every evening."

"I cannot, and I will not, believe it!" cried the banker with an ashen face.

"I will tell you, then, what occurred in your house that night. Your niece, when you had, as she thought, gone to your room, slipped down and talked to her lover through the window which leads into the stable lane. His footmarks had pressed right through the snow, so long had he stood there. She told him of the coronet. His wicked lust for gold kindled at the news, and he bent her to his will. I have no doubt that she loved you, but there are women in whom the love of a lover extinguishes all other loves, and I think that she must have been one. She had hardly listened to his instructions when she saw you coming downstairs, on which she closed the window rapidly, and told you about one of the servants' escapade with her wooden-legged lover, which was all perfectly true.

"Your boy, Arthur, went to bed after his interview with you, but he slept badly on account of his uneasiness about his club debts. In the middle of the night he heard a soft tread pass his door, so he rose, and looking out, was surprised to see his cousin walking very stealthily along the passage, until she disappeared into your dressing-room. Petrified with astonishment the lad slipped on some clothes, and waited there in the dark to see what would come of this strange affair. Presently she emerged from the room again, and in the light of the passage lamp your son saw that she carried the precious coronet in her hands. She passed down the stairs, and he, thrilling with horror, ran along and slipped behind the curtain near your door whence he could see what passed in the hall beneath. He saw her stealthily open the window, hand out the coronet to someone in the gloom, and then closing it once more hurry back to her room, passing quite close to where he stood hid behind the curtain.

"As long as she was on the scene he could not take any action without a horrible exposure of the woman whom he loved. But the instant she was gone he realized how crushing a misfortune this would be for you, and how all-important it was to set it right. He rushed down, just as he was, in his bare feet, opened the window, sprang out into the snow, and ran down the lane, where he could see a
dark figure in the moonlight. Sir George Burnwell tried 8
to get away, but Arthur caught him, and there was a struggle between them, your lad tugging at one side of the coronet, and his opponent at the other. In the scuffle, your son struck Sir George, and cut him over the eye. Then something suddenly snapped, and your son, finding that he had the coronet in his hands, rushed back, closed the window, ascended to your room, and had just observed that the coronet had been twisted in the struggle and was endeavouring to straighten it, when you appeared upon the scene."

7 *a man without heart or conscience.* The late Robert R. Pattrick maintained ("Moriarty Was There") that "the entire affair of the Beryl Coronet has sinister overtones which have never been properly examined. Burnwell's careful cultivation of the friendships of both Arthur and Mary smacks of a devious plot being brewed. Surely it was not entirely by chance he was lurking outside the house the very night the Coronet was brought there. It seems probable that [Burnwell] was a Moriarty agent assigned especially to confiscate the Coronet."

8 *a dark figure in the moonlight.* It must be admitted that the moon was wrong for both of the dates suggested by the snowfall (March 17, 1887, and December 18, 1890). The moon did not rise until 3:09 on the morning of Friday, March 18, 1887; it set at 11:46 on the night of Thursday, December 18, 1890, to rise again at 12:51 P.M. on Friday, December 19th.

. . . ARTHUR CAUGHT HIM . . .

Illustration by Sidney Paget for the *Strand Magazine*, May, 1892.

" Is it possible ? " gasped the banker.

" You then roused his anger by calling him names at a moment when he felt that he had deserved your warmest thanks. He could not explain the true state of affairs without betraying one who certainly deserved little enough consideration at his hands. He took the more chivalrous view, however, and preserved her secret."

" And that was why she shrieked and fainted when she saw the coronet," cried Mr. Holder. " Oh, my God ! what a blind fool I have been. And his asking to be allowed to go out for five minutes ! The dear fellow wanted to see if the missing piece were at the scene of the struggle. How cruelly I have misjudged him ! "

" When I arrived at the house," continued Holmes, " I at once went very carefully round it to observe if there were any traces in the snow which might help me. I knew that none had fallen since the evening before, and also that there had been a strong frost to preserve impressions. I passed along the tradesmen's path, but found it all trampled down and indistinguishable. Just beyond it, however, at the far side of the kitchen door, a woman had stood and talked with a man, whose round impression on one side showed that he had a wooden leg. I could even tell that they had been disturbed, for the woman had run back swiftly to the door, as was shown by the deep toe and light heel-marks, while Wooden-leg had waited a little, and then had gone away. I thought at the time that this might be the maid and her sweetheart, of whom you had already spoken to me, and inquiry showed it was so. I passed round the garden without seeing anything more than random tracks, which I took to be the police ; but when I got into the stable lane a very long and complex story was written in the snow in front of me.

" There was a double line of tracks of a booted man, and a second double line which I saw with delight belonged to a man with naked feet. I was at once convinced from what you had told me that the latter was your son. The first had walked both ways, but the other had run swiftly, and, as his tread was marked in places over the depression of the boot, it was obvious that he had passed after the other. I followed them up, and found that they led to the hall window, where Boots had worn all the snow away while waiting. Then I walked to the other end, which was a hundred yards or more down the lane. I saw where Boots had faced round, where the snow was cut up, as though there had been a struggle, and, finally, where a few drops of blood had fallen, to show me that I was not mistaken. Boots had then run down the lane, and another little smudge of blood showed that it was he who had been hurt. When he came to the high-road at the other end, I found that the pavement had been cleared, so there was an end to that clue.

" On entering the house, however, I examined, as you remember, the sill and framework of the hall window with my lens, and I could at once see that someone had passed out. I could distinguish the outline of an instep where the wet foot had been placed in coming in. I was then beginning to be able to form an opinion as to what had occurred. A man had waited outside the window, someone had brought him the gems ; the deed had been overseen by your son, he had pursued the thief, had struggled with him, they had each tugged at the coronet, their united strength causing injuries which neither alone could have effected. He had returned with the prize, but had left a fragment in the grasp of his opponent. So far I was clear. The question now was, who was the man, and who was it brought him the coronet ?

" It is an old maxim of mine that when you have excluded the impossible, whatever remains, however improbable, must be the truth. Now, I knew that it was not you who had brought it down, so there only remained your niece and the maids. But if it were the maids, why should your son allow himself to be accused in their place ? There could be no possible reason. As he loved his cousin, however, there was an excellent explanation why he should retain her secret—the more so as the secret was a disgraceful one. When I remembered that you had seen her at that window, and how she had fainted on seeing the coronet again, my conjecture became a certainty.

" And who could it be who was her confederate ? A lover evidently, for who else could outweigh the love and gratitude which she must feel to you ? I knew that you went out little, and that your circle of friends was a very limited one. But among them was Sir George Burnwell. I had heard of him before as being a man of evil reputation among women. It must have been he who wore those boots, and retained the missing gems. Even though he knew that Arthur had discovered him, he might still flatter himself that he was safe, for the lad could not say a word without compromising his own family.

" Well, your own good sense will suggest what measures I took next. I went in the shape of a loafer to Sir George's house, managed to pick up an acquaintance with his valet, learned that his master had cut his head the night before, and finally, at the expense of six shillings, made all sure by buying a pair of his cast-off shoes. With these I journeyed down to Streatham, and saw that they exactly fitted the tracks."

" I saw an ill-dressed vagabond in the lane yesterday 9
evening," said Mr. Holder.

" Precisely. It was I. I found that I had my man, so I came home and changed my clothes. It was a delicate part which I had to play then, for I saw that a prosecution must be avoided to avert scandal, and I knew that so astute a villain would see that our hands were tied in the matter. I went and saw him. At first, of course, he denied everything. But when I gave him every particular that had occurred, he tried to bluster, and took down a life-preserver from the wall. I knew my man, however, and I clapped a pistol to his head before he could strike. Then he became a little more reasonable. I told him that we would give him a price for the stones he held—a thousand pounds apiece. That brought out the first signs of grief he had shown. ' Why, dash it all ! ' said he, ' I've let them go at

". . . I CLAPPED A PISTOL TO HIS HEAD . . ."

Illustration by Sidney Paget for the *Strand Magazine*, May, 1892. As Mr. Robert Keith Leavitt has observed ("Annie Oakley in Baker Street") "whenever [Holmes] had occasion to pull a gun on a really desperate character, he got as near as possible to his man before showing his weapon. His standard practice of clapping a pistol right against his captive's head [see also "The Adventure of the Dancing Men" and "The Adventure of the Mazarin Stone"] is ample evidence of awareness of personal fallability with the handgun."

9 *an ill-dressed vagabond.* "One might wonder if there was such a thing as a 'well-dressed vagabond' in those days," the late Page Heldenbrand commented in "Sherlock Holmes in Disguise."

six hundred for the three!' I soon managed to get the address of the receiver who had them, on promising him that there would be no prosecution. Off I set to him, and after much chaffering I got our stones at a thousand apiece. Then I looked in upon your son, told him that all was right, and eventually got to my bed about two o'clock, after what I may call a really hard day's work."

"A day which has saved England from a great public
10 scandal," said the banker, rising. "Sir, I cannot find
words to thank you, but you shall not find me ungrateful for what you have done. Your skill has indeed exceeded all that I have ever heard of it. And now I must fly to my dear boy to apologize to him for the wrong which I have done him. As to what you tell me of poor Mary, it goes to my heart. Not even your skill can inform me where she is now."

"I think that we may safely say," returned Holmes, "that she is wherever Sir George Burnwell is. It is equally certain, too, that whatever her sins are, they will soon receive a more than sufficient punishment."

10 "*A day which has saved England from a great public scandal.*" "The injuries to the coronet pose a problem for which there seems to be no solution," the late A. Carson Simpson wrote in "Whose Was It? Conjectures on a Coronet." "We are told that 'any injury' to it would be almost as serious as its complete loss.' But it was in fact injured, being twisted out of shape and having a piece broken off. How did Alexander Holder expect to get it made as good as new between Saturday morning, when he got back the missing piece, and the following Monday, when the borrower would return to reclaim it? If this could not be done, how did he expect to placate the borrower on Monday, unless by a little genteel blackmail? Apparently he did not worry about these questions, for his first act, after getting back the missing piece, was to rush off—not to the nearest goldsmith, as one might expect, but—to make his peace with his son Arthur."

47

THE FINAL PROBLEM

[Friday, April 24, to Monday, May 4, 1891]

IT is with a heavy heart that I take up my pen to write these the last words in which I shall ever record the singular gifts by which my friend Mr. Sherlock Holmes was distinguished. In an incoherent and, as I deeply feel, an entirely inadequate fashion, I have endeavoured to give some account of my strange experiences in his company from the chance which first brought us together at the period of the "Study in Scarlet," up to the time of his interference in the matter
of the "Naval Treaty"—an interference which had the 1
unquestionable effect of preventing a serious international complication. It was my intention to have stopped there, and to have said nothing of that event which has created a void in my life which the lapse of two years has done little to fill. My hand has been forced, however, by the recent letters in which Colonel James Moriarty defends the memory of his brother, and I have no choice but to lay the facts before the public exactly as they occurred. I alone know the absolute truth of the matter, and I am satisfied that the time has come when no good purpose is to be served by its suppression. As far as I know, there have been only three accounts in the public Press: that in the *Journal de Genève* upon May 6th, 1891, the Reuter's despatch in the English papers upon May 7th, and finally the recent letters to which I have alluded. Of these the first and second were extremely condensed, while the last is, as I shall now show, an absolute perversion of the facts. It lies with me to tell for the first time what really took place between Professor Moriarty and Mr. Sherlock Holmes.

It may be remembered that after my marriage, and my subsequent start in private practice, the very intimate relations which had existed between Holmes and myself became to some extent modified. He still came to me from time to time when he desired a companion in his investigations, but these occasions grew more and more seldom, until I find that in the year 1890 there were only
three cases of which I retain any record. During the 2
winter of that year and the early spring of 1891, I saw in
the papers that he had been engaged by the French
Government upon a matter of supreme importance, and I 3
received two notes from Holmes, dated from Narbonne 4
and from Nîmes, from which I gathered that his stay in
France was likely to be a long one. It was with some 5

1 *in the matter of the "Naval Treaty."* As the late Dr. Ernest Bloomfield Zeisler wrote (*Baker Street Chronology*): "Watson was obviously thinking of the dates of publication, as we see that 'The Naval Treaty' was the last case published before the publication of 'The Final Problem.'"

2 *there were only three cases of which I retain any record.* The three cases, as we have seen, were "The Adventure of Wisteria Lodge," "Silver Blaze" and "The Adventure of the Beryl Coronet."

3 *a matter of supreme importance.* In his prize-winning essay, "Study of an Untold Tale," Mr. Edward F. Clark, Jr., has shown that Holmes' service to the French Government was to recover a famous painting stolen from the Louvre by the English Napoleon of Crime, Professor James Moriarty, and his gang. The recovery was made in the south of France on or about February 15th—i.e., "the middle of February" in Moriarty's later complaint to Holmes.

4 *Narbonne.* Since Narbonne is famous for its honey, it has been suggested that Holmes may have got his first interest in beekeeping there.

5 *his stay in France was likely to be a long one.* Mrs. Winifred M. Christie has noted ("On the Remarkable Explorations of Sigerson") that Holmes "was necessarily much in France" in the early months of 1891. "On January 31, 1891, Monsieur Gabriel Bonvalot, Prince Henry of Orleans and Father Dedeken gave an illustrated talk on their work in Tibet to the French Geographical Society in Paris. Mr. Holmes may easily have heard their lecture." This, Mrs. Christie suggests, may have been one of the factors that led Holmes, during the years of the Great Hiatus, to travel for two years in Tibet.

6 *the 24th of April.* A Friday in 1891.

7 "*Of air-guns.*" Not to be confused with the air rifles so dear to the heart of the American boy. As Mr. William Perceval wrote in "Sherlock Holmes and Air-Guns": "The first known example of an air-gun was a single shot model made by Güter of Nuremberg as long ago as 1530. Other German gunsmiths, such as Lobsinger (1550) and Mavin (1600), then developed a repeating air-gun. One maker at this period, Dumbler, even perfected a gun which could fire through a 1-inch plank, but was forbidden to market it on the ground that it was 'a murderous weapon with which a man might be killed and yet not know what hit him.' Indeed so unsporting was the weapon thought to be that gunmakers made air-guns resemble ordinary muskets as much as possible."

. . . I SAW IN THE LIGHT OF THE LAMP THAT TWO OF HIS KNUCKLES WERE BURST AND BLEEDING.

Illustration by Sidney Paget for the *Strand Magazine*, December, 1893.

"AYE, THERE'S THE GENIUS AND THE WONDER OF THE THING!" HE CRIED.

Illustration by Harry C. Edwards for *McClure's Magazine*, December, 1893.

surprise, therefore, that I saw him walk into my consult-
6 ing-room upon the evening of the 24th of April. It struck me that he was looking even paler and thinner than usual.

"Yes, I have been using myself up rather too freely," he remarked, in answer to my look rather than to my words; "I have been a little pressed of late. Have you any objection to my closing your shutters?"

The only light in the room came from the lamp upon the table at which I had been reading. Holmes edged his way round the wall, and flinging the shutters together, he bolted them securely.

"You are afraid of something?" I asked.

"Well, I am."

"Of what?"

7 "Of air-guns."

"My dear Holmes, what do you mean?"

"I think that you know me well enough, Watson, to understand that I am by no means a nervous man. At the same time, it is stupidity rather than courage to refuse to recognize danger when it is close upon you. Might I trouble you for a match?" He drew in the smoke of his cigarette as if the soothing influence was grateful to him.

"I must apologize for calling so late," said he, "and I must further beg you to be so unconventional as to allow me to leave your house presently by scrambling over your back garden wall."

"But what does it all mean?" I asked.

He held out his hand, and I saw in the light of the lamp that two of his knuckles were burst and bleeding.

"It's not an airy nothing, you see," said he, smiling. "On the contrary, it is solid enough for a man to break his hand over. Is Mrs. Watson in?"

"She is away upon a visit."

"Indeed! You are alone?"

"Quite."

"Then it makes it the easier for me to propose that you should come away with me for a week on to the Continent."

"Where?"

"Oh, anywhere. It's all the same to me."

There was something very strange in all this. It was not Holmes' nature to take an aimless holiday, and something about his pale, worn face told me that his nerves were at their highest tension. He saw the question in my eyes, and, putting his finger-tips together and his elbows upon his knees, he explained the situation.

"You have probably never heard of Professor Moriarty?" said he.

8 "Never."

"Aye, there's the genius and the wonder of the thing!" he cried. "The man pervades London, and no one has heard of him. That's what puts him on a pinnacle in the records of crime. I tell you, Watson, in all seriousness, that if I could beat that man, if I could free society of him, I should feel that my own career had reached its summit, and I should be prepared to turn to some more placid line in life. Between ourselves, the recent cases in

which I have been of assistance to the Royal Family of Scandinavia, and to the French Republic, have left me in such a position that I could continue to live in the quiet fashion which is most congenial to me, and to concentrate my attention upon my chemical researches. But I could 9
not rest, Watson, I could not sit quiet in my chair, if I thought that such a man as Professor Moriarty were walking the streets of London unchallenged."

" What has he done, then ? "

" His career has been an extraordinary one. He is a man of good birth and excellent education, endowed by Nature with a phenomenal mathematical faculty. At the age of twenty-one he wrote a treatise upon the Binomial Theorem, which has had a European vogue. On the strength of it, he won the Mathematical Chair at one of our smaller Universities, and had, to all appearance, a most brilliant career before him. But the man had hereditary tendencies of the most diabolical kind. A criminal strain ran in his blood, which, instead of being modified, was increased and rendered infinitely more dangerous by his extraordinary mental powers. Dark rumours gathered round him in the University town, and eventually he was compelled to resign his Chair and to come down to London, where he set up as an Army coach. So much is known to the world, but what I am telling you now is what I have myself discovered.

" As you are aware, Watson, there is no one who knows the higher criminal world of London so well as I do. For years past I have continually been conscious of some power behind the malefactor, some deep organizing power which for ever stands in the way of the law, and throws its shield over the wrong-doer. Again and again in cases of the most varying sorts—forgery cases, robberies, murders—I have felt the presence of this force, and I have deduced its action in many of those undiscovered crimes in which I have not been personally consulted. For years I have endeavoured to break through the veil which shrouded it, and at last the time came when I seized my thread and followed it, until it led me, after a thousand cunning windings, to ex-Professor Moriarty of mathematical celebrity.

" He is the Napoleon of crime, Watson. He is the organizer of half that is evil and of nearly all that is undetected in this great city. He is a genius, a philosopher, an abstract thinker. He has a brain of the first order. He sits motionless, like a spider in the centre of its web, but that web has a thousand radiations, and he knows well every quiver of each of them. He does little himself. He only plans. But his agents are numerous and splendidly organized. Is there a crime to be done, a paper to be abstracted, we will say, a house to be rifled, a man to be removed—the word is passed to the Professor, the matter is organized and carried out. The agent may be caught. In that case money is found for his bail or his defence. But the central power which uses the agent is never caught—never so much as suspected. This was the organization which I deduced, Watson, and which I devoted my whole energy to exposing and breaking up.

8 "*Never.*" It must be remembered that "The Final Problem" was written and published *before The Valley of Fear*. Therefore, as Dr. John Dardess long ago pointed out ("On the Dating of *The Valley of Fear*), Watson's negative here was "merely literary license, necessary for the properly dramatic introduction of Moriarty to the public: if Watson had replied in the affirmative to Holmes' question, there would be no reason for his ensuing description of the professor. Hence, the . . . passage may deal with something that never actually took place, both question and answer being purely rhetorical, and the interpolated description probably recorded on some earlier occasion."

This same view has been expressed by Mr. G. B. Newton ("The Date of *The Valley of Fear*") and by Mr. James Buchholtz ("A Tremor at the Edge of the Web"): "The description of Moriarty [Watson] puts into the mouth of Holmes had doubtless been made on an earlier occasion but its transposition becomes *artistically* necessary as Watson, the practiced story-teller, instantly and rightly recognized." "By professing to be ignorant of Moriarty's existence, Watson was able to sketch in the background for the dramatic Reichenbach Falls incident. He had only to alter the time of a well-remembered conversation which may have taken place any time prior to 1891 between Holmes and his Boswell."

9 *to concentrate my attention upon my chemical researches.* But let us note here that Holmes, when he did come to retire in the October of 1903, turned his attention, not to chemical researches, but to philosophy and agriculture.

"HE IS THE NAPOLEON OF CRIME, WATSON."

Portrait of Professor James Moriarty by Sidney Paget for the *Strand Magazine*, December, 1893.

"... PROFESSOR MORIARTY STOOD BEFORE ME."

Illustration by Harry C. Edwards for *McClure's Magazine*, December, 1893.

"HE PEERED AT ME WITH GREAT CURIOSITY IN HIS PUCKERED EYES."

In "Chip Off the Old Block?" the late James Montgomery noted the extraordinary resemblance between Professor James Moriarty and Fernand De Brinon, Vichy representative to German-occupied France during World War II. The fact that there is, in New Orleans, a Moriarty Monument in Metairie Cemetery, led Mr. Montgomery to the conclusion that Moriarty had issue through a marriage with a French Creole lady, which would "account for a French traitor son, who carried on [the Professor's] reprehensible career under the thinly-disguised alias of De Brinon."

" But the Professor was fenced round with safeguards so cunningly devised that, do what I would, it seemed impossible to get evidence which could convict in a court of law. You know my powers, my dear Watson, and yet at the end of three months I was forced to confess that I had at last met an antagonist who was my intellectual equal. My horror at his crimes was lost in my admiration at his skill. But at last he made a trip—only a little, little trip—but it was more than he could afford, when I was so close upon him. I had my chance, and, starting from that point, I have woven my net round him until now it is all ready to close. In three days, that is to say on Monday next, matters will be ripe, and the Professor, with all the principal members of his gang, will be in the hands of the police. Then will come the greatest criminal trial of the century, the clearing up of over forty mysteries, and the rope for all of them—but if we move at all prematurely, you understand, they may slip out of our hands even at the last moment.

" Now, if I could have done this without the knowledge of Professor Moriarty, all would have been well. But he was too wily for that. He saw every step which I took to draw my toils round him. Again and again he strove to break away, but I as often headed him off. I tell you, my friend, that if a detailed account of that silent contest could be written, it would take its place as the most brilliant bit of thrust-and-parry work in the history of detection. Never have I risen to such a height, and never have I been so hard pressed by an opponent. He cut deep, and yet I just undercut him. This morning the last steps were taken, and three days only were wanted to complete the business. I was sitting in my room thinking the matter over, when the door opened and Professor Moriarty stood before me.

" My nerves are fairly proof, Watson, but I must confess to a start when I saw the very man who had been so much in my thoughts standing there on my threshold. His appearance was quite familiar to me. He is extremely tall and thin, his forehead domes out in a white curve, and his two eyes are deeply sunken in his head. He is clean-shaven, pale, and ascetic-looking, retaining something of the professor in his features. His shoulders are rounded from much study, and his face protrudes forward, and is for ever slowly oscillating from side to side in a curiously reptilian fashion. He peered at me with great curiosity in his puckered eyes.

" ' You have less frontal development than I should have expected,' said he at last. ' It is a dangerous habit to finger loaded firearms in the pocket of one's dressing-gown.'

" The fact is that upon his entrance I had instantly recognized the extreme personal danger in which I lay. The only conceivable escape for him lay in silencing my tongue. In an instant I had slipped the revolver from the drawer into my pocket, and was covering him through the cloth. At his remark I drew the weapon out and laid it cocked upon the table. He still smiled and blinked, but there was something about his eyes which made me feel very glad that I had it there.

" ' You evidently don't know me,' said he.

" 'On the contrary,' I answered, 'I think it is fairly evident that I do. Pray take a chair. I can spare you five minutes if you have anything to say.'

" 'All that I have to say has already crossed your mind,' said he.

" 'Then possibly my answer has crossed yours,' I replied.

" 'You stand fast?'

" 'Absolutely.'

" He clapped his hand into his pocket, and I raised the pistol from the table. But he merely drew out a memorandum-book in which he had scribbled some dates.

" 'You crossed my path on the 4th of January,' said he. **10**
'On the 23rd you incommoded me; by the middle of February I was seriously inconvenienced by you; at the end of March I was absolutely hampered in my plans; and now, at the close of April, I find myself placed in such a position through your continual persecution that I am in positive danger of losing my liberty. The situation is becoming an impossible one.'

" 'Have you any suggestion to make?' I asked.

" 'You must drop it, Mr. Holmes,' said he, swaying his face about. 'You really must, you know.'

" 'After Monday,' said I.

" 'Tut, tut!' said he. 'I am quite sure that a man of your intelligence will see that there can be but one outcome to this affair. It is necessary that you should withdraw. You have worked things in such a fashion that we have only one resource left. It has been an intellectual treat to me to see the way in which you have grappled with this affair, and I say, unaffectedly, that it would be a grief to me to be forced to take any extreme measure. You smile, sir, but I assure you that it really would.'

" 'Danger is part of my trade,' I remarked.

" 'This is not danger,' said he. 'It is inevitable destruction. You stand in the way not merely of an individual, but of a mighty organization, the full extent of which you, with all your cleverness, have been unable to realize. You must stand clear, Mr. Holmes, or be trodden under foot.'

" 'I am afraid,' said I, rising, 'that in the pleasure of this conversation I am neglecting business of importance which awaits me elsewhere.'

" He rose also and looked at me in silence, shaking his head sadly.

" 'Well, well,' said he at last. 'It seems a pity, but I have done what I could. I know every move of your game. You can do nothing before Monday. It has been a duel between you and me, Mr. Holmes. You hope to place me in the dock. I tell you that I will never stand in the dock. You hope to beat me. I tell you that you will never beat me. If you are clever enough to bring destruction upon me, rest assured that I shall do as much to you.'

" 'You have paid me several compliments, Mr. Moriarty,' said I. 'Let me pay you one in return when I say that if I were assured of the former eventuality I would, in the interests of the public, cheerfully accept the latter.'

"I CAN SPARE YOU FIVE MINUTES IF YOU HAVE ANYTHING TO SAY."

A flesh-and-blood Holmes, in the person of William Gillette, gets the drop on his archenemy, Professor James Moriarty, on the Garrick stage in 1899.

10 " '*You crossed my path on the 4th of January.*' "There is not the slightest doubt in my mind that what Moriarty actually said was 'the 7th of January,' and that the '4' is but another example of Watson's careless handwriting," Mr. Nathan L. Bengis wrote in "What Was the Month?" "The two digits are easily confused in any case. I know that the chronological experts will be up in arms against me, but I cannot help feeling that here we have the best of all possible reasons for assigning The Valley of Fear [which, as we have seen, began on a 7th of January] to January, 1891."

This is tempting, as Mr. T. S. Blakeney earlier wrote (*Sherlock Holmes: Fact or Fiction?*), "but the objections . . . are considerable. Moriarty's phrase 'crossed my path' must be taken to mean that Holmes had in some degree, not perhaps very large, *hampered* the professor's activities, but he cannot be said to have done so in *The Valley of Fear*, since Douglas was 'removed' quite satisfactorily some little time later. Moriarty was bound to know of Holmes, as did most London criminals, long before the clash came, and on the latter's own showing in *The Valley of Fear* he knew all about Moriarty, and had warned Scotland Yard accordingly. What seems most plausible is that Holmes worked quietly and waited patiently for many months . . . before he was in a position to start his contest with Moriarty on 4th January, 1891."

". . . AND SO HE TURNED HIS ROUNDED BACK UPON ME AND WENT PEERING AND BLINKING OUT OF THE ROOM."

Illustration by Sidney Paget for the *Strand Magazine*, December, 1893.

" ' I can promise you the one but not the other,' he snarled, and so turned his rounded back upon me and went peering and blinking out of the room.

" That was my singular interview with Professor Moriarty. I confess that it left an unpleasant effect upon my mind. His soft, precise fashion of speech leaves a conviction of sincerity which a mere bully could not produce. Of course, you will say : ' Why not take police precautions against him ? ' The reason is that I am well convinced that it is from his agents the blow would fall. I have the best of proofs that it would be so."

" You have already been assaulted ? "

" My dear Watson, Professor Moriarty is not a man who lets the grass grow under his feet. I went out about midday to transact some business in Oxford Street. As I passed the corner which leads from Bentinck Street on to the Welbeck Street crossing a two-horse van furiously driven whizzed round and was on me like a flash. I sprang for the footpath and saved myself by the fraction of a second. The van dashed round from Marylebone Lane and was gone in an instant. I kept to the pavement after that, Watson, but as I walked down Vere Street a brick
11 came down from the roof of one of the houses, and was shattered to fragments at my feet. I called the police and had the place examined. There were slates and bricks piled upon the roof preparatory to some repairs, and they would have me believe that the wind had toppled over one of these. Of course I knew better, but I could prove nothing. I took a cab after that and reached my brother's rooms in Pall Mall, where I spent the day. Now I have come round to you, and on my way I was attacked by a rough with a bludgeon. I knocked him down, and the police have him in custody ; but I can tell you with the most absolute confidence that no possible connection will ever be traced between the gentleman upon whose front teeth I have barked my knuckles and the retiring mathematical coach, who is, I dare say, working out problems upon a blackboard ten miles away. You will not wonder, Watson, that my first act on entering your rooms was to close your shutters, and that I have been compelled to ask your permission to leave the house by some less conspicuous exit than the front door."

I had often admired my friend's courage, but never more than now, as he sat quietly checking off a series of incidents which must have combined to make up a day of horror.

" You will spend the night here ? " I said.

" No, my friend ; you might find me a dangerous guest. I have my plans laid, and all will be well. Matters have gone so far now that they can move without my help as far as the arrest goes, though my presence is necessary for a conviction. It is obvious, therefore, that I cannot do better than get away for the few days which remain before the police are at liberty to act. It would be a
12 great pleasure to me, therefore, if you could come on to the Continent with me."

" The practice is quiet," said I, " and I have an accommodating neighbour. I should be glad to come."

11 *a brick came down from the roof of one of the houses.* The building was perhaps the big department store, Marshall & Snelgrove, established in 1837; it fronts on Oxford Street.

12 *if you could come on to the Continent with me."* Holmes suggests—to Watson, at least—that his prime purpose in leaving for the Continent is to escape the unwelcome attentions of the Moriarty gang. As Mr. Walter P. Armstrong, Jr., has written ("The Truth About Sherlock Holmes"): "To those of us who know Holmes this is incredible. He was never one to shirk danger, as he had told Moriarty himself in no uncertain terms a short time before. The only possible conclusion is that . . . Sherlock Holmes was luring Professor Moriarty into a trap."

Mr. Jerry Neal Williamson, on the other hand, has come to the conclusion that Professor James "Moriarty" was in fact Professor James *Holmes*, an elder brother of Sherlock's, a younger brother of Mycroft's ("'There Was Something Very Strange'"). "The flight from England must have been made to give James a chance to escape with his life. . . . Acting as a decoy, Sherlock Holmes 'fled,' vanished, and lived on the funds of his honest brother [Mycroft] until the gang was gone and James a free but broken man. Just as he found compassion for James Ryder ["The Adventure of the Blue Carbuncle"], the detective found compassion for his criminal brother."

" And to start to-morrow morning ? "

" If necessary."

" Oh yes, it is most necessary. Then these are your instructions, and I beg, my dear Watson, that you will obey them to the letter, for you are now playing a double-handed game with me against the cleverest rogue and the most powerful syndicate of criminals in Europe. Now listen ! You will despatch whatever luggage you intend to take by a trusty messenger unaddressed to Victoria to-night. In the morning you will send for a hansom, desiring your man to take neither the first nor the second which may present itself. Into this hansom you will jump, and you will drive to the Strand end of the Lowther Arcade, handing the address to the cabman upon a slip of paper, with a request that he will not throw it away. Have your fare ready, and the instant that your cab stops, dash through the Arcade, timing yourself to reach the other side at a quarter-past nine. You will find a small brougham waiting close to the kerb, driven by a fellow with a heavy black cloak tipped at the collar with red. Into this you will step, and you will reach Victoria in time for the Continental express."

" Where shall I meet you ? "

" At the station. The second first-class carriage from the front will be reserved for us."

" The carriage is our rendezvous, then ? "

" Yes."

It was in vain that I asked Holmes to remain for the evening. It was evident to me that he thought he might bring trouble to the roof he was under, and that that was the motive which impelled him to go. With a few hurried words as to our plans for the morrow he rose and came out with me into the garden, clambering over the wall
which leads into Mortimer Street, and immediately **13**
whistling for a hansom, in which I heard him drive away.

In the morning I obeyed Holmes' injunctions to the **14**
letter. A hansom was procured with such precautions as would prevent its being one which was placed ready for us, and I drove immediately after breakfast to the Lowther Arcade, through which I hurried at the top of my speed. A brougham was waiting with a very massive driver wrapped in a dark cloak, who, the instant that I had stepped in, whipped up the horse and rattled off to Victoria Station. On my alighting there he turned the carriage, and dashed away without so much as a look in my direction.

So far all had gone admirably. My luggage was waiting for me, and I had no difficulty in finding the carriage in which Holmes had indicated, the less so as it was the only one in the train which was marked " Engaged." My only source of anxiety now was the non-appearance of Holmes. The station clock marked only seven minutes from the time when we were due to start. In vain I searched among the groups of travellers and leave-takers for the lithe figure of my friend. There was no sign of him. I spent a few minutes in assisting a venerable Italian priest, who was endeavouring to make a porter understand, in his broken English, that his luggage was to be booked through to Paris. Then, having taken

". . . YOU WILL DRIVE TO THE STRAND END OF THE LOWTHER ARCADE . . ."

". . . the most historic, and rather dubious of reputation [of London's bazaars] was the Lowther Arcade—built 1830," Mr. Michael Harrison wrote (*In the Footsteps of Sherlock Holmes*). "The exiled Louis Philippe used to stroll through the Lowther Arcade, ogling the pretty assistants who were the famous principal attraction of this Victorian shopping-centre."

13 *Mortimer Street.* Mortimer Street runs parallel to Oxford Street, connecting Goodge Street on the east with the north side of Cavendish Square and Wigmore Street on the west. Its appearance here is a little mysterious, to say the least: it would not seem to fit in with either of Watson's practices, that in Kensington or that in the Paddington district.

14 *In the morning.* The morning of Saturday, April 25, 1891.

. . . MY DECREPIT ITALIAN FRIEND . . .

Illustration by Sidney Paget for the *Strand Magazine*, December, 1893.

another look round, I returned to my carriage, where I found that the porter, in spite of the ticket, had given me my decrepit Italian friend as a travelling companion. It was useless for me to explain to him that his presence was an intrusion, for my Italian was even more limited than his English, so I shrugged my shoulders resignedly and continued to look out anxiously for my friend. A chill of fear had come over me, as I thought that his absence might mean that some blow had fallen during the night. Already the doors had all been shut and the whistle blown, when——

" My dear Watson," said a voice, " you have not even condescended to say good morning."

I turned in incontrollable astonishment. The aged ecclesiastic had turned his face towards me. For an instant the wrinkles were smoothed away, the nose drew away from the chin, the lower lip ceased to protrude and the mouth to mumble, the dull eyes regained their fire, the drooping figure expanded. The next the whole frame
15 collapsed, and Holmes had gone as quickly as he had come.

" Good heavens ! " I cried. " How you startled me ! "

16 " Every precaution is still necessary," he whispered.
" I have reason to think that they are hot upon our trail. Ah, there is Moriarty himself."

17 The train had already begun to move as Holmes spoke.
Glancing back I saw a tall man pushing his way furiously through the crowd and waving his hand as if he desired to have the train stopped. It was too late, however, for we were rapidly gathering momentum, and an instant later had shot clear of the station.

" With all our precautions, you see that we have cut it rather fine," said Holmes, laughing. He rose, and throwing off the black cassock and hat which had formed his disguise, he packed them away in a hand-bag.

" Have you seen the morning paper, Watson ? "

" No."

" You haven't seen about Baker Street, then ? "

" Baker Street ? "

" They set fire to our rooms last night. No great harm was done."

" Good heavens, Holmes ! This is intolerable."

" They must have lost my track completely after their bludgeon-man was arrested. Otherwise they could not have imagined that I had returned to my rooms. They have evidently taken the precaution of watching you, however, and that is what has brought Moriarty to Victoria. You could not have made any slip in coming ? "

" I did exactly what you advised."

" Did you find your brougham ? "

" Yes, it was waiting."

" Did you recognize your coachman ? "

" No."

" It was my brother Mycroft. It is an advantage to get about in such a case without taking a mercenary into your confidence. But we must plan what we are to do about Moriarty now."

" As this is an express, and as the boat runs in connection with it, I should think we have shaken him off very effectively."

15 *Holmes had gone as quickly as he had come.* ". . . for a second time," the Reverend Otis R. Rice wrote in "Clergymen in the Canon," "it was a little unchivalrous of Holmes to avoid legal culpability by impersonating a Roman Catholic priest, an act for which there was at the time the same immunity as in the previous impersonation of a Nonconformist minister ["A Scandal in Bohemia"]. Holmes, a consummate actor, seems to have played the part well. Yet he, who usually had such an eye for complete disguise, neglected to provide himself on this occasion with the breviary and beads, without which no venerable Italian priest would ever have traveled. Watson, as a Protestant and not recognizing the discrepancy, reports the only accoutrement as a 'black cassock and hat which had formed his disguise.' "

16 "*Every precaution is still necessary.*" "It is a logical supposition," Mr. Walter P. Armstrong, Jr., wrote in "The Truth About Sherlock Holmes," "that by [this] date it was fairly well known that Watson and Holmes were closely associated, as Watson had published accounts of several of their joint adventures. Surely Moriarty must have known it. Then why did not Holmes go to the Continent alone? Why assume an elaborate disguise and have as his travelling companion a man who was himself a dead giveaway? Obviously because he *wanted* Moriarty to follow him. The disguise, the change of trains, the altered itinerary, simply served to keep the whole thing from being too transparent. Holmes never for a moment

" My dear Watson, you evidently did not realize my meaning when I said that this man may be taken as being quite on the same intellectual plane as myself. You do not imagine that if I were the pursuer I should allow myself to be baffled by so slight an obstacle. Why, then, should you think so meanly of him ? "

" What will he do ? "

" What I should do."

" What would you do, then ? "

" Engage a special."

" But it must be late."

" By no means. This train stops at Canterbury ; and **18** there is always at least a quarter of an hour's delay at the boat. He will catch us there."

" One would think that we were the criminals. Let us have him arrested on his arrival."

" It would be to ruin the work of three months. We should get the big fish, but the smaller would dart right and left out of the net. On Monday we should have them all. No, an arrest is inadmissible."

" What then ? "

" We shall get out at Canterbury."

" And then ? "

" Well, then we must make a cross-country journey to Newhaven, and so over to Dieppe. Moriarty will again do what I should do. He will get on to Paris, mark down

thought that Moriarty would fail to see through them. Holmes was fully aware that the official police were incapable of dealing with such a man. The only solution was to give him his personal attention. And yet he could hardly shoot him down in cold blood in law-abiding England. So step by step he enticed him out of the country to as lonely a spot as could be found, and then he deliberately offered himself as bait for the trap which he was about to spring."

17 *The train had already begun to move.* As the late Professor Jay Finley Christ pointed out in *Finch's Final Fling*, Von Neumann and Morgenstern, in *Theory of Games and Economic Behavior* (Princeton Press, 1944) analyze the mathematical probabilities in the business. They show that Holmes had a 60 percent chance of success if he stopped, while the professor had the same chance of winning if Holmes went on. A footnote, however, says that the mathematical odds were definitely in favor of the pursuer and that Holmes "is as good as 48 percent dead when his train pulls out."

18 *Canterbury.* Canterbury, the "Mother of England," is not elsewhere mentioned in the Chronicles.

"IT WAS MY BROTHER MYCROFT."

Illustration by Harry C. Edwards for *McClure's Magazine*, December, 1893.

"ENGAGE A SPECIAL."

"A purse deep enough for the suitably grand fare—usually five shillings [$1.25] a mile—could command a first-class carriage, a light engine, and a line cleared of slower traffic," Mr. Bernard Davies wrote in "Canonical Connections." But "Professor Moriarty's dramatic chase . . . must have been a superlative triumph of organization of the London, Chatham & Dover Railway Co.," as Mr. E. P. Greenwood wrote in "Some Random Thoughts on Railway Journeys by Holmes and Watson." "Think of the many signalmen between London and Dover who had to be informed at very short notice and the many train movements which had to be suspended; to say nothing of all the complicated signal and point operations which had to be made to let Moriarty's special through. Without a doubt the Traffic Superintendent was one of Moriarty's creatures and most of the railway company's servants concerned were part of his sinister and complex organisation; all the same, they must have been pretty hard put to it!" The photograph, from Mr. Michael Harrison's *In the Footsteps of Sherlock Holmes*, shows a "special" of the old South-Eastern Railway. In the background is a London Board School: what Holmes, in "The Naval Treaty," called "a beacon of the future."

". . . AND MAKE OUR WAY AT OUR LEISURE INTO SWITZERLAND . . ."

Dr. Julian Wolff's map of "Operation Reichenbach," from his *Sherlockian Atlas.*

our luggage, and wait for two days at the depot. In the meantime we shall treat ourselves to a couple of carpet bags, encourage the manufactures of the countries through which we travel, and make our way at our leisure into Switzerland, via Luxembourg and Basle."

I am too old a traveller to allow myself to be seriously inconvenienced by the loss of my luggage, but I confess that I was annoyed at the idea of being forced to dodge and hide before a man whose record was black with unutterable infamies. It was evident, however, that Holmes understood the situation more clearly than I did. At
19 Canterbury, therefore, we alighted, only to find that we should have to wait an hour before we could get a train to Newhaven.

I was still looking rather ruefully after the rapidly disappearing luggage van which contained my wardrobe, when Holmes pulled my sleeve and pointed up the line.

"Already, you see," said he.

Far away from among the Kentish woods there arose a thin spray of smoke. A minute later a carriage and engine could be seen flying along the open curve which leads to the station. We had hardly time to take our places behind a pile of luggage when it passed with a rattle and a roar, beating a blast of hot air into our faces.

"There he goes," said Holmes, as we watched the carriage swing and rock over the points. "There are limits, you see, to our friend's intelligence. It would have been a *coup de maître* had he deduced what I would deduce and acted accordingly."

"And what would he have done had he overtaken us?"

"There cannot be the least doubt that he would have made a murderous attack upon me. It is, however, a game at which two may play. The question now is whether we should take a premature lunch here, or run our chance of starving before we reach the buffet at
20 Newhaven."

We made our way to Brussels that night and spent two days there, moving on upon the third day as far as Stras-
21 burg. On the Monday morning Holmes had telegraphed

19 *At Canterbury, therefore, we alighted.* Although it has generally been assumed that Holmes and Watson were making for Paris via the Dover-Calais route, Mr. Bernard Davies has shown ("Can-

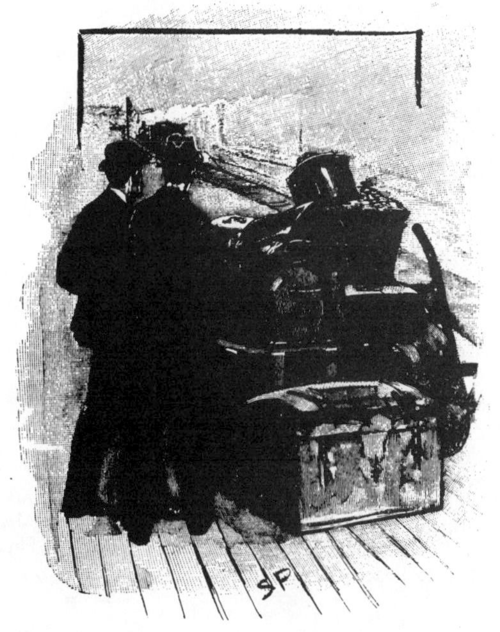

WE HAD HARDLY TIME TO TAKE OUR PLACES BEHIND A PILE OF LUGGAGE WHEN IT PASSED WITH A RATTLE AND A ROAR . . .

Illustration by Sidney Paget for the *Strand Magazine*, December, 1893. Harry C. Edwards illustrated the same scene for *McClure's Magazine*, December, 1893.

to the London police, and in the evening we found a reply waiting for us at our hotel. Holmes tore it open, and then with a bitter curse hurled it into the grate.

"I might have known it," he groaned. "He has escaped!"

"Moriarty!"

"They have secured the whole gang with the exception of him. He has given them the slip. Of course, **22** when I had left the country there was no one to cope with him. But I did think that I had put the game in their hands. I think that you had better return to England, Watson."

"Why?"

"Because you will find me a dangerous companion now. This man's occupation is gone. He is lost if he returns to London. If I read his character right he will devote his whole energies to revenging himself upon me. He said as much in our short interview, and I fancy that he meant it. I should certainly recommend you to return to your practice."

WE MADE OUR WAY TO BRUSSELS THAT NIGHT . . .

Could they have caught a boat that night? Mr. Davies continues: "In April, 1891, the L.B.S.C.R. ran only one boat a day to Dieppe. This left Newhaven at 11 P.M. following the arrival of the 9 P.M. express from London Bridge. It was the only boat they could have caught, so their three-and-a-half-hour journey from Canterbury could have been taken at a much more leisurely pace. The boat, one of the Brighton's fleet of four steel-built, electrically-lighted paddle-steamers:—*Normandy*, *Brittany*, *Paris* and *Rouen* [the *Paris* is shown above]—took almost five and a half hours on the crossing, docking in Dieppe at 4:23 in the morning. If they were lucky enough to secure unbooked cabins they could have snatched a few hours sleep. . . . The final problem . . . is:—How did they go from Dieppe to Brussels, avoiding Paris? This takes us on a Continental ramble and, at the same time, introduces us to a delightfully colourful work, *Bradshaw's Continental Railway, Steam Navigation and Conveyance Guide*. . . . There were several possible cross-country routes avoiding Paris, all of them via Arras, but none which would have got them to Brussels earlier than 6:05 that evening. No doubt they took the best of a bad lot by taking the Paris train as far as Rouen and alighting there at 5:41 A.M. From there they would catch the 6:30 to Amiens, via Serqueux, then another arriving at 11:02. An hour's wait and they could leave for Brussels by the 12:07 via Douai, Valenciennes and Mons. It was certainly gone six on the Sunday evening by the time they arrived in the Belgian capital."

onical Connections") that Holmes' intended destination must have been Ostend, regardless of where he sent their luggage: ". . . if we consult *Bradshaw's Monthly Railway Guide* for April, 1891, we find the following morning boat-trains: —an 8:30 and an 11 o'clock, both for Calais, and a 10 o'clock for Ostend, all first- and second-class only. As regards departure time the Ostend Boat Express is the only one that qualifies, but if any doubts remain as to which train Holmes and Watson travelled by, they are soon dispelled by a glance down the columns of Bradshaw. . . . The 10 A.M. Ostend train . . . had a two-hour timing, stopping at Herne Hill, Chatham, Canterbury and Dover Priory, five minutes before the Harbour, where it arrived at 12 noon. It was the only morning boat-express to do so, and therefore the only possible train on which Holmes and Watson could have commenced their cross-country wanderings."

20 *the buffet at Newhaven.*" Could Holmes and Watson have made the cross-country journey satisfactorily to Newhaven? Again, Mr. Bernard Davies has shown that they could: "The boat-train stopped at Herne Hill at 10:12 and at Chatham at 10:51 and reached Canterbury at its appointed time at 11:29. . . . In actual fact the next train on the South Eastern branch to Ashford left in about forty minutes, at 12:08, but it probably seemed the best part of an hour [to Watson] in restrospect. It ran via Chatham, Chilham and Wye, arriving at Ashford Junction at 12:40. After a twenty-minute wait the South Eastern dispatched a slow Hastings train at 1:00 P.M. . . . Holmes and Watson trundled along in easy stages via Ham Street, Appledore, Rye and Winchelsea, arriving at Hastings at 2:03. Here there was a smart change to the London, Brighton and South Coast Railway train, with its mustard-yellow engine and crimson-ended brake-van, running as it did non-stop from Bexhill to Lewes where it pulled in at 3:05. At Lewes, where they changed once more, they had a wait of twenty-five minutes, as the local for Newhaven left at 3:30 and deposited them at the Harbour at 3:45."

21 *upon the third day as far as Strasburg.* Holmes and Watson presumably spent Monday, April 27th, and Tuesday, April 28th, in Brussels, moving to Strasburg on Wednesday, April 29th. ". . . intensive research of hotel registers shows that the great detective [stopped] at the very best hotel in Strasburg—the Maison Rouge," Mr. Thayer Cumings wrote in "Don't Write—Telegraph!"

22 "*'They have secured the whole gang with the exception of him.* We learn in "The Adventure of the Empty House" that this was not true, since the notorious Colonel Sebastian Moran, next to Moriarty the most dangerous man in London, was still very much at large, as was one other member of the gang. The London police, in 1891, evidently did not know these two as criminals—or, if they did, as members of the Moriarty gang.

It was hardly an appeal to be successful with one who
was an old campaigner as well as an old friend. We sat
23 in the Strasburg *salle-à-manger* arguing the question for
half an hour, but the same night we had resumed our
24 journey and were well on our way to Geneva.

25 For a charming week we wandered up the Valley of the
Rhone, and then, branching off at Leuk, we made our way
over the Gemmi Pass, still deep in snow, and so, by way
26 of Interlaken, to Meiringen. It was a lovely trip, the
dainty green of the spring below, the virgin white of the
winter above ; but it was clear to me that never for one
instant did Holmes forget the shadow which lay across
him. In the homely Alpine villages or in the lonely
mountain passes, I could still tell, by his quick glancing
eyes and his sharp scrutiny of every face that passed us,
that he was well convinced that, walk where we would,
we could not walk ourselves clear of the danger which was
dogging our footsteps.

Once, I remember, as we passed over the Gemmi, and walked along the border of the melancholy Daubensee, a large rock which had been dislodged from the ridge upon our right clattered down and roared into the lake behind us. In an instant Holmes had raced up on to the ridge, and, standing upon a lofty pinnacle, craned his neck in every direction. It was in vain that our guide assured him that a fall of stones was a common chance in the spring-time at that spot. He said nothing, but he smiled at me with the air of a man who sees the fulfilment of that which he had expected.

And yet for all his watchfulness he was never depressed. On the contrary, I can never recollect having seen him in such exuberant spirits. Again and again he recurred to the fact that if he could be assured that society was freed from Professor Moriarty, he would cheerfully bring his own career to a conclusion.

" I think that I may go so far as to say, Watson, that I
have not lived wholly in vain," he remarked. " If my
record were closed to-night I could still survey it with
27 equanimity. The air of London is the sweeter for my
presence. In over a thousand cases I am not aware that I
have ever used my powers upon the wrong side. Of late
I have been tempted to look into the problems furnished
by Nature rather than those more superficial ones for
which our artificial state of society is responsible. Your
memoirs will draw to an end, Watson, upon the day that
I crown my career by the capture or extinction of the
most dangerous and capable criminal in Europe."

I shall be brief, and yet exact, in the little which remains for me to tell. It is not a subject on which I would willingly dwell, and yet I am conscious that a duty devolves upon me to omit no detail.

It was upon the 3rd of May that we reached the little
village of Meiringen, where we put up at the 'Englischer
28 Hof, then kept by Peter Steiler the elder. Our landlord
was an intelligent man, and spoke excellent English,
having served for three years as waiter at the Grosvenor
29 Hotel in London. At his advice, upon the afternoon of
the 4th we set off together with the intention of crossing
the hills and spending the night at the Hamlet of Rosen-

23 *the Strasburg* salle-à-manger. "The dining room of their hotel," the late Christopher Morley wrote in *Sherlock Holmes and Dr. Watson: A Textbook of Friendship.* "Under less anxious circumstances Holmes, who enjoyed good food, would have taken time to enjoy Strasburg's world-famous goose-liver pie . . . , but it cannot be digested in haste."

24 *and were well on our way to Geneva.* "The keenness with which Holmes pursued Moriarty is clear from the fact that the departure to which Watson casually refers . . . was a departure in the small hours (3:55 A.M.), since there was no evening train on the 1890–91 winter timetable," Mr. Michael C. Kaser wrote in "Sherlock Holmes on the Continent." "They reached Geneva via Colmar, Basel, Biel and Lausanne, at 3:18 the following afternoon (the 30th), and we know they passed the night at Geneva, probably at the Hôtel de l'Écu, the most patronised by literary Englishmen at that time."

25 *For a charming week.* "The night that Holmes and Watson spent in Geneva can be dated as that of the 30th of April without shadow of doubt," Mr. Kaser continued. "The date is important, for the 'week' they spent in 'wandering up the valley of the Rhone' shrinks upon such investigation to be no more than Thursday, May 1st, since by the 3rd they had reached Meiringen. When Watson writes of a 'week wandering up the valley,' it is obviously a sarcastic reference to the easy pace of the train, for while from Geneva the slowest train of the day took eight and three-quarter hours, even the fastest took six hours to reach Leuk: today the journey is less than three hours."

26 *and so, by way of Interlaken, to Meiringen.* "The line to Leukerbad, at the foot of the Gemmi Pass, had not been built, and obviously they must have left Leuk on 2nd May," Mr. Kaser continued. "A study of the map Holmes must have used for his fateful journey—Blatt 17 of the *Topgraphische Karte der Schweiz,* in the revision of 1882—shows clearly the path from Leukerbad to the Gemmi and its bifurcation before the Daubensee. . . . It is obvious that Holmes followed the right bank, since the rock dislodged in a presumed attempt on his life came from the *right,* and fell thence into the lake behind him. Moreover, the right bank path is shown on the map as the better one. They would have reached Kandersteg very late; with no train on the Leuk side and no cable car on the Kandersteg side as there is today, it is a full day's walk. The railway from Kandersteg to Spiez was not built until much later, and the regular diligence service in that year did not operate until 1st June. They were perhaps able to hire a carriage and catch the 10:05 A.M. boat from Spiez, which, via Interlaken, connected with the train leaving Brienz at 1:00 P.M."

Reproduced from a contemporary steel engraving by the late James Montgomery.

A panoramic view of Meiringen and the Hasli Valley from a brochure distributed by Popularis Tours, Inc., of New York City. Copyright Brügger S.A., Ltd., Meiringen.

WE REACHED THE LITTLE VILLAGE OF MEIRINGEN . . .

The population of Meiringen was then under 3,000. "Prior to the great fire of 1891, which almost demolished the village, Meiringen was a little, old-world place consisting of quaint cottages round a little Swiss Church erected in the early pre-Reformation period," says the *Guide Through Europe*, published by the Hamburg-American Line in 1905. "The church escaped the flames; and, together with a few wooden structures and the Austrian Tower that stands out among the woods to the right of the Mühlbach, it still tells of the middle-age appearance worn by the hamlet within the last few years. At the present time, it possesses a number of fine hotels and boarding houses, which give it the character of a modern health-resort. It is the principal village in the narrow and fertile Hasli Valley, whose beauty has won for the spot the title of the 'Front Garden of the Bernese Oberland.' Through this valley flows the river Aare, flanked by wooded steeps. To the S., the river forms the Reichenbach Falls . . ."

"The destruction of Meiringen [by fire] so soon after the epic event that transpired nearby suggests its immolation at the hand of [a Moriarty henchman], enraged as he must have been at the death of his leader and the escape of his intended victim," the late James Montgomery wrote in "Meiringen Musings."

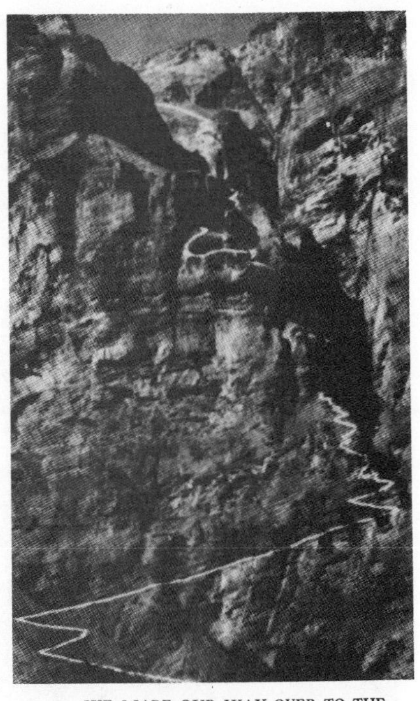

. . . WE MADE OUR WAY OVER TO THE GEMMI PASS . . .

Photograph by Lord Donegall, who writes: "Watson deserves credit for making the 2¾ hrs. up this path with his game leg. (Or perhaps his wound was in his shoulder on that day!)."

. . . A LARGE ROCK . . . CLATTERED DOWN AND ROARED INTO THE LAKE BEHIND US.

Illustration by Sidney Paget for the *Strand Magazine*, December, 1893. Harry C. Edwards illustrated the same scene for *McClure's Magazine,* December, 1893.

IT IS, INDEED, A FEARFUL PLACE.

". . . the Fall of Reichenbach is not actually a single fall, even though it is labeled as such," Messrs. Bryce Crawford, Jr., and R. C. Moore wrote in "The Final Problem—Where?" "Actually, it is three falls. . . From the beginning of the upper falls, the water plunges down into a pool not far above the viewing platform [that now exists on the west or right side of the falls as one faces it]. From this upper segment the water plunges, not in a single sheer drop but with several minor cascades caused by rocks in the path of the fall which have not completely washed away. The middle segment is by far the most spectacular, with its several interruptions, its roar of waters rushing against the containing cliffs, and its end in a pool of great depth and magnitude. . . . The first question therefore [is]: Did Holmes and Moriarty struggle at the upper segment and did Moriarty fall into the pool at the bottom of it; or was the struggle at the middle segment? . . . The middle segment fits the [Canonical] description perfectly. . . . But here again the question arises, exactly where? One must rule out the possibility of the struggle having taken place on the west side of the falls . . . For . . . in 1891 . . . [there was no] path up the right side of the mountain. The presumption therefore is that the struggle took place on the left side of the fall. There is indeed a path that leads up the left side of the mountain. It goes clear to the top and crosses over the upper segment via a foot bridge before taking off to Rosenlaui. . . . There is no . . . ledge there today, [but] there [was] one in 1891 . . . about two-thirds of the way up. Appearances strongly suggest that part of the cliff fell away . . . in March, 1944, [when] there was a substantial erosion and fall of rock at the middle segment."

laui. We had strict injunctions, however, on no account to pass the falls of Reichenbach, which are about half-way up the hill, without making a small detour to see them.

It is, indeed, a fearful place. The torrent, swollen by the melting snow, plunges into a tremendous abyss, from which the spray rolls up like the smoke from a burning house. The shaft into which the river hurls itself is an immense chasm, lined by glistening, coal-black rock, and narrowing into a creaming, boiling pit of incalculable depth, which brims over and shoots the stream onward over its jagged lip. The long sweep of green water roaring for ever down, and the thick flickering curtain of spray hissing for ever upwards, turn a man giddy with their constant whirl and clamour. We stood near the edge peering down at the gleam of the breaking water far below us against the black rocks, and listening to the half-human shout which came booming up with the spray out of the abyss.

The path has been cut half-way round the fall to afford a complete view, but it ends abruptly, and the traveller has to return as he came. We had turned to do so, when we saw a Swiss lad come running along it with a letter in his hand. It bore the mark of the hotel which we had just left, and was addressed to me by the landlord. It appeared that within a very few minutes of our leaving, an English lady had arrived who was in the last stage of
30-31 consumption. She had wintered at Davos Platz, and was journeying now to join her friends at Lucerne, when a sudden hæmorrhage had overtaken her. It was thought that she could hardly live a few hours, but it would be a great consolation to her to see an English doctor, and, if I would only return, etc. etc. The good Steiler assured me in a postscript that he would himself look upon my

. . . WE SAW A SWISS LAD COME RUNNING ALONG IT WITH A LETTER IN HIS HAND.

Illustration by Harry C. Edwards for *McClure's Magazine*, December, 1893.

compliance as a very great favour, since the lady absolutely refused to see a Swiss physician, and he could not but feel that he was incurring a great responsibility.

The appeal was one which could not be ignored. It was impossible to refuse the request of a fellow-countrywoman dying in a strange land. Yet I had my scruples about leaving Holmes. It was finally agreed, however, that he should retain the young Swiss messenger with him as guide and companion while I returned to Meiringen. My friend would stay some little time at the fall, he said, and would then walk slowly over the hill to Rosenlaui, where I was to rejoin him in the evening. As I turned away I saw Holmes with his back against a rock and his arms folded, gazing down at the rush of the waters. It was the last that I was ever destined to see of him in this world.

When I was near the bottom of the descent I looked back. It was impossible, from that position, to see the fall, but I could see the curving path which winds over the shoulder of the hill and leads to it. Along this a man was, I remember, walking very rapidly. I could see his black figure clearly outlined against the green behind him. I noted him, and the energy with which he walked, but he passed from my mind again as I hurried on upon my errand.

It may have been a little over an hour before I reached Meiringen. Old Steiler was standing at the porch of his hotel.

" Well," said I, as I came hurrying up, " I trust that she is no worse ? "

A look of surprise passed over his face, and at the first quiver of his eyebrows my heart turned to lead in my breast.

" You did not write this ? " I said, pulling the letter from my pocket. " There is no sick Englishwoman in the hotel ? "

" Certainly not," he cried. " But it has the hotel mark upon it ! Ha ! it must have been written by that tall Englishman who came in after you had gone. He said——"

But I waited for none of the landlord's explanations. In a tingle of fear I was already running down the village street, and making for the path which I had so lately descended. It had taken me an hour to come down. For all my efforts, two more had passed before I found myself at the fall of Reichenbach once more. There was Holmes' alpenstock still leaning against the rock by which I had left him. But there was no sign of him, and it was in vain that I shouted. My only answer was my own voice reverberating in a rolling echo from the cliffs around me.

It was the sight of that alpenstock which turned me cold and sick. He had not gone to Rosenlaui, then. He had remained on that three-foot path, with sheer wall on one side and sheer drop upon the other, until his enemy had overtaken him. The young Swiss had gone too. He had probably been in the pay of Moriarty, and had left the two men together. And then what had happened ? Who was to tell us what had happened then ?

27 *survey it with equanimity*. Mr. Morris Rosenblum has suggested ("The Horatian Spirit in Holmes") that "Sherlock was obviously recalling appropriate lines from the *Odes* of Horace. The first passage that comes to mind is: *Aequam memento rebus in arduis / Servare mentem. . . . Odes*, 11, 3. 'Remember to keep your "equanimity" when you are in trouble.' "

28 *Peter Steiler the elder*. "No such hotel [as the Englischer Hoff] exists today," Mr. Michael C. Kaser wrote in "Sherlock Holmes on the Continent," "but there are Steiners (a slip of Watson's pen there) still tradesmen in Meiringen—one a tobacconist and another a haberdasher."

29 *the Grosvenor Hotel*. The Grosvenor Hotel, which was opened in 1861, shortly after the completion of Victoria Station, is a handsome building 300 feet long and 100 feet high, with its main frontage to the Buckingham Palace Road.

30 *the last stage of consumption*. If Mary Morstan Watson suffered from (and shortly died of) consumption, as many commentators believe, "the genius of Moriarty is here revealed that he chose the surest way of decoying Watson away from Holmes, knowing from his dossier on Watson that Mrs. Watson was herself a consumptive in an advanced stage."—Dr. Ebbe Curtis Hoff, "The Adventure of John and Mary."

31 *Davos Platz*. A town in the east of Switzerland. It is, in fact, a health resort for consumptives.

. . . I SAW HOLMES WITH HIS BACK AGAINST A ROCK AND HIS ARMS FOLDED, GAZING DOWN AT THE RUSH OF THE WATERS.

Illustration by Harry C. Edwards for *McClure's Magazine*, December, 1893. Sidney Paget illustrated the same scene for the *Strand Magazine*, December, 1893.

I stood for a minute or two to collect myself, for I was dazed with the horror of the thing. Then I began to think of Holmes' own methods and to try to practise them in reading this tragedy. It was, alas ! only too easy to do. During our conversation we had not gone to the end of the path, and the alpenstock marked the place where we had stood. The blackish soil is kept for ever soft by the incessant drift of spray, and a bird would leave its tread upon it. Two lines of footmarks were clearly marked along the further end of the path, both
32 leading away from me. There were none returning. A few yards from the end the soil was all ploughed up into a patch of mud, and the brambles and ferns which fringed the chasm were torn and bedraggled. I lay upon my face and peered over, with the spray spouting up all around me. It had darkened since I had left, and now I could only see here and there the glistening of moisture upon the black walls, and far away down at the end of the shaft the gleam of the broken water. I shouted ; but only that same half-human cry of the fall was borne back to my ears.

But it was destined that I should after all have a last word of greeting from my friend and comrade. I have said that his alpenstock had been left leaning against a rock which jutted on to the path. From the top of this boulder the gleam of something bright caught my eye, and, raising my hand, I found that it came from the silver cigarette-case which he used to carry. As I took it up a small square of paper upon which it had lain fluttered down on to the ground. Unfolding it I found that it consisted of three pages torn from his notebook and addressed to me. It was characteristic of the man that the direction was as precise, and the writing as firm and clear, as though it had been written in his study.

" My dear Watson," he said, " I write these few lines through the courtesy of Mr. Moriarty, who awaits my convenience for the final discussion of those questions which lie between us. He has been giving me a sketch of the methods by which he avoided the English police and kept himself informed of our movements. They certainly confirm the very high opinion which I had formed of his abilities. I am pleased to think that I shall be able to free society from any further effects of his presence, though I fear that it is at a cost which will give pain to my friends, and especially, my dear Watson, to you. I have already explained to you, however, that my career had in any case reached its crisis, and that no possible conclusion to it could be more congenial to me than this. Indeed, if I may make a full confession to you, I was quite convinced that the letter from Meiringen

. . . A SMALL SQUARE OF PAPER . . . FLUTTERED DOWN ON TO THE GROUND.

Illustration by Sidney Paget for the *Strand Magazine*, December, 1893.

32 *Two lines of footmarks were clearly marked along the further end of the path, both leading away from me.* Mr. Pope R. Hill, Sr., has written (in "The Final Problem") that "The crowning absurdity in the published account is shown by the tracks. On the three-foot ledge, Holmes is supposed to have walked *with his back to Moriarty.* This would have meant certain death for Holmes, with absolutely no chance for him to bring about the death of Moriarty. . . . If Holmes had backed away from Moriarty, one set of tracks would be pointing forward and the other backward. Both sets were said to lead in the same direction toward the end of the path, which meant one man was walking in front of the other *with his back turned.* Neither man would have walked in front of the other like that, for it would have meant *his* certain death and the escape of his opponent."

But the late A. Carson Simpson wrote ("The Curious Incident of the Missing Corpse"): "The writer likes to think that the best traditions of British sportsmanship were observed by both sides in the epochal struggle. There are several indications of this. Holmes, an expert singlestick player and swordsman, no doubt had a useful knowledge of the quarter-staff; his six-foot alpenstock would have been perfect for such play, while the crook at its end offered some of the advantages of a medieval bill—yet he did not use it. Likewise, Moriarty allowed the note to Watson to be written and left under the cigarette case. Everything points to a mutual decision to fight it out on a man-to-man basis."

And Mr. Webster Evans has added ("Sherlock Holmes and Sport."): "Personally I have always thought that, considering his skill with the singlestick, Holmes was more than sporting in leaving his stick with the cigarette box. Moriarty, however, with equal nicety [as we learn later], 'drew no weapon.' "

was a hoax, and I allowed you to depart on that errand under the persuasion that some development of this sort would follow. Tell Inspector Patterson that the papers which he needs to convict the gang are in pigeon-hole M., done up in a blue envelope and inscribed ' Moriarty.' I made every disposition of my property before leaving England, and handed it to my brother Mycroft. Pray give my greetings to Mrs. Watson, and believe me to be, my dear fellow,

" Very sincerely yours,
" SHERLOCK HOLMES." 33

A few words may suffice to tell the little that remains. An examination by experts leaves little doubt that a personal contest between the two men ended, as it could hardly fail to end in such a situation, in their reeling over, locked in each other's arms. Any attempt at
recovering the bodies was absolutely hopeless, and there, 34
deep down in that dreadful cauldron of swirling water and seething foam, will lie for all time the most dangerous criminal and the foremost champion of the law of their generation. The Swiss youth was never found again, and there can be no doubt that he was one of the numerous agents whom Moriarty kept in his employ. As to the gang, it will be within the memory of the public how completely the evidence which Holmes had accumulated exposed their organization, and how heavily the hand of the dead man weighed upon them. Of their terrible chief few details came out during the proceeding, and if I have now been compelled to make a clear statement of his career, it is due to those injudicious champions who have endeavoured to clear his memory by attacks upon him whom I shall ever regard as the best and the wisest man
whom I have ever known. 35

33 "*SHERLOCK HOLMES.*" Mr. Lorenzo J. Chieco, Certified Grapho-Analytical Psychologist, has reconstructed from Holmes' known traits of character and personality the signature reproduced here:

Sherlock Holmes.

34 *Any attempt at recovering the bodies was absolutely hopeless.* Why? "The Reichenbach, it is true, is a brawling stream in its upper reaches, but, below the Falls, it settles down for its last short flow into the Aare at Meiringen," the late A. Carson Simpson wrote in "The Curious Incident of the Missing Corpse." "The Aare, in turn, travels fairly calmly for seven or eight miles until it empties into the Lake of Brienz. Moriarty's corpse should have been found floating in the lake or in one of the streams, but was not. This cannot have been for lack of searching, since, when the in-

"I MADE EVERY DISPOSITION OF MY PROPERTY BEFORE LEAVING ENGLAND . . ."

In the *London Mystery Magazine* for June, 1955, a document purporting to be the last will and testament of Mr. Sherlock Holmes was reproduced in facsimile, with a prefatory note, unsigned, ascribing the discovery of the paper to Mr. Nathan L. Bengis, Keeper of the Crown of the Musgrave Ritualists of New York. Although strong doubts have been raised as to its genuineness, notably by Professor Jacques Barzun in "Sherlock Holmes' Will—A Forgery," Mr. Bengis has made a spirited rebuttal in "Where There's a Will, There's a Pay."

This is the last Will and Testament

of me Sherlock Holmes
of 221B. Baker Street in the parish of St. Marylebone
in the County of London made this Sixteenth
day of April, 1891 in the year of our Lord

I hereby revoke all former testamentary dispositions made by me and declare this to be my last Will.

I appoint my brother
Mycroft Holmes

to be my Executor and direct that all my just Debts and Funeral and Testamentary Expenses shall be paid as soon as conveniently may be after my decease.

I give and bequeath unto

my devoted friend and associate, Dr John H. Watson, often tried, sometimes trying, but never found wanting in loyalty; my well-intentioned though unavailing mentor against the blandishments of vice; my indispensable foil and whetstone; the perfect sop to my wounded vanity and too tactful to whisper Norbury in my ear when necessary; the ideal listener and the audience par excellence for those little tricks which others more discerning might well have deemed meretricious; the faithful Boswell to whose literary efforts - despite my occasional unkindly gibes - I owe whatever little fame I have enjoyed: in short, to the one true friend I have ever had, the sum of £5,000; also the choice of any books in my personal library (with such reservations as are mentioned below), including my commonplace books and the complete file of my cases, published and unpublished, with the sole exception of the papers in pigeonhole M. contained in a blue envelope and marked Moriarty which the proper authorities will take over in the event my demise should make it impossible for me to hand them over in person.

— To George Lestrade, of Scotland Yard, my gilt-edged German dictionary, in the hope he will find it useful should he again see the handwriting of Miss Rachel on the wall.

— To Tobias Gregson, ditto; my leatherbound Hafiz, the study of whose poetry may supply a dash of that imagination so necessary to the ideal reasoner.

— To the authorities of Scotland Yard, one copy of each of my trifling monographs on crime detection, unless happily they shall feel they have outgrown the need for the elementary suggestions of an amateur detective.

— To my good brother, Mycroft Holmes, the remainder and residue of my estate, which he will be agreeably surprised to find, even after the foregoing bequests, to be not inconsiderable, and which will enable him, I hope, to take a much needed holiday from governmental cares to surroundings more congenial than those of the Diogenes Club; in the expectation that he will remain celibate for the rest of his natural life — and unnatural too, for that matter.

Sherlock Holmes

Signed by the Testator in the presence of us, present at the same time, who at his request, in his presence, and in the presence of each other, have subscribed our names as Witnesses .. .. ..

1st WITNESS—Name Thomas P. Stockton
Address Staple Inn, Holborn
Occupation Solicitor

2nd WITNESS—Name Philip H Maas
Address Staple Inn, Holborn
Occupation Solicitor

N.B.—The person making the will should sign it at the end of the Will itself, that is, immediately at the end of the writing.

cident occurred, it was believed that there were two bodies to look for—Holmes' as well as the Professor's. Although the distraught Dr. Watson considered that 'any attempt at recovering the bodies was absolutely hopeless,' the Swiss, more experienced in such matters, and accustomed to seeing the corpse of a mountaineer emerge from a glacier some decades after he fell into a crevasse, would know better, and would not fail to make a thorough search."

In Mr. Simpson's view, the corpse of Professor Moriarty was not found because he had developed an Atomic Accelerator, a weapon more terrible than the atomic or hydrogen-bomb, which he turned upon himself as a last resort. But Mr. Poul Anderson ("A Treatise on the Binomial Theorem") has taken issue with Mr. Simpson: "the theory overlooks one basic item: that in order to accelerate mass, and so shrink it, energy must be applied. A shrinkage of one-half through velocity would require an energy equivalent to the original mass. Thus, to reduce, let us say, a 6-foot, 170-pound man to three feet, an energy of 170 pounds must be applied. Now a mass of one gram is equivalent to 9×10^{20} ergs, sufficient to raise a 30,000-ton ship more than 19 miles into the air. Mass-energy to the amount of 170 pounds, necessarily applied to Moriarty's body through the law of equal and opposite reaction, would not only have destroyed the Reichenbach Falls in one annihilating blow but probably would have left a large hole in place of the entire Republic of Switzerland. Mr. Simpson goes yet further: postulating that objects were shrunk to nearly zero size. In order to do this, Moriarty would have to convert the entire sidereal universe into energy, a project somewhat too large even for his ambitious nature."

35 *the best and the wisest man whom I have ever known.* "Watson's words," Mr. Morris Rosenblum wrote in "Foreign Language Quotations in the Canon," "are an echo of the final paragraph of [Plato's] *Phaedo*, describing the death of Socrates: 'Such was the end, Echecrates, of our friend, who was, as we may say, of all those of his time whom we have ever known, the best and wisest and most righteous man.' "

Auctorial and Bibliographical Note: Conan Doyle's own opinion of "The Final Problem" was a high one: he placed it No. 4 on his "twelve best" list of the short stories. Of the original manuscript, only "a noble fragment" is recorded, the "original autograph manuscript of Sherlock Holmes' letter to Dr. Watson, regarding his last meeting with Professor Moriarty." The fragment was auctioned in Philadelphia on December 8, 1915; its present location is unknown.

. . . A PERSONAL CONTEST BETWEEN THE TWO MEN ENDED . . . IN THEIR REELING OVER, LOCKED IN EACH OTHER'S ARMS

Illustration by Sidney Paget for the *Strand Magazine*, December, 1893. Harry C. Edwards illustrated the same sad scene for *McClure's Magazine*, December, 1893.

VII. FROM HOLMES' RETURN TO DR. WATSON'S THIRD MARRIAGE

[Thursday, April 5, 1894 to October, 1902]

"Once again Mr. Sherlock Holmes is free to devote his life to examining those interesting little problems which the complex life of London so plentifully presents."

—"The Adventure of the Empty House"

48

"YOU MAY HAVE READ OF THE REMARKABLE EXPLORATIONS OF A NORWEGIAN NAMED SIGERSON . . ."

We must here anticipate Holmes' Return to examine critically what has aptly been termed the Great Hiatus—the three years, May, 1891, to April, 1894, when all the world, except his brother Mycroft, thought Sherlock Holmes dead.

In "The Adventure of the Empty House," Holmes tells Watson (and us): "I travelled for two years in Tibet . . . , and amused myself by visiting Lhassa and spending some days with the head Llama. . . . I then passed through Persia, looked in at Mecca, and paid a short but interesting visit to the Khalifa at Khartoum. . . . Returning to France, I spent some months in a research into the coal-tar derivatives, which I conducted at a laboratory at Montpelier, in the south of France."

Now, "here . . . is a tale compounded of fallacy, anachronism and paradox," the late Edgar W. Smith wrote in "Sherlock Holmes and the Great Hiatus"; "an itinerary that starts from the realm of the merely improbable and carries us swiftly to the never-never land of the globally impossible; a fantasy that rivals the most befuddled denizen of Upper Swandam Lane. The doings at Reichenbach, we may all agree, are veiled in a mist of considerable doubt. But the Years of the Hiatus which lie beyond are enshrouded in a fog so thick that the streets of London itself have never known its like."

These are strong words, trebly strong in coming from one of the most distinguished of all Sherlockian scholars, past or present, and we must first of all see upon what grounds Mr. Smith (and many other commentators) have based their doubts about the Holmes itinerary as Watson has given it to us.

Let us look at the Master Detective's statements, one by one:

1. *"I travelled for two years in Tibet . . . and amused myself by visiting Lhassa and spending some days with the head Llama."* As Mr. Ogden Nash has so delightfully pointed out in *Many Long Years Ago:*

> The one-l lama,
> He's a priest,
> The two-l llama,
> He's a beast . . .

and it is most unfortunate that our text here reads *Llama* and not *Lama.* Since it is highly unlikely that Holmes, confusing Tibet with Peru, spent some days with a high-ranking llama, he presumably passed his time with one of the dignitaries of

Tibetan Lamaism, probably not the Dalai Lama, then a youth who lived in much seclusion, but perhaps either the Pan-chen Rim-Poche (the Tashai or Teshai Lama) or the Regent, abbot of the great Ten-gye-ling Monastery in Lhassa, then one of the four major monasteries in Tibet. The late A. Carson Simpson, in Volume Two of his great work, *Sherlock Holmes' Wanderjahre,* voted for the Regent, who has been called "the head Lama" by no less an authority than Sir Charles Bell (*Tibet, Past and Present,* Oxford, 1924); although Mrs. Winifred M. Christie ("On the Remarkable Explorations of Sigerson") thought it more likely that Holmes' host was the Pan-chen Lama, who outranked the Dalai Lama spiritually although subordinate to him in worldly matters. But here Mr. Smith entered his first objection: *no* European, Norwegian or otherwise, he pointed out, "came anywhere near the forbidden city of Lhassa until 1903, when a military mission under Lt. Col. Younghusband battered its way into the Lama's presence by force of arms. Two Englishmen, Captain Bower and Dr. Thorold, crossed the borders of Tibet in 1891; and in 1892—by which time Holmes must have begun to tire of the amusement his visit was affording him—an Englishwoman, Miss Taylor, came within 150 miles of the holy of holies. The record for peaceful penetration—still as far from Lhassa itself as Philadelphia from New York—was established by a Mr. and Mrs. Littledale in 1895; but from that point on all foreigners, including the Scandinavian, seem to have given up the idea of carrying European culture to the innocent Tibetans until, nearly a decade later, the task was finally and successfully accomplished with benefit of Gatling gun and other light artillery. There can be no confusion in all of this: Holmes was neither a woman nor a soldier, and we must be constrained now to believe that he was not even a Norwegian. The first two years of his reputed itinerary we may, therefore, dismiss as a figment."

Dr. John D. Clark, in his paper, "Some Notes Relating to a Preliminary Investigation into the Paternity of Nero Wolfe," has expressed his agreement with this position: "Holmes' account of his travels in Tibet and through Persia are the purest invention on his part. . . . The mention of the 'Norwegian traveller Sigerson' is cleverly designed to lead to a degree of confusion in Watson's mind between the mythical Norwegian and the very real Sven Hedin who was at that time starting his Central Asian researches. . . ."

And Mr. H. B. Williams has added that Holmes "could have found no better method of informing the Moriarty organization of his whereabouts [than through his letters to the London newspapers, concerning the remarkable explorations of which Watson "may have read"]. Proof of this . . . is to be had in the consideration of the short biography of Colonel Moran included in Holmes' fine collection of *M*'s ["The Adventure of the Empty House"]. Colonel Moran is therein listed as the author of *Heavy Game of the Western Himalayas.* Any exploration of the Himalayas and Tibet would be of intense interest to him. Holmes having no time to build up [his] alter ego, [Sigerson], the exploits of this hereto unknown explorer meant that Moran would explore the background of this newcomer being chronicled in the daily press. It would not be long before Holmes' disguise would have been penetrated."[1]

1 But the late A. Carson Simpson shortly afterwards pointed out that in Tibet at that time the postal system, such as it was, was strictly for government officials; there were no postage stamps until 1913, and then for internal use only. "Such being the case, there is little force in the suggestion that newspaper accounts of Sigerson's explorations would have alerted Col. Moran to investigate; these could not even have been started on their way to the papers until after Holmes was safely out of Tibet."

2. "*I then passed through Persia . . .*" "It is to be hoped" (Mr. Smith continued) "that this transit, if it really occurred, was both rapid and discreet, and that Holmes did not tarry long in search of a mate to the slipper which still, we may suppose, was hanging by the fireplace in the empty room at Baker Street. For Persia, in the year 1893, was seething with unrest, and all strangers, particularly Englishmen and Russians, whose governments were even then sparring for political advantage in this ancient land, were regarded with suspicion."

3. ". . . *looked in at Mecca . . .*" "There, too, if [Holmes] arrived early in the summer of 1893" (we are still quoting Mr. Smith), "he would have run into trouble in the form of a modest civil war. Mecca itself was probably sanctuary to all the faithful in common, but in nearby Mulaida a fierce battle had recently been waged between overzealous Mohammedan factions and, in crossing from the western borders of Persia to the ultimate shrine of Islam, Holmes would have had to pass through territory which was still witness to brisk if sporadic skirmishing. . . . It is to be earnestly doubted, in view of the excitements prevailing, that Holmes' 'look-in' at Mecca was from any very close point of vantage."

4. ". . . *paid a short but interesting visit to the Khalifa at Khartoum . . .*" The Khalifa, we may note to begin with, was the Mohammedan ruler of the Sudan south of Egypt and Libya, a region which was a storm center of British foreign policy in the 'eighties and 'nineties. And now let us return to Mr. Smith: ". . . the curious incident of the Khalifa at Khartoum, in the year 1893, is that the Khalifa was not at Khartoum. That historic city on the banks of the Nile had been leveled to the ground in 1885, and the Mahdist government had taken up its residence in nearby Omdurman, where the Calif ["Khalifa"] Abdullah held forth embattled until 1888, when Kitchener overthrew him and returned the seat of Sudanese affairs once more to Khartoum."

5. ". . . *spent some months in a research into the coal-tar derivatives, which I conducted in a laboratory at Montpelier, in the south of France.*" It is again to be deeply regretted that our text here reads *Montpelier*, for Montpelier—with one *l* —is 1) a city in Bear Lake County, Idaho; 2) a city in Blockford County, Indiana; 3) a village in Williams County, Ohio; 4) the county seat of Washington County, Vermont, and the capital of that state. We assume that Watson meant *Montpellier*, with two *l*'s, which, happily, *is* a city in the south of France. Aside from Watson's spelling, little exception can be taken to this statement, although—as Professor Remsen Ten Eyck Schenck pointed out in "Baker Street Fables"—"no chemist would be guilty of making it. At least 80% of all the research work in chemistry done by thousands of men in the last hundred years could be so described, since about that proportion of the known organic compounds are coal-tar derivatives. The remark is therefore windy, grandiose and so diffuse as to be practically devoid of meaning."

Despite these formidable objections, there exists a highly articulate group of Sherlockian commentators—the Apologistic, or Fundamentalist, School—which maintains that Holmes did almost exactly what he said he did at the time of the Great Hiatus: visited the head Lama in Lhassa, passed through Persia, looked in at Mecca, and interviewed the Khalifa (but not, perhaps, at Khartoum).

Let us briefly review the opinions of this school, starting with its views on Tibet.

1. *On Tibet.* Here our outstanding authority is certainly Mr. Simpson, who has traced virtually every step of Holmes' explorations in the Forbidden Land in his monumental study of *Sherlock Holmes' Wanderjahre.* Mr. Simpson demonstrates with considerable believeability that Holmes outfitted his expedition at Darjeeling, made the eighteen-mile trip by cart-road to the valley of the Teesta River, crossed the river by means of the Teesta Bridge, and started a sixty-mile trip over a narrow and crude pony-track to the Tibetan frontier. This was probably the most uncomfortable part of the trip because of the Himalayan leeches. Contending with leeches all the way, Holmes followed the pony-track through Kalimpong, gradually climbing along the river to Rangpo, where he left it and entered Native Sikkim. Here began the steep climb to the Tibetan frontier. The Master crossed the Jelep La (Pass) on the frontier and made the steep ascent to the Chumbi Valley. The beginning of the climb up the Chumbi Valley to the settlement of Chumbi was easy. From there the way climbed to Phari Dzong, forty miles from the Jelep La. Holmes had to cross several other passes before reaching Lhassa, over 210 miles away. "There [Holmes'] first act would be to call on the Head Lama and to present him with the traditional white scarf." It is Mr. Simpson's hypothesis that the "head Lama" (Regent, in his view) then commissioned Holmes to solve the mystery of the Abominable Snowman, then known only by his footprints in the snow. This would take Holmes into the Everest region. His interest in Buddhism would of course lead him to visit the Rocky Valley Inner Monastery (Rongbuk), sixteen miles from Mount Everest, and the Monastery of the Mount of Blessing—Ta-shi Lhun-po, at Shigaste. In the course of his Snowman researches he would investigate the whole vicinity of Everest, as well as the slopes of the mountain itself. "This made him the first European—and probably the first man—to set foot on the sacred ground of the highest mountain in the world. To the British Empire, therefore, belongs the credit for the first partial ascent, as well as for finishing the job on that memorable May 29, 1953, over sixty years later." It is at this time that Holmes would naturally visit the Kharta Valley, to the eastward (*see below*). His Snowman researches completed, Holmes moved westward to Ladakh, under British protection, to replenish his funds. "After travelling around Ladakh for a time, he no doubt headed east for his researches into the geology of Central Tibet,"**2** returning by a more northerly course to Toghral Ombo, where his homeward journey, via Persia, Mecca, Khartoum and the south of France began.

2. *On Persia.* Here a correspondent (and a considerable authority on both Persia and Mecca), Mr. Benson Murray, writes: "Persia in [1893] may have been 'seething with unrest,' but I doubt that this would have bothered a man of Holmes' accomplishments. Sykes makes mention of the cancellation of the tobacco *régie* in 1892 'after disturbances had broken out and intense hostility had been displayed towards

2 As mentioned by Mr. P. M. Stone in his "Sussex Interview" with Holmes.

Europeans' (*History of Persia,* II, 373). Browne characterizes the period from 1890 to 1896 as 'notable for political fermentation which brought on revolution' (*Literary History of Persia,* IV, 156). Shuster (*The Strangling of Persia*) makes no particular mention of unrest. Certainly Gertrude Bell's *Persian Pictures* (trip made 1892; work first published with additional material 1894) shows no seething unrest."

3. *On Mecca.* "I do not remember" (we are again quoting our authority on the history of the Middle East, Mr. Benson Murray) "that either Hurgronje, who visited Mecca in 1885, or Gervais-Courtellement, who was there in 1894, mentions civil war. Neither of these accounts is presently at hand to me, but a check of de Gaury's *Rulers of Mecca* (London, 1951) and Hogarth's *History of Arabia* (Oxford, 1922) indicates nothing more than a struggle between the Ottoman administration and the Sherif. I would scarcely call this civil war."**3**

4. *On Khartoum.* "One would think," the late Dr. Ernest Bloomfield Zeisler wrote in *Baker Street Chronology,* "that Khartoum and Omdurman are at opposite poles of the earth. As a matter of fact they are only a mile or two apart, Khartoum being on the right bank of the Nile and Omdurman on the left bank directly opposite. It is true that the Khalifa's capital was at that time not Khartoum but Omdurman. The former had been besieged by the Mahdists and captured on January 26, 1885, the day they killed General Gordon. Almost every building in Khartoum was destroyed. On June 22, 1885, the Mahdi died and was succeeded by the Khalifa, whose capital was Omdurman. It was not until September of 1898 that Omdurman was captured by General Kitchener, and the capital was transferred back to Khartoum. The Master's visit to the Khalifa was probably late in 1893, at which time Khartoum had been partly rebuilt, and it is quite possible that the Khalifa actually was in Khartoum when the Master saw him, though it is more likely that it was in Omdurman rather than in Khartoum. It was probably either a slip of the tongue by the Master or a slip of the pen by Watson which led to this slight error in the account. But this cannot stamp the entire story as untrue. The two cities were joined by much history and by a bridge, and it would have been easy to mis-speak or mis-write one for the other. Indeed, this very slip speaks rather potently for the truth of the story, for if the Master had been trying to deceive the public he would have been careful to avoid so obvious an error."

And the late A. Carson Simpson added: "Indeed, the 'Khalifa-Khartoum' error, rightly understood, *confirms* the visit to Tibet. Service in Afghanistan would not familiarize Watson with the name of every region in the far end of Tibet, especially one not on a recognized trade-route. So when Holmes referred to passing through *Kharta,* the name was unknown to the Doctor, who confused it with Khartoum —a place only too well known to every Britisher at that time. He did not realize that the Master was referring to a district in south-eastern Tibet, just north of the eastern end of Nepal. Instead, Watson erroneously associated it with the Sudan, probably misled by the reference to the Khalifa, and misunderstood Kharta as Khartoum, which the Master un-

3 Mr. Murray adds: "In spite of [very strict] restrictions [against the visits of non-Muslims to Mecca] a number of people have visited Mecca and left reports. The classic reports are probably those of Burckhardt (in Mecca 1814) and Burton (in Mecca 1853). Including Holmes . . . I am aware of 28 visitors, mostly of European origin, who have left accounts in European languages. These accounts range from that of Ludovico Varthema who visited the city in 1503 to H. B. St. J. Philby who made the pilgrimage in 1931. I question the veracity of the account of a visit made to Mecca by Arnold von Harff. If his account is true he would be the first western visitor —1496."

Mr. Murray also suggests an interesting *reason* for Holmes' visit: "In 1877 'an Englishman professing Mohammedanism' visited Mecca. He resided there for some six months, and his account (which appeared in 1881) is of considerable interest. . . . In this work he makes mention of an Englishwoman in Mecca. Upon his return from Mecca he attempted to make contact with her to see if she could be brought from Mecca to England. The material in the appendix of the book casts some doubt on whether she really was English although all reports indicate that her command of the language was very good. In 1877 she had been residing in Mecca since the Indian Mutiny of 1857. Shortly after 1877 she appears to have been taken back to India, and it was reported that she did not want 'rescue.' I know nothing of her subsequent history but it is possible that by 1893 she had been once again taken to Mecca and by that time she desired to spend her last years in England. At the time of Holmes' visit [presumably to affect her rescue] she would have been in her sixties. The book in question is (J.) T. F. Keane, *Six Months in Mecca,* London, 1881."

doubtedly never mentioned at all in speaking of his 'short but interesting visit to the Khalifa.' "

Opposed to the Apologistic, or Fundamentalist, School of Sherlockian Commentary, however, is a group we may call the Interpretive School. This group holds that Holmes, for one reason or another, was not being entirely frank with Watson in his brief description of his travels—or, alternatively, that Watson, for one reason or another, was not being entirely frank with his readers.

In this latter vein, for example, Mr. Walter P. Armstrong, Jr., writes (in "The Truth About Sherlock Holmes"): "Not only was Holmes in London [during the entire period 1891–1894], but he was living in the same house with Watson all the time. . . . So it becomes apparent that Watson never believed that Holmes lay at the bottom of the Reichenbach Fall; that on the contrary he helped him to lay a false trail and later published an account of his death which he knew to be false; that during the three years during which he was supposed to be traveling under the name of Sigerson, Holmes was in fact in London waiting for Colonel Moran to make a false move, and Watson knew it; that after the apprehension of Colonel Moran [Holmes] assumed his true character; and that Watson then, in order to conceal his lapse from the strictest veracity, composed a fictional account of his escape and return. . . . Watson has deceived us. But we cannot blame him, for the deception was necessary in order to trap the wily members of the Moriarty gang who remained."**4**

Mr. Edgar W. Smith, on the other hand, noting that Holmes in "The Adventure of the Dancing Men" "made reference in familiar terms to 'my friend Wilson Hargreave, of the New York Police Bureau' " and spoke confidently, in that same adventure, of "my knowledge of the crooks of Chicago," wrote that: "Such friendships and such knowledge are not credibly acquired, even by a man of Holmes' attainments, on a mail-order basis, and in both instances the statements as he made them have a ring of authority which speaks eloquently of first-hand acquaintance and information." In the Smith view, then, Holmes spent the years of the Great Hiatus, not in Tibet, Persia, Arabia, the Egyptian Sudan, and the south of France, but in the United States of America. Indeed, he concluded that: "It is obvious [in the murders of Andrew Jackson Borden and his wife, Abby Durfee Borden, at Fall River, Massachusetts, on the fourth of August in the year 1892] that some unseen hand was steadily at work in the weaving of [the] net [that caught and held Lizzie Borden, who was indicted on December 2, 1892], and it should be equally obvious to us whose hand that was. Confronted as they were by the bloodiest and most blood-curdling murder in the annals of crime, it is wholly reasonable to suppose that the police of Fall River . . . should have appealed to the closest thing there is in America to a Scotland Yard—the New York Police Bureau. And in rallying to meet that appeal it would be incredible that Wilson Hargreave should have failed to call in turn upon the aid and counsel of the greatest criminal investigator of all time, who sat beside him at the moment—or that Sherlock Holmes should have refused to heed that call."

A third view, popular with this school, holds that Holmes

4 The late Gavin Brend agreed with Mr. Armstrong that Holmes was in London all the time—but Mr. Brend went on to suggest (*My Dear Holmes*) that Colonel James Moriarty took over the gang after his brother's death and that Sherlock Holmes joined the gang in disguise in order to break it up; it was during this period, Mr. Brend held, that Mycroft communicated with Sherlock by the "second stain" code through Watson's reports of "The Yellow Face" and "The Naval Treaty."

during the years of the Great Hiatus was acting as a secret agent for the Allies and was therefore circumspect with Watson about the areas he actually visited. "In the Far East he must have observed with sage foreboding Japan's preparations for the Chinese war of 1894 that would begin the march of Japanese imperialism," Mr. Manly Wade Wellman wrote in "Scoundrels in Bohemia." "His other activities concentrated on Persia, the East African Coast, and France—hot spots of international dispute then and later."

Nor should we forget here those who believe that the Great Hiatus was a period when Love at last Conquered All. Here is Mr. Stanley McComas, speaking for this group in his essay, "Love at Lhassa": ". . . after Reichenbach, Holmes met Irene Adler in Florence and married her without delay. He was in a hurry to get there, too. Can anyone believe that a man, torn and bleeding from a nasty adventure on a ledge over the Reichenbach Falls, would do 'ten miles over the mountains in the darkness' [see "The Adventure of the Empty House"] merely out of fear of an old man with an air gun?"**5**

And now we must consider the speculations of still a third group of commentators—the Sensationalist School—whose theories may be conveniently grouped under three major headings:

1. *Both Holmes and Moriarty survived Reichenbach.*

a. Holmes survived (said the late A. G. Macdonell**6**) because he was a pure invention of Holmes', part of an elaborate hoax. In Mr. Macdonell's view, "Holmes selected a perfectly ordinary ex-professor and fastened on to the unfortunate man the fearful reputation which has dogged him ever since." Holmes did this, we are told, because in the late 'eighties he found himself slipping. To explain his failures, he therefore invented a supercriminal. At Reichenbach, Holmes clung to one rock and Moriarty to another; Moriarty was then resuscitated in 1899 (Mr. Macdonell's date) to play his part in *The Valley of Fear.*

b. Or Moriarty survived because he and Holmes were one and the same man. In *Sherlock Holmes: Fact or Fiction?*, Mr. T. S. Blakeney reported this as the "very subtle suggestion . . . thrown out in private by a distinguished writer whose name cannot be divulged." The evidence for the hypothesis is: 1) Holmes' testimony that Moriarty existed is all we have; 2) Holmes was a master at disguise; 3) Holmes had someone impersonate Moriarty at Reichenbach. Mr. Blakeney then commented: "The more we reflect on this Holmes-Moriarty hypothesis the more we are convinced that it is adequately answered in Holmes' own words: 'it seems to have only one drawback, and that is that it is intrinsically impossible.' "

c. Or Moriarty survived because he used a double at Reichenbach. "Is it not logical," Mr. H. B. Williams wrote in "A Non-Canonical Clue," "that Moriarty would pit one of greater physical ability than he possessed to engage in a hand-to-hand struggle with Holmes? There must have been times in the pursuance of his nefarious doings that the employment of a double was mandatory. Why not at this time use one whose strength could cope with Holmes' bodily powers?"**7**

5 But the late Elmer Davis commented (*Introducing Mr. Sherlock Holmes*): "If any such interlude of dalliance is admissible at all, which I doubt, it is more likely to have lasted three weeks than three years. What a three weeks! you may say. What, indeed." And Dean Theodore C. Blegen wrote ("These Were Hidden Fires, Indeed"): "The theory is engaging and cannot be dismissed lightly, but there is no documentation . . ."

6 In "The Truth About Moriarty," which has also appeared under the title of "Mr. Moriarty."

7 Moriarty not only survived, he reformed, in the view of Miss Ruth Berman. She has suggested that some evidence of this may be found in the Periodic Chart of the Elements, which shows that Element 67, one of the rare earths, was called *Holmium* by its discoverer, as a tribute to Holmes by the reformed Moriarty.

2. *Neither Holmes nor Moriarty survived Reichenbach.* The late Monsignor Ronald A. Knox was forced to conclude his *Studies in the Literature of Sherlock Holmes* with the solemn thought that Holmes had indeed been killed at Reichenbach, and that—while "all the stories were written by Watson"—they consisted in part of a "genuine cycle [which] actually happened" and in part of "spurious adventures [which were] the lucubrations of his own unaided invention."

The late Page Heldenbrand was another who believed that Holmes perished at the Reichenbach. Some of the later-chronicled adventures, he contended in "The Adventures of the Dead Detective," took place before Holmes' demise ("The Adventure of Charles Augustus Milverton," "The Second Stain," "The Adventure of the Dying Detective," *The Valley of Fear*), while others were fictions concocted by Watson for his personal gain.

And Mr. Rolfe Boswell has agreed that a rock "carried both Holmes and Moriarty over the falls—a strike without a spare." The later Holmes, he holds ("Sarasate, Sherlock and Shaw"), was a fictive creature, "recreated from the chasm to line the pockets" of writers other than Watson.

Writing in "Who Killed Holmes?", Mr. Marvin Grasse has answered his own question by suggesting that it was Watson and Mycroft. This theory runs as follows: Watson had a long-smoldering hatred for Holmes, who had taunted him repeatedly, and finally had wrecked his marriage; Mycroft, too, was jealous of his younger brother and anxious to inherit his wealth. So Watson and Mycroft connived together, Mycroft being the tall Englishman hurrying to meet Sherlock. And Watson, after helping Mycroft to bash in Holmes' brains, not only scribbled the cunning alibi note that recalled him to the hotel, but composed Sherlock's death message as well.

And Mr. Anthony Boucher, writing in "Was the Later Holmes an Imposter?", has based his case that the later Holmes *was* an imposter on these four points:

a. "The protero-Holmes announced his intended retirement after the triumph over Moriarty. . . . The returned Holmes continues in practice for almost a decade after the complete annihilation of the Moriarty gang."

b. "The original Holmes plays the violin frequently. . . . The deutero-Holmes never once plays the violin.**8** . . . [He] is apparently more interested in vocal music . . ."

c. "Holmes I was addicted to the use of cocaine and morphine. Holmes II uses no stronger stimulant than shag."

d. ". . . the *ur*-Holmes knows off-hand [the names of] the three leading free-lance spies in London ["The Second Stain"] . . . Holmes [in 1895, in "The Adventure of the Bruce-Partington Plans"] is forced to appeal to Mycroft for their names . . ."

Other commentators, notably Mr. Eustace Portugal and Professor John B. Wolf, have added to Mr. Boucher's list:

e. Holmes I and II are inconsistent in respect to their attitudes to the law.**9**

f. In later cases, Holmes shows a tendency to gibe at his opponents; this would be like Moriarty, but unlike Holmes.

8 Mr. Boucher is not quite correct here. In "The Adventure of the Norwood Builder" (August, 1895), Watson wrote: "For two hours he [Holmes] droned away upon his violin . . ."

9 A point on which Magistrate S. Tupper Bigelow has expanded in his essay, "Sherlock Holmes Was No Burglar": ". . . what of Holmes' colossal ignorance of the law of burglary and unlawful entry after the Return? . . . It would appear . . . that this . . . provides powerful ammunition for those who espouse the theory of [a] deutero-Holmes. There is no instance in the Canon before the Return, for example, in which Holmes revealed his contempt for what he believed to be the law so far as burglary was concerned. Nor is there a case in which he thought he had committed burglary or even unlawful entry, before the Return. On the contrary, compare Holmes' respect for a search-warrant in 'The Greek Interpreter' with his utter disdain for such a scrap of paper in 'The Disappearance of Lady Frances Carfax.' Furthermore, it must be pointed out, Holmes' sublimated yearnings for a criminal career are made evident in the Canon only after the Return."

g. Holmes I quotes both German and French several times; Holmes II never does.

h. Holmes I demonstrates a considerable knowledge of horse racing ("Silver Blaze"); Holmes II has to make Watson his "Handy Guide to the Turf" ("The Adventure of Shoscombe Old Place").

Mr. Boucher concluded that "Mycroft saw to it that there should be a Sherlock Holmes. He found a cousin, markedly similar to the lost brother and possessed of some of the intellectual attainments characteristic of the Vernet strain of blood. He would be capable of playing the role of Sherlock reasonably well on his own, and if need be, he could always call upon Mycroft. . . . The three *Wanderjahre*, 1891–1894, were doubtless spent, not in Tibet nor in the ruins of Khartoum, but in the Pall Mall lodgings opposite the Diogenes Club under the careful tutelage of Mycroft, with visits (no doubt in disguise) to the empty lodgings in Baker Street, where files and scrapbooks might be consulted and memorized. The Adair murder provided the perfect moment for the resurrection, and Sherlock Holmes once more walked the streets of London."

This is an ingenious theory, argued with much plausibility —but we must add that Mr. Boucher himself later abandoned it, in favor of the Armstrong Holmes-Never-Left-London Theory.

3. *Moriarty alone survived Reichenbach.* This is the view of Mr. Eustace Portugal, who, like Mr. Boucher, based his case largely on the changes in Holmes' nature after the Return. "It is my opinion," Mr. Portugal wrote in "The Holmes-Moriarty Duel," "that it is Professor Moriarty who keeps bees on the Sussex Downs, and that the body of Sherlock Holmes lies in the Reichenbach abyss."

But—as Mr. Boucher has written—Mr. Portugal's evidence "amounts to hardly more than the fact that the mathematician [like Holmes] was . . . tall and thin. This solution, though pleasantly outrageous, has little to recommend it."

Let us conclude our examination of the years of the Great Hiatus with this quotation from Mr. E. W. McDiarmid ("Reichenbach and Beyond"):

"No conclusive evidence has appeared to make one believe that Holmes lies buried in the chasm at Reichenbach. Nor is there conclusive evidence to suggest that the period of the Great Hiatus was not just that: the interlude between the early practice and some later events. And finally, we must agree that whether or not Holmes returned to active practice,**10** he *did* return—and, at least by 1903, had fulfilled his dream of retiring to a Sussex bee farm."

10 Mr. McDiarmid argues that Holmes actually did retire after vanquishing Moriarty and that the later cases are either 1) special cases, which Holmes felt he had to undertake (e.g., "His Last Bow"); or 2) reports of earlier cases issued by Watson, who for some reason wished to maintain the fiction that Holmes was in active practice until 1903.

49

THE ADVENTURE OF THE EMPTY HOUSE

[Thursday, April 5, 1894]

IT was in the spring of the year 1894 that all London was interested, and the fashionable world dismayed,
by the murder of the Honourable Ronald Adair, 1
under most unusual and inexplicable circumstances. The public has already learned those particulars of the crime which came out in the police investigation ; but a good deal was suppressed upon that occasion, since the case for the prosecution was so overwhelmingly strong that it was not necessary to bring forward all the facts.
Only now, at the end of nearly ten years, am I allowed 2
to supply those missing links which make up the whole of that remarkable chain. The crime was of interest in itself, but that interest was as nothing to me compared to the inconceivable sequel, which afforded me the greatest shock and surprise of any event in my adventurous life. Even now, after this long interval, I find myself thrilling as I think of it, and feeling once more that sudden flood of joy, amazement, and incredulity which utterly submerged my mind. Let me say to that public which has shown some interest in those glimpses which I have occasionally given them of the thoughts and actions of a very remarkable man that they are not to blame me if I have not shared my knowledge with them, for I should have considered it my first duty to have done so had I not been barred by a positive prohibition from his own lips, which was only withdrawn upon the third of last
month. 3

It can be imagined that my close intimacy with Sherlock Holmes had interested me deeply in crime, and that after his disappearance I never failed to read with care the various problems which came before the public and I even attempted more than once for my own private satisfaction to employ his methods in their solution, though with indifferent success. There was none, however, which appealed to me like this tragedy of Ronald Adair. As I read the evidence at the inquest, which led up to a verdict of wilful murder against some person or persons unknown, I realized more clearly than I had ever done the loss which the community had sustained by the death of Sherlock Holmes. There were points about this strange business which would, I was sure, have specially appealed to him, and the efforts of the police would have been supplemented, or more probably anticipated, by the trained observation and the alert mind of the first criminal agent in Europe. All day as I drove

1 *the Honourable Ronald Adair.* "British conventions in regard to titles are sometimes puzzling to the American reader," the late Christopher Morley wrote in *Sherlock Holmes and Dr. Watson: A Textbook of Friendship.* "Young Ronald Adair has the courtesy prefix The Honourable because he is the child of a 'peer' (viz., a nobleman; there are five degrees of nobility: duke, marquis, earl, viscount, baron). Similarly his sister Hilda would be known as The Honourable Hilda Adair. The prefix Honourable is also given by courtesy to judges of the higher courts and some government officials, as is also done, though more casually, in the U.S. This attribution of honor is not acquired by marriage: if Ronald had married Miss Woodley they would have been announced by the butler as The Honourable Ronald Adair and Mrs. Adair. The most frequent error made by those unfamiliar with these traditional labels is to use the title of honor as a substitute for Mister. When Dr. Doyle was knighted and became Sir Arthur Conan Doyle it would be wrong to refer to him as 'Sir Doyle,' just as you would never call Sir Walter Scott 'Sir Scott.' Sir Walter Scott, Bart., means Sir Walter Scott, Baronet; the Baronet's title is hereditary and passes to his son. The order of simple knighthood, as in the case of Doyle, is personal and not hereditary. In these innocent old formalities are many entertaining distinctions. For instance the formal address for the Earl of Maynooth would be Right Honourable the Earl of Maynooth. His wife would be The Countess of Maynooth, but referred to informally as Lady Maynooth. Perhaps it was the complexity of all this that discouraged plain Miss Edith Woodley."

2 *at the end of nearly ten years.* "The Adventure of the Empty House" was published in the *Strand Magazine*, October, 1903, and in *Collier's Magazine*, September 26, 1903.

3 *the third of last month.* Allowing for magazine printing schedules, the time Watson would have needed to write his account of the adventure, and the time required by the artists to prepare illustrations, it is probable that "the third of last month" was no later than the third of June, 1903, some four months before Holmes' retirement.

upon my round I turned over the case in my mind, and found no explanation which appeared to me to be adequate. At the risk of telling a twice-told tale I will recapitulate the facts as they were known to the public at the conclusion of the inquest.

The Honourable Robert Adair was the second son of the Earl of Maynooth, at that time Governor of one of the Australian colonies. Adair's mother had returned from
4 Australia to undergo an operation for cataract, and she, her son Ronald, and her daughter Hilda were living together at 427 Park Lane. The youth moved in the best society, had, so far as was known, no enemies, and no particular vices. He had been engaged to Miss Edith Woodley, of Carstairs, but the engagement had been broken off by mutual consent some months before, and there was no sign that it had left any very profound feeling behind it. For the rest, the man's life moved in a narrow and conventional circle, for his habits were quiet and his nature unemotional. Yet it was upon this easy-going young aristocrat that death came in most strange and unexpected form between the hours of ten and eleven-
5 twenty on the night of March 30, 1894.

Ronald Adair was fond of cards, playing continually, but never for such stakes as would hurt him. He was a
6-7-8 member of the Baldwin, the Cavendish, and the Bagatelle Card Clubs. It was shown that after dinner on the day of his death he had played a rubber of whist at the latter club. He had also played there in the afternoon. The evidence of those who had played with him—Mr. Murray, Sir John Hardy, and Colonel Moran—showed that the game was whist, and that there was a fairly equal fall of the cards. Adair might have lost five pounds, but not more. His fortune was a considerable one, and such a loss could not in any way affect him. He had played nearly every day at one club or other, but he was a cautious player, and usually rose a winner. It came out in evidence that in partnership with Colonel Moran he had
9 actually won as much as £420 in a sitting some weeks before from Godfrey Milner and Lord Balmoral. So much for his recent history, as it came out at the inquest.

On the evening of the crime he returned from the club exactly at ten. His mother and sister were out spending the evening with a relation. The servant deposed that she heard him enter the front room on the second floor, generally used as his sitting-room. She had lit a fire there, and as it smoked she had opened the window. No sound was heard from the room until eleven-twenty, the hour of the return of Lady Maynooth and her daughter. Desiring to say good night, she had attempted to enter her son's room. The door was locked on the inside, and no answer could be got to their cries and knocking. Help was obtained, and the door forced. The unfortunate young man was found lying near the table. His head had been horribly mutilated by an expanded revolver bullet, but no weapon of any sort was to be found in the room. On the table lay two bank-notes for
10 £10 each and £17 10*s.* in silver and gold, the money arranged in little piles of varying amount. There were some figures also upon a sheet of paper with the names of some club friends opposite to them, from which it was

ALL DAY AS I DROVE UPON MY ROUND . . .

Here Dr. Joseph Bell of Edinburgh, the prototype of Sherlock Holmes, makes *his* daily round.

4 *an operation for cataract.* "The Australian colonies were Victoria, New South Wales, South Australia, West Australia and Queensland; but they also included the 'two adjacent islands' of Tasmania and New Zealand," Mrs. Jennifer Chorley wrote in "Some Diggings Down Under." "Taking these seven, three (Victoria-Hopetown; South Australia-Kintore; New Zealand-Glasgow) were governed by earls. But Tasmania had Viscount Gormansion—not an earl but the only Irish peer. My mother is a Tasmanian by birth and judging from accounts of Tasmania at this time by my late grandmother, it is surprising that the Adairs could not enjoy this beautiful place in preference to Park Lane. I have a great-uncle, now in his 90's, still living in Melbourne, where he was practicing medicine, in 1893–4. I am sure he would agree that a cataract operation could have been performed in Melbourne or Sydney. But Tasmania might not have had the facilities so perhaps the Countess had some justification for returning to England."

5 *March 30, 1894.* A Friday. Watson has said that he would "recapitulate the facts as they were known to the public at the time of the inquest." The inquest cannot have been before, or long after, Monday, April 2, 1894.

6 *the Baldwin.* A "card-playing club, which . . . admits no strangers, is the Baldwin, in Pall Mall, which opens at two o'clock in the afternoon. The stakes here are very small," Mr. Ralph Nevill wrote in *London Clubs, Their History and Treasures,* London: Chatto & Windus, 1911.

7 *the Cavendish.* The Cavendish Club, on the north side of Piccadilly, between Down Street and Park Lane, was later taken over by the Cavalry Club.

conjectured that before his death he was endeavouring to make out his losses or winnings at cards.

A minute examination of the circumstances served only to make the case more complex. In the first place, no reason could be given why the young man should have fastened the door upon the inside. There was the possibility that the murderer had done this and had afterwards escaped by the window. The drop was at least twenty feet, however, and a bed of crocuses in full bloom **11**
lay beneath. Neither the flowers nor the earth showed any sign of having been disturbed, nor were there any marks upon the narrow strip of grass which separated the house from the road. Apparently, therefore, it was the young man himself who had fastened the door. But how did he come by his death? No one could have climbed up to the window without leaving traces. Suppose a man had fired through the window, it would indeed be a remarkable shot who could with a revolver inflict so deadly a wound. Again, Park Lane is a frequented thoroughfare, and there is a cab-stand within a hundred yards of the house. No one had heard a shot. And yet there was the dead man, and there the revolver bullet, which had mushroomed out, as soft-nosed bullets will, and so inflicted a wound which must have caused instantaneous death. Such were the circumstances of the Park Lane Mystery, which were further complicated by entire absence of motive, since, as I have said, young Adair was not known to have any enemy, and no attempt had been made to remove the money or valuables in the room.

All day I turned these facts over in my mind, endeavouring to hit upon some theory which could reconcile them all, and to find that line of least resistance which my poor friend had declared to be the starting-point of every investigation. I confess that I made little progress. In the evening I strolled across the Park, and found myself about six o'clock at the Oxford Street end of Park Lane. A group of loafers upon the pavements, all staring up at a particular window, directed me to the house which I had come to see. A tall, thin man with coloured glasses, whom I strongly suspected of being a plain-clothes detective, was pointing out some theory of his own, while the others crowded round to listen to what he said. I got as near as I could, but his observations seemed to me to be absurd, so I withdrew again in some disgust. As I did so I struck against an elderly deformed man, who had been behind me, and I knocked down several books which he was carrying. I remember that as I picked them up I observed the title of one of them, *The Origin of Tree Worship*, and it struck me that the fellow must be some **12**
poor bibliophile who, either as a trade or as a hobby, was a collector of obscure volumes. I endeavoured to apologize for the accident, but it was evident that these books which I had so unfortunately maltreated were very precious objects in the eyes of their owner. With a snarl of contempt he turned upon his heel, and I saw his curved back and white side-whiskers disappear among the throng.

My observations of No. 427 Park Lane did little to clear up the problem in which I was interested. The house

8 *the Bagatelle.* Watson has presumably masked the actual name of the club at which Adair played on the day of his death.

9 *£420.* About $2,100 U.S. at the time.

10 *£17 10s. in silver and gold.* About $187.50 in all.

11 *a bed of crocuses in full bloom.* Watson evidently confused crocuses with another flower, for, as the late Gavin Brend pointed out in *My Dear Holmes,* "the crocus is hardly likely to be blooming [in England] at the end of March, and it would seem that January 30th would be a more appropriate date."

12 The Origin of Tree Worship. "Everywhere and, before the world was laicized, at all times, trees have been worshipped," Mr. Aldous Huxley has written. "It is not to be wondered at. . . . Half hidden in the darkness, half displayed in the air of heaven, the tree stands there, magnificent, a manifest god. . . . Trees in the mass can be almost terrible."

. . . I KNOCKED DOWN SEVERAL BOOKS WHICH HE WAS CARRYING.

A popular scene with the Canonical artists: it has been depicted by Sidney Paget in the *Strand Magazine*, October, 1903; by Frederic Dorr Steele in *Collier's Magazine*, September 26, 1903; by Charles Raymond Macauley in *The Return of Sherlock Holmes*, New York: McClure, Phillips & Co., 1905.

was separated from the street by a low wall and railing, the whole not more than five feet high. It was perfectly easy, therefore, for anyone to get into the garden ; but the window was entirely inaccessible, since there was no water-pipe or anything which could help the most active man to climb it. More puzzled than ever, I retraced
13 my steps to Kensington. I had not been in my study five minutes when the maid entered to say that a person desired to see me. To my astonishment, it was none other than my strange old book-collector, his sharp, wizened face peering out from a frame of white hair, and his precious volumes, a dozen of them at least, wedged under his right arm.

" You're surprised to see me, sir," said he, in a strange, croaking voice.

I acknowledged that I was.

" Well, I've a conscience, sir, and when I chanced to see you go into this house, as I came hobbling after you, I thought to myself, I'll just step in and see that kind gentleman, and tell him that if I was a bit gruff in my manner there was not any harm meant, and that I am much obliged to him for picking up my books."

" You make too much of a trifle," said I. " May I ask how you knew who I was ? "

" Well, sir, if it isn't too great a liberty, I am a neighbour of yours, for you'll find my little bookshop at the
14 corner of Church Street, and very happy to see you, I am
15 sure. Maybe you collect yourself, sir ; here's *British*
16-17-18 *Birds*, and *Catullus*, and *The Holy War*—a bargain every one of them. With five volumes you could just fill that gap on that second shelf. It looks untidy, does it not, sir ? "

I moved my head to look at the cabinet behind me. When I turned again Sherlock Holmes was standing smiling at me across my study table. I rose to my feet,

. . . SHERLOCK HOLMES WAS STANDING SMILING AT ME ACROSS MY STUDY TABLE.

Illustration by Frederic Dorr Steele for *Collier's Magazine*, September 26, 1903. Sidney Paget illustrated the same dramatic scene for the *Strand Magazine*, October, 1903.

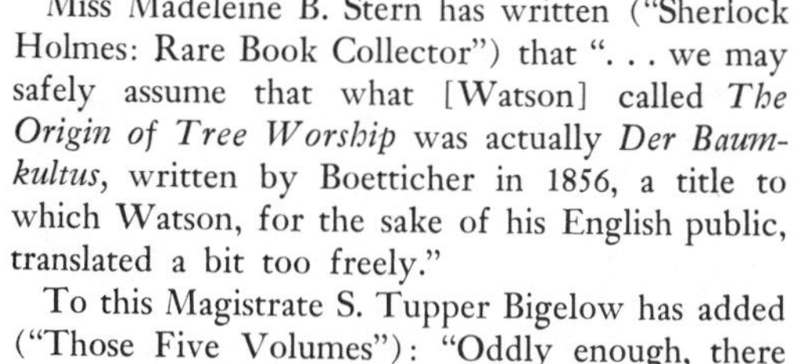

Miss Madeleine B. Stern has written ("Sherlock Holmes: Rare Book Collector") that ". . . we may safely assume that what [Watson] called *The Origin of Tree Worship* was actually *Der Baumkultus*, written by Boetticher in 1856, a title to which Watson, for the sake of his English public, translated a bit too freely."

To this Magistrate S. Tupper Bigelow has added ("Those Five Volumes"): "Oddly enough, there is not a book ever written in the English language called *The Origin of Tree Worship*. About the closest we can get to it is *Tree and Serpent Worship*, James Ferguson, London, 1873, and *The Sacred Tree in Religion and Myth*, Philpot, London, 1897. The latter can be ruled out at once, of course, as it was published after 1894." But see also Note 17.

13 *I retraced my steps to Kensington.* But Watson's practice in the years 1889–1891 was in *Paddington.* Why has he now returned to Kensington, the scene of his earlier (1886–1887) practice? In our view, the answer is to be found in Watson's career as a writer. As the late Edgar W. Smith wrote in "Dr. Watson and the Great Censorship": "Watson returned to England [from Switzerland], heartbroken, weary, and mourning the death of the best and wisest man whom he had ever known. He sought to lose himself in work, apparently. . . . Almost immediately the stories that had been simmering in his brain for so long began to pour forth in a great flood. The world was electrified by the appearance in the *Strand Magazine* for July, 1891, not two months after Holmes' disappearance, of the first of these long-suppressed adventures, given under the fetching title of 'A Scandal in Bohemia.' From then until December, 1893, they came in a steady stream, two round dozen in all."

Now, how could a doctor with a successful practice ("The Boscombe Valley Mystery") which "steadily increased" ("The Engineer's Thumb") find the time and energy needed to pour forth "two round dozen" chronicles in "a great flood," "a steady stream"? *Some* of them we know had been written as early as May, 1887 ("A Scandal in Bohemia"), but many of the cases Watson related in the *Strand* during the period of the Great Hiatus occurred much later in the partnership; with Watson so busy with his Paddington practice from May, 1889, on, they simply could not have been committed to paper until shortly before publication. What Watson did now seems clear: he sold the Paddington practice and with the proceeds repurchased the "small Kensington practice" of his first marriage—a practice which was "never very absorbing" ("The Red-Headed League")—a

stared at him for some seconds in utter amazement, and
then it appears that I must have fainted for the first and
the last time in my life. Certainly a grey mist swirled **19**
before my eyes, and when it cleared I found my collar-
ends undone and the tingling after-taste of brandy upon
my lips. Holmes was bending over my chair, his flask
in his hand. **20**

"My dear Watson," said the well-remembered voice, "I owe you a thousand apologies. I had no idea that you would be so affected."

I gripped him by the arm.

"Holmes!" I cried. "Is it really you? Can it indeed be that you are alive? Is it possible that you succeeded in climbing out of that awful abyss?"

"Wait a moment!" said he. "Are you sure that you are really fit to discuss things? I have given you a serious shock by my unnecessarily dramatic appearance."

"I am all right; but indeed, Holmes, I can hardly believe my eyes. Good heavens, to think that you—you of all men—should be standing in my study!" Again I gripped him by the sleeve and felt the thin, sinewy arm beneath it. "Well, you're not a spirit, anyhow," said I. "My dear chap, I am overjoyed to see you. Sit down, and tell me how you came alive out of that dreadful chasm."

He sat opposite to me and lit a cigarette in his old non-
chalant manner. He was dressed in the seedy frock-coat
of the book merchant, but the rest of that individual lay
in a pile of white hair and old books upon the table.
Holmes looked even thinner and keener than of old, but
there was a dead-white tinge in his aquiline face which **21**
told me that his life recently had not been a healthy
one.

"I am glad to stretch myself, Watson," said he. "It is no joke when a tall man has to take a foot off his stature for several hours on end. Now, my dear fellow, in the matter of these explanations we have, if I may ask for your co-operation, a hard and dangerous night's work in front of us. Perhaps it would be better if I gave you an account of the whole situation when that work is finished."

"I am full of curiosity. I should much prefer to hear now."

"You'll come with me to-night?"

"When you like and where you like."

"This is indeed like the old days. We shall have time for a mouthful of dinner before we need go. Well, then, about that chasm. I had no serious difficulty in getting out of it, for the very simple reason that I never was in it."

"You never were in it?"

"No, Watson, I never was in it. My note to you was absolutely genuine. I had little doubt that I had come to the end of my career when I perceived the somewhat sinister figure of the late Professor Moriarty standing upon the narrow pathway which led to safety. I read an inexorable purpose in his grey eyes. I exchanged some remarks with him, therefore, and obtained his courteous permission to write the short note which you afterwards received. I left it with my cigarette-box and my stick, and I walked along the pathway, Moriarty still

practice he knew from experience would provide a livelihood and *still give him time* for his writing.

14 *at the corner of Church Street.* As Miss Madeleine B. Stern has shown ("Sherlock Holmes: Rare Book Collector"), Holmes on this occasion assumed the guise of his bookdealer, Alfred B. Clementson, who plied his trade at 73 Church Street, Kensington, W. (*London Post-Office Directory* for 1890). Church Street, we may add, leads north to Notting Hill, where Selden (*The Hound of the Baskervilles*) committed his brutal murder. The street takes its name from the Carmelite Church, an unfinished early Gothic building by E. W. Pugin, begun in 1865.

15 *Maybe you collect yourself, sir.* The old bookseller now mentions three titles. Then he says: "With five volumes you could just fill that gap on the second shelf." Obviously, two of the three titles must have been two-volume editions or one of the three titles must have been a three-volume edition—a point which seems to have been made for the first time by Magistrate S. Tupper Bigelow in "Those Five Volumes."

16 British Birds. ". . . not a minor nineteenth-century work, but the fine *History of British Birds* with the Bewick wood engravings printed in two volumes at Newcastle in 1797 and 1804," Miss Stern wrote.

To this, Miss Lisa McGaw added ("Some Trifling Notes on Sherlock Holmes and Ornithology"): "A perusal of Raymond Irwin's *British Bird Books: An Index to British Ornithology, A.D. 1481 to A.D. 1948* (London: Grafton & Co., 1951) reveals no volume entitled simply *British Birds* prior to early 1894. There is, however, a six-volume work by Francis O. Morris entitled *A History of British Birds* (Groombridge, 1851–57) and bearing on its spine the label *Morris' British Birds*. Could that have been what Holmes was carrying? It seems likely, although it would have been nearly an armful in itself if he had all six volumes. To suggest that this work was obscure is misleading because, in its day, it was well known in its field. Three reissues of the first edition, four revised editions, and two cabinet editions attest to its popularity among persons interested in birds. Its 357 hand-colored plates, all rather good, greatly enhanced the work in an era when accurate bird drawings were rare, and that helped to counteract the fact that the information in the text was not too reliable. If this is the work referred to, Holmes undoubtedly possessed a first edition, which would have increased its value as a collector's item."

But to both these commentators, Magistrate Bigelow responded: "An equally good guess would be Robert Mudie's *The Feathered Tribes of the British Islands*, lettered on its spine *Mudie's British Birds*, the first edition of which appeared in London in 1853, and a fourth edition . . . , similarly spine-lettered, in 1878. . . . Furthermore, Bewick's two volumes were spine-lettered *History of British Birds,* so as between Bewick and Mudie, it would appear that Mudie has the slight advantage. . . . Both books are in two volumes. What we must have, obviously, is a book on British birds in three volumes. We are bound, therefore, to discard Morris' *History of British Birds,* 1878, in six volumes; and A. Thorburn's *British Birds,* 1915, in one volume. . . . We are not assisted, either, by the three-volume *British Birds and Their Nests* by Vesey B. Fitzgerald, London, 1953, nor the three-volume *British Birds, Trees and Wild Flowers* by Walter M. Gallichan, London, 1915. There seems, indeed, to be only one possible solution. William Yarrell's *A History of British Birds* was first published in London by John Van Voorst in 1843; a second edition appeared in 1845 and a third in 1846. Each edition was published in three volumes. On the spine of each volume of all editions is lettered *Yarrell's British Birds.*"

17 Catullus. "The first Aldine Catullus: *Catullus, Tibulius, Propertius,* printed in italic letter by Aldus at Venice in 1502, with the title-page in the first state, reading *Propetius* for *Propertius*—a rare edition though, of course, not under the circumstances, an incunable," Miss Stern wrote.

"Mr. Norman Dodge of Goodspeed's Bookshop in Boston believes the Catullus was the one printed by the noted typographer John Baskerville, 1706–1765," the late Christopher Morley added.

But Mr. Bliss Austin (in "Two Bibliographical Footnotes") held that "the Catullus and *The Origin of Tree Worship* were one and the same book! It is a work by Grant Allen, entitled *The Attis of Caius Valerius Catullus, Translated into English Verse, with Dissertations on the Myth of Attis, on the Origin of Tree-Worship, and on the Galliambic Metre.* It was published, in an edition limited to 550 copies, as Volume VI of the *Bibliotheque de Carabas* in London in 1892 by David Nutt."

18 The Holy War. To Miss Stern, this was ". . . obviously a copy of the 1639 first edition of Thomas Fuller's *History of the Holy Warre,* and not one of the numerous reprints of that popular work on the Crusades."

Mr. Austin wrote: ". . . I should like to suggest as a possible alternative John Bunyan's *The Holy War,* which bears the subtitle: 'Made by King Shaddai upon Diabolus for the Regaining of the Metropolis of the World; or the Losing and Taking Again of the Town of Mansoul.' This, the second most famous of Bunyan's works, was first published in 1682 in a small octavo volume which was quite handsome by the standards of the day. It was, within a few years, translated into Dutch, German, Gaelic, Portugese and Turkish. The first edition would, I am certain, have been an item worthy of Holmes' attention."

Magistrate Bigelow wrote: "*The Holy War* must surely have been some edition of Bunyan's famous work, first published in 1682. Sherlock Holmes' copy could scarcely have been a first edi-

at my heels. When I reached the end I stood at bay. He drew no weapon, but he rushed at me and threw his long arms around me. He knew that his own game was up, and was only anxious to revenge himself upon me. We tottered together upon the brink of the fall. I have some knowledge, however, of baritsu, or the Japanese
22 system of wrestling, which has more than once been very useful to me. I slipped through his grip, and he with a horrible scream kicked madly for a few seconds and clawed the air with both his hands. But for all his efforts he could not get his balance, and over he went. With my face over the brink I saw him fall for a long way. Then he struck a rock, bounded off, and splashed into the water."

I listened with amazement to this explanation, which Holmes delivered between the puffs of his cigarette.

"But the tracks!" I cried. "I saw with my own eyes that two went down the path and none returned."

"It came about in this way. The instant that the professor had disappeared it struck me what a really extraordinarily lucky chance Fate had placed in my way. I knew that Moriarty was not the only man who had sworn my death. There were at least three others whose desire for vengeance upon me would only be increased by the
23 death of their leader. They were all most dangerous

WE TOTTERED TOGETHER UPON THE BRINK OF THE FALL.

"The death of Sherlock Holmes" as seen by two different artists (and compare with Paget's illustration of the same scene in "The Final Problem"). The first illustration shown here is by Arthur Twidle, from the 1903 "Author's Edition" of *The Memoirs of Sherlock Holmes;* the second is by John Nunney from *Look and Learn,* issue of June 23, 1962. It will be noted that the artists did not agree on which bank of the falls the struggle took place (Paget and Twidle, left bank; Nunney, right bank).

men. One or other would certainly get me. On the other hand, if all the world was convinced that I was dead they would take liberties, these men ; they would lay themselves open, and sooner or later I could destroy them. Then it would be time for me to announce that I was still in the land of the living. So rapidly does the brain act that I believe I had thought this all out before Professor Moriarty had reached the bottom of the Reichenbach Fall.

" I stood up and examined the rocky wall behind me. In your picturesque account of the matter, which I read with great interest some months later, you assert that the wall was sheer. This was not literally true. A few small footholds presented themselves, and there was some indication of a ledge. The cliff is so high that to climb it all was an obvious impossibility, and it was equally impossible to make my way along the wet path without leaving some tracks. I might, it is true, have reversed my boots, as I have done on similar occasions, but the **24**
sight of three sets of tracks in one direction would certainly have suggested a deception. On the whole, then, it was best that I should risk the climb. It was not a pleasant business, Watson. The fall roared beneath me. I am not a fanciful person, but I give you my word that I seemed to hear Moriarty's voice screaming at me out of the abyss. A mistake would have been fatal.

"WITH MY FACE OVER THE BRINK I SAW HIM FALL FOR A LONG WAY."

Cover illustration by Frederic Dorr Steele for *Collier's Magazine*, September 26, 1903. "The resultant print of [Holmes'] prone body in the moist earth should have betrayed his escape to the Swiss experts," Mr. Anthony Boucher wrote in "Was the Later Holmes an Imposter?", "but it is conceivable that Watson's similar print overlay his."

tion, as there is no first edition of this work in the United States . . . and the only first edition [the *Encyclopædia Britannica*'s Library Research Service] knows about is in the British Museum. . . . No known edition . . . was published in two volumes [although] there were no less than 44 editions of *The Holy War* published in England and the United States from 1682 to 1795 inclusive . . ."

To this Professor David A. Randall has added ("The Adventure of the Notorious Forger") that Holmes offered *British Birds* and *The Holy War* "out of all the millions [of volumes] he could have possessed" because his true reason for returning to England was to unmask Thomas James Wise, the great literary forger, and "he naturally had with him some volumes in which the forger also would be interested."

19 *for the first and the last time in my life.* "It is true that the manner of Holmes' return was sufficiently melodramtic to accelerate the most sluggish pulse," Mr. S. C. Roberts wrote in *Doctor Watson,* "but it is hardly enough to account for an old campaigner like Watson falling into a dead faint. Clearly, his constitution had not fully recovered from the ravages of recent grief and worry [caused by the final illness and subsequent death of Mary Morstan Watson]."

And Mr. Walter P. Armstrong, Jr., has written ("The Truth About Sherlock Holmes"): "This was such an uncharacteristic act that it has led to the wildest conjectures. It is a weakness to which old soldiers are seldom addicted; but it is one which is all too apparent to writers of fiction. A Watson who in real life had never fainted might easily in composing an imaginative account of an emotional scene which never happened depict Watson as fainting."

20 *his flask in his hand.* "Did Sherlock Holmes, as one of the properties in his character of an aged bibliophile, carry a hip flask?" Mr. Armstrong asked. "It does not seem likely."

21 *a dead-white tinge in his aquiline face.* "This is hardly what would be expected of a man who has been wandering in unknown portions of Tibet and under the burning sun of the Egyptian Sudan," Mr. Armstrong continued. "But it is exactly what we would expect of a man who has been spending much time indoors and venturing out only in a heavy disguise." (Mr. Armstrong, we will remember, holds that Holmes spent the entire period of the Great Hiatus in London.)

22 *baritsu, or the Japanese system of wrestling.* In his article, "The Mystery of Baritsu: A Sidelight Upon Sherlock Holmes' Accomplishments," Mr. Ralph Judson has shown that a Mr. E. W. Barton-Wright had published in *Pearson's Magazine* in the March and April, 1899, issues, an article called "The New Art of Self-Defence." He "described therein a few of the three hundred methods of attack and counter-attack that comprise the New

Art of Self-Defence, to which I have given the name of Bartisu . . ." (after Barton). "In giving the name Bartisu to a number of selected methods of Ju-Jutsu, adapted to European needs and costume, Mr. Barton-Wright followed a well-established precedent," Mr. Judson wrote. "Many of the exponents of this art in Japan founded their own schools and gave their own names to the methods they taught. . . . Dr. Watson must have read Mr. Barton-Wright's article in the *Pearson's Magazine* in 1899, got the word 'Bartisu' stuck in his mind, and, in describing, in 1903, the return of his friend, inadvertently written 'Baritsu' . . . instead of Ju-Jutsu"—the system of Japanese wrestling by which Holmes actually overcame Professor Moriarty. Since Holmes knew a Japanese system of wrestling in 1891, and since it takes roughly seven years to become proficient in this art and reach instinctive actions and reactions to every kind of attack, it is likely that he started his training around 1883–1884. When Holmes shortly tells us that he slipped through Moriarty's grip, this is what he is likely to have done: "In one fast and smooth movement, dropping on one knee, [Holmes] gripped with one hand Moriarty's heel, which was closer to the abyss, and lifting the heel and with it the foot, diagonally, away from himself, he pushed hard, at the same time, with his other hand, into the groin of the captured leg, applying terrific leverage."

23 *at least three others whose desire for vengeance upon me would only be increased by the death of their leader.* "The reasons given by Holmes . . . for his daring ascent of the rock-wall above the Reichenbach are unsatisfactory," Mr. T. S. Blakeney wrote in *Sherlock Holmes: Fact or Fiction?* "If he were believed dead, he affirmed, his enemies in Moriarty's gang would drop their caution, commit indiscretions, and leave themselves open to his attack. But at the time he was excogitating these considerations, he was unaware that any of Moriarty's followers were at large! On the contrary, he had recently had a wire from the London police saying (not quite accurately, as events were to prove) that they had secured the whole organization. Holmes did not become aware of Colonel Moran's presence [*see below*] till after he had acted upon his idea, and his statement of his thoughts, as given by Watson, must have been coloured by wisdom after the event."

24 *I might, it is true, have reversed my boots.* ". . . a trick that is common enough practice among horsethieves, but is somewhat impractical here in view of the shape of the human foot," Mr. Anthony Boucher wrote in "Was the Later Holmes an Imposter?"

"If Holmes could, or ever did, put his shoes on backwards, volumes could be written on the physiology of his foot," Mr. Walter P. Armstrong, Jr., commented in "The Truth About Sherlock Holmes." "It would never have occurred to Holmes, the detective; but it did to Watson, the writer of fiction."

More than once, as tufts of grass came out in my hand or my foot slipped in the wet notches of the rock, I thought that I was gone. But I struggled upwards, and at last I reached a ledge several feet deep and covered with soft green moss, where I could lie unseen in the most perfect comfort. There I was stretched when you, my dear Watson, and all your following were investigating in the most sympathetic and inefficient manner the circumstances of my death.

"At last, when you had all formed your inevitable and totally erroneous conclusions, you departed for the hotel, and I was left alone. I had imagined that I had reached the end of my adventures, but a very unexpected occurrence showed me that there were surprises still in store for me. A huge rock, falling from above, boomed past me, struck the path, and bounded over into the chasm. For an instant I thought that it was an accident; but a
moment later, looking up, I saw a man's head against the
25 darkening sky, and another stone struck the very ledge
upon which I was stretched, within a foot of my head. Of course, the meaning of this was obvious. Moriarty had not been alone. A confederate—and even that one glance had told me how dangerous a man that confederate was—had kept guard while the professor had attacked
me. From a distance, unseen by me, he had been a wit-
26 ness of his friend's death and of my escape. He had
waited, and then, making his way round to the top of the cliff, he had endeavoured to succeed where his comrade had failed.

"I did not take long to think about it, Watson. Again I saw that grim face look over the cliff, and I knew that it was the precursor of another stone. I scrambled down on to the path. I don't think I could have done it in cold blood. It was a hundred times more difficult than getting up. But I had no time to think of the danger, for
27 another stone sang past me as I hung by my hands from
the edge of the ledge. Half-way down I slipped, but by the blessing of God I landed, torn and bleeding, upon the path. I took to my heels, did ten miles over the mountains in the darkness, and a week later I found myself in Florence, with the certainty that no one in the world knew what had become of me.

"I had only one confidant—my brother Mycroft. I owe you many apologies, my dear Watson, but it was all-important that it should be thought I was dead, and it is quite certain that you would not have written so convincing an account of my unhappy end had you not yourself thought that it was true. Several times during the last three years I have taken up my pen to write to you, but always I feared lest your affectionate regard for me should tempt you to some indiscretion which would betray my secret. For that reason I turned away from you this evening when you upset my books, for I was in danger at the time, and any show of surprise and emotion upon your
part might have drawn attention to my identity and led to
28 the most deplorable and irreparable results. As to My-
croft, I had to confide in him in order to obtain the money which I needed. The course of events in London did not run so well as I had hoped, for the trial of the Moriarty gang left two of its most dangerous members, my own

most vindictive enemies, at liberty. I travelled for two 29
years in Tibet, therefore, and amused myself by visiting Lhassa and spending some days with the head Llama. You may have read of the remarkable explorations of a Norwegian named Sigerson, but I am sure that it never occurred to you that you were receiving news of your friend. I then passed through Persia, looked in at Mecca, and paid a short but interesting visit to the Khalifa at Khartoum, the results of which I have communicated to the Foreign Office. Returning to France, I spent some months in a research into the coal-tar derivatives, which I conducted in a laboratory at Montpelier, in the south of France. Having concluded this to my satisfaction, and learning that only one of my enemies was now left in London, I was about to return, when my movements were hastened by the news of this remarkable Park Lane Mystery, which not only appealed to me by its own merits, but which seemed to offer some most peculiar personal opportunities. I came over at once to London, called in my own person at Baker Street, threw Mrs. Hudson into violent hysterics, and found that Mycroft had preserved my rooms and my papers exactly as they had
always been. So it was, my dear Watson, that at two 30
o'clock to-day I found myself in my old arm-chair in my own old room, and only wishing that I could have seen my old friend Watson in the other chair which he has so often adorned."

Such was the remarkable narrative to which I listened on that April evening—a narrative which would have been utterly incredible to me had it not been confirmed by the actual sight of the tall, spare figure and the keen, eager face which I had never thought to see again. In some manner he had learned of my own sad bereavement, and his sympathy was shown in his manner rather than in his words. "Work is the best antidote to sorrow, my dear Watson," said he, "and I have a piece of work for us both to-night which, if we can bring it to a successful conclusion, will in itself justify a man's life on this planet." In vain I begged him to tell me more. "You will hear and see enough before morning," he answered. "We have three years of the past to discuss. Let that suffice until half-past nine, when we start upon the notable adventure of the empty house."

It was indeed like old times when, at that hour, I found myself seated beside him in a hansom, my revolver in my pocket and the thrill of adventure in my heart. Holmes was cold and stern and silent. As the gleam of the street-lamps flashed upon his austere features, I saw that his brows were drawn down in thought and his thin lips compressed. I knew not what wild beast we were about to hunt down in the dark jungle of criminal London, but I was well assured from the bearing of this master huntsman that the adventure was a most grave one, while the sardonic smile which occasionally broke through his ascetic gloom boded little good for the object of our quest.

I had imagined that we were bound for Baker Street, but Holmes stopped the cab at the corner of Cavendish
Square. I observed that as he stepped out he gave a 31
most searching glance to right and left, and at every

To comments like these the Fundamentalists have responded: "You can't easily put boots on backward, the uppers crumple and hamper; but *shoes* . . . are easily reversed and can be walked in, with care, far enough to leave a misleading spoor. You trample down the flanges of the shoe, and tie the laces over your ankle" (the late Christopher Morley). "It is very easy to put one's shoes on backwards to reverse the direction in which they point; it is merely necessary to cut the toe and part of the shoe directly back of this, and then to put the feet into the shoes from the toe end" (the late Dr. Ernest Bloomfield Zeisler).

25 *the darkening sky*. Watson's (and Holmes') time references in "The Final Problem" and "The Adventure of the Empty House" have been severely criticized by Mr. Anthony Boucher and Mr. Walter P. Armstrong, Jr.; as stoutly defended by the late Dr. Ernest Bloomfield Zeisler, the late A. Carson Simpson, and the late Professor Jay Finley Christ.

Let us first present the case *against* (Mr. Boucher in "Was the Later Holmes an Imposter?"):

"In 'The Final Problem,' we have Watson's statement that the trip from Meiringen to the Reichenbach Fall takes two hours uphill and one hour down. Holmes and Watson leave Meiringen 'in the afternoon,' which cannot mean earlier than one o'clock; we shall see . . . that it must have been closer to two. They arrived at the Fall, then, at four; and Watson leaves, allowing for his awed inspection of the Fall and his conversation with the bearer of the false message, around four fifteen. His trip to Meiringen and back adds another three hours so that he discovers the tragedy at a quarter past seven. In the latitude of Meiringen (46° 45′ N.), the sun sets on May 4th at about seven ten, with slight variations for local standard time. When Watson leans over the brim, 'it had darkened since I left, and now I could only see here and there the glistening of moisture upon the black walls, and far away down at the end of the shaft the gleam of broken water.' Watson makes a careful study of the scene and of Holmes' note and leaves at about seven–thirty. It is probably quite dark by then; night comes quickly in high mountains. Now it is highly unlikely that 'experts,' who, as Watson informs us, examined the ground, were on call in 'the little village of Meiringen,' on a May evening. But even granting the deutero-Holmes' assertion that this examination took place on the same day, the experts could not have reached the site in less than three hours after Watson left to summon them—in other words, at ten–thirty. It would take them at least half an hour to reach 'their inevitable and totally erroneous conclusions.' Holmes cannot have been left alone, then, before eleven o'clock, by which time he has been lying on the ledge for almost seven hours. It is therefore some time after eleven when Holmes recognizes Colonel Sebastian Moran as the rock-throwing confederate. Conceivably Moran's 'thin, projecting nose' and 'high bald forehead' might have been recognizable in silhouette at night, but Holmes describes 'a man's head against the darkening sky.'

In short, that sky had been darkening from seven-fifteen until some minutes after eleven—a meteorological phenomena surely deserving some Holmesian contribution to the literature of the subject."

But the late A. Carson Simpson replied (*Sherlock Holmes' Wanderjahre*, Vol. I) that Watson "says it took him an hour to get down to Meiringen and, 'for all his efforts,' two more hours to get back to the Fall. On the contrary, Baedeker, whose timing is always on the conservative side, says that it takes only three-quarters of an hour to walk up from Meiringen to the Upper Fall; the whole trip to Rosenlaui requires only three. . . . Actually, the good Doctor's trip downhill to Meiringen cannot have taken more than a half-hour at an ordinary pace, and we may be sure that, exerting 'all his efforts,' he got back up to the Fall in about the same length of time. After vainly seeking for Holmes, he would have walked or run down to Meiringen in some twenty minutes, to raise a search-party. A simple arithmetical calculation will demonstrate that the various trips to and fro could easily be made, with ample margins between trips, before sunset at 7:10 P.M."

And Dr. Zeisler has added (*Baker Street Chronology*): "There is not the slightest indication that Watson made the upward journey *three* times. When Watson learned from Steiler that the letter had been a hoax he rushed back up to the Fall, and there is no reason at all to think that he made another trip down to fetch the police; indeed, we can be certain that he did *not* do this. Watson told Steiler that he suspected foul play, and Steiler surely fetched the police and sent them up after Watson without delay, so that they probably arrived at the Fall shortly after Watson. It took Watson two hours to rush up to the top, so that we may allow a longer time for the trip up by the Master and Watson, who did not rush. If we allow two and a half hours for the first trip up, then it was about five and a half hours from the time they left the hotel together until Watson returned to the Fall. If they left the hotel at 2:00 P.M., . . . then Watson and the police would have made their investigations between 7:30 and 8:30 P.M. It is true that sunset was a few minutes past seven, but it is not true that it was dark at 8:30 P.M. Twilight at that season and place lasts a good two hours, so that it is not really dark until 9:00 P.M. or after. . . ."

Professor Christ agreed that there is not "the slightest suggestion or basis for an assumption that Watson made *three* trips to the Fall, nor that he brought experts 'later,'" and he presented the following suggested time schedule ("The Later Holmes an Imposter: A Sequel"):

2:00 Holmes and Watson left the inn.
4:00 Holmes and Watson reach the Fall.
4:15 The messenger reaches the Fall.
4:20 Watson leaves the Fall.
4:45 Holmes struggles with Moriarty.
5:20 Watson reaches the inn.
5:25 Watson leaves the inn, running, with guides following shortly thereafter.

subsequent street corner he took the utmost pains to assure that he was not followed. Our route was certainly a singular one. Holmes' knowledge of the by-ways of London was extraordinary, and on this occasion he passed rapidly, and with an assured step, through a network of mews and stables the very existence of which I had never known. We emerged at last into a small road, lined with old, gloomy houses, which led us into Manchester Street, and so to Blandford Street. Here he turned swiftly down a narrow passage, passed through a wooden gate into a deserted yard, and then opened with a key the back door of a house. We entered together, and he closed it behind us.

The place was pitch dark, but it was evident to me that it was an empty house. Our feet creaked and crackled over the bare planking, and my outstretched hand touched a wall from which the paper was hanging in ribbons. Holmes' cold, thin fingers closed round my wrist and led me forward down a long hall, until I dimly saw the murky fanlight over the door. Here Holmes turned suddenly to the right, and we found ourselves in a large, square, empty room, heavily shadowed in the corners, but faintly lit in the centre from the lights of the street beyond. There was no lamp near, and the window was thick with dust, so that we could only just discern each other's figures within. My companion put his hand upon my shoulder, and his lips close to my ear.

"Do you know where we are?" he whispered.

"Surely that is Baker Street," I answered, staring through the dim window.

"Exactly. We are in Camden House, which stands opposite to our own old quarters."

"But why are we here?"

"WE ARE IN CAMDEN HOUSE, WHICH STANDS OPPOSITE TO OUR OWN OLD QUARTERS."

"The empty house"—the present No. 32 Baker Street—as photographed for your editor's biography, *Sherlock Holmes.*

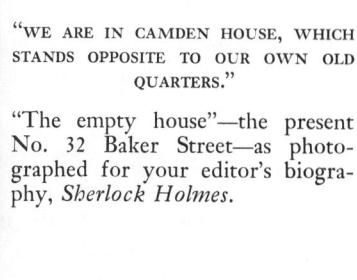

" Because it commands so excellent a view of that picturesque pile. Might I trouble you, my dear Watson, to draw a little nearer to the window, taking every precaution not to show yourself, and then to look up at our old rooms—the starting-point of so many of our little adventures ? We will see if my three years of absence have entirely taken away my power to surprise you."

I crept forward and looked across at the familiar window. As my eyes fell upon it I gave a gasp and a cry of amazement. The blind was down, and a strong light was burning in the room. The shadow of a man who was seated in a chair within was thrown in hard, black outline upon the luminous screen of the window. There was no mistaking the poise of the head, the squareness of the shoulders, the sharpness of the features. The face was turned half-round, and the effect was that of one of those black silhouettes which our grandparents loved to frame. It was a perfect reproduction of Holmes. So amazed was I that I threw out my hand to make sure that the man himself was standing beside me. He was quivering with silent laughter.

" Well ? " said he.

" Good heavens ! " I cried. " It's marvellous."

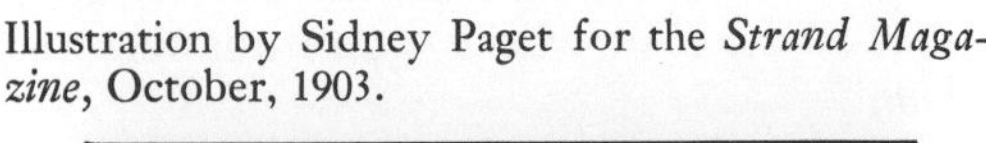

I CREPT FORWARD AND LOOKED ACROSS AT THE FAMILIAR WINDOW.

Illustration by Sidney Paget for the *Strand Magazine*, October, 1903.

7:25 Watson reaches the Fall.
7:30 Guides reach the Fall. Sunset, moon about 30 degrees west of meridian.
8:00 Party left the Fall.
8:15 Holmes saw head against the darkening sky.
8:30 Holmes descended from the cliff.

26 *he had been a witness of his friend's death and of my escape.* "In other words," Mr. Stanley McComas wrote in "Love at Lhassa," "Moran *saw him alive*, so Moran will *believe he is dead*. Every underworld character in London must have known Holmes was alive. Watson's acceptance of this incongruous tale can only be put down to his shock at seeing Holmes again."

And Mr. Boucher wrote ("Was the Later Holmes an Imposter?"): "Holmes' purported motive in going underground and allowing Watson to believe him dead was to trap the remaining Moriartists. But his own account makes nonsense of that motive; the one person, aside from Mycroft, who knew that he was certainly not dead, and who had seen him alive after the destruction of Moriarty, was the new chief of the gang, Colonel Sebastian Moran."

27 *another stone sang past me.* "Why"—the late Edgar W. Smith asked in "The Old Shikari"—"why, when Moriarty had fallen to his death, and Holmes had scrambled up to the ledge again, did the best rifle shot in all India resort to hurling rocks at his intended victim? . . . We may be sure that it was not with a view to giving Holmes an even break. It is obvious that the plotters had forgotten to bring a suitable weapon with them, and that Moran found himself, in his extremity, reduced to only such expedients as nature could provide. There are those who have contended that this was not an oversight, but a matter of necessity, and that the pursuers went weaponless into battle because of the great difficulties, in those days, attendant upon importing firearms into law-abiding Switzerland. To them I say that the ingenuity which permitted a lethal air-gun to be disguised effectively as a walking-stick would not have boggled at the project of masking that same air-gun to even better advantage, in the guise of an alpenstock. No—both Moriarty and Moran were off their feed that day, and we, in common with Sherlock Holmes, must be ever grateful for it."

28 *led to the most deplorable and irreparable results.* "Will this explanation hold water?" Mr. Armstrong wrote. "I doubt it. In the first place, Holmes said he turned away in order that Watson should not recognize him and give the game away. And yet, hardly more than a few minutes later, he voluntarily came to Watson and revealed himself. True, he may have wished to avoid a scene in public; but if he had so little confidence in Watson's self-control, why did he come to him at all? . . . Above all, why did he turn aside? On numerous occasions when he knew Holmes to be alive

" I trust that age doth not wither nor custom stale my
32 infinite variety," said he, and I recognized in his voice the
joy and pride which the artist takes in his own creation.
" It really is rather like me, is it not ? "

" I should be prepared to swear that it was you."

" The credit of the execution is due to Monsieur Oscar
33 Meunier, of Grenoble, who spent some days in doing the
moulding. It is a bust in wax. The rest I arranged
myself during my visit to Baker Street this afternoon."

" But why ? "

" Because, my dear Watson, I had the strongest possible reason for wishing certain people to think that I was there when I was really elsewhere."

" And you thought the rooms were watched ? "

" I *knew* that they were watched."

" By whom ? "

" By my old enemies, Watson. By the charming
society whose leader lies in the Reichenbach Fall. You
must remember that they knew, and only they knew,
that I was still alive. Sooner or later they believed that
I should come back to my rooms. They watched them
34 continuously, and this morning they saw me arrive."

" How do you know ? "

" Because I recognized their sentinel when I glanced out of my window. He is a harmless enough fellow, Parker by name, a garrotter by trade, and a remarkable performer upon the jews' harp. I cared nothing for him. But I cared a great deal for the much more formidable person who was behind him, the bosom friend of Moriarty, the man who dropped the rocks over the cliff, the most cunning and dangerous criminal in London. That is the man who is after me to-night, Watson, and that is the man who is quite unaware that we are after *him.*"

My friend's plans were gradually revealing themselves.
From this convenient retreat the watchers were being
watched and the trackers tracked. That angular shadow
up yonder was the bait, and we were the hunters. In
silence we stood together in the darkness and watched the
hurrying figures who passed and repassed in front of us.
Holmes was silent and motionless ; but I could tell that
he was keenly alert, and that his eyes were fixed intently
upon the stream of passers-by. It was a bleak and
35 boisterous night, and the wind whistled shrilly down the
long street. Many people were moving to and fro, most
of them muffled in their coats and cravats. Once or twice
it seemed to me that I had seen the same figure before,
and I especially noticed two men who appeared to be
sheltering themselves from the wind in the doorway of a
house some distance up the street. I tried to draw my
companion's attention to them, but he gave a little
ejaculation of impatience, and continued to stare into the
street. More than once he fidgeted with his feet and
tapped rapidly with his fingers upon the wall. It was
evident to me that he was becoming uneasy, and that his
plans were not working out altogether as he had hoped.
At last, as midnight approached and the street gradually
cleared, he paced up and down the room in uncontrollable
agitation. I was about to make some remark to him,
when I raised my eyes to the lighted window, and again

Watson had failed to penetrate his various disguises. In fact, Holmes delighted in trying them on him and made some very cutting remarks upon his failure to see through them. It is incredible that his confidence in his art of make-up had grown so weak that he was afraid Watson would recognize in the aged bookseller a man whom he thought long dead."

29 *left two of its most dangerous members, my own most vindictive enemies, at liberty.* "But Holmes could not have known that before the trial, and even before he had seen Colonel Moran against the darkening sky" (Boucher).

30 *exactly as they had always been.* "Yet in another place," Mr. Armstrong wrote, "[Holmes] makes the statement that Mycroft had only visited his rooms once, and a second visit is a cause for great excitement ("The Adventure of the Bruce-Partington Plans"). Mycroft could hardly have kept the rooms up without visiting them, especially as they had been burned shortly prior to Holmes' departure; for although the damage was slight, it was sufficient to deserve notice in the press. Nor could he restore them to their former state on the basis of a single visit, even though his powers of observation were admittedly great. Neither could Mrs. Hudson, unfamiliar with many of the esoteric devices which her distinguished lodger employed in his trade. In fact, only one man could have done it, and that man was Watson. Naturally he did not want his name to appear, because he is supposed to have thought that Holmes was dead."

31 *Cavendish Square.* Cavendish Square, laid out in 1717, takes its name from Lady Henrietta Cavendish Holles, as does the adjoining Henrietta Street and Holles Street. It stands directly opposite Hanover Square on the south side of Oxford Street.

32 *age doth nor wither nor custom stale my infinite variety.*" Holmes paraphrases Shakespeare's *Antony and Cleopatra:* "Age cannot wither her, nor custom stale her infinite variety . . ."—Act II, Scene 2, lines 241–242.

33 *Grenoble.* "Presumably, in the intervals between sittings, the Master of Baker Street found much to interest him in that ancient town, not the least being the famous 'hanging bridges,' one over the Isère and the other over the Drac," Mr. Belden Wigglesworth wrote in "The French Background of Sherlock Holmes."

34 *They watched them continuously.* "*Credat Judaeus Apella*" the late Monsignor Ronald A. Knox wrote in "The Mystery of Mycroft"; "you do not really watch a house on the chance of its being revisited, for three years on end. No, Colonel Moran's information will have come, as usual, from Mycroft; Sherlock, as usual, conceals the equivocal

experienced almost as great a surprise as before. I clutched Holmes' arm and pointed upwards.

"The shadow has moved!" I cried.

It was, indeed, no longer the profile, but the back, which was turned towards us.

Three years had certainly not smoothed the asperities of his temper, or his impatience with a less active intelligence than his own.

"Of course it has moved," said he. "Am I such a farcical bungler, Watson, that I should erect an obvious dummy and expect that some of the sharpest men in Europe would be deceived by it? We have been in this room two hours, and Mrs. Hudson has made some change in that figure eight times, or once every quarter of an hour. She works it from the front, so that her shadow may never be seen. Ah!" He drew in his breath with a shrill, excited intake. In the dim light I saw his head thrown forward, his whole attitude rigid with attention. Those two men might still be crouching in the doorway, but I could no longer see them. All was still and dark, save only that brilliant yellow screen in front of us with the black figure outlined upon its centre. Again in the utter silence I heard that thin, sibilant note which spoke of intense suppressed excitement. An instant later he pulled me back into the blackest corner of the room, and I felt his warning hand upon my lips. The fingers which clutched me were quivering. Never had I known my friend more moved, and yet the dark street still stretched lonely and motionless before us.

But suddenly I was aware of that which his keener senses had already distinguished. A low, stealthy sound came to my ears, not from the direction of Baker Street, but from the back of the very house in which we lay concealed. A door opened and shut. An instant later steps crept down the passage—steps which were meant to be silent, but which reverberated harshly through the empty house. Holmes crouched back against the wall, and I did the same, my hand closing upon the handle of my revolver. Peering through the gloom, I saw the vague outline of a man a shade blacker than the blackness of the open door. He stood for an instant, and then he crept forward, crouching, menacing, into the room. He was within three yards of us, this sinister figure, and I had braced myself to meet his spring, before I realized that he had no idea of our presence. He passed close beside us, stole over to the window, and very softly and noiselessly raised it for half a foot. As he sank to the level of this opening the light of the street, no longer dimmed by the dusty glass, fell full upon his face. The man seemed to be beside himself with excitement. His two eyes shone like stars, and his features were working convulsively. He was an elderly man, with a thin projecting nose, a high, bald forehead, and a huge grizzled moustache. An opera-hat was pushed to the back of his head, and an evening dress shirt-front gleamed out through his
open overcoat. His face was gaunt and swarthy, scored **36**
with deep, savage lines. In his hand he carried what appeared to be a stick, but as he laid it down upon the floor it gave a metallic clang. Then from the pocket of his overcoat he drew a bulky object, and he busied

part his brother has been playing in the drama, and fobs off his credulous biographer with a manifest lie."

35 *It was a bleak and boisterous night.* The only day in early April, 1894, that could possibly be called both bleak and windy was Thursday, April 5th. On that day the temperature fell to a low of 36.7° (fifty-year average for the day, 45°) and the wind achieved a pressure of 4.7 pounds. (We must remember what Watson tells us in "The Cardboard Box": "For myself, my term of service in India had trained me to stand heat better than cold . . ." What might have been brisk, even bracing, to another may well have been bleak, even bitter, to Watson.) The inquest on the Honourable Ronald Adair must therefore have concluded on Wednesday, April 4, 1894.

36 *an evening dress shirt-front gleamed out through his open overcoat.* "But why was [Colonel Moran] thus attired for a sniping expedition in an empty house?" Colonel Ronald Sherbrooke-Walker asked in "Clothes Canonical." "Perhaps like Mr. Holmes and Dr. Watson in their foray on Appledore Towers ["The Adventure of Charles Augustus Milverton"] he thought he would fit better into the landscape than he would in battle-dress."

. . . THE LIGHT OF THE STREET . . . FELL FULL UPON HIS FACE.

Illustration by Sidney Paget for the *Strand Magazine*, October, 1903.

THEN HIS FINGER TIGHTENED ON THE TRIGGER.

Illustration by Joseph Camana from *Cases of Sherlock Holmes*, St. Louis: Webster Publishing Company, 1947.

. . . WITH CONVULSIVE STRENGTH HE SEIZED HOLMES BY THE THROAT; BUT I STRUCK HIM ON THE HEAD WITH THE BUTT OF MY REVOLVER . . .

Illustration by Sidney Paget for the *Strand Magazine*, October, 1903.

himself in some task which ended with a loud, sharp click, as if a spring or bolt had fallen into its place. Still kneeling upon the floor, he bent forward and threw all his weight and strength upon some lever, with the result that there came a long, whirling, grinding noise, ending once more in a powerful click. He straightened himself then, and I saw that what he held in his hand was a sort of a gun, with a curiously misshapen butt. He opened it at the breech, put something in, and snapped the breech-block. Then, crouching down, he rested the end of the barrel upon the ledge of the open window, and I saw his long moustache droop over the stock and his eye gleam as it peered along the sights. I heard a little sigh of satisfaction as he cuddled the butt into his shoulder, and saw that amazing target, the black man on the yellow ground, standing clear at the end of his foresight. For an instant he was rigid and motionless. Then his finger tightened
on the trigger. There was a strange, loud whiz and a
37 long, silvery tinkle of broken glass. At that instant
Holmes sprang like a tiger on to the marksman's back and hurled him flat upon his face. He was up again at a moment, and with convulsive strength he seized Holmes by the throat; but I struck him on the head with the butt of my revolver, and he dropped again upon the floor. I fell upon him, and as I held him my comrade blew a shrill call upon a whistle. There was the clatter of running feet upon the pavement, and two policemen in uniform, with one plain-clothes detective, rushed through the front entrance and into the room.

"That you, Lestrade ?" said Holmes.

"Yes, Mr. Holmes. I took the job myself. It's good to see you back in London, sir."

"I think you want a little unofficial help. Three undetected murders in one year won't do, Lestrade. But you handled the Molesey Mystery with less than your usual—that's to say, you handled it fairly well."

We had all risen to our feet, our prisoner breathing hard, with a stalwart constable on each side of him. Already a few loiterers had begun to collect in the street. Holmes stepped up to the window, closed it, and dropped the blinds. Lestrade had produced two candles, and the policemen had uncovered their lanterns. I was able at last to have a good look at our prisoner.

It was a tremendously virile and yet sinister face which was turned towards us. With the brow of a philosopher above and the jaw of a sensualist below, the man must have started with great capacities for good or for evil. But one could not look upon his cruel blue eyes, with their drooping, cynical lids, or upon the fierce, aggressive nose and the threatening, deep-lined brow, without reading Nature's plainest danger-signals. He took no heed of any of us, but his eyes were fixed upon Holmes' face with an expression in which hatred and amazement were equally blended. "You fiend !" he kept on muttering —"you clever, clever fiend !"

"Ah, colonel," said Holmes, arranging his rumpled
collar, "'journeys end in lovers' meetings,' as the old
38 play says. I don't think I have had the pleasure of
seeing you since you favoured me with those attentions

as I lay on the ledge above the Reichenbach Fall."

The colonel still stared at my friend like a man in a trance. "You cunning, cunning fiend!" was all that he could say.

"I have not introduced you yet," said Holmes. This, gentlemen, is Colonel Sebastian Moran, once of Her Majesty's Indian Army, and the best heavy game shot that our Eastern Empire has ever produced. I believe I am correct, colonel, in saying that your bag of tigers still remain unrivalled?"

The fierce old man said nothing, but still glared at my companion; with his savage eyes and bristling moustache, he was wonderfully like a tiger himself.

"I wonder that my very simple stratagem could
deceive so old a shikari," said Holmes. "It must be 39
very familiar to you. Have you not tethered a young kid under a tree, lain above it with your rifle, and waited for the bait to bring up your tiger? This empty house is my tree, and you are my tiger. You have possibly had other guns in reserve in case there should be several tigers, or in the unlikely supposition of your own aim failing you. These," he pointed around, "are my other guns. The parallel is exact."

Colonel Moran sprang forward with a snarl of rage, but the constables dragged him back. The fury upon his face was terrible to look at.

"I confess that you had one small surprise for me," said Holmes. "I did not anticipate that you would yourself make use of this empty house and this convenient front window. I had imagined you as operating from the street, where my friend Lestrade and his merry men were awaiting you. With that exception, all has gone as I expected."

Colonel Moran turned to the official detective.

"You may or may not have just cause for arresting me," said he, "but at least there can be no reason why I should submit to the gibes of this person. If I am in the hands of the law, let things be done in a legal way."

"Well, that's reasonable enough," said Lestrade. "Nothing further you have to say, Mr. Holmes, before we go?"

Holmes had picked up the powerful air-gun from the floor, and was examining its mechanism.

"An admirable and unique weapon," said he, "noise-

37 *a long, silvery tinkle of broken glass.* "Does a revolver bullet, fired from an air-gun across a street through a window, cause a 'long, silvery tinkle of broken glass'?" Magistrate S. Tupper Bigelow asked in "Two Canonical Problems Solved." "All the ones I've ever seen or heard about drill a neat hole even through plate glass."

38 *as the old play says.* Holmes slightly misquotes *Twelfth Night*, Act II, Scene 3, line 46: "Journeys end in lovers meeting." As we have previously noted, *Twelfth Night* is the only one of Shakespeare's works which Holmes quotes twice (see "The Adventure of the Red Circle," Note 10).

39 *shikari.* Hindu word for a sportsman or hunter.

THE FIERCE OLD MAN SAID NOTHING, BUT STILL GLARED AT MY COMPANION . . .

Illustration by Frederic Dorr Steele for *Collier's Magazine*, September 26, 1903.

COLONEL MORAN SPRANG FORWARD WITH A SNARL OF RAGE . . .

Illustration by Sidney Paget for the *Strand Magazine*, October, 1903.

less and of tremendous power. I knew Von Herder, the
40 blind German mechanic, who constructed it to the order of the late Professor Moriarty. For years I have been aware of its existence, though I have never before had an opportunity of handling it. I commend it very specially to your attention, Lestrade, and also the bullets which fit it."

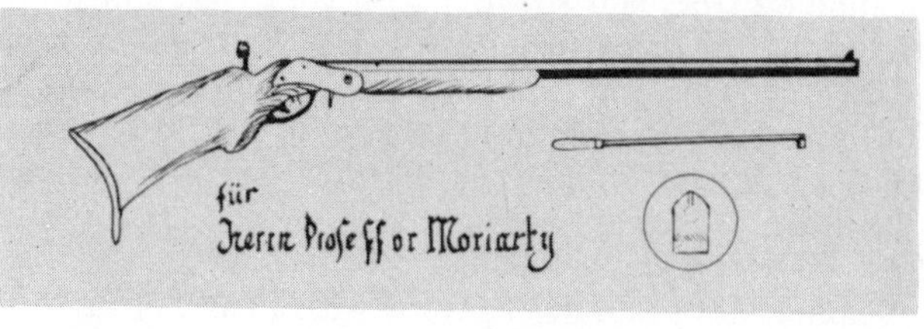

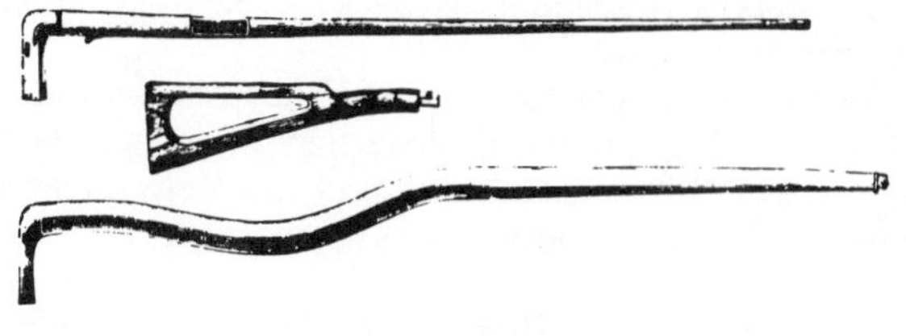

"I COMMEND IT VERY SPECIALLY TO YOUR ATTENTION . . ."

There existed, from the middle of the eighteenth century, a rare arm, the Blozenbüchse, a breech-loading air-powered rifle designed to shoot darts over a range of about 10 meters. It was unerringly accurate; it was virtually noiseless. Mr. Ashton has suggested ("Colonel Moran's Infamous Air Rifle") that von Herder adapted this gun to meet the two other specifications set up by Professor Moriarty: first, he bored the Bolzenbüchse to carry a revolver bullet of sufficient caliber to kill; second, to make the gun portable, and in a form unrecognizable as a gun, he redesigned the one-piece Bolzenbüchse rifle into a two-piece take-down model. "Von Herder didn't create anything. He merely adapted an existing type of firearm. It is interesting to note that this was not lost on Holmes, who did not classify von Herder as a master gunsmith. He called him a blind German mechanic."

On the other hand, Mr. William Percival has written ("Sherlock Holmes and Air-Guns") that "there can be little doubt that [Colonel Moran's air-gun] was of the air chamber walking stick air rifle type. The walking stick air rifle was an exclusively English invention, first made in the early 1840's. Messrs. Townsend and Reilly were the most prolific makers. These guns ceased to be made in the early 1900's and good examples are now both rare and expensive. They closely resembled ordinary walking sticks

40 *Von Herder, the blind German mechanic.* "How did a mechanic come to have a title of nobility?" the late Elmer Davis asked in his introduction to *The Return of Sherlock Holmes.* "Even big industrialists found them hard to come by, in the Kaiserreich. Or, alternatively, how did a nobleman happen to become a mechanic?"

Mr. Ralph A. Ashton has given us an answer in his biography of Von Herder (from "Colonel Moran's Infamous Air Rifle")" "Augustus Heinrich Friedrich Kartiffelschale von Herder was born Vienna 1 April 1803. Mother: Fräulein Schmutzi Liebelnhastic von Herder. Father: unknown. Knighted by Friedrich Wilhelm IV (date unknown) for research into problems of using dehydrated water as a propellant in place of gunpowder. (By removing all traces of moisture from water, it could be concentrated into a very small place; when reconstituted, it expanded and forced the bullet from the barrel with explosive energy.) Blinded by acid in 1839 while experimenting with poisoned bullets. Died by gunshot wounds 1 April 1901, believed to have been inflicted by a jealous husband.—Unpublished notes of Rudolf von Esche."

" You can trust us to look after that, Mr. Holmes," said Lestrade, as the whole party moved towards the door. " Anything further to say ? "

" Only to ask what charge you intend to prefer ? "

" What charge, sir ? Why, of course, the attempted murder of Mr. Sherlock Holmes."

" Not so, Lestrade. I do not propose to appear in the matter at all. To you, and to you only, belongs the credit of the remarkable arrest which you have effected. Yes, Lestrade, I congratulate you ! With your usual happy mixture of cunning and audacity you have got him."

" Got him ! Got whom, Mr. Holmes ? "

" The man whom the whole Force has been seeking in vain—Colonel Sebastian Moran, who shot the Honourable Ronald Adair with an expanding bullet from an air-gun through the open window of the second-floor
front of No. 427 Park Lane, upon the 30th of last month. **41**
That's the charge, Lestrade. And now, Watson, if you can endure the draught from a broken window, I think that half an hour in my study over a cigar may afford you some profitable amusement."

Our old chambers had been left unchanged, through the supervision of Mycroft Holmes and the immediate care of Mrs. Hudson. As I entered I saw, it is true, an unwonted tidiness, but the old landmarks were all in their places. There were the chemical corner and the
acid-stained deal-topped table. There upon a shelf **42**
was the row of formidable scrap-books and books of reference which many of our fellow-citizens would have been so glad to burn. The diagrams, the violin-case,

and would be murderous weapons in the wrong hands. As there was no recoil, the firing position was to hold the knob against the cheek and sight along the stick, but some sticks (such as that used by Colonel Moran) had a crooked handle and were fired from the shoulder. They operated at a pressure of 400–500 pounds per square inch or more, being pumped up manually by a separate pump. (It has been queried whether Watson's description of Moran's method of loading did not indicate a spring-operated air gun. The answer is probably that in the semi-darkness, Watson confused the loading of the gun with the operation of the air pump. No spring-operated air gun could have been of the requisite power.) One pumping sufficed for at least 20 shots and, by means of compensating valves, the power did not greatly diminish as the pressure fell. The extreme range was about 350 yards, and at 50 yards bullets (soft-nosed expanding revolver bullets, if desired) would easily penetrate a 1-inch wooden plank."

Shown here are, first, the Bolzenbüchse and, second, the von Herder adaptation according to Mr. Ashton (each with its ammunition, slightly reduced in size) and its lever or *Hebel.* The following illustration shows walking-stick guns from a catalogue of W. W. Greener, Birmingham and London, about 1900. The first is for .410 shotgun shells. The second is an air rifle to be used with a pump (not shown).

41 *through the open window of the second-floor front.* Since Park Lane fronts on Hyde Park for its entire length, the question arises: Where was the Colonel when he shot? As Mr. Russell McLauchlin wrote, in his "Ballade on a Daring Theme":

> Across the way the land is stark,
> Of building there is not a trace,
> Only the semi-rural Park
> Confronts the fatal mansion's face;
> The fence, the trees which interlace
> Their branches in that sightly spot,
> These occupy the total space.
> Where was the Colonel when he shot?

Mr. Percival Wilde, in "The Bust in the Window," wrote that "Colonel Moran must have fired from a spot near the Marble Arch entrance of Hyde Park, in the Park itself, and must have done so without attracting the least attention from the masses of humanity which are so much in evidence 'between the hours of ten and eleven-twenty' P.M. A comparable shot would be one fired into a third-story window of the Astor Hotel by a marksman standing on the east side of Broadway at an identical time of night."

The late Edgar W. Smith, writing in "The Old Shikari," thought that Moran must have "climbed a strategically-placed tree in the park to put himself on a level with the second-storey window at 427 Park Lane (two flights up, mind you), behind which young Adair was sitting."

And Magistrate S. Tupper Bigelow, in "Two Canonical Problems Solved," asked: "If Moran killed [Adair], where was Moran when he fired the shot—in a helicopter?"

42 *the acid-stained deal-topped table.* "Deal, in British usage, means simply lumber or timber," Mr. D. A. Redmond wrote in "Some Chemical Problems in the Canon." "Critics have suggested that a plain softwood table, or bench, would be unsuited for chemical use, and soon pitted by the Master's experiments [but] the description 'acid-stained' has been misinterpreted. A standard method of acid-proofing wooden laboratory bench tops is to coat them successively with potassium nitrate solution and with boiling aniline and hydrocholoric acid. This spectacular process produces a dense black stain. Here is our 'acid-stained deal-topped table'—a properly finished laboratory bench."

43 *Here it is!*" In *Design for Murder*, a detective novel by Percival Wilde, published by Random House, one Mary Ashton finds fault with "The Adventure of the Empty House." A bullet fired from the ground floor of a house on one side of the street, could not, she claims: 1) penetrate both the shadow and the bust of Sherlock Holmes which is casting it, since the bust must be at some distance from its shadow; or 2) if it struck both shadow and bust, it should strike the lamp which is in a straight line with them; and 3) it would, in any event, because of the elevation of the gun's muzzle, finally strike the ceiling and not the far wall of the room which is the starting point for so many of Dr. Watson's stories.

Mr. Robert S. Schultz, however, writing in "The Ballistics of the Empty House," refused to admit any of these claims: 1) "the distance of the bust from the window cannot have been great: in Watson's words, the shadow 'was thrown in hard, black outline upon the luminous screen of the window.' Consideration of the most elementary laws of optics shows that, had the bust been at any distance from the window, and particularly, had it been closer to the lamp than to the window, the shadow would have been large and fuzzy, with features indistinct. . . . The present writer concludes that the bust could not have been much more than one foot from the window." 2) "The four objects (lamp, bust, shadow and gun) could have been in a straight line relationship to each other only if Moran had fired from the first floor instead of from the ground floor. In this event, the lamp would obviously have been smashed. The point is, of course, inconsistent with Wilde's other two points. . . . Needless to say, all this talk about straight lines is misleading; one would think it was well known that the path of a bullet is a parabola, not a straight line." 3) After an elaborate analysis of the heights and distances involved, Mr. Schultz concluded that "We have only Mrs. Hudson's word that the bullet 'flattened itself against the wall,' and in the midst of the excitement she might not have observed correctly." The bullet, Mr. Schultz thought, more probably hit the ceiling.

To the first of these points, Mr. Wilde replied ("The Bust in the Window"): "With a large light source there would have been both umbra and penumbra, and the shadow would have been indistinct; with a point-source such as the lamp we know so well, there was no penumbra, and the shadow was sharp for all positions of the bust." To the second: "The height of the shadow above the muzzle of the gun was far more than [Mr. Schultz] admits, and while I rule that Mary Ashton . . . was liberal when she referred to 'thirty degrees,' I decline to find that the angle was so small that it was inconsequential." To the third: "One concludes that only in a room of the most palatial dimensions could this ungracious bullet have hit the ceiling; one descries that Martha Hudson's observations were also accurate."

and the pipe-rack—even the Persian slipper which contained the tobacco—all met my eye as I glanced round me. There were two occupants of the room—one Mrs. Hudson, who beamed upon us both as we entered ; the other, the strange dummy which had played so important a part in the evening's adventures. It was a wax-coloured model of my friend, so admirably done that it was a perfect facsimile. It stood on a small pedestal table with an old dressing-gown of Holmes' so draped round it that the illusion from the street was absolutely perfect.

" I hope you preserved all precautions, Mrs. Hudson ? " said Holmes.

" I went to it on my knees, sir, just as you told me."

" Excellent. You carried the thing out very well. Did you observe where the bullet went ? "

" Yes, sir. I'm afraid it has spoilt your beautiful bust, for it passed right through the head and flattened itself
on the wall. I picked it up from the carpet. Here it
43 is ! "

Holmes held it out to me. " A soft revolver bullet, as you perceive, Watson. There's genius in that—for who would expect to find such a thing fired from an air-gun ? All right, Mrs. Hudson, I am much obliged for your assistance. And now, Watson, let me see you in your old seat once more, for there are several points which I should like to discuss with you."

He had thrown off the seedy frock-coat, and now he was the Holmes of old, in the mouse-coloured dressing-gown which he took from his effigy.

" The old shikari's nerves have not lost their steadiness nor his eyes their keenness," said he, with a laugh, as he inspected the shattered forehead of his bust.

" Plumb in the middle of the back of the head and smack through the brain. He was the best shot in India, and I expect that there are few better in London. Have you heard the name ? "

" No, I have not."

" Well, well, such is fame ! But then, if I remember aright, you had not heard the name of Professor James Moriarty, who had one of the great brains of the century. Just give me down my index of biographies from the shelf."

He turned over the pages lazily, leaning back in his chair and blowing great clouds of smoke from his cigar.

" My collection of M's is a fine one," said he. " Moriarty himself is enough to make any letter illustrious, and here is Morgan the poisoner, and Merridew of
abominable memory, and Mathews, who knocked out
44 my left canine in the waiting-room at Charing Cross, and,
finally, here is our friend of to-night."

He handed over the book, and I read : " *Moran,*
Sebastian, Colonel. Unemployed. Formerly 1st Ben-
45 galore Pioneers. Born London, 1840. Son of Sir
Augustus Moran, C.B., once British Minister to Persia.
46 Educated Eton and Oxford. Served in Jowaki Campaign, Afghan Campaign, Charasiab (dispatches), Sher-
47 pur, and Cabul. Author of *Heavy Game of the Western*
Himalayas, 1881 ; *Three Months in the Jungle*, 1884.

"MY COLLECTION OF M'S IS A FINE ONE," SAID HE.

Illustration by Frederic Dorr Steele for *Collier's Magazine*, September 26, 1903. Sidney Paget illustrated the same scene for the *Strand Magazine*, October, 1903.

"SON OF SIR AUGUSTUS MORAN, C.B. . . ."

Companion of the Bath, a member of the Honorary Order of the Bath, founded in 1725; so called from the ceremonial cleansing performed by members before joining. As the onetime British Minister to Persia, Sir Augustus Moran would have received the Civil rather than the Military Order of the Bath; the badge of the Civil Order is shown above.

Address: Conduit Street. Clubs: The Anglo-Indian, 48
the Tankerville, the Bagatelle Card Club."

On the margin was written in Holmes' precise hand:
"The second most dangerous man in London." 49

"This is astonishing," said I, as I handed back the volume. "The man's career is that of an honourable soldier."

"It is true," Holmes answered. "Up to a certain point he did well. He was always a man of iron nerve, and the story is still told in India how he crawled down a drain after a wounded man-eating tiger. There are some trees, Watson, which grow to a certain height and then suddenly develop some unsightly eccentricity. You will see it often in humans. I have a theory that the individual represents in his development the whole procession of his ancestors, and that such a sudden turn to good or evil stands for some strong influence which came into the line of his pedigree. The person becomes, as it were, the epitome of the history of his own family."

"It is surely rather fanciful."

"Well, I don't insist upon it. Whatever the cause, Colonel Moran began to go wrong. Without any open scandal, he still made India too hot to hold him. He retired, came to London, and again acquired an evil name. It was at this time that he was sought out by Professor Moriarty, to whom for a time he was chief of the staff. Moriarty supplied him liberally with money, and used him only in one or two very high-class jobs which no ordinary criminal could have undertaken. You
may have some recollection of the death of Mrs. Stewart,
of Lauder, in 1887. Not? Well, I am sure Moran 50
was at the bottom of it; but nothing could be proved. So cleverly was the colonel concealed that even when the Moriarty gang was broken up we could not incriminate

But Mr. Schultz stuck to his air guns: "Moran sighted at the shadow thrown upon the screen, allowing for the fact that there was a distance of about one foot or so from the shadow to the actual target. . . . The angle of fire was somewhat over eleven degrees. The bullet rose, following a parabola. By the time it had passed through the wax bust its initial velocity was somewhat retarded, both because of the pull of gravity and because of the resistance of the wax. Nevertheless, the remaining velocity was adequate to carry the bullet above the lamp, which was not smashed, and on across the room."

44 *who knocked out my left canine.* "Of course, we in the dental profession know that under normal conditions [Holmes'] canine tooth could never have been easily 'knocked out,'" Dr. Charles Goodman wrote in "The Dental Holmes." "Even the dental surgeon, equipped with specially devised forceps, must exert unusual leverage and force to remove that type of tooth. I am advised by one of my colleagues, who is also an official examiner of the Royal Boxing Commission, that in all his wide experience he never saw a normal canine knocked out in a boxing match. Therefore I am sure that . . . Holmes had pyorrhea."

We may also note that Dr. Jay Weiss, in "Holmes As a Patient," came to this identical conclusion independently. In addition, research by the late Rudolph Elie ("The Battle of Charing Cross") has enabled him to pinpoint Holmes' encounter with Mathews to the night of November 12, 1878. On that night, according to the London *Times* of January 3, 1879, one *Thomas Mathews* took part in a riot in which a detective named James Hand attributed the saving of his life to the fortunate intervention of an unidentified person, unquestionably Holmes. Mathews, we are glad to learn, was sentenced to 15 months' imprisonment with hard labor.

45 *1st Bengalore Pioneers. Bangalore* Pioneers in some American editions. Neither the Bengalore nor the Bangalore Pioneers ever existed, but, as Mrs. Crighton Sellars has written in "Dr. Watson and the British Army," "there was a very famous Corps in the Indian Army called The Corps of Madras Sappers and Miners (The Queen's Own), which consisted of two separate bodies, the Engineers and the Pioneers, whose history, dating from capture of Seringapatam, closely parallels Moran's service during his time with it. Bangalor, near the eastern boundary of Mysore, is just next to the district of Madras, and this may account for the association of the districts in Watson's mind when he came to paraphrasing the name of the real regiment to which his knave belonged. The Madras Pioneers served in the Afghan Campaign, Sherpur and Cabul, and had detachments in the Jowaki Campaign; also at [Charasiab]."

46 *Educated Eton and Oxford.* "It has often been noticed," the late Christopher Morley wrote in *Sherlock Holmes and Dr. Watson: A Textbook of Friendship,* "that this education can produce some notable results. In Holmes' experience both [Colonel Moran], 'the second most dangerous man in London' and [John Clay of "The Red-Headed League"], 'the fourth smartest man in London' had studied at Eton and Oxford."

47 *Sherpur, and Cabul.* "The first of these [campaigns]," the late Edgar W. Smith wrote in "The Old Shikari," "was against the Jowaki Afridis in the northern fastnesses, where, under Colonel Mocatta, [Moran] was one of a force of 1,500 sent to punish these wild Pathan tribesmen for the recalcitrant attitude they were showing toward the British. The Afghan campaign itself came upon the heels of a contre-temps with Russia which has had familiar echoes since, and it was precipitated by the rough treatment given to a British diplomatic mission at the hands of the Amir of the tribes. When the armies marched to avenge these insults and to hold the gem of India secure in Victoria's crown, Moran found himself embroiled in the gruesome doings around Kabul. At Sherpur, he served under General Frederick S. L. Roberts, later Earl Roberts; and at [Charasiab, more properly Charasia or Charasiah], he found himself under the direct command of General T. D. Baker. In this last battle, as Holmes' index of biographies confirms, Moran's bravery was so exceptional that he was mentioned in the dispatches."

48 *Conduit Street.* One of the tributary thoroughfares leading out of Regent Street, and today perhaps the most imposing from a shopping point of view. It takes its name from Conduit Mead, an open field of 27 acres until 1713. In this street Charles James Fox was born on January 24, 1749.

him. You remember at that date, when I called upon you in your rooms, how I put up the shutters for fear of air-guns? No doubt you thought me fanciful. I knew exactly what I was doing, for I knew of the existence of this remarkable gun, and I knew also that one of the best shots in the world would be behind it. When we were in Switzerland he followed us with Moriarty, and it was undoubtedly he who gave me that evil five minutes on the Reichenbach ledge.

"You may think that I read the papers with some attention during my sojourn in France, on the look-out for any chance of laying him by the heels. So long as he was free in London my life would really not have been worth living. Night and day the shadow would have been over me, and sooner or later his chance must have come. What could I do? I could not shoot him at sight, or I should myself be in the dock. There was no use appealing to a magistrate. They cannot interfere on the strength of what would appear to them to be a wild suspicion. So I could do nothing. But I watched the criminal news, knowing that sooner or later I should get him. Then came the death of this Ronald Adair. My chance had come at last! Knowing what I did, was it not certain that Colonel Moran had done it? He had played cards with the lad; he had followed him home from the club; he had shot him through the open window. There was not a doubt of it. The bullets
51 alone are enough to put his head in a noose. I came over at once. I was seen by the sentinel, who would, I knew, direct the colonel's attention to my presence. He could not fail to connect my sudden return with his crime, and to be terribly alarmed. I was sure that he would make an attempt to get me out of the way *at once*, and would bring round his murderous weapon for that purpose. I left him an excellent mark in the window, and, having warned the police that they might be needed—by the way, Watson, you spotted their presence in that doorway with unerring accuracy—I took up what seemed to me to be a judicious post for observation, never dreaming that he would choose the same spot for his attack. Now, my dear Watson, does anything remain for me to explain?"

"Yes," said I. "You have not made it clear what was Colonel Moran's motive in murdering the Honourable Ronald Adair."

"Ah! my dear Watson, there we come into those realms of conjecture where the most logical mind may be at fault. Each may form his own hypothesis upon the present evidence, and yours is as likely to be correct as mine."

"You have formed one, then?"

"I think that is not difficult to explain the facts. It came out in evidence that Colonel Moran and young Adair had between them won a considerable amount of money. Now, Moran undoubtedly played foul—of that I have long been aware. I believe that on the day of the murder, Adair had discovered that Moran was cheating. Very likely he had spoken to him privately, and had threatened to expose him unless he voluntarily resigned his membership of the club and promised not to play cards again. It is unlikely that a youngster like Adair would at once make a hideous scandal by exposing a well-known man so much older than himself. Probably he acted as I suggest. The exclusion from his clubs would mean ruin to Moran, who lived by his ill-gotten card gains. He therefore murdered Adair, who at the time was endeavouring to work out how much money he should himself return, since he could not profit by his partner's foul play. He locked the door, lest the ladies should surprise him and insist upon knowing what he was doing with these names and coins. Will it pass ? "

" I have no doubt that you have hit upon the truth."

" It will be verified or disproved at the trial. Meanwhile, come what may, Colonel Moran will trouble us no
more, the famous air-gun of Von Herder will embellish the **52**
Scotland Yard Museum, and once again Mr. Sherlock Holmes is free to devote his life to examining those interesting little problems which the complex life of London so plentifully presents."

49 *"The second most dangerous man in London."* The most dangerous man in London had of course been Professor James Moriarty; the worst man in London we will meet in "The Adventure of Charles Augustus Milverton."

50 *Lauder.* A town in Berwickshire, Scotland.

51 *The bullets alone are enough to put his head in a noose.* Not so, as we shall see shortly. In making this statement, Holmes was anticipating by about fifteen years the part that ballistics would play in the investigation of crime. In 1894, ballistics was unknown at Scotland Yard, or, for that matter, at any police department in the world. The police became aware of its possibilities no earlier than 1909. By 1910 all modern police forces were using it in their investigation of crimes committed with the aid of firearms.

52 *Colonel Moran will trouble us no more.* The fact remains that Holmes referred to "the living Sebastian Moran" in 1902 ("The Adventure of the Illustrious Client") and implied that he was alive and at liberty as late as the outbreak of World War I ("His Last Bow"): "The old sweet song. It was a favorite ditty of the late lamented Professor Moriarty. Colonel Sebastian Moran *has* also been known to warble it." This is not at all as unlikely as it may sound. We have the opinion of Magistrate S. Tupper Bigelow ("Two Canonical Problems Solved") that the case against Moran "boils down to this: Adair was killed; the expanding revolver bullet that killed him was similar to one that was shot from Moran's air-gun; therefore Moran killed Adair." It is interesting in this connection to note that the villain of the play *The Crown Diamond*, from which Conan Doyle fashioned the Sherlock Holmes short story "The Adventure of the Mazarin Stone" was *Colonel Sebastian Moran.* "The Adventure of the Mazarin Stone," virtually all commentators are agreed, took place in the summer of 1903.

Auctorial Note: It has been said that Sir Arthur Conan Doyle's second wife supplied him with the idea for "The Adventure of the Empty House," and how Sherlock Holmes could safely and "logically" be brought back to life in the pages of *Collier's* and the *Strand.* In any case, the story ranked high with Sir Arthur himself, who placed it No. 6 on his list of the "twelve best" Sherlock Holmes short stories.

50

THE ADVENTURE OF THE GOLDEN PINCE-NEZ

[Wednesday, November 14, to Thursday, November 15, 1894]

WHEN I look at the three massive manuscript volumes which contain our work for the year 1894 I confess that it is very difficult for me, out of such a wealth of material, to select the cases which are most interesting in themselves and at the same time most conducive to a display of those peculiar powers for which my friend was famous. As I turn over the
pages I see my notes upon the repulsive story of the
1 red leech and the terrible death of Crosby the banker.
2 Here also I find an account of the Addleton tragedy and
3 the singular contents of the ancient British barrow. The
famous Smith-Mortimer succession case comes also within
this period, and so does the tracking and arrest of Huret,
the Boulevard assassin—an exploit which won for Holmes
4 an autograph letter of thanks from the French President
and the Order of the Legion of Honour. Each of these
would furnish a narrative, but on the whole I am of
opinion that none of them unite so many singular points
5 of interest as the episode of Yoxley Old Place, which
includes, not only the lamentable death of young Willoughby Smith, but also those subsequent developments which threw so curious a light upon the causes of the crime.

It was a wild, tempestuous night towards the close of
November. Holmes and I sat together in silence all the
6 evening, he engaged with a powerful lens deciphering the
7 remains of the original inscription upon a palimpsest, I
8 deep in a recent treatise upon surgery. Outside the wind
howled down Baker Street, while the rain beat fiercely against the windows. It was strange there in the very depths of the town, with ten miles of man's handiwork on every side of us, to feel the iron grip of Nature, and to be conscious that to the huge elemental forces all London was no more than the molehills that dot the fields. I walked to the window and looked out on the deserted street.

. . . AN EXPLOIT WHICH WON FOR HOLMES . . . THE ORDER OF THE LEGION OF HONOUR.

1 *the red leech.* ". . . most leeches are not red, but olive-green to brown in colour," Mr. Paul H. Gore-Booth wrote in "The Journeys of Sherlock Holmes." "The inference may be that Watson was referring to one of the red-*blooded* leeches (e.g. *Hirudo medicinalis,* the medicinal leech or *Haemopsis* (*aulastomum*) *gulo,* the horseleech, both of which are common in the British Isles); alternatively he may have meant *Pontobdella muricata,* also green in colour but identified by Professor [F. E.] Beddard [of Oxford, England, a leading contemporary expert] also as a large red-coloured leech occasionally observed by fishermen on the basking shark."

The late A. Carson Simpson submitted (*Sherlock Holmes' Wanderjahre,* Vol. III) that Holmes' experience with Himalayan leeches during his stay in Tibet peculiarly qualified him to uncover the truth of this case. "If there are red leeches anywhere in the world, they must have at least a token representation in the Teesta Valley and Sikkim. Of course, many leeches, when engorged, have their skins so far distended that the color of their blood-meal shows through, giving them a reddish tone. Perhaps poor Crosby encountered a gigantic leech—a mutation or a 'sport,' if you will —that was able to drain *all* the blood from his system, leaving only a shrunken corpse."

Mr. Simpson did not, however, exclude the possibility that "the term 'leech' was used in its extended meaning of 'physician,' and that the 'red' refers to 1) the color of his hair (as Eric the Red); or 2) the color of his clothes (as Count Amadeo VII of Saxony—*il Conte Rosso*—who affected a red costume in tournaments); or 3) his association with blood-letting (as 'Red' or 'Bloody' Jeffreys); or 4) his political complexion, in which case he would naturally select the capitalist Crosby as his victim."

2 *the Addleton tragedy.* "The 'Addleton' tragedy is probably a misunderstanding for 'Addlestone,'" Mr. Paul H. Gore-Booth wrote, "a conjecture founded on no hypothesis save that, while Addleton does not, as far as I know, exist, Addlestone is in Surrey, which was the scene of many of Holmes' exploits. We may justifiably suspect a printer's error faithfully repeated in subsequent editions."

The occasional lamps gleamed on the expanse of muddy road and shining pavement. A single cab was splashing
its way from the Oxford Street end. 9
" Well, Watson, it's as well we have not to turn out tonight," said Holmes, laying aside his lens and rolling up the palimpsest. " I've done enough for one sitting. It is trying work for the eyes. So far as I can make out, it is nothing more exciting than an Abbey's accounts dating from the second half of the fifteenth century. Halloa ! halloa ! halloa ! What's this ? "

Amid the droning of the wind there had come the stamping of a horse's hoofs and the long grind of a wheel as it rasped against the kerb. The cab which I had seen had pulled up at our door.

" What can he want ? " I ejaculated, as a man stepped out of it.

" Want ! He wants us. And we, my poor Watson, want overcoats and cravats and goloshes, and every aid that man ever invented to fight the weather. Wait a bit, though ! There's the cab off again ! There's hope yet. He'd have kept it if he had wanted us to come. Run down, my dear fellow, and open the door, for all virtuous folk have been long in bed."

When the light of the hall lamp fell upon our midnight visitor, I had no difficulty in recognizing him. It was young Stanley Hopkins, a promising detective, in whose career Holmes had several times shown a very practical interest.

"The Adventure of the Foulkes Rath," a pastiche stemming from this reference of Dr. Watson's, by Adrian M. Conan Doyle, appears in *The Exploits of Sherlock Holmes.*

3 *the singular contents of the ancient British barrow.* "While no hint is vouchsafed us of its contents and circumstances, it is unlikely that anyone could open one of the ancient burial places of the original inhabitants of Britain without acquiring or having acquired a first-hand knowledge of Britain's pre-history," Mr. Whitfield J. Bell, Jr., noted in "Holmes and History."

We may also note that Watson's phrase has been enlarged upon by Mr. Poul Anderson in "Time Patrol," in which Holmes himself makes a brief anonymous appearance.

4 *the French President.* M. Jean-Paul-Pierre Casimir-Perier, 1847–1907, was the President of France in 1894. Mr. Svend Petersen has pointed out, in his *Sherlock Holmes Almanac*, that M. Casimer-Perier's predecessor, Marie François Sadi-Carnot, was assassinated, which may have accounted for the former's gratitude toward Sherlock Holmes.

5 *Yoxley Old Place.* We are shortly told that Yoxley Old Place was "down in Kent, seven miles from Chatham and three from the railway line." This may be, but Mr. Humfrey Michell has pointed out that there is a very real Yoxley Old *Hall* near Bury St. Edmunds in Suffolk.

6 *Holmes and I sat together in silence all the evening.* "I . . . sold my practice and returned to share the old quarters at Baker Street," Watson tells us in "The Adventure of the Norwood Builder," the second-*published* adventure in *The Return* series. "A young doctor named Verner . . . purchased my small Kensington practice, and [gave] with astonishingly little demur the highest price that I ventured to ask—an incident which only explained itself some years later, when I found that Verner was a distant relation of Holmes' and that it was my friend who had really found the money."

IT WAS YOUNG STANLEY HOPKINS, A PROMISING DETECTIVE . . .

Illustration by Sidney Paget for the *Strand Magazine*, July, 1904. We shall meet Stanley Hopkins again—in "The Adventure of Black Peter," "The Adventure of the Missing Three-Quarter," and "The Adventure of the Abbey Grange." As we have previously noted, Mr. Marion Prince has advanced the theory that Stanley Hopkins was the son of Sherlock Holmes.

" Is he in ? " he asked eagerly.

" Come up, my dear sir," said Holmes' voice from above. " I hope you have no designs upon us on such a night as this."

The detective mounted the stairs, and our lamp gleamed upon his shining waterproof. I helped him out of it, while Holmes knocked a blaze out of the logs in the grate.

" Now, my dear Hopkins, draw up and warm your toes," said he. " Here's a cigar, and the doctor has a prescription containing hot water and a lemon which is good medicine on a night like this. It must be something important which has brought you out in such a gale."

" It is indeed, Mr. Holmes. I've had a bustling afternoon, I promise you. Did you see anything of the Yoxley case in the latest editions ? "

" I've seen nothing later than the fifteenth century to-day."

" Well, it was only a paragraph, and all wrong at that, so you have not missed anything. I haven't let the grass grow under my feet. It's down in Kent, seven miles from Chatham and three from the railway line. I was wired for at three-fifteen, reached Yoxley Old Place at five, conducted my investigation, was back at Charing Cross by the last train and straight to you by cab."

" Which means, I suppose, that you are not quite clear about your case ? "

" It means that I can make neither head nor tail of it. So far as I can see it is just as tangled a business as ever I handled, and yet at first it seemed so simple that one couldn't go wrong. There's no motive, Mr. Holmes. That's what bothers me—I can't put my hand on a motive. Here's a man dead—there's no denying that —but, so far as I can see, no reason on earth why anyone should wish him harm."

Holmes lit his cigar and leaned back in his chair.

" Let us hear about it," said he.

" I've got my facts pretty clear," said Stanley Hopkins. " All I want now is to know what they all mean. The story, so far as I can make it out, is like this. Some years ago this country house, Yoxley Old Place, was taken by an elderly man, who gave the name of Professor Coram. He was an invalid, keeping his bed half the time, and the other half hobbling round the house with a stick, or being pushed about the grounds by the gardener in a bath-chair. He was well liked by the few neighbours who called upon him, and he has the reputation down there of being a very learned man. His household used to consist of an elderly housekeeper, Mrs. Marker, and of a maid, Susan Tarlton. These have both been with him since his arrival, and they seem to be women of excellent character. The professor is writing a learned book, and he found it necessary about a year ago to engage a secretary. The first two that he tried were not successes ; but the third, Mr. Willoughby Smith, a very young man straight from the University, seems to have been just what his employer wanted. His work consisted in writing all the morning to the professor's dictation, and he usually spent the evening in hunting up

7 *the original inscription upon a palimpsest.* A parchment or other writing material, written upon twice, the original having been erased in whole or in part to make room for the second. Valuable fragments of ancient literature have been recovered in manuscripts by the use of chemical reagents, and Holmes was almost certainly making use of his chemical corner in this instance. Mr. Morris Rosenblum has noted ("Some Latin By-ways in the Canon") that Holmes "must have possessed an intimate knowledge of post-classical Latin to decipher 'the remains of the original inscription upon a palimpsest' and to pursue 'some laborious researches into early English charters ["The Adventure of the Three Students"], since these documents were undoubtedly written in late Latin, intelligible only to expert philologists."

8 *a recent treatise upon surgery.* "Doctor Watson has been rated somewhere between the extremes of merely a good First Aid man and a well trained surgeon," the late Dr. Roland Hammond wrote in "The Surgeon Probes Doctor Watson's Wound." "The proper level of his competence would probably be that of an average general practitioner of medicine. There is no evidence of any outstanding ability as a surgeon in spite of the fact that he was reading a recent treatise on surgery."

And Mr. A. S. Galbraith has added ("The Real Moriarty"): "It is clear from the stories that Watson can write, and write very well, and that he is reasonably well read. He is a capable physician, with the scientific knowledge appropriate to the general practitioner of his day, and he tries by reading to keep up to date in his work."

9 *splashing its way from the Oxford Street end.* Dr. Watson would not be able to see such a sight today: an experimental one-way traffic scheme in the Baker Street-Gloucester Place area has now been made permanent.

references and passages which bore upon the next day's work. This Willoughby Smith has nothing against
him either as a boy at Uppingham or as a young man at **10**
Cambridge. I have seen his testimonials, and from the first he was a decent, quiet, hard-working fellow, with no weak spot in him at all. And yet this is the lad who has met his death this morning in the professor's study under circumstances which can point only to murder."

The wind howled and screamed at the windows. Holmes and I drew closer to the fire while the young inspector slowly and point by point developed his singular narrative.

"If you were to search all England," said he, "I don't suppose you could find a household more self-contained or free from outside influences. Whole weeks would pass and not one of them go past the garden gate. The professor was buried in his work, and existed for nothing else. Young Smith knew nobody in the neighbourhood, and lived very much as his employer did. The two women had nothing to take them from the house. Mortimer, the gardener, who wheels the bath-chair, is an Army pensioner—an old Crimean man of excellent character. He does not live in the house, but in a three-roomed cottage at the other end of the garden. Those are the only people that you would find within the grounds of Yoxley Old Place. At the same time, the gate of the garden is a hundred yards from the main London to Chatham road. It opens with a latch, and there is nothing to prevent anyone from walking in.

"Now I will give you the evidence of Susan Tarlton, who is the only person who can say anything positive about the matter. It was in the forenoon, between eleven and twelve. She was engaged at the moment in hanging some curtains in the upstairs front bedroom. Professor Coram was still in bed, for when the weather is bad he seldom rises before midday. The housekeeper was busied with some work in the back of the house. Willoughby Smith had been in his bedroom, which he uses as a sitting-room; but the maid heard him at that moment pass along the passage and descend to the study immediately below her. She did not see him, but she says that she could not be mistaken in his quick, firm tread. She did not hear the study door close, but a minute or so later there was a dreadful cry in the room below. It was a wild, hoarse scream, so strange and unnatural that it might have come either from a man or a woman. At the same instant there was a heavy thud, which shook the whole house, and then all was silence. The maid stood petrified for a moment, and then, recovering her courage, she ran downstairs. The study door was shut, and she opened it. Inside young Mr. Willoughby Smith was stretched upon the floor. At first she could see no injury, but as she tried to raise him she saw that blood was pouring from the under side of his neck. It was pierced by a very small but very deep wound, which had divided the carotid artery. The instrument with which the injury had been inflicted lay upon the carpet beside him. It was one of those small sealing-wax knives to be found on old-fashioned writing-tables, with

10 *Uppingham.* An ancient public school in Rutlandshire.

an ivory handle and a stiff blade. It was part of the fittings of the professor's own desk.

" At first the maid thought that young Smith was already dead, but on pouring some water from the carafe over his forehead, he opened his eyes for an instant. ' The professor,' he murmured—' it was she.' The maid is prepared to swear that those were the exact words. He tried desperately to say something else, and he held his right hand up in the air. Then he fell back dead.

" In the meantime the housekeeper had also arrived upon the scene, but she was just too late to catch the young man's dying words. Leaving Susan with the body, she hurried to the professor's room. He was sitting up in bed, horribly agitated, for he had heard enough to convince him that something terrible had occurred. Mrs. Marker is prepared to swear that the professor was still in his night-clothes, and, indeed, it was impossible for him to dress without the help of Mortimer, whose orders were to come at twelve o'clock. The professor declares that he heard the distant cry, but that he knows nothing more. He can give no explanation of the young man's last words, ' The professor—it was she,' but imagines that they were the outcome of delirium. He believes that Willoughby Smith had not an enemy in the world, and can give no reason for the crime. His first action was to send Mortimer, the gardener, for the local police. A little later the chief constable sent for me. Nothing was moved before I got there, and strict orders were given that no one should walk upon the paths leading to the house. It was a splendid chance of putting your theories into practice, Mr. Sherlock Holmes. There was really nothing wanting."

" Except Mr. Sherlock Holmes ! " said my companion, with a somewhat bitter smile. " Well, let us hear about it. What sort of job did you make of it ? "

" I must ask you first, Mr. Holmes, to glance at this rough plan, which will give you a general idea of the

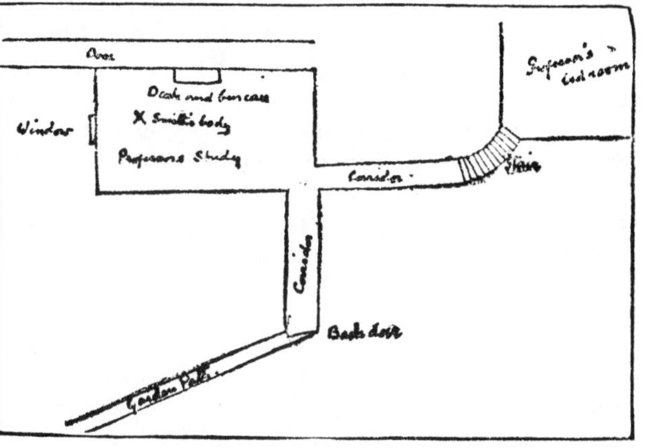

position of the professor's study and the various points of the case. It will help you in following my investigations."

He unfolded the rough chart, which I here reproduce, and he laid it across Holmes' knee. I rose, and, standing behind Holmes, I studied it over his shoulder.

" It is very rough, of course, and it only deals with the points which seem to me to be essential. All the rest you will see later for yourself. Now, first of all, presuming that the assassin entered the house, how did he or she come in ? Undoubtedly by the garden path and the back door, from which there is direct access to the study. Any other way would have been exceedingly complicated. The escape must also have been made along that line, for of the two other exits from the room one was blocked by Susan as she ran downstairs, and the other leads straight to the professor's bedroom. I therefore directed my attention at once to the garden path, which was saturated with recent rain and would certainly show any footmarks.

" My examination showed me that I was dealing with a cautious and expert criminal. No footmarks were to be found on the path. There could be no question, however, that someone had passed along the grass border which lines the path, and that he had done so in order to avoid leaving a track. I could not find anything in the nature of a distinct impression, but the grass was trodden down and someone had undoubtedly passed. It could only have been the murderer, since neither the gardener nor anyone else had been there that morning, and the rain had only begun during the night."

" One moment," said Holmes. " Where does this path lead to ? "

" To the road."

" How long is it ? "

" A hundred yards or so."

" At the point where the path passes through the gate you could surely pick up the tracks ? "

" Unfortunately the path was tiled at that point."

" Well, on the road itself ? "

" No ; it was all trodden into mire."

" Tut-tut ! Well, then, these tracks upon the grass—were they coming or going ? "

" It was impossible to say. There was never any outline."

" A large foot or a small ? "

" You could not distinguish."

Holmes gave an ejaculation of impatience. " It has been pouring rain and blowing a hurricane ever since," said he. " It will be harder to read now than that palimpsest. Well, well, it can't be helped. What did you do, Hopkins, after you had made certain that you had made certain of nothing ? "

" I think I made certain of a good deal, Mr. Holmes. I knew that someone had entered the house cautiously from without. I next examined the corridor. It is lined with coconut matting, and had taken no impression of any kind. This brought me into the study itself. It is a scantily furnished room. The main article is a large writing-table with a fixed bureau. This bureau consists of a double column of drawers with a central small cupboard between them. The drawers were open, the cupboard locked. The drawers, it seems, were always open, and nothing of value was kept in them. There were some papers of importance in the cupboard, but there

"IT WAS FOUND NEAR THE BUREAU, AND JUST TO THE LEFT OF IT, AS MARKED UPON THE CHART."

Illustration by Sidney Paget for the *Strand Magazine*, July, 1904.

were no signs that this had been tampered with, and the professor assures me that nothing was missing. It is certain that no robbery had been committed.

" I come now to the body of the young man. It was found near the bureau, and just to the left of it, as marked upon that chart. The stab was on the right side of the neck and from behind forwards, so that it is almost impossible that it could have been self-inflicted."

" Unless he fell upon the knife," said Holmes.

" Exactly. The idea crossed my mind. But we found the knife some feet away from the body, so that seems impossible. Then, of course, there are the man's own dying words. And, finally, there was this very important piece of evidence which was found clasped in the dead man's right hand."

From his pocket Stanley Hopkins drew a small paper packet. He unfolded it, and disclosed a golden pince-nez, with two broken ends of black silk cord dangling from the end of it. " Willoughby Smith had excellent sight," he added. " There can be no question that this was snatched from the face or the person of the assassin."

Sherlock Holmes took the glasses into his hand and examined them with the utmost attention and interest. He held them on his nose, endeavoured to read through them, went to the window and stared up the street with them, looked at them most minutely in the full light of the lamp, and finally, with a chuckle, seated himself at the table and wrote a few lines upon a sheet of paper, which he tossed across to Stanley Hopkins.

"That's the best I can do for you," said he. "It may prove to be of some use."

The astonished detective read the note aloud. It ran as follows :

" Wanted, a woman of good address, attired like a lady. She has a remarkably thick nose, with eyes which are set close upon either side of it. She has a puckered forehead, a peering expression, and probably rounded shoulders. There are indications that she has had recourse to an optician at least twice during the last few months. As her glasses are of remarkable strength, and as opticians are not very numerous, there should be no difficulty in tracing her."

HE HELD THEM ON HIS NOSE, ENDEAVOURED TO READ THROUGH THEM . . .

Cover illustration by Frederic Dorr Steele for *Collier's Magazine*, October 29, 1904. Sidney Paget illustrated the same scene for the *Strand Magazine*, July, 1904.

Holmes smiled at the astonishment of Hopkins, which must have been reflected upon my features.

" Surely my deductions are simplicity itself," said he. " It would be difficult to name any articles which afford a finer field for inference than a pair of glasses, especially so remarkable a pair as these. That they belong to a woman I infer from their delicacy, and also, of course, from the last words of the dying man. As to her being a person of refinement and well dressed, they are, as you perceive, handsomely mounted in solid gold, and it is inconceivable that anyone who wore such glasses could be slatternly
11 in other respects. You will find that the clips are too wide for your nose, showing that the lady's nose was very broad at the base. This sort of nose is usually a short

and coarse one, but there are a sufficient number of exceptions to prevent me from being dogmatic or from insisting upon this point in my description. My own face is a narrow one, and yet I find that I cannot get my eyes into the centre, or near the centre, of these glasses. Therefore, the lady's eyes are set very near to the sides of the nose. You will perceive, Watson, that the glasses are concave and of unusual strength. A lady whose vision has been so extremely contracted all her life is sure to have the physical characteristics of such vision, which are seen in the forehead, the eyelids, and the shoulders."

"Yes," I said, "I can follow each of your arguments. I confess, however, that I am unable to understand how you arrive at the double visit to the optician."

Holmes took the glasses into his hand.

"You will perceive," he said, "that the clips are lined with tiny bands of cork to soften the pressure upon the nose. One of these is discoloured and worn to some slight extent, but the other is new. Evidently one has fallen off and been replaced. I should judge that the older of them has not been there more than a few months. They exactly correspond, so I gather that the lady went back to the same establishment for the second."

"By George, it's marvellous!" cried Hopkins, in an ecstasy of admiration. "To think that I had all that evidence in my hand and never knew it! I had intended, however, to go the round of the London opticians."

"Of course you would. Meanwhile, have you anything more to tell us about the case?"

"Nothing, Mr. Holmes. I think that you know as much as I do now—probably more. We have had inquiries made as to any stranger seen on the country roads or at the railway station. We have heard of none. What beats me is the utter want of all object in the crime. Not a ghost of a motive can anyone suggest."

"Ah! there I am not in a position to help you. But I suppose you want us to come out to-morrow?"

"If it is not asking too much, Mr. Holmes. There's a
train from Charing Cross to Chatham at six in the morning, 12
and we should be at Yoxley Old Place between eight and nine."

"Then we shall take it. Your case has certainly some features of great interest, and I shall be delighted to look into it. Well, it's nearly one, and we had best get a few hours' sleep. I dare say you can manage all right on the
sofa in front of the fire. I'll light my spirit-lamp and 13
give you a cup of coffee before we start."

The gale had blown itself out next day, but it was a bitter morning when we started upon our journey. We saw the cold winter sun rise over the dreary marshes of the Thames and the long, sullen reaches of the river, which I shall ever associate with our pursuit of the
Andaman Islander in the earlier days of our career. 14
After a long and weary journey we alighted at a small
station some miles from Chatham. While a horse was 15
being put into a trap at the local inn we snatched a hurried breakfast, and so we were all ready for business when we at last arrived at Yoxley Old Place. A constable

11 *could be slatternly in other respects.* "The conclusion that a woman who wears gold pince-nez must be well-dressed is unconvincing," Mr. Vernon Rendall wrote in "The Limitations of Sherlock Holmes." "People, when they first buy glasses, know nothing of the price, and the vendor naturally provides them with the most expensive form of eyewear. Vanity also induces them to have gold fittings, and they may insist on a detail which concerns their face, even if they cannot run to good clothes. Forty years ago, it must be remembered, horn spectacles had not come into fashion, and glasses, being regarded as a disfigurement, were not so often worn as they are to-day. Gold-rimmed glasses may have been bought during a period of prosperity which in later life the owner no longer enjoyed. . . . As I write, a notice appears in the papers of a woman with gold-rimmed glasses whose dull, if not slatternly clothing, as described, resembles that of a charwoman rather than what is prescribed by the 'dictates of fashion.'"

12 *at six in the morning.* There was, in fact, such a train at 6:12 A.M. They would have traveled by the old Southeastern and Chatham line.

13 *I'll light my spirit-lamp.* Why a spirit-lamp, when we know very well that the sitting room at 221B had gas laid on? And, as Mr. D. A. Redmond noted in "Some Chemical Problems in the Canon," "it is not likely that in a private lodging, for which he was paying 'princely' rentals, Holmes' gas supply would be equipped with a shilling-in-the-slot meter and his pockets empty of coins. Had he not paid his gas bill?"

14 *in the earlier days of our career.* Watson in this adventure must be speaking of the night of *November 14th*, a day on which the wind achieved a pressure of 29.5 pounds to the inch and there was 0.35 inch of rain, and the morning of *November 15th*, when the wind slackened to only 1.9 pounds and the temperature was 42.1 degrees. (We have already noted that Watson was unusually sensitive to drops in the temperature. In addition, as the late Professor Jay Finley Christ noted, "We are further entitled to doubt [Watson's impressions of bitter weather here] because he said that the streets were muddy and the pavement shiny as he looked out the window, and the men 'loitered the morning away in the garden,' at Coram's.") These two days were a Wednesday and Thursday. The late Dr. Ernest Bloomfield Zeisler chose to date this case October, 1894. He rightly said that November 14th–15th are not "towards the close of November." We, on the other hand, would sacrifice Watson's "towards the close" of November to preserve both his "November" and his "winter sun" (October is not "winter" in either the popular or the astronomical sense of the word). Dr. Zeisler also held that the month could not be November because: 1) Watson saw the sun rise after the start of their journey, which we know began at six; 2) the time of sunrise cannot be long after six because Watson, seeing the Thames, was reminded of the pursuit of the Islander and therefore could not have been long upon his journey. Certainly Watson saw the sun rise between the start of the journey and its close between eight and nine (on November 15, 1895, sunrise was at 7:20 A.M.); certainly he glimpsed the Thames and was reminded of the adventure of *The Sign of the Four*. But there is nothing in Watson's statement to lead us to believe that these incidents were *simultaneous*.

15 *a small station some miles from Chatham.* Mr. Michael Harrison has suggested (*In the Footsteps of Sherlock Holmes*) that the station was Higham. Of Yoxley Old Place, he writes: "It can only have been just off the main Gravesend-Chatham road, at the village of Shorne, only a few yards from Dickens' old house, Gadshill, and equally near to the famed Falstaff Inn, at the summit of Gadshill itself—that long slope which leads down to the Medway—at whose top Prince Hal, and Falstaff, and Nym and the rest, used to waylay travellers."

met us at the garden gate.

"Well, Wilson, any news?"

"No, sir, nothing."

"No reports of any stranger seen?"

"No, sir. Down at the station they are certain that no stranger either came or went yesterday."

"Have you had inquiries made at inns and lodgings?"

"Yes, sir; there is no one that we cannot account for."

"Well, it's only a reasonable walk to Chatham. Anyone might stay there, or take a train without being observed. This is the garden path of which I spoke, Mr. Holmes. I'll pledge my word there was no mark on it yesterday."

"On which side were the marks on the grass?"

"This side, sir. This narrow margin of grass between the path and the flower-bed. I can't see the traces now, but they were clear to me then."

"Yes, yes; someone has passed along," said Holmes, stooping over the grass border. "Our lady must have picked her steps carefully, must she not, since on the one side she would leave a track on the path, and on the other an even clearer one on the soft bed?"

"Yes, sir, she must have been a cool hand."

I saw an intent look pass over Holmes' face.

"You say that she must have come back this way?"

"Yes, sir; there is no other."

"On this strip of grass?"

"Certainly, Mr. Holmes."

"Hum! It was a very remarkable performance—very remarkable. Well, I think we have exhausted the path. Let us go farther. This garden door is usually kept open, I suppose? Then this visitor had nothing to do but to walk in. The idea of murder was not in her mind, or she would have provided herself with some sort of weapon, instead of having to pick this knife off the writing-table. She advanced along this corridor, leaving no traces upon the coconut matting. Then she found herself in this study. How long was she there? We have no means of judging."

"Not more than a few minutes, sir. I forgot to tell you that Mrs. Marker, the housekeeper, had been in there tidying not very long before—about a quarter of an hour she says."

"Well, that gives us a limit. Our lady enters this room, and what does she do? She goes over to the writing-table. What for? Not for anything in the drawers. If there had been anything worth her taking it would scarcely have been locked up. No; it was for something in that wooden bureau. Halloa! what is that scratch upon the face of it? Just hold a match, Watson. Why did you not tell me of this, Hopkins?"

The mark which he was examining began upon the brasswork on the right-hand side of the keyhole, and extended for about four inches, where it had scratched the varnish from the surface.

"I noticed it, Mr. Holmes. But you'll always find scratches round a keyhole."

"This is recent—quite recent. See how the brass

shines where it is cut. An old scratch would be the same colour as the surface. Look at it through my lens. There's the varnish, too, like earth on each side of a furrow. Is Mrs. Marker there ? "

A sad-faced, elderly woman came into the room.

" Did you dust this bureau yesterday morning ? "

" Yes, sir."

" Did you notice this scratch ? "

" No, sir, I did not."

" I am sure you did not, for a duster would have swept away these shreds of varnish. Who has the key of this bureau ? "

" The professor keeps it on his watch-chain."

" Is it a simple key ? "

" No, sir ; it is a Chubb's key."

" Very good. Mrs. Marker, you can go. Now we are making a little progress. Our lady enters the room, advances to the bureau, and either opens it or tries to do so. While she is thus engaged young Willoughby Smith enters the room. In her hurry to withdraw the key she makes this scratch upon the door. He seizes her, and she, snatching up the nearest object, which happens to be this knife, strikes at him in order to make him let go his hold. The blow is a fatal one. He falls and she escapes, either with or without the object for which she has come. Is Susan the maid there ? Could anyone have got away through that door after the time that you heard the cry, Susan ? "

" No, sir ; it is impossible. Before I got down the stair I'd have seen anyone in the passage. Besides, the door never opened, for I would have heard it."

" That settles this exit. Then no doubt the lady went out the way she came. I understand that this other passage leads only to the professor's room. There is no exit that way ? "

" No, sir."

" We shall go down it and make the acquaintance of the professor. Halloa, Hopkins ! this is very important, very important indeed. The professor's corridor is also lined with coconut matting."

" Well, sir, what of that ? "

" Don't you see any bearing upon the case ? Well, well, I don't insist upon it. No doubt I am wrong. And yet it seems to me to be suggestive. Come with me and introduce me."

We passed down the passage, which was of the same length as that which led to the garden. At the end was a short flight of steps ending in a door. Our guide knocked, and then ushered us into the professor's bedroom.

It was a very large chamber, lined with innumerable volumes, which had overflowed from the shelves and lay in piles in the corners, or were stacked all round at the base of the cases. The bed was in the centre of the room, and in it, propped up with pillows, was the owner of the house. I have seldom seen a more remarkable-looking person. It was a gaunt, aquiline face which was turned towards us, with piercing dark eyes, which lurked in deep hollows under overhung and tufted brows. His hair and beard were white, save that the latter was curiously stained with

"DID YOU DUST THIS BUREAU YESTERDAY MORNING?"

Illustration by Sidney Paget for the *Strand Magazine*, July, 1904.

"YES, SIR, IT IS A CRUSHING BLOW," SAID THE OLD MAN.

Illustration by Frederic Dorr Steele for *Collier's Magazine*, October 29, 1904.

yellow around his mouth. A cigarette glowed amid the tangle of white hair, and the air of the room was fetid with stale tobacco smoke. As he held out his hand to Holmes I perceived that it also was stained yellow with nicotine.

" A smoker, Mr. Holmes ? " said he, speaking well-chosen English with a curious little mincing accent. " Pray take a cigarette. And you, sir ? I can recommend them, for I have them especially prepared by Ionides of Alexandria. He sends me a thousand at a time, and I grieve to say that I have to arrange for a fresh supply every fortnight. Bad, sir, very bad ; but an old man has few pleasures. Tobacco and my work—that is all that is left to me."

Holmes had lit a cigarette, and was shooting little darting glances all over the room.

" Tobacco and my work, but now only tobacco," the old man exclaimed. " Alas, what a fatal interruption ! Who could have foreseen such a terrible catastrophe ? So estimable a young man ! I assure you that after a few months' training he was an admirable assistant. What do you think of the matter, Mr. Holmes ? "

" I have not yet made up my mind."

" I shall indeed be indebted to you if you can throw a light where all is so dark to us. To a poor bookworm and invalid like myself such a blow is paralysing. I seem to have lost the faculty of thought. But you are a man of action—you are a man of affairs. It is part of the every-day routine of your life. You can preserve your balance in every emergency. We are fortunate indeed in having you at our side."

Holmes was pacing up and down on one side of the room whilst the old professor was talking. I observed that he was smoking with extraordinary rapidity. It was evident that he shared our host's liking for the fresh Alexandrian cigarettes.

" Yes, sir, it is a crushing blow," said the old man. " That is my *magnum opus*—the pile of papers on the side-table yonder. It is my analysis of the documents found in the Coptic monasteries of Syria and Egypt, a work which will cut deep at the very foundations of revealed religion. With my enfeebled health I do not know whether I shall ever be able to complete it now that my assistant has been taken from me. Dear me, Mr. Holmes ; why, you are even a quicker smoker than I am myself."

Holmes smiled.

" I am a connoisseur," said he, taking another cigarette from the box—his fourth—and lighting it from the stub of that which he had finished. " I will not trouble you with any lengthy cross-examination, Professor Coram, since I gather that you were in bed at the time of the crime and could know nothing about it. I would only ask this—What do you imagine that this poor fellow meant by his last words : ' The professor—it was she ' ? "

The professor shook his head.

" Susan is a country girl," said he, " and you know the incredible stupidity of that class. I fancy that the poor fellow murmured some incoherent, delirious words, and that she twisted them into this meaningless message."

" I see. You have no explanation yourself of the tragedy ? "

" Possibly an accident ; possibly—I only breathe it among ourselves—a suicide. Young men have their hidden troubles—some affair of the heart, perhaps, which we have never known. It is a more probable supposition than murder."

" But the eyeglasses ? "

" Ah ! I am only a student—a man of dreams. I cannot explain the practical things of life. But still, we are aware, my friend, that love-gages may take strange shapes. By all means take another cigarette. It is a pleasure to see anyone appreciate them so. A fan, a glove, glasses—who knows what article may be carried as a token or treasured when a man puts an end to his life ? This gentleman speaks of footsteps on the grass ; but, after all, it is easy to be mistaken on such a point. As to the knife, it might well be thrown far from the unfortunate man as he fell. It is possible that I speak as a child, but to me it seems that Willoughby Smith has met his fate by his own hand."

Holmes seemed struck by the theory thus put forward, and he continued to walk up and down for some time, lost in thought and consuming cigarette after cigarette.

" Tell me, Professor Coram," he said at last, " what is in that cupboard in the bureau ? "

" Nothing that would help a thief. Family papers, letters from my poor wife, diplomas of Universities which have done me honour. Here is the key. You can look for yourself."

Holmes picked up the key and looked at it for an instant ; then he handed it back.

" No ; I hardly think that it would help me," said he. " I should prefer to go quietly down to your garden and turn the whole matter over in my head. There is something to be said for the theory of suicide which you have put forward. We must apologize for having intruded upon you, Professor Coram, and I promise that we won't disturb you until after lunch. At two o'clock we will come again and report to you anything which may have happened in the interval."

Holmes was curiously distrait, and we walked up and down the garden path for some time in silence.

" Have you a clue ? " I asked at last.

" It depends upon those cigarettes that I smoked," said he. " It is possible that I am utterly mistaken. The cigarettes will show me."

" My dear Holmes," I exclaimed, " how on earth——"

" Well, well, you may see for yourself. If not, there's no harm done. Of course, we always have the optician clue to fall back upon, but I take a short cut when I can
get it. Ah, here is the good Mrs. Marker ! Let us **16**
enjoy five minutes of instructive conversation with her."

I may have remarked before that Holmes had, when he liked, a peculiarly ingratiating way with women, and that he very readily established terms of confidence with them. In half the time which he had named he had captured the housekeeper's goodwill, and was chatting with her as if he had known her for years.

" Yes, Mr. Holmes, it is as you say, sir. He does smoke

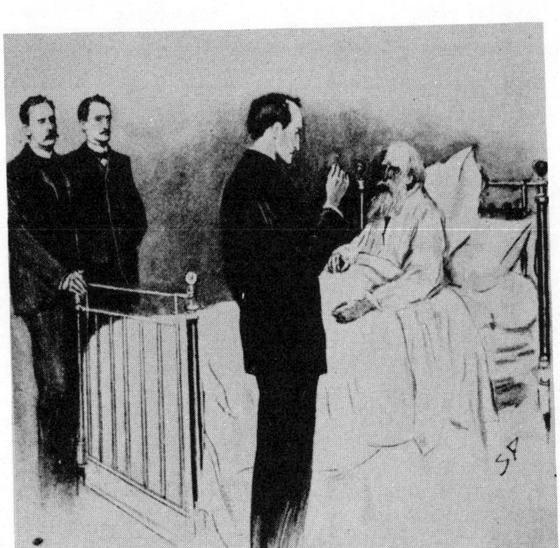

HOLMES PICKED UP THE KEY AND LOOKED AT IT FOR AN INSTANT . . .

Illustration by Sidney Paget for the *Strand Magazine*, July, 1904.

16 *I take a short cut when I can get it.* How truly the "short cut" Holmes used in this case was inspired may be seen by a comparison of "The Adventure of the Golden Pince-Nez" with the first episode in "The History of the Destruction of Bel and the Dragon" as recorded in the Old Testament Apocrypha. "Of course the stories are different, but the pivotal points are the same," Professor Stephen F. Crocker wrote in his "Pseudepigraphical Matter in the Holmesian Canon." Another commentator, Professor Clarke Olney, has suggested ("The Literacy of Sherlock Holmes") that the trick used by Holmes here was adapted from the artifice of Frocin, the evil-minded dwarf who sprinkled flour between the beds occupied by Tristram and Isolde.

something terrible. All day and sometimes all night, sir. I've seen that room of a morning—well, sir, you'd have thought it was a London fog. Poor young Mr. Smith, he was a smoker also, but not as bad as the professor. His health—well, I don't know that it's better nor worse for the smoking."

"Ah !" said Holmes, "but it kills the appetite."

"Well, I don't know about that, sir."

"I suppose the professor eats hardly anything ?"

"Well, he is variable. I'll say that for him."

"I'll wager he took no breakfast this morning, and won't face his lunch after all the cigarettes I saw him consume."

"Well, you're out there, sir, as it happens, for he ate a remarkably big breakfast this morning. I don't know when I've known him make a better one, and he's ordered a good dish of cutlets for his lunch. I'm surprised myself, for since I came into that room yesterday and saw young Mr. Smith lying there on the floor I couldn't bear to look at food. Well, it takes all sorts to make a world, and the professor hasn't let it take his appetite away."

We loitered the morning away in the garden. Stanley Hopkins had gone down to the village to look into some rumours of a strange woman who had been seen by some children on the Chatham road the previous morning. As to my friend, all his usual energy seemed to have deserted him. I had never known him handle a case in such a half-hearted fashion. Even the news brought back by Hopkins that he had found the children and that they had undoubtedly seen a woman exactly corresponding with Holmes' description, and wearing either spectacles or eyeglasses, failed to rouse any sign of keen interest. He was more attentive when Susan, who waited upon us at lunch, volunteered the information that she believed Mr. Smith had been out for a walk yesterday morning, and that he had only returned half an hour before the tragedy occurred. I could not myself see the bearing of this incident, but I clearly perceived that Holmes was weaving it into the general scheme which he had formed in his brain. Suddenly he sprang from his chair, and glanced at his watch. "Two o'clock, gentlemen," said he. "We must go up and have it out with our friend the professor."

The old man had just finished his lunch, and certainly his empty dish bore evidence to the good appetite with which his housekeeper had credited him. He was, indeed, a weird figure as he turned his white mane and his glowing eyes towards us. The eternal cigarette smouldered in his mouth. He had been dressed and was seated in an arm-chair by the fire.

"Well, Mr. Holmes, have you solved this mystery yet ?" He shoved the large tin of cigarettes which stood on a table beside him towards my companion. Holmes stretched out his hand at the same moment, and between them they tipped the box over the edge. For a minute or two we were all on our knees retrieving stray cigarettes from impossible places. When we rose again I observed that Holmes' eyes were shining and his cheeks tinged with colour. Only at a crisis have I seen those battle-signals flying.

" Yes," said he, " I have solved it."

Stanley Hopkins and I stared in amazement. Something like a sneer quivered over the gaunt features of the old professor.

" Indeed ! In the garden ? "

" No, here."

" Here ! When ? "

" This instant."

" You are surely joking, Mr. Sherlock Holmes. You compel me to tell you that this is too serious a matter to be treated in such a fashion."

" I have forged and tested every link of my chain, Professor Coram, and I am sure that it is sound. What your motives are, or what exact part you play in this strange business, I am not yet able to say. In a few minutes I shall probably hear it from your own lips. Meanwhile, I will reconstruct what is past for your benefit, so that you may know the information which I still require.

" A lady yesterday entered your study. She came with the intention of possessing herself of certain documents which were in your bureau. She had a key of her own. I have had an opportunity of examining yours, and I do not find that slight discoloration which the scratch made upon the varnish would have produced. You were not an accessory, therefore, and she came, so far as I can read the evidence, without your knowledge to rob you."

The professor blew a cloud from his lips.

" This is most interesting and instructive," said he. " Have you no more to add ? Surely, having traced this lady so far, you can also say what has become of her."

" I will endeavour to do so. In the first place, she was seized by your secretary, and stabbed him in order to escape. This catastrophe I am inclined to regard as an unhappy accident, for I am convinced that the lady had no intention of inflicting so grievous an injury. An assassin does not come unarmed. Horrified by what she had done, she rushed wildly away from the scene of the tragedy. Unfortunately for her she had lost her glasses in the scuffle, and as she was extremely short-sighted she was really helpless without them. She ran down a corridor, which she imagined to be that by which she had come—both were lined with coconut matting—and it was only when it was too late that she understood that she had taken the wrong passage and that her retreat was cut off behind her. What was she to do ? She could not go back. She could not remain where she was. She must go on. She went on. She mounted a stair, pushed open a door, and found herself in your room."

The old man sat with his mouth open staring wildly at Holmes. Amazement and fear were stamped upon his expressive features. Now, with an effort, he shrugged his shoulders and burst into insincere laughter.

" All very fine, Mr. Holmes," said he. " But there is one little flaw in a splendid theory. I was myself in my room, and I never left it during the day."

" I am aware of that, Professor Coram."

" And you mean to say that I could lie upon that bed and not be aware that a woman had entered my room ? "

" I never said so. You *were* aware of it. You spoke

with her. You recognized her. You aided her to escape."

Again the professor burst into high-keyed laughter. He had risen to his feet, and his eyes glowed like embers.

"You are mad!" he cried. "You are talking insanely. I helped her to escape? Where is she now?"

"She is there," said Holmes, and he pointed to a high bookcase in the corner of the room.

I saw the old man throw up his arms, a terrible convulsion passed over his grim face, and he fell back in his chair. At the same instant the bookcase at which Holmes pointed swung round upon a hinge, and a woman rushed out into the room.

"You are right," she cried, in a strange foreign voice. "You are right! I am here."

. . . A WOMAN RUSHED OUT INTO THE ROOM.

Illustration by Sidney Paget for the *Strand Magazine*, July, 1904.

She was brown with the dust and draped with the cobwebs which had come from the walls of her hiding-place. Her face, too, was streaked with grime, and at the best she could have never been handsome, for she had the exact physical characteristics which Holmes had divined, with, in addition, a long and obstinate chin. What with her natural blindness, and what with the change from dark to light, she stood as one dazed, blinking about her to see where and who we were. And yet, in spite of all these disadvantages, there was a certain nobility in the woman's bearing, a gallantry in the defiant chin and in the upraised head, which compelled something of respect and admiration. Stanley Hopkins had laid his hand upon her arm and claimed her as his prisoner, but she waved him aside gently, and yet with an overmastering dignity which compelled obedience. The old man lay back in his chair, with a twitching face, and stared at her with brooding eyes.

"Yes, sir, I am your prisoner," she said. "From where I stood I could hear everything, and I know that you have learned the truth. I confess it all. It was I who killed the young man. But you are right, you who say that it was an accident. I did not even know that it was a knife which I held in my hand, for in my despair I snatched anything from the table and struck at him to make him let me go. It is the truth that I tell."

"Madame," said Holmes, "I am sure that it is the truth. I fear that you are far from well."

She had turned a dreadful colour, the more ghastly under the dark dust-streaks upon her face. She seated herself on the side of the bed; then she resumed.

"I have only a little time here," she said, "but I would have you to know the whole truth. I am this man's wife. He is not an Englishman. He is a Russian. His name I will not tell."

For the first time the old man stirred. "God bless you, Anna!" he cried. "God bless you!"

She cast a look of the deepest disdain in his direction. "Why should you cling so hard to that wretched life of yours, Sergius?" said she. "It has done harm to many and good to none—not even to yourself. However, it is not for me to cause the frail thread to be snapped before God's time. I have enough already upon my soul since I crossed the threshold of this cursed house. But I must speak, or I shall be too late.

" I have said, gentlemen, that I am this man's wife. He was fifty and I a foolish girl of twenty when we married. It was in a city of Russia, a University—I will not name the place."

" God bless you, Anna ! " murmured the old man again.

" We were reformers—revolutionists—Nihilists, you understand. He and I and many more. Then there
came a time of trouble, a police officer was killed, many **17**
were arrested, evidence was wanted, and in order to save his own life and to earn a great reward my husband betrayed his own wife and his companions. Yes ; we were all arrested upon his confession. Some of us found our way to the gallows and some to Siberia. I was among these last but my term was not for life. My husband came to England with his ill-gotten gains, and has lived in quiet ever since, knowing well that if the Brotherhood knew where he was not a week would pass before justice would be done."

The old man reached out a trembling hand and helped himself to a cigarette. " I am in your hands, Anna," said he. " You were always good to me."

" I have not yet told you the height of his villainy ! " said she. " Among our comrades of the Order there was one who was the friend of my heart. He was noble, unselfish, loving—all that my husband was not. He hated violence. We were all guilty—if that is guilt—but he was not. He wrote for ever dissuading me from such a course. These letters would have saved him. So would my diary, in which from day to day I had entered both my feelings towards him and the view which each of us had taken. My husband found and kept both diary and letters. He hid them, and he tried hard to swear away the young man's life. In this he failed, but Alexis was sent a convict to Siberia, where now, at this moment, he works in a salt mine. Think of that, you villain, you villain ; now, now, at this very moment, Alexis, a man whose name you are not worthy to speak, works and lives like a slave, and yet I have your life in my hands and I let you go ! "

" You were always a noble woman, Anna," said the old man, puffing at his cigarette.

She had risen, but she fell back again with a little cry of pain.

" I must finish," she said. " When my term was over I set myself to get the diary and letters, which if sent to the Russian Government, would procure my friend's release. I knew that my husband had come to England. After months of searching I discovered where he was. I knew that he still had the diary, for when I was in Siberia I had a letter from him once reproaching me and quoting some passages from its pages. Yet I was sure that with his revengeful nature he would never give it to me of his own free will. I must get it for myself. With this object I engaged an agent from a private detective firm, who entered my husband's house as secretary—it was your second secretary, Sergius, the one who left you so hurriedly. He found that papers were kept in the cupboard, and he got an impression of

17 *Then there came a time of trouble.* See Job 38:23; Psalms 9:9, 27:5; Jeremiah 2:27. "Strange phrasing for a Russian revolutionist," Professor Crocker wrote, "but perhaps she had a Christian upbringing!"

"I AM IN YOUR HANDS, ANNA," SAID HE.

Illustration by Sidney Paget for the *Strand Magazine*, July, 1904.

the key. He would not go farther. He furnished me with a plan of the house, and he told me that in the forenoon the study was always empty, as the secretary was employed up here. So at last I took my courage in both hands and I came down to get the papers for myself. I succeeded, but at what a cost!

"I had just taken the papers and was locking the cupboard when the young man seized me. I had seen him already that morning. He had met me in the road, and I had asked him to tell me where Professor Coram lived, not knowing that he was in his employ."

"Exactly! exactly!" said Holmes. "The secretary came back and told his employer of the woman he had met. Then in his last breath he tried to send a message that it was she—the she whom he had just discussed with him."

"You must let me speak," said the woman, in an imperative voice, and her face contracted as if in pain. "When he had fallen I rushed from the room, chose the wrong door, and found myself in my husband's room. He spake of giving me up. I showed him that if he did so his life was in my hands. If he gave me to the law I could give him to the Brotherhood. It was not that I wished to live for my own sake, but it was that I desired to accomplish my purpose. He knew that I would do what I said—that his own fate was involved in mine. For that reason, and for no other, he shielded me. He thrust me into that dark hiding-place, a relic of old days, known only to himself. He took his meals in his own room, and so was able to give me part of his food. It was agreed that when the police left the house I should slip away by night and come back no more. But in some way you have read our plans." She tore from the bosom of her dress a small packet. "These are my last words," said she; "here is the packet which will save Alexis. I confide it to your honour and to your love of justice. Take it! You will deliver it at the Russian Embassy. Now I have done my duty, and——"

"Stop her!" cried Holmes. He had bounded across the room and had wrenched a small phial from her hand.

"Too late!" she said, sinking back on the bed. "Too
18 late! I took the poison before I left my hiding-place. My head swims! I am going! I charge you, sir, to remember the packet."

HE HAD BOUNDED ACROSS THE ROOM AND HAD WRENCHED A SMALL PHIAL FROM HER HAND.

Illustration by Sidney Paget for the *Strand Magazine*, July, 1904.

"A simple case, and yet in some ways an instructive one," Holmes remarked as we travelled back to town. "It hinged from the outset upon the pince-nez. But for the fortunate chance of the dying man having seized these I am not sure that we could ever have reached our solution. It was clear to me from the strength of the glasses that the wearer must have been very blind and helpless when deprived of them. When you asked me to believe that she walked along a narrow strip of grass without once making a false step I remarked, as you may remember, that it was a noteworthy performance. In my mind, I set it down as an impossible performance, save in the unlikely case that she had a second pair of glasses. I was forced, therefore, to seriously consider the hypothesis that she

18 *I took the poison.* "Tr. Aconite is believed to be the suicide weapon of Anna Coram," Dr. J. W. Sovine wrote in "The Toxicanon." "She swallowed the poison from a small phial, which suggests a potent liquid. She lived about fifteen minutes . . . and was conscious and able to talk correctly until nearly the end, which rules out hypnotics, opium derivatives and corrosive poisons. The poison was too slow for cyanide."

had remained within the house. On perceiving the similarity of the two corridors, it became clear that she might very easily have made such a mistake, and in that case it was evident that she must have entered the professor's room. I was keenly on the alert, therefore, for whatever would bear out this supposition, and I examined the room narrowly for anything in the shape of a hiding-place. The carpet seemed continuous and firmly nailed, so I dismissed the idea of a trap-door. There might well be a recess behind the books. As you are aware, such devices are common in old libraries. I observed that books were piled on the floor at all other points, but that one bookcase was left clear. This, then, might be the door. I could see no marks to guide me, but the carpet was of a dun colour, which lends itself very well to examination. I therefore smoked a great number of those excellent cigarettes, and I dropped the ash all over the space in front of the suspected bookcase. It was a simple trick, but exceedingly effective. I then went downstairs, and I ascertained in your presence, Watson, without your quite perceiving the drift of my remarks, that Professor Coram's consumption of food had increased—as one would expect when he is supplying a second person. We then ascended to the room again, when, by upsetting the cigarette-box, I obtained a very excellent view of the floor, and was able to see quite clearly, from the traces upon the cigarette ash, that the prisoner had, in our absence, come out from her retreat. Well, Hopkins, here we are at Charing Cross, and I congratulate you on having brought your case to a successful conclusion. You are going to headquarters, no doubt. I think, Watson, you and I will drive together to the Russian Embassy."

Bibliographical Note: Inscribed "Sherlock Holmes original manuscript from Arthur Conan Doyle to H. Greenhough Smith, a souvenir of 20 years of collaboration. Feb. 8/16," the original manuscript of this story, in 53 pages, 4to, is believed to be the only presentation by the author of one of his manuscript-writings. The manuscript was auctioned in London on March 26, 1934, bringing £120. Its present location is unknown.

51

THE ADVENTURE OF THE THREE STUDENTS

[Friday, April 5, to Saturday, April 6, 1895]

IT was in the year '95 that a combination of events, into
which I need not enter, caused Mr. Sherlock
Holmes and myself to spend some weeks in one of
1 our great University towns, and it was during this time
that the small but instructive adventure which I am about to relate befell us. It will be obvious that any details which would help the reader to exactly identify the college or the criminal would be injudicious and offensive. So painful a scandal may well be allowed to die out. With due discretion the incident itself may, however, be described, since it serves to illustrate some of those qualities for which my friend was remarkable. I will endeavour in my statement to avoid such terms as would serve to limit the events to any particular place, or give a clue as to the people concerned.

We were residing at the time in furnished lodgings close
to a library where Sherlock Holmes was pursuing some
2 laborious researches in Early English charters—re-
searches which led to results so striking that they may be the subject of one of my future narratives. Here it was that one evening we received a visit from an acquaintance, Mr. Hilton Soames, tutor and lecturer at the College of St. Luke's. Mr. Soames was a tall, spare man, of a nervous and excitable temperament. I had always known him to be restless in his manner, but on this particular occasion he was in such a state of uncontrollable agitation that it was clear something very unusual had occurred.

"I trust, Mr. Holmes, that you can spare me a few hours of your valuable time. We have had a very painful incident at St. Luke's, and really, but for the happy chance of your being in the town, I should have been at a loss what to do."

"I am very busy just now, and I desire no distractions,' my friend answered. "I should much prefer that you called in the aid of the police."

"No, no, my dear sir; such a course is utterly impossible. When once the law is evoked it cannot be stayed again, and this is just one of those cases where, for the credit of the college, it is most essential to avoid scandal. Your discretion is as well known as your powers, and you

1 *one of our great University towns.* Oxford or Cambridge? The debate has been a prolonged one, and we shall try here to give the case for and against each university as fairly as we can. We may note, to begin with, that Watson's use of the word *town* speaks for Cambridge: Oxford in 1895 was a city, Cambridge still a town.

2 *some laborious researches in Early English charters.* "It is significant of [Holmes] and the quality of his historical knowledge and interest that [he] chose for his most original and serious work this very field of history which Charles Gross said was at the time 'so sadly neglected in England' (*Sources and Literature of English History, from the earliest times to about 1485*, London, 1900, p. 28)," Mr. Whitfield J. Bell, Jr., wrote in "Holmes and History."

And Mr. T. S. Blakeney has noted ("The Location of 'The Three Students'") that Holmes' study shows that he could read court hand, the Gothic or Saxon writing used in English public records. ". . . I submit," Mr. Blakeney continued, "that the probabilities are almost overwhelming that it would be to Oxford, not to Cambridge, that a student in 1895 would most naturally gravitate for the study of Early English charters. Bishop Stubbs had, as Regius Professor of History, established the Oxford historical school as predominant in England at that time. And Stubbs had given a particular impetus to medieval history studies, and had himself, in 1870, issued his 'Select Charters and other Illustrations of English Constitutional History from the Earliest Times to the Reign of Edward I.' Furthermore, in 1878, Mr. W. H. Turner had published his 'Calendar of Charters and Rolls' in the Bodleian Library, just the sort of volume that an amateur historian, as Holmes was, would find invaluable. Against this solidly enthroned tradition of the Oxford Medieval History School, what had Cambridge to offer? The Historical Tripos there was only established in 1875 (the Law and History Tripos had begun in 1870) and in Dr. G. P. Gooch's view (*Studies in Modern History*, p. 314) Seeley was the first scholar of the

"I TRUST, MR. HOLMES, THAT YOU CAN SPARE ME A FEW HOURS OF YOUR VALUABLE TIME."

Illustration by Frederic Dorr Steele for *Collier's Magazine*, September 24, 1904.

are the one man in the world who can help me. I beg you, Mr. Holmes, to do what you can."

My friend's temper had not improved since he had been
deprived of the congenial surroundings of Baker Street.
Without his scrap-books, his chemicals, and his homely
untidiness, he was an uncomfortable man. He shrugged
his shoulders in ungracious acquiescence, while our 3
visitor in hurried words and with much excitable gesticu-
lation poured forth his story.

" I must explain to you, Mr. Holmes, that to-morrow is the first day of the examination for the Fortescue Scholarship. I am one of the examiners. My subject is Greek, and the first of the papers consists of a large passage of Greek translation which the candidate has not seen. This passage is printed on the examination paper, and it would naturally be an immense advantage if the candidate could prepare it in advance. For this reason great care is taken to keep the paper secret.

" To-day about three o'clock the proofs of this paper
arrived from the printers. The exercise consists of half
a chapter of Thucydides. I had to read it over carefully, 4
as the text must be absolutely correct. At four-thirty my
task was not yet completed. I had, however, promised
to take tea in a friend's rooms, so I left the proof upon my
desk. I was absent rather more than an hour. You are
aware, Mr. Holmes, that our college doors are double—a
green baize one within and a heavy oak one without. As 5
I approached my outer door I was amazed to see a key in
it. For an instant I imagined that I had left my own
there, but on feeling in my pocket I found that it was all
right. The only duplicate which existed, so far as I
knew, was that which belonged to my servant, Bannister, 6
a man who has looked after my room for ten years, and
whose honesty is absolutely above suspicion. I found that
the key was indeed his, that he had entered my room to
know if I wanted tea, and that he had very carelessly left
the key in the door when he came out. His visit to my
room must have been within a very few minutes of my

front rank to hold the Cambridge Chair of History. He was Regius Professor from 1869–95; but it seems fair to say that medieval history was somewhat in abeyance during this period, as compared with Oxford, and Maitland only made his great influence felt from the 1890s onwards. There was nothing comparable to Turner's 'Calendar,' nor was the University Library at Cambridge so well endowed with early charters as was the Bodleian. If it be objected that Holmes might have studied in a Cambridge College library, and not at the University library, one must point out that the late Dr. M. R. James only began to publish his volumes of Catalogues of Western MSS in Cambridge college libraries in 1895—too late to be of service to Holmes. even had they contained the sort of material he needed. And that Holmes would have required all such aids as could be given him may be regarded as certain. . . . His real intellectual gifts were scientific rather than historical, and Miss Dorothy Sayers (*Unpopular Opinions*, pp. 142, 899) has made out a good case for his having, when at the University himself, taken the Natural Sciences Tripos rather than any other. Medieval history studies would be a learned hobby of his and he would stand in need of any help that scholars might have prepared to guide the inexpert student. Beyond question, Oxford in the year 1895 would have been the most probable centre at which to study early charters . . ."

The late Christopher Morley was in complete agreement with Mr. Blakeney. In *Sherlock Holmes and Dr. Watson: A Textbook of Friendship*, he wrote: ". . . Holmes is (1895) visiting one of the Universities to do research in Early English charters. My own theory is that he was at Oxford consulting the excellent Stubbs, Bishop of Oxford and Regius Professor of History, who was in that year preparing his 8th edition of the *Select Charters*, a classic among historical students. Holmes' special interest may have been the 10th section of the famous Dialogue de Scaccario or Dialogue on the Exchequer (c. 1200). This section deals with murder which it defines thus: *Murdrum proprie dicitur mors alicujus occulta, cujus interfector ignoratur.* (Murder, properly so-called, is the secret death of anyone whose slayer is not known.) This is not the same as the modern definition of murder, which distinguishes it from manslaughter and homicide by the element of 'malice aforethought.' "

On the other hand, Dr. W. S. Bristowe writes ("Oxford or Cambridge?") that Mr. Blakeney "is entirely fair, as always, in his erudite review of charters at each University, but the story he unfolds is of a later development of historical research at Cambridge and of a growing recognition of their neglected wealth of old documents. Indeed at the very time of Holmes' visit to Cambridge in 1895, Mr. Blakeney tells us that the late Dr. M. R. James was starting to publish his volumes of Catalogues of Western MSS in Cambridge college libraries. This surely would be the very moment when a man interested in research in the same field would be eager to meet Dr. James and to examine documents freshly coming to light."

To this the late A. Carson Simpson added: "I had always assumed that it was at Oxford that the Master pursued his study of Early English charters . . . perhaps because of the trail-blazing work in that field done by Canon Stubbs. While this volume (F. E. Harmer, *Anglo-Saxon Writs;* Manchester University Press, 1952) is on writs, rather than on charters, it is significant, that a large proportion of the material came from various libraries in Cambridge. The distinction between writs and charters has only been recognized quite recently, and it may be that the 'striking results' of Holmes' researches, to which Watson makes reference, were the beginning of the recognition of this distinction."

3 *He shrugged his shoulders in ungracious acquiescence.* "Scarcely had ["The Adventure of the Three Students"] appeared in the June number of the *Strand Magazine* of 1904," Mr. Roger Lancelyn Green wrote in "Dr. Watson's First Critic," "when Andrew Lang . . . subjected it to careful analysis in his monthly *causerie* 'At the Sign of the Ship' in *Longman's Magazine* (July, 1904), and put forward an interesting theory. . . . Lang's contention was that Holmes and Watson were, in this case, made victims of an elaborate hoax prepared, and brilliantly acted, by Mr. Hilton Soames the tutor, with the aid and connivance of Gilchrist, if not of Bannister the gyp. Playing on Holmes' complete ignorance of Greek literature, Soames of St. Luke's came to [Holmes] with a cock-and-bull story, which would not have taken in a Fifth Form boy.' "

Holmes was indeed the victim of an elaborate hoax, but Watson was not, in the view of Mr. Vernon Rendall (*The London Nights of Belsize*). As Mr. T. S. Blakeney wrote in *Sherlock Holmes: Fact or Fiction?*, Rendall "boldly claims that Watson deliberately hoodwinked Holmes . . . with the aid of Soames, Gilchrist and Bannister. Holmes, it is suggested, was worried over his charters, and to prevent his finding solace in drugs, Watson arranged a spoof job for him to investigate. . . . Mr. [S. C.] Roberts has characterized the theory of a put-up job as 'interesting, though not wholly convincing' ('A Note on the Watson Problem'). To Father Ronald Knox the solecisms in this adventure are one of three lines of evidence that the stories in the collection known as *The Return of Sherlock Holmes* are 'lucubrations of his [Watson's] own unaided invention' (*Essays in Satire*). . . . Upon the general theory of a spoof job, we may observe that Watson and his confederates would need to have been consummate actors to humbug Holmes. We have no special reason to think Watson was a good deceiver: on the contrary, Holmes told him that his features were very expressive ["The Cardboard Box"], and his strongly individual characteristics more than once betrayed him [*The Hound of the Baskervilles* (Watson's cigarette); "The Crooked Man" (habit of carrying his handkerchief in his sleeve); "The Disap-

leaving it. His forgetfulness about the key would have mattered little upon any other occasion, but on this one day it has produced the most deplorable consequences.

" The moment I looked at my table I was aware that some one had rummaged among my papers. The proof
7 was in three long slips. I had left them all together. Now I found that one of them was lying on the floor, one was on the side-table near the window, and the third was where I had left it."

Holmes stirred for the first time.

" The first page on the floor, the second in the window, and the third where you left it," said he.

" Exactly, Mr. Holmes. You amaze me. How could you possibly know that ? "

" Pray continue your very interesting statement."

" For an instant I imagined that Bannister had taken the unpardonable liberty of examining my papers. He denied it, however, with the utmost earnestness, and I am convinced that he was speaking the truth. The alternative was that someone passing had observed the key in the door, had known that I was out, and had entered to look at the papers. A large sum of money is at stake, for the scholarship is a very valuable one, and an unscrupulous man might very well run a risk in order to gain advantage over his fellows.

" Bannister was very much upset by the incident. He had nearly fainted when we found that the papers had undoubtedly been tampered with. I gave him a little brandy and left him collapsed in a chair while I made a most careful examination of the room. I soon saw that the intruder had left other traces of his presence besides the rumpled papers. On the table in the window were

"HOW COULD YOU POSSIBLY KNOW THAT?"

Illustration by Sidney Paget for the *Strand Magazine*, June, 1904.

several shreds from a pencil which had been sharpened. A broken tip of lead was lying there also. Evidently the
rascal had copied the paper in a great hurry, had broken 8
his pencil, and had been compelled to put a fresh point to it."

"Excellent!" said Holmes, who was recovering his good humour as his attention became more engrossed by the case. "Fortune has been your friend."

"This was not all. I have a new writing-table with a fine surface of red leather. I am prepared to swear, and so is Bannister, that it was smooth and unstained. Now I found a clean cut in it about three inches long—not a mere scratch, but a positive cut. Not only this, but on the table I found a small ball of black dough, or clay, with specks of something which looks like sawdust in it. I am convinced that these marks were left by the man who rifled the papers. There were no footmarks and no other evidence as to his identity. I was at my wits' end, when suddenly the happy thought occurred to me that you were in the town, and I came straight round to put the matter into your hands. Do help me, Mr. Holmes! You see my dilemma. Either I must find the man, or else the examination must be postponed until fresh papers are prepared, and since this cannot be done without explanation, there will ensue a hideous scandal, which will throw a cloud not only on the college but on the University. Above all things, I desire to settle the matter
quietly and discreetly." 9

"I shall be happy to look into it and to give you such advice as I can," said Holmes, rising and putting on his overcoat. "This case is not entirely devoid of interest. Had anyone visited you in your room after the papers came to you?"

"Yes; young Daulat Ras, an Indian student who lives on the same stair, came in to ask me some particulars about the examination."

"For which he was entered?"

"Yes."

"And the papers were on your table?"

"To the best of my belief they were rolled up."

"But might be recognized as proofs?"

"Possibly."

"No one else in your room?"

"No."

"Did anyone know that these proofs would be there?"

"No one save the printer."

"Did this man Bannister know?"

"No, certainly not. No one knew."

"Where is Bannister now?"

"He was very ill, poor fellow! I left him collapsed in the chair. I was in such a hurry to come to you."

"You left your door open?"

"I locked the papers up first."

"Then it amounts to this, Mr. Soames, that unless the Indian student recognized the roll as being proofs, the man who tampered with them came upon them accidentally without knowing that they were there."

"So it seems to me."

Holmes gave an enigmatic smile.

pearance of Lady Frances Carfax" (method of tying his bootlaces)]. Again, although Watson was not averse to 'taking a rise' out of Holmes if he had the chance [*The Valley of Fear*], his straightforward character and complete honesty do not fit him for any high degree of deception. Moreover, the need of such deception is not established; so far, indeed, from Holmes appearing to be worried over his charters, we are told he reached some striking results—evidence of success than otherwise."

4 *half a chapter of Thucydides.* One of the greatest of ancient historians, c. 460–400 B.C. His one work is his history of the Peloponnesian War to 411 B.C.

But "every man who went in [for the Fortescue Scholarship] (they were not schoolboys but senior men) had read the whole of Thucydides," Andrew Lang complained in his July, 1904, article in *Longman's Magazine.* To set Thucydides for an "unseen," Lang continued, "would be the act of an idiot."

"As the description indicates, an 'unseen' is a passage with which it should be reasonably certain that no candidate will be familiar," Lord Donegall added in "Lunatic Banker's Royal Client—Dr. Watson Tries Semi-Fiction." "But any candidate for the Fortescue Scholarship would know his Thucydides as well as an Honours Student in English Literature knows his *Hamlet.*"

5 *a green baize one within and a heavy oak one without.*" Dr. W. S. Bristowe has pointed out that "This system of doors is common to both [Oxford and Cambridge]. Furthermore, Watson remarked . . . that 'we received a visit from an acquaintance,' so it is not unlikely that they had both been to [Soames'] rooms during their stay of 'some weeks.'"

6 *my servant, Bannister.* If the University is Oxford, Bannister would be known as "the scout"; if Cambridge, as "the gyp."

7 *The proof was in three long slips.* But no "half a chapter" of Thucydides would take up three long "slips"—galley proofs. No whole chapter, even, is as long as that.

8 *Evidently the rascal had copied the paper in a great hurry.* "There had never been any need to copy the portion of Thucydides set for the examination," Mr. Richard S. Schwartz wrote in "Three Students in Search of a Scholar." "All serious editions of Thucydides have an index of proper names, and only a glance at the set piece is necessary to note the odd names in it. A glance at the index, in turn, and a check through the text, and the passage is located. The sense of the first and last sentence completes the location. Nothing could be more useless than copying the entire passage, since the text was either owned by the student or available in the college library. I have checked on the most important editions of Thucydides published in the nineteenth century before the year '95. All but one, a cheap German edition, had such an index. Even if this was the one owned by [the copier], he would have had easy access to one with an index."

9 *Above all things, I desire to settle the matter quietly and discreetly.*" ". . . at Cambridge," Mr. N. P. Metcalfe wrote in "Oxford or Cambridge or Both?", "there are always duplicate papers for each examination which are only printed the night before, and Oxford would surely have a similar scheme; so it is difficult to understand why Soames did not quietly 'make the switch," after notifying his fellow examiners of the occurrence."

10 *It was already twilight.* It was "at four-thirty" that Hilton Soames says he "left the proof upon his desk" and "was absent for more than an hour." Thus he returned to his room after 5:30. He found a key in his door and the examination papers tampered with; he called and questioned Bannister, gave him brandy, and "made a most careful examination of the room." He then "came straight around to put the matter" into Holmes' hands, and "poured forth his story." All of this—especially the "most careful examination" of Soames' room—took time; he can hardly have concluded his story much before 6:30, after which Holmes and Watson went directly to St. Luke's, evidently a short walk from their lodgings. We conclude that twilight on that day must have fallen close to 6:40 P.M.; it can hardly have been much later, for Holmes said, "It is nearly nine" at the close of an investigation that included a careful examination of Soames' room, interviews with Bannister, Gilchrist and Daulat Ras, an attempt to visit McClaren, and calls on four stationers. The term, as we shall see, was the Lent term. This ended at Oxford on April 6th, at Cambridge on March 27th in the year 1895. March 27th is too early in the year for twilight at approximately 6:40 P.M., and therefore indicates to your editor that the University of "The Three Students" was *Oxford*, not Cambridge. Twilight close to 6:40 P.M. indicates the latest possible date in Oxford's Lent term. In addition, it is our opinion that the Fortescue examination would most probably be given on the closing day of the term—*Saturday, April 6, 1895.* We conclude that the case ended on that day and began on the preceding day, *Friday, April 5th*, a day on which the sun set (and twilight began) at 6:37 P.M.

" Well," said he, " let us go round. Not one of your cases, Watson—mental, not physical. All right ; come if you want to. Now, Mr. Soames—at your disposal ! "

The sitting-room of our client opened by a long, low, latticed window on to the ancient lichen-tinted court of the old college. A Gothic arched door led to a worn stone staircase. On the ground floor was the tutor's room. Above were three students, one on each story.
10 It was already twilight when we reached the scene of our problem. Holmes halted and looked earnestly at the window. Then he approached it, and, standing on tiptoe, with his neck craned, he looked into the room.

" He must have entered through the door. There is no opening except the one pane," said our learned guide.

" Dear me ! " said Holmes, and he smiled in a singular way as he glanced at our companion. " Well, if there is nothing to be learned here we had best go inside."

The lecturer unlocked the outer door and ushered us into his room. We stood at the entrance while Holmes made an examination of the carpet.

" I am afraid there are no signs here," said he. " One could hardly hope for any upon so dry a day. Your servant seems to have quite recovered. You left him in a chair, you say ; which chair ? "

" By the window there."

" I see. Near this little table. You can come in now. I have finished with the carpet. Let us take the little table first. Of course, what has happened is very clear. The man entered and took the papers, sheet by sheet, from the central table. He carried them over to the window table, because from there he could see if you came across the courtyard, and so could effect an escape."

" As a matter of fact, he could not," said Soames, " for I entered by the side-door."

. . . WITH HIS NECK CRANED, HE LOOKED INTO THE ROOM.

Illustration by Sidney Paget for the *Strand Magazine*, June, 1904.

" Ah, that's good ! Well, anyhow, that was in his mind. Let me see the three strips. No finger impressions—no ! Well, he carried over this one first and he copied it. How long would it take him to do that, using every possible contraction ? A quarter of an hour, not less. Then he tossed it down and seized the next. He was in the midst of that when your return caused him to make a very hurried retreat—*very* hurried, since he had not time to replace the papers which would tell you that he had been there. You were not aware of any hurrying feet on the stair as you entered the outer door ? "

" No, I can't say I was."

" Well, he wrote so furiously that he broke his pencil, and had, as you observe, to sharpen it again. This is of interest, Watson. The pencil was not an ordinary one. It was about the usual size with a soft lead ; the outer colour was dark blue, the maker's name was printed in silver lettering, and the piece remaining is only about an inch and a half long. Look for such a pencil, Mr. Soames, and you have got your man. When I add that he possesses a large and very blunt knife, you have an additional aid."

Mr. Soames was somewhat overwhelmed by this flood of information. " I can follow the other points," said he, " but really in this matter of the length——"

Holmes held out a small chip with the letters NN and a space of clear wood after them.

" You see ? "

" No, I fear that even now——"

" Watson, I have always done you an injustice. There
are others. What could this NN be ? It is at the end
of a word. You are aware that Johann Faber is the most **11**
common maker's name. Is it not clear that there is just
as much of the pencil left as usually follows the Johann ? "
He held the small table sideways to the electric light. " I **12**
was hoping that if the paper on which he wrote was thin some trace of it might come through upon this polished surface. No, I see nothing. I don't think there is anything more to be learned here. Now for the central table. This small pellet is, I presume, the black doughy mass you spoke of. Roughly pyramidal in shape and hollowed out, I perceive. As you say, there appear to be grains of sawdust in it. Dear me, this is very interesting. And the cut—a positive tear, I see. It began with a thin scratch and ended in a jagged hole. I am much indebted to you for directing my attention to this case, Mr. Soames. Where does that door lead to ? "

" To my bedroom."

" Have you been in it since your adventure ? "

" No ; I came straight away for you."

" I should like to have a glance round. What a charming, old-fashioned room ! Perhaps you will kindly wait a minute until I have examined the floor. No, I see nothing. What about this curtain ? You hang your clothes behind it. If anyone were forced to conceal himself in this room he must do it there, since the bed is too low and the wardrobe too shallow. No one there, I suppose ? "

As Holmes drew the curtain I was aware, from some little rigidity and alertness of his attitude, that he was

11 *Johann Faber.* Johann Lothar von Faber, of Germany, 1817–1896.

12 *to the electric light.* The reader may wonder if colleges at Oxford (or Cambridge) were equipped with electric light in 1895. The answer is that most Oxford colleges were so equipped and so were at least some of the Cambridge colleges. Dr. Bristowe, who plumps for Cambridge as the University of "The Three Students," rather hoped that he might identify "St. Luke's" as Cambridge's St. John's—"the only college in Cambridge bearing the name of an apostle and to alter the name to that of another apostle represented a fairly obvious mental process when a change in name was under consideration by Watson." "But," he continued, "the insurmountable difficulty then arose that electric light was confined to the Hall, Chapel and lamps in First Court in 1895 and was not installed in rooms until 1911." Dr. Bristowe was nonetheless capable of throwing out a subtle hint about "St. Luke's" if that college were indeed at Cambridge: "Rooms in Caius had electric light by 1895 and it was to Caius that Watson's close friend, Mr. Conan Doyle, sent his sons through Watson's introduction, perhaps, to Hilton Soames." Those who hold that the University of "The Three Students" was Oxford will side with Mr. Metcalfe, who wrote that "St. Luke's" was perhaps "the most 'medical' of the Oxford colleges, for St. Paul (Colossians, 4.14) speaks of St. Luke as 'the beloved physician.' "

"... THE THREE MEN WHO INHABIT THESE ROOMS."

Illustration by Frederic Dorr Steele for *Collier's Magazine*, September 24, 1904.

prepared for an emergency. As a matter of fact the drawn curtain disclosed nothing but three or four suits of clothes hanging from a line of pegs. Holmes turned away, and stooped suddenly to the floor.

"Halloa! What's this?" said he.

It was a small pyramid of black, putty-like stuff, exactly like the one upon the table of the study. Holmes held it out on his open palm in the glare of the electric light.

"Your visitor seems to have left traces in your bedroom as well as in your sitting-room, Mr. Soames."

"What could he have wanted there?"

"I think it is clear enough. You came back by an unexpected way, and so he had no warning until you were at the very door. What could he do? He caught up everything which would betray him, and he rushed into your bedroom to conceal himself."

"Good gracious, Mr. Holmes, do you mean to tell me that all the time I was talking to Bannister in this room we had the man prisoner if we had only known it?"

"So I read it."

"Surely there is another alternative, Mr. Holmes? I don't know whether you observed my bedroom window."

"Lattice-paned, lead framework, three separate windows, one swinging on hinge and large enough to admit a man."

"Exactly. And it looks out on an angle of the courtyard so as to be partly invisible. The man might have effected his entrance there, left traces as he passed through the bedroom, and, finally, finding the door open, have escaped that way."

Holmes shook his head impatiently.

"Let us be practical," said he. "I understand you to say that there are three students who use this stair and are in the habit of passing your door?"

"Yes, there are."

"And they are all in for this examination?"

"Yes."

"Have you any reason to suspect any one of them more than the others?"

Soames hesitated.

"It is a very delicate question," said he. "One hardly likes to throw suspicion where there are no proofs."

"Let us hear the suspicions. I will look after the proofs."

"I will tell you, then, in a few words, the character of the three men who inhabit these rooms. The lower of the three is Gilchrist, a fine scholar and athlete; plays in the Rugby team and the cricket team for the college, and got
13 his Blue for the hurdles and the long jump. He is a fine, manly fellow. His father was the notorious Sir Jabez Gilchrist, who ruined himself on the Turf. My scholar has been left very poor, but he is hard-working and industrious. He will do well.

"The second floor is inhabited by Daulat Ras, the Indian. He is a quiet, inscrutable fellow, as most of those Indians are. He is well up in his work, though his Greek is his weak subject. He is steady and methodical.

"The top floor belongs to Miles McLaren. He is a brilliant fellow when he chooses to work—one of the brightest intellects of the University; but he is wayward,

13 *got his Blue for the hurdles and the long jump.* At both Oxford and Cambridge, anyone who represented the University at sport was commonly referred to—but quite incorrectly—as a "Blue." There was no true Blue for the long jump at Cambridge in 1895, but at Oxford there was: he was the late Captain C. B. Fry who represented Oxford in this event throughout the period 1892 to 1895. If we can rely on Watson's data, Gilchrist must therefore have been either C. B. Fry's second string at Oxford or else his opponent from Cambridge. ". . . C. B. Fry's second string, W. J. Oaklet, was a Blue for both [the hurdles and the long jump] in 1895 and in fact got his Blue for them in 1894," Dr. Bristowe wrote. There seems little doubt that Gilchrist at this time (April 5th) would be training for the Amateur Athletic Championships and other important athletic events which took place in the summer.

dissipated, and unprincipled. He was nearly expelled over a card scandal in his first year. He has been idling all this term, and he must look forward with dread to the 14
examination."

" Then it is he whom you suspect ? "

" I dare not go so far as that. But of the three he is perhaps the least unlikely."

" Exactly. Now, Mr. Soames, let us have a look at your servant, Bannister."

He was a little, white-faced, clean-shaven, grizzly haired fellow of fifty. He was still suffering from this sudden disturbance of the quiet routine of his life. His plump face was twitching with his nervousness, and his fingers could not keep still.

" We are investigating this unhappy business, Bannister," said his master.

" Yes, sir."

" I understand," said Holmes, " that you left your key in the door ? "

" Yes, sir."

" Was it not very extraordinary that you should do this on the very day when there were these papers inside ? "

" It was most unfortunate, sir. But I have occasionally done the same thing at other times."

" When did you enter the room ? "

" It was about half-past four. That is Mr. Soames' tea-time."

" How long did you stay ? "

" When I saw that he was absent I withdrew at once."

" Did you look at these papers on the table ? "

" No, sir ; certainly not."

" How came you to leave the key in the door ? "

" I had the tea-tray in my hand. I thought I would come back for the key. Then I forgot."

" Has the outer door a spring lock ? "

" No, sir."

" Then it was open all the time ? "

" Yes, sir."

" Any one in the room could get out ? "

" Yes, sir."

" When Mr. Soames returned and called for you, you were very much disturbed ? "

" Yes, sir. Such a thing has never happened during the many years that I have been here. I nearly fainted, sir."

" So I understand. Where were you when you began to feel bad ? "

" Where was I, sir ? Why, here, near the door."

" That is singular, because you sat down in that chair over yonder near the corner. Why did you pass these other chairs ? "

" I don't know, sir. It didn't matter to me where I sat."

" I really don't think he knew much about it, Mr. Holmes. He was looking very bad—quite ghastly."

" You stayed here when your master left ? "

" Only for a minute or so. Then I locked the door and went to my room."

" Whom do you suspect ? "

" Oh, I would not venture to say, sir. I don't believe

14 *He has been idling all this term.* Another indication that "The Adventure of the Three Students" took place at the very end of a term—in our view, the Lent term.

"HOW CAME YOU TO LEAVE THE KEY IN THE DOOR?"

Illustration by Sidney Paget for the *Strand Magazine*, June, 1904.

15 *we will take a walk in the quadrangle.* At Oxford it is a "quadrangle," at Cambridge it is a "court," and it has been said that Holmes' use of the word "quadrangle" here is a powerful argument for Oxford. But both Watson and Soames, in this same adventure, use the word "court" or "courtyard" (Watson also uses "quadrangle"). In fact, Holmes himself also refers to the "quadrangle" as the "courtyard"—thus, as the Reverend Stephen Adams wrote in "Holmes: A Student of London?", "displaying a nice disregard for the better feelings of either University."

THREE YELLOW SQUARES OF LIGHT SHONE ABOVE US IN THE GATHERING GLOOM.

Illustration by Charles Raymond Macauley for *The Return of Sherlock Holmes*, New York: McClure, Phillips & Co., 1905. Alert students will note that Mr. Macauley has placed two of the students on the same floor, whereas the text tells us that their rooms were on three separate floors, one above another.

there is any gentleman in this University who is capable of profiting by such an action. No, sir, I'll not believe it."

"Thank you; that will do," said Holmes. "Oh, one more word. You have not mentioned to any of the three gentlemen whom you attend that anything is amiss?"

"No, sir; not a word."

"You haven't seen any of them?"

"No, sir."

"Very good. Now, Mr. Soames, we will take a walk
15 in the quadrangle, if you please."

Three yellow squares of light shone above us in the gathering gloom.

"Your three birds are all in their nests," said Holmes, looking up. "Halloa! What's that? One of them seems restless enough."

It was the Indian, whose dark silhouette appeared suddenly upon the blind. He was pacing swiftly up and down his room.

"I should like to have a peep at each of them," said Holmes. "Is it possible?"

"No difficulty in the world," Soames answered. "This set of rooms is quite the oldest in the college, and it is not unusual for visitors to go over them. Come along, and I will personally conduct you."

"No names, please!" said Holmes, as we knocked at Gilchrist's door. A tall, flaxen-haired, slim young fellow opened it, and made us welcome when he understood our errand. There were some really curious pieces of mediæval domestic architecture within. Holmes was so charmed with one of them that he insisted on drawing it on his notebook, broke his pencil, had to borrow one from our host, and finally borrowed a knife to sharpen his own. The same curious accident happened to him in the rooms of the Indian—a silent little hook-nosed fellow, who eyed us askance and was obviously glad when Holmes' architectural studies had come to an end. I could not see that in either case Holmes had come upon

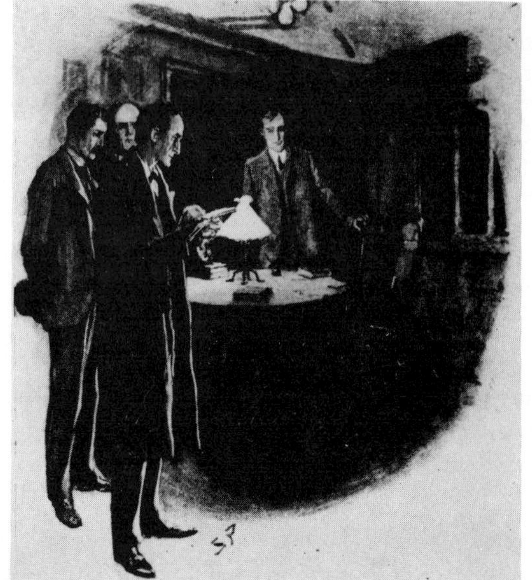

. . . HE INSISTED ON DRAWING IT ON HIS NOTEBOOK . . .

Illustration by Sidney Paget for the *Strand Magazine*, June, 1904.

the clue for which he was searching. Only at the third did our visit prove abortive. The outer door would not open to our knock, and nothing more substantial than a torrent of bad language came from behind it. " I don't care who you are. You can go to blazes ! " roared the angry voice. " To-morrow's the exam., and I won't be drawn by anyone."

" A rude fellow," said our guide, flushing with anger as we withdrew down the stair. " Of course, he did not realize that it was I who was knocking, but none the less his conduct was very uncourteous, and, indeed, under the circumstances, rather suspicious."

Holmes' response was a curious one.

" Can you tell me his exact height ? " he asked.

" Really, Mr. Holmes, I cannot undertake to say. He is taller than the Indian, not so tall as Gilchrist. I suppose five foot six would be about it."

" That is very important," said Holmes. " And now, Mr. Soames, I wish you good night."

Our guide cried aloud in his astonishment and dismay. " Good gracious, Mr. Holmes, you are surely not going to leave me in this abrupt fashion ! You don't seem to realize the position. To-morrow is the examination. I must take some definite action to-night. I cannot allow the examination to be held if one of the papers has been tampered with. The situation must be faced."

" You must leave it as it is. I shall drop round early to-morrow morning and chat the matter over. It is possible that I may be in a position then to indicate some course of action. Meanwhile you change nothing—nothing at all."

" Very good, Mr. Holmes."

" You can be perfectly easy in your mind. We shall certainly find some way out of your difficulties. I will take the black clay with me, also the pencil cuttings. Good-bye."

When we were out in the darkness of the quadrangle we again looked up at the windows. The Indian still paced his room. The others were invisible.

" Well, Watson, what do you think of it ? " Holmes asked as we came out into the main street. " Quite a little parlour game—sort of three-card trick, is it not ? There are your three men. It must be one of them. You take your choice. Which is yours ? "

" The foul-mouthed fellow at the top. He is the one with the worst record. And yet that Indian was a sly fellow also. Why should he be pacing his room all the time ? "

" There is nothing in that. Many men do it when they are trying to learn anything by heart."

" He looked at us in a queer way."

" So would you if a flock of strangers came in on you when you were preparing for an examination next day, and every moment was of value. No, I see nothing in that. Pencils, too, and knives—all was satisfactory. But that fellow *does* puzzle me."

" Who ? "

" Why, Bannister, the servant. What's his game in the matter ? "

" He impressed me as being a perfectly honest man."

" So he did me. That's the puzzling part. Why should a perfectly honest man—well, well, here's a large stationer's. We shall begin our researches here."

There were only four stationers of any consequence in
16 the town, and at each Holmes produced his pencil chips and bid high for a duplicate. All were agreed that one could be ordered, but that it was not a usual size of pencil, and that it was seldom kept in stock. My friend did not appear to be depressed by his failure, but shrugged his shoulders in half-humorous resignation.

" No good, my dear Watson. This, the best and only final clue, has run to nothing. But, indeed, I have little doubt that we can build up a sufficient case without it. By Jove ! my dear fellow, it is nearly nine, and the land-
17 lady babbled of green peas at seven-thirty. What with your eternal tobacco, Watson, and your irregularity at meals, I expect that you will get notice to quit, and that I shall share your downfall—not, however, before we have solved the problem of the nervous tutor, the careless servant, and the three enterprising students."

Holmes made no further allusion to the matter that day, though he sat lost in thought for a long time after our belated dinner. At eight in the morning he came into my room just as I finished my toilet.

" Well, Watson," said he, " it is time we went down to St. Luke's. Can you do without breakfast ? "

" Certainly."

" Soames will be in a dreadful fidget until we are able to tell him something positive."

" Have you anything positive to tell him ? "

" I think so."

" You have formed a conclusion ? "

" Yes, my dear Watson ; I have solved the mystery."

" But what fresh evidence could you have got ? "

" Aha ! It is not for nothing that I have turned myself out of bed at the untimely hour of six. I have put in two hours' hard work and covered at least five miles, with something to show for it. Look at that ! "

He held out his hand. On the palm were three little
18 pyramids of black, doughy clay.

" Why, Holmes, you had only two yesterday ! "

" And one more this morning. It is a fair argument, that wherever No. 3 came from is also the source of Nos. 1 and 2. Eh, Watson ? Well, come along and put friend Soames out of his pain."

The unfortunate tutor was certainly in a state of pitiable agitation when we found him in his chambers. In a few hours the examinations would commence and he was still in the dilemma between making the facts public and allowing the culprit to compete for the valuable scholarship. He could hardly stand still, so great was his mental agitation, and he ran towards Holmes with two eager hands outstretched.

" Thank Heaven that you have come ! I feared that you had given it up in despair. What am I to do ? Shall the examination proceed ? "

" Yes ; let it proceed, by all means."

16 *There were only four stationers of any consequence in the town.* The late Gavin Brend felt that Holmes' knowledge of all four stationers was an indication that he himself had been a student at the University of "The Three Students." Since we know that Holmes was a student at *both* Oxford and Cambridge, it is of course only natural that he should have known his way about at either University.

17 *the landlady babbled of green peas.* ". . . surely an oblique allusion to Falstaff, who, it will be recalled, 'babbled of green fields' on his deathbed [*Henry V*]," Professor Clarke Olney wrote in "The Literacy of Sherlock Holmes."

There is, moreover, a chronological significance to the statement. In England, green peas are usually a June delicacy. How to reconcile this with a sunset appropriate to April, the need for Holmes to wear an overcoat and Gilchrist to wear gloves in the afternoon? "As for Holmes wearing an overcoat and Gilchrist gloves, we have to take changed fashions into account as well as the risk of April showers or the cold East wind for which Cambridge, at least, is notorious," Dr. Bristowe wrote. "Green peas [in April] are not so easy, but it is clear from their being the only item on the menu to be mentioned that they were a special delicacy and horticulturists tell me that limited quantities grown under glass can be supplied even in March."

18 *three little pyramids of black, doughy clay.* We soon learn that they came from the University jumping pit—another indication, Mr. Brend pointed out, that Holmes was well acquainted with the University of "The Three Students," since he found the jumping pit shortly after "the untimely hour of six"—an hour when there would certainly have been few people about from whom to ask directions.

Dr. Bristowe disagreed: the Iffley Road running track at Oxford, he pointed out, is only a mile from a central point like Carfax "so why did [Holmes] have to walk five miles if he is in his own University town of Oxford? Even allowing for some exaggeration in order to impress Watson, the discrepancy is too great. Fenners' at Cambridge is even closer to the center of town. It is just over three-quarters of a mile from the Market Place (close to the University Library) and it is not easy to find. Surely we are forced to conclude that Holmes got lost . . ."

That, your editor holds, could happen at either Oxford or Cambridge; let us remember that "bar boxing and fencing," neither of which is done in a jumping pit, Holmes in his University days indulged in no sports.

But there is even greater significance to those "three little pyramids of black, doughy clay": they provide the most powerful argument for those who hold that the University of the "Three Students" was Cambridge. The point is perhaps best made by Dr. Bristowe in his illuminating article, "The Three Students in Limelight, Electric Light and Daylight":

" But this rascal—— ? "

" He shall not compete."

" You know him ? "

" I think so. If this matter is not to become public we must give ourselves certain powers, and resolve ourselves into a small private court-martial. You there, if you please, Soames ! Watson, you here ! I'll take the arm-chair in the middle. I think that we are now sufficiently imposing to strike terror into a guilty breast. Kindly ring the bell ! "

Bannister entered, and shrank back in evident surprise and fear at our judicial appearance.

" You will kindly close the door," said Holmes. " Now, Bannister, will you please tell us the truth about yesterday's incident ? "

The man turned white to the roots of his hair.

" I have told you everything, sir."

" Nothing to add ? "

" Nothing at all, sir."

" Well, then, I must make some suggestions to you. When you sat down on that chair yesterday, did you do so in order to conceal some object which would have shown who had been in the room ? "

Bannister's face was ghastly.

" No, sir ; certainly not."

" It is only a suggestion," said Holmes suavely. " I frankly admit that I am unable to prove it. But it seems probable enough, since the moment that Mr. Soames' back was turned you released the man who was hiding in that bedroom."

Bannister licked his dry lips.

" There was no man, sir."

" Ah, that's a pity, Bannister. Up to now you may have spoken the truth, but now I know that you have lied."

The man's face set in sullen defiance.

" There was no man, sir."

" Come, come, Bannister."

" No, sir ; there was no one."

" In that case you can give us no further information. Would you please remain in the room ? Stand over there near the bedroom door. Now, Soames, I am going to ask you to have the great kindness to go up to the room of young Gilchrist, and to ask him to step down into yours."

An instant later the tutor returned, bringing with him the student. He was a fine figure of a man, tall, lithe, and agile, with a springy step and a pleasant, open face. His troubled blue eyes glanced at each of us, and finally rested with an expression of blank dismay upon Bannister in the farther corner.

" Just close the door," said Holmes. " Now, Mr. Gilchrist, we are all quite alone here, and no one need ever know one word of what passes between us. We can be perfectly frank with each other. We want to know, Mr. Gilchrist, how you, an honourable man, ever came to commit such an action as that of yesterday ? "

The unfortunate young man staggered back, and cast a look full of horror and reproach at Bannister.

" No, no, Mr. Gilchrist, sir ; I never said a word—never one word ! " cried the servant.

" No, but you have now," said Holmes. " Now, sir,

"Remembering an article on athletics by C. B. Fry in the *Strand Magazine* in 1902, I found an interesting comment that 'a kind of clay [had been] invented by the groundsman at Fenners' and that this invention had just been imitated in 1902 by the Queen's Club, London, for their long jump pit. I wrote to Captain Fry and in his reply of 21st December, 1955, he confirmed that throughout his time at Oxford he always had to jump into a soft sandy material. 'I saw no damped semi-clay soil in the Long Jump pit till at Queens in 1903,' he wrote. 'It was introduced there, I fancy, by Mr. Clement Jackson, the Hertford (Oxford) don ex-hurdle A. A. champion after I did the World Records 23 ft. 6½ in. in 1902, because the Americans did not make allowance for breakaway behind the heel mark. I really did 24 ft. 2½ in.' Here, I submit, we have positive proof from this distinguished contemporary of Gilchrist that the mud which led to his detection was invented by the Cambridge groundsman and was unique to Cambridge in 1895."

AN INSTANT LATER THE TUTOR RETURNED . . .

Illustration by Sidney Paget for the *Strand Magazine*, June, 1904.

"NO, BUT YOU HAVE NOW," SAID HOLMES.

Cover illustration by Frederic Dorr Steele for *Collier's Magazine*, September 24, 1904.

you must see that after Bannister's words your position is hopeless, and that your only chance lies in a frank confession."

For a moment Gilchrist, with upraised hand, tried to control his writhing features. The next he had thrown himself on his knees beside the table, and, burying his face in his hands, he burst into a storm of passionate sobbing.

" Come, come," said Holmes kindly ; " it is human to err, and at least no one can accuse you of being a callous criminal. Perhaps it would be easier for you if I were to tell Mr. Soames what occurred, and you can check me where I am wrong. Shall I do so ? Well, well, don't trouble to answer. Listen, and see that I do you no injustice.

" From the moment, Mr. Soames, that you said to me that no one, not even Bannister, could have told that the papers were in your room, the case began to take a definite shape in my mind. The printer one could, of course, dismiss. He could examine the papers in his own office. The Indian I also thought nothing of. If the proofs were in roll he could not possibly know what they were. On the other hand, it seemed an unthinkable coincidence that a man should dare to enter the room, and that by chance on that very day the papers were on the table. I dismissed that. The man who entered knew that the papers were there. How did he know ?

" When I approached your room I examined the window. You amused me by supposing that I was contemplating the possibility of someone having in broad daylight, under the eyes of all these opposite rooms, forced himself through it. Such an idea was absurd. I was measuring how tall a man would need to be in order to see as he passed what papers were on the central table. I am six feet high, and I could do it with an effort. No one less than that would have a chance. Already, you see, I had reason to think that if one of your three students was a man of unusual height he was the most worth watching of the three.

" I entered, and I took you into my confidence as to the suggestions of the side-table. Of the centre table I

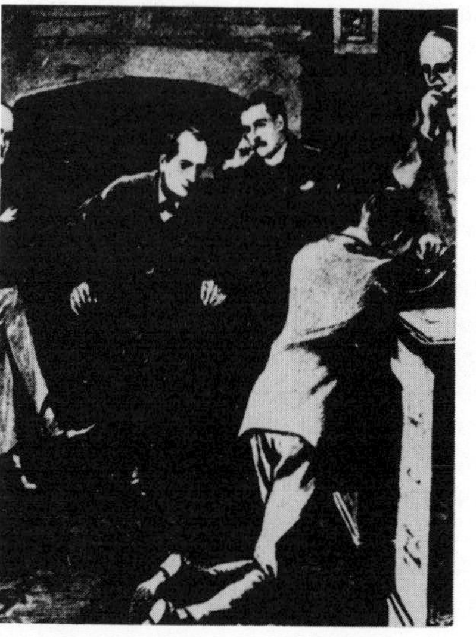

"COME, COME," SAID HOLMES KINDLY; "IT IS HUMAN TO ERR . . ."

Illustration by Sidney Paget for the *Strand Magazine*, June, 1904.

could make nothing, until in your description of Gilchrist you mentioned that he was a long-distance jumper. Then the whole thing came to me in an instant, and I only needed certain corroborative proofs, which I speedily obtained.

" What happened was this. This young fellow had employed his afternoon at the athletic grounds, where he had been practising the jump. He returned carrying his jumping-shoes, which are provided, as you are aware, with several spikes. As he passed your window he saw, **19**
by means of his great height, these proofs upon your table, and conjectured what they were. No harm would have been done had it not been that as he passed your door he perceived the key which had been left by the carelessness of your servant. A sudden impulse came over him to enter and see if they were indeed the proofs. It was not a dangerous exploit, for he could always pretend that he had simply looked in to ask a question.

" Well, when he saw that they were indeed the proofs, it was then that he yielded to temptation. He put his shoes on the table. What was it you put on that chair near the window ? "

" Gloves," said the young man.

Holmes looked triumphantly at Bannister.

" He put his gloves on the chair, and he took the proofs, sheet by sheet, to copy them. He thought the tutor must return by the main gate, and that he would see him. As we know, he came back by the side-gate. Suddenly he heard him at the very door. There was no possible escape. He forgot his gloves, but he caught up his shoes and darted into the bedroom. You observe that the scratch on that table is slight at one side, but deepens in the direction of the bedroom door. That in itself is enough to show us that the shoes had been drawn in that direction, and that the culprit had taken refuge there. The earth round the spike had been left on the table, and a second sample was loosened and fell in the bedroom. I may add that I walked out to the athletic grounds this morning, saw that tenacious black clay is used in the jumping-pit, and carried away a specimen of it, together with some of the fine tan or sawdust which is strewn over it to prevent the athlete from slipping. Have I told the truth, Mr. Gilchrist ? "

The student had drawn himself erect.

" Yes, sir, it is true," said he.

" Good heavens, have you nothing to add ?" cried Soames.

" Yes, sir, I have, but the shock of this disgraceful exposure has bewildered me. I have a letter here, Mr. Soames, which I wrote to you early this morning in the middle of a restless night. It was before I knew that my sin had found me out. Here it is, sir. You will see that I have said, ' I have determined not to go in for the examination. I have been offered a commission in the Rhodesian Police, and I am going out to South Africa at once.' "

" I am indeed pleased to hear that you did not intend to profit by your unfair advantage," said Soames. " But why did you change your purpose ? "

Gilchrist pointed to Bannister.

19 *which are provided, as you are aware, with several spikes.* Did track athletes in 1895 wear spiked shoes? They did, as Dr. Bristowe has shown. In "The Three Students in Limelight, Electric Light and Daylight," he has called attention to a book published in 1887 which advised "spikes of less than half an inch for cinder tracks at the universities but spikes up to three-quarters of an inch for use on grass." Dr. Bristowe also reported that Captain C. B. Fry recalled a detail of singular interest—those who went in for field sports at Oxford in 1895 got their spiked running shoes "from a small cobbler near Dorset Square, *Baker Street.*"

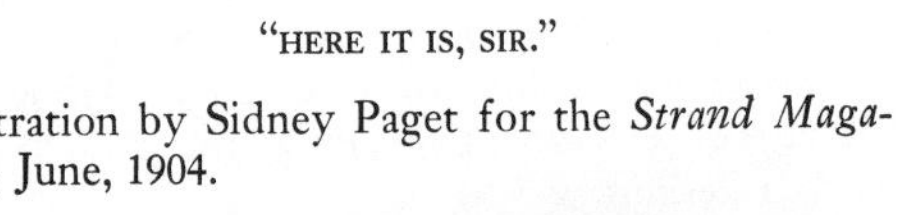

"HERE IT IS, SIR."

Illustration by Sidney Paget for the *Strand Magazine*, June, 1904.

" There is the man who sent me in the right path," said he.

" Come now, Bannister," said Holmes. " It will be clear to you from what I have said that only you could have let this young man out, since you were left in the room and must have locked the door when you went out. As to his escaping by that window, it was incredible. Can you not clear up the last point in this mystery, and tell us the reason for your action ? "

" It was simple enough, sir, if you only had known ; but with all your cleverness it was impossible that you could know. Time was, sir, when I was butler to old Sir Jabez Gilchrist, this young gentleman's father. When he was ruined I come to the college as servant, but I never forgot my old employer because he was down in the world. I watched his son all I could for the sake of the old days. Well, sir, when I came into this room yesterday when the alarm was given, the first thing I saw was Mr. Gilchrist's tan gloves a-lying in that chair. I knew those gloves well, and I understood their message. If Mr. Soames saw them the game was up. I flopped down into that chair, and nothing would budge me until Mr. Soames he went for you. Then out came my poor young master, whom I had dandled on my knee, and confessed it all to me. Wasn't it natural, sir, that I should save him, and wasn't it natural also that I should try to speak to him as his dead father would have done, and make him understand that he could not profit by such a deed ? Could you blame me, sir ? "

" No, indeed ! " said Holmes heartily, springing to his feet. " Well, Soames, I think we have cleared your little problem up, and our breakfast awaits us at home. Come, Watson ! As to you, sir, I trust that a bright future awaits you in Rhodesia. For once you have fallen low.
20 Let us see in the future how high you can rise."

20 *Let us see in the future how high you can rise.*" "Since we have had no news of Gilchrist in South Africa," Dr. Bristowe wrote, "it may be worth mentioning that J. L. B. Smith (the discoverer of the coelocanth) writes in his book, *Old Fourlegs* (1956) that the most important collection of South African fishes up to 1930 was made by the late J. D. F. Gilchrist, who was a Professor and a man 'with a great heart and great mind.' "

Bibliographical Note: The original manuscript of "The Adventure of the Three Students," 224 to leaves, white vellum, is owned by the Houghton Library of Harvard University, the gift of Mr. Norton Perkins.

52

THE ADVENTURE OF THE SOLITARY CYCLIST

[Saturday, April 13, to Saturday, April 20, 1895]

FROM the years 1894 to 1901 inclusive, Mr. Sherlock Holmes was a very busy man. It is safe to
say that there was no public case of any difficulty
in which he was not consulted during those eight years,
and there were hundreds of private cases, some of them
of the most intricate and extraordinary character, in
which he played a prominent part. Many startling
successes and a few unavoidable failures were the outcome of this long period of continuous work. As I have
preserved very full notes of all these cases, and was
myself personally engaged in many of them, it may be
imagined that it is no easy task to know which I should
select to lay before the public. I shall, however, preserve my former rule, and give the preference to those
cases which derive their interest not so much from the
brutality of the crime as from the ingenuity and dramatic
quality of the solution. For this reason I will now lay
before the reader the facts connected with Miss Violet
Smith, the solitary cyclist of Charlington, and the curious 1
sequel of our investigation, which culminated in unexpected tragedy. It is true that the circumstances did
not permit of any striking illustration of those powers for
which my friend was famous, but there were some points
about the case which made it stand out in those long
records of crime from which I gather the material for
these little narratives.

On referring to my notebook for the year 1895, I find
that it was upon Saturday, April 23, that we first heard of 2
Miss Violet Smith. Her visit was, I remember, extremely unwelcome to Holmes, for he was immersed at
the moment in a very abstruse and complicated problem
concerning the peculiar persecution to which John Vincent Harden, the well-known tobacco millionaire, had 3
been subjected. My friend, who loved above all things
precision and concentration of thought, resented anything which distracted his attention from the matter
in hand. And yet without harshness which was foreign
to his nature it was impossible to refuse to listen to the
story of the young and beautiful woman, tall, graceful,
and queenly, who presented herself at Baker Street late
in the evening and implored his assistance and advice.

1 *Charlington.* Near Farnham, in Surrey.

2 *Saturday, April 23.* Something is clearly wrong here, since April 23, 1895, was a *Tuesday*. Is Watson's "Saturday" wrong? Hardly. Miss Violet Smith came to town every Saturday forenoon and returned to Chiltern Grange on Monday; she says on the day of her visit to Holmes: "Again I had to cycle to the station. That was this morning." Is Watson's "April" wrong? Hardly. Miss Smith says her interview with Carruthers and Woodley took place "Last December—four months ago." Watson speaks of "golden patches of flowering gorse," "the bright spring sunshine," "the freshness of the spring," "the budding green of the woods." Is his "23" wrong? If so, the date must be April 6th, 13th, 20, or 27th. Of these, the 13th is certainly the most likely to be mistaken for his "23." Or is his "1895" wrong? If so, the date must be April 23, 1898, for 1898 is the only year from 1894 to 1901, the limits set by Watson, in which the 23rd of April fell on a Saturday. Holmes and Watson journeyed to Chiltern Grange on the Saturday following Miss Smith's visit, and Watson tells us that "A rainy night had been followed by a glorious morning." The possible dates are: 1) Friday, April 12–Saturday, April 13, 1895; 2) Friday, April 19–Saturday, April 20, 1895; 3) Friday, April 26–Saturday, April 27, 1895; 4) Friday, May 3–Saturday, May 4, 1895; 5) Friday, April 29–Saturday, April 30, 1898. Of these, only Friday, April 19–Saturday, April 20, 1895, answer Watson's description. Miss Violet Smith's call on Holmes must therefore have been on *Saturday, April 13, 1895*. This, as we have seen, was the date most likely to have been mistaken by the typesetter as "23."

3 *John Vincent Harden.* Properly, John Vincent *Hardin,* as Mr. William D. Jenkins has shown in his remarkable study, "A Peculiar Persecution." John Vincent Hardin was a cousin of John Wesley Hardin, "probably the most deadly gunman the American West ever produced," whose plan to visit England with the Buffalo Bill Wild West

Show subjected his socially ambitious cousin, the tobacco millionaire, to his peculiar persecution. Mr. Jenkins' essay also provides a new solution for the "Missing Year" late 1895–late 1896, a period during much of which (Mr. Jenkins suggests) Watson was in Texas preparing for publication the manuscript called *The Life of John Wesley Hardin, As Written by Himself* (reissued in 1961 by the University of Oklahoma Press).

4 *Archie Stamford, the forger.* Mr. Jerry Neal Williamson has speculated that he was the "Archie" of "The Red-Headed League" and also the young Stamford who introduced Holmes to Watson ("The Sad Case of Young Stamford").

MY FRIEND TOOK THE LADY'S UNGLOVED HAND . . .

Illustration by Sidney Paget for the *Strand Magazine*, January, 1904.

It was vain to urge that his time was already fully occupied, for the young lady had come with the determination to tell her story, and it was evident that nothing short of force could get her out of the room until she had done so. With a resigned air and a somewhat weary smile, Holmes begged the beautiful intruder to take a seat and to inform us what it was that was troubling her.

" At least it cannot be your health," said he, as his keen eyes darted over her ; " so ardent a bicyclist must be full of energy."

She glanced down in surprise at her own feet, and I observed the slight roughening of the side of the sole caused by the friction of the edge of the pedal.

" Yes, I bicycle a good deal, Mr. Holmes, and that has something to do with my visit to you to-day."

My friend took the lady's ungloved hand and examined it with as close an attention and as little sentiment as a scientist would show to a specimen.

" You will excuse me, I am sure. It is my business," said he, as he dropped it. " I nearly fell into the error of supposing that you were typewriting. Of course, it is obvious that it is music. You observe the spatulate finger-end, Watson, which is common to both professions ? There is a spirituality about the face, however " —he gently turned it towards the light—" which the typewriter does not generate. This lady is a musician."

" Yes, Mr. Holmes, I teach music."

" In the country, I presume, from your complexion."

" Yes, sir ; near Farnham, on the borders of Surrey."

" A beautiful neighbourhood, and full of the most interesting associations. You remember, Watson, that it was
4 near there that we took Archie Stamford, the forger. Now, Miss Violet, what has happened to you near Farnham, on the borders of Surrey ? "

The young lady, with great clearness and composure, made the following curious statement :

". . . NEAR FARNHAM, ON THE BORDERS OF SURREY."

Photograph by Reece Winston, A.P.P.S., of Bristol, from *Surrey*, by Eric Parker; London: Robert Hale, Ltd. Farnham lies to the extreme west of the county of Surrey, almost on the border of Hampshire, on the edge of the New Forest, for which Watson longed in "The Cardboard Box." It is ten miles southwest of Guildford, and but three miles to the south of the famous military center of Aldershot, well known to Holmes and Watson from the adventure of "The Crooked Man."

"My father is dead, Mr. Holmes. He was James
Smith, who conducted the orchestra at the old Imperial
Theatre. My mother and I were left without a relation 5
in the world except one uncle, Ralph Smith, who went to Africa twenty-five years ago, and we have never had a word from him since. When father died we were left very poor, but one day we were told that there was an advertisement in *The Times* inquiring for our whereabouts. You can imagine how excited we were, for we thought that someone had left us a fortune. We went at once to the lawyer whose name was given in the paper. There we met two gentlemen, Mr. Carruthers and Mr. Woodley, who were home on a visit from South Africa. They said that my uncle was a friend of theirs, that he died some months before in poverty in Johannesburg, and that he had asked them with his last breath to hunt up his relations and see that they were in no want. It seemed strange to us that Uncle Ralph, who took no notice of us when he was alive, should be so careful to look after us when he was dead; but Mr. Carruthers explained that the reason was that my uncle had just heard of the death of his brother, and so felt responsible for our fate."

"Excuse me," said Holmes; "when was this interview?"

"Last December—four months ago."

"Pray proceed."

"Mr. Woodley seemed to me to be a most odious person. He was for ever making eyes at me—a coarse, puffy-faced, red-moustached young man, with his hair plastered down on each side of his forehead. I thought that he was perfectly hateful—and I was sure that Cyril would not wish me to know such a person."

"Oh, Cyril is his name!" said Holmes, smiling.

The young lady blushed and laughed.

"Yes, Mr. Holmes; Cyril Morton, an electrical engineer, and we hope to be married at the end of the summer. Dear me, how *did* I get talking about him? What I wished to say was that Mr. Woodley was perfectly odious, but that Mr. Carruthers, who was a much older man, was more agreeable. He was a dark, sallow, clean-shaven, silent person; but he had polite manners and a pleasant smile. He inquired how we were left, and on finding that we were very poor he suggested that I should come and teach music to his only daughter, aged ten. I said that I did not like to leave my mother, on which he suggested that I should go home to her every week-end, and he offered me a hundred a year, which was certainly splendid pay. So it ended by my accepting, and I went down to Chiltern Grange, about six miles from Farnham. Mr. Carruthers was a widower, but he had engaged a lady-housekeeper, a very respectable, elderly person, called Mrs. Dixon, to look after his establishment. The child was a dear, and everything promised well. Mr. Carruthers was very kind and very musical, and we had most pleasant evenings together. Every week-end I went home to my mother in town.

"The first flaw in my happiness was the arrival of the red-moustached Mr. Woodley. He came for a visit of a week, and oh, it seemed three months to me! He was a

5 *the old Imperial Theatre*. Erected in 1875, it once covered (with the adjoining Westminster Aquarium) the site now occupied by the Wesleyan Central Hall on the north side of Tothill Street. The Imperial was leased during its later years to Mrs. Lily Langtry, and this brought it more popularity with the London public than had hitherto been the case.

dreadful person, a bully to everyone else, but to me something infinitely worse. He made odious love to me, boasted of his wealth, said that if I married him I would have the finest diamonds in London, and finally, when I would have nothing to do with him, he seized me in his arms one day after dinner—he was hideously strong—and he swore that he would not let me go until I had kissed him. Mr. Carruthers came in, and tore him off from me, on which he turned upon his own host, knocking him down and cutting his face open. That was the end of his visit, as you can imagine. Mr. Carruthers apologized to me next day, and assured me that I should never be exposed to such an insult again. I have not seen Mr. Woodley since.

" And now, Mr. Holmes, I come at last to the special thing which has caused me to ask your advice to-day. You must know that every Saturday forenoon I ride on my bicycle to Farnham Station in order to get the 12.22
6 to town. The road from Chiltern Grange is a lonely one, and at one spot it is particularly so, for it lies for over a mile between Charlington Heath upon one side and the woods which lie round Charlington Hall upon the other. You could not find a more lonely tract of road anywhere, and it is quite rare to meet so much as a cart, or a peasant, until you reach the high-road near Crooks-
7 bury Hill. Two weeks ago I was passing this place when I chanced to look back over my shoulder, and about two hundred yards behind me I saw a man, also on a bicycle. He seemed to be a middle-aged man, with a short, dark beard. I looked back before I reached Farnham, but the man was gone, so I thought no more about it. But you can imagine how surprised I was, Mr. Holmes, when on my return on the Monday I saw the same man on the same stretch of road. My astonishment was increased when the incident occurred again, exactly as before, on the following Saturday and Monday. He always kept his distance, and did not molest me in any way, but still it certainly was very odd. I mentioned it to Mr. Carruthers, who seemed interested in what I said, and told me that he had ordered a horse and trap, so that in future I should not pass over these lonely roads without some companion.

" The horse and trap were to have come this week, but for some reason they were not delivered, and again I had to cycle to the station. That was this morning. You can think that I looked out when I came to Charlington Heath, and there, sure enough, was the man, exactly as he had been the two weeks before. He always kept so far from me that I could not clearly see his face, but it was certainly someone whom I did not know. He was dressed in a dark suit with a cloth cap. The only thing about his face that I could clearly see was his dark beard. To-day I was not alarmed, but I was filled with curiosity, and I determined to find out who he was and what he wanted. I slowed down my machine, but he slowed down his. Then I stopped altogether, but he stopped also. Then I laid a trap for him. There is a sharp turning of the road, and I pedalled very quickly round this, and then I stopped and waited. I expected him to shoot round and pass me before he could stop. But he never

6 *the 12.22 to town.* There was, unhappily, no such train.

7 *Crooksbury Hill.* ". . . only one district," Mr. Michael Harrison wrote (*In the Footsteps of Sherlock Holmes*) "can meet all [the] requirements of distance, direction, and having 'Crooksbury Hill' between it and Farnham: that is Charleshill, which lies on the north side of the main road from Farnham to Milford, and has its boundaries marked by the bend that the River Wey takes after it has crossed the main road at a point just slightly west of Elstead. 'Crooksbury Hill' may be either Crooksbury Heath, which could be called a hill, or it may be that part of Crooksbury Common known as Monk's Hill. I feel that the latter is more likely."

"I SLOWED DOWN MY MACHINE . . ."

Illustration by Sidney Paget for the *Strand Magazine*, January, 1904.

appeared. Then I went back and looked round the corner. I could see a mile of road, but he was not on it. To make it the more extraordinary there was no side-road at this point down which he could have gone."

Holmes chuckled and rubbed his hands.

" This case certainly presents some features of its own," said he. " How much time elapsed between your turning the corner and your discovery that the road was clear ? "

" Two or three minutes."

" Then he could not have retreated down the road, and you say that there are no side-roads ? "

" None."

" Then he certainly took a footpath on one side or the other."

" It could not have been on the side of the heath or I should have seen him."

" So by the process of exclusion we arrive at the fact that he made his way towards Charlington Hall, which, as I understand, is situated in its own grounds on one side of the road. Anything else ? "

" Nothing, Mr. Holmes, save that I was so perplexed that I felt I should not be happy until I had seen you and had your advice."

Holmes sat in silence for some little time.

" Where is the gentleman to whom you are engaged ? " he asked at last.

" He is in the Midland Electric Company, at Coventry."

" He would not pay you a surprise visit ? "

" Oh, Mr. Holmes ! As if I should not know him ! "

" Have you had any other admirers ? "

" Several before I knew Cyril."

" And since ? "

" There was this dreadful man, Woodley, if you can call him an admirer."

" No one else ? "

Our fair client seemed a little confused.

" Who was he ? " asked Holmes.

" Oh, it may be a mere fancy of mine ; but it has seemed to me sometimes that my employer, Mr. Carruthers, takes a great deal of interest in me. We are thrown rather together. I play his accompaniments in the evening. He has never said anything. He is a perfect gentleman. But a girl always knows."

" Ha ! " Holmes looked grave. " What does he do for a living ? "

" He is a rich man."

" No carriages or horses ? "

" Well, at least he is fairly well-to-do. But he goes into the city two or three times a week. He is deeply interested in South African gold shares."

" You will let me know any fresh development, Miss Smith. I am very busy just now, but I will find time to make some inquiries into your case. In the meantime, take no step without letting me know. Good-bye, and I trust that we shall have nothing but good news from you."

" It is part of the settled order of Nature that such a girl should have followers," said Holmes, as he pulled at his meditative pipe, " but for choice not on bicycles in

"IT IS PART OF THE SETTLED ORDER OF NATURE THAT SUCH A GIRL SHOULD HAVE FOLLOWERS," SAID HOLMES, AS HE PULLED AT HIS MEDITATIVE PIPE . . .

Cover illustration by Frederic Dorr Steele for *Collier's Magazine*, December 26, 1903.

lonely country roads. Some secretive lover, beyond all doubt. But there are curious and suggestive details about the case, Watson."

"That he should appear only at that point?"

"Exactly. Our first effort must be to find who are the tenants of Charlington Hall. Then, again, how about the connection between Carruthers and Woodley, since they appear to be men of such different types? How came they *both* to be so keen upon looking up Ralph Smith's relations? One more point. What sort of a
8 *ménage* is it which pays double the market price for a governess, but does not keep a horse although six miles from the station? Odd, Watson—very odd."

"You will go down?"

"No, my dear fellow, *you* will go down. This may be some trifling intrigue, and I cannot break my other important research for the sake of it. On Monday you will arrive early at Farnham; you will conceal yourself near Charlington Heath; you will observe these facts for yourself, and act as your own judgment advises. Then, having inquired as to the occupants of the Hall, you will come back to me and report. And now, Watson, not another word of the matter until we have a few solid stepping-stones on which we may hope to get across to our solution."

We had ascertained from the lady that she went down upon the Monday by the train which leaves Waterloo at
9 9.50, so I started early and caught the 9.13. At Farnham Station I had no difficulty in being directed to Charlington Heath. It was impossible to mistake the scene of the young lady's adventure, for the road runs between the open heath on one side, and an old yew hedge upon the other, surrounding a park which is studded with magnificent trees. There was a main gateway of lichen-studded stone, each side-pillar surmounted by mouldering heraldic emblems; but besides this central carriage-drive I observed several points where there were gaps in the hedge and paths leading through them. The house was invisible from the road, but the surroundings all spoke of gloom and decay.

The heath was covered with golden patches of flowering gorse, gleaming magnificently in the light of the bright spring sunshine. Behind one of these clumps I took up my position, so as to command both the gateway of the Hall and a long stretch of the road upon either side. It had been deserted when I left it, but now I saw a cyclist riding down it from the opposite direction to that in which I had come. He was clad in a dark suit, and I saw that he had a black beard. On reaching the end of the Charlington grounds he sprang from his machine and led it through a gap in the hedge, disappearing from my view.

A quarter of an hour passed and then a second cyclist appeared. This time it was the young lady coming from the station. I saw her look about her as she came to the Charlington hedge. An instant later the man emerged from his hiding-place, sprang upon his bicycle, and followed her. In all the broad landscape those were the only moving figures, the graceful girl sitting very straight upon her machine, and the man behind her bending low

8 ménage. French: the persons taken collectively who occupy one house; a household.

9 *so I started early and caught the 9.13.* There were 9:15 and 9:45 trains, but no trains at 9:13 or 9:50 Waterloo to Farnham.

over his handle-bar, with a curiously furtive suggestion in every movement. She looked back at him and slowed her pace. He slowed also. She stopped. He at once stopped, too, keeping two hundred yards behind her. Her next movement was as unexpected as it was spirited. She suddenly whisked her wheels round and dashed straight at him! He was as quick as she, however, and darted off in desperate flight. Presently she came back up the road again, her head haughtily in the air, not deigning to take further notice of her silent attendant. He had turned also, and still kept his distance until the curve of the road hid them from my sight.

I remained in my hiding-place, and it was well that I did so, for presently the man reappeared cycling slowly back. He turned in at the Hall gates and dismounted from his machine. For some few minutes I could see him standing among the trees. His hands were raised, and he seemed to be settling his necktie. Then he mounted his bicycle and rode away from me down the drive towards the Hall. I ran across the heath and peered through the trees. Far away I could catch glimpses of the old grey building with its bristling Tudor chimneys, but the drive ran through a dense shrubbery, and I saw no more of my man.

However, it seemed to me that I had done a fairly good morning's work, and I walked back in high spirits to Farnham. The local house agent could tell me nothing about Charlington Hall, and referred me to a well-known firm in Pall Mall. There I halted on my way home, and met with courtesy from the representative. No, I could not have Charlington Hall for the summer. I was just too late. It had been let about a month ago. Mr. Williamson was the name of the tenant. He was a respectable elderly gentleman. The polite agent was afraid he could say no more, as the affairs of his clients were not matters which he could discuss.

Mr. Sherlock Holmes listened with attention to the long report which I was able to present to him that evening, but it did not elicit that word of curt praise which I had hoped for and should have valued. On the contrary, his austere face was even more severe than usual as he commented upon the things that I had done and the things that I had not.

"Your hiding-place, my dear Watson, was very faulty. You should have been behind the hedge; then you would have had a close view of this interesting person. As it is you were some hundreds of yards away, and can tell me even less than Miss Smith. She thinks she does not know the man; I am convinced she does. Why, otherwise, should he be so desperately anxious that she should not get so near him as to see his features? You describe him as bending over the handle-bar. Concealment again, you see. You really have done remarkably badly. He returns to the house, and you want to find out who he is. You come to a London house agent!"

"What should I have done?" I cried, with some heat.

"Gone to the nearest public-house. That is the centre of country gossip. They would have told you every name, from the master to the scullery-maid. Williamson! It conveys nothing to my mind. If he is an elderly man he is not this active cyclist who sprints away from that athletic young lady's pursuit. What have we gained by your expedition? The knowledge that the girl's story is true. I never doubted it. That there is a connection between the cyclist and the Hall. I never doubted that either. That the Hall is tenanted by Williamson. Who's the better for that? Well, well, my dear sir, don't look so depressed. We can do little more until next Saturday, and in the meantime I may make one or two inquiries myself."

Next morning we had a note from Miss Smith, recounting shortly and accurately the very incidents which I had seen, but the pith of the letter lay in the postscript:

"I am sure that you will respect my confidence, Mr. Holmes, when I tell you that my place here has become difficult owing to the fact that my employer has proposed marriage to me. I am convinced that his feelings are most deep and most honourable. At the same time my promise is, of course, given. He took my refusal very seriously, but also very gently. You can understand, however, that the situation is a little strained."

"Our young friend seems to be getting into deep waters," said Holmes thoughtfully, as he finished the letter. "The case certainly presents more features of interest and more possibility of development than I had originally thought. I should be none the worse for a quiet, peaceful day in the country, and I am inclined to run down this afternoon and test one or two theories which I have formed."

Holmes' quiet day in the country had a singular termination, for he arrived at Baker Street late in the evening with a cut lip and a discoloured lump upon his forehead, besides a general air of dissipation which would have made his own person the fitting object of a Scotland Yard investigation. He was immensely tickled by his own adventures, and laughed heartily as he recounted them.

"I get so little active exercise that it is always a treat," said he. "You are aware that I have some proficiency in the good old British sport of boxing. Occasionally it is of service. To-day, for example, I should have come to very ignominious grief without it."

I begged him to tell me what had occurred.

"I found that country pub which I had already recommended to your notice, and there I made my discreet inquiries. I was in the bar, and a garrulous landlord was giving me all that I wanted. Williamson is a white-bearded man, and he lives alone with a small staff of servants at the Hall. There is some rumour that he is or has been a clergyman; but one or two incidents of his short residence at the Hall struck me as peculiarly unecclesiastical. I have already made some inquiries at a clerical agency, and they tell me that there *was* a man of that name in orders whose career has been a singularly dark one. The landlord further informed me that there are usually week-end visitors—'a warm lot, sir'—at the Hall, and especially one gentleman with a red moustache, Mr. Woodley by name, who was always there. We had got as far as this when who should walk in but the gentleman himself, who had been drinking his beer in the taproom, and had heard the whole conversation. Who was I? What did I want? What did I mean by asking questions? He had a fine flow of language, and his adjectives were very vigorous. He ended a string of abuse by a vicious back-hander, which I failed to entirely avoid. The next few minutes were delicious. It was a straight left against a slogging ruffian. I emerged as you see me. Mr. Woodley went home in a cart. So ended my country trip, and it must be confessed that, however enjoyable, my day on the Surrey border has not been much more profitable than your own."

The Thursday brought us another letter from our client.

"IT WAS A STRAIGHT LEFT AGAINST A SLOGGING RUFFIAN."

Illustration by Sidney Paget for the *Strand Magazine*, January, 1904.

" You will not be surprised, Mr. Holmes (said she), to hear that I am leaving Mr. Carruthers' employment. Even the high pay cannot reconcile me to the discomforts of my situation. On Saturday I come up to town, and I do not intend to return. Mr. Carruthers has got a trap, and so the dangers of the lonely road, if there ever were any dangers, are now over.

" As to the special cause of my leaving, it is not merely the strained situation with Mr. Carruthers, but it is the reappearance of that odious man, Mr. Woodley. He was always hideous, but he looks more awful than ever now, for he appears to have had an accident and he is much disfigured. I saw him out of the window, but I am glad to say I did not meet him. He had a long talk with Mr. Carruthers, who seemed much excited afterwards. Woodley must be staying in the neighbourhood, for he did not sleep here, and yet I caught a glimpse of him again this morning slinking about in the shrubbery. I would sooner have a savage wild animal loose about the place. I loathe and fear him more than I can say. How *can* Mr. Carruthers endure such a creature for a moment? However, all my troubles will be over on Saturday."

"I EMERGED AS YOU SEE ME. MR. WOODLEY WENT HOME IN A CART."

Illustration by Frederic Dorr Steele for *Collier's Magazine*, December 26, 1903.

" So I trust, Watson, so I trust," said Holmes gravely. " There is some deep intrigue going on round that little woman, and it is our duty to see that no one molests her upon that last journey. I think, Watson, that we must spare time to run down together on Saturday morning, and make sure that this curious and inconclusive investigation has no untoward ending."

I confess that I had not up to now taken a very serious view of the case, which had seemed to me rather grotesque and bizarre than dangerous. That a man should lie in wait for and follow a very handsome woman is no unheard-of thing, and if he had so little audacity that he not only dared not address her, but even fled from her approach, he was not a very formidable assailant. The ruffian Woodley was a very different person, but, except on the one occasion, he had not molested our client, and now he visited the house of Carruthers without intruding upon her presence. The man on the bicycle was doubtless a member of those week-end parties at the Hall of which the publican had spoken ; but who he was or what he wanted was as obscure as ever. It was the severity

"TOO LATE, WATSON; TOO LATE!" CRIED HOLMES . . .

Illustration by Sidney Paget for the *Strand Magazine,* January, 1904.

of Holmes' manner and the fact that he slipped a revolver into his pocket before leaving our rooms which impressed me with the feeling that tragedy might prove to lurk behind this curious train of events.

A rainy night had been followed by a glorious morning, and the heath-covered country-side, with the glowing clumps of flowering gorse, seemed all the more beautiful to eyes which were weary of the duns and drabs and slate-greys of London. Holmes and I walked along the broad, sandy road inhaling the fresh morning air, and rejoicing in the music of the birds and the fresh breath of the spring. From a rise of the road on the shoulder of Crooksbury Hill we could see the grim Hall bristling out from amidst the ancient oaks, which, old as they were, were still younger than the building which they surrounded. Holmes pointed down the long tract of road which wound, a reddish-yellow band, between the brown of the heath and the budding green of the woods. Far away, a black dot, we could see a vehicle moving in our direction. Holmes gave an exclamation of impatience.

" I had given a margin of half an hour," said he. " If that is her trap she must be making for the earlier train. I fear, Watson, that she will be past Charlington before we can possibly meet her."

From the instant that we passed the rise we could no longer see the vehicle, but we hastened onwards at such a pace that my sedentary life began to tell upon me, and I was compelled to fall behind. Holmes, however, was always in training, for he had inexhaustible stores of nervous energy upon which to draw. His springy step never slowed, until suddenly, when he was a hundred yards in front of me, he halted, and I saw him throw up his hand with a gesture of grief and despair. At the same instant an empty dog-cart, the horse cantering, the reins trailing, appeared round the curve of the road and rattled swiftly towards us.

" Too late, Watson ; too late ! " cried Holmes, as I ran panting to his side. " Fool that I was not to allow for the earlier train ! It's abduction, Watson—abduction ! Murder ! Heaven knows what ! Block the road ! Stop the horse ! That's right. Now jump in, and let us see if I can repair the consequences of my own blunder."

We had sprung into the dog-cart, and Holmes, after turning the horse, gave it a sharp cut with the whip, and we flew back along the road. As we turned the curve the whole stretch of road between the Hall and the heath was opened up. I grasped Holmes' arm.

" That's the man ! " I gasped.

A solitary cyclist was coming towards us. His head was down and his shoulders rounded as he put every ounce of energy that he possessed on to the pedals. He was flying like a racer. Suddenly he raised his bearded face, saw us close to him, and pulled up, springing from his machine. That coal-black beard was in singular contrast to the pallor of his face, and his eyes were as bright as if he had a fever. He stared at us and at the dog-cart. Then a look of amazement came over his face.

" Halloa ! Stop there ! " he shouted, holding his bicycle to block our road. " Where did you get that dog-cart ? Pull up, man ! " he yelled, drawing a pistol from his side-pocket. " Pull up, I say, or, by George, I'll put a bullet into your horse ! "

Holmes threw the reins into my lap and sprang down from the cart.

" You're the man we want to see. Where is Miss Violet Smith ? " he said in his quick, clear way.

" That's what I am asking you. You're in her dog-cart. You ought to know where she is."

" We met the dog-cart on the road. There was no one in it. We drove back to help the young lady."

" Good Lord ! Good Lord ! What shall I do ? " cried the stranger, in an ecstasy of despair. " They've got her, that hellhound Woodley and the blackguard parson. Come, man, come, if you really are her friend. Stand by me and we'll save her, if I have to leave my carcass in Charlington Wood."

He ran distractedly, his pistol in his hand, towards a gap in the hedge. Holmes followed him, and I, leaving the horse grazing beside the road, followed Holmes.

" This is where they came through," said he, pointing to the marks of several feet upon the muddy path. " Halloa ! Stop a minute ! Who's this in the bush ? "

It was a young fellow about seventeen, dressed like an ostler, with leather cords and gaiters. He lay upon his back, his knees drawn up, a terrible cut upon his head. He was insensible, but alive. A glance at his wound told me that it had not penetrated the bone.

" That's Peter, the groom," cried the stranger. " He drove her. The beasts have pulled him off and clubbed him. Let him lie ; we can't do him any good, but we may save her from the worst fate that can befall a woman."

We ran frantically down the path, which wound among the trees. We had reached the shrubbery which surrounded the house when Holmes pulled up.

" They didn't go to the house. Here are their marks on the left—here, beside the laurel bushes ! Ah, I said so ! "

As he spoke a woman's shrill scream—a scream which vibrated with a frenzy of horror—burst from the thick green clump of bushes in front of us. It ended suddenly on its highest note with a choke and a gurgle.

" This way ! This way ! They are in the bowling alley," cried the stranger, darting through the bushes. " Ah, the cowardly dogs ! Follow me, gentlemen ! Too late ! too late ! by the living Jingo ! "

We had broken suddenly into a lovely glade of greensward surrounded by ancient trees. On the farther side of it, under the shadow of a mighty oak, there stood a singular group of three people. One was a woman, our client, drooping and faint, a handkerchief round her mouth. Opposite her stood a brutal, heavy-faced, red-moustached young man, his gaitered legs parted wide, one arm akimbo, the other waving a riding-crop, his whole attitude suggestive of triumphant bravado. Between them an elderly, grey-bearded man, wearing a short surplice over a light tweed suit, had evidently just com- **10**
pleted the wedding service, for he pocketed his Prayer Book as we appeared, and slapped the sinister bridegroom upon the back in jovial congratulation.

" They're married ! " I gasped.

10 *a short surplice.* "It appears that there are two patterns of short surplice in Dress Regulations—the Cotta, which has short sleeves, and the Roman Alb, with longer sleeves," Colonel Ronald D. Sherbrooke-Walker wrote in "Clothes Canonical." "We have no information as to which 'the old reprobate' was wearing."

AS WE APPROACHED, THE LADY STAGGERED AGAINST THE TRUNK OF THE TREE FOR SUPPORT.

Illustration by Sidney Paget for the *Strand Magazine*, January, 1904.

HE SPUN ROUND WITH A SCREAM AND FELL UPON HIS BACK . . .

Illustration by Sidney Paget for the *Strand Magazine*, January, 1904.

"Come on!" cried our guide; "come on!" He rushed across the glade, Holmes and I at his heels. As we approached, the lady staggered against the trunk of the tree for support. Williamson, the ex-clergyman, bowed to us with mock politeness, and the bully Woodley advanced with a shout of brutal and exultant laughter.

"You can take your beard off, Bob," said he. "I know you right enough. Well, you and your pals have just come in time for me to be able to introduce you to Mrs. Woodley."

Our guide's answer was a singular one. He snatched off the dark beard which had disguised him and threw it on the ground, disclosing a long, sallow, clean-shaven face below it. Then he raised his revolver and covered the young ruffian, who was advancing upon him with his dangerous riding-crop swinging in his hand.

"Yes," said our ally, "I *am* Bob Carruthers, and I'll see this woman righted if I have to swing for it. I told you what I'd do if you molested her, and, by the Lord, I'll be as good as my word!"

"You're too late. She's my wife!"

"No, she's your widow."

His revolver cracked, and I saw the blood spurt from the front of Woodley's waistcoat. He spun round with a scream and fell upon his back, his hideous red face turning suddenly to a dreadful mottled pallor. The old man, still clad in his surplice, burst into such a string of foul oaths as I have never heard, and pulled out a revolver of his own, but before he could raise it he was looking down the barrel of Holmes' weapon.

"Enough of this," said my friend coldly. "Drop that pistol! Watson, pick it up! Hold it to his head! Thank you. You, Carruthers, give me that revolver. We'll have no more violence. Come, hand it over!"

"Who are you, then?"

"My name is Sherlock Holmes."

"Good Lord!"

"You have heard of me, I see. I will represent the official police until their arrival. Here, you!" he shouted to the frightened groom, who had appeared at the edge of the glade. "Come here. Take this note as hard as you can ride to Farnham." He scribbled a few words upon a leaf from his notebook. "Give it to the superintendent at the police-station. Until he comes, I must detain you all under my personal custody."

The strong, masterful personality of Holmes dominated the tragic scene, and all were equally puppets in his hands. Williamson and Carruthers found themselves carrying the wounded Woodley into the house, and I gave my arm to the frightened girl. The injured man was laid on his bed, and at Holmes' request I examined him. I carried my report to where he sat in the old tapestry-hung dining-room with his two prisoners before him.

"He will live," said I.

"What!" cried Carruthers, springing out of his chair. "I'll go upstairs and finish him first. Do you tell me that that girl, that angel, is to be tied to Roaring Jack Woodley for life?"

"You need not concern yourself about that," said Holmes. "There are two very good reasons why she should under no circumstances be his wife. In the first place, we are very safe in questioning Mr. Williamson's right to solemnize a marriage."

"I have been ordained," cried the old rascal.

"And also unfrocked." 11

"Once a clergyman, always a clergyman."

"I think not. How about the licence?"

"We had a licence for the marriage. I have it here in my pocket."

"Then you got it by a trick. But in any case a forced
marriage is no marriage, but it is a very serious felony, as 12
you will discover before you have finished. You'll have time to think the point out during the next ten years or so, unless I am mistaken. As to you, Carruthers, you would have done better to keep your pistol in your pocket."

"I begin to think so, Mr. Holmes; but when I thought of all the precaution I had taken to shield this girl—for I loved her, Mr. Holmes, and it is the only time that ever I knew what love was—it fairly drove me mad to think that she was in the power of the greatest brute and bully in South Africa, a man whose name is a holy terror from Kimberley to Johannesburg. Why, Mr. Holmes, you'll hardly believe it, but ever since that girl has been in my employment I never once let her go past this house, where I knew these rascals were lurking, without following her on my bicycle just to see that she came to no harm. I kept my distance from her, and I wore a beard so that she should not recognize me, for she is a good and high-spirited girl, and she wouldn't have stayed in my employment long if she had thought that I was following her about the country roads."

"Why didn't you tell her of her danger?"

"Because then, again, she would have left me, and I couldn't bear to face that. Even if she couldn't love me it was a great deal to me just to see her dainty form about the house, and to hear the sound of her voice."

"Well," said I, "you call that love, Mr. Carruthers, but I should call it selfishness."

"Maybe the two things go together. Anyhow, I couldn't let her go. Besides, with this crowd about, it was well that she should have someone near to look after her. Then when the cable came I knew they were bound to make a move."

"What cable?"

Carruthers took a telegram from his pocket.

"That's it!" said he. It was short and concise:

"The old man is dead."

"Hum!" said Holmes. "I think I see how things worked, and I can understand how this message would, as you say, bring them to a head. But while we wait, you might tell me what you can."

The old reprobate with the surplice burst into a volley of bad language.

"By Heaven," said he, "if you squeal on us, Bob Carruthers, I'll serve you as you served Jack Woodley! You can bleat about the girl to your heart's content, for that's your own affair, but if you round on your pals to this

11 *"And also unfrocked."* "What [Holmes] meant was 'deposed,'" the Reverend Otis R. Rice wrote in "Clergymen in the Canon." "This is the correct term of this form of ecclesiastical demise."

12 *a very serious felony*. Holmes was correct. As the Reverend Otis R. Rice continued: "The sacraments and sacramentals administered by a priest are valid whether he is inhibited, deposed, or not. In this respect Williamson's flippant remark, 'Once a clergyman, always a clergyman' was in a sense true. He was accountable for such an act and open to ecclesiastical and civil action for solemnizing any marriage after his deposition. Religiously, morally and legally, however, this mock ceremony was no marriage because of the lack of *intention* and *consent* upon the part of Violet Smith. The very fact that she was gagged was presumptive proof of her lack of 'free consent.' Unlike any other sacrament, the priest in solemnizing Holy Matrimony as practiced by the Church of England, is not the minister of the rite. The *bride and groom* themselves are its ministers. The officiating divine, in the name of the Church, blesses and attests the marriage, which the couple themselves perform. Without Miss Smith's *intention* and *willingness* to perform the marriage, it was in the eyes of the Church invalid. One wonders why Williamson did not know this. Possibly his theological education had been as fragmentary as had been his liturgical training. What informed Anglican clergyman would have believed he was 'solemnizing a marriage' while wearing 'a short surplice over a light tweed suit'?"

plain-clothes copper it will be the worst day's work that ever you did "

" Your reverence need not be excited," said Holmes, lighting a cigarette. " The case is clear enough against you, and all I ask is a few details for my private curiosity. However, if there's any difficulty in your telling me I'll do the talking, and then you will see how far you have a chance of holding back your secrets. In the first place, three of you came from South Africa on this game—you, Williamson, you, Carruthers, and Woodley."

" Lie number one," said the old man ; " I never saw either of them until two months ago, and I have never been in Africa in my life, so you can put that in your pipe and smoke it, Mr. Busybody Holmes ! "

" What he says is true," said Carruthers.

" Well, well, two of you came over. His reverence is our own home-made article. You had known Ralph Smith in South Africa. You had reason to believe he would not live long. You found out that his niece would inherit his fortune. How's that—eh ? "

Carruthers nodded, and Williamson swore.

" She was next-of-kin, no doubt, and you were aware that the old fellow would make no will."

" Couldn't read or write," said Carruthers.

" So you came over, the two of you, and hunted up the girl. The idea was that one of you was to marry her, and the other have a share of the plunder. For some reason Woodley was chosen as the husband. Why was that ? "

" We played cards for her on the voyage. He won."

" I see. You got the young lady into your service, and there Woodley was to do the courting. She recognized the drunken brute that he was, and would have nothing to do with him. Meanwhile, your arrangement was rather upset by the fact that you had yourself fallen in love with the lady. You could no longer bear the idea of this ruffian owning her."

" No, by George, I couldn't ! "

" There was a quarrel between you. He left you in a rage, and began to make his own plans independently of you."

" It strikes me, Williamson, there isn't very much that we can tell this gentleman," cried Carruthers, with a bitter laugh. " Yes, we quarrelled, and he knocked me down. I am level with him on that, anyhow. Then I lost sight of him. That was when he picked up with this cast padre here. I found that they had set up housekeeping together at this place on the line that she had to pass for the station. I kept my eye on her after that, for I knew there was some devilry in the wind. I saw them from time to time, for I was anxious to know what they were after. Two days ago Woodley came up to my house with this cable, which showed that Ralph Smith was dead. He asked me if I would stand by the bargain. I said I would not. He asked me if I would marry the girl myself and give him a share. I said I would willingly do so, but that she would not have me. He said, ' Let us get her married first, and after a week or two she may see things a bit different.' I said I would have nothing to do with violence. So he went off cursing, like the foul-mouthed blackguard that he was, and swearing that he would have her yet. She was leaving me this week-end, and I had got a trap to take her to the station, but I was so uneasy in my mind that I followed her on my bicycle. She had got a start, however, and before I could catch her the mischief was done. The first thing I knew about it was when I saw you two gentlemen driving back in her dog-cart."

Holmes rose and tossed the end of his cigarette into the grate. "I have been very obtuse, Watson," said he. "When in your report you said that you had seen the cyclist as you thought arrange his necktie in the shrubbery, that alone should have told me all. However, we may congratulate ourselves upon a curious and in some respects a unique case. I perceive three of the county constabulary in the drive, and I am glad to see that the little ostler is able to keep pace with them ; so it is likely that neither he nor the interesting bridegroom will be permanently damaged by their morning's adventures. I think, Watson, that in your medical capacity you might wait upon Miss Smith and tell her that if she is sufficiently recovered we shall be happy to escort her to her mother's home. If she is not quite convalescent you will find that a hint that we were about to telegraph to a young electrician in the Midlands would probably complete the cure. As to you, Mr. Carruthers, I think that you have done what you could to make amends for your share in an evil plot. There is my card, sir, and if my evidence can be of help to you in your trial it shall be at your disposal."

In the whirl of our incessant activity it has often been difficult for me, as the reader has probably observed, to round off my narratives, and to give those final details which the curious might expect. Each case has been the prelude to another, and the crisis once over, the actors have passed for ever out of our busy lives. I find, however, a short note at the end of my manuscripts dealing with this case, in which I have put it upon record that Miss Violet Smith did indeed inherit a large fortune, and that she is now the wife of Cyril Morton, the senior partner of Morton and Kennedy, the famous Westminster electricians. Williamson and Woodley were both tried for abduction and assault, the former getting seven years and the latter ten. Of the fate of Carruthers I have no record, but I am sure that his assault was not viewed very gravely by the Court, since Woodley had the reputation of being a most dangerous ruffian, and I think that a few months were sufficient to satisfy the demands of justice.

HOLMES ROSE AND TOSSED THE END OF HIS CIGARETTE INTO THE GRATE.

Illustration by Sidney Paget for the *Strand Magazine*, January, 1904.

Bibliographical Note: The manuscript of "The Adventure of the Solitary Cyclist," about 7,000 words, with cancellations and insertions in two exercise books, 8vo, vellum by Spealls, was auctioned in New York City on January 26, 1922, bringing $120. It was auctioned again in London on January 28, 1935; sold in one lot with "The Adventure of the Priory School" and "The Adventure of the Dancing Men" for £66. It was auctioned for a third time in New York City on April 26, 1927, ringing $160. Its present location is unknown.

53

THE ADVENTURE OF BLACK PETER

[Wednesday, July 3, to Friday, July 5, 1895]

I HAVE never known my friend to be in better form,
both mental and physical, than in the year '95.
His increasing fame had brought with it an immense
practice, and I should be guilty of an indiscretion if I
were even to hint at the identity of some of the illustrious
clients who crossed our humble threshold in Baker
Street. Holmes, however, like all great artists, lived
for his art's sake, and, save in the case of the Duke of
1 Holdernesse, I have seldom known him claim any large
reward for his inestimable services. So unworldly was
he—or so capricious—that he frequently refused his
help to the powerful and wealthy where the problem
made no appeal to his sympathies, while he would devote
weeks of most intense application to the affairs of some
humble client whose case presented those strange and
dramatic qualities which appealed to his imagination and
challenged his ingenuity.

2 In this memorable year '95 a curious and incongruous
succession of cases had engaged his attention, ranging
from his famous investigation of the sudden death of
3 Cardinal Tosca—an inquiry which was carried out by
him at the express desire of his Holiness the Pope—down
4 to his arrest of Wilson, the notorious canary-trainer,
which removed a plague-spot from the East End of London.
Close on the heels of these two famous cases came
5 the tragedy of Woodman's Lee, and the very obscure
circumstances which surrounded the death of Captain
Peter Carey. No record of the doings of Mr. Sherlock
Holmes would be complete which did not include some
account of this very unusual affair.

During the first week of July my friend had been absent
so often and so long from our lodgings that I knew he had
something on hand. The fact that several rough-looking
men called during that time and inquired for Captain
Basil made me understand that Holmes was working
somewhere under one of the numerous disguises and
names with which he concealed his own formidable
identity. He had at least five small refuges in different
6 parts of London in which he was able to change his
personality. He said nothing of his business to me, and

1 *the Duke of Holdernesse.* Watson refers to "The Adventure of the Priory School." He must have written his account of "The Adventure of Black Peter" some years after the event, since "The Adventure of the Priory School" did not take place until May, 1901.

2 *In this memorable year '95.* There is no reason to doubt that the year *was* 1895: Inspector Stanley Hopkins tells us later that Captain Carey "was born in '45—fifty years of age."

3 *the sudden death of Cardinal Tosca.* Cardinal "Tosca" has been identified by Mr. Francis Albert Young ("Upon the Identification of Cardinal Tosca") as Cardinal Luigi Ruffo-Scilla, whose collapse and death, at the age of fifty-five, in Rome on May 29, 1895, came as a great surprise to many.

A pastiche stemming from this reference of Dr. Watson's, by Mr. Issac S. George, appeared in the *Baker Street Journal,* Vol. III, No. 1, Old Series, January, 1946, pp. 72-82.

4 *Wilson, the notorious canary-trainer.* At their 1949 dinner, The Speckled Band of Boston announced a prize competition for the best attempt at writing the story of "the arrest of Wilson." The winning entry, a playlet, was "The Yellow Birds," by Mr. Roger T. Clapp, published in *The Third Cab,* Boston: Privately printed, 1960, pp. 64–80.

Dr. Watson's reference also served to inspire a pastiche by Adrian M. Conan Doyle in *The Exploits of Sherlock Holmes;* it is titled "The Adventure of the Deptford Horror."

But: "How could a canary trainer become notorious if he stayed with canaries?" Mr. "Red" Smith asked in "The Nefarious Holmes." "There is absolutely nothing whatsoever in any way, shape, or form notorious about canaries. A bird trainer, however, can branch out, as Hirsch Jacobs has demonstrated in our day; Mr. Jacobs began with pigeons and went on to become America's leading

it was not my habit to force a confidence. The first positive sign which he gave me of the direction which his investigation was taking was an extraordinary one. He had gone out before breakfast, and I had sat down to mine, when he strode into the room, his hat upon his head, and a huge, barb-headed spear tucked like an umbrella under his arm.

"Good gracious, Holmes!" I cried. "You don't mean to say that you have been walking about London with that thing?"

"I drove to the butcher's and back."

"The butcher's?"

"And I return with an excellent appetite. There can be no question, my dear Watson, of the value of exercise before breakfast. But I am prepared to bet that you will not guess the form that my exercise has taken."

"I will not attempt it."

He chuckled as he poured out the coffee.

"If you could have looked into Allardyce's back shop you would have seen a dead pig swung from a hook in the ceiling, and a gentleman in his shirt-sleeves furiously stabbing at it with this weapon. I was that energetic person, and I have satisfied myself that by no exertion of my strength can I transfix the pig with a single blow. Perhaps you would care to try?"

"Not for worlds. But why were you doing this?"

"Because it seemed to me to have an indirect bearing upon the mystery of Woodman's Lee. Ah, Hopkins, I got your wire last night, and I have been expecting you. Come and join us."

Our visitor was an exceedingly alert man, thirty years of age, dressed in a quiet tweed suit, but retaining the erect bearing of one who was accustomed to official uniform. I recognized him at once as Stanley Hopkins, a young police inspector for whose future Holmes had high hopes, while he in turn professed the admiration and respect of a pupil for the scientific methods of the famous amateur. Hopkins' brow was clouded and he sat down with an air of deep dejection.

"No, thank you, sir. I breakfasted before I came round. I spent the night in town, for I came up yesterday to report."

"And what had you to report?"

"Failure, sir—absolute failure."

"You have made no progress?"

"None."

"Dear me! I must have a look at the matter."

"I wish to heavens that you would, Mr. Holmes. It's my first big chance, and I am at my wits' end. For goodness' sake come down and lend me a hand."

"Well, well, it happens that I have already read all the available evidence, including the report of the inquest, with some care. By the way, what do you make of that tobacco-pouch found on the scene of the crime? Is there no clue there?"

Hopkins looked surprised.

"It was the man's own pouch, sir. His initials were inside it. And it was of sealskin—and he an old sealer."

"But he had no pipe."

horse-trainer in eleven of twelve consecutive years. It stands to reason that Holmes' man, Wilson, followed a similar course . . ."

5 *Woodman's Lee.* Mr. Michael Harrison (*In the Footsteps of Sherlock Holmes*) has suggested that "Woodman's Lee" is Coleman's Hatch, near Forest Row in Sussex.

6 *He had at least five small refuges in different parts of London.* "The reference is tantalizing and obscure," Mr. Vincent Starrett wrote in *The Private Life of Sherlock Holmes.* "The rooms of Mycroft Holmes, opposite the Diogenes Club, would certainly be one of them; but it would be satisfying to know the others. . . . It may be assumed that in all of his five refuges he stored the materials of deception, as well as quantities of shag tobacco."

"YOU DON'T MEAN TO SAY THAT YOU HAVE BEEN WALKING ABOUT LONDON WITH THAT THING?"

Illustration by Sidney Paget for the *Strand Magazine*, March, 1904.

" No, sir, we could find no pipe ; indeed, he smoked very little. And yet he might have kept some tobacco for his friends."

" No doubt. I only mention it because if I had been handling the case I should have been inclined to make that the starting-point of my investigation. However, my friend Dr. Watson knows nothing of this matter, and I should be none the worse for hearing the sequence of events once more. Just give us some short sketch of the essentials."

Stanley Hopkins drew a slip of paper from his pocket.

" I have a few dates here which will give you the career of the dead man, Captain Peter Carey. He was born in '45—fifty years of age. He was a most daring and successful seal and whale fisher. In 1883 he commanded the steam sealer *Sea Unicorn*, of Dundee. He had then had several successful voyages in succession, and in the following year, 1884, he retired. After that he travelled for some years, and finally he bought a small place called Woodman's Lee, near Forest Row, in Sussex. There he has lived for six years, and there he died just a week ago to-day.

" There were some most singular points about the man. In ordinary life he was a strict Puritan—a silent, gloomy fellow. His household consisted of his wife, his daughter, aged twenty, and two female servants. These last were continually changing, for it was never a very cheery situation, and sometimes it became past all bearing. The man was an intermittent drunkard, and when he had the fit on him he was a perfect fiend. He has been known to drive his wife and his daughter out of doors in the middle of the night, and flog them through the park until the whole village outside the gates was aroused by their screams.

" He was summoned once for a savage assault upon the old vicar, who had called upon him to remonstrate with him upon his conduct. In short, Mr. Holmes, you would go far before you found a more dangerous man than Peter Carey, and I have heard that he bore the same character when he commanded his ship. He was known in the trade as Black Peter, and the name was given him, not only on account of his swarthy features and the colour of his huge beard, but for the humours which were the terror of all around him I need not say that he was loathed and avoided by every one of his neighbours, and that I have not heard one single word of sorrow about his terrible end.

" You must have read in the account of the inquest about the man's cabin, Mr. Holmes ; but perhaps your friend here has not heard of it. He had built himself a wooden outhouse—he always called it ' the cabin '—a few hundred yards from his house, and it was here that he slept every night. It was a little, single-roomed hut, sixteen feet by ten. He kept the key in his pocket, made his own bed, cleaned it himself, and allowed no other foot to cross the threshold. There are small windows on each side, which were covered by curtains, and never opened. One of these windows was turned towards the high-road, and when the light burned in it at night the folk used to point it out to each other, and wonder what Black Peter was doing in there. That's the window, Mr. Holmes, which gave us one of the few bits of positive evidence that came out at the inquest.

" You remember that a stonemason, named Slater, walking from Forest Row about one o'clock in the morning —two days before the murder—stopped as he passed the grounds and looked at the square of light still shining among the trees. He swears that the shadow of a man's head turned sideways was clearly visible on the blind, and that this shadow was certainly not that of Peter Carey, whom he knew well. It was that of a bearded man, but the beard was short, and bristled forwards in a way very different from that of the captain. So he says, but he had been two hours in the public-house, and it is some distance from the road to the window. Besides, this refers to the Monday, and the crime was done upon the Wednesday. 7

" On the Tuesday Peter Carey was in one of his blackest moods, flushed with drink and as savage as a dangerous wild beast. He roamed about the house, and the women ran for it when they heard him coming. Late in the evening he went down to his own hut. About two o'clock the following morning his daughter, who slept with her window open, heard a most fearful yell from that direction, but it was no unusual thing for him to bawl and shout when he was in drink, so no notice was taken. On rising at seven one of the maids noticed that the door of the hut was open, but so great was the terror which the man caused that it was midday before anyone would venture down to see what had become of him. Peeping into the open door, they saw a sight which sent them flying with white faces into the village. Within an hour I was on the spot, and had taken over the case.

" Well, I have fairly steady nerves, as you know, Mr. Holmes, but I give you my word that I got a shake when I put my head into that little house. It was droning like a harmonium with the flies and bluebottles, and the floor and walls were like a slaughter-house. He had called it a cabin, and a cabin it was, sure enough, for you would have thought that you were in a ship. There was a bunk at one end, a sea-chest, maps and charts, a picture of the *Sea Unicorn*, a line of log-books on a shelf, all exactly as one would expect to find it in a captain's room. And there in the middle of it was the man himself, his face twisted like a lost soul in torment, and his great brindled beard stuck upwards in his agony. Right through his broad breast a steel harpoon had been driven, and it had sunk deep into the wood of the wall behind him. He was pinned like a beetle on a card. Of course, he was quite dead, and had been so from the instant that he uttered that last yell of agony.

" I know your methods, sir, and I applied them. Before I permitted anything to be moved I examined most carefully the ground outside, and also the floor of the room. There were no footmarks."

" Meaning that you saw none ? "

" I assure you, sir, that there were none."

" My good Hopkins, I have investigated many crimes, but I have never yet seen one which was committed by a flying creature. As long as the criminal remains upon

7 *the crime was done upon the Wednesday.* Since Captain Peter Carey died "just a week ago to-day," and since we are in "the first week of July" "in the year '95," the opening day of the adventure must be *Wednesday, July 3, 1895*. It ended two days later—on the morning of *Friday, July 5, 1895*.

two legs so long must there be some indentation, some abrasion, some trifling displacement which can be detected by the scientific searcher. It is incredible that this blood-bespattered room contained no trace which could have aided us. I understand, however, from the inquest that there were some objects which you failed to overlook?"

The young inspector winced at my companion's ironical comments.

"I was a fool not to call you in at the time, Mr. Holmes. However, that's past praying for now. Yes, there were several objects in the room which called for special attention. One was the harpoon with which the deed was committed. It had been snatched down from a rack on the wall. Two others remained there, and there was a vacant place for the third. On the stock was engraved 'S.s. *Sea Unicorn*, Dundee.' This seemed to establish that the crime had been done in a moment of fury, and that the murderer had seized the first weapon which came in his way. The fact that the crime was committed at two in the morning, and yet Peter Carey was fully dressed, suggested that he had an appointment with the murderer, which is borne out by the fact that a bottle of rum and two dirty glasses stood upon the table."

HOLMES LAID IT ON THE TABLE AND EXAMINED IT IN HIS MINUTE WAY . . .

Illustration by Sidney Paget for the *Strand Magazine*, March, 1904.

"Yes," said Holmes; "I think that both inferences are permissible. Was there any other spirit but rum in the room?"

"Yes; there was a tantalus containing brandy and whisky on the sea-chest. It is of no importance to us, however, since the decanters were full and it had therefore not been used."

"For all that its presence has some significance," said Holmes. "However, let us hear some more about the objects which do seem to you to bear upon the case."

"There was this tobacco-pouch upon the table."

"What part of the table?"

"It lay in the middle. It was of coarse sealskin—the straight-haired skin, with a leather thong to bind it. Inside was 'P. C.' on the flap. There was half an ounce of strong ship's tobacco in it."

"Excellent! What more?"

Stanley Hopkins drew from his pocket a drab-covered notebook. The outside was rough and worn, the leaves were discoloured. On the first page were written the initials "J. H. N." and the date "1883." Holmes laid it on the table and examined it in his minute way, while Hopkins and I gazed over each shoulder. On the second page were printed the letters "C. P. R.," and then came several sheets of numbers. Another heading was Argentine, another Costa Rica, and another San Paulo, each with pages of signs and figures after it.

"What do you make of these?" asked Holmes.

"They appear to be lists of Stock Exchange securities. I thought that 'J. H. N.' were the initials of a broker, and that 'C. P. R.' may have been his client."

"Try Canadian Pacific Railway," said Holmes.

Stanley Hopkins swore between his teeth, and struck his thigh with his clenched hand.

"What a fool I have been!" he cried. "Of course

it is as you say. Then 'J. H. N.' are the only initials we have to solve. I have already examined the old Stock Exchange lists, and I can find no one in 1883 either in the House or among the outside brokers whose initials 8
correspond with these. Yet I feel that the clue is the most important one that I hold. You will admit, Mr. Holmes, that there is a possibility that these initials are those of the second person who was present—in other words, of the murderer. I would also urge that the introduction into the case of a document relating to large masses of valuable securities gives us for the first time some indication of a motive for the crime."

Sherlock Holmes' face showed that he was thoroughly taken aback by this new development.

"I must admit both your points," said he. "I confess that the notebook, which did not appear at the inquest, modifies any views which I may have formed. I had come to a theory of the crime in which I can find no place for this. Have you endeavoured to trace any of the securities here mentioned?"

"Inquiries are now being made at the offices, but I fear that the complete register of the stock-holders of these South American concerns is in South America, and that some weeks must elapse before we can trace the shares."

Holmes had been examining the cover of the notebook with his magnifying lens.

"Surely there is some discoloration here," said he.

"Yes, sir, it is a blood-stain. I told you that I picked the book off the floor."

"Was the blood-stain above or below?"

"On the side next the boards."

"Which proves, of course, that the book was dropped after the crime was committed."

"Exactly, Mr. Holmes. I appreciated that point, and I conjectured that it was dropped by the murderer on his hurried flight. It lay near the door."

"I suppose that none of these securities have been found among the property of the dead man?"

"No, sir."

"Have you any reason to suspect robbery?"

"No, sir. Nothing seemed to have been touched."

"Dear me, it is certainly a very interesting case. Then there was a knife, was there not?"

"A sheath-knife, still in its sheath. It lay at the feet of the dead man. Mrs. Carey has identified it as being her husband's property."

Holmes was lost in thought for some time.

"Well," said he at last, "I suppose I shall have to come out and have a look at it."

Stanley Hopkins gave a cry of joy.

"Thank you, sir. That will indeed be a weight off my mind."

Holmes shook his finger at the Inspector.

"It would have been an easier task a week ago," said he. "But even now my visit may not be entirely fruitless. Watson, if you can spare the time, I should be very glad of your company. If you will call a four-wheeler, Hopkins, we shall be ready to start for Forest Row in a quarter of an hour."

8 *the House.* Hopkins presumably refers to the London Stock Exchange, which had its first home in Jonathan's Coffee House in Change Alley.

"SOMEONE HAS BEEN TAMPERING WITH IT," HE SAID.

Illustration by Sidney Paget for the *Strand Magazine*, March, 1904.

Alighting at the small wayside station, we drove for some miles through the remains of widespread woods, which were once part of that great forest which for so long held the Saxon invaders at bay—the impenetrable "weald," for sixty years the bulwark of Britain. Vast sections of it have been cleared, for this is the seat of the first ironworks of the country, and the trees have been felled to smelt the ore. Now the richer fields of the North have absorbed the trade, and nothing save these ravaged groves and great scars in the earth show the work of the past. Here in a clearing upon the green slope of a hill stood a long, low stone house, approached by a curving drive running through the fields. Nearer the road, and surrounded on three sides by bushes, was a small outhouse, one window and the door facing in our direction. It was the scene of the murder.

Stanley Hopkins led us first to the house, where he introduced us to a haggard, grey-haired woman, the widow of the murdered man, whose gaunt and deep-lined face, with the furtive look of terror in the depths of her red-rimmed eyes, told of the years of hardship and ill-usage which she had endured. With her was her daughter, a pale, fair-haired girl, whose eyes blazed defiantly at us as she told us that she was glad that her father was dead, and that she blessed the hand which had struck him down. It was a terrible household that Black Peter Carey had made for himself, and it was with a sense of relief that we found ourselves in the sunlight again and making our way along the path which had been worn across the fields by the feet of the dead man.

The outhouse was the simplest of dwellings, wooden-walled, single-roofed, one window beside the door, and one on the farther side. Stanley Hopkins drew the key from his pocket, and had stooped to the lock, when he paused with a look of attention and surprise upon his face.

"Someone has been tampering with it," he said.

There could be no doubt of the fact. The woodwork was cut, and the scratches showed white through the paint, as if they had been that instant done. Holmes had been examining the window.

"Someone has tried to force this also. Whoever it was has failed to make his way in. He must have been a very poor burglar."

"This is a most extraordinary thing," said the Inspector; "I could swear that these marks were not here yesterday evening."

"Some curious person from the village, perhaps," I suggested.

"Very unlikely. Few of them would dare to set foot in the grounds, far less try to force their way into the cabin. What do you think of it, Mr. Holmes?"

"I think that fortune is very kind to us."

"You mean that the person will come again?"

"It is very probable. He came expecting to find the door open. He tried to get in with the blade of a very small penknife. He could not manage it. What would he do?"

"Come again next night with a more useful tool."

"So I should say. It will be our fault if we are not

there to receive him. Meanwhile, let me see the inside of the cabin."

The traces of the tragedy had been removed, but the furniture of the little room still stood as it had been on the night of the crime. For two hours, with the most intense concentration, Holmes examined every object in turn, but his face showed that his quest was not a successful one. Once only he paused in his patient investigation.

"Have you taken anything off this shelf, Hopkins?"

"No; I have moved nothing."

"Something has been taken. There is less dust in this corner of the shelf than elsewhere. It may have been a book lying on its side. It may have been a box. Well, well, I can do nothing more. Let us walk in these beautiful woods, Watson, and give a few hours to the birds and the flowers. We shall meet you here later, Hopkins, and see if we can come to closer quarters with the gentleman who has paid this visit in the night."

It was past eleven o'clock when we formed our little ambuscade. Hopkins was for leaving the door of the hut open, but Holmes was of opinion that this would rouse the suspicions of the stranger. The lock was a perfectly simple one, and only a strong blade was needed to push it back. Holmes also suggested that we should wait, not inside the hut, but outside it among the bushes which grew round the farther window. In this way we should be able to watch our man if he struck a light, and see what his object was in this stealthy nocturnal visit.

It was a long and melancholy vigil, and yet it brought with it something of the thrill which the hunter feels when he lies beside the water-pool and waits for the coming of the thirsty beast of prey. What savage creature was it which might steal upon us out of the darkness? Was it a fierce tiger of crime, which could only be taken fighting hard with flashing fang and claw, or would it prove to be some skulking jackal, dangerous only to the weak and unguarded? In absolute silence we crouched amongst the bushes, waiting for whatever might come. At first the steps of a few belated villagers, or the sound of voices from the village, lightened our vigil; but one by one these interruptions died away, and an absolute stillness fell upon us, save for the chimes of the distant church, which told us of the progress of the night, and for the rustle and whisper of a fine rain falling amid the foliage which roofed us in.

Half-past two had chimed, and it was the darkest hour which precedes the dawn, when we all started as a low but sharp click came from the direction of the gate. Someone had entered the drive. Again there was a long silence, and I had begun to fear that it was a false alarm, when a stealthy step was heard upon the other side of the hut, and a moment later a metallic scraping and clicking. The man was trying to force the lock! This time his skill was greater or his tool was better, for there was a sudden snap and the creak of the hinges. Then a match was struck, and next instant the steady light from a candle filled the interior of the hut. Through the gauze curtain our eyes were all riveted upon the scene within.

. . . HOLMES EXAMINED EVERY OBJECT IN TURN . . .

Cover illustration by Frederic Dorr Steele for *Collier's Magazine*, February 27, 1904.

HE SANK DOWN UPON THE SEA-CHEST . . .

Illustration by Sidney Paget for the *Strand Magazine*, March, 1904.

The nocturnal visitor was a young man, frail and thin, with black moustache which intensified the deadly pallor of his face. He could not have been much above twenty years of age. I have never seen any human being who appeared to be in such a pitiable fright, for his teeth were visibly chattering, and he was shaking in every limb. He was dressed like a gentleman, in Norfolk jacket and knickerbockers, with a cloth cap upon his head. We watched him staring round with frightened eyes. Then he laid the candle-end upon the table and disappeared from our view into one of the corners. He returned with a large book, one of the log-books which formed a line upon the shelves. Leaning on the table, he rapidly turned over the leaves of this volume until he came to the entry which he sought. Then, with an angry gesture of his clenched hand, he closed the book, replaced it in the corner, and put out the light. He had hardly turned to leave the hut when Hopkins' hand was on the fellow's collar, and I heard his loud gasp of terror as he understood that he was taken. The candle was relit, and there was our wretched captive shivering and cowering in the grasp of the detective. He sank down upon the sea-chest, and looked helplessly from one of us to the other.

" Now, my fine fellow," said Stanley Hopkins, " who are you, and what do you want here ? "

The man pulled himself together and faced us with an effort at self-composure.

" You are detectives, I suppose ? " said he. " You imagine I am connected with the death of Captain Peter Carey. I assure you that I am innocent."

" We'll see about that," said Hopkins. " First of all, what is your name ? "

" It is John Hopley Neligan."

I saw Holmes and Hopkins exchange a quick glance.

" What are you doing here ? "

" Can I speak confidentially ? "

" No, certainly not."

" Why should I tell you ? "

" If you have no answer it may go badly with you at the trial."

The young man winced.

" Well, I will tell you," he said. " Why should I not ? And yet I hate to think of this old scandal gaining a new lease of life. Did you ever hear of Dawson & Neligan ? "

I could see from Hopkins' face that he never had ; but Holmes was keenly interested.

" You mean the West Country bankers," said he. " They failed for a million, ruined half the county families of Cornwall, and Neligan disappeared."

" Exactly. Neligan was my father."

At last we were getting something positive, and yet it seemed a long gap between an absconding banker and Captain Peter Carey pinned against the wall with one of his own harpoons. We all listened intently to the young man's words.

" It was my father who was really concerned. Dawson had retired. I was only ten years of age at the time, but I

was old enough to feel the shame and horror of it all. It has always been said that my father stole all the securities and fled. It is not true. It was his belief that if he were given time in which to realize them all would be well, and
every creditor paid in full. He started in his little yacht 9
for Norway just before the warrant was issued for his arrest. I can remember that last night when he bade farewell to my mother. He left us a list of the securities he was taking, and he swore that he would come back with his honour cleared, and that none who had trusted him would suffer. Well, no word was ever heard from him again. Both the yacht and he vanished utterly. We believed, my mother and I, that he and it, with the securities that he had taken with him, were at the bottom of the sea. We had a faithful friend, however, who is a business man, and it was he who discovered some time ago that some of the securities which my father had with him have reappeared on the London market. You can imagine our amazement. I spent months in trying to trace them, and at last, after many doublings and difficulties, I discovered that the original seller had been Captain Peter Carey, the owner of this hut.

" Naturally I made some inquiries about the man. I found that he had been in command of a whaler which was due to return from the Arctic seas at the very time when my father was crossing to Norway. The autumn of that year was a stormy one, and there was a long succession of southerly gales. My father's yacht may well have been blown to the north, and there met by Captain Peter Carey's ship. If that were so, what had become of my father ? In any case, if I could prove from Peter Carey's evidence how these securities came on the market, it would be a proof that my father had not sold them, and that he had no view to personal profit when he took them.

" I came down to Sussex with the intention of seeing the captain, but it was at this moment that his terrible death occurred. I read at the inquest a description of his cabin, in which it stated that the old log-books of his vessel were preserved in it. It struck me that if I could see what occurred in the month of August, 1883, on board the *Sea Unicorn*, I might settle the mystery of my father's fate. I tried last night to get at these log-books, but was unable to open the door. To-night I tried again, and succeeded ; but I find that the pages which deal with that month have been torn from the book. It was at that moment I found myself a prisoner in your hands."

" Is that all ? " asked Hopkins.

" Yes, that is all." His eyes shifted as he said it.

" You have nothing else to tell us ? "

He hesitated.

" No ; there is nothing."

" You have not been here before last night ? "

" No."

" Then how do you account for *that* ? " cried Hopkins, as he held up the damning notebook, with the initials of our prisoner on the first leaf, and the blood-stain on the cover.

The wretched man collapsed. He sank his face in his hands and trembled all over.

9 *and every creditor paid in full.* "What I do not quite grasp is what the Receiver in Bankruptcy of the defunct banking firm of Dawson and Neligan had been doing all these years?" Mr. Humfrey Michell wrote in a "Letter to Baker Street." "It would have been a simple matter for him to obtain the record of the missing securities from the family and take the appropriate steps to obtain title to them for the benefit of the creditors. The only explanation I can think of, and I admit it is very improbable, is that young Neligan was a liar and was after something else than share certificates. If so, he was a very successful one, because he bamboozled Sherlock Holmes."

" Where did you get it ? " he groaned. " I did not know. I thought I had lost it at the hotel."

" That is enough," said Hopkins sternly. " Whatever else you have to say you must say in court. You will walk down with me now to the police-station. Well, Mr. Holmes, I am very much obliged to you and to your friend for coming down to help me. As it turns out your presence was unnecessary, and I would have brought the case to this successful issue without you ; but none the less I am very grateful. Rooms have been reserved for you at the Brambletye Hotel, so we can all walk down to the village together."

" Well, Watson, what do you think of it ? " asked Holmes as we travelled back next morning.

" I can see that you are not satisfied."

" Oh, yes, my dear Watson, I am perfectly satisfied. At the same time Stanley Hopkins' methods do not commend themselves to me. I am disappointed in Stanley Hopkins. I had hoped for better things from him. One should always look for a possible alternative and provide against it. It is the first rule of criminal investigation."

" What, then, is the alternative ? "

" The line of investigation which I have myself been pursuing. It may give nothing. I cannot tell. But at least I shall follow it to the end."

Several letters were waiting for Holmes at Baker Street. He snatched one of them up, opened it, and burst out into a triumphant chuckle of laughter.

" Excellent, Watson. The alternative develops. Have you telegraph forms ? Just write a couple of messages for me : ' Sumner, Shipping Agent, Ratcliff Highway. Send three men on, to arrive ten to-morrow morning.—Basil.' That's my name in those parts. The other is ' Inspector Stanley Hopkins, 46 Lord Street, Brixton. Come breakfast to-morrow at nine-thirty. Important. Wire if unable to come.—Sherlock Holmes.' There, Watson, this infernal case had haunted me for ten days. I hereby banish it completely from my presence. To-morrow I trust that we shall hear the last of it for ever."

Sharp at the hour named Inspector Stanley Hopkins appeared, and we sat down together to the excellent breakfast which Mrs. Hudson had prepared. The young detective was in high spirits at his success.

" You really think that your solution must be correct ? " asked Holmes.

" I could not imagine a more complete case."

" It did not seem to me conclusive."

" You astonish me, Mr. Holmes. What more could one ask for ? "

" Does your explanation cover every point ? "

" Undoubtedly. I find that young Neligan arrived at the Brambletye Hotel on the very day of the crime. He came on the pretence of playing golf. His room was on the ground floor, and he could get out when he liked. That very night he went down to Woodman's Lee, saw Peter Carey at the hut, quarrelled with him, and killed him with the harpoon. Then, horrified by what he had done, he fled out of the hut, dropping the notebook which he had brought with him in order to question Peter Carey about these different securities. You may have observed that some of them were marked with ticks, and the others—the great majority—were not. Those which are ticked have been traced on the London market ; but the others presumably were still in the possession of Carey, and young Neligan, according to his own account, was anxious to recover them in order to do the right thing by his father's creditors. After his flight he did not dare to approach the hut again for some time ; but at last he forced himself to do so in order to obtain the information which he needed. Surely that is all simple and obvious ? "

Holmes smiled and shook his head.

" It seems to me to have only one drawback, Hopkins, and that is that it is intrinsically impossible. Have you tried to drive a harpoon through a body ? No ? Tut, tut, my dear sir, you must really pay attention to these details. My friend Watson could tell you that I spent a whole morning in that exercise. It is no easy matter, and requires a strong and practised arm. But this blow was delivered with such violence that the head of the weapon sank deep into the wall. Do you imagine that this anæmic youth was capable of so frightful an assault ? Is he the man who hob-nobbed in rum and water with Black Peter in the dead of the night ? Was it his profile that was seen on the blind two nights before ? No, no, Hopkins ; it is another and a more formidable person for whom we must seek."

The detective's face had grown longer and longer during Holmes' speech. His hopes and his ambitions were all crumbling about him. But he would not abandon his position without a struggle.

" You can't deny that Neligan was present that night, Mr. Holmes. The book will prove that. I fancy that I have evidence enough to satisfy a jury, even if you are able to pick a hole in it. Besides, Mr. Holmes, I have laid my hand upon *my* man. As to this terrible person of yours, where is he ? "

" I rather fancy that he is on the stair," said Holmes serenely. " I think, Watson, that you would do well to put that revolver where you can reach it." He rose, and laid a written paper upon a side-table. " Now we are ready," said he.

There had been some talking in gruff voices outside, and now Mrs. Hudson opened the door to say that there were three men inquiring for Captain Basil.

" Show them in one by one," said Holmes.

The first who entered was a little ribston-pippin of a **10**
man, with ruddy cheeks and fluffy white side-whiskers. Holmes had drawn a letter from his pocket.

" What name ? " he asked.

" James Lancaster."

" I am sorry, Lancaster, but the berth is full. Here is half a sovereign for your trouble. Just step into this
room and wait there for a few minutes." **11**

The second man was a long, dried-up creature, with lank hair and sallow cheeks. His name was Hugh

10 *ribston-pippin.* A variety of apple.

11 *this room.* Holmes' bedroom.

"SHALL I SIGN HERE?" HE ASKED . . .

Illustration by Sidney Paget for the *Strand Magazine*, March, 1904.

Pattins. He also received his dismissal, his half-sovereign, and the order to wait.

The third applicant was a man of remarkable appearance. A fierce, bull-dog face was framed in a tangle of hair and beard, and two bold dark eyes gleamed behind the cover of thick, tufted, overhung eyebrows. He saluted and stood sailor-fashion, turning his cap round in his hands.

" Your name ? " asked Holmes.

" Patrick Cairns."

" Harpooner ? "

" Yes, sir. Twenty-six voyages."

" Dundee, I suppose ? "

" Yes, sir."

" And ready to start with an exploring ship ? "

" Yes, sir."

" What wages ? "

" Eight pounds a month."

" Could you start at once ? "

" As soon as I get my kit."

" Have you your papers ? "

" Yes, sir." He took a sheaf of worn and greasy forms from his pocket. Holmes glanced over them and returned them.

" You are just the man I want," said he. " Here's the agreement on the side-table. If you sign it the whole matter will be settled."

The seaman lurched across the room and took up the pen.

" Shall I sign here ? " he asked, stooping over the table.

Holmes leaned over his shoulder and passed both hands over his neck.

" This will do," said he.

I heard a click of steel and a bellow like an enraged bull. The next instant Holmes and the seaman were rolling on the ground together. He was a man of such gigantic strength that, even with the handcuffs which Holmes had so deftly fastened upon his wrists, he would have quickly overpowered my friend had Hopkins and I not rushed to his rescue. Only when I pressed the cold muzzle of the revolver to his temple did he at last understand that resistance was vain. We lashed his ankles with cord and rose breathless from the struggle.

" I must really apologize, Hopkins," said Sherlock Holmes ; " I fear that the scrambled eggs are cold. However, you will enjoy the rest of your breakfast all the better, will you not, for the thought that you have brought your case to a triumphant conclusion ? "

Stanley Hopkins was speechless with amazement.

" I don't know what to say, Mr. Holmes," he blurted out at last, with a very red face. " It seems to me that I have been making a fool of myself from the beginning. I understand now, what I should never have forgotten, that I am the pupil and you are the master. Even now I see what you have done, but I don't know how you did it, or what it signifies."

" Well, well," said Holmes good-humouredly. " We all learn by experience, and your lesson this time is that you should never lose sight of the alternative. You were so absorbed in young Neligan that you could not spare a thought to Patrick Cairns, the true murderer of Peter Carey."

The hoarse voice of the seaman broke in on our conversation.

" See here, mister," said he, " I make no complaint of being man-handled in this fashion, but I would have you call things by their right names. You say I murdered Peter Carey ; I say I *killed* Peter Carey, and there's all the difference. Maybe you don't believe what I say. Maybe you think I am just slinging you a yarn."

" Not at all," said Holmes. " Let us hear what you have to say."

" It's soon told, and, by the Lord, every word of it is truth. I knew Black Peter, and when he pulled out his knife I whipped a harpoon through him sharp, for I knew that it was him or me. That's how he died. You can call it murder. Anyhow, I'd as soon die with a rope round my neck as with Black Peter's knife in my heart."

" How came you there ? " asked Holmes.

" I'll tell it you from the beginning. Just sit me up a little so as I can speak easy. It was in '83 that it happened—August of that year. Peter Carey was master of the *Sea Unicorn*, and I was spare harpooner. We were coming out of the ice-pack on our way home, with head winds and a week's southerly gale, when we picked up a little craft that had been blown north. There was one man on her—a landsman. The crew had thought she would founder, and had made for the Norwegian coast in the dinghy. I guess they were all drowned. Well, we took him on board, this man, and he and the skipper had some long talks in the cabin. All the baggage we took off with him was one tin box. So far as I know the man's name was never mentioned, and on the second night he disappeared as if he had never been. It was given out that he had either thrown himself overboard or fallen overboard in the heavy weather that we were having. Only one man knew what had happened to him, and that was me, for with my own eyes I saw the skipper tip up his heels and put him over the rail in the middle watch of a dark night, two days before we sighted the Shetland lights.

" Well, I kept my knowledge to myself and waited to see what would come of it. When we got back to Scotland it was easily hushed up, and nobody asked any questions. A stranger died by an accident, and it was nobody's business to inquire. Shortly after Peter Carey gave up the sea, and it was long years before I could find where he was. I guessed that he had done the deed for the sake of what was in that tin box, and that he could afford now to pay me well for keeping my mouth shut.

" I found out where he was through a sailor man that had met him in London, and down I went to squeeze him. The first night he was reasonable enough, and was ready to give me what would make me free of the sea for life. We were to fix it all two nights later. When I came I found him three-parts drunk and in a vile temper. We sat down and we drank and we yarned about old times, but the more he drank the less I liked the look on his face. I spotted that harpoon upon the wall, and I thought I

"WE SAT DOWN AND WE DRANK AND WE YARNED ABOUT OLD TIMES . . ."

Illustration by Sidney Paget for the *Strand Magazine*, March, 1904.

might need it before I was through. Then at last he broke out at me, spitting and cursing, with murder in his eyes and a great clasp-knife in his hand. He had not time to get it from the sheath before I had the harpoon through him. Heavens ! what a yell he gave ; and his face gets between me and my sleep ! I stood there, with his blood splashing round me, and I waited for a bit ; but all was quiet, so I took heart once more. I looked round, and there was the tin box on a shelf. I had as much right to it as Peter Carey, anyhow, so I took it with me and left the hut. Like a fool I left my baccy-pouch upon the table.

" Now I'll tell you the queerest part of the whole story. I had hardly got outside the hut when I heard someone coming, and I hid among the bushes. A man came slinking along, went into the hut, gave a cry as if he had seen a ghost, and legged it as hard as he could run until he was out of sight. Who he was or what he wanted is more than I can tell. For my part, I walked ten miles, got a train at Tunbridge Wells, and so reached London, and no one the wiser.

" Well, when I came to examine the box I found there was no money in it, and nothing but papers that I would not dare to sell. I had lost my hold on Black Peter, and was stranded in London without a shilling. There was only my trade left. I saw these advertisements about harpooners and high wages, so I went to the shipping agents, and they sent me here. That's all I know, and I say again that if I killed Black Peter the law should give me thanks, for I saved them the price of a hempen rope."

" A very clear statement," said Holmes, rising and lighting his pipe. " I think, Hopkins, that you should lose no time in conveying your prisoner to a place of safety. This room is not well adapted for a cell, and Mr. Patrick Cairns occupies too large a portion of our carpet."

" Mr. Holmes," said Hopkins, " I do not know how to express my gratitude. Even now I do not understand how you attained this result."

" Simply by having the good fortune to get the right clue from the beginning. It is very possible that if I had known about this notebook it might have led away my thoughts, as it did yours. But all I heard pointed in the one direction. The amazing strength, the skill in the use of the harpoon, the rum and water, the sealskin tobacco-pouch, with the coarse tobacco—all these pointed to a seaman, and one who had been a whaler. I was convinced that the initials ' P. C.' upon the pouch were a coincidence, and not those of Peter Carey, since he seldom smoked, and no pipe was found in his cabin. You remember that I asked whether whisky and brandy were in the cabin. You said they were. How many landsmen are there who would drink rum when they could get these other spirits ? Yes, I was certain it was a seaman."

" And how did you find him ? "

" My dear sir, the problem had become a very simple one. If it were a seaman, it could only be a seaman who

had been with him on the *Sea Unicorn.* So far as I could learn, he had sailed in no other ship. I spent three days in wiring to Dundee, and at the end of that time I had 12
ascertained the names of the crew of the *Sea Unicorn* in 1883. When I found Patrick Cairns among the harpooners my research was nearing its end. I argued that the man was probably in London, and that he would desire to leave the country for a time. I therefore spent some days in the East End, devised an Arctic expedition, put forward tempting terms for harpooners who would serve under Captain Basil—and behold the result!"

"Wonderful!" cried Hopkins. "Wonderful!"

"You must obtain the release of young Neligan as soon as possible," said Holmes. "I confess that I think you owe him some apology. The tin box must be returned to him, but, of course, the securities which Peter Carey has sold are lost for ever. There's the cab, Hopkins, and you can remove your man. If you want me for the trial, my address and that of Watson will be somewhere in Norway—I'll send particulars later."

12 *I spent three days in wiring to Dundee.* ". . . since there was a telephone across the road [*The Sign of the Four*], it would have been simpler to call Hopkins at the Brixton Police Station [rather than to telegraph him to come to breakfast], and should he have been absent, the police would have delivered the message and forwarded his reply at once," Colonel E. Ennalls Berl wrote in "Sherlock Holmes and the Telephone." "But, worst of all, Holmes 'spent three days in wiring to Dundee' to get crew lists of the *Sea Unicorn* when it seems almost certain that a much shorter telephone struggle through the Dundee police would have given him the information."

Or, as the late Fletcher Pratt suggested in "Holmes and the Royal Navy," "Admiralty records would have supplied the necessary information in the matter . . . without the necessity of Holmes spending three days in wiring to Dundee."

54

THE ADVENTURE OF THE NORWOOD BUILDER

[Tuesday, August 20, to Wednesday, August 21, 1895]

"FROM the point of view of the criminal expert," said Mr. Sherlock Holmes, "London has become a singularly uninteresting city since the death of the late lamented Professor Moriarty."

"I can hardly think that you would find many decent citizens to agree with you," I answered.

"Well, well, I must not be selfish," said he, with a smile, as he pushed back his chair from the breakfast-table. "The community is certainly the gainer, and no one the loser, save the poor out-of-work specialist, whose occupation has gone. With that man in the field one's morning paper presented infinite possibilities. Often it was only the smallest trace, Watson, the faintest indication, and yet it was enough to tell me that the great malignant brain was there, as the gentlest tremors of the edges of the web remind one of the foul spider which lurks in the centre. Petty thefts, wanton assaults, purposeless outrage—to the man who held the clue all could be worked into one connected whole. To the scientific student of the higher criminal world no capital in Europe offered the advantages which London then possessed. But now——" He shrugged his shoulders in humorous deprecation of the state of things which he had himself done so much to produce.

At the time of which I speak, Holmes had been back for
1 some months, and I, at his request, had sold my practice and returned to share the old quarters in Baker Street. A young doctor, named Verner, had purchased my small Kensington practice, and given with astonishingly little demur the highest price that I ventured to ask—an incident which only explained itself some years later, when I found that Verner was a distant relation of Holmes', and that it was my friend who had really found the
2 money.

Our months of partnership had not been so uneventful as he had stated, for I find, on looking over my notes, that this period includes the case of the papers of ex-President Murillo, and also the shocking affair of the Dutch steamship, *Friesland*, which so nearly cost us both
3 our lives. His cold and proud nature was always averse, however, to anything in the shape of public applause, and he bound me in the most stringent terms to say no further

1 *some months.* We soon learn that the month was August (Holmes "crawled about the lawn with an August sun" on his back), the weather had been "very warm these past few days" and there had been no rain for some days: "This drought has made everything as hard as iron." Watson can not mean 1894: there was no period in the August of that year in which the weather was both dry and hot. In August, 1895, on the other hand, there was no rain from Wednesday, August 14 (when there was a meager 0.01 inches), to Tuesday, August 22. From Tuesday, August 13, when the maximum temperature was 64.8°, it rose steadily to a high of 82.2° on Monday, August 19th. But the case did not open on a Monday: Mr. John Hector McFarlane "was very surprised . . . when yesterday, about three o'clock in the afternoon" Mr. Jonas Oldacre "walked into my office in the City." We believe that the case took place on *Tuesday, August 20, and Wednesday, August 21, 1895.* The selection of 1895 over 1894 is strengthened by the fact that Watson did not include "The Adventure of the Norwood Builder" in his list of important cases of 1894 ("The Adventure of the Golden Pince-Nez").

2 *it was my friend who had really found the money.* "The connection between the younger doctor and that grandmother [of Holmes] who was the sister of Vernet is obvious," Mr. Vincent Starrett wrote in *The Private Life of Sherlock Holmes.* "Verner would be the English form of Vernet, or a corruption of the French name after a year or so in England. And Dr. Verner would be a cousin of the detective, twice or thrice removed."

"Since the money for the purchase was provided by Holmes who, unworldly as he was in the matter of payment for his services, could certainly at this period command high fees when he chose, we may assume that it was not less than Watson had given in the first place, i.e., about £1,000 [$5,000]," Miss Helen Simpson wrote in "Medical Career and Capacities of Dr. J. H. Watson."

word of himself, his methods, or his successes—a prohibition which, as I have explained, has only now been removed.

Mr. Sherlock Holmes was leaning back in his chair after his whimsical protest, and was unfolding his morning paper in a leisurely fashion, when our attention was arrested by a tremendous ring at the bell, followed immediately by a hollow drumming sound, as if someone were beating on the outer door with his fist. As it opened there came a tumultuous rush into the hall, rapid feet clattered up the stair, and an instant later a wild-eyed and frantic young man, pale, dishevelled, and palpitating, burst into the room. He looked from one to the other of us, and under our gaze of inquiry he became conscious that some apology was needed for this unceremonious entry.

" I'm sorry, Mr. Holmes," he cried. " You mustn't blame me. I am nearly mad. Mr. Holmes, I am the unhappy John Hector McFarlane."

He made the announcement as if the name alone would explain both his visit and its manner, but I could see by my companion's unresponsive face that it meant no more to him than to me.

" Have a cigarette, Mr. McFarlane," said he, pushing his case across. " I am sure that with your symptoms my friend Dr. Watson here would prescribe a sedative. The weather has been so very warm these last few days. Now, if you feel a little more composed, I should be glad if you would sit down in that chair and tell us very slowly and quietly who you are and what it is that you want. You mentioned your name as if I should recognize it, but I assure you that, beyond obvious facts that you are a bachelor, a solicitor, a Freemason, and an asthmatic, I know nothing whatever about you."

Familiar as I was with my friend's methods, it was not difficult for me to follow his deductions, and to observe the untidiness of attire, the sheaf of legal papers, the watch-charm, and the breathing which had prompted them. Our client, however, stared in amazement.

" Yes, I am all that, Mr. Holmes, and in addition I am the most unfortunate man at this moment in London. For Heaven's sake don't abandon me, Mr. Holmes! If they come to arrest me before I have finished my story, make them give me time, so that I may tell you the whole truth. I could go to gaol happy if I knew that you were working for me outside."

" Arrest you ! " said Holmes. " This is really most grati—most interesting. On what charge do you expect to be arrested ? "

" Upon the charge of murdering Mr. Jonas Oldacre, of Lower Norwood."

My companion's expressive face showed a sympathy which was not, I am afraid, unmixed with satisfaction.

The reader interested in the later career of young Dr. Verner is recommended to Mr. Anthony Boucher's "The Anomoly of the Empty Man," in his collection *Far and Away* (New York: Ballantine Books, 1953).

3 *which so nearly cost us both our lives.* The *Friesland*, a real ship, was located by Mr. Richard W. Clarke ("On the Nomenclature of Watson's Ships") "under Belgian rather than French registry." The late Christopher Morley, who crossed in her on one of her later voyages, Philadelphia to Liverpool, September, 1910, described her as "a beauty, a smart little Red Star liner."

Mr. Ray Kierman, noting that it was "the SS *Friesland*, a Dutch-American liner," which sighted Professor Challenger's pterodactyl when it escaped from the Queen's Hall (*The Lost World*) suggested, in "A Shocking Affair," that Holmes and Watson, retained by Challenger, had chartered the steamship and "placed the vessel in the very path [Holmes'] matchless brain told him the beast would pursue [on its flight back to Maple White Land]. . . . There seems no doubt that Holmes lured the monster to the very decks of the vessel, and there . . . fought it out. . . . There seems little doubt, either, that Watson, in the nick of time, when the pterodactyl had Holmes down for the last prod of its vile and lethal beak, stepped forward and sent a bullet through the brainless skull of the creature . . ."

But Mr. T. S. Blakeney objected ("Some Disjecta Membra") that: "Unfortunately, the dates do not appear to agree. Holmes' affair on the *Friesland* was after The Return and before 'The Adventure of the Norwood Builder' [which Mr. Blakeney places in August, 1894], and this would give us Spring/Summer of 1894. This was not the time of year when Challenger's pterodactyl left England; Malone gives the date as November 7th/8th, though closer examination makes it clear that the month could not have been earlier than December. The year of *The Lost World* would seem to be 1906 . . ."

. . . A WILD-EYED AND FRANTIC YOUNG MAN, PALE, DISHEVELLED, AND PALPITATING, BURST INTO THE ROOM.

Illustration by Sidney Paget for the *Strand Magazine*, November, 1903.

" Dear me ! " said he ; " it was only this moment at breakfast that I was saying to my friend, Dr. Watson, that sensational cases had disappeared out of our papers."

Our visitor stretched forward a quivering hand and picked up the *Daily Telegraph*, which still lay upon Holmes' knee.

" If you had looked at it, sir, you would have seen at a glance what the errand is on which I have come to you this morning. I feel as if my name and my misfortune must be in every man's mouth." He turned it over to expose the central page. " Here it is, and with your permission I will read it to you. Listen to this, Mr. Holmes. The headlines are : 'Mysterious affair at Lower Norwood. Disappearance of a Well-known Builder. Suspicion of Murder and Arson. A Clue to the Criminal.' That is the clue which they are already following, Mr. Holmes, and I know that it leads infallibly to me. I have been followed from London Bridge Station, and I am sure that they are only waiting for the warrant to arrest me. It will break my mother's heart—it will break her heart ! " He wrung his hands in an agony of apprehension, and swayed backwards and forwards in his chair.

"I HAVE BEEN FOLLOWED FROM LONDON BRIDGE STATION . . ."

The approach to London Bridge Station, in a photograph taken about 1880. From Michael Harrison's *In the Footsteps of Sherlock Holmes.*

I looked with interest upon this man, who was accused of being the perpetrator of a crime of violence. He was flaxen-haired and handsome in a washed-out negative fashion, with frightened blue eyes and a clean-shaven face, with a weak, sensitive mouth. His age may have been about twenty-seven ; his dress and bearing, that of a gentleman. From the pocket of his light summer overcoat protruded the bundle of endorsed papers which proclaimed his profession.

" We must use what time we have," said Holmes. " Watson, would you have the kindness to take the paper and to read me the paragraph in question ? "

Underneath the vigorous headlines which our client had quoted I read the following suggestive narrative :

4 Late last night, or early this morning, an incident occurred at Lower Norwood which points, it is feared, to a serious crime. Mr. Jonas Oldacre is a well-known resident of that suburb, where he has carried on his business as a builder for many years. Mr. Oldacre is a bachelor, fifty-two years of age, and lives in Deep Dene House, at the Sydenham end of the road of that name. He has had the reputation of being a man of eccentric habits, secretive and retiring. For some years he has practically withdrawn from the business, in which he is said to have amassed considerable wealth. A small timber-yard still exists, however, at the back of the house, and last night, about twelve o'clock, an alarm was given that one of the stacks was on fire. The engines were soon upon the spot, but the dry wood burned with great fury, and it was impossible to arrest the conflagration until the stack had been entirely consumed. Up to this point the incident bore the appearance of an ordinary accident, but fresh indications seem to point to serious crime. Surprise was expressed at the absence of the master of the establishment from the scene of the fire, and an inquiry followed which showed that he had disappeared from the house. An examination of his room revealed that the bed had not been slept in, that a safe which stood in it was open, that a number of important papers were scattered about the room, and, finally, that there were signs of a murderous struggle, slight traces of blood being found within the room,

4 *Late last night, or early this morning.* "Now this really was swift work in the *Telegraph* office," Mr. John Hyslop wrote in "Sherlock Holmes and the Press." "The murder took place, said the newspaper, last night or in the early morning. Yet here was the *Telegraph* with a full story . . ."

and an oaken walking-stick which also showed stains of blood upon the handle. It is known that Mr. Jonas Oldacre had received a late visitor in his bedroom upon that night, and the stick found has been identified as the property of this person, who is a young London solicitor named John Hector McFarlane, junior partner of Graham & McFarlane, of 426 Gresham Buildings, E.C. The police believe that they have evidence in their possession which supplies a very convincing motive for the crime, and altogether it cannot be doubted that sensational developments will follow.

Later.—It is rumoured as we go to press that Mr. John Hector McFarlane has actually been arrested on the charge of the murder of Mr. Jonas Oldacre. It is at least certain that a warrant has been issued. There have been further and sinister developments in the investigation at Norwood. Besides the signs of a struggle in the room of the unfortunate builder, it is now known that the French windows of his bedroom (which is on the ground floor) were found to be open, that there were marks as if some bulky object had been dragged across to the wood-pile, and, finally, it is asserted that charred remains have been found among the charcoal ashes of the fire The police theory is that a most sensational crime has been committed, that the victim was clubbed to death in his own bedroom, his papers rifled, and his dead body dragged across to the wood-stack, which was then ignited so as to hide all traces of the crime. The conduct of the criminal investigation has been left in the experienced hands of Inspector Lestrade, of Scotland Yard, who is following up the clues with his accustomed energy and sagacity.

Sherlock Holmes listened with closed eyes and finger-tips together to this remarkable account.

" The case has certainly some points of interest," said he, in his languid fashion. " May I ask, in the first place, Mr. McFarlane, how it is that you are still at liberty, since there appears to be enough evidence to justify your arrest ? "

" I live at Torrington Lodge, Blackheath, with my **5**
parents, Mr. Holmes ; but last night, having to do business very late with Mr. Jonas Oldacre, I stayed at an
hotel in Norwood, and came to my business from there. **6**
I knew nothing of this affair until I was in the train, when I read what you have just heard. I at once saw the horrible danger of my position, and I hurried to put the case into your hands. I have no doubt that I should have been arrested either at my City office or at my home. A man followed me from London Bridge Station, and I have no doubt—— Great heaven, what is that ? "

It was a clang of the bell, followed instantly by heavy steps upon the stair. A moment later our old friend Lestrade appeared in the doorway. Over his shoulder I caught a glimpse of one or two uniformed policemen outside.

" Mr. John Hector McFarlane," said Lestrade.

Our unfortunate client rose with a ghastly face.

" I arrest you for the wilful murder of Mr. Jonas Oldacre, of Lower Norwood."

McFarlane turned to us with a gesture of despair, and sank into his chair once more like one who is crushed.

" One moment, Lestrade," said Holmes. " Half an hour more or less can make no difference to you, and the gentleman was about to give us an account of this very interesting affair, which might aid us in clearing it up."

" I think there will be no difficulty in clearing it up,"

5 *Blackheath.* In Lewisham, Blackheath is one of the most agreeable of the London suburbs. Blackheath Common, comprising 267 acres, is known as the place where Wat Tyler in 1381 and Jack Cade in 1450 marshaled their hosts; here, too, once took place many highway robberies; here, too, the game of golf was introduced to an unappreciative London public by James I.

6 *and came to my business from there.* "It has always bothered me," the late Christopher Morley wrote, "why could not the unhappy John Hector McFarlane get back from Lower Norwood to Blackheath that night? It was 'between eleven and twelve' when he and Jonas Oldacre finished their business. Young McFarlane said that it was so late he couldn't get back to Blackheath. . . . He could certainly have got back to Blackheath that night if he had really wanted to. It was only four miles if he wanted to walk."

"MR. JOHN HECTOR MCFARLANE," SAID LESTRADE.

Illustration by Frederic Dorr Steele for *Collier's Magazine*, October 31, 1903.

said Lestrade grimly.

"None the less, with your permission, I should be much interested to hear his account."

"Well, Mr. Holmes, it is difficult for me to refuse you anything, for you have been of use to the Force once or twice in the past, and we owe you a good turn at Scotland Yard," said Lestrade. "At the same time, I must remain with my prisoner, and I am bound to warn him that anything he may say will appear in evidence against him."

"I wish nothing better," said our client. "All I ask is that you should hear and recognize the absolute truth."

Lestrade looked at his watch. "I'll give you half an hour," said he.

"I must explain first," said McFarlane, "that I knew nothing of Mr. Jonas Oldacre. His name was familiar to me; for many years ago my parents were acquainted with him, but they drifted apart. I was very much surprised, therefore, when yesterday, about three o'clock in the afternoon, he walked into my office in the City. But I was still more astonished when he told me the object of his visit. He had in his hand several sheets of a note-book, covered with scribbled writing—here they are—and he laid them on my table.

"'Here is my will,' said he. 'I want you, Mr. McFarlane, to cast it into proper legal shape. I will sit here while you do so.'

"I set myself to copy it, and you can imagine my astonishment when I found that, with some reservations, he had left all his property to me. He was a strange, little, ferret-like man, with white eyelashes, and when I looked up at him I found his keen grey eyes fixed upon me with an amused expression. I could hardly believe my own senses as I read the terms of the will; but he explained that he was a bachelor with hardly any living relation, that he had known my parents in his youth, and that he had always heard of me as a very deserving young man, and was assured that his money would be in worthy hands. Of course, I could only stammer out my thanks. The will was duly finished, signed, and witnessed by my clerk. This is it on the blue paper, and
7 these slips, as I have explained, are the rough draft. Mr. Jonas Oldacre then informed me that there were a number of documents—building leases, title-deeds, mortgages, scrip, and so forth—which it was necessary that I should see and understand. He said that his mind would not be easy until the whole thing was settled, and he begged me to come out to his house at Norwood that night, bringing the will with me, and to arrange matters. 'Remember, my boy, not one word to your parents about the affair until everything is settled. We will keep it as a little surprise for them.' He was very insistent upon this point, and made me promise it faithfully.

"You can imagine, Mr. Holmes, that I was not in a humour to refuse him anything that he might ask. He was my benefactor, and all my desire was to carry out his wishes in every particular. I sent a telegram home, therefore, to say that I had important business on hand,

7 *are the rough draft.* ". . . an English will, to be valid, requires two witnesses," Mr. S. T. L. Harbottle wrote in "Sherlock Holmes and the Law." "If it be supposed that McFarlane himself was the second witness then this would have invalidated the bequest of almost all Oldacre's property to McFarlane (Wills Act of 1837). In either case the will's main object was defeated. . . . Either [McFarlane] was a most unreliable solicitor who had acted in error, or he intended to defraud his client. . . . I fear McFarlane deliberately planned that the will should be ineffective. The fact that it was written on blue paper (at that time universally used for drafts and not for final copies or engrossments) then assumes a sinister significance."

and that it was impossible for me to say how late I might be. Mr. Oldacre had told me that he would like me to have supper with him at nine, as he might not be home before that hour. I had some difficulty in finding his house, however, and it was nearly half-past before I reached it. I found him——"

"One moment!" said Holmes. "Who opened the door?"

"A middle-aged woman, who was, I suppose, his housekeeper."

"And it was she, I presume, who mentioned your name?"

"Exactly," said McFarlane.

"Pray proceed."

Mr. McFarlane wiped his damp brow, and then continued his narrative:

"I was shown by this woman into a sitting-room, where a frugal supper was laid out. Afterwards Mr. Jonas Oldacre led me into his bedroom, in which there stood a heavy safe. This he opened and took out a mass of documents, which we went over together. It was between eleven and twelve when we finished. He remarked that we must not disturb the housekeeper. He showed me out through his own French window, which had been open all this time."

"Was the blind down?" asked Holmes.

"I will not be sure, but I believe that it was only half down. Yes, I remember how he pulled it up in order to swing open the window. I could not find my stick, and he said, 'Never mind, my boy; I shall see a good deal of you now, I hope, and I will keep your stick until you come back to claim it.' I left him there, the safe open, and the papers made up in packets upon the table. It was so late that I could not get back to Blackheath, so I spent the night at the 'Anerley Arms,' and I knew nothing more until I read of this horrible affair in the morning."

"Anything more that you would like to ask, Mr. Holmes?" said Lestrade, whose eyebrows had gone up once or twice during this remarkable explanation.

"Not until I have been to Blackheath."

"You mean to Norwood," said Lestrade.

"Oh, yes; no doubt that is what I must have meant," said Holmes, with his enigmatical smile. Lestrade had learned by more experiences than he would care to acknowledge that that razor-like brain could cut through that which was impenetrable to him. I saw him look curiously at my companion.

"I think I should like to have a word with you presently, Mr. Sherlock Holmes," said he. "Now, Mr. McFarlane, two of my constables are at the door, and there is a four-wheeler waiting." The wretched young man arose, and with a last beseeching glance at us he walked from the room. The officers conducted him to the cab, but Lestrade remained.

Holmes had picked up the pages which formed the rough draft of the will, and was looking at them with the keenest interest upon his face.

"There are some points about that document, Lestrade, are there not?" said he pushing them over.

THE WRETCHED YOUNG MAN AROSE . . .

Illustration by Sidney Paget for the *Strand Magazine*, November, 1903.

The official looked at them with a puzzled expression.

" I can read the first few lines, and these in the middle of the second page, and one or two at the end. Those are as clear as print," said he ; " but the writing in between is very bad, and there are three places where I cannot read it at all."

" What do you make of that ? " said Holmes.

" Well, what do *you* make of it ? "

" That it was written in a train ; the good writing represents stations, the bad writing movement, and the very bad writing passing over points. A scientific expert would pronounce at once that this was drawn up on a suburban line, since nowhere save in the immediate vicinity of a great city could there be so quick a succession of points. Granting that his whole journey was occupied in drawing up the will, then the train was an express, only stopping once between Norwood and London Bridge."

Lestrade began to laugh.

" You are too many for me when you begin to get on your theories, Mr. Holmes," said he. " How does this bear on the case ? "

" Well, it corroborates the young man's story to the extent that the will was drawn up by Jonas Oldacre in his journey yesterday. It is curious—is it not ?—that a man should draw up so important a document in so haphazard a fashion. It suggests that he did not think it was going to be of much practical importance. If a man drew up a will which he did not intend ever to be effective he might do it so."

" Well, he drew up his own death-warrant at the same time," said Lestrade.

" Oh, you think so ? "

" Don't you ? "

" Well, it is quite possible ; but the case is not clear to me yet."

" Not clear ? Well, if that isn't clear, what *could* be clearer ? Here is a young man who learns suddenly that if a certain older man dies he will succeed to a fortune. What does he do ? He says nothing to anyone but he arranges that he shall go out on some pretext to see his client that night ; he waits until the only other person in the house is in bed, and then in the solitude of the man's room he murders him, burns his body in the wood-pile, and departs to a neighbouring hotel. The blood-stains in the room and also on the stick are very slight. It is probable that he imagined his crime to be a bloodless one, and hoped that if the body were consumed it would hide all traces of the method of his death—traces which for some reason must have pointed to him. Is all this not obvious ? "

" It strikes me, my good Lestrade, as being just a trifle too obvious," said Holmes. " You do not add imagination to your other great qualities ; but if you could for one moment put yourself in the place of this young man, would you choose the very night after the will had been made to commit your crime ? Would it not seem dangerous to you to make so very close a relation between the two incidents ? Again, would you choose an occasion when you are known to be in the house, when a servant has let you in? And, finally, would you take the great pains to conceal the body and yet leave your own stick as a sign that you were the criminal? Confess, Lestrade, that all this is very unlikely."

"As to the stick, Mr. Holmes, you know as well as I do that a criminal is often flurried and does things which a cool man would avoid. He was very likely afraid to go back to the room. Give me another theory that would fit the facts."

"I could very easily give you half a dozen," said Holmes. "Here, for example, is a very possible and even probable one. I make you a free present of it. The older man is showing documents which are of evident value. A passing tramp sees them through the window, the blind of which is only half down. Exit the solicitor. Enter the tramp! He seizes a stick, which he observes there, kills Oldacre, and departs after burning the body."

"Why should the tramp burn the body?"

"For the matter of that, why should McFarlane?"

"To hide some evidence."

"Possibly the tramp wanted to hide that any murder at all had been committed."

"And why did the tramp take nothing?"

"Because they were papers that he could not negotiate."

Lestrade shook his head, though it seemed to me that his manner was less absolutely assured than before.

"Well, Mr. Sherlock Holmes, you may look for your tramp, and while you are finding him we will hold on to our man. The future will show which is right. Just notice this point, Mr. Holmes—that so far as we know none of the papers were removed, and that the prisoner is the one man in the world who had no reason for removing them since he was heir-at-law and would come into them in any case."

My friend seemed struck by this remark.

"I don't mean to deny that the evidence is in some ways very strongly in favour of your theory," said he. "I only wish to point out that there are other theories possible. As you say, the future will decide. Good morning! I dare say that in the course of the day I shall drop in at Norwood and see how you are getting on."

When the detective departed my friend rose and made his preparations for the day's work with the alert air of a man who has a congenial task before him.

"My first movement, Watson," said he, as he bustled into his frock-coat, "must, as I said, be in the direction of Blackheath."

"And why not Norwood?"

"Because we have in this case one singular incident coming close to the heels of another singular incident. The police are making the mistake of concentrating their attention upon the second because it happens to be the one which is actually criminal. But it is evident to me that the logical way to approach the case is to begin by trying to throw some light upon the first incident—the curious will, so suddenly made, and to so unexpected an heir. It may do something to simplify what followed. No, my dear fellow, I don't think you can help me. There is no prospect of danger, or I should not dream of stir-

"MY FIRST MOVEMENT, WATSON, . . . MUST . . . BE IN THE DIRECTION OF BLACKHEATH."

Illustration by Sidney Paget for the *Strand Magazine*, November, 1903.

ring out without you. I trust that when I see you in the evening I will be able to report that I have been able to do something for this unfortunate youngster who has thrown himself upon my protection."

It was late when my friend returned, and I could see by a glance at his haggard and anxious face that the high hopes with which he had started had not been fulfilled. For an hour he droned away upon his violin, endeavouring to soothe his own ruffled spirits. At last he flung down the instrument and plunged into a detailed account of his misadventures.

" It's all going wrong, Watson—all as wrong as it can go. I kept a bold face before Lestrade, but, upon my soul, I believe that for once the fellow is on the right track and we are on the wrong. All my instincts are one way, and all the facts are the other, and I much fear that British juries have not yet attained that pitch of intelligence when they will give the preference to my theories over Lestrade's facts."

" Did you go to Blackheath ? "

" Yes, Watson, I went there, and I found very quickly that the late lamented Oldacre was a pretty considerable blackguard. The father was away in search of his son. The mother was at home—a little, fluffy, blue-eyed person, in a tremor of fear and indignation. Of course, she would not admit even the possibility of his guilt. But she would not express either surprise or regret over the fate of Oldacre. On the contrary, she spoke of him with such bitterness that she was unconsciously considerably strengthening the case of the police ; for, of course, if her son had heard her speak of the man in that fashion it would predispose him towards hatred and violence. ' He was more like a malignant and cunning ape than a human being,' said she, ' and he always was, ever since he was a young man.'

" ' You knew him at the time ? ' said I.

" ' Yes, I knew him well ; in fact, he was an old suitor of mine. Thank Heaven that I had the sense to turn away from him and to marry a better, if a poorer, man. I was engaged to him, Mr. Holmes, when I heard a shocking story of how he had turned a cat loose in an aviary, and I was so horrified at his brutal cruelty that I would have nothing more to do with him.' She rummaged in a bureau, and presently she produced a photograph of a woman, shamefully defaced and mutilated with a knife. ' That is my own photograph,' said she. ' He sent it to me in that state, with his curse, upon my wedding morning.'

" ' Well,' said I, ' at least he has forgiven you now, since he has left all his property to your son.'

" ' Neither my son nor I want anything from Jonas Oldacre, dead or alive,' she cried, with a proper spirit. ' There is a God in heaven, Mr. Holmes, and that same God who has punished that wicked man will show in His own good time that my son's hands are guiltless of his blood.'

" Well, I tried one or two leads, but could get at nothing which would help our hypothesis, and several points which would make against it. I gave it up at last, and off I went to Norwood.

" 'HE SENT IT TO ME IN THAT STATE, WITH HIS CURSE, UPON MY WEDDING MORNING.' "

Illustration by Sidney Paget for the *Strand Magazine*, November, 1903.

" This place, Deep Dene House, is a big modern villa of staring brick, standing back in its own grounds, with a laurel-clumped lawn in front of it. To the right and some distance back from the road was the timber-yard which had been the scene of the fire. Here's a rough plan on a leaf of my notebook. This window on the left is the one which opens into Oldacre's room. You can look into it from the road, you see. That is about the only bit of consolation I have had to-day. Lestrade was not there, but his head constable did the honours. They had just made a great treasure-trove. They had spent the morning raking among the ashes of the burned wood-pile, and besides the charred organic remains they had secured several discoloured metal discs. I examined them with care, and there was no doubt that they were trouser buttons. I even distinguished that one of them was marked with the name of ' Hyams,' who was Oldacre's tailor. I then worked the lawn very carefully for signs and traces, but this drought has made everything as hard as iron. Nothing was to be seen save that somebody or a bundle had been dragged through a low privet hedge which is in a line with the wood-pile. All that, of course, fits in with the official theory. I crawled about the lawn with an August sun on my back. But I got up at the end of an hour no wiser than before.

" Well, after this fiasco I went into the bedroom and examined that also. The blood-stains were very slight, mere smears and discolorations, but undoubtedly fresh. The stick had been removed, but there also the marks were slight. There is no doubt about the stick belonging to our client. He admits it. Footmarks of both men could be made out on the carpet, but none of any third person, which again is a trick for the other side. They were piling up their score all the time, and we were at a standstill.

" Only one little gleam of hope did I get—and yet it amounted to nothing. I examined the contents of the safe, most of which had been taken out and left on the table. The papers had been made up into sealed envelopes, one or two of which had been opened by the police. They were not, so far as I could judge, of any great value, nor did the bank book show that Mr. Oldacre was in such very affluent circumstances. But it seemed to me that all the papers were not there. There were allusions to some deeds—possibly the more valuable—which I could not find. This, of course, if we could definitely prove it, would turn Lestrade's argument against himself, for who would steal a thing if he knew that he would shortly inherit it ?

" Finally, having drawn every other cover and picked up no scent, I tried my luck with the housekeeper. Mrs. Lexington is her name, a little, dark, silent person, with suspicious and sidelong eyes. She could tell us something if she would—I am convinced of it. But she was as close as wax. Yes, she had let Mr. McFarlane in at half-past nine. She wished her hand had withered before she had done so. She had gone to bed at half-past ten. Her room was at the other end of the house, and she could hear nothing of what passed. Mr. McFarlane had left his hat, and to the best of her

8 *who wanted us to get him off in '87?* The late H. W. Bell thought that Stevens was perhaps the murderer in the Camberwell Poisoning Case, referred to in "The Five Orange Pips."

belief his stick, in the hall. She had been awakened by the alarm of fire. Her poor, dear master had certainly been murdered. Had he any enemies? Well, every man had enemies, but Mr. Oldacre kept himself very much to himself, and only met people in the way of business. She had seen the buttons, and was sure that they belonged to the clothes which he had worn last night. The wood-pile was very dry, for it had not rained for a month. It burned like a tinder, and by the time she reached the spot nothing could be seen but flames. She and all the firemen smelled the burned flesh from inside it. She knew nothing of the papers, nor of Mr. Oldacre's private affairs.

"So, my dear Watson, there's my report of a failure. And yet—and yet"—he clenched his thin hands in a paroxysm of conviction—"I *know* it's all wrong. I feel it in my bones. There is something that has not come out, and that housekeeper knows it. There was a sort of sulky defiance in her eyes which only goes with guilty knowledge. However, there's no good talking any more about it, Watson; but unless some lucky chance comes our way I fear that the Norwood Disappearance Case will not figure in that chronicle of our successes which I foresee that a patient public will sooner or later have to endure."

"Surely," said I, "the man's appearance would go far with any jury?"

"That is a dangerous argument, my dear Watson. You remember that terrible murderer, Bert Stevens, who
8 wanted us to get him off in '87? Was there ever a more mild-mannered, Sunday-school young man?"

"It is true."

"Unless we succeed in establishing an alternative theory, this man is lost. You can hardly find a flaw in the case which can now be presented against him, and all further investigation has served to strengthen it. By the way, there is one curious little point about those papers which may serve us as the starting-point for an inquiry. On looking over the bank book I found that the low state of the balance was principally due to large cheques which have been made out during the last year to Mr. Cornelius. I confess that I should be interested to know who this Mr. Cornelius may be with whom a retired builder has such very large transactions. Is it possible that he has had a hand in the affair? Cornelius might be a broker, but we have found no scrip to correspond with these large payments. Failing any other indication, my researches must now take the direction of an inquiry at the bank for the gentleman who has cashed these cheques. But I fear, my dear fellow, that our case will end ingloriously by Lestrade hanging our client, which will certainly be a triumph for Scotland Yard."

I do not know how far Sherlock Holmes took any sleep that night, but when I came down to breakfast I found him pale and harassed, his bright eyes the brighter for the dark shadows round them. The carpet round his chair was littered with cigarette ends, and with the early editions of the morning papers. An open telegram lay upon the table.

" What do you think of this, Watson ? " he asked, tossing it across.

It was from Norwood, and ran as follows :

" Important fresh evidence to hand. McFarlane's guilt definitely established. Advise you to abandon case.—LESTRADE."

" This sounds serious," said I.

" It is Lestrade's little cock-a-doodle of victory," Holmes answered with a bitter smile. " And yet it may be premature to abandon the case. After all, important fresh evidence is a two-edged thing, and may possibly cut in a very different direction to that which Lestrade imagines. Take your breakfast, Watson, and we will go out together and see what we can do. I feel as if I shall need your company and your moral support to-day."

My friend had no breakfast himself, for it was one of his peculiarities that in his more intense moments he would permit himself no food, and I have known him presume upon his iron strength until he has fainted from pure inanition. " At present I cannot spare energy and nerve force for digestion," he would say, in answer to my medical remonstrances. I was not surprised, therefore, when this morning he left his untouched meal behind him and started with me for Norwood. A crowd of morbid sightseers were still gathered round Deep Dene House, which was just such a suburban villa as I had pictured. Within the gates Lestrade met us, his face flushed with victory, his manner grossly triumphant.

" Well, Mr. Holmes, have you proved us to be wrong yet ? Have you found your tramp ? " he cried.

" I have formed no conclusion whatever," my companion answered.

" But we formed ours yesterday, and now it proves to be correct ; so you must acknowledge that we have been a little in front of you this time, Mr. Holmes."

" You certainly have the air of something unusual having occurred," said Holmes.

Lestrade laughed loudly.

" You don't like being beaten any more than the rest of us do," said he. " A man can't expect always to have it his own way—can he, Dr. Watson ? Step this way, if you please, gentlemen, and I think I can convince you once for all that it was John McFarlane who did this crime."

He led us through the passage and out into a dark hall beyond.

" This is where young McFarlane must have come out to get his hat after the crime was done," said he. " Now look at this." With dramatic suddenness he struck a match, and by its light exposed a stain of blood upon the whitewashed wall. As he held the match nearer I saw that it was more than a stain. It was the well-marked print of a thumb.

" Look at that with your magnifying glass, Mr. Holmes."

" Yes, I am doing so."

" You are aware that no two thumb-marks are alike ? "

" I have heard something of the kind." 9

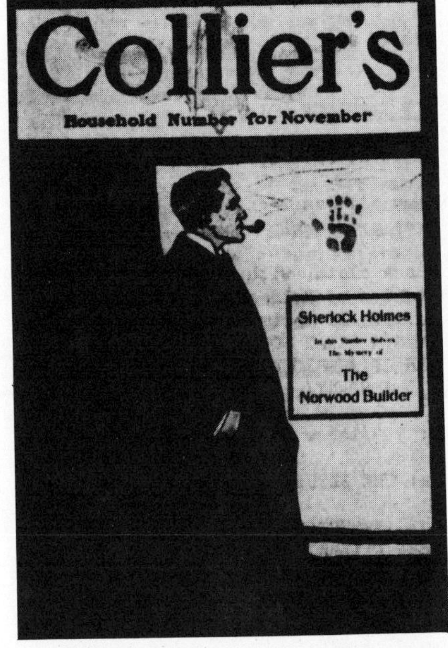

IT WAS THE WELL-MARKED PRINT OF A THUMB.

The cover of *Collier's Magazine* for October 31, 1903, showing Frederic Dorr Steele's illustration. We see that Holmes for some reason has chosen to wear his dressing gown to Deep Dene House. In addition, "the well-marked print of a thumb" has grown into the bloody print of an entire hand. Sidney Paget illustrated the same scene for the *Strand Magazine*, November, 1903.

9 *"I have heard something of the kind."* "It is odd," Mr. Vernon Rendall wrote in "The Limitations of Sherlock Holmes," "since [Holmes] admired the work of Bertillon ["The Naval Treaty"], that he did not discover the important paper which Galton gave to the British Association in 1899 on *Finger-prints and the Detection of Crime in India.* Galton's method was examined by a committee appointed by Asquith, in 1894. . . . Finger-prints as a means of detecting criminals were first used by Sir William Herschel of the I.C.S. in the district of Hooghli, in Bengal. They were recognized as superior to Bertillon's anthropometry, and were recommended for all India in a report of 1896. All one can suggest is that Holmes was not eager to take up other people's methods. With his vanity, he found it difficult to use another expert to help him."

But Mr. Rendall is clearly in error here. Since "The Adventure of the Norwood Builder" took place in 1895, it is hardly odd that Holmes had not read a paper given in 1899. On the contrary, the obviously sarcastic tone of Holmes' "I have heard something of the kind" clearly indicates that he had studied fingerprints and was aware of their importance in the detection of crime. It is more difficult to explain how Lestrade, in 1895, was aware that "no two thumb-prints are alike," since the system was not adopted by Scotland Yard until 1901.

" Well, then, will you please compare that print with this wax impression of young McFarlane's right thumb, taken by my orders this morning ? "

As he held the waxen print close to the blood-stain it did not take a magnifying glass to see that the two were undoubtedly from the same thumb. It was evident to me that our unfortunate client was lost.

" That is final," said Lestrade.

" Yes, that is final," I voluntarily echoed.

" It is final," said Holmes.

Something in his tone caught my ear, and I turned to look at him. An extraordinary change had come over his face. It was writhing with inward merriment.

His two eyes were shining like stars. It seemed to me that he was making desperate efforts to restrain a convulsive attack of laughter.

" Dear me ! Dear me ! " he said at last. " Well, now, who would have thought it ? And how deceptive appearances may be, to be sure ! Such a nice young man to look at ! It is a lesson to us not to trust our own judgment—is it not, Lestrade ? "

" Yes, some of us are a little too much inclined to be cocksure, Mr. Holmes," said Lestrade. The man's insolence was maddening, but we could not resent it.

" What a providential thing that this young man should press his right thumb against the wall in taking his hat from the peg ! Such a very natural action, too, if you come to think of it." Holmes was outwardly calm, but his whole body gave a wriggle of suppressed excitement as he spoke. " By the way, Lestrade, who made this remarkable discovery ? "

" It was the housekeeper, Mrs. Lexington, who drew the night constable's attention to it ? "

" Where was the night constable ? "

" He remained on guard in the bedroom where the crime was committed, so as to see that nothing was touched."

" But why didn't the police see this mark yesterday ? "

" Well, we had no particular reason to make a careful examination of the hall. Besides, it's not in a very prominent place, as you see."

" No, no, of course not. I suppose there is no doubt that the mark was there yesterday ? "

Lestrade looked at Holmes as if he thought he was going out of his mind. I confess that I was myself surprised both at his hilarious manner and at his rather wild observation.

" I don't know whether you think that McFarlane came out of gaol in the dead of the night in order to strengthen the evidence against himself," said Lestrade. " I leave it to any expert in the world whether that is not the mark of his thumb."

" It is unquestionably the mark of his thumb."

" There, that's enough," said Lestrade. " I am a practical man, Mr. Holmes, and when I have got my evidence I come to my conclusions. If you have anything to say you will find me writing my report in the sitting-room."

Holmes had recovered his equanimity, though I still seemed to detect gleams of amusement in his expression.

" Dear me, this is a very sad development, Watson, is it not ? " said he. " And yet there are singular points about it which hold out some hopes for our client."

" I am delighted to hear it," said I heartily. " I was afraid it was all up with him."

" I would hardly go so far as to say that, my dear Watson. The fact is that there is one really serious flaw in this evidence to which our friend attaches so much importance."

" Indeed, Holmes ! What is it ? "

" Only this—that I *know* that that mark was not there when I examined the hall yesterday. And now, Watson, let us have a little stroll round in the sunshine."

With a confused brain, but with a heart into which some warmth of hope was returning, I accompanied my friend in a walk round the garden. Holmes took each face of the house in turn and examined it with great interest. He then led the way inside, and went over the whole building from basement to attics. Most of the rooms were unfurnished, but none the less Holmes inspected them all minutely. Finally, on the top corridor, which ran outside three untenanted bedrooms, he again was seized with a spasm of merriment.

" There are really some very unique features about this case, Watson," said he. " I think it is time now that we took our friend Lestrade into our confidence. He has had his little smile at our expense, and perhaps we may do as much by him if my reading of this problem proves to be correct. Yes, yes ; I think I see how we should approach it."

The Scotland Yard inspector was still writing in the parlour when Holmes interrupted him.

" I understood that you were writing a report of this case," said he.

" So I am."

" Don't you think it may be a little premature ? I can't help thinking that your evidence is not complete."

Lestrade knew my friend too well to disregard his words. He laid down his pen and looked curiously at him.

What do you mean, Mr. Holmes ? "

" Only that there is an important witness whom you have not seen."

" Can you produce him ? "

" I think I can."

" Then do so."

" I will do my best. How many constables have you ? "

" There are three within call."

" Excellent ! " said Holmes. " May I ask if they are all large, able-bodied men with powerful voices ? "

" I have no doubt they are, though I fail to see what their voices have to do with it."

" Perhaps I can help you to see that, and one or two other things as well," said Holmes. " Kindly summon your men, and I will try."

. . . A LITTLE WIZENED MAN DARTED OUT . . .

Illustration by Sidney Paget for the *Strand Magazine*, November, 1903.

Five minutes later three policemen had assembled in the hall.

" In the outhouse you will find a considerable quantity of straw," said Holmes. " I will ask you to carry in two bundles of it. I think it will be of the greatest assistance in producing the witness whom I require. Thank you very much. I believe you have some matches in your pocket, Watson. Now, Mr. Lestrade, I will ask you all to accompany me to the top landing."

As I have said, there was a broad corridor there, which ran outside three empty bedrooms. At one end of the corridor we were all marshalled by Sherlock Holmes, the constables grinning, and Lestrade staring at my friend with amazement, expectation, and derision chasing each other across his features. Holmes stood before us with an air of a conjurer who is performing a trick.

" Would you kindly send one of your constables for two buckets of water ? Put the straw on the floor here, free from the wall on either side. Now I think that we are all ready."

Lestrade's face had begun to grow red and angry.

" I don't know whether you are playing a game with us, Mr. Sherlock Holmes," said he. " If you know anything, you can surely say it without all this tomfoolery."

" I assure you, my good Lestrade, that I have an excellent reason for everything that I do. You may possibly remember that you chaffed me a little some hours ago, when the sun seemed on your side of the hedge, so you must not grudge me a little pomp and ceremony now. Might I ask you, Watson, to open that window, and then to put a match to the edge of the straw ? "

I did so, and, driven by the draught, a coil of grey smoke swirled down the corridor, while the dry straw crackled and flamed.

" Now we must see if we can find this witness for you, Lestrade. Might I ask you all to join in the cry of 'Fire'? Now, then : one, two, three——"

" Fire ! " we all yelled.

" Thank you. I will trouble you once again."

" Fire ! "

" Just once more, gentlemen, and all together."

" Fire ! " The shout must have rung over Norwood.

It had hardly died away when an amazing thing happened. A door suddenly flew open out of what appeared to be solid wall at the end of the corridor, and a little wizened man darted out of it, like a rabbit out of its burrow.

" Capital ! " said Holmes calmly. " Watson, a bucket of water over the straw. That will do ! Lestrade, allow me to present you with your principal missing witness, Mr. Jonas Oldacre."

The detective stared at the new-comer with blank amazement. The latter was blinking in the bright light of the corridor, and peering at us and at the smouldering fire. It was an odious face—crafty, vicious, malignant, with shifty, light-grey eyes and white eyelashes.

" What's this, then ? " said Lestrade at last. " What have you been doing all this time, eh ? "

Oldacre gave an uneasy laugh, shrinking back from the furious red face of the angry detective.

"I have done no harm."

"No harm? You have done your best to get an innocent man hanged. If it wasn't for this gentleman here, I am not sure that you would not have succeeded."

The wretched creature began to whimper.

"I am sure, sir, it was only my practical joke."

"Oh! a joke, was it? You won't find the laugh on your side, I promise you. Take him down and keep him in the sitting-room until I come. Mr. Holmes," he continued, when they had gone, "I could not speak before the constables, but I don't mind saying, in the presence of Dr. Watson, that this is the brightest thing that you have done yet, though it is a mystery to me how you did it. You have saved an innocent man's life, and you have prevented a very grave scandal, which would have ruined my reputation in the Force."

Holmes smiled and clapped Lestrade upon the shoulder.

"Instead of being ruined, my good sir, you will find that your reputation has been enormously enhanced. Just make a few alterations in that report which you were writing, and they will understand how hard it is to throw dust in the eyes of Inspector Lestrade."

"And you don't want your name to appear?"

"Not at all. The work is its own reward. Perhaps I shall get the credit also at some distant day when I permit my zealous historian to lay out his foolscap once more—eh, Watson? Well, now, let us see where this rat has been lurking."

A lath-and-plaster partition had been run across the passage six feet from the end, with a door cunningly concealed in it. It was lit within by slits under the eaves. A few articles of furniture and a supply of food and water were within, together with a number of books and papers.

"There's the advantage of being a builder," said Holmes as we came out. "He was able to fix up his own little hiding-place without any confederate—save, of course, that precious housekeeper of his, whom I should lose no time in adding to your bag, Lestrade."

"I will take your advice. But how did you know of this place, Mr. Holmes?"

"I made up my mind that the fellow was in hiding in the house. When I paced one corridor and found it six feet shorter than the corresponding one below, it was pretty clear where he was. I thought he had not the nerve to lie quiet before an alarm of fire. We could, of course, have gone in and taken him, but it amused me to make him reveal himself; besides, I owed you a little mystification, Lestrade, for your chaff in the morning."

"Well, sir, you certainly got equal with me on that. But how in the world did you know that he was in the house at all?"

"The thumb-mark, Lestrade. You said it was final; and so it was, in a very different sense. I knew it had not been there the day before. I pay a good deal of attention to matters of detail, as you may have observed, and I had examined the hall, and was sure that the wall was clear. Therefore, it had been put on during the night."

HOLMES SMILED AND CLAPPED LESTRADE UPON THE SHOULDER.

Illustration by Sidney Paget for the *Strand Magazine*, November, 1903.

" But how ? "

" Very simply. When those packets were sealed up, Jonas Oldacre got McFarlane to secure one of the seals by putting his thumb upon the soft wax. It would be done so quickly and so naturally that I dare say the young man himself has no recollection of it. Very likely it just so happened, and Oldacre had himself no notion of the use he would put it to. Brooding over the case in that den of his, it suddenly struck him what absolutely damning evidence he could make against McFarlane by using that thumb-mark. It was the simplest thing in the world for him to take a wax impression from the seal, to moisten it in as much blood as he could get from a pin-prick, and to put the mark upon the wall during the night, either with his own hand or with that of his housekeeper. If you examine among these documents which he took with him into his retreat, I will lay you a wager that you find the seal with the thumb-mark upon it."

" Wonderful ! " said Lestrade. " Wonderful ! It's all as clear as crystal, as you put it. But what is the object of this deep deception, Mr. Holmes ? "

It was amusing to me to see how the detective's overbearing manner had changed suddenly to that of a child asking questions of its teacher.

" Well, I don't think that is very hard to explain. A very deep, malicious, vindictive person is the gentleman who is now awaiting us downstairs. You know that he was once refused by McFarlane's mother ? You don't ! I told you that you should go to Blackheath first and Norwood afterwards. Well, this injury, as he would consider it, has rankled in his wicked, scheming brain, and all his life he has longed for vengeance, but never seen his chance. During the last year or two things have gone against him—secret speculation, I think—and he finds himself in a bad way. He determines to swindle his creditors, and for this purpose he pays large cheques to a certain Mr. Cornelius, who is, I imagine, himself under another name. I have not traced these cheques yet, but I have no doubt that they were banked under that name at some provincial town where Oldacre from time to time led a double existence. He intended to change his name altogether, draw this money, and vanish, starting life again elsewhere."

" Well, that's likely enough."

" It would strike him that in disappearing he might throw all pursuit off his track, and at the same time have an ample and crushing revenge upon his old sweetheart, if he could give the impression that he had been murdered by her only child. It was a masterpiece of villainy, and he carried it out like a master. The idea of the will, which would give an obvious motive for the crime, the secret visit unknown to his own parents, the retention of the stick, the blood, and the animal remains and buttons in the wood-pile, all were admirable. It was a net from which it seemed to me a few hours ago that there was no possible escape. But he had not that supreme gift of the artist, the knowledge of when to stop. He wished to improve that which was already perfect—to draw the rope tighter yet round the neck of his unfortunate victim—and so he ruined all. Let us descend, Lestrade. There are just one or two questions that I would ask him."

The malignant creature was seated in his own parlour with a policeman upon each side of him.

" It was a joke, my good sir ; a practical joke, nothing more," he whined incessantly. " I assure you, sir, that I simply concealed myself in order to see the effect of my disappearance, and I am sure that you would not be so unjust as to imagine that I would have allowed any harm to befall poor young Mr. McFarlane."

" That's for the jury to decide," said Lestrade. " Anyhow, we shall have you on a charge of conspiracy, if not for attempted murder."

" And you'll probably find that your creditors will impound the banking account of Mr. Cornelius," said Holmes.

The little man started and turned his malignant eyes upon my friend.

" I have to thank you for a good deal," said he. " Perhaps I'll pay my debt some day."

Holmes smiled indulgently.

" I fancy that for some few years you will find your time very fully occupied," said he. " By the way, what was it you put into the wood-pile besides your old trousers ? A dead dog, or rabbits, or what ? You won't tell ? Dear me, how very unkind of you ! Well, well, I dare say that a couple of rabbits would account both for the blood and for the charred ashes. If ever you write an account, Watson, you can make rabbits serve your turn."

Bibliographical Note: The original manuscript of "The Adventure of the Norwood Builder," 50 pages, with numerous corrections, was donated by Sir Arthur Conan Doyle to a Red Cross Charity Sale and auctioned in London, April 22, 1918, bringing £12. It was auctioned again in New York City on February 13, 1923, bringing $100, and again in New York City, February 8, 1926, bringing only $60. It is presently owned by the New York Public Library.

55

THE ADVENTURE OF THE BRUCE-PARTINGTON PLANS

[Thursday, November 21, to Saturday, November 23, 1895]

IN the third week of November, in the year 1895, a dense yellow fog settled down upon London. From
1 the Monday to the Thursday I doubt whether it was ever possible from our windows in Baker Street to see the loom of the opposite houses. The first day Holmes had spent in cross-indexing his huge book of references. The second and third had been patiently occupied upon a subject which he had recently made his hobby—the music of
2 the Middle Ages. But when, for the fourth time, after pushing back our chairs from breakfast we saw the greasy, heavy brown swirl still drifting past us and condensing in oily drops upon the window-panes, my comrade's impatient and active nature could endure this drab existence no longer. He paced restlessly about our sitting-room in a fever of suppressed energy, biting his nails, tapping the furniture, and chafing against inaction.

" Nothing of interest in the paper, Watson ? " he said.

I was aware that by anything of interest, Holmes meant anything of criminal interest. There was the news of a revolution, of a possible war, and of an impending change
3 of Government ; but these did not come within the horizon of my companion. I could see nothing recorded in the shape of crime which was not commonplace and futile. Holmes groaned and resumed his restless meanderings.

" The London criminal is certainly a dull fellow," said he, in the querulous voice of the sportsman whose game has failed him. " Look out of this window, Watson. See how the figures loom up, are dimly seen, and then blend once more into the cloud-bank. The thief or the murderer could roam London on such a day as the tiger does the jungle, unseen until he pounces, and then evident only to his victim."

" There have," said I, " been numerous petty thefts."

Holmes snorted his contempt.

" This great and sombre stage is set for something more worthy than that," said he. " It is fortunate for this community that I am not a criminal."

" It is, indeed ! " said I, heartily.

" Suppose that I were Brooks or Woodhouse, or any of the fifty men who have good reason for taking my life, how long could I survive against my own pursuit ? A summons, a bogus appointment, and all would be over.

1 *From the Monday to the Thursday.* Watson in this adventure is unusually precise in his dating, and there is no reason to doubt him: the meteorological reports for the period are quite compatible with his description of the weather. The case opened on *Thursday, November 21, 1895;* it closed on *Saturday, November 23, 1895.*

2 *the music of the Middle Ages.* ". . . it is strongly to be doubted that the word *recently* is accurate, for one does not suddenly become an authority in this field in a short time simply by adopting a hobby and with little or no technical study," Mr. Benjamin Grosbayne wrote in "Sherlock Holmes —Musician."

3 *an impending change of Government.* "There was indeed a 'revolution' (Turkey), 'a possible war' (troops left for Ashanti) and 'an impending change of Government' (Bechuanaland became part of Cape Colony)," Mrs. Jennifer Chorley wrote in "1896–1964, 'The Wheel Has Come Full Circle.' "

But the "impending change of Government" was probably much closer to Baker Street than Bechuanaland, as Mr. Owen F. Grazebrook pointed out in his essay on "Royalty" (in the Sherlockian Canon): "It was in July '95 that Lord Roseberry retired, after the country had thrown from office the remnants of the Liberal Party; it was the first among many of the Liberal debacles, and the corridors of Hatfield were full of rejoicing and bicycles. There can be no question that in November '95, 'an impending change of Government' in the ordinary sense of the words, would *not* be filling the columns of the Press. The only event of any importance in Court and political circles that Autumn was the substitution of the Duke of Cambridge by Lord Wolseley as Commander-in-Chief. An affair which needed a delicate hand, for it was Mr. Broderick's vote of censure, nominally on the supply of cordite, but in reality on the personality of the Commander-in-Chief, which had brought down the Government. Queen Victoria was not very fond of Wolseley, and very fond of the

It is well they don't have days of fog in the Latin countries—the countries of assassination. By Jove! here comes something at last to break our dead monotony."

It was the maid with a telegram. Holmes tore it open and burst out laughing.

"Well, well! What next?" said he. "Brother Mycroft is coming round."

"Why not?" I asked.

"Why not? It is as if you met a tram-car coming down a country lane. Mycroft has his rails and he runs on them. His Pall Mall lodgings, the Diogenes Club, Whitehall—that is his cycle. Once, and only once, he has been here. What upheaval can possibly have derailed him?"

"Does he not explain?"

Holmes handed me his brother's telegram.

"Must see you over Cadogan West. Coming at once.
MYCROFT."

"Cadogan West? I have heard the name."

"It recalls nothing to my mind. But that Mycroft should break out in this erratic fashion! A planet might as well leave its orbit. By the way, do you know what Mycroft is?"

I had some vague recollection of an explanation at the time of the Adventure of the Greek Interpreter.

"You told me that he had some small office under the British Government."

Holmes chuckled.

"I did not know you quite so well in those days. One
has to be discreet when one talks of high matters of state. 4
You are right in thinking that he is under the British Government. You would also be right in a sense if you said that occasionally he *is* the British Government."

"My dear Holmes!"

"I thought I might surprise you. Mycroft draws four
hundred and fifty pounds a year, remains a subordinate, 5
has no ambitions of any kind, will receive neither honour nor title, but remains the most indispensable man in the country."

"But how?"

"Well, his position is unique. He has made it for himself. There has never been anything like it before, nor will be again. He has the tidiest and most orderly brain, with the greatest capacity for storing facts, of any man living. The same great powers which I have turned to the detection of crime he has used for this particular business. The conclusions of every department are passed to him, and he is the central exchange, the clearing-house,
which makes out the balance. All other men are special- 6
ists, but his specialism is omniscience. We will suppose that a Minister needs information as to a point which involves the Navy, India, Canada and the bi-metallic question; he could get his separate advices from various 7
departments upon each, but only Mycroft can focus them all, and say off-hand how each factor would affect the other. They began by using him as a short-cut, a convenience; now he has made himself an essential. In that great brain of his everything is pigeon-holed, and can be

Duke. It may well be that in Dr. Watson's somewhat slipshod mind, *and being an old Army veteran*, the office of Commander-in-Chief *was* connected with the governance of the country, and that the substitution of the Duke by Wolseley meant, to him at any rate, 'an impending change of Government.' If this is so, November, 1895, may stand as being correct, for in November of that year the Queen graciously received Lord Wolseley and, to continue a military metaphor, 'buried the hatchet.'"

4 *One has to be discreet when one talks of high matters of state.* Dr. Felix Morley has written ("The Significance of the Second Stain") that "much can be read into Sherlock's tactful remark to Watson at this time." One can understand, Dr. Morley holds, that Watson's wound or wounds may have developed in him an isolationist attitude that could "stir a subconscious resentment whenever Holmes seemed inclined to endorse the principles of collective action. And we know that Holmes realized this idiosyncracy in his friend and as a result deliberately concealed many of the very important international undertakings to which his practice led. Thus Watson only knew from newspaper references that . . . Holmes was 'engaged by the French Government upon a matter of supreme importance' ["The Final Problem"]. The doctor was never told of the very delicate matter in which Holmes . . . had served the reigning family of Holland ["A Case of Identity"]. And more than five years passed after Watson's introduction to Mycroft Holmes before Sherlock thought it wise to give the doctor any indication of the enormous importance of his brother's governmental post."

5 *four hundred and fifty pounds a year.* About $2,250 in U.S. currency at the time.

6 *the clearing-house, which makes out the balance.* "Mycroft's curious position in the Government would seem to have points in common with that of his German contemporary, Holstein." Mr. T. S. Blakeney noted in *Sherlock Holmes: Fact or Fiction?*

7 *the bi-metallic question.* The ratio between gold and silver as legal tender. It was at that time an important political topic, particularly in the United States.

handed out in an instant. Again and again his word has decided the national policy. He lives in it. He thinks of nothing else save when, as an intellectual exercise, he unbends if I call upon him and ask him to advise me on one of my little problems. But Jupiter is descending to-day. What on earth can it mean? Who is Cadogan
8 West, and what is he to Mycroft?"

"I have it," I cried, and plunged among the litter of papers upon the sofa. "Yes, yes, here he is, sure enough! Cadogan West was the young man who was found dead on the Underground on Tuesday morning."

Holmes sat up at attention, his pipe half-way to his lips.

"This must be serious, Watson. A death which has caused my brother to alter his habits can be no ordinary one. What in the world can he have to do with it? The case was featureless as I remember it. The young man had apparently fallen out of the train and killed himself. He had not been robbed, and there was no particular reason to suspect violence. Is that not so?"

"There has been an inquest," said I, "and a good many fresh facts have come out. Looked at more closely, I should certainly say that it was a curious case."

"Judging by its effect upon my brother, I should think it must be a most extraordinary one." He snuggled down in his arm-chair. "Now, Watson, let us have the facts."

"The man's name was Arthur Cadogan West. He was twenty-seven years of age, unmarried, and a clerk at
9 Woolwich Arsenal."

"Government employ. Behold the link with brother Mycroft!"

"He left Woolwich suddenly on Monday night. Was last seen by his fiancée, Miss Violet Westbury, whom he left abruptly in the fog about 7.30 that evening. There was no quarrel between them and she can give no motive for his action. The next thing heard of him was when his dead body was discovered by a platelayer named Mason,
10 just outside Aldgate Station on the Underground system in London."

"When?"

"The body was found at six on the Tuesday morning. It was lying wide of the metals upon the left hand of the
11 track as one goes eastward, at a point close to the station, where the line emerges from the tunnel in which it runs. The head was badly crushed—an injury which might well have been caused by a fall from the train. The body could only have come on the line in that way. Had it been carried down from any neighbouring street, it must have passed the station barriers, where a collector is always standing. This point seems absolutely certain."

"Very good. The case is definite enough. The man, dead or alive, either fell or was precipitated from a train. So much is clear to me. Continue."

"The trains which traverse the lines of rail beside which the body was found are those which run from west to east,
12 some being purely Metropolitan, and some from Willesden and outlying junctions. It can be stated for certain that this young man, when he met his death, was travelling in this direction at some late hour of the night, but at what point he entered the train it is impossible to state."

8 *and what is he to Mycroft?"* ". . . an instinctive paraphrase of Hamlet's 'What's Hecuba to him or he to Hecuba,'" Professor Clarke Olney wrote in "The Literacy of Sherlock Holmes."

9 *Woolwich Arsenal."* Woolwich, then part of Kent, has not changed much since Holmes *floruit.* Mr. Michael Harrison described it well (*In the Footsteps of Sherlock Holmes*): "Arsenal buildings, barracks, Georgian houses of senior officials, and miles of drab two-stories for the workers."

10 *Aldgate Station.* Not to be confused with Aldersgate, from which Holmes and Watson descended from the Underground during their reconnoitering mission at the time of "The Red-Headed League."

11 *wide of the metals upon the left hand of the track.* "The metals" is English for *rails;* in Britain, it should be remembered, all traffic moves on the left.

12 *Willesden.* A century ago Willesden, then called Wilsdon, was a retired village five miles from Oxford Street; today the borough of Willesden includes Brondesbury, Harlesden, Kensal Rise, and part of Cricklewood, and is an important railway junction of British Railways, Midland Region.

" His ticket, of course, would show that."

" There was no ticket in his pockets."

" No ticket ! Dear me, Watson, this is really very singular. According to my experience it is not possible to reach the platform of a Metropolitan train without exhibiting one's ticket. Presumably, then, the young man had one. Was it taken from him in order to conceal the station from which he came ? It is possible. Or did he drop it in the carriage ? That also is possible. But the point is of curious interest. I understand that there was no sign of robbery ? "

" Apparently not. There is a list here of his possessions. His purse contained two pounds fifteen. He had **13**
also a cheque-book on the Woolwich branch of the Capital and Counties Bank. Through this his identity was established. There were also two dress-circle tickets for the Woolwich Theatre, dated for that very evening. Also a small packet of technical papers."

Holmes gave an exclamation of satisfaction.

" There we have it at last, Watson ! British Government—Woolwich Arsenal—Technical papers—Brother Mycroft, the chain is complete. But here he comes, if I am not mistaken, to speak for himself."

A moment later the tall and portly form of Mycroft Holmes was ushered into the room. Heavily built and massive, there was a suggestion of uncouth physical inertia in the figure, but above this unwieldy frame there was perched a head so masterful in its brow, so alert in its steel-grey, deep-set eyes, so firm in its lips, and so subtle in its play of expression, that after the first glance one forgot the gross body and remembered only the dominant mind.

At his heels came our old friend Lestrade, of Scotland Yard—thin and austere. The gravity of both their faces foretold some weighty quest. The detective shook hands without a word. Mycroft Holmes struggled out of his overcoat and subsided into an arm-chair.

" A most annoying business, Sherlock," said he. " I extremely dislike altering my habits, but the powers that be would take no denial. In the present state of Siam it is most awkward that I should be away from the office. But it is a real crisis. I have never seen the Prime Minister so upset. As to the Admiralty—it is buzzing like an **14**
overturned beehive. Have you read up the case ? "

" We have just done so. What were the technical papers ? "

" Ah, there's the point ! Fortunately, it has not come out. The Press would be furious if it did. The papers which this wretched youth had in his pocket were the plans of the Bruce-Partington submarine."

Mycroft Holmes spoke with a solemnity which showed his sense of the importance of the subject. His brother and I sat expectant.

" Surely you have heard of it ? I thought everyone had heard of it."

" Only as a name."

" Its importance can hardly be exaggerated. It has
been the most jealously guarded of all Government secrets. **15**
You may take it from me that naval warfare becomes impos-

13 *two pounds fifteen.* About $13.

14 *I have never seen the Prime Minister so upset.* The Prime Minister at the time was Lord Salisbury, and Mr. T. S. Blakeney has remarked (*Sherlock Holmes: Fact or Fiction?*) that "The seriousness of the theft may be realized less from the peculiar properties of a Bruce-Partington submarine than from the fact that even Lord Salisbury had been shaken out of his habitual imperturbability. The loss of a very secret report on the possibility of forcing the Dardanelles could leave him unmoved (*Secret and Confidential,* by Brigadier-General W. H.-H. Waters, pp. 53–4), but Mycroft had seldom seen [him] so upset as over the Cadogan West mystery."

15 *the most jealously guarded of all Government secrets.* How to reconcile this remark with Mycroft's previous "I thought everyone had heard of it" is something we will not attempt.

A MOMENT LATER THE TALL AND PORTLY FORM OF MYCROFT HOLMES WAS USHERED INTO THE ROOM.

Illustration by Arthur Twidle for the *Strand Magazine*, December, 1908.

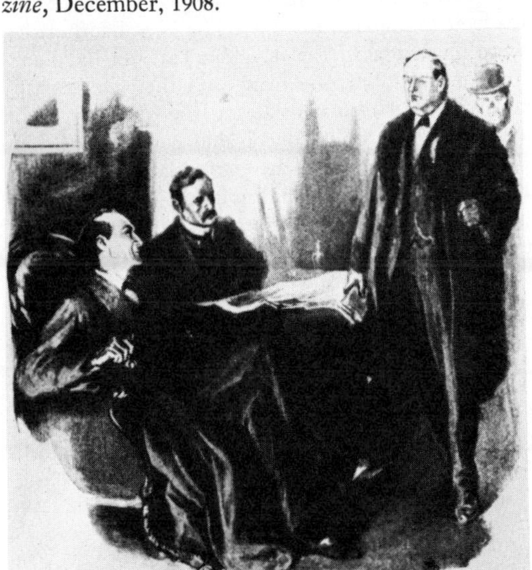

16 *naval warfare becomes impossible within the radius of a Bruce-Partington's operation.* But there is not much doubt that Mycroft Holmes' hopes were completely disappointed, as the late Fletcher Pratt pointed out in "Holmes and the Royal Navy." "The date was 1895; and not for a decade and a half thereafter was any submarine produced which made the operations of surface ships even dangerous, to say nothing of impossible. As a matter of fact England herself built no submarines of any kind until 1903, eight years after the recovery of the plans of the wonder-working Bruce-Partington, and the submarines built by the Royal Navy at that time were from the designs of John Holland, the plans themselves being purchased in America." France, on the other hand, Mr. Pratt continued, only a year later, in 1896, laid down a new submarine of revolutionary design named the *Morse*. The *Morse* turned out to be a miserable failure and never made more than a couple of voyages at sea, but the suspicion will not rest that she was designed from the stolen Bruce-Partington plans. It should be noted here that Conan Doyle, in a story called "Danger!", written in 1913, predicted with great prophetic accuracy, even in small details, the consequences of a submarine blockade which would prevent any food-ship of any nationality from reaching the British Isles. When it appeared in the *Strand Magazine* for July, 1914, naval officialdom dismissed the threat as meaningless. Admiral Sir Compton Domville, K.C.B., in an extraordinary instance of unintentional and exact compliment, felt "compelled to say that I think it most improbable, and more like one of Jules Verne's stories than any other author I know."

17 *even he was forced to go to the Woolwich office.* Mrs. Crighton Sellars seems to have been the first to point out that "Woolwich . . . since 1869 has been an *Army* arsenal." Commenting on this in a letter to Mrs. Sellars, Captain P. C. W. Howe of the Royal Navy wrote: "As far as the Navy was concerned no [submarine plans were being made at Woolwich in 1895]. The Naval authorities were quite against the development and introduction of the submarine boat until they were practically forced into considering the question about 1900. . . . The only conceivable connection I can think of was that in the early days of torpedo development, the Royal Engineers had a torpedo of the Brennan type which could be directed from the shore and was used to protect the entrance to naval harbors, and these torpedos were dealt with at Woolwich Arsenal."

18 *"I play the game for the game's own sake."* As we know, Holmes accepted the Legion of Honor from France ("The Adventure of Wisteria Lodge") but was later to decline a knighthood from England ("The Adventure of the Three Garridebs").

16 sible within the radius of a Bruce-Partington's operation. Two years ago a very large sum was smuggled through the Estimates and was expended in acquiring a monopoly of the invention. Every effort has been made to keep the secret. The plans, which are exceedingly intricate, comprising some thirty separate patents, each essential to the working of the whole, are kept in an elaborate safe in a confidential office adjoining the Arsenal, with burglar-proof doors and windows. Under no conceivable circumstances were the plans to be taken from the office. If the Chief Constructor of the Navy desired to consult them,
17 even he was forced to go to the Woolwich office for the purpose. And yet here we find them in the pockets of a dead junior clerk in the heart of London. From an official point of view it's simply awful."

"But you have recovered them?"

"No, Sherlock, no! That's the pinch. We have not. Ten papers were taken from Woolwich. There were seven in the pockets of Cadogan West. The three most essential are gone—stolen, vanished. You must drop everything, Sherlock. Never mind your usual petty puzzles of the police-court. It's a vital international problem that you have to solve. Why did Cadogan West take the papers, where are the missing ones, how did he die, how came his body where it was found, how can the evil be set right? Find an answer to all these questions, and you will have done good service for your country."

"Why do you not solve it yourself, Mycroft? You can see as far as I."

"Possibly, Sherlock. But it is a question of getting details. Give me your details, and from an arm-chair I will return you an excellent expert opinion. But to run here and run there, to cross-question railway guards, and lie on my face with a lens to my eye—it is not my *métier*. No, you are the one man who can clear the matter up. If you have a fancy to see your name in the next honours list——"

My friend smiled and shook his head.

18 "I play the game for the game's own sake," said he. "But the problem certainly presents some points of interest, and I shall be very pleased to look into it. Some more facts, please."

"I have jotted down the more essential ones upon this sheet of paper, together with a few addresses which you will find of service. The actual official guardian of the papers is the famous Government expert, Sir James Walter, whose decorations and sub-titles fill two lines of a book of reference. He has grown grey in the service, is a gentleman, a favoured guest in the most exalted houses, and above all a man whose patriotism is beyond suspicion. He is one of two who have a key of the safe. I may add that the papers were undoubtedly in the office during working hours on Monday, and that Sir James left for London about three o'clock taking his key with him. He
19 was at the house of Admiral Sinclair at Barclay Square during the whole of the evening when this incident occurred."

"Has the fact been verified?"

"Yes; his brother, Colonel Valentine Walter, has testified to his departure from Woolwich, and Admiral Sinclair to his arrival in London ; so Sir James is no longer a direct factor in the problem."

" Who was the other man with a key ? "

" The senior clerk and draughtsman, Mr. Sidney Johnson. He is a man of forty, married, with five children.
He is a silent, morose man, but he has, on the whole, an **20**
excellent record in the public service. He is unpopular with his colleagues, but a hard worker. According to his own account, corroborated only by the word of his wife, he was at home the whole of Monday evening after office hours, and his key has never left the watch-chain upon which it hangs."

" Tell us about Cadogan West."

" He has been ten years in the Service, and has done good work. He has the reputation of being hot-headed and impetuous, but a straight, honest man. We have nothing against him. He was next Sidney Johnson in the office. His duties brought him into daily personal contact with the plans. No one else had the handling of them."

" Who locked the plans up that night ? "

" Mr. Sidney Johnson, the senior clerk."

" Well, it is surely perfectly clear who took them away. They are actually found upon the person of this junior clerk, Cadogan West. That seems final, does it not ? "

" It does, Sherlock, and yet it leaves so much unexplained. In the first place, why did he take them ? "

" I presume they were of value ? "

" He could have got several thousands for them very easily."

" Can you suggest any possible motive for taking the papers to London except to sell them ? "

" No, I cannot."

" Then we must take that as our working hypothesis. Young West took the papers. Now this could only be done by having a false key——"

" Several false keys. He had to open the building and the room."

" He had, then, several false keys. He took the papers to London to sell the secret, intending, no doubt, to have the plans themselves back in the safe next morning before they were missed. While in London on this treasonable mission he met his end."

" How ? "

" We will suppose that he was travelling back to Woolwich when he was killed and thrown out of the compartment."

" Aldgate, where the body was found, is considerably past the station for London Bridge, which would be his route to Woolwich."

" Many circumstances could be imagined under which he would pass London Bridge. There was someone in the carriage, for example, with whom he was having an absorbing interview. This interview led to a violent scene, in which he lost his life. Possibly he tried to leave the carriage, fell out on the line, and so met his end. The other closed the door. There was a thick fog, and nothing could be seen."

19 *Barclay Square.* Watson for some unspecified reason of his own seems to have chosen this phonetic spelling of London's famous Berkeley Square, built 1698, named from Berkeley House in Piccadilly. In Holmes' and Watson's day it had the best trees of any square in London: all planes (sycamores), "the only trees" (wrote Augustus J. C. Hare in his *Walks in London*, Vol. II), "which thoroughly enjoy a smoky atmosphere." It was in No. 11 Berkeley Square that Horace Walpole died in 1797. In No. 45 the great Lord Clive, founder of the British Empire in India, committed suicide, November 22, 1774. No. 50 had at this time a great notoriety as a haunted house, and was a source of many strange stories and surmises.

20 *He is a silent, morose man.* "The humorous effect of this rhetorical device (known as 'amphibology') was characteristic of the Holmes family," the late Christopher Morley noted in *Sherlock Holmes and Dr. Watson: A Textbook of Friendship*, and cited Sherlock Holmes' famous riposte in "Silver Blaze" *re* the curious incident of the dog in the nighttime.

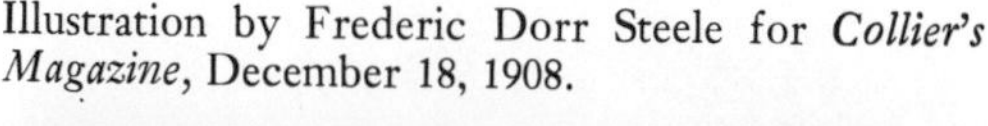

"THIS IS WHERE THE YOUNG MAN'S BODY LAY," SAID HE . . .

Illustration by Frederic Dorr Steele for *Collier's Magazine,* December 18, 1908.

" No better explanation can be given with our present knowledge; and yet consider, Sherlock, how much you leave untouched. We will suppose, for argument's sake, that young Cadogan West *had* determined to convey these papers to London. He would naturally have made an appointment with the foreign agent and kept his evening clear. Instead of that he took two tickets for the theatre, escorted his fiancée half-way there, and then suddenly disappeared."

" A blind," said Lestrade, who had sat listening with some impatience to the conversation.

" A very singular one. That is objection No. 1. Objection No. 2: We will suppose that he reaches London and sees the foreign agent. He must bring back the papers before morning or the loss will be discovered. He took away ten. Only seven were in his pocket. What had become of the other three? He certainly would not leave them of his own free will. Then, again, where is the price of his treason? One would have expected to find a large sum of money in his pocket."

" It seems to me perfectly clear," said Lestrade. " I have no doubt at all as to what occurred. He took the papers to sell them. He saw the agent. They could not agree as to price. He started home again, but the agent went with him. In the train the agent murdered him, took the more essential papers, and threw his body from the carriage. That would account for everything, would it not?"

" Why had he no ticket?"

" The ticket would have shown which station was nearest the agent's house. Therefore he took it from the murdered man's pocket."

" Good, Lestrade, very good," said Holmes. " Your theory holds together. But if this is true, then the case is at an end. On the one hand the traitor is dead. On the other the plans of the Bruce-Partington submarine are presumably already on the Continent. What is there for us to do?"

" To act, Sherlock—to act!" cried Mycroft, springing to his feet. " All my instincts are against this explanation. Use your powers! Go to the scene of the crime! See the people concerned! Leave no stone unturned! In all your career you have never had so great a chance of serving your country."

" Well, well!" said Holmes, shrugging his shoulders. " Come, Watson! And you, Lestrade, could you favour us with your company for an hour or two? We will begin our investigation by a visit to Aldgate Station. Good-bye, Mycroft. I shall let you have a report before evening, but I warn you in advance that you have little to expect."

An hour later, Holmes, Lestrade and I stood upon the underground railroad at the point where it emerges from the tunnel immediately before Aldgate Station. A courteous red-faced old gentleman represented the railway company.

" This is where the young man's body lay," said he, indicating a spot about three feet from the metals. " It could not have fallen from above, for these, as you see, are all blank walls. Therefore, it could only have come from a train, and that train, so far as we can trace it, must have passed about midnight on Monday."

"Have the carriages been examined for any sign of violence?"

"There are no such signs, and no ticket has been found."

"No record of a door being found open?"

"None."

"We have had some fresh evidence this morning," said Lestrade. "A passenger who passed Aldgate in an ordinary Metropolitan train about 11.40 on Monday night declares that he heard a heavy thud, as of a body striking the line, just before the train reached the station. There was dense fog, however, and nothing could be seen. He made no report of it at the time. Why, whatever is the matter with Mr. Holmes?"

My friend was standing with an expression of strained intensity upon his face, staring at the railway metals where they curved out of the tunnel. Aldgate is a junction, and there was a network of points. On these his eager, questioning eyes were fixed, and I saw on his keen, alert face that tightening of the lips, that quiver of the nostrils, and concentration of the heavy tufted brows which I knew so well.

"Points," he muttered; "the points."

"What of it? What do you mean?"

"I suppose there are no great number of points on a system such as this?"

"No; there are very few."

"And a curve, too. Points, and a curve. By Jove! if it were only so."

"What is it, Mr. Holmes? Have you a clue?"

"An idea—an indication, no more. But the case certainly grows in interest. Unique, perfectly unique, and yet why not? I do not see any indications of bleeding on the line."

"There were hardly any."

"But I understand that there was a considerable wound."

"The bone was crushed, but there was no great external injury."

"And yet one would have expected some bleeding. Would it be possible for me to inspect the train which contained the passenger who heard the thud of a fall in the fog?"

"I fear not, Mr. Holmes. The train has been broken up before now, and the carriages redistributed."

"I can assure you, Mr. Holmes," said Lestrade, "that every carriage has been carefully examined. I saw to it myself."

It was one of my friend's most obvious weaknesses that he was impatient with less alert intelligences than his own.

"Very likely," said he, turning away. "As it happens, it was not the carriages which I desired to examine. Watson, we have done all we can here. We need not trouble you any further, Mr. Lestrade. I think our investigations must now carry us to Woolwich."

At London Bridge, Holmes wrote a telegram to his

MY FRIEND WAS STANDING WITH AN EXPRESSION OF STRAINED INTENSITY UPON HIS FACE . . .

Illustration by Arthur Twidle for the *Strand Magazine*, December, 1908.

brother, which he handed to me before dispatching it. It ran thus:

" See some light in the darkness, but it may possibly flicker out. Meanwhile, please send by messenger, to await return at Baker Street, a complete list of all foreign
21 spies or international agents known to be in England, with full address.—SHERLOCK."

" That should be helpful, Watson," he remarked, as we took our seats in the Woolwich train. " We certainly owe brother Mycroft a debt for having introduced us to what promises to be a really very remarkable case."

His eager face still wore that expression of intense and high-strung energy, which showed me that some novel and suggestive circumstance had opened up a stimulating line of thought. See the foxhound with hanging ears and drooping tail as it lolls about the kennels, and compare it with the same hound as, with gleaming eyes and straining muscles, it runs upon a breast-high scent—such was the change in Holmes since the morning. He was a different man to the limp and lounging figure in the mouse-coloured dressing-gown who had prowled so restlessly only a few hours before round the fog-girt room.

" There is material here. There is scope," said he. " I am dull indeed not to have understood its possibilities."

" Even now they are dark to me."

" The end is dark to me also, but I have hold of one idea which may lead us far. The man met his death elsewhere,
22 and his body was on the *roof* of a carriage."

" On the roof ! "

" Remarkable, is it not ? But consider the facts. Is it a coincidence that it is found at the very point where the train pitches and sways as it comes round on the points ? Is not that the place where an object upon the roof might be expected to fall off ? The points would affect no object inside the train. Either the body fell from the roof, or a very curious coincidence has occurred. But now consider the question of the blood. Of course, there was no bleeding on the line if the body had bled elsewhere. Each fact is suggestive in itself. Together they have a cumulative force."

" And the ticket, too ! " I cried.

" Exactly. We could not explain the absence of a ticket. This would explain it. Everything fits together."

" But suppose it were so, we are still as far as ever from unravelling the mystery of his death. Indeed, it becomes not simpler, but stranger."

" Perhaps," said Holmes, thoughtfully ; " perhaps." He relapsed into a silent reverie, which lasted until the slow train drew up at last in Woolwich Station. There he called a cab and drew Mycroft's paper from his pocket.

" We have quite a little round of afternoon calls to make," said he. " I think that Sir James Walter claims our first attention."

The house of the famous official was a fine villa with green lawns stretching down to the Thames. As we reached it the fog was lifting, and a thin, watery sunshine was breaking through. A butler answered our ring.

21 *a complete list of all foreign spies or international agents known to be in England.* Much has been made of the point that Holmes, at the time of "The Adventure of the Second Stain," knew offhand the names of the principal foreign spies in London, but that here he had to call on brother Mycroft's help. If the former occasion was in 1886 and the latter not until 1895, however, a lapse of memory is understandable. But it is by no means clear that any such lapse of memory existed. As Mr. Walter P. Armstrong, Jr., wrote in "The Truth About Sherlock Holmes": "Even supposing that Holmes was fully aware of [the identities of important foreign spies or international agents] this poses three additional questions: Were they in England? What were their addresses? Were there any others who might undertake so ambitious a plot as that involved in the theft of the Bruce-Partington plans? Of course it was the addresses in which he was particularly interested, and it was certainly logical to assume that in [almost ten] years men in such an uncertain line of business might have moved. Mycroft understood all this, for in his reply he said, 'There are numerous small fry, but few who would handle so big an affair.' . . . No doubt Holmes could have acquired [his] information through his own resources, but it was easier to wire Mycroft and time was pressing."

22 *his body was on the* roof *of a carriage.*" Holmes' "recognition of the fact that West's body was on the roof of the carriage seems a very long shot in the dark," Mr. T. S. Blakeney wrote in *Sherlock Holmes: Fact or Fiction?*, "and one cannot but feel that this was Holmes' lucky day. 'A single blunder on the part of the guilty man would have thrown all Holmes' deductions out of joint'—Father Knox's rather sweeping generalization—certainly applies to 'The Bruce-Partington Plans.' "

" Sir James, sir ! " said he, with solemn face. " Sir James died this morning."

" Good heavens ! " cried Holmes, in amazement. " How did he die ? "

" Perhaps you would care to step in, sir, and see his brother, Colonel Valentine ? " **23**

" Yes, we had best do so."

We were ushered into a dim-lit drawing-room, where an instant later we were joined by a very tall, handsome, light-bearded man of fifty, the younger brother of the dead scientist. His wild eyes, stained cheeks, and unkempt hair all spoke of the sudden blow which had fallen upon the household. He was hardly articulate as he spoke of it.

" It was this horrible scandal," said he. " My brother, Sir James, was a man of very sensitive honour, and he could not survive such an affair. It broke his heart. He was always so proud of the efficiency of his department, and this was a crushing blow."

" We had hoped that he might have given us some indications which would have helped us to clear the matter up."

" I assure you that it was all a mystery to him as it is to you and to all of us. He had already put all his knowledge at the disposal of the police. Naturally, he had no doubt that Cadogan West was guilty. But all the rest was inconceivable."

" You cannot throw any new light upon the affair ? "

" I know nothing myself save what I have read or heard. I have no desire to be discourteous, but you can understand, Mr. Holmes, that we are much disturbed at present, and I must ask you to hasten this interview to an end."

" This is indeed an unexpected development," said my friend when we had regained the cab. " I wonder if the death was natural, or whether the poor old fellow killed himself ! If the latter, may it be taken as some sign of self-reproach for duty neglected ? We must leave that question to the future. Now we shall turn to the Cadogan Wests."

A small but well-kept house in the outskirts of the town sheltered the bereaved mother. The old lady was too dazed with grief to be of any use to us, but at her side was a white-faced young lady, who introduced herself as Miss Violet Westbury, the fiancée of the dead man, and the last to see him upon that fatal night.

" I cannot explain it, Mr. Holmes," she said. " I have not shut an eye since the tragedy, thinking, thinking, thinking, night and day, what the true meaning of it can be. Arthur was the most single-minded, chivalrous, patriotic man upon earth. He would have cut his right hand off before he would sell a State secret confided to his keeping. It is absurd, impossible, preposterous to anyone who knew him."

" But the facts, Miss Westbury ? "

" Yes, yes ; I admit I cannot explain them."

" Was he in any want of money ? "

" No ; his needs were very simple and his salary ample. He had saved a few hundreds, and we were to marry at the New Year."

" No signs of any mental excitement ? Come, Miss

23 *his brother, Colonel Valentine?"* "Does—or did—a well-trained British butler refer to his employer's brother by his first name—Colonel Valentine?" Dr. Felix Morley asked in "The Bruce-Partington Keys."

Westbury, be absolutely frank with us."

The quick eye of my companion had noted some change in her manner. She coloured and hesitated.

" Yes," she said, at last. " I had a feeling that there was something on his mind."

" For long ? "

" Only for the last week or so. He was thoughtful and worried. Once I pressed him about it. He admitted that there was something, and that it was concerned with his official life. ' It is too serious for me to speak about, even to you,' said he. I could get nothing more."

Holmes looked grave.

" Go on, Miss Westbury. Even if it seems to tell against him, go on. We cannot say what it may lead to."

" Indeed I have nothing more to tell. Once or twice it seemed to me that he was on the point of telling me something. He spoke one evening of the importance of the secret, and I have some recollection that he said that no doubt foreign spies would pay a great deal to have it."

My friend's face grew graver still.

" Anything else ? "

" He said that we were slack about such matters—that it would be easy for a traitor to get the plans."

" Was it only recently that he made such remarks ? "

" Yes, quite recently."

" Now tell us of that last evening."

" We were to go to the theatre. The fog was so thick that a cab was useless. We walked, and our way took us close to the office. Suddenly he darted away into the fog."

" Without a word ? "

" He gave an exclamation ; that was all. I waited but he never returned. Then I walked home. Next morning, after the office opened, they came to inquire. About twelve o'clock we heard the terrible news. Oh, Mr. Holmes, if you could only, only save his honour ! It was so much to him."

Holmes shook his head sadly.

" Come, Watson," said he, " our ways lie elsewhere. Our next station must be the office from which the papers were taken."

" It was black enough before against this young man, but our inquiries make it blacker," he remarked, as the cab lumbered off. " His coming marriage gives a motive for the crime. He naturally wanted money. The idea was in his head, since he spoke about it. He nearly made the girl an accomplice in the treason by telling her his plans. It is all very bad."

" But surely, Holmes, character goes for something ? Then, again, why should he leave the girl in the street and dart away to commit a felony ? "

" Exactly ! There are certainly objections. But it is a formidable case which they have to meet."

Mr. Sidney Johnson, the senior clerk, met us at the office, and received us with that respect which my companion's card always commanded. He was a thin, gruff, bespectacled man of middle age, his cheeks haggard, and his hands twitching from the nervous strain to which he had been subjected.

" It is bad, Mr. Holmes, very bad ! Have you heard of the death of the Chief ? "

" We have just come from his house."

" The place is disorganized. The Chief dead, Cadogan West dead, our papers stolen. And yet, when we closed our door on Monday evening we were as efficient an office as any in the Government service. Good God, it's dreadful to think of ! That West, of all men, should have done such a thing ! "

" You are sure of his guilt, then ? "

" I can see no other way out of it. And yet I would have trusted him as I trust myself."

" At what hour was the office closed on Monday ? "

" At five."

" Did you close it ? "

" I am always the last man out."

" Where were the plans ? "

" In that safe. I put them there myself."

" Is there no watchman to the building ? "

" There is ; but he has other departments to look after as well. He is an old soldier and a most trustworthy man. He saw nothing that evening. Of course, the fog was very thick."

" Suppose that Cadogan West wished to make his way into the building after hours ; he would need three keys, would he not, before he could reach the papers ? "

" Yes, he would. The key of the outer door, the key of the office, and the key of the safe."

" Only Sir James Walter and you had those keys ? "

" I had no keys of the doors—only of the safe."

" Was Sir James a man who was orderly in his habits ? "

" Yes, I think he was. I know that so far as those three keys are concerned he kept them on the same ring. I have often seen them there."

" And that ring went with him to London ? "

" He said so."

" And your key never left your possession ? "

" Never." **24**

" Then West, if he is the culprit, must have had a duplicate. And yet none was found upon his body. One other point : if a clerk in this office desired to sell the plans, would it not be simpler to copy the plans for himself than to take the originals, as was actually done ? "

" It would take considerable technical knowledge to copy the plans in an effective way."

" But I suppose either Sir James, or you, or West had that technical knowledge ? "

" No doubt we had, but I beg you won't try to drag me into the matter, Mr. Holmes. What is the use of our speculating in this way when the original plans were actually found on West ? "

" Well, it is certainly singular that he should run the risk of taking originals, if he could safely have taken copies, which would have equally served his turn."

" Singular, no doubt—and yet he did so."

" Every inquiry in this case reveals something inexplicable. Now there are three papers still missing. They are, as I understand, the vital ones."

" Yes, that is so."

24 *"Never."* Wrote the editors of the *Sherlock Holmes Journal* in their issue of December, 1954: "[Reuben] Kelf-Cohen, a senior Civil Servant, recently discovered that the keys mentioned [in "The Adventure of the Bruce-Partington Plans"] just didn't add up. He thereupon wrote to Paul Gore-Booth, now H. M. Ambassador at Rangoon, for an explanation. Their letters . . . are given below. . . .

R. Kelf-Cohen to Paul Gore-Booth: "The safe in which the Plans were kept had two keys, one kept by Sir James Walter and the other by Mr. Sidney Johnson, the Senior Clerk at Woolwich—a typical Civil Servant. Sir James had three keys on his ring—the key of the outer door, the key of the office and the key of the safe. Mr. Sidney Johnson, *according to his own statement,* had only the key of the safe. Yet, according to the story told by Mycroft, 'Sir James left for London about three o'clock, taking his keys with him.' Mr. Johnson, on the other hand, informed Sherlock Holmes that the office closed on Monday at five o'clock and that he was, as always, 'the last man out.' How could Mr. Johnson let himself out without a complete set of keys? Why did he conceal the fact that he had such a set? You will agree that it is normal Civil Service practice for Sidney Johnson, the Senior Clerk, to be responsible for closing the office and making everything secure. Would the Head of Chancery leave it to the Ambassador to secure everything in the Chancery at the end of the day? And yet this is what Mycroft suggested and Sherlock Holmes swallowed."

Paul Gore-Booth to R. Kelf-Cohen: "'All my instincts are against this explanation,' as a better man than I am said in the same context. We clearly cannot infer that Mr. Johnson was lying. Civil Servants do not—but need I say more. We must therefore seek the solution elsewhere. Two possibilities suggest themselves. 1. The offices had spring locks. I do not know whether spring locks had been invented in 1895, but there is a pretty little problem to examine. 2. The offices, as opposed to the safe, were closed with keys on one of those clumsy bits of wood which, in my day when I was 'twenty-seven years of age, unmarried and a clerk,' were handed in at some central point and were not taken home. 1. is the obvious first resort, but I don't like it much. Supposing the door blew shut in office hours and Mr. Johnson had gone out for natural purposes, could he only get in by summoning Sir James to open the door? Nothing is impossible—only that doesn't seem likely. The advantage of 2. is that it is good Civil Servant practice, or was, anyway. The Head of the Department probably would have his private keys of the doors but there was no good reason to make a lot of spares, if there was some way of getting at the Departmental set. Perhaps they were left with the 'old soldier and . . . most trustworthy man.' The weakness of 2. is that, if it is correct, it was all taken for granted in rather a surprising way. But what seems to me much more surprising was the way Colonel Valentine Walter was allowed to go messing about the place within reach of the documents; no wonder Sir J. found it all a crushing blow."

25 *after he had left the lady about 7.30.* "This was doubly not true," Mr. Roger Clapp wrote in "The Curious Problem of the Railway Timetables," "since there was no 8.15 train and there were two earlier trains at 7.44 and 8.04."

"DO YOU MEAN TO SAY THAT ANYONE HOLDING THESE THREE PAPERS . . . COULD CONSTRUCT A BRUCE-PARTINGTON SUBMARINE?"

Illustration by Arthur Twidle for the *Strand Magazine*, December, 1908.

" Do you mean to say that anyone holding these three papers, and without the seven others, could construct a Bruce-Partington submarine ? "

" I reported to that effect to the Admiralty. But to-day I have been over the drawings again, and I am not so sure of it. The double valves with the automatic self-adjusting slots are drawn in one of the papers which have been returned. Until the foreigners had invented that for themselves they could not make the boat. Of course, they might soon get over the difficulty."

" But the three missing drawings are the most important ? "

" Undoubtedly."

" I think, with your permission, I will now take a stroll round the premises. I do not recall any other question which I desired to ask."

He examined the lock of the safe, the door of the room, and finally the iron shutters of the window. It was only when we were on the lawn outside that his interest was strongly excited. There was a laurel bush outside the window, and several of the branches bore signs of having been twisted or snapped. He examined them carefully with his lens, and then some dim and vague marks upon the earth beneath. Finally he asked the chief clerk to close the iron shutters, and he pointed out to me that they hardly met in the centre, and that it would be possible for anyone outside to see what was going on within the room.

" The indications are ruined by the three days' delay. They may mean something or nothing. Well, Watson, I do not think that Woolwich can help us further. It is a small crop which we have gathered. Let us see if we can do better in London."

Yet we added one more sheaf to our harvest before we left Woolwich Station. The clerk in the ticket office was able to say with confidence that he saw Cadogan West—whom he knew well by sight—upon the Monday night, and that he went to London by the 8.15 to London Bridge. He was alone, and took a single third-class ticket. The clerk was struck at the time by his excited and nervous manner. So shaky was he that he could hardly pick up his change, and the clerk had helped him with it. A reference to the time-table showed that the 8.15 was the first train which it was possible for West to take after he had
25 left the lady about 7.30.

" Let us reconstruct, Watson," said Holmes, after half an hour of silence. " I am not aware that in all our joint researches we have ever had a case which was more difficult to get at. Every fresh advance which we make only reveals a fresh ridge beyond. And yet we have surely made some appreciable progress.

" The effect of our inquiries at Woolwich has in the main been against young Cadogan West ; but the indications at the window would lend themselves to a more favourable hypothesis. Let us suppose, for example, that he had been approached by some foreign agent. It might have been done under such pledges as would have prevented him from speaking of it, and yet would have affected his thoughts in the direction indicated by his remarks to his fiancée. Very good. We will now suppose that as he went to the theatre with the young lady he suddenly, in the fog, caught a glimpse of this same agent going in the direction of the office. He was an impetuous man, quick in his decisions. Everything gave way to his duty. He followed the man, reached the window, saw the abstraction of the documents, and pursued the thief. In this way we get over the objection that no one would take originals when he could make copies. This outsider had to take originals. So far it holds together."

"What is the next step?"

"Then we come into difficulties. One would imagine that under such circumstances the first act of young Cadogan West would be to seize the villain and raise the alarm. Why did he not do so? Could it have been an official superior who took the papers? That would explain West's conduct. Or could the Chief have given West the slip in the fog, and West started at once to London to head him off from his own rooms, presuming that he knew where the rooms were? The call must have been very pressing, since he left his girl standing in the fog, and made no effort to communicate with her. Our scent runs cold here, and there is a vast gap between either hypothesis and the laying of West's body, with seven papers in his pocket, on the roof of a Metropolitan train. My instinct now is to work from the other end. If Mycroft has given us the list of addresses we may be able to pick our man, and follow two tracks instead of one."

Surely enough, a note awaited us at Baker Street. A Government messenger had brought it post-haste. Holmes glanced at it and threw it over to me.

"There are numerous small fry, but few who would
handle so big an affair. The only men worth considering
are Adolph Meyer, of 13 Great George Street, West- **26**
minster; Louis La Rothière, of Campden Mansions,
Notting Hill; and Hugo Oberstein, 13 Caulfield Gardens, Kensington. The latter was known to be in town **27**
on Monday, and is now reported as having left. Glad to hear you have seen some light. The Cabinet awaits your final report with the utmost anxiety. Urgent representations have arrived from the very highest quarter. The whole force of the State is at your back if you should need it.—MYCROFT."

"I'm afraid," said Holmes, smiling, "that all the Queen's horses and all the Queen's men cannot avail in this matter." He had spread out his big map of London, and leaned eagerly over it. "Well, well," said he presently, with an exclamation of satisfaction, "things are turning a little in our direction at last. Why, Watson, I do honestly believe that we are going to pull it off after all." He slapped me on the shoulder with a sudden burst of hilarity. "I am going out now. It is only a reconnaissance. I will do nothing serious without my trusted comrade and biographer at my elbow. Do you stay here, and the odds are that you will see me again in an hour or two. If time hangs heavy get foolscap and a pen, and

26 *13 Great George Street.* Great George Street runs from the corner of Birdcage Walk and Prince Street to the corner of Parliament Square. "Talk about squatting on the enemy's doorstep!" Mr. Michael Harrison wrote (*In the Footsteps of Sherlock Holmes*). "Mr. Meyer had almost taken up his quarters in the enemy's office!"

27 *13 Caulfield Gardens.* The late Christopher Morley thought that "Caulfield Gardens" was probably "Courtfield Road or Courtfield Gardens." But Mr. Michael Harrison suggests that "Caulfield Gardens" should be read "Cornwall Gardens." Oberstein's house, he writes, must have lain "at the southern side of the western half . . . , for here the back of the houses overlook a vast, open cutting in which the District and Metropolitan lines are joined."

begin your narrative of how we saved the State."

I felt some reflection of his elation in my own mind, for I knew well that he would not depart so far from his usual austerity of demeanour unless there was good cause for exultation. All the long November evening I waited, filled with impatience for his return. At last, shortly after nine o'clock there arrived a messenger with a note :

" Am dining at Goldini's Restaurant, Gloucester Road, Kensington. Please come at once and join me there. Bring with you a jemmy, a dark lantern, a chisel, and a revolver.—S.H."

It was a nice equipment for a respectable citizen to carry through the dim, fog-draped streets. I stowed them all discreetly away in my overcoat, and drove straight to the address given. There sat my friend at a little round table near the door of the garish Italian restaurant.

" Have you had something to eat ? Then join me in a coffee and curaçao. Try one of the proprietor's cigars. They are less poisonous than one would expect. Have you the tools ? "

" They are here, in my overcoat."

" Excellent. Let me give you a short sketch of what I have done, with some indication of what we are about to do. Now it must be evident to you, Watson, that this young man's body was *placed* on the roof of the train. That was clear from the instant that I determined the fact that it was from the roof, and not from a carriage, that he had fallen."

" Could it not have been dropped from a bridge ? "

" I should say it was impossible. If you examine the roofs you will find that they are slightly rounded, and there is no railing round them. Therefore, we can say for certain that young Cadogan West was placed on it."

" How could he be placed there ? "

" That was the question which we had to answer. There is only one possible way. You are aware that the Underground runs clear of tunnels at some points in the West End. I had a vague memory that as I have travelled by it I have occasionally seen windows just above my head. Now, suppose that a train halted under such a window, would there be any difficulty in laying a body upon the roof ? "

" It seems most improbable."

" We must fall back upon the old axiom that when all other contingencies fail, whatever remains, however improbable, must be the truth. Here all other contingencies *have* failed. When I found that the leading international agent, who had just left London, lived in a row of houses which abutted upon the Underground, I was so pleased that you were a little astonished at my sudden frivolity."

" Oh, that was it, was it ? "

" Yes, that was it. Mr. Hugo Oberstein, of 13 Caulfield Gardens, had become my objective. I began my operations at Gloucester Road Station, where a very helpful official walked with me along the track, and allowed me to satisfy myself, not only that the back-stair windows of

Caulfield Gardens open on the line, but the even more essential fact that, owing to the intersection of one of the larger railways, the Underground trains are frequently held motionless for some minutes at that very spot."

" Splendid, Holmes ! You have got it ! "

" So far—so far, Watson. We advance, but the goal is afar. Well, having seen the back of Caulfield Gardens, I visited the front and satisfied myself that the bird was indeed flown. It is a considerable house, unfurnished, so far as I could judge, in the upper rooms. Oberstein lived there with a single valet, who was probably a confederate entirely in his confidence. We must bear in mind that Oberstein has gone to the Continent to dispose of his booty, but not with any idea of flight ; for he had no reason to fear a warrant, and the idea of an amateur domiciliary visit would certainly never occur to him. Yet that is precisely what we are about to make."

" Could we not get a warrant and legalize it ? "

" Hardly on the evidence." 28

" What can we hope to do ? "

" We cannot tell what correspondence may be there."

" I don't like it, Holmes."

" My dear fellow, you shall keep watch in the street. I'll do the criminal part. It's not a time to stick at trifles. Think of Mycroft's note, of the Admiralty, the Cabinet, the exalted person who waits for news. We are bound to go."

My answer was to rise from the table.

" You are right, Holmes. We are bound to go."

He sprang up and shook me by the hand.

" I knew you would not shrink at the last," said he, and for a moment I saw something in his eyes which was nearer to tenderness than I had ever seen. The next instant he was his masterful, practical self once more.

" It is nearly half a mile, but there is no hurry. Let us walk," said he. " Don't drop the instruments, I beg. Your arrest as a suspicious character would be a most unfortunate complication." 29

Caulfield Gardens was one of those lines of flat-faced, pillared, and porticoed houses which are so prominent a product of the middle Victorian epoch in the West End of London. Next door there appeared to be a children's party, for the merry buzz of young voices and the clatter of a piano resounded through the night. The fog still hung about and screened us with its friendly shade. Holmes had lit his lantern and flashed it upon the massive door.

" This is a serious proposition," said he. " It is certainly bolted as well as locked. We would do better in the area. There is an excellent archway down yonder in case a too zealous policeman should intrude. Give me a hand, Watson, and I'll do the same for you."

A minute later we were both in the area. Hardly had we reached the dark shadows before the step of the policeman was heard in the fog above. As its soft rhythm died away, Holmes set to work upon the lower door. I saw him stoop and strain until with a sharp crash it flew open. We sprang through into the dark passage, closing the area

28 *"Hardly on the evidence."* Again "the reader gets a chance to see the detective's legal mind at work," Mr. Albert P. Blaustein wrote in "Sherlock Holmes As a Lawyer."

29 *a most unfortunate complication."* Again "Holmes' knowledge of the British law [is] in evidence, for he was well aware that it is a serious offense to be caught in possession of housebreaking tools by night," Mr. Doyle W. Beckemeyer commented in "The Irregular Holmes."

door behind us. Holmes led the way up the curving, uncarpeted stair. His little fan of yellow light shone
30 upon a low window.

"Here we are, Watson—this must be the one." He threw it open, and as he did so there was a low, harsh murmur, growing steadily into a loud roar as a train dashed past us in the darkness. Holmes swept his light along the window-sill. It was thickly coated with soot from the passing engines, but the black surface was blurred and rubbed in places.

"You can see where they rested the body. Halloa, Watson! what is this? There can be no doubt that it is a blood mark." He was pointing to faint discolorations along the woodwork of the window. "Here it is on the stone of the stair also. The demonstration is complete. Let us stay here until a train stops."

We had not long to wait. The very next train roared from the tunnel as before, but slowed in the open, and then, with a creaking of brakes, pulled up immediately beneath us. It was not four feet from the window-ledge to the roof of the carriages. Holmes softly closed the window.

"So far we are justified," said he. "What do you think of it, Watson?"

"A masterpiece. You have never risen to a greater height."

"I cannot agree with you there. From the moment that I conceived the idea of the body being upon the roof, which surely was not a very abstruse one, all the rest was inevitable. If it were not for the grave interests involved the affair up to this point would be insignificant. Our difficulties are still before us. But perhaps we may find something here which may help us."

We had ascended the kitchen stair and entered the suite of rooms upon the first floor. One was a dining-room, severely furnished and containing nothing of interest. A second was a bedroom, which also drew blank. The remaining room appeared more promising, and my companion settled down to a systematic examination. It was littered with books and papers, and was evidently used as a study. Swiftly and methodically Holmes turned over the contents of drawer after drawer and cupboard after cupboard, but no gleam of success came to brighten his austere face. At the end of an hour he was no further than when he started.

"The cunning dog has covered his tracks," said he. "He has left nothing to incriminate him. His dangerous correspondence has been destroyed or removed. This is our last chance."

It was a small tin cash-box which stood upon the writing-desk. Holmes prised it open with his chisel. Several rolls of paper were within, covered with figures and calculations, without any note to show to what they referred. The recurring words, "Water pressure," and "Pressure to the square inch" suggested some possible relation to a submarine. Holmes tossed them all impatiently aside. There only remained an envelope with some small newspaper slips inside it. He shook them out on the table, and at once I saw by his eager face that his hopes had been raised.

30 *His little fan of yellow light shone upon a low window.* "It should be pointed out that the expression . . . 'His little fan of yellow light' is not merely a phrase to catch the fancy," Mr. Melvin Cross wrote in "The Lantern of Sherlock Holmes." "With many lanterns, an inverted, more or less indistinct image of the flame is actually projected, let us say, upon the wall; it is roughly triangular, with the base of the triangle at the top. So Dr. Watson's metaphor 'fan' is quite precise. To the general reader this will not be worth notice, but to an 'Irregular' it will be considered a technical detail drawn to a nicety." Mr. Cross pointed out in this same article that the most satisfactory illuminant for a dark lantern is signal oil; this, undoubtedly, was what Holmes used: "It gives a rather yellow light."

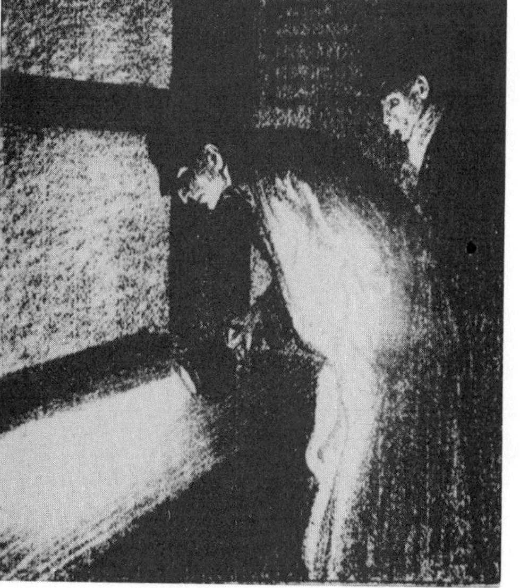

HOLMES SWEPT HIS LIGHT ALONG THE WINDOW-SILL.

The same scene as depicted by two different artists: *Above*, by Frederic Dorr Steele for *Collier's Magazine,* December 18, 1908; *Below*, by Arthur Twidle for the *Strand Magazine*, December, 1908.

" What's this, Watson ? Eh ? What's this ? Record of a series of messages in the advertisements of a paper. *Daily Telegraph* agony column by the print and paper. Right-hand top corner of a page. No dates—but messages arrange themselves. This must be the first :

" ' Hoped to hear sooner. Terms agreed to. Write fully to address given on card.—Pierrot.'

" Next comes : ' Too complex for description. Must have full report. Stuff awaits you when goods delivered. —Pierrot.'

" Then comes : ' Matter presses. Must withdraw offer unless contract completed. Make appointment by letter. Will confirm by advertisement.—Pierrot.'

" Finally : ' Monday night after nine. Two taps. Only ourselves. Do not be so suspicious. Payment in hard cash when goods delivered.—Pierrot.'

" A fairly complete record, Watson ! If we could only get at the man at the other end ! " He sat lost in thought, tapping his fingers on the table. Finally he sprang to his feet.

" Well, perhaps it won't be so difficult after all. There is nothing more to be done here, Watson. I think we might drive round to the offices of the *Daily Telegraph*, and so bring a good day's work to a conclusion."

Mycroft Holmes and Lestrade had come round by appointment after breakfast next day and Sherlock Holmes had recounted to them our proceedings of the day before. The professional shook his head over our confessed
burglary. 31

" We can't do these things in the force, Mr. Holmes," said he. " No wonder you get results that are beyond us. But some of these days you'll go too far, and you'll find yourself and your friend in trouble."

" For England, home and beauty—eh, Watson ? Mar- 32
tyrs on the altar of our country. But what do you think of it, Mycroft ? "

" Excellent, Sherlock ! Admirable ! But what use will you make of it ? "

Holmes picked up the *Daily Telegraph* which lay upon the table.

" Have you seen Pierrot's advertisement to-day ? "

" What ! Another one ? "

" Yes, here it is : ' To-night. Same hour. Same place. Two taps. Most vitally important. Your own safety at stake.—Pierrot.' "

" By George ! " cried Lestrade. " If he answers that we've got him ! "

" That was my idea when I put it in. I think if you could both make it convenient to come with us about eight o'clock to Caulfield Gardens we might possibly get a little nearer to a solution."

One of the most remarkable characteristics of Sherlock Holmes was his power of throwing his brain out of action and switching all his thoughts on to lighter things whenever he had convinced himself that he could no longer work to advantage. I remember that during the whole of that memorable day he lost himself in a monograph which
he had undertaken upon the Polyphonic Motets of Lassus. 33

31 *our confessed burglary.* But Magistrate S. Tupper Bigelow has shown ("Sherlock Holmes Was No Burglar") that, under the letter of British law, Holmes and Watson were guilty of neither burglary nor unlawful entry.

32 *"For England, home and beauty.* A traditional toast in the British Navy.

33 *the Polyphonic Motets of Lassus.* "Briefly, [a motet] is a musical composition not very different from an anthem," Mr. Richard Wait wrote in "The Case of the Neophyte and the Motet." "Its words generally have a biblical origin and are in continuous or prose form (although there are motets which are metrical and rhymed) and it is usually founded upon Gregorian tones. Originally it was sung between the *credo* and the *sanctus* in the mass. The words of the motets which Holmes fancied were Latin but some may be found in the vulgar tongue. The motet is polyphonic when composed for several voices."

Orlando or Orlande or Orlandus (or Roland or Robert) Lassus or di Lasso or de Lattre was born at Mons in 1532 and died at Munich, June 14, 1594. If not the greatest composer of the sixteenth century he was undoubtedly one of the greatest influences in sixteenth-century music. His first book of motets, dedicated to Antoine Perrenet, Bishop of Arras, was published at Antwerp in 1556. On December 7, 1570, at the Diet of Spires, the Emperor Maximilian ennobled Lassus and his posterity, and gave the eminent musician a grant of arms. Two years earlier, in 1568, Lassus had published two comprehensive collections of motets at Nuremberg.

"Musicians have often wondered why Holmes evinced special interest in the motets and seemingly paid no attention to the approximately 2,500 other liturgical and secular works with which this master enriched our musical heritage," Mr. Benjamin Grosbayne wrote in "Sherlock Holmes—Musician." "Perhaps Holmes returned to Lassus on his bee farm and wrote other monographs on the masses, the madrigals, the villanelles, the chansons, and especially, on the Psalmi Davidis poenitentiales."

In any case, only a Watson could have described a monograph on Lassus as one of the "lighter things," fit only for one who "could no longer work," as the late Harvey Officer pointed out in "Sherlock Holmes and Music." "The motets of di Lasso number five hundred and ten, filling eleven volumes of the great Breitkopf and Härtel edition. They are written for voices ranging in number from two to twelve. One cannot hear these motets today anywhere in the world. One cannot play them, for they are meant for voices only, and would be meaningless if played on instruments. One can only do what Sherlock Holmes must have been able to do, i.e., read them, and then with the ear of the mind hear their complicated web of sounds."

BEFORE OUR PRISONER HAD RECOVERED HIS BALANCE THE DOOR WAS SHUT AND HOLMES STANDING WITH HIS BACK AGAINST IT.

Illustration by Arthur Twidle for the *Strand Magazine,* December, 1908.

For my own part I had none of this power of detachment, and the day, in consequence, appeared to be interminable. The great national importance of the issue, the suspense in high quarters, the direct nature of the experiment which we were trying—all combined to work upon my nerve. It was a relief to me when at last, after a light dinner, we set out upon our expedition. Lestrade and Mycroft met us by appointment at the outside of Gloucester Road Station. The area door of Oberstein's house had been left open the night before, and it was necessary for me, as Mycroft Holmes absolutely and indignantly declined to climb the railings, to pass in and open the hall door. By nine o'clock we were all seated in the study, waiting patiently for our man.

An hour passed and yet another. When eleven struck,
34 the measured beat of the great church clock seemed to sound the dirge of our hopes. Lestrade and Mycroft were fidgeting in their seats and looking twice a minute at their watches. Holmes sat silent and composed, his eyelids half shut, but every sense on the alert. He raised his head with a sudden jerk.

" He is coming," said he.

There had been a furtive step past the door. Now it returned. We heard a shuffling sound outside, and then two sharp taps with the knocker. Holmes rose, motioning to us to remain seated. The gas in the hall was a mere point of light. He opened the outer door, and then as a dark figure slipped past him he closed and fastened it. " This way ! " we heard him say, and a moment later our man stood before us. Holmes had followed him closely, and as the man turned with a cry of surprise and alarm he caught him by the collar and threw him back into the room. Before our prisoner had recovered his balance the door was shut and Holmes standing with his back against it. The man glared round him, staggered, and fell senseless upon the floor. With the shock, his broad-brimmed hat flew from his head, his cravat slipped down from his lips, and there was the long light beard and the soft, handsome delicate features of Colonel Valentine Walter.

Holmes gave a whistle of surprise.

" You can write me down an ass this time, Watson,"
35 said he. " This was not the bird that I was looking for."

" Who is he ? " asked Mycroft eagerly.

" The younger brother of the late Sir James Walter, the head of the Submarine Department. Yes, yes ; I see the fall of the cards. He is coming to. I think that you had best leave his examination to me."

We had carried the prostrate body to the sofa. Now our prisoner sat up, looked round him with a horror-stricken face, and passed his hand over his forehead, like one who cannot believe his own senses.

" What is this ? " he asked. " I came here to visit Mr. Oberstein."

" Everything is known, Colonel Walter," said Holmes. " How an English gentleman could behave in such a manner is beyond my comprehension. But your whole correspondence and relations with Oberstein are within our knowledge. So also are the circumstances connected with the death of young Cadogan West. Let me advise you to gain at least the small credit for repentance and confession,

34 *the great church clock.* Probably St. Stephen's Church on Gloucester Road.

35 *"This was not the bird that I was looking for."* ". . . who, if not Walter, was the 'bird' Holmes was expecting?" Mr. Nathan L. Bengis has asked. "There can be little doubt that the man Holmes had in mind was Sidney Johnson, the senior clerk. Logically, indeed, he was the ideal suspect, as all indications point to him, whereas few if any point to Colonel Walter: Johnson had locked up the plans for the night, he was always the last man out, and he was known to have a key to the safe."

since there are still some details which we can only learn from your lips."

The man groaned and sank his face in his hands. We waited, but he was silent.

" I can assure you," said Holmes, " that every essential is already known. We know that you were pressed for money ; that you took an impress of the keys which your brother held ; and that you entered into a correspondence with Oberstein, who answered your letters through the advertisement columns of the *Daily Telegraph*. We are aware that you went down to the office in the fog on Monday night, but that you were seen and followed by young Cadogan West, who had probably some previous reason to suspect you. He saw your theft, but could not give the alarm, as it was just possible that you were taking the papers to your brother in London. Leaving all his private concerns, like the good citizen that he was, he followed you closely in the fog, and kept at your heels until you reached this very house. There he intervened, and then it was, Colonel Walter, that to treason you added the more terrible crime of murder."

" I did not ! I did not ! Before God I swear that I did not ! " cried our wretched prisoner.

" Tell us, then, how Cadogan West met his end before you laid him upon the roof of a railway carriage."

" I will. I swear to you that I will. I did the rest. I confess it. It was just as you say. A Stock Exchange debt had to be paid. I needed the money badly. Oberstein offered me five thousand. It was to save myself from ruin. But as to murder, I am as innocent as you."

" What happened then ? "

" He had his suspicions before, and he followed me as you describe. I never knew it until I was at the very door. It was thick fog, and one could not see three yards. I had given two taps and Oberstein had come to the door. The young man rushed up and demanded to know what we were about to do with the papers. Oberstein had a short life-preserver. He always carried it with him. As West forced his way after us into the house Oberstein struck him on the head. The blow was a fatal one. He was dead within five minutes. There he lay in the hall, and we were at our wits' end what to do. Then Oberstein had this idea about the trains which halted under his back window. But first he examined the papers which I had brought. He said that three of them were essential, and that he must keep them. ' You cannot keep them,' said I. ' There will be a dreadful row at Woolwich if they are not returned.' ' I must keep them,' said he, ' for they are so technical that it is impossible in the time to make copies.' ' Then they must all go back together to-night,' said I. He thought for a little, and then he cried out that he had it. ' Three I will keep,' said he. ' The others we will stuff into the pocket of this young man. When he is found the whole business will assuredly be put to his account.' I could see no other way out of it, so we did as he suggested. We waited half an hour at the window before a train stopped. It was so thick that nothing could be seen, and we had no difficulty in lowering West's body on to the train. That was the end of the matter so far as I was concerned." **36**

"THAT WAS THE END OF THE MATTER"

Illustration by Arthur Twidle for the *Strand Magazine*, December, 1908.

36 *That was the end of the matter so far as I was concerned.*" But the question remains: did Cadogan West's body travel from Gloucester Road to Aldgate on the "inner rail" (that is, via Victoria), or on the "outer rail" (that is, via Baker Street)? In October, 1951, the late Norman Crump went over the same ground as Sherlock Holmes and concluded that "the inner rail is the most probable, in all respects save one. This is the absence of any windows overlooking it between High Street and Gloucester Road. Therefore it looks like the outer rail [although] this postulates [six] extreme improbabilities . . ."

On the other hand, Mr. Cornelis Helling, referring to *The Railways of Britain, Past and Present*, by O. S. Nock (London: B. T. Batsford, Ltd., Second Edition, 1949) has written that "an Inner Circle train was concerned, and at that time, of course, it would have been steam hauled, by one of those supremely ugly, yet most efficient Beyer-Peacock tank engines. Had the train chanced instead to be one on the Outer Circle service, the body, far from remaining on the roof all the way

"And your brother?"

"He said nothing, but he had caught me once with his keys, and I think that he suspected. I read in his eyes that he suspected. As you know, he never held up his head again."

There was silence in the room. It was broken by Mycroft Holmes.

"Can you not make reparation? It would ease your conscience, and possibly your punishment."

"What reparation can I make?"

"Where is Oberstein with the papers?"

"I do not know."

"Did he give you no address?"

"He said that letters to the Hôtel du Louvre, Paris, would eventually reach him."

"Then reparation is still within your power," said Sherlock Holmes.

"I will do anything I can. I owe this fellow no particular goodwill. He has been my ruin and my downfall."

"Here are paper and pen. Sit at this desk and write to my dictation. Direct the envelope to the address given. That is right. Now the letter: 'Dear Sir,—With regard to our transaction, you will no doubt have observed by now that one essential detail is missing. I have a tracing which will make it complete. This has involved me in extra trouble, however, and I must ask you for a further advance of five hundred pounds. I will not trust it to the post, nor will I take anything but gold or notes. I would come to you abroad, but it would excite remark if I left the country at present. Therefore I shall expect to meet you in the smoking-room of the Charing Cross Hotel at noon on Saturday. Remember that only English notes, or gold, will be taken.' That will do very well. I shall be very much surprised if it does not fetch our man."

And it did! It is a matter of history—that secret history of a nation which is often so much more intimate and interesting than its public chronicles—that Oberstein, eager to complete the coup of his lifetime, came to the lure
37 and was safely engulfed for fifteen years in a British prison. In his trunk were found the invaluable Bruce-Partington plans, which he had put up for auction in all the naval centres of Europe.

Colonel Walter died in prison towards the end of the second year of his sentence. As to Holmes, he returned refreshed to his monograph upon the Polyphonic Motets of Lassus, which has since been printed for private circulation, and is said by experts to be the last word upon the subject. Some weeks afterwards I learned incidentally that my friend spent a day at Windsor, whence he returned with a remarkably fine emerald tie-pin. When I asked him if he had bought it, he answered that it was a present from a certain gracious lady in whose interests he had once been fortunate enough to carry out a small commission. He said no more; but I fancy that I could guess at that lady's august name, and I have little doubt that the emerald pin will for ever recall to my friend's memory the adventure of the Bruce-Partington plans.

from Gloucester Road till the sharp curve at Minories Junction, might have rolled off at the very first start with [that] one particular engine. The 'Outer Circle' was not really a circle at all, but merely a horseshoe as it consisted of a shuttle service between Broad Street and Mansion House, by way of Hampstead Heath, Willesden and Earl's Court. It was operated by the London and North Western Railway, utilizing running powers over the Underground line from Earl's Court to Mansion House."

37 *was safely engulfed for fifteen years in a British prison.* "What were the extenuating circumstances whereby Oberstein got only fifteen years for as cold-blooded and indefensible a murder as can be found?" Dr. Felix Morley asked in "The Bruce-Partington Keys."

56

THE ADVENTURE OF THE VEILED LODGER

[*October, 1896; one day*]

WHEN one considers that Mr. Sherlock Holmes was in active practice for twenty-three years, and that during seventeen of these I was allowed to co-operate with him and to keep notes of his doings, it will be clear that I have a mass of material at my command. The problem has always been, not to find, but to choose. There is the long row of year-books which fill a shelf, and there are the dispatch-cases filled with documents, a perfect quarry for the student, not only of crime, but of the social and official scandals of the late Victorian era. Concerning these latter, I may say that the writers of agonized letters, who beg that the honour of their families or the reputation of famous forbears may not be touched, have nothing to fear. The discretion and high sense of professional honour which have always distinguished my friend are still at work in the choice of these memoirs, and no confidence will be abused. I deprecate, however, in the strongest way the attempts which have been made lately to get at and to destroy these papers. The source of these outrages is known, and if they are repeated I have Mr. Holmes' authority for saying that the whole story concerning the
politician, the lighthouse and the trained cormorant will **1**
be given to the public. There is at least one reader who will understand.

It is not reasonable to suppose that every one of these cases gave Holmes the opportunity of showing those curious gifts of instinct and observation which I have endeavoured to set forth in these memoirs. Sometimes he had with much effort to pick the fruit, sometimes it fell easily into his lap. But the most terrible human tragedies were often involved in these cases which brought him the fewest personal opportunities, and it is one of these which I now desire to record. In telling it, I have made a slight change of name and place, but otherwise the facts are as stated.

One forenoon—it was late in 1896—I received a hur- **2**
ried note from Holmes asking for my attendance. When I arrived, I found him seated in a smoke-laden atmosphere, with an elderly, motherly woman of the buxom landlady type in the corresponding chair in front of him.

1 *the politician, the lighthouse and the trained cormorant.* "The training of cormorants is not widely practiced in Britain," Mr. Paul H. Gore-Booth wrote in "The Journeys of Sherlock Holmes." "But it is a well-known Far Eastern custom to train cormorants to catch fish in such a way that they are not swallowed, but are brought back to the owner (of the cormorant), and this suggests that there may have been a Chinese or Japanese involved in the case. A lighthouse suggests a shipwreck, and the significance of the title must suddenly dawn on us when we remember that the first Japanese (Nippon Yusen Kaisha) steamship came to Europe in 1895. There we have the whole scene; Japan emerging as a modern power (she had just defeated China in the war of 1894 and the era of the Russo-Japanese War and the Anglo-Japanese Alliance was fast approaching); a prominent Japanese politician embarks secretly on one of the new Japanese ships for England; there is a mishap in a storm or a fog; the ship and the politician disappear within hail of the lighthouse, and all that is left as material for Mr. Holmes is the trained cormorant. A fascinating case."

It has fascinated, among others, Mr. Ralph A. Ashton, whose pastiche, "The Adventure of the Pius Missal," appeared in the *Baker Street Journal*, Vol. VII, No. 3, New Series, July, 1957, pp. 149–52; and Mr. Howard Collins, whose pastiche, "The Affair of the Politician, the Lighthouse, and the Trained Cormorant," appeared in the *Baker Street Journal*, Vol. II, No. 2, Old Series, April, 1947, pp. 195–204.

2 *it was late in 1896.* Mrs. Ronder had been a lodger at Mrs. Merrilow's "for seven years," before which she had suffered "for many a weary month" as a result of the Abbas Parva tragedy. Watson had no recollection of that case, although Holmes had been brought into it by young Edmunds of the Berkshire Constabulary and Watson was with Holmes at the time. The Abbas Parva tragedy would seem to have taken place early in 1889 or late in 1888, and Watson, as we have seen, was with Holmes all through the year 1888 and the first four months of 1889. Watson's date of 1896 for "The Adventure of the Veiled Lodger" would seem to be substantiated.

" This is Mrs. Merrilow, of South Brixton," said my friend, with a wave of the hand. " Mrs. Merrilow does not object to tobacco, Watson, if you wish to indulge your filthy habits. Mrs. Merrilow has an interesting story to tell which may well lead to further developments in which your presence may be useful."

" Anything I can do——"

" You will understand, Mrs. Merrilow, that if I come to Mrs. Ronder I should prefer to have a witness. You will make her understand that before we arrive."

" Lord bless you, Mr. Holmes," said our visitor; " she is that anxious to see you that you might bring the whole parish at your heels ! "

" Then we shall come early in the afternoon. Let us see that we have our facts correct before we start. If we go over them it will help Dr. Watson to understand the situation. You say that Mrs. Ronder has been your lodger for seven years and that you have only once seen her face."

" And I wish to God I had not ! " said Mrs. Merrilow.

" It was, I understand, terribly mutilated."

" Well, Mr. Holmes, you would hardly say it was a face at all. That's how it looked. Our milkman got a glimpse of her once peeping out of the upper window, and he dropped his tin and the milk all over the front garden. That is the kind of face it is. When I saw her—I happened on her unawares—she covered up quick, and then she said, ' Now, Mrs. Merrilow, you know at last why it is that I never raise my veil.' "

" Do you know anything about her history ? "

" Nothing at all."

" Did she give references when she came ? "

" No, sir, but she gave hard cash, and plenty of it. A quarter's rent right down on the table in advance and no arguing about terms. In these times a poor woman like me can't afford to turn down a chance like that."

" Did she give any reason for choosing your house ? "

" Mine stands well back from the road and is more private than most. Then, again, I only take the one, and I have no family of my own. I reckon she had tried others and found that mine suited her best. It's privacy she is after, and she is ready to pay for it."

" You say that she never showed her face from first to last save on the one accidental occasion. Well, it is a very remarkable story, most remarkable, and I don't wonder that you want it examined."

" I don't, Mr. Holmes. I am quite satisfied so long as I get my rent. You could not have a quieter lodger or one who gives less trouble."

" Then what has brought matters to a head ? "

" Her health, Mr. Holmes. She seems to be wasting away. And there's something terrible on her mind. ' Murder ! ' she cries. ' Murder ! ' And once I heard her, ' You cruel beast ! You monster ! ' she cried. It was in the night, and it fair rang through the house and sent the shivers through me. So I went to her in the morning. ' Mrs. Ronder,' I says, ' if you have anything that is troubling your soul, there's the clergy,' I says, ' and there's the police. Between them you should get some help.' ' For God's sake, not the police ! ' says she, 'and the clergy can't change what is past. And yet,' she says, 'it would ease my mind if someone knew the truth before I died.' 'Well,' says I, 'if you won't have the regulars, there is this detective man what we read about '—beggin' your pardon, Mr. Holmes. And she, she fair jumped at it. 'That's the man,' says she. 'I wonder I never thought of it before. Bring him here, Mrs. Merrilow, and if he won't come, tell him I am the wife of Ronder's wild beast show. Say that, and give him the name Abbas Parva. Here it is as she wrote it, Abbas Parva. 'That will bring him, if he's the man I think he is.' "

" And it will, too," remarked Holmes. " Very good, Mrs. Merrilow. I should like to have a little chat with Dr. Watson. That will carry us till lunch-time. About three o'clock you may expect to see us at your house in Brixton."

Our visitor had no sooner waddled out of the room —no other verb can describe Mrs. Merrilow's method of progression—than Sherlock Holmes threw himself with fierce energy upon the pile of commonplace books in the corner. For a few minutes there was a constant swish of the leaves, and then with a grunt of satisfaction he came upon what he sought. So excited was he that he did not rise, but sat upon the floor like some strange Buddha, with crossed legs, the huge books all round him, and one open upon his knees.

" The case worried me at the time, Watson. Here are my marginal notes to prove it. I confess that I could make nothing of it. And yet I was convinced that the coroner was wrong. Have you no recollection of the Abbas Parva tragedy ? "

" None, Holmes."

" And yet you were with me then. But certainly my own impression was very superficial, for there was nothing to go by, and none of the parties had engaged my services. Perhaps you would care to read the papers ? "

" Could you not give me the points ? "

" That is very easily done. It will probably come back to your memory as I talk. Ronder, of course, was a household word. He was the rival of Wombwell, and of Sanger, one of the greatest showmen of his day. **3** There is evidence, however, that he took to drink, and that both he and his show were on the down grade at the time of the great tragedy. The caravan had halted for the night at Abbas Parva, which is a small village in Berkshire, when this horror occurred. They were on their way to Wimbledon, travelling by road, and they were simply camping, and not exhibiting, as the place is so small a one that it would not have paid them to open.

" They had among their exhibits a very fine North African lion. Sahara King was its name, and it was the habit, both of Ronder and his wife, to give exhibitions inside its cage. Here, you see, is a photograph of the performance, by which you will perceive that Ronder was a huge porcine person and that his wife was a very magnificent woman. It was deposed at the inquest that there had been some signs that the lion was dangerous, but, as usual, familiarity begat contempt, and no

. . . HE DID NOT RISE, BUT SAT UPON THE FLOOR LIKE SOME STRANGE BUDDHA . . .

Illustration by Frank Wiles for the *Strand Magazine*, February, 1927.

"SAHARA KING WAS ITS NAME . . ."

Illustration by Frederic Dorr Steele for *Liberty Magazine*, January 22, 1927.

3 *the rival of Wombwell, and of Sanger.* Wombwell's Traveling Menagerie and the circus of "Lord" George Sanger were two of the best-known shows of the day.

notice was taken of the fact.

" It was usual for either Ronder or his wife to feed the lion at night. Sometimes one went, sometimes both, but they never allowed anyone else to do it, for they believed that so long as they were the food-carriers he would regard them as benefactors, and would never molest them. On this particular night, seven years ago, they both went, and a very terrible happening followed, the details of which have never been made clear.

" It seems that the whole camp was roused near midnight by the roars of the animal and the screams of the woman. The different grooms and *employés* rushed from their tents, carrying lanterns, and by their light an awful sight was revealed. Ronder lay, with the back of his head crushed in and deep claw-marks across his scalp, some ten yards from the cage, which was open. Close to the door of the cage lay Mrs. Ronder, upon her back, with the creature squatting and snarling above her. It had torn her face in such a fashion that it was never thought that she could live. Several of the circus men, headed by Leonardo, the strong man, and Griggs, the clown, drove the creature off with poles, upon which it sprang back into the cage, and was at once locked in. How it had got loose was a mystery. It was conjectured that the pair intended to enter the cage, but that when the door was loosed the creature bounded out upon them. There was no other point of interest in the evidence, save that the woman in a delirium of agony kept screaming, ' Coward ! Coward ! ' as she was carried back to the van in which they lived. It was six months before she was fit to give evidence, but the inquest was duly held, with the obvious verdict of death from misadventure."

" What alternative could be conceived ? " said I.

" You may well say so. And yet there were one or two points which worried young Edmunds, of the Berkshire Constabulary. A smart lad that ! He was sent later to Allahabad. That was how I came into the matter, for he dropped in and smoked a pipe or two over it."

" A thin, yellow-haired man ? "

" Exactly. I was sure you would pick up the trail presently."

" But what worried him ? "

" Well, we were both worried. It was so deucedly difficult to reconstruct the affair. Look at it from the lion's point of view. He is liberated. What does he do ? He takes half a dozen bounds forward, which brings him to Ronder. Ronder turns to fly—the claw-marks were on the back of his head—but the lion strikes him down. Then, instead of bounding on and escaping, he returns to the woman, who was close to the cage, and he knocks her over and chews her face up. Then, again, those cries of hers would seem to imply that her husband had in some way failed her. What could the poor devil have done to help her ? You see the difficulty ? "

" Quite."

" And then there was another thing. It comes back

to me now as I think it over. There was some evidence that, just at the time the lion roared and the woman screamed, a man began shouting in terror."

" This man Ronder, no doubt."

" Well, if his skull was smashed in you would hardly expect to hear from him again. There were at least two witnesses who spoke of the cries of a man being mingled with those of a woman."

" I should think the whole camp was crying out by then. As to the other points, I think I could suggest a solution."

" I should be glad to consider it."

" The two were together, ten yards from the cage, when the lion got loose. The man turned and was struck down. The woman conceived the idea of getting into the cage and shutting the door. It was her only refuge. She made for it, and just as she reached it the beast bounded after her and knocked her over. She was angry with her husband for having encouraged the beast's rage by turning. If they had faced it, they might have cowed it. Hence her cries of ' Coward ! ' "

" Brilliant, Watson ! Only one flaw in your diamond."

" What is the flaw, Holmes ? "

" If they were both ten paces from the cage, how came the beast to get loose ? "

" Is it possible that they had some enemy who loosed it ? "

" And why should it attack them savagely when it was in the habit of playing with them, and doing tricks with them inside the cage ? "

" Possibly the same enemy had done something to enrage it."

Holmes looked thoughtful and remained in silence for some moments.

" Well, Watson, there is this to be said for your theory. Ronder was a man of many enemies. Edmunds told me that in his cups he was horrible. A huge bully of a man, he cursed and slashed at everyone who came in his way. I expect those cries about a monster, of which our visitor has spoken, were nocturnal reminiscences of the dear departed. However, our speculations are futile until we have all the facts. There is a cold partridge on the sideboard, Watson, and a bottle of Montrachet. **4** Let us renew our energies before we make a fresh call upon them."

When our hansom deposited us at the house of Mrs. Merrilow, we found that plump lady blocking up the open door of her humble but retired abode. It was very clear that her chief preoccupation was lest she should lose a valuable lodger, and she implored us, before showing us up, to say and do nothing which could lead to so undesirable an end. Then, having reassured her, we followed her up the straight, badly-carpeted staircase and were shown into the room of the mysterious lodger.

It was a close, musty, ill-ventilated place, as might be expected, since its inmate seldom left it. From keeping beasts in a cage, the woman seemed, by some retribution of Fate, to have become herself a beast in a

4 *a bottle of Montrachet.* "Why a white Burgundy could be found here is still an unsolved problem," Mr. Jørgen Cold wrote in "What Did Sherlock Holmes Drink?" "Holmes may have bought it before he sent for Watson in order to take it with the cold partridge which was there also."

cage. She sat now in a broken arm-chair in the shadowy corner of the room. Long years of inaction had coarsened the lines of her figure, but at some period it must have been beautiful, and was still full and voluptuous. A thick dark veil covered her face, but it was cut off close at her upper lip, and disclosed a perfectly-shaped mouth and a delicately-rounded chin. I could well conceive that she had indeed been a very remarkable woman. Her voice, too, was well-modulated and pleasing.

"My name is not unfamiliar to you, Mr. Holmes," said she. "I thought that it would bring you."

"That is so, madam, though I do not know how you are aware that I was interested in your case."

"I learned it when I had recovered my health and was examined by Mr. Edmunds, the County detective. I fear I lied to him. Perhaps it would have been wiser had I told the truth."

"It is usually wiser to tell the truth. But why did you lie to him?"

"Because the fate of someone else depended upon it. I know that he was a very worthless being, and yet I would not have his destruction upon my conscience. We had been so close—so close!"

"But has this impediment been removed?"

"Yes, sir. The person that I allude to is dead."

"Then why should you not now tell the police anything you know?"

"Because there is another person to be considered. That other person is myself. I could not stand the scandal and publicity which would come from a police examination. I have not long to live, but I wish to die undisturbed. And yet I wanted to find one man of judgment to whom I could tell my terrible story, so that when I am gone all might be understood."

"THAT IS LEONARDO," SHE SAID.

Illustration by Frederic Dorr Steele for *Liberty Magazine*, January 22, 1927.

"You compliment me, madam. At the same time, I am a responsible person. I do not promise you that when you have spoken I may not myself think it my duty to refer the case to the police."

"I think not, Mr. Holmes. I know your character and methods too well, for I have followed your work for some years. Reading is the only pleasure which Fate has left me, and I miss little which passes in the world. But in any case, I will take my chance of the use which you may make of my tragedy. It will ease my mind to tell it."

"My friend and I would be glad to hear it."

The woman rose and took from a drawer the photograph of a man. He was clearly a professional acrobat, a man of magnificent physique, taken with his huge arms folded across his swollen chest and a smile breaking from under his heavy moustache—the self-satisfied smile of the man of many conquests.

"That is Leonardo," she said.

"Leonardo, the strong man, who gave evidence?"

"The same. And this—this is my husband."

It was a dreadful face—a human pig, or rather a human wild boar, for it was formidable in its bestiality. One could imagine that vile mouth champing and foaming in its rage, and one could conceive those small, vicious eyes darting pure malignancy as they looked forth upon the world. Ruffian, bully, beast—it was all written on that heavy-jowled face.

"Those two pictures will help you, gentlemen, to understand the story. I was a poor circus girl brought up on the sawdust, and doing springs through the hoop before I was ten. When I became a woman this man loved me, if such lust as his can be called love, and in an evil moment I became his wife. From that day I was in hell, and he the devil who tormented me. There was no one in the show who did not know of his treatment. He deserted me for others. He tied me down and lashed me with his riding-whip when I complained. They all pitied me and they all loathed him, but what could they do? They feared him, one and all. For he was terrible at all times, and murderous when he was drunk. Again and again he was had for assault, and for cruelty to the beasts, but he had plenty of money and the fines were nothing to him. The best men all left us and the show began to go downhill. It was only Leonardo and I who kept it up—with little Jimmy Griggs, the clown. Poor devil, he had not much to be funny about, but he did what he could to hold things together.

"Then Leonardo came more and more into my life. You see what he was like. I know now the poor spirit that was hidden in that splendid body, but compared to my husband he seemed like the Angel Gabriel. He pitied me and helped me, till at last our intimacy turned to love—deep, deep, passionate love, such love as I had dreamed of but never hoped to feel. My husband suspected it, but I think that he was a coward as well as a bully, and that Leonardo was the one man that he was afraid of. He took revenge in his own way by torturing me more than ever. One night my cries brought Leonardo to the door of our van. We were near tragedy that night, and soon my lover and I understood that it could not be avoided. My husband was not fit to live. We planned that he should die.

"Leonardo had a clever, scheming brain. It was he who planned it. I do not say that to blame him, for I was ready to go with him every inch of the way. But I should never have had the wit to think of such a plan. We made a club—Leonardo made it—and in the leaden head he fastened five long steel nails, the points outwards, with just such a spread as the lion's paw. This was to give my husband his death-blow, and yet to leave the evidence that it was the lion which we would loose who had done the deed.

"It was a pitch-dark night when my husband and I went down, as was our custom, to feed the beast. We carried with us the raw meat in a zinc pail. Leonardo was waiting at the corner of the big van which we should have to pass before we reached the cage. He was too slow, and we walked past him before he could strike, but he followed us on tiptoe and I heard the crash as the club smashed my husband's skull. My heart leaped with joy at the sound. I sprang forward, and I undid the catch which held the door of the great lion's cage.

"And then the terrible thing happened. You may have heard how quick these creatures are to scent human

"AS I SLIPPED THE BARS IT BOUNDED OUT, AND WAS ON ME IN AN INSTANT."

Illustration by Frank Wiles for the *Strand Magazine*, February, 1927.

blood, and how it excites them. Some strange instinct had told the creature in one instant that a human being had been slain. As I slipped the bars it bounded out, and was on me in an instant. Leonardo could have saved me. If he had rushed forward and struck the beast with his club he might have cowed it. But the man lost his nerve. I heard him shout in his terror, and then I saw him turn and fly. At the same instant the teeth of the lion met in my face. Its hot, filthy breath had already poisoned me and I was hardly conscious of pain. With the palms of my hands I tried to push the great steaming, blood-stained jaws away from me, and I screamed for help. I was conscious that the camp was stirring, and then dimly I remember a group of men, Leonardo, Griggs and others, dragging me from under the creature's paws. That was my last memory, Mr. Holmes, for many a weary month. When I came to myself, and saw myself in the mirror, I cursed that lion—oh, how I cursed him !—not because he had torn away my beauty, but because he had not torn away my life. I had but one desire, Mr. Holmes, and I had enough money to gratify it. It was that I should cover myself so that my poor face should be seen by none, and that I should dwell where none whom I had ever known should find me. That was all that was left to me to do—and that is what I have done. A poor wounded beast that has crawled into its hole to die—that is the end of Eugenia Ronder."

We sat in silence for some time after the unhappy woman had told her story. Then Holmes stretched out his long arm and patted her hand with such a show of sympathy as I had seldom known him to exhibit.

" Poor girl ! " he said. " Poor girl ! The ways of Fate are indeed hard to understand. If there is not some compensation hereafter, then the world is a cruel jest. But what of this man Leonardo ? "

" I never saw him or heard from him again. Perhaps I have been wrong to feel so bitterly against him. He might as soon have loved one of the freaks whom we carried round the country as the thing which the lion had left. But a woman's love is not so easily set aside. He had left me under the beast's claws, he had deserted me in my need, and yet I could not bring myself to give him to the gallows. For myself, I cared nothing what became of me. What could be more dreadful than my actual life ? But I stood between Leonardo and his fate."

" And he is dead ? "

" He was drowned last month when bathing near
5 Margate. I saw his death in the paper."

" And what did he do with this five-clawed club, which is the most singular and ingenious part of all your story ? "

" I cannot tell, Mr. Holmes. There is a chalk-pit by the camp, with a deep green pool at the base of it. Perhaps in the depths of that pool——"

" Well, well, it is of little consequence now. The case is closed."

" Yes," said the woman, " the case is closed."

We had risen to go, but there was something in the

5 *when bathing near Margate.* Even a strong man would hardly have gone bathing at Margate after September; our month would seem to be October. The day was probably not a Friday ("Two days later," when Watson called on Holmes, he found that a small blue bottle had come by post, presumably on the day of his call), but there does not seem to be any other evidence by which one can determine the day of the month.

woman's voice which arrested Holmes' attention. He turned swiftly upon her.

" Your life is not your own," he said. " Keep your hands off it."

" What use is it to anyone ? "

" How can you tell ? The example of patient suffering is in itself the most precious of all lessons to an impatient world."

The woman's answer was a terrible one. She raised her veil and stepped forward into the light.

" I wonder if you would bear it," she said.

It was horrible. No words can describe the framework of a face when the face itself is gone. Two living and beautiful brown eyes looking sadly out from that grisly ruin did but make the view more awful. Holmes held up his hand in a gesture of pity and protest, and together we left the room.

Two days later, when I called upon my friend, he pointed with some pride to a small blue bottle upon his mantelpiece. I picked it up. There was on it a red poison label. A pleasant almondy odour rose when I opened it.

" Prussic acid ? " said I.

" Exactly. It came by post. ' I send you my temptation.' I will follow your advice.' That was the message. I think, Watson, we can guess the name of the brave woman who sent it."

On the Canonicity of "The Adventure of the Veiled Lodger": Commentators have questioned the "Canonicity" of some of the adventures supposedly narrated by Watson in *The Case-Book of Sherlock Holmes.* But Mr. D. Martin Dakin has written of this adventure ("The Problem of the Case-Book") that it is "in all probability genuine. Holmes' own part in it is so unsensational that there would be no reason for inventing it. His advice to Mrs. Ronder to keep her hands off her life shows him at his best as a good man as well as a good detective (compare his treatment of Ryder at the end of 'The Adventure of the Blue Carbuncle'), and his comment 'The ways of Fate are indeed hard to understand. If there is not some compensation hereafter, then the world is a cruel jest'—is parallel to his philosophic collections on the same theme in 'The Boscombe Valley Mystery' and 'The Cardboard Box.' Indeed his whole conversation reads like the authentic Holmes. But above all we have the unmistakable mark of Watsonian authorship in the passage at the beginning with the dark hints of the unpublished cases, particularly that most tantalising of them all, the 'story concerning the politician, the lighthouse and the trained cormorant' . . ."

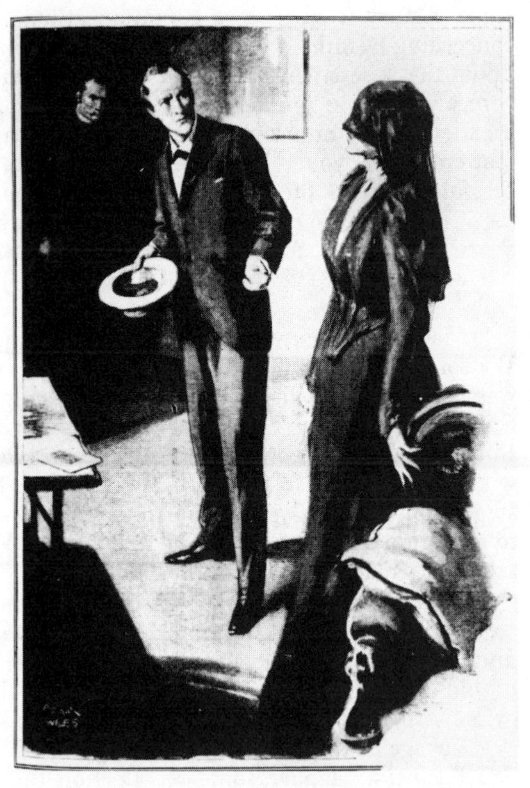

. . . THERE WAS SOMETHING IN THE WOMAN'S VOICE WHICH ARRESTED HOLMES' ATTENTION.

Illustration by Frank Wiles for the *Strand Magazine*, February, 1927.

57

THE ADVENTURE OF THE SUSSEX VAMPIRE

[Thursday, November 19, to Saturday, November 21, 1896]

HOLMES had read carefully a note which the last post had brought him. Then, with the dry chuckle which was his nearest approach to a laugh, he tossed it over to me.

" For a mixture of the modern and the mediæval, of the practical and of the wildly fanciful, I think this is surely the limit," said he. " What do you make of it, Watson ? "

I read as follows :

1 46 OLD JEWRY,
Nov. 19th.

Re Vampires.

SIR,—

Our client, Mr. Robert Ferguson, of Ferguson &
2 Muirhead, tea brokers, of Mincing Lane, has made
some inquiry from us in a communication of even date concerning vampires. As our firm specializes entirely upon the assessment of machinery the matter hardly comes within our purview, and we have therefore recommended Mr. Ferguson to call upon you and lay the matter before you. We have not forgotten your successful action in the case of Matilda Briggs.

We are, Sir, faithfully yours,
MORRISON, MORRISON, AND DODD.
per E. J. C.

" Matilda Briggs was not the name of a young woman,
Watson," said Holmes, in a reminiscent voice. " It
3 was a ship which is associated with the giant rat of
4 Sumatra, a story for which the world is not yet prepared.
But what do we know about vampires ? Does it come within our purview either ? Anything is better than stagnation, but really we seem to have been switched on to a Grimm's fairy tale. Make a long arm, Watson, and see what V has to say."

I leaned back and took down the great index volume to which he referred. Holmes balanced it on his knee and his eyes moved slowly and lovingly over the record of old cases, mixed with the accumulated information of a lifetime.

" Voyage of the *Gloria Scott,*" he read. " That was a bad business. I have some recollection that you made

1 *Old Jewry.* Old Jewry, in the City, on the north side of Cheapside, was the street where the original synagogue of the Jews was erected, and was their headquarters till their expulsion in 1291.

2 *Mincing Lane.* Named from houses which belonged to the Minchuns or nuns of St. Helen's.

3 *"It was a ship.* And a real ship, identified by Mr. Richard W. Clarke ("On the Nomenclature of Watson's Ships") as having been owned by the Oriental Trading Company of Shanghai. " I fear she came to her end in the East," the late Christopher Morley wrote, "for my grand old Findlay's *Sailing Directory of the Indian Archipelago and China and Japan* (1878 edition, the one used by Conrad) lists on p. 679 as a hazard of Batavia Bay the Matilda Rock. According to the custom of marine geographers, a reef or shoal is named for the vessel that first ran upon it, or surveyed it." And the late Edgar W. Smith once noted that the ill-fated *Mary Celeste,* found abandoned for no known reason, in a high running sea between the Azores and Portugal in the year 1872, "was commanded . . . by Captain Benjamin Spooner Briggs, and aboard her when she sailed from New York—in addition to a first and second mate, a cook, and four seamen—were the captain's wife and his two-year-old daughter. The wife's name was Sarah Elizabeth Briggs. The daughter's name . . . was Sophia Matilda Briggs."

4 *the giant rat of Sumatra. Rhizomys sumatrensis,* the great Sumatran bamboo rat, which may attain a length of nineteen inches excluding the tail. The world's largest rats, however, are three-foot-long animals from the Caroline Islands in the Pacific. They weigh twenty pounds and have black and yellow stomachs. Their teeth are yellow in front, white behind, and are shaped like tusks, 1½ inches long. The animals have sealed throats which permit them to eat under water without strangling.

a record of it, Watson, though I was unable to con- 5
gratulate you upon the result. Victor Lynch, the forger. 6-7
Venomous lizard or gila. Remarkable case, that! 8
Vittoria, the circus belle. Vanderbilt and the Yeggman.
Vipers. Vigor, the Hammersmith wonder. Hullo!
Hullo! Good old index. You can't beat it. Listen to
this, Watson. Vampirism in Hungary. And again,
Vampires in Transylvania." He turned over the pages 9
with eagerness, but after a short intent perusal he threw
down the great book with a snarl of disappointment.

"Rubbish, Watson, rubbish! What have we to do with walking corpses who can only be held in their grave by stakes driven through their hearts? It's pure lunacy."

"But surely," said I, "the vampire was not necessarily a dead man? A living person might have the habit. I have read, for example, of the old sucking the blood of the young in order to retain their youth."

"You are right, Watson. It mentions the legend
in one of these references. But are we to give serious
attention to such things? This Agency stands flat-
footed upon the ground, and there it must remain. 10
The world is big enough for us. No ghosts need apply.
I fear that we cannot take Mr. Robert Ferguson very
seriously. Possibly this note may be from him, and
may throw some light upon what is worrying him."

He took up a second letter which had lain unnoticed upon the table whilst he had been absorbed with the first. This he began to read with a smile of amusement upon his face which gradually faded away into an expression of intense interest and concentration. When he had finished he sat for some little time lost in thought with the letter dangling from his fingers. Finally, with a start, he aroused himself from his reverie.

"Cheeseman's, Lamberley. Where is Lamberley, Watson?"

"It is in Sussex, south of Horsham."

"Not very far, eh? And Cheeseman's?"

"I know that country, Holmes. It is full of old houses which are named after the men who built them centuries ago. You get Odley's and Harvey's and Carriton's—the folk are forgotten but their names live in their houses."

"Precisely," said Holmes coldly. It was one of the peculiarities of his proud, self-contained nature that, though he docketed any fresh information very quickly and accurately in his brain, he seldom made any acknowledgment to the giver. "I rather fancy we shall know a good deal more about Cheeseman's, Lamberley, before we are through. The letter is, as I had hoped, from Robert Ferguson. By the way, he claims acquaintance with you."

"With me!"

"You had better read it."

He handed the letter across. It was headed with the address quoted.

DEAR MR. HOLMES, (it said)—I have been recommended to you by my lawyers, but indeed the matter is so extraordinarily delicate that it is most difficult to discuss.

5 *I have some recollection that you made a record of it, Watson.* "The Adventure of the Sussex Vampire" cannot be earlier than November, 1894, or later than November, 1899: 1) Holmes speaks of Watson's "record" of the voyage of the *Gloria Scott*, published in April, 1893. 2) Watson, as we shall see, played rugby for Blackheath when Ferguson was three-quarter for Richmond. Thus the two men were much of an age. Since Watson took his medical degree in 1878, 1852 is a probable year for his birth. Ferguson was twice married; he had a fifteen-year-old son by his first wife and had married his second wife "some five years ago." He cannot have been less than forty at the time of "The Sussex Vampire," and he was most probably some years older than that. 3) Billy the page was on duty at Baker Street from October, 1900, on ("The Problem of Thor Bridge"). But there is no page boy at Baker Street at the time of "The Sussex Vampire"; Holmes, having written a telegram, says to Watson, "Take a wire down, like a good fellow." The year was not 1894: "The Sussex Vampire" is not mentioned in the list of important cases for that year given in "The Adventure of the Golden Pince-Nez"; also, it would have come too soon after that case for Holmes to say to Ferguson: "There is a lull at present." The year was not 1895: in that year Holmes spent the three days November 18th–20th in his rooms, as we know from "The Adventure of the Bruce-Partington Plans." The year was not 1897: Holmes wrote his reply to Morrison, Morrison, and Dodd's letter of the 19th on the 21st; he would not have written a business communication on a Sunday. The year was not 1898 nor 1899: the letter from Morrison, Morrison, and Dodd, dated the 19th, arrived by "the last post" and was therefore dispatched that day. November 19th is therefore not a Sunday and almost certainly not a Saturday. As the late H. W. Bell wrote: "If [the letter] had been dispatched before one o'clock it would have been delivered earlier in the day." We therefore date the adventure *Thursday, November 19, to Saturday, November 21, 1896.*

6 *I was unable to congratulate you upon the result.* ". . . one would not expect [Holmes] to . . . tell Watson he could not congratulate him on his record of a case which (as we know) consists almost entirely of narrative by Holmes himself," Mr. D. Martin Dakin commented in "Second Thoughts on the Case-Book."

7 *Victor Lynch, the forger.* "Sherlock Holmes' method of indexing 'Victor Lynch' under 'V' has aroused nasty sniggers and smiles among the up-to-date experts in cataloguing," Mr. Humfrey Michell wrote. "But I perceive from indexes of various volumes of the *Strand* that this method, if not standard, was at least quite common. E.g., Vol. 6: 'Charles Kean, an unpublished letter of' is included under 'C.' 'Martin Hewitt, Investigator' is put under 'M.' So Sherlock Holmes was following a sound tradition when in 'the good old index' Victor Lynch went into 'V.'"

"Holmes had no time to waste on the nice gradation of alphabetic initials," "A Penang Lawyer" wrote in "The Name's the Same." "He just stuck a case under the letter which first occurred to his curiously ill-balanced mind, and relied on his remarkable memory of association of ideas when he needed to refer to the subject again."

8 *Venomous lizard or gila.* "The Gila, or *Heloderma suspectum* . . . is of course a native of Arizona and New Mexico," Mr. Paul H. Gore-Booth wrote in "The Journeys of Sherlock Holmes." "Unfortunately, this does not enable us to deduce a visit to one of these states, since it appears that the creature thrives in captivity . . . and the specimen in question may well have been a captive brought to Britain for some sinister purpose by a countryman of Killer Evans or Jefferson Hope. But what a loss this case is! 'It is well,' says a leading authority (Raymond L. Ditmars, *Reptiles of the World*, Pitman, 1910, p. 164), 'to rate this species as among the reptiles highly dangerous to man.' And there, alas, our knowledge ends."

9 *Vampires in Transylvania.*" Under "Vampirism in London" Holmes' scrapbooks would surely have contained cuttings which appeared in the *Daily-graph* of August 5, 1890, the *Pall Mall Gazette* of September 18, 1890, and the *Westminster Gazette* of September 25, 1890, all describing the outrages perpetrated by Count Voivode Dracula (of Bram Stoker's *Dracula*, 1879). Whether Holmes—disguised, perhaps, as the mysterious Dr. Adolph Von Helsing, ostensibly of Amsterdam—actually participated in the hunt for the monster is a point debated by scholars, as is the theory that Count Dracula and Professor James Moriarty were one and the same man. The most convincing elucidation of this interesting theory is to be found in Mr. William Leonard's "Re: Vampires."

10 *This Agency stands flatfooted upon the ground.* "The most interesting feature of 'The Adventure of the Sussex Vampire' is Holmes' reference on two separate occasions to his 'Agency,' the word being spelt each time with a capital 'A,'" the late Gavin Brend wrote in *My Dear Holmes*. "Search where we will there is no mention of the Agency elsewhere, and it must be something more than a coincidence that the only two references to it should both occur in the same case. Can the explanation have something to do with the missing year 1896?"

It concerns a friend for whom I am acting. This gentleman married some five years ago a Peruvian lady, the daughter of a Peruvian merchant, whom he had met in connection with the importation of nitrates. The lady was very beautiful, but the fact of her foreign birth and of her alien religion always caused a separation of interests and of feelings between husband and wife, so that after a time his love may have cooled towards her and he may have come to regard their union as a mistake. He felt there were sides of her character which he could never explore or understand. This was the more painful as she was as loving a wife as a man could have—to all appearance absolutely devoted.

Now for the point which I will make more plain when we meet. Indeed, this note is merely to give you a general idea of the situation and to ascertain whether you would care to interest yourself in the matter. The lady began to show some curious traits, quite alien to her ordinarily sweet and gentle disposition. The gentleman had been married twice and he had one son by the first wife. This boy was now fifteen, a very charming and affectionate youth, though unhappily injured through an accident in childhood. Twice the wife was caught in the act of assaulting this poor lad in the most unprovoked way. Once she struck him with a stick and left a great weal on his arm.

This was a small matter, however, compared with her conduct to her own child, a dear boy just under one year of age. On one occasion about a month ago this child had been left by its nurse for a few minutes. A loud cry from the baby, as of pain, called the nurse back. As she ran into the room she saw her employer, the lady, leaning over the baby and apparently biting his neck. There was a small wound in the neck, from which a stream of blood had escaped. The nurse was so horrified that she wished to call the husband, but the lady implored her not to do so, and actually gave her five pounds as a price for her silence. No explanation was ever given, and for the moment the matter was passed over.

It left, however, a terrible impression upon the nurse's mind, and from that time she began to watch her mistress closely, and to keep a closer guard upon the baby, whom she tenderly loved. It seemed to her that even as she watched the mother, so the mother watched her, and that every time she was compelled to leave the baby alone the mother was waiting to get at it. Day and night the nurse covered the child, and day and night the silent, watchful mother seemed to be lying in wait as a wolf waits for a lamb. It must read most incredible to you, and yet I beg you to take it seriously, for a child's life and a man's sanity may depend upon it.

At last there came one dreadful day when the facts could no longer be concealed from the husband. The nurse's nerve had given way; she could stand the strain no longer, and she made a clean breast of it all to the man. To him it seemed as wild a tale as it may now seem to you. He knew his wife to be a loving wife, and, save for the assaults upon her stepson, a loving mother. Why, then, should she wound her own dear little baby? He told the nurse that she was dreaming, that her suspicions were those of a lunatic, and that such libels upon her mistress were not to be tolerated. Whilst they were talking, a sudden cry of pain was heard. Nurse and master rushed together to the nursery. Imagine his feelings, Mr. Holmes, as he saw his wife rise from a kneeling position beside the cot, and saw blood upon the child's exposed neck and upon the sheet. With a cry of horror, he turned his wife's face to the light and saw blood all round her lips. It was she—she beyond all question—who had drunk the poor baby's blood.

So the matter stands. She is now confined to her room. There has been no explanation. The husband is half demented. He knows, and I know, little of Vampirism beyond the name. We had thought it was some wild tale of foreign parts. And yet here in the very heart of the English Sussex—well, all this can be discussed with you in the morning. Will you see me? Will you use your great powers in aiding a distracted man? If so, kindly wire to Ferguson, Cheeseman's, Lamberley, and I will be at your rooms by ten o'clock.

Yours faithfully,
ROBERT FERGUSON.

PS.—I believe your friend Watson played Rugby for Blackheath when I was three-quarter for Richmond. It is the only personal introduction which I can 11
give.

"Of course I remember him," said I, as I laid down the letter. "Big Bob Ferguson, the finest three-quarter Richmond ever had. He was always a good-natured chap. It's like him to be so concerned over a friend's case."

Holmes looked at me thoughtfully and shook his head.

"I never get your limits, Watson," said he. "There are unexplored possibilities about you. Take a wire down, like a good fellow. 'Will examine your case with pleasure.'"

"*Your* case!"

"We must not let him think that this Agency is a home for the weak-minded. Of course it is his case. Send him that wire and let the matter rest till morning."

Promptly at ten o'clock next morning Ferguson strode into our room. I had remembered him as a long, slab-sided man with loose limbs and a fine turn of speed, which had carried him round many an opposing back. There is surely nothing in life more painful than to meet the wreck of a fine athlete whom one has known in his prime. His great frame had fallen in, his flaxen hair was scanty, and his shoulders were bowed. I fear that I roused corresponding emotions in him.

"Hullo, Watson," said he, and his voice was still deep and hearty. "You don't look quite the man you did when I threw you over the ropes into the crowd at the
Old Deer Park. I expect I have changed a bit also. 12
But it's this last day or two that has aged me. I see by

11 *three-quarter for Richmond.* Football, played at an earlier period as a rough country game without any fixed rules, had fallen into disrepute by 1801. Then the public schools revived it on their playing fields. Rugger came into existence at Rugby, where, in 1823, William Webb Ellis first took the ball into his arms and ran with it. Blackheath, for which Watson played, was an amateur Rugby club which in 1871 was one of the founders of the Rugby Football Union; Richmond was another club in the same Union. "Watson had to be a forward," Mr. Frederick Byran-Brown wrote in "Sherlockian Schools and Schoolmasters"; "he was a man of action and common sense but his best friends would hardly call him a schemer. In those days the game was less complex and law-bound and would have suited his qualities well: Watson was probably captain and certainly leader of the pack. After his five years with the Barts' XV he established himself in the leading London Club side, perhaps with international hopes, which were to be foiled by his Army service abroad."

"NURSE AND MASTER RUSHED TOGETHER TO THE NURSERY."

Illustration by W. T. Benda for *Hearst's International*, January, 1924.

12 *the Old Deer Park.* At Richmond. It contains the Kew Observatory built by Sir William Chambers in 1769, the Mid-Surrey Golf Course, and a large public recreation ground fronting the Great Chertsey Road. Here George II set up a court of his own when he was Prince of Wales.

your telegram, Mr. Holmes, that it is no use my pretending to be anyone's deputy."

"It is simpler to deal direct," said Holmes.

"Of course it is. But you can imagine how difficult it is when you are speaking of the one woman whom you are bound to protect and help. What can I do? How am I to go to the police with such a story? And yet the kiddies have got to be protected. Is it madness, Mr. Holmes? Is it something in the blood? Have you any similar case in your experience? For God's sake, give me some advice, for I am at my wits' end."

"Very naturally, Mr. Ferguson. Now sit here and pull yourself together and give me a few clear answers. I can assure you that I am very far from being at my wits' end, and that I am confident we shall find some solution. First of all, tell me what steps you have taken. Is your wife still near the children?"

"We had a dreadful scene. She is a most loving woman, Mr. Holmes. If ever a woman loved a man with all her heart and soul, she loves me. She was cut to the heart that I should have discovered this horrible, this incredible, secret. She would not even speak. She gave no answer to my reproaches, save to gaze at me with a sort of wild, despairing look in her eyes. Then she rushed to her room and locked herself in. Since then she has refused to see me. She has a maid who was with her before her marriage, Dolores by name—a friend rather than a servant. She takes her food to her."

"Then the child is in no immediate danger?"

"Mrs. Mason, the nurse, has sworn that she will not leave it night or day. I can absolutely trust her. I am more uneasy about poor little Jack, for, as I told you in my note, he has twice been assaulted by her."

"But never wounded?"

"No; she struck him savagely. It is the more terrible as he is a poor little inoffensive cripple." Ferguson's gaunt features softened as he spoke of his boy. "You would think that the dear lad's condition would soften anyone's heart. A fall in childhood and a twisted spine, Mr. Holmes. But the dearest, most loving heart within."

"FOR GOD'S SAKE, GIVE ME SOME ADVICE, FOR I AM AT MY WITS' END."

Illustration by Howard K. Elcock for the *Strand Magazine*, January, 1924.

Holmes had picked up the letter of yesterday and was reading it over. "What other inmates are there in your house, Mr. Ferguson?"

"Two servants who have not been long with us. One stable-hand, Michael, who sleeps in the house. My wife, myself, my boy Jack, baby, Dolores, and Mrs. Mason. That is all."

"I gather that you did not know your wife well at the time of your marriage?"

"I had only known her a few weeks."

"How long had this maid Dolores been with her?"

"Some years."

"Then your wife's character would really be better known by Dolores than by you?"

"Yes, you may say so."

Holmes made a note.

"I fancy," said he, "that I may be of more use at Lamberley than here. It is eminently a case for personal investigation. If the lady remains in her room, our presence could not annoy or inconvenience her. Of course, we would stay at the inn."

Ferguson gave a gesture of relief.

"It is what I hoped, Mr. Holmes. There is an excellent train at two from Victoria, if you could come." **13**

"Of course we could come. There is a lull at present. I can give you my undivided energies. Watson, of course, comes with us. But there are one or two points upon which I wish to be very sure before I start. This unhappy lady, as I understand it, has appeared to assault both the children, her own baby and your little son?"

"That is so."

"But the assaults take different forms, do they not? She has beaten your son."

"Once with a stick and once very savagely with her hands."

"Did she give no explanation why she struck him?"

"None, save that she hated him. Again and again she said so."

"Well, that is not unknown among stepmothers. A posthumous jealousy, we will say. Is the lady jealous by nature?"

"Yes, she is very jealous—jealous with all the strength of her fiery tropical love."

"But the boy—he is fifteen, I understand, and probably very developed in mind, since his body has been circumscribed in action. Did he give you no explanation of these assaults?"

"No; he declared there was no reason."

"Were they good friends at other times?"

"No; there was never any love between them."

"Yet you say he is affectionate?"

"Never in the world could there be so devoted a son. My life is his life. He is absorbed in what I say or do."

Once again Holmes made a note. For some time he sat lost in thought.

"No doubt you and the boy were great comrades before this second marriage. You were thrown very close together, were you not?"

"Very much so."

"And the boy, having so affectionate a nature, was devoted, no doubt, to the memory of his mother?"

"Most devoted."

"He would certainly seem to be a most interesting lad. There is one other point about these assaults. Were the strange attacks upon the baby and the assaults upon your son at the same period?"

"In the first case it was so. It was as if some frenzy had seized her, and she had vented her rage upon both. In the second case it was only Jack who suffered. Mrs. Mason had no complaint to make about the baby."

"That certainly complicates matters."

"I don't quite follow you, Mr. Holmes."

"Possibly not. One forms provisional theories and

13 *There is an excellent train at two from Victoria.* There was no 2:00 o'clock train from Victoria to Lamberley, but a train to Horsham left Victoria at 1:45.

waits for time or fuller knowledge to explode them. A bad habit, Mr. Ferguson ; but human nature is weak. I fear that your old friend here has given an exaggerated view of my scientific methods. However, I will only say at the present stage that your problem does not appear to me to be insoluble, and that you may expect to find us at Victoria at two o'clock."

It was evening of a dull, foggy November day when, having left our bags at the "Chequers," Lamberley, we drove through the Sussex clay of a long winding lane, and finally reached the isolated and ancient farm-house in which Ferguson dwelt. It was a large, straggling building, very old in the centre, very new at the wings, with towering Tudor chimneys and a lichen-spotted, high-pitched roof of Horsham slabs. The doorsteps were worn into curves, and the ancient tiles which lined the porch were marked with the rebus of a cheese and a man, after the original builder. Within, the ceilings were corrugated with heavy oaken beams, and the uneven floors sagged into sharp curves. An odour of age and decay pervaded the whole crumbling building.

There was one very large central room, into which Ferguson led us. Here, in a huge old-fashioned fireplace with an iron screen behind it dated 1670, there blazed and spluttered a splendid log fire.

The room, as I gazed round, was a most singular mixture of dates and of places. The half-panelled walls may well have belonged to the original yeoman farmer of the seventeenth century. They were ornamented, however, on the lower part by a line of well-chosen modern water-colours ; while above, where yellow plaster took the place of oak, there was hung a fine collection of South American utensils and weapons, which had been brought, no doubt, by the Peruvian lady upstairs. Holmes rose, with that quick curiosity which sprang from his eager mind, and examined them with some care. He returned with his eyes full of thought.

"Hullo ! " he cried. "Hullo ! "

A spaniel had lain in a basket in the corner. It came slowly forward towards its master, walking with difficulty. Its hind-legs moved irregularly and its tail was on the
14 ground. It licked Ferguson's hand.

"What is it, Mr. Holmes ? "

"The dog. What's the matter with it ? "

"That's what puzzled the vet. A sort of paralysis. Spinal meningitis, he thought. But it is passing. He'll be all right soon—won't you, Carlo ? "

A shiver of assent passed through the drooping tail. The dog's mournful eyes passed from one of us to the other. He knew that we were discussing his case.

"Did it come on suddenly ? "

"In a single night."

"How long ago ? "

"It may have been four months ago."

"Very remarkable. Very suggestive."

"What do you see in it, Mr. Holmes ? "

"A confirmation of what I had already thought."

"For God's sake, what *do* you think, Mr. Holmes ?

HOLMES ROSE, WITH THAT QUICK CURIOSITY WHICH SPRANG FROM HIS EAGER MIND, AND EXAMINED THEM WITH SOME CARE.

Illustration by W. T. Benda for *Hearst's International*, January, 1924.

14 *and its tail was on the ground.* "Since spaniels of all types have tails shortened very early in life to approximately two or three inches, the position assumed by this unhappy spaniel must have been an extremely odd one," Mr. Stuart Palmer commented in "Notes on Certain Evidences of Caniphobia in Mr. Sherlock Holmes and His Associates."

It may be a mere intellectual puzzle to you, but it is life and death to me! My wife a would-be murderer—my child in constant danger! Don't play with me, Mr. Holmes. It is too terribly serious."

The big Rugby three-quarter was trembling all over. Holmes put his hand soothingly upon his arm.

"I fear that there is pain for you, Mr. Ferguson, whatever the solution may be," said he. "I would spare you all I can. I cannot say more for the instant, but before I leave this house I hope I may have something definite."

"Please God you may! If you will excuse me, gentlemen, I will go up to my wife's room and see if there has been any change."

He was away some minutes, during which Holmes resumed his examination of the curiosities upon the wall. When our host returned it was clear from his downcast face that he had made no progress. He brought with him a tall, slim, brown-faced girl.

"The tea is ready, Dolores," said Ferguson. "See that your mistress has everything she can wish."

"She verra ill," cried the girl, looking with indignant eyes at her master. "She no ask for food. She verra ill. She need doctor. I frightened stay alone with her without doctor."

Ferguson looked at me with a question in his eyes.

"I should be so glad if I could be of use."

"Would your mistress see Dr. Watson?"

"I take him. I no ask leave. She needs doctor."

"Then I'll come with you at once."

I followed the girl, who was quivering with strong emotion, up the staircase and down an ancient corridor. At the end was an iron-clamped and massive door. It struck me as I looked at it that if Ferguson tried to force his way to his wife he would find it no easy matter. The girl drew a key from her pocket, and the heavy oaken planks creaked upon their old hinges. I passed in and she swiftly followed, fastening the door behind her.

On the bed a woman was lying who was clearly in a high fever. She was only half conscious, but as I entered she raised a pair of frightened but beautiful eyes and glared at me in apprehension. Seeing a stranger, she appeared to be relieved, and sank back with a sigh upon the pillow. I stepped up to her with a few reassuring words, and she lay still while I took her pulse and temperature. Both were high, and yet my impression was that the condition was rather that of mental and nervous excitement than of any actual seizure.

"She lie like that one day, two day. I 'fraid she die," said the girl.

The woman turned her flushed and handsome face towards me.

"Where is my husband?"

"He is below, and would wish to see you."

"I will not see him. I will not see him." Then she seemed to wander off into delirium. "A fiend! A fiend! Oh, what shall I do with this devil?"

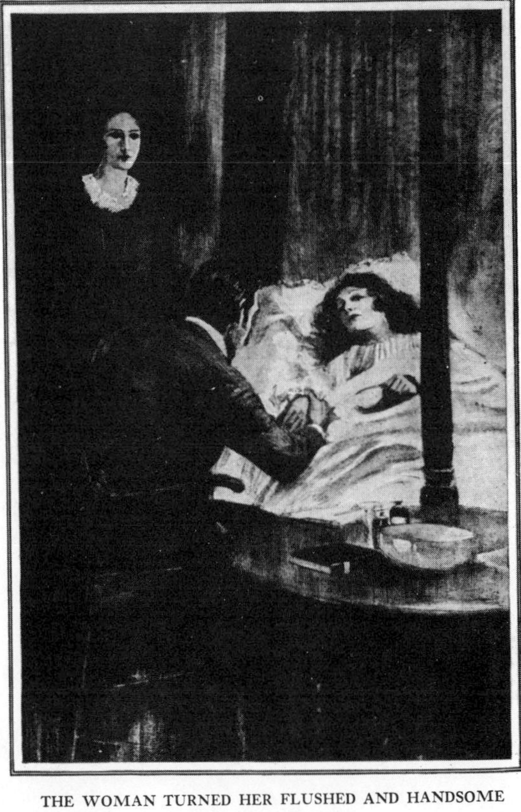

THE WOMAN TURNED HER FLUSHED AND HANDSOME FACE TOWARDS ME.

Illustration by Howard K. Elcock for the *Strand Magazine*, January, 1924.

" Can I help you in any way ? "

" No. No one can help. It is finished. All is destroyed. Do what I will, all is destroyed."

The woman must have some strange delusion. I could not see honest Bob Ferguson in the character of fiend or devil.

" Madame," I said, " your husband loves you dearly. He is deeply grieved at this happening."

Again she turned on me those glorious eyes.

" He loves me. Yes. But do I not love him ? Do I not love him even to sacrifice myself rather than break his dear heart. That is how I love him. And yet he could think of me—he could speak of me so."

" He is full of grief, but he cannot understand."

" No, he cannot understand. But he should trust."

" Will you not see him ? " I suggested.

" No, no ; I cannot forget those terrible words nor the look upon his face. I will not see him. Go now. You can do nothing for me. Tell him only one thing. I want my child. I have a right to my child. That is the only message I can send him." She turned her face to the wall and would say no more.

I returned to the room downstairs, where Ferguson and Holmes still sat by the fire. Ferguson listened moodily to my account of the interview.

" How can I send her the child ? " he said. " How do I know what strange impulse might come upon her ? How can I ever forget how she rose from beside it with its blood upon her lips ? " He shuddered at the recollection. " The child is safe with Mrs. Mason, and there he must remain."

A smart maid, the only modern thing which we had seen in the house, had brought in some tea. As she was serving it the door opened and a youth entered the room. He was a remarkable lad, pale-faced and fair-haired, with excitable light blue eyes which blazed into a sudden flame of emotion and joy as they rested upon his father. He rushed forward and threw his arms round his neck with the abandon of a loving girl.

" Oh, daddy," he cried, " I did not know that you were due yet. I should have been here to meet you. Oh, I am so glad to see you ! "

Ferguson gently disengaged himself from the embrace with some little show of embarrassment.

" Dear old chap," said he, patting the flaxen head with a very tender hand. " I came early because my friends, Mr. Holmes and Dr. Watson, have been persuaded to come down and spend an evening with us."

" Is that Mr. Holmes, the detective ? "

" Yes."

The youth looked at us with a very penetrating and, as it seemed to me, unfriendly gaze.

" What about your other child, Mr. Ferguson ? " asked Holmes. " Might we make the acquaintance of the baby ? "

" Ask Mrs. Mason to bring baby down," said Ferguson. The boy went off with a curious, shambling gait which told my surgical eyes that he was suffering
15 from a weak spine. Presently he returned, and behind

15 *which told my surgical eyes that he was suffering from a weak spine.* "Watson is always careful not to use expressions which may puzzle the layman," Miss Helen Simpson wrote in "Medical Career and Capacities of Dr. J. H. Watson," "but these simplifications make interpretation difficult for the commentator. Had he used the words 'ataxic gait,' we might have known that the boy suffered from some congenital syphilitic affliction; but had he spoken of a 'spastic gait,' we should have pictured some trouble as that which afflicted Byron. A gait showing signs of paralysis of one or more muscles is probably what he meant, but he is evidently mistaken in suggesting spinal injury as the cause. Any injury sufficient to affect the walk would certainly not permit the boy to 'rush,' and would be far more likely to involve complete paralysis below the waist."

him came a tall, gaunt woman bearing in her arms a very beautiful child, dark-eyed, golden-haired, a wonderful mixture of the Saxon and the Latin. Ferguson was evidently devoted to it, for he took it into his arms and fondled it most tenderly.

"Fancy anyone having the heart to hurt him," he muttered, as he glanced down at the small, angry red pucker upon the cherub throat.

It was at this moment that I chanced to glance at Holmes, and saw a most singular intentness in his expression. His face was as set as if it had been carved out of old ivory, and his eyes, which had glanced for a moment at father and child, were now fixed with eager curiosity upon something at the other side of the room. Following his gaze I could only guess that he was looking out through the window at the melancholy, dripping garden. It is true that a shutter had half closed outside and obstructed the view, but none the less it was certainly at the window that Holmes was fixing his concentrated attention. Then he smiled, and his eyes came back to the baby. On its chubby neck there was this small puckered mark. Without speaking, Holmes examined it with care. Finally he shook one of the dimpled fists which waved in front of him.

"Good-bye, little man. You have made a strange start in life. Nurse, I should wish to have a word with you in private."

He took her aside and spoke earnestly for a few minutes. I only heard the last words, which were: "Your anxiety will soon, I hope, be set at rest." The woman, who seemed to be a sour, silent kind of creature, withdrew with the child.

"What is Mrs. Mason like?" asked Holmes.

"Not very prepossessing externally, as you can see, but a heart of gold, and devoted to the child."

"FANCY ANYONE HAVING THE HEART TO HURT HIM," HE MUTTERED . . .

(*Above*) Illustration by Howard K. Elcock for the Louisville *Courier-Journal*, March 8, 1925. (*Below*) W. T. Benda illustrated the same scene for *Hearst's International*, January, 1924.

IT WAS AT THIS MOMENT THAT I CHANCED TO GLANCE AT HOLMES . . .

Illustration by Howard K. Elcock for the *Strand Magazine*, January, 1924.

" Do you like her, Jack ? " Holmes turned suddenly upon the boy. His expressive mobile face shadowed over, and he shook his head.

" Jacky has very strong likes and dislikes," said Ferguson, putting his arm round the boy. " Luckily I am one of his likes."

The boy cooed and nestled his head upon his father's breast. Ferguson gently disengaged him.

" Run away, little Jacky," said he, and he watched his son with loving eyes until he disappeared. " Now, Mr. Holmes," he continued, when the boy was gone, " I really feel that I have brought you on a fool's errand, for what can you possibly do, save give me your sympathy ? It must be an exceedingly delicate and complex affair from your point of view."

" It is certainly delicate," said my friend, with an amused smile, " but I have not been struck up to now with its complexity. It has been a case for intellectual deduction, but when this original intellectual deduction is confirmed point by point by quite a number of independent incidents, then the subjective becomes objective and we can say confidently that we have reached our goal. I had, in fact, reached it before we left Baker Street, and the rest has merely been observation and confirmation."

Ferguson put his big hand to his furrowed forehead.

" For Heaven's sake, Holmes," he said hoarsely, " if you can see the truth in this matter, do not keep me in suspense. How do I stand ? What shall I do ? I care nothing as to how you have found your facts so long as you have really got them."

" Certainly I owe you an explanation, and you shall have it. But you will permit me to handle the matter in my own way ? Is the lady capable of seeing us, Watson ? "

" She is ill, but she is quite rational."

" Very good. It is only in her presence that we can clear the matter up. Let us go up to her."

" She will not see me," cried Ferguson.

" Oh, yes, she will," said Holmes. He scribbled a few lines upon a sheet of paper. " You at least have the *entrée*, Watson. Will you have the goodness to give the lady this note ? "

I ascended again and handed the note to Dolores, who cautiously opened the door. A minute later I heard a cry from within, a cry in which joy and surprise seemed to be blended. Dolores looked out.

" She will see them. She will leesten," said she.

At my summons Ferguson and Holmes came up. As we entered the room Ferguson took a step or two towards his wife, who had raised herself in the bed, but she held out her hand to repulse him. He sank into an arm-chair, while Holmes seated himself beside him, after bowing to the lady, who looked at him with wide-eyed amazement.

" I think we can dispense with Dolores," said Holmes. " Oh, very well, madame, if you would rather she stayed I can see no objection. Now, Mr. Ferguson, I am a busy man with many calls, and my methods have to be short and direct. The swiftest surgery is the least painful. Let me first say what will ease your mind. Your wife is a very good, a very loving, and a very ill-used woman."

Ferguson sat up with a cry of joy.

"Prove that, Mr. Holmes, and I am your debtor for ever."

"I will do so, but in doing so I must wound you deeply in another direction."

"I care nothing so long as you clear my wife. Everything on earth is insignificant compared to that."

"Let me tell you, then, the train of reasoning which passed through my mind in Baker Street. The idea of a vampire was to me absurd. Such things do not happen in criminal practice in England. And yet your observation was precise. You had seen the lady rise from beside the child's cot with the blood upon her lips."

"I did."

"Did it not occur to you that a bleeding wound may be sucked for some other purpose than to draw the blood from it? Was there not a Queen in English history
who sucked such a wound to draw poison from it?" 16

"Poison!"

"A South American household. My instinct felt the presence of those weapons upon the wall before my eyes ever saw them. It might have been other poison, but that was what occurred to me. When I saw that little empty quiver beside the small bird-bow, it was just what I expected to see. If the child were pricked with one of those arrows dipped in curare or some other devilish drug, it would mean death if the venom were not sucked out.

"And the dog! If one were to use such a poison, would one not try it first in order to see that it had not lost its power? I did not foresee the dog, but at least
I understood him and he fitted into my reconstruction. 17

"Now do you understand? Your wife feared such an attack. She saw it made and saved the child's life, and yet she shrank from telling you all the truth, for she knew how you loved the boy and feared lest it break your heart."

"Jacky!"

"I watched him as you fondled the child just now. His face was clearly reflected in the glass of the window where the shutter formed a background. I saw such jealousy, such cruel hatred, as I have seldom seen in a human face."

"My Jacky!"

"You have to face it, Mr. Ferguson. It is the more painful because it is a distorted love, a maniacal exaggerated love for you, and possibly for his dead mother, which has prompted his action. His very soul is consumed with hatred for this splendid child, whose health and beauty are a contrast to his own weakness."

"Good God! It is incredible!"

"Have I spoken the truth, madame?"

The lady was sobbing, with her face buried in the pillows. Now she turned to her husband.

"How could I tell you, Bob? I felt the blow it

16 *who sucked such a wound to draw poison from it?"* Holmes refers to Eleanor of Castile, Queen of England, 1272–1290. But in his *Popular Fallacies,* Alfred S. E. Ackermann denies that "the Queen Eleanor, Consort of Edward I, sucked poison from the arm of her husband while he was on his Palestine expedition."

17 *he fitted into my reconstruction.* Curare works by paralyzing the thorax and chest muscles, not the legs, and it kills within minutes or has no effect at all.

"The spaniel Carlo should have died at once, when pierced by a poison dart, for, if 'it would mean death if the venom were not sucked out' for the baby, it would certainly mean the same for the dog, which did not weigh as much," Mrs. Eleanor S. Cole wrote in "Holmes, Watson and the K'9's." "It is safe to surmise that the demonic little Jackie, filled with unusual remorse, sucked some of the poison from the dog's wound, yet not enough to leave him completely unimpaired."

And F. A. Allen, M.P.S., has written in "Devilish Drugs": "The persistence of the paralytic effect . . . must be taken as traumatic or infective. This was strangely localized in the hind quarters of [the] dog, following the would-be murderer's preliminary experiment on the animal—a clumsy job in the back, near the cord, with a dirty half-scraped arrow-tip."

To this, Dr. George B. Koelle has added ("The Poisons of the Canon"): ". . . the effects of a non-fatal dose of [curare] should wear off in a day. Consequently, the protracted lameness which the dog Carlo developed was probably due to spinal meningitis . . . or to mechanical injury or secondary infection of the sciatic nerve, as a result of the arrow-puncture. Curare is very poorly absorbed when taken by mouth; hence Mrs. Ferguson actually did not expose herself to serious risk when she immediately sucked the wound inflicted on her child."

would be to you. It was better that I should wait and that it should come from some other lips than mine. When this gentleman, who seems to have powers of magic, wrote that he knew all, I was glad."

" I think a year at sea would be my prescription for Master Jacky," said Holmes, rising from his chair. " Only one thing is still clouded, madame. We can quite understand your attacks upon Master Jacky. There is a limit to a mother's patience. But how did you dare to leave the child these last two days ? "

" I had told Mrs. Mason. She knew."

" Exactly. So I imagined."

Ferguson was standing by the bed, choking, his hands outstretched and quivering.

" This, I fancy, is the time for our exit, Watson," said Holmes in a whisper. " If you will take one elbow of the too faithful Dolores, I will take the other. There, now," he added, as he closed the door behind him. " I think we may leave them to settle the rest among themselves."

I have only one further note of this case. It is the letter which Holmes wrote in final answer to that with which the narrative begins. It ran thus :

BAKER STREET,
Nov. 21st.

Re Vampires.

SIR,—

Referring to your letter of the 19th, I beg to state that I have looked into the inquiry of your client, Mr. Robert Ferguson, of Ferguson & Muirhead, tea brokers, of Mincing Lane, and that the matter has been brought to a satisfactory conclusion. With thanks for your recommendation,

I am, Sir,
Faithfully yours,
SHERLOCK HOLMES.

A Note on the "Canonicity" of "The Adventure of the Sussex Vampire": Mr. D. Martin Dakin, who rejects from the Canon many of the stories in *The Case-Book of Sherlock Holmes,* accepts "The Sussex Vampire" as genuine. "The trivial details about the Doctor's early life are not such as would occur to a pseudo-Watson," he writes, "and Holmes' contemptuous dismissal of the vampire superstitions is thoroughly characteristic. 'I never get your limits, Watson . . . There are unexplored possibilities about you. . . . We must not let him think that this Agency is a home for the weakminded.' This is Holmes in his genuinely satirical vein. It is true that some have seen a suspicious similarity between the lame spaniel and the famous sheep in the paddock [in "Silver Blaze"], but we need not assume that there were never any similar features in Holmes' cases, and perhaps Jack Ferguson had even been reading 'Silver Blaze' himself? It is true that many critics have raised their eyebrows at Holmes' indexing system, but it is possible that we have here another instance of Watson's faulty memory . . ."

58

THE ADVENTURE OF THE MISSING THREE-QUARTER

[Tuesday, December 8, to Thursday, December 10, 1896]

WE were fairly accustomed to receive weird telegrams at Baker Street, but I have a particular recollection of one which reached us on a gloomy February morning some seven or eight
years ago, and gave Mr. Sherlock Holmes a puzzled 1
quarter of an hour. It was addressed to him, and ran thus :

" Please await me. Terrible misfortune. Right wing three-quarter missing ; indispensable to-morrow.—OVER-
TON." 2

" Strand postmark, and despatched ten thirty-six," said Holmes, reading it over and over. " Mr. Overton was evidently considerably excited when he sent it, and somewhat incoherent in consequence. Well, well, he will be here, I dare say, by the time I have looked through *The Times*, and then we shall know all about it. Even the most insignificant problem would be welcome in these stagnant days."

Things had indeed been very slow with us, and I had learned to dread such periods of inaction, for I knew by experience that my companion's brain was so abnormally active that it was dangerous to leave it without material upon which to work. For years I had gradually weaned him from that drug mania which had threatened once to check his remarkable career. Now I knew that under ordinary conditions he no longer craved for this artificial stimulus ; but I was well aware that the fiend was not dead, but sleeping ; and I have known that the sleep was a light one and the waking near when in periods of idleness I have seen the drawn look upon Holmes' ascetic face, and the brooding of his deep-set and inscrutable eyes. Therefore I blessed this Mr. Overton, whoever he might be, since he had come with his enigmatic message to break that dangerous calm which brought more peril to my friend than all the storms of his tempestuous life.

As we expected, the telegram was soon followed by its sender, and the card of Mr. Cyril Overton, of Trinity College, Cambridge, announced the arrival of an enormous young man, sixteen stone of solid bone and muscle, who spanned the doorway with his broad shoulders and looked

1 *a gloomy February morning some seven or eight years ago.* The year was not earlier than 1894: Holmes later says of Dr. Leslie Armstrong, "I have not seen a man . . . more calculated to fill the gap left by the illustrious Moriarty." Nor was it later than mid-1897: while we cannot say with any degree of certainty when the case was *chronicled*, it was certainly *published* in August, 1904, and Watson tells us that it began "some seven or eight years ago." But Watson's "February" is clearly an error. As the late Professor Jay Finley Christ wrote, the game of Rugby employs the three-quarter line, as Association football, or soccer, does not. The game of importance in this adventure is Rugby, then—and in the nineties, the Cambridge-Oxford Rugby matches were always played at the Queen's Club in December, on a Wednesday, usually the second Wednesday in the month. The month, therefore, is December, and the year is 1894, 1895, or 1896; we shall shortly determine which.

2 OVERTON." ". . . if Watson were the old rugger player that he claimed to be [in "The Adventure of the Sussex Vampire"]—big-time rugger, at that—the name of Cyril Overton would hardly have been unknown to him; nor would there have been anything enigmatic about Overton's telegram to Holmes," the late Elmer Davis commented in his introduction to *The Return of Sherlock Holmes*. "Accordingly J. P. Mallalieu, M.P.—himself an old Oxford rugger Blue—has argued (in the London *Tribune*) that Watson's story of his own football prowess was not merely sheer invention, but invention in an alcoholic haze. Watson, says Mallalieu, was a dipsomaniac, at least between his marriages. This accounts for his lapses of memory—dates and details jotted down in his notebook while he was drunk; accounts for his not knowing the name of so celebrated a medical man as Dr. Leslie Armstrong; and probably explains the quarrel with Holmes which . . . occasioned his leaving Baker Street in 1896."

from one of us to the other with a comely face which was
3 haggard with anxiety.

"Mr. Sherlock Holmes?"

My companion bowed.

"I've been down to Scotland Yard, Mr. Holmes. I saw Inspector Stanley Hopkins. He advised me to come to you. He said the case, so far as he could see, was more in your line than in that of the regular police."

"Pray sit down and tell me what is the matter."

"It's awful, Mr. Holmes, simply awful! I wonder my hair isn't grey. Godfrey Staunton—you've heard of him, of course? He's simply the hinge that the whole team turns on. I'd rather spare two from the pack and have Godfrey for my three-quarter line. Whether it's passing,
4 or tackling, or dribbling, there's no one to touch him; and then, he's got the head and can hold us all together. What am I to do? That's what I ask you, Mr. Holmes. There's Moorhouse, first reserve, but he is trained as a half, and he always edges right in on to the scrum instead of keeping out on the touch-line. He's a fine place-kick, it's true, but, then, he has no judgment, and he can't sprint for nuts. Why, Morton or Johnson, the Oxford fliers, could romp round him. Stevenson is fast enough, but he couldn't drop from the twenty-five line, and a three-quarter who can't either punt or drop isn't worth a place for pace alone. No, Mr. Holmes, we are done unless you can help me to find Godfrey Staunton."

My friend had listened with amused surprise to this long speech, which was poured forth with extraordinary vigour and earnestness, every point being driven home by the slapping of a brawny hand upon the speaker's knee. When our visitor was silent Holmes stretched out his hand and took down letter "S" of his commonplace book. For once he dug in vain into that mine of varied information.

"There is Arthur H. Staunton, the rising young forger," said he, "and there was Henry Staunton, whom
5 I helped to hang, but Godfrey Staunton is a new name to me."

It was our visitor's turn to look surprised.

"Why, Mr. Holmes, I thought you knew things," said he. "I suppose, then, if you have never heard of Godfrey Staunton you don't know Cyril Overton either?"

Holmes shook his head good-humouredly.

"Great Scott!" cried the athlete. "Why, I was first reserve for England against Wales, and I've skippered the 'Varsity all this year. But that's nothing. I didn't think there was a soul in England who didn't know Godfrey Staunton, the crack three-quarter, Cambridge, Blackheath, and five Internationals. Good Lord! Mr. Holmes, where *have* you lived?"

Holmes laughed at the young giant's naïve astonishment.

"You live in a different world to me, Mr. Overton, a sweeter and healthier one. My ramifications stretch out into many sections of society, but never, I am happy to say, into amateur sport, which is the best and soundest thing in England. However, your unexpected visit this morning shows me that even in that world of fresh air and

3 *a comely face which was haggard with anxiety.* As we have seen, Mr. Rolfe Boswell has suggested that *this* was the adventure to which Watson alluded, in "The Naval Treaty," as "The Adventure of the Tired Captain."

4 *or dribbling.* "Is there dribbling in *rugby* football?" the late Christopher Morley asked. "It is an expertise in soccer, of course. I know nothing of rugger, but I am wondering whether it is possible, in any exact sense, to dribble the oval ball?"

5 *Henry Staunton, whom I helped to hang.* Historically, there was also Louis Staunton, who starved his half-witted wife to death in the gray dreariness of Penge.

"WHY, MR. HOLMES, I THOUGHT YOU KNEW THINGS," SAID HE.

Illustration by Sidney Paget for the *Strand Magazine*, August, 1904.

fair play there may be work for me to do ; so now, my good sir, I beg you to sit down and to tell me slowly and quietly exactly what it is that has occurred, and how you desire that I should help you."

Young Overton's face assumed the bothered look of the man who is more accustomed to using his muscles than his wits ; but by degrees, with many repetitions and obscurities which I may omit from his narrative, he laid his strange story before us.

" It's this way, Mr. Holmes. As I have said, I am the skipper of the Rugger team of Cambridge 'Varsity, and Godfrey Staunton is my best man. To-morrow we play Oxford. Yesterday we all came up and we settled at Bentley's private hotel. At ten o'clock I went round and saw that all the fellows had gone to roost, for I believe in strict training and plenty of sleep to keep a team fit. I had a word or two with Godfrey before he turned in. He seemed to me to be pale and bothered. I asked him what was the matter. He said he was all right—just a touch of headache. I bade him good night and left him. Half an hour later the porter tells me that a rough-looking man with a beard called with a note for Godfrey. He had not gone to bed, and the note was taken to his room. Godfrey read it and fell back in a chair as if he had been pole-axed. The porter was so scared that he was going to fetch me, but Godfrey stopped him, had a drink of water, and pulled himself together. Then he went downstairs, said a few words to the man who was waiting in the hall, and the two of them went off together. The last that the porter saw of them, they were almost running down the street in the direction of the Strand. This morning Godfrey's room was empty, his bed had never been slept in, and his things were all just as I had seen them the night before. He had gone off at a moment's notice with this stranger, and no word has come from him since. I don't believe he will ever come back. He was a sportsman, was Godfrey, down to his marrow, and he wouldn't have stopped his training and let in his skipper if it were not for some cause that was too strong for him. No ; I feel as if he were gone for good and we should never see him again."

Sherlock Holmes listened with the deepest attention to this singular narrative.

" What did you do ? " he asked.

" I wired to Cambridge to learn if anything had been heard of him there. I have had an answer. No one has seen him."

" Could he have got back to Cambridge ? "

" Yes, there is a late train—quarter-past eleven." **6**

" But, so far as you can ascertain, he did not take it ? "

" No, he has not been seen."

" What did you do next ? "

" I wired to Lord Mount-James."

" Why to the Lord Mount-James ? "

" Godfrey is an orphan, and Lord Mount-James is his nearest relative—his uncle, I believe."

" Indeed. This throws new light upon the matter.

6 *"Yes, there is a late train—quarter-past eleven."* The fact that Holmes did not know whether or not there was a late train to Cambridge has been scored as a point against his having himself attended that great University. "It may be, however, in this particular case, that the difficulty can be removed by assuming that this late train was not in existence in Holmes' time but was put on at some later date," the late Gavin Brend wrote in *My Dear Holmes*.

In any case, however, as the late Christopher Morley pointed out, there never *was* an 11:15 train to Cambridge either from King's Cross or from Liverpool Station. "There would be no point, and no passengers, for such a train. The whole purpose of the late trains (10:02 from Liverpool Station, and 10:25 from King's Cross, per Bradshaw, July, 1894) was, and still is, to get students back to the university before midnight, by order of the Vice Chancellor and Proctors."

"DID YOU TAKE ANY MESSAGE TO MR. STAUNTON?"

Illustration by Sidney Paget for the *Strand Magazine*, August, 1904.

Lord Mount-James is one of the richest men in England."

"So I've heard Godfrey say."

"And your friend was closely related?"

"Yes, he was his heir, and the old boy is nearly eighty—cram full of gout, too. They say he could chalk his billiard-cue with his knuckles. He never allowed Godfrey a shilling in his life, for he is an absolute miser, but it will all come to him right enough."

"Have you heard from Lord Mount-James?"

"No."

"What motive could your friend have in going to Lord Mount-James?"

"Well, something was worrying him the night before, and if it was to do with money it is possible that he would make for his nearest relative who had so much of it, though from all I have heard he would not have much chance of getting it. Godfrey was not fond of the old man. He would not go if he could help it."

"Well, we can soon determine that. If your friend was going to his relative Lord Mount-James, you have then to explain the visit of this rough-looking fellow at so late an hour, and the agitation that was caused by his coming."

Cyril Overton pressed his hands to his head. "I can make nothing of it!" said he.

"Well, well, I have a clear day, and I shall be happy to look into the matter," said Holmes. "I should strongly recommend you to make your preparations for your match without reference to this young gentleman. It must, as you say, have been an overpowering necessity which tore him away in such a fashion, and the same necessity is likely to hold him away. Let us step round together to this hotel, and see if the porter can throw any fresh light upon the matter."

Sherlock Holmes was a past master in the art of putting a humble witness at his ease, and very soon, in the privacy of Godfrey Staunton's abandoned room, he had extracted all that the porter had to tell. The visitor of the night before was not a gentleman, neither was he a working man. He was simply what the porter described as a "medium-looking chap"; a man of fifty, beard grizzled, pale face, quietly dressed. He seemed himself to be agitated. The porter had observed his hand trembling when he had held out the note. Godfrey Staunton had crammed the note into his pocket. Staunton had not shaken hands with the man in the hall. They had exchanged a few sentences, of which the porter had only distinguished the one word "time." Then they had hurried off in the manner described. It was just half-past ten by the hall clock.

"Let me see," said Holmes, seating himself on Staunton's bed. "You are the day porter, are you not?"

"Yes, sir; I go off duty at eleven."

"The night porter saw nothing, I suppose?"

"No, sir; one theatre party came in late. No one else."

"Were you on duty all day yesterday?"

"Yes, sir."

"Did you take any message to Mr. Staunton?"

"Yes, sir; one telegram."

" Ah ! that is interesting. What o'clock was this ? "

" About six."

" Where was Mr. Staunton when he received it ? "

" Here in his room."

" Were you present when he opened it ? "

" Yes, sir ; I waited to see if there was an answer."

" Well, was there ? "

" Yes, sir. He wrote an answer."

" Did you take it ? "

" No ; he took it himself."

" But he wrote it in your presence ? "

" Yes, sir. I was standing by the door, and he with his back turned at that table. When he had written it he said, ' All right, porter, I will take this myself.' "

" What did he write it with ? "

" A pen, sir."

" Was the telegraphic form one of these on the table ? "

" Yes, sir ; it was the top one."

Holmes rose. Taking the forms, he carried them over to the window and carefully examined that which was uppermost.

" It is a pity he did not write in pencil," said he, throwing them down again with a shrug of disappointment. " As you have no doubt frequently observed, Watson, the impression usually goes through—a fact which has dissolved many a happy marriage. However, I can find no trace here. I rejoice, however, to perceive that he wrote with a broad-pointed quill pen, and I can hardly doubt that we will find some impression upon this blotting-pad. Ah, yes, surely this is the very thing ! "

He tore off a strip of the blotting-paper and turned towards us the following hieroglyphic :

Cyril Overton was much excited. " Hold it to the glass," he cried.

" That is unnecessary," said Holmes. " The paper is thin, and the reverse will give the message. Here it is." He turned it over, and we read :

" So that is the tail end of the telegram which Godfrey Staunton despatched within a few hours of his disappearance. There are at least six words of the message which have escaped us ; but what remains—' Stand by us for God's sake ! '—proves that this young man saw a formidable danger which approached him, and from which someone else could protect him. ' *Us*,' mark you ! Another person was involved. Who should it be but the pale-faced, bearded man who seemed himself in so nervous a state ? What, then, is the connection between Godfrey Staunton and the bearded man ? And what is the third source from which each of them sought for help against pressing danger ? Our inquiry has already narrowed down to that."

"We have only to find to whom that telegram is addressed," I suggested.

"Exactly, my dear Watson. Your reflection, though profound, had already crossed my mind. But I dare say it may have come to your notice that if you walk into a post-office and demand to see the counterfoil of another man's message there may be some disinclination on the part of the officials to oblige you. There is so much red tape in these matters! However, I have no doubt that with a little delicacy and finesse the end may be attained. Meanwhile, I should like in your presence, Mr. Overton, to go through these papers which have been left upon the table."

There were a number of letters, bills, and notebooks, which Holmes turned over and examined with quick, nervous fingers and darting, penetrating eyes. "Nothing here," he said at last. "By the way, I suppose your friend was a healthy young fellow—nothing amiss with him?"

"Sound as a bell."

"Have you ever known him ill?"

7 "Not a day. He has been laid up with a hack, and
once he slipped his knee-cap, but that was nothing."

"Perhaps he was not so strong as you suppose. I should think he may have had some secret trouble. With your assent I will put one or two of these papers in my pocket, in case they should bear upon our future inquiry."

"One moment, one moment!" cried a querulous voice, and we looked up to find a queer little old man jerking and twitching in the doorway. He was dressed in rusty black, with a very broad-brimmed top-hat and a loose white necktie—the whole effect being that of a very rustic parson or of an undertaker's mute. Yet, in spite of his shabby and even absurd appearance, his voice had a sharp crackle, and his manner a quick intensity which commanded attention.

"Who are you, sir, and by what right do you touch this gentleman's papers?" he asked.

"I am a private detective, and I am endeavouring to explain his disappearance."

"Oh, you are, are you? And who instructed you, eh?"

"This gentleman, Mr. Staunton's friend, was referred to me by Scotland Yard."

"Who are you, sir?"

"I am Cyril Overton."

"Then it is you who sent me a telegram. My name
is Lord Mount-James. I came round as quickly as the
8 Bayswater bus would bring me. So you have instructed
a detective?"

"Yes, sir."

"And are you prepared to meet the cost?"

"I have no doubt, sir, that my friend Godfrey, when we find him, will be prepared to do that."

"But if he is never found, eh? Answer me that?"

"In that case no doubt his family——"

"Nothing of the sort, sir!" screamed the little man. "Don't look to me for a penny—not a penny! You

7 *He has been laid up with a back.* Laid up with a *back* in some editions. Overton means, not a hacking cough, but a gash on the shin.

8 *Bayswater.* The name given to a district between the north side of Hyde Park and Notting Hill Gate. Bayswater has always been a favorite abode of foreigners of every nationality; today many of its shops are owned by foreigners, and its restaurants are amongst the best in London.

"ONE MOMENT, ONE MOMENT!" CRIED A QUERULOUS VOICE . . .

Illustration by Frederic Dorr Steele for *Collier's Magazine*, November 26, 1904. Sidney Paget illustrated the same scene for the *Strand Magazine*, August, 1904.

understand that, Mr. Detective! I am all the family that this young man has got, and I tell you that I am not responsible. If he has any expectations it is due to the fact that I have never wasted money, and I do not propose to begin to do so now. As to those papers with which you are making so free, I may tell you that in case there should be anything of any value among them you will be held strictly to account for what you do with them."

"Very good, sir," said Sherlock Holmes. "May I ask in the meanwhile whether you have yourself any theory to account for this young man's disappearance?"

"No, sir, I have not. He is big enough and old enough to look after himself, and if he is so foolish as to lose himself I entirely refuse to accept the responsibility of hunting for him."

"I quite understand your position," said Holmes, with a mischievous twinkle in his eyes. "Perhaps you don't quite understand mine. Godfrey Staunton appears to have been a poor man. If he has been kidnapped it could not have been for anything which he himself possesses. The fame of your wealth has gone abroad, Lord Mount-James, and it is entirely possible that a gang of thieves has secured your nephew in order to gain from him some information as to your house, your habits, and your treasure."

The face of our unpleasant little visitor turned as white as his neckcloth.

"Heavens, sir, what an idea! I never thought of such villainy! What inhuman rogues there are in the world! But Godfrey is a fine lad—a staunch lad. Nothing would induce him to give his old uncle away. I'll have the plate moved over to the bank this evening. In the meantime spare no pains, Mr. Detective. I beg you to leave no stone unturned to bring him safely back. As to money, well, so far as a fiver, or even a tenner, goes, you can always look to me."

Even in his chastened frame of mind the noble miser could give us no information which could help us, for he knew little of the private life of his nephew. Our only clue lay in the truncated telegram, and with a copy of this in his hand Holmes set forth to find a second link for his chain. We had shaken off Lord Mount-James, and Overton had gone to consult with the other members of his team over the misfortune which had befallen them.

There was a telegraph office at a short distance from the hotel. We halted outside it.

"It's worth trying, Watson," said Holmes. "Of course, with a warrant we could demand to see the counterfoils, but we have not reached that stage yet. I don't suppose they remember faces in so busy a place. Let us venture it."

"I am sorry to trouble you," said he in his blandest manner to the young woman behind the grating; "there is some small mistake about a telegram I sent yesterday. I have had no answer, and I very much fear that I must have omitted to put my name at the end. Could you tell me if this was so?"

The young lady turned over a sheaf of counterfoils.

"What o'clock was it?" she asked.

"A little after six."

"Whom was it to?"

Holmes put his finger to his lips and glanced at me. "The last words in it were 'for God's sake,'" he whispered confidentially; "I am very anxious at getting no answer."

The young woman separated one of the forms..

"This is it. There is no name," said she, smoothing it out upon the counter.

"Then that, of course, accounts for my getting no answer," said Holmes. "Dear me, how very stupid of me, to be sure! Good morning, miss, and many thanks for having relieved my mind." He chuckled and rubbed his hands when we found ourselves in the street once more.

"Well?" I asked.

"We progress, my dear Watson, we progress. I had seven different schemes for getting a glimpse of that
9 telegram, but I could hardly hope to succeed the very first time."

"And what have you gained?"

"A starting-point for our investigation." He hailed
10 a cab. "King's Cross Station," said he.

"We have a journey, then?"

11 "Yes, I think we must run down to Cambridge together. All the indications seem to point in that direction."

12 "Tell me," I asked as we rattled up Gray's Inn Road, "have you any suspicion yet as to the cause of the disappearance? I don't think that among all our cases I have known one where the motives were more obscure. Surely you don't really imagine that he may be kidnapped in order to give information against his wealthy uncle?"

"I confess, my dear Watson, that that does not appeal to me as a very probable explanation. It struck me, however, as being the one which was most likely to interest that exceedingly unpleasant old person."

"It certainly did that. But what are your alternatives?"

"I could mention several. You must admit that it is curious and suggestive that this incident should occur on the eve of this important match, and should involve the only man whose presence seems essential to the success of the side. It may, of course, be coincidence, but it is interesting. Amateur sport is free from betting, but a good deal of outside betting goes on among the public, and it is possible that it might be worth someone's while
13 to get at a player as the ruffians of the Turf get at a racehorse. There is one explanation. A second very obvious one is that this young man really is the heir of a great property, however modest his means may be at present, and it is not impossible that a plot to hold him for ransom might be concocted."

"These theories take no account of the telegram."

"Quite true, Watson. The telegram still remains the only solid thing with which we have to deal, and we must not permit our attention to wander away from it. It is to

9 *I had seven different schemes for getting a glimpse of that telegram.* Mr. Colin Prestige has noted that "It was reported in the *Daily Telegraph* of June 2, 1955, that a Post Office telegraphist . . . residing at Hove, Sussex . . . was, on the previous day, fined £5 with costs for disclosing the contents of a telegram. . . . The above news item, and particularly the penalty imposed, are of obvious interest since Dr. Watson recorded a similar instance of telegram disclosure in 'The Adventure of the Missing Three-Quarter.' . . . Presumably the persuasive charm ('bland,' as Watson puts it) of Mr. Holmes was in itself sufficient to overcome any question of scruple or conscience or fear of dismissal on the part of the young lady concerned."

10 *"King's Cross Station," said he.* In fact, a quicker and more direct route to Cambridge would have been from Liverpool Street Station.

11 *I think we must run down to Cambridge.* It has been said (by Sir Sydney Roberts) that this statement is another indication that Holmes was an Oxford, never a Cambridge, man. "You talk about going up to Cambridge," said Sir Sydney in a newspaper interview (Cambridge *Daily News*, March 23, 1962).

12 *Gray's Inn Road.* One of the principal thoroughfares leading north from High Holborn, so called because it contains on the west side Gray's Inn, one of the four great Inns of Court, originally founded for the education and lodging of law students. Gray's Inn Road from Holborn to Theobald's Road was considerably widened in Holmes' and Watson's day; before then it was called Gray's Inn Lane.

13 *it might be worth someone's while to get at a player.* "Worth someone's while, eh?" Mr. "Red" Smith commented in "The Game's Afoot." "Almost from the outset, Holmes was aware that Dr. Armstrong . . . held the key to the puzzle. Yet when he questioned Armstrong he allowed himself to be put off with windy bluff, learning nothing. Shadowing Armstrong to locate the missing man's hideout, he managed to lose sight of a carriage in a Cambridgeshire landscape 'as flat and clean as the palm of your hand.' Finally when Watson wanted to grab a bike and chase the doctor's carriage to the place of concealment, Holmes flatly forbade it. Why? Well, the match hadn't been played yet [and Holmes knew that Cambridge would stand no chance against Oxford without Staunton. He] was busy in Cambridge sending and receiving telegrams. Not until word was received of Oxford's victory . . . did the great detective strike upon an elementary device that should have occurred to anybody hours earlier . . ."

gain light upon the purpose of this telegram that we are now upon our way to Cambridge. The path of our investigation is at present obscure, but I shall be very much surprised if before evening we have not cleared it up or made a considerable advance along it."

It was already dark when we reached the old University city. Holmes took a cab at the station, and ordered the man to drive to the house of Dr. Leslie Armstrong. A few minutes later we had stopped at a large mansion in the busiest thoroughfare. We were shown in, and after a long wait were admitted into the consulting-room, where we found the doctor seated behind his table.

It argues the degree in which I had lost touch with my profession that the name of Leslie Armstrong was unknown to me. Now I am aware that he is not only one of the heads of the medical school of the University, but a thinker of European reputation in more than one branch of science. Yet even without knowing his brilliant record one could not fail to be impressed by a mere glance at the man—the square, massive face, the brooding eyes under the thatched brows, and the granite moulding of the inflexible jaw. A man of deep character, a man with an alert mind, grim, ascetic, self-contained, formidable—so I read Dr. Leslie Armstrong. He held my friend's card in his hand, and he looked up with no very pleased expression upon his dour features.

"I have heard your name, Mr. Sherlock Holmes, and I am aware of your profession, one of which I by no means approve."

"In that, doctor, you will find yourself in agreement with every criminal in the country," said my friend quietly.

"So far as your efforts are directed towards the suppression of crime, sir, they must have the support of every reasonable member of the community, though I cannot doubt that the official machinery is amply sufficient for the purpose. Where your calling is more open to criticism is when you pry into the secrets of private individuals, when you rake up family matters which are better hidden, and when you incidentally waste the time of men who are more busy than yourself. At the present moment, for example, I should be writing a treatise instead of conversing with you."

"No doubt, doctor; and yet the conversation may prove more important than the treatise. Incidentally I may tell you that we are doing the reverse of what you very justly blame, and that we are endeavouring to prevent anything like public exposure of private matters which must necessarily follow when once the case is fairly in the hands of the official police. You may look upon me simply as an irregular pioneer who goes in front of the regular force of the country. I have come to ask you about Mr. Godfrey Staunton."

"What about him?"

"You know him, do you not?"

"He is an intimate friend of mine."

"You are aware that he has disappeared?"

"Ah, indeed!" There was no change of expression in the rugged features of the doctor.

. . . HE LOOKED UP WITH NO VERY PLEASED EXPRESSION UPON HIS DOUR FEATURES.

Illustration by Sidney Paget for the *Strand Magazine*, August, 1904.

" He left his hotel last night. He has not been heard of."

" No doubt he will return."

" To-morrow is the 'Varsity football match."

" I have no sympathy with these childish games. The young man's fate interests me deeply, since I know him and like him. The football match does not come within my horizon at all."

" I claim your sympathy, then, in my investigation of Mr. Staunton's fate. Do you know where he is ? "

" Certainly not."

" You have not seen him since yesterday ? "

" No, I have not."

" Was Mr. Staunton a healthy man ? "

" Absolutely."

" Did you ever know him ill ? "

" Never."

Holmes popped a sheet of paper before the doctor's eyes. " Then perhaps you will explain this receipted bill for thirteen guineas, paid by Mr. Godfrey Staunton last month to Dr. Leslie Armstrong, of Cambridge. I picked it out from among the papers upon his desk."

The doctor flushed with anger.

" I do not feel that there is any reason why I should render an explanation to you, Mr. Holmes."

Holmes replaced the bill in his notebook.

" If you prefer a public explanation it must come sooner or later," said he. " I have already told you that I can hush up that which others will be bound to publish, and you would really be wiser to take me into your complete confidence."

" I know nothing about it."

" Did you hear from Mr. Staunton in London ? "

" Certainly not."

" Dear me, dear me !—the post office again ! " Holmes sighed wearily. " A most urgent telegram was despatched to you from London by Godfrey Staunton at six-fifteen yesterday evening—a telegram which is undoubtedly associated with his disappearance—and yet you have not had it. It is most culpable. I shall certainly go down to the office here and register a complaint."

Dr. Leslie Armstrong sprang up from behind his desk, and his dark face was crimson with fury.

" I'll trouble you to walk out of my house, sir," said he. " You can tell your employer, Lord Mount-James, that I do not wish to have anything to do either with him or with his agents. No, sir, not another word ! " He rang the bell furiously. " John, show these gentlemen out." A pompous butler ushered us severely to the door, and we found ourselves in the street. Holmes burst out laughing.

" Dr. Leslie Armstrong is certainly a man of energy and character," said he. " I have not seen a man who, if he turned his talents that way, was more calculated to fill the gap left by the illustrious Moriarty. And now, my poor Watson, here we are, stranded and friendless, in this
14 inhospitable town, which we cannot leave without abandoning our case. This little inn just opposite

14 *this inhospitable town.* Why does Holmes call Cambridge an "inhospitable town"? Perhaps, as a student, he had considerable trouble finding lodgings after he had given up living in college there.

Armstrong's house is singularly adapted to our needs. If you would engage a front room and purchase the necessaries for the night, I may have time to make a few inquiries."

These few inquiries proved, however, to be a more lengthy proceeding than Holmes had imagined, for he did not return to the inn until nearly nine o'clock. He was pale and dejected, stained with dust, and exhausted with hunger and fatigue. A cold supper was ready upon the table, and when his needs were satisfied and his pipe alight he was ready to take that half-comic and wholly philosophic view which was natural to him when his affairs were going awry. The sound of carriage wheels caused him to rise and glance out of the window. A brougham and pair of greys under the glare of a gas-lamp stood before the doctor's door.

"It's been out three hours," said Holmes; "started at half-past six, and here it is back again. That gives a radius of ten or twelve miles, and he does it once, or sometimes twice, a day."

"No unusual thing for a doctor in practice."

"But Armstrong is not really a doctor in practice. He is a lecturer and a consultant, but he does not care for general practice, which distracts him from his literary work. Why, then, does he make these long journeys, which must be exceedingly irksome to him, and who is it that he visits?"

"His coachman——"

"My dear Watson, can you doubt that it was to him that I first applied? I do not know whether it came from his own innate depravity or from the promptings of his master, but he was rude enough to set a dog at me. Neither dog nor man liked the look of my stick, however, and the matter fell through. Relations were strained after that, and further inquiries out of the question. All that I have learned I got from a friendly native in the yard of our own inn. It was he who told me of the doctor's habits and of his daily journey. At that instant, to give point to his words, the carriage came round to the door."

"Could you not follow it?"

"Excellent, Watson! You are scintillating this evening. The idea did cross my mind. There is, as you may have observed, a bicycle shop next to our inn. Into this I rushed, engaged a bicycle, and was able to get started before the carriage was quite out of sight. I rapidly overtook it, and then, keeping at a discreet distance of a hundred yards or so, I followed its lights until we were clear of the town. He had got well out on the country road when a somewhat mortifying incident occurred. The carriage stopped, the doctor alighted, walked swiftly back to where I had also halted, and told me in an excellent sardonic fashion that he feared the road was narrow, and that he hoped his carriage did not impede the passage of my bicycle. Nothing could have been more admirable than his way of putting it. I at once rode past the carriage, and, keeping to the main road, I went on for a few miles, and then halted in a convenient place to see if the carriage passed. There was no sign of it, however, and so it became evident that it had turned down one of several side-roads which I had observed. I rode back, but again saw nothing of the carriage, and now, as you perceive, it has returned after me. Of course, I had at the outset no particular reason to connect these journeys with the disappearance of Godfrey Staunton, and was only inclined to investigate them on the general grounds that everything which concerns Dr. Armstrong is at present of interest to us ; but, now that I find he keeps so keen a lookout upon anyone who may follow him on these excursions, the affair appears more important, and I shall not be satisfied until I have made the matter clear."

" We can follow him to-morrow."

" Can we ? It is not so easy as you seem to think.
You are not familiar with Cambridgeshire scenery, are
15 you ? It does not lend itself to concealment. All
this country that I passed over to-night is as flat and clean as the palm of your hand, and the man we are following is no fool, as he very clearly showed to-night. I have wired to Overton to let us know any fresh London developments at this address, and in the meantime we can only concentrate our attention upon Dr. Armstrong, whose name the obliging young lady at the office allowed me to read upon the counterfoil of Staunton's urgent message. He knows where that young man is—to that I'll swear—and if he knows, then it must be our own fault if we cannot manage to know also. At present it must be admitted that the odd trick is in his possession, and, as you are aware, Watson, it is not my habit to leave the game in that condition."

And yet the next day brought us no nearer to the solution of the mystery. A note was handed in after breakfast, which Holmes passed across to me with a smile.

Sir [it ran],—I can assure you that you are wasting your time in dogging my movements. I have, as you discovered last night, a window at the back of my brougham, and if you desire a twenty-mile ride which will lead you to the spot from which you started, you have only to follow me. Meanwhile, I can inform you that no spying upon me can in any way help Mr. Godfrey Staunton, and I am convinced that the best service you can do to that gentleman is to return at once to London and to report to your employer that you are unable to trace him. Your time in Cambridge will certainly be wasted.—Yours faithfully,

" Leslie Armstrong."

" An outspoken, honest antagonist is the doctor," said Holmes. " Well, well, he excites my curiosity, and I must really know more before I leave him."

" His carriage is at his door now," said I. " There he is stepping into it. I saw him glance up at our window as he did so. Suppose I try my luck upon the bicycle ? "

" No, no, my dear Watson ! With all respect for your natural acumen, I do not think that you are quite a match for the worthy doctor. I think that possibly I can attain our end by some independent explorations of my own. I

15 *You are not familiar with Cambridgeshire scenery, are you?* Holmes implies that he, Holmes, *is* familiar with Cambridgeshire scenery. "But in that case," the late Gavin Brend wrote in *My Dear Holmes*, "why does Holmes even undertake a pursuit which was foredoomed to failure? The answer would appear to be that having never been in Cambridge before he was in the same state of lamentable ignorance as to the distinctive peculiarities of Cambridgeshire scenery. We now see the significance of Watson's remark that it was after dark when they first arrived in Cambridge. Had they arrived by daylight, Holmes would have seen the difficulties from the window of his train, but as it was, they only became apparent after he had actually started out."

The fact of the matter is, however, that Holmes would have been familiar with the Fens scenery whether or not he was ever a student at Cambridge: in the 1870's he would almost certainly have had to travel to Donnithorpe ("The *Gloria Scott*") via Cambridge to get there, as the University town was on the main line from London (Liverpool Street Station) to Ely, Norwich, Yarmouth and Cromer.

There is a further point here of interest to students: if Watson was not familiar with Cambridgeshire scenery, as Holmes implies, then (it has been said) the University of "The Three Students," where Watson had previously spent "some weeks," must be Oxford. But Dr. W. S. Bristowe has answered this as follows: "Cambridge is a town full of interesting things to do and see and I, for one, would not have recommended Watson to foresake its hospitality in April for a country walk. If he had expressed a desire to go for a walk I would have directed him to the Gogamog Hills which would not have taught him of the flatness of the countryside in other directions of which he appears to be ignorant a few years later."

am afraid that I must leave you to your own devices, as the appearance of *two* inquiring strangers upon a sleepy country-side might excite more gossip than I care for. No doubt you will find some sights to amuse you in this venerable city, and I hope to bring back a more favourable report to you before evening."

Once more, however, my friend was destined to be disappointed. He came back at night weary and unsuccessful.

"I have had a blank day, Watson. Having got the doctor's general direction, I spent the day in visiting all the villages upon that side of Cambridge, and comparing notes with publicans and other local news agencies. I have covered some ground: Chesterton, Histon, Waterbeach, and Oakington have each been explored, and have each proved disappointing. The daily appearance of a brougham and pair could hardly have been overlooked in such Sleepy Hollows. The doctor has scored once more. Is there a telegram for me?"

"Yes; I opened it. Here it is: 'Ask for Pompey from Jeremy Dixon, Trinity College.' I don't understand it."

"Oh, it is clear enough. It is from our friend Overton, and is in answer to a question from me. I'll just send round a note to Mr. Jeremy Dixon, and then I have no doubt that our luck will turn. By the way, is there any news of the match?"

"Yes, the local evening paper has an excellent account in its last edition. Oxford won by a goal and two tries. **16**
The last sentences of the description say: 'The defeat of the Light Blues may be entirely attributed to the unfortunate absence of the crack International, Godfrey Staunton, whose want was felt at every instant of the game. The lack of combination in the three-quarter line and their weakness both in attack and defence more than neutralized the efforts of a heavy and hard-working pack.'"

"Then our friend Overton's forebodings have been justified," said Holmes. "Personally I am in agreement with Dr. Armstrong, and football does not come within my horizon. Early to bed to-night, Watson, for I foresee that to-morrow may be an eventful day."

I was horrified by my first glimpse of Holmes next morning, for he sat by the fire holding his tiny hypodermic syringe. I associated that with the single weakness of his nature, and I feared the worst when I saw it glittering in his hand. He laughed at my expression of dismay, and laid it upon the table.

"No, no, my dear fellow, there is no cause for alarm. It is not upon this occasion the instrument of evil, but it will rather prove to be the key which will unlock our mystery. On this syringe I base all my hopes. I have just returned from a small scouting expedition, and everything is favourable. Eat a good breakfast, Watson, for I propose to get upon Dr. Armstrong's trail to-day, and once on it I will not stop for rest or food until I run him to his burrow."

"In that case," said I, "we had best carry our breakfast with us, for he is making an early start. His car-

16 *Oxford won by a goal and two tries.* The year of "The Adventure of the Missing Three-Quarter," as we have seen, was 1894, 1895, or 1896. In 1894, the Cambridge-Oxford Rugby match was *drawn;* this is clearly not the year. In 1895, *Cambridge* won the match—again, this cannot be the year. In 1896, on the other hand, Oxford won—with a score of two goals to Cambridge's score of a goal and a try. In other words, as the late Dr. Ernest Bloomfield Zeisler so shrewdly observed, Oxford *won* by a goal, as Watson says it did. The Cambridge-Oxford game of 1896 was played on December 9th. The case, as we have seen, began on the preceding day, *Tuesday, December 8, 1896.* It closed on the day following the game—*Thursday, December 10, 1896.*

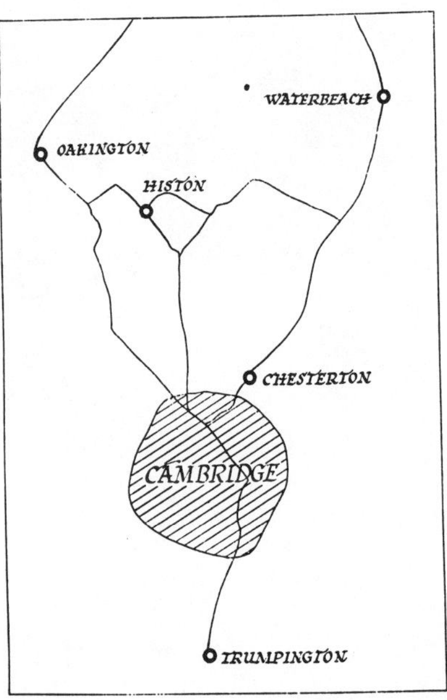

"I HAVE COVERED SOME GROUND: CHESTERTON, HISTON, WATERBEACH, AND OAKINGTON . . ."

Our map is from *My Dear Holmes*, by the late Gavin Brend. "Note the order," Mr. Brend wrote, "for it is a rather peculiar one. Presumably [Holmes] visited them in the order in which he names them, particularly in view of the certainty that in any circumstances Chesterton would obviously come first. But consider the position of the other three. From Cambridge or from Chesterton, Histon lies to the northwest, Oakington is still further northwest, but Waterbeach is to the northeast. So that if he went to Waterbeach after Histon he would probably come back again through Histon in order to get to Oakington. The obvious route which anyone familiar with the neighbourhood would take would be Chesterton, Waterbeach, Histon, Oakington, and the route actually taken reveals the Oxonian in a hurry who has not yet had time to procure a map."

17 *loose-box.* An enclosure in a stable in which a horse is kept unhaltered.

18 *no very great flier.* "Flier," as Mrs. Eleanor S. Cole noted in "Holmes, Watson and the K-9's," is "a word in common parlance today among dog fanciers to denote one which flies through to his champion title."

19 *John o' Groats.* John o' Groat, a Dutchman, was said to have settled in the north of Scotland in the year 1489. His house was near Dunscansby Head, the northernmost point of the British Isles.

THE DOG SNIFFED ROUND FOR AN INSTANT, AND THEN WITH A SHRILL WHINE OF EXCITEMENT STARTED OFF DOWN THE STREET . . .

(*Above*) Cover illustration by Frederic Dorr Steele for *Collier's Magazine*, November 26, 1904.

(*Below*) Illustration by Sidney Paget for the *Strand Magazine*, August, 1904.

riage is at the door."

" Never mind. Let him go. He will be clever if he can drive where I cannot follow him. When you have finished come downstairs with me, and I will introduce you to a detective who is a very eminent specialist in the work that lies before us."

When we descended I followed Holmes into the stable-
17 yard, where he opened the door of a loose-box and led out a squat, lop-eared, white-and-tan dog, something between a beagle and a foxhound.

" Let me introduce you to Pompey," said he. " Pompey is the pride of the local draghounds, no very great
18 flier, as his build will show, but a staunch hound on a scent. Well, Pompey, you may not be fast, but I expect you will be too fast for a couple of middle-aged London gentlemen, so I will take the liberty of fastening this leather leash to your collar. Now, boy, come along, and show what you can do." He led him across to the doctor's door. The dog sniffed round for an instant, and then with a shrill whine of excitement started off down the street, tugging at his leash in his efforts to go faster. In half an hour we were clear of the town and hastening down a country road.

" What have you done, Holmes ? " I asked.

" A threadbare and venerable device, but useful upon occasion. I walked into the doctor's yard this morning and shot my syringe full of aniseed over the hind wheel. A draghound will follow aniseed from here to John o'
19 Groats, and our friend Armstrong would have to drive through the Cam before he would shake Pompey off his trail. Oh, the cunning rascal ! This is how he gave me the slip the other night."

The dog had suddenly turned out of the main road into a grass-grown lane. Half a mile farther this opened into another broad road, and the trail turned hard to the right in the direction of the town, which we had just quitted. The road took a sweep to the south of the town and continued in the opposite direction to that in which we started.

" This detour has been entirely for our benefit, then ? " said Holmes. " No wonder that my inquiries among those villages led to nothing. The doctor has certainly played the game for all it is worth, and one would like to know the reason for such elaborate deception. This
20 should be the village of Trumpington to the right of us. And, by Jove ! here is the brougham coming round the corner ! Quick, Watson, quick, or we are done ! "

He sprang through a gate into a field, dragging the reluctant Pompey after him. We had hardly got under the shelter of the hedge when the carriage rattled past. I caught a glimpse of Dr. Armstrong within, his shoulders bowed, his head sunk on his hands, the very image of distress. I could tell by my companion's graver face that he also had seen.

" I fear there is some dark ending to our quest," said he. " It cannot be long before we know it. Come, Pompey ! Ah, it is the cottage in the field."

There could be no doubt that we had reached the end of our journey. Pompey ran about and whined eagerly outside the gate, where the marks of the brougham's wheels were still to be seen. A footpath led across to the lonely cottage. Holmes tied the dog to the hedge, and we hastened onwards. My friend knocked at the little rustic door, and knocked again without response. And yet the cottage was not deserted, for a low sound came to our ears—a kind of drone of misery and despair, which was indescribably melancholy. Holmes paused irresolute, and then he glanced back at the road which we had just traversed. A brougham was coming down it, and there could be no mistaking those grey horses.

" By Jove, the doctor is coming back ! " cried Holmes. " That settles it. We are bound to see what it means before he comes."

He opened the door, and we stepped into the hall. The droning sound swelled louder upon our ears, until it became one long, deep wail of distress. It came from upstairs. Holmes darted up, and I followed him. He pushed open a half-closed door, and we both stood appalled at the sight before us.

A woman, young and beautiful, was lying dead upon the bed. Her calm, pale face, with dim, wide-opened blue eyes, looked upwards from amid a great tangle of golden hair. At the foot of the bed, half sitting, half kneeling, his face buried in the clothes, was a young man, whose frame was racked by his sobs. So absorbed was he by his bitter grief that he never looked up until Holmes' hand was on his shoulder.

" Are you Mr. Godfrey Staunton ? "

" Yes, yes ; I am—but you are too late. She is dead."

The man was so dazed that he could not be made to understand that we were anything but doctors who had been sent to his assistance. Holmes was endeavouring to utter a few words of consolation, and to explain the alarm which had been caused to his friends by his sudden disappearance, when there was a step upon the stairs, and there was the heavy, stern, questioning face of Dr. Armstrong at the door.

" So, gentlemen," said he, " you have attained your end, and have certainly chosen a particularly delicate moment for your intrusion. I would not brawl in the presence of death, but I can assure you that if I were a younger man your monstrous conduct would not pass with impunity."

" Excuse me, Dr. Armstrong, I think we are a little at cross purposes," said my friend with dignity. " If you could step downstairs with us we may each be able to give some light to the other upon this miserable affair."

20 *This should be the village of Trumpington.* Holmes, the late Gavin Brend wrote, "could hardly have been at Cambridge without visiting a place so near. The Cantab would certainly say 'This *is* Trumpington.' The 'should be' is the mark of the Oxonian. So too we suggest is the expression 'the village of Trumpington' as opposed to mere 'Trumpington.' The former suggests the stranger, the latter the neighbour."

I CAUGHT A GLIMPSE OF DR. ARMSTRONG WITHIN . . .

Illustration by Sidney Paget for the *Strand Magazine*, August, 1904. Charles Raymond Macauley illustrated the same scene for *The Return of Sherlock Holmes*, New York: McClure, Phillips & Co., 1905.

. . . HE NEVER LOOKED UP UNTIL HOLMES' HAND WAS ON HIS SHOULDER.

Illustration by Sidney Paget for the *Strand Magazine*, August, 1904.

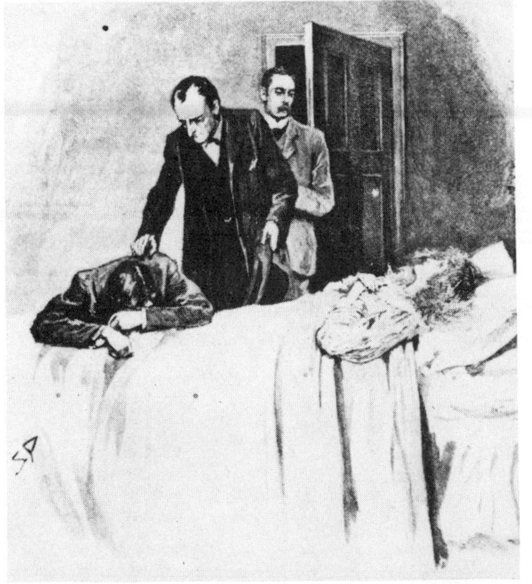

Bibliographical Note: The original manuscript of "The Adventure of the Missing Three-Quarter," about 8,000 words in 25 folio pages, white vellum by Spealls, was auctioned in New York City on January 30, 1923, bringing $130. It was listed in Scribner's Sherlock Holmes Catalogue at $450. At one time owned by Mr. Vincent Starrett of Chicago, it became the first Conan Doyle manuscript to become vested in the British people when it was presented in 1959 to the British Museum by the Sherlock Holmes Society of London, aided by generous donations from the Friends of the National Libraries and five American donors, J. Bliss Austin, Lew David Feldman, E. T. Guymon, Jr., Rollin V. N. Hadley, Jr., and the late Edgar W. Smith. The purchase price was $1,000.

The Adventure of the Missing Three Quarter.

We were fairly accustomed to receive weird telegrams at Baker Street but I have a particular recollection of one which reached us on a gloomy February morning some seven or eight years ago and gave Mr. Sherlock Holmes a puzzled quarter of an hour. It was addressed to him and ran thus

"Please await me. Terrible misfortune. Right wing three quarter missing indispensable tomorrow. Overton"

"Strand post mark and dispatched 10.36" said Holmes, reading it over and over. "Mr. Overton was evidently considerably excited when he sent it and somewhat incoherent in consequence. Well, well, he will be here I dare say by the time I have looked through the Times and then we shall know all about it. Even the most insignificant problem would be welcome in these stagnant times."

Things had indeed been very slow with us, and I had learned to dread such periods of inaction for I knew by experience that my companion's brain was so abnormally active that it was dangerous to leave it without material upon which to work. For years I had gradually weaned him from that drug mania which had threatened once to check his remarkable career. Now I knew that under ordinary conditions he no longer craved for this artificial stimulus but I was well aware that the fiend was not dead but sleeping, and I have known that the sleep was a light one and the waking near when in periods of idleness I have seen the drawn look upon Holmes' ascetic face, and the brooding of his deep set and inscrutable eyes. Therefore I blessed Mr. Overton, whoever he might be, since he had come with his enigmatic message to break that dangerous calm which brought more danger to my friend than all the storms of his tempestuous life.

A minute later the grim doctor and ourselves were in the sitting-room below.

"Well, sir?" said he.

"I wish you to understand, in the first place, that I am not employed by Lord Mount-James, and that my sympathies in this matter are entirely against that nobleman. When a man is lost it is my duty to ascertain his fate, but having done so the matter ends so far as I am concerned; and so long as there is nothing criminal, I am much more anxious to hush up private scandals than to give them publicity. If, as I imagine, there is no breach of the law in this matter, you can absolutely depend upon my discretion and my co-operation in keeping the facts out of the papers!"

Dr. Armstrong took a quick step forward and wrung Holmes by the hand.

"You are a good fellow," said he. "I had misjudged you. I thank Heaven that my compunction at leaving poor Staunton all alone in this plight caused me to turn my carriage back, and so to make your acquaintance. Knowing as much as you do, the situation is very easily explained. A year ago Godfrey Staunton lodged in London for a time, and became passionately attached to his landlady's daughter, whom he married. She was as good as she was beautiful, and as intelligent as she was good. No man need be ashamed of such a wife. But Godfrey was the heir to this crabbed old nobleman, and it was quite certain that the news of his marriage would have been the end of his inheritance. I knew the lad well, and I loved him for his many excellent qualities. I did all I could to help him to keep things straight. We did our very best to keep the thing from everyone, for when once such a whisper gets about it is not long before everyone has heard it. Thanks to this lonely cottage and his own discretion, Godfrey has up to now succeeded. Their secret was known to no one save to me and to one excellent servant who has at present gone for assistance to Trumpington. But at last there came a terrible blow in the shape of dangerous illness to his wife. It was consumption of the most virulent kind. The poor boy was half crazed with grief, and yet he had to go to London to play this match, for he could not get out of it without explanations which would expose the secret. I tried to cheer him up by a wire, and he sent me one in reply imploring me to do all I could. This was the telegram which you appear in some inexplicable way to have seen. I did not tell him how urgent the danger was, for I knew that he could do no good here, but I sent the truth to the girl's father, and he very injudiciously communicated to Godfrey. The result was that he came straight away in a state bordering on frenzy, and has remained in the same state, kneeling at the end of her bed, until this morning death put an end to her sufferings. That is all, Mr. Holmes, and I am sure that I can rely upon your discretion and that of your friend."

Holmes grasped the doctor's hand.

"Come, Watson," said he, and we passed from that house of grief into the pale sunlight of the winter day.

59

THE ADVENTURE OF THE ABBEY GRANGE

[*Saturday, January 23, 1897*]

IT was on a bitterly cold and frosty morning during the winter of '97 that I was wakened by a tugging at my shoulder. It was Holmes. The candle in his hand shone upon his eager, stooping face, and told me at a glance that something was amiss.

" Come, Watson, come ! " he cried. " The game is afoot. Not a word ! Into your clothes and come ! "

Ten minutes later we were both in a cab and rattling through the silent streets on our way to Charing Cross Station. The first faint winter's dawn was beginning to appear, and we could dimly see the occasional figure of an early workman as he passed us, blurred and indistinct in the opalescent London reek. Holmes nestled in silence into his heavy coat, and I was glad to do the same, for the air was most bitter, and neither of us had broken our fast. It was not until we had consumed some hot tea at the station, and taken our places in the Kentish train, that we were sufficiently thawed, he to speak and I to listen. Holmes drew a note from his pocket and read it aloud :

" ABBEY GRANGE, MARSHAM, KENT, 3.30 a.m.

" MY DEAR MR. HOLMES,—I should be very glad of your immediate assistance in what promises to be a most remarkable case. It is something quite in your line. Except for releasing the lady I will see that everything is kept exactly as I have found it, but I beg you not to lose an instant, as it is difficult to leave Sir Eustace there.—Yours faithfully,

" STANLEY HOPKINS.

" Hopkins has called me in seven times, and on each **1** occasion his summons has been entirely justified," said Holmes. " I fancy that every one of his cases has found its way into your collection, and I must admit, Watson, that you have some power of selection which atones for much which I deplore in your narratives. Your fatal habit of looking at everything from the point of view of a story instead of as a scientific exercise has ruined what might have been an instructive and even classical series of demonstrations. You slur over work of the utmost finesse and delicacy in order to dwell upon sensational details which may excite but cannot possibly instruct the reader."

1 "*Hopkins has called me in seven times.* Holmes helped Hopkins in "The Adventure of the Golden Pince-Nez," "The Adventure of Black Peter" and "The Adventure of the Missing Three-Quarter" prior to the time he made this statement. But what were the other four cases?

"COME, WATSON, COME!" HE CRIED. "THE GAME IS AFOOT."

Holmes quotes Shakespeare: *The First Part of Henry the Fourth*, Act I, Scene 3, line 276: "Before the game's afoot . . ." and *The Life of Henry the Fifth*, Act III, Scene 1, line 32: "The game's afoot!" His words epitomize the whole Saga. With the possible exception of the obnoxious—and wholly apocryphal—"Quick, Watson, the needle!"—they are no doubt more often quoted than any other Holmes-Watson expression. The illustration by Sidney Paget was drawn for the *Strand Magazine*, September, 1904.

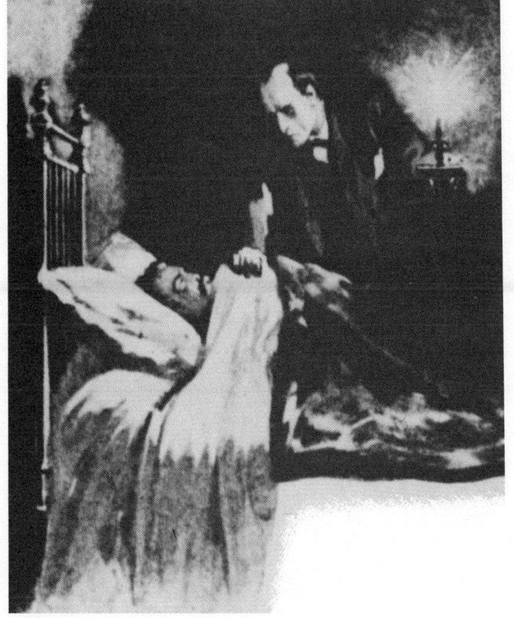

" Why do you not write them yourself ? " I said, with some bitterness.

2 " I will, my dear Watson, I will. At present I am, as you know, fairly busy, but I propose to devote my declining years to the composition of a textbook which shall focus the whole art of detection into one volume. Our present research appears to be a case of murder."

" You think this Sir Eustace is dead, then ? "

" I should say so. Hopkins' writing shows considerable agitation, and he is not an emotional man. Yes, I gather there has been violence, and that the body is left for our inspection. A mere suicide would not have caused him to send for me. As to the release of the lady, it would appear that she has been locked in her room during the tragedy. We are moving in high life. Watson—crackling paper, 'E.B.' monogram, coat-of-arms, picturesque address. I think that friend Hopkins will live up to his reputation, and that we shall have an interesting morning. The crime was committed before twelve last night."

" How can you possibly tell ? "

" By an inspection of the trains and by reckoning the time. The local police had to be called in, they had to communicate with Scotland Yard, Hopkins had to go out, and he in turn had to send for me. All that makes a fair night's work. Well, here we are at Chislehurst Station, and we shall soon set our doubts at rest."

A drive of a couple of miles through narrow country
3 lanes brought us to a park gate, which was opened for us by an old lodge-keeper, whose haggard face bore the reflection of some great disaster. The avenue ran through a noble park, between lines of ancient elms, and ended in a low, widespread house, pillared in front after the
4 fashion of Palladio. The central part was evidently of a great age and shrouded in ivy, but the large windows showed that modern changes had been carried out, and one wing of the house appeared to be entirely new. The youthful figure and alert, eager face of Inspector Stanley Hopkins confronted us in the open doorway.

" I'm very glad you have come, Mr. Holmes. And you, too, Dr. Watson ! But, indeed, if I had my time over again I should not have troubled you, for since the lady has come to herself she has given so clear an account of the affair that there is not much left for us to do. You remember that Lewisham gang of burglars ? "

" What, the three Randalls ? "

" Exactly ; the father and two sons. It's their work. I have not a doubt of it. They did a job at Sydenham a fortnight ago, and were seen and described. Rather cool to do another so soon and so near ; but it is they, beyond all doubt. It's a hanging matter this time."

" Sir Eustace is dead, then ? "

" Yes ; his head was knocked in with his own poker."

" Sir Eustace Brackenstall, the driver tells me."

" Exactly—one of the richest men in Kent. Lady Brackenstall is in the morning-room. Poor lady, she has had a most dreadful experience. She seemed half dead when I saw her first. I think you had best see her and hear her account of the facts. Then we will examine the dining-room together."

2 *"I will, my dear Watson, I will.* And he did, at the age of 72, in 1926, with the appearance of "The Adventure of the Blanched Soldier" and "The Adventure of the Lion's Mane."

3 *brought us to a park gate.* Mr. Michael Harrison believes that "Marsham, Kent" may reasonably be identified with St. Mary Cray. In *In the Footsteps of Sherlock Holmes* he wrote: "Most of the old houses in this once most select of all London's suburbs remain: turned . . . into golf-clubs, or hospitals or schools or lunatic asylums . . . if 'Abbey Grange' . . . still survives, it will no longer be in private occupation."

4 *the fashion of Palladio.* Andrea Palladio, 1518–1580, was an Italian architect of the Renaissance, known for formal, grandiose designs based on the Roman style. The Palladian style, characterized by arches supported by minor columns and framed between larger columns, was followed by architects of the Georgian period.

Lady Brackenstall was no ordinary person. Seldom have I seen so graceful a figure, so womanly a presence, and so beautiful a face. She was a blonde, golden-haired, blue-eyed, and would, no doubt, have had the perfect complexion which goes with such colouring had not her recent experience left her drawn and haggard. Her sufferings were physical as well as mental, for over one eye rose a hideous, plum-coloured swelling, which her maid, a tall, austere woman, was bathing assiduously with vinegar and water. The lady lay back exhausted upon a couch, but her quick, observant gaze as we entered the room, and the alert expression of her beautiful features, showed that neither her wits nor her courage had been shaken by her terrible experience. She was enveloped in a loose dressing-gown of blue and silver, but a black sequin-covered dinner-dress was hung upon the couch beside her.

" I have told you all that happened, Mr. Hopkins," she said wearily ; " could you not repeat it for me ? Well, if you think it necessary, I will tell these gentlemen what occurred. Have they been in the dining-room yet ? "

" I thought they had better hear your ladyship's story first."

" I shall be glad when you can arrange matters. It is horrible to me to think of him still lying there." She shuddered and buried her face for a moment in her hands. As she did so the loose gown fell back from her fore-arm. Holmes uttered an exclamation.

" You have other injuries, madam ! What is this ? " Two vivid red spots stood out on one of the white, round limbs. She hastily covered it.

" It is nothing. It has no connection with the hideous business of last night. If you and your friend will sit down I will tell you all I can.

" I am the wife of Sir Eustace Brackenstall. I have been married about a year. I suppose that it is no use 5 my attempting to conceal that our marriage has not been a happy one. I fear that all our neighbours would tell you that, even if I were to attempt to deny it. Perhaps the fault may be partly mine. I was brought up in the freer, less conventional atmosphere of South Australia, and this English life, with its proprieties and its primness, is not congenial to me. But the main reason lies in the one fact which is notorious to everyone, and that is that Sir Eustace was a confirmed drunkard. To be with such a man for an hour is unpleasant. Can you imagine what it means for a sensitive and high-spirited woman to be tied to him for day and night ? It is a sacrilege, a crime, a villainy to hold that such a marriage is binding. I say that these monstrous laws of yours will bring a curse upon the land—Heaven will not let such wickedness endure." For an instant she sat up, her cheeks flushed, and her eyes blazing from under the terrible mark upon her brow. Then the strong, soothing hand of the austere maid drew her head down on to the cushion, and the wild anger died away into passionate sobbing. At last she continued :

" I will tell you about last night. You are aware, perhaps, that in this house all servants sleep in the modern

THE LADY LAY BACK EXHAUSTED UPON A COUCH . . .

Illustration by Frederic Dorr Steele for *Collier's Magazine*, December 31, 1904. Sidney Paget portrayed the same scene for the *Strand Magazine*, September, 1904.

5 *I have been married about a year.* Watson's dating of this adventure—"the winter of '97"—could mean that it took place in the January, February, or December of that year. The correct month, as we shall see, is *January:* the manager of the steamer line later told Holmes that the *Rock of Gibralter*, on which Miss Mary Fraser (later Lady Brackenstall) sailed to England, docked at a home port in "June of '95." Miss Fraser had "only just arrived in London," according to Theresa Wright, when she met Sir Eustace Brackenstall. This was "only eighteen months ago." "They first left Australia eighteen months ago," Stanley Hopkins later tells Holmes, and Theresa Wright adds: "We arrived in June, and it was July [when Miss Fraser and Sir Eustace met]. They were married in January of last year." "I have been married about a year," Lady Brackenstall says here. It is clear that Miss Fraser and Theresa Wright arrived in England in June, 1895; in July, Miss Fraser and Sir Eustace met; in January, 1896, they were married, bringing us to a date eighteen months after July, 1895, twelve months after January, 1896: to *January, 1897*.

wing. This central block is made up of the dwelling-rooms, with the kitchen behind and our bedroom above. My maid Theresa sleeps above my room. There is no one else, and no sound could alarm those who are in the farther wing. This must have been well known to the robbers, or they would not have acted as they did.

" Sir Eustace retired about half-past ten. The servants had already gone to their quarters. Only my maid was up, and she had remained in her room at the top of the house until I needed her services. I sat until after eleven in this room, absorbed in a book. Then I walked round to see that all was right before I went upstairs. It was my custom to do this myself, for, as I have explained, Sir Eustace was not always to be trusted. I went into the kitchen, the butler's pantry, the gun-room, the billiard-room, the drawing-room, and finally the dining-room. As I approached the window, which is covered with thick curtains, I suddenly felt the wind blow upon my face, and realized that it was open. I flung the curtain aside, and found myself face to face with a broad-shouldered, elderly man who had just stepped into the room. The window is a long French one, which really forms a door leading to the lawn. I held my bedroom candle lit in my hand, and, by its light, behind the first man I saw two others, who were in the act of entering. I stepped back, but the fellow was on me in an instant. He caught me first by the wrist and then by the throat. I opened my mouth to scream, but he struck me a savage blow with his fist over the eye, and felled me to the ground. I must have been unconscious for a few minutes, for when I came to myself I found that they had torn down the bell-rope and had secured me tightly to the oaken chair which stands at the head of the dining-room table. I was so firmly bound that I could not move, and a handkerchief round my mouth prevented me from uttering any sound. It was at this instant that my unfortunate husband entered the room. He had evidently heard some suspicious sounds, and he came prepared for such a scene as he found. He was dressed in his shirt and trousers, with his favourite blackthorn cudgel in his hand. He rushed at one of the burglars, but another--it was the elderly man—stooped, picked the poker out of the grate, and struck him a terrible blow as he passed. He fell without a groan, and never moved again. I fainted once more, but again it could only have been a very few minutes during which I was insensible. When I opened my eyes I found that they had collected the silver from the sideboard, and they had drawn a bottle of wine which stood there. Each of them had a glass in his hand. I have already told you, have I not, that one was elderly, with a beard, and the others young, hairless lads. They might have been a father with his two sons. They talked together in whispers. Then they came over and made sure that I was still securely bound. Finally they withdrew, closing the window after them. It was quite a quarter of an hour before I got my mouth free. When I did so my screams brought the maid to my assistance. The other servants were soon alarmed, and we sent for the local police, who instantly communicated with

London. That is really all I can tell you, gentlemen, and I trust that it will not be necessary for me to go over so painful a story again."

"Any questions, Mr. Holmes?" asked Hopkins.

"I will not impose any further tax upon Lady Brackenstall's patience and time," said Holmes. "Before I go into the dining-room I should be glad to hear your experience." He looked at the maid.

"I saw the men before ever they came into the house," said she. "As I sat by my bedroom window I saw three men in the moonlight down by the lodge gate yonder, 6 but I thought nothing of it at the time. It was more than an hour after that I heard my mistress scream, and down I ran, to find her, poor lamb, just as she says, and him on the floor with his blood and brains over the room. It was enough to drive a woman out of her wits, tied there, and her very dress spotted with him; but she never wanted courage, did Miss Mary Fraser of Adelaide, and Lady Brackenstall of Abbey Grange hasn't learned new ways. You've questioned her long enough, you gentlemen, and now she is coming to her own room, just with her old Theresa, to get the rest that she badly needs."

With a motherly tenderness the gaunt woman put her arm round her mistress and led her from the room.

"She has been with her all her life," said Hopkins. "Nursed her as a baby, and came with her to England when they first left Australia eighteen months ago. Theresa Wright is her name, and the kind of maid you don't pick up nowadays. This way, Mr. Holmes, if you please!"

The keen interest had passed out of Holmes' expressive face, and I knew that with the mystery all the charm of the case had departed. There still remained an arrest to be effected, but what were these commonplace rogues that he should soil his hands with them? An abstruse and learned specialist who finds that he has been called in for a case of measles would experience something of the annoyance which I read in my friend's eyes. Yet the scene in the dining-room of the Abbey Grange was sufficiently strange to arrest his attention and to recall his waning interest.

It was a very large and high chamber, with carved oak ceiling, oaken panelling, and a fine array of deers' heads and ancient weapons around the walls. At the farther end from the door was the high French window of which we had heard. Three smaller windows on the right-hand side filled the apartment with cold winter sunshine. On the left was a large, deep fireplace, with a massive overhanging oak mantelpiece. Beside the fireplace was a heavy oaken chair with arms and cross-bars at the bottom. In and out through the open woodwork was woven a crimson cord, which was secured at each side to the crosspiece below. In releasing the lady the cord had been slipped off her, but the knots with which it had been secured still remained. These details only struck our attention afterwards, for our thoughts were entirely absorbed by the terrible object which lay spread upon the tiger-skin hearthrug in front of the fire.

6 *in the moonlight.* The maid, as we shall learn, lied about the three men but she would not have lied about something on which Holmes, Watson, and even Hopkins could at once have caught her out. The moon must therefore have been shining at about 11:00 P.M. on the night of the murder. As the late Dr. Ernest Bloomfield Zeisler wrote (*Baker Street Chronology*): "In January of 1897 the moon had set before 11:00 P.M. on the 1st to the 8th and did not rise until after 11:00 P.M. on the 24th to the 31st. Hence the murder must have been on one of the 9th to the 23rd, inclusive." To this the late Professor Jay Finley Christ added (*An Irregular Chronology*): "January, 1897, was nearly 100 per cent cloudy until the 22nd. The moon probably was not visible until midnight on the 21st, at the earliest." The murder must therefore have taken place on the night of the 22nd (a Friday) or the 23rd (a Saturday); Holmes solved it the next day (a Saturday or a Sunday). But the day was not a Sunday: at dawn, Holmes and Watson "could dimly see an occasional figure of an early workman as he passed us . . . in the opalescent London reek." We can now say with some confidence that Holmes' investigation of the Abbey Grange affair took place on *Saturday, January 23, 1897.*

IT WAS THE BODY OF A TALL, WELL-MADE MAN, ABOUT FORTY YEARS OF AGE.

Illustration by Sidney Paget for the *Strand Magazine*, September, 1904.

"WHAT ARE YOU LOOKING AT NOW?"

Cover illustration by Frederic Dorr Steele for *Collier's Magazine*, December 31, 1904.

It was the body of a tall, well-made man, about forty years of age. He lay upon his back, his face upturned, with his white teeth grinning through his short, black beard. His two clenched hands were raised above his head, and a heavy blackthorn stick lay across them. His dark, handsome, aquiline features were convulsed into a spasm of vindictive hatred, which had set his dead face in a terribly fiendish expression. He had evidently been in his bed when the alarm had broken out, for he wore a foppish, embroidered night-shirt, and his bare feet projected from his trousers. His head was horribly injured, and the whole room bore witness to the savage ferocity of the blow which had struck him down. Beside him lay the heavy poker, bent into a curve by the concussion. Holmes examined both it and the indescribable wreck which it had wrought.

"He must be a powerful man, this elder Randall," he remarked.

"Yes," said Hopkins. "I have some record of the fellow, and he is a rough customer."

"You should have no difficulty in getting him."

"Not the slightest. We have been on the look-out for him, and there was some idea that he had got away to America. Now that we know the gang are here I don't see how they can escape. We have the news at every seaport already, and a reward will be offered before evening. What beats me is how they could have done so mad a thing, knowing that the lady would describe them, and that we could not fail to recognize the description."

"Exactly. One would have expected that they would have silenced Lady Brackenstall as well."

"They may not have realized," I suggested, "that she had recovered from her faint."

"That is likely enough. If she seemed to be senseless they would not take her life. What about this poor fellow, Hopkins? I seem to have heard some queer stories about him."

"He was a good-hearted man when he was sober, but a perfect fiend when he was drunk, or rather when he was half drunk, for he seldom really went the whole way. The devil seemed to be in him at such times, and he was capable of anything. From what I hear, in spite of all his wealth and his title, he very nearly came our way once or twice. There was a scandal about his drenching a dog with petroleum and setting it on fire—her ladyship's dog, to make the matter worse—and that was only hushed up with difficulty. Then he threw a decanter at that maid Theresa Wright; there was trouble about that. On the whole, and between ourselves, it will be a brighter house without him. What are you looking at now?"

Holmes was down on his knees examining with great attention the knots upon the red cord with which the lady had been secured. Then he carefully scrutinized the broken and frayed end where it had snapped off when the burglar had dragged it down.

"When this was pulled down the bell in the kitchen must have rung loudly," he remarked.

" No one could hear it. The kitchen stands right at the back of the house."

" How did the burglar know no one would hear it? How dare he pull at a bell-rope in that reckless fashion?"

" Exactly, Mr. Holmes, exactly. You put the very question which I have asked myself again and again. There can be no doubt that this fellow must have known the house and its habits. He must have perfectly understood that the servants would all be in bed at that comparatively early hour, and that no one could possibly hear a bell ring in the kitchen. Therefore he must have been in close league with one of the servants. Surely that is evident. But there are eight servants, and all of good character."

" Other things being equal," said Holmes, " one would suspect the one at whose head the master threw a decanter. And yet that would involve treachery towards the mistress to whom this woman seems devoted. Well, well, the point is a minor one, and when you have Randall you will probably find no difficulty in securing his accomplices. The lady's story certainly seems to be corroborated, if it needed corroboration, by every detail which we see before us." He walked to the French window and threw it open. " There are no signs here, but the ground is iron hard, and one would not expect them. I see that these candles on the mantelpiece have been lighted."

" Yes, it was by their light and that of the lady's bedroom candle that the burglars saw their way about."

" And what did they take?"

" Well, they did not take much—only half a dozen articles of plate off the sideboard. Lady Brackenstall thinks that they were themselves so disturbed by the death of Sir Eustace that they did not ransack the house as they would otherwise have done."

" No doubt that is true. And yet they drank some wine, I understand."

" To steady their own nerves."

" Exactly. These three glasses upon the sideboard have been untouched, I suppose?"

" Yes; and the bottle stands as they left it."

" Let us look at it. Halloa, halloa! what is this?"

The three glasses were grouped together, all of them tinged with wine, and one of them containing some dregs
of beeswing. The bottle stood near them, two-thirds 7
full, and beside it lay a long, deeply stained cork. Its appearance and the dust upon the bottle showed that it was no common vintage which the murderers had enjoyed.

A change had come over Holmes' manner. He had lost his listless expression, and again I saw an alert light of interest in his keen deep-set eyes. He raised the cork and examined it minutely.

" How did they draw it?" he asked.

Hopkins pointed to a half-opened drawer. In it lay some table linen and a large corkscrew.

" Did Lady Brackenstall say that screw was used?"

" No; you remember that she was senseless at the moment when the bottle was opened."

"THESE THREE GLASSES UPON THE SIDEBOARD HAVE BEEN UNTOUCHED, I SUPPOSE?"

Illustration by Charles Raymond Macauley for *The Return of Sherlock Holmes*, New York: McClure, Phillips & Co., 1905.

7 *beeswing*. "This word may occasion a trifle of difficulty among Americans, in its syllabic division," Mr. Cyrus Durgin noted in "The Speckled Band." "It is not bee-swing . . . but 'bee's-wing,' or 'bees'-wing,' depending upon how much sediment is in the bottle. Scant, fine sediment would take the singular possessive, large, plentiful sediment the plural."

"HALLOA, HALLOA! WHAT IS THIS?"

Illustration by Sidney Paget for the *Strand Magazine*, September, 1904.

"BUT THESE GLASSES DO PUZZLE ME, I CONFESS."

Illustration by Frederic Dorr Steele for *Collier's Magazine*, December 31, 1904.

" Quite so. As a matter of fact, that screw was *not* used. This bottle was opened by a pocket-screw, probably contained in a knife, and not more than an inch and a half long. If you examine the top of the cork you will observe that the screw was driven in three times before the cork was extracted. It has never been transfixed. This long screw would have transfixed it and drawn it with a single pull. When you catch this fellow you will find that he has one of these multiplex knives in his possession."

" Excellent ! " said Hopkins.

" But these glasses do puzzle me, I confess. Lady Brackenstall actually *saw* the three men drinking, did she not ? "

" Yes ; she was clear about that."

" Then there is an end of it. What more is to be said ? And yet you must admit that the three glasses are very remarkable, Hopkins. What, you see nothing remarkable ! Well, well, let it pass. Perhaps when a man has special knowledge and special powers like my own it rather encourages him to seek a complex explanation when a simpler one is at hand. Of course, it must be a mere chance about the glasses. Well, good morning, Hopkins. I don't see that I can be of any use to you, and you appear to have your case very clear. You will let me know when Randall is arrested, and any further developments which may occur. I trust that I shall soon have to congratulate you upon a successful conclusion. Come, Watson, I fancy that we may employ ourselves more profitably at home."

During our return journey I could see by Holmes' face that he was much puzzled by something which he had observed. Every now and then, by an effort, he would throw off the impression and talk as if the matter were clear, but then his doubts would settle down upon him again, and his knitted brows and abstracted eyes would show that his thoughts had gone back once more to the great dining-room of the Abbey Grange in which this midnight tragedy had been enacted. At last, by a sudden impulse, just as our train was crawling out of a suburban station, he sprang on to the platform and pulled me out after him.

" Excuse me, my dear fellow," said he, as we watched the rear carriages of our train disappearing round a curve ; " I am sorry to make you the victim of what may seem a mere whim, but on my life, Watson, I simply *can't* leave that case in this condition. Every instinct that I possess cries out against it. It's wrong—it's all wrong—I'll swear that it's wrong. And yet the lady's story was complete, the maid's corroboration was sufficient, the detail was fairly exact. What have I to put against that ? Three wine-glasses, that is all. But if I had not taken things for granted, if I had examined everything with the care which I would have shown had
8 we approached the case *de novo* and had no cut-and-dried story to warp my mind, would I not then have found something more definite to go upon ? Of course I should. Sit down on this bench, Watson, until a train for Chislehurst arrives, and allow me to lay the evidence

8 de novo. Latin: new; afresh.

before you, imploring you in the first instance to dismiss from your mind the idea that anything which the maid or mistress may have said must necessarily be true. The lady's charming personality must not be permitted to warp our judgment.

" Surely there are details in her story which, if we look at it in cold blood, would excite our suspicion. These burglars made a considerable haul at Sydenham a fortnight ago. Some account of them and their appearance was in the papers, and would naturally occur to anyone who wished to invent a story in which imaginary robbers should play a part. As a matter of fact, burglars who have done a good stroke of business are, as a rule, only too glad to enjoy the proceeds in peace and quiet without embarking on another perilous undertaking. Again, it is unusual for burglars to operate at so early an hour ; it is unusual for burglars to strike a lady to prevent her screaming, since one would imagine that was the sure way to make her scream ; it is unusual for them to commit murder when their numbers are sufficient to overpower one man ; it is unusual for them to be content with a limited plunder when there is much more within their reach ; and, finally, I should say that it was very unusual for such men to leave a bottle half empty. How do all these unusuals strike you, Watson ? "

" Their cumulative effect is certainly considerable, and yet each of them is quite possible in itself. The most unusual thing of all, as it seems to me, is that the lady should be tied to the chair."

" Well, I am not so sure about that, Watson, for it is evident that they must either kill her or else secure her in such a way that she could not give immediate notice of their escape. But at any rate I have shown, have I not, that there is a certain element of improbability about the lady's story ? And now on the top of this comes the incident of the wine-glasses."

" What about the wine-glasses ? "

" Can you see them in your mind's eye ? "

" I see them clearly."

" We are told that three men drank from them. Does that strike you as likely ? "

" Why not ? There was wine in each glass."

" Exactly ; but there was beeswing only in one glass. You must have noticed that fact. What does that suggest to your mind ? "

" The last glass filled would be most likely to contain beeswing."

" Not at all. The bottle was full of it, and it is inconceivable that the first two glasses were clear and the third heavily charged with it. There are two possible explanations, and only two. One is that after the second glass was filled the bottle was violently agitated, and so the third glass received the beeswing. That does not appear probable. No, no ; I am sure that I am right."

" What, then, do you suppose ? "

" That only two glasses were used, and that the dregs of both were poured into a third glass, so as to give the false impression that three people had been there. In that way all the beeswing would be in the last glass, would it

DURING OUR RETURN JOURNEY I COULD SEE BY HOLMES' FACE THAT HE WAS MUCH PUZZLED . . .

Illustration by Sidney Paget for the *Strand Magazine*, September, 1904.

not? Yes, I am convinced that this is so. But if I have hit upon the true explanation of this one small phenomenon, then in an instant the case rises from the commonplace to the exceedingly remarkable, for it can only mean that Lady Brackenstall and her maid have deliberately lied to us, that not one word of their story is to be believed, that they have some very strong reason for covering the real criminal, and that we must construct our case for ourselves without any help from them. That is the mission which now lies before us, and here, Watson, is the Chislehurst train."

The household of the Abbey Grange were much surprised at our return, but Sherlock Holmes, finding that Stanley Hopkins had gone off to report to headquarters, took possession of the dining-room, locked the door upon the inside and devoted himself for two hours to one of those minute and laborious investigations which formed the solid basis on which his brilliant edifices of deduction were reared. Seated in a corner like an interested student who observes the demonstration of his professor, I followed every step of that remarkable research. The window, the curtains, the carpet, the chair, the rope—each in turn was minutely examined and duly pondered. The body of the unfortunate baronet had been removed, but all else remained as we had seen it in the morning. Then, to my astonishment, Holmes climbed up on to the massive mantelpiece. Far above his head hung the few inches of red cord which were still attached to the wire. For a long time he gazed upwards at it, and then in an attempt to get nearer to it he rested his knee upon a wooden bracket on the wall. This brought his hand within a few inches of the broken end of the rope; but it was not this so much as the bracket itself which seemed to engage his attention. Finally he sprang down with an ejaculation of satisfaction.

"It's all right, Watson," said he. "We have got our case—one of the most remarkable in our collection. But, dear me, how slow-witted I have been, and how nearly I have committed the blunder of my lifetime! Now, I think that with a few missing links my chain is almost complete."

"You have got your men?"

"Man, Watson, man. Only one, but a very formidable person. Strong as a lion—witness the blow which bent that poker. Six foot three in height, active as a squirrel, dexterous with his fingers; finally, remarkably quick-witted, for this whole ingenious story is of his concoction. Yes, Watson, we have come upon the handiwork of a very remarkable individual. And yet in that bell-rope he has given us a clue which should not have left us a doubt."

"Where was the clue?"

"Well, if you were to pull down a bell-rope, Watson, where would you expect it to break? Surely at the spot where it is attached to the wire. Why should it break three inches from the top as this one has done?"

"Because it is frayed there?"

"Exactly. This end, which we can examine, is frayed. He was cunning enough to do that with his knife. But the other end is not frayed. You could not observe that from here, but if you were on the mantelpiece you would see that it is cut clean off without any mark of fraying whatever. You can reconstruct what occurred. The man needed the rope. He would not tear it down for fear of giving the alarm by ringing the bell. What did he do? He sprang up on the mantelpiece, could not quite reach it, put his knee on the bracket—you will see the impression in the dust—and got his knife to bear upon the cord. I could not reach the place by at least three inches, from which I infer that he is at least three inches a bigger man than I. Look at that mark upon the seat of the oaken chair! What is it?"

"Blood."

"Undoubtedly it is blood. This alone puts the lady's story out of court. If she were seated on the chair when the crime was done, how comes that mark? No, no; she was placed in the chair *after* the death of her husband. I'll wager that the black dress shows a corresponding mark to this. We have not yet met our Waterloo,
Watson, but this is our Marengo, for it begins in defeat 9
and ends in victory. I should like now to have a few words with the nurse Theresa. We must be wary for a while, if we are to get the information which we want."

She was an interesting person, this stern Australian nurse. Taciturn, suspicious, ungracious, it took some time before Holmes' pleasant manner and frank acceptance of all that she said thawed her into a corresponding amiability. She did not attempt to conceal her hatred for her late employer.

"Yes, sir, it is true that he threw the decanter at me. I heard him call my mistress a name, and I told him that he would not dare to speak so if her brother had been there. Then it was that he threw it at me. He might have thrown a dozen if he had but left my bonny bird alone. He was for ever ill-treating her, and she was too proud to complain. She will not even tell me all that he has done to her. She never told me of those marks on her arm that you saw this morning, but I know very well that they come from a stab with a hat-pin. The sly fiend—Heaven forgive me that I should speak of him so, now that he is dead, but a fiend he was if ever one walked the earth. He was all honey when first we met him, only eighteen months ago, and we both feel as if it were eighteen years. She had only just arrived in London. Yes, it was her first voyage—she had never been from home before. He won her with his title and his money and his false London ways. If she made a mistake she has paid for it, if ever a woman did. What month did we meet him? Well, I tell you it was just after we arrived. We arrived in June, and it was July. They were married in January of last year. Yes, she is down in the morning-room again, and I have no doubt she will see you, but you must not ask too much of her, for she has gone through all that flesh and blood will stand."

Lady Brackenstall was reclining on the same couch, but looked brighter than before. The maid had entered with us, and began once more to foment the bruise upon her mistress's brow.

9 *We have not yet met our Waterloo, Watson, but this is our Marengo.* "The reference . . . is very apt," Mr. T. S. Blakeney wrote in *Sherlock Holmes: Fact or Fiction?*, "and Holmes must surely have devoted some attention to Napoleonic history, for the remark is not one to occur to anybody."

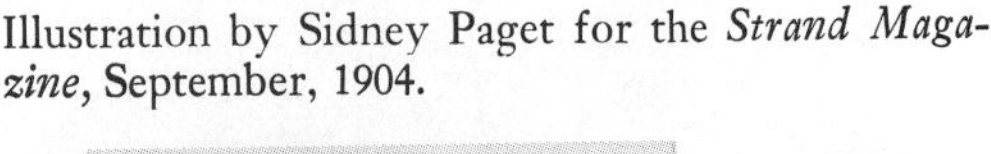

"LOOK AT THAT MARK UPON THE SEAT OF THE OAKEN CHAIR!"

Illustration by Sidney Paget for the *Strand Magazine*, September, 1904.

"I hope," said the lady, "that you have not come to cross-examine me again?"

"No," Holmes answered, in his gentlest voice, "I will not cause you any unnecessary trouble, Lady Brackenstall, and my whole desire is to make things easy for you, for I am convinced that you are a much-tried woman. If you will treat me as a friend and trust me, you may find that I will justify your trust."

"What do you want me to do?"

"To tell me the truth."

"Mr. Holmes!"

"No, no, Lady Brackenstall, it is no use. You may have heard of any little reputation which I possess. I will stake it all on the fact that your story is an absolute fabrication."

Mistress and maid were both staring at Holmes with pale faces and frightened eyes.

"You are an impudent fellow!" cried Theresa. "Do you mean to say that my mistress has told a lie?"

Holmes rose from his chair.

"Have you nothing to tell me?"

"I have told you everything."

"Think once more, Lady Brackenstall. Would it not be better to be frank?"

For an instant there was hesitation in her beautiful face. Then some new strong thought caused it to set like a mask.

"I have told you all I know."

Holmes took his hat and shrugged his shoulders. "I am sorry," he said, and without another word we left the room and the house. There was a pond in the park, and to this my friend led the way. It was frozen over, but a single hole was left for the convenience of a solitary swan. Holmes gazed at it, and then passed on to the lodge gate. There he scribbled a short note for Stanley Hopkins, and left it with the lodge-keeper.

"It may be a hit, or it may be a miss, but we are bound to do something for friend Hopkins, just to justify this second visit," said he. "I will not quite take him into my confidence yet. I think our next scene of operations must be the shipping office of the Adelaide-Southampton
10 line, which stands at the end of Pall Mall, if I remember right. There is a second line of steamers which connect South Australia with England, but we will draw the larger cover first."

Holmes' card sent in to the manager ensured instant attention, and he was not long in acquiring all the information which he needed. In June of '95 only one of their line had reached a home port. It was the *Rock of Gibraltar*, their largest and best boat. A reference to the passenger list showed that Miss Fraser of Adelaide, with her maid, had made the voyage in her. The boat was now on her way to Australia, somewhere to the south of the Suez Canal. Her officers were the same as in '95, with one exception. The first officer, Mr. Jack Croker, had been made a captain, and was to take charge of their
11 new ship, the *Bass Rock*, sailing in two days' time from Southampton. He lived at Sydenham, but he was likely to be in that morning for instructions, if we cared to wait for him.

IT WAS FROZEN OVER, BUT A SINGLE HOLE WAS LEFT FOR THE CONVENIENCE OF A SOLITARY SWAN.

The day, Watson has already told us, was "bitterly cold and frosty." In January, 1897, the temperature was below freezing every day from the 15th to the 29th—corroboration that we have correctly assigned the date of this adventure to Saturday, the 23rd. The illustration, by Sidney Paget, is from the *Strand Magazine*, September, 1904.

10 *which stands at the end of Pall Mall.* The main Australian shipping line of the day was the Orient Line, with offices "at the end of Pall Mall" at 16 Cockspur Street.

11 *their new ship, the* Bass Rock. In "Some Diggings Down Under," Mrs. Jennifer Chorley has pointed out that the "new ship" of the Orient Line was "the glorious *Ophir*, known as the Queen of the Indian Ocean, the first twin-screw liner on the Australian run, built in 1891. Electric lighting and hot and cold baths were part of the luxuries offered." Apart from the *Ophir*, the "largest and best boat" of the Orient Line was the *Orizaba*, which we may take to have been the *Rock of Gibraltar*. Watson's ships sailed from Southampton, but the Orient Line used Tilbury (a village and docks in Essex, north of the Thames, and within the Port of London), as did all the larger ships bound for Australia at the time.

No ; Mr. Holmes had no desire to see him, but would be glad to know more about his record and character.

His record was magnificent. There was not an officer in the fleet to touch him. As to his character, he was reliable on duty, but a wild, desperate fellow off the deck of his ship, hot-headed, excitable, but loyal, honest, and kind-hearted. That was the pith of the information with which Holmes left the office of the Adelaide-Southampton Company. Thence he drove to Scotland Yard, but instead of entering he sat in his cab, with his brows drawn down, lost in profound thought. Finally he drove round to the Charing Cross telegraph office, sent off a message, and then, at last, we made for Baker Street once more.

" No, I couldn't do it, Watson," said he, as we re-entered our room. " Once that warrant was made out nothing on earth would save him. Once or twice in my career I feel that I have done more real harm by my discovery of the criminal than ever he had done by his crime. I have learned caution now, and I had rather play tricks with the law of England than with my own conscience. Let us know a little more before we act."

Before evening we had a visit from Inspector Stanley Hopkins. Things were not going very well with him.

" I believe that you are a wizard, Mr. Holmes. I really do sometimes think that you have powers that are not human. Now, how on earth could you know that the stolen silver was at the bottom of that pond ? "

" I didn't know it."

" But you told me to examine it."

" You got it then ? "

" Yes, I got it."

" I am very glad if I have helped you."

" But you haven't helped me. You have made the affair far more difficult. What sort of burglars are they who steal silver and then throw it into the nearest pond ? "

" It was certainly rather eccentric behaviour. I was merely going on the idea that if the silver had been taken by persons who did not want it, who merely took it for a blind, as it were, then they would naturally be anxious to get rid of it."

" But why should such an idea cross your mind ? "

" Well, I thought it was possible. When they came out through the French window there was the pond, with one tempting little hole in the ice right in front of their noses. Could there be a better hiding-place ? "

" Ah, a hiding-place—that is better ! " cried Stanley Hopkins. " Yes, yes, I see it all now ! It was early, there were folk upon the roads, they were afraid of being seen with the silver, so they sank it in the pond, intending to return for it when the coast was clear. Excellent, Mr. Holmes—that is better than your idea of a blind."

" Quite so ; you have got an admirable theory. I have no doubt that my own ideas were quite wild, but you must admit that they have ended in discovering the silver."

" Yes, sir ; yes. It was all your doing. But I have had a bad set-back."

" A set-back ? "

" Yes, Mr. Holmes. The Randall gang were arrested

. . . HE STOOD WITH CLENCHED HANDS AND HEAVING BREAST . . .

Illustration by Frederic Dorr Steele for *Collier's Magazine*, December 31, 1904. Note the copy of *Punch*. The cover illustration indicated here—used on every issue of *Punch* for many years—was drawn by Richard Doyle, artist, man-about-town —and Conan Doyle's uncle. Again, Sidney Paget chose to illustrate this same scene for the *Strand Magazine*, September, 1904.

in New York this morning."

" Dear me, Hopkins. That is certainly rather against your theory that they committed a murder in Kent last night."

" It is fatal, Mr. Holmes, absolutely fatal. Still, there are other gangs of three besides the Randalls, or it may be some new gang of which the police have never heard."

" Quite so ; it is perfectly possible. What, are you off ? "

" Yes, Mr. Holmes ; there is no rest for me until I have got to the bottom of the business. I suppose you have no hint to give me ? "

" I have given you one."

" Which ? "

" Well, I suggested a blind."

" But why, Mr. Holmes, why ! "

" Ah, that's the question, of course. But I commend the idea to your mind. You might possibly find that there was something in it. You won't stop for dinner ? Well, good-bye, and let us know how you get on."

Dinner was over and the table cleared before Holmes alluded to the matter again. He had lit his pipe, and held his slippered feet to the cheerful blaze of the fire. Suddenly he looked at his watch.

" I expect developments, Watson."

" When ? "

" Now—within a few minutes. I dare say you thought I acted rather badly to Stanley Hopkins just now ? "

" I trust your judgment."

" A very sensible reply, Watson. You must look at it this way : what I know is unofficial ; what he knows is official. I have the right to private judgment, but he has none. He must disclose all, or he is a traitor to his service. In a doubtful case I would not put him in so painful a position, and so I reserve my information until my own mind is clear upon the matter."

" But when will that be ? "

" The time has come. You will now be present at the last scene of a remarkable little drama."

There was a sound upon the stairs, and our door was opened to admit as fine a specimen of manhood as ever passed through it. He was a very tall young man, golden-moustached, blue-eyed, with a skin which had been burned by tropical suns, and a springy step which showed that the huge frame was as active as it was strong. He closed the door behind him, and then he stood with clenched hands and heaving breast, choking down some overmastering emotion.

" Sit down, Captain Croker. You got my telegram ? "

Our visitor sank into an arm-chair and looked from one to the other of us with questioning eyes.

" I got your telegram, and I came at the hour you said. I heard that you had been down to the office. There was no getting away from you. Let's hear the worst. What are you going to do with me ? Arrest me ? Speak out, man ! You can't sit there and play with me like a cat with a mouse."

" Give him a cigar," said Holmes. " Bite on that, Captain Croker, and don't let your nerves run away with you. I should not sit here smoking with you if I thought that you were a common criminal, you may be sure of that. Be frank with me, and we may do some good. Play tricks with me, and I'll crush you."

" What do you wish me to do ? "

" To give me a true account of all that happened at the Abbey Grange last night—a *true* account, mind you, with nothing added and nothing taken off. I know so much already that if you go one inch off the straight I'll blow this police whistle from my window and the affair goes out of my hands for ever."

The sailor thought for a little. Then he struck his leg with his great sunburnt hand.

" I'll chance it," he cried. " I believe you are a man of your word, and a white man, and I'll tell you the whole story. But one thing I will say first. So far as I am concerned, I regret nothing and I fear nothing, and I would do it all again and be proud of the job. Curse the beast—if he had as many lives as a cat he would owe them all to me ! But it's the lady, Mary—Mary Fraser—for never will I call her by that accursed name. When I think of getting her into trouble, I who would give my life just to bring one smile to her dear face, it's that that turns my soul into water. And yet—and yet—what less could I do ? I'll tell you my story, gentlemen, and then I'll ask you as man to man what less could I do.

" I must go back a bit. You seem to know everything, so I expect that you know that I met her when she was a passenger and I was first officer of the *Rock of Gibraltar*. From the first day I met her she was the only woman to me. Every day of that voyage I loved her more, and many a time since have I kneeled down in the darkness of the night watch and kissed the deck of that ship because I knew her dear feet had trod it. She was never engaged to me. She treated me as fairly as ever a woman treated a man. I have no complaint to make. It was all love on my side, and all good comradeship and friendship on hers. When we parted she was a free woman, but I could never again be a free man.

" Next time I came back from sea I heard of her marriage. Well, why shouldn't she marry whom she liked ? Title and money—who could carry them better than she ? She was born for all that is beautiful and dainty. I didn't grieve over her marriage. I was not such a selfish hound as that. I just rejoiced that good luck had come her way, and that she had not thrown herself away on a penniless sailor. That's how I loved Mary Fraser.

" Well, I never thought to see her again ; but last voyage I was promoted, and the new boat was not yet launched, so I had to wait for a couple of months with my people at Sydenham. One day out in a country lane I met Theresa Wright, her old maid. She told me about her, about him, about everything. I tell you, gentlemen, it nearly drove me mad. This drunken hound, that he should dare to raise his hand to her whose boots he was not worthy to lick ! I met Theresa again. Then I met Mary herself—and met her again. Then she would meet me no more. But the other day I had a notice that I was to start on my voyage within a week, and I determined that I would see her once before I left. Theresa was always my friend, for she loved Mary and hated this villain almost as much as I did. From her I learned the ways of the house. Mary used to sit up reading in her own little room downstairs. I crept round there last night and scratched at the window. At first she would not open to me, but in her heart I know that now she loves me, and she could not leave me in the frosty night. She whispered to me to come round to the big front window, and I found it open before me so as to let me into the dining-room. Again I heard from her own lips things that made my blood boil, and again I cursed this brute who mishandled the woman that I loved. Well, gentlemen, I was standing with her just inside the window, in all innocence, as Heaven is my judge, when he rushed like a madman into the room, called her the vilest name that a man could use to a woman, and welted her across the face with the stick he had in his hand. I had sprung for the poker, and it was a fair fight between us. See here on my arm where his first blow fell. Then it was my turn, and I went through him as if he had been a rotten pumpkin. Do you think I was sorry? Not I! It was his life or mine; but far more than that—it was his life or hers, for how could I leave her in the power of this madman? That was how I killed him. Was I wrong? Well, then, what would either of you gentlemen have done if you had been in my position?

"She had screamed when he struck her, and that brought old Theresa down from the room above. There was a bottle of wine on the sideboard, and I opened it and poured a little between Mary's lips, for she was half dead with the shock. Then I took a drop myself. Theresa was as cool as ice, and it was her plot as much as mine. We must make it appear that burglars had done the thing. Theresa kept on repeating our story to her mistress, while I swarmed up and cut the rope of the bell. Then I lashed her in her chair, and frayed out the end of the rope to make it look natural, else they would wonder how in the world a burglar could have got up there to cut it. Then I gathered up a few plates and pots of silver, to carry out the idea of a robbery, and there I left them, with orders to give the alarm when I had a quarter of an hour's start. I dropped the silver into the pond and made off for Sydenham, feeling that for once in my life I had done a real good night's work. And that's the truth and the whole truth, Mr. Holmes, if it costs me my neck."

Holmes smoked for some time in silence. Then he crossed the room and shook our visitor by the hand.

"That's what I think," said he. "I know that every word is true, for you have hardly said a word which I did not know. No one but an acrobat or a sailor could have got up to that bell-rope from the bracket, and no one but a sailor could have made the knots with which the cord was fastened to the chair. Only once had this lady been brought into contact with sailors, and that was on her voyage, and it was someone of her own class of life, since she was trying hard to shield him and so showing that she loved him. You see how easy it was for me to lay my hands upon you when once I had started upon the right trail."

" I thought the police never could have seen through our dodge."

" And the police haven't; nor will they, to the best of my belief. Now, look here, Captain Croker, this is a very serious matter, though I am willing to admit that you acted under the most extreme provocation to which any man could be subjected. I am not sure that in defence of your own life your action will not be pronounced legitimate. However, that is for a British jury to decide. Meanwhile I have so much sympathy for you that if you choose to disappear in the next twenty-four hours I will promise you that no one will hinder you."

" And then it will all come out?"

" Certainly it will come out."

The sailor flushed with anger.

" What sort of proposal is that to make to a man? I know enough of law to understand that Mary would be had as accomplice. Do you think I would leave her alone to face the music while I slunk away? No, sir; let them do their worst upon me, but for Heaven's sake, Mr. Holmes, find some way of keeping my poor Mary out of the courts."

Holmes for the second time held out his hand to the sailor.

" I was only testing you, and you ring true every time. Well, it is a great responsibility that I take upon myself, but I have given Hopkins an excellent hint, and if he can't avail himself of it I can do no more. See here, Captain Croker, we'll do this in due form of law. You are the prisoner. Watson, you are a British jury, and I never met a man who was more eminently fitted to represent one. I am the judge. Now, gentlemen of the jury, you have heard the evidence. Do you find the prisoner guilty or not guilty?"

" Not guilty, my lord," said I.

" *Vox populi, vox Dei.* You are acquitted, Captain **12**
Croker. So long as the law does not find some other victim, you are safe from me. Come back to this lady in a year, and may her future and yours justify us in the judgment which we have pronounced this night."

12 "Vox populi, vox Dei. "The voice of the people is the voice of God"—a phrase first used by the English scholar, educator and ecclesiastical reformer Albinus Flaccus, called Alcuin or Alchuine, 735–804, in his Epistle to his friend Charlemagne.

Bibliographical Note: The original manuscript of "The Adventure of the Abbey Grange," consisting of 26 folio leaves, was auctioned in New York City on February 13, 1923, bringing $105. Once owned by the late James Montgomery of Philadelphia, it is now the property of Mr. Rollin V. Hadley, Jr., of Corning, New York.

60

THE ADVENTURE OF THE DEVIL'S FOOT

[*Tuedsay, March 16, to Saturday, March 20, 1897*]

IN recording from time to time some of the curious experiences and interesting recollections which I associate with my long and intimate friendship with Mr. Sherlock Holmes, I have continually been faced by difficulties caused by his own aversion to publicity. To his sombre and cynical spirit all popular applause was always abhorrent, and nothing amused him more at the end of a successful case than to hand over the actual exposure to some orthodox official, and to listen with a mocking smile to the general chorus of misplaced congratulation. It was indeed, this attitude upon the part of my friend, and certainly not any lack of interesting material which has caused me of late years to lay very few of my records before the public. My participation in some of his adventures was always a privilege which entailed discretion and reticence upon me.

It was, then, with considerable surprise that I received a telegram from Holmes last Tuesday—he has never been known to write where a telegram would serve—in the following terms: "Why not tell them of the Cornish horror—strangest case I have handled." I have no idea what backward sweep of memory had brought the matter fresh to his mind, or what freak had caused him to desire that I should recount it; but I hasten, before another cancelling telegram may arrive, to hunt out the notes which give me the exact details of the case, and to lay the narrative before my readers.

1 It was, then, in the spring of the year 1897 that Holmes' iron constitution showed some symptoms of giving way in the face of constant hard work of a most exacting kind, aggravated, perhaps, by occasional indiscretions of his own. In March of that year Dr. Moore Agar, of Harley Street, whose dramatic introduction to Holmes I may some day recount, gave positive injunctions that the famous private agent would lay aside all his cases and surrender himself to complete rest if he wished to avert an absolute break-down. The state of his health was not a matter in which he himself took the faintest interest, for his mental detachment was absolute, but he was induced at last, on the threat of being permanently disqualified from work, to give himself a complete change of scene and air. Thus it was that in the early spring of that year we found ourselves together in a small cottage near Poldhu Bay, at the further extremity of the Cornish peninsula.

1 *in the spring of the year 1897*. The month was "March," by three mentions. It has been objected that March is not "spring" in the astronomical sense, but we know that there were other occasions on which both Holmes and Watson spoke of the seasons in other than the astronomical sense. To cite only two: Holmes used "autumn" in the popular sense in "The *Gloria Scott*"; November was "winter" to Watson in "The Adventure of the Golden Pince-Nez." It has also been said that the month must be later than March because Holmes expressed surprise at finding that there had been a fire in the Tregennis grate "on a spring evening." But the March of 1897 must have been an exceptionally mild one in Cornwall—Watson speaks of "the glorious sunshine," and he says the Tregennis garden was "*already* well-filled with spring flowers." These evidences of unusually fine weather make Holmes' surprise as apropos in March as it would have been, say, in April. (Despite the fineness of the days, it would grow chilly at night. The Tregennis family lit a fire because, as Mortimer explains, "the night was cold and damp." A cold, damp night is of course more likely to occur in March than in April.)

It was a singular spot, and one peculiarly well suited to the grim humour of my patient. From the windows of our little whitewashed house, which stood high upon a grassy headland, we looked down upon the whole sinister semicircle of Mounts Bay, that old death trap of sailing vessels, with its fringe of black cliffs and surge-swept reefs on which innumerable seamen have met their end. With a northerly breeze it lies placid and sheltered, inviting the storm-tossed craft to tack into it for rest and protection.

Then comes the sudden swirl round of the wind, the blustering gale from the south-west, the dragging anchor, the lee shore, and the last battle in the creaming breakers. The wise mariner stands far out from that evil place.

On the land side our surroundings were as sombre as on the sea. It was a country of rolling moors, lonely and dun-coloured, with an occasional church tower to mark the site of some old-world village. In every direction upon these moors there were traces of some vanished race which had passed utterly away, and left as its sole record strange monuments of stone, irregular mounds which contained the burned ashes of the dead, and curious earthworks which hinted at prehistoric strife. The glamour and mystery of the place, with its sinister atmosphere of forgotten nations, appealed to the imagination of my friend, and he spent much of his time in long walks and solitary meditations upon the moor. The ancient Cornish language had also arrested his attention, and he had, I remember, conceived the idea that it was akin to the Chaldean, and had been largely derived from the Phœnician traders in tin. He had received a consignment of books
upon philology and was settling down to develop this 2
thesis, when suddenly, to my sorrow and to his unfeigned delight, we found ourselves, even in that land of dreams, plunged into a problem at our very doors which was more intense, more engrossing, and infinitely more mysterious than any of those which had driven us from London. Our simple life and peaceful, healthy routine were violently interrupted, and we were precipitated into the midst of a series of events which caused the utmost excitement not only in Cornwall, but throughout the whole West of England. Many of my readers may retain some recollection of what was called at the time "The Cornish Horror," though a most imperfect account of the matter reached the
London Press. Now, after thirteen years, I will give the 3
true details of this inconceivable affair to the public.

I have said that scattered towers marked the villages which dotted this part of Cornwall. The nearest of these
was the hamlet of Tredannick Wollas, where the cottages 4
of a couple of hundred inhabitants clustered round an ancient, moss-grown church. The vicar of the parish, Mr. Roundhay, was something of an archæologist, and as such Holmes had made his acquaintance. He was a middle-aged man, portly and affable, with a considerable fund of local lore. At his invitation we had taken tea at the vicarage, and had come to know, also, Mr. Mortimer Tregennis, an independent gentleman, who increased the clergyman's scanty resources by taking rooms in his large straggling house. The vicar, being a bachelor, was glad to come to such an arrangement, though he had little in

. . . HE SPENT MUCH OF HIS TIME IN LONG WALKS . . .

Illustration by Gilbert Holiday for the *Strand Magazine*, December, 1910.

2 *a consignment of books upon philology*. "Among them," Miss Madeleine B. Stern wrote in "Sherlock Holmes: Rare Book Collector," "was surely to be found a copy of Lhuyd's *Archaeologica Britannica* of 1707, a work containing a grammar of the language. There also must have been included . . . Edward Norris' *Ancient Cornish Drama* printed in Penzance in 1859, to which a 'Sketch of Cornish Grammar' is added as an appendix. Nor could the collection have been complete without Jago's *Dialect of Cornwall* printed at Truro in 1882, Williams' *Lexicon Cornu-Britannicum* (Landovery, 1865), Bannister's *Glossary of Cornish Names* (Truro, 1871) and the Courtney and Couch *Glossary of Words in Use in Cornwall* (Penzance, 1880)."

3 *Now, after thirteen years*. "The Adventure of the Devil's Foot" was published in December, 1910—confirming Watson's "1897" as the year of the adventure.

4 *the hamlet of Tredannick Wollas*. There is a hamlet called Predannack Wollas near Poldhu Bay in Cornwall, and the nearby village of Cwry answers closely to Watson's description of "Tredannick Wollas."

5 *Tuesday, March the 16th.* And the 16th of March, 1897, *did*, curiously enough, fall on a Tuesday.

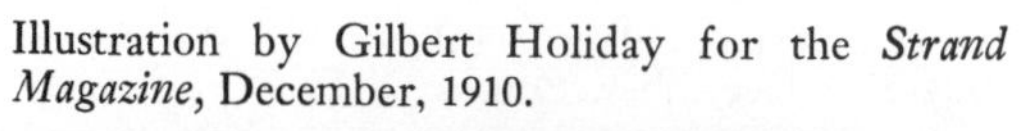

"THE MOST EXTRAORDINARY AND TRAGIC AFFAIR HAS OCCURRED DURING THE NIGHT."

Illustration by Gilbert Holiday for the *Strand Magazine*, December, 1910.

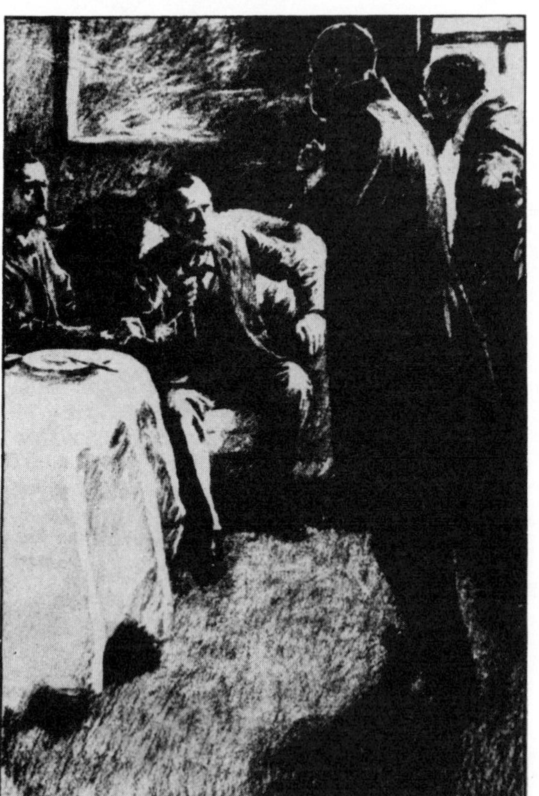

common with his lodger, who was a thin, dark, spectacled man, with a stoop which gave the impression of actual physical deformity. I remember that during our short visit we found the vicar garrulous, but his lodger strangely reticent, a sad-faced, introspective man, sitting with averted eyes, brooding apparently upon his own affairs.

These were the two men who entered abruptly into our
5 little sitting-room on Tuesday, March the 16th, shortly after our breakfast hour, as we were smoking together, preparatory to our daily excursion upon the moors.

"Mr. Holmes," said the vicar, in an agitated voice, "the most extraordinary and tragic affair has occurred during the night. It is the most unheard-of business. We can only regard it as a special Providence that you should chance to be here at the time, for in all England you are the one man we need."

I glared at the intrusive vicar with no very friendly eyes; but Holmes took his pipe from his lips and sat up in his chair like an old hound who hears the view-holloa. He waved his hand to the sofa, and our palpitating visitor with his agitated companion sat side by side upon it. Mr. Mortimer Tregennis was more self-contained than the clergyman, but the twitching of his thin hands and the brightness of his dark eyes showed that they shared a common emotion.

"Shall I speak or you?" he asked of the vicar.

"Well, as you seem to have made the discovery, whatever it may be, and the vicar to have had it second-hand, perhaps you had better do the speaking," said Holmes.

I glanced at the hastily-clad clergyman, with the formally-dressed lodger seated beside him, and was amused at the surprise which Holmes' simple deduction had brought to their faces.

"Perhaps I had best say a few words first," said the vicar, "and then you can judge if you will listen to the details from Mr. Tregennis, or whether we should not hasten at once to the scene of this mysterious affair. I may explain, then, that our friend here spent last evening in the company of his two brothers, Owen and George, and of his sister Brenda, at their house of Tredannick Wartha, which is near the old stone cross upon the moor. He left them shortly after ten o'clock, playing cards round the dining-room table, in excellent health and spirits. This morning, being an early riser, he walked in that direction before breakfast, and was overtaken by the carriage of Dr. Richards, who explained that he had just been sent for on a most urgent call to Tredannick Wartha. Mr. Mortimer Tregennis naturally went with him. When he arrived at Tredannick Wartha he found an extraordinary state of things. His two brothers and his sister were seated round the table exactly as he had left them, the cards still spread in front of them and the candles burned down to their sockets. The sister lay back stone-dead in her chair, while the two brothers sat on each side of her laughing, shouting, and singing, the senses stricken clean out of them. All three of them, the dead woman and the two demented men, retained upon their faces an expression of the utmost horror—a convulsion of terror which was dreadful to look upon. There was no sign of the presence of anyone in the house, except Mrs. Porter, the old cook and housekeeper, who declared that she had slept deeply and heard no sound during the night. Nothing had been stolen or disarranged, and there is absolutely no explanation of what the horror can be which has frightened a woman to death and two strong men out of their senses. There is the situation, Mr. Holmes, in a nutshell and if you can help us to clear it up you will have done a great work."

I had hoped that in some way I could coax my companion back into the quiet which had been the object of our journey ; but one glance at his intense face and contracted eyebrows told me how vain was now the expectation. He sat for some little time in silence, absorbed in the strange drama which had broken in upon our peace.

" I will look into this matter," he said at last. " On the face of it, it would appear to be a case of a very exceptional nature. Have you been there yourself, Mr. Roundhay ? "

" No, Mr. Holmes. Mr. Tregennis brought back the account to the vicarage, and I at once hurried over with him to consult you."

" How far is it to the house where this singular tragedy occurred ? "

" About a mile inland."

" Then we shall walk over together. But, before we start, I must ask you a few questions, Mr. Mortimer Tregennis."

The other had been silent all this time, but I had observed that his more controlled excitement was even greater than the obtrusive emotion of the clergyman. He sat with a pale, drawn face, his anxious gaze fixed upon Holmes, and his thin hands clasped convulsively together. His pale lips quivered as he listened to the dreadful experience which had befallen his family, and his dark eyes seemed to reflect something of the horror of the scene.

" Ask what you like, Mr. Holmes," said he eagerly. " It is a bad thing to speak of, but I will answer you the truth."

" Tell me about last night."

" Well, Mr. Holmes, I supped there, as the vicar has said, and my elder brother George proposed a game of whist afterwards. We sat down about nine o'clock. It was a quarter-past ten when I moved to go. I left them all round the table, as merry as could be."

" Who let you out ? "

" Mrs. Porter had gone to bed, so I let myself out. I shut the hall door behind me. The window of the room in which they sat was closed, but the blind was not drawn down. There was no change in door or window this morning, nor any reason to think that any stranger had been to the house. Yet there they sat, driven clean mad with terror, and Brenda lying dead of fright, with her head hanging over the arm of the chair. I'll never get the sight of that room out of my mind so long as I live."

" The facts, as you state them, are certainly most remarkable," said Holmes. " I take it that you have no theory yourself which can in any way account for them ? "

" It's devilish, Mr. Holmes ; devilish ! " cried Mortimer Tregennis. " It is not of this world. Something has come into that room which has dashed the light of reason from their minds. What human contrivance could do that ? "

" I fear," said Holmes, " that if the matter is beyond humanity it is certainly beyond me. Yet we must exhaust all natural explanations before we fall back upon such a theory as this. As to yourself, Mr. Tregennis, I take it you were divided in some way from your family, since they lived together and you had rooms apart ? "

" That is so, Mr. Holmes, though the matter is past and done with. We were a family of tin-miners at Redruth, but we sold out our venture to a company, and so retired with enough to keep us. I won't deny that there was some feeling about the division of the money and it stood between us for a time, but it was all forgiven and forgotten, and we were the best of friends together."

" Looking back at the evening which you spent together, does anything stand out in your memory as throwing any possible light upon the tragedy ? Think carefully, Mr. Tregennis, for any clue which can help me."

" There is nothing at all, sir."

" Your people were in their usual spirits ? "

" Never better."

" Were they nervous people ? Did they ever show any apprehension of coming danger ? "

" Nothing of the kind."

" You have nothing to add then, which could assist me ? "

Mortimer Tregennis considered earnestly for a moment.

" There is one thing occurs to me," said he at last. " As we sat at the table my back was to the window, and my brother George, he being my partner at cards, was facing it. I saw him once look hard over my shoulder, so I turned round and looked also. The blind was up and the window shut, but I could just make out the bushes on the lawn, and it seemed to me for a moment that I saw something moving among them. I couldn't even say if it were man or animal, but I just thought there was something there. When I asked him what he was looking at, he told me that he had the same feeling. That is all that I can say."

" Did you not investigate ? "

" No ; the matter passed as unimportant."

" You left them, then, without any premonition of evil ? "

" None at all."

" I am not clear how you came to hear the news so early this morning."

" I am an early riser, and generally take a walk before breakfast. This morning I had hardly started when the doctor in his carriage overtook me. He told me that old Mrs. Porter had sent a boy down with an urgent message. I sprang in beside him and we drove on. When we got there we looked into that dreadful room. The candles and the fire must have burned out hours before, and they had been sitting there in the dark until dawn had broken. The doctor said Brenda must have been dead at least six hours. There were no signs of violence. She just lay

across the arm of the chair with that look on her face. George and Owen were singing snatches of songs and gibbering like two great apes. Oh, it was awful to see! I couldn't stand it, and the doctor was as white as a sheet. Indeed, he fell into a chair in a sort of faint, and we nearly had him on our hands as well."

"Remarkable—most remarkable!" said Holmes, rising and taking his hat. "I think, perhaps, we had better go down to Tredannick Wartha without further delay. I confess that I have seldom known a case which at first sight presented a more singular problem."

Our proceedings of that first morning did little to advance the investigation. It was marked, however, at the outset by an incident which left the most sinister impression upon my mind. The approach to the spot at which the tragedy occurred is down a narrow winding country lane. While we made our way along it we heard the rattle of a carriage coming towards us, and stood aside to let it pass. As it drove by us I caught a glimpse through the closed window of a horribly contorted, grinning face glaring out at us. Those staring eyes and gnashing teeth flashed past us like a dreadful vision.

"My brothers!" cried Mortimer Tregennis, white to his lips. "They are taking them to Helston."

We looked with horror after the black carriage, lumbering upon its way. Then we turned our steps towards this ill-omened house in which they had met their strange fate.

It was a large and bright dwelling, rather a villa than a cottage, with a considerable garden which was already, in that Cornish air, well filled with spring flowers. Towards this garden the window of the sitting-room fronted, and from it, according to Mortimer Tregennis, must have come that thing of evil which had by sheer horror in a single instant blasted their minds. Holmes walked slowly and thoughtfully among the flower-pots and along the path before we entered the porch. So absorbed was he in his thoughts, I remember, that he stumbled over the watering-pot, upset its contents, and deluged both our feet and the garden path. Inside the house we were met by the elderly Cornish housekeeper, Mrs. Porter, who, with the aid of a young girl, looked after the wants of the family. She readily answered all Holmes' questions. She had heard nothing in the night. Her employers had all been in excellent spirits lately, and she had never known them more cheerful and prosperous. She had fainted with horror upon entering the room in the morning and seeing that dreadful company round the table. She had, when she recovered, thrown open the window to let the morning air in, and had run down to the lane, whence she sent a farm-lad for the doctor. The lady was on her bed upstairs, if we cared to see her. It took four strong men to get the brothers into the asylum carriage. She would not herself stay in the house another day, and was starting that very afternoon to rejoin her family at St. Ives.

We ascended the stairs and viewed the body. Miss Brenda Tregennis had been a very beautiful girl, though now verging upon middle age. Her dark, clear-cut face was handsome, even in death, but there still lingered upon it something of that convulsion of horror which had been

THOSE STARING EYES AND GNASHING TEETH FLASHED PAST US LIKE A DREADFUL VISION.

Illustration by Gilbert Holiday for the *Strand Magazine,* December, 1910.

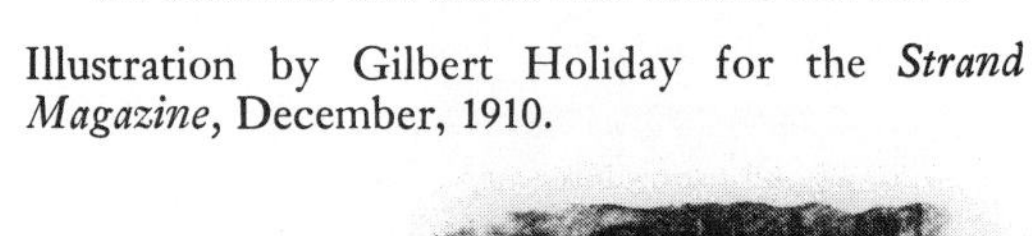

WE ASCENDED THE STAIRS AND VIEWED THE BODY.

Illustration by Gilbert Holiday for the *Strand Magazine,* December, 1910.

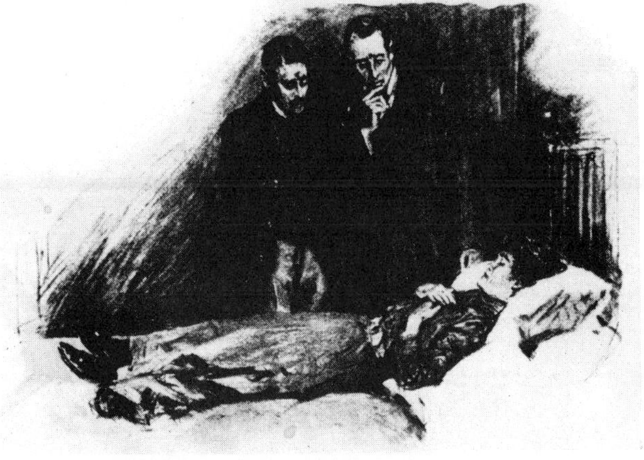

her last human emotion. From her bedroom we descended to the sitting-room where this strange tragedy had actually occurred. The charred ashes of the overnight fire lay in the grate. On the table were the four guttered and burned-out candles, with the cards scattered over its surface. The chairs had been moved back against the walls, but all else was as it had been the night before. Holmes paced with light, swift steps about the room ; he sat in the various chairs, drawing them up and reconstructing their positions. He tested how much of the garden was visible ; he examined the floor, the ceiling, and the fireplace ; but never once did I see that sudden brightening of his eyes and tightening of his lips which would have told me that he saw some gleam of light in this utter darkness.

" Why a fire ? " he asked once. Had they always a fire in this small room on a spring evening ? "

Mortimer Tregennis explained that the night was cold and damp. For that reason, after his arrival, the fire was lit. " What are you going to do now, Mr. Holmes ? " he asked.

My friend smiled and laid his hand upon my arm. " I think, Watson, that I shall resume that course of tobacco-poisoning which you have so often and so justly condemned," said he. " With your permission, gentlemen, we will now return to our cottage, for I am not aware that any new factor is likely to come to our notice here. I will turn the facts over in my mind, Mr. Tregennis, and should anything occur to me I will certainly communicate with you and the vicar. In the meantime I wish you both good morning."

It was not until long after we were back in Poldhu Cottage that Holmes broke his complete and absorbed silence. He sat coiled in his arm-chair, his haggard and ascetic face hardly visible amid the blue swirl of his tobacco smoke, his black brows drawn down, his forehead contracted, his eyes vacant and far away. Finally, he laid down his pipe and sprang to his feet.

" It won't do, Watson ! " said he, with a laugh. " Let us walk along the cliffs together and search for flint arrows. We are more likely to find them than clues to this problem. To let the brain work without sufficient material is like racing an engine. It racks itself to pieces. The sea air, sunshine, and patience, Watson—all else will come.

" Now, let us calmly define our position, Watson," he continued, as we skirted the cliffs together. " Let us get a firm grip of the very little which we *do* know, so that when fresh facts arise we may be ready to fit them into their places. I take it, in the first place, that neither of us is prepared to admit diabolical intrusions into the affairs of men. Let us begin by ruling that entirely out of our minds. Very good. There remain three persons who have been grievously stricken by some conscious or unconscious human agency. That is firm ground. Now, when did this occur ? Evidently, assuming his narrative to be true, it was immediately after Mr. Mortimer Tregennis had left the room. That is a very important point. The presumption is that it was within a few minutes afterwards. The cards still lay upon the table. It was already past their usual hour for bed. Yet they had not changed their position or pushed back their chairs. I repeat, then, that the occurrence was immediately after his departure, and not later than eleven o'clock last night.

" Our next obvious step is to check, so far as we can, the movements of Mortimer Tregennis after he left the room. In this there is no difficulty, and they seem to be above suspicion. Knowing my methods as you do, you were, of course, conscious of the somewhat clumsy water-pot expedient by which I obtained a clearer impress of his foot than might otherwise have been possible. The wet sandy path took it admirably. Last night was also wet, you will remember, and it was not difficult—having obtained a sample print—to pick out his track among others and to follow his movements. He appears to have walked away swiftly in the direction of the vicarage.

" If, then, Mortimer Tregennis disappeared from the scene, and yet some outside person affected the card-players, how can we reconstruct that person, and how was such an impression of horror conveyed ? Mrs. Porter may be eliminated. She is evidently harmless. Is there any evidence that someone crept up to the garden window and in some manner produced so terrific an effect that he drove those who saw it out of their senses ? The only suggestion in this direction comes from Mortimer Tregennis himself, who says that his brother spoke about some movement in the garden. That is certainly remarkable, as the night was rainy, cloudy, and dark. Anyone who had the design to alarm these people would be compelled to place his very face against the glass before he could be seen. There is a three-foot flower-border outside this window, but no indication of a footmark. It is difficult to imagine, then, how an outsider could have made so terrible an impression upon the company, nor have we found any possible motive for so strange and elaborate an attempt. You perceive our difficulties, Watson ? "

" They are only too clear," I answered, with conviction.

" And yet, with a little more material, we may prove that they are not insurmountable," said Holmes. " I fancy that among your extensive archives, Watson, you may find some which were nearly as obscure. Meanwhile, we shall put the case aside until more accurate data are available, and devote the rest of our morning to the pursuit of neolithic man."

I may have commented upon my friend's power of mental detachment, but never have I wondered at it more than upon that spring morning in Cornwall when for two hours he discoursed upon celts, arrowheads, and shards, as lightly as if no sinister mystery was waiting for his solution. It was not until we had returned in the afternoon to our cottage that we found a visitor awaiting us, who soon brought our minds back to the matter in hand. Neither of us needed to be told who that visitor was. The huge body, the craggy and deeply-seamed face with the fierce eyes and hawk-like nose, the grizzled hair which nearly brushed our cottage ceiling, the beard—golden at the fringes and white near the lips, save for the nicotine stain from his perpetual cigar—all these were as well known in London as in Africa, and could only be associated with the tremendous personality of Dr. Leon Sterndale, the great lion-hunter and explorer.

We had heard of his presence in the district, and had once or twice caught sight of his tall figure upon the moorland paths. He made no advances to us, however, nor would we have dreamed of doing so to him, as it was well known that it was his love of seclusion which caused him to spend the greater part of the intervals between his journeys in a small bungalow buried in the lonely wood of Beauchamp Arriance. Here, amid his books and his maps, he lived an absolutely lonely life, attending to his own simple wants, and paying little apparent heed to the affairs of his neighbours. It was a surprise to me, therefore. to hear him asking Holmes in an eager voice, whether he had made any advance in his reconstruction of this mysterious episode. " The county police are utterly at fault," said he ; " but perhaps your wider experience has suggested some conceivable explanation. My only claim to being taken into your confidence is that during my many residences here I have come to know this family of Tregennis very well—indeed, upon my Cornish mother's side I could call them cousins—and their strange fate has naturally been a great shock to me. I may tell you that I had got as far as Plymouth upon my way to Africa, but the news reached me this morning, and I came straight back again to help in the inquiry."

Holmes raised his eyebrows.

" Did you lose your boat through it ? "

" I will take the next."

" Dear me ! that is friendship indeed."

" I tell you they were relatives."

" Quite so—cousins of your mother. Was your baggage aboard the ship ? "

" Some of it, but the main part at the hotel.'

" I see. But surely this event could not have found its way into the Plymouth morning papers ? "

" No, sir ; I had a telegram."

" Might I ask from whom ? "

A shadow passed over the gaunt face of the explorer.

" You are very inquisitive, Mr. Holmes."

" It is my business."

With an effort, Dr. Sterndale recovered his ruffled composure.

" I have no objection to telling you," he said. " It was Mr. Roundhay, the vicar, who sent me the telegram which recalled me."

" Thank you," said Holmes. " I may say in answer to your original question, that I have not cleared my mind entirely on the subject of this case, but that I have every hope of reaching some conclusion. It would be premature to say more."

" Perhaps you would not mind telling me if your suspicions point in any particular direction ? "

" No, I can hardly answer that."

" Then I have wasted my time, and need not prolong my visit." The famous doctor strode out of our cottage in considerable ill-humour, and within five minutes Holmes had followed him. I saw him no more until the evening, when he returned with a slow step and haggard face which assured me that he had made no great progress with his investigation. He glanced at a telegram which awaited him, and threw it into the grate.

"From the Plymouth hotel, Watson," he said. "I learned the name of it from the vicar, and I wired to make certain that Dr. Leon Sterndale's account was true. It appears that he did indeed spend last night there, and that he has actually allowed some of his baggage to go on to Africa, while he returned to be present at this investigation. What do you make of that, Watson?"

"He is deeply interested."

"Deeply interested—yes. There is a thread here which we have not yet grasped, and which might lead us through the tangle. Cheer up, Watson, for I am very sure that our material has not yet all come to hand. When it does, we may soon leave our difficulties behind us."

Little did I think how soon the words of Holmes would be realized, or how strange and sinister would be that new development which opened up an entirely fresh line of investigation. I was shaving at my window in the morning when I heard the rattle of hoofs, and, looking up, saw a dog-cart coming at a gallop down the road. It pulled up at our door, and our friend the vicar sprang from it and rushed up our garden path. Holmes was already dressed, and we hastened down to meet him.

Our visitor was so excited that he could hardly articulate, but at last in gasps and bursts his tragic story came out of him.

"We are devil-ridden, Mr. Holmes! My poor parish is devil-ridden!" he cried. "Satan himself is loose in it! We are given over into his hands!" He danced about in his agitation, a ludicrous object if it were not for his ashy face and startled eyes. Finally he shot out his terrible news.

"Mr. Mortimer Tregennis died during the night, and with exactly the same symptoms as the rest of his family."

Holmes sprang to his feet, all energy in an instant.

"Can you fit us both into your dog-cart?"

"Yes, I can."

"Then, Watson, we will postpone our breakfast. Mr. Roundhay, we are entirely at your disposal. Hurry—hurry, before things get disarranged."

The lodger occupied two rooms at the vicarage, which were in an angle by themselves, the one above the other. Below was a large sitting-room; above, his bedroom. They looked out upon a croquet lawn which came up to the windows. We had arrived before the doctor or the police, so that everything was absolutely undisturbed. Let me describe exactly the scene as we saw it upon that misty March morning. It has left an impression which can never be effaced from my mind.

The atmosphere of the room was of a horrible and depressing stuffiness. The servant who had first entered had thrown up the window, or it would have been even more intolerable. This might partly be due to the fact that a lamp stood flaring and smoking on the centre table. Beside it sat the dead man, leaning back in his chair, his thin beard projecting, his spectacles pushed up on to his forehead, and his lean, dark face turned towards the window and twisted into the same distortion of terror which had marked the features of his dead sister. His

BESIDE IT SAT THE DEAD MAN, LEANING BACK IN HIS CHAIR . . .

Illustration by Gilbert Holiday for the *Strand Magazine*, U.S. edition only, February, 1911. The late James Montgomery wrote (*A Study in Pictures*) that "This is the only instance on record where the *Strand* reproduced two different pictures to portray the same episode, and undoubtedly came about through the necessity of providing a full page frontispiece for the second part when the story was split into two installments in America." (The original illustration, in the London *Strand*, was a half-page sketch of the body.)

limbs were convulsed and his fingers contorted as though he had died in a very paroxysm of fear. He was fully clothed, though there were signs that his dressing had been done in a hurry. We had already learned that his bed had been slept in, and that the tragic end had come to him in the early morning.

One realized the red-hot energy which underlay Holmes' phlegmatic exterior when one saw the sudden change which came over him from the moment that he entered the fatal apartment. In an instant he was tense and alert, his eyes shining, his face set, his limbs quivering with eager activity. He was out on the lawn, in through the window, round the room, and up into the bedroom, for all the world like a dashing foxhound drawing a cover. In the bedroom he made a rapid cast around, and ended by throwing open the window, which appeared to give him some fresh cause for excitement, for he leaned out of it with loud ejaculations of interest and delight. Then he rushed down the stair, out through the open window, threw himself upon his face on the lawn, sprang up and into the room once more, all with the energy of the hunter who is at the very heels of his quarry. The lamp, which was an ordinary standard, he examined with minute care, making certain measurements upon its bowl. He carefully scrutinized with his lens the talc shield which covered the top of the chimney, and scraped off some ashes which adhered to its upper surface, putting some of them into an envelope, which he placed in his pocket-book. Finally, just as the doctor and the official police put in an appearance, he beckoned to the vicar and we all three went out upon the lawn.

" I am glad to say that my investigation has not been entirely barren," he remarked. " I cannot remain to discuss the matter with the police, but I should be exceedingly obliged, Mr. Roundhay, if you would give the inspector my compliments and direct his attention to the bedroom window and to the sitting-room lamp. Each is suggestive, and together they are almost conclusive. If the police would desire further information I shall be happy to see any of them at the cottage. And now, Watson, I think that, perhaps, we shall be better employed elsewhere."

It may be that the police resented the intrusion of an amateur, or that they imagined themselves to be upon some hopeful line of investigation ; but it is certain that we
6 heard nothing from them for the next two days. During this time Holmes spent some of his time smoking and dreaming in the cottage ; but a greater portion in country walks which he undertook alone, returning after many hours without remark as to where he had been. One experiment served to show me the line of his investigation. He had bought a lamp which was the duplicate of the one which had burned in the room of Mortimer Tregennis on the morning of the tragedy. This he filled with the same oil as that used at the vicarage, and he carefully timed the period which it would take to be exhausted. Another experiment which he made was of a more unpleasant nature, and one which I am not likely ever to forget.

" You will remember, Watson," he remarked one after-

6 *the next two days.* It is probable, but not certain, that this adventure ended on *Saturday, March 20th.* The "two days" of which Watson speaks would be the Thursday and Friday following Wednesday the 17th; it was "one afternoon" after Friday the 19th that Holmes made the experiment that solved the case.

noon, " that there is a single common point of resemblance in the varying reports which have reached us. This concerns the effect of the atmosphere of the room in each case upon those who had first entered it. You will recollect that Mortimer Tregennis, in describing the episode of his last visit to his brothers' house, remarked that the doctor on entering the room fell into a chair? You had forgotten? Well, I can answer for it that it was so. Now, you will remember also that Mrs. Porter, the housekeeper, told us that she herself fainted upon entering the room and had afterwards opened the window. In the second case—that of Mortimer Tregennis himself—you cannot have forgotten the horrible stuffiness of the room when we arrived, though the servant had thrown open the window. That servant, I found upon inquiry, was so ill that she had gone to her bed. You will admit, Watson, that these facts are very suggestive. In each case there is evidence of a poisonous atmosphere. In each case, also, there is combustion going on in the room—in the one case a fire, in the other a lamp. The fire was needed, but the lamp was lit—as a comparison of the oil consumed will show—long after it was broad daylight. Why? Surely because there is some connection between three things—the burning, the stuffy atmosphere, and, finally, the madness or death of those unfortunate people. That is clear, is it not? "

" It would appear so."

" At least we may accept it as a working hypothesis. We will suppose, then, that something was burned in each case which produced an atmosphere causing strange toxic effects. Very good. In the first instance—that of the Tregennis family—this substance was placed in the fire. Now the window was shut, but the fire would naturally carry fumes to some extent up the chimney. Hence one would expect the effects of the poison to be less than in the second case, where there was less escape for the vapour. The result seems to indicate that it was so, since in the first case only the woman, who had presumably the more sensitive organism, was killed, the others exhibiting that temporary or permanent lunacy which is evidently the first effect of the drug. In the second case the result was complete. The facts, therefore, seem to bear out the theory of a poison which worked by combustion. 7

" With this train of reasoning in my head I naturally looked about in Mortimer Tregennis' room to find some remains of this substance. The obvious place to look was the talc shield or smoke-guard of the lamp. There, sure enough, I perceived a number of flaky ashes, and round the edges a fringe of brownish powder, which had not yet been consumed. Half of this I took, as you saw, and I placed it in an envelope."

" Why half, Holmes? "

" It is not for me, my dear Watson, to stand in the way of the official police force. I leave them all the evidence which I found. The poison still remained upon the talc, had they the wit to find it. Now, Watson, we will light our lamp; we will, however, take the precaution to open our window to avoid the premature decease of two deserving members of society, and you will seat yourself near

7 *a poison which worked by combustion.* In "Tregennis and Poe," Mr. Stephen Saxe has suggested that the murderer in this adventure must have derived his idea for the murder from reading Edgar Allan Poe's story, "The Imp of the Perverse," just as the murderer in Poe's story got the idea from reading some French memoirs.

. . . TOGETHER WE LURCHED THROUGH THE DOOR . . .

Illustration by Gilbert Holiday for the *Strand Magazine*, December, 1910.

that open window in an arm-chair, unless, like a sensible man, you determine to have nothing to do with the affair. Oh, you will see it out, will you ? I thought I knew my Watson. This chair I will place opposite yours, so that we may be the same distance from the poison, and face to face. The door we will leave ajar. Each is now in a position to watch the other and to bring the experiment to an end should the symptoms seem alarming. Is that all clear ? Well, then, I take our powder—or what remains of it—from the envelope, and I lay it above the burning lamp. So ! Now, Watson, let us sit down and await developments."

They were not long in coming. I had hardly settled in my chair before I was conscious of a thick, musky odour, subtle and nauseous. At the very first whiff of it my brain and my imagination were beyond all control. A thick, black cloud swirled before my eyes, and my mind told me that in this cloud, unseen as yet, but about to spring out upon my appalled senses, lurked all that was vaguely horrible, all that was monstrous and inconceivably wicked in the universe. Vague shapes swirled and swam amid the dark cloud-bank, each a menace and a warning of something coming, the advent of some unspeakable dweller upon the threshold, whose very shadow would blast my soul. A freezing horror took possession of me. I felt that my hair was rising, that my eyes were protruding, that my mouth was opened, and my tongue like leather. The turmoil within my brain was such that something must surely snap. I tried to scream, and was vaguely aware of some hoarse croak which was my own voice, but distant and detached from myself. At the same moment, in some effort of escape, I broke through that cloud of despair, and had a glimpse of Holmes' face, white, rigid, and drawn with horror—the very look which I had seen upon the features of the dead. It was that vision which gave me an instant of sanity and of strength. I dashed from my chair, threw my arms round Holmes, and together we lurched through the door, and an instant afterwards had thrown ourselves down upon the grass plot and were lying side by side, conscious only of the glorious sunshine which was bursting its way through the hellish cloud of terror which had girt us in. Slowly it rose from our souls like the mists from a landscape, until peace and reason had returned, and we were sitting upon the grass, wiping our clammy foreheads, and looking with apprehension at each other to mark the last traces of that terrific experience which we had undergone.

"Upon my word, Watson !" said Holmes at last, with an unsteady voice ; "I owe you both my thanks and an apology. It was an unjustifiable experiment even for oneself, and doubly so for a friend. I am really very sorry."

"You know," I answered, with some emotion, for I had never seen so much of Holmes' heart before, "that it is my greatest joy and privilege to help you."

He relapsed at once into the half-humorous, half-cynical vein which was his habitual attitude to those about him. "It would be superfluous to drive us mad, my dear Watson," said he. "A candid observer would certainly declare that we were so already before we embarked upon so wild an experiment. I confess that I never imagined that the effect could be so sudden and so severe." He dashed into the cottage, and reappearing with the burning lamp held at full arm's length, he threw it among a bank of brambles. "We must give the room a little time to clear. I take it, Watson, that you have no longer a shadow of a doubt as to how these tragedies were produced?"

"None whatever."

"But the cause remains as obscure as before. Come into the arbour here, and let us discuss it together. That villainous stuff seems still to linger round my throat. I think we must admit that all the evidence points to this man, Mortimer Tregennis, having been the criminal in the first tragedy, though he was the victim in the second one. We must remember, in the first place, that there is some story of a family quarrel, followed by a reconciliation. How bitter that quarrel may have been, or how hollow the reconciliation we cannot tell. When I think of Mortimer Tregennis, with the foxy face and the small shrewd, beady eyes behind the spectacles, he is not a man whom I should judge to be of a particularly forgiving disposition. Well, in the next place, you will remember that this idea of someone moving in the garden, which took our attention for a moment from the real cause of the tragedy, emanated from him. He had a motive in misleading us. Finally, if he did not throw this substance into the fire at the moment of leaving the room, who did do so? The affair happened immediately after his departure. Had anyone else come in, the family would certainly have risen from the table. Besides, in peaceful Cornwall, visitors do not arrive after ten o'clock at night. We may take it, then, that all the evidence points to Mortimer Tregennis as the culprit."

"Then his own death was suicide!"

"Well, Watson, it is on the face of it a not impossible supposition. The man who had the guilt upon his soul of having brought such a fate upon his own family might well be driven by remorse to inflict it upon himself. There are, however, some cogent reasons against it. Fortunately, there is one man in England who knows all about it, and I have made arrangements by which we shall hear the facts this afternoon from his own lips. Ah! he is a little before his time. Perhaps you would kindly step this way, Dr. Leon Sterndale. We have been conducting a chemical experiment indoors which has left our little room hardly fit for the reception of so distinguished a visitor."

I had heard the click of the garden gate, and now the majestic figure of the great African explorer appeared upon the path. He turned in some surprise towards the rustic arbour in which we sat.

"You sent for me, Mr. Holmes. I had your note about an hour ago, and I have come, though I really do not know why I should obey your summons."

"Perhaps we can clear the point up before we separate," said Holmes. "Meanwhile, I am much obliged to you for your courteous acquiescence. You will excuse this informal reception in the open air, but my friend Watson and I have nearly furnished an additional chapter to what the papers call the ' Cornish Horror,' and we prefer a clear atmosphere for the present. Perhaps, since the matters which we have to discuss will affect you personally in a very intimate fashion, it is as well that we should talk where there can be no eavesdropping."

The explorer took his cigar from his lips and gazed sternly at my companion.

" I am at a loss to know, sir," he said, " what you can have to speak about which affects me personally in a very intimate fashion."

" The killing of Mortimer Tregennis," said Holmes.

For a moment I wished that I were armed. Sterndale's fierce face turned to a dusky red, his eyes glared, and the knotted, passionate veins started out in his forehead, while he sprang forward with clenched hands towards my companion. Then he stopped, and with a violent effort he resumed a cold, rigid calmness which was, perhaps, more suggestive of danger than his hot-headed outburst.

" I have lived so long among savages and beyond the law," said he, " that I have got into the way of being a law to myself. You would do well, Mr. Holmes, not to forget it, for I have no desire to do you an injury."

" Nor have I any desire to do you an injury, Dr. Sterndale. Surely the clearest proof of it is that, knowing what I know, I have sent for you and not for the police."

Sterndale sat down with a gasp, overawed for, perhaps, the first time in his adventurous life. There was a calm assurance of power in Holmes' manner which could not be withstood. Our visitor stammered for a moment, his great hands opening and shutting in his agitation.

. . . HE SPRANG FORWARD WITH CLENCHED HANDS TOWARDS MY COMPANION.

Illustration by Gilbert Holiday for the *Strand Magazine*, December, 1910.

" What do you mean ? " he asked, at last. " If this is bluff upon your part, Mr. Holmes, you have chosen a bad man for your experiment. Let us have no more beating about the bush. What *do* you mean ? "

" I will tell you," said Holmes, " and the reason why I tell you is that I hope frankness may beget frankness. What my next step may be will depend entirely upon the nature of your own defence."

" My defence ? "

" Yes, sir."

" My defence against what ? "

" Against the charge of killing Mortimer Tregennis."

Sterndale mopped his forehead with his handkerchief. " Upon my word, you are getting on," said he. " Do all your successes depend upon this prodigious power of bluff ? "

" The bluff," said Holmes, sternly, " is upon your side, Dr. Leon Sterndale, and not upon mine. As a proof I will tell you some of the facts upon which my conclusions are based. Of your return from Plymouth, allowing much of your property to go on to Africa, I will say nothing save that it first informed me that you were one of the factors which had to be taken into account in reconstructing this drama——"

" I came back——"

" I have heard your reasons and regard them as unconvincing and inadequate. We will pass that. You came down here to ask me whom I suspected. I refused to answer you. You then went to the vicarage, waited outside it for some time, and finally returned to your cottage."

"How do you know that?"

"I followed you."

"I saw no one."

"That is what you may expect to see when I follow you. You spent a restless night at your cottage, and you formed certain plans, which in the early morning you proceeded to put into execution. Leaving your door just as day was breaking, you filled your pocket with some reddish gravel that was lying heaped beside your gate."

Sterndale gave a violent start and looked at Holmes in amazement.

"You then walked swiftly for the mile which separated you from the vicarage. You were wearing, I may remark, the same pair of ribbed tennis shoes which are at the present moment upon your feet. At the vicarage you passed through the orchard and the side hedge, coming out under the window of the lodger Tregennis. It was now daylight, but the household was not yet stirring. You drew some of the gravel from your pocket, and you threw it up at the window above you."

Sterndale sprang to his feet.

"I believe that you are the devil himself!" he cried.

Holmes smiled at the compliment. "It took two, or possibly three, handfuls before the lodger came to the window. You beckoned him to come down. He dressed hurriedly and descended to his sitting-room. You entered by the window. There was an interview—a short one—during which you walked up and down the room. Then you passed out and closed the window, standing on the lawn outside smoking a cigar and watching what occurred. Finally, after the death of Tregennis, you withdrew as you had come. Now, Dr. Sterndale, how do you justify such conduct, and what were the motives for your actions? If you prevaricate or trifle with me, I give you my assurance that the matter will pass out of my hands for ever."

Our visitor's face had turned ashen grey as he listened to the words of his accuser. Now he sat for some time in thought with his face sunk in his hands. Then with a sudden impulsive gesture he plucked a photograph from his breast-pocket and threw it on the rustic table before us.

"That is why I have done it," said he.

It showed the bust and face of a very beautiful woman. Holmes stooped over it.

"Brenda Tregennis," said he.

"Yes, Brenda Tregennis," repeated our visitor. "For years I have loved her. For years she has loved me. There is the secret of that Cornish seclusion which people have marvelled at. It has brought me close to the one thing on earth that was dear to me. I could not marry her, for I have a wife who has left me for years and yet whom, by the deplorable laws of England, I could not divorce. For years Brenda waited. For years I waited. And this is what we have waited for." A terrible sob shook his great frame, and he clutched his throat under his brindled beard. Then with an effort he mastered himself and spoke on.

"The vicar knew. He was in our confidence. He would tell you that she was an angel upon earth. That was why he telegraphed to me and I returned. What was my baggage or Africa to me when I learned that such a fate had come upon my darling? There you have the missing clue to my action, Mr. Holmes."

"Proceed," said my friend.

Dr. Sterndale drew from his pocket a paper packet and laid it upon the table. On the outside was written, "*Radix pedis diaboli*" with a red poison label beneath it. He pushed it towards me. "I understand that you are a doctor, sir. Have you ever heard of this preparation?"

"Devil's-foot root! No, I have never heard of it."

"It is no reflection upon your professional knowledge," said he, "for I believe that, save for one sample in a laboratory at Buda, there is no other specimen in Europe. It has not yet found its way either into the pharmacopœia
8 or into the literature of toxicology. The root is shaped like a foot, half human, half goat-like; hence the fanciful name given by a botanical missionary. It is used as an ordeal poison by the medicine-men in certain districts of West Africa, and is kept as a secret among them. This particular specimen I obtained under very extraordinary circumstances in the Ubanghi country." He opened the paper as he spoke, and disclosed a heap of reddish-brown, snuff-like powder.

"Well, sir?" asked Holmes sternly.

"I am about to tell you, Mr. Holmes, all that actually occurred, for you already know so much that it is clearly to my interest that you should know all. I have already explained the relationship in which I stood to the Tregennis family. For the sake of the sister I was friendly with the brothers. There was a family quarrel about money which estranged this man Mortimer, but it was supposed to be made up, and I afterwards met him as I did the others. He was a sly, subtle, scheming man, and several things arose which gave me a suspicion of him, but I had no cause for any positive quarrel.

"One day, only a couple of weeks ago, he came down to my cottage and I showed him some of my African curiosities. Among other things I exhibited this powder, and I told him of its strange properties, how it stimulates those brain centres which control the emotion of fear, and how either madness or death is the fate of the unhappy native who is subjected to the ordeal by the priest of his tribe. I told him also how powerless European science would be to detect it. How he took it I cannot say, for I never left the room, but there is no doubt that it was then, while I was opening cabinets and stooping to boxes, that he managed to abstract some of the devil's-foot root. I well remember how he plied me with questions as to the amount and the time that was needed for its effect, but I little dreamed that he could have a personal reason for asking.

"I thought no more of the matter until the vicar's telegram reached me at Plymouth. This villain had thought that I would be at sea before the news could reach me, and that I should be lost for years in Africa. But I returned at once. Of course, I could not listen to the details without feeling assured that my poison had been used. I came round to see you on the chance that some other explana-

8 *or into the literature of toxicology*. Dr. George B. Koelle has commented ("The Poisons in the Canon"): "The situation has not changed since Dr. Leon Sterndale stated, over a half century ago, that [*radix pedis diaboli*] is not to be found in any pharmacopeia; in fact, it is not yet known to modern science. Until recently, skeptics might have questioned the possible existence of a drug which could produce such bizarre effects. . . . Recent discoveries have shed new light on the matter. A few days ago two Swiss chemists, Stoll and Hoffmann, synthesized a remarkable compound known as lysergic acid diethylamide, or LSD-25. . . . In doses of less than one-thousandth of a grain, it causes strange hallucinations, visions and fantasies, not unlike those presumably experienced by the ill-fated members of the Tregennis family. . . . The compound used in the synthesis of LSD-25 is lysergic acid, which is prepared from a natural alkaloid. Thus it is not difficult to conceive of the presence of a compound similar to or more potent than LSD-25 itself in some unidentified root. Time alone can establish the validity of this hypothesis."

On the other hand, F. A. Allen, M.P.S., has written in "Devilish Drugs" that while "the poison in . . . 'The Adventure of the Devil's Foot,' is, on a first impression virtually unknown to science . . . rauwolfia species, suitably trimmed, suggest themselves. There are the recent reports of acute depression following large doses of reserpine. In fact, [authorities] explicitly list *nightmares* among its undesirable possible side-effects. *Rauwolfia serpentina* is an Asiatic plant; *radix pedis diaboli* was obtained 'in curious circumstances,' from the Ubangi district of the Congo where, as an ordeal poison, it could well be a secret and nightmare-enhanced African species."

tion had suggested itself to you. But there could be none. I was convinced that Mortimer Tregennis was the murderer ; that for the sake of money, and with the idea, perhaps, that if the other members of his family were all insane he would be the sole guardian of their joint property, he had used the devil's-foot powder upon them, driven two of them out of their senses, and killed his sister Brenda, the one human being whom I have ever loved or who has ever loved me. There was his crime ; what was to be his punishment ?

" Should I appeal to the law ? Where were my proofs ? I knew that the facts were true, but could I help to make a jury of countrymen believe so fantastic a story ? I might or I might not. But I could not afford to fail. My soul cried out for revenge. I have said to you once before, Mr. Holmes, that I have spent much of my life outside the law, and that I have come at last to be a law to myself. So it was now. I determined that the fate which he had given to others should be shared by himself. Either that or I would do justice upon him with my own hand. In all England there can be no man who sets less value upon his own life than I do at the present moment.

" Now I have told you all. You have yourself supplied the rest. I did, as you say, after a restless night, set off early from my cottage. I foresaw the difficulty of arousing him, so I gathered some gravel from the pile which you have mentioned, and I used it to throw up to his window. He came down and admitted me through the window of the sitting-room. I laid his offence before him. I told him that I had come both as judge and executioner. The wretch sank into a chair paralysed at the sight of my revolver. I lit the lamp, put the powder above it, and stood outside the window, ready to carry out my threat to shoot him should he try to leave the room. In five minutes he died. My God ! how he died ! But my heart was flint, for he endured nothing which my innocent darling had not felt before him. There is my story, Mr. Holmes. Perhaps, if you loved a woman, you would have done as much yourself. At any rate, I am in your hands. You can take what steps you like. As I have already said, there is no man living who can fear death less than I do."

Holmes sat for some little time in silence.

" What were your plans ? " he asked, at last.

" I had intended to bury myself in Central Africa. My work there is but half finished."

" Go and do the other half," said Holmes. " I, at least, am not prepared to prevent you."

Dr. Sterndale raised his giant figure, bowed gravely, and walked from the arbour. Holmes lit his pipe and handed me his pouch.

" Some fumes which are not poisonous would be a welcome change," said he. " I think you must agree, Watson, that it is not a case in which we are called upon to interfere. Our investigation has been independent, and our action shall be so also. You would not denounce the man ? "

" Certainly not," I answered.

" I have never loved, Watson, but if I did and if the

woman I loved had met such an end, I might act even as our lawless lion-hunter has done. Who knows? Well, Watson, I will not offend your intelligence by explaining what is obvious. The gravel upon the window-sill was, of course, the starting-point of my research. It was unlike anything in the vicarage garden. Only when my attention had been drawn to Dr. Sterndale and his cottage did I find its counterpart. The lamp shining in broad daylight and the remains of powder upon the shield were successive links in a fairly obvious chain. And now, my dear Watson, I think we may dismiss the matter from our mind, and go back with a clear conscience to the study of those Chaldean roots which are surely to be traced in the Cornish branch of the great Celtic speech."

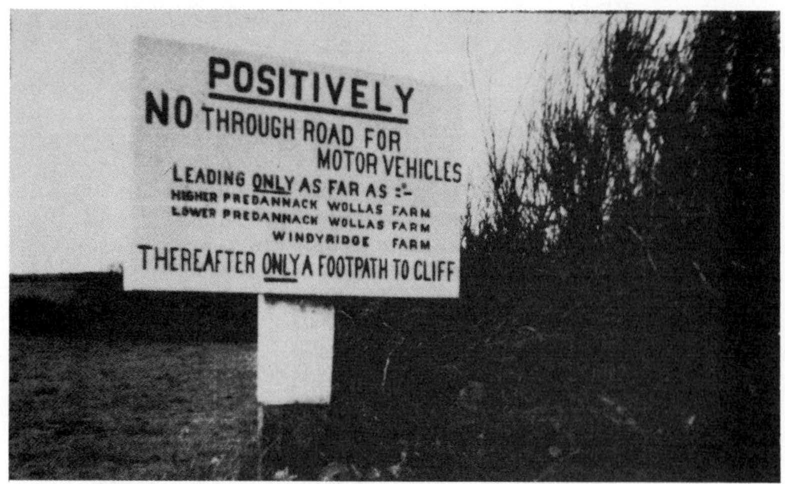

THE ROAD TO "TREDANNICK WOLLAS"

The photograph is by Mr. C. O. Merriman of the Sherlock Holmes Society of London, who adds this informative note: "A hamlet of Tredannick Wartha exists. I think the name given of Tredannick Wartha to the house where the Cornish Horror took place probably is that of Predannack Manor Farm which is one of the major farms in the hamlet of Predannack Wartha. The origin of the Wollas and Wartha is that at one time Predannack consisted of fourteen small holdings which formed two hamlets, High Predannack (Wartha) and Lower Predannack (Wollas). The larger farms took over the smaller but the names remained."

Auctorial and Bibliographical Note: Conan Doyle ranked "The Adventure of the Devil's Foot" No. 9 on his list of the "twelve best" Sherlock Holmes short stories, excluding those in *The Case-Book*. The original manuscript, 58 4to pages written in two exercise books, white vellum, is owned by the New York Public Library, the gift of Lucius Wilmerding.

61

THE ADVENTURE OF THE DANCING MEN

[Wednesday, July 27, to Wednesday, August 10, and Saturday, August 13, 1898]

HOLMES had been seated for some hours in silence, with his long, thin back curved over a chemical vessel in which he was brewing a particularly malodorous product. His head was sunk upon his breast, and he looked from my point of view like a strange, lank bird, with dull grey plumage and a black top-knot.

" So, Watson," said he suddenly, " you do not propose to invest in South African securities ? " 1

I gave a start of astonishment. Accustomed as I was to Holmes' curious faculties, this sudden intrusion into my most intimate thoughts was utterly inexplicable.

" How on earth do you know that ? " I asked.

He wheeled round upon his stool, with a steaming test-tube in his hand and a gleam of amusement in his deep-set eyes.

" Now, Watson, confess yourself utterly taken aback," said he.

" I am."

" I ought to make you sign a paper to that effect."

" Why ? "

" Because in five minutes you will say that it is all so absurdly simple."

" I am sure that I shall say nothing of the kind."

" You see, my dear Watson "—he propped his test-tube in the rack and began to lecture with the air of a professor addressing his class—" it is not really difficult to construct a series of inferences, each dependent upon its predecessor and each simple in itself. If, after doing so, one simply knocks out all the central inferences and presents one's audience with the starting-point and the conclusion, one may produce a startling, though possibly a meretricious, effect. Now, it was not really difficult, by an inspection of the groove between your left forefinger and thumb, to feel sure that you did *not* propose to invest your small capital in the goldfields."

" I see no connection."

" Very likely not ; but I can quickly show you a close connection. Here are the missing links of the very simple chain : 1. You had chalk between your left finger and thumb when you returned from the club last night. 2. You put chalk there when you play 2

1 *"you do not propose to invest in South African securities?"* Dr. Felix Morley has suggested ("The Significance of the Second Stain") that here is an indication that Dr. Watson's isolationist attitude (noted in "The Adventure of the Bruce-Partington Plans") continued: ". . . the doctor, although possessed of a strong gambling instinct, refused pointblank to take an inside tip for investment in South African gold fields. Had Watson taken advantage of [this] advice . . . the speculation would by this time have richly retrieved the shattered fortunes of the family. But it was a foreign commitment with political implications, and the doctor would have none of it."

2 *when you returned from the club last night.* "It is hard to believe," the late Edgar W. Smith commented, "that a man with medical training . . . could so far depart from the elementary principles of hygiene as to forget to wash his hands."

JOHN THURSTON,
Superior Billiard Table Manufacturer.
14, Catherine Street, Strand, London.
AT VERY REDUCED PRICES.

"YOU NEVER PLAY BILLIARDS EXCEPT WITH THURSTON."

Thurston is a famous name in the world of billiards. John Thurston of 78 Margaret Street, Cavendish Square, started making "superior" billiard tables sometime prior to 1814. A few years later he moved to 14 Catherine Street, The Strand. In 1869, Messrs. Thurston & Coy, still on Catherine Street, were one of the chief table-makers in England. As Mr. Ralph Hodgson once wrote to the late Christopher Morley: "Dr. Watson *may* have had a friend of the name, who though a billiards player was not a member of the illustrious family. He *may* have had. There *were* other Thurstons." "Playing with Thurston would not have been outrageously expensive," Mr. Michael Harrison noted (*In the Footsteps of Sherlock Holmes*): "The standard charge for billiards in the 1880's was 1s [25¢] an hour by the day, or 1s 6d [about 37¢] an hour by gas-light."

billiards to steady the cue. 3. You never play billiards except with Thurston. 4. You told me four weeks ago that Thurston had an option on some South African property which would expire in a month, and which he desired you to share with him. 5. Your
3 cheque-book is locked in my drawer, and you have not asked for the key. 6. You do not propose to invest your money in this manner."

"How absurdly simple!" I cried.

"Quite so!" said he, a little nettled. "Every problem becomes very childish when once it is explained to you. Here is an unexplained one. See what you can make of that, friend Watson." He tossed a sheet of paper upon the table, and turned once more to his chemical analysis.

I looked with amazement at the absurd hieroglyphics upon the paper.

"Why, Holmes, it is a child's drawing!" I cried.

"Oh, that's your idea!"

"What else should it be?"

"That is what Mr. Hilton Cubitt, of Ridling Thorpe
4 Manor, Norfolk, is very anxious to know. This little conundrum came by the first post, and he was to follow by the next train. There's a ring at the bell, Watson. I should not be very much surprised if this were he."

A heavy step was heard upon the stairs, and an instant later there entered a tall, ruddy, clean-shaven gentleman, whose clear eyes and florid cheeks told of a life led far from the fogs of Baker Street. He seemed to bring a whiff of his strong, fresh, bracing, east-coast air with him as he entered. Having shaken hands with each of us, he was about to sit down, when his eye rested upon the paper with the curious markings, which I had just examined and left upon the table.

"Well, Mr. Holmes, what do you make of these?" he cried. "They told me that you were fond of queer mysteries, and I don't think you can find a queerer one than that. I sent the paper on ahead so that you might have time to study it before I came."

"It is certainly rather a curious production," said Holmes. "At first sight it would appear to be some childish prank. It consists of a number of absurd little figures dancing across the paper upon which they are drawn. Why should you attribute any importance to so grotesque an object?"

"I never should, Mr. Holmes. But my wife does. It is frightening her to death. She says nothing, but I can see terror in her eyes. That's why I want to sift the matter to the bottom."

Holmes held up the paper so that the sunlight shone full upon it. It was a page torn from a notebook. The markings were done in pencil, and ran in this way:

Holmes examined it for some time, and then, folding it carefully up, he placed it in his pocket-book.

"This promises to be a most interesting and unusual case," said he. "You gave me a few particulars in your

3 *Your cheque-book is locked in my drawer.* "It is evident . . . that Holmes kept the watchful eye of an elder brother upon Watson's gambling propensities," Mr. S. C. Roberts commented in *Doctor Watson.*

4 *Ridling Thorpe Manor. Riding Thorp* or plain *Ridling* in other editions. "If you will open your Batholomew survey map of Norfolk, and study the neighborhood of North Walsham," the late Christopher Morley wrote, "you will see that it was only a short drive from there to the house of Hilton Cubitt, Esq. He lived either at *Edingthorp* or at *Ridlington,* which accounts for the confusion of the . . . texts."

letter, Mr. Hilton Cubitt, but I should be very much obliged if you would kindly go over it all again for the benefit of my friend, Dr. Watson."

" I'm not much of a story-teller," said our visitor, nervously clasping and unclasping his great, strong hands. " You'll just ask me anything that I don't make clear. I'll begin at the time of my marriage last year ; but I want to say first of all that, though I'm not a rich man, my people have been at Ridling Thorpe for a matter of five centuries, and there is no better-known family in the county of Norfolk. Last year I came up to London
for the Jubilee, and I stopped at a boarding-house in 5
Russell Square, because Parker, the vicar of our parish, 6
was staying in it. There was an American young lady there—Patrick was the name—Elsie Patrick. In some way we became friends, until before my month was up I was as much in love as a man could be. We were quietly married at a registry office, and we returned to Norfolk a wedded couple. You'll think it very mad, Mr. Holmes, that a man of a good old family should marry a wife in this fashion, knowing nothing of her past or of her people ; but if you saw her and knew her it would help you to understand.

" She was very straight about it, was Elsie. I can't say that she did not give me every chance of getting out of it if I wished to do so. ' I have had some very disagreeable associations in my life,' said she ; ' I wish to forget all about them. I would rather never allude to the past, for it is very painful to me. If you take me, Hilton, you will take a woman who has nothing that she need be personally ashamed of ; but you will have to be content with my word for it, and to allow me to be silent as to all that passed up to the time when I became yours. If these conditions are too hard, then go back to Norfolk and leave me to the lonely life in which you found me.' It was only the day before our wedding that she said those very words to me. I told her that I was content to take her on her own terms, and I have been as good as my word.

" Well, we have been married now for a year, and very happy we have been. But about a month ago, at the end of June, I saw for the first time signs of trouble. One day my wife received a letter from America. I saw the American stamp. She turned deadly white, read the letter, and threw it into the fire. She made no allusion to it afterwards, and I made none, for a promise is a

HOLMES HELD UP THE PAPER SO THAT THE SUNLIGHT SHONE FULL UPON IT.

Illustration by Sidney Paget for the *Strand Magazine*, December, 1903.

5 *Last year I came up to London for the Jubilee.* The year is therefore 1888, the year after the Golden Jubilee of 1887, or 1898, the year after the Diamond Jubilee of 1897.

6 *Russell Square.* ". . . a name which will recall to many minds the homes of the Selbys and Osbornes in Thackeray's *Vanity Fair*," Augustus J. C. Hare wrote in *Walks in London*, Vol. II. "On its north side is a seated statue of Francis Russell, Duke of Bedford, by Westmacott. It was in No. 21 that Sir Samuel Romilly died by his own hand in 1818. In No. 66, Sir Thomas Lawrence, who had lived and painted in that house for twenty-five years, died January 7, 1830. Cossacks 'mounted on their small white horses, with their long spears grounded,' stood sentinels at its door while he was painting their general, Platoff."

". . . THERE IS NO BETTER-KNOWN FAMILY IN THE COUNTY OF NORFOLK."

"There is only one Cubitt listed in Robson's *British Heraldry*, published in 1830," Dr. Julian Wolff wrote in his *Practical Guide to Sherlockian Heraldry*. "The arms are: 'ermine a lion's head erased azure.' "

7 *it was the Tuesday of last week—.* Since Tuesday was not "a week ago" but "about a week ago," the day of Hilton Cubitt's visit to Holmes must have been a Monday or a Wednesday. But Holmes deduced that Watson had been playing billiards with Thurston at his club the night before the day of Cubitt's visit. That day was therefore not a Sunday and the day of Cubitt's visit not a Monday. We are at the end of July or early in August: the Wednesdays in that period in 1888 and 1898 are Wednesday, July 25, 1888; Wednesday, August 1, 1888; Wednesday, July 27, 1898; and Wednesday, August 3, 1898.

promise ; but she has never known an easy hour from that moment. There is always a look of fear upon her face—a look as if she were waiting and expecting. She would do better to trust me. She would find that I was her best friend. But until she speaks I can say nothing. Mind you, she is a truthful woman, Mr. Holmes, and whatever trouble there may have been in her past life, it has been no fault of hers. I am only a simple Norfolk squire, but there is not a man in England who ranks his family honour more highly than I do. She knows it well, and she knew it well before she married me. She would never bring any stain upon it—of that I am sure.

" Well, now I come to the queer part of my story.
7 About a week ago—it was the Tuesday of last week—I found on one of the window-sills a number of absurd little dancing figures, like these upon the paper. They were scrawled with chalk. I thought that it was the stable-boy who had drawn them, but the lad swore he knew nothing about it. Anyhow, they had come there during the night. I had them washed out, and I only mentioned the matter to my wife afterwards. To my surprise she took it very seriously, and begged me if any more came to let her see them. None did come for a week, and then yesterday morning I found this paper lying on the sun-dial in the garden. I showed it to Elsie, and down she dropped in a dead faint. Since then she has looked like a woman in a dream, half dazed, and with terror always lurking in her eyes. It was then that I wrote and sent the paper to you, Mr. Holmes. It was not a thing that I could take to the police, for they would have laughed at me, but you will tell me what to do. I am not a rich man ; but if there is any danger threatening my little woman, I would spend my last copper to shield her."

He was a fine creature, this man of the old English soil, simple, straight, and gentle, with his great, earnest blue eyes and broad, comely face. His love for his wife and his trust in her shone in his features. Holmes had listened to his story with the utmost attention, and now he sat for some time in silent thought.

" Don't you think, Mr. Cubitt," said he at last, " that your best plan would be to make a direct appeal to your wife, and to ask her to share her secret with you ? "

Hilton Cubitt shook his massive head.

" A promise is a promise, Mr. Holmes. If Elsie wished to tell me, she would. If not, it is not for me to force her confidence. But I am justified in taking my own line—and I will."

" Then I will help you with all my heart. In the first place, have you heard of any strangers being seen in your neighbourhood ? "

" No."

" I presume that it is a very quiet place. Any fresh face would cause comment ? "

" In the immediate neighbourhood, yes. But we have several small watering-places not very far away. And the farmers take in lodgers."

" These hieroglyphics have evidently a meaning. If it is a purely arbitrary one, it may be impossible for us to solve it. If, on the other hand, it is systematic, I have no doubt that we shall get to the bottom of it. But this particular sample is so short that I can do nothing, and the facts which you have brought me are so indefinite that we have no basis for an investigation. I would suggest that you return to Norfolk, that you keep a keen look-out, and that you take an exact copy of any fresh dancing men which may appear. It is a thousand pities that we have not a reproduction of those which were done in chalk upon the window-sill. Make a discreet inquiry, also, as to any strangers in the neighbourhood. When you have collected some fresh evidence, come to me again. That is the best advice which I can give you, Mr. Hilton Cubitt. If there are any pressing fresh developments, I shall be always ready to run down and see you in your Norfolk home."

The interview left Sherlock Holmes very thoughtful, and several times in the next few days I saw him take his slip of paper from his notebook and look long and earnestly at the curious figures inscribed upon it. He made no allusion to the affair, however, until one afternoon a fortnight or so later. I was going out, when he called me back.

"You had better stay here, Watson."

"Why?"

"Because I had a wire from Hilton Cubitt this morning—you remember Hilton Cubitt, of the dancing men? He was to reach Liverpool Street at one-twenty. He may be here at any moment. I gather from his wire that there have been some new incidents of importance."

We had not long to wait, for our Norfolk squire came straight from the station as fast as a hansom could bring him. He was looking worried and depressed, with tired eyes and a lined forehead.

"It's getting on my nerves, this business, Mr. Holmes," said he, as he sank, like a wearied man, into an arm-chair. "It's bad enough to feel that you are surrounded by unseen, unknown folk, who have some kind of design upon you; but when, in addition to that, you know that it is just killing your wife by inches, then it becomes as much as flesh and blood can endure. She's wearing away under it—just wearing away before my eyes."

"Has she said anything yet?"

"No, Mr. Holmes, she has not. And yet there have been times when the poor girl has wanted to speak, and yet could not quite bring herself to take the plunge. I have tried to help her; but I dare say I did it clumsily, and scared her off from it. She has spoken about my old family, and our reputation in the county, and our pride in our unsullied honour, and I always felt it was leading to the point; but somehow it turned off before we got there."

"But you have found out something for yourself?"

"A good deal, Mr. Holmes. I have several fresh dancing men pictures for you to examine, and, what is more important, I have seen the fellow."

"What—the man who draws them?"

"Yes, I saw him at his work. But I will tell you everything in order. When I got back after my visit to you, the

8 *I saw her white face grow whiter yet in the moonlight.* On Cubitt's second visit to Holmes—"a fortnight or so" after his first visit—he says the first thing he saw on the morning of the day after his return to Norfolk—a Thursday morning, then—was another row of dancing men. "Two mornings later"—a Saturday—a fresh inscription appeared. "Three days later"—a Tuesday—a message on paper was placed upon the sundial. That night Cubitt lay in wait; "about two o'clock in the morning"—a Wednesday morning—all was dark "save for the moonlight outside" and Cubitt saw his wife's "white face grow whiter yet in the moonlight." Of the four Wednesdays under consideration, only one will serve—the morning of Wednesday, August 3, 1898: there was a full moon on the night of the 2nd–3rd, and it did not set until 4:38 A.M. The day of Cubitt's first visit to Holmes was therefore Wednesday, July 27, 1898; his second visit was on Wednesday, August 10, or a few days thereafter; "two days of impatience followed"; "on the evening of the second there came a letter from Hilton Cubitt"; Holmes went to Ridling Thorpe Manor the next morning—Saturday, August 13th, or a few days thereafter (but not on Sunday, August 14th—on the journey from town he "turned over the morning papers with anxious attention").

"... MY WIFE THREW HER ARMS ROUND ME ..."

Illustration by Sidney Paget for the *Strand Magazine*, December, 1903.

very first thing I saw next morning was a fresh crop of dancing men. They had been drawn in chalk upon the black wooden door of the tool-house, which stands beside the lawn in full view of the front windows. I took an exact copy, and here it is." He unfolded a paper and laid it upon the table. Here is a copy of the hieroglyphics :

" Excellent ! " said Holmes. " Excellent ! Pray continue."

" When I had taken the copy I rubbed out the marks ; but two mornings later a fresh inscription had appeared. I have a copy of it here " :

Holmes rubbed his hands and chuckled with delight.

" Our material is rapidly accumulating," said he.

" Three days later a message was left scrawled upon paper, and placed under a pebble upon the sundial. Here it is. The characters are, as you see, exactly the same as the last one. After that I determined to lie in wait ; so I got out my revolver and I sat up in my study, which overlooks the lawn and garden. About two in the morning I was seated by the window, all being dark save for the moonlight outside, when I heard steps behind me, and there was my wife in her dressing-gown. She implored me to come to bed. I told her frankly that I wished to see who it was who played such absurd tricks upon us. She answered that it was some senseless practical joke, and that I should not take any notice of it.

" ' If it really annoys you, Hilton, we might go and travel, you and I, and so avoid this nuisance.'

" ' What, be driven out of our own house by a practical joker ? ' said I. ' Why, we should have the whole county laughing at us ! '

" ' Well, come to bed,' said she, ' and we can discuss it in the morning.'

" Suddenly, as she spoke, I saw her white face grow
8 whiter yet in the moonlight, and her hand tightened upon my shoulder. Something was moving in the shadow of the tool-house. I saw a dark, creeping figure which crawled round the corner and squatted in front of the door. Seizing my pistol I was rushing out, when my wife threw her arms round me and held me with convulsive strength. I tried to throw her off, but she clung to me most desperately. At last I got clear, but by the time I had opened the door and reached the house the creature was gone. He had left a trace of his presence, however, for there on the door was the very same arrangement of dancing men which had already twice appeared, and which I have copied on that paper. There was no other sign of the fellow anywhere, though I ran all over the grounds. And yet the amazing thing is that

he must have been there all the time, for when I examined the door again in the morning he had scrawled some more of his pictures under the line which I had already seen."

"Have you that fresh drawing?"

"Yes; it is very short, but I made a copy of it, and here it is."

Again he produced a paper. The new dance was in this form:

"Tell me," said Holmes—and I could see by his eyes that he was much excited—"was this a mere addition to the first, or did it appear to be entirely separate?"

"It was on a different panel of the door."

"Excellent! This is far the most important of all for our purpose. It fills me with hopes. Now, Mr. Hilton Cubitt, please continue your most interesting statement."

"I have nothing more to say, Mr. Holmes, except that I was angry with my wife that night for having held me back when I might have caught the skulking rascal. She said that she feared that I might come to harm. For an instant it had crossed my mind that perhaps what she really feared was that *he* might come to harm, for I could not doubt that she knew who this man was and what he meant by these strange signals. But there is a tone in my wife's voice, Mr. Holmes, and a look in her eyes which forbid doubt, and I am sure that it was indeed my own safety that was in her mind. There's the whole case, and now I want your advice as to what I ought to do. My own inclination is to put half a dozen of my farm lads in the shrubbery, and when this fellow comes again to give him such a hiding that he will leave us in peace for the future."

"I fear it is too deep a case for such simple remedies," said Holmes. "How long can you stop in London?"

"I must go back to-day. I would not leave my wife alone at night for anything. She is very nervous and begged me to come back."

"I dare say you are right. But if you could have stopped I might possibly have been able to return with you in a day or two. Meanwhile, you will leave me these papers, and I think that it is very likely that I shall be able to pay you a visit shortly and to throw some light upon your case."

Sherlock Holmes preserved his calm professional manner until our visitor had left us, although it was easy for me, who knew him so well, to see that he was profoundly excited. The moment that Hilton Cubitt's broad back had disappeared through the door my comrade rushed to the table, laid out all the slips of paper containing dancing men in front of him, and threw himself into an intricate and elaborate calculation.

For two hours I watched him as he covered sheet after sheet of paper with figures and letters, so completely absorbed in his task that he had evidently forgotten my

"I SUPPOSE THAT YOU ARE THE DETECTIVES FROM LONDON?" SAID HE.

Illustration by Sidney Paget for the *Strand Magazine*, December, 1903.

presence. Sometimes he was making progress, and whistled and sang at his work; sometimes he was puzzled and would sit for a long spell with a furrowed brow and a vacant eye. Finally he sprang from his chair with a cry of satisfaction, and walked up and down the room rubbing his hands together. Then he wrote a long telegram upon a cable form. "If my answer to this is as I hope, you will have a very pretty case to add to your collection, Watson," said he. "I expect that we shall be able to go down to Norfolk to-morrow, and to take our friend some very definite news as to the secret of his annoyance."

I confess that I was filled with curiosity, but I was aware that Holmes liked to make his disclosures at his own time and in his own way; so I waited until it should suit him to take me into his confidence.

But there was a delay in that answering telegram, and two days of impatience followed, during which Holmes pricked up his ears at every ring of the bell. On the evening of the second there came a letter from Hilton Cubitt. All was quiet with him, save that a long inscription had appeared that morning upon the pedestal of the sundial. He enclosed a copy of it, which is here reproduced:

Holmes bent over this grotesque frieze for some minutes and then suddenly sprang to his feet with an exclamation of surprise and dismay. His face was haggard with anxiety.

"We have let this affair go far enough," said he. "Is there a train to North Walsham to-night?"

I turned up the time-table. The last had just gone.

"Then we shall breakfast early and take the very first in the morning," said Holmes. "Our presence is most urgently needed. Ah, here is our expected cablegram. One moment, Mrs. Hudson—there may be an answer. No, that is quite as I expected. This message makes it even more essential that we should not lose an hour in letting Hilton Cubitt know how matters stand, for it is a singular and dangerous web in which our simple Norfolk squire is entangled."

So, indeed, it proved, and as I come to the dark conclusion of a story which had seemed to me to be only childish and bizarre, I experience once again the dismay and horror with which I was filled. Would that I had some brighter ending to communicate to my readers; but these are the chronicles of facts, and I must follow to their dark crisis the strange chain of events which for some days made Ridling Thorpe Manor a household word through the length and breadth of England.

We had hardly alighted at North Walsham, and mentioned the name of our destination, when the stationmaster hurried towards us. "I suppose that you are the detectives from London?" said he.

A look of annoyance passed over Holmes' face.

"What makes you think such a thing?"

"Because Inspector Martin from Norwich has just

passed through. But maybe you are the surgeons. She's not dead—or wasn't by last accounts. You may be in time to save her yet—though it be for the gallows."

Holmes' brow was dark with anxiety.

"We are going to Ridling Thorpe Manor," said he, "but we have heard nothing of what has passed there."

"It's a terrible business," said the station-master. "They are shot, both Mr. Hilton Cubitt and his wife. She shot him and then herself—so the servants say. He's dead, and her life is despaired of. Dear, dear! one of the oldest families in the county of Norfolk, and one of the most honoured."

Without a word Holmes hurried to a carriage, and during the long seven-miles drive he never opened his mouth. Seldom have I seen him so utterly despondent. He had been uneasy during all our journey from town, and I had observed that he had turned over the morning papers with anxious attention; but now this sudden realization of his worst fears left him in a blank melancholy. He leaned back in his seat, lost in gloomy speculation. Yet there was much around us to interest us, for we were passing through as singular a country-
side as any in England, where a few scattered cottages 9
represented the population of to-day, while on every hand enormous square-towered churches bristled up from the flat, green landscape and told of the glory and prosperity of old East Anglia. At last the violet rim of the German Ocean appeared over the green edge of the Norfolk coast, and the driver pointed with his whip to two old brick-and-timber gables which projected from a grove of trees. "That's Ridling Thorpe Manor," said he.

As we drove up to the porticoed front door I observed in front of it, beside the tennis lawn, the black tool-house and the pedestalled sundial with which we had such strange associations. A dapper little man, with a quick, alert manner and a waxed moustache, had just descended from a high dog-cart. He introduced himself as Inspector Martin, of the Norfolk Constabulary, and he was considerably astonished when he heard the name of my companion.

"Why, Mr. Holmes, the crime was only committed at three this morning! How could you hear of it in London and get to the spot as soon as I?"

"I anticipated it. I came in the hope of preventing it."

"Then you must have important evidence of which we are ignorant, for they were said to be a most united couple."

"I have only the evidence of the dancing men," said Holmes. "I will explain the matter to you later. Meanwhile, since it is too late to prevent this tragedy, I am very anxious that I should use the knowledge which I possess in order to ensure that justice be done. Will you associate me in your investigation, or will you prefer that I should act independently?"

"I should be proud to feel that we were acting together, Mr. Holmes," said the Inspector earnestly.

"In that case I should be glad to hear the evidence and to examine the premises without an instant of unnecessary delay."

9 *as singular a countryside as any in England.* Watson's description remains true today with the square-towered churches prominent on the horizon and with Norfolk farms reputed to be among the most prosperous in Great Britain. The term "German Ocean" was—before the first World War—an alternative name for the North Sea. On maps of this period "the North Sea or German Ocean" was always given.

"THAT'S RIDLING THORPE MANOR," SAID HE.

"Walcott is a small village near the North Sea and lies approximately seven miles from North Walsham, on the road to Happisburgh," Miss Shirley Sanderson wrote in "Another Case of Identity." "If Holmes and Watson approached Walcott via Keswick, 'the violet rim of the German Ocean' would be very apparent. Two or three miles south of Walcott lies East Ruston, where the villain, Mr. Abe Slaney, lived at Elrige's Farm (as yet unidentified by us). The main house in the village is Walcott House, owned by a Miss Wenn . . ."

Inspector Martin had the good sense to allow my friend to do things in his own fashion, and contented himself with carefully noting the results. The local surgeon, an old, white-haired man, had just come down from Mrs. Hilton Cubitt's room, and he reported that her injuries were serious, but not necessarily fatal. The bullet had passed through the front of her brain, and it would probably be some time before she could regain consciousness. On the question of whether she had been shot or had shot herself he would not venture to express any decided opinion. Certainly the bullet had been discharged at very close quarters. There was only the one pistol found in the room, two barrels of which had been emptied. Mr. Hilton Cubitt had been shot through the heart. It was equally conceivable that he had shot her and then himself, or that she had been the criminal, for the revolver lay upon the floor midway between them.

"Has he been moved?" asked Holmes.

"We have moved nothing except the lady. We could not leave her lying wounded upon the floor."

"How long have you been here, doctor?"

"Since four o'clock."

"Anyone else?"

"Yes, the constable here."

"And you have touched nothing?"

"Nothing."

"You have acted with great discretion. Who sent for you?"

"The housemaid, Saunders."

"Was it she who gave the alarm?"

"She and Mrs. King, the cook."

"Where are they now?"

"In the kitchen, I believe."

"Then I think we had better hear their story at once."

The old hall, oak-panelled and high-windowed, had been turned into a court of investigation. Holmes sat in a great, old-fashioned chair, his inexorable eyes gleaming out of his haggard face. I could read in them a set purpose to devote his life to this quest until the client whom he had failed to save should at last be avenged. The trim Inspector Martin, the old grey-bearded country doctor, myself, and a stolid village policeman made up the rest of that strange company.

The two women told their story clearly enough. They had been aroused from their sleep by the sound of an explosion, which had been followed a minute later by a second one. They slept in adjoining rooms, and Mrs. King had rushed in to Saunders. Together they had descended the stairs. The door of the study was open and a candle was burning upon the table. Their master lay upon his face in the centre of the room. He was quite dead. Near the window his wife was crouching, her head leaning against the wall. She was horribly wounded, and the side of the face was red with blood. She breathed heavily, but was incapable of saying anything. The passage, as well as the room, was full of smoke and the smell of powder. The window was certainly shut and fastened upon the inside. Both women were positive upon the point. They had at once sent for the doctor and for the constable. Then, with the aid of the groom and the stable-boy, they had conveyed their injured mistress to her room. Both she and her husband had occupied the bed. She was clad in her dress—he in his dressing-gown, over his night-clothes. Nothing had been moved in the study. So far as they knew, there had never been any quarrel between husband and wife. They had always looked upon them as a very united couple.

These were the main points of the servants' evidence. In answer to Inspector Martin they were clear that every door was fastened upon the inside and that no one could have escaped from the house. In answer to Holmes, they both remembered that they were conscious of the smell of powder from the moment that they ran out of their rooms upon the top floor. " I commend that fact very carefully to your attention," said Holmes to his professional colleague. " And now I think that we are in a position to undertake a thorough examination of the room."

The study proved to be a small chamber, lined on three sides with books, and with a writing-table facing an ordinary window, which looked out upon the garden. Our first attention was given to the body of the unfortunate squire, whose huge frame lay stretched across the room. His disordered dress showed that he had been hastily aroused from sleep. The bullet had been fired at him from the front, and had remained in his body after penetrating the heart. His death had certainly been instantaneous and painless. There was no powder-marking either upon his dressing-gown or on his hands. According to the country surgeon, the lady had stains upon her face, but none upon her hand.

" The absence of the latter means nothing, though its presence may mean everything," said Holmes. " Unless the powder from a badly fitting cartridge happens to spurt backwards, one may fire many shots without leaving a sign. I would suggest that Mr. Cubitt's body may now be removed. I suppose, doctor, you have not recovered the bullet which wounded the lady ? "

" A serious operation will be necessary before that can be done. But there are still four cartridges in the revolver. Two have been fired and two wounds inflicted, so that each bullet can be accounted for."

" So it would seem," said Holmes. " Perhaps you can account also for the bullet which has so obviously struck the edge of the window ? "

He had turned suddenly, and his long, thin finger was pointing to a hole which had been drilled right through the lower window-sash about an inch above the bottom.

" By George ! " cried the Inspector. " How ever did you see that ? "

" Because I looked for it."

" Wonderful ! " said the country doctor. " You are certainly right, sir. Then a third shot has been fired, and therefore a third person must have been present. But who could that have been, and how could he have got away ? "

. . . THEY BOTH REMEMBERED THAT THEY WERE CONSCIOUS OF THE SMELL OF POWDER . . .

Illustration by Sidney Paget for the *Strand Magazine*, December, 1903.

OUR FIRST ATTENTION WAS GIVEN TO THE BODY OF THE UNFORTUNATE SQUIRE . . .

Illustration by Frederic Dorr Steele for *Collier's Magazine*, December 5, 1903.

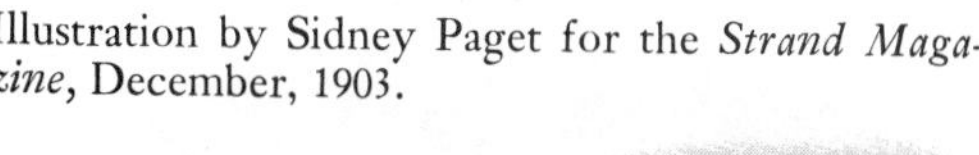

. . . HE BENT FORWARD AND PICKED UP A LITTLE BRAZEN CYLINDER.

Illustration by Sidney Paget for the *Strand Magazine,* December, 1903.

" That is the problem which we are now about to solve," said Sherlock Holmes. " You remember, Inspector Martin, when the servants said that on leaving their room they were at once conscious of a smell of powder, I remarked that the point was an extremely important one ? "

" Yes, sir ; but I confess I did not quite follow you."

" It suggested that at the time of the firing the window as well as the door of the room had been open. Otherwise the fumes of powder could not have been blown so rapidly through the house. A draught in the room was necessary for that. Both door and window were only open for a short time, however."

" How do you prove that ? "

" Because the candle has not gutted."

" Capital ! " cried the Inspector. " Capital ! "

" Feeling sure that the window had been open at the time of the tragedy, I conceived that there might have been a third person in the affair, who stood outside this opening and fired through it. Any shot directed at this person might hit the sash. I looked, and there, sure enough, was the bullet mark ! "

" But how came the window to be shut and fastened ? "

" The woman's first instinct would be to shut and fasten the window. But, halloa ! what is this ? "

It was a lady's hand-bag which stood upon the study table—a trim little hand-bag of crocodile-skin and silver. Holmes opened it and turned the contents out. There were twenty fifty-pound notes of the Bank of England, held together by an india-rubber band—nothing else.

" This must be preserved, for it will figure in the trial," said Holmes, as he handed the bag with its contents to the Inspector. " It is now necessary that we should try to throw some light upon this third bullet, which has clearly, from the splintering of the wood, been fired from inside the room. I should like to see Mrs. King, the cook, again. . . . You said, Mrs. King, that you were awakened by a *loud* explosion. When you said that, did you mean that it seemed to you to be louder than the second one ? "

" Well, sir, it wakened me from my sleep, and so it is hard to judge. But it did seem very loud."

" You don't think that it might have been two shots fired almost at the same instant ? "

" I am sure I couldn't say, sir."

" I believe that it was undoubtedly so. I rather think, Inspector Martin, that we have now exhausted all that this room can teach us. If you will kindly step round with me we shall see what fresh evidence the garden has to offer."

A flower-bed extended up to the study window, and we all broke into an exclamation as we approached it. The flowers were trampled down, and the soft soil was imprinted all over with footmarks. Large, masculine feet they were, with peculiarly long, sharp toes. Holmes hunted about among the grass and leaves like a retriever after a wounded bird. Then, with a cry of satisfaction, bent forward and picked up a little brazen cylinder.

" I thought so," said he ; " the revolver had an ejector, and here is the third cartridge. I really think, Inspector Martin, that our case is almost complete."

The country inspector's face had shown his intense amazement at the rapid and masterful progress of Holmes' investigations. At first he had shown some disposition to assert his own position ; but now he was overcome with admiration, and ready to follow without question wherever Holmes led.

" Whom do you suspect ? " he asked.

" I'll go into that later. There are several points in this problem which I have not been able to explain to you yet. Now that I have got so far I had best proceed on my own lines, and then clear the whole matter up once and for all."

" Just as you wish, Mr. Holmes, so long as we get our man."

" I have no desire to make mysteries, but it is impossible at the moment of action to enter into long and complex explanations. I have the threads of this affair all in my hand. Even if this lady should never recover consciousness we can still reconstruct the events of last night and ensure that justice be done. First of all I wish to know whether there is any inn in this neighbourhood known as ' Elrige's ' ? "

The servants were cross-questioned, but none of them had heard of such a place. The stable-boy threw a light upon the matter by remembering that a farmer of that name lived miles off in the direction of East Rust

" Is it a lonely farm ? "

" Very lonely, sir."

" Perhaps they have not heard yet of all that happened here during the night ? "

" Maybe not, sir."

Holmes thought for a little, and then a curious smile played over his face.

" Saddle a horse, my lad," said he. " I shall wish you to take a note to Elrige's Farm."

He took from his pocket the various slips of the dancing men. With these in front of him he worked for some time at the study table. Finally he handed a note to the boy, with directions to put it into the hands of the person to whom it was addressed, and especially to answer no questions of any sort which might be put to him. I saw the outside of the note, addressed in straggling, irregular characters, very unlike Holmes' usual precise hand. It was consigned to Mr. Abe Slaney, Elrige's Farm, East Ruston, Norfolk.

" I think, Inspector," Holmes remarked, " that you would do well to telegraph for an escort, as, if my calculations prove to be correct, you may have a particularly dangerous prisoner to convey to the county gaol. The boy who takes this note could no doubt forward your telegram. If there is an afternoon train to town, Watson, I think we should do well to take it, as I have a chemical analysis of some interest to finish, and this investigation draws rapidly to a close."

When the youth had been despatched with the note, Sherlock Holmes gave his instructions to the servants.

10 *a trifling monograph upon the subject.* Holmes' "little collection on ciphers and secret writings . . . undoubtedly included two fine seventeenth-century works: Falconer's *Cryptomenysis Patefacta* (London, 1685), on such pertinent subjects as deciphering secret writings, Bacon's cipher and the systems used by the Turks, as well as that ingenious volume on cryptography, John Wilkins' *Mercury* (London, 1694)," Miss Madeleine B. Stern wrote in "Sherlock Holmes: Rare Book Collector." "Eighteenth-century researches in the field were represented among the Holmes sources by John Lockington's edition of Bowle's *New and Complete Book of Cyphers* (1795), illustrated with plates of ciphers. Holmes' shelf undoubtedly also contained the study of Thomas Young, who deciphered the Rosetta Stone: *An Account of some Recent Discoveries in Hieroglyphical Literature* (London, 1823) as well as Champollion's *Précis du Système Hiéroglyphique des Anciens Égyptiens* (Paris, 1828), with its useful plates of hieroglyphic alphabets."

11 *I confess that this is entirely new to me.* Holmes of course meant that the symbols of the Dancing Men were new to him, not the cipher system itself, which is simple substitution.

"The fact that a code of such transparent simplicity baffled the Master for a time has long been a matter of wonder," Mr. Ed S. Woodhead wrote in "In Defense of Dr. Watson." "Is it not obvious that he suppressed the true code as too abstruse, substituting a type which would baffle the reader of his day but would not require a treatise to explain it?"

The late Fletcher Pratt was in complete agreement with this view: "We are driven almost irresistibly to the conclusion that the cipher in the printed account was no more the one actually used than Upper Swandam Lane was actually named Upper Swandam Lane," he wrote in "The Secret Message of the Dancing Men." "The internal evidence points to the same conclusion. If the cipher of the dancing men is far too simple for practical use, with its single unvarying character for each letter, it is also far too complex for simple substitution cipher. It offers too many opportunities for variation of which no advantage has been taken. Let us consider the little mannikins in detail. . . . When we combine the various leg possibilities with the various arm possibilities the result is represented by the multiplication of the possible arm and leg types and we obtain the astonishing figure of 784 possible little dancing men to be made with the elements shown in those few messages. But this is not all: D, G and T show the little figures standing on their heads, and T is simply an E in reverse. Obviously the meaning of any one of the 784 characters can be changed by turning it upside down, which doubles the total, giving 1,568 characters. . . . The discovered messages in the Great Cipher [compiled by Rossignol in the reign of Louis XIV] show a total of 587

If any visitor were to call asking for Mrs. Hilton Cubitt no information should be given as to her condition, but he was to be shown at once into the drawing-room. He impressed these points upon them with the utmost earnestness. Finally he led the way into the drawing-room, with the remark that the business was now out of our hands, and that we must while away the time as best we might until we could see what was in store for us. The doctor had departed to his patients, and only the Inspector and myself remained.

" I think I can help you to pass an hour in an interesting and profitable manner," said Holmes, drawing his chair up to the table and spreading out in front of him the various papers upon which were recorded the antics of the dancing men. " As to you, friend Watson, I owe you every atonement for having allowed your natural curiosity to remain so long unsatisfied. To you, Inspector, the whole incident may appeal as a remarkable professional study. I must tell you first of all the interesting circumstances connected with the previous consultations which Mr. Hilton Cubitt has had with me in Baker Street." He then shortly recapitulated the facts which have already been recorded.

" I have here in front of me these singular productions, at which one might smile had they not proved themselves to be the forerunners of so terrible a tragedy. I am fairly familiar with all forms of secret writings, and am myself
10 the author of a trifling monograph upon the subject, in
which I analyse one hundred and sixty separate ciphers ;
11 but I confess that this is entirely new to me. The object of
those who invented the system has apparently been to conceal that these characters convey a message, and to give the idea that they are the mere random sketches of children.

" Having once recognized, however, that the symbols stood for letters, and having applied the rules which guide us in all forms of secret writings, the solution was easy enough. The first message submitted to me was so short that it was impossible for me to do more than to say with some confidence that the symbol stood for E. As you are aware, E is the most common letter in the English alphabet and it predominates to so marked an extent that even in a short sentence one would expect to find it most often. Out of fifteen symbols in the first message four were the same, so it was reasonable to set this down as E. It is true that in some cases the figure was bearing a flag, and in some cases not, but it was probable from the way in which the flags were distributed that they were used to break the sentence up into words. I accepted this as an hypothesis, and noted that E was represented by

" But now came the real difficulty of the inquiry. The order of the English letters after E is by no means well-marked, and any preponderance which may be shown in an average of a printed sheet may be reversed in a single short sentence. Speaking roughly,
T, A, O, I, N, S, H, R, D, and L are the numerical
12 order in which letters occur ; but T, A, O, and I are
very nearly abreast of each other, and it would be an endless task to try each combination until a meaning was

arrived at. I, therefore, waited for fresh material. In my second interview with Mr. Hilton Cubitt he was able to give me two other short sentences and one message, which appeared—since there was no flag—to be a single word. Here are the symbols. Now, in the single word I have already got the two E's coming second and fourth in a word of five letters. It might be ' sever,' or ' lever,'
or ' never.' There can be no question that the latter as a 13
reply to an appeal is far the most probable, and the circumstances pointed to its being a reply written by the lady. Accepting it as correct, we are now able to say that the symbols stand respectively for
N, V, and R. 14

" Even now I was in considerable difficulty, but a happy thought put me in possession of several other letters. It occurred to me that if these appeals came, as I expected, from someone who had been intimate with the lady in her early life, a combination which contained two E's with three letters between might very well stand for the name ' ELSIE.' On examination I found that such a combination formed the termination of the message which was three times repeated. It was certainly some appeal to ' Elsie.' In this way I had got my L, S, and I. But what appeal could it be ? There were only four letters in the word which preceded ' Elsie,' and it ended in E. Surely the word must be ' COME.' I tried all other four letters ending in E, but could find none to fit the case. So now I was in possession of C, O, and M, and I was in a position to attack the first message once more, dividing it into words and putting dots for each symbol which was still unknown. So treated it worked out in this fashion :

. M . ERE . . E SL . NE .

" Now, the first letter can only be A, which is a most useful discovery, since it occurs no fewer than three times in this short sentence, and the H is also apparent in the second word. Now it becomes :

AM HERE A . E SLANE .

Or, filling in the obvious vacancies in the name :

AM HERE ABE SLANEY.

I had so many letters now that I could proceed with considerable confidence to the second message, which worked out in this fashion :

A . ELRI . ES.

Here I could only make sense by putting T and G for the missing letters, and supposing that the name was that of some house or inn at which the writer was staying."

Inspector Martin and I had listened with the utmost interest to the full and clear account of how my friend had produced results which had led to so complete a command over our difficulties.

" What did you do then, sir ? " asked the Inspector.

" I had every reason to suppose that this Abe Slaney was an American, since Abe is an American contraction, and since a letter from America had been the starting-

different characters; but not all the possible characters are used, and when the permutations and combinations were studied by Bazéries he reported that the possible total of characters was exactly *1,568*. The long arm of coincidence would have to stretch itself right out of joint to cover such a set of figures if it were accidental. We have good reason to believe that it was not accidental; that with the connivance of Holmes, Watson deliberately eliminated from the record the cipher used by Abe Slaney (probably . . . a root cipher or a variant on the Vigenère tableau) and inserted in its place this other."

12 *Speaking roughly, T, A, O, I, N, S, H, R, D, and L are the numerical order in which letters occur.* The order of frequency of single letters in English is given as follows by Mr. Laurence Dwight Smith in his fascinating little book *Cryptography: The Science of Secret Writing,* New York: Dover Publications, Inc., 1955: E T O A N I : R S H : D L : C W U M : F Y G P B : V K : X Q J Z. The table of frequency in normal *literary* text and in normal *telegraphic* text appears as follows in Miss Eugenia Williams' *An Invitation to Cryptograms;* New York: Simon and Schuster, 1959:

Literary: E T A O I N S R H L D C U M F W G Y P B V K X J Q Z

Telegraphic: E O A N I R S T D L H U C M P Y F G W B V K X J Q Z

13 *It might be 'sever,' or 'lever,' or 'never.'* "This dictum implies that the five-letter word *must* be one of these alternatives," Mr. Colin Prestige wrote in "Agents of Evil." "Never! A simple mental exercise reveals more than 30 alternatives, some possible and some improbable."

14 *stand respectively for N, V, and R.* But the symbol used for V in message No. IV is the same as that used for P in message No. V in all the texts which your editor has examined, including the original publication in the *Strand Magazine.* In some texts, in addition, the symbol used for C in message No. VI is the same as that used for M throughout, and different from that used for C in Message No. III. We may note here that a number of Sherlockian scholars have amused themselves by devising complete alphabets in the "Dancing Men" cipher.

15 *the New York Police Bureau.* "This was Watson's error; it was even then the New York Police *Department,*" the late Fletcher Pratt wrote in "The Secret Message of the Dancing Men."

point of all the trouble. I had also every cause to think that there was some criminal secret in the matter. The lady's allusions to her past and her refusal to take her husband into her confidence both pointed in that direction. I therefore cabled to my friend, Wilson Har-
15 greave, of the New York Police Bureau, who has more than once made use of my knowledge of London crime. I asked him whether the name of Abe Slaney was known to him. Here is his reply: 'The most dangerous crook in Chicago.' On the very evening upon which I had his answer Hilton Cubitt sent me the last message from Slaney. Working with known letters it took this form:

ELSIE . RE . ARE TO MEET THY GO .

The addition of a P and a D completed a message which showed me that the rascal was proceeding from persuasion to threats, and my knowledge of the crooks of Chicago prepared me to find that he might very rapidly put his words into action. I at once came to Norfolk with my friend and colleague, Dr. Watson, but, unhappily, only in time to find that the worst had already occurred."

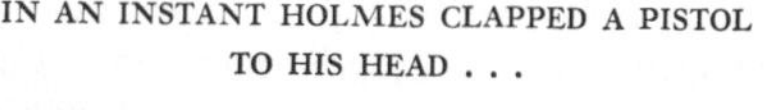

IN AN INSTANT HOLMES CLAPPED A PISTOL TO HIS HEAD . . .

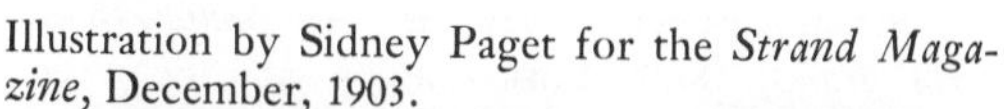

Illustration by Sidney Paget for the *Strand Magazine*, December, 1903.

"It is a privilege to be associated with you in the handling of a case," said the Inspector warmly. "You will excuse me, however, if I speak frankly to you. You are only answerable to yourself, but I have to answer to my superiors. If this Abe Slaney, living at Elrige's, is indeed the murderer, and if he has made his escape while I am seated here, I should certainly get into serious trouble."

"You need not be uneasy. He will not try to escape."

"How do you know?"

"To fly would be a confession of guilt."

"Then let us go to arrest him."

"I expect him here every instant."

"But why should he come?"

"Because I have written and asked him."

"But this is incredible, Mr. Holmes! Why should he come because you have asked him? Would not such a request rather rouse his suspicions and cause him to fly?"

"I think I have known how to frame the letter," said Sherlock Holmes. "In fact, if I am not very much mistaken, here is the gentleman himself coming up the drive."

A man was striding up the path which led to the door. He was a tall, handsome, swarthy fellow, clad in a suit of grey flannel, with a Panama hat, a bristling black beard, and a great, aggressive, hooked nose, and flourishing a cane as he walked. He swaggered up the path as if the place belonged to him, and we heard his loud, confident peal at the bell.

"I think, gentlemen," said Holmes quietly, "that we had best take up our position behind the door. Every precaution is necessary when dealing with such a fellow. You will need your handcuffs, Inspector. You can leave the talking to me."

We waited in silence for a minute—one of those minutes which one can never forget. Then the door opened, and the man stepped in. In an instant Holmes clapped a pistol to his head, and Martin slipped the handcuffs over his wrists. It was all done so swiftly and deftly that the fellow was helpless before he knew that he was attacked.

He glared from one to the other of us with a pair of blazing black eyes. Then he burst into a bitter laugh.

" Well, gentlemen, you have the drop on me this time. I seem to have knocked up against something hard. But I came here in answer to a letter from Mrs. Hilton Cubitt. Don't tell me that she is in this ? Don't tell me that she helped to set a trap for me ? "

" Mrs. Hilton Cubitt was seriously injured, and is at death's door."

The man gave a hoarse cry of grief which rang through the house.

" You're crazy ! " he cried fiercely. " It was he that was hurt, not she. Who would have hurt little Elsie ? I may have threatened her, God forgive me, but I would not have touched a hair of her pretty head. Take it back—you ! Say that she is not hurt ! "

" She was found badly wounded by the side of her dead husband."

He sank with a deep groan on to the settee, and buried his face in his manacled hands. For five minutes he was silent. Then he raised his face once more, and spoke with the cold composure of despair.

" I have nothing to hide from you, gentlemen," said he. " If I shot the man he had his shot at me, and there's no murder in that. But if you think I could have hurt that woman, then you don't know either me or her. I tell you there was never a man in this world loved a woman more than I loved her. I had a right to her. She was pledged to me years ago. Who was this Englishman that he should come between us ? I tell you that I had the first right to her, and that I was only claiming my own."

" She broke away from your influence when she found the man that you are," said Holmes sternly. "She fled from America to avoid you, and she married an honourable gentleman in England. You dogged her and followed her, and made her life a misery to her in order to induce her to abandon the husband whom she loved and respected in order to fly with you, whom she feared and hated. You have ended by bringing about the death of a noble man and driving his wife to suicide. That is your record in this business, Mr. Abe Slaney, and you will answer for it to the law."

" If Elsie dies I care nothing what becomes of me," said the American. He opened one of his hands and looked at a note crumpled up in his palm. " See here, mister," he cried, with a gleam of suspicion in his eyes, " you're not trying to scare me over this, are you ? If the lady is hurt as bad as you say, who was it that wrote this note ? " He tossed it forward on to the table.

" I wrote it to bring you here."

" You wrote it ? There was no one on earth outside the Joint who knew the secret of the dancing men. How came you to write it ? "

" What one man can invent another can discover," said Holmes. " There is a cab coming to convey you to Norwich, Mr. Slaney. But, meanwhile, you have time to make some small reparation for the injury you have wrought. Are you aware that Mrs. Hilton Cubitt has herself lain under grave suspicion of the murder of her

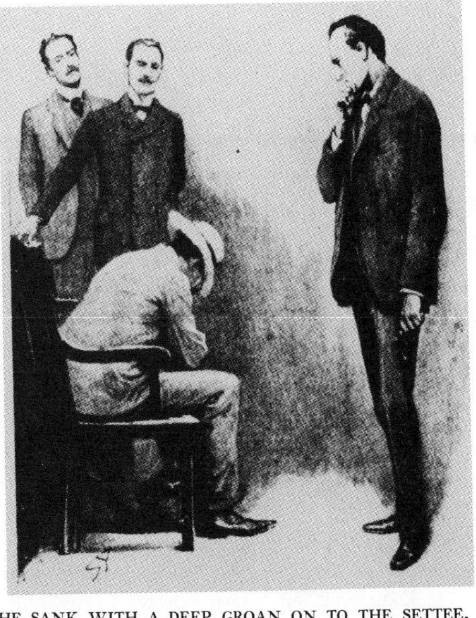

HE SANK WITH A DEEP GROAN ON TO THE SETTEE, AND BURIED HIS FACE IN HIS MANACLED HANDS.

Illustration by Sidney Paget for the *Strand Magazine*, December, 1903.

husband, and that it was only my presence here and the knowledge which I happened to possess which has saved her from the accusation ? The least that you owe her is to make it clear to the whole world that she was in no way directly or indirectly responsible for his tragic end."

" I ask nothing better," said the American. " I guess the very best case I can make for myself is the absolute naked truth."

" It is my duty to warn you that it will be used against you," cried the Inspector, with the magnificent fair-play of the British criminal law.

Slaney shrugged his shoulders.

" I'll chance that," said he. " First of all, I want you gentlemen to understand that I have known this lady since she was a child. There were seven of us in a gang in Chicago, and Elsie's father was the boss of the Joint. He was a clever man, was old Patrick. It was he who
16 invented that writing, which would pass as a child's scrawl unless you just happened to have the key to it. Well, Elsie learned some of our ways ; but she couldn't stand the business, and she had a bit of honest money of her own, so she gave us all the slip and got away to London. She had been engaged to me, and she would have married me, I believe, if I had taken over another profession ; but she would have nothing to do with anything on the cross. It was only after her marriage to this Englishman that I was able to find out where she was. I wrote to her, but got no answer. After that I came over, and, as letters were of no use, I put my messages where she could read them.

" Well, I have been here a month now. I lived in that farm, where I had a room down below, and could get in and out every night, and no one the wiser. I tried all I could to coax Elsie away. I knew that she read the messages, for once she wrote an answer under one of them. Then my temper got the better of me, and I began to threaten her. She sent me a letter then, imploring me to go away, and saying that it would break her heart if any scandal should come upon her husband. She said that she would come down when her husband was asleep at three in the morning, and speak with me through the end window, if I would go away afterwards and leave her in peace. She came down and brought money with her, trying to bribe me to go. This made me mad, and I caught her arm and tried to pull her through the window. At that moment in rushed the husband with his revolver in his hand. Elsie had sunk down upon the floor, and we were face to face. I was heeled also, and I held up my gun to scare him off and let me get away. He fired and missed me. I pulled off almost at the same instant, and down he dropped. I made away across the garden, and as I went I heard the window shut behind me. That's God's truth, gentlemen, every word of it, and I heard no more about it until that lad came riding up with a note which made me walk in here, like a jay, and give myself into your hands."

16 *It was he who invented that writing.* In the year 1903, Sir Arthur Conan Doyle stayed briefly at Hill House Hotel at Happisburgh, near Norwich. Asked to sign an autograph book, he saw in it a signature and address written in "dancing men" by G. J. Cubitt, the proprietor's son, then about seven. Conan Doyle then and there set to work upon "The Adventure of the Dancing Men," using not only the cipher but the name Cubitt for the central character in his tale. Neither Mr. Cubitt nor Sir Arthur ever claimed to have *invented* the cipher, and it is certainly possible, as some commentators have claimed, that it originated with the "Restless Imps" which appeared in *St. Nicholas Magazine* for June, 1874. On the other hand, the late Professor Jay Finley Christ demonstrated ("The Dancing Men") that "there is only one instance in which even approximately similar characters are used in the two alphabets." A cipher very similar to *St. Nicholas*' "Restless Imps" is also said to have appeared in the *Boy's Own Paper* in 1881 as "The Restless Fays." It is interesting to note that Conan Doyle contributed at least two stories to the *Boy's Own Paper:* "The Fate of the *Evangeline*" appeared in the Christmas number for 1885 and "The Stone of Boxman's Drift" somewhat later on. The late William Swift Dalliba found still another possible source of the "dancing men" in the book *Secret Missions of the Civil War*, by Philip Van Doren Stern, New York: Bonanza Books, 1959: "Major Alfred J. Meyer, Signal Corps of the Union Army . . . wrote a book, *A Manual of Signals,* in 1864. In this second edition, 1866, he described various methods of transferring letters of the alphabet into signals that can be sent by flags, etc. Then in order to show that practically anything can be used to convey a secret message, he printed a pictograph based on what he calls 'ludicrous sketches of little figures of men.' A similar device was used by Conan Doyle in his Sherlock Holmes story 'The Adventure of the Dancing Men'; Doyle is said to have gotten the idea for his grotesque cipher from the Carbonari, an early nineteenth-century Italian secret society, but he may very well have seen Meyer's book." To add to the confusion, Professor Christ also noted similarities between the Dancing Men cipher and a tree alphabet and "Alphabet of Hermes" illustrated in Albert Mackey's *Encyclopedia of Freemasonry* (1874).

A cab had driven up whilst the American had been talking. Two uniformed policemen sat inside. Inspector Martin rose and touched his prisoner on the shoulder.

" It is time for us to go."

" Can I see her first ? "

" No, she is not conscious. Mr. Sherlock Holmes, I only hope that if ever again I have an important case I shall have the good fortune to have you by my side."

We stood at the window and watched the cab drive away. As I turned back my eye caught the pellet of paper which the prisoner had tossed upon the table. It was the note with which Holmes had decoyed him.

" See if you can read it, Watson," said he, with a smile.

It contained no word, but this little line of dancing men :

" If you use the code which I have explained," said Holmes, " you will find that it simply means ' Come here at once.' I was convinced that it was an invitation which he would not refuse, since he could never imagine that it could come from anyone but the lady. And so, my dear Watson, we have ended by turning the dancing men to good when they have so often been the agents of evil, and I think that I have fulfilled my promise of giving you something unusual for your notebook. Three-
forty is our train, and I fancy we should be back in **17**
Baker Street for dinner."

Only one word of epilogue.

The American, Abe Slaney, was condemned to death at the winter assizes at Norwich ; but his penalty was changed to penal servitude in consideration of mitigating circumstances, and the certainty that Hilton Cubitt had fired the first shot.

Of Mrs. Hilton Cubitt I only know that I have heard she recovered entirely, and that she still remains a widow, devoting her whole life to the care of the poor and to the administration of her husband's estate.

17 *Three-forty is our train.* There unhappily was no such train—nor was there the earlier "one-twenty" to Liverpool Street.

Auctorial and Bibliographical Note: Conan Doyle placed "The Adventure of the Dancing Men" high on his "twelve best" list—he rated it No. 3. The original manuscript, donated by Sir Arthur to a Red Cross Charity Sale, was auctioned in London on April 22, 1918, bringing £10 10s. It was auctioned again in New York City on February 13, 1923, bringing $105, and again in London on January 28, 1925, where it was sold in one lot with "The Adventure of the Priory School" and "The Adventure of the Solitary Cyclist" for £66. Its present location is unknown.

62

THE ADVENTURE OF THE RETIRED COLOURMAN

[Thursday, July 28, to Saturday, July 30, 1898]

SHERLOCK HOLMES was in a melancholy and philosophic mood that morning. His alert practical nature was subject to such reactions.

" Did you see him ? " he asked.

" You mean the old fellow who has just gone out ? "

" Precisely."

" Yes, I met him at the door."

" What did you think of him ? "

" A pathetic, futile, broken creature."

" Exactly, Watson. Pathetic and futile. But is not all life pathetic and futile ? Is not his story a microcosm of the whole ? We reach. We grasp. And what is left in our hands at the end ? A shadow. Or worse than a
1 shadow—misery."

" Is he one of your clients ? "

" Well, I suppose I may call him so. He has been sent on by the Yard. Just as medical men occasionally send their incurables to a quack. They argue that they can do nothing more, and that whatever happens the patient can be no worse than he is."

" What is the matter ? "

Holmes took a rather soiled card from the table. " Josiah Amberley. He says he was junior partner of Brickfall & Amberley, who are manufacturers of artistic materials. You will see their names upon paint-boxes. He made his little pile, retired from business at the age
2 of sixty-one, bought a house at Lewisham, and settled down to rest after a life of ceaseless grind. One would think his future was tolerably assured."

" Yes, indeed."

Holmes glanced over some notes which he had scribbled upon the back of an envelope.

" Retired in 1896, Watson. Early in 1897 he married a woman twenty years younger than himself—a good-looking woman, too, if the photograph does not flatter. A competence, a wife, leisure—it seemed a straight road
3 which lay before him. And yet within two years he is, as you have seen, as broken and miserable a creature as crawls beneath the sun."

" But what has happened ? "

" The old story, Watson. A treacherous friend and a fickle wife. It would appear that Amberley has one hobby in life, and it is chess. Not far from him at Lewisham there lives a young doctor who is also a chess-

1 *Or worse than a shadow—misery.*" "These depressing reflections are not typical of Holmes, although the tragic might move him to philosophic melancholy, as we see in the Boscombe Valley case, and over the wretched story of Browner in 'The Cardboard Box,' " Mr. T. S. Blakeney wrote in *Sherlock Holmes: Fact or Fiction?*

2 *Lewisham.* An extensive metropolitan borough of London, now the third largest borough in area of the County of London. A century ago it was an attractive village, with a branch of the River Ravensbourne running alongside its main street. With the land rising gently on either side of the stream, it was then a very pleasant rural district.

3 *And yet within two years.* The year of the adventure, then, is 1898.

player. I have noted his name as Dr. Ray Ernest. Ernest was frequently in the house, and an intimacy between him and Mrs. Amberley was a natural sequence, for you must admit that our unfortunate client has few outward graces, whatever his inner virtues may be. The couple went off together last week—destination untraced. What is more, the faithless spouse carried off the old man's deed-box as her personal luggage with a good part of his life's savings within. Can we find the lady ? Can we save the money ? A commonplace problem so far as it has developed, and yet a vital one for Josiah Amberley."

" What will you do about it ? "

" Well, the immediate question, my dear Watson, happens to be, What will *you* do ?—if you will be good enough to understudy me. You know that I am preoccupied with this case of the two Coptic Patriarchs, 4
which should come to a head to-day. I really have not time to go out to Lewisham, and yet evidence taken on the spot has a special value. The old fellow was quite insistent that I should go, but I explained my difficulty. He is prepared to meet a representative."

" By all means," I answered. " I confess I don't see that I can be of much service, but I am willing to do my best." And so it was that on a summer afternoon I set forth to Lewisham, little dreaming that within a week the affair in which I was engaging would be the eager debate of all England.

It was late that evening before I returned to Baker Street and gave an account of my mission. Holmes lay with his gaunt figure stretched in his deep chair, his pipe curling forth slow wreaths of acrid tobacco, while his eyelids drooped over his eyes so lazily that he might almost have been asleep were it not that at any halt or questionable passage of my narrative they half lifted, and two grey eyes, as bright and keen as rapiers, transfixed me with their searching glance.

" The Haven is the name of Mr. Josiah Amberley's house," I explained. " I think it would interest you, Holmes. It is like some penurious patrician who has sunk into the company of his inferiors. You know that particular quarter, the monotonous brick streets, the weary suburban highways. Right in the middle of them, a little island of ancient culture and comfort, lies this old home, surrounded by a high sun-baked wall mottled with lichens and topped with moss, the sort of wall ——"

" Cut out the poetry, Watson," said Holmes severely. " I note that it was a high brick wall."

" Exactly. I should not have known which was The Haven had I not asked a lounger who was smoking in the street. I have a reason for mentioning him. He was a tall, dark, heavily-moustached, rather military-looking man. He nodded in answer to my inquiry and gave me a curiously questioning glance, which came back to my memory a little later.

" I had hardly entered the gateway before I saw Mr. Amberley coming down the drive. I only had a glimpse

4 *this case of the two Coptic Patriarchs.* "Patriarchs of the Coptic Church must by rule and tradition be plain, hard-working monks, chosen from the desert monasteries," Mr. John A. Wilson noted in a pastiche stemming from this reference of Holmes' ("The Case of the Two Coptic Patriarchs," The *Baker Street Journal*, Vol. IV, No. 1, Old Series, January, 1949, pp. 74–85).

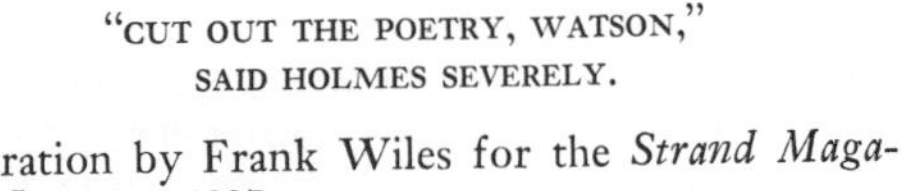

"CUT OUT THE POETRY, WATSON," SAID HOLMES SEVERELY.

Illustration by Frank Wiles for the *Strand Magazine*, January, 1927.

of him this morning, and he certainly gave me the impression of a strange creature, but when I saw him in full light his appearance was even more abnormal."

"I have, of course, studied it, and yet I should be interested to have your impression," said Holmes.

"He seemed to me like a man who was literally bowed down by care. His back was curved as though he carried a heavy burden. Yet he was not the weakling that I had at first imagined, for his shoulders and chest have the framework of a giant, though his figure tapers away into a pair of spindled legs."

"Left shoe wrinkled, right one smooth."

"I did not observe that."

"No, you wouldn't. I spotted his artificial limb. But proceed."

"I was struck by the snaky locks of grizzled hair which curled from under his old straw hat, and his face with its fierce, eager expression and the deeply-lined features."

"Very good, Watson. What did he say?"

"He began pouring out the story of his grievances. We walked down the drive together, and of course I took a good look round. I have never seen a worse-kept place. The garden was all running to seed, giving me an impression of wild neglect in which the plants had been allowed to find the way of nature rather than of art. How any decent woman could have tolerated such a state of things, I don't know. The house, too, was slatternly to the last degree, but the poor man seemed himself to be aware of it and to be trying to remedy it, for a great pot of green paint stood in the centre of the hall and he was carrying a thick brush in his left hand. He had been working on the woodwork.

"He took me into his dingy sanctum, and we had a long chat. Of course, he was disappointed that you had not come yourself. 'I hardly expected,' he said, 'that so humble an individual as myself, especially after my heavy financial loss, could obtain the complete attention of so famous a man as Mr. Sherlock Holmes.'

"I assured him that the financial question did not arise. 'No, of course, it is art for art's sake with him,' said he; 'but even on the artistic side of crime he might have found something here to study. And human nature, Dr. Watson—the black ingratitude of it all! When did I ever refuse one of her requests? Was ever a woman so pampered? And that young man—he might have been my own son. He had the run of my house. And yet see how they have treated me! Oh, Dr. Watson, it is a dreadful, dreadful world!'

"That was the burden of his song for an hour or more. He had, it seems, no suspicion of an intrigue. They lived alone save for a woman who comes in by the day and leaves every evening at six. On that particular evening old Amberley, wishing to give his wife a treat, had taken two upper circle seats at the Haymarket
5 Theatre. At the last moment she had complained of a headache and had refused to go. He had gone alone. There seemed to be no doubt about the fact, for he produced the unused ticket which he had taken for his wife."

"That is remarkable—most remarkable," said Holmes,

5 *the Haymarket Theatre.* Opened December, 1720, the Haymarket Theatre stood on the right of the Haymarket, the street so called from the market for hay and straw which was held there in the reign of Elizabeth I, and was not finally abolished until 1830. Addison lived in the Haymarket, and wrote his *Campaign* there; certainly Holmes' records of crime would have included an account of the murder, at the foot of the Haymarket, of Thomas Thynne of Longleat on Sunday, February 12, 1681; the villain in the case was Count Königsmarck, who hoped, when Thynne was out of the way, to ingratiate himself with his affianced bride, the rich, young Lady Elizabeth Percy, already, in her sixteenth year, the widow of Lord Ogle.

The late H. W. Bell noted that the Haymarket Theatre, in the summer of 1898, was playing Sir James M. Barrie's *The Little Minister. But the play closed on Friday, July 22nd.* The "sun-baked wall" around Amberley's house, the "garden . . . all running to seed" point to late July; almost certainly, Amberley must have purchased his seats for a night in the closing week of the play, Monday, July 18th, to Friday, July 22nd. Mrs. Amberley and her lover "disappeared" on the night for which the tickets were purchased—and Holmes tells us that "The couple went off together last week." The case began, then, on a day in the week of Monday, July 25, to Saturday, July 30, 1898. It occupied three days—none of which would seem to have been a Sunday: 1) On the evening of the first day, Holmes invited Watson to hear Carina sing at the Albert Hall—an event which would not have taken place on a Sunday in the 1890's. 2) On the second day, Watson and Amberley paid a call on Vicar Elman, something Holmes would not have suggested their doing on a Sunday. 3) On the third day, Watson asked Amberley to "take Baker Street as we pass . . . Mr. Holmes may have fresh instructions." Watson would not have made such a suggestion on a Sunday. The three-day period under consideration is therefore: Monday-Wednesday; Tuesday-Thursday; Wednesday-Friday; Thursday-Saturday. Monday-Wednesday is extremely unlikely: this would place both the taking of Amberley and Holmes' interview with Hilton Cubitt ("The Adventure of the Dancing Men") on Wednesday, July 27th. Tuesday-Thursday is quite impossible: the interview with Cubitt could not have taken place on the second day of "The Adventure of the Retired Colourman," when Watson did not see Holmes until three o'clock in the afternoon, and then proceeded to pay his call on Vicar Elman with Amberley, not returning to Baker Street until the following morning. We may also eliminate Wednesday-Friday: the by-weekly North Surrey *Observer* reported the solution of the case "a couple of days" after the concluding day; on whatever day the *Observer* was published, it was certainly not Sunday. In short, our vote is cast for *Thursday, July 28–Saturday, July 30, 1898.*

whose interest in the case seemed to be rising. " Pray continue, Watson. I find your narrative most arresting. Did you personally examine this ticket ? You did not, perchance, take the number ? "

" It so happens that I did," I answered with some pride. " It chanced to be my old school number, thirty-one, and so it stuck in my head."

" Excellent, Watson ! His seat, then, was either thirty or thirty-two."

" Quite so," I answered, with some mystification. " And on B row."

" That is most satisfactory. What else did he tell you ? "

" He showed me his strong-room, as he called it. It really is a strong-room—like a bank—with iron door and shutter—burglar-proof, as he claimed. However, the woman seems to have had a duplicate key, and between them they had carried off some seven thousand pounds' worth of cash and securities."

" Securities ! How could they dispose of those ? "

" He said that he had given the police a list and that he hoped they would be unsaleable. He had got back from the theatre about midnight, and found the place plundered, the door and window open and the fugitives gone. There was no letter or message, nor has he heard a word since. He at once gave the alarm to the police."

Holmes brooded for some minutes.

" You say he was painting. What was he painting ? "

" Well, he was painting the passage. But he had already painted the door and woodwork of this room I spoke of."

" Does it not strike you as a strange occupation in the circumstances ? "

" ' One must do something to ease an aching heart.' That was his own explanation. It was eccentric, no doubt, but he is clearly an eccentric man. He tore up one of his wife's photographs in my presence—tore it up furiously in a tempest of passion. ' I never wish to see her damned face again,' he shrieked."

" Anything more, Watson ? "

" Yes, one thing which struck me more than anything else. I had driven to the Blackheath Station and had caught my train there, when just as it was starting I saw a man dart into the carriage next to my own. You know that I have a quick eye for faces, Holmes. It was undoubtedly the tall, dark man whom I had addressed in the street. I saw him once more at London Bridge, and then I lost him in the crowd. But I am convinced that he was following me."

" No doubt ! No doubt ! " said Holmes. " A tall, dark, heavily-moustached man, you say, with grey-tinted sun-glasses ? "

" Holmes, you are a wizard. I did not say so, but he *had* grey-tinted sun-glasses."

" And a Masonic tie-pin ? "

" Holmes ! "

" Quite simple, my dear Watson. But let us get down to what is practical. I must admit to you that the case, which seemed to me to be so absurdly simple as to be hardly worth my notice, is rapidly assuming a very

"HE TORE UP ONE OF HIS WIFE'S PHOTOGRAPHS IN MY PRESENCE . . ."

Illustration by Frank Wiles for the *Strand Magazine*, January, 1927. Frederic Dorr Steele illustrated the same scene for *Liberty Magazine*, December 18, 1926.

different aspect. It is true that though in your mission you have missed everything of importance, yet even those things which have obtruded themselves upon your notice give rise to serious thought."

"What have I missed?"

"Don't be hurt, my dear fellow. You know that I am quite impersonal. No one else would have done better. Some possibly not so well. But clearly you have missed some vital points. What is the opinion of the neighbours about this man Amberley and his wife? That surely is of importance. What of Dr. Ernest? Was he the gay Lothario one would expect? With your natural advantages, Watson, every lady is your helper and accomplice. What about the girl at the post office, or the wife of the greengrocer? I can picture you whispering soft nothings with the young lady at the 'Blue Anchor,' and receiving hard somethings in exchange. All this you have left undone."

"It can still be done."

6 "It has been done. Thanks to the telephone and the help of the Yard, I can usually get my essentials without leaving this room. As a matter of fact, my information confirms the man's story. He has the local repute of being a miser as well as a harsh and exacting husband. That he had a large sum of money in that strong-room of his is certain. So also is it that young Dr. Ernest, an unmarried man, played chess with Amberley, and probably played the fool with his wife. All this seems plain sailing, and one would think that there was no more to be said—and yet!—and yet!"

"Where lies the difficulty?"

"In my imagination, perhaps. Well, leave it there, Watson. Let us escape from this weary workaday world by the side door of music. Carina sings to-night at the
7 Albert Hall, and we still have time to dress, dine and enjoy."

In the morning I was up betimes, but some toast crumbs and two empty egg-shells told me that my companion was earlier still. I found a scribbled note upon the table.

DEAR WATSON,—

There are one or two points of contact which I should wish to establish with Mr. Josiah Amberley. When I have done so we can dismiss the case—or not. I would only ask you to be on hand about three o'clock, as I conceive it possible that I may want you.

S. H.

I saw nothing of Holmes all day, but at the hour named he returned, grave, preoccupied and aloof. At such times it was wiser to leave him to himself.

"Has Amberley been here yet?"

"No."

"Ah! I am expecting him."

He was not disappointed, for presently the old fellow arrived with a very worried and puzzled expression upon his austere face.

"I've had a telegram, Mr. Holmes. I can make

". . . YOUNG DR. ERNEST . . . PLAYED CHESS WITH AMBERLEY . . ."

Mr. Nathan L. Bengis, in his fascinating article, "Smothered Mate," has expressed his conviction that the Amberley tragedy was foreshadowed in two chess games played between Amberley and Dr. Ernest a month previous to Holmes' investigation. In them, Dr. Ernest won Amberley's queen (that is, his wife) and in retaliation Amberley sacrificed his queen (that is, his wife) to inflict death by suffocation (that is, smothered mate) on both her and her king (that is, Dr. Ernest). The end-positions of the two games are shown here.

6 *Thanks to the telephone.* Here is the telephone in Baker Street at last. And once installed, it was evidently there to stay: in "The Adventure of the Three Garridebs," in 1902, Watson writes: "the telephone directory lay on the table beside me . . ." "Just ring him up, Watson," says Sherlock Holmes. In "The Adventure of the Illustrious Client," also in 1902, Holmes says that "the General 'phoned that all was ready" and adds "but, in case of emergency, there is a private telephone call, XX.31."

7 *Carina sings to-night at the Albert Hall.* The Albert Hall, a vast elliptical building of brick, with terra-cotta decorations, was commenced in 1867. "This huge pile has no beauty, except in the

nothing of it." He handed it over, and Holmes read it aloud.

" Come at once without fail. Can give you information as to your recent loss.—ELMAN. The Vicarage."

" Dispatched at two-ten from Little Purlington," said Holmes. " Little Purlington is in Essex, I believe, not far from Frinton. Well, of course you will start at once. This is evidently from a responsible person, the vicar of
the place. Where is my Crockford ? Yes, here we have 8
him. J. C. Elman, M.A., Living of Mossmoor-cum-Little Purlington. Look up the trains, Watson."

" There is one at five-twenty from Liverpool Street." 9

" Excellent. You had best go with him, Watson. He may need help or advice. Clearly we have come to a crisis in this affair."

But our client seemed by no means eager to start.

" It's perfectly absurd, Mr. Holmes," he said. " What can this man possibly know of what has occurred ? It is waste of time and money."

" He would not have telegraphed to you if he did not know something. Wire at once that you are coming."

" I don't think I shall go."

Holmes assumed his sternest aspect.

" It would make the worst possible impression both on the police and upon myself, Mr. Amberley, if when so obvious a clue arose you should refuse to follow it up. We should feel that you were not really in earnest in this investigation."

Our client seemed horrified at the suggestion.

" Why, of course I shall go if you look at it in that way," said he. " On the face of it, it seems absurd to suppose that this parson knows anything, but if you think——"

" I *do* think," said Holmes, with emphasis, and so we were launched upon our journey. Holmes took me aside before we left the room and gave me one word of counsel which showed that he considered the matter to be of importance. " Whatever you do, see that he really *does* go," said he. " Should he break away or return, get to the nearest telephone exchange and send the single word ' Bolted.' I will arrange here that it shall reach me wherever I am."

Little Purlington is not an easy place to reach, for it is on a branch line. My remembrance of the journey is not a pleasant one, for the weather was hot, the train slow, and my companion sullen and silent, hardly talking at all, save to make an occasional sardonic remark as to the futility of our proceedings. When we at last reached the little station it was a two-mile drive before we came to the Vicarage, where a big, solemn, rather pompous clergyman received us in his study. Our telegram lay before him.

" Well, gentlemen," he asked, " what can I do for you ? "

" We came," I explained, " in answer to your wire."

" My wire ! I sent no wire."

" I mean the wire which you sent to Mr. Josiah Amberley about his wife and his money."

porches, which are exceedingly grandiose in form and effective in shadow and colour," Augustus J. C. Hare wrote in his *Walks in London*, Vol. II.

As for Carina—all scholars to date have unanimously failed to identify any singer of the period with that name. Mr. Guy Warrack's attempt (*Sherlock Holmes and Music*) to identify her with Annie Louise Cary is, as he says, "tempting" but inconclusive. However, Mr. Anthony Boucher has written ("The Records of Baker Street"): "Observe three things—1) that every other musician referred to in the Canon is of great historical eminence; 2) that all research has thus far failed to unearth a singer named Carina; 3) that *carina* is a common enough Italian term of endearment, roughly equivalent to *darling*. Who this *carina* of Holmes' was can never be ascertained certainly." But may we surmise again that Watson was wrong in calling *the* woman "the late" Irene Adler?

8 *Where is my Crockford?* "Crockford's *Clerical Directory* was on Holmes' shelf by 1898, when he took the name of J. C. Elman from it in connection with 'The Adventure of the Retired Colourman,'" Miss Madeleine B. Stern noted in "Sherlock Holmes: Rare Book Collector."

9 *"There is one at five-twenty from Liverpool Street."* Watson's Bradshaw is playing him false again: there was no 5:20 train from Liverpool Street to Little Purlington—perhaps because there was no Little Purlington.

"IF THIS IS A JOKE, SIR, IT IS A VERY QUESTIONABLE ONE," SAID THE VICAR ANGRILY.

Illustration by Frank Wiles for the *Strand Magazine*, January, 1927.

" If this is a joke, sir, it is a very questionable one," said the vicar angrily. " I have never heard of the gentleman you name, and I have not sent a wire to anyone."

Our client and I looked at each other in amazement.

" Perhaps there is some mistake," said I ; " are there perhaps two vicarages ? Here is the wire itself, signed Elman, and dated from the Vicarage."

" There is only one vicarage, sir, and only one vicar, and this wire is a scandalous forgery, the origin of which shall certainly be investigated by the police. Meanwhile, I can see no possible object in prolonging this interview."

So Mr. Amberley and I found ourselves on the road-
side in what seemed to me to be the most primitive
10 village in England. We made for the telegraph office,
but it was already closed. There was a telephone, however, at the little ' Railway Arms,' and by it I got into touch with Holmes, who shared in our amazement at the result of our journey.

" Most singular ! " said the distant voice. " Most remarkable ! I much fear, my dear Watson, that there is no return train to-night. I have unwittingly condemned you to the horrors of a country inn. However, there is always Nature, Watson—Nature and Josiah Amberley—you can be in close commune with both." I heard his dry chuckle as he turned away.

It was soon apparent to me that my companion's reputation as a miser was not undeserved. He had grumbled at the expense of the journey, had insisted upon travelling third-class, and was now clamorous in his objections to the hotel bill. Next morning, when we did at last arrive in London, it was hard to say which of us was in the worse humour.

" You had best take Baker Street as we pass," said I. " Mr. Holmes may have some fresh instructions."

" If they are not worth more than the last ones they
are not of much use," said Amberley, with a malevolent
scowl. None the less, he kept me company. I had
11 already warned Holmes by telegram of the hour of our
arrival, but we found a message waiting that he was at Lewisham, and would expect us there. That was a surprise, but an even greater one was to find that he was not alone in the sitting-room of our client. A stern-looking, impassive man sat beside him, a dark man with grey-tinted glasses and a large Masonic pin projecting from his tie.

" This is my friend Mr. Barker," said Holmes. " He has been interesting himself also in your business, Mr. Josiah Amberley, though we have been working independently. But we both have the same question to ask you ! "

Mr. Amberley sat down heavily. He sensed impending danger. I read it in his straining eyes and his twitching features.

" What is the question, Mr. Holmes ? "

" Only this : What did you do with the bodies ? "

The man sprang to his feet with a hoarse scream. He

10 *We made for the telegraph office.* "We get the impression that [the telephone] is like a new toy to the Master. It is not so with Watson, however," Colonel E. Ennalls Berl wrote in "Sherlock Holmes and the Telephone."

11 *I had already warned Holmes by telegram.* Again, Watson's ingrained instinct leads him to the Post Office to handle the matter by telegram rather than by resorting once more to the telephone at the little Railway Arms.

clawed into the air with his bony hands. His mouth was open, and for the instant he looked like some horrible bird of prey. In a flash we got a glimpse of the real Josiah Amberley, a misshapen demon with a soul as distorted as his body. As he fell back into his chair he clapped his hand to his lips as if to stifle a cough. Holmes sprang at his throat like a tiger, and twisted his face towards the ground. A white pellet fell from between his gasping lips. 12

" No short cuts, Josiah Amberley. Things must be done decently and in order. What about it, Barker ? " 13

" I have a cab at the door," said our taciturn companion.

" It is only a few hundred yards to the station. We will go together. You can stay here, Watson. I shall be back within half an hour."

The old colourman had the strength of a lion in that great trunk of his, but he was helpless in the hands of the two experienced man-handlers. Wriggling and twisting he was dragged to the waiting cab, and I was left to my solitary vigil in the ill-omened house. In less time than he had named, however, Holmes was back, in company with a smart young police inspector.

" I've left Barker to look after the formalities," said Holmes. " You had not met Barker, Watson. He is my hated rival upon the Surrey shore. When you said a tall, dark man it was not difficult for me to complete the picture. He has several good cases to his credit, has he not, Inspector ? "

" He has certainly interfered several times," the Inspector answered with reserve.

" His methods are irregular, no doubt, like my own. The irregulars are useful sometimes, you know. You, for example, with your compulsory warning about whatever he said being used against him, could never have bluffed this rascal into what is virtually a confession." 14

" Perhaps not. But we get there all the same, Mr. Holmes. Don't imagine that we had not formed our own views of this case, and that we would not have laid our

THE MAN SPRANG TO HIS FEET WITH A HOARSE SCREAM.

Illustration by Frank Wiles for the *Strand Magazine*, January, 1927.

HOLMES SPRANG AT HIS THROAT LIKE A TIGER . . .

Illustration by Frederic Dorr Steele for *Liberty Magazine*, December 18, 1926.

12 *A white pellet fell from between his gasping lips.* "Cyanide of potassium is believed to be the intended suicide vehicle of Josiah Amberley," Dr. J. W. Sovine wrote in "The Toxicanon." "His poison was contained in a white pellet. Only an extremely rapid deadly poison effective in small dose would suffice for Josiah's purpose. Cyanide of potassium qualifies. In addition, as a colourman, Mr. Amberley would have had access to potassium cyanide or to potassium ferrocyanide, from which the cyanide can be easily prepared."

13 *Things must be done decently and in order.* "Let all things be done decently and in order."—I Corinthians 14.40.

14 *could never have bluffed this rascal into what is virtually a confession.*" "In England," Mr. Doyle W. Beckemeyer wrote in "The Irregular Holmes," "private detectives are . . . without [the] official status they have in the United States, because they are not licensed as they are here. Thus, they are not bound by Judges' Rules, nor by the laws of the land. . . . The English Police [on the other hand] operate under conditions designed to be so scrupulously fair to the suspect that one wonders how they ever get their man at all. In Holmes' day they often didn't; but they were wise enough to condone the irregular methods employed by Sherlock Holmes . . ."

15 *this man's mentality.* "It should be noted that Watson's account of the case was written long after the event," the late H. W. Bell noted in *Sherlock Holmes and Dr. Watson: The Chronology of Their Adventures.* "He puts into Holmes' mouth the neologism 'this man's mentality,' which could not possibly have been uttered in 1898." And Mr. D. Martin Dakin has added ("The Problem of the Case-Book"): "Mr. Bell has . . . pointed out that in 1895–9 Holmes could never have referred to 'this man's mentality,' and I have confirmed this from the Oxford Dictionary."

16 *one mark, Watson, of a scheming mind.*" We have noted that most students do not believe that Holmes was himself a player, although he studded his talk with chess terms and expressions. However, a very different view is held by Mr. Harold Schonberg, the music critic of *The New York Times.* Mr. Schonberg has shown ("Yet Another Case of Identity") that Holmes had good reasons for not wanting anyone to think that he knew the game: it was in 1895, Mr. Schonberg has pointed out, that the Brooklyn Chess Club sent young Harry Nelson Pillsbury to England to participate in the great tournament at Hastings. To everybody's amazement, Pillsbury took first prize. He never again won a major tournament, dying in 1906. "Nobody can understand this sudden flash of greatness. . . . A twenty-two-year-old unknown licked the cream of Europe's experts, trouncing such formidable masters as Lasker, Tarrasch, Tchigorin, Gunsberg and Mieses." The mystery is easily solved, Mr. Schonberg explained, if we suppose that it was not Pillsbury but "the finest analytical mind in Europe, the mind of one who had genius, infinite capacity for concentration, and a brilliant insight into chess. Suppose that it was Sherlock Holmes, the master of disguise, who impersonated Pillsbury [whom Holmes somewhat resembled] at Hastings, letting Pillsbury, on his own after that, sink to his normal level."

hands on our man. You will excuse us for feeling sore when you jump in with methods which we cannot use, and so rob us of the credit."

"There shall be no such robbery, MacKinnon. I assure you that I efface myself from now onwards, and as to Barker, he has done nothing save what I told him."

The Inspector seemed considerably relieved.

"That is very handsome of you, Mr. Holmes. Praise or blame can matter little to you, but it is very different to us when the newspapers begin to ask questions."

"Quite so. But they are pretty sure to ask questions anyhow, so it would be as well to have answers. What will you say, for example, when the intelligent and enterprising reporter asks you what the exact points were which aroused your suspicion, and finally gave you a certain conviction as to the real facts?"

The Inspector looked puzzled.

"We don't seem to have got any real facts yet, Mr. Holmes. You say that the prisoner, in the presence of three witnesses, practically confessed, by trying to commit suicide, that he had murdered his wife and her lover. What other facts have you?"

"Have you arranged for a search?"

"There are three constables on their way."

"Then you will soon get the clearest fact of all. The bodies cannot be far away. Try the cellars and the garden. It should not take long to dig up the likely places. This house is older than the water-pipes. There must be a disused well somewhere. Try your luck there."

"But how did you know of it, and how was it done?"

"I'll show you first how it was done, and then I
will give the explanation which is due to you, and even
more to my long-suffering friend here, who has been
invaluable throughout. But, first, I would give you an
15 insight into this man's mentality. It is a very unusual
one—so much so that I think his destination is more
likely to be Broadmoor than the scaffold. He has, to a
high degree, the sort of mind which one associates with the
mediæval Italian nature rather than with the modern
Briton. He was a miserable miser who made his wife
so wretched by his niggardly ways that she was a ready
prey for any adventurer. Such a one came upon the
scene in the person of this chess-playing doctor. Amberley excelled at chess—one mark, Watson, of a scheming
16 mind. Like all misers, he was a jealous man, and his
jealousy became a frantic mania. Rightly or wrongly,
he suspected an intrigue. He determined to have his
revenge, and he planned it with diabolical cleverness.
Come here!"

Holmes led us along the passage with as much certainty as if he had lived in the house, and halted at the open door of the strong-room.

"Pooh! What an awful smell of paint!" cried the Inspector.

"That was our first clue," said Holmes. "You can thank Dr. Watson's observation for that, though he failed to draw the inference. It set my foot upon the trail. Why should this man at such a time be filling his house with strong odours? Obviously, to cover some other smell which he wished to conceal—some guilty smell which would suggest suspicions. Then came the idea of a room such as you see here with iron door and shutter—a hermetically sealed room. Put those two facts together, and whither do they lead? I could only determine that by examining the house myself. I was already certain that the case was serious, for I had examined the box-office chart at the Haymarket Theatre—another of Dr. Watson's bull's-eyes—and ascertained that neither B thirty nor thirty-two of the upper circle had been occupied that night. Therefore, Amberley had not been to the theatre, and his alibi fell to the ground. He made a bad slip when he allowed my astute friend to notice the number of the seat taken for his wife. The question now arose how I might be able to examine the house. I sent an agent to the most impossible village I could think of, and summoned my man to it at such an hour that he could not possibly get back. To prevent any miscarriage, Dr. Watson accompanied him. The good vicar's name I took, of course, out of my Crockford. Do I make it all clear to you?"

"It is masterly," said the Inspector, in an awed voice.

"There being no fear of interruption I proceeded to
burgle the house. Burglary has always been an alter- 17
native profession, had I cared to adopt it, and I have little doubt that I should have come to the front. Observe what I found. You see the gas-pipe along the skirting here. Very good. It rises in the angle of the wall, and there is a tap here in the corner. The pipe runs out into the strong-room, as you can see, and ends in that plaster rose in the centre of the ceiling, where it is concealed by the ornamentation. That end is wide open. At any moment by turning the outside tap the room could be flooded with gas. With door and shutter closed and the tap full on I would not give two minutes of conscious sensation to anyone shut up in that little chamber. By what devilish device he decoyed them there I do not know, but once inside the door they were at his mercy."

17 *I proceeded to burgle the house.* But again Magistrate S. Tupper Bigelow has shown ("Sherlock Holmes Was No Burglar") that under the letter of the British law Holmes was guilty of neither burglary nor unlawful entry.

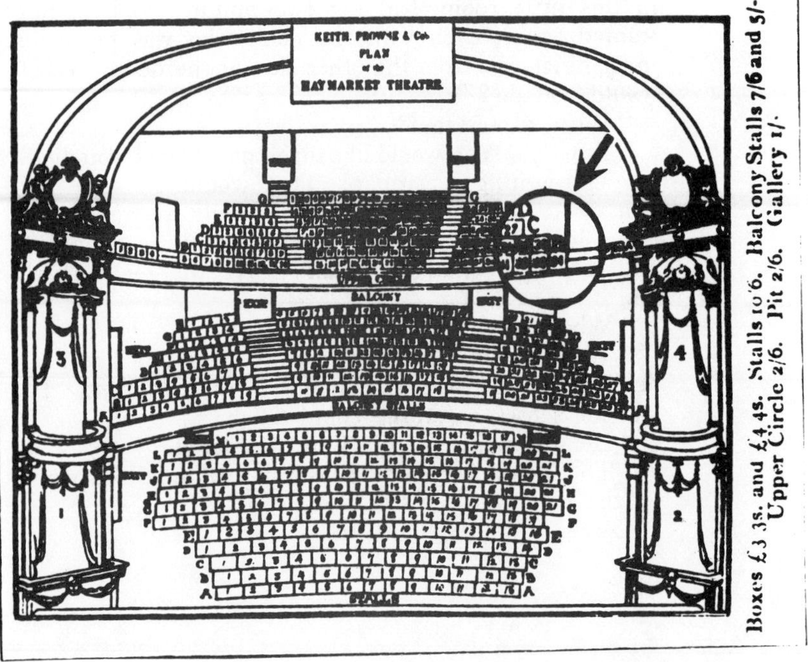

"... I HAD EXAMINED THE BOX-OFFICE CHART AT THE HAYMARKET THEATRE ..."

There is no seat numbered 31 (30 is the last number) in B row of the upper circle at the Haymarket Theatre—in spite of the fact that Watson told Holmes he had seen Josiah Amberley's unused ticket for that very seat. The diagram is from *The Combined Atlas and Guide of London*, H. Grube, Ltd., *c.* 1900.

"... I FELT A HAND INSIDE MY COLLAR ..."

Illustration by Frank Wiles for the *Strand Magazine*, January, 1927.

The Inspector examined the pipe with interest. "One of our officers mentioned the smell of gas," said he, "but, of course, the window and door were open then, and the paint—or some of it—was already about. He had begun the work of painting the day before, according to his story. But what next, Mr. Holmes?"

"Well, then came an incident which was rather unexpected to myself. I was slipping through the pantry window in the early dawn when I felt a hand inside my collar, and a voice said: 'Now, you rascal, what are you doing in there?' When I could twist my head round I looked into the tinted spectacles of my friend and rival, Mr. Barker. It was a curious forgathering, and set us both smiling. It seems that he had been engaged by Dr. Ray Ernest's family to make some investigations, and had come to the same conclusion as to foul play. He had watched the house for some days, and had spotted Dr. Watson as one of the obviously suspicious characters who had called there. He could hardly arrest Watson, but when he saw a man actually climbing out of the pantry window there came a limit to his restraint. Of course, I told him how matters stood and we continued the case together."

"Why him? Why not us?"

"Because it was in my mind to put that little test which answered so admirably. I fear you would not have gone so far."

The Inspector smiled.

"Well, maybe not. I understand that I have your word, Mr. Holmes, that you step right out of the case now and that you turn all your results over to us."

"Certainly, that is always my custom."

"Well, in the name of the Force I thank you. It seems a clear case, as you put it, and there can't be much difficulty over the bodies."

"I'll show you a grim little bit of evidence," said Holmes, "and I am sure Amberley himself never observed it. You'll get results, Inspector, by always putting yourself in the other fellow's place, and thinking what you would do yourself. It takes some imagination, but it pays. Now, we will suppose that you were shut up in this little room, had not two minutes to live, but wanted to get even with the fiend who was probably mocking at you from the other side of the door. What would you do?"

"Write a message."

"Exactly. You would like to tell people how you died. No use writing on paper. That would be seen. If you wrote on the wall some eye might rest upon it. Now, look here! Just above the skirting is scribbled with a purple indelible pencil: 'We we——' That's all."

"What do you make of that?"

"Well, it's only a foot above the ground. The poor devil was on the floor and dying when he wrote it. He lost his senses before he could finish."

"He was writing, 'We were murdered.'"

"That's how I read it. If you find an indelible pencil
18 on the body——"

18 *If you find an indelible pencil on the body—"* But how could the indelible pencil have found "a place on the *body* of the deceased Dr. Ray, as he himself could not be in a position to place it there as he gave up the ghost even before writing *four letters*," Mr. T. V. Ramamurthy has asked. "The chances of Amberley picking it up and placing the same on the body of Dr. Ray is most preposterous and unbelievable, as it will not do credit to the scheming brain of Amberley who has dared to consult not only the police but even Sherlock Holmes." We may add that the offending words "on the body" were wisely deleted by the editors of *Liberty Magazine* when "The Adventure of the Retired Colourman" appeared in that periodical.

" We'll look out for it, you may be sure. But those securities? Clearly there was no robbery at all. And yet he *did* possess those bonds. We verified that."

" You may be sure he has them hidden in a safe place. When the whole elopement had passed into history he would suddenly discover them, and announce that the guilty couple had relented and sent back the plunder or had dropped it on the way."

" You certainly seem to have met every difficulty," said the Inspector. " Of course, he was bound to call us in, but why he should have gone to you I can't understand."

" Pure swank!" Holmes answered. " He felt so clever and so sure of himself that he imagined no one could touch him. He could say to any suspicious neighbour, ' Look at the steps I have taken. I have consulted not only the police, but even Sherlock Holmes.' "

The Inspector laughed.

" We must forgive you your ' even,' Mr. Holmes," said he; " it's as workmanlike a job as I can remember."

A couple of days later my friend tossed across to me a copy of the bi-weekly *North Surrey Observer*. Under a series of flaming headlines, which began with " The Haven Horror " and ended with " Brilliant Police Investigation," there was a packed column of print which gave the first consecutive account of the affair. The concluding paragraph is typical of the whole. It ran thus:

" The remarkable acumen by which Inspector MacKinnon deduced from the smell of paint that some other smell, that of gas, for example, might be concealed; the bold deduction that the strong-room might also be the death-chamber, and the subsequent inquiry which led to the discovery of the bodies in a disused well, cleverly concealed by a dog-kennel, should live in the history of crime as a standing example of the intelligence of our professional detectives."

" Well, well, MacKinnon is a good fellow," said Holmes, with a tolerant smile. " You can file it in our archives, Watson. Some day the true story may be **19**
told."

19 *"You can file it in our archives, Watson.* Mr. D. Martin Dakin has questioned the "Canonicity" of this adventure "partly as it is a rather loosely constructed, inconsequential story and partly owing to the ambiguous part played by Barker—it is never quite clear whether he was an agent of Holmes' or a rival practitioner."

Bibliographical Note: The manuscript of "The Adventure of the Retired Colourman" was lent by Jean Conan Doyle to the Abbey House Sherlock Holmes Exhibition in 1951; it is presumably still in the possession of the Doyle Estate.

63

THE ADVENTURE OF CHARLES AUGUSTUS MILVERTON

[Thursday, January 5, to Saturday, January 14, 1899]

IT is years since the incidents of which I speak took place, and yet it is with diffidence that I allude to them. For a long time, even with the utmost discretion and reticence, it would have been impossible to make the facts public ; but now the principal person concerned is beyond the reach of human law, and with due suppression the story may be told in such fashion as to injure no one. It records an absolutely unique experience in the career both of Mr. Sherlock Holmes and of myself. The reader will excuse me if I conceal the date or any other fact by which he might trace the actual
1 occurrence.

We had been out for one of our evening rambles, Holmes and I, and had returned about six o'clock on a cold, frosty winter's evening. As Holmes turned up the lamp the light fell upon a card on the table. He glanced at it, and then, with an ejaculation of disgust, threw it on the floor. I picked it up and read :

CHARLES AUGUSTUS MILVERTON,
APPLEDORE TOWERS,
HAMPSTEAD.

Agent.

" Who is he ? " I asked.

" The worst man in London," Holmes answered, as he sat down and stretched his legs before the fire. " Is anything on the back of the card ? "

I turned it over.

" Will call at 6.30.—C. A. M.," I read.

" Hum ! He's about due. Do you feel a creeping, shrinking sensation, Watson, when you stand before the
2 serpents in the Zoo and see the slithery, gliding, venomous creatures, with their deadly eyes and wicked, flattened faces ? Well, that's how Milverton impresses me. I've
3 had to do with fifty murderers in my career, but the worst of them never gave me the repulsion which I have for this fellow. And yet I can't get out of doing business with him—indeed, he is here at my invitation."

" But who is he ? "

" I'll tell you, Watson. He is the king of all the blackmailers. Heaven help the man, and still more the woman, whose secret and reputation come into the power

1 *by which he might trace the actual occurrence.* Watson has to a great extent succeeded: there are few adventures about which chronologists are in greater disagreement (their suggested dates range from 1882 to 1899). "The Adventure of Charles Augustus Milverton" is thought by some to be one of the earliest adventures shared by Holmes and Watson; as many hold, and for good reasons, that it was one of the latest adventures.

Watson in this paragraph tells us that "It is years since the incidents of which I speak took place . . ." Since his account of the case was first published in *Collier's Magazine* for March 26, 1904, this statement, taken by itself, would seem to indicate that the adventure took place before or very soon after the Return.

Watson says he alludes to the incidents "with diffidence"—and Lawyer Irving M. Fenton has shown ("An Analysis of the Crimes and Near-Crimes at Appledore Towers in the Light of the English Criminal Law") that his phrase is well chosen: "In the light of the present English criminal law, we are presented [in this case] with what might be paradoxically termed a miniature omnibus of crime. All the principals are involved in one way or another."

Watson tells us that the principal person concerned "is beyond the reach of human law." It has usually been taken to mean that this implied the recent death of Milverton's executor, but Mr. L. W. Bailey has pointed out ("The Dark Lady of Appledore Towers") that "Watson's words could bear a more subtle explanation. The story was first published in April, 1904 [Mr. Bailey is speaking of its first *English* appearance—in the *Strand Magazine*]. Allowing for customary publication delays, therefore, it is likely Watson started to write it early in 1903. On the 26th of June, 1902, Edward VII had been crowned King of England, and had thus become technically above the law and so 'beyond its reach.' Is it not possible that by his choice of words Watson was hinting at a truth he dare not reveal, and into which even now it would be indelicate to probe any further?"

"THE WORST MAN IN LONDON . . ."

Two portraits of Charles Augustus Milverton: the first, by Sidney Paget, for the *Strand Magazine*, April, 1904; the second, by Frederic Dorr Steele, for *Collier's Magazine*, March 26, 1904. We may note, in addition, that Holmes in "The Adventure of the Empty House" (April, 1894) remarked to Watson that his collection of M's was a fine one. He named Moriarty and Moran, Morgan, Merridew and Mathews. If "The Adventure of Charles Augustus Milverton" took place *before* that time, it is curious that Holmes made no mention of "the worst man in London" as well as "the second most dangerous man in London."

of Milverton. With a smiling face and a heart of marble he will squeeze and squeeze until he has drained them dry. The fellow is a genius in his way, and would have made his mark in some more savoury trade. His method is as follows : He allows it to be known that he is prepared to pay very high sums for letters which compromise people of wealth or position. He receives these wares not only from treacherous valets or maids, but frequently from genteel ruffians who have gained the confidence and affection of trusting women. He deals with no niggard hand. I happen to know that he paid seven hundred pounds to a footman for a note two lines in length, and that the ruin of a noble family was the result. Everything which is in the market goes to Milverton, and there are hundreds in this great city who turn white at his name. No one knows where his grip may fall, for he is far too rich and far too cunning to work from hand to mouth. He will hold a card back for years in order to play it at the moment when the stake is best worth winning. I have said that he is the worst man in London, and I would ask you how could one compare the ruffian who in hot blood bludgeons his mate with this man, who methodically and at his leisure tortures the soul and wrings the nerves in order to add to his already swollen money-bags ? "

I had seldom heard my friend speak with such intensity of feeling.

" But surely," said I, " the fellow must be within the grasp of the law ? "

" Technically, no doubt, but practically not. What would it profit a woman, for example, to get him a few months' imprisonment if her own ruin must immediately follow ? His victims dare not hit back. If ever he blackmailed an innocent person, then, indeed, we should have him ; but he is as cunning as the Evil One. No, no ; we must find other ways to fight him."

" And why is he here ? "

" Because an illustrious client has placed her piteous case in my hands. It is the Lady Eva Brackwell, the most beautiful *débutante* of last season. She is to be married

2 *the Zoo.* Holmes refers to the wonderful Zoological Gardens on the northeast side of Regent's Park, founded in 1826. Admission in his day was 1s (6d on Mondays and holidays). The Gardens comprise thirty-four acres and have one of the largest and finest exhibits in the world; today they are visited annually by about two million people. It is unfortunate that the Zoo, in Holmes' day, did not have a panda on display, for it seems likely that Holmes would have encountered the animal during his Tibetan expedition, and would have been happy to renew its acquaintance.

3 *I've had to do with fifty murderers in my career.* Since Holmes had dealt with five hundred cases of capital importance by the autumn of 1888 (*The Hound of the Baskervilles*) and over a thousand cases by the spring of 1891 ("The Final Problem"), this case would seem to have taken place very soon after he and Watson began to share the rooms at 221B Baker Street. We take Holmes' statement here to be a red herring, deliberately inserted into the text by Watson to confuse the chronology of "Charles Augustus Milverton."

in a fortnight to the Earl of Dovercourt. This fiend has several imprudent letters—imprudent, Watson, nothing worse—which were written to an impecunious young squire in the country. They would suffice to break off the match. Milverton will send the letters to the earl unless a large sum of money is paid him. I have been commissioned to meet him, and—to make the best terms I can."

At that instant there was a clatter and a rattle in the street below. Looking down I saw a stately carriage and pair, the brilliant lamps gleaming on the glossy haunches of the noble chestnuts. A footman opened the door, and a small, stout man in a shaggy astrachan overcoat descended. A minute later he was in the room.

Charles Augustus Milverton was a man of fifty, with a large, intellectual head, a round, plump, hairless face, a perpetual frozen smile, and two keen grey eyes, which gleamed brightly from behind broad, golden-rimmed glasses. There was something of Mr. Pickwick's benevolence in his appearance, marred only by the insincerity of the fixed smile and by the hard glitter of those restless and penetrating eyes. His voice was as smooth and suave as his countenance, as he advanced with a plump little hand extended, murmuring his regret for having missed us at his first visit.

Holmes disregarded the outstretched hand and looked at him with a face of granite. Milverton's smile broadened ; he shrugged his shoulders, removed his overcoat, folded it with great deliberation over the back of a chair, and then took a seat.

" This gentleman," said he, with a wave in my direction. " Is it discreet ? Is it right ? "

" Dr. Watson is my friend and partner."

" Very good, Mr. Holmes. It is only in your client's interests that I protested. The matter is so very delicate——"

" Dr. Watson has already heard of it."

" Then we can proceed to business. You say that you are acting for Lady Eva. Has she empowered you to accept my terms ? "

" What are your terms ? "

4 " Seven thousand pounds."

" And the alternative ? "

" My dear sir, it is painful to me to discuss it ; but if the money is not paid on the 14th there certainly will be no
5 marriage on the 18th." His insufferable smile was more complacent than ever. Holmes thought for a little.

" You appear to me," he said at last, " to be taking matters too much for granted. I am, of course, familiar with the contents of these letters. My client will certainly do what I may advise. I shall counsel her to tell her future husband the whole story and to trust to his generosity."

Milverton chuckled.

" You evidently do not know the earl," said he.

From the baffled look upon Holmes' face I could clearly see that he did.

" What harm is there in the letters ? " he asked.

" They are sprightly—very sprightly," Milverton

4 "*Seven thousand pounds.*" "Milverton's insistence on £7,000 'or there will be no marriage on the 18th' falls into [the category of attempted extortion]. 'Attempt' is, of course, a crime per se," Lawyer Fenton noted.

5 *no marriage on the 18th.*" Watson has told us that the season was "winter." Milverton now tells us that Lady Eva Brackwell was to be married "on the 18th." That the month was December or March is possible but unlikely: December 18th would fall in Advent, March 18th in Lent, seasons in which marriages are frowned upon by the Church. Nevertheless, in the interest of complete accuracy, we will consider December and March with January and February in attempting to date this case. We have also seen (in "The Adventure of the Golden Pince-Nez") that Watson at least once spoke of November as a "winter" month. We must therefore take November, as well as December and March, into our calculations.

Since the marriage was to take place on the 18th, that day was not a Sunday. This eliminates December, 1898; February, 1900; March, 1900; and January, 1903.

answered. " The lady was a charming correspondent. But I can assure you that the Earl of Dovercourt would fail to appreciate them. However, since you think otherwise, we will let it rest at that. It is purely a matter of business. If you think that it is in the best interests of your client that these letters should be placed in the hands of the earl, then you would indeed be foolish to pay so large a sum of money to regain them." He rose and seized his astrachan coat.

Holmes was grey with anger and mortification.

" Wait a little," he said. " You go too fast. We would certainly make every effort to avoid scandal in so delicate a matter."

Milverton relapsed into his chair.

" I was sure that you would see it in that light," he purred.

" At the same time," Holmes continued, " Lady Eva is not a wealthy woman. I assure you that two thousand pounds would be a drain upon her resources, and that the sum you name is utterly beyond her power. I beg, therefore, that you will moderate your demands, and that you will return the letters at the price I indicate, which is, I assure you, the highest that you can get."

Milverton's smile broadened and his eyes twinkled humorously.

" I am aware that what you say is true about the lady's resources," said he. " At the same time, you must admit that the occasion of a lady's marriage is a very suitable time for her friends and relatives to make some little effort upon her behalf. They may hesitate as to an acceptable wedding present. Let me assure them that this little bundle of letters would give more joy than all the candelabra and butter-dishes in London."

" It is impossible," said Holmes.

" Dear me, dear me, how unfortunate ! " cried Milverton, taking out a bulky pocket-book. " I cannot help thinking that ladies are ill-advised in not making an effort. Look at this ! " He held up a little note with a coat-of-
arms upon the envelope. " That belongs to—well, 6
perhaps it is hardly fair to tell the name until to-morrow morning. But at that time it will be in the hands of the lady's husband. And all because she will not find a beggarly sum which she could get in an hour by turning her diamonds into paste. It *is* such a pity. Now, you remember the sudden end of the engagement between the Honourable Miss Miles and Colonel Dorking ? Only two days before the wedding there was a paragraph in the *Morning Post* to say that it was all off. And why ? It is almost incredible, but the absurd sum of twelve hundred pounds would have settled the whole question. Is it not pitiful ? And there I find you, a man of sense, boggling about terms when your client's future and honour are at stake. You surprise me, Mr. Holmes."

" What I say is true," Holmes answered. " The money cannot be found. Surely it is better for you to take the substantial sum which I offer than to ruin this woman's career, which can profit you in no way ? "

" There you make a mistake, Mr. Holmes. An exposure would profit me indirectly to a considerable

6 *with a coat-of-arms upon the envelope.* Mr. Russell L. Merritt has suggested ("Re: The Adventure of the Worst Man in London") that it well may be that Holmes immediately recognized the coat-of-arms, and that his future course in this adventure was dictated by his knowledge of the bearer, the bearer's wife, and what that lady was capable of.

7 extent. I have eight or ten similar cases maturing. If it was circulated among them that I had made a severe example of the Lady Eva I should find all of them much more open to reason. You see my point ?"

Holmes sprang from his chair.

"Get behind him, Watson. Don't let him out!
8 Now, sir, let us see the contents of that notebook."

Milverton had glided as quick as a rat to the side of the room, and stood with his back against the wall.

"Mr. Holmes, Mr. Holmes!" he said, turning the front of his coat and exhibiting the butt of a large revolver, which projected from the inside pocket. "I have been expecting you to do something original. This has been done so often, and what good has ever come from it? I assure you that I am armed to the teeth, and I am perfectly prepared to use my weapon, knowing that the law will support me. Besides, your supposition that I would bring the letters here in a notebook is entirely mistaken. I would do nothing so foolish. And now, gentlemen, I have one or two little interviews this evening, and it is a long drive to Hampstead." He stepped forward, took up his coat, laid his hand on his revolver, and turned to the door. I picked up a chair, but Holmes shook his head, and I laid it down again. With a bow, a smile, and a twinkle Milverton was out of the room, and a few moments after we heard the slam of the carriage door and the rattle of the wheels as he drove away.

Holmes sat motionless by the fire, his hands buried deep in his trouser pockets, his chin sunk upon his breast, his eyes fixed upon the glowing embers. For half an hour he was silent and still. Then, with the gesture of a man who has taken his decision, he sprang to his feet and passed into his bedroom. A little later a rakish young workman with a goatee beard and a swagger lit his clay pipe at the lamp before descending into the street. "I'll be back some time, Watson," said he, and vanished into the night. I understood that he had opened his campaign against Charles Augustus Milverton; but I little dreamed the strange shape which that campaign was destined to take.

For some days Holmes came and went at all hours in this attire, but beyond a remark that his time was spent at Hampstead, and that it was not wasted, I knew nothing of what he was doing. At last, however, on a wild, tempestuous evening, when the wind screamed and rattled against the windows, he returned from his last expedition, and, having removed his disguise, he sat before the fire and laughed heartily in his silent, inward fashion.

"You would not call me a marrying man, Watson?"

"No, indeed!"

"You will be interested to hear that I am engaged."

"My dear fellow! I congrat——"

"To Milverton's housemaid."

"Good heavens, Holmes!"

9 "I wanted information, Watson."

"Surely you have gone too far?"

"It was a most necessary step. I am a plumber with

7 *I have eight or ten similar cases maturing.* "Contemporary philanderers whose first principle is never to commit anything to writing may find this *penchant* for exchanging passionate *billets-doux* incomprehensible, but two points should be considered," Mr. L. W. Bailey wrote in "The Dark Lady of Appledore Towers." "As there were no private telephones the only means of communication and of making appointments between two people living in separate establishments was the written word, and as letters could not be safely posted and dropped naked on the matrimonial mat, they had to be entrusted for personal delivery to a valet or lady's maid. These servants, alas, were perpetually tempted by scoundrels like Milverton with large sums of money, and too often, as in other fields of human activity, avarice proved stronger than loyalty. The second point is that what seems to us a perfectly innocent message could at that time be construed as a confession of guilt. Lax though the standards of actual behaviour were, the outward appearance had to be rigidly correct, and an appointment between a man and a woman (especially if one or both were married to someone else) to meet alone was considered sufficient evidence of a 'guilty' accusation."

"MR. HOLMES, MR. HOLMES!" HE SAID, TURNING THE FRONT OF HIS COAT AND EXHIBITING THE BUTT OF A LARGE REVOLVER . . .

Illustration by Sidney Paget for the *Strand Magazine*, April, 1904.

a rising business, Escott by name. I have walked out with her each evening, and I have talked with her.
Good heavens, those talks! However, I have got all I **10**
wanted. I know Milverton's house as I know the palm of my hand."

"But the girl, Holmes?"

He shrugged his shoulders.

"You can't help it, my dear Watson. You must play your cards as best you can when such a stake is on the table. However, I rejoice to say that I have a hated rival who will certainly cut me out the instant that my back is turned. What a splendid night it is!"

"You like this weather?"

"It suits my purpose. Watson, I mean to burgle Milverton's house to-night."

I had a catching of the breath, and my skin went cold at the words, which were slowly uttered in a tone of concentrated resolution. As a flash of lightning in the night shows up in an instant every detail of a wide landscape, so at one glance I seemed to see every possible result of such an action—the detection, the capture, the honoured career ending in irreparable failure and disgrace, my friend himself lying at the mercy of the odious Milverton.

"For Heaven's sake, Holmes, think what you are
doing!" I cried. **11**

"My dear fellow, I have given it every consideration. I am never precipitate in my actions, nor would I adopt so energetic and indeed so dangerous a course if any other were possible. Let us look at the matter clearly and fairly. I suppose that you will admit that the action is morally justifiable, though technically criminal. To burgle his house is no more than to forcibly take his pocket-book—an action in which you were prepared to aid me."

I turned it over in my mind.

"Yes," I said; "it is morally justifiable so long as our object is to take no articles save those which are used for an illegal purpose."

"Exactly. Since it is morally justifiable, I have only to consider the question of personal risk. Surely a gentleman should not lay much stress upon this when a lady is in most desperate need of his help?"

"You will be in such a false position."

"Well, that is part of the risk. There is no other possible way of regaining these letters. The unfortunate lady has not the money, and there are none of her people in whom she could confide. To-morrow is the last day of grace, and unless we can get the letters to-night this villain will be as good as his word, and will bring about her ruin. I must, therefore, abandon my client to her fate, or I must play this last card. Between ourselves, Watson, it's a sporting duel between this fellow Milverton and me. He had, as you saw, the best of the first exchanges; but my self-respect and my reputation are concerned to fight it to a finish."

"Well, I don't like it; but I suppose it must be," said I. "When do we start?

"You are not coming."

"Then you are not going," said I. "I give you my

8 *Now, sir, let us see the contents of that notebook.*" Lawyer Fenton: "Holmes' counter-offer of £2,000 made for the purpose of disentangling Lady Eva Brackwell from the slimy Milverton's meshes does not make him a *particeps criminis*, for his purpose is not criminal—but he is treading on thin ice. When, however, he tries to detain Milverton in order to take away his notebook he is guilty of attempted 'unlawful detention,' a crime in itself, and 'taking and carrying away'—larceny, in fact. 'Taking' includes possession by intimidation. . . . 'Carrying away' presupposes the permanent removal of anything from the place it occupies. It is indisputable that Holmes and Watson had no intention of returning the notebook to Milverton. Nor could Holmes and Watson plead as a valid defense that the blackmailer intended to use the documents it contained for improper purposes. It would still be a technical larceny."

9 "*Surely you have gone too far?*" Lawyer Fenton: "Holmes is guilty here of no more than the commission of a tort. The Larceny Act of 1916, codifying the criminal law, provides that 'every person who by any false pretence, with intent to defraud, obtains from any other person, any chattel, money or valuable security . . . shall be guilty . . .' Holmes had no intention of depriving Agatha of money or valuable security, neither of which she appears to have had to offer. The common law generally afforded little protection against fraud, holding it no crime for a man to make a fool of another man (or woman either, for that matter). This would not have prevented the maid of Hampstead, however, from suing for breach of promise in what is strangely referred to as a civil action."

10 *Good heavens, those talks!* "Is it not a tribute to Holmes' versatility," Dr. Richard Asher wrote in "Holmes and the Fair Sex," "that he, a man accustomed to discourse upon the Chaldean roots of the ancient Cornish language and the Polyphonic Motets of Lassus, should be equally capable of love talk with a housemaid? Is it not remarkable that a man accustomed to the company of khalifas, dukes, headmasters and llamas should be such a success with a servant?"

11 "*For Heaven's sake, Holmes, think what you are doing!*" Compare Watson's reaction to Holmes' suggestion that they spend the night in Stoke Moran without the sinister Dr. Roylott's permission or knowledge in "The Adventure of the Speckled Band," which we know took place in 1883: "I have really some scruples as to taking you tonight. There is a distinct element of danger." "Can I be of assistance?" "Your presence might be invaluable." "Then I shall certainly come." As the late Gavin Brend noted, it is curious that Watson should react so violently to Holmes' suggestion in this adventure *unless it were their first experience in lawbreaking together*. In so doing, he provided a powerful argument for placing the adventure earlier rather than later. But Mr. Brend himself provided an alternative explanation: that Watson, at the time of this adventure, had recently suffered a shocking experience which had left him shaken and totally unnerved for any form of housebreaking. In Mr. Brend's view, this experience was Watson's recent encounter on the moor with that dreadful apparition, the Hound of the Baskervilles.

12 *we have shared the same room for some years.* Holmes *could* have made this statment as early as 1883 (although he would have been more likely to say "two years" in that year). Taken by itself, however, the statment indicates a later rather than an earlier year for this adventure.

13 *I would have made a highly efficient criminal.* Lawyer Fenton: "Freudians may make what they will of Holmes' often-expressed desire to become a highly efficient criminal, a burglar by choice. The casual reader detects a note of yearning, but a closer examination discloses a substantial fulfillment."

14 *"I have rubber-soled tennis shoes."* If Watson's presumptive leg wound was bothering him so little at this period that he was able to enjoy a game of tennis, "The Adventure of Charles Augustus Milverton" must be 1) prior to the time that he supposedly sustained his leg wound; or 2) very late in his career. It is otherwise difficult to see what use he could have made of tennis shoes—they are not worn ordinarily for comfort, certainly.

15 *we shall drive as far as Church Row.* This beautiful road of old houses in Hampstead has hardly changed through the years and, apart from the cars that now line its pavements, Holmes and Watson would find little difference in the street if they visited Church Row today.

16 *so that we might appear to be two theatre-goers homeward bound.* The money was to be paid "on the 14th." On the preceding night—"To-morrow is the last day of grace"—"Holmes and I put on our dress-clothes, so that we might appear to be two theatre-goers homeward bound." The 13th was therefore not a Sunday. This eliminates January, 1895; December, 1896; February, 1898; March, 1898; January, 1901; December, 1903; and March, 1904.

17 *In Oxford Street we picked up a hansom.* But "why did Holmes and Watson [go] into Oxford Street on a bitterly cold night in order to pick up a hansom to take them to Hampstead?" Mr. James Edward Holroyd has asked. "They would be walking *away* from their destination no matter in which part of Baker Street 221B lay."

To this, Mr. Humphrey Morton has replied ("A Long Drive to Hampstead"): "Obviously, one presumes, with Holmes' customary thoroughness and attention to detail he desired to make the entire

word of honour—and I never broke it in my life—that I will take a cab straight to the police-station and give you away unless you let me share this adventure with you."

"You can't help me."

"How do you know that? You can't tell what may happen. Anyway, my resolution is taken. Other people besides you have self-respect and even reputations."

Holmes had looked annoyed, but his brow cleared, and he clapped me on the shoulder.

"Well, well, my dear fellow, be it so. We have shared
12 the same room for some years, and it would be amusing if
we ended by sharing the same cell. You know, Watson,
I don't mind confessing to you that I have always had an
13 idea that I would have made a highly efficient criminal.
This is the chance of my lifetime in that direction. See here!" He took a neat little leather case out of a drawer, and opening it he exhibited a number of shining instruments. "This is a first-class, up-to-date burgling kit, with nickel-plated jemmy, diamond-tipped glass cutter, adaptable keys, and every modern improvement which the march of civilization demands. Here, too, is my dark lantern. Everything is in order. Have you a pair of silent shoes?"

14 "I have rubber-soled tennis shoes."

"Excellent. And a mask?"

"I can make a couple out of black silk."

"I can see that you have a strong natural turn for this sort of thing. Very good; do you make the masks. We shall have some cold supper before we start. It is now
nine-thirty. At eleven we shall drive as far as Church
15 Row. It is a quarter of an hour's walk from there to
Appledore Towers. We shall be at work before midnight. Milverton is a heavy sleeper, and retires punctually at ten-thirty. With any luck we should be back here by two, with the Lady Eva's letters in my pocket."

Holmes and I put on our dress-clothes, so that we might
16 appear to be two theatre-goers homeward bound. In
17 Oxford Street we picked up a hansom and drove to an
address in Hampstead. Here we paid off our cab, and with our greatcoats buttoned up—for it was bitterly cold, and the wind seemed to blow through us—we walked along the edge of the Heath.

"It's a business that needs delicate treatment," said Holmes. "These documents are contained in a safe in the fellow's study, and the study is the ante-room of his bedchamber. On the other hand, like all these stout, little men who do themselves well, he is a plethoric sleeper. Agatha—that's my fiancée—says it is a joke in the servants' hall that it's impossible to wake the master. He has a secretary who is devoted to his interests, and never budges from the study all day. That's why we are going at night. Then he has a beast of a dog which roams the garden. I met Agatha late the last two evenings, and she locks the brute up so as to give me a clear run. This is the house, this big one in its own grounds. Through the gate—now to the right among the laurels. We might put on our masks here, I think. You see, there is not a glimmer of light in any of the windows, and everything is working splendidly."

With our black silk face-coverings, which turned us into two of the most truculent figures in London, we stole up to the silent, gloomy house. A sort of tiled veranda extended along one side of it, lined by several windows and two doors.

" That's his bedroom," Holmes whispered. " This door opens straight into the study. It would suit us best, but it is bolted as well as locked, and we should make too much noise getting in. Come round here. There's a greenhouse which opens into the drawing-room."

The place was locked, but Holmes removed a circle of
glass and turned the key from the inside. An instant 18
afterwards he had closed the door behind us, and we had
become felons in the eyes of the law. The thick warm
air of the conservatory and the rich, choking fragrance
of exotic plants took us by the throat. He seized my
hand in the darkness and led me swiftly past banks of
shrubs which brushed against our faces. Holmes had
remarkable powers, carefully cultivated, of seeing in the
dark. Still holding my hand in one of his, he opened a
door, and I was vaguely conscious that we had entered a
large room in which a cigar had been smoked not long
before. He felt his way among the furniture, opened
another door, and closed it behind us. Putting out my
hand I felt several coats hanging from the wall, and I
understood that I was in a passage. We passed along
it, and Holmes very gently opened a door upon the right-
hand side. Something rushed out at us, and my heart
sprang into my mouth, but I could have laughed when I
realized that it was the cat. A fire was burning in this
new room, and again the air was heavy with tobacco
smoke. Holmes entered on tiptoe, waited for me to
follow, and then very gently closed the door. We were
in Milverton's study, and a *portière* at the farther side
showed the entrance to his bedroom.

It was a good fire, and the room was illuminated by it.
Near the door I saw the gleam of an electric switch, but 19
it was unnecessary, even if it had been safe, to turn it on.
At one side of the fireplace was a heavy curtain, which
covered the bay window we had seen from outside. On
the other side was the door which communicated with the
veranda. A desk stood in the centre, with a turning chair
of shining red leather. Opposite was a large bookcase,
with a marble bust of Athene on the top. In the corner
between the bookcase and the wall there stood a tall green
safe, the firelight flashing back from the polished brass
knobs upon its face. Holmes stole across and looked at
it. Then he crept to the door of the bedroom, and stood
with slanting head listening intently. No sound came
from within. Meanwhile it had struck me that it would
be wise to secure our retreat through the outer door, so
I examined it. To my amazement it was neither locked
nor bolted ! I touched Holmes on the arm, and he
turned his masked face in that direction. I saw him
start, and he was evidently as surprised as I.

" I don't like it," he whispered, putting his lips to my very ear. " I can't quite make it out. Anyhow, we have no time to lose."

"THIS IS THE HOUSE, THIS BIG ONE IN ITS OWN GROUNDS."

"There are varied theories as to which house is Appledore Towers," Mr. Humphrey Morton wrote in " 'A Long Drive to Hampstead!' " "Mr. Ivor Brown thinks there is a case for citing the big house on the corner of Spaniards Road and North End Road, but to reach that from Church Row does not entail walking along the edge of the heath. The direct route to this house would be to walk straight up Heath Street, where Holmes and Watson were now near, and the house would have been facing them with the heath upon *either* side, and with Jack Straw's Castle on the left. One is inclined to assume, therefore, that they did indeed walk up Heath Street, and then to the right down East Heath Road (along the edge of the heath) and so to the 'silent, gloomy house,' let us say, at the corner of Well Road."

Elsewhere (in "A Milvertonian Identification"), Mr. Morton identified "Appledore Towers" as the house now known as "The Logs." At the east end of Well Walk, he wrote, East Heath Road is reached. At the corner of Well Road stands The Logs. "The house was designed by J. S. Nightingale and built in 1868. There appears to be no record of its first owner, but it was occupied by Edward Gotto from 1873 until 1896. Following this lengthy occupation there is a mysterious gap of two years, from 1896 to 1898, during which period it is said that the house was 'apparently empty.' . . . Cannot we assume . . . that Milverton moved to The Logs in 1896, changed its name to Appledore Towers and was in residence until his timely and unlamented death a year or two later?"

journey to Hampstead appear convincing from the start. There might be a chance of suspicion falling on them had they hailed a cab outside 221B. C. A. M. might have had Holmes' movements watched. Theatre-goers. Right. Now in Oxford Street in the '80s and '90s the nearest theatre to Baker Street was the old Princess's, which stood upon the north side of Oxford Street between what is now Upper Regent Street and Tottenham Court Road. Suppose that they hailed their hansom outside the Princess's Theatre, which route to Hampstead would they take? Either via Tottenham Court Road, through Hampstead Road, Camden Town and thus, on to Haverstock Hill, Rosslyn Hill and Hampstead High Street *or* via Portland Place, the Outer Circle of Regent's Park, Avenue Road and so up to Fitzjohn's Avenue to Church Row. One is inclined to accept the former theory, and surely it would have been superfluous to return westward along Oxford Street and into Baker Street once more and north from there."

18 *Holmes removed a circle of glass and turned the key from the inside.* Lawyer Fenton: "At this point 'breaking and entering are complete. Burglary has, in fact, been committed. Section 25 of the Larceny Act states, 'Every person who breaks and enters the dwelling house of another with intent to commit a felony therein . . . shall be guilty of burglary.' It has been held that the insertion of any part of the intruder's body, even a finger or part of a finger, will suffice for 'entry.' Burglary here is limited to dwelling houses and only is committed between the hours of 9 P.M. and 6 A.M. The crime is triable at assizes and quarter-sessions and is punishable by imprisonment for life. Housebreaking, not essentially a nocturnal activity, carries a maximum penalty of 14 years."

19 *Near the door I saw the gleam of an electric switch.* This is the first of many references to electricity in Appledore Towers, and it raises, chronologically, a most interesting point. Appledore Towers, it will be remembered, was in Hampstead. Your editor is indebted to the late Gavin Brend for the following information, communicated to him in a letter from Mr. Brend dated June 27, 1954: "The position as regards electricity in England at that time was briefly as follows. It would have been theoretically possible at any time after 1880 but in practice it was most unlikely, for the original legislation was most restrictive and the first supply companies found it practically impossible to function. Only later in the eighties

"Can I do anything?"

"Yes; stand by the door. If you hear anyone come, bolt it on the inside, and we can get away as we came. If they come the other way, we can get through the door if our job is done, or hide behind these window curtains if it is not. Do you understand?"

I nodded and stood by the door. My first feeling of fear had passed away, and I thrilled now with a keener zest than I had ever enjoyed when we were the defenders of the law instead of its defiers. The high object of our mission, the consciousness that it was unselfish and chivalrous, the villainous character of our opponent, all added to the sporting interest of the adventure. Far from feeling guilty, I rejoiced and exulted in our dangers. With a glow of admiration I watched Holmes unrolling his case of instruments and choosing his tool with the calm, scientific accuracy of a surgeon who performs a delicate operation. I knew that the opening of safes was a particular hobby with him, and I understood the joy which it gave him to be confronted with this green and gold monster, the dragon which held in its maw the reputations of many fair ladies. Turning up the cuffs of his dress-coat—he had placed his overcoat on a chair—Holmes laid out two drills, a jemmy, and several skeleton keys. I stood at the centre door with my eyes glancing at each of the others, ready for any emergency; though, indeed, my plans were somewhat vague as to what I should do if we were interrupted. For half an hour Holmes worked with concentrated energy, laying down one tool, picking up another, handling each with the strength and delicacy of the trained mechanic. Finally I heard a click, the broad green door swung open, and inside I had a glimpse of a number of paper packets, each tied, sealed, and inscribed. Holmes picked one out, but it was hard to read by the flickering fire, and he drew out his little dark lantern, for it was too dangerous, with

THEN HE CREPT TO THE DOOR OF THE BEDROOM, AND STOOD WITH SLANTING HEAD LISTENING INTENTLY.

Illustration by Sidney Paget for the *Strand Magazine*, April, 1904.

Milverton in the next room, to switch on the electric light. Suddenly I saw him halt, listen intently, and then in an instant he had swung the door of the safe to, picked up his coat, stuffed his tools into the pockets, and darted behind the window curtain, motioning me to do the same.

It was only when I had joined him there that I heard what had alarmed his quicker senses. There was a noise somewhere within the house. A door slammed in the distance. Then a confused, dull murmur broke itself into the measured thud of heavy footsteps rapidly approaching. They were in the passage outside the room. They paused at the door. The door opened. There was a sharp snick as the electric light was turned on. The door closed once more, and the pungent reek of a strong cigar was borne to our nostrils. Then the footsteps continued backwards and forwards, backwards and forwards, within a few yards of us. Finally, there was a creak from a chair, and the footsteps ceased. Then a key clicked in a lock, and I heard the rustle of papers. So far I had not dared to look out, but now I gently parted the division of the curtains in front of me and peeped through. From the pressure of Holmes' shoulder against mine I knew that he was sharing my observations. Right in front of us, and almost within our reach, was the broad, rounded back of Milverton. It was evident that we had entirely miscalculated his movements, that he had never been to his bedroom, but that he had been sitting up in some smoking- or billiard-room in the farther wing of the house, the windows of which we had not seen. His broad, grizzled head, with its shining patch of baldness, was in the immediate foreground of our vision. He was leaning far back in the red leather chair, his legs outstretched, a long black cigar projecting at an angle from his mouth. He wore a semi-military smoking-jacket, claret-coloured, with a black velvet collar. In his hand he held a long legal document, which he was reading in an indolent fashion, blowing rings of tobacco smoke from his lips as he did so. There was no promise of a speedy departure in his composed bearing and his comfortable attitude.

I felt Holmes' hand steal into mine and give me a reassuring shake, as if to say that the situation was within his powers, and that he was easy in his mind. I was not sure whether he had seen what was only too obvious from my position—that the door of the safe was imperfectly closed, and that Milverton might at any moment observe it. In my own mind I had determined that if I were sure, from the rigidity of his gaze, that it had caught his eye, I would at once spring out, throw my greatcoat over his head, pinion him, and leave the rest to Holmes. But Milverton never looked up. He was languidly interested by the papers in his hand, and page after page was turned as he followed the argument of the lawyer. At least, I thought, when he has finished the document and the cigar he will go to his room ; but before he had reached the end of either there came a remarkable development which turned our thoughts into quite another channel.

were the restrictions removed. For some time I left it at that. After all, Milverton was a blackmailer. Perhaps he had jumped the queue, although obviously this would take a bit of doing. But finally I decided I ought to look further into it. It so happens that I too live in Hampstead. When paying my electricity bill I asked the authority The London Electricity Board (North Western Sub-Area), when electricity was first installed in Hampstead. *The reply was in 1894.*"

This seemed to Mr. Brend, and to your editor, to prove conclusively that "The Adventure of Charles Augustus Milverton" belongs to the period after the Return. Still, a Sherlockian whose opinion is always to be highly respected, Mr. Elliot Kimball, has written that: "The fact that public electrical supply did not become available at Hampstead until 1894 does not apply with exclusive force. Milverton was a sybarite, and would be precisely the sort of an individual who would avail himself of a Swan System, providing himself with electric light by means of a privately-operated plant. Such apparatus might have been installed as early as 1880. No necessity arises to assign the Milverton adventure to a period after the Return."

In rebuttal, your editor would submit the following statement from Mr. William E. Plimental: "This . . . accessory [the electric switch, which we are later told operated with "a sharp snick"] is very much more recent that the date usually given to Milverton's crimes. The two accessories in use at the time accepted by most authorities were the little square attached to a table lamp, and the push-button in the wall for a chandelier, neither of which gave what might be called a 'snick.' If I am correct, the date for ["The Adventure of Charles Augustus Milverton"] would be around 1900 or 1901."

Several times I had observed that Milverton looked at his watch, and once he had risen and sat down again, with a gesture of impatience. The idea, however, that he might have an appointment at so strange an hour never occurred to me until a faint sound reached my ears from the veranda outside. Milverton dropped his papers and sat rigid in his chair. The sound was repeated, and then there came a gentle tap at the door. Milverton rose and opened it.

" Well," said he curtly, " you are nearly half an hour late."

So this was the explanation of the unlocked door and of the nocturnal vigil of Milverton. There was the gentle rustle of a woman's dress. I had closed the slit between the curtains as Milverton's face turned in our direction, but now I ventured very carefully to open it once more. He had resumed his seat, the cigar still projecting at an insolent angle from the corner of his mouth. In front of him, in the full glare of the electric light, there stood a tall, slim, dark woman, a veil over her face, a mantle drawn round her chin. Her breath came quick and fast, and every inch of the lithe figure was quivering with strong emotion.

" Well," said Milverton, " you've made me lose a good night's rest, my dear. I hope you'll prove worth it. You couldn't come any other time—eh ? "

The woman shook her head.

" Well, if you couldn't you couldn't. If the countess is a hard mistress you have your chance to get level with her now. Bless the girl, what are you shivering about ? That's right ! Pull yourself together ! Now, let us get down to business." He took a note from the drawer of his desk. " You say that you have five letters which compromise the Countess d'Albert. You want to sell them. I want to buy them. So far so good. It only remains to fix a price. I should want to inspect the letters, of course. If they are really good specimens—— Great heavens, is it you ? "

The woman without a word had raised her veil and dropped the mantle from her chin. It was a dark, handsome, clear-cut face which confronted Milverton, a face with a curved nose, strong, dark eyebrows, shading hard, glittering eyes, and a straight, thin-lipped mouth set
20 in a dangerous smile.

" It is I," she said—" the woman whose life you have ruined."

Milverton laughed, but fear vibrated in his voice. " You were so very obstinate," said he. " Why did you drive me to such extremities ? I assure you I wouldn't hurt a fly of my own accord, but every man has his business, and what was I to do ? I put the price well within your means. You would not pay."

" So you sent the letters to my husband, and he—the noblest gentleman that ever lived, a man whose boots I was never worthy to lace—he broke his gallant heart and died. You remember that last night when I came through that door I begged and prayed you for mercy, and you laughed in my face as you are trying to laugh now, only your coward heart cannot keep your lips from twitching ?

"YOU COULDN'T COME ANY OTHER TIME—EH?"

Illustration by Frederic Dorr Steele for *Collier's Magazine*, March 26, 1904. Sidney Paget illustrated the same scene for the *Strand Magazine*, April, 1904.

20 *and a straight, thin-lipped mouth set in a dangerous smile.* "It is surprising," Mr. L. W. Bailey wrote in "The Dark Lady of Appledore Towers," "that Watson should so stress the facial contours of one whose identity he is anxious to hide, but unless he is deliberately misleading us, we must accept his description and surmise that the lady was probably a member of one of the wealthy Jewish titled families of the period. These were quite a recent phenomena. Until the rise of the Rothschilds, Jews had not been accepted into aristocratic circles, and in 1869 Queen Victoria had refused to grant a peerage to Baron Lionel Rothschild, saying, 'To make a Jew a peer is a step the Queen could not assent to.' By the eighteen-eighties, however, the picture had changed radically. A Jew —D'Israeli—had been Prime Minister and the intimate confidant of the Queen herself, and was eventually ennobled as Lord Beaconsfield. In 1885 the Queen conferred a peerage on Nathaniel Rothschild, and against much opposition from the landed aristocracy the Prince of Wales had become intimate with the Rothschild family and admitted them into his circle. If the lady was of Jewish extraction it is quite clear that her husband was not, since he had a 'time-honoured title.' One may surmise therefore that he had married into one of the Jewish families he had met through the Prince of Wales . . ."

Yes; you never thought to see me here again, but it was that night which taught me how I could meet you face to face, and alone. Well, Charles Milverton, what have you to say?"

"Don't imagine that you can bully me," said he, rising to his feet. "I have only to raise my voice, and I could call my servants and have you arrested. But I will make allowance for your natural anger. Leave the room at once as you came, and I will say no more."

The woman stood with her hand buried in her bosom, and the same deadly smile on her thin lips.

"You will ruin no more lives as you ruined mine. You will wring no more hearts as you wrung mine. I will free the world of a poisonous thing. Take that, you hound, and that!—and that!—and that!—and that!"

She had drawn a little gleaming revolver, and emptied
barrel after barrel into Milverton's body, the muzzle 21
within two feet of his shirt-front. He shrank away, and then fell forward upon the table, coughing furiously and clawing among the papers. Then he staggered to his feet, received another shot, and rolled upon the floor. "You've done me," he cried, and lay still. The woman looked at him intently and ground her heel into his upturned face. She looked again, but there was no sound or movement. I heard a sharp rustle, the night air blew into the heated room, and the avenger was gone.

No interference upon our part could have saved the man from his fate; but as the woman poured bullet after bullet into Milverton's shrinking body, I was about to spring out, when I felt Holmes' cold, strong grasp upon my wrist. I understood the whole argument of that firm, restraining grip—that it was no affair of ours; that justice had overtaken a villain; that we had our own duties and our own objects which were not to be lost sight of. But hardly had the woman rushed from the room when Holmes, with swift, silent steps, was over at the other door. He turned the key in the lock. At the same instant we heard voices in the house and the sound of hurrying feet. The revolver shots had roused the household. With perfect coolness Holmes slipped across to the safe, filled his two arms with bundles of letters, and poured them all into the fire.
Again and again he did it, until the safe was empty. 22
Someone turned the handle and beat upon the outside of the door. Holmes looked swiftly round. The letter which had been the messenger of death for Milverton lay, all mottled with his blood, upon the table. Holmes tossed it in among the blazing papers. Then he drew the key from the outer door, passed through after me, and locked it on the outside. "This way, Watson," said he; "we can scale the garden wall in this direction."

I could not have believed that an alarm could have spread so swiftly. Looking back, the huge house was one blaze of light. The front door was open, and figures were rushing down the drive. The whole garden was alive with people, and one fellow raised a view-halloa as we emerged from the veranda and followed hard at our heels. Holmes seemed to know the ground perfectly, and he threaded his way swiftly among a plantation of small trees, I close at his heels, and our foremost pursuer

21 *emptied barrel after barrel into Milverton's body*. Surely Watson meant "chamber after chamber" instead of "barrel after barrel"? Still, there was, as Professor Remsen Ten Eyck Schenck once pointed out, "a type of revolver, now obsolete, called . . . a 'pepperbox'; the antique was no more than an elongated cylinder revolving before the hammer, and may be variously considered to have either no barrel or a separate barrel for each chamber, however you choose to regard it." But this was a gun of great weight and could hardly have been called "a little gleaming revolver."

22 *Again and again he did it.* Lawyer Fenton: "A fairly clear case of malicious damage, and actionable at law."

But there is (perhaps) more to Holmes' action than this. As Dr. Richard Asher wrote, in "Holmes and the Fair Sex," "Was he doing this purely for his client Lady Eva Brackwell whose sprightly, very sprightly, letters to an impecunious country squire were endangering her impending marriage with the Earl of Dovercourt? Surely Lady Eva was quite safe once Milverton was dead. The letters could only have come into the hands of the police. Was it possible that among the papers in the safe there were some sprightly, very sprightly, letters from Holmes himself—perhaps to the woman who poisoned children for their insurance money [*The Sign of the Four*]. Perhaps to Milverton's housemaid, but in any case letters which had they reached Scotland Yard might have caused Holmes as much embarrassment as he usually gave to them?"

. . . RECEIVED ANOTHER SHOT, AND ROLLED UPON THE FLOOR.

Illustration by Sidney Paget for the *Strand Magazine*, April, 1904.

panting behind us. It was a six-foot wall which barred
our path, but he sprang to the top and over. As I did the
same I felt the hand of the man behind me grab at my
23 ankle ; but I kicked myself free, and scrambled over a
glass-strewn coping. I fell upon my face among some
bushes ; but Holmes had me on my feet in an instant, and
together we dashed away across the huge expanse of
24 Hampstead Heath. We had run two miles, I suppose,
before Holmes at last halted and listened intently. All
was absolutely silence behind us. We had shaken off our
pursuers, and were safe.

We had breakfasted and were smoking our morning pipe, on the day after the remarkable experience which I have recorded, when Mr. Lestrade, of Scotland Yard, very solemn and impressive, was ushered into our modest sitting-room.

" Good morning, Mr. Holmes," said he—" good morning. May I ask if you are very busy just now ? "

" Not too busy to listen to you."

" I thought that, perhaps, if you had nothing particular on hand, you might care to assist us in a most remarkable case which occurred only last night at Hampstead."

" Dear me ! " said Holmes. " What was that ? "

" A murder—a most dramatic and remarkable murder. I know how keen you are upon these things, and I would take it as a great favour if you would step down to Appledore Towers and give us the benefit of your advice. It is no ordinary crime. We have had our eyes upon this Mr. Milverton for some time, and, between ourselves, he was a bit of a villain. He is known to have held papers which he used for blackmailing purposes. These papers have all been burned by the murderers. No article of value was taken, as it is probable that the criminals were men of good position, whose sole object was to prevent social exposure."

" Criminals ! " exclaimed Holmes. " Plural ! "

" Yes, there were two of them. They were, as nearly as possible, captured red-handed. We have their footmarks, we have their description ; it's ten to one that we trace them. The first fellow was a bit too active, but the second was caught by the under-gardener, and only got away after a struggle. He was a middle-sized, strongly built man—square jaw, thick neck, moustache, a mask over his eyes."

" That's rather vague," said Sherlock Holmes. " Why, it might be a description of Watson ! "

" It's true," said the Inspector, with much amusement. " It might be a description of Watson."

" Well, I am afraid I can't help you, Lestrade," said Holmes. " The fact is that I knew this fellow Milverton, that I considered him one of the most dangerous men in London, and that I think there are certain crimes which the law cannot touch, and which therefore, to some extent, justify private revenge. No, it's no use arguing. I have made up my mind. My sympathies are with the criminals rather than with the victim, and I will not handle this case."

Holmes had not said one word to me about the tragedy

23 *but I kicked myself free.* Lawyer Fenton: "Watson kicks himself free from the arresting under-gardener and flees safely, terminating an incredibly felonious night by committing a technical battery on a citizen and violating the Persons Act of 1861 which brands as a crime 'an assault upon any constable in the execution of his duty or upon any person acting in aid of such a constable; an assault with intent to prevent the lawful apprehension either of the assailant himself or of any other person.' Lestrade, that odd mixture of obstinacy and futility, had of course placed a constable there, for he [later] tells Holmes, 'We have had our eyes on this Mr. Milverton for some time.' "

24 *We had run two miles, I suppose.* The late H. W. Bell was perhaps the first to say that this feat alone should indicate that this adventure took place some years before the duel at the Reichenbach Falls, when Holmes and Watson were both young men. But many other commentators have doubted that the two-mile run ever took place. "For," as the late Gavin Brend wrote, "apparently [Holmes and Watson] were not pursued out of the garden and although a man might run for a quarter of a mile before he realized that he was not being followed, a two-mile run in these circumstances would be fantastic." Indeed, as Mr. Michael Harrison pointed out (*In the Footsteps of Sherlock Holmes*) *it is not possible* "to run for two miles across the Heath; not even by loosely calling Parliament Hill and Ken Wood part of Hampstead Heath. The overall breadth of the Heath is just about one mile, only; while the maximum width across the open area comprising Hampstead Heath, Parliament Hill and Ken Wood is only about one and a half miles."

which we had witnessed, but I observed all the morning that he was in the most thoughtful mood, and he gave me the impression, from his vacant eyes and his abstracted manner, of a man who is striving to recall something to his memory. We were in the middle of our lunch, when he suddenly sprang to his feet. " By Jove, Watson ! I've got it ! " he cried. " Take your hat ! Come with me ! " He hurried at his top speed down Baker Street and along Oxford Street, until we had almost reached Regent Circus. Here on the left hand there
stands a shop window filled with photographs of the **25**
celebrities and beauties of the day. Holmes' eyes fixed themselves upon one of them, and following his gaze I saw the picture of a regal and stately lady in Court dress, with a high diamond tiara upon her noble head. I looked at that delicately curved nose, at the marked eyebrows, at the straight mouth, and the strong little chin beneath it. Then I caught my breath as I read the time-honoured title of the great nobleman and statesman whose wife she had been. My eyes met those of Holmes, and he put his finger to his lips as we turned away from the window.

. . . I SAW THE PICTURE OF A REGAL AND STATELY LADY . . .

Illustration by Sidney Paget for the *Strand Magazine*, April, 1904.

25 *a shop window filled with photographs.* This day, if we can believe Watson, was the 14th of the month—and no shop window, in the eighties, would be unshuttered on the Sabbath. Since the 14th of the month in question was not a Sunday, this eliminates February, 1897; March, 1897; January, 1900; December, 1902; and February, 1904—and we must now ask the thorny question: in what month of what year did "The Adventure of Charles Augustus Milverton" take place? Watson has told us that the evening of the 13th was "a wild, tempestuous evening, when the wind screamed and rattled against the windows"; "it was bitterly cold, and the wind seemed to blow through us." Milverton, we know, called on Holmes "on a cold, frosty winter's evening"; on that evening, Holmes said: "She [Lady Eva] is to be married in a fortnight." As the late Dr. Ernest Bloomfield Zeisler wrote, Holmes may not have meant a fortnight to the day, but Milverton's call on Holmes must certainly have been within a day or two at the most of the 4th of the month in question. A careful examination of the meteorological records of all the months remaining to us has dictated your editor's choice of *January, 1899.* In that month, the temperature fell to 31.3° on the 5th (a Thursday). On the 13th (a Friday) the wind achieved a pressure of 15.9 pounds to the inch. The minimum temperature was 39.6°—not, perhaps, as bitter as we would like to have it, but uncomfortable enough in such a gale, and within eight degrees of freezing. The fact that Holmes and Watson burgled Appledore Towers on the night of *Friday the 13th* leads us to wonder if the date itself could have been the cause of Watson's uneasiness. Was the good doctor by any chance exceptionally superstitious?

Bibliographical Note: The original manuscript of this chronicle, titled "The Adventure of the Worst Man in London," about 6,800 words in 21 folio pages, vellum by Spealls, was auctioned in New York City on January 30, 1923, bringing $70. It was listed in Scribner's Sherlock Holmes Catalogue at $450. Its owner, at one time, was the late Edgar W. Smith. It was sold, on Mr. Smith's death, to Mr. Carl Anderson of Philadelphia as part of Mr. Smith's Sherlockian estate.

64

THE ADVENTURE OF THE SIX NAPOLEONS

[*Friday, June 8, to Sunday, June 10, 1900*]

LESTRADE TOOK OUT HIS OFFICIAL NOTEBOOK . . .

Illustration by Sidney Paget for the *Strand Magazine*, May, 1904.

IT was no very unusual thing for Mr. Lestrade, of Scotland Yard, to look in upon us of an evening, and his visits were welcome to Sherlock Holmes, for they enabled him to keep in touch with all that was going on at the police headquarters. In return for the news which Lestrade would bring, Holmes was always ready to listen with attention to the details of any case upon which the detective was engaged, and was able occasionally, without any active interference, to give some hint or suggestion drawn from his own vast knowledge and experience.

On this particular evening Lestrade had spoken of the weather and the newspapers. Then he had fallen silent, puffing thoughtfully at his cigar. Holmes looked keenly at him.

" Anything remarkable on hand ? " he asked.

" Oh, no, Mr. Holmes, nothing very particular."

" Then tell me all about it."

Lestrade laughed.

" Well, Mr. Holmes, there is no use denying that there *is* something on my mind. And yet it is such an absurd business that I hesitated to bother you about it. On the other hand, although it is trivial, it is undoubtedly queer, and I know that you have a taste for all that is out of the common. But in my opinion it comes more in Dr. Watson's line than ours."

" Disease ? " said I.

" Madness, anyhow. And a queer madness too ! You wouldn't think there was anyone living at this time of day who had such a hatred of Napoleon the First that he would break any image of him that he could see."

Holmes sank back in his chair.

" That's no business of mine," said he.

" Exactly. That's what I said. But then, when the man commits burglary in order to break images which are not his own, that brings it away from the doctor and on to the policeman."

Holmes sat up again.

" Burglary ! This is more interesting. Let me hear the details."

Lestrade took out his official notebook and refreshed his memory from its pages.

" The first case reported was four days ago," said he.
" It was at the shop of Morse Hudson, who has a place 1
for the sale of pictures and statues in the Kennington Road. The assistant had left the front shop for an instant, when he heard a crash, and, hurrying in, found a plaster bust of Napoleon, which stood with several other works of art upon the counter, lying shivered into fragments. He rushed out into the road, but, although several passers-by declared that they had noticed a man run out of the shop, he could neither see anyone nor could he find any means of identifying the rascal. It seemed to be one of those senseless acts of hooliganism which occur from time to time, and it was reported to the constable on the beat as such. The plaster cast was not worth more than a few shillings, and the whole affair appeared to be too childish for any particular investigation.

" The second case, however, was more serious and also more singular. It occurred only last night.

" In Kennington Road, and within a few hundred yards of Morse Hudson's shop, there lives a well-known medical practitioner, named Dr. Barnicot, who has one of the largest practices upon the south side of the Thames. His residence and principal consulting-room is at Kennington Road, but he has a branch surgery and dispensary at Lower Brixton Road, two miles away. This Dr. Barnicot is an enthusiastic admirer of Napoleon, and his house is full of books, pictures, and relics of the French Emperor. Some little time ago he purchased from Morse Hudson two duplicate plaster casts of the famous head of Napoleon by the French sculptor Devine. One of these he placed in his hall in the house at Kennington Road, and the other on the mantelpiece of the surgery at Lower Brixton. Well, when Dr. Barnicot came down this morning he was astonished to find that his house had been burgled during the night, but that nothing had been taken save the plaster head from the hall. It had been carried out, and had been dashed savagely against the garden wall, under which its splintered fragments were discovered."

Holmes rubbed his hands.

" This is certainly very novel," said he.

" I thought it would please you. But I have not got to the end yet. Dr. Barnicot was due at his surgery at twelve o'clock, and you can imagine his amazement when, on arriving there, he found that the window had been opened in the night, and that the broken pieces of his second bust were strewn all over the room. It had been smashed to atoms where it stood. In neither case were there any signs which could give us a clue as to the criminal or lunatic who had done the mischief. Now, Mr. Holmes, you have got the facts."

" They are singular, not to say grotesque," said Holmes. " May I ask whether the two busts smashed in Dr. Barnicot's rooms were the exact duplicates of the one which was destroyed in Morse Hudson's shop ? "

" They were taken from the same mould."

" Such a fact must tell against the theory that the man

1 *Morse Hudson.* As we have previously noted, Mr. Manly Wade Wellman, in "The Great Man's Great Son," has identified Morse Hudson both as the Hudson who blackmailed Squire Trevor ("The *Gloria Scott*") and the estranged husband of Holmes' landlady, Mrs. Hudson.

who breaks them is influenced by any general hatred of Napoleon. Considering how many hundreds of statues of the great Emperor must exist in London, it is too much to suppose such a coincidence as that a promiscuous iconoclast should chance to begin upon three specimens of the same bust."

"Well, I thought as you do," said Lestrade. "On the other hand, this Morse Hudson is the purveyor of busts in that part of London, and these three were the only ones which had been in his shop for years. So although, as you say, there are many hundreds of statues in London, it is very probable that these three were the only ones in that district. Therefore a local fanatic would begin with them. What do you think, Dr. Watson?"

"There are no limits to the possibilities of monomania," I answered. "There is the condition which the modern French psychologists have called the '*idée fixe*,' which may be trifling in character, and accompanied by complete sanity in every other way. A man who had read deeply about Napoleon, or who had possibly received some hereditary family injury through the great war, might conceivably form such an '*idée fixe*,' and under its influence be capable of any fantastic outrage."

"That won't do, my dear Watson," said Holmes, shaking his head; "for no amount of '*idée fixe*' would enable your interesting monomaniac to find out where these busts were situated."

"Well, how do *you* explain it?"

"I don't attempt to do so. I would only observe that there is a certain method in the gentleman's eccentric proceedings. For example, in Dr. Barnicot's hall where a sound might arouse the family, the bust was taken outside before being broken, whereas in the surgery, where there was less danger of an alarm, it was smashed where it stood. The affair seems absurdly trifling, and yet I dare call nothing trivial when I reflect that some of my most classic cases have had the least promising commencement. You will remember, Watson, how the dreadful business of the Abernetty family was first brought to my notice by the depth which the parsley had
2 sunk into the butter upon a hot day. I can't afford, therefore, to smile at your three broken busts, Lestrade, and I shall be very much obliged to you if you will let me hear of any fresh developments of so singular a chain of events."

The development for which my friend had asked came in a quicker and an infinitely more tragic form than he could have imagined. I was still dressing in my bedroom next morning, when there was a tap at the door, and Holmes entered, a telegram in his hand. He read it aloud:

"Come instantly, 131 Pitt Street, Kensington.—LESTRADE."

"What is it, then?" I asked.

"Don't know—may be anything. But I suspect it is the sequel of the story of the statues. In that case our friend the image-breaker has begun operations in another

2 *by the depth which the parsley had sunk into the butter upon a hot day*. "We may compare a somewhat similar example in the career of Sergt. Cuff—see Wilkie Collins, *The Moonstone*, chap. xii," Mr. T. S. Blakeney commented. For a pastiche by Mr. Richard W. Clarke stemming from this reference of Holmes', see "The Dreadful Business of the Abernetty Family" in the *Baker Street Journal*, Vol. XI, No. 1, New Series, January, 1961, pp. 13–26.

quarter of London. There's coffee on the table, Watson, and I have a cab at the door."

In half an hour we had reached Pitt Street, a quiet little backwater just beside one of the briskest currents of London life. No. 131 was one of a row, all flat-chested, 3
respectable, and most unromantic dwellings. As we drove up we found the railings in front of the house lined by a curious crowd. Holmes whistled.

"By George! it's attempted murder at the least. Nothing less will hold the London message boy. There's a deed of violence indicated in that fellow's round shoulders and outstretched neck. What's this, Watson? The top step swilled down and the other ones dry. Footsteps enough, anyhow! Well, well, there's Lestrade at the front window, and we shall soon know all about it."

The official received us with a very grave face and showed us into a sitting-room, where an exceedingly unkempt and agitated elderly man, clad in a flannel dressing-gown, was pacing up and down. He was introduced to us as the owner of the house—Mr. Horace Harker, of the
Central Press Syndicate. 4

"It's the Napoleon bust business again," said Lestrade. "You seemed interested last night, Mr. Holmes, so I thought perhaps you would be glad to be present now that the affair has taken a very much graver turn."

"What has it turned to, then?"

"To murder. Mr. Harker, will you tell these gentlemen exactly what has occurred?"

The man in the dressing-gown turned upon us with a most melancholy face.

"It's an extraordinary thing," said he, "that all my life I have been collecting other people's news, and now that a real piece of news has come my own way I am so confused and bothered that I can't put two words together. If I had come in here as a journalist I should have interviewed
myself and had two columns in every evening paper. 5
As it is, I am giving away valuable copy by telling my story over and over to a string of different people, and I can make no use of it myself. However, I've heard your name, Mr. Sherlock Holmes, and if you'll only explain this queer business I shall be paid for my trouble in telling you the story."

Holmes sat down and listened.

"It all seems to centre round that bust of Napoleon which I bought for this very room about four months ago. I picked it up cheap from Harding Brothers, two doors from the High Street Station. A great deal of my journalistic work is done at night, and I often write until the early morning. So it was to-day. I was sitting in my den, which is at the back of the top of the house, about three o'clock, when I was convinced that I heard some sounds downstairs. I listened, but they were not repeated, and I concluded that they came from outside. Then suddenly, about five minutes later, there came a most horrible yell—the most dreadful sound, Mr. Holmes, that ever I heard. It will ring in my ears as long as I live. I sat frozen with horror for a minute or two. Then I seized the poker and went downstairs. When I entered this room I found the window wide open, and I at once observed that the bust was gone from the mantel-

3 *No. 131 was one of a row.* "There are not many houses [in Pitt Street]," the late H. W. Bell wrote in "Three Identifications," "—they are numbered 1–13, and 2–18—and most of them have bow-windows and a low balustraded front; but a group of five (Nos. 10–18) corresponds in every way to Watson's account. . . . The number as reported is a disguise. Perhaps it stands for No. 14."

4 *the Central Press Syndicate.* In fact, the Central News Agency. It was to the Central News Agency that Jack the Ripper mailed two horribly jocund notes in late September and early October, 1888. In "A Challenge from Baker Street," Mr. Charles Fisher has set forth the interesting hypothesis that Mr. Horace Harker was himself Jack the Ripper.

5 *in every evening paper.* "How was Mr. Harker going to do this?" John Hyslop asked in "Sherlock Holmes and the Press." "Two columns amounted to about 2,000 words, and even with 'his pen travelling shrilly over the foolscap' that would have taken Mr. Harker two hours to write. He would then have to get it across London to Fleet Street, and it would have to be duplicated and delivered to . . . six or seven newspaper offices. Nevertheless, he did succeed in getting something into the evening papers, including a few sly paragraphs suggested by Holmes . . ."

HE WAS INTRODUCED TO US AS THE OWNER OF THE HOUSE . . .

Illustration by Sidney Paget for the *Strand Magazine*, May, 1904.

piece. Why any burglar should take such a thing passes my understanding, for it was only a plaster cast, and of no real value whatever.

" You can see for yourself that anyone going out through that open window could reach the front doorstep by taking a long stride. This was clearly what the burglar had done, so I went round and opened the door. Stepping out into the dark I nearly fell over a dead man who was lying there. I ran back for a light, and there was the poor fellow, a great gash in his throat and the whole place swimming in blood. He lay on his back, his knees drawn up, and his mouth horribly open. I shall see him in my dreams. I had just time to blow on my police whistle, and then I must have fainted, for I knew nothing more until I found the policeman standing over me in the hall."

" Well, who was the murdered man ? " asked Holmes.

" There's nothing to show who he was," said Lestrade. " You shall see the body at the mortuary, but we have made nothing of it up to now. He is a tall man, sunburnt, very powerful, not more than thirty. He is poorly dressed, and yet does not appear to be a labourer. A horn-handled clasp-knife was lying in a pool of blood beside him. Whether it was the weapon which did the deed, or whether it belonged to the dead man, I do not know. There was no name on his clothing, and nothing in his pockets save an apple, some string, a shilling map of London, and a photograph. Here it is."

It was evidently taken by a snap-shot from a small camera. It represented an alert, sharp-featured simian man with thick eyebrows, and a very peculiar projection of the lower part of the face like the muzzle of a baboon.

" And what became of the bust ? " asked Holmes, after a careful study of this picture.

" We had news of it just before you came. It has been
found in the front garden of an empty house in Campden
6 House Road. It was broken into fragments. I am going
round now to see it. Will you come ? "

" Certainly. I must just take one look round." He examined the carpet and the window. " The fellow had either very long legs or was a most active man," said he. " With an area beneath it was no mean feat to reach that window-ledge and open that window. Getting back was comparatively simple. Are you coming with us to see the remains of your bust, Mr. Harker ? "

The disconsolate journalist had seated himself at a writing-table.

" I must try and make something of it," said he, " though I have no doubt that the first editions of the evening papers are out already with full details. It's
like my luck ! You remember when the stand fell at
7 Doncaster ! Well, I was the only journalist in the stand,
and my journal the only one that had no account of it, for I was too shaken to write it. And now I'll be too late with a murder done on my own doorstep."

As we left the room we heard his pen travelling shrilly over the foolscap.

The spot where the fragments of the bust had been found was only a few hundred yards away. For the first

6 *Campden House Road.* "There is no Campden *House* Road," Mr. Bell wrote in "Three Identifications." "Watson certainly meant to write Campden Hill Road, but his eye was caught by the word 'house' immediately before, in the same sentence. In this long street only two houses (Nos. 49 and 51) within a reasonable distance of Pitt Street possess front grass-plots; the others are separated from the pavement by narrow sunken areas. On the pavement before one of them, No. 51, is a lamppost, as required by the narrative. It is less than 400 yards from the group of five houses in Pitt Street."

7 *You remember when the stand fell at Doncaster!* The late Professor Jay Finley Christ believed that the news current at the time he was writing had a considerable effect on Watson. "The Adventure of the Six Napoleons" was first published in the spring of 1904, and "In Whitaker for 1903, one finds that a stand had fallen in April, 1902, at Glasgow, killing some 21 persons."

time our eyes rested upon this presentment of the great Emperor, which seemed to raise such frantic and destructive hatred in the mind of the unknown. It lay scattered in splintered shards upon the grass. Holmes picked up several of them and examined them carefully. I was convinced from his intent face and his purposeful manner that at last he was upon a clue.

"Well ?" asked Lestrade.

Holmes shrugged his shoulders.

"We have a long way to go yet," said he. "And yet—and yet—well, we have some suggestive facts to act upon. The possession of this trifling bust was worth more in the eyes of this strange criminal than a human life. That is one point. Then there is the singular fact that he did not break it in the house, or immediately outside the house, if to break it was his sole object."

"He was rattled and bustled by meeting this other fellow. He hardly knew what he was doing."

"Well, that's likely enough. But I wish to call your attention very particularly to the position of this house in the garden of which the bust was destroyed."

Lestrade looked about him.

"It was an empty house, and so he knew that he would not be disturbed in the garden."

"Yes, but there is another empty house farther up the street which he must have passed before he came to this one. Why did he not break it there, since it is evident that every yard that he carried it increased the risk of someone meeting him ?"

"I give it up," said Lestrade.

Holmes pointed to the street lamp above our heads.

"He could see what he was doing here, and he could not there. That was the reason."

"By Jove ! that's true," said the detective. "Now that I come to think of it, Mr. Barnicot's bust was broken not far from his red lamp. Well, Mr. Holmes, what are we to do with that fact ?"

"To remember it—to docket it. We may come on something later which will bear upon it. What steps do you propose to take now, Lestrade ?"

"The most practical way of getting at it, in my opinion, is to identify the dead man. There should be no difficulty about that. When we have found who he is and who his associates are, we should have a good start in learning what he was doing in Pitt Street last night, and who it was who met him and killed him on the doorstep of Mr. Horace Harker. Don't you think so ?"

"No doubt ; and yet it is not quite the way in which I should approach the case."

"What would you do then ?"

"Oh, you must not let me influence you in any way. I suggest that you go on your line and I on mine. We can compare notes afterwards, and each will supplement the other."

"Very good," said Lestrade.

"If you are going back to Pitt Street you might see Mr. Horace Harker. Tell him from me that I have quite made up my mind, and that it is certain that a dangerous homicidal lunatic with Napoleonic delusions was in his

HOLMES POINTED TO THE STREET LAMP ABOVE OUR HEADS.

Illustration by Sidney Paget for the *Strand Magazine*, May, 1904.

house last night. It will be useful for his article."

Lestrade stared.

"You don't seriously believe that?"

Holmes smiled.

"Don't I? Well, perhaps I don't. But I am sure that it will interest Mr. Horace Harker and the subscribers of the Central Press Syndicate. Now, Watson, I think that we shall find that we have a long and rather complex day's work before us. I should be glad, Lestrade, if you could make it convenient to meet us at Baker Street at six o'clock this evening. Until then I should like to keep
8 this photograph found in the dead man's pocket. It is possible that I may have to ask your company and assistance upon a small expedition which will have to be undertaken to-night, if my chain of reasoning should prove to be correct. Until then, good-bye, and good luck."

Sherlock Holmes and I walked together to the High Street, where he stopped at the shop of Harding Brothers, whence the bust had been purchased. A young assistant informed us that Mr. Harding would be absent until afternoon, and that he was himself a new-comer, who could give us no information. Holmes' face showed his disappointment and annoyance.

"Well, well, we can't expect to have it all our own way, Watson," he said at last. "We must come back in the afternoon, if Mr. Harding will not be here until then. I am, as you have no doubt surmised, endeavouring to trace these busts to their source, in order to find if there is not something peculiar which may account for their remarkable fate. Let us make for Mr. Morse Hudson, of the Kennington Road, and see if he can throw any light upon the problem."

A drive of an hour brought us to the picture-dealer's establishment. He was a small, stout man with a red face and a peppery manner.

"Yes, sir. On my very counter, sir," said he. "What we pay rates and taxes for I don't know, when any ruffian can come in and break one's goods. Yes, sir, it was I who sold Dr. Barnicot his two statues. Disgraceful, sir! A Nihilist plot, that's what I make it. No one but an Anarchist would go about breaking statues. Red republicans, that's what I call 'em. Who did I get the statues from? I don't see what that has to do with it. Well, if you really want to know, I got them from Gelder & Co.,
9 in Church Street, Stepney. They are a well-known house in the trade, and have been this twenty years. How many had I? Three—two and one are three—two of Dr. Barnicot's and one smashed in broad daylight on my own counter. Do I know that photograph? No, I don't. Yes, I do, though. Why, it's Beppo! He was a kind of Italian piecework man, who made himself useful in the shop. He could carve a bit, and gild a frame, and do odd jobs. The fellow left me last week, and I've heard nothing of him since. No, I don't know where he came from nor where he went to. I have nothing against him while he was here. He was gone two days before the bust was smashed."

"Well, that's all we could reasonably expect to get

8 *Until then I should like to keep this photograph.* ". . . how frightfully irregular of Holmes to ask to keep the photograph found in the dead man's pocket and of Lestrade to allow him to do!" Mr. James Edward Holroyd commented. "One feels that if the Commissioner of the time had heard of this misdemeanour he would have 'snapped at it like a hungry wolf.' "

9 *Stepney.* Stepney is "the Stibbenhidde or Stebenheth of early deeds: the affix indicating the *hid* or Haeredium of a Saxon freeman," wrote Augustus J. C. Hare in *Walks in London*, Vol. I. One of the largest of the metropolitan boroughs, it extends from the City boundary to Poplar from west to east and from the Thames to Bethnal Green from south to north.

from Morse Hudson," said Holmes, as we emerged from the shop. "We have this Beppo as a common factor, both in Kennington and in Kensington, so that is worth a ten-mile drive. Now, Watson, let us make for Gelder & Co., of Stepney, the source and origin of busts. I shall be surprised if we don't get some help down there."

In rapid succession we passed through the fringe of fashionable London, hotel London, theartical London, literary London, commercial London, and, finally, maritime London, till we came to a river-side city of a hundred 10
thousand souls, where the tenement houses swelter and reek with the outcasts of Europe. Here, in a broad thoroughfare, once the abode of wealthy city merchants, we found the sculptor works for which we searched. Outside was a considerable yard full of monumental masonry. Inside was a large room in which fifty workers were carving or moulding. The manager, a big blond German, received us civilly, and gave a clear answer to all Holmes' questions. A reference to his books showed that hundreds of casts had been taken from a marble copy of Devine's head of Napoleon, but that the three which had been sent to Morse Hudson a year or so before had been half of a batch of six, the other three being sent to Harding Brothers, of Kensington. There was no reason why those six should be different to any of the other casts. He could suggest no possible cause why anyone should wish to destroy them—in fact, he laughed at the idea. Their wholesale price was six shillings, but the retailer would get twelve or more. The cast was taken in two moulds from each side of the face, and then these two profiles of plaster of Paris were joined together to make the complete bust. The work was usually done by Italians in the room we were in. When finished the busts were put on a table in the passage to dry, and afterwards stored. That was all he could tell us.

But the production of the photograph had a remarkable effect upon the manager. His face flushed with anger, and his brows knotted over his blue Teutonic eyes.

"Ah, the rascal!" he cried. "Yes, indeed, I know him very well. This has always been a respectable establishment, and the only time that we have ever had the police in it was over this very fellow. It was more than a year ago now. He knifed another Italian in the street, and then he came to the works with the police on his heels, and he was taken here. Beppo was his name—his second name I never knew. Serve me right for engaging a man with such a face. But he was a good workman—one of the best."

"What did he get?"

"The man lived, and he got off with a year. I have no doubt he is out now; but he has not dared to show his nose here. We have a cousin of his here, and I dare say he could tell you where he is."

"No, no," cried Holmes, "not a word to the cousin—not a word, I beg you. The matter is very important, and the farther I go with it the more important it seems to grow. When you referred in your ledger to the sale of

10 *and, finally, maritime London.* "How, in driving from Kennington to Stepney, would you pass successively through fashionable London, hotel London, theatrical London and literary London?" Mr. James Edward Holroyd has asked. "All these quarters are on the north side of the river, whereas the map suggests that the shorter and more obvious way would have been to continue on the south side, crossing at London Bridge."

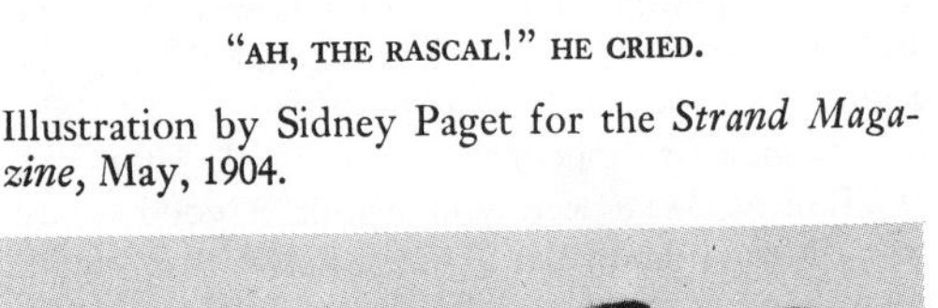

"AH, THE RASCAL!" HE CRIED.

Illustration by Sidney Paget for the *Strand Magazine*, May, 1904.

11 "*Yes," he continued, after some turning over of pages.* ". . . although the manager of Gelder & Co. . . . had never known Beppo's second name, he was able to spot him immediately in the firm's paylist," Mr. Holroyd continued. "I should like to have seen the index to that pay-list. How do you enter the name of a man who has no surname? As Beppo 'X'? Or was the index conducted on the simple Holmesian principle of first names first as in Victor Lynch, the forger?"

12 *May 20.*" Since May 20th was a payday, it must have been a Saturday; May 20th fell on a Saturday in 1882, 1893, and 1899; "The Adventure of the Six Napoleons" took place somewhat "more than a year" later, so the year in which the case took place is 1883, 1894, or 1900. It was not 1883, for two reasons: 1) Holmes later says to Watson: "If ever I permit you to chronicle any more of my little problems . . ." Watson evidently did not begin to chronicle Holmes' problems until 1887 ("A Scandal in Bohemia"). 2) Lestrade later says to Holmes: "I've seen you handle a good many cases, Mr. Holmes, but I don't know that I ever knew a more workmanlike one than that. We're not jealous of you at Scotland Yard. No sir, we are very proud of you, and if you come down tomorrow there is not a man, from the oldest inspector to the youngest constable, who wouldn't be glad to shake you by the hand." It was not until 1888–1889, as we have seen (*The Hound of the Baskervilles*), that Lestrade and other Scotland Yarders began to adopt a "reverential" attitude toward Holmes. Nor is the year 1894: the famous black pearl of the Borgias (we later learn) disappeared "exactly two days before the arrest of Beppo," and this, as we have seen, was "roughly" around "May 20." The disappearance created a sensation and Holmes says "I was myself consulted upon the case." But in late May, 1893, Holmes was believed dead beneath the Reichenbach. The year, then, was 1900. To determine the month of the adventure we must start with the date of Beppo's arrest—shortly after Saturday, May 20, 1889. It was not Sunday, May 21—his arrest "took place in the factory . . . at the very moment when [the] busts were being made"—and it was before Saturday, May 26th, since he was *not* paid on that day. His arrest was therefore on one of the five days Monday, May 22nd to Friday, May 26th, inclusive. We are justified in assuming that Beppo was sentenced very soon after his arrest, for the police only wished to determine whether or not his victim would live. The date of Beppo's sentencing cannot be much earlier than Thursday, May 25th, or much later than Monday, May 29th. Beppo got a year; he was therefore released from prison between May 25th and May 29, 1900. Certainly he would lose no time in looking up his cousin and obtaining employment at Morse Hudson's shop, and we know he worked for Hudson during the week preceding the week in which the adventure began: "The

those casts I observed that the date was June 3 of last year. Could you give me the date when Beppo was arrested ? "

" I could tell you roughly by the pay-list," the manager answered. " Yes," he continued, after some turning
11-12 over of pages, " he was paid last on May 20."

" Thank you," said Holmes. " I don't think that I need intrude upon your time and patience any more." With a last word of caution that he should say nothing as to our researches we turned our faces westward once more.

The afternoon was far advanced before we were able to snatch a hasty luncheon at a restaurant. A news-bill at the entrance announced " Kensington Outrage. Murder by a Madman," and the contents of the paper showed that Mr. Horace Harker had got his account into print after all. Two columns were occupied with a highly sensational and flowery rendering of the whole incident. Holmes propped it against the cruet-stand and read it while he ate. Once or twice he chuckled.

" This is all right, Watson," said he. " Listen to this : ' It is satisfactory to know that there can be no difference of opinion upon this case, since Mr. Lestrade, one of the most experienced members of the official force, and Mr. Sherlock Holmes, the well-known consulting expert, have each come to the conclusion that the grotesque series of incidents, which have ended in so tragic a fashion, arise from lunacy rather than from deliberate crime. No explanation save mental aberration can cover the facts.' The Press, Watson, is a most valuable institution, if you only know how to use it. And now, if you have quite finished, we will hark back to Kensington, and see what the manager of Harding Brothers has to say to the matter."

The founder of that great emporium proved to be a brisk, crisp little person, very dapper and quick, with a clear head and a ready tongue.

" Yes, sir, I have already read the account in the evening papers. Mr. Horace Harker is a customer of ours. We supplied him with the busts some months ago. We ordered three busts of that sort from Gelder & Co., of Stepney. They are all sold now. To whom ? Oh, I dare say by consulting our sales book we could very easily tell you. Yes, we have the entries here. One to Mr. Harker, you see, and one to Mr. Josiah Brown, of Laburnum Lodge, Laburnum Vale, Chiswick, and one to Mr. Sandeford, of Lower Grove Road, Reading. No, I have never seen this face which you show me in the photograph. You would hardly forget it—would you, sir ?—for I've seldom seen an uglier. Have we any Italians on the staff ? Yes, sir, we have several among our workpeople and cleaners. I dare say they might get a peep at that sales book if they wanted to. There is no particular reason for keeping a watch upon that book. Well, well, it's a very strange business, and I hope that you'll let me know if anything comes of your inquiries."

Holmes had taken several notes during Mr. Harding's evidence, and I could see that he was thoroughly satisfied by the turn which affairs were taking. He made no remark, however, save that, unless we hurried, we should be late for our appointment with Lestrade. Sure enough, when we reached Baker Street the detective was already there, and we found him pacing up and down in a fever of impatience. His look of importance showed that his day's work had not been in vain.

"Well?" he asked. "What luck, Mr. Holmes?"

"We have had a very busy day, and not entirely a wasted one," my friend explained. "We have seen both the retailers and also the wholesale manufacturers. I can trace each of the busts now from the beginning."

"The busts!" cried Lestrade. "Well, well, you have your own methods, Mr. Sherlock Holmes, and it is not for me to say a word against them, but I think I have done a better day's work than you. I have identified the dead man."

"You don't say so!"

"And found a cause for the crime."

"Splendid!"

"We have an inspector who makes a speciality of
Saffron Hill and the Italian quarter. Well, this dead **13**
man had some Catholic emblem round his neck, and that, along with his colour, made me think he was from the South. Inspector Hill knew him the moment he caught sight of him. His name is Pietro Venucci, from Naples, and he is one of the greatest cut-throats in London. He is connected with the Mafia, which, as you know, is a secret political society, enforcing its decrees by murder. Now you see how the affair begins to clear up. The other fellow is probably an Italian also, and a member of the Mafia. He has broken the rules in some fashion. Pietro is set upon his track. Probably the photograph we found in his pocket is the man himself, so that he may not knife the wrong person. He dogs the fellow, he sees him enter a house, he waits outside for him, and in the scuffle he receives his own death-wound. How is that, Mr. Sherlock Holmes?"

Holmes clapped his hands approvingly.

"Excellent, Lestrade, excellent!" he cried. "But I didn't quite follow your explanation of the destruction of the busts."

"The busts! You never can get those busts out of your head. After all, that is nothing; petty larceny, six months at the most. It is the murder that we are really investigating, and I tell you that I am gathering all the threads into my hands."

"And the next stage?"

"Is a very simple one. I shall go down with Hill to the Italian quarter, find the man whose photograph we have got, and arrest him on the charge of murder. Will you come with us?"

"I think not. I fancy we can attain our end in a simpler way. I can't say for certain, because it all depends—well, it all depends upon a factor which is completely outside our control. But I have great hopes—in fact, the betting is exactly two to one—that if you will come with us to-night I shall be able to help you to lay him by the heels."

"In the Italian quarter?"

fellow left me last week. . . . He was gone two days when the bust was smashed." It is extremely unlikely that Beppo left Hudson without collecting his pay for a week's work—to do so would be to arouse suspicion and perhaps investigation of his activities, the last thing he would want. We deduce that he worked for Hudson from Monday, May 28th, to Saturday, June 2nd, collected his pay on the Saturday and left. (To suppose that Beppo worked for Hudson from Monday, June 4th, to Saturday, June 9th, leaves much too long a gap between his release from prison and his obtaining employment at Hudson's shop.) It is not clear from Mr. Hudson's account whether the first bust was smashed on the second or third day after Beppo's departure; in either case, the day must be Monday, June 4th, or Tuesday, June 5th. On the first day of the case, Lestrade told Holmes that the first instance of bust-smashing was reported "four days ago." The case must therefore open on Friday, June 8th, or Saturday, June 9th. We know that the first day was not Saturday, June 9th, since on the *second* day evening newspapers were published; the shop of Harding Brothers was open, as was Morse Hudson's, as was Gelder & Co. Furthermore, as we learn later, Mr. Sandeford of Reading sold his bust of Napoleon to Holmes on the third day of the case. "Not a very rich man," he could hardly have afforded to take time from work to journey from Reading to Baker Street. Almost certainly, he would have called on Holmes on a Sunday—and this is substantiated by his remark that "the trains were awkward"; they would hardly have been so on a weekday. We conclude that the case began on *Friday, June 8*, and ended on *Sunday, June 10, 1900.*

13 *Saffron Hill.* So called because saffron once grew in the garden of Ely House, the old palace of the Bishops of Ely, built in 1388 by Bishop Arundel.

. . . HE CARRIED SOMETHING WHITE UNDER HIS ARM.

Illustration by Charles Raymond Macauley for *The Return of Sherlock Holmes*, New York: McClure, Phillips & Co., 1905.

WITH THE BOUND OF A TIGER HOLMES WAS ON HIS BACK . . .

Illustration by Sidney Paget for the *Strand Magazine*, May, 1904.

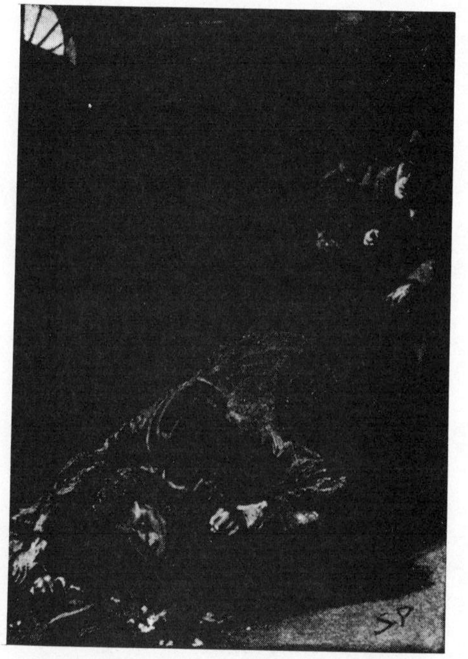

"No; I fancy Chiswick is an address which is more likely to find him. If you will come with me to Chiswick to-night, Lestrade, I'll promise to go to the Italian quarter with you to-morrow, and no harm will be done by the delay. And now I think that a few hours' sleep would do us all good, for I do not propose to leave before eleven o'clock, and it is unlikely that we shall be back before morning. You'll dine with us, Lestrade, and then you are welcome to the sofa until it is time for us to start. In the meantime, Watson, I should be glad if you would ring for an express messenger, for I have a letter to send, and it is important that it should go at once."

Holmes spent the evening in rummaging among the files of the old daily papers with which one of our lumber-rooms was packed. When at last he descended it was with triumph in his eyes, but he said nothing to either of us as to the result of his researches. For my own part, I had followed step by step the methods by which he had traced the various windings of this complex case, and, though I could not yet perceive the goal which we would reach, I understood clearly that Holmes expected this grotesque criminal to make an attempt upon the two remaining busts, one of which, I remember, was at Chiswick. No doubt the object of our journey was to catch him in the very act, and I could not but admire the cunning with which my friend had inserted a wrong clue in the evening paper so as to give the fellow the idea that he could continue his scheme with impunity. I was not surprised when Holmes suggested that I should take my revolver with me. He had himself picked up the loaded hunting-crop which was his favourite weapon.

A four-wheeler was at the door at eleven, and in it we drove to a spot at the other side of Hammersmith Bridge. Here the cabman was directed to wait. A short walk brought us to a secluded road fringed with pleasant houses, each standing in its own grounds. In the light of a street lamp we read "Laburnum Villa" upon the gate-post of one of them. The occupants had evidently retired to rest, for all was dark save for a fanlight over the hall door, which shed a single blurred circle on to the garden path. The wooden fence which separated the grounds from the road threw a dense black shadow upon the inner side, and here it was that we crouched.

"I fear that you'll have a long time to wait," Holmes whispered. "We may thank our stars that it is not raining. I don't think we can even venture to smoke to pass the time. However, it's a two to one chance that we get something to pay us for our trouble."

It proved, however, that our vigil was not to be so long as Holmes had led us to fear, and it ended in a very sudden and singular fashion. In an instant, without the least sound to warn us of his coming, the garden gate swung open, and a lithe, dark figure, as swift and active as an ape, rushed up the garden path. We saw it whisk past the light thrown from over the door and disappear against the black shadow of the house. There was a long pause, during which we held our breath, and then a very gentle creaking sound came to our ears. The window was being opened. The noise ceased, and again there was a long silence. The fellow was making his way into the house. We saw the sudden flash of a dark lantern inside the room. What he sought was evidently not there, for again we saw the flash through another blind, and then through another.

"Let us get to the open window. We will nab him as he climbs out," Lestrade whispered.

But before we could move the man had emerged again. As he came out into the glimmering patch of light we saw that he carried something white under his arm. He looked stealthily all round him. The silence of the deserted street reassured him. Turning his back upon us, he laid down his burden, and the next instant there was the sound of a sharp tap, followed by a clatter and rattle. The man was so intent upon what he was doing that he never heard our steps as we stole across the grass plot. With the bound of a tiger Holmes was on his back, and an instant later Lestrade and I had him by either wrist, and the handcuffs had been fastened. As we turned him over I saw a hideous, sallow face, with writhing, furious features glaring up at us, and I knew that it was indeed the man of the photograph whom we had secured.

But it was not our prisoner to whom Holmes was giving his attention. Squatted on the doorstep, he was engaged in most carefully examining that which the man had brought from the house. It was a bust of Napoleon like the one which we had seen that morning, and it had been broken into similar fragments. Carefully Holmes held each separate shard to the light, but in no way did it differ from any other shattered piece of plaster. He had just completed his examination, when the hall lights flew up, the door opened, and the owner of the house, a jovial, rotund figure in shirt and trousers, presented himself.

"Mr. Josiah Brown, I suppose?" said Holmes.

"Yes, sir; and you no doubt are Mr. Sherlock Holmes? I had the note which you sent by the express messenger, and I did exactly what you told me. We locked every door on the inside and awaited developments. Well, I'm very glad to see that you have got the rascal. I hope, gentlemen, that you will come in and have some refreshment."

However, Lestrade was anxious to get his man into safe quarters, so within a few minutes our cab had been summoned and we were all four upon our way to London. Not a word would our captive say; but he glared at us from the shadow of his matted hair, and once, when my hand seemed within his reach, he snapped at it like a hungry wolf. We stayed long enough at the police-station to learn that a search of his clothing revealed nothing save a few shillings and a long sheath knife, the handle of which bore copious traces of recent blood.

"That's all right," said Lestrade, as we parted. "Hill knows all these gentry, and he will give a name to him. You'll find that my theory of the Mafia will work out all right. But I'm sure I am exceedingly obliged to you, Mr. Holmes, for the workmanlike way in which you laid hands upon him. I don't quite understand it all yet."

HE HAD JUST COMPLETED HIS EXAMINATION, WHEN THE HALL LIGHTS FLEW UP . . .

Illustration by Frederic Dorr Steele for *Collier's Magazine*, April 30, 1904.

. . . THE DOOR OPENED, AND THE OWNER OF THE HOUSE . . . PRESENTED HIMSELF.

Illustration by Sidney Paget for the *Strand Magazine*, May, 1904.

" I fear it is rather too late an hour for explanations," said Holmes. " Besides, there are one or two details which are not finished off, and it is one of those cases which are worth working out to the very end. If you will come round once more to my rooms at six o'clock to-morrow I think I shall be able to show you that even now you have not grasped the entire meaning of this business, which presents some features which make it absolutely original in the history of crime. If ever I permit you to chronicle any more of my little problems, Watson, I foresee that you will enliven your pages by an account of the singular adventure of the Napoleonic busts."

When we met again next evening, Lestrade was furnished with much information concerning our prisoner. His name, it appeared, was Beppo, second name unknown. He was a well-known ne'er-do-well among the Italian colony. He had once been a skilful sculptor and had earned an honest living, but he had taken to evil courses, and had twice already been in gaol—once for a petty theft and once, as we had already heard, for stabbing a fellow-countryman. He could talk English perfectly well. His reasons for destroying the busts were still unknown, and he refused to answer any questions upon the subject ; but the police had discovered that these same busts might very well have been made by his own hands, since he was engaged in this class of work at the establishment of Gelder & Co. To all this information, much of which we already knew, Holmes listened with polite attention ; but I, who knew him so well, could clearly see that his thoughts were elsewhere, and I detected a mixture of mingled uneasiness and expectation beneath that mask which he was wont to assume. At last he started in his chair and his eyes brightened. There had been a ring at the bell. A minute later we heard steps upon the stairs, and an elderly, red-faced man with grizzled side-whiskers was ushered in. In his right hand he carried an old-fashioned carpet-bag, which he placed upon the table.

" Is Mr. Sherlock Holmes here ? "

My friend bowed and smiled. " Mr. Sandeford, of Reading, I suppose ? " said he.

" Yes, sir. I fear that I am a little late ; but the trains were awkward. You wrote to me about a bust that is in my possession."

" Exactly."

" I have your letter here. You said, ' I desire to possess a copy of Devine's Napoleon, and am prepared to pay you ten pounds for the one which is in your possession.' Is that right ? "

" Certainly."

" I was very much surprised at your letter, for I could not imagine how you knew that I owned such a thing."

" Of course you must have been surprised, but the explanation is very simple. Mr. Harding, of Harding Brothers, said that they had sold you their last copy, and he gave me your address."

" Oh, that was it, was it ? Did he tell you what I paid for it ? "

" No, he did not."

" Well, I am an honest man, though not a very rich one. I only gave fifteen shillings for the bust, and I think you ought to know that before I take ten pounds from you."

" I am sure the scruple does you honour, Mr. Sandeford. But I have named that price, so I intend to stick to it."

" Well, it is very handsome of you, Mr. Holmes. I brought the bust up with me, as you asked me to do. Here it is ! "

He opened his bag, and at last we saw placed upon our table a complete specimen of that bust which we had already seen more than once in fragments.

Holmes took a paper from his pocket and laid a ten-pound note upon the table.

" You will kindly sign that paper, Mr. Sandeford, in the presence of these witnesses. It is simply to say that you transfer every possible right that you ever had in the bust to me. I am a methodical man, you see, and you never know what turn events might take afterwards. Thank you, Mr. Sandeford ; here is your money, and I wish you a very good evening."

When our visitor had disappeared Sherlock Holmes' movements were such as to rivet our attention. He began by taking a clean white cloth from a drawer and laying it over the table. Then he placed his newly acquired bust in the centre of the cloth. Finally he picked up his hunting-crop and struck Napoleon a sharp blow on the top of the head. The figure broke into fragments, and Holmes bent eagerly over the shattered remains. Next instant, with a loud shout of triumph, he held up one splinter, in which a round, dark object was fixed like a plum in a pudding.

" Gentlemen," he cried, " let me introduce you to the famous black pearl of the Borgias ! "

Lestrade and I sat silent for a moment, and then, with a spontaneous impulse, we both broke out clapping as at the well-wrought crisis of a play. A flush of colour sprang to Holmes' pale cheeks, and he bowed to us like the master dramatist who receives the homage of his audience. It was at such moments that for an instant he ceased to be a reasoning machine, and betrayed his human love for admiration and applause. The same singularly proud and reserved nature which turned away with disdain from popular notoriety was capable of being moved to its depths by spontaneous wonder and praise from a friend.

" Yes, gentlemen," said he, " it is the most famous pearl now existing in the world, and it has been my good fortune by a connected chain of inductive reasoning, to trace it from the Prince of Colonna's bedroom at the Dacre Hotel, where it was lost, to the interior of this, the last of the six busts of Napoleon which were manufactured by Gelder & Co., of Stepney. You will remember, Lestrade, the sensation caused by the disappearance of this valuable jewel, and the vain efforts of the London police to recover it. I was myself consulted upon the case ; but I was unable to throw any light upon it. Suspicion fell upon the maid of the Princess, who was an Italian, and it was proved that she had a brother in London, but

"I BROUGHT THE BUST UP WITH ME, AS YOU ASKED ME TO DO."

Illustration by Sidney Paget for the *Strand Magazine*, May, 1904.

we failed to trace any connection between them. The maid's name was Lucretia Venucci, and there is no doubt in my mind that this Pietro who was murdered two nights ago was the brother. I have been looking up the dates in the old files of the paper, and I find that the disappearance of the pearl was exactly two days before the arrest of Beppo for some crime of violence—an event which took place in the factory of Gelder & Co., at the very moment when these busts were being made. Now you clearly see the sequence of events, though you see them, of course, in the inverse order to the way in which they presented themselves to me. Beppo had the pearl in his possession. He may have stolen it from Pietro, he may have been Pietro's confederate, he may have been the go-between of Pietro and his sister. It is of no consequence to us which is the correct solution.

" The main fact is that he *had* the pearl, and at that moment, when it was on his person, he was pursued by the police. He made for the factory in which he worked, and he knew that he had only a few minutes in which to conceal this enormously valuable prize, which would otherwise be found on him when he was searched. Six plaster casts of Napoleon were drying in the passage. One of them was still soft. In an instant Beppo, a skilful workman, made a small hole in the wet plaster, dropped in the pearl, and with a few touches covered over the aperture once more. It was an admirable hiding-place. No one could possibly find it. But Beppo was condemned to a year's imprisonment, and in the meanwhile his six busts were scattered over London. He could not tell which contained his treasure. Only by breaking them could he see. Even shaking would tell him nothing for as the plaster was wet it was probable that the pearl would adhere to it—as, in fact, it has done. Beppo did not despair, and he conducted his search with considerable ingenuity and perseverance. Through a cousin who works with Gelder he found out the retail firms who had bought the busts. He managed to find employment with Morse Hudson, and in that way tracked down three of them. The pearl was not there. Then with the help of some Italian employé, he succeeded in finding out where the other three busts had gone. The first was at Harker's. There he was dogged by his confederate, who held Beppo responsible for the loss of the pearl, and he stabbed him in the scuffle which followed."

" If he was his confederate, why should he carry his photograph ? " I asked.

" As a means of tracing him if he wished to inquire about him from any third person. That was the obvious reason. Well, after the murder I calculated that Beppo would probably hurry rather than delay his movements. He would fear that the police would read his secret, and so he hastened on before they should get ahead of him. Of course, I could not say that he had not found the pearl in Harker's bust. I had not even concluded for certain that it was the pearl ; but it was evident to me that he was looking for something, since he carried the bust past the other houses in order to break it in the garden which had a lamp overlooking it. Since Harker's bust was one in three, the chances were exactly as I told you—two to one against the pearl being inside it. There remained two busts, and it was obvious that he would go for the London one first. I warned the inmates of the house, so as to avoid a second tragedy, and we went down, with the happiest results. By that time, of course, I knew for certain that it was the Borgia pearl that we were after. The name of the murdered man linked the one event with the other. There only remained a single bust—the Reading one—and the pearl must be there. I bought it in your presence from the owner—and there it lies."

We sat in silence for a moment.

"Well," said Lestrade, "I've seen you handle a good many cases, Mr. Holmes, but I don't know that I ever knew a more workmanlike one than that. We're not jealous of you at Scotland Yard. No, sir, we are very proud of you, and if you come down to-morrow there's not a man, from the oldest inspector to the youngest constable, who wouldn't be glad to shake you by the hand."

"Thank you!" said Holmes. "Thank you!" and as he turned away it seemed to me that he was more nearly moved by the softer human emotions than I had ever seen him. A moment later he was the cold and practical thinker once more. "Put the pearl in the
safe, Watson," said he, "and get out the papers of the **14**
Conk-Singleton forgery case. Good-bye, Lestrade. If **15**
any little problem comes your way I shall be happy, if I can, to give you a hint or two as to its solution."

14 *"Put the pearl in the safe, Watson."* "The pearl after all had been stolen," Mr. S. T. L. Harbottle wrote in "Sherlock Holmes and the Law." "The thief had no right to it and could give no one else any right to it. Sandeford was not the owner, and, as against the Prince of Colonna who was, Holmes had no title to the pearl at all. He was in fact a receiver of stolen goods. There was no suggestion of returning the pearl to the Prince—far from it. 'Put the pearl in the safe, Watson,' said Holmes quite unblushingly."

15 *the papers of the Conk-Singleton forgery case.* A version of this unreported case, in the form of a playlet, was enacted in 1948 at the Mystery Writers of America Edgar Award Dinner, with the following cast: Clayton Rawson as Sherlock Holmes, Lawrence G. Blochman as Dr. Watson, John Dickson Carr as The Visitor. The playlet—as "by Dr. John H. Watson"—was published in the *Unicorn Mystery Book Club News*, Vol. I, No. 9, pp. 8–9, 16. Of interest here also is the late Gavin Brend's "Prooimion" to this case, as published in the *Sherlock Holmes Journal*, Vol. I, No. 4, December, 1953, pp. 2–4.

65

THE PROBLEM OF THOR BRIDGE

[*Thursday, October 4, to Friday, October 5, 1900*]

SOMEWHERE in the vaults of the bank of Cox
& Co., at Charing Cross, there is a travel-
1 worn and battered tin dispatch-box with my name,
2 John H. Watson, M.D., Late Indian Army, painted
upon the lid. It is crammed with papers, nearly all
of which are records of cases to illustrate the curious
problems which Mr. Sherlock Holmes had at various
times to examine. Some, and not the least interesting,
were complete failures, and as such will hardly bear
narrating, since no final explanation is forthcoming. A
problem without a solution may interest the student,
but can hardly fail to annoy the casual reader. Among
these unfinished tales is that of Mr. James Phillimore,
who, stepping back into his own house to get his
3 umbrella, was never more seen in this world. No less
remarkable is that of the cutter *Alicia*, which sailed one
spring morning into a small patch of mist from where she
never again emerged, nor was anything further ever heard
4 of herself and her crew. A third case worthy of note is
that of Isadora Persano, the well-known journalist and
duellist, who was found stark staring mad with a match-
box in front of him which contained a remarkable worm,
5 said to be unknown to science. Apart from these
unfathomed cases, there are some which involve the
secrets of private families to an extent which would mean
consternation in many exalted quarters if it were thought
possible that they might find their way into print. I
need not say that such a breach of confidence is unthinkable, and that these records will be separated and
destroyed now that my friend has time to turn his energies to the matter. There remain a considerable residue
of cases of greater or less interest which I might have
edited before had I not feared to give the public a surfeit
which might react upon the reputation of the man whom
above all others I revere. In some I was myself concerned and can speak as an eye-witness, while in others I
was either not present or played so small a part that they
6 could only be told as by a third person. The following
narrative is drawn from my own experience.

It was a wild morning in October, and I observed as I
was dressing how the last remaining leaves were being
7 whirled from the solitary plane tree which graces the

1 *tin dispatch-box with my name.* To the never-ending regret of all Sherlockians, the Charing Cross banking firm of Cox & Co. was wiped out in the World War II bombings that so badly damaged that section of London.

2 *Late Indian Army.* If Watson's service with the Berkshires and the Northumberland Fusiliers was all the army service he had, he was never in the Indian Army (as we have previously noted), for those two regiments are part of the regular establishment of the British Army and were merely ordered to India, while the Indian Army, as an organization, is an entirely separate thing.

3 *was never more seen in this world.* A pastiche of this adventure by the late Edgar W. Smith has appeared in *A Baker Street Four-Wheeler;* a second, titled "Sunshine, Sunshine," by Mr. Benjamin S. Clark, has appeared in the *Baker Street Journal Christmas Annual* for 1960; and a third, titled "The Adventure of the Highgate Miracle," by Adrian M. Conan Doyle and John Dickson Carr has appeared in *The Exploits of Sherlock Holmes.*

4 *nor was anything further ever heard of herself and her crew.* Watson's reference here reminded both Mr. T. S. Blakeney and the late Edgar W. Smith of the mystery of the *Mary Celeste:* "Perhaps Holmes' failure over the cutter *Alicia* decided him not to add to the number of would-be solvers of the mystery of the *Mary Celeste*" (Blakeney); "The fate of the *Alicia* reminds us, somehow, of what befell the brigantine *Mary Celeste* . . . which was found abandoned, for no known reason, in a high-running sea between the Azores and Portugal in the year 1872" (Smith). In addition, Mr. Richard W. Clarke has speculated that "the cutter *Alicia* was so named by Watson for a Miss Alicia Cutter of New York City, whom Watson met in Lausanne during the search for Lady Frances Carfax, and whom he later married ("On the Nomenclature of Watson's Ships").

yard behind our house. I descended to breakfast prepared to find my companion in depressed spirits, for, like all great artists, he was easily impressed by his surroundings. On the contrary, I found that he had nearly finished his meal, and that his mood was particularly bright and joyous, with that somewhat sinister cheerfulness which was characteristic of his lighter moments.

" You have a case, Holmes ? " I remarked.

" The faculty of deduction is certainly contagious, Watson," he answered. " It has enabled you to probe my secret. Yes, I have a case. After a month of trivialities and stagnation the wheels move once more."

" Might I share it ? "

" There is little to share, but we may discuss it when you have consumed the two hard-boiled eggs with which our new cook has favoured us. Their condition may not be unconnected with the copy of the *Family Herald* which I observed yesterday upon the hall-table. Even so trivial a matter as cooking an egg demands an attention which is conscious of the passage of time, and incompatible with the love romance in that excellent periodical."

A quarter of an hour later the table had been cleared and we were face to face. He had drawn a letter from his pocket.

" You have heard of Neil Gibson, the Gold King ? " he said.

" You mean the American Senator ? "

" Well, he was once Senator for some Western State, but is better known as the greatest gold-mining magnate in the world."

" Yes, I know of him. He has surely lived in England for some time. His name is very familiar."

" Yes ; he bought a considerable estate in Hampshire some five years ago. Possibly you have already heard of the tragic end of his wife ? "

" Of course. I remember it now. That is why the name is familiar. But I really know nothing of the details."

Holmes waved his hand towards some papers on a chair. " I had no idea that the case was coming my way or I should have had my extracts ready," said he. " The fact is that the problem, though exceedingly sensational, appeared to present no difficulty. The interesting personality of the accused does not obscure the clearness of the evidence. That was the view taken by the coroner's jury and also in the police-court proceedings. It is now referred to the Assizes at Winchester. I fear it is a thankless business. I can discover facts, Watson, but I cannot change them. Unless some entirely new and unexpected ones come to light I do not see what my client can hope for."

" Your client ? '

" Ah, I forgot I had not told you. I am getting into your involved habit, Watson, of telling a story backwards. You had best read this first."

The letter which he handed to me, written in a bold, masterful hand, ran as follows :

CLARIDGE'S HOTEL, *October 3rd.* **8**

DEAR MR. SHERLOCK HOLMES,—

5 *said to be unknown to science.* "One optical illusion used in the German *Gestalt-Psycholgie* is a spiral, a line beginning with a central dot and forming a whirling curve until the whole is approximately an inch in diameter," Mr. Rolfe Boswell once wrote. "Intense concentration upon this optical cynosure induces self-hypnosis. Prolonged concentration might cause madness. The same effect might be caused by prolonged gazing at a tightly coiled watch spring. The *Shorter Oxford English Dictionary* gives this definition of worm: III. g. A spring or strip of metal of spiral shape 1724. Presumably, if you gaze at such a *worm* long enough, you'll be *Persano non grata,* if not 'stark staring mad.' "

"In a work entitled *A Voyage of Discovery, made under the Orders of the Admiralty, in His Majesty's Ships Isabella and Alexander, for the Purpose of Exploring Baffin's Bay and Enquiring into the Probability of a North-West Passage,* written by Sir John Ross in 1819, one finds the statement: '. . . it fell bearly calm for a short time and we sounded with the deepsea clamms, which brought up a quantity of mud, in which were *five worms of a species that had not been seen before,*' " Mr. R. P. Graham wrote. "Who of Ross's crew . . . preserved these Baffin Bay worms, and who put one of their descendants into a match-box to help drive poor Isadora Persano 'stark staring mad'?"

And Mr. James Edward Holroyd has added that: "Isadora Persano was not the first journalist to be confronted with a remarkable worm said to be unknown to science. I find that a correspondent wrote to Dr. Johnson in No. 82 of *The Rambler,* December 29, 1750: 'I have three species of earthworms not known to the naturalists . . .' "

We should also note here that Mr. Stuart Palmer has written a pastiche stemming from this reference of Dr. Watson's which Ellery Queen has called "utterly delightful and satisfying"; see *The Misadventures of Sherlock Holmes.*

6 *they could only be told as by a third person.* Of the sixty Canonical Tales, two—"The Adventure of the Mazarin Stone" and "His Last Bow" —are told in the third person. There has been much controversy as to the authorship of these two adventures. Some students have advanced the theory that they were written by Mycroft Holmes; others have maintained that their authoress was the second, or third, Mrs. Watson; still others have claimed that they were written by Sir Arthur Conan Doyle. In the view of other commentators Watson's statement here, properly interpreted, can point to only one conclusion: both cases were recorded by none other than Watson.

7 *the solitary plane tree.* Americans would call the plane tree a sycamore.

8 CLARIDGE'S HOTEL. On Brook Street, at the south corner of Davies Street, stands the world-famous Claridge's Hotel. This hotel, formerly Mivart's, was opened in 1808 by M. Mivart, a Frenchman, at a time when sumptuous accommodation was very much lacking in the metropolis. So well did M. Mivart prosper that he added four adjoining houses to the one originally leased before he sold the business to Mr. and Mrs. Claridge in the middle of the last century. In 1895, after the death of Mr. Claridge, the old premises were pulled down and the present magnificent hotel erected.

9 *I'll come at eleven to-morrow.* J. Neil Gibson therefore called on Holmes on October 4th. On this day Holmes complained that the breakfast eggs were hard-boiled; the new cook had been reading the love romance in her copy of the *Family Herald,* which Holmes had "observed yesterday upon the hall-table." The late H. W. Bell long ago demonstrated that the *Family Herald,* a weekly publication, was published on *Wednesdays.* The case therefore opened on Thursday, October 4th—but in what year? The case is obviously a late one: 1) Watson calls Holmes "my famous friend." And, as Mr. Bell wrote, "Judging from Senator Gibson's letter, in which he writes: 'If ever in your life you showed your powers, put them now into this case,' Holmes must have been in practice for years and have acquired an immense reputation." 2) Holmes speaks of Watson's "annals," and says that he, Holmes, is "getting into your involved habit, Watson, of telling a story backwards." 3) Holmes says he has been threatened often. 4) To these evidences of "lateness," add the fact that Billy the page opened the door to Mr. Marlow Bates. This cannot be the Billy of *The Valley of Fear;* it must therefore be the Billy of "The Adventure of the Mazarin Stone," which took place, as we shall see, in the summer of 1903. A subtle point, provided by the late Gavin Brend, furnishes further evidence that the case began in fact on *Thursday, October 4, 1900.* (It ended the next day.) "1901," Mr. Brend wrote (a year suggested by some commentators), "can be deleted on account of Holmes' grandiloquent remark to Neil Gibson, 'My professional charges are upon a fixed scale. I do not vary them save when I remit them altogether.' In the case of 'The Priory School' which . . . occurred in May, 1901, Holmes received for his services the sum of £6,000, which was paid to him by the Duke of Holdernesse. . . . It is true that the initiative came from the Duke, but even so, [Holmes] would hardly be justified in making the above remark in the month of October after pocketing the Duke's cheque in the month of May. Accordingly we are left with October, 1900, as the only possible date for 'Thor Bridge.' "

I can't see the best woman God ever made go to her death without doing all that is possible to save her. I can't explain things—I can't even try to explain them, but I know beyond all doubt that Miss Dunbar is innocent. You know the facts—who doesn't? It has been the gossip of the country. And never a voice raised for her! It's the damned injustice of it all that makes me crazy. That woman has a heart that wouldn't let her
9 kill a fly. Well, I'll come at eleven to-morrow and see if you can get some ray of light in the dark. Maybe I have a clue and don't know it. Anyhow, all I know and all I have and all I am are for your use if only you can save her. If ever in your life you showed your powers, put them now into this case.

Yours faithfully,
J. Neil Gibson.

" There you have it," said Sherlock Holmes, knocking out the ashes of his after-breakfast pipe and slowly refilling it. " That is the gentleman I await. As to the story, you have hardly time to master all these papers, so I must give it to you in a nutshell if you are to take an intelligent interest in the proceedings. This man is the greatest financial power in the world, and a man, as I understand, of most violent and formidable character. He married a wife, the victim of this tragedy, of whom I know nothing save that she was past her prime, which was the more unfortunate as a very attractive governess superintended the education of two young children. These are the three people concerned, and the scene is a grand old manor-house, the centre of an historical English estate. Then as to the tragedy. The wife was found in the grounds nearly half a mile from the house, late at night, clad in her dinner dress, with a shawl over her shoulders and a revolver bullet through her brain. No weapon was found near her and there was no local clue as to the murder. No weapon near her, Watson—mark that! The crime seems to have been committed late in the evening, and the body was found by a gamekeeper about eleven o'clock, when it was examined by the police and by a doctor before being carried up to the house. Is this too condensed, or can you follow it clearly? "

" It is all very clear. But why suspect the governess? "

" Well, in the first place there is some very direct evidence. A revolver with one discharged chamber and a calibre which corresponded with the bullet was found on the floor of her wardrobe." His eyes fixed and he repeated in broken words, " On—the—floor—of—her—wardrobe." Then he sank into silence, and I saw that some train of thought had been set moving which I should be foolish to interrupt. Suddenly with a start he emerged into brisk life once more. " Yes, Watson, it was found. Pretty damning, eh? So the two juries thought. Then the dead woman had a note upon her making an appointment at that very place and signed by the governess. How's that? Finally, there is the motive. Senator Gibson is an attractive person. If his wife dies, who more likely to succeed her than the young lady who had already by all accounts received pressing attentions from her employer. Love, fortune, power, all depending upon one middle-aged life. Ugly, Watson—very ugly!"

"Yes, indeed, Holmes."

"Nor could she prove an alibi. On the contrary, she had to admit that she was down near Thor Bridge—that was the scene of the tragedy—about that hour. She couldn't deny it, for some passing villager had seen her there."

"That really seems final."

"And yet, Watson—and yet! This bridge—a single broad span of stone with balustraded sides—carries the drive over the narrowest part of a long, deep, reed-girt sheet of water. Thor Mere it is called. In the mouth of the bridge lay the dead woman. Such are the main facts. But here, if I mistake not, is our client, considerably before his time."

Billy had opened the door, but the name which he announced was an unexpected one. Mr. Marlow Bates was a stranger to both of us. He was a thin, nervous wisp of a man with frightened eyes, and a twitching, hesitating manner—a man whom my own professional eye would judge to be on the brink of an absolute nervous breakdown.

"You seem agitated, Mr. Bates," said Holmes. "Pray sit down. I fear I can only give you a short time, for I have an appointment at eleven."

"I know you have," our visitor gasped, shooting out short sentences like a man who is out of breath. "Mr. Gibson is coming. Mr. Gibson is my employer. I am manager of his estate. Mr. Holmes, he is a villain—an infernal villain."

"Strong language, Mr. Bates."

"I have to be emphatic, Mr. Holmes, for the time is so limited. I would not have him find me here for the world. He is almost due now. But I was so situated that I could not come earlier. His secretary, Mr. Ferguson, only told me this morning of his appointment with you."

"And you are his manager?"

"I have given him notice. In a couple of weeks I shall have shaken off his accursed slavery. A hard man, Mr. Holmes, hard to all about him. Those public charities are a screen to cover his private iniquities. But his wife was his chief victim. He was brutal to her—yes, sir, brutal! How she came by her death I do not know, but I am sure that he had made her life a misery to her. She was a creature of the Tropics, a Brazilian by birth, as no doubt you know?"

"No; it had escaped me."

"Tropical by birth and tropical by nature. A child of the sun and of passion. She had loved him as such women can love, but when her own physical charms had faded—I am told that they once were great—there was nothing to hold him. We all liked her and felt for her and hated him for the way that he treated her. But he is plausible and cunning. That is all I have to say to you. Don't take him at his face value. There is more behind. Now I'll go. No, no, don't detain me! He is almost due."

With a frightened look at the clock our strange visitor

"THE WIFE WAS FOUND IN THE GROUNDS NEARLY HALF A MILE FROM THE HOUSE, LATE AT NIGHT . . ."

Illustration by A. Gilbert for the *Strand Magazine*, February, 1922. G. Patrick Nelson illustrated the same scene for *Hearst's International*, February, 1922.

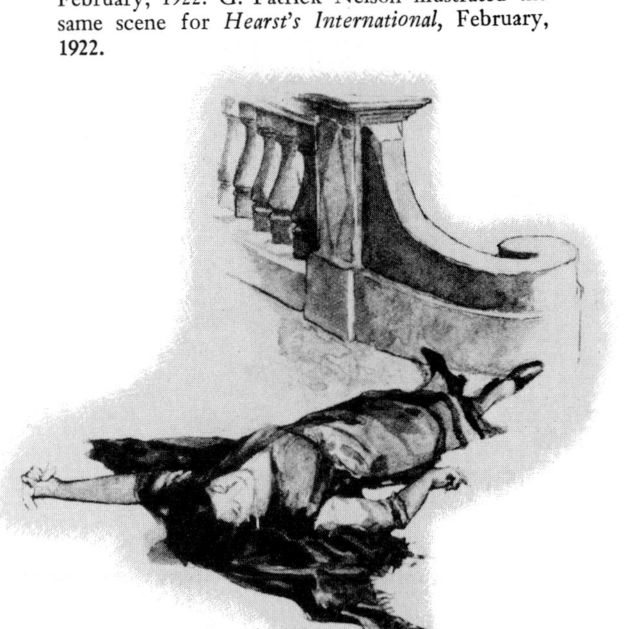

literally ran to the door and disappeared.

" Well! Well!" said Holmes, after an interval of silence. " Mr. Gibson seems to have a nice loyal household. But the warning is a useful one, and now we can only wait till the man himself appears."

Sharp at the hour we heard a heavy step upon the stairs and the famous millionaire was shown into the room. As I looked upon him I understood not only the fears and dislike of his manager, but also the execrations which so many business rivals have heaped upon his head. If I were a sculptor and desired to idealize the successful man of affairs, iron of nerve and leathery of conscience, I should choose Mr. Neil Gibson as my model. His tall, gaunt craggy figure had a suggestion of hunger and rapacity. An Abraham Lincoln keyed to base uses instead of high ones would give some idea of the man. His face might have been chiselled in granite, hard-set, craggy, remorseless, with deep lines upon it, the scars of many a crisis. Cold grey eyes, looking shrewdly out from under bristling brows, surveyed us each in turn. He bowed in perfunctory fashion as Holmes mentioned my name, and then with a masterful air of possession he drew a chair up to my companion and seated himself with his bony knees almost touching him.

" Let me say right here, Mr. Holmes," he began, " that money is nothing to me in this case. You can burn it if it's any use in lighting you to the truth. This woman is innocent and this woman has to be cleared, and it's up to you to do it. Name your figure!"

10 " My professional charges are upon a fixed scale," said Holmes coldly. " I do not vary them, save when I remit them altogether."

" Well, if dollars make no difference to you, think of the reputation. If you pull this off every paper in England and America will be booming you. You'll be the talk of two continents."

" Thank you, Mr. Gibson, I do not think that I am in need of booming. It may surprise you to know that I prefer to work anonymously, and that it is the problem itself which attracts me. But we are wasting time. Let us get down to the facts."

" I think that you will find all the main ones in the Press reports. I don't know that I can add anything which will help you. But if there is anything you would wish more light upon—well, I am here to give it."

" Well, there is just one point."

" What is it?"

" What were the exact relations between you and Miss Dunbar?"

The Gold King gave a violent start, and half rose from his chair. Then his massive calm came back to him.

" I suppose you are within your rights—and maybe doing your duty—in asking such a question, Mr. Holmes."

" We will agree to suppose so," said Holmes.

" Then I can assure you that our relations were entirely and always those of an employer towards a young lady whom he never conversed with, or ever saw, save when

10 "*My professional charges are upon a fixed scale.*" "On what was [this "fixed scale"] to be based?" Mr. S. T. L. Harbottle asked in "'My Charges Are Upon a Fixed Scale—' ". "On the value of property recovered? But few would care to put a price on the Naval Treaty or the ancient crown of England, to take but two examples. On the time taken by the investigation? But are we to equate, for instance, the 4½ hours in the train on the way to Boscombe Valley with the 4½ hours spent in vigil at Stoke Moran? The only thing clear about this scale is that it cannot have been fixed."

she was in the company of his children."

Holmes rose from his chair.

"I am a rather busy man, Mr. Gibson," said he, "and I have no time or taste for aimless conversations. I wish you good morning."

Our visitor had risen also and his great loose figure towered above Holmes. There was an angry gleam from under those bristling brows and a tinge of colour in the sallow cheeks.

"What the devil do you mean by this, Mr. Holmes? Do you dismiss my case?"

"Well, Mr. Gibson, at least I dismiss you. I should have thought my words were plain."

"Plain enough, but what's at the back of it? Raising the price on me, or afraid to tackle it, or what? I've a right to a plain answer."

"Well, perhaps you have," said Holmes. "I'll give you one. This case is quite sufficiently complicated to start with, without the further difficulty of false information."

"Meaning that I lie."

"Well, I was trying to express it as delicately as I could, but if you insist upon the word I will not contradict you."

I sprang to my feet, for the expression upon the millionaire's face was fiendish in its intensity, and he had raised his great knotted fist. Holmes smiled languidly, and reached his hand out for his pipe.

"Don't be noisy, Mr. Gibson. I find that after breakfast even the smallest argument is unsettling. I suggest that a stroll in the morning air and a little quiet thought will be greatly to your advantage."

With an effort the Gold King mastered his fury. I could not but admire him, for by a supreme self-command he had turned in a minute from a hot flame of anger to a frigid and contemptuous indifference.

"Well, it's your choice. I guess you know how to run your own business. I can't make you touch the case against your will. You've done yourself no good this morning, Mr. Holmes, for I have broken stronger men than you. No man ever crossed me and was the better for it."

"So many have said so, and yet here I am," said Holmes, smiling. "Well, good morning, Mr. Gibson. You have a good deal yet to learn."

Our visitor made a noisy exit, but Holmes smoked in imperturbable silence with dreamy eyes fixed upon the ceiling.

"Any views, Watson?" he asked at last.

"Well, Holmes, I must confess that when I consider that this is a man who would certainly brush any obstacle from his path, and when I remember that his wife may have been an obstacle and an object of dislike, as that man Bates plainly told us, it seems to me——"

"Exactly. And to me also."

"But what were his relations with the governess, and how did you discover them?"

"Bluff, Watson, bluff! When I considered the passionate, unconventional, unbusiness-like tone of his letter, and contrasted it with his self-contained manner

I SPRANG TO MY FEET, FOR THE EXPRESSION UPON THE MILLIONAIRE'S FACE WAS FIENDISH IN ITS INTENSITY . . .

How two artists depicted the same scene: *above*, G. Patrick Nelson for *Hearst's International*, February, 1922; *below*, A. Gilbert for the *Strand Magazine*, February, 1922.

and appearance, it was pretty clear that there was some deep emotion which centred upon the accused woman rather than upon the victim. We've got to understand the exact relations of those three people if we are to reach the truth. You saw the frontal attack which I made upon him and how imperturbably he received it. Then I bluffed him by giving him the impression that I was absolutely certain, when in reality I was only extremely suspicious."

"Perhaps he will come back?"

"He is sure to come back. He *must* come back. He can't leave it where it is Ha! isn't that a ring? Yes, there is his footstep. Well, Mr. Gibson, I was just saying to Dr. Watson that you were somewhat overdue."

The Gold King had re-entered the room in a more chastened mood than he had left it. His wounded pride still showed in his resentful eyes, but his common sense had shown him that he must yield if he would attain his end.

"I've been thinking it over, Mr. Holmes, and I feel that I have been hasty in taking your remarks amiss. You are justified in getting down to the facts, whatever they may be, and I think the more of you for it. I can assure you, however, that the relations between Miss Dunbar and me don't really touch this case."

"That is for me to decide, is it not?"

"Yes, I guess that is so. You're like a surgeon who wants every symptom before he can give his diagnosis."

"Exactly. That expresses it. And it is only a patient who has an object in deceiving his surgeon who would conceal the facts of his case."

"That may be so, but you will admit, Mr. Holmes, that most men would shy off a bit when they are asked point-blank what their relations with a woman may be —if there is really some serious feeling in the case. I guess most men have a little private reserve of their own in some corner of their souls where they don't welcome intruders. And you burst suddenly into it. But the object excuses you, since it was to try and save her. Well, the stakes are down and the reserve open and you can explore where you will. What is it you want?"

"The truth."

The Gold King paused for a moment, as one who marshals his thoughts. His grim, deep-lined face had become even sadder and more grave.

"I can give it to you in a very few words, Mr. Holmes," said he at last. "There are some things that are painful as well as difficult to say, so I won't go deeper than is needful. I met my wife when I was gold-hunting in Brazil. Maria Pinto was the daughter of a Government official at Manaos, and she was very beautiful. I was young and ardent in those days, but even now, as I look back with colder blood and a more critical eye, I can see that she was rare and wonderful in her beauty. It was a deep rich nature, too, passionate, wholehearted, tropical, ill-balanced, very different from the American women whom I had known. Well, to make a long story short, I loved her and I married her. It was only when the romance had passed—and it lingered for years—that I realized that we had nothing—absolutely nothing—in common. My love faded. If hers had faded also it might have been easier. But you know the wonderful way of women! Do what I might nothing could turn her from me. If I have been harsh to her, even brutal as some have said, it has been because I knew that if I could kill her love, or if it turned to hate, it would be easier for both of us. But nothing changed her. She adored me in those English woods as she had adored me twenty years ago on the banks of the Amazon. Do what I might, she was as devoted as ever.

" Then came Miss Grace Dunbar. She answered our advertisement and became governess to our two children. Perhaps you have seen her portrait in the papers. The whole world has proclaimed that she also is a very beautiful woman. Now, I make no pretence to be more moral than my neighbours, and I will admit to you that I could not live under the same roof with such a woman and in daily contact with her without feeling a passionate regard for her. Do you blame me, Mr. Holmes? "

" I do not blame you for feeling it. I should blame you if you expressed it, since this young lady was in a sense under your protection."

" Well, maybe so," said the millionaire, though for a moment the reproof had brought the old angry gleam into his eyes. " I'm not pretending to be any better than I am. I guess all my life I've been a man that reached out his hand for what he wanted, and I never wanted anything more than the love and possession of that woman. I told her so."

" Oh, you did, did you? "

Holmes could look very formidable when he was moved.

" I said to her that if I could marry her I would, but that it was out of my power. I said that money was no object and that all I could do to make her happy and comfortable would be done."

" Very generous, I am sure," said Holmes, with a sneer.

" See here, Mr. Holmes. I came to you on a question of evidence, not on a question of morals. I'm not asking for your criticism."

" It is only for the young lady's sake that I touch your case at all," said Holmes sternly. " I don't know that anything she is accused of is really worse than what you have yourself admitted, that you have tried to ruin a defenceless girl who was under your roof. Some of you rich men have to be taught that all the world cannot be bribed into condoning your offences."

To my surprise the Gold King took the reproof with equanimity.

" That's how I feel myself about it now. I thank God that my plans did not work out as I intended. She would have none of it, and she wanted to leave the house instantly."

" Why did she not? "

" Well, in the first place, others were dependent upon her, and it was no light matter for her to let them all down by sacrificing her living. When I had sworn—as I did—that she should never be molested again, she consented to remain. But there was another reason. She knew the influence she had over me, and that it was stronger than any other influence in the world. She wanted to use it for good."

"How?"

"Well, she knew something of my affairs. They are large, Mr. Holmes—large beyond the belief of an ordinary man. I can make or break—and it is usually break. It wasn't individuals only. It was communities, cities, even nations. Business is a hard game, and the weak go to the wall. I played the game for all it was worth. I never squealed myself and I never cared if the other fellow squealed. But she saw it different. I guess she was right. She believed and said that a fortune for one man that was more than he needed should not be built on ten thousand ruined men who were left without the means of life. That was how she saw it, and I guess she could see past the dollars to something that was more lasting. She found that I listened to what she said, and she believed she was serving the world by influencing my actions. So she stayed—and then this came along."

"Can you throw any light upon that?"

The Gold King paused for a minute or more, his head sunk in his hands, lost in deep thought.

"It's very black against her. I can't deny that. And women lead an inward life and may do things beyond the judgment of a man. At first I was so rattled and taken aback that I was ready to think she had been led away in some extraordinary fashion that was clean against her usual nature. One explanation came into my head. I give it to you, Mr. Holmes, for what it is worth. There is no doubt that my wife was bitterly jealous. There is a soul-jealousy that can be as frantic as any body-jealousy, and though my wife had no cause—and I think she understood this—for the latter, she was aware that this English girl exerted an influence upon my mind and my acts that she herself never had. It was an influence for good, but that did not mend the matter. She was crazy with hatred, and the heat of the Amazon was always in her blood. She might have planned to murder Miss Dunbar—or we will say to threaten her with a gun and so frighten her into leaving us. Then there might have been a scuffle and the gun gone off and shot the woman who held it."

"That possibility had already occurred to me," said Holmes. "Indeed, it is the only obvious alternative to deliberate murder."

"But she utterly denies it."

"Well, that is not final—is it? One can understand that a woman placed in so awful a position might hurry home still in her bewilderment holding the revolver. She might even throw it down among her clothes, hardly knowing what she was doing, and when it was found she might try to lie her way out by a total denial, since all explanation was impossible. What is against such a supposition?"

"Miss Dunbar herself."

" Well, perhaps."

Holmes looked at his watch. " I have no doubt we can get the necessary permits this morning and reach Winchester by the evening train. When I have seen this young lady, it is very possible that I may be of more use to you in the matter, though I cannot promise that my conclusions will necessarily be such as you desire."

There was some delay in the official pass, and instead of reaching Winchester that day we went down to Thor Place, the Hampshire estate of Mr. Neil Gibson. He did not accompany us himself, but we had the address of Sergeant Coventry, of the local police, who had first examined into the affair. He was a tall, thin, cadaverous man, with a secretive and mysterious manner, which conveyed the idea that he knew or suspected a very great deal more than he dared say. He had a trick, too, of suddenly sinking his voice to a whisper as if he had come upon something of vital importance, though the information was usually commonplace enough. Behind these tricks of manner he soon showed himself to be a decent, honest fellow who was not too proud to admit that he was out of his depth and would welcome any help.

" Anyhow, I'd rather have you than Scotland Yard, Mr. Holmes," said he. " If the Yard gets called into a case, then the local loses all credit for success and may be blamed for failure. Now, you play straight, so I've heard."

" I need not appear in the matter at all," said Holmes, to the evident relief of our melancholy acquaintance. " If I can clear it up I don't ask to have my name mentioned."

" Well, it's very handsome of you, I am sure. And your friend, Dr. Watson, can be trusted, I know. Now, Mr. Holmes, as we walk down to the place there is one question I should like to ask you. I'd breathe it to no soul but you." He looked round as though he hardly dare utter the words. " Don't you think there might be a case against Mr. Neil Gibson himself ? "

" I have been considering that."

" You've not seen Miss Dunbar. She is a wonderfully fine woman in every way. He may well have wished his wife out of the road. And these Americans are readier with pistols than our folk are. It was *his* pistol, you know."

" Was that clearly made out ? "

" Yes, sir. It was one of a pair that he had."

" One of a pair ? Where is the other ? "

" Well, the gentleman has a lot of fire-arms of one sort and another. We never quite matched that particular pistol—but the box was made for two."

" If it was one of a pair you should surely be able to match it."

" Well, we have them all laid out at the house if you would care to look them over."

" Later, perhaps. I think we will walk down together and have a look at the scene of the tragedy."

This conversation had taken place in the little front room of Sergeant Coventry's humble cottage which served as the local police-station. A walk of half a mile or so

OUR GUIDE PAUSED AT THE MOUTH OF THIS BRIDGE, AND HE POINTED TO THE GROUND.

Illustration by A. Gilbert for the *Strand Magazine*, February, 1922.

across a wind-swept heath, all gold and bronze with the fading ferns, brought us to a side-gate opening into the grounds of the Thor Place estate. A path led us through the pheasant preserves, and then from a clearing we saw the widespread, half-timbered house, half Tudor and half Georgian, upon the crest of the hill. Beside us there was a long, reedy pool, constricted in the centre where the main carriage drive passed over a stone bridge, but swelling into small lakes on either side. Our guide paused at the mouth of this bridge, and he pointed to the ground.

" That was where Mrs. Gibson's body lay. I marked it by that stone."

" I understand that you were there before it was moved ? "

" Yes ; they sent for me at once."

" Who did ? "

" Mr. Gibson himself. The moment the alarm was given and he had rushed down with others from the house, he insisted that nothing should be moved until the police should arrive."

" That was sensible. I gathered from the newspaper report that the shot was fired from close quarters."

" Yes, sir, very close."

" Near the right temple ? "

" Just behind it, sir."

" How did the body lie ? "

" On the back, sir. No trace of a struggle. No marks. No weapon. The short note from Miss Dunbar was clutched in her left hand."

" Clutched, you say ? "

" Yes, sir ; we could hardly open the fingers."

" That is of great importance. It excludes the idea that anyone could have placed the note there after death in order to furnish a false clue. Dear me ! The note, as I remember, was quite short. ' I will be at Thor Bridge at nine o'clock.—G. Dunbar.' Was that not so ? "

" Yes, sir."

" Did Miss Dunbar admit writing it ? "

" Yes, sir."

" What was her explanation ? "

" Her defence was reserved for the Assizes. She would say nothing."

" The problem is certainly a very interesting one. The point of the letter is very obscure, is it not ? "

" Well, sir," said the guide, " it seemed, if I may be so bold as to say so, the only really clear point in the whole case."

Holmes shook his head.

" Granting that the letter is genuine and was really written, it was certainly received some time before—say one hour or two. Why, then, was this lady still clasping it in her left hand ? Why should she carry it so carefully ? She did not need to refer to it in the interview. Does it not seem remarkable ? "

" Well, sir, as you put it, perhaps it does."

" I think I should like to sit quietly for a few minutes and think it out." He seated himself upon the stone ledge of the bridge, and I could see his quick grey eyes darting their questioning glances in every direction.

Suddenly he sprang up again and ran across to the opposite parapet, whipped his lens from his pocket, and began to examine the stonework.

"This is curious," said he.

"Yes, sir ; we saw the chip on the ledge. I expect it's been done by some passer-by."

The stonework was grey, but at this one point it showed white for a space not larger than a sixpence. When examined closely one could see that the surface was chipped as by a sharp blow.

"It took some violence to do that," said Holmes thoughtfully. With his cane he struck the ledge several times without leaving a mark. "Yes, it was a hard knock. In a curious place, too. It was not from above but from below, for you see that it is on the *lower* edge of the parapet."

"But it is at least fifteen feet from the body."

"Yes, it is fifteen feet from the body. It may have nothing to do with the matter, but it is a point worth noting. I do not think that we have anything more to learn here. There were no footsteps, you say ?"

"The ground was iron hard, sir. There were no traces at all."

"Then we can go. We will go up to the house first and look over these weapons of which you speak. Then we shall get on to Winchester, for I should desire to see Miss Dunbar before we go farther."

Mr. Neil Gibson had not returned from town, but we saw in the house the neurotic Mr. Bates who had called upon us in the morning. He showed us with a sinister relish the formidable array of fire-arms of various shapes and sizes which his employer had accumulated in the course of an adventurous life.

"Mr. Gibson has his enemies, as anyone would expect who knew him and his methods," said he. "He sleeps with a loaded revolver in the drawer beside his bed. He is a man of violence, sir, and there are times when all of us are afraid of him. I am sure that the poor lady who has passed was often terrified."

"Did you ever witness physical violence towards her ?"

"No, I cannot say that. But I have heard words which were nearly as bad—words of cold, cutting contempt, even before the servants."

"Our millionaire does not seem to shine in private life," remarked Holmes, as we made our way to the station. "Well, Watson, we have come on a good many facts, some of them new ones, and yet I seem some way from my conclusion. In spite of the very evident dislike which Mr. Bates has to his employer, I gather from him that when the alarm came he was undoubtedly in his library. Dinner was over at eight-thirty and all was normal up to then. It is true that the alarm was somewhat late in the evening, but the tragedy certainly occurred about the hour named in the note. There is no evidence at all that Mr. Gibson had been out of doors since his return from town at five o'clock. On the other hand, Miss Dunbar, as I understand it, admits that she had made an appointment to meet Mrs. Gibson at the bridge. Beyond this she would say nothing, as her

WITH HIS CANE HE STRUCK THE LEDGE SEVERAL TIMES WITHOUT LEAVING A MARK.

Illustration by A. Gilbert for the *Strand Magazine*, February, 1922.

lawyer had advised her to reserve her defence. We have several very vital questions to ask that young lady, and my mind will not be easy until we have seen her. I must confess that the case would seem to me to be very black against her if it were not for one thing."

"And what is that, Holmes?"

"The finding of the pistol in her wardrobe."

"Dear me, Holmes!" I cried, "that seemed to me to be the most damning incident of all."

"Not so, Watson. It had struck me even at my first perfunctory reading as very strange, and now that I am in closer touch with the case it is my only firm ground for hope. We must look for consistency. Where there is a want of it we must suspect deception."

"I hardly follow you."

"Well now, Watson, suppose for a moment that we visualize you in the character of a woman who, in a cold, premeditated fashion, is about to get rid of a rival. You have planned it. A note has been written. The victim has come. You have your weapon. The crime is done. It has been workmanlike and complete. Do you tell me that after carrying out so crafty a crime you would now ruin your reputation as a criminal by forgetting to fling your weapon into those adjacent reed-beds which would forever cover it, but you must needs carry it carefully home and put it in your own wardrobe, the very first place that would be searched? Your best friends would hardly call you a schemer, Watson, and yet I could not picture you doing anything so crude as that."

"In the excitement of the moment——"

"No, no, Watson, I will not admit that it is possible. Where a crime is coolly premeditated, then the means of covering it are coolly premeditated also. I hope, therefore, that we are in the presence of a serious misconception."

"But there is so much to explain."

"Well, we shall set about explaining it. When once your point of view is changed, the very thing which was so damning becomes a clue to the truth. For example, there is this revolver. Miss Dunbar disclaims all knowledge of it. On our new theory she is speaking truth when she says so. Therefore, it was placed in her wardrobe. Who placed it there? Someone who wished to incriminate her. Was not that person the actual criminal? You see how we come at once upon a most fruitful line of inquiry."

We were compelled to spend the night at Winchester, as the formalities had not yet been completed, but next morning, in the company of Mr. Joyce Cummings, the rising barrister who was entrusted with the defence, we were allowed to see the young lady in her cell. I had expected from all that we had heard to see a beautiful woman, but I can never forget the effect which Miss Dunbar produced upon me. It was no wonder that even the masterful millionaire had found in her something more powerful than himself—something which could control and guide him. One felt, too, as one looked at that strong, clear-cut, and yet sensitive face, that even should she be capable of some impetuous deed, none the less there was an innate nobility of character which would make her influence always for the good. She was a brunette, tall, with a noble figure and commanding presence, but her dark eyes had in them the appealing, helpless expression of the hunted creature who feels the nets around it, but can see no way out from the toils. Now, as she realized the presence and the help of my famous friend, there came a touch of colour in her wan cheeks and a light of hope began to glimmer in the glance which she turned upon us.

" Perhaps Mr. Neil Gibson has told you something of what occurred between us ? " she asked, in a low, agitated voice.

" Yes," Holmes answered ; " you need not pain yourself by entering into that part of the story. After seeing
you, I am prepared to accept Mr. Gibson's statement both **11**
as to the influence which you had over him and as to the innocence of your relations with him. But why was the whole situation not brought out in court ? "

" It seemed to me incredible that such a charge could be sustained. I thought that if we waited the whole thing must clear itself up without our being compelled to enter into painful details of the inner life of the family. But I understand that far from clearing it has become even more serious."

" My dear young lady," cried Holmes earnestly, " I beg you to have no illusions upon the point. Mr. Cummings here would assure you that all the cards are at present against us, and that we must do everything that is possible if we are to win clear. It would be a cruel deception to pretend that you are not in very great danger. Give me all the help you can, then, to get at the truth."

" I will conceal nothing."

" Tell us, then, of your true relations with Mr. Gibson's wife."

" She hated me, Mr. Holmes. She hated me with all the fervour of her tropical nature. She was a woman who would do nothing by halves, and the measure of her love for her husband was the measure also of her hatred for me. It is probable that she misunderstood our relations. I would not wish to wrong her, but she loved so vividly in a physical sense that she could hardly understand the mental, and even spiritual, tie which held her husband to me, or imagine that it was only my desire to influence his power to good ends which kept me under his roof. I can see now that I was wrong. Nothing could justify me in remaining where I was a cause of unhappiness, and yet it is certain that the unhappiness would have remained even if I had left the house."

" Now, Miss Dunbar," said Holmes, " I beg you to tell us exactly what occurred that evening."

" I can tell you the truth so far as I know it, Mr. Holmes, but I am in a position to prove nothing, and there are points—the most vital points—which I can neither explain nor can I imagine any explanation."

" If you will find the facts, perhaps others may find the explanation."

" With regard, then, to my presence at Thor Bridge

11 *After seeing you, I am prepared to accept Mr. Gibson's statement.* "We all know that Holmes often cautioned Watson against being unduly impressed by the appearance of a client," Mr. Nathan L. Bengis wrote in "Sherlock Stays After School." "It is more than slightly remarkable that the same Holmes who failed to see the naive sweetness of Mary Morstan should be able to tell from one look at Grace Dunbar that her relations with Neil Gibson had been completely innocent. Is this the same man who boasted of never making exceptions?"

"SHE POURED HER WHOLE WILD FURY OUT IN BURNING AND HORRIBLE WORDS."

Illustration by A. Gilbert for the *Strand Magazine*, March, 1922. G. Patrick Nelson illustrated the same scene for *Hearst's International*, February, 1922.

that night, I received a note from Mrs. Gibson in the morning. It lay on the table of the schoolroom, and it may have been left there by her own hand. It implored me to see her there after dinner, said she had something important to say to me, and asked me to leave an answer on the sundial in the garden, as she desired no one to be in our confidence. I saw no reason for such secrecy, but I did as she asked, accepting the appointment. She asked me to destroy her note and I burned it in the schoolroom grate. She was very much afraid of her husband, who treated her with a harshness for which I frequently reproached him, and I could only imagine that she acted in this way because she did not wish him to know of our interview."

"Yet she kept your reply very carefully?"

"Yes. I was surprised to hear that she had it in her hand when she died."

"Well, what happened then?"

"I went down as I had promised. When I reached the bridge she was waiting for me. Never did I realize till that moment how this poor creature hated me. She was like a mad woman—indeed, I think she *was* a mad woman, subtly mad with the deep power of deception which insane people may have. How else could she have met me with unconcern every day and yet had so raging a hatred of me in her heart? I will not say what she said. She poured her whole wild fury out in burning and horrible words. I did not even answer—I could not. It was dreadful to see her. I put my hands to my ears and rushed away. When I left her she was standing still shrieking out her curses at me, in the mouth of the bridge."

"Where she was afterwards found?"

"Within a few yards from the spot."

"And yet, presuming that she met her death shortly after you left her, you heard no shot?"

"No, I heard nothing. But, indeed, Mr. Holmes, I was so agitated and horrified by this terrible outbreak that I rushed to get back to the peace of my own room, and I was incapable of noticing anything which happened."

"You say that you returned to your room. Did you leave it again before next morning?"

"Yes; when the alarm came that the poor creature had met her death I ran out with the others."

"Did you see Mr. Gibson?"

"Yes; he had just returned from the bridge when I saw him. He had sent for the doctor and the police."

"Did he seem to you much perturbed?"

"Mr. Gibson is a very strong, self-contained man. I do not think that he would ever show his emotions on the surface. But I, who knew him so well, could see that he was deeply concerned."

"Then we come to the all-important point. This pistol that was found in your room. Had you ever seen it before?"

"Never, I swear it."

"When was it found?"

"Next morning, when the police made their search."

"Among your clothes?"

"Yes; on the floor of my wardrobe under my dresses."

" You could not guess how long it had been there ? "

" It had not been there the morning before."

" How do you know ? "

" Because I tidied out the wardrobe."

" That is final. Then someone came into your room and placed the pistol there in order to inculpate you."

" It must have been so."

" And when ? "

" It could only have been at meal-time, or else at the hours when I would be in the schoolroom with the children."

" As you were when you got the note ? "

" Yes ; from that time onwards for the whole morning."

" Thank you, Miss Dunbar. Is there any other point which could help me in the investigation ? "

" I can think of none."

" There was some sign of violence on the stonework of the bridge—a perfectly fresh chip just opposite the body. Could you suggest any possible explanation of that ? "

" Surely it must be a mere coincidence."

" Curious, Miss Dunbar, very curious. Why should it appear at the very time of the tragedy and why at the very place ? "

" But what could have caused it ? Only great violence could have such an effect."

Holmes did not answer. His pale, eager face had suddenly assumed that tense, far-away expression which I had learned to associate with the supreme manifestations of his genius. So evident was the crisis in his mind that none of us dared to speak, and we sat, barrister, prisoner, and myself, watching him in a concentrated and absorbed silence. Suddenly he sprang from his chair, vibrating with nervous energy and the pressing need for action.

" Come, Watson, come ! " he cried.

" What is it, Mr. Holmes ? "

" Never mind, my dear lady. You will hear from me, Mr. Cummings. With the help of the God of justice I will give you a case which will make England ring. You will get news by to-morrow, Miss Dunbar, and meanwhile take my assurance that the clouds are lifting and that I have every hope that the light of truth is breaking through."

SUDDENLY HE SPRANG FROM HIS CHAIR . . .

Illustration by A. Gilbert for the *Strand Magazine*, March, 1922.

It was not a long journey from Winchester to Thor Place, but it was long to me in my impatience, while for Holmes it was evident that it seemed endless ; for, in his nervous restlessness, he could not sit still, but paced the carriage or drummed with his long, sensitive fingers upon the cushions beside him. Suddenly, however, as we neared our destination he seated himself opposite to me—we had a first-class carriage to ourselves—and laying a hand upon each of my knees he looked into my eyes with the peculiarly mischievous gaze which was characteristic of his more imp-like moods.

" Watson," said he, " I have some recollection that you go armed upon these excursions of ours."

It was as well for him that I did so, for he took little care for his own safety when his mind was once absorbed by a problem, so that more than once my revolver had been a good friend in need. I reminded him of the fact.

" Yes, yes, I am a little absent-minded in such matters. But have you your revolver on you ? "

I produced it from my hip-pocket, a short, handy,
12 but very serviceable little weapon. He undid the catch, shook out the cartridges, and examined it with care.

" It's heavy—remarkably heavy," said he.

" Yes, it is a solid bit of work."

He mused over it for a minute.

" Do you know, Watson," said he, " I believe your revolver is going to have a very intimate connection with the mystery which we are investigating."

" My dear Holmes, you are joking."

" No, Watson, I am very serious. There is a test before us. If the test comes off, all will be clear. And the test will depend upon the conduct of this little weapon. One cartridge out. Now we will replace the other five and put on the safety-catch. So ! That increases the weight and makes it a better reproduction."

I had no glimmer of what was in his mind nor did he enlighten me, but sat lost in thought until we pulled up in the little Hampshire station. We secured a ramshackle trap and in a quarter of an hour were at the house of our confidential friend, the sergeant.

" A clue, Mr. Holmes ? What is it ? "

" It all depends upon the behaviour of Dr. Watson's revolver," said my friend. " Here it is. Now, officer, can you give me ten yards of string ? "

The village shop provided a ball of stout twine.

" I think that this is all we will need," said Holmes. " Now, if you please, we will get off on what I hope is the last stage of our journey."

The sun was setting and turning the rolling Hampshire moor into a wonderful autumnal panorama. The sergeant, with many critical and incredulous glances, which showed his deep doubts of the sanity of my companion, lurched along beside us. As we approached the scene of the crime I could see that my friend under all his habitual coolness was in truth deeply agitated.

" Yes," he said, in answer to my remark, " you have seen me miss my mark before, Watson. I have an instinct for such things, and yet it has sometimes played me false. It seemed a certainty when first it flashed across my mind in the cell at Winchester, but one drawback of an active mind is that one can always conceive alternative explanations which would make our scent a false one. And yet—and yet—— Well, Watson, we can but try."

As he walked he had firmly tied one end of the string to the handle of the revolver. We had now reached the scene of the tragedy. With great care he marked out under the guidance of the policeman the exact spot where the body had been stretched. He then hunted among the heather and the ferns until he found a considerable stone. This he secured to the other end of his line of string, and he hung it over the parapet of the bridge so that it swung clear above the water. He then stood on the fatal spot, some distance from the edge of the bridge, with my revolver in his hand, the string being

12 *a short, handy, but very serviceable little weapon.* The description, thought the editors of the Catalogue of the Sherlock Holmes Exhibition, "can only refer to the Webley hammerless .320, which is not common today. It had six chambers whereas most .32 revolvers have only five; and it had a stirrup catch without the familiar thumb lever, and a shot-gun type 'safety catch.' "

taut between the weapon and the heavy stone on the farther side.

"Now for it!" he cried.

At the words he raised the pistol to his head, and then let go his grip. In an instant it had been whisked away by the weight of the stone, had struck with a sharp crack against the parapet and had vanished over the side into the water. It had hardly gone before Holmes was kneeling beside the stonework, and a joyous cry showed that he had found what he expected.

"Was there ever a more exact demonstration?" he cried. "See, Watson, your revolver has solved the problem!" As he spoke he pointed to a second chip of the exact size and shape of the first which had appeared on the under edge of the stone balustrade.

"We'll stay at the inn to-night," he continued, as he rose and faced the astonished sergeant. "You will, of course, get a grappling-hook and you will easily restore my friend's revolver. You will also find beside it the revolver, string and weight with which this vindictive woman attempted to disguise her own crime and to
fasten a charge of murder upon an innocent victim. You 13
can let Mr. Gibson know that I will see him in the morning, when steps can be taken for Miss Dunbar's vindication."

Late that evening, as we sat together smoking our pipes in the village inn, Holmes gave me a brief review of what had passed.

"I fear, Watson," said he, "that you will not improve any reputation which I may have acquired by adding the Case of the Thor Bridge Mystery to your annals. I have been sluggish in mind and wanting in that mixture of imagination and reality which is the basis of my art. I confess that the chip in the stonework was a sufficient clue to suggest the true solution, and that I blame myself for not having attained it sooner.

"It must be admitted that the workings of this unhappy woman's mind were deep and subtle, so that it was no very simple matter to unravel her plot. I do not think that in our adventures we have ever come across a stranger example of what perverted love can bring about. Whether Miss Dunbar was her rival in a physical or in a merely mental sense seems to have been equally unforgivable in her eyes. No doubt she blamed this innocent lady for all those harsh dealings and unkind words with which her husband tried to repel her too demonstrative affection. Her first resolution was to end her own life. Her second was to do it in such a way as to involve her victim in a fate which was worse far than any sudden death could be.

"We can follow the various steps quite clearly, and they show a remarkable subtlety of mind. A note was extracted very cleverly from Miss Dunbar which would make it appear that she had chosen the scene of the crime. In her anxiety that it should be discovered she somewhat overdid it, by holding it in her hand to the last. This alone should have excited my suspicions earlier than it did.

"Then she took one of her husband's revolvers—there

IT HAD HARDLY GONE BEFORE HOLMES WAS KNEELING BESIDE THE STONEWORK . . .

Two artists depict the same scene: *above*, G. Patrick Nelson for *Hearst's International*, March, 1922; *below*, A. Gilbert for the *Strand Magazine*, March, 1922.

13 *to fasten a charge of murder upon an innocent victim.* There seems little doubt that Conan Doyle's inspiration for this adventure came from Dr. Hans Gross, Professor of Criminology at the University of Prague, whose great work on criminal investigation, *System der Kriminalistik*, was published in 1893.

was, as you saw, an arsenal in the house—and kept it for her own use. A similar one she concealed that morning in Miss Dunbar's wardrobe after discharging one barrel, which she could easily do in the woods without attracting attention. She then went down to the bridge where she had contrived this exceedingly ingenious method for getting rid of her weapon. When Miss Dunbar appeared she used her last breath in pouring out her hatred, and then, when she was out of hearing, carried out her terrible purpose. Every link is now in its place and the chain is complete. The papers may ask why the mere was not dragged in the first instance, but it is easy to be wise after the event, and in any case the expanse of a reed-filled lake is no easy matter to drag unless you have a clear perception of what you are looking for, and where. Well, Watson, we have helped a remarkable woman, and also a formidable man. Should they in the future join their forces, as seems not unlikely, the financial world may find that Mr. Neil Gibson has learned something in that schoolroom of Sorrow where our earthly lessons are taught."

. . .

14 *A similar one she concealed that morning.* At the Sherlock Holmes Exhibition, a matched pair of small revolvers, lent by Major Hugh Pollard, was exhibited, with the comment, in the Catalogue: "These ivory-handled Whitneyville armoury revolvers are more powerful than the saloon pistol as they take the standard .22 rimfire short case; at close range they are fatal. First developed by Smith and Wesson in 1856 these little .22 revolvers were made in many types and patterns by both English and American makers. They were almost invariably 'seven-shooters,' as are the specimens shown. These represent an improved model which was made with little variation from about 1875 to the close of the century, and are of American origin."

A Note on the "Canonicity" of "The Problem of Thor Bridge": Mr. D. Martin Dakin, who has decisively rejected from the Canon many of the adventures that appear in *The Case-Book of Sherlock Holmes*, has written that "there are others in the collection that bear just as clearly the stamp of authenticity. 'Thor Bridge' is one. The plot and style are excellent, and it shows in every line the marks of a genuine Watson reminiscence. Holmes dealing with Mr. Neil Gibson, the Gold King, is Holmes at his best. . . ."

Bibliographical Note: The manuscript of "The Problem of Thor Bridge" is owned by Mr. Adrian M. Conan Doyle.

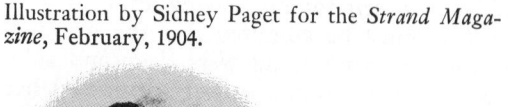

THE HEAVY WHITE FACE WAS SEAMED WITH LINES OF TROUBLE . . .

Illustration by Sidney Paget for the *Strand Magazine*, February, 1904.

66

THE ADVENTURE OF THE PRIORY SCHOOL

[Thursday, May 16, to Saturday, May 18, 1901]

WE have had some dramatic entrances and exits upon our small stage at Baker Street, but I cannot recollect anything more sudden and startling than the first appearance of Dr. Thorneycroft Huxtable, M.A., Ph.D., etc. His card, which **1**
seemed too small to carry the weight of his academic distinctions, preceded him by a few seconds, and then he entered himself—so large, so pompous, and so dignified that he was the very embodiment of self-possession and solidity. And yet his first action when the door had closed behind him was to stagger against the table, whence he slipped down upon the floor, and there was that majestic figure prostrate and insensible upon our bearskin hearth-rug.

We had sprung to our feet, and for a few moments we stared in silent amazement at this ponderous piece of wreckage, which told of some sudden and fatal storm far out on the ocean of life. Then Holmes hurried with a cushion for his head, and I with brandy for his lips. The heavy white face was seamed with lines of trouble, the hanging pouches under the closed eyes were leaden in colour, the loose mouth drooped dolorously at the corners, the rolling chins were unshaven. Collar and shirt bore the grime of a long journey, and the hair bristled unkempt from the well-shaped head. It was a sorely stricken man who lay before us.

"What is it, Watson?" asked Holmes.

"Absolute exhaustion—possibly mere hunger and fatigue," said I, with my finger on the thready pulse, where the stream of life trickled thin and small.

"Return ticket from Mackleton, in the North of England," said Holmes, drawing it from the watch-pocket. **2**
"It is not twelve o'clock yet. He has certainly been an early starter."

The puckered eyelids had begun to quiver, and now a pair of vacant grey eyes looked up at us. An instant later the man had scrambled on to his feet, his face crimson with shame.

"Forgive this weakness, Mr. Holmes; I have been a little overwrought. Thank you, if I might have a glass of milk and a biscuit I have no doubt that I should be better. I came personally, Mr. Holmes, in order to ensure that you would return with me. I feared that no telegram would convince you of the absolute urgency of the case."

1 *M.A., Ph.D., etc.* "Except apparently at the Court of Siam," Mr. Frederick Bryan-Brown wrote in "Sherlockian Schools and Schoolmasters," "'etc.' is not a word well thought of in educational circles, being normally interpreted as 'I don't know any more' or 'I can't be bothered to put any more.' . . . Also the Dr. in front, when the Ph.D. is behind, is somewhat redundant and merely to impress credulous parents. True Classical scholars from the major universities go for Doctor of Letters or nothing, and one suspects Huxtable of travelling to Europe in the summer vacation to buy his Doctorate . . ."

2 *Mackleton, in the North of England.* ". . . we must identify 'Mackleton' with the well known Derbyshire spa of Matlock, some ten miles from Chesterfield," Mr. Michael Harrison wrote (*In the Footsteps of Sherlock Holmes*). "It was at Chesterfield, by the way, that Neville St. Clair, the Man with the Twisted Lip, was at school. The nearby town of Alfreton, distant 11 miles from Chesterfield, 9 miles from Matlock, will explain the construction of 'Mackleton': Ma(tlo)ck—(A)l(fr)eton." But the problem remains: why did Holmes call Derbyshire, the epitome of the Midlands, the "North of England"?

" When you are quite restored——"

" I am quite well again. I cannot imagine how I came to be so weak. I wish you, Mr. Holmes, to come to Mackleton with me by the next train."

My friend shook his head.

" My colleague, Dr. Watson, could tell you that we are very busy at present. I am retained in this case of the
3-4 Ferrers Documents, and the Abergavenny murder is coming up for trial. Only a very important issue could call me from London at present."

" Important ! " Our visitor threw up his hands. " Have you heard nothing of the abduction of the only son of the Duke of Holdernesse ? "

" What ! the late Cabinet Minister ? "

" Exactly. We had tried to keep it out of the papers, but there was some rumour in the *Globe* last night. I thought it might have reached your ears."

Holmes shot out his long, thin arm and picked out Volume " H " in his encyclopædia of reference.

5 " ' Holdernesse, sixth Duke, K.G., P.C.'—half the alphabet ! ' Baron Beverley, Earl of Carston '—dear me, what a list ! ' Lord-Lieutenant of Hallamshire since 1900. Married Edith, daughter of Sir Charles Appledore, 1888. Heir and only child, Lord Saltire. Owns about two hundred and fifty thousand acres. Minerals in Lancashire and Wales. Address : Carlton House Ter-
6 race ; Holdernesse Hall, Hallamshire ; Carston Castle, Bangor, Wales. Lord of the Admiralty, 1872 ; Chief Secretary of State for——' Well, well, this man is
7 certainly one of the greatest subjects of the Crown ! "

" The greatest and perhaps the wealthiest. I am aware, Mr. Holmes, that you take a very high line in professional matters, and that you are prepared to work for the work's

3 *this case of the Ferrers Documents.* For a pastiche stemming from this reference of Holmes', see "The Adventure of the Dark Angels," by Adrian M. Conan Doyle in *The Exploits of Sherlock Holmes.*

4 *the Abergavenny murder.* "The Abergavenny murder presumably took place at Abergavenny," Mr. Paul H. Gore-Booth wrote in "The Journeys of Sherlock Holmes," "(it does not seem to have been the murder of Lord or Mr. Abergavenny, as far as we can tell) so that implies a visit to Monmouthshire."

5 *K.G., P.C.'* "The K.G., of course, stands for Knight of the Garter, while the P.C. is presumably for Privy Councillor, rather than Police Constable, for which it is used elsewhere in the Sacred Writings," the late A. Carson Simpson wrote in *Numismatics in the Canon,* Part III. "This Order, originally known as the Society (or Fraternity) of St. George, is generally said to date back to 1349; probably it began between 1346 and 1348. . . . As originally constituted, the Order of the Garter consisted of the sovereign (Edward III) and 25 Knights (including the Prince of Wales). Later, important foreign rulers were admitted, then lineal descendants of George I; certain clerical and heraldic officials were attached for administrative purposes. Until after the Napoleonic Wars, all members were nobles, generally of no less degree than an earl, but later a few distinguished commoners (e.g., Austin Chamberlain) were admitted to what came to be known as the Most Noble Order of the Garter. The original

"I CANNOT IMAGINE HOW I CAME TO BE SO WEAK."

Illustration by Frederic Dorr Steele for *Collier's Magazine,* January 30, 1904.

" 'LORD-LIEUTENANT OF HALLAMSHIRE SINCE 1900.' "

Hallamshire, though not a county of England, is a well-known district—as Mr. T. H. B. Symons has pointed out in "Some Notes on the Sixth Duke of Holdernesse": "Watson's Hallamshire, like Hardy's Wessex and Trollope's Barsetshire, may be identified fairly readily. The ancient lordship of Hallamshire embraced parts of Yorkshire and Derbyshire, and this historic place name is preserved in the community of West Hallam which still remains in Derbyshire." By law (sec. 3 [1] of the Criminal Justice Administration Act), Hallamshire "is to include Sheffield, Doncaster, Barnsley and Rotherham," Magistrate S. Tupper Bigelow wrote in "Hallamshire Revisited."

sake. I may tell you, however, that his Grace has already intimated that a cheque for five thousand pounds will be handed over to the person who can tell him where his son is, and another thousand to him who can name the man, or men, who have taken him."

"It is a princely offer," said Holmes. "Watson, I think that we shall accompany Dr. Huxtable back to the North of England. And now, Dr. Huxtable, when you have consumed that milk you will kindly tell me what has happened, when it happened, how it happened, and, finally, what Dr. Thorneycroft Huxtable, of the Priory School, near Mackleton, has to do with the matter, and why he comes three days after an event—the state of your chin gives the date—to ask for my humble services."

Our visitor had consumed his milk and biscuits. The light had come back to his eyes and the colour to his cheeks as he set himself with great vigour and lucidity to explain the situation.

"I must inform you, gentlemen, that the Priory is a preparatory school, of which I am the founder and principal. *Huxtable's Sidelights on Horace* may possibly **8**
recall my name to your memories. The Priory is, without exception, the best and most select preparatory school in England. Lord Leverstoke, the Earl of Blackwater, Sir Cathcart Soames—they all have entrusted their sons to me. But I felt that my school had reached its zenith when, three weeks ago, the Duke of Holdernesse sent Mr. James Wilder, his secretary, with the intimation that young Lord Saltire, ten years old, his only son and heir, was about to be committed to my charge. Little did I think that this would be the prelude to the most crushing misfortune of my life.

"On May 1 the boy arrived, that being the beginning of the summer term. He was a charming youth, and he soon fell into our ways. I may tell you—I trust that I am not indiscreet; half-confidences are absurd in such a case—that he was not entirely happy at home. It is an open secret that the duke's married life had not been a peaceful one, and the matter had ended in a separation by mutual consent, the duchess taking up her residence in the South of France. This had occurred very shortly before, and the boy's sympathies are known to have been strongly with his mother. He moped after her departure from Holdernesse Hall, and it was for this reason that the duke desired to send him to my establishment. In a fortnight the boy was quite at home with us, and was apparently absolutely happy.

"He was last seen on the night of May 13—that is, the night of last Monday. His room was on the second floor, and was approached through another larger room in which two boys were sleeping. These boys saw and heard nothing, so that it is certain that young Saltire did not pass out that way. His window was open, and there is a stout ivy plant leading to the ground. We could trace no footmarks below, but it is sure that this is the only possible exit.

"His absence was discovered at seven o'clock on Tuesday morning. His bed had been slept in. He had dressed himself fully before going off in his usual school suit of black Eton jacket and dark grey trousers. There

insigne of the Order was the blue silk buckled Garter with the motto HONI SOIT QUI MAL Y PENSE embroidered on it with gold thread. About 1503 the Collar was added, consisting of 24 Tudor roses enamelled red and white, each surrounded by a buckled Garter with motto; these are linked together by 'lover's knots' of heavy gold wire. From this hung the 'Great George,' a gold and enamel equestrian figure of the Order's patron saint killing the dragon. The Collar is today generally worn only on occasions of great moment, such as coronations, etc. Instead, the 'Lesser George'—a smaller copy of the 'Great George,' but enclosed in an enamel Garter—is worn attached to a wide deep-blue ribbon slung over the left shoulder. The Knights also wear the Garter Star on their robes. It is an enamelled radiate St. George's Cross within a Garter with motto, all surrounded by silver rays. A curious feature of the Order of the Garter is that all the insignia must be returned on the death of a member. The Garter and the Collar (including the Great George) must be turned in to the Central Chancery of the Orders of Knighthood, while the heir of the Knight must deliver the Star and Badge (the Lesser George) direct to the Sovereign. These articles are later reissued to subsequently-created Knights, hence they may pass through many hands over the centuries. Only the shoulder-ribbon, apparently, remains with the family."

6 *Carlton House Terrace.* The two handsome blocks of houses, known as Carlton House Terrace, adorn the north side of the Mall. They were completed about 1831, and occupy the site of Carlton House and its grounds, the residence of George IV when Prince Regent. Among the Duke of Holdernesse's onetime neighbors were Lord Goderich, who paid £25,000 for his house, and the Count de Salis, who gave £10,000 for his. At Number 13, and afterwards Number 11, Mr. W. E. Gladstone resided for many years. Carlton House Terrace was badly damaged in the blitz but its houses have been repaired and repainted.

7 *Well, well, this man is certainly one of the greatest subjects of the Crown!"* In a thoughtful and persuasive paper delivered to the Society of Baker Street Squires of Toronto, Mr. Gordon Macpherson has suggested that it was the Sixth Duke of Northumberland who figures in "The Adventure of the Priory School."

On the other hand, Dr. Julian Wolff, in his *Practical Handbook of Sherlockian Heraldry*, has written that "In view of the fact that his son was called Lord Saltire, it would seem likely that the Duke of Holdernesse belonged to the great family of Neville, since a saltire [a diagonal cross] is prominent in their arms. However, none of them can be fitted into the frame provided and one more coruscation is necessary. Careful study of the problem suggests . . . the 8th Duke of Devonshire . . ."

Dr. Wolff's identification has received the

wholehearted support of Mr. T. H. B. Symons, who wrote, in "Some Notes on the Sixth Duke of Holdernesse," "a number of considerations suggest that the person disguised as the sixth Duke of Holdernesse by Watson was in fact the Eighth Duke of Devonshire. [He] was in fact the Lord-Lieutenant [of Derbyshire], and in this shire were his ancestral estates. Such a location of Holdernesse Hall, in Hallamshire, in Derbyshire, would seem to fit in with a number of other geographic facts noted in 'The Adventure of the Priory School.' Like Holdernesse Hall, the Devonshire estates are set in the Peak country. . . . Nearby is Chesterfield . . . and close by in other directions is Macclesfield, which may be the Mackleton near which the Priory School was located. . . . There is strong heraldic support for [this] view. . . . Hardwick Hall [one of the two famous Devonshire estates owned by the Duke of Devonshire] is enriched at many points, in panel, fireplace and lock, with the arms of [Bess of Hardwick, who married William Cavendish, whose son was the first Earl of Devonshire]: 'a saltire engrailed azure; on a chief of the second three cinquefoils of the field,' set in a lozenge-shaped shield and bearing the coronet. The supporters are two 'stags proper, each gorged with a chaplet of roses, argent, between two bars azure.' . . . It is not surprising that Dr. Watson, who was we know impressed by the entrance to the Hall should be struck at once by these fine emblazonments and that they should suggest to him the idea of disguising the heir to the estate under the title of Lord Saltire. . . . The Duke of Devonshire was very much 'the late Cabinet Minister' at the time of 'The Adventure of the Priory School,' having resigned from Balfour's Cabinet a few months before as the result of a celebrated row with Joseph Chamberlain over the comparative merits of free trade and imperial preference. His earlier political career was one of great distinction which matched very closely that of the Duke of Holdernesse."

It is equally understandable that Watson should have disguised his great northern magnate under the title of *Holdernesse*. As Mr. Symons has also pointed out: "In bygone centuries, the great northern family of d'Arcy held the earldom of Holderness. From a medieval house, the d'Arcy's had developed into one of the powerful landowning Whig families. Their Yorkshire estates drew praise from Arthur Young when he wrote of his northern town in 1768. Robert d'Arcy, the Fourth Earl, was Lord-Lieutenant of the North Riding of Yorkshire, and Secretary for the North in Pitt's administration. On his death, predeceased by his two sons, the ancient barony of d'Arcy and the earldom of Holderness became extinct. But the d'Arcy pride and the family's tradition of participation in public affairs had become a legend, and the title of Holderness had been at times almost synonymous with the north of England. When the direct male line, and with it the title of Holderness, disappeared, there remained many remind-

were no signs that anyone had entered the room, and it is quite certain that anything in the nature of cries or a struggle would have been heard, since Caunter, the elder boy in the inner room, is a very light sleeper.

" When Lord Saltire's disappearance was discovered I at once called a roll of the whole establishment—boys, masters, and servants. It was then that we ascertained that Lord Saltire had not been alone in his flight. Heidegger, the German master, was missing. His room was on the second floor, at the farther end of the building, facing the same way as Lord Saltire's. His bed had also been slept in ; but he had apparently gone away partly dressed, since his shirt and socks were lying on the floor. He had undoubtedly let himself down by the ivy, for we could see the marks of his feet where he had landed on the lawn. His bicycle was kept in a small shed beside this lawn, and it also was gone.

" He had been with me for two years, and came with the best references ; but he was a silent, morose man, not very popular either with masters or boys. No trace could be found of the fugitives, and now on Thursday
9 morning we are as ignorant as we were on Tuesday. Inquiry was, of course, made at once at Holdernesse Hall. It is only a few miles away, and we imagined that in some sudden attack of home-sickness he had gone back to his father ; but nothing had been heard of him. The duke is greatly agitated—and as to me, you have seen yourselves the state of nervous prostration to which the suspense and the responsibility have reduced me. Mr. Holmes, if ever you put forward your full powers, I implore you to do so now, for never in your life could you have a case which is more worthy of them."

Sherlock Holmes had listened with the utmost intentness to the statement of the unhappy schoolmaster. His drawn brows and the deep furrow between them showed that he needed no exhortation to concentrate all his attention upon a problem which, apart from the tremendous interests involved, must appeal so directly to his love of the complex and the unusual. He now drew out his notebook and jotted down one or two memoranda.

" You have been very remiss in not coming to me sooner," said he severely. " You start me on my investigation with a very serious handicap. It is inconceivable, for example, that this ivy and this lawn would have yielded nothing to an expert observer."

" I am not to blame, Mr. Holmes. His Grace was extremely desirous to avoid all public scandal. He was afraid of his family unhappiness being dragged before the world. He has a deep horror of anything of the kind."

" But there has been some official investigation ? "

" Yes, sir, and it has proved most disappointing. An apparent clue was at once obtained, since a boy and a young man were reported to have been seen leaving a neighbouring station by an early train. Only last night we had news that the couple had been hunted down in Liverpool, and they prove to have no connection whatever with the matter in hand. Then it was that in my despair and disappointment, after a sleepless night, I came straight to you by the early train."

" I suppose the local investigation was relaxed while this false clue was being followed up ? "

" It was entirely dropped."

" So that three days have been wasted. The affair has been most deplorably handled."

" I feel it, and admit it."

" And yet the problem should be capable of ultimate solution. I shall be very happy to look into it. Have you been able to trace any connection between the missing boy and this German master ? "

" None at all."

" Was he in the master's class ? "

" No ; he never exchanged a word with him, so far as I know."

" That is certainly very singular. Had the boy a bicycle ? "

" No."

" Was any other bicycle missing ? "

" No."

" Is that certain ? "

" Quite."

" Well, now, you do not mean to seriously suggest that this German rode off upon a bicycle in the dead of the night bearing the boy in his arms ? "

" Certainly not."

" Then what is the theory in your mind ? "

" The bicycle may have been a blind. It may have been hidden somewhere, and the pair gone off on foot."

" Quite so ; but it seems rather an absurd blind, does it not ? Were there other bicycles in this shed? "

" Several."

" Would he not have hidden a *couple* had he desired to give the idea that they had gone off upon them ? "

" I suppose he would."

" Of course he would. The blind theory won't do. But the incident is an admirable starting-point for an investigation. After all, a bicycle is not an easy thing to conceal or to destroy. One other question. Did any-one call to see the boy on the day before he disappeared ? "

" No."

" Did he get any letters ? "

" Yes ; one letter."

" From whom ? "

" From his father."

" Do you open the boys' letters ? "

" No."

" How do you know it was from the father ? "

" The coat-of-arms was on the envelope, and it was addressed in the duke's peculiar stiff hand. Besides, the duke remembers having written."

" When had he a letter before that ? "

" Not for several days."

" Had he ever one from France ? "

" No ; never."

" You see the point of my questions, of course. Either the boy was carried off by force or he went of his own free will. In the latter case you would expect that some prompting from outside would be needed to make so young a lad do such a thing. If he has had no visitors, that prompting must have come in letters. Hence I

ers and historical echoes from the activities of this famous house. Its honours and line are examined in the *Official Baronage of England*, published in 1888. This magnificent classic of genealogy was the product of thirteen years of scholarly endeavour by James Doyle, the uncle of . . . Arthur Conan Doyle."

8 Huxtable's Sidelights on Horace. "So elusive is this rarest of all Horatiana that many a scholar would be willing to part with his Aldine in exchange," Mr. Morris Rosenblum wrote in "Hafiz and Horace, Huxtable and Holmes."

9 *and now on Thursday morning.* The case began, according to Dr. Thorneycroft Huxtable's statement, on Thursday, May 16. Young Lord Saltire "was last seen on the night of May 13—that is, the night of last Monday." "His absence was discovered at seven o'clock on Tuesday morning." "And now on Thursday we are as ignorant as we were on Tuesday." It has been suggested that the year was 1900, but we very much doubt it: Holmes' encyclopedia of reference read: "Holdernesse, sixth Duke . . . Lord-Lieutenant of Hallamshire since 1900." Were this account written in the year 1900, it is hardly likely that the word "since" would have been included. On the other hand, the case cannot have taken place long after 1900: the Duke of Holdernesse had married in 1888; Lord Saltire was ten years old; "the duke's married life had not been a peaceful one"—Lord Saltire's birth must have come earlier rather than later in the duke's married life. Indeed, the latest possible date for the case is May, 1903: "The Adventure of the Priory School" was published in *Collier's Magazine* for January 30, 1904, the *Strand Magazine* for February, 1904. In 1901, the earliest year for the case if we discard 1900, the 16th of May *was* a Thursday. We accordingly date the case *Thursday, May 16, to Saturday, May 18, 1901.*

"THEN WHAT IS THE THEORY IN YOUR MIND?"

Illustration by Sidney Paget for the *Strand Magazine*, February, 1904.

try to find out who were his correspondents."

" I fear I cannot help you much. His only correspondent, so far as I know, was his own father."

" Who wrote to him on the very day of his disappearance. Were the relations between father and son very friendly ? "

" His Grace is never very friendly with anyone. He is completely immersed in large public questions, and is rather inaccessible to all ordinary emotions. But he was always kind to the boy in his own way."

" But the sympathies of the latter were with the mother ? "

" Yes."

" Did he say so ? "

" No."

" The duke, then ? "

" Good heavens, no ! "

" Then how could you know ? "

" I have had some confidential talk with Mr. James Wilder, his Grace's secretary. It was he who gave me the information about Lord Saltire's feelings."

" I see. By the way, that last letter of the duke's—was it found in the boy's room after he was gone ? "

" No ; he had taken it with him. I think, Mr. Holmes,
10 it is time that we were leaving for Euston."

" I will order a four-wheeler. In a quarter of an hour we shall be at your service. If you are telegraphing home, Mr. Huxtable, it would be well to allow the people in your neighbourhood to imagine that the inquiry is still going on in Liverpool, or wherever else that red herring led your pack. In the meantime, I will do a little quiet work at your own doors, and perhaps the scent is not so cold but that two old hounds like Watson and myself may get a sniff of it."

That evening found us in the cold, bracing atmosphere of the Peak country, in which Dr. Huxtable's famous school is situated. It was already dark when we reached it. A card was lying on the hall table, and the butler whispered something to his master, who turned to us with agitation in every heavy feature.

" The duke is here," said he. " The duke and Mr. Wilder are in the study. Come, gentlemen, and I will introduce you."

I was, of course, familiar with the pictures of the famous statesman, but the man himself was very different from his representation. He was a tall and stately person, scrupulously dressed, with a drawn, thin face, and a nose which was grotesquely curved and long. His complexion was of a dead pallor, which was more startling by contrast with a long, dwindling beard of vivid red, which flowed down over his white waistcoat, with his watch-chain gleaming through its fringe. Such was the stately presence who looked stonily at us from the centre of Dr. Huxtable's hearthrug. Beside him stood a very young man, whom I understood to be Wilder, the private secretary. He was small, nervous, alert, with intelligent, light blue eyes and mobile features. It was he who at once, in an incisive and positive tone, opened the conversation.

10 *it is time that we were leaving for Euston."* ". . . no mean feat as the Derbyshire Peak District, where the Priory School was obviously situated, can only be reached from St. Pancras and that part of the country is still the preserve of the old Midland Railway," Mr. E. P. Greenwood commented in "Some Random Thoughts on Railway Journeys by Holmes and Watson."

BESIDE HIM STOOD A VERY YOUNG MAN . . .

Illustration by Sidney Paget for the *Strand Magazine*, February, 1904. Frederic Dorr Steele illustrated the same scene for *Collier's Magazine*, January 30, 1904.

" I called this morning, Dr. Huxtable, too late to prevent you from starting for London. I learned that your object was to invite Mr. Sherlock Holmes to undertake the conduct of this case. His Grace is surprised, Dr. Huxtable, that you should have taken such a step without consulting him."

" When I learned the police had failed——"

" His Grace is by no means convinced that the police have failed."

" But surely, Mr. Wilder——"

" You are well aware, Dr. Huxtable, that his Grace is particularly anxious to avoid all public scandal. He prefers to take as few people as possible into his confidence."

" The matter can be easily remedied," said the browbeaten doctor. " Mr. Sherlock Holmes can return to London by the morning train."

" Hardly that, doctor, hardly that," said Holmes, in his blandest voice. " This northern air is invigorating and pleasant, so I propose to spend a few days upon your moors, and to occupy my mind as best I may. Whether I have the shelter of your roof or of the village inn is, of course, for you to decide."

I could see that the unfortunate doctor was in the last stage of indecision, from which he was rescued by the deep, sonorous voice of the red-bearded duke, which boomed out like a dinner-gong.

" I agree with Mr. Wilder, Dr. Huxtable, that you would have done wisely to consult me. But since Mr. Holmes has already been taken into your confidence, it would indeed be absurd that we should not avail our selves of his services. Far from going to the inn, Mr. Holmes, I should be pleased if you would come and stay with me at Holdernesse Hall ? "

" I thank your Grace. For the purposes of my investigation I think that it would be wiser for me to remain at the scene of the mystery."

" Just as you like, Mr. Holmes. Any information which Mr. Wilder or I can give you is, of course, at your disposal."

" It will probably be necessary for me to see you at the Hall," said Holmes. " I would only ask you now, sir, whether you have formed any explanation in your own mind as to the mysterious disappearance of your son ? "

" No, sir, I have not."

" Excuse me if I allude to that which is painful to you, but I have no alternative. Do you think that the duchess had anything to do with the matter ? "

The great minister showed perceptible hesitation.

" I do not think so," he said at last.

" The other most obvious explanation is that the child had been kidnapped for the purpose of levying ransom. You have not had any demand of the sort ? "

" No, sir."

" One more question, your Grace. I understand that you wrote to your son upon the day when this incident occurred."

" No ; I wrote upon the day before."

" Exactly. But he received it on that day ? "

" Yes."

" Was there anything in your letter which might have unbalanced him or induced him to take such a step ? "

" No, sir, certainly not."

" Did you post that letter yourself ? "

The nobleman's reply was interrupted by his secretary, who broke in with some heat.

" His Grace is not in the habit of posting letters himself," said he. " This letter was laid with others upon the study table, and I myself put them in the post-bag."

" You are sure this one was among them ? "

" Yes ; I observed it."

" How many letters did your Grace write that day ? "

" Twenty or thirty. I have a large correspondence. But surely this is somewhat irrelevant ? "

" Not entirely," said Holmes.

" For my own part," the duke continued, " I have advised the police to turn their attention to the South of France. I have already said that I do not believe that the duchess would encourage so monstrous an action, but the lad had the most wrong-headed opinions, and it is possible that he may have fled to her, aided and abetted by this German. I think, Dr. Huxtable, that we will now return to the Hall."

I could see that there were other questions which Holmes would have wished to put ; but the nobleman's abrupt manner showed that the interview was at an end. It was evident that to his intensely aristocratic nature this discussion of his intimate family affairs with a stranger was most abhorrent, and that he feared lest every fresh question would throw a fiercer light into the discreetly shadowed corners of his ducal history.

When the nobleman and his secretary had left, my friend flung himself at once with characteristic eagerness into the investigation.

The boy's chamber was carefully examined, and yielded nothing save the absolute conviction that it was only through the window that he could have escaped. The German master's room and effects gave no further clue. In his case a trailer of ivy had given way under his weight, and we saw by the light of a lantern the mark on the lawn where his heels had come down. That one dent in the short green grass was the only material witness left of this inexplicable nocturnal flight.

Sherlock Holmes left the house alone, and only returned after eleven. He had obtained a large ordnance map of the neighbourhood, and this he brought into my room, where he laid it out on the bed, and, having balanced the lamp in the middle of it, he began to smoke over it, and occasionally to point out objects of interest with the reeking amber of his pipe.

" This case grows upon me, Watson," said he. " There are decidedly some points of interest in connection with it. In this early stage I want you to realize these geographical features, which may have a good deal to do with our investigation.

" Look at this map. This dark square is the Priory School. I'll put a pin in it. Now, this line is the main road. You see that it runs east and west past the school, and you see also there is no side-road for a mile either way. If these two folk passed away by road it was *this* road."

" Exactly."

" By a singular and happy chance we are able to some extent to check what passed along this road during the night in question. At this point, where my pipe is now resting, a country constable was on duty from twelve to six. It is, as you perceive, the first cross-road on the east side. This man declares that he was not absent from his post for an instant, and he is positive that neither boy nor man could have gone that way unseen. I have

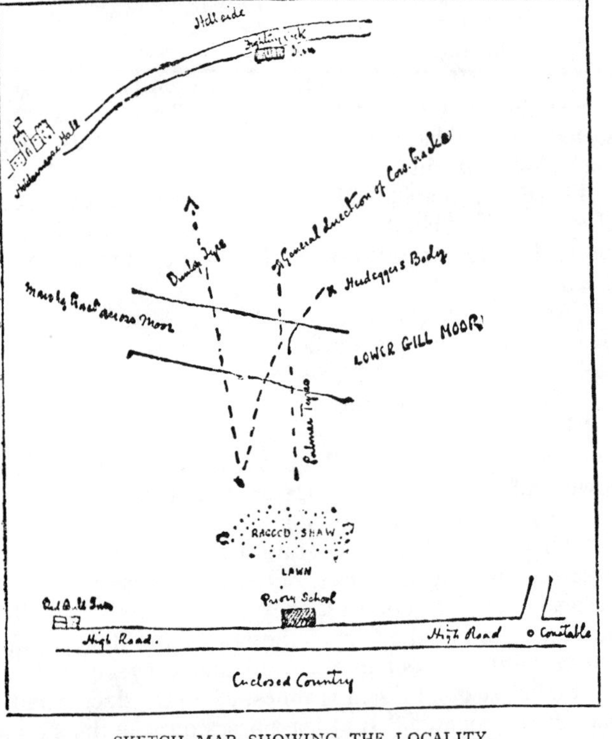

SKETCH MAP SHOWING THE LOCALITY.

spoken with this policeman to-night, and he appears to me to be a perfectly reliable person. That blocks this end. We have now to deal with the other. There is an inn here, the ' Red Bull,' the landlady of which was ill. She had sent to Mackleton for a doctor, but he did not arrive until morning, being absent at another case. The people at the inn were alert all night, awaiting his coming, and one or other of them seems to have continually had an eye upon the road. They declare that no one passed. If their evidence is good, then we are fortunate enough to be able to block the west, and also to be able to say that the fugitives did *not* use the road at all."

" But the bicycle ? " I objected.

" Quite so. We will come to the bicycle presently. To continue our reasoning : if these people did not go by the road, they must have traversed the country to the north of the house or to the south of the house. That is certain. Let us weigh the one against the other. On the south of the house is, as you perceive, a large district of arable land, cut up into small fields, with stone walls between them. There, I admit that a bicycle is impossible. We can dismiss the idea. We turn to the country on the north. Here there lies a grove of trees, marked as the ' Ragged Shaw,' and on the farther side stretches a great rolling moor, Lower Gill Moor, extending for ten miles, and sloping gradually upwards. Here, at one side of this wilderness, is Holdernesse Hall, ten miles by road, but only six across the moor. It is a peculiarly desolate plain. A few moor farmers have small holdings, where they rear sheep and cattle. Except these, the plover and the curlew are the only inhabitants until you come to the Chesterfield high road. There is a church there, you see, a few cottages, and an inn. Beyond that the hills become precipitous. Surely it is here to the north that our quest must lie."

"But the bicycle?" I persisted.

"Well, well!" said Holmes impatiently. "A good cyclist does not need a high road. The moor is inter-
11 sected with paths, and the moon was at the full. Halloa! What is this?"

There was an agitated knock at the door, and an instant afterwards Dr. Huxtable was in the room. In his hand he held a blue cricket-cap, with a white chevron on the peak.

"At last we have a clue!" he cried. "Thank Heaven, at last we are on the dear boy's track! It is his cap."

"Where was it found?"

"In the van of the gipsies who camped on the moor. They left on Tuesday. To-day the police traced them down and examined their caravan. This was found."

"How do they account for it?"

"They shuffled and lied—said that they found it on the moor on Tuesday morning. They know where he is, the rascals! Thank goodness, they are all safe under lock and key. Either the fear of the law or the duke's purse will certainly get out of them all that they know."

"So far, so good," said Holmes, when the doctor had at last left the room. "It at least bears out the theory that it is on the side of the Lower Gill Moor that we must hope for results. The police have really done nothing locally, save the arrest of these gipsies. Look here, Watson! There is a watercourse across the moor. You see it marked here in the map. In some parts it widens into a morass. This is particularly so in the region between Holdernesse Hall and the school. It is vain to look else-
12 where for tracks in this dry weather; but at *that* point there is certainly a chance of some record being left. I will call you early to-morrow morning, and you and I will try if we can throw some light upon the mystery."

The day was just breaking when I woke to find the long, thin form of Holmes by my bedside. He was fully dressed, and had apparently already been out.

"I have done the lawn and the bicycle shed," said he. "I have also had a ramble through the Ragged Shaw. Now, Watson, there is cocoa ready in the next room. I must beg you to hurry, for we have a great day before us."

His eyes shone, and his cheek was flushed with the exhilaration of the master workman who sees his work lies ready before him. A very different Holmes, this active, alert man, from the introspective and pallid dreamer of Baker Street. I felt, as I looked upon that

11 *the moon was at the full.* There is one objection to 1901 as the year of the case: Holmes said the moon was at the full "on the night the boy disappeared," and the moon was *not* at the full on the night of Monday, May 13, 1901; it was ten days past the full. This led the late Dr. Ernest Bloomfield Zeisler to conclude that the case must have taken place in May, 1900.

12 *in this dry weather.* Unhappily, this is of little help to us in dating the adventure: before the 16th of the month, it rained on only four days in *both* the May of 1900 and the May of 1901. In the entire month of May, 1900, it rained on nine days for a total fall of 1.32 inch, 0.68 inch below the 1841–1890 average; in the entire month of May, 1901, it rained on five days for a total fall of 1.79 inch, 0.18 inch below the 1841–1890 average.

supple figure, alive with nervous energy, that it was indeed a strenuous day that awaited us.

And yet it opened in the blackest disappointment. With high hopes we struck across the peaty, russet moor, intersected with a thousand sheep-paths, until we came to the broad light green-belt which marked the morass between us and Holdernesse. Certainly, if the lad had gone homewards, he must have passed this, and he would not pass it without leaving his trace. But no sign of him or the German could be seen. With a darkening face my friend strode along the margin, eagerly observant of every muddy stain upon the mossy surface. Sheep-marks there were in profusion, and at one place, some miles down, cows had left their tracks. Nothing more.

"Check number one," said Holmes, looking gloomily over the rolling expanse of the moor. "There is another morass down yonder, and a narrow neck between. Halloa! halloa! halloa! What have we here?"

We had come on a small black ribbon of pathway. In the middle of it, clearly marked on the sodden soil, was the track of a bicycle.

"Hurrah!" I cried. "We have it."

But Holmes was shaking his head, and his face was puzzled and expectant rather than joyous.

"A bicycle certainly, but not *the* bicycle," said he. "I am familiar with forty-two different impressions left by
tyres. This, as you perceive, is a Dunlop, with a patch **13**
upon the outer cover. Heidegger's tyres were Palmer's, leaving longitudinal stripes. Aveling, the mathematical master, was sure upon the point. Therefore it is not Heidegger's track."

"The boy's, then?"

"Possibly, if we could prove a bicycle to have been in his possession. But this we have utterly failed to do. This track, as you perceive, was made by a rider who was going from the direction of the school."

"Or towards it?"

"No, no, my dear Watson. The more deeply sunk impression is, of course, the hind wheel, upon which the weight rests. You perceive several places where it has passed across and obliterated the more shallow mark of the front one. It was undoubtedly heading
away from the school. It may or may not be connected **14**
with our inquiry, but we will follow it backwards before we go any farther."

We did so, and at the end of a few hundred yards lost the tracks as we emerged from the boggy portion of the moor. Following the path backwards, we picked out another spot, where a spring trickled across it. Here, once again, was the mark of the bicycle, though nearly obliterated by the hoofs of cows. After that there was no sign, but the path ran right on into Ragged Shaw, the wood which backed on to the school. From this wood the cycle must have emerged. Holmes sat down on a boulder and rested his chin in his hands. I had smoked two cigarettes before he moved.

"Well, well," said he at last. "It is, of course, possible that a cunning man might change the tyre of his bicycle in order to leave unfamiliar tracks. A criminal

13 *a Dunlop.* Named for its developer, John Boyd Dunlop, 1840–1921.

14 *It was undoubtedly heading away from the school.* Much, perhaps too much, has been written about these tire tracks. Holmes' deduction has been challenged by Mr. A. D. Galbraith ("The Real Moriarty") and Mr. Stuart C. Rand ("What Sherlock Didn't Know"), among others; defended by Mr. T. S. Blakeney (*Sherlock Holmes: Fact or Fiction?*) and Mr. George K. Gardner ("What Sherlock Did Know"), among others. "But it is clear that the tracks would look the same both ways, unless the tread had some lack of symmetry, or other peculiarity, and the manner of mounting it on the wheel were known," Mr. Galbraith wrote. ". . . the depth of the mark of the rear wheel, when the bicycle was going uphill, would indicate the direction of travel, for on the down slope it is markedly less," Mr. Blakeney wrote. "In any case, Holmes probably had a dozen other small indications to guide him; though he might mention only one factor, he usually had others in reserve as evidenced by the twenty-three additional points of difference in the joint letter of the Cunninghams ["The Reigate Squires"]."

"CHECK NUMBER ONE," SAID HOLMES, LOOKING GLOOMILY OVER THE ROLLING EXPANSE OF THE MOOR.

Cover illustration by Frederic Dorr Steele for *Collier's Magazine*, January 30, 1904.

AN IMPRESSION LIKE A FINE BUNDLE OF TELEGRAPH WIRES RAN DOWN THE CENTRE OF IT.

Illustration by Sidney Paget for the *Strand Magazine*, February, 1904.

WE RAN ROUND, AND THERE LAY THE UNFORTUNATE RIDER.

Illustration by Sidney Paget for the *Strand Magazine*, February, 1904.

who was capable of such a thought is a man whom I should be proud to do business with. We will leave this question undecided and hark back to our morass again, for we have left a good deal unexplored."

We continued our systematic survey of the edge of the sodden portion of the moor, and soon our perseverance was gloriously rewarded.

Right across the lower part of the bog lay a miry path. Holmes gave a cry of delight as he approached it. An impression like a fine bundle of telegraph wires ran down the centre of it. It was the Palmer tyre.

"Here is Herr Heidegger, sure enough!" cried Holmes exultantly. "My reasoning seems to have been pretty sound, Watson."

"I congratulate you."

"But we have a long way still to go. Kindly walk clear of the path. Now let us follow the trail. I fear that it will not lead very far."

We found, however, as we advanced, that this portion of the moor is intersected with soft patches, and, though we frequently lost sight of the track, we always succeeded in picking it up once more.

"Do you observe," said Holmes, "that the rider is now undoubtedly forcing the pace? There can be no doubt of it. Look at this impression, where you get both tyres clear. The one is as deep as the other. That can only mean that the rider is throwing his weight on to the handlebar as a man does when he is sprinting. By Jove! he has had a fall."

There was a broad, irregular smudge covering some yards of the track. Then there were a few footmarks, and the tyre reappeared once more.

"A side-slip," I suggested.

Holmes held up a crumpled branch of flowering gorse. To my horror I perceived that the yellow blossoms were all dabbled with crimson. On the path, too, and among the heather were dark stains of clotted blood.

"Bad!" said Holmes. "Bad! Stand clear, Watson! Not an unnecessary footstep! What do I read here? He fell wounded, he stood up, he remounted, he proceeded. But there is no other track. Cattle on this side-path. He was surely not gored by a bull? Impossible! But I see no traces of anyone else. We must push on, Watson. Surely, with stains as well as the track to guide us, he cannot escape us now."

Our search was not a very long one. The tracks of the tyre began to curve fantastically upon the wet and shining path. Suddenly, as I looked ahead, the gleam of metal caught my eye from amid the thick gorse bushes. Out of them we dragged a bicycle, Palmer-tyred, one pedal bent, and the whole front of it horribly smeared and slobbered with blood. On the other side of the bushes a shoe was projecting. We ran round, and there lay the unfortunate rider. He was a tall man, full bearded, with spectacles, one glass of which had been knocked out. The cause of his death was a frightful blow upon the head, which had crushed in part of his skull. That he could have gone on after receiving such an injury said much for the vitality and courage of the man. He wore shoes, but no socks, and his open coat disclosed a night-shirt beneath it. It was undoubtedly the German master.

Holmes turned the body over reverently, and examined it with great attention. He then sat in deep thought for a time, and I could see by his ruffled brow that this grim discovery had not, in his opinion, advanced us much in our inquiry.

" It is a little difficult to know what to do, Watson," said he, at last. " My own inclinations are to push this inquiry on, for we have already lost so much time that we cannot afford to waste another hour. On the other hand, we are bound to inform the police of this discovery, and to see that this poor fellow's body is looked after."

" I could take a note back."

" But I need your company and assistance. Wait a bit! There is a fellow cutting peat up yonder. Bring him over here, and he will guide the police."

I brought the peasant across, and Holmes despatched the frightened man with a note to Dr. Huxtable.

" Now, Watson," said he, " we have picked up two clues this morning. One is the bicycle with the Palmer tyre, and we see what that has led to. The other is the bicycle with the patched Dunlop. Before we start to investigate that, let us try to realize what we *do* know, so as to make the most of it, and to separate the essential from the accidental.

" First of all, I wish to impress upon you that the boy certainly left of his own free will. He got down from his window and he went off, either alone or with someone. That is sure."

I assented.

" Well, now, let us turn to this unfortunate German master. The boy was fully dressed when he fled. Therefore he foresaw what he would do. But the German went without his socks. He certainly acted on very short notice."

" Undoubtedly."

" Why did he go? Because, from his bedroom window, he saw the flight of the boy. Because he wished to overtake him and bring him back. He seized his bicycle, pursued the lad, and in pursuing him met his death."

" So it would seem."

" Now I come to the critical part of my argument. The natural action of a man in pursuing a little boy would be to run after him. He would know that he could overtake him. But the German does not do so. He turns to his bicycle. I am told that he was an excellent cyclist. He would not do this if he did not see that the boy had some swift means of escape."

" The other bicycle."

" Let us continue our reconstruction. He meets his death five miles from the school—not by a bullet, mark you, which even a lad might conceivably discharge, but by a savage blow dealt by a vigorous arm. The lad, then, *had* a companion in his flight. And the flight was a swift one, since it took five miles before an expert cyclist could overtake them. Yet we survey the ground round the scene of the tragedy. What do we find? A few cattle tracks, nothing more. I took a wide sweep round,

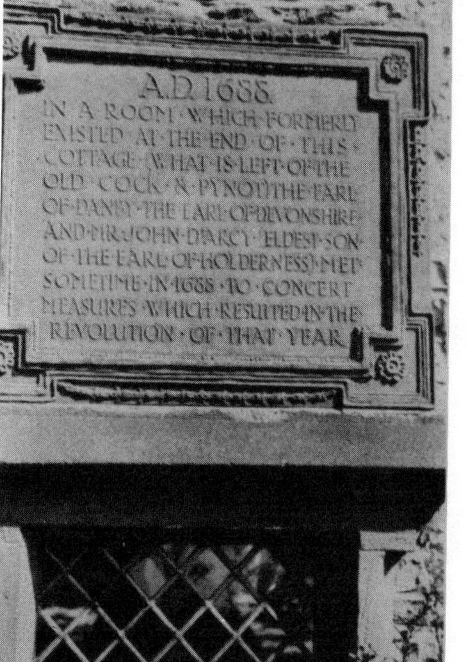

. . . THE FORBIDDING AND SQUALID INN, WITH THE SIGN OF A GAMECOCK ABOVE THE DOOR . . .

To Mr. Charles O. Merriman of the Sherlock Holmes Society of London goes the credit for identifying what must have been the Fighting Cock Inn. He found it at the proper location, in Old Whittington, on the high road, four miles from Chesterfield, and it bears a plaque which reads: A.D. 1688 / IN A ROOM WHICH FORMERLY / EXISTED AT THE END OF THIS / COTTAGE (WHAT IS LEFT OF THE / OLD COCK & PYNOT) THE EARL / OF DANBY THE EARL OF DEVONSHIRE / AND MR. JOHN D'ARCY (ELDEST SON / OF THE EARL OF HOLDERNESS) MET / SOMETIME IN 1688 TO CONCERT / MEASURES WHICH RESULTED IN THE / REVOLUTION OF THAT YEAR.

and there is no path within fifty yards. Another cyclist could have had nothing to do with the actual murder. Nor were there any human footmarks."

"Holmes," I cried, "this is impossible."

"Admirable!" he said. "A most illuminating remark. It *is* impossible as I state it, and therefore I must in some respect have stated it wrong. Yet you saw for yourself. Can you suggest any fallacy?"

"He could not have fractured his skull in a fall?"

"In a morass, Watson?"

"I am at my wits' end."

"Tut, tut; we have solved some worse problems. At least we have plenty of material, if we can only use it. Come, then, and, having exhausted the Palmer, let us see what the Dunlop with the patched cover has to offer us."

We picked up the track and followed it onwards for some distance; but soon the moor rose into a long, heather-tufted curve, and we left the watercourse behind us. No further help from tracks could be hoped for. At the spot where we saw the last of the Dunlop tyre it might equally have led to Holdernesse Hall, the stately towers of which rose some miles to our left, or to a low, grey village which lay in front of us, and marked the position of the Chesterfield high-road.

As we approached the forbidding and squalid inn, with the sign of a game-cock above the door, Holmes gave a sudden groan and clutched me by the shoulder to save himself from falling. He had had one of those violent strains of the ankle which leave a man helpless. With difficulty he limped up to the door, where a squat, dark, elderly man was smoking a black clay pipe.

"How are you, Mr. Reuben Hayes?" said Holmes.

"Who are you, and how do you get my name so pat?" the countryman answered, with a suspicious flash of a pair of cunning eyes.

"Well, it's printed on the board above your head. It's easy to see a man who is master of his own house. I suppose you haven't such a thing as a carriage in your stables?"

"No; I have not."

"I can hardly put my foot to the ground."

"Don't put it to the ground."

"But I can't walk."

"Well, then, hop."

Mr. Reuben Hayes' manner was far from gracious, but Holmes took it with admirable good humour.

"Look here, my man," said he. "This is really rather an awkward fix for me. I don't mind how I get on."

"Neither do I," said the morose landlord.

"The matter is very important. I would offer you a sovereign for the use of a bicycle."

The landlord pricked up his ears.

"Where do you want to go?"

"To Holdernesse Hall."

"Pals of the dook, I suppose?" said the landlord, surveying our mud-stained garments with ironical eyes.

Holmes laughed good-naturedly.

"He'll be glad to see us, anyhow."

"Why?"

"Because we bring him news of his lost son."

The landlord gave a very visible start.

"What, you're on his track?"

"He has been heard of in Liverpool. They expect to get him every hour."

Again a swift change passed over the heavy, unshaven face. His manner was suddenly genial.

"I've less reason to wish the dook well than most men," said he, "for I was his head coachman once, and cruel bad he treated me. It was him that sacked me without a character on the word of a lying corn-chandler. But I'm glad to hear that the young lord was heard of in Liverpool, and I'll help you to take the news to the Hall."

"Thank you," said Holmes. "We'll have some food first. Then you can bring round the bicycle."

"I haven't got a bicycle."

Holmes held up a sovereign.

"I tell you, man, that I haven't got one. I'll let you have two horses as far as the Hall."

"Well, well," said Holmes, "we'll talk about it when we've had something to eat."

When we were left alone in the stone-flagged kitchen it was astonishing how rapidly that sprained ankle recovered. It was nearly nightfall, and we had eaten nothing since early morning, so that we spent some time over our meal. Holmes was lost in thought, and once or twice he walked over to the window and stared earnestly out. It opened on to a squalid courtyard. In the far corner was a smithy, where a grimy lad was at work. On the other side were the stables. Holmes had sat down again after one of these excursions, when he suddenly sprang out of his chair with a loud exclamation.

"By Heaven, Watson, I believe that I've got it!" he cried. "Yes, yes, it must be so. Watson, do you remember seeing any cow-tracks to-day?"

"Yes, several."

"Where?"

"Well, everywhere. They were at the morass, and again on the path, and again near where poor Heidegger met his death."

"Exactly. Well, now, Watson, how many cows did you see on the moor?"

"I don't remember seeing any."

"Strange, Watson, that we should see tracks all along our line, but never a cow on the whole moor; very strange, Watson, eh?"

"Yes, it is strange."

"Now, Watson, make an effort; throw your mind back! Can you see those tracks upon the path?"

"Yes, I can."

"Can you recall that the tracks were sometimes like that, Watson"—he arranged a number of breadcrumbs in this fashion—: : : : :—"and sometimes like this"—: · : · : · : ·—"and occasionally like this—. · . · . · . ·

"Can you remember that?" **15**

"No, I cannot."

"But I can. I could swear to it. However, we will go back at our leisure and verify it. What a blind beetle I have been not to draw my conclusion?"

WITH DIFFICULTY HE LIMPED UP TO THE DOOR . . .

Illustration by Sidney Paget for the *Strand Magazine*, February, 1904.

15 *"Can you remember that?"* In his searching and prize-winning study of "The Hoof-Marks in 'The Priory School,'" Magistrate S. Tupper Bigelow has shown that the walk of a horse is more correctly depicted in dots as:

: :   : :   : :   : :

the canter as

. .   .   .   . .

and the gallop more or less as Holmes has it in our text and in most, but not all, other editions.

WE HAD HARDLY SUNK FROM VIEW WHEN THE MAN FLEW PAST US ON THE ROAD.

Illustration by Sidney Paget for the *Strand Magazine*, February, 1904.

" And what is your conclusion ? "

" Only that it is a remarkable cow which walks, canters, and gallops. By George, Watson, it was no brain of a country publican that thought out such a blind as that! The coast seems to be clear, save for that lad in the smithy. Let us slip out and see what we can see."

There were two rough-haired, unkempt horses in the tumble-down stable. Holmes raised the hind-leg of one of them and laughed aloud.

" Old shoes, but newly shod—old shoes, but new nails. This case deserves to be a classic. Let us go across to the smithy."

The lad continued his work without regarding us. I saw Holmes' eye darting to right and left among the litter of iron and wood, which was scattered about the floor. Suddenly, however, we heard a step behind us, and there was the landlord, his heavy eyebrows drawn down over his savage eyes, his swarthy features convulsed with passion.

He held a short metal-headed stick in his hand, and he advanced in so menacing a fashion that I was right glad to feel the revolver in my pocket.

" You infernal spies ! " the man cried. " What are you doing there ? "

" Why, Mr. Reuben Hayes," said Holmes coolly, " one might think that you were afraid of our finding something out."

The man mastered himself with a violent effort, and his grim mouth loosened into a false laugh, which was more menacing than his frown.

" You're welcome to all you can find out in my smithy," said he. " But look here, mister, I don't care for folk poking about my place without my leave, so the sooner you pay your score and get out of this the better I shall be pleased."

" All right, Mr. Hayes—no harm meant," said Holmes. " We have been having a look at your horses ; but I think I'll walk after all. It's not far, I believe."

" Not more than two miles to the Hall gates. That's the road to the left." He watched us with sullen eyes until we had left his premises.

We did not go very far along the road, for Holmes stopped the instant that the curve hid us from the landlord's view.

" We were warm, as the children say, at that inn," said he. " I seem to grow colder every step that I take away from it. No, no ; I can't possibly leave it."

" I am convinced," said I, " that this Reuben Hayes knows all about it. A more self-evident villain I never saw."

" Oh ! he impressed you in that way, did he ? There are the horses, there is the smithy. Yes, it is an interesting place, this 'Fighting Cock.' I think we shall have another look at it in an unobtrusive way."

A long, sloping hill-side, dotted with grey limestone boulders, stretched behind us. We had turned off the road, and were making our way up the hill, when, looking in the direction of Holdernesse Hall, I saw a cyclist coming swiftly along.

" Get down, Watson ! " cried Holmes, with a heavy hand upon my shoulder. We had hardly sunk from view when the man flew past us on the road. Amid a rolling cloud of dust I caught a glimpse of a pale, agitated face—a face with horror in every lineament, the mouth open, the eyes staring wildly in front. It was like some strange caricature of the dapper James Wilder whom we had seen the night before.

" The duke's secretary ! " cried Holmes. " Come, Watson, let us see what he does."

We scrambled from rock to rock until in a few moments we had made our way to a point from which we could see the front door of the inn. Wilder's bicycle was leaning against the wall beside it. No one was moving about the house, nor could we catch a glimpse of any faces at the windows. Slowly the twilight crept down as the sun sank behind the high towers of Holdernesse Hall. Then in the gloom we saw the two side-lamps of a trap light up in the stable-yard of the inn, and shortly afterwards heard the rattle of hoofs, as it wheeled out into the road and tore off at a furious pace in the direction of Chesterfield.

" What do you make of that, Watson ? " Holmes whispered.

" It looks like a flight."

" A single man in a dog-cart, so far as I could see. Well, it certainly was not Mr. James Wilder, for there he is at the door."

A red square of light had sprung out of the darkness. In the middle of it was the black figure of the secretary, his head advanced, peering out into the night. It was evident that he was expecting some one. Then at last there were steps in the road, a second figure was visible for an instant against the light, the door shut, and all was black once more. Five minutes later a lamp was lit in a room upon the first floor.

" It seems to be a curious class of custom that is done by the ' Fighting Cock,' " said Holmes.

" The bar is on the other side."

" Quite so. These are what one may call the private guests. Now, what in the world is Mr. James Wilder doing in that den at this hour of night, and who is the companion who comes to meet him there ? Come, Watson, we must really take a risk and try to investigate this a little more closely."

Together we stole down to the road and crept across to the door of the inn. The bicycle still leaned against the wall. Holmes struck a match and held it to the back wheel, and I heard him chuckle as the light fell upon a patched Dunlop tyre. Up above us was the lighted window.

" I must have a peep through that, Watson. If you bend your back and support yourself upon the wall, I think that I can manage."

An instant later his feet were on my shoulders. But he was hardly up before he was down again.

" Come, my friend," said he, " our day's work has been quite long enough. I think that we have gathered all that we can. It's a long walk to the school, and the sooner we get started the better."

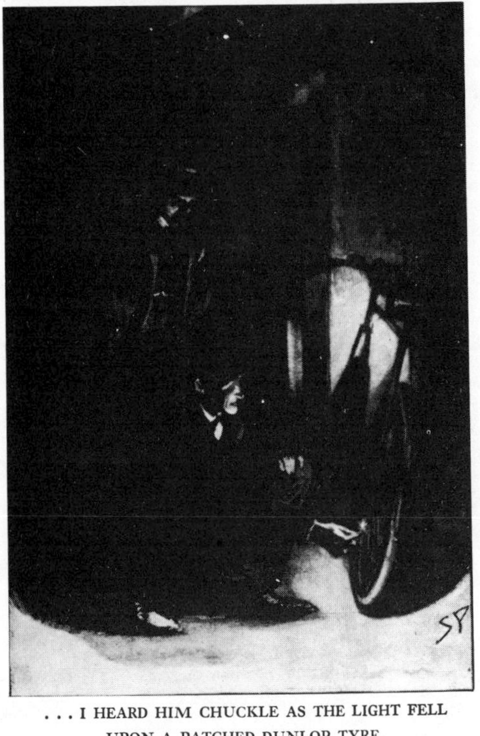

. . . I HEARD HIM CHUCKLE AS THE LIGHT FELL UPON A PATCHED DUNLOP TYRE.

Illustration by Sidney Paget for the *Strand Magazine*, February, 1904.

AN INSTANT LATER HIS FEET WERE ON MY SHOULDERS.

Illustration by Charles Raymond Macauley for *The Return of Sherlock Holmes*, New York: McClure, Phillips & Co., 1905.

He hardly opened his lips during that weary trudge across the moor, nor would he enter the school when he reached it, but went on to Mackleton Station, whence he could send some telegrams. Late at night I heard him consoling Dr. Huxtable, prostrated by the tragedy of his master's death, and later still he entered my room as alert and vigorous as he had been when he started in the morning. "All goes well, my friend," said he. "I promise that before to-morrow evening we shall have reached the solution of the mystery."

At eleven o'clock next morning my friend and I were walking up the famous yew avenue of Holdernesse Hall. We were ushered through the magnificent Elizabethan doorway and into his Grace's study. There we found Mr. James Wilder, demure and courtly, but with some trace of that wild terror of the night before still lurking in his furtive eyes and in his twitching features.

"You have come to see his Grace? I am sorry; but the fact is that the duke is far from well. He has been very much upset by the tragic news. We received a telegram from Dr. Huxtable yesterday afternoon, which told us of your discovery."

"I must see the duke, Mr. Wilder."

"But he is in his room."

"Then I must go to his room."

"I believe he is in his bed."

"I will see him there."

Holmes' cold and inexorable manner showed the secretary that it was useless to argue with him.

"Very good, Mr. Holmes; I will tell him that you are here."

After half an hour's delay the great nobleman appeared. His face was more cadaverous than ever, his shoulders had rounded, and he seemed to me to be an altogether older man than he had been the morning before. He greeted us with a stately courtesy, and seated himself at his desk, his red beard streaming down on to the table.

"Well, Mr. Holmes?" said he.

But my friend's eyes were fixed upon the secretary, who stood by his master's chair.

"I think, your Grace, that I could speak more freely in Mr. Wilder's absence."

The man turned a shade paler and cast a malignant glance at Holmes.

"If your Grace wishes——"

"Yes, yes; you had better go. Now, Mr. Holmes, what have you to say?"

My friend waited until the door had closed behind the retreating secretary.

"The fact is, your Grace," said he, "that my colleague, Dr. Watson, and myself had an assurance from Dr. Huxtable that a reward had been offered in this case. I should like to have this confirmed from your own lips."

"Certainly, Mr. Holmes."

"It amounted, if I am correctly informed, to five thousand pounds to anyone who will tell you where your son is?"

"Exactly."

"And another thousand to the man who will name

the person or persons who keep him in custody ? "

" Exactly."

" Under the latter heading is included, no doubt, not only those who may have taken him away, but also those who conspire to keep him in his present position ? "

" Yes, yes," cried the duke impatiently. " If you do your work well, Mr. Sherlock Holmes, you will have no reason to complain of niggardly treatment."

My friend rubbed his thin hands together with an appearance of avidity which was a surprise to me, who knew his frugal tastes.

" I fancy that I see your Grace's cheque-book upon the table," said he. " I should be glad if you would make me out a cheque for six thousand pounds. It would be as
well, perhaps, for you to cross it. The Capital and **16**
Counties Bank, Oxford Street branch, are my agents." **17**

His Grace sat very stern and upright in his chair, and looked stonily at my friend.

" Is this a joke, Mr. Holmes ? It is hardly a subject for pleasantry."

" Not at all, your Grace. I was never more earnest in my life."

" What do you mean, then ? "

" I mean that I have earned the reward. I know where your son is, and I know some, at least, of those who are holding him."

The duke's beard had turned more aggressively red than ever against his ghastly white face.

" Where is he ? " he gasped.

" He is, or was last night, at the Fighting Cock Inn, about two miles from your park gate."

The duke fell back in his chair.

" And whom do you accuse ? "

Sherlock Holmes' answer was an astounding one. He stepped swiftly forward and touched the duke upon the shoulder.

" I accuse *you*," said he. " And now, your Grace, I'll trouble you for that cheque."

Never shall I forget the duke's appearance as he sprang up and clawed with his hand like one who is sinking into an abyss. Then, with an extraordinary effort of aristocratic self-command, he sat down and sank his face in his hands. It was some minutes before he spoke.

" How much do you know ? " he asked at last, without raising his head.

" I saw you together last night."

" Does anyone else besides your friend know ? "

" I have spoken to no one."

The duke took a pen in his quivering fingers and opened his cheque-book.

" I shall be as good as my word, Mr. Holmes. I am about to write your cheque, however unwelcome the information which you have gained may be to me. When the offer was first made I little thought the turn which events would take. But you and your friend are men of discretion, Mr. Holmes ? "

" I hardly understand your Grace."

" I must put it plainly, Mr. Holmes. If only you two know of the incident, there is no reason why it should go
any farther. I think twelve thousand pounds is the sum **18**

16 *to cross it.* To write something, such as the name of a bank, across the face of the check, requiring its deposit in the bank by the payee before collection.

17 *The Capital and Counties Bank, Oxford Street branch.* In Holmes' day, the Oxford Street branch of the Capital and Counties Bank was located at No. 125.

18 *twelve thousand pounds.* "The Duke, when it came to paying, spoke of £12,000 being the sum owed, presumably intending to give the promised reward of £6,000 to Watson as well, unless, indeed, he was hoping to purchase Holmes' silence by doubling the amount due to him," Mr. T. S. Blakeney commented in *Sherlock Holmes: Fact or Fiction?*

"NO; THE MURDERER HAS ESCAPED."

Illustration by Sidney Paget for the *Strand Magazine*, February, 1904.

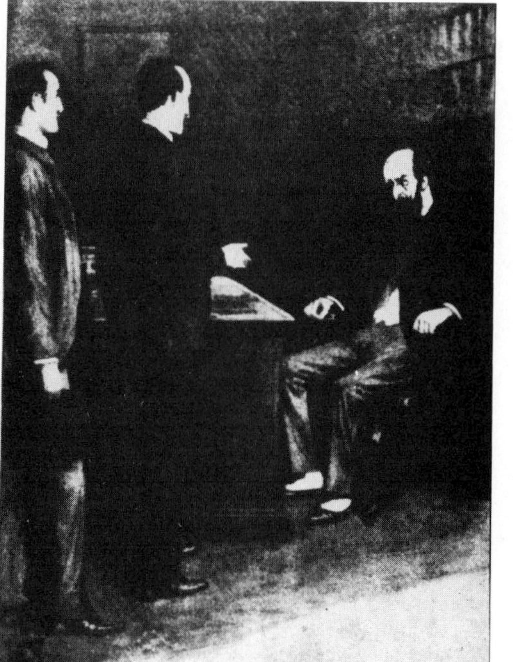

that I owe you, is it not ? "

But Holmes smiled, and shook his head.

" I fear, your Grace, that matters can hardly be arranged so easily. There is the death of this schoolmaster to be accounted for."

" But James knew nothing of that. You cannot hold him responsible for that. It was the work of this brutal ruffian whom he had the misfortune to employ."

" I must take the view, your Grace, that when a man embarks upon a crime he is morally guilty of any other crime which may spring from it."

" Morally, Mr. Holmes. No doubt you are right. But surely not in the eyes of the law. A man cannot be condemned for a murder at which he was not present, and which he loathes and abhors as much as you do. The instant that he heard of it he made a complete confession to me, so filled was he with horror and remorse. He lost not an hour in breaking entirely with the murderer. Oh, Mr. Holmes, you must save him—you must save him ! I tell you that you must save him ! " The duke had dropped the last attempt at self-command, and was pacing the room with a convulsed face and with his clenched hands raving in the air. At last he mastered himself and sat down once more at his desk. " I appreciate your conduct in coming here before you spoke to anyone else," said he. " At least we may take counsel how far we can minimize this hideous scandal."

" Exactly," said Holmes. " I think, your Grace, that this can only be done by absolute and complete frankness between us. I am disposed to help your Grace to the best of my ability ; but in order to do so I must understand to the last detail how the matter stands. I realize that your words applied to Mr. James Wilder, and that he is not the murderer."

" No ; the murderer has escaped."

Sherlock Holmes smiled demurely.

" Your Grace can hardly have heard of any small reputation which I possess, or you would not imagine that it is so easy to escape me. Mr. Reuben Hayes was arrested at Chesterfield on my information at eleven o'clock last night. I had a telegram from the head of the local police before I left the school this morning."

The duke leaned back in his chair and stared with amazement at my friend.

" You seem to have powers that are hardly human," said he. " So Reuben Hayes is taken ? I am right glad to hear it, if it will not react upon the fate of James."

" Your secretary ? "

" No, sir ; my son."

It was Holmes' turn to look astonished.

" I confess that this is entirely new to me, your Grace. I must beg of you to be more explicit."

" I will conceal nothing from you. I agree with you that complete frankness, however painful it may be to me, is the best policy in this desperate situation to which James' folly and jealousy have reduced us. When I was a young man, Mr. Holmes, I loved with such a love as comes only once in a lifetime. I offered the lady marriage, but she refused it on the grounds that such a match might mar my career. Had she lived I would certainly never have married anyone else. She died, and left this one child, whom for her sake I have cherished and cared for. I could not acknowledge the paternity to the world; but I gave him the best of educations, and since he came to manhood I have kept him near my person. He surprised my secret, and has presumed ever since upon the claim which he has upon me and upon his power of provoking a scandal, which would be abhorrent to me. His presence had something to do with the unhappy issue of my marriage. Above all, he hated my young legitimate heir from the first with a persistent hatred. You may well ask me why, under these circumstances, I still kept James under my roof. I answer that it was because I could see his mother's face in his, and that for her dear sake there was no end to my long-suffering. All her pretty ways, too—there was not one of them which he could not suggest and bring back to my memory. I *could* not send him away. But I feared so lest he should do Arthur—that is, Lord Saltire—a mischief that I despatched him for safety to Dr. Huxtable's school.

"James came into contact with this fellow Hayes because the man was a tenant of mine, and James acted as agent. The fellow was a rascal from the beginning; but in some extraordinary way James became intimate with him. He had always a taste for low company. When James determined to kidnap Lord Saltire it was of this man's service that he availed himself. You remember that I wrote to Arthur upon that last day. Well, James opened the letter and inserted a note asking Arthur to meet him in a little wood called the Ragged Shaw which is near to the school. He used the duchess' name, and in that way got the boy to come. That evening James cycled over—I am telling you what he has himself confessed to me—and he told Arthur, whom he met in the wood, that his mother longed to see him, that she was awaiting him on the moor, and that if he would come back into the wood at midnight he would find a man with a horse, who would take him to her. Poor Arthur fell into the trap. He came to the appointment, and found this fellow Hayes with a led pony. Arthur mounted, and they set off together. It appears—though this James only heard yesterday—that they were pursued, that Hayes struck the pursuer with his stick, and that the man died of his injuries. Hayes brought Arthur to his public-house, the 'Fighting Cock,' where he was confined in an upper room, under the care of Mrs. Hayes, who is a kindly woman, but entirely under the control of her brutal husband.

"Well, Mr. Holmes, that was the state of affairs when I first saw you two days ago. I had no more idea of the truth than you. You will ask me what was James' motive in doing such a deed. I answer that there was a great deal which was unreasoning and fanatical in the hatred which he bore my heir. In his view he should himself have been heir of all my estates, and he deeply resented those social laws which made it impossible. At the same time, he had a definite motive also. He was eager that I should break the entail, and he was of opinion that it lay in my power to do so. He intended to make a bargain with me—to restore Arthur if I would break the entail, and so make it possible for the estate to be left to him by will. He knew well that I should never willingly invoke the aid of the police against him. I say that he would have proposed such a bargain to me, but he did not actually do so, for events moved too quickly for him, and he had not time to put his plans into practice.

" What brought all his wicked scheme to wreck was your discovery of this man Heidegger's dead body. James was seized with horror at the news. It came to us yesterday as we sat together in this study. Dr. Huxtable had sent a telegram. James was so overwhelmed with grief and agitation that my suspicions, which had never been entirely absent, rose instantly to a certainty, and I taxed him with the deed. He made a complete voluntary confession. Then he implored me to keep his secret for three days longer, so as to give his wretched accomplice a chance of saving his guilty life. I yielded—as I have always yielded—to his prayers, and instantly James hurried off to the 'Fighting Cock' to warn Hayes and give him the means of flight. I could not go there by daylight without provoking comment, but as soon as night fell I hurried off to see my dear Arthur. I found him safe and well, but horrified beyond expression by the dreadful deed he had witnessed. In deference to my promise, and much against my will, I consented to leave him there for three days under the charge of Mrs. Hayes, since it was evident that it was impossible to inform the police where he was without telling them also who was the murderer, and I could not see how that murderer could be punished without ruin to my unfortunate James. You asked for frankness, Mr. Holmes, and I have taken you at your word, for I have now told you everything without an attempt at circumlocution or concealment. Do you in your turn be as frank with me."

" I will," said Holmes. " In the first place, your Grace, I am bound to tell you that you have placed yourself in a most serious position in the eyes of the law. You have condoned a felony, and you have aided the escape of a murderer; for I cannot doubt that any money which was taken by James Wilder to aid his accomplice in his flight came from your Grace's purse."

The duke bowed his assent.

" This is indeed a most serious matter. Even more culpable, in my opinion, your Grace, is your attitude towards your younger son. You leave him in this den for three days."

" Under solemn promises——"

" What are promises to such people as these? You have no guarantee that he will not be spirited away again. To humour your guilty elder son you have exposed your innocent younger son to imminent and unnecessary danger. It was a most unjustifiable action."

The proud lord of Holdernesse was not accustomed to be so rated in his own ducal hall. The blood flushed into his high forehead, but his conscience held him dumb.

" I will help you, but on one condition only. It is that you ring for the footman and let me give such orders as I like."

Without a word the duke pressed the electric button. A servant entered.

" You will be glad to hear," said Holmes, " that your young master is found. It is the duke's desire that the carriage shall go at once to the Fighting Cock Inn to bring Lord Saltire home."

" Now," said Holmes, when the rejoicing lackey had disappeared, " having secured the future we can afford to be more lenient with the past. I am not in an official position, and there is no reason, so long as the ends of justice are served, why I should disclose all that I know. As to Hayes I say nothing. The gallows awaits him, and I would do nothing to save him from it. What he will divulge I cannot tell, but I have no doubt that your Grace could make him understand that it is to his interest to be silent. From the police point of view he will **19** have kidnapped the boy for the purpose of ransom. If they do not themselves find it out I see no reason why I should prompt them to take a broader view. I would warn your Grace, however, that the continued presence of Mr. James Wilder in your household can only lead to misfortune."

" I understand that, Mr. Holmes, and it is already settled that he shall leave me for ever and go to seek his fortune in Australia."

" In that case, your Grace, since you have yourself stated that any unhappiness in your married life was caused by his presence, I would suggest that you make such amends as you can to the duchess, and that you try to resume those relations which have been so unhappily interrupted."

" That also I have arranged, Mr. Holmes. I wrote to the duchess this morning."

" In that case," said Holmes, rising, " I think that my friend and I can congratulate ourselves upon several most happy results from our little visit to the North. There is one other small point upon which I desire some light. This fellow Hayes had shod his horses with shoes which counterfeited the tracks of cows. Was it from Mr. Wilder that he learned so extraordinary a device ? "

The duke stood in thought for a moment, with a look of intense surprise on his face. Then he opened a door and showed us into a large room furnished as a museum. He led the way to a glass case in a corner, and pointed to the inscription.

" These shoes," it ran, " were dug up in the moat of Holdernesse Hall. They are for the use of horses ; but they are shaped below with a cloven foot of iron, so as to **20** throw pursuers off the track. They are supposed to have belonged to some of the marauding Barons of Holdernesse in the Middle Ages."

Holmes opened the case, and, moistening his finger, he passed it along the shoe. A thin film of recent mud was left upon his skin.

" Thank you," said he, as he replaced the glass. " It is the second most interesting object that I have seen in the North."

" And the first ? "

Holmes folded up his cheque, and placed it carefully **21** in his notebook. " I am a poor man," said he, as he patted it affectionately, and thrust it into the depths of his inner pocket.

19 *it is to his interest to be silent.* "Whether Reuben Hayes was able to see that it would serve his interest to keep his tongue quiet appears a little questionable," Mr. T. S. Blakeney wrote in *Sherlock Holmes: Fact or Fiction?* "One would have thought that, with the scaffold in prospect, he might consider it worth while to do all the harm he could to others, for though it would not help him, it would at least hurt them, and particularly the Duke, for whom he had a strong dislike. It is true he would have to make his damaging statements at the trial, or they were not likely to be made public at all, and to do this would involve admitting his guilt. We presume that the Crown so presented their case as to leave out all possible mention of the Duke, though one hardly sees how they could avoid bringing in Mr. Wilder's complicity in the abduction of Lord Saltire. If not, Mr. Wilder probably found himself unable to leave for Australia."

20 *a cloven foot of iron.* "The Adventure of the Priory School" first appeared in the *Strand Magazine* in February, 1904. Nine months before—in its May, 1903, number—the *Strand* had carried a brief paragraph in a letter from a correspondent, reproducing a photograph of two ancient horseshoes recently found in the moat at Birtsmorton Court, near Tewkesbury. One was so contrived as to make the imprint of a child's foot; the other counterfeited the mark of a cloven hoof. It seems reasonable to suppose that the *Strand* paragraph provided in part at least Conan Doyle's inspiration for the plot of "The Priory School."

21 *Holmes folded up his cheque.* This is one of the few Canonical occasions on which Holmes accepted payment for his services. He perhaps had good reason to: as the late Gavin Brend pointed out in *My Dear Holmes*, the British Government, in 1901, raised the rate of income tax from one shilling to one and two-pence on the pound. "When we recall that 'The Priory School,' being in the month of May, would come just after the Budget, we realize the significance of Holmes' comment, 'I am a poor man.' "

Auctorial and Bibliographical Note: Conan Doyle ranked "The Adventure of the Priory School" No. 10 on his list of the "twelve best" Sherlock Holmes short stories. The original manuscript, about 13,500 words in 71 4to pages with corrections and cancellations in the author's hand, vellum, was auctioned in New York City on January 26, 1922, bringing $155. It was auctioned again in London on January 28, 1925, when it was sold in one lot with "The Adventure of the Dancing Men" and "The Adventure of the Solitary Cyclist" for £66. In October, 1946, it was owned by Mr. Leigh Block of Chicago.

67

THE ADVENTURE OF SHOSCOMBE OLD PLACE

[*Tuesday, May 6, to Wednesday, May 7, 1902*]

SHERLOCK HOLMES had been bending for a long time over a low-power microscope. Now he straightened himself up and looked round at me in triumph.

" It is glue, Watson," said he. " Unquestionably it is glue. Have a look at these scattered objects in the field ! "

I stooped to the eyepiece and focused for my vision.

" Those hairs are threads from a tweed coat. The
irregular grey masses are dust. There are epithelial
scales on the left. Those brown blobs in the centre are
1 undoubtedly glue."

" Well," I said, laughing, " I am prepared to take your word for it. Does anything depend upon it ? "

" It is a very fine demonstration," he answered. " In
2 the St. Pancras case you may remember that a cap was
found beside the dead policeman. The accused man
denies that it is his. But he is a picture-frame maker who
habitually handles glue."

" Is it one of your cases ? "

" No ; my friend, Merivale of the Yard, asked me
to look into the case. Since I ran down that coiner
3 by the zinc and copper filings in the seam of his cuff
they have begun to realize the importance of the microscope." He looked impatiently at his watch. " I had a
new client calling, but he is overdue. By the way, Watson, you know something of racing ? "

" I ought to. I pay for it with about half my wound pension."

4 " Then I'll make you my ' Handy Guide to the Turf.'
What about Sir Robert Norberton ? Does the name
recall anything ? "

" Well, I should say so. He lives at Shoscombe Old Place, and I know it well, for my summer quarters were down there once. Norberton nearly came within your province once."

" How was that ? "

" It was when he horsewhipped Sam Brewer, the well-
5 known Curzon Street moneylender, on Newmarket
Heath. He nearly killed the man."

" Ah, he sounds interesting ! Does he often indulge in that way ? "

1 *Those brown blobs in the centre are undoubtedly glue.*" "Glue it may well have been, but neither Holmes nor anyone else ever made the identification in such a manner," Professor Remsen Ten Eyck Schenck wrote in "Baker Street Fables." "Glue, which is an amorphous, impure form of gelatin, can exist in particles of any size and shape and could be positively identified only by chemical means. Microscopically it would be quite indistinguishable from rosin, shellac or any one of dozens of physically similar substances."

2 *St. Pancras.* This metropolitan borough, which extends from Islington to Marylebone east to west, and from Holborn to Hampstead and Hornsey south to north, derives its name from a youthful nobleman of Phrygia who suffered martyrdom at Rome by order of Diocletian. Until about two hundred years ago St. Pancras was a spa containing mineral springs which attracted many visitors. Not only were digestive troubles alleged to be removed by a cure at St. Pancras, but even leprosy, scurvy, and cancer. The site of St. Pancras Wells is now occupied by British Railways, Midland Region.

3 *by the zinc and copper filings in the seam of his cuff.* Zinc and copper filings "could be unequivocally identified even in minute amounts by a chemical analysis, [but] visual examination would reveal no more than that they were probably (but not certainly) metallic," Professor Schenck wrote. "No slightest clue as to the metal of which they were composed could be hoped for."

To this, Mr. Leon S. Holstein has replied ("'7. Knowledge of Chemistry—Profound'"): "I personally have seen and recognized as such, zinc and copper filings under a microscope—and if an amateur can do so today, surely the outstanding professional of all time should have had no trouble in doing so . . ."

SHERLOCK HOLMES HAD BEEN BENDING FOR A LONG TIME OVER A LOW-POWER MICROSCOPE.

Illustration by Frederic Dorr Steele for *Liberty Magazine*, March 5, 1927.

"IT IS GLUE, WATSON," SAID HE.

Illustration by Frank Wiles for the *Strand Magazine*, April, 1927.

" Well, he has the name of being a dangerous man. He is about the most daredevil rider in England—second in the Grand National a few years back. He is one of those men who have overshot their true generation. He should have been a buck in the days of the Regency —a boxer, an athlete, a plunger on the Turf, a lover of fair ladies, and, by all account, so far down Queer Street that he may never find his way back again."

" Capital, Watson ! A thumb-nail sketch. I seem to know the man. Now, can you give me some idea of Shoscombe Old Place ? "

" Only that it is in the centre of Shoscombe Park, and that the famous Shoscombe stud and training quarters are to be found there."

" And the head trainer," said Holmes, " is John Mason. You need not look surprised at my knowledge, Watson, for this is a letter from him which I am unfolding. But let us have some more about Shoscombe. I seem to have struck a rich vein."

" There are the Shoscombe spaniels," said I. " You
hear of them at every dog show. The most exclusive
breed in England. They are the special pride of the **6**
lady of Shoscombe Old Place."

" Sir Robert Norberton's wife, I presume ! "

" Sir Robert has never married. Just as well, I think, considering his prospects. He lives with his widowed sister, Lady Beatrice Falder."

" You mean that she lives with him ? "

" No, no. The place belonged to her late husband, Sir James. Norberton has no claim on it at all. It is only a life interest and reverts to her husband's brother. Meantime, she draws the rents every year."

" And brother Robert, I suppose, spends the said rents ? "

" That is about the size of it. He is a devil of a fellow and must lead her a most uneasy life. Yet I have heard that she is devoted to him. But what is amiss at Shoscombe ? "

" Ah, that is just what I want to know. And here, I expect, is the man who can tell us."

The door had opened and the page had shown in a tall, clean-shaven man with the firm, austere expression which is only seen upon those who have to control horses or boys. Mr. John Mason had many of both under his sway, and he looked equal to the task. He bowed with cold self-possession and seated himself upon the chair to which Holmes had waved him.

4 *my 'Handy Guide to the Turf.'* " Holmes, once so knowledgeable about racing matters ("Silver Blaze") now seems to have lost all interest in the Sport of Kings. This is perhaps balanced by Watson: although the doctor showed an almost complete ignorance of racing in 1890, at the time of the Wessex Cup (or Plate), he now reveals himself as a slave to the turf. On the other hand, Mr. R. M. McLaren has expressed considerable doubt that Watson in fact paid for racing with about half of his wound pension. In "Doctor Watson—Punter or Speculator?", he wrote: "[Watson] spent half his wound pension on gambling—not on the Turf but on the Stock Exchange. In sharp contrast to his fumbling approach to the Turf is his interest, and to some extent his informed interest, about the Stock Exchange. On this subject he wrote with a much surer and more certain hand. He was clearly familiar with the circumstances under which Coxon and Woodhouse failed through the Venezuelan loan ["The Stockbroker's Clerk"]. In reporting 'A Case of Identity' the exact investment of Miss Mary Sutherland's inheritance from her Uncle Ned had no bearing on Holmes' investigation, but Watson duly recorded that it was in New Zealand 4½ per cent. He remembered exactly the prices of three of the securities quoted by Hall Pycroft in reply to the questions of Mr. Arthur Pinner. It appears probable, though he does not claim it, that it was he who suggested to Holmes that Cornelius to whom Jonas Oldacre was making large payments was a broker ["The Adventure of the Norwood Builder"]. He was immensely impressed by Sir Charles Baskerville having made ¾ million pounds in South African speculation."

" You had my note, Mr. Holmes ? "

" Yes, but it explained nothing."

" It was too delicate a thing for me to put the details on paper. And too complicated. It was only face to face I could do it."

" Well, we are at your disposal."

" First of all, Mr. Holmes, I think that my employer, Sir Robert, has gone mad."

Holmes raised his eyebrows. " This is Baker Street, not Harley Street," said he. " But why do you say so ? "

" Well, sir, when a man does one queer thing, or two queer things, there may be a meaning to it, but when everything he does is queer, then you begin to wonder. I believe Shoscombe Prince and the Derby have turned his brain."

" That is a colt you are running ? "

7 " The best in England, Mr. Holmes. I should know, if anyone does. Now, I'll be plain with you, for I know you are gentlemen of honour and that it won't go beyond the room. Sir Robert has got to win this Derby. He's up to the neck, and it's his last chance. Everything he could raise or borrow is on the horse—and at fine odds, too ! You can get forties now, but it was nearer the hundred when he began to back him."

" But how is that, if the horse is so good ? "

" The public don't know how good he is. Sir Robert has been too clever for the touts. He has the Prince's half-brother out for spins. You can't tell 'em apart. But there are two lengths in a furlong between them when it comes to a gallop. He thinks of nothing but the horse and the race. His whole life is on it. He's holding off the Jews till then. If the Prince fails him, he is done."

" It seems a rather desperate gamble, but where does the madness come in ? "

" Well, first of all, you have only to look at him. I don't believe he sleeps at night. He is down at the stables at all hours. His eyes are wild. It has all been too much for his nerves. Then there is his conduct to Lady Beatrice ! "

" Ah ! what is that ? "

" They have always been the best of friends. They had the same tastes, the two of them, and she loved the horses as much as he did. Every day at the same hour she would drive down to see them—and, above all, she loved the Prince. He would prick up his ears when he heard the wheels on the gravel, and he would trot out each morning to the carriage to get his lump of sugar. But that's all over now."

" Why ? "

" Well, she seems to have lost all interest in the horses. For a week now she has driven past the stables with never so much as ' good morning ' ! "

" You think there has been a quarrel ? "

" And a bitter, savage, spiteful quarrel at that. Why else would he give away her pet spaniel that she loved as if he were her child ? He gave it a few days ago to old Barnes, what keeps the ' Green Dragon,' three miles off, at Crendall."

5 *Curzon Street.* Named for George Augustus Curzon, third Viscount Howe, Curzon Street, Augustus J. C. Hare tells us in *Walks in London,* Vol. II, was "associated in the recollection of so many living persons with the charming parties of the sisters Mary and Agnes Berry, who died in 1852 equally honoured and beloved. They lived at No. 8, where Murrell, their servant, used to set up a lamp over their door, as a sign when they had 'too many women' at their parties: a few habitues of the male sex, however, knew that thev could still come in, whether the lamp was lighted or not. 'The day may be distant,' says Lord Houghton, 'before social tradition forgets the house in Curzon Street where dwelt the Berrys.' . . . Chantrey lived in an attic of No. 24, Curzon Street, and modelled several of his busts there."

6 *The most exclusive breed in England.* "Of course [Watson] means *strain,*" Mrs. Eleanor S. Cole wrote in "Holmes, Watson and the K-9's," "for the breed is spaniel, although he neglects to tell us which kind. We may safely assume they were English cocker spaniels, although they could have been Brittany, Clumber, English springer, field, Irish water, Sussex, or Welsh springer spaniels."

7 "*The best in England, Mr. Holmes.* The late Gavin Brend wrote:

"I'm Shoscombe Prince and I'd have you know
That I won the Derby long ago.
So I can't understand this ridiculous craze
For that fatuous animal, Silver Blaze.
Isonomy's son is so stuck up
Yet all he has won is the Wessex Cup.
(The Wessex Cup, or, as some relate,
A piffling affair called the Wessex Plate.)
But *I* came first in a classic race
And saved Sir Robert from dire disgrace.
I repeat that I can't understand this craze
For that ludicrous quadruped, Silver Blaze."

"That certainly did seem strange."

"Of course, with her weak heart and dropsy one couldn't expect that she could get about with him, but he spent two hours every evening in her room. He might well do what he could, for she has been a rare good friend to him. But that's all over, too. He never goes near her. And she takes it to heart. She is brooding and sulky and drinking, Mr. Holmes—drinking like a fish."

"Did she drink before this estrangement?"

"Well, she took her glass, but now it is often a whole bottle of an evening. So Stephens, the butler, told me. It's all changed, Mr. Holmes, and there is something damned rotten about it. But then, again, what is master doing down at the old church crypt at night? And who is the man that meets him there?"

Holmes rubbed his hands.

"Go on, Mr. Mason. You get more and more interesting."

"It was the butler who saw him go. Twelve o'clock at night and raining hard. So next night I was up at the house and, sure enough, master was off again. Stephens and I went after him, but it was jumpy work, for it would have been a bad job if he had seen us. He's a terrible man with his fists if he gets started, and no respecter of persons. So we were shy of getting too near, but we marked him down all right. It was the haunted crypt that he was making for, and there was a man waiting for him there."

"What is this haunted crypt?"

"Well, sir, there is an old ruined chapel in the park. It is so old that nobody could fix its date. And under it there's a crypt which has a bad name among us. It's a dark, damp, lonely place by day, but there are few in that county that would have the nerve to go near it at night. But master's not afraid. He never feared anything in his life. But what is he doing there in the night-time?"

"Wait a bit!" said Holmes. "You say there is another man there. It must be one of your own stablemen, or someone from the house! Surely you have only to spot who it is and question him?"

"It's no one I know."

"How can you say that?"

"Because I have seen him, Mr. Holmes. It was on that second night. Sir Robert turned and passed us—me and Stephens, quaking in the bushes like two bunny-rabbits, for there was a bit of moon that night. But we could hear the other moving about behind. We were not afraid of him. So we up when Sir Robert was gone and pretended we were just having a walk like in the moonlight, and so we came right on him as casual and innocent as you please. 'Hullo, mate! who may you be?' says I. I guess he had not heard us coming, so he looked over his shoulder with a face as if he had seen the Devil coming out of Hell. He let out a yell, and away he went as hard as he could lick it in the darkness. He could run!—I'll give him that. In a minute he was out of sight and hearing, and who he was, or what he was, we never found."

"But you saw him clearly in the moonlight?"

"Yes, I would swear to his yellow face—a mean dog,

"I GUESS HE HAD NOT HEARD US COMING . . ."

Illustration by Frank Wiles for the *Strand Magazine*, April, 1927.

I should say. What could he have in common with Sir Robert ? "

Holmes sat for some time lost in thought.

" Who keeps Lady Beatrice Falder company ? " he asked at last.

" There is her maid, Carrie Evans. She has been with her this five years."

" And is, no doubt, devoted ? "

Mr. Mason shuffled uncomfortably.

" She's devoted enough," he answered at last. " But I won't say to whom."

" Ah ! " said Holmes.

" I can't tell tales out of school."

" I quite understand, Mr. Mason. Of course, the situation is clear enough. From Dr. Watson's description of Sir Robert I can realize that no woman is safe from him. Don't you think the quarrel between brother and sister may lie there ? "

" Well, the scandal has been pretty clear for a long time."

" But she may not have seen it before. Let us suppose that she has suddenly found it out. She wants to get rid of the woman. Her brother will not permit it. The invalid, with her weak heart and inability to get about, has no means of enforcing her will. The hated maid is still tied to her. The lady refuses to speak, sulks, takes to drink. Sir Robert in his anger takes her pet spaniel away from her. Does not all this hang together ? "

" Well, it might do—so far as it goes."

" Exactly ! As far as it goes. How would all that bear upon the visits by night to the old crypt ? We can't fit that into our plot."

" No, sir, and there is something more that I can't fit in. Why should Sir Robert want to dig up a dead body ? "

Holmes sat up abruptly.

" We only found it out yesterday—after I had written to you. Yesterday Sir Robert had gone to London, so Stephens and I went down to the crypt. It was all in order, sir, except that in one corner was a bit of a human body."

" You informed the police, I suppose ? "

Our visitor smiled grimly.

" Well, sir, I think it would hardly interest them. It was just the head and a few bones of a mummy. It may have been a thousand years old. But it wasn't there before. That I'll swear, and so will Stephens. It had been stowed away in a corner and covered over with a board, but that corner had always been empty before."

" What did you do with it ? "

" Well, we just left it there."

" That was wise. You say Sir Robert was away yesterday. Has he returned ? "

" We expect him back to-day."

" When did Sir Robert give away his sister's dog ? "

" It was just a week ago to-day. The creature was howling outside the old well-house, and Sir Robert was in one of his tantrums that morning. He caught it up and I thought he would have killed it. Then he gave it to Sandy Bain, the jockey, and told him to take the dog to old Barnes at the 'Green Dragon,' for he never wished to see it again."

Holmes sat for some time in silent thought. He had lit the oldest and foulest of his pipes. **8**

"I am not clear yet what you want me to do in this matter, Mr. Mason," he said at last. "Can't you make it more definite?"

"Perhaps this will make it more definite, Mr. Holmes," said our visitor.

He took a paper from his pocket and, unwrapping it carefully, he exposed a charred fragment of bone.

Holmes examined it with interest.

"Where did you get it?"

"There is a central heating furnace in the cellar under Lady Beatrice's room. It's been off for some time, but Sir Robert complained of cold and had it on again. Harvey runs it—he's one of my lads. This very morning he came to me with this which he found raking out the cinders. He didn't like the look of it."

"Nor do I," said Holmes. "What do you make of it, Watson?"

It was burned to a black cinder, but there could be no question as to its anatomical significance.

"It's the upper condyle of a human femur," said I. **9**

"Exactly!" Holmes had become very serious. "When does this lad attend to the furnace?"

"He makes it up every evening and then leaves it."

"Then anyone could visit it during the night?"

"Yes, sir."

"Can you enter it from outside?"

"There is one door from outside. There is another which leads up by a stair to the passage in which Lady Beatrice's room is situated."

"These are deep waters, Mr. Mason; deep and rather dirty. You say that Sir Robert was not at home last night?"

"No, sir."

"Then, whoever was burning bones, it was not he."

"That's true, sir."

"What is the name of that inn you spoke of?"

"The 'Green Dragon.'"

"Is there good fishing in that part of Berkshire?"

The honest trainer showed very clearly upon his face that he was convinced that yet another lunatic had come into his harassed life.

"Well, sir, I've heard there are trout in the mill-stream and pike in the Hall lake."

"That's good enough. Watson and I are famous fishermen—are we not, Watson? You may address us in future at the 'Green Dragon.' We should reach it to-night. I need not say that we don't want to see you, Mr. Mason, but a note will reach us, and no doubt I could find you if I want you. When we have gone a little further into the matter I will let you have a considered opinion."

Thus it was that on a bright May evening Holmes and I found ourselves alone in a first-class carriage and bound for the little "halt-on-demand" station of Shoscombe. The rack above us was covered with a for-

8 *the oldest and foulest of his pipes.* "One can hardly doubt that when . . . Holmes lit 'the oldest and foulest of his pipes,' he was lighting the 'old briar pipe' of 'The Man with the Twisted Lip'—a pipe mellowed by years of devoted attention," Mr. John L. Hicks wrote in "No Fire Without Some Smoke."

9 *the upper condyle of a human femur.*" Watson's "anatomy was rusty . . . in point of fact there is no such part," Dr. Samuel R. Meaker wrote in "Watson Medicus."

midable litter of rods, reels and baskets. On reaching our destination a short drive took us to an old-fashioned tavern, where a sporting host, Josiah Barnes, entered eagerly into our plans for the extirpation of the fish of the neighbourhood.

" What about the Hall lake and the chance of a pike ? " said Holmes.

The face of the innkeeper clouded.

" That wouldn't do, sir. You might chance to find yourself in the lake before you were through."

" How's that, then ? "

" It's Sir Robert, sir. He's terrible jealous of touts. If you two strangers were as near his training quarters as that he'd be after you as sure as fate. He ain't taking no chances, Sir Robert ain't."

" I've heard he has a horse entered for the Derby."

" Yes, and a good colt, too. He carries all our money for the race, and all Sir Robert's into the bargain. By the way "—he looked at us with thoughtful eyes—" I suppose you ain't on the Turf yourselves ? "

" No, indeed. Just two weary Londoners who badly need some good Berkshire air."

" Well, you are in the right place for that. There is a deal of it lying about. But mind what I have told you about Sir Robert. He's the sort that strikes first and speaks afterwards. Keep clear of the park."

" Surely, Mr. Barnes ! We certainly shall. By the way, that was a most beautiful spaniel that was whining in the hall."

" I should say it was. That was the real Shoscombe breed. There ain't a better in England."

" I am a dog-fancier myself," said Holmes. " Now, if it is a fair question, what would a prize dog like that cost ? "

" More than I could pay, sir. It was Sir Robert himself who gave me this one. That's why I have to keep it on a lead. It would be off to the Hall in a jiffy if I gave it its head."

" We are getting some cards in our hand, Watson," said Holmes, when the landlord had left us. " It's not an easy one to play, but we may see our way in a day or two. By the way, Sir Robert is still in London, I hear. We might, perhaps, enter the sacred domain to-night without fear of bodily assault. There are one or two points on which I should like reassurance."

" Have you any theory, Holmes ? "

" Only this, Watson, that something happened a week or so ago which has cut deep into the life of the Shoscombe household. What is that something ? We can only guess at it from its effects. They seem to be of a curiously mixed character. But that should surely help us. It is only the colourless, uneventful case which is hopeless."

" Let us consider our data. The brother no longer visits the beloved invalid sister. He gives away her favourite dog. Her dog, Watson ! Does that suggest nothing to you ? "

" Nothing but the brother's spite."

" Well, it might be so. Or—well, there is an alternative. Now to continue our review of the situation from the time that the quarrel, if there is a quarrel, began. The lady keeps her room, alters her habits, is not seen save when she drives out with her maid, refuses to stop at the stables to greet her favourite horse, and apparently takes to drink. That covers the case, does it not ? "

" Save for the business in the crypt."

" That is another line of thought. There are two, and I beg you will not tangle them. Line A, which concerns Lady Beatrice, has a vaguely sinister flavour, has it not ? "

" I can make nothing of it."

" Well, now, let us take up line B, which concerns Sir Robert. He is mad keen upon winning the Derby. He is in the hands of the Jews, and may at any moment be sold up and his racing stables seized by his creditors. He is a daring and desperate man. He derives his income from his sister. His sister's maid is his willing tool. So far we seem to be on fairly safe ground, do we not ? "

" But the crypt ? "

" Ah, yes, the crypt ! Let us suppose, Watson—it is merely a scandalous supposition, a hypothesis put forward for argument's sake—that Sir Robert has done away with his sister."

" My dear Holmes, it is out of the question."

" Very possibly, Watson. Sir Robert is a man of an honourable stock. But you do occasionally find a carrion crow among the eagles. Let us for a moment argue upon this supposition. He could not fly the country until he had realized his fortune, and that fortune could only be realized by bringing off this coup with Shoscombe Prince. Therefore, he has still to stand his ground. To do this he would have to dispose of the body of his victim, and he would also have to find a substitute who would impersonate her. With the maid as his confidante that would not be impossible. The woman's body might be conveyed to the crypt, which is a place so seldom visited, and it might be secretly destroyed at night in the furnace, leaving behind it such evidence as we have already seen. What say you to that, Watson ? "

" Well, it is all possible if you grant the original monstrous supposition."

" I think that there is a small experiment which we may try to-morrow, Watson, in order to throw some light on the matter. Meanwhile, if we mean to keep up our characters, I suggest that we have our host in for a glass of his own wine and hold some high converse upon eels and dace, which seems to be the straight road to his affections. We may chance to come upon some useful local gossip in the process."

In the morning Holmes discovered that we had come without our spoon-bait for jack, which absolved us from fishing for the day. About eleven o'clock we started for a walk, and he obtained leave to take the black spaniel with us.

" This is the place," said he, as we came to two high park gates with heraldic griffins towering above them. " About midday, Mr. Barnes informs me, the old lady

. . . WITH HERALDIC GRIFFINS TOWERING ABOVE THEM.

"At the outset it must be acknowledged that it has not been possible to find any Berkshire family that fulfills all the requirements of the Canon," Dr. Julian Wolff wrote in his *Practical Handbook of Sherlockian Heraldry*. "But some interesting information presents itself when the base of operations is slightly shifted to the adjacent county of Hampshire. Burke's *Visitation of Seats and Arms* has an extensive description of Highclere in Hampshire, the estate of the old and honoured Herbert family. . . . 'The Herbert griffin' [Burke wrote] 'holding in its mouth the bloody hand appears beautifully carved in stone in every variety of attitude.' . . . After all this talk of griffins, by both Watson and Burke, it comes as a shock to learn that the creature of the family crest is not a griffin at all, but is actually a wyvern—but vert, and so accounting for the Green Dragon Inn at Crendall (or is it really Kendall?) three miles off. But this mistake is not a fatal one, and certainly Watson may be excused when the Great Burke himself made the same error. The arms are: Per pale, azure and gules three lions rampant argent. Crest—a wyvern, wings elevated, vert, holding in the mouth a sinister hand couped at the wrist, gules.' . . . The Norberton arms have not been found and it is not discreet to enquire too deeply in view of Sir Robert's escapades. The matter must rest here and readers will have to be content with the arms of the Falders alone—the dexter half of the lady's lozenge [reproduced above]."

takes a drive, and the carriage must slow down while the gates are opened. When it comes through, and before it gathers speed, I want you, Watson, to stop the coachman with some question. Never mind me. I shall stand behind this holly-bush and see what I can see."

It was not a long vigil. Within a quarter of an hour
10 we saw the big open yellow barouche coming down the
long avenue, with two splendid, high-stepping grey
carriage horses in the shafts. Holmes crouched behind
his bush with the dog. I stood unconcernedly swinging
a cane in the roadway. A keeper ran out and the gates
swung open.

The carriage had slowed to a walk and I was able to get a good look at the occupants. A highly-coloured young woman with flaxen hair and impudent eyes sat on the left. At her right was an elderly person with rounded back and a huddle of shawls about her face and shoulders which proclaimed the invalid. When the horses reached the high road I held up my hand with an authoritative gesture, and as the coachman pulled up I inquired if Sir Robert was at Shoscombe Old Place.

At the same moment Holmes stepped out and released the spaniel. With a joyous cry it dashed forward to the carriage and sprang upon the step. Then in a moment its eager greeting changed to furious rage, and it snapped at the black skirt above it.

" Drive on! Drive on!" shrieked a harsh voice. The coachman lashed the horses, and we were left standing in the roadway.

" Well, Watson, that's done it," said Holmes, as he
fastened the lead to the neck of the excited spaniel.
" He thought it was his mistress and he found it was a
11 stranger. Dogs don't make mistakes."

" But it was the voice of a man!" I cried.

" Exactly! We have added one card to our hand, Watson, but it needs careful playing, all the same."

My companion seemed to have no further plans for the day, and we did actually use our fishing tackle in the mill-stream, with the result that we had a dish of trout for our supper. It was only after that meal that Holmes showed signs of renewed activity. Once more we found ourselves upon the same road as in the morning, which led us to the park gates. A tall, dark figure was awaiting us there, who proved to be our London acquaintance, Mr. John Mason, the trainer.

" Good evening, gentlemen," said he. " I got your note, Mr. Holmes. Sir Robert has not returned yet, but I hear that he is expected to-night."

" How far is this crypt from the house?" asked Holmes.

" A good quarter of a mile."

" Then I think we can disregard him altogether."

" I can't afford to do that, Mr. Holmes. The moment he arrives he will want to see me to get the last news of Shoscombe Prince."

" I see! In that case we must work without you, Mr. Mason. You can show us the crypt and then leave us."

It was pitch-dark and without a moon, but Mason led us over the grass-lands until a dark mass loomed up in front of us which proved to be the ancient chapel.

10 *barouche.* A four-wheeled carriage with a seat in front for the driver, two double seats inside, one facing back and the other front and facing each other, with a folding top over the back seat which may be raised to cover the occupants, but not the driver.

11 *Dogs don't make mistakes."* No dog, particularly a spaniel, would be fooled into thinking that it *saw* his or her mistress. Or so Mr. Stuart Palmer claimed in "Notes on Certain Evidences of Caniphobia in Mr. Sherlock Holmes and His Associates": "Anyone who has had even a passing acquaintance with dogs knows that their eyesight is extremely poor (except for the greyhound) and that most dogs rely almost entirely on their senses of smell and hearing. No dog, for instance, ever paid any attention to his image in a mirror. The image has no smell or sound; therefore it isn't there. We must reluctantly conclude that the spaniel fell into a rage about something else, or was troubled by worms."

AT THE SAME MOMENT HOLMES STEPPED OUT AND RELEASED THE SPANIEL.

Illustration by Frank Wiles for the *Strand Magazine*, April, 1927.

We entered the broken gap which was once the porch, and our guide, stumbling among heaps of loose masonry, picked his way to the corner of the building, where a steep stair led down into the crypt. Striking a match, he illuminated the melancholy place—dismal and evil-smelling, with ancient crumbling walls of rough-hewn stone, and piles of coffins, some of lead and some of stone, extending upon one side right up to the arched and groined roof which lost itself in the shadows above our heads. Holmes had lit his lantern, which shot a tiny tunnel of vivid yellow light upon the mournful scene. Its rays were reflected back from the coffin-plates, many of them adorned with the griffin and coronet of this old family which carried its honours even to the gate of Death.

" You spoke of some bones, Mr. Mason. Could you show them before you go ? "

" They are here in this corner." The trainer strode across and then stood in silent surprise as our light was turned upon the place. " They are gone," said he.

" So I expected," said Holmes, chuckling. " I fancy the ashes of them might even now be found in that oven which had already consumed a part."

" But why in the world would anyone want to burn the bones of a man who has been dead a thousand years ? " asked John Mason.

" That is what we are here to find out," said Holmes. " It may mean a long search, and we need not detain you. I fancy that we shall get our solution before morning."

When John Mason had left us, Holmes set to work making a very careful examination of the graves, ranging from a very ancient one, which appeared to be Saxon, in the centre, through a long line of Norman Hugos and Odos, until we reached the Sir William and Sir Denis Falder of the eighteenth century. It was an hour or more before Holmes came to a leaden coffin standing on end before the entrance to the vault. I heard his little cry of satisfaction, and was aware from his hurried but purposeful movements that he had reached a goal. With his lens he was eagerly examining the edges of the heavy lid. Then he drew from his pocket a short jemmy, a box-opener, which he thrust into a chink, levering back the whole front, which seemed to be secured by only a couple of clamps. There was a rending, tearing sound as it gave way, but it had hardly hinged back and partly revealed the contents before we had an unforeseen interruption.

Someone was walking in the chapel above. It was the firm, rapid step of one who came with a definite purpose and knew well the ground upon which he walked. A light streamed down the stairs, and an instant later the man who bore it was framed in the Gothic archway. He was a terrible figure, huge in stature and fierce in manner. A large stable-lantern which he held in front of him shone upwards upon a strong, heavily-moustached face and angry eyes, which glared round him into every recess of the vault, finally fixing themselves with a deadly stare upon my companion and myself.

HOLMES HAD LIT HIS LANTERN . . .

Illustration by Frank Wiles for the *Strand Magazine*, April, 1927.

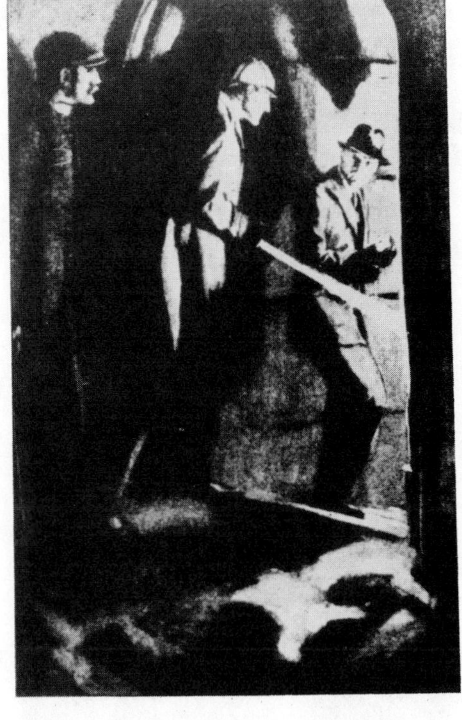

"WHO THE DEVIL ARE YOU?" HE THUNDERED.
"AND WHAT ARE YOU DOING UPON
MY PROPERTY?"

Illustration by Frederic Dorr Steele for *Liberty Magazine,* March 5, 1927.

"I ALSO HAVE A QUESTION TO ASK YOU, SIR ROBERT,"
HE SAID IN HIS STERNEST TONE.

Illustration by Frank Wiles for the *Strand Magazine,* April, 1927.

" Who the devil are you ? " he thundered. " And what are you doing upon my property ? " Then, as Holmes returned no answer, he took a couple of steps forward and raised a heavy stick which he carried. " Do you hear me ? " he cried. " Who are you ? What are you doing here ? " His cudgel quivered in the air.

But instead of shrinking, Holmes advanced to meet him.

" I also have a question to ask you, Sir Robert," he said in his sternest tone. " Who is this ? And what is it doing here ? "

He turned and tore open the coffin-lid behind him. In the glare of the lantern I saw a body swathed in a sheet from head to foot, with dreadful, witch-like features, all nose and chin, projecting at one end, the dim, glazed eyes staring from a discoloured and crumbling face.

The Baronet had staggered back with a cry and supported himself against a stone sarcophagus.

" How came you to know of this ? " he cried. And then, with some return of his truculent manner : " What business is it of yours ? "

" My name is Sherlock Holmes," said my companion. " Possibly it is familiar to you. In any case, my business is that of every other good citizen—to uphold the law. It seems to me that you have much to answer for."

Sir Robert glared for a moment, but Holmes' quiet voice and cool, assured manner had their effect.

" 'Fore God, Mr. Holmes, it's all right," said he. " Appearances are against me, I'll admit, but I could act no otherwise."

" I should be happy to think so, but I fear your explanations must be for the police."

Sir Robert shrugged his broad shoulders.

" Well, if it must be, it must. Come up to the house and you can judge for yourself how the matter stands."

Quarter of an hour later we found ourselves in what I judge, from the lines of polished barrels behind glass covers, to be the gun-room of the old house. It was comfortably furnished, and here Sir Robert left us for a few moments. When he returned he had two companions with him ; the one, the florid young woman whom we had seen in the carriage ; the other, a small rat-faced man with a disagreeably furtive manner. These two wore an appearance of utter bewilderment, which showed that the Baronet had not yet had time to explain to them the turn events had taken.

" There," said Sir Robert, with a wave of his hand, " are Mr. and Mrs. Norlett. Mrs. Norlett, under her maiden name of Evans, has for some years been my sister's confidential maid. I have brought them here because I feel that my best course is to explain the true position to you, and they are the two people upon earth who can substantiate what I say."

" Is this necessary, Sir Robert ? Have you thought what you are doing ? " cried the woman.

" As to me, I entirely disclaim all responsibility," said her husband.

Sir Robert gave him a glance of contempt. " I will take all responsibility," said he. " Now, Mr. Holmes, listen to a plain statement of the facts.

" You have clearly gone pretty deeply into my affairs or I should not have found you where I did. Therefore, you know already, in all probability, that I am running a dark horse for the Derby and that everything depends upon my success. If I win, all is easy. If I lose—well, I dare not think of that ! "

" I understand the position," said Holmes.

" I am dependent upon my sister, Lady Beatrice, for everything. But it is well known that her interest in the estate is for her own life only. For myself, I am deeply in the hands of the Jews. I have always known that if my sister were to die my creditors would be on to my estate like a flock of vultures. Everything would be seized ; my stables, my horses—everything. Well, Mr. Holmes, my sister *did* die just a week ago."

" And you told no one ! "

" What could I do ? Absolute ruin faced me. If I
could stave things off for three weeks all would be well. 12
Her maid's husband—this man here—is an actor. It came into our heads—it came into my head—that he could for that short period personate my sister. It was but a case of appearing daily in the carriage, for no one need enter her room save the maid. It was not difficult to arrange. My sister died of the dropsy which had long afflicted her."

" That will be for a coroner to decide."

" Her doctor would certify that for months her symptoms have threatened such an end."

" Well, what did you do ? "

" The body could not remain there. On the first night Norlett and I carried it out to the old well-house, which is now never used. We were followed, however, by her pet spaniel, which yapped continually at the door, so I felt some safer place was needed. I got rid of the spaniel and we carried the body to the crypt of the church. There was no indignity or irreverence, Mr. Holmes. I do not feel that I have wronged the dead."

" Your conduct seems to me inexcusable, Sir Robert."

The Baronet shook his head impatiently. " It is easy to preach," said he. " Perhaps you would have felt differently if you had been in my position. One cannot see all one's hopes and all one's plans shattered at the last moment and make no effort to save them. It seemed to me that it would be no unworthy resting-place if we put her for the time in one of the coffins of her husband's ancestors lying in what is still consecrated ground. We opened such a coffin, removed the contents, and placed her as you have seen her. As to the old relics which we took out, we could not leave them on the floor of the crypt. Norlett and I removed them, and he descended at night and burned them in the central furnace. There is my story, Mr. Holmes, though how you forced my hand so that I have to tell it is more than I can say."

Holmes sat for some time lost in thought.

" There is one flaw in your narrative, Sir Robert,"

12 *If I could stave things off for three weeks.* The month we know was May—but what was the year? It must have been after Holmes' Return: Watson, so ignorant of racing matters in 1890 is now Holmes' "Handy Guide to the Turf." On the other hand, the year cannot be long before Holmes' retirement: 1) Holmes on the opening day was using a microscope, and says that Scotland Yard is beginning to appreciate its importance. In none of the other chronicles is a microscope mentioned, as it almost certainly would have been if it had come into general use in detection shortly after Holmes' Return. 2) "The page had shown in a tall, clean-shaven man . . ." This page must have been none other than the later Billy, introduced to us as a member of the Baker Street staff in "Thor Bridge," which, as we have seen, took place in October, 1900. The year was not 1903, however: Watson was married again in the last quarter of 1902, and he is clearly living at Baker Street at the time of this adventure. Derby Day was three weeks away. If the year were 1900, then, when Derby Day fell on June 6th, the concluding night must have been May 29th. But this would make the opening day of the case as chronicled by Watson the *thirteenth* day, counting the day of Lady Beatrice's death as the first day, and this is impossible by *either* Mason's or Sir Robert's statements. If the year were 1901, when Derby Day fell on May 29th, the concluding night must have been May 18th, and the opening day of the case was the *tenth* day. This comes very close to the situation *according to Mason*, and it would mean that Sir Robert was speaking approximately rather than literally when he said that Derby Day was "three weeks" after his sister's death. If the year were 1902, when Derby Day fell on May 21st, the concluding night must have been May 7th, and the opening day of the case the *seventh* day. This is *precisely* the situation *according to Sir Robert*, and—as the late Dr. Ernest Bloomfield Zeisler wrote—"There was one thing about which [Sir Robert] would be quite certain not to be mistaken, and that was the date of the coming Derby." In addition, we know that Holmes and Watson, from Thursday, May 16, to Saturday, May 18, 1901, were engaged in "The Adventure of the Priory School." The adventure of Shoscombe Old Place therefore began on *Tuesday, May 6,* and ended on *Wednesday, May 7, 1902.*

he said at last. " Your bets on the race, and therefore your hopes for the future, would hold good even if your creditors seized your estate."

" The horse would be part of the estate. What do they care for my bets ? As likely as not they would not run him at all. My chief creditor is, unhappily, my most bitter enemy—a rascally fellow, Sam Brewer, whom I was once compelled to horsewhip on Newmarket Heath. Do you suppose that he would try to save me ? "

" Well, Sir Robert," said Holmes, rising, " this matter must, of course, be referred to the police. It was my duty to bring the facts to light and there I must leave it. As to the morality or decency of your own conduct, it is not for me to express an opinion. It is nearly midnight, Watson, and I think we may make our way back to our humble abode."

13 It is generally known now that this singular episode
ended upon a happier note than Sir Robert's actions
deserved. Shoscombe Prince did win the Derby, the
14 sporting owner did net eighty thousand pounds in bets,
and the creditors did hold their hand until the race was over, when they were paid in full, and enough was left to re-establish Sir Robert in a fair position in life. Both police and coroner took a lenient view of the transaction, and beyond a mild censure for the delay in registering the lady's decease, the lucky owner got away scatheless from this strange incident in a career which has now outlived its shadows and promises to end in an honoured old age.

13 *this singular episode.* Mr. D. Martin Dakin, writing on the "Canonicity" of "The Adventure of Shoscombe Old Place," inclined to accept it as genuine, "as there seems to be no particular reason for doubting it, in spite of its distressing revelations as to some of the sources of Watson's income."

14 *eighty thousand pounds.* About $400,000.

Bibliographical Note: The manuscript of "The Adventure of Shoscombe Old Place," the property of Mr. Adrian M. Conan Doyle, reveals that Conan Doyle originally intended to call the tale "The Adventure of Shoscombe *Abbey*." The change was perhaps made to avoid confusion with "The Adventure of the Abbey Grange." Something of the same thought seems to have occurred to the editors of the *Strand Magazine:* they announced the story as "The Adventure of the Black Spaniel."

68

THE ADVENTURE OF THE THREE GARRIDEBS

[*Thursday, June 26, to Friday, June 27, 1902*]

IT may have been a comedy, or it may have been a tragedy. It cost one man his reason, it cost me a blood-letting, and it cost yet another man the penalties of the law. Yet there was certainly an element of comedy. Well, you shall judge for yourselves.

I remember the date very well, for it was in the same month that Holmes refused a knighthood for services 1 which may perhaps some day be described. I only refer to the matter in passing, for in my position of partner and confidant I am obliged to be particularly careful to avoid any indiscretion. I repeat, however, that this enables me to fix the date, which was the latter end of June, 1902, shortly after the conclusion of the South African War. Holmes had spent several days in bed, as was his habit from time to time, but he emerged that morning with a long foolscap document in his hand and a twinkle of amusement in his austere grey eyes.

"There is a chance for you to make some money, friend Watson," said he. "Have you ever heard the name of Garrideb?"

I admitted that I had not.

"Well, if you can lay your hand upon a Garrideb, there's money in it."

"Why?"

"Ah, that's a long story—rather a whimsical one, too. I don't think in all our explorations of human complexities we have ever come upon anything more singular. The fellow will be here presently for cross-examination, so I won't open the matter up till he comes. But meanwhile, that's the name we want."

The telephone directory lay on the table beside me, and I turned over the pages in a rather hopeless quest. But to my amazement there was this strange name in its due place. I gave a cry of triumph.

"Here you are, Holmes! Here it is!"

Holmes took the book from my hand.

"'Garrideb, N.,'" he read, "'136 Little Ryder Street, W.' Sorry to disappoint you, my dear Watson, but this is the man himself. That is the address upon his letter. We want another to match him."

1 *the same month that Holmes refused a knighthood.* Miss Marcella Holmes, in "Sherlock Holmes and the Prime Ministers," has noted that "Lord Salisbury's resignation [as Prime Minister of Britain] occurred in early July [1902], and as retiring Prime Ministers often recommend well-deserving friends and supporters for honours before relinquishing office, was this a belated acknowledgment of Holmes' invaluable work in 'The Second Stain'? . . . For what else would knighthood have been given but for Holmes' work in his most important international case?"

But why was it that Holmes declined a knighthood or even mention in the Honours List, though he accepted the Legion of Honour from France and a remarkably fine emerald tie-pin from a certain gracious lady? We must remember that Edward VII was on the throne at this time, Queen Victoria having died on January 22, 1901. If Edward VII was that Prince of Wales who once masqueraded as "the King of Bohemia," we have, perhaps, the reason why Holmes declined to accept a knighthood from him.

The late A. Carson Simpson pointed out that it was nevertheless *Sir* Sherlock, for even members of the lowest grade of the Legion of Honour were known as "Chevaliers," anglicized "Knights." Chevalier Holmes, therefore, in France, is Sir Sherlock Holmes in England.

Mrs. Hudson had come in with a card upon a tray. I took it up and glanced at it.

"Why, here it is!" I cried in amazement. "This is a different initial. John Garrideb, Counsellor at Law,
2 Moorville, Kansas, U.S.A."

Holmes smiled as he looked at the card. "I am afraid you must make yet another effort, Watson," said he. "This gentleman is also in the plot already, though I certainly did not expect to see him this morning. However, he is in a position to tell us a good deal which I want to know."

A moment later he was in the room. Mr. John Garrideb, Counsellor at Law, was a short, powerful man with the round, fresh, clean-shaven face characteristic of so many American men of affairs. The general effect was chubby and rather childlike, so that one received the impression of quite a young man with a broad set smile upon his face. His eyes, however, were arresting. Seldom in any human head have I seen a pair which bespoke a more intense inward life, so bright were they, so alert, so responsive to every change of thought. His accent was American, but was not accompanied by any eccentricity of speech.

"Mr. Holmes?" he asked, glancing from one to the other. "Ah, yes! Your pictures are not unlike you, sir, if I may say so. I believe you have had a letter from my namesake, Mr. Nathan Garrideb, have you not?"

"Pray sit down," said Sherlock Holmes. "We shall, I fancy, have a good deal to discuss." He took up his sheets of foolscap. "You are, of course, the Mr. John Garrideb mentioned in this document. But surely you have been in England some time?"

"Why do you say that, Mr. Holmes?" I seemed to read sudden suspicion in those expressive eyes.

"Your whole outfit is English."

Mr. Garrideb forced a laugh. "I've read of your tricks, Mr. Holmes, but I never thought I would be the subject of them. Where do you read that?"

"The shoulder cut of your coat, the toes of your boots—could anyone doubt it?"

"Well, well, I had no idea I was so obvious a Britisher. But business brought me over here some time ago, and so, as you say, my outfit is nearly all London. However, I guess your time is of value, and we did not meet to talk about the cut of my socks. What about getting down to that paper you hold in your hand?"

Holmes had in some way ruffled our visitor, whose chubby face had assumed a far less amiable expression.

"Patience! Patience, Mr. Garrideb!" said my friend in a soothing voice. "Dr. Watson would tell you that these little digressions of mine sometimes prove in the end to have some bearing on the matter. But why did Mr. Nathan Garrideb not come with you?"

"Why did he ever drag you into it at all?" asked our visitor, with a sudden outflame of anger. "What in thunder had you to do with it? Here was a bit of professional business between two gentlemen, and one of them must needs call in a detective! I saw him this

2 *Moorville, Kansas, U.S.A.*" "In Kansas there is no Moorville. There are no moors," Mr. Willis B. Wood wrote in "Sherlock in Kansas."

"WHY DID HE EVER DRAG YOU INTO IT AT ALL?" ASKED OUR VISITOR . . .

Illustration by Howard K. Elcock for the *Strand Magazine*, January, 1925.

morning, and he told me this fool-trick he had played me, and that's why I am here. But I feel bad about it, all the same."

"There was no reflection upon you, Mr. Garrideb. It was simply zeal upon his part to gain your end—an end which is, I understand, equally vital for both of you. He knew that I had means of getting information, and, therefore, it was very natural that he should apply to me."

Our visitor's angry face gradually cleared.

"Well, that puts it different," said he. "When I went to see him this morning and he told me he had sent to a detective, I just asked for your address and came right away. I don't want police butting into a private matter. But if you are content just to help us find the man, there can be no harm in that."

"Well, that is just how it stands," said Holmes. "And now, sir, since you are here, we had best have a clear account from your own lips. My friend here knows nothing of the details."

Mr. Garrideb surveyed me with not too friendly a gaze.

"Need he know?" he asked.

"We usually work together."

"Well, there's no reason it should be kept a secret. I'll give you the facts as short as I can make them. If you came from Kansas I would not need to explain to you who Alexander Hamilton Garrideb was. He made his money in real estate, and afterwards in the wheat pit at Chicago, but he spent it in buying up as much land as would make one of your counties, lying along the Arkansas River, west of Fort Dodge. It's grazing-land and lumber-land and arable-land and mineralized-land, and just every sort of land that brings dollars to the man that owns it.

"He had no kith nor kin—or, if he had, I never heard of it. But he took a kind of pride in the queerness of his name. That was what brought us together. I was in the law at Topeka, and one day I had a visit from the old man, and he was tickled to death to meet another man with his own name. It was his pet fad, and he was dead set to find out if there were any more Garridebs in the world. 'Find me another!' said he. I told him I was a busy man and could not spend my life hiking round the world in search of Garridebs. 'None the less,' said he, 'that is just what you will do if things pan out as I planned them.' I thought he was joking, but there was a powerful lot of meaning in the words, as I was soon to discover.

"For he died within a year of saying them, and he left a will behind him. It was the queerest will that has ever been filed in the State of Kansas. His property was divided into three parts, and I was to have one on condition that I found two Garridebs who would share the remainder. It's five million dollars for each if it is a cent, but we can't lay a finger on it until we all three stand in a row.

"It was so big a chance that I just let my legal practice slide and I set forth looking for Garridebs. There is not one in the United States. I went through it, sir, with a fine-toothed comb and never a Garrideb could I catch. Then I tried the old country. Sure enough there was the name in the London Telephone Directory. I went after him two days ago and explained the whole matter to him. But he is a lone man, like myself, with some women relations, but no men. It says three adult men in the will. So you see we still have a vacancy, and if you can help to fill it we will be very ready to pay your charges."

"Well, Watson," said Holmes, with a smile, "I said it was rather whimsical, did I not? I should have thought, sir, that your obvious way was to advertise in the agony columns of the papers."

"I have done that, Mr. Holmes. No replies."

"Dear me! Well, it is certainly a most curious little problem. I may take a glance at it in my leisure. By the way, it is curious that you should have come from Topeka. I used to have a correspondent—he is
3 dead now—old Dr. Lysander Starr, who was Mayor in 1890."

"Good old Dr. Starr!" said our visitor. "His name is still honoured. Well, Mr. Holmes, I suppose all we can do is to report to you and let you know how we progress. I reckon you will hear within a day or two." With this assurance our American bowed and departed.

Holmes had lit his pipe, and he sat for some time with a curious smile upon his face.

"Well?" I asked at last.

"I am wondering, Watson—just wondering!"

"At what?"

Holmes took his pipe from his lips.

"I was wondering, Watson, what on earth could be the object of this man in telling us such a rigmarole of lies. I nearly asked him so—for there are times when a brutal frontal attack is the best policy—but I judged it better to let him think he had fooled us. Here is a man with an English coat frayed at the elbow and trousers bagged at the knee with a year's wear, and yet by this document and by his own account he is a provincial American lately landed in London. There have been no advertisements in the agony columns. You know that I miss nothing there. They are my favourite covert for putting up a bird, and I would never have over-looked such a cock pheasant as that. I never knew a Dr. Lysander Starr of Topeka. Touch him where you would he was false. I think the fellow is really an American, but he has worn his accent smooth with years of London. What is his game, then, and what motive lies behind this preposterous search for Garridebs? It's worth our attention, for, granting that the man is a rascal, he is certainly a complex and ingenious one. We must now find out if our other correspondent is a fraud also. Just ring him up, Watson."

I did so, and heard a thin, quavering voice at the other end of the line.

"Yes, yes, I am Mr. Nathan Garrideb. Is Mr. Holmes there? I should very much like to have a word with Mr. Holmes."

My friend took the instrument and I heard the usual syncopated dialogue.

3 *old Dr. Lysander Starr.* Holmes, groping for a fictitious name, comes up with a minor variant on Lysander Stark, the alias of the elusive counterfeiter in "The Adventure of the Engineer's Thumb." For the sake of the record, as Mr. Bliss Austin noted in "Thumbing His Way to Fame," the Mayor of Topeka in 1890 was the Honorable Roswell F. Cofran.

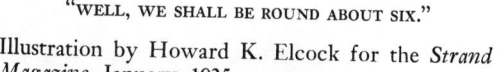

"WELL, WE SHALL BE ROUND ABOUT SIX."

Illustration by Howard K. Elcock for the *Strand Magazine*, January, 1925.

" Yes, he has been here. I understand that you don't know him. . . . How long ? . . . Only two days ! . . . Yes, yes, of course, it is a most captivating prospect. Will you be at home this evening ? I suppose your namesake will not be there ? . . . Very good, we will come then, for I would rather have a chat without him. . . . Dr. Watson will come with me. . . . I understood from your note that you did not go out often. . . . Well, we shall be round about six. You need not mention it to the American lawyer. . . . Very good. Good-bye ! "

It was twilight of a lovely spring evening, and even Little Ryder Street, one of the smaller offshoots from the Edgware Road, within a stone-cast of old Tyburn Tree of evil memory, looked golden and wonderful 4
in the slanting rays of the setting sun. The particular house to which we were directed was a large, old-fashioned, Early Georgian edifice with a flat brick face broken only by two deep bay windows on the ground floor. It was on this ground floor that our client lived, and, indeed, the low windows proved to be the front of the huge room in which he spent his waking hours. Holmes pointed as we passed to the small brass plate which bore the curious name.

" Up some years, Watson," he remarked, indicating its discoloured surface. " It's *his* real name, anyhow, and that is something to note."

The house had a common stair, and there were a number of names painted in the hall, some indicating offices and some private chambers. It was not a collection of residential flats, but rather the abode of Bohemian bachelors. Our client opened the door for us himself and apologized by saying that the woman in charge left at four o'clock. Mr. Nathan Garrideb proved to be a very tall, loose-jointed, round-backed person, gaunt and bald, some sixty-odd years of age. He had a cadaverous face, with the dull dead skin of a man to whom exercise was unknown. Large round spectacles and a small projecting goat's beard combined with his stooping attitude to give him an expression of peering curiosity. The general effect, however, was amiable, though eccentric.

The room was as curious as its occupant. It looked like a small museum. It was both broad and deep, with cupboards and cabinets all round, crowded with specimens, geological and anatomical. Cases of butterflies and moths flanked each side of the entrance. A large table in the centre was littered with all sorts of debris, while the tall brass tube of a powerful microscope bristled up amongst them. As I glanced round I was surprised at the universality of the man's interests. Here was a case of ancient coins. There was a cabinet of flint instruments. Behind his central table was a large cupboard of fossil bones. Above was a line of plaster skulls with such names as " Neanderthal," " Heidelberg," " Cromagnon " printed beneath them. It was clear that he was a student of many subjects. As he stood in front of us now, he held a piece of chamois leather in his
right hand with which he was polishing a coin. 5

" Syracusan—of the best period," he explained, holding it up. " They degenerated greatly towards the end.

4 *old Tyburn Tree of evil memory.* "At [the] corner of Hyde Park, where the angle of Connaught Place now stands, was the famous 'Tyburn Tree,' sometimes called the 'Three-Legged Mare,' being a triangle on three legs, where the public executions took place till they were transferred to Newgate in 1783," Augustus J. C. Hare wrote in *Walks in London*, Vol. II. "The manor of Tyburn took its name from the Tye Bourne or brook, which rose under Primrose Hill, and the place was originally chosen for executions because, though on the highroad to Oxford, it was remote from London. The condemned were brought hither in a cart from Newgate—'thief and parson in a Tyburn cart' [Dryden, 1684]—the prisoner usually carrying the immense nosegay which, by old custom, was presented to him on the steps of St. Sepulchre's Church, and having been refreshed with a bowl of ale at St. Gile's. The cart was driven underneath the gallows, and, after the noose was adjusted, was driven quickly away by Jack Ketch, the hangman, so that the prisoner was left suspended. (The scene is depicted in Hogarth's 'Idle Apprentice Executed at Tyburn.') Death by this method was much slower and more uncertain than it has been since the drop was invented, and there have been several cases in which animation has been restored after the prisoner was cut down. Around the place of execution were raised galleries which were let to spectators; they were destroyed by the disappointed mob who had engaged them when Dr. Henesey was reprieved in 1758. One Mammy Douglas, who kept the key of the boxes, bore the name of the 'Tyburn Pewopener.' The bodies of Cromwell, Ireton, and Bradshaw were buried under the tyburn tree after hanging there for a day. Some bones discovered in 1840, on removing the pavement close to Arklow House, at the southwest angle of the Edgware Road, are supposed to have been theirs. On the corner of Upper Bryanston Street and the Edgware Road the iron balconies remained till 1785, whence the sheriffs used to watch the executions . . ." Jonathan Wild, whom Holmes mentioned in *The Valley of Fear*, was hanged from Tyburn Tree on May 24, 1725; at his execution he "picked the parson's pocket of his corkscrew, which he carried out of the world in his hand."

5 *he was polishing a coin.* The late Professor Jay Finley Christ, in his article, "Glittering Golden Guineas," doubted Nathan's right to be called a "numismatist," as distinct from a collector of coins. "His misgivings are due to the strong feeling of a large group of numismatists—especially in England —that coins should never be cleaned," the late A. Carson Simpson wrote in *Numismatics in the Canon*, Part II. "An equally large group takes the view that such cleaning as will bring out the design clearly is desirable; careful polishing, so long as it does not scratch the coin or impair its 'tone,' would be acceptable to them. We should give Nathan the benefit of the doubt and assume he was proceeding with due care."

At their best I hold them supreme, though some prefer
6 the Alexandrian school. You will find a chair here, Mr. Holmes. Pray allow me to clear these bones. And you, sir—ah, yes, Dr. Watson—if you would have the goodness to put the Japanese vase to one side. You see round me my little interests in life. My doctor lectures me about never going out, but why should I go out when I have so much to hold me here ? I can assure you that the adequate cataloguing of one of those cabinets would take me three good months."

Holmes looked round him with curiosity.

" But do you tell me that you *never* go out ? " he said.

7 " Now and again I drive down to Sotheby's or Christie's. Otherwise I very seldom leave my room. I am not too strong, and my researches are very absorbing. But you can imagine, Mr. Holmes, what a terrific shock—pleasant but terrific—it was for me when I heard of this unparalleled good fortune. It only needs one more Garrideb to complete the matter, and surely we can find one. I had a brother, but he is dead, and female relatives are disqualified. But there must surely be others in the world. I had heard that you handled strange cases, and that was why I sent to you. Of course, this American gentleman is quite right, and I should have taken his advice first, but I acted for the best."

" I think you acted very wisely indeed," said Holmes. " But are you really anxious to acquire an estate in America ? "

" Certainly not, sir. Nothing would induce me to leave my collection. But this gentleman has assured me that he will buy me out as soon as we have established our claim. Five million dollars was the sum named. There are a dozen specimens in the market at the present moment which fill gaps in my collection, and which I am unable to purchase for want of a few hundred pounds. Just think what I could do with five million dollars. Why, I have the nucleus of a national collection. I shall
8 be the Hans Sloane of my age."

His eyes gleamed behind his great spectacles. It was very clear that no pains would be spared by Mr. Nathan Garrideb in finding a namesake.

" I merely called to make your acquaintance, and there is no reason why I should interrupt your studies," said Holmes. " I prefer to establish personal touch with those with whom I do business. There are few questions I need ask, for I have your very clear narrative in my pocket, and I filled up the blanks when this American gentleman called. I understand that up to this week you were unaware of his existence."

9 " That is so. He called last Tuesday."

" Did he tell you of our interview to-day ? "

" Yes, he came straight back to me. He had been very angry."

" Why should he be angry ? "

" He seemed to think it was some reflection on his honour. But he was quite cheerful again when he returned."

" Did he suggest any course of action ? "

6 *the Alexandrian school.* "Nathan's high esteem for the coins of Syracuse is generally shared by numismatists," Mr. Simpson continued, "even those whose activities do not fall in the ancient field. They were, of course, Greek coins, and the period 400–336 B.C. is generally accepted as that in which the numismatic art reached the highest point of excellence it ever attained. Thereafter, although portraiture on coins became more lifelike and individual, the general level of artistic treatment declined. . . . Garrideb's remark that 'some prefer the Alexandrian school' is perhaps not as clear as it seems to be. Taken literally, it would refer to the 'school of Alexandria,' that is to say, to coins struck in that city. There were, of course, several Alexandrians, but the coinages of the smaller ones are not of especial numismatic importance. The greater city of Alexandria, Egypt, produced coins chiefly notable for their number and variety, rather than for their artistry."

7 *Sotheby's or Christie's.* Two of London's great sales rooms celebrated for their picture and china sales.

8 *the Hans Sloane of my age."* Sir Hans Sloane, 1660–1753, naturalist, physician, collector, and benefactor. The late A. Carson Simpson noted that Nathan Garrideb's ambition recalls another connection between Holmes and Montpellier, for Sir Hans Sloane studied there also. Like Holmes, he was interested in poisons, and witnessed the opening of the body of the tragedian, Barton Booth, who had died of excessive doses of mercury. Again, among his numerous "trifling monographs" published in the *Transactions of the Royal Philosophical Society* was one on "Poisoning from the Ingestion of Henbane Seeds." In his medical practice he was accustomed to prescribe viper's fat for all sorts of ailments, and he was a Governor of Bart's Hospital. Like the Master, he too was interested in America, for he helped General Oglethorpe to promote the settlement of Captain James Calhoun's destination ("The Five Orange Pips") and was made a Commissioner of the Colony of Georgia.

9 *He called last Tuesday."* It was on a day in "the latter end of June, 1902" that "John Garrideb, Counsellor at Law," called upon Sherlock Holmes. He said to Holmes: "I went after [Mr. Nathan Garrideb] two days ago and explained the whole matter to him." On the evening of that day, Holmes said to Nathan Garrideb: "I understand that up to this week you were unaware of [John Garrideb's] existence." "That is so," Nathan replied. "He called last Tuesday." The case opened, then, on a Thursday that can only be *Thursday, June 26, 1902.* It ended the next day.

" No, sir, he did not."

" Has he had, or asked for, any money from you ? "

" No, sir, never ! "

" You see no possible object he has in view ? "

" None, except what he states."

" Did you tell him of our telephone appointment ? "

" Yes, sir, I did."

Holmes was lost in thought. I could see that he was puzzled.

" Have you any articles of great value in your collection ? "

" No, sir. I am not a rich man. It is a good collection, but not a very valuable one."

" You have no fear of burglars ? "

" Not the least."

" How long have you been in these rooms ? "

" Nearly five years."

Holmes' cross-examination was interrupted by an imperative knocking at the door. No sooner had our client unlatched it than the American lawyer burst excitedly into the room.

" Here you are ! " he cried, waving a paper over his head. " I thought I should be in time to get you. Mr. Nathan Garrideb, my congratulations ! You are a rich man, sir. Our business is happily finished and all is well. As to you, Mr. Holmes, we can only say we are sorry if we have given you any useless trouble."

He handed over the paper to our client, who stood staring at a marked advertisement. Holmes and I leaned forward and read it over his shoulder. This is how it ran :

> HOWARD GARRIDEB.
>
> Constructor of Agricultural Machinery.
>
> Binders, reapers' steam and hand plows, drills, harrows, farmers' carts, buckboards, and all other appliances.
>
> Estimates for Artesian Wells.
>
> Apply Grosvenor Buildings, Aston.

" Glorious ! " gasped our host. " That makes our third man."

" I had opened up inquiries in Birmingham," said the American, " and my agent there has sent me this advertisement from a local paper. We must hustle and put the thing through. I have written to this man and told him that you will see him in his office to-morrow afternoon at four o'clock."

" You want *me* to see him ? "

" What do you say, Mr. Holmes ? Don't you think it would be wiser ? Here am I, a wandering American with a wonderful tale. Why should he believe what I tell him ? But you are a Britisher with solid references, and he is bound to take notice of what you say. I would go with you if you wished, but I have a very busy day to-morrow, and I could always follow you if you are in any trouble."

"HERE YOU ARE!" HE CRIED, WAVING A PAPER OVER HIS HEAD.

Illustration by Howard K. Elcock for the *Strand Magazine*, January, 1925.

" Well, I have not made such a journey for years."

" It is nothing, Mr. Garrideb. I have figured out your connections. You leave at twelve and should be there soon after two. Then you can be back the same night. All you have to do is to see this man, explain the matter, and get an affidavit of his existence. By the Lord ! " he added hotly, " considering I've come all the way from the centre of America, it is surely little enough if you go a hundred miles in order to put this matter through."

" Quite so," said Holmes. " I think what this gentleman says is very true."

Mr. Nathan Garrideb shrugged his shoulders with a disconsolate air. " Well, if you insist I shall go," said he. " It is certainly hard for me to refuse you anything, considering the glory of hope that you have brought into my life."

" Then that is agreed," said Holmes, " and no doubt you will let me have a report as soon as you can."

" I'll see to that," said the American. " Well," he added, looking at his watch, " I'll have to get on. I'll call to-morrow, Mr. Nathan, and see you off to Birmingham. Coming my way, Mr. Holmes ? Well, then, good-bye, and we may have good news for you to-morrow night."

I noticed that my friend's face cleared when the American left the room, and the look of thoughtful perplexity had vanished.

" I wish I could look over your collection, Mr. Garrideb," said he. " In my profession all sorts of odd knowledge comes useful, and this room of yours is a storehouse of it."

Our client shone with pleasure and his eyes gleamed from behind his big glasses.

" I had always heard, sir, that you were a very intelligent man," said he. " I could take you round now, if you have the time."

" Unfortunately, I have not. But these specimens are so well labelled and classified that they hardly need your personal explanation. If I should be able to look in to-morrow, I presume that there would be no objection to my glancing over them ? "

" None at all. You are most welcome. The place will, of course, be shut up, but Mrs. Saunders is in the basement up to four o'clock and would let you in with her key."

" Well, I happen to be clear to-morrow afternoon. If you would say a word to Mrs. Saunders it would be quite in order. By the way, who is your house-agent ? "

Our client was amazed at the sudden question.

" Holloway and Steele, in the Edgware Road. But why ? "

" I am a bit of an archæologist myself when it comes to houses," said Holmes, laughing. " I was wondering if this was Queen Anne or Georgian."

" Georgian, beyond doubt."

" Really. I should have thought a little earlier. However, it is easily ascertained. Well, good-bye, Mr. Garrideb, and may you have every success in your Birmingham journey."

The house-agent's was close by, but we found that it was closed for the day, so we made our way back to Baker Street. It was not till after dinner that Holmes reverted to the subject.

" Our little problem draws to a close," said he. " No doubt you have outlined the solution in your own mind."

" I can make neither head nor tail of it."

" The head is surely clear enough and the tail we should see to-morrow. Did you notice nothing curious about that advertisement ? "

" I saw that the word ' plough ' was mis-spelt."

" Oh, you did notice that, did you ? Come, Watson, you improve all the time. Yes, it was bad English but good American. The printer had set it up as received. Then the buckboards. That is American also. And artesian wells are commoner with them than with us. It was a typical American advertisement, but purporting to be from an English firm. What do you make of that ? "

" I can only suppose that this American lawyer put it in himself. What his object was I fail to understand."

" Well, there are alternative explanations. Anyhow, he wanted to get this good old fossil up to Birmingham. That is very clear. I might have told him that he was clearly going on a wild-goose chase, but, on second thoughts, it seemed better to clear the stage by letting him go. To-morrow, Watson—well, to-morrow will speak for itself."

Holmes was up and out early. When he returned at lunch-time I noticed that his face was very grave.

" This is a more serious matter than I had expected, Watson," said he. " It is fair to tell you so, though I know it will only be an additional reason to you for running your head into danger. I should know my Watson by now. But there *is* danger, and you should know it."

" Well, it is not the first we have shared, Holmes. I hope it may not be the last. What is the particular danger this time ? "

" We are up against a very hard case. I have identified Mr. John Garrideb, Counsellor at Law. He is none other than ' Killer ' Evans, of sinister and murderous reputation."

" I fear I am none the wiser."

" Ah, it is not part of your profession to carry about a portable Newgate Calendar in your memory. I have been down to see friend Lestrade at the Yard. There **10** may be an occasional want of imaginative intuition down there, but they lead the world for thoroughness and method. I had an idea that we might get on the track of our American friend in their records. Sure enough, I found his chubby face smiling up at me from the Rogues' Portrait Gallery. James Winter, *alias* Morecroft, *alias* Killer Evans, was the inscription below." Holmes drew an envelope from his pocket. " I scribbled down a few points from his dossier. Aged forty-four. Native of Chicago. Known to have shot three men in the States. Escaped from penitentiary through political influence. Came to London in 1893. Shot a man

10 *I have been down to see friend Lestrade at the Yard.* "After twenty years of more-or-less congenial association between [Holmes and Lestrade], during which time Lestrade repeatedly went out of his way to let Holmes 'in' on strange and bizarre problems, Holmes deliberately by-passes Lestrade, even after the Scotland Yarder has kindly supplied Sherlock with a complete biography of 'Killer' Evans," the late Clifton R. Andrew wrote in "That Scotland Yarder, Gregson—What a Help (?) He Was." "Holmes, apparently, gave Lestrade no inkling of what he [Holmes] was up to. Instead, with the information that the Scotland Yard Inspector gave them, Holmes and Watson slipped out themselves to apprehend the vicious criminal without asking Lestrade to assist them in the potential 'pinch.' A little unappreciative, I call it—and it doesn't seem as if Lestrade merited a 'go-by' such as that."

over cards in a night club in the Waterloo Road in January, 1895. Man died, but he was shown to have been the aggressor in the row. Dead man was identified as Rodger Prescott, famous as forger and coiner in Chicago. Killer Evans released in 1901. Has been under police supervision since, but so far as known has led an honest life. Very dangerous man, usually carries arms and is prepared to use them. That is our bird, Watson—a sporting bird, as you must admit."

" But what is his game ? "

" Well, it begins to define itself. I have been to the house-agents. Our client, as he told us, has been there five years. It was unlet for a year before then. The previous tenant was a gentleman at large named Waldron. Waldron's appearance was well remembered at the office. He had suddenly vanished and nothing more been heard of him. He was a tall, bearded man with very dark features. Now, Prescott, the man whom Killer Evans had shot, was, according to Scotland Yard, a tall, dark man with a beard. As a working hypothesis, I think we may take it that Prescott, the American criminal, used to live in the very room which our innocent friend now devotes to his museum. So at last we get a link, you see."

" And the next link ? "

" Well, we must go now and look for that."

He took a revolver from the drawer and handed it to me.

11 " I have my old favourite with me. If our Wild West friend tries to live up to his nickname, we must be ready for him. I'll give you an hour for a siesta, Watson, and then I think it will be time for our Ryder Street adventure."

It was just four o'clock when we reached the curious apartment of Nathan Garrideb. Mrs. Saunders, the caretaker, was about to leave, but she had no hesitation in admitting us, for the door shut with a spring lock and Holmes promised to see that all was safe before we left. Shortly afterwards the outer door closed, her bonnet passed the bow window, and we knew that we were alone in the lower floor of the house. Holmes made a rapid examination of the premises. There was one cupboard in a dark corner which stood out a little from the wall. It was behind this that we eventually crouched, while Holmes in a whisper outlined his intentions.

" He wanted to get our amiable friend out of his room—that is very clear, and, as the collector never went out, it took some planning to do it. The whole of this Garrideb invention was apparently for no other end. I
12 must say, Watson, that there is a certain devilish ingenuity about it even if the queer name of the tenant did give him an opening which he could hardly have expected. He wove his plot with remarkable cunning."

" But what did he want ? "

" Well, that is what we are here to find out. It has nothing whatever to do with our client, so far as I can read the situation. It is something connected with the man he murdered—the man who may have been his

11 *"I have my old favourite.* Mr. Robert Keith Leavitt has assumed that the weapon to which Holmes refers here is still the impractical little Webley of his early days. But, as the late H. T. Webster wrote in "Observations on Sherlock Holmes as an Athlete and Sportsman," "such a weapon would make a very inefficient bludgeon [as Holmes later in this case had to make use of it]. What, then, is more probable that Sir Henry Baskerville or some other grateful transatlantic client had presented Holmes with a Colt Frontier Model .45, or some other well-designed American arm which would have been a practical substitute for either a rifle or a loaded hunting crop?"

12 *a certain devilish ingenuity.* "There is something very curious about this affair," the late Gavin Brend wrote in *My Dear Holmes* "The crime is a work of art, but the criminal seems to fall far below the level of the crime. Could Killer Evans, who appears to be rather a humdrum personality, have invented this very ingenious scheme? It certainly looks as if it were a one-man job, but it may be that the Killer sought out one of his associates, explained his difficulties and asked for advice. The advice was given, the adviser taking care to keep well in the background, so that when the Killer was arrested he escaped. There exists a theory that most criminals repeat certain details every time they commit a crime, so that they may be said to write their signatures across it. If this be so then the signature on 'The Adventure of the Three Garridebs' can easily be read. It is one that we have met before . . . in the matter of 'The Red-Headed League.' It is the signature of the most interesting of all Holmes' opponents, our old acquaintance, John Clay, once of Eton and Oxford, the grandson of a Royal Duke."

confederate in crime. There is some guilty secret in the room. That is how I read it. At first I thought our friend might have something in his collection more valuable than he knew—something worth the attention of a big criminal. But the fact that Rodger Prescott of evil memory inhabited these rooms points to some deeper reason. Well, Watson, we can but possess our souls in patience and see what the hour may bring."

That hour was not long in striking. We crouched closer in the shadow as we heard the outer door open and shut. Then came the sharp, metallic snap of a key, and the American was in the room. He closed the door softly behind him, took a sharp glance around him to see that all was safe, threw off his overcoat, and walked up to the central table with the brisk manner of one who knows exactly what he has to do and how to do it. He pushed the table to one side, tore up the square of carpet on which it rested, rolled it completely back, and then, drawing a jemmy from his inside pocket, he knelt down and worked vigorously upon the floor. Presently we heard the sound of sliding boards, and an instant later a square had opened in the planks. Killer Evans struck a match, lit a stump of candle, and vanished from our view.

Clearly our moment had come. Holmes touched my wrist as a signal, and together we stole across to the open trap-door. Gently as we moved, however, the old floor must have creaked under our feet, for the head of our American, peering anxiously round, emerged suddenly from the open space. His face turned upon us with a glare of baffled rage, which gradually softened into a rather shamefaced grin as he realized that two pistols were pointed at his head.

" Well, well ! " said he, coolly, as he scrambled to the surface. " I guess you have been one too many for me, Mr. Holmes. Saw through my game, I suppose, and played me for a sucker from the first. Well, sir, I hand it to you ; you have me beat and——"

In an instant he had whisked out a revolver from his breast and had fired two shots. I felt a sudden hot sear as if a red-hot iron had been pressed to my thigh. There was a crash as Holmes' pistol came down on the man's head. I had a vision of him sprawling upon the floor with blood running down his face while Holmes rummaged him for weapons. Then my friend's wiry arms were round me and he was leading me to a chair.

" You're not hurt, Watson ? For God's sake, say that you are not hurt ! "

It was worth a wound—it was worth many wounds—to know the depth of loyalty and love which lay behind that cold mask. The clear, hard eyes were dimmed for a moment, and the firm lips were shaking. For the one and only time I caught a glimpse of a great heart as well as of a great brain. All my years of humble but **13**
single-minded service culminated in that moment of revelation.

" It's nothing, Holmes. It's a mere scratch."

He had ripped up my trousers with his pocket-knife.

" You are right," he cried, with an immense sigh of

HIS FACE TURNED UPON US WITH A GLARE OF BAFFLED RAGE . . .

Illustration by Howard K. Elcock for the *Strand Magazine*, January, 1925.

13 *a great heart as well as of a great brain.* Mr. T. S. Blakeney has made an apt comparison between Holmes and the Iron Duke of Wellington: "In both, despite an outwardly cold aspect, we are vouchsafed glimpses of an emotional (not sentimental) nature kept in strong control, repressed, perhaps, from a sense that any display was a sign of weakness. Both were keen musicians, and music is the most emotional of all the arts; both could be delightful with children, who instinctively know real from feigned affability. The Iron Duke broke down seldom, but those breaks were very complete; the other side of Holmes' nature peeps through even less thoroughly, but not less certainly."

THERE WAS A CRASH AS HOLMES' PISTOL CAME DOWN ON THE MAN'S HEAD.

Illustration by Howard K. Elcock for the *Strand Magazine*, January, 1925. "Holmes' return shot was as curious an incident as that of the dog in the nighttime," Mr. Robert Keith Leavitt wrote in "Annie Oakley in Baker Street." "There *was* no return shot from Holmes. That was the curious incident. Instead, the great detective, confronted with a life-and-death emergency, at the muzzle of an armed opponent going full blast, *hit that opponent over the head*. . . . Effective though such a crack could be—and was—nothing could more completely reveal Holmes' distrust of his own markmanship with the pistol."

relief. " It is quite superficial." His face set like flint as he glared at our prisoner, who was sitting up with a dazed face. " By the Lord, it is as well for you. If you had killed Watson, you would not have got out of this room alive. Now, sir, what have you to say for yourself ? "

He had nothing to say for himself. He only lay and scowled. I leaned on Holmes' arm, and together we looked down into the small cellar which had been disclosed by the secret flap. It was still illuminated by the candle which Evans had taken down with him. Our eyes fell upon a mass of rusted machinery, great rolls of paper, a litter of bottles, and, neatly arranged upon a small table, a number of neat little bundles.

" A printing press—a counterfeiter's outfit," said Holmes.

" Yes, sir," said our prisoner, staggering slowly to his feet and then sinking into the chair. " The greatest counterfeiter London ever saw. That's Prescott's machine, and those bundles on the table are two thousand of Prescott's notes worth a hundred each and fit to pass anywhere. Help yourselves, gentlemen. Call it a deal and let me beat it."

Holmes laughed.

" We don't do things like that, Mr. Evans. There is no bolt-hole for you in this country. You shot this man Prescott, did you not ? "

" Yes, sir, and got five years for it, though it was he who pulled on me. Five years—when I should have had a medal the size of a soup plate. No living man could tell a Prescott from a Bank of England, and if I hadn't put him out he would have flooded London with them. I was the only one in the world who knew where he made them. Can you wonder that I wanted to get to the place ? And can you wonder that when I found this crazy boob of a bug-hunter with the queer name squatting right on the top of it, and never quitting his room, I had to do the best I could to shift him ? Maybe I would have been wiser if I had put him away. It would have been easy enough, but I'm a soft-hearted guy that can't begin shooting unless the other man has a gun also. But say, Mr. Holmes, what have I done wrong, anyhow ? I've not used this plant. I've not hurt this old stiff. Where do you get me ? "

" Only attempted murder, so far as I can see," said Holmes. " But that's not our job. They take that at the next stage. What we wanted at present was just your sweet self. Please give the Yard a call, Watson. It won't be entirely unexpected."

So those were the facts about Killer Evans and his remarkable invention of the three Garridebs. We heard later that our poor old friend never got over the shock of his dissipated dreams. When his castle in the air fell down, it buried him beneath the ruins. He was last heard of at a nursing-home in Brixton. It was a glad day at the Yard when the Prescott outfit was discovered, for, though they knew that it existed, they had never been able, after the death of the man, to find out where it was. Evans had indeed done great service and caused several worthy C.I.D. men to sleep the sounder, for the counterfeiter stands in a class by himself as a public danger. They would willingly have subscribed to that soup-plate medal of which the criminal had spoken, but an unappreciative Bench took a less favourable view, and the Killer returned to those shades from which he had just emerged.

"A PRINTING PRESS—A COUNTERFEITER'S OUTFIT," SAID HOLMES.

Illustration by John Richard Flanagan for *Collier's Magazine*, October 25, 1924.

A Note on the "Canonicity" of "The Adventure of the Three Garridebs": Mr. Russell McLauchlin feels that it is time "to call into serious question the Canonicity of [this adventure]. . . . I suggest that it was the work of a well-known hand. We are aware that the literary agent, who served Dr. Watson effectively for many years, was himself a writer of some repute in other fields. It is by no means improbable that, after long association with the doctor, he was tempted to compose a pastiche."

On the other hand, Mr. D. Martin Dakin, who rejects from the Canon many of the adventures in *The Case-Book,* accepts "The Adventure of the Three Garridebs" as genuine. "[It] is a story told in Watson's best manner," he wrote in "The Problem of the Case-Book." "There can be few Baker Street enthusiasts who would sacrifice the account of the supreme moment in the Doctor's life when Killer Evans' bullet-wound was the means of revealing to him the depth of Holmes' devotion to him." Later, in "Second Thoughts on the Case-Book," Mr. Dakin wrote: "I must add that it is a little startling to learn that, if Evans had killed Watson, Holmes proposed to take the law into his own hands and murder him in retaliation. Still we should probably not take too seriously a remark that escaped him in the heat of his indignation for his friend."

Bibliographical Note: The manuscript of "The Adventure of the Three Garridebs" is the property of Mr. Adrian M. Conan Doyle.

69

THE DISAPPEARANCE OF LADY FRANCES CARFAX

[*Tuesday, July 1, to Friday, July 18, 1902*]

"BUT why Turkish ?" asked Mr. Sherlock Holmes, gazing fixedly at my boots. I was reclining in a cane-backed chair at the moment, and my protruded feet had attracted his ever-active attention.

"English," I answered, in some surprise. "I got them at Latimer's, in Oxford Street."

Holmes smiled with an expression of weary patience.

"The bath !" he said ; "the bath ! Why the relaxing and expensive Turkish rather than the invigorating home-made article ?"

"Because for the last few days I have been feeling
1 rheumatic and old. A Turkish bath is what we call an alterative in medicine—a fresh starting-point, a cleanser of the system.

"By the way, Holmes," I added, "I have no doubt the connection between my boots and a Turkish bath is a perfectly self-evident one to a logical mind, and yet I should be obliged to you if you would indicate it."

"The train of reasoning is not very obscure, Watson," said Holmes, with a mischievous twinkle. "It belongs to the same elementary class of deduction which I should illustrate if I were to ask you who shared your cab in your drive this morning."

"I don't admit that a fresh illustration is an explanation," said I, with some asperity.

"Bravo, Watson ! A very dignified and logical remonstrance. Let me see, what were the points ? Take the last one first—the cab. You observe that you have some splashes on the left sleeve and shoulder of your coat. Had you sat in the centre of a hansom you would probably have had no splashes, and if you had they would certainly have been symmetrical. Therefore it is clear that you sat at the side. Therefore it is equally clear that you had a
2 companion."

"That is very evident."

"Absurdly commonplace, is it not ?"

"But the boots and the bath ?"

"Equally childish. You are in the habit of doing up your boots in a certain way. I see them on this occasion fastened with an elaborate double bow, which is not your usual method of tying them. You have, therefore, had

1 *I have been feeling rheumatic and old.* Your editor, while acknowledging that this case is a chronologist's nightmare, has nevertheless dated it more or less to his own satisfaction as having taking place between Tuesday, July 1st, and Friday, July 18th, in the year 1902. It is clearly a late case: 1) Certainly it was after 1889, because Holy Peters' ear "was badly bitten in a saloon-fight in Adelaide" in that year. 2) Watson's account of the adventure was not published until December, 1911. 3) Watson has just said that he was feeling "rheumatic and old." 4) Holmes introduces Watson as his "old friend and associate." 5) Watson says: "But neither the official police nor Holmes' own small, but every efficient organization sufficed to clear away the mystery." Except for Holmes' references to his "Agency" in "The Adventure of the Sussex Vampire" this is the first we have heard of an organization supporting Holmes, apart from the Baker Street Irregulars. Did the case take place in 1890? Surely not: 1) Holmes would have said that Peters' ear had been bitten "last year" instead of "in '89." 2) Watson was married to Mary Morstan in 1890; it is unthinkable that Holmes under those conditions would twit Watson about riding in a hansom cab with a lady. 3) Finally, "in the year 1890 there were only three cases of which [Watson retained] any record"—and these, as we have seen, were "The Adventure of Wisteria Lodge," "Silver Blaze," and "The Adventure of the Beryl Coronet." The Great Hiatus makes 1891, 1892, and 1893 quite impossible. Watson did not mention the case in "The Adventure of the Golden Pince-Nez" as one of the important cases of 1894—we must discard this year also. "The Adventure of Black Peter" beginning on Wednesday, July 3, 1895, makes that year dubious but not impossible. For the present, let us say only that the years between 1896 and Holmes' retirement in late 1904 provide the *probable* period—and add the fact that Watson having been shot in the thigh on Friday, June 27, 1902 ("The Adventure of the Three Garridebs") may have accounted in part for his feeling "rheumatic and old."

them off. Who has tied them? A bootmaker—or the boy at the bath. It is unlikely that it is the bootmaker, since your boots are nearly new. Well, what remains? The bath. Absurd, is it not? But, for all that, the Turkish bath has served a purpose."

"What is that?"

"You say that you have had it because you need a change. Let me suggest that you take one. How would Lausanne do, my dear Watson—first-class tickets and all expenses paid on a princely scale?"

"Splendid! But why?"

Holmes leaned back in his arm-chair and took his note-book from his pocket.

"One of the most dangerous classes in the world," said he, "is the drifting and friendless woman. She is the most harmless, and often the most useful of mortals, but
she is the inevitable inciter of crime in others. She is **3**
helpless. She is migratory. She has sufficient means to take her from country to country and from hotel to hotel. She is lost, as often as not, in a maze of obscure *pensions* and boarding-houses. She is a stray chicken in a world of foxes. When she is gobbled up she is hardly missed. I much fear that some evil has come to the Lady Frances
Carfax." **4**

I was relieved at this sudden descent from the general to the particular. Holmes consulted his notes.

"Lady Frances," he continued, "is the sole survivor of the direct family of the late Earl of Rufton. The estates went, as you may remember, in the male line. She was left with limited means, but with some very remarkable old Spanish jewellery of silver and curiously-cut diamonds to which she was fondly attached—too attached, for she refused to leave them with her banker and always carried them about with her. A rather pathetic figure, the Lady Frances, a beautiful woman, still in fresh middle age, and yet, by a strange chance, the last derelict of what only twenty years ago was a goodly fleet."

"What has happened to her, then?"

"Ah, what has happened to the Lady Frances? Is she alive or dead? There is our problem. She is a lady of precise habits, and for four years it has been her invariable custom to write every second week to Miss Dobney, her old governess, who has long retired, and lives in Camberwell. It is this Miss Dobney who has consulted me. Nearly five weeks have passed without a word. The last
letter was from the Hôtel National at Lausanne. Lady **5**
Frances seems to have left there and given no address. The family are anxious, and, as they are exceedingly wealthy, no sum will be spared if we can clear the matter up."

"Is Miss Dobney the only source of information? Surely she had other correspondents?"

"There is one correspondent who is a sure draw, Watson. That is the bank. Single ladies must live, and their pass-books are compressed diaries. She banks at Silvester's. I have glanced over her account. The last cheque but one paid her bill at Lausanne, but it was a large one and probably left her with cash in hand. Only one cheque has been drawn since."

2 *you had a companion.*" The late H. W. Bell pointed out that Watson would have sat upon the left side of the cab if his companion had been a lady, and saw in this incident "an unmistakable hint [that Watson is] preparing his readers for a change in his circumstances." We later learn that Watson married for a third time in the last quarter of 1902; it seems logical to think that he might well be sharing his cab with his bride-to-be a few months before the marriage took place.

3 *the inevitable inciter of crime in others.* "Holmes' experience of women was, of course, limited, and perhaps if he had had experience of life in a London boarding-house he might have altered somewhat the first half of his sentence," Mr. T. S. Blakeney commented in *Sherlock Holmes: Fact or Fiction?*

4 *the lady Frances Carfax.*" "In . . . 'The Disappearance of Lady Frances Carfax' [Watson] is guilty of calling her, and of making Holmes call her, at least once, *the* Lady Frances Carfax; which is wrong," Dr. William Braid White wrote in "Dr. Watson and the Peerage." "She could have been *the* Lady Frances Carfax, but actually she was not. She was Lady Frances Carfax. I shall leave it to another scholar to supply the reason for this subtle distinction."

Another scholar, Mr. Humfrey Michell, was quick to disagree with Dr. White: "The lady in question was the sole survivor of the late Earl of Rufton, 'the last derelict of what only twenty years ago was a goodly fleet.' As the daughter of an earl she ranked with her father, and since the prefix 'the' is the equivalent of 'Right Honourable' she was entitled to be called 'the Lady Frances Carfax,' as Holmes correctly calls her when first speaking of her to Watson. In all, the right appellation is used nine times during the story and the incorrect 'Lady Frances Carfax' twelve times."

On the postulation that Holmes instructed Watson to conceal the Lady Frances Carfax's real identity, and that he personally selected the pseudonym for this unfortunate lady, Lord Donegall has insisted that Holmes identifies himself irrevocably as an Oxford man. No Cantabrigian, he asserts, would ever have thought of this appellation which attaches to the main square in the town of Oxford.

5 *the Hôtel National at Lausanne.* Mr. Michael Kaser has pointed out in a paper on the dating of this case that the Hôtel National at Lausanne was open between 1886 and 1951 and that it did possess "luxurious rooms overlooking the lake" as Watson later described the Lady Frances' suite. "Slight evidence for a later [rather than an earlier] dating may be found in the absence of the Hôtel from the 1896 edition of Baedeker's *Switzerland*," he wrote, "whereas it was listed in the 1902 edition. One could surmise that the Lady Frances, of wealthy and noble family, would have selected for

"To whom, and where?"

"To Miss Marie Devine. There is nothing to show where the cheque was drawn. It was cashed at the Crédit Lyonnais at Montpelier less than three weeks ago. The sum was fifty pounds."

"And who is Miss Marie Devine?"

"That also I have been able to discover. Miss Marie Devine was the maid of Lady Frances Carfax. Why she should have paid her this cheque we have not yet determined. I have no doubt, however, that your researches will soon clear the matter up."

"*My* researches!"

"Hence the health-giving expedition to Lausanne. You know that I cannot possibly leave London while old Abrahams is in such mortal terror of his life. Besides, on general principles it is best that I should not leave the country. Scotland Yard feels lonely without me, and it causes an unhealthy excitement among the criminal classes. Go, then, my dear Watson, and if my humble counsel can
6 ever be valued at so extravagant a rate as twopence a word,
it waits your disposal night and day at the end of the Continental wire."

Two days later found me at the National Hotel at Lausanne, where I received every courtesy at the hands of M. Moser, the well-known manager. Lady Frances, as he informed me, had stayed there for several weeks. She had been much liked by all who met her. Her age was not more than forty. She was still handsome, and bore every sign of having in her youth been a very lovely woman. M. Moser knew nothing of any valuable jewellery, but it had been remarked by the servants that the heavy trunk in the lady's bedroom was always scrupulously locked. Marie Devine, the maid, was as popular as her mistress. She was actually engaged to one of the head waiters in the hotel, and there was no difficulty in
7 getting her address. It was 11 Rue de Trajan, Montpelier.
All this I jotted down, and felt that Holmes himself could not have been more adroit in collecting his facts.

Only one corner still remained in the shadow. No light which I possessed could clear up the cause for the lady's sudden departure. She was very happy at Lausanne. There was every reason to believe that she intended to remain for the season in her luxurious rooms overlooking the lake. And yet she had left at a single day's notice, which involved her in the useless payment of a week's rent. Only Jules Vibart, the lover of the maid, had any suggestion to offer. He connected the sudden departure with the visit to the hotel a day or two before of a tall, dark, bearded man. "*Un sauvage—un véritable sauvage!*" cried Jules Vibart. The man had rooms somewhere in the town. He had been seen talking earnestly to madame on the promenade by the lake. Then he had called. She had refused to see him. He was English, but of his name there was no record. Madame had left the place immediately afterwards. Jules Vibart, and, what was of more importance, Jules Vibart's sweetheart, thought that this call and this departure were cause and effect. Only one thing Jules could not discuss. That

her season's stay a hotel of confirmed international standing, and that so far as Baedeker (then virtually the only reliable guide) went, that standing was not ratified until 1902."

There is every reason to believe that the Lady Frances intended to remain for the season in her luxurious rooms; since the Continental "season" is from May 1st to October 1st, and the Lady Frances had not been heard from for "nearly five weeks," it seems logical to surmise that the case opened no earlier than June 30th, no later than July 7th. Watson's bullet wound on Friday, June 27, 1902, coupled with his phrase "the last few days," added to the fact that the closing day of the case was neither a Sunday nor a Monday, lead us to *Tuesday, July 1, 1902*, as the opening day of the case; it ended, we think, on *Friday, July 18, 1902*.

6 *at so extravagant a rate as twopence a word.* Mr. Kaser has noted that: "The telegram rate to France of twopence a word was introduced in 1889 and continued until 1920, when it changed to twopence halfpenny; the rate to Switzerland at the time was threepence a word (it dropped to twopence halfpenny in 1909 but reverted to threepence in 1926). Leaving aside the query why Holmes should have referred to the rate to France and not to Switzerland, which was Watson's immediate destination (one could suppose intuition on Holmes' part that the trail would lead out of Switzerland into France; Holmes did not in fact send any telegram to Watson in Switzerland—only to Baden and Montpellier), it is clear that any dating beyond 1889 would satisfy the evidence of the telegram charge."

7 *11 Rue de Trajan.* "No 'Rue de Trajan' is to be found on the maps of Montpellier in the 1897 edition of Baedeker's guide to that region of France, but the street, patently a minor one, was of insufficient importance for depiction on such a map," Mr. Kaser wrote.

was the reason why Marie had left her mistress. Of that he could or would say nothing. If I wished to know, I must go to Montpelier and ask her.

So ended the first chapter of my inquiry. The second was devoted to the place which Lady Frances Carfax had sought when she left Lausanne. Concerning this there had been some secrecy, which confirmed the idea that she had gone with the intention of throwing someone off her track. Otherwise why should not her luggage have been openly labelled for Baden? Both she and it reached the Rhenish spa by some circuitous route. Thus much I
gathered from the manager of Cook's local office. So to **8**
Baden I went, after dispatching to Holmes an account of all my proceedings, and receiving in reply a telegram of half-humorous commendation.

At Baden the track was not difficult to follow. Lady
Frances had stayed at the Englischer Hof for a fortnight. **9**
Whilst there she had made the acquaintance of a Dr. Shlessinger and his wife, a missionary from South America. Like most lonely ladies, Lady Frances found her comfort and occupation in religion. Dr. Shlessinger's remarkable personality, his whole-hearted devotion, and the fact that he was recovering from a disease contracted in the exercise of his apostolic duties, affected her deeply. She had helped Mrs. Shlessinger in the nursing of the convalescent saint. He spent his day, as the manager described it to me, upon a lounge-chair on the verandah, with an attendant lady upon either side of him. He was preparing a map of the Holy Land, with special reference to the kingdom of the Midianites, upon which he was writing a monograph. Finally, having improved much in health, he and his wife had returned to London, and Lady Frances had started thither in their company. This was just three weeks before, and the manager had heard nothing since. As to the maid, Marie, she had gone off some days beforehand in floods of tears, after informing the other maids that she was leaving service for ever. Dr. Shlessinger had paid the bill of the whole party before his departure.

"By the way," said the landlord, in conclusion, "you are not the only friend of Lady Frances Carfax who is inquiring after her just now. Only a week or so ago we had a man here upon the same errand."

"Did he give a name?" I asked.

"None; but he was an Englishman, though of an unusual type."

"A savage?" said I, linking my facts after the fashion of my illustrious friend.

"Exactly. That describes him very well. He is a bulky, bearded, sunburned fellow, who looks as if he would be more at home in a farmers' inn than in a fashionable hotel. A hard, fierce man, I should think, and one whom I should be sorry to offend."

Already the mystery began to define itself, as figures grow clearer with the lifting of a fog. Here was this good and pious lady pursued from place to place by a sinister and unrelenting figure. She feared him, or she would not have fled from Lausanne. He had still followed. Sooner or later he would overtake her. Had he already overtaken her? Was *that* the secret of her continued silence?

8 *Cook's local office.* "Thomas Cook's office in Lausanne was opened April, 1891, at No. 1 Rue Pépinet; consequently any date beyond 1891 is satisfactory," Mr. Kaser wrote.

9 *the Englischer Hof.* "The Englischer Hof in Baden . . . is listed in both the 1893 and 1902 edition's of Baedeker's *Southern Germany,*" Mr. Kaser wrote, adding in a footnote: "The Hotel changed its name during the First World War for obvious reasons."

HE SPENT HIS DAY . . . UPON A LOUNGE-CHAIR ON THE VERANDAH . . .

Illustration by Alec Ball for the *Strand Magazine,* December, 1911. Here is additional evidence that Watson's trip to the Continent was made in the early summer.

Could the good people who were her companions not screen her from his violence or his blackmail? What horrible purpose, what deep design, lay behind this long pursuit? There was the problem which I had to solve.

10 To Holmes I wrote showing how rapidly and surely I had got down to the roots of the matter. In reply I had a telegram asking for a description of Dr. Shlessinger's left ear. Holmes' ideas of humour are strange and occasionally offensive, so I took no notice of his ill-timed jest—indeed, I had already reached Montpelier in my pursuit of the maid, Marie, before his message came.

I had no difficulty in finding the ex-servant and in learning all that she could tell me. She was a devoted creature, who had only left her mistress because she was sure that she was in good hands, and because her own approaching marriage made a separation inevitable in any case. Her mistress had, as she confessed with distress, shown some irritability of temper towards her during their stay in Baden, and had even questioned her once as if she had suspicions of her honesty, and this had made the parting easier than it would otherwise have been. Lady Frances had given her fifty pounds as a wedding-present. Like me, Marie viewed with deep distrust the stranger who had driven her mistress from Lausanne. With her own eyes she had seen him seize the lady's wrist with great violence on the public promenade by the lake. He was a fierce and terrible man. She believed that it was out of dread of him that Lady Frances had accepted the escort of the Shlessingers to London. She had never spoken to Marie about it, but many little signs had convinced the maid that her mistress lived in a state of continual nervous apprehension. So far she had got in her narrative, when suddenly she sprang from her chair and her face was convulsed with surprise and fear. "See!" she cried. "The miscreant follows still! There is the very man of whom I speak."

Through the open sitting-room window I saw a huge, swarthy man with a bristling black beard walking slowly down the centre of the street and staring eagerly at the numbers of the houses. It was clear that, like myself, he was on the track of the maid. Acting upon the impulse of the moment, I rushed out and accosted him.

"You are an Englishman," I said.

"What if I am?" he asked, with a most villainous scowl.

"May I ask what your name is?"

"No, you may not," said he, with decision.

The situation was awkward, but the most direct way is often the best.

"Where is the Lady Frances Carfax?" I asked.

He stared at me in amazement.

"What have you done with her? Why have you pursued her? I insist upon an answer!" said I.

The fellow gave a bellow of anger and sprang upon me like a tiger. I have held my own in many a struggle, but the man had a grip of iron and the fury of a fiend. His
11 hand was on my throat and my senses were nearly gone
12 before an unshaven French *ouvrier*, in a blue blouse,

10 *To Holmes I wrote.* "It would appear that [Watson's information] was fairly vital," Mr. Benjamin Clark, Jr., wrote in "Holmes on the Range," "and yet, although he had been advised before leaving to call on Holmes' aid if needed via the Continental wire (at twopence a word), Watson nevertheless saw fit to report his findings by letter. If, however, one feels that Watson was dilatory in this action, how about Holmes? Might he not himself, before sending Watson abroad ('First class tickets and all expenses paid on a princely scale') have tried to get a little information via this same Continental wire? As it turned out, Watson's information could have been produced by telegrams in half the time, and at a fraction of the expense."

11 *my senses were nearly gone.* "This is an unusual incident and Watson must have been unprepared, for in a rough-and-tumble fight he could take care of himself in fast company," Dr. Edward J. Van Liere wrote in "Sherlock Holmes and Doctor Watson, Perennial Athletes." "He had the courage and tenacity of an English bulldog, and, what is more important, knew how to use his strength."

THE FELLOW GAVE A BELLOW OF ANGER AND SPRANG UPON ME LIKE A TIGER.

Illustration by Alec Ball for the *Strand Magazine*, December, 1911.

darted out from a *cabaret* opposite, with a cudgel in his hand, and struck my assailant a sharp crack over the forearm, which made him leave go his hold. He stood for an instant fuming with rage and uncertain whether he should not renew his attack. Then, with a snarl of anger, he left me and entered the cottage from which I had just come. I turned to thank my preserver, who stood beside me in the roadway.

" Well, Watson," said he, " a very pretty hash you have
made of it ! I rather think you had better come back with 13
me to London by the night express."

An hour afterwards Sherlock Holmes, in his usual garb and style, was seated in my private room at the hotel. His explanation of his sudden and opportune appearance was
simplicity itself, for, finding that he could get away from 14
London, he determined to head me off at the next obvious point of my travels. In the disguise of a working-man he had sat in the *cabaret* waiting for my appearance.

" And a singularly consistent investigation you have made, my dear Watson," said he. " I cannot at the moment recall any possible blunder which you have omitted. The total effect of your proceedings has been to give the alarm everywhere and yet to discover nothing."

" Perhaps you would have done no better," I answered, 15
bitterly.

" There is no ' perhaps ' about it. I *have* done better. Here is the Hon. Philip Green, who is a fellow-lodger with you in this hotel, and we may find in him the starting-point for a more successful investigation."

A card had come up on a salver, and it was followed by the same bearded ruffian who had attacked me in the street. He started when he saw me.

" What is this, Mr. Holmes ? " he asked. " I had your note and I have come. But what has this man to do with the matter ? "

" This is my old friend and associate, Dr. Watson, who is helping us in this affair."

The stranger held out a huge, sunburned hand, with a few words of apology.

" I hope I didn't harm you. When you accused me of hurting her I lost my grip of myself. Indeed, I'm not responsible in these days. My nerves are like live wires. But this situation is beyond me. What I want to know, in the first place, Mr. Holmes, is, how in the world you came to hear of my existence at all."

" I am in touch with Miss Dobney, Lady Frances' governess."

" Old Susan Dobney with the mob cap ! I remember her well."

" And she remembers you. It was in the days before—before you found it better to go to South Africa."

" Ah, I see you know my whole story. I need hide nothing from you. I swear to you, Mr. Holmes, that there never was in this world a man who loved a woman with a more whole-hearted love than I had for Frances. I was a wild youngster, I know—not worse than others of my class. But her mind was pure as snow. She could not bear a shadow of coarseness. So, when she came to hear of things that I had done, she would have no more to

12 ouvrier. French: workman.

13 *"a very pretty hash you have made of it!* "If Holmes' conduct of the case up to now has been illogical," Mr. Benjamin Clark, Jr., wrote, "it assumes aspects from here on that are both illogical and bizarre. So far as the detective knows, the Lady Frances Carfax was last seen headed for London in the company of, as Holmes strongly suspects . . . one Holy Peters—that is, the Rev. Shlessinger. Under these circumstances, why should Holmes take such pains to conceal his identity in Montpellier? Surely there was no reason for believing that Peters was anywhere near that city, and yet the detective chose this moment to indulge his craving for fancy dress by disguising himself as a French workman. Was his only purpose in doing so to have the pleasure of startling Watson? Certainly one can think of no other plausible reason."

14 *was simplicity itself*. "Of Holmes' next move," Mr. Clark continued, "we can only say, like Alice, 'curiouser and curiouser,' for certainly it is an extraordinary *non sequitur* for the detective, having just received information from Watson placing the Lady Frances in London with the Shlessingers, to up and *leave* London."

15 *"Perhaps you would have done no better.* "Now the facts of the matter are" (we are still quoting Mr. Benjamin Clark, Jr.) "that if poor Watson had not been so in awe of the detective he could have availed himself of an unparalleled opportunity to indulge in one of his rare flashes of . . . 'pawky humour,' instead of his feeble 'perhaps you would have done no better.' What Watson could have said would have been something along the following lines: 'Holmes, your accusations are so easily refuted that it is ridiculous. In the first place, I have picked up the Lady Frances' trail. I have found out in whose company she left Baden for London. What is more, if what I have discovered is true, I have given no alarm, because the criminals left the Continent over three weeks ago. You, on the other hand, for some obscure reason of your own, have seen fit to completely disregard my information placing the Lady Frances in London, and you now appear in Montpellier unaccountably disguised as a French *ouvrier*. You must have good reasons for acting in this strange fashion, but at the moment they escape me.' "

16 *Barberton.* A gold-mining town in the Transvaal, South Africa.

say to me. And yet she loved me—that is the wonder of it !—loved me well enough to remain single all her sainted days just for my sake alone. When the years had passed
16 and I had made my money at Barberton I thought perhaps I could seek her out and soften her. I had heard that she was still unmarried. I found her at Lausanne, and tried all I knew. She weakened, I think, but her will was strong, and when next I called she had left the town. I traced her to Baden, and then after a time heard that her maid was here. I'm a rough fellow, fresh from a rough life, and when Dr. Watson spoke to me as he did I lost hold of myself for a moment. But for God's sake tell me what has become of the Lady Frances."

" That is for us to find out," said Sherlock Holmes, with peculiar gravity. " What is your London address, Mr. Green ? "

" The Langham Hotel will find me."

" Then may I recommend that you return there and be on hand in case I should want you ? I have no desire to encourage false hopes, but you may rest assured that all that can be done will be done for the safety of Lady Frances. I can say no more for the instant. I will leave you this card so that you may be able to keep in touch with us. Now, Watson, if you will pack your bag I will cable to Mrs. Hudson to make one of her best efforts for two hungry travellers at seven-thirty to-morrow."

A telegram was awaiting us when we reached our Baker Street rooms, which Holmes read with an exclamation of interest and threw across to me. " Jagged or torn," was the message, and the place of origin Baden.

" What is this ? " I asked.

" It is everything," Holmes answered. " You may remember my seemingly irrelevant question as to this clerical gentleman's left ear. You did not answer it."

" I had left Baden, and could not inquire."

" Exactly. For this reason I sent a duplicate to the manager of the Englischer Hof, whose answer lies here."

" What does it show ? "

" It shows, my dear Watson, that we are dealing with an exceptionally astute and dangerous man. The Rev. Dr. Shlessinger, missionary from South America, is none other than Holy Peters, one of the most unscrupulous rascals that Australia has ever evolved—and for a young country it has turned out some very finished types. His particular speciality is the beguiling of lonely ladies by playing upon their religious feelings, and his so-called wife, an Englishwoman named Fraser, is a worthy helpmate. The nature of his tactics suggested his identity to me, and this physical peculiarity—he was badly bitten in a saloon-fight at Adelaide in '89—confirmed my suspicion. This poor lady is in the hands of a most infernal couple, who will stick at nothing, Watson. That she is already dead is a very likely supposition. If not, she is undoubtedly in some sort of confinement, and unable to write to Miss Dobney or her other friends. It is always possible that she never reached London, or that she has passed through it, but the former is improbable, as, with their system of registration, it is not easy for foreigners to play tricks with the Continental police ; and the latter is also unlikely, as these rogues could not hope to find any other place where it would be as easy to keep a person under restraint. All my instincts tell me that she is in London, but, as we have at present no possible means of telling where, we can only take the obvious steps, eat our dinner, and possess our souls in patience. Later in the evening I will stroll down and have a word with friend Lestrade at Scotland Yard."

But neither the official police nor Holmes' own small, but very efficient, organization sufficed to clear away the mystery. Amid the crowded millions of London the three persons we sought were as completely obliterated as if they had never lived. Advertisements were tried, and failed. Clues were followed, and led to nothing. Every criminal resort which Shlessinger might frequent was drawn in vain. His old associates were watched, but they kept clear of him. And then suddenly, after a week of helpless suspense, there came a flash of light. A silver-and-brilliant pendant of old Spanish design had been pawned at Bevington's, in Westminster Road. The pawner was a large, clean-shaven man of clerical appearance. His name and address were demonstrably false. The ear had escaped notice, but the description was surely that of Shlessinger.

Three times had our bearded friend from the Langham called for news—the third time within an hour of this fresh development. His clothes were getting looser on his great body. He seemed to be wilting away in his anxiety. " If you will only give me something to do ! " was his constant wail. At last Holmes could oblige him.

" He has begun to pawn the jewels. We should get him now."

" But does this mean that any harm has befallen the Lady Frances ? "

Holmes shook his head very gravely.

" Supposing that they have held her prisoner up to now, it is clear that they cannot let her loose without their own destruction. We must prepare for the worst."

" What can I do ? "

" These people do not know you by sight ? "

" No."

" It is possible that he will go to some other pawnbroker in the future. In that case, we must begin again. On the other hand, he has had a fair price and no questions asked, so if he is in need of ready money he will probably come back to Bevington's. I will give you a note to them, and they will let you wait in the shop. If the fellow comes
you will follow him home. But no indiscretion, and, **17**
above all, no violence. I put you on your honour that you will take no step without my knowledge and consent."

For two days the Hon. Philip Green (he was, I may mention, the son of the famous admiral of that name who commanded the Sea of Azof fleet in the Crimean War) brought us no news. On the evening of the third he rushed into our sitting-room, pale, trembling, with every muscle of his powerful frame quivering with excitement.

" We have him ! We have him ! " he cried.

He was incoherent in his agitation. Holmes soothed him with a few words, and thrust him into an arm-chair.

17 *you will follow him home.* "One might query this use of the Honourable Philip Green to detect Holy Peters on his expected second visit to the pawnshop, inasmuch as, of all concerned in the case, he, it would appear, was the most likely to have been seen by the Shlessingers on the Continent," Mr. Benjamin Clark, Jr., wrote. "The selection of Green must have been quite a slap in the face to Scotland Yard, whose men Holmes apparently did not consider good enough for the job, and may possibly explain the unconscionable delay shortly after in the procuring of a search warrant—a delay which . . . came close to costing the Lady Frances her life."

"WE HAVE HIM! WE HAVE HIM!" HE CRIED.

Illustration by Alec Ball for the *Strand Magazine*, December, 1911.

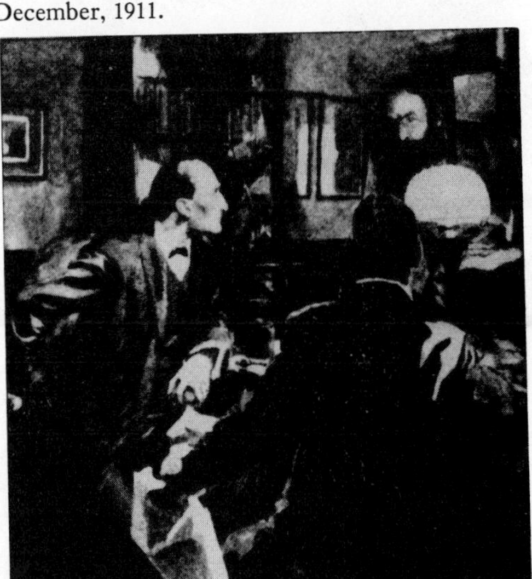

" Come, now, give us the order of events," said he.

" She came only an hour ago. It was the wife, this time, but the pendant she brought was the fellow of the other. She is a tall, pale woman, with ferret eyes."

" That is the lady," said Holmes.

" She left the office and I followed her. She walked up the Kennington Road, and I kept behind her. Presently she went into a shop. Mr. Holmes, it was an undertaker's."

My companion started. " Well ? " he asked, in that vibrant voice which told of the fiery soul behind the cold, grey face.

" She was talking to the woman behind the counter. I entered as well. ' It is late,' I heard her say, or words to that effect. The woman was excusing herself. ' It should be there before now,' she answered. ' It took longer, being out of the ordinary.' They both stopped and looked at me, so I asked some question and then left the shop."

" You did excellently well. What happened next ? "

" The woman came out, but I had hid myself in a doorway. Her suspicions had been aroused, I think, for she looked round her. Then she called a cab and got in. I was lucky enough to get another and so to follow her. She got down at last at No. 36 Poultney Square, Brixton. I drove past, left my cab at the corner of the square, and watched the house."

" Did you see anyone ? "

" The windows were all in darkness save one on the lower floor. The blind was down, and I could not see in. I was standing there, wondering what I should do next, when a covered van drove up with two men in it. They descended, took something out of the van, and carried it up the steps to the hall door. Mr. Holmes, it was a coffin."

" Ah ! "

" For an instant I was on the point of rushing in. The door had been opened to admit the men and their burden. It was the woman who had opened it. But as I stood there she caught a glimpse of me, and I think that she recognized me. I saw her start, and she hastily closed the door. I remembered my promise to you, and here I am."

" You have done excellent work," said Holmes, scribbling a few words upon a half-sheet of paper. " We can do nothing legal without a warrant, and you can serve the cause best by taking this note down to the authorities and getting one. There may be some difficulty, but I should think that the sale of the jewellery should be sufficient. Lestrade will see to all details."

" But they may murder her in the meanwhile. What could the coffin mean, and for whom could it be but for her ? "

" We will do all that can be done, Mr. Green. Not a moment will be lost. Leave it in our hands. Now, Watson," he added, as our client hurried away, " he will set the regular forces on the move. We are, as usual, the irregulars, and we must take our own line of action. The situation strikes me as so desperate that the most extreme measures are justified. Not a moment is to be lost in
18 getting to Poultney Square."

18 *Not a moment is to be lost in getting to Poultney Square.*" Noting that "Holmes did not use the telephone in order to alert someone who could have reached Poultney Square more promptly than they could," Dr. Theodore Gibson of the University of Virginia, in a letter to Mr. Michael Kaser, pointed out that he was not inclined to date "The Disappearance of Lady Frances Carfax" subsequent to July, 1898 ("The Adventure of the Retired Colourman"), by which time, as we know, a telephone had been installed at 221B Baker Street. Dr. Gibson has certainly put his finger on an important clue, and one which has led Mr. Kaser to date "The Disappearance of Lady Frances Carfax" to the early summer of 1897.

" Let us try to reconstruct the situation," said he, as we drove swiftly past the Houses of Parliament and over Westminster Bridge. " These villains have coaxed this unhappy lady to London, after first alienating her from her faithful maid. If she has written any letters they have been intercepted. Through some confederate they have engaged a furnished house. Once inside it, they have made her a prisoner, and they have become possessed of the valuable jewellery which has been their object from the first. Already they have begun to sell part of it, which seems safe enough to them, since they have no reason to
think that anyone is interested in the lady's fate. When 19
she is released she will, of course, denounce them. Therefore, she must not be released. But they cannot keep her under lock and key for ever. So murder is their only solution."

" That seems very clear."

" Now we will take another line of reasoning. When you follow two separate chains of thought, Watson, you will find some point of intersection which should approximate to the truth. We will start now, not from the lady, but from the coffin, and argue backwards. That incident proves, I fear, beyond all doubt that the lady is dead. It points also to an orthodox burial with proper accompaniment of medical certificate and official sanction. Had the lady been obviously murdered, they would have buried her in a hole in the back garden. But here all is open and regular. What does that mean? Surely that they have done her to death in some way which has deceived the doctor, and simulated a natural end—poisoning, perhaps. And yet how strange that they should ever let a doctor approach her unless he were a confederate, which is hardly a credible proposition."

" Could they have forged a medical certificate ? "

" Dangerous, Watson, very dangerous. No, I hardly see them doing that. Pull up, cabby ! This is evidently the undertaker's, for we have just passed the pawnbroker's. Would you go in, Watson ? Your appearance inspires confidence. Ask what hour the Poultney Square funeral takes place to-morrow."

The woman in the shop answered me without hesitation that it was to be at eight o'clock in the morning.

" You see, Watson, no mystery ; everything above-board ! In some way the legal forms have undoubtedly been complied with, and they think that they have little to fear. Well, there's nothing for it now but a direct frontal attack. Are you armed ? "

" My stick ! "

" Well, well, we shall be strong enough. Thrice is he
armed who hath his quarrel just.' We simply can't afford 20
to wait for the police, or to keep within the four corners of the law. You can drive off, cabby. Now, Watson, we'll just take our luck together, as we have occasionally done in the past."

He had rung loudly at the door of a great dark house in the centre of Poultney Square. It was opened immediately, and the figure of a tall woman was outlined against the dim-lit hall.

" Well, what do you want ? " she asked, sharply, peering at us through the darkness.

19 *they have no reason to think that anyone is interested in the lady's fate.* "No reason to think anyone is interested in the lady's fate!" Mr. Benjamin Clark, Jr., wrote. "Why, for a week, Holmes, with what he describes as his own small but very efficient organization, together with Scotland Yard, has been investigating, advertising, combing Shlessinger's haunt, watching his old associates, and heaven knows what else. . . . No! If Peters failed to be alarmed under the above-described conditions, he certainly does not deserve the title of astute. Nor was it astute to pawn the two pendants, and separately at that, thereby running a double risk which in the end was his undoing. As a matter of fact, if Peters had not outbungled Holmes, the Lady Frances would have long since been buried before the detective ever reached the scene."

20 *'Thrice is he armed who hath his quarrel just.'* Holmes quotes from *King Henry VI*, Act III, Scene 2, line 233.

"THERE IS SURELY SOME MISTAKE HERE, GENTLEMEN," HE SAID . . .

Illustration by Frederic Dorr Steele for the *American Magazine,* December, 1911.

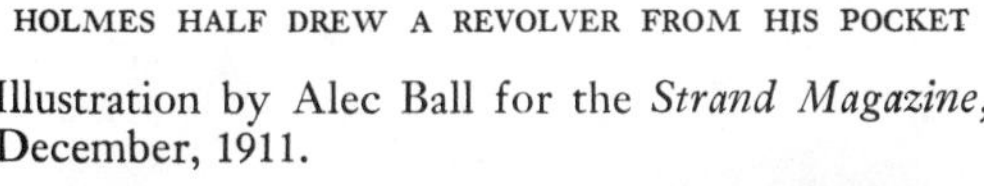

HOLMES HALF DREW A REVOLVER FROM HIS POCKET

Illustration by Alec Ball for the *Strand Magazine,* December, 1911.

"I want to speak to Dr. Shlessinger," said Holmes.

"There is no such person here," she answered, and tried to close the door, but Holmes had jammed it with his foot.

"Well, I want to see the man who lives here, whatever he may call himself," said Holmes, firmly.

She hesitated. Then she threw open the door. "Well, come in!" said she. "My husband is not afraid to face any man in the world." She closed the door behind us, and showed us into a sitting-room on the right side of the hall, turning up the gas as she left us. "Mr. Peters will be with you in an instant," she said.

Her words were literally true, for we had hardly time to look round the dusty and moth-eaten apartment in which we found ourselves before the door opened and a big, clean-shaven, bald-headed man stepped lightly into the room. He had a large red face, with pendulous cheeks, and a general air of superficial benevolence which was marred by a cruel, vicious mouth.

"There is surely some mistake here, gentlemen," he said, in an unctuous, make-everything-easy voice. "I fancy that you have been misdirected. Possibly if you tried farther down the street——"

"That will do; we have no time to waste," said my companion, firmly. "You are Henry Peters, of Adelaide, late the Rev. Dr. Shlessinger, of Baden and SouthAmerica. I am as sure of that as that my own name is Sherlock Holmes."

Peters, as I will now call him, started and stared hard at his formidable pursuer. "I guess your name does not frighten me, Mr. Holmes," said he, coolly. "When a man's conscience is easy you can't rattle him. What is your business in my house?"

"I want to know what you have done with the Lady Frances Carfax, whom you brought away with you from Baden."

"I'd be very glad if you could tell me where that lady may be," Peters answered, coolly. "I've a bill against her for nearly a hundred pounds, and nothing to show for it but a couple of trumpery pendants that the dealer would hardly look at. She attached herself to Mrs. Peters and me at Baden (it is a fact that I was using another name at the time), and she stuck on to us until we came to London. I paid her bill and her ticket. Once in London, she gave us the slip, and, as I say, left these out-of-date jewels to pay her bills. You find her, Mr. Holmes, and I'm your debtor."

"*I mean* to find her," said Sherlock Holmes. "I'm going through this house till I do find her."

"Where is your warrant?"

Holmes half drew a revolver from his pocket. "This will have to serve till a better one comes."

"Why, you are a common burglar."

"So you might describe me," said Holmes, cheerfully. "My companion is also a dangerous ruffian. And together we are going through your house."

Our opponent opened the door.

"Fetch a policeman, Annie!" said he. There was a

whisk of feminine skirts down the passage, and the hall door was opened and shut.

" Our time is limited, Watson," said Holmes. " If you try to stop us, Peters, you will most certainly get hurt. Where is that coffin which was brought into your house ? "

" What do you want with the coffin ? It is in use. There is a body in it."

" I must see that body."

" Never with my consent."

" Then without it." With a quick movement Holmes pushed the fellow to one side and passed into the hall. A door half-open stood immediately before us. We entered. It was the dining-room. On the table, under a half-lit chandelier, the coffin was lying. Holmes turned up the gas and raised the lid. Deep down in the recesses of the coffin lay an emaciated figure. The glare from the lights above beat down upon an aged and withered face. By no possible process of cruelty, starvation, or disease could this worn-out wreck be the still beautiful Lady Frances. Holmes' face showed his amazement, and also his relief.

" Thank God ! " he muttered. " It's someone else."

" Ah, you've blundered badly for once, Mr. Sherlock Holmes," said Peters, who had followed us into the room.

" Who is this dead woman ? "

" Well, if you really must know, she is an old nurse of my wife's, Rose Spender her name, whom we found in the Brixton Workhouse Infirmary. We brought her round here, called in Dr. Horsom, of 13 Firbank Villas—mind you take the address, Mr. Holmes—and had her carefully tended, as Christian folk should. On the third day she died—certificate says senile decay—but that's only the doctor's opinion, and, of course, you know better. We ordered her funeral to be carried out by Stimson & Co., of the Kennington Road, who will bury her at eight o'clock to-morrow morning. Can you pick any hole in that, Mr. Holmes ? You've made a silly blunder, and you may as well own up to it. I'd give something for a photograph of your gaping, staring face when you pulled aside that lid expecting to see the Lady Frances Carfax, and only found a poor old woman of ninety."

Holmes' expression was as impassive as ever under the jeers of his antagonist, but his clenched hands betrayed his acute annoyance.

" I am going through your house," said he.

" Are you, though ! " cried Peters, as a woman's voice and heavy steps sounded in the passage. " We'll soon see about that. This way, officers, if you please. These men have forced their way into my house, and I cannot get rid of them. Help me to put them out."

A sergeant and a constable stood in the doorway. Holmes drew his card from his case.

" This is my name and address. This is my friend, Dr. Watson."

" Bless you, sir, we know you very well," said the sergeant, " but you can't stay here without a warrant."

" Of course not. I quite understand that."

" Arrest him ! " cried Peters.

" We know where to lay our hands on this gentleman if he is wanted," said the sergeant, majestically ; " but you'll have to go, Mr. Holmes."

"Yes, Watson, we shall have to go."

A minute later we were in the street once more. Holmes was as cool as ever, but I was hot with anger and humiliation. The sergeant had followed us.

"Sorry, Mr. Holmes, but that's the law."

"Exactly, sergeant; you could not do otherwise."

"I expect there was good reason for your presence there. If there is anything I can do——"

"It's a missing lady, sergeant, and we think she is in that house. I expect a warrant presently."

"Then I'll keep my eye on the parties, Mr. Holmes. If anything comes along, I will surely let you know."

It was only nine o'clock, and we were off full cry upon the trail at once. First we drove to Brixton Workhouse Infirmary, where we found that it was indeed the truth that a charitable couple had called some days before, that they had claimed an imbecile old woman as a former servant, and that they had obtained permission to take her away with them. No surprise was expressed at the news that she had since died.

The doctor was our next goal. He had been called in, had found the woman dying of pure senility, had actually seen her pass away, and had signed the certificate in due form. "I assure you that everything was perfectly normal and there was no room for foul play in the matter," said he. Nothing in the house had struck him as suspicious, save that for people of their class it was remarkable that they should have no servant. So far and no farther went the doctor.

Finally, we found our way to Scotland Yard. There had been difficulties of procedure in regard to the warrant. Some delay was inevitable. The magistrate's signature might not be obtained until next morning. If Holmes would call about nine he could go down with Lestrade and see it acted upon. So ended the day, save that near midnight our friend, the sergeant, called to say that he had seen flickering lights here and there in the windows of the great dark house, but that no one had left it and none had entered. We could but pray for patience, and wait for the morrow.

Sherlock Holmes was too irritable for conversation and too restless for sleep. I left him smoking hard, with his heavy, dark brows knotted together, and his long, nervous fingers tapping upon the arms of his chair, as he turned over in his mind every possible solution of the mystery. Several times in the course of the night I heard him prowling about the house. Finally, just after I had been called in the morning, he rushed into my room. He was in his dressing-gown, but his pale, hollow-eyed face told me that his night had been a sleepless one.

"What time was the funeral? Eight, was it not?" he asked, eagerly. "Well, it is seven-twenty now. Good heavens, Watson, what has become of any brains that God has given me? Quick, man, quick! It's life or death—a hundred chances on death to one on life. I'll never forgive myself, never, if we are too late!"

Five minutes had not passed before we were flying in a hansom down Baker Street. But even so it was twenty-five to eight as we passed Big Ben, and eight struck as we tore down the Brixton Road. But others were late as well as we. Ten minutes after the hour the hearse was still standing at the door of the house, and even as our foaming horse came to a halt the coffin, supported by three men, appeared on the threshold. Holmes darted forward and barred their way.

" Take it back ! " he cried, laying his hand on the breast of the foremost. " Take it back this instant ! "

" What the devil do you mean ? Once again I ask you, where is your warrant ? " shouted the furious Peters, his big red face glaring over the farther end of the coffin.

" The warrant is on its way. This coffin shall remain in the house until it comes."

The authority in Holmes' voice had its effect upon the bearers. Peters had suddenly vanished into the house, and they obeyed these new orders. " Quick, Watson, quick ! Here is a screw-driver ! " he shouted, as the coffin was replaced upon the table. " Here's one for you, my man : a sovereign if the lid comes off in a minute ! Ask no questions—work away ! That's good ! Another ! And another ! Now pull all together ! It's giving ! It's giving ! Ah, that does it at last ! "

With a united effort we tore off the coffin-lid. As we did so there came from the inside a stupefying and overpowering smell of chloroform. A body lay within, its head all wreathed in cotton-wool, which had been soaked in the narcotic. Holmes plucked it off and disclosed the statuesque face of a handsome and spiritual woman of middle age. In an instant he had passed his arm round the figure and raised her to a sitting position.

" Is she gone, Watson ? Is there a spark left ? Surely we are not too late ! "

For half an hour it seemed that we were. What with actual suffocation, and what with the poisonous fumes of the chloroform, the Lady Frances seemed to have passed the last point of recall. And then, at last, with artificial
respiration, with injected ether, with every device that **21**
science could suggest, some flutter of life, some quiver of the eyelids, some dimming of a mirror, spoke of the slowly returning life. A cab had driven up, and Holmes, parting the blind, looked out at it. " Here is Lestrade with his warrant," said he. " He will find that his birds have flown. And here," he added, as a heavy step hurried along the passage, " is someone who has a better right to nurse this lady than we have. Good morning, Mr. Green ; I think that the sooner we can move the Lady Frances the better. Meanwhile, the funeral may proceed, and the poor old woman who still lies in that coffin may go to her last resting-place alone."

" Should you care to add the case to your annals, my dear Watson," said Holmes that evening, " it can only be as an example of that temporary eclipse to which even the best-balanced mind may be exposed. Such slips are common to all mortals, and the greatest is he who can recognize and repair them. To this modified credit I may, perhaps, make some claim. My night was haunted by the thought that somewhere a clue, a strange sentence, a

21 *with injected ether.* "This . . . was rather startling treatment for a patient already over-dosed with chloroform," Dr. Samuel R. Meaker noted in "Watson Medicus."

HOLMES DARTED FORWARD AND BARRED THEIR WAY.

Illustration by Alec Ball for the *Strand Magazine*, December, 1911.

curious observation, had come under my notice and had been too easily dismissed. Then, suddenly, in the grey of the morning, the words came back to me. It was the remark of the undertaker's wife, as reported by Philip Green. She had said, ' It should be there before now. It took longer, being out of the ordinary.' It was the coffin of which she spoke. It had been out of the ordinary. That could only mean that it had been made to some special measurement. But why? Why? Then in an instant I remembered the deep sides, and the little wasted figure at the bottom. Why so large a coffin for so small a body? To leave room for another body. Both would be buried under the one certificate. It had all been so clear, if only my own sight had not been dimmed. At eight the Lady Frances would be buried. Our one chance was to stop the coffin before it left the house.

" It was a desperate chance that we might find her alive, but it *was* a chance, as the result showed. These people had never, to my knowledge, done a murder. They might shrink from actual violence at the last. They could bury her with no sign of how she met her end, and even if she were exhumed there was a chance for them. I hoped that such considerations might prevail with them. You can reconstruct the scene well enough. You saw the horrible den upstairs, where the poor lady had been kept so long. They rushed in and overpowered her with their chloroform, carried her down, poured more into the coffin to ensure against her waking, and then screwed down the
22 lid. A clever device, Watson. It is new to me in the annals of crime. If our ex-missionary friends escape the clutches of Lestrade, I shall expect to hear of some brilliant incidents in their future career."

. . .

. . . FOR ANSWER HE HAD SHOT HIS LONG, THIN, NERVOUS ARM OUT OF THE SHEETS . . .

Illustration by Howard K. Elcock for the *Strand Magazine*, February, 1925.

22 *A clever device, Watson.* "'Unusual' might have been a better adjective," Mr. Benjamin Clark, Jr., wrote. "Surely it was a device with truly extraordinary risks. In the first place, the extraction from the workhouse had to be done in an innocent and plausible manner. Then it was important that the Shlessingers pick an inmate who had to be, one might say, 'just right'—not yet dead, but *awful close;* and yet not so close but what she could be moved. A very 'nice' calculation, all things considered." Mr. Clark was forced to conclude that Holmes in this adventure was still feeling the effect of the deadly fumes of *radix pedis diaboli* ("The Adventure of the Devil's Foot")—another vote, it would seem, for dating "The Disappearance of Lady Frances Carfax" in the early summer of 1897.

Bibliographical Note: The original manuscript of this adventure, about 7,500 words in 28 pages, 4to, white vellum, was auctioned in New York City on February 5, 1929, bringing $285. Its present location is unknown.

70

THE ADVENTURE OF THE ILLUSTRIOUS CLIENT

[*Wednesday, September 3, to Tuesday, September 16, 1902*]

"IT can't hurt now," was Mr. Sherlock Holmes'
comment when, for the tenth time in as many
years, I asked his leave to reveal the following 1
narrative. So it was that at last I obtained permission
to put on record what was, in some ways, the supreme
moment of my friend's career. 2
Both Holmes and I had a weakness for the Turkish
Bath. It was over a smoke in the pleasant lassitude of the
drying-room that I have found him less reticent and more
human than anywhere else. On the upper floor of the
Northumberland Avenue establishment there is an 3
isolated corner where two couches lie side by side, and
it was on these that we lay upon September 3, 1902, the 4
day when my narrative begins. I had asked him whether anything was stirring, and for answer he had shot his long, thin, nervous arm out of the sheets which enveloped him and had drawn an envelope from the inside pocket of the coat which hung beside him.

"It may be some fussy, self-important fool, it may be a matter of life or death," said he, as he handed me the note. "I know no more than this message tells me."

It was from the Carlton Club, and dated the evening before. This is what I read:

"Sir James Damery presents his compliments to Mr. Sherlock Holmes, and will call upon him at 4.30 to-morrow. Sir James begs to say that the matter upon which he desires to consult Mr. Holmes is very delicate, and also very important. He trusts, therefore, that Mr. Holmes will make every effort to grant this interview, and that he will confirm it over the telephone to the Carlton Club."

"I need not say that I have confirmed it, Watson," said Holmes, as I returned the paper. "Do you know anything of this man Damery?"

"Only that his name is a household word in Society."

"Well, I can tell you a little more than that. He has rather a reputation for arranging delicate matters which are to be kept out of the papers. You may remember his negotiations with Sir George Lewis over the Hammerford Will case. He is a man of the world with a natural

1 *for the tenth time in as many years.* Watson presumably chronicled "The Adventure of the Illustrious Client" in 1912, although it was not published until twelve years after that.

2 *the supreme moment of my friend's career.* Watson exaggerates when he calls this adventure the supreme moment of Holmes' career. As Mr. T. S. Blakeney wrote in *Sherlock Holmes: Fact or Fiction?:* "Baron Gruner had achieved a European reputation, it is true, but the successful breaking off of his engagement with Miss de Merville can hardly be considered as of prime importance save to the small circle of individuals concerned. If, as Watson is probably implying, it was the exalted standing of the Illustrious Client that gave the case its significance, there could only be one person in England whose position would suit the requirements, and seeing that that person's interests were only involved as a matter of friendly concern, we cannot surely rate this case above the services rendered by Holmes to the nation in 'The Naval Treaty,' 'The Second Stain,' or 'The Bruce-Partington Plans,' or to the royal houses of Holland, Scandinavia and Bohemia. Indeed, from what we learn of Baron Gruner, he was not in the same class as Professor Moriarty or even Colonel Moran, nor did he give Holmes so good a run for his money as did Stapleton."

3 *the Northumberland Avenue establishment.* Identified by Mr. Michael Harrison (*In the Footsteps of Sherlock Holmes*) as Nevill's, at the corner of Craven Passage. Before 7 P.M. Holmes and Watson would have paid 3s 6d. (about 87½¢) each; after, the charge would have been reduced to 2s (50¢).

4 *September 3, 1902.* A Wednesday.

THE BIG, MASTERFUL ARISTOCRAT DOMINATED THE LITTLE ROOM.

"The go-between used by the illustrious client was an arranger of delicate matters, and as such, may have been descended from Sir Amery of Pavia, the Lombard, who also tried to arrange a very delicate matter—the betrayal of Calais to the French in 1348," Dr. Julian Wolff wrote in his *Practical Handbook of Sherlockian Heraldry*. "His story appears in both Conan Doyle's *Sir Nigel* and in Froissart's *Chronycles*. . . . It seems more worthy of belief, however, that Sir James was descended from an honourable man, Sir Thomas Dammery, who was knighted by the Duke of Lancaster in the Spanish war, as related by Froissart. His arms were blazoned: Barry wavy argent and gules, a bend or."

COLONEL DAMERY THREW UP HIS KID-GLOVED HANDS WITH A LAUGH.

Illustration by Howard K. Elcock for the *Strand Magazine*, February, 1925.

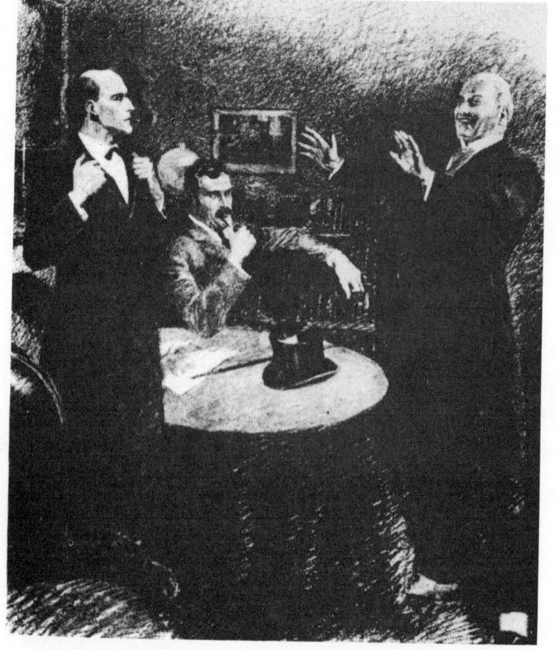

turn for diplomacy. I am bound, therefore, to hope that it is not a false scent and that he has some real need for our assistance."

" Our ? "

" Well, if you will be so good, Watson."

" I shall be honoured."

" Then you have the hour—four-thirty. Until then we can put the matter out of our heads."

5 I was living in my own rooms in Queen Anne Street at the time, but I was round at Baker Street before the time named. Sharp to the half-hour, Colonel Sir James Damery was announced. It is hardly necessary to describe him, for many will remember that large, bluff, honest personality, that broad, clean-shaven face, above all, that pleasant, mellow voice. Frankness shone from his grey Irish eyes, and good humour played round his mobile, smiling lips. His lucent top-hat, his dark frock-coat, indeed, every detail, from the pearl pin in the black satin cravat to the lavender spats over the varnished shoes, spoke of the meticulous care in dress for which he was famous. The big, masterful aristocrat dominated the little room.

" Of course, I was prepared to find Dr. Watson," he remarked, with a courteous bow. " His collaboration may be very necessary, for we are dealing on this occasion, Mr. Holmes, with a man to whom violence is familiar and who will, literally, stick at nothing. I should say that there is no more dangerous man in Europe."

" I have had several opponents to whom that flattering term has been applied," said Holmes, with a smile.
" Don't you smoke ? Then you will excuse me if I
6 light my pipe. If your man is more dangerous than
the late Professor Moriarty, or than the living Colonel
7 Sebastian Moran, then he is indeed worth meeting.
May I ask his name ? "

" Have you ever heard of Baron Gruner ? "

" You mean the Austrian murderer ? "

Colonel Damery threw up his kid-gloved hands with a laugh. " There is no getting past you, Mr. Holmes ! Wonderful ! So you have already sized him up as a murderer ? "

" It is my business to follow the details of Continental crime. Who could possibly have read what happened at Prague and have any doubts as to the man's guilt ! It was a purely technical legal point and the suspicious death of a witness that saved him ! I am as sure that
he killed his wife when the so-called ' accident ' happened
8 in the Splügen Pass as if I had seen him do it. I knew,
also, that he had come to England, and had a presentiment that sooner or later he would find me some work to do. Well, what has Baron Gruner been up to ? I presume it is not this old tragedy which has come up again ? "

" No, it is more serious than that. To revenge crime is important, but to prevent it is more so. It is a terrible thing, Mr. Holmes, to see a dreadful event, an atrocious situation, preparing itself before your eyes, to clearly understand whither it will lead and yet to be utterly unable to avert it. Can a human being be placed in a more trying position ? "

" Perhaps not."

" Then you will sympathize with the client in whose interests I am acting."

" I did not understand that you were merely an intermediary. Who is the principal ? "

" Mr. Holmes, I must beg you not to press that question. It is important that I should be able to assure him that his honoured name has been in no way dragged into the matter. His motives are, to the last degree, honourable and chivalrous, but he prefers to remain unknown. I need not say that your fees will be assured and that you will be given a perfectly free hand. Surely the actual name of your client is immaterial ? "

" I am sorry," said Holmes. " I am accustomed to have mystery at one end of my cases, but to have it at both ends is too confusing. I fear, Sir James, that I must decline to act."

Our visitor was greatly disturbed. His large, sensitive face was darkened with emotion and disappointment.

" You hardly realize the effect of your own action, Mr. Holmes," said he. " You place me in a most serious dilemma, for I am perfectly certain that you would be proud to take over the case if I could give you the facts, and yet a promise forbids me from revealing them all. May I, at least, lay all that I can before you ? "

" By all means, so long as it is understood that I commit myself to nothing."

" That is understood. In the first place, you have no doubt heard of General de Merville ? "

" De Merville of Khyber fame ? Yes, I have heard of him."

" He has a daughter, Violet de Merville, young, rich, beautiful, accomplished, a wonder-woman in every way. It is this daughter, this lovely, innocent girl, whom we are endeavouring to save from the clutches of a fiend."

" Baron Gruner has some hold over her, then ? "

" The strongest of all holds where a woman is concerned—the hold of love. The fellow is, as you may have heard, extraordinarily handsome, with a most fascinating manner, a gentle voice, and that air of romance and mystery which means so much to a woman. He is said to have the whole sex at his mercy and to have made ample use of the fact."

" But how came such a man to meet a lady of the standing of Miss Violet de Merville ? "

5 *my own rooms in Queen Anne Street.* Another sure indication that Watson is preparing the reader to hear of another marriage. The new address, Queen Anne Street, with Weymouth Street and Portland Place, are suburbs of Harley Street, the highest *geographical qualification* for a doctor in London. "That very citadel of medicine," Dr. Vernon Pennell calls the area in his "Resumé of the Medical Life of John H. Watson, M.D., Late of the Army Medical Department"; he adds that even today "the ability to pay rent for the occasional use of a room and a half, and part salary of a receptionist in Harley Street or Queen Anne Street is considered by many of the lay public to be the highest qualification that medicine or surgery has to offer."

6 *Then you will excuse me if I light my pipe.* "This case provides one of the best examples of Holmes' subtle wit, directed, in this instance, at Colonel James Damery, though ineffectively, as it turned out, because of that worthy's impenetrable stuffiness," Mr. Bliss Austin wrote in "Three Footnotes to 'The Adventure of the Illustrious Client.' " "The appearance of this fop must have been enough to tempt any man of Holmes' sensitivity. Thus, it is recorded that he wore a lucent top-hat, a dark frock coat, a black satin cravat complete with pearl pin and—believe it or not—lavender spats over varnished shoes. But what of his manners? Judge for yourself. It is stated that on meeting Holmes and Watson, he made a courteous bow —nothing more. Later, after a bit of conversation, we learn that 'Colonel Damery threw up his kid-gloved hands with a laugh.' Imagine it! The elegant lout had not yet removed his gloves, from which one infers that he did not altogether approve of the general state of cleanliness at 221B, Baker Street; also, that he had not shaken hands with Holmes. One would hardly expect Sherlock to overlook these nuances and he did not, for one finds him baiting the Colonel. 'Don't you smoke?' he asks slyly. The trap was not obvious but it was there. Unless the Colonel refused altogether, he must either remove his gloves or treat Holmes to the delicious sight of a man in lavender spats smoking with kid gloves on. But refuse he did, so Holmes continued: 'Then you will excuse me if I light my pipe.' And one can be certain that he smiled as he said it."

"DE MERVILLE OF KHYBER FAME?"

"Indian and Afghan wars in the nineteenth century produced many great English soldiers," Dr. Julian Wolff wrote in his *Practical Handbook of Sherlockian Heraldry.* "The entry under the name of one of the Goughs in a standard work of reference possibly indicates he whom Dr. Watson had in mind when he wrote of General de Merville: K.C.B., C.B.; entered the Bengal cavalry as cornet in 1848; colonel in 1875; Punjab campaign; battle of Chilian Wallah; Indian mutiny, capture at Delhi and Lucknow; commanded a brigade at Jugdullak Pass during Afghan War, V.C.; brigadier-general, 1881. The slight discrepancy between Jugdullak Pass and Khyber Pass, mentioned by Holmes, is just sufficient to give the identification the proper Canonical touch . . . The arms: a lion passant on a fess between three boars' heads couped. The tinctures differ for each branch of the family."

" It was on a Mediterranean yachting voyage. The company, though select, paid their own passages. No doubt the promoters hardly realized the Baron's true character until it was too late. The villain attached himself to the lady, and with such effect that he has completely and absolutely won her heart. To say that she loves him hardly expresses it. She dotes upon him, she is obsessed by him. Outside of him there is nothing on earth. She will not hear one word against him. Everything has been done to cure her of her madness, but in vain. To sum up, she proposes to marry him next month. As she is of age and has a will of iron, it is hard to know how to prevent her."

" Does she know about the Austrian episode ? "

" The cunning devil has told her every unsavoury public scandal of his past life, but always in such a way as to make himself out to be an innocent martyr. She absolutely accepts his version and will listen to no other."

" Dear me ! But surely you have inadvertently let out the name of your client ? It is no doubt General de Merville."

Our visitor fidgeted in his chair.

" I could deceive you by saying so, Mr. Holmes, but it would not be true. De Merville is a broken man. The strong soldier has been utterly demoralized by this incident. He has lost the nerve which never failed him on the battlefield and has become a weak, doddering old man, utterly incapable of contending with a brilliant, forceful rascal like this Austrian. My client, however, is an old friend, one who has known the General intimately for many years and taken a paternal interest in this young girl since she wore short frocks. He cannot see this tragedy consummated without some attempt to stop it. There is nothing in which Scotland Yard can act. It was his own suggestion that you should be called in, but it was, as I have said, on the express stipulation that he should not be personally involved in the matter. I have no doubt, Mr. Holmes, with your great powers you could easily trace my client back through me, but I must ask you, as a point of honour, to refrain from doing so, and not to break in upon his incognito."

Holmes gave a whimsical smile.

" I think I may safely promise that," said he. " I may add that your problem interests me, and that I shall be prepared to look into it. How shall I keep in touch with you ? "

" The Carlton Club will find me. But, in case of emergency, there is a private telephone call, ' XX.31.' "

Holmes noted it down and sat, still smiling, with the open memorandum-book upon his knee.

" The Baron's present address, please ? "

9 " Vernon Lodge, near Kingston. It is a large house. He has been fortunate in some rather shady speculations and is a rich man, which, naturally, makes him a more dangerous antagonist."

" Is he at home at present ? "

" Yes."

" Apart from what you have told me, can you give

7 *the living Colonel Sebastian Moran.* Mr. O. F. Grazebrook, writing in "Royalty," states his conviction that Watson's phrase "the supreme moment of my friend's career" dates "The Adventure of the Illustrious Client" *before* "The Adventure of the Bruce-Partington Plans" (November, 1895), and that Holmes' phrase "the living Sebastian Moran" dates the adventure *shortly after* "The Adventure of the Empty House" (April, 1894). Watson's reference to "September 3, 1902, the day when my narrative begins" indicates to Mr. Grazebrook only that that was the day of the Turkish bath shared by Holmes and Watson.

8 *the so-called 'accident' happened in the Splügen Pass.* Mr. Bliss Austin ("Three Footnotes to 'The Adventure of the Illustrious Client' ") and Mr. Michael Kayser ("Sherlock Holmes on the Continent") both have a fault to find with Holmes' statement. "Holmes refers to Baron Gruner's trial in Prague for the alleged murder of his wife at the Splügen Pass," Mr. Kaser wrote. "But why, the reader asks, should a Prague court have had jurisdiction in a crime committed on the Swiss-Trentino (then, of course, Austrian) frontier?"

9 *Kingston.* The Royal Borough of Kingston, including the district of Norbiton. Kingston-on-Thames was already in existence a thousand years ago, and King Edward the Elder was crowned there in 900.

10 *Hurlingham.* The grounds used by the Polo Club have since been acquired by the London County Council, partly for a housing estate and partly for a park.

11 *Wainwright was no mean artist.* Holmes refers to Thomas Griffiths Wainwright, who poisoned George Edward Griffiths and others (including, for esthetic reasons, a girl whose ankles he found too thick). The reader is recommended to "Pen, Pencil, and Poison," by Oscar Wilde (in *The Pocket Book of True Crime Stories*, edited by Anthony Boucher) for an excellent account of this poisoner and "no mean artist."

12 *he became a valuable assistant.* Shinwell Johnson was obviously a part of that "small, but very efficient" organization to which Watson referred in "The Disappearance of Lady Frances Carfax." We learn now that this organization was formed "During the first years of the century"—a point in favor of dating "The Disappearance of Lady Frances Carfax" (as we have) in 1902.

13 *looking down at the rushing stream of life in the Strand.* "The description no longer applies," as Mr. Michael Harrison noted (*In the Footsteps of Sherlock Holmes*): "there are no front windows at Simpson's now—through which the customers can look—as well as be looked at. The rebuilding was completed in 1904."

me any further information about the man?"

"He has expensive tastes. He is a horse fancier. For
a short time he played polo at Hurlingham, but then this 10
Prague affair got noised about and he had to leave. He collects books and pictures. He is a man with a considerable artistic side to his nature. He is, I believe, a recognized authority upon Chinese pottery, and has written a book upon the subject."

"A complex mind," said Holmes. "All great criminals have that. My old friend Charlie Peace was a
violin virtuoso. Wainwright was no mean artist. I 11
could quote many more. Well, Sir James, you will inform your client that I am turning my mind upon Baron Gruner. I can say no more. I have some sources of information of my own, and I dare say we may find some means of opening the matter up."

When our visitor had left us, Holmes sat so long in deep thought that it seemed to me that he had forgotten my presence. At last, however, he came briskly back to earth.

"Well, Watson, any views?" he asked.

"I should think you had better see the young lady herself."

"My dear Watson, if her poor old broken father cannot move her, how shall I, a stranger, prevail? And yet there is something in the suggestion if all else fails. But I think we must begin from a different angle. I rather fancy that Shinwell Johnson might be a help."

I have not had occasion to mention Shinwell Johnson in these memoirs because I have seldom drawn my cases from the latter phases of my friend's career. During the first years of the century he became a valuable assistant. Johnson, I grieve to say, made his name first as 12
a very dangerous villain and served two terms at Parkhurst. Finally, he repented and allied himself to Holmes, acting as his agent in the huge criminal underworld of London, and obtaining information which often proved to be of vital importance. Had Johnson been a "nark" of the police he would soon have been exposed, but as he dealt with cases which never came directly into the courts, his activities were never realized by his companions. With the glamour of his two convictions upon him, he had the *entrée* of every night-club, doss-house, and gambling-den in the town, and his quick observation and active brain made him an ideal agent for gaining information. It was to him that Sherlock Holmes now proposed to turn.

It was not possible for me to follow the immediate steps taken by my friend, for I had some pressing professional business of my own, but I met him by appointment that evening at Simpson's, where, sitting at a small table in the front window, and looking down at the
rushing stream of life in the Strand, he told me some- 13
thing of what had passed.

"Johnson is on the prowl," said he. "He may pick up some garbage in the darker recesses of the underworld, for it is down there, amid the black roots of crime, that we must hunt for this man's secrets."

"MY OLD FRIEND CHARLIE PEACE . . ."

Mr. Vernon Rendall ("The Limitations of Sherlock Holmes"), the late Clifton R. Andrew ("My Old Friend Charlie Peace") and Mr. Irving Fenton ("On Friendship") have all given us illuminating comments on Holmes' statement.

"Charles Peace—burglar, murderer, liar, wife-beater, braggart, actor, inventor, violin virtuoso and old friend of Sherlock Holmes—was born in Sheffield, England, on May 14, 1832, of respectable parents," Mr. Fenton wrote. "He received no formal education, but was endowed with intelligence, a mechanical bent, and an inventive genius. One of his early accomplishments was to fashion the tools of his trade, a burglar's kit. In prison at Dartmoor he suggested some improvements in the machinery then in use which Dartmoor and some other English prisons adopted. . . . While engaged in a burglary in a suburb of Manchester, Peace shot and killed Constable Cook, whose sense of duty outweighed his discretion when he closed in, unarmed, on this dangerous jailbird. He committed his second murder when he shot Arthur Dyson, who resented Peace's attentions to Dyson's wife. . . . He got safely away with both murders, but had to keep constantly on the move. Yet, about this time, he patented an invention for raising sunken vessels and worked on a smoke helmet for firemen. . . . Peace was finally captured during a burglary in Blackheath in 1878 and recognized as the murderer of Arthur Dyson. After a sensational trial during which he almost succeeded in escaping, he was sentenced to death (the jury was out ten minutes), and on February 25, 1879, the law ended his terrestrial friendship, at least, with Sherlock Holmes."

Mr. Andrew added that Peace was "minus the forefinger of his left hand, and after he left Sheffield on 29th November, 1876, his description was posted at every police station in the country. So he made himself [a false arm] which he placed in his sleeve, hanging his violin on the hook . . . and screwing in a fork in the place of the hook for use at meals. For something like two years, the irrepressible Peace walked this earth short of a hand, while the police were looking for a man short of a finger."

Mr. Rendall inclined to the belief that Holmes had no personal acquaintance with Peace, and referred to him as his "old friend" only because Holmes was familiar with all the famous trials of the century.

The illustration is from *The Fifty Most Amazing Crimes of the Last 100 Years*, edited by J. M. Parrish and John R. Crossland, London: Odhams Press, Ltd., 1936.

" But, if the lady will not accept what is already known, why should any fresh discovery of yours turn her from her purpose ? "

" Who knows, Watson ? Woman's heart and mind are insoluble puzzles to the male. Murder might be condoned or explained, and yet some smaller offence might rankle. Baron Gruner remarked to me——"

" He remarked to you ! "

" Oh, to be sure, I had not told you of my plans ! Well, Watson, I love to come to close grips with my man. I like to meet him eye to eye and read for myself the stuff that he is made of. When I had given Johnson his instructions, I took a cab out to Kingston and found the Baron in a most affable mood."

" Did he recognize you ? "

" There was no difficulty about that, for I simply sent in my card. He is an excellent antagonist, cool as ice, silky voiced and soothing as one of your fashionable consultants and poisonous as a cobra. He has breed in him, a real aristocrat of crime, with a superficial suggestion of afternoon tea and all the cruelty of the grave behind it. Yes, I am glad to have had my attention called to Baron Adelbert Gruner."

" You say he was affable ? "

" A purring cat who thinks he sees prospective mice. Some people's affability is more deadly than the violence of coarser souls. His greeting was characteristic. ' I rather thought I should see you sooner or later, Mr. Holmes,' said he. ' You have been engaged, no doubt, by General de Merville to endeavour to stop my marriage with his daughter, Violet. That is so, is it not ? '

" I acquiesced.

" ' My dear man,' said he, ' you will only ruin your own well-deserved reputation. It is not a case in which you can possibly succeed. You will have barren work, to say nothing of incurring some danger. Let me very strongly advise you to draw off at once.'

" ' It is curious,' I answered, ' but that was the very advice which I had intended to give you. I have a respect for your brains, Baron, and the little which I have seen of your personality has not lessened it. Let me put it to you as man to man. No one wants to rake up your past and make you unduly uncomfortable. It is over, and you are now in smooth waters, but if you persist in this marriage you will raise up a swarm of powerful enemies who will never leave you alone until they have made England too hot to hold you. Is the game worth it ? Surely you would be wiser if you left the lady alone. It would not be pleasant for you if these facts of your past were brought to her notice.'

" The Baron has little waxed tips of hair under his nose, like the short antennæ of an insect. These quivered with amusement as he listened, and he finally broke into a gentle chuckle.

" ' Excuse my amusement, Mr. Holmes,' said he, ' but it is really funny to see you trying to play a hand with no cards in it. I don't think anyone could do it better, but it is rather pathetic, all the same. Not a colour card there, Mr. Holmes, nothing but the smallest of the small.'

" 'So you think.'

" 'So I know. Let me make the thing clear to you, for my own hand is so strong that I can afford to show it. I have been fortunate enough to win the entire affection of this lady. This was given to me in spite of the fact that I told her very clearly of all the unhappy incidents in my past life. I also told her that certain wicked and designing persons—I hope you recognize yourself—would come to her and tell her these things, and I warned her how to treat them. You have heard of post-hypnotic suggestion, Mr. Holmes? Well, you will see how it works, for a man of personality can use hypnotism without any vulgar passes or tomfoolery. So she is ready for you and, I have no doubt, would give you an appointment, for she is quite amenable to her father's will—save only in the one little matter.'

" Well, Watson, there seemed to be no more to say, so I took my leave with as much cold dignity as I could summon, but, as I had my hand on the door-handle, he stopped me.

" 'By the way, Mr. Holmes,' said he, 'did you know Le Brun, the French agent?'

" 'Yes,' said I.

" 'Do you know what befell him?'

" 'I heard that he was beaten by some Apaches in the Montmartre district and crippled for life.'

" 'Quite true, Mr. Holmes. By a curious coincidence he had been inquiring into my affairs only a week before. Don't do it, Mr. Holmes; it's not a lucky thing to do. Several have found that out. My last word to you is, go your own way and let me go mine. Good-bye!'

" So there you are, Watson. You are up to date now."

" The fellow seems dangerous."

" Mighty dangerous. I disregard the blusterer, but this is the sort of man who says rather less than he means."

" Must you interfere? Does it really matter if he marries the girl?"

" Considering that he undoubtedly murdered his last wife, I should say it mattered very much. Besides, the client! Well, well, we need not discuss that. When you have finished your coffee you had best come home with me, for the blithe Shinwell will be there with his report."

We found him sure enough, a huge, coarse, red-faced, scorbutic man, with a pair of vivid black eyes which were the only external sign of the very cunning mind within. It seems that he had dived down into what was peculiarly his kingdom, and beside him on the settee was a brand which he had brought up in the shape of a slim, flame-like young woman with a pale, intense face, youthful, and yet so worn with sin and sorrow that one read the terrible years which had left their leprous mark upon her.

" This is Miss Kitty Winter," said Shinwell Johnson, waving his fat hand as an introduction. " What she don't know—well, there, she'll speak for herself. Put

AS I HAD MY HAND ON THE DOOR HANDLE, HE STOPPED ME.

Illustration by Howard K. Elcock for the *Strand Magazine*, February, 1925.

my hand right on her, Mr. Holmes, within an hour of your message."

" I'm easy to find," said the young woman. " Hell, London, gets me every time. Same address for Porky Shinwell. We're old mates, Porky, you and I. But, by Cripes ! there is another who ought to be down in a lower hell than we if there was any justice in the world ! That is the man you are after, Mr. Holmes."

Holmes smiled. " I gather we have your good wishes, Miss Winter."

" If I can help to put him where he belongs, I'm yours to the rattle," said our visitor, with fierce energy. There was an intensity of hatred in her white, set face and her blazing eyes such as woman seldom and man never can attain. " You needn't go into my past, Mr. Holmes. That's neither here nor there. But what I am Adelbert Gruner made me. If I could pull him down ! " She clutched frantically with her hands into the air. " Oh, if I could only pull him into the pit where he has pushed so many ! "

" You know how the matter stands ? "

" Porky Shinwell has been telling me. He's after some other poor fool and wants to marry her this time. You want to stop it. Well, you surely know enough about this devil to prevent any decent girl in her senses wanting to be in the same parish with him."

" She is not in her senses. She is madly in love. She has been told all about him. She cares nothing."

" Told about the murder ? "

" Yes."

" My Lord, she must have a nerve ! "

" She puts them all down as slanders."

" Couldn't you lay proofs before her silly eyes ? "

" Well, can you help us do so ? "

" Ain't I a proof myself ? If I stood before her and told her how he used me——"

" Would you do this ? "

" Would I ? Would I not ! "

" Well, it might be worth trying. But he has told her most of his sins and had pardon from her, and I understand she will not reopen the question."

" I'll lay he didn't tell her all," said Miss Winter. " I caught a glimpse of one or two murders besides the one that made such a fuss. He would speak of someone in his velvet way and then look at me with a steady eye and say : 'He died within a month.' It wasn't hot air, either. But I took little notice—you see, I loved him myself at that time. Whatever he did went with me, same as with this poor fool ! There was just one thing that shook me. Yes, by Cripes ! if it had not been for his poisonous, lying tongue that explains and soothes, I'd have left him that very night. It's a book he has—a brown leather book with a lock, and his arms in gold on the outside. I think he was a bit drunk that night, or he would not have shown it to me."

" What was it, then ? "

" I tell you, Mr. Holmes, this man collects women, and takes a pride in his collection, as some men collect moths or butterflies. He had it all in that book. Snap-shot photographs, names, details, everything about them. It was a beastly book—a book no man, even if he had come from the gutter, could have put together. But it was Adelbert Gruner's book all the same. 'Souls I have ruined.' He could have put that on the outside if he had been so minded. However, that's neither here nor there, for the book would not serve you, and, if it would, you can't get it."

"Where is it?"

"How can I tell you where it is now? It's more than a year since I left him. I know where he kept it then. He's a precise, tidy cat of a man in many of his ways, so maybe it is still in the pigeon-hole of the old bureau in the inner study. Do you know his house?"

"I've been in the study," said Holmes.

"Have you, though? You haven't been slow on the job if you only started this morning. Maybe dear Adelbert has met his match this time. The outer study is the one with the Chinese crockery in it—big glass cupboard between the windows. Then behind his desk is the door that leads to the inner study—a small room where he keeps papers and things."

"Is he not afraid of burglars?"

"Adelbert is no coward. His worst enemy couldn't say that of him. He can look after himself. There's a burglar alarm at night. Besides, what is there for a burglar—unless they got away with all this fancy crockery?"

"No good," said Shinwell Johnson, with the decided voice of the expert. "No fence wants stuff of that sort that you can neither melt nor sell."

"Quite so," said Holmes. "Well, now, Miss Winter, if you would call here to-morrow evening at five, I would consider in the meanwhile whether your suggestion of seeing this lady personally may not be arranged. I am exceedingly obliged to you for your co-operation. I need not say that my clients will consider liberally——"

"None of that, Mr. Holmes," cried the young woman. "I am not out for money. Let me see this man in the mud, and I've got all I worked for—in the mud with my foot on his cursed face. That's my price. I'm with you to-morrow or any other day so long as you are on his track. Porky here can tell you always where to find me."

I did not see Holmes again until the following evening, when we dined once more at our Strand restaurant. He shrugged his shoulders when I asked him what luck he had had in his interview. Then he told the story, which I would repeat in this way. His hard, dry statement needs some little editing to soften it into the terms of real life.

"There was no difficulty at all about the appointment," said Holmes, "for the girl glories in showing abject filial obedience in all secondary things in an attempt to atone for her flagrant breach of it in her engagement. The General 'phoned that all was ready and the fiery Miss W. turned up according to schedule, so that at half-past five a cab deposited us outside 104 Berkeley Square, where the old soldier resides—one of those awful grey London castles which would make a church seem frivolous. A footman showed us into a great yellow-curtained drawing-room, and there was the lady awaiting us, demure, pale, self-contained, as inflexible and remote as a snow image on a mountain.

"I don't quite know how to make her clear to you, Watson. Perhaps you may meet her before we are through, and you can use your own gift of words. She is beautiful, but with the ethereal other-world beauty of some fanatic whose thoughts are set on high. I have seen such faces in the pictures of the old masters of the Middle Ages. How a beast-man could have laid his vile paws upon such a being of the beyond I cannot imagine. You may have noticed how extremes call to each other, the spiritual to the animal, the cave-man to the
14 angel. You never saw a worse case than this.

"She knew what we had come for, of course—that villain had lost no time in poisoning her mind against us. Miss Winter's advent rather amazed her, I think, but she waved us into our respective chairs like a reverend abbess receiving two rather leprous mendicants. If your head is inclined to swell, my dear Watson, take a course of Miss Violet de Merville.

"'Well, sir,' said she, in a voice like the wind from an iceberg, 'your name is familiar to me. You have called, as I understand, to malign my fiancé, Baron Gruner. It is only by my father's request that I see you at all, and I warn you in advance that anything you can say could not possibly have the slightest effect upon my mind.'

"I was sorry for her, Watson. I thought of her for the moment as I would have thought of a daughter of my own. I am not often eloquent. I use my head, not my heart. But I really did plead with her with all the warmth of words that I could find in my nature. I pictured to her the awful position of the woman who only wakes to a man's character after she is his wife—a woman who has to submit to be caressed by bloody hands and lecherous lips. I spared her nothing—the shame, the fear, the agony, the hopelessness of it all. All my hot words could not bring one tinge of colour to those ivory cheeks or one gleam of emotion to those abstracted eyes. I thought of what the rascal had said about a post-hypnotic influence. One could really believe that she was living above the earth in some ecstatic dream. Yet there was nothing indefinite in her replies.

"'I have listened to you with patience, Mr. Holmes,' said she. 'The effect upon my mind is exactly as predicted. I am aware that Adelbert, that my fiancé, has had a stormy life in which he has incurred bitter hatreds and most unjust aspersions. You are only the last of a series who have brought their slanders before me. Possibly you mean well, though I learn that you are a paid agent who would have been equally willing to act for the Baron as against him. But in any case I wish you to understand once for all that I love him and that he loves me, and that the opinion of all the world is no more to me than the twitter of those birds outside the window. If his noble nature has ever for an instant fallen, it may be that I have been specially sent to raise it to its true and lofty level. I am not clear,' here she

14 *the cave-man to the angel.* Dr. Richard Asher has deduced from Holmes' remarks on this occasion ("Holmes and the Fair Sex") that it "seems highly probable that Holmes the scholar and aesthete had suffered the mortifying experience of being attracted to one who was intellectually and socially below him. His antagonism to sentiment and his support of pure reasoning against emotional thinking no doubt sprang from his youthful suffering (a type of suffering so brilliantly portrayed by Mr. Somerset Maugham in *Of Human Bondage* and again in *His Excellency*), and his immediate success with Milverton's housemaid no doubt reflects his previous experience in that field."

turned her eyes upon my companion, 'who this young lady may be.'

" I was about to answer when the girl broke in like a whirlwind. If ever you saw flame and ice face to face, it was those two women.

" 'I'll tell you who I am,' she cried, springing out of her chair, her mouth all twisted with passion—' I am his last mistress. I am one of a hundred that he has tempted and used and ruined and thrown into the refuse heap, as he will you also. *Your* refuse heap is more likely to be a grave, and maybe that's the best. I tell you, you foolish woman, if you marry this man he'll be the death of you. It may be a broken heart or it may be a broken neck, but he'll have you one way or the other. It's not out of love for you I'm speaking. I don't care a tinker's curse whether you live or die. It's out of hate for him and to spite him and to get back on him for what he did to me. But it's all the same, and you needn't look at me like that, my fine lady, for you may be lower than I am before you are through with it.'

" 'I should prefer not to discuss such matters,' said Miss de Merville coldly. 'Let me say once for all that I am aware of three passages in my fiancé's life in which he became entangled with designing women, and that I am assured of his hearty repentance for any evil that he may have done.'

" 'Three passages!' screamed my companion. 'You fool! You unutterable fool!'

" 'Mr. Holmes, I beg that you will bring this interview to an end,' said the icy voice. 'I have obeyed my father's wish in seeing you, but I am not compelled to listen to the ravings of this person.'

" With an oath Miss Winter darted forward, and if I had not caught her wrist she would have clutched this maddening woman by the hair. I dragged her towards the door, and was lucky to get her back into the cab without a public scene, for she was beside herself with rage. In a cold way I felt pretty furious myself, Watson, for there was something indescribably annoying in the calm aloofness and supreme self-complaisance of the woman whom we were trying to save. So now once again you know exactly how we stand, and it is clear that I must plan some fresh opening move, for this gambit won't work. I'll keep in touch with you, Watson, for it is more than likely that you will have your part to play, though it is just possible that the next move may lie with them rather than with us."

" 'MR. HOLMES, I BEG THAT YOU WILL BRING THIS INTERVIEW TO AN END,' SAID THE ICY VOICE."

Illustration by Howard K. Elcock for the *Strand Magazine*, February, 1925.

And it did. Their blow fell—or his blow rather, for never could I believe that the lady was privy to it. I think I could show you the very paving-stone upon which I stood when my eyes fell upon the placard, and a pang of horror passed through my very soul. It was between
15 the Grand Hotel and Charing Cross Station, where a one-legged newsvendor displayed his evening papers. The date was just two days after the last conversation. There, black upon yellow, was the terrible news-sheet :

MURDEROUS
ATTACK
UPON
SHERLOCK
HOLMES.

I think I stood stunned for some moments. Then I have a confused recollection of snatching at a paper, of the remonstrance of the man, whom I had not paid, and, finally, of standing in the doorway of a chemist's shop while I turned up the fateful paragraph. This was how it ran :

" We learn with regret that Mr. Sherlock Holmes, the well-known private detective, was the victim this morning of a murderous assault which has left him in a precarious position. There are no exact details to hand, but the event seems to have occurred about twelve o'clock in Regent Street, outside the Café Royal. The attack was made by two men armed with sticks, and Mr. Holmes was beaten about the head and body, receiving injuries which the doctors describe as most serious. He was carried to Charing Cross Hospital, and afterwards insisted upon being taken to his rooms in Baker Street. The miscreants who attacked him appear to have

15 *the Grand Hotel.* In Trafalgar Square; it has now been converted into business premises.

MURDEROUS ATTACK UPON SHERLOCK HOLMES.

Illustration by Howard K. Elcock for the *Strand Magazine*, February, 1925.

"... OUTSIDE THE CAFÉ ROYAL."

The illustration shows the Regent Street entrance to the Café Royal, London. The Café lies only a hundred yards from the Criterion Restaurant, across the width of Piccadilly Circus. Mr. Michael Harrison has called it "the nearest thing London has ever had to the artist-patronized restaurants and cafés of the better class with which Paris is still well-provided. . . . The original Café Royal was opened by a Frenchman, Monsieur Nicol, in 1865, in Glasshouse Street. . . . When M. Nicol died, in 1907, the Café Royal was established as the most popular restaurant-café with the artist and writer of London."

been respectably dressed men, who escaped from the bystanders by passing through the Café Royal and out into Glasshouse Street behind it. No doubt they belonged to that criminal fraternity which has so often had occasion to bewail the activity and ingenuity of the injured man."

I need not say that my eyes had hardly glanced over the paragraph before I had sprung into a hansom and was on my way to Baker Street. I found Sir Leslie Oakshott, the famous surgeon, in the hall and his brougham waiting at the kerb.

"No immediate danger," was his report. "Two lacerated scalp wounds and some considerable bruises. Several stitches have been necessary. Morphine has been injected and quiet is essential, but an interview of a few minutes would not be absolutely forbidden."

With this permission I stole into the darkened room. The sufferer was wide awake, and I heard my name in a hoarse whisper. The blind was three-quarters down, but one ray of sunlight slanted through and struck the bandaged head of the injured man. A crimson patch
had soaked through the white linen compress. I sat 16
beside him and bent my head.

"All right, Watson. Don't look so scared," he muttered in a very weak voice. "It's not as bad as it seems."

"Thank God for that!"

"I'm a bit of a single-stick expert, as you know. I took most of them on my guard. It was the second man that was too much for me."

"What can I do, Holmes? Of course, it was that damned fellow who set them on. I'll go and thrash the hide off him if you give the word."

"Good old Watson! No, we can do nothing there unless the police lay their hands on the men. But their get-away had been well prepared. We may be sure of that. Wait a little. I have my plans. The first thing is to exaggerate my injuries. They'll come to you for news. Put it on thick, Watson. Lucky if I live the week out—concussion—delirium—what you like! You can't overdo it."

"But Sir Leslie Oakshott?"

"Oh, he's all right. He shall see the worst side of me. I'll look after that."

"Anything else?"

"Yes. Tell Shinwell Johnson to get that girl out of the way. Those beauties will be after her now. They know, of course, that she was with me in the case. If they dared to do me in it is not likely they will neglect her. That is urgent. Do it to-night."

"I'll go now. Anything more?"

"Put my pipe on the table—and the tobacco-slipper. Right! Come in each morning and we will plan our campaign."

I arranged with Johnson that evening to take Miss Winter to a quiet suburb and see that she lay low until the danger was past.

For six days the public were under the impression that Holmes was at the door of death. The bulletins were very grave and there were sinister paragraphs in the papers. My continual visits assured me that it was

"THE ATTACK WAS MADE BY TWO MEN ARMED WITH STICKS . . ."

Illustration by Howard K. Elcock for the *Strand Magazine*, March, 1925.

16 *A crimson patch had soaked through the white linen compress.* "It would seem that [Sir Leslie Oakshott, the famous surgeon] did a pretty poor job of suturing, for the dressing was blood-soaked almost before he got out of the house, and an even worse job of after-care, for eight days later Holmes' head was still girt with bloody bandages," Dr. Samuel R. Meaker commented in "Watson Medicus."

not so bad as that. His wiry constitution and his determined will were working wonders. He was recovering fast, and I had suspicions at times that he was really finding himself faster than he pretended, even to me. There was a curious secretive streak in the man which led to many dramatic effects, but left even his closest friend guessing as to what his exact plans might be. He pushed to an extreme the axiom that the only safe plotter was he who plotted alone. I was nearer him than anyone else, and yet I was always conscious of the gap between.

On the seventh day the stitches were taken out, in spite of which there was a report of erysipelas in the evening papers. The same evening papers had an announcement which I was bound, sick or well, to carry to my friend. It was simply that among the passengers on the Cunard boat *Ruritania*, starting from Liverpool on Friday, was the Baron Adelbert Gruner, who had some important financial business to settle in the States before his impending wedding to Miss Violet de Merville, only daughter of, etc., etc. Holmes listened to the news with a cold, concentrated look upon his pale face, which told me that it hit him hard.

17 " Friday ! " he cried. " Only three clear days. I believe the rascal wants to put himself out of danger's way. But he won't, Watson ! By the Lord Harry, he won't ! Now, Watson, I want you to do something for me."

" I am here to be used, Holmes."

" Well, then, spend the next twenty-four hours in an intensive study of Chinese pottery."

He gave no explanations and I asked for none. By long experience I had learned the wisdom of obedience. But when I had left his room I walked down Baker Street, revolving in my head how on earth I was to carry out so strange an order. Finally I drove to the London
18 Library in St. James' Square, put the matter to my friend Lomax, the sub-librarian, and departed to my rooms with a goodly volume under my arm.

It is said that the barrister who crams up a case with such care that he can examine an expert witness upon the Monday has forgotten all his forced knowledge before the Saturday. Certainly I should not like now to pose as an authority upon ceramics. And yet all that evening, and all that night with a short interval for rest, and all next morning I was sucking in knowledge and committing names to memory. There I learned of the hall-marks of the great artist-decorators, of the mystery of cyclical dates, the marks of the Hung-wu and the beauties of the Yung-lo, the writings of Tang-ying, and the glories of the primitive period of the Sung and the Yuan. I was charged with all this information when I called upon Holmes next evening. He was out of bed now, though you would not have guessed it from the published reports, and he sat with his much-bandaged head resting upon his hand in the depth of his favourite arm-chair.

" Why, Holmes," I said, " if one believed the papers you are dying."

" That," said he, " is the very impression which I

17 *"Friday!" he cried. "Only three clear days.* Something is clearly wrong here, and there would seem to be two alternatives: 1) Holmes and Kitty Winter saw Violet de Merville on Thursday, September 4; Holmes and Watson dined that night; Holmes was attacked on the following Monday, September 8th, just *four*—not *two*—days "after the last conversation." 2) Holmes and Kitty Winter saw Violet de Merville on Saturday, September 6th; Holmes and Watson dined that night —the following *Saturday* evening, *not* "the following evening"; Holmes was attacked on the following Monday, September 8th. We believe the second alternative to be the correct one. Had Holmes and Kitty Winter seen Violet de Merville on Thursday, Baron Adelbert Gruner would hardly have waited until the following Monday morning to launch his attack on Holmes. In brief, we believe that Watson is once again up to his literary trick of telescoping a time period to create a more dramatic effect. We have seen that he did just this in *A Study in Scarlet*. We shall see that he will do it again in "The Adventure of the Creeping Man." Clearly, Holmes spent *several days* considering whether or not it would be wise to arrange an appointment between Miss de Merville and Miss Winter: "I would consider in the meanwhile whether your suggestion of seeing this lady personally may not be arranged." When Holmes decided, *on the Saturday*, that the suggestion was a good one, "There was no difficulty at all about the appointment." It was on the evening of Monday, September 15th, then—*not* the evening of Saturday, September 13th—that Holmes said: "Friday! Only three clear days."

18 *St. James's Square.* St. James's Square dates from the time of Charles II, when the adjoining King Street and Charles Street were named in honor of the Duke of York. Formerly consisting mostly of aristocratic private residences, this square now contains several large office buildings and several of the leading West End clubs.

intended to convey. And now, Watson, have you learned your lessons ? "

" At least I have tried to."

" Good. You could keep up an intelligent conversation on the subject ? "

" I believe I could."

" Then hand me that little box from the mantelpiece."

He opened the lid and took out a small object most carefully wrapped in some fine Eastern silk. This he unfolded, and disclosed a delicate little saucer of the most beautiful deep-blue colour.

" It needs careful handling, Watson. This is the real
egg-shell pottery of the Ming dynasty. No finer piece 19
ever passed through Christie's. A complete set of this would be worth a king's ransom—in fact, it is doubtful if there is a complete set outside the Imperial palace of Peking. The sight of this would drive a real connoisseur wild."

" What am I to do with it ? "

Holmes handed me a card upon which was printed :
" Dr. Hill Barton, 369 Half Moon Street." 20

" That is your name for the evening, Watson. You will call upon Baron Gruner. I know something of his habits, and at half-past eight he would probably be disengaged. A note will tell him in advance that you are about to call, and you will say that you are bringing him a specimen of an absolutely unique set of Ming china. You may as well be a medical man, since that is a part which you can play without duplicity. You are a collector, this set has come your way, you have heard of the Baron's interest in the subject, and you are not averse to selling at a price."

" What price ? "

" Well asked, Watson. You would certainly fall down badly if you did not know the value of your own wares. This saucer was got for me by Sir James, and comes, I understand, from the collection of his client. You will not exaggerate if you say that it could hardly be matched in the world."

" I could perhaps suggest that the set should be valued by an expert."

" Excellent, Watson ! You scintillate to-day. Suggest Christie or Sotheby. Your delicacy prevents your putting a price for yourself."

" But if he won't see me ? "

" Oh, yes, he will see you. He has the collection mania in its most acute form—and especially on this subject, on which he is an acknowledged authority. Sit down, Watson, and I will dictate the letter. No answer needed. You will merely say that you are coming, and why."

It was an admirable document, short, courteous, and stimulating to the curiosity of the connoisseur. A district messenger was duly dispatched with it. On the same evening, with the precious saucer in my hand and the card of Dr. Hill Barton in my pocket, I set off on my own adventure.

The beautiful house and grounds indicated that Baron

"IT NEEDS CAREFUL HANDLING, WATSON."

Illustration by John Richard Flanagan for *Collier's Magazine*, November 8, 1924.

19 *This is the real egg-shell pottery of the Ming dynasty*. In his autobiography, *Those Days* (London, 1940), Mr. E. C. Bentley tells of an early dinner of the original Sherlock Holmes Society at which Sir Eric MacLaglan, the Director of the Victoria and Albert Museum, declared that there *is no* Ming pottery of a "deep-blue colour."

20 *Half Moon Street*." So called from a tavern located there. Half Moon Street leads into Curzon Street.

"VERY FINE—VERY FINE INDEED!" HE SAID AT LAST.

Illustration by Howard K. Elcock for the *Strand Magazine*, March, 1925.

Gruner was, as Sir James had said, a man of considerable wealth. A long winding drive, with banks of rare shrubs on either side, opened out into a great gravelled square adorned with statues. The place had been built by a South African gold king in the days of the great boom, and the long, low house with the turrets at the corners, though an architectural nightmare, was imposing in its size and solidity. A butler who would have adorned a bench of bishops showed me in, and handed me over to a plush-clad footman, who ushered me into the Baron's presence.

He was standing at the open front of a great case which stood between the windows, and which contained part of his Chinese collection. He turned as I entered, with a small brown vase in his hand.

" Pray sit down, doctor," said he. " I was looking over my own treasures and wondering whether I could really afford to add to them. This little Tang specimen, which dates from the seventh century, would probably interest you. I am sure you never saw finer workmanship or a richer glaze. Have you the Ming saucer with you of which you spoke ? "

I carefully unpacked it and handed it to him. He seated himself at his desk, pulled over the lamp, for it was growing dark, and set himself to examine it. As he did so the yellow light beat upon his own features, and I was able to study them at my ease.

He was certainly a remarkably handsome man. His European reputation for beauty was fully deserved. In figure he was not more than of middle size, but was built upon graceful and active lines. His face was swarthy, almost Oriental, with large, dark, languorous eyes which might easily hold an irresistible fascination for women. His hair and moustache were raven black : the latter short, pointed, and carefully waxed. His features were regular and pleasing, save only his straight, thin-lipped mouth. If ever I saw a murderer's mouth it was there—a cruel, hard gash in the face, compressed, inexorable, and terrible. He was ill-advised to train his moustache away from it, for it was Nature's danger-signal, set as a warning to his victims. His voice was engaging and his manners perfect. In age I should have put him at little over thirty, though his record afterwards showed that he was forty-two.

" Very fine—very fine indeed ! " he said at last. " And you say you have a set of six to correspond. What puzzles me is that I should not have heard of such magnificent specimens. I only know of one in England to match this, and it is certainly not likely to be in the market. Would it be indiscreet if I were to ask you, Dr. Hill Barton, how you obtained this ? "

" Does it really matter ? " I asked, with as careless an air as I could muster. " You can see that the piece is genuine, and, as to the value, I am content to take an expert's valuation."

" Very mysterious," said he, with a quick, suspicious flash of his dark eyes. " In dealing with objects of such value, one naturally wishes to know all about the transaction. That the piece is genuine is certain. I have no doubts at all about that. But suppose—I am bound to take every possibility into account—that it should prove afterwards that you had no right to sell ? "

" I would guarantee you against any claim of the sort."

" That, of course, would open up the question as to what your guarantee was worth."

" My bankers would answer that."

" Quite so. And yet the whole transaction strikes me as rather unusual."

" You can do business or not," said I, with indifference. " I have given you the first offer, as I understood that you were a connoisseur, but I shall have no difficulty in other quarters."

" Who told you I was a connoisseur ? "

" I was aware that you had written a book upon the subject."

" Have you read the book ? "

" No."

" Dear me, this becomes more and more difficult for me to understand ! You are a connoisseur and collector with a very valuable piece in your collection, and yet you have never troubled to consult the one book which would have told you of the real meaning and value of what you held. How do you explain that ? "

" I am a very busy man. I am a doctor in practice."

" That is no answer. If a man has a hobby he follows it up, whatever his other pursuits may be. You said in your note that you were a connoisseur."

" So I am."

" Might I ask you a few questions to test you ? I am obliged to tell you, doctor—if you are indeed a doctor—that the incident becomes more and more suspicious. I would ask you what do you know of the Emperor Shomu and how do you associate him with the Shoso-in near Nara ? Dear me, does that puzzle you ? Tell me a little about the Northern Wei dynasty and its place in the history of ceramics."

I sprang from my chair in simulated anger.

" This is intolerable, sir," said I. " I came here to do you a favour, and not to be examined as if I were a schoolboy. My knowledge on these subjects may be second only to your own, but I certainly shall not answer questions which have been put in so offensive a way."

He looked at me steadily. The languor had gone from his eyes. They suddenly glared. There was a gleam of teeth from between those cruel lips.

" What is the game ? You are here as a spy. You are an emissary of Holmes. This is a trick that you are playing upon me. The fellow is dying, I hear, so he sends his tools to keep watch upon me. You've made your way in here without leave, and, by God ! you may find it harder to get out than to get in."

He had sprung to his feet, and I stepped back, bracing myself for an attack, for the man was beside himself with rage. He may have suspected me from the first ; certainly this cross-examination had shown him the truth ; but it was clear that I could not hope to deceive him. He dived his hand into a side-drawer and rummaged furiously. Then something struck upon his ear, for he stood listening intently.

"Ah!" he cried. "Ah!" and dashed into the room behind him.

Two steps took me to the open door, and my mind will ever carry a clear picture of the scene within. The window leading out to the garden was wide open. Beside it, looking like some terrible ghost, his head girt with bloody bandages, his face drawn and white, stood Sherlock Holmes. The next instant he was through the gap, and I heard the crash of his body among the laurel bushes outside. With a howl of rage the master of the house rushed after him to the open window.

And then! It was done in an instant, and yet I clearly saw it. An arm—a woman's arm—shot out from among the leaves. At the same instant the Baron uttered a horrible cry—a yell which will always ring in my memory. He clapped his two hands to his face and rushed round the room, beating his head horribly against the walls. Then he fell upon the carpet, rolling and writhing, while scream after scream resounded through the house.

"Water! For God's sake, water!" was his cry.

I seized a carafe from a side-table and rushed to his aid. At the same moment the butler and several footmen ran in from the hall. I remember that one of them fainted as I knelt by the injured man and turned that awful face to the light of the lamp. The vitriol was eating into it everywhere and dripping from the ears and the chin. One eye was already white and glazed. The other was red and inflamed. The features which I had admired a few minutes before were now like some beautiful painting over which the artist has passed a wet and foul sponge. They were blurred, discoloured, inhuman, terrible.

In a few words I explained exactly what had occurred, so far as the vitriol attack was concerned. Some had climbed through the window and others had rushed out on to the lawn, but it was dark and it had begun to rain. Between his screams the victim raged and raved against the avenger. "It was that hell-cat, Kitty Winter!" he cried. "Oh, the she-devil! She shall pay for it! She shall pay! Oh, God in heaven, this pain is more than I can bear!"

I bathed his face in oil, put cotton wadding on the
21 raw surfaces, and administered a hypodermic of morphia.
All suspicion of me had passed from his mind in the presence of this shock, and he clung to my hands as if I might have the power even yet to clear those dead-fish eyes which gazed up at me. I could have wept over the ruin had I not remembered very clearly the vile life which had led up to so hideous a change. It was loathsome to feel the pawing of his burning hands, and I was relieved when his family surgeon, closely followed by a specialist, came to relieve me of my charge. An inspector of police had also arrived, and to him I handed my real card. It would have been useless as well as foolish to do otherwise, for I was nearly as well known by sight at the Yard as Holmes himself. Then I left that

"AH!" HE CRIED. "AH!" AND DASHED INTO THE ROOM BEHIND HIM.

Illustration by Howard K. Elcock for the *Strand Magazine*, March, 1925.

21 *a hypodermic of morphia.* "Perfectly reasonable treatment at that time but where, oh, where did Dr. Hill Barton, Watson's alias and disguise, carry his oil, wadding and morphia?" Dr. Vernon Pennell asked in his "Resume of the Medical Life of John H. Watson, M.D., Late of the Army Medical Department." "Why on earth should he take these with him on an expedition to one with whom he only expected a discussion on ceramics?"

house of gloom and terror. Within an hour I was at Baker Street.

Holmes was seated in his familiar chair, looking very pale and exhausted. Apart from his injuries, even his iron nerves had been shocked by the events of the evening, and he listened with horror to my account of the Baron's transformation.

" The wages of sin, Watson—the wages of sin ! " said 22
he. " Sooner or later it will always come. God knows, there was sin enough," he added, taking up a brown volume from the table. " Here is the book the woman talked of. If this will not break off the marriage, nothing ever could. But it will, Watson. It must. No self-respecting woman could stand it."

" It is his love diary ? "

" Or his lust diary. Call it what you will. The moment the woman told us of it I realized what a tremendous weapon was there, if we could but lay our hands on it. I said nothing at the time to indicate my thoughts, for this woman might have given it away. But I brooded over it. Then this assault upon me gave me the chance of letting the Baron think that no precautions need be taken against me. That was all to the good. I would have waited a little longer, but his visit to America forced my hand. He would never have left so compromising a document behind him. Therefore we had to act at once. Burglary at night is impossible. He takes precautions. But there was a chance in the evening if I could only be sure that his attention was engaged. That was where you and your blue saucer came in. But I had to be sure of the position of the book, and I knew I had only a few minutes in which to act, for my time was limited by your knowledge of Chinese pottery. Therefore I gathered the girl up at the last moment. How could I guess what the little packet was that she carried so carefully under her cloak ? I thought she had come altogether on my business, but it seems she had some of her own."

" He guessed I came from you."

" I feared he would. But you held him in play just long enough for me to get the book, though not long enough for an unobserved escape. Ah, Sir James, I am very glad you have come ! "

Our courtly friend had appeared in answer to a previous summons. He listened with the deepest attention to Holmes' account of what had occurred.

" You have done wonders—wonders ! " he cried, when he had heard the narrative. " But if these injuries are as terrible as Dr. Watson describes, then surely our purpose of thwarting the marriage is sufficiently gained without the use of this horrible book."

Holmes shook his head.

" Women of the de Merville type do not act like that. She would love him the more as a disfigured martyr. No, no. It is his moral side, not his physical, which we have to destroy. That book will bring her back to earth—and I know nothing else that could. It is in his own writing. She cannot get past it."

Sir James carried away both it and the precious saucer.
As I was myself overdue, I went down with him into 23

22 *"The wages of sin, Watson—the wages of sin!"* Holmes draws upon Romans, 6.23.

23 *As I was myself overdue.* "Overdue where?" the late Elmer Davis asked in his essay, "On the Emotional Geology of Baker Street." "Not at the bedside of a patient; since Holmes' distant cousin Dr. Verner had bought up his practice, eight years earlier, he had not returned to his profession. Overdue, obviously, (in view of his marriage soon after) in the drawing-room of a fiancée who did not take his involvement in Holmes' affairs as lightly as did Mary Morstan Watson."

the street. A brougham was waiting for him. He sprang in, gave a hurried order to the cockaded coachman, and drove swiftly away. He flung his overcoat half out of the window to cover the armorial bearings upon the panel, but I had seen them in the glare of our fanlight none the less. I gasped with surprise. Then I turned back and ascended the stair to Holmes' room.

" I have found out who our client is," I cried, bursting with my great news. " Why, Holmes, it is——"

24 " It is a loyal friend and a chivalrous gentleman," said Holmes, holding up a restraining hand. " Let that now and for ever be enough for us."

I do not know how the incriminating book was used. Sir James may have managed it. Or it is more probable that so delicate a task was entrusted to the young lady's father. The effect, at any rate, was all that could be desired. Three days later appeared a paragraph in the *Morning Post* to say that the marriage between Baron Adelbert Gruner and Miss Violet de Merville would not take place. The same paper had the first police-court hearing of the proceedings against Miss Kitty Winter on the grave charge of vitriol-throwing. Such extenuating circumstances came out in the trial that the sentence, as will be remembered, was the lowest that was
25 possible for such an offence. Sherlock Holmes was threatened with a prosecution for burglary, but when an object is good and a client is sufficiently illustrious, even the rigid British law becomes human and elastic. My friend has not yet stood in the dock.

24 *a loyal friend and a chivalrous gentleman."* We see that King Edward VII continued to give evidence of his faith in Holmes' powers. We see also that Holmes, since his refusal to accept a knighthood, has mellowed somewhat in his personal attitude toward King Edward.

25 *the lowest that was possible for such an offence.* "Of all the persons involved in this sordid affair," Mr. Bliss Austin wrote in "Three Footnotes to 'The Adventure of the Illustrious Client,' " "the one who makes the greatest claim to our sympathies is Kitty Winter, the lass who went to see Baron Gruner's etchings and then repaid him by etching his face with acid. Was she English and descended from that branch of the family which lost a pair of brothers in Guy Fawkes' plot? Perhaps, but her experience with the Baron suggests that her origin was Central European. It is possible that she was a relative of Zigmund Winter, the great Czech novelist, whose historical fiction is described by the *Encyclopædia Britannica* as possessing artistic force and delicacy of treatment. Since the gentleman was born in 1846, Kitty might even have been his daughter. It is difficult to prove this, however, because of the lack of data about her. For, in spite of Watson's statement that her first police-court trial was reported by the papers, a search through the dailies of the day fails to reveal anything of the kind. Apparently the patronage of the Illustrious Client carried great weight with the press."

A Note on the "Canonicity" of "The Adventure of the Illustrious Client": Mr. D. Martin Dakin writes: "Of 'The Illustrious Client' it is . . . difficult to speak with confidence. Mr. Blakeney has seen in Holmes' remarks to Sir James Damery ("I am accustomed to have mystery at one end of my cases, but to have it at both ends is too confusing')—an echo of what he said in 'The Second Stain,' and felt it was unlike him to yield so easily and not insist on the complete confidence of his client as he did to Lord Bellinger and Mr. Trelawney Hope. Yet the story is well-written. Holmes' account of his impression of Miss Violet de Merville is admirable, and the description of the vitriol-throwing, horrible as it is, shows Watson at his most powerful as a word-painter. I am inclined to think that the story as a whole is by Watson, but that the editor of the series has added paragraphs at the beginning and end—possibly the title also—to exaggerate its importance. It is absurd to describe it as 'the supreme moment of my friend's career,' for even if we assume the Client to have been Edward VII, Holmes had already rendered services to the reigning families of Holland and Scandinavia, not to speak of the Pope, and possessed an amethyst-and-gold snuff-box from the King of Bohemia and an emerald tie-pin from Queen Victoria herself for his services in the matter of the Bruce-Partington plans, while the issues at stake, however charming Miss de Merville may have been, must be counted trivial indeed compared with those in, say, 'The Second Stain.' "

We may add that Conan Doyle's own opinion of "The Adventure of the Illustrious Client" was a high one: ". . . not remarkable for plot," he wrote in the *Strand Magazine*, March, 1927, "but it has a certain quality and moves adequately in lofty circles . . ." And in a letter to John Gore (1926), Conan Doyle wrote: "If I were to choose the six best Holmes stories I should certainly include 'The Illustrious Client.' "

71

THE ADVENTURE OF THE RED CIRCLE

[*Wednesday, September 24, to Thursday, September 25, 1902*]

I

"WELL, Mrs. Warren, I cannot see that you have any particular cause for uneasiness, nor do I understand why I, whose time is of some value, should interfere in the matter. I really have other things to engage me." So spoke Sherlock Holmes, and turned back to the great scrap-book in which he was arranging and indexing some of his recent material.

But the landlady had the pertinacity, and also the cunning, of her sex. She held her ground firmly.

"You arranged an affair for a lodger of mine last year," she said—"Mr. Fairdale Hobbs."

"Ah, yes—a simple matter."

"But he would never cease talking of it—your kindness, sir, and the way in which you brought light into the darkness. I remembered his words when I was in doubt and darkness myself. I know you could if you only would."

Holmes was accessible upon the side of flattery, and also, to do him justice, upon the side of kindliness. The two forces made him lay down his gum-brush with a sigh of resignation and push back his chair.

"Well, well, Mrs. Warren, let us hear about it, then. You don't object to tobacco, I take it? Thank you, Watson—the matches! You are uneasy, as I understand, because your new lodger remains in his rooms and you cannot see him. Why, bless you, Mrs. Warren, if I were your lodger you often would not see me for weeks on end."

"No doubt, sir; but this is different. It frightens me, Mr. Holmes. I can't sleep for fright. To hear his quick step moving here and moving there from early morning to late at night, and yet never to catch so much as a glimpse of him—it's more than I can stand. My husband is as nervous over it as I am, but he is out at his work all day, while I get no rest from it. What is he hiding for? What has he done? Except for the girl, I am all alone in the house with him, and it's more than my nerves can stand."

Holmes leaned forward and laid his long, thin fingers upon the woman's shoulder. He had an almost hypnotic power of soothing when he wished. The scared look faded from her eyes, and her agitated features smoothed into their usual commonplace. She sat down in the chair which he had indicated.

1 *fifty shillings a week.* About $12.50 U.S. at the time.

2 *five pounds a week.* About $25.

"If I take it up I must understand every detail," said he. "Take time to consider. The smallest point may be the most essential. You say that the man came ten days ago, and paid you for a fortnight's board and lodging?"

1 "He asked my terms, sir. I said fifty shillings a week. There is a small sitting-room and bedroom, and all complete, at the top of the house."

"Well?"

2 "He said, 'I'll pay you five pounds a week if I can have it on my own terms.' I'm a poor woman, sir, and Mr. Warren earns little, and the money meant much to me. He took out a ten-pound note, and he held it out to me then and there. 'You can have the same every fortnight for a long time to come if you keep the terms,' he said. 'If not, I'll have no more to do with you.'"

"What were the terms?"

"Well, sir, they were that he was to have a key of the house. That was all right. Lodgers often have them. Also, that he was to be left entirely to himself, and never, upon any excuse, to be disturbed."

"Nothing wonderful in that, surely?"

"Not in reason, sir. But this is out of all reason. He has been there for ten days, and neither Mr. Warren, nor I, nor the girl has once set eyes upon him. We can hear that quick step of his pacing up and down, up and down, night, morning, and noon; but except on that first night he has never once gone out of the house."

"Oh, he went out the first night, did he?"

"Yes, sir, and returned very late—after we were all in bed. He told me after he had taken the rooms that he would do so, and asked me not to bar the door. I heard him come up the stair after midnight."

"But his meals?"

"It was his particular direction that we should always, when he rang, leave his meal upon a chair, outside his door. Then he rings again when he has finished, and we take it down from the same chair. If he wants anything else he prints it on a slip of paper and leaves it."

"Prints it?"

"Yes, sir; prints it in pencil. Just the word, nothing more. Here's one I brought to show you—SOAP. Here's another—MATCH. This is one he left the first morning—DAILY GAZETTE. I leave that paper with his breakfast every morning."

"Dear me, Watson," said Holmes, staring with great curiosity at the slips of foolscap which the landlady had handed to him, "this is certainly a little unusual. Seclusion I can understand; but why print? Printing is a clumsy process. Why not write? What would it suggest, Watson?"

"That he desired to conceal his handwriting."

"But why? What can it matter to him that his landlady should have a word of his writing? Still, it may be as you say. Then, again, why such laconic messages?"

"I cannot imagine."

"It opens a pleasing field for intelligent speculation. The words are written with a broad-pointed, violet-tinted pencil of a not unusual pattern. You will observe that the

"DEAR ME, WATSON," SAID HOLMES, STARING WITH GREAT CURIOSITY AT THE SLIPS OF FOOLSCAP . . .

Illustration by Joseph Simpson for the *Strand Magazine*, March, 1911.

paper is torn away at the side here after the printing was done, so that the ' S ' of ' SOAP ' is partly gone. Suggestive, Watson, is it not ? "

" Of caution ? "

" Exactly. There was evidently some mark, some thumb-print, something which might give a clue to the person's identity. Now, Mrs. Warren, you say that the **3**
man was of middle size, dark, and bearded. What age would he be ? "

" Youngish, sir—not over thirty."

" Well, can you give me no further indications ? "

" He spoke good English, sir, and yet I thought he was a foreigner by his accent."

" And he was well dressed ? "

" Very smartly dressed, sir—quite the gentleman. Dark clothes—nothing you would note."

" He gave no name ? "

" No, sir."

" And has had no letters or callers ? "

" None."

" But surely you or the girl enter his room of a morning ? "

" No, sir ; he looks after himself entirely."

" Dear me ! that is certainly remarkable. What about his luggage ? "

" He had one big brown bag with him—nothing else."

" Well, we don't seem to have much material to help us. Do you say nothing has come out of that room—absolutely nothing ? "

The landlady drew an envelope from her bag ; from it she shook out two burnt matches and a cigarette-end upon the table.

" They were on his tray this morning. I brought them because I had heard that you can read great things out of small ones."

Holmes shrugged his shoulders.

" There is nothing here," said he. " The matches have, of course, been used to light cigarettes. That is obvious from the shortness of the burnt end. Half the match is consumed in lighting a pipe or cigar. But, dear me ! this cigarette stub is certainly remarkable. The gentleman was bearded and moustached, you say ? "

" Yes, sir."

" I don't understand that. I should say that only a clean-shaven man could have smoked this. Why, Watson, even your modest moustache would have been singed."

" A holder ? " I suggested.

" No, no ; the end is matted. I suppose there could not be two people in your rooms, Mrs. Warren ? "

" No, sir. He eats so little that I often wonder it can keep life in one."

" Well, I think we must wait for a little more material. After all, you have nothing to complain of. You have received your rent, and he is not a troublesome lodger, though he is certainly an unusual one. He pays you well, and if he chooses to lie concealed it is no direct business of yours. We have no excuse for an intrusion upon his privacy until we have some reason to think that there

3 *some thumb-print, something which might give a clue to the person's identity*. Mr. Rolfe Boswell, in his article, "Squaring the Red Circle," provides chronologists with a valuable clue to the proper dating of this adventure: "It was Sir Francis Galton (b. 1822, Birmingham; d. 1911, London) famous British anthropologist, who worked out the foundations of the Galton-Henry system of fingerprint classification. Final touches were added by Sir Edward Richard Henry, the knight with no last name, who later became police commissioner for the metropolitan district of London. This system was adopted by Scotland Yard in 1901. . . . The point here is that few criminals were aware of the evidential utility of fingerprints before the turn of this century. Certainly non-criminals . . . would not have known earlier about such police methods for establishing identities. Therefore, the [mysterious lodger] in 'The Adventure of the Red Circle' case tore off the corner of [the] notepaper because, during 1901, or thereafter, [that lodger] had read magazine or newspaper articles about Scotland Yard's fingerprint system, newly-introduced." The year, then, was not before 1901.

is a guilty reason for it. I've taken up the matter, and I won't lose sight of it. Report to me if anything fresh occurs, and rely upon my assistance if it should be needed."

"There are certainly some points of interest in this case, Watson," he remarked, when the landlady had left us. "It may, of course, be trivial—individual eccentricity; or it may be very much deeper than appears on the surface. The first thing that strikes one is the obvious possibility that the person now in the rooms may be entirely different from the one who engaged them."

"Why should you think so?"

"Well, apart from this cigarette-end, was it not suggestive that the only time the lodger went out was immediately after his taking the rooms? He came back—or someone came back—when all witnesses were out of the way. We have no proof that the person who came back was the person who went out. Then, again, the man who took the rooms spoke English well. This other, however, prints 'match' when it should have been 'matches.' I can imagine that the word was taken out of a dictionary, which would give the noun but not the plural. The laconic style may be to conceal the absence of knowledge of English. Yes, Watson, there are good reasons to suspect that there has been a substitution of lodgers."

"But for what possible end?"

"Ah! there lies our problem. There is one rather obvious line of investigation." He took down the great book in which, day by day, he filed the agony columns of the various London journals. "Dear me!" said he, turning over the pages, "what a chorus of groans, cries, and bleatings! What a rag-bag of singular happenings! But surely the most valuable hunting-ground that ever was given to a student of the unusual! This person is alone, and cannot be approached by letter without a breach of that absolute secrecy which is desired. How is any news or any message to reach him from without? Obviously by advertisement through a newspaper. There seems no other way, and fortunately we need concern ourselves with the one paper only. Here are the *Daily Gazette* extracts of the last fortnight. 'Lady with a black boa at Prince's Skating Club'—that we may pass. 'Surely Jimmy will not break his mother's heart'—that appears to be irrelevant. 'If the lady who fainted in the Brixton bus'—she does not interest me. 'Every day my heart longs——' Bleat, Watson—unmitigated bleat! Ah! this is a little more possible. Listen to this: 'Be patient. Will find some sure means of communication. Meanwhile, this column.—G.' That is two days after Mrs. Warren's lodger arrived. It sounds plausible, does it not? The mysterious one could understand English, even if he could not print it. Let us see if we can pick up the trace again. Yes, here we are—three days later. 'Am making successful arrangements. Patience and prudence. The clouds will pass.—G.' Nothing for a week after that. Then comes something much more definite: 'The path is clearing. If I find chance signal message remember code agreed—one A, two B, and so on. You will hear soon.—G.' That was in yesterday's paper, and there is nothing
4 in to-day's. It's all very appropriate to Mrs. Warren's

4 *nothing in to-day's.* It should be noted that there is a discrepancy between Mrs. Warren's statement regarding the length of time her lodger had occupied the "small sitting-room and bedroom, and all complete" ("He has been there for ten days"), and Holmes' comments while searching the file of the *Daily Gazette.* The schedule is clearly as follows: First day—lodger arrives. Third day—first advertisement appears ("two days after Mrs. Warren's lodger arrived"). Sixth day—second advertisement appears ("three days later"). "Nothing for a week after that." Fourteenth day—third advertisement appears ("yesterday's paper"). Fifteenth day—"nothing in to-day's." By the days on which the newspapers were published, we see that "to-day" was not Sunday, Monday, Tuesday, or Friday; it follows that it must be Wednesday, Thursday, or Saturday. But it was not Saturday: on the *second* day Holmes picked up the morning newspaper from the table; Mr. Warren was on his way to work at Morton & Waylight's when he was assaulted. The second day was certainly not a Sunday. The case opened, then, on a Wednesday or a Thursday.

lodger. If we wait a little, Watson, I don't doubt that the affair will grow more intelligible."

So it proved; for in the morning I found my friend standing on the hearthrug with his back to the fire, and a 5
smile of complete satisfaction upon his face.

"How's this, Watson?" he cried, picking up the paper from the table. "'High red house with white stone facings. Third floor. Second window left. After dusk. —G.' That is definite enough. I think after breakfast we must make a little reconnaissance of Mrs. Warren's neighbourhood. Ah, Mrs. Warren! what news do you bring us this morning?"

Our client had suddenly burst into the room with an explosive energy which told of some new and momentous development.

"It's a police matter, Mr. Holmes!" she cried. "I'll have no more of it! He shall pack out of that with his baggage. I would have gone straight up and told him so, only I thought it was but fair to you to take your opinion first. But I'm at the end of my patience, and when it comes to knocking my old man about——"

"Knocking Mr. Warren about?"

"Using him roughly, anyway."

"But who used him roughly?"

"Ah! that's what we want to know! It was this morning, sir. Mr. Warren is a timekeeper at Morton & Waylight's, in Tottenham Court Road. He has to be out of the house before seven. Well, this morning he had not got ten paces down the road when two men came up behind him, threw a coat over his head, and bundled him into a cab that was beside the kerb. They drove him an hour, and then opened the door and shot him out. He lay in the roadway so shaken in his wits that he never saw what became of the cab. When he picked himself up he found he was on Hampstead Heath; so he took a bus home, and there he lies now on the sofa, while I came straight round to tell you what had happened."

"Most interesting," said Holmes. "Did he observe the appearance of these men—did he hear them talk?"

"No; he is clean dazed. He just knows that he was lifted up as if by magic and dropped as if by magic. Two at least were in it, and maybe three."

"And you connect this attack with your lodger?"

"Well, we've lived there fifteen years and no such happenings ever came before. I've had enough of him. Money's not everything. I'll have him out of my house before the day is done."

"Wait a bit, Mrs. Warren. Do nothing rash. I begin to think that this affair may be very much more important than appeared at first sight. It is clear now that some danger is threatening your lodger. It is equally clear that his enemies, lying in wait for him near your door, mistook your husband for him in the foggy morning light. On discovering their mistake they released him. What they would have done had it not been a mistake, we can only conjecture."

"Well, what am I to do, Mr. Holmes?"

"I have a great fancy to see this lodger of yours, Mrs. Warren."

5 *I found my friend standing on the hearthrug.* As the late Professor Jay Finley Christ was one of the first to point out, "It is uncertain whether or not Watson was living at Baker Street [at this time]. On the second morning he 'found Holmes waiting,' and Holmes made reference to 'our quarters.' These things are not conclusive; they might have been said in either case." We shall see that "The Adventure of the Red Circle" was subsequent to "The Adventure of the Illustrious Client"; Watson was therefore in his rooms in Queen Anne Street at this time.

". . . TWO MEN CAME UP BEHIND HIM, THREW A COAT OVER HIS HEAD, AND BUNDLED HIM INTO A CAB . . ."

Illustration by H. M. Brock for the *Strand Magazine*, March, 1911.

"I don't see how that is to be managed, unless you break in the door. I always hear him unlock it as I go down the stair after I leave the tray."

"He has to take the tray in. Surely we could conceal ourselves and see him do it."

The landlady thought for a moment.

"Well, sir, there's the box-room opposite. I could arrange a looking-glass, maybe, and if you were behind the door——"

"Excellent!" said Holmes. "When does he lunch?"

"About one, sir."

"Then Dr. Watson and I will come round in time. For the present, Mrs. Warren, good-bye."

At half-past twelve we found ourselves upon the steps of Mrs. Warren's house—a high, thin, yellow-brick edifice in Great Orme Street, a narrow thoroughfare at the north-east side of the British Museum. Standing as it does near the corner of the street, it commands a view down Howe
6 Street, with its more pretentious houses. Holmes pointed with a chuckle to one of these, a row of residential flats, which projected so that they could not fail to catch the eye.

"See, Watson!" said he. "'High red house with stone facings.' There is the signal station all right. We know the place, and we know the code; so surely our task should be simple. There's a 'To Let' card in that window. It is evidently an empty flat to which the confederate has access. Well, Mrs. Warren, what now?"

"I have it all ready for you. If you will both come up and leave your boots below on the landing, I'll put you there now."

It was an excellent hiding-place which she had arranged. The mirror was so placed that, seated in the dark, we could very plainly see the door opposite. We had hardly settled down in it, and Mrs. Warren left us, when a distant tinkle announced that our mysterious neighbour had rung. Presently the landlady appeared with the tray, laid it down upon a chair beside the closed door, and then, treading heavily, departed. Crouching together in the angle of the door, we kept our eyes fixed upon the mirror. Suddenly, as the landlady's footsteps died away, there was the creak of a turning key, the handle revolved, and two thin hands darted out and lifted the tray from the chair. An instant later it was hurriedly replaced, and I caught a glimpse of a dark, beautiful, horrified face glaring at the narrow opening of the box-room. Then the door crashed to, the key turned once more, and all was silence. Holmes twitched my sleeve, and together we stole down the stair.

"I will call again in the evening," said he to the expectant landlady. "I think, Watson, we can discuss this business better in our own quarters."

"My surmise, as you saw, proved to be correct," said he, speaking from the depths of his easy-chair. "There has been a substitution of lodgers. What I did not foresee is that we should find a woman, and no ordinary woman, Watson."

"She saw us."

"Well, she saw something to alarm her. That is certain. The general sequence of events is pretty clear, is it

6 *Howe Street.* "Watson's 'Great Orme Street . . . at the northeast side of the British Museum' identifies itself so readily with Great Ormond Street, which ends a very few blocks to the northeast of the Museum, that it is disappointing to find no Howe Street running into it, or any street with a name in any way suggesting Howe," Mr. S. F. Blake wrote in "Sherlock Holmes and the Italian Cipher." "In fact, no Howe Street or Place is listed for the entire London area in the City Council's 'List of streets and places within the administrative county of London' (1901)."

. . . I CAUGHT A GLIMPSE OF A DARK, BEAUTIFUL, HORRIFIED FACE . . .

Illustration by H. M. Brock for the *Strand Magazine*, March, 1911.

not ? A couple seek refuge in London from a very terrible and instant danger. The measure of that danger is the rigour of their precautions. The man, who has some work which he must do, desires to leave the woman in absolute safety while he does it. It is not an easy problem, but he solved it in an original fashion, and so effectively that her presence was not even known to the landlady who supplies her with food. The printed messages, as is now evident, were to prevent her sex being discovered by her writing. The man cannot come near the woman, or he will guide their enemies to her. Since he cannot communicate with her direct, he has recourse to the agony column of a paper. So far all is clear."

" But what is at the root of it ? "

" Ah, yes, Watson—severely practical, as usual ! What is at the root of it all ? Mrs. Warren's whimsical problem enlarges somewhat and assumes a more sinister aspect as we proceed. This much we can say : that it is no ordinary love escapade. You saw the woman's face at the sign of danger. We have heard, too, of the attack upon the landlord, which was undoubtedly meant for the lodger. These alarms, and the desperate need for secrecy, argue that the matter is one of life or death. The attack upon Mr. Warren further shows that the enemy, whoever they are, are themselves not aware of the substitution of the female lodger for the male. It is very curious and complex, Watson."

" Why should you go further in it ? What have you to gain from it ? "

" What, indeed ? It is Art for Art's sake, Watson. I suppose when you doctored you found yourself studying cases without thought of a fee ? "

" For my education, Holmes."

" Education never ends, Watson. It is a series of lessons, with the greatest for the last. This is an instructive case. There is neither money nor credit in it, and yet one would wish to tidy it up. When dusk comes we should find ourselves one stage advanced in our investigation."

When we returned to Mrs. Warren's rooms, the gloom of a London winter evening had thickened into one grey curtain, a dead monotone of colour, broken only by the sharp yellow squares of the windows and the blurred haloes of the gas-lamps. As we peered from the darkened sitting-room of the lodging-house, one more dim light glimmered high up through the obscurity.

" Someone is moving in that room," said Holmes in a whisper, his gaunt and eager face thrust forward to the window-pane. " Yes, I can see his shadow. There he is again ! He has a candle in his hand. Now he is peering across. He wants to be sure that she is on the look-out. Now he begins to flash. Take the message also, Watson, that we may check each other. A single flash—that is 'A,' surely. Now, then. How many did you make it ? Twenty. So did I. That should mean 'T.' A T— [7] that's intelligible enough ! Another 'T.' Surely this is the beginning of a second word. Now, then—TENTA. Dead stop. That can't be all, Watson ? 'ATTENTA' gives no sense. Nor is it any better as three words—

7 *Twenty*. The manuscript of "The Adventure of the Red Circle" reads here: *Nineteen*.

8 *'PERI.'* Almost half a century after the event, the late Professor Louis E. Lord of the Classics Department at Oberlin College pointed out that the Italian alphabet contains no K (and, he might have added, no W, X, or Y, and precious little of J). His argument, as reported by Mr. Vincent Starrett in his "Explanation" (Introduction) to *221B: Studies in Sherlock Holmes,* was as follows: "The language used is Italian, we are informed, although Holmes and Watson, who are intercepting the message, do not at first suspect it. The first letter of the message is a single flash, A, and the next is twenty flashes—'T' says Holmes. But, alas, the Italian alphabet has no letter K. . . . and so its twentieth letter is U. The full message as read by Holmes is 'Attenta, pericolo.' Yet the omission of K must have misplaced every letter below it, and Holmes should have read, not 'Attenta pericolo,' but 'Assemsa, oeqicnkn.' Or, if Signor Lucca, sending his warning, had—for the convenience of Holmes and Watson—used the English alphabet, his wife, who knew little English and was expecting the message in Italian, would have read 'Auueoua, qesicpmp.' Well, it is a sufficiently startling message, either way; and it is no slight testimony to the ability of Sherlock Holmes that he brought off the case with honors."

To this, Mr. S. F. Blake has responded that ". . . it is unfortunately necessary for me to point out [an error] which Prof. Lord himself committed. He says that Holmes should have read the message "Assemsa, oeqicnkn.' Since Holmes counted the first three series of flashes as 1, 20, 20, and then translated them A, T, T, we have to infer that he counted the other flashes in this word as 5, 14, 20, 1 in order to translate it as 'attenta.' But 1, 20, 20, 5, 14, 20, 1 flashes do not spell out 'assemsa' in any language known to me, certainly not in English or Italian, the only two in question here. They spell 'attenta' in the English alphabet and 'auueoua' in the Italian. In the English alphabet, 'assemsa' would call for 1, 19, 19, 5, 13, 19, 1 flashes, and in Italian, 1, 18, 18, 5, 12, 18, 1. A similar situation holds, obviously, with regard to the word 'pericolo' (or oeqicnkn). It is clearly *lèse majesté,* or something approaching it, to accuse the keen-eyed Holmes of being unable to count up to 20."

We have noted above that the manuscript of the adventure *does* read *Nineteen* for *Twenty* (enabling Holmes to spell out "assemsa" *in English,* and Mr. Donald A. Yates has expressed his view that the code agreed upon must have been *to spell Italian in the English alphabet* ("A Final Illumination of the Lucca Code'). But this still leaves an element of mystery in the situation: Holmes did not know that the message was in Italian when he was counting to 19; he realized that later. Thus neither a *Nineteen* or a *Twenty* will fully resolve the problem. We may conclude this note by adding that Mr. Blake's own experiments in flashing messages by means of a lighted candle have convinced him that it would have taken at least 477 waves of the candle, occupying about 4¾ minutes, to deliver the message.

'AT. TEN. TA,' unless 'T.A.' are a person's initials. There it goes again! What's that? ATTE—why, it is the same message over again. Curious, Watson, very curious! Now he is off once more! AT—why, he is repeating it for the third time. 'ATTENTA' three times! How often will he repeat it? No, that seems to be the finish. He has withdrawn from the window. What do you make of it, Watson?"

"A cipher message, Holmes."

My companion gave a sudden chuckle of comprehension. "And not a very obscure cipher, Watson," said he. "Why, of course, it is Italian! The 'A' means that it is addressed to a woman. 'Beware! Beware! Beware!' How's that, Watson?"

"I believe you have hit it."

"Not a doubt of it. It is a very urgent message, thrice repeated to make it more so. But beware of what? Wait a bit; he is coming to the window once more."

Again we saw the dim silhouette of a crouching man and the whisk of the small flame across the window, as the signals were renewed. They came more rapidly than before—so rapid that it was hard to follow them.

"'PERICOLO'—'Pericolo'—Eh, what's that, Watson? Danger, isn't it? Yes, by Jove! it's a danger signal.
8 There he goes again! 'PERI.' Halloa, what on earth——"

The light had suddenly gone out, the glimmering square of window had disappeared, and the third floor formed a dark band round the lofty building, with its tiers of shining casements. That last warning cry had been suddenly cut short. How, and by whom? The same thought occurred on the instant to us both. Holmes sprang up from where he crouched by the window.

"This is serious, Watson," he cried. "There is some devilry going forward! Why should such a message stop in such a way? I should put Scotland Yard in touch with this business—and yet, it is too pressing for us to leave."

"Shall I go for the police?"

"We must define the situation a little more clearly. It may bear some more innocent interpretation. Come, Watson, let us go across ourselves and see what we can make of it."

II

As we walked rapidly down Howe Street I glanced back at the building which we had left. There, dimly outlined at the top window, I could see the shadow of a head, a woman's head, gazing tensely, rigidly, out into the night, waiting with breathless suspense for the renewal of that interrupted message. At the doorway of the Howe Street flats a man, muffled in a cravat and greatcoat, was leaning against the railing. He started as the hall-light fell upon our faces.

"Holmes!" he cried.

9 "Why, Gregson!" said my companion, as he shook
hands with the Scotland Yard detective. "Journeys end
10 with lovers' meetings. What brings you here?"

"The same reasons that bring you, I expect," said Gregson. "How you got on to it I can't imagine."

"Different threads, but leading up to the same tangle.

I've been taking the signals."

" Signals ? "

" Yes, from that window. They broke off in the middle. We came over to see the reason. But since it is safe in your hands I see no object in continuing the business."

" Wait a bit ! " cried Gregson, eagerly. " I'll do you this justice, Mr. Holmes, that I was never in a case yet that I didn't feel stronger for having you on my side. There's only the one exit to these flats, so we have him safe."

" Who is he ? "

" Well, well, we score over you for once, Mr. Holmes. You must give us best this time." He struck his stick sharply upon the ground, on which a cabman, his whip in his hand, sauntered over from a four-wheeler which stood on the far side of the street. " May I introduce you to Mr. Sherlock Holmes ? " he said to the cabman. " This is Mr. Leverton, of Pinkerton's American Agency."

" The hero of the Long Island Cave mystery ? " said **11**
Holmes. " Sir, I am pleased to meet you."

The American, a quiet, business-like young man, with a clean-shaven, hatchet face, flushed up at the words of commendation. " I am on the trail of my life now, Mr. Holmes," said he. " If I can get Gorgiano——"

" What ! Gorgiano of the Red Circle ? "

" Oh, he has a European fame, has he ? Well, we've learned all about him in America. We *know* he is at the bottom of fifty murders, and yet we have nothing positive we can take him on. I tracked him over from New York, and I've been close to him for a week in London, waiting some excuse to get my hand on his collar. Mr. Gregson and I ran him to ground in that big tenement house, and there's only the one door, so he can't slip us. There's three folk come out since he went in, but I'll swear he wasn't one of them."

" Mr. Holmes talks of signals," said Gregson. " I expect, as usual, he knows a good deal that we don't."

In a few clear words Holmes explained the situation as it had appeared to us. The American struck his hands together with vexation.

" He's on to us ! " he cried.

" Why do you think so ? "

" Well, it figures out that way, does it not ? Here he is, sending out messages to an accomplice—there are several of his gang in London. Then suddenly, just as by your own account he was telling them that there was danger, he broke short off. What could it mean except that from the window he had suddenly either caught sight of us in the street, or in some way come to understand how close the danger was, and that he must act right away, if he was to avoid it ? What do you suggest, Mr. Holmes ? "

" That we go up at once and see for ourselves."

" But we have no warrant for his arrest."

" He is in unoccupied premises under suspicious circumstances," said Gregson. " That is good enough for the moment. When we have him by the heels we can see if New York can't help us to keep him. I'll take the responsibility of arresting him now."

9 "*Why, Gregson!*" Mr. T. S. Blakeney has noted that we "so seldom see [Inspector Gregson] in late years that an early date may be assumed for most of his cases." "The Adventure of the Red Circle" must therefore be taken as an indication that Inspector Gregson's tenure at Scotland Yard (like Inspector Lestrade's) was a lengthy one.

10 "*Journeys end with lovers' meetings.* For the second time, Holmes slightly misquotes *Twelfth Night,* Act II, Scene 3, line 46.

11 "*The hero of the Long Island Cave mystery?*" "The mystery, on true Sherlockian principles, is that there are no caves on Long Island," the late Christopher Morley wrote in "Was Sherlock Holmes an American?"

"BY GEORGE! IT'S BLACK GORGIANO HIMSELF!" CRIED THE AMERICAN DETECTIVE.

Illustration by H. M. Brock for the *Strand Magazine*, April, 1911.

HOLMES . . . WAS PASSING IT BACKWARDS AND FORWARDS ACROSS THE WINDOW-PANES.

Illustration by H. M. Brock for the *Strand Magazine*, April, 1911.

Our official detectives may blunder in the matter of intelligence, but never in that of courage. Gregson climbed the stair to arrest this desperate murderer with the same absolutely quiet and business-like bearing with which he would have ascended the official staircase of Scotland Yard. The Pinkerton man had tried to push past him, but Gregson had firmly elbowed him back. London dangers were the privilege of the London force.

The door of the left-hand flat upon the third landing was standing ajar. Gregson pushed it open. Within all was absolute silence and darkness. I struck a match, and lit the detective's lantern. As I did so, and as the flicker steadied into a flame, we all gave a gasp of surprise. On the deal boards of the carpetless floor there was outlined a fresh track of blood. The red steps pointed towards us, and led away from an inner room, the door of which was closed. Gregson flung it open and held his light full blaze in front of him, whilst we all peered eagerly over his shoulders.

In the middle of the floor of the empty room was huddled the figure of an enormous man, his clean-shaven, swarthy face grotesquely horrible in its contortion, and his head encircled by a ghastly crimson halo of blood, lying in a broad wet circle upon the white woodwork. His knees were drawn up, his hands thrown out in agony, and from the centre of his broad, brown, upturned throat there projected the white haft of a knife driven blade-deep into his body. Giant as he was, the man must have gone down like a pole-axed ox before that terrific blow. Beside his right hand a most formidable horn-handled, two-edged dagger lay upon the floor, and near it a black kid glove.

" By George ! it's Black Gorgiano himself ! " cried the American detective. " Someone has got ahead of us this time."

" Here is the candle in the window, Mr. Holmes," said Gregson. " Why, whatever are you doing ? "

Holmes had stepped across, had lit the candle, and was passing it backwards and forwards across the window-panes. Then he peered into the darkness, blew the candle out, and threw it on the floor.

" I rather think that will be helpful," said he. He came over and stood in deep thought while the two professionals were examining the body. " You say that three people came out from the flat while you were waiting downstairs," said he, at last. " Did you observe them closely ? "

" Yes, I did."

" Was there a fellow about thirty, black-bearded, dark, of middle size ? "

" Yes ; he was the last to pass me."

" That is your man, I fancy. I can give you his description, and we have a very excellent outline of his footmark. That should be enough for you."

" Not much, Mr. Holmes, among the millions of London."

" Perhaps not. That is why I thought it best to summon this lady to your aid."

We all turned round at the words. There, framed in the doorway, was a tall and beautiful woman—the mysterious lodger of Bloomsbury. Slowly she advanced, her face pale and drawn with a frightful apprehension, her eyes fixed and staring, her terrified gaze riveted upon the dark figure on the floor.

" You have killed him ! " she muttered. " Oh, *Dio mio*, you have killed him ! " Then I heard a sudden sharp intake of her breath, and she sprang into the air with a cry of joy. Round and round the room she danced, her hands clapping, her dark eyes gleaming with delighted wonder, and a thousand pretty Italian exclamations pouring from her lips. It was terrible and amazing to see such a woman so convulsed with joy at such a sight. Suddenly she stopped and gazed at us all with a questioning stare.

" But you ! You are police, are you not ? You have killed Giuseppe Gorgiano. Is it not so ? "

" We are police, madam."

She looked round into the shadows of the room.

" But where, then, is Gennaro ? " she asked. " He is my husband, Gennaro Lucca. I am Emilia Lucca, and we are both from New York. Where is Gennaro ? He called me this moment from this window, and I ran with all my speed."

" It was I who called," said Holmes.

" You ! How could you call ? "

" Your cipher was not difficult, madam. Your presence here was desirable. I knew that I had only to flash ' *Vieni* ' and you would surely come."

The beautiful Italian looked with awe at my companion.

" I do not understand how you know these things," she said. " Giuseppe Gorgiano—how did he——" She paused, and then suddenly her face lit up with pride and delight. " Now I see it ! My Gennaro ! My splendid, beautiful Gennaro, who has guarded me safe from all harm, he did it, with his own strong hand he killed the monster ! Oh, Gennaro, how wonderful you are ! What woman could ever be worthy of such a man ? "

" Well, Mrs. Lucca," said the prosaic Gregson, laying his hand upon the lady's sleeve with as little sentiment as if she were a Notting Hill hooligan, " I am not very clear yet who you are or what you are ; but you've said enough to make it very clear that we shall want you at the Yard."

" One moment, Gregson," said Holmes. " I rather fancy that this lady may be as anxious to give us information as we can be to get it. You understand, madam, that your husband will be arrested and tried for the death of the man who lies before us ? What you say may be used
in evidence. But if you think that he has acted from **12**
motives which are not criminal, and which he would wish to have known, then you cannot serve him better than by telling us the whole story."

" Now that Gorgiano is dead we fear nothing," said the lady. " He was a devil and a monster, and there can be no judge in the world who would punish my husband for having killed him."

" In that case," said Holmes, " my suggestion is that we lock this door, leave things as we found them, go with this lady to her room, and form our opinion after we have heard what it is that she has to say to us."

SLOWLY SHE ADVANCED, HER FACE PALE AND DRAWN WITH A FRIGHTFUL APPREHENSION . . .

Illustration by H. M. Brock for the *Strand Magazine*, April, 1911.

12 *What you say may be used in evidence.* We note that Holmes here uses the correct formula—not the "used in evidence against you" favored by some writers of fictional detective stories.

Half an hour later we were seated, all four, in the small sitting-room of Signora Lucca, listening to her remarkable narrative of those sinister events, the ending of which we had chanced to witness. She spoke in rapid and fluent but very unconventional English, which, for the sake of clearness, I will make grammatical.

" I was born in Posilippo, near Naples," said she, " and was the daughter of Augusto Barelli, who was the chief lawyer and once the deputy of that part. Gennaro was in my father's employment, and I came to love him, as any woman must. He had neither money nor position—nothing but his beauty and strength and energy—so my father forbade the match. We fled together, were married at Bari, and sold my jewels to gain the money which would take us to America. This was four years ago, and we have been in New York ever since.

" Fortune was very good to us at first. Gennaro was able to do a service to an Italian gentleman—he saved him from some ruffians in the place called the Bowery, and so made a powerful friend. His name was Tito Castalotte, and he was the senior partner of the great firm of Castalotte & Zamba, who are the chief fruit importers of New York. Signor Zamba is an invalid, and our new friend Castalotte has all power within the firm, which employs more than three hundred men. He took my husband into his employment, made him head of a department, and showed his goodwill towards him in every way. Signor Castalotte was a bachelor, and I believe that he felt as if Gennaro was his son, and both my husband and I loved him as if he were our father. We had taken and furnished a little house in Brooklyn, and our whole future seemed assured, when that black cloud appeared which was soon to overspread our sky.

" One night, when Gennaro returned from his work, he brought a fellow-countryman back with him. His name was Gorgiano, and he had come also from Posilippo. He was a huge man, as you can testify, for you have looked upon his corpse. Not only was his body that of a giant, but everything about him was grotesque, gigantic, and terrifying. His voice was like thunder in our little house. There was scarce room for the whirl of his great arms as he talked. His thoughts, his emotions, his passions, all were exaggerated and monstrous. He talked, or rather roared, with such energy that others could but sit and listen, cowed with the mighty stream of words. His eyes blazed at you and held you at his mercy. He was a terrible and wonderful man. I thank God that he is dead !

" He came again and again. Yet I was aware that Gennaro was no more happy than I was in his presence. My poor husband would sit pale and listless, listening to the endless raving upon politics and upon social questions which made up our visitor's conversation. Gennaro said nothing, but I who knew him so well could read in his face some emotion which I had never seen there before. At first I thought that it was dislike. And then, gradually, I understood that it was more than dislike. It was fear—a deep, secret, shrinking fear. That night—the night that I read his terror—I put my arms round him and I implored him by his love for me and by all that he held dear to hold nothing from me, and to tell me why this huge man overshadowed him so.

" He told me, and my own heart grew cold as ice as I listened. My poor Gennaro, in his wild and fiery days, when all the world seemed against him and his mind was driven half mad by the injustices of life, had joined a Neapolitan society, the Red Circle, which was allied to the
old Carbonari. The oaths and secrets of this brotherhood **13**
were frightful ; but once within its rule no escape was possible. When we had fled to America Gennaro thought that he had cast it all off for ever. What was his horror one evening to meet in the streets the very man who had initiated him in Naples, the giant Gorgiano, a man who had earned the name of ' Death ' in the South of Italy, for he was red to the elbow in murder ! He had come to New York to avoid the Italian police, and he had already planted a branch of this dreadful society in his new home. All this Gennaro told me, and showed me a summons which he had received that very day, a Red Circle drawn upon the head of it, telling him that a lodge would be held upon a certain date, and that his presence at it was required and ordered.

" That was bad enough, but worse was to come. I had noticed for some time that when Gorgiano came to us, as he constantly did, in the evening, he spoke much to me ; and even when his words were to my husband those terrible, glaring, wild-beast eyes of his were always turned upon me. One night his secret came out. I had awakened what he called ' love ' within him—the love of a brute—a savage. Gennaro had not yet returned when he came. He pushed his way in, seized me in his mighty arms, hugged me in his bear's embrace, covered me with kisses, and implored me to come away with him. I was struggling and screaming when Gennaro entered and attacked him. He struck Gennaro senseless and fled from the house which he was never more to enter. It was a deadly enemy that we made that night.

" A few days later came the meeting. Gennaro returned from it with a face which told me that something dreadful had occurred. It was worse than we could have imagined possible. The funds of the society were raised by blackmailing rich Italians and threatening them with violence should they refuse the money. It seems that Castalotte, our dear friend and benefactor, had been approached. He had refused to yield to threats, and he had handed the notices to the police. It was resolved now that such an example should be made of him as would prevent any other victim from rebelling. At the meeting it was arranged that he and his house should be blown up with dynamite. There was a drawing of lots as to who should carry out the deed. Gennaro saw our enemy's cruel face smiling at him as he dipped his hand in the bag. No doubt it had been prearranged in some fashion, for it was the fatal disc with the Red Circle upon it, the mandate for murder, which lay upon his palm. He was to kill his best friend, or he was to expose himself and me to the vengeance of his comrades. It was part of their fiendish system to punish those whom they feared or hated by injuring not only their own persons, but those whom they

13 *the old Carbonari.* The manuscript reads here *the famous Camorra.*

loved, and it was the knowledge of this which hung as a terror over my poor Gennaro's head and drove him nearly crazy with apprehension.

" All that night we sat together, our arms round each other, each strengthening each for the troubles that lay before us. The very next evening had been fixed for the attempt. By midday my husband and I were on our way to London, but not before he had given our benefactor full warning of his danger, and had also left such information for the police as would safeguard his life for the future.

" The rest, gentlemen, you know for yourselves. We were sure that our enemies would be behind us like our own shadows. Gorgiano had his private reasons for vengeance, but in any case we knew how ruthless, cunning, and untiring he could be. Both Italy and America are full of stories of his dreadful powers. If ever they were exerted it would be now. My darling made use of the few clear days which our start had given us in arranging for a refuge for me in such a fashion that no possible danger could reach me. For his own part, he wished to be free that he might communicate both with the American and with the Italian police. I do not myself know where he lived, or how. All that I learned was through the columns of a newspaper. But once, as I looked through my window, I saw two Italians watching the house, and I understood that in some way Gorgiano had found out our retreat. Finally Gennaro told me, through the paper, that he would signal to me from a certain window, but when the signals came they were nothing but warnings, which were suddenly interrupted. It is very clear to me now that he knew Gorgiano to be close upon him, and that, thank God ! he was ready for him when he came. And now, gentlemen, I would ask you whether we have anything to fear from the Law, or whether any judge upon earth would condemn my Gennaro for what he has done ? "

" Well, Mr. Gregson," said the American, looking across at the official, " I don't know what your British point of view may be, but I guess that in New York this lady's husband will receive a pretty general vote of thanks."

" She will have to come with me and see the Chief," Gregson answered. " If what she says is corroborated, I do not think she or her husband has much to fear. But what I can't make head or tail of, Mr. Holmes, is how on earth *you* got yourself mixed up in the matter."

" Education, Gregson, education. Still seeking knowledge at the old university. Well, Watson, you have one more specimen of the tragic and grotesque to add to your collection. By the way, it is not eight o'clock, and a
14 Wagner night at Covent Garden ! If we hurry, we might be in time for the second act."

14 *a Wagner night at Covent Garden!* Again, Mr. Rolfe Boswell, an eminent musicologist, has proved himself invaluable in dating "The Adventure of the Red Circle." His essay on the case continues: "There were no winter performances of opera at Covent Garden in those times: there was, in 1901, only a summer season. In 1902 an autumnal series was added, and there were several Wagner nights, the last of which was on Thursday, 25 September, when Philip Brozel and Blanch Marchesi were starred in *Tristan and Isolda* with Marie Alexander as Brängane. Bearing in mind that London's equinoctial gales, as Watson remarked in 'The Five Orange Pips,' often are 'very long and very severe,' he can be excused for believing, nearly a decade later ["The Adventure of the Red Circle" was published in March–April, 1911], when he wrote up the case, that he became an Imperfect Wagnerite in 'the gloom of a London winter evening.' " We have said that the case opened on a Wednesday or a Thursday. Since Holmes' Wagner night at Covent Garden was the night of the second day, and Mr. Boswell's Wagner night at Covent Garden was Thursday, September 25, 1902, we hold that the case opened on *Wednesday, September 24, 1902.*

Bibliographical Note: As the opening page of the manuscript of this adventure attests, Conan Doyle's first thought was to call it "The Adventure of the Bloomsbury Lodger." The manuscript consists of 23 pages, folio, white vellum; it was listed in Scribner's Sherlock Holmes Catalogue at $450; in October, 1946, it was owned by Mr. Vincent Starrett of Chicago; in April, 1947, it was listed for sale by the House of El Dieff at $600; it is presently owned by Mr. J. Bliss Austin of Philadelphia.

The Adventure of the ~~Bloomsbury Lodger~~ Red Circle

"Well, Mrs Warren, I cannot see that you have any particular cause for uneasiness, nor do I understand why I, whose time is of some value, should interfere in the matter. I really have other things to engage me". So spoke Sherlock Holmes, and turned back to the great scrap book in which he was arranging and indexing some of his recent material.

But the landlady had the pertinacity, and also the cunning of her sex. She held her ground firmly.

"You arranged an affair for a lodger of mine last year" she said "Mr Fairdale Hobbs"

"Ah yes – a simple matter"

"But he would never cease talking of it – your

VIII. THE PARTNERSHIP COMES TO A CLOSE

[January to October, 1903]

The good Watson had at that time deserted me for a wife.
—Sherlock Holmes,
"The Adventure of the Blanched Soldier"

The relations between us in those latter days were peculiar.
—John H. Watson, M.D.,
"The Adventure of the Creeping Man"

72

THE ADVENTURE OF THE BLANCHED SOLDIER

[*Wednesday, January* 7, *to Monday, January 12, 1903*]

THE ideas of my friend Watson, though limited, are exceedingly pertinacious. For a long time he has worried me to write an experience of
my own. Perhaps I have rather invited this persecu- 1
tion, since I have often had occasion to point out to him how superficial are his own accounts and to accuse him of pandering to popular taste instead of confining himself rigidly to facts and figures. "Try it yourself, Holmes!" he has retorted, and I am compelled to admit that, having taken my pen in my hand, I do begin to realize that the matter must be presented in such a way as may interest the reader. The following case can hardly fail to do so, as it is among the strangest happenings in my collection, though it chanced that Watson had no note of it in his collection. Speaking of my old friend and biographer, I would take this opportunity to remark that if I burden myself with a companion in my various little inquiries it is not done out of sentiment or caprice, but it is that Watson has some remarkable characteristics of his own, to which in his modesty he has given small attention amid his exaggerated estimates of my own performances. A confederate who foresees your conclusions and course of action is always dangerous, but one to whom each development comes as a perpetual surprise, and to whom the future is always a closed book, is, indeed, an ideal helpmate.

I find from my notebook that it was in January, 1903, just after the conclusion of the Boer War, that I had my visit from Mr. James M. Dodd, a big, fresh, sunburned, upstanding Briton. The good Watson had at that time deserted me for a wife, the only selfish action which I can recall in our association. I was alone.

It is my habit to sit with my back to the window and to place my visitors in the opposite chair, where the light falls full upon them. Mr. James M. Dodd seemed somewhat at a loss how to begin the interview. I did not attempt to help him, for his silence gave me more time for observation. I have found it wise to impress clients with a sense of power, and so I gave him some of my conclusions.

"From South Africa, sir, I perceive."

"Yes, sir," he answered, with some surprise.

1 *to write an experience of my own.* "The Adventure of the Blanched Soldier" and a later adventure, "The Lion's Mane," are both ostensibly from the pen of Holmes, not Watson. But critics have found reason to doubt that he really wrote them.

"It seems very unlikely that he would start to record his cases at this stage in his career," the late Gavin Brend commented in *My Dear Holmes.* "Moreover, if he were the author the style would surely be quite different. The probability is that Watson was the author of both ["The Adventure of the Blanched Soldier" and "The Adventure of the Lion's Mane," as well as the "third-person narrative, "The Adventure of the Mazarin Stone."]"

And D. Martin Dakin has written ("The Problem of the Case-Book"): "After [Holmes'] caustic comments on Watson's attempt at popular stories, is it credible that he would have tried to write in the same vein himself? (The excuses for doing so prefaced to 'The Adventure of the Blanched Soldier' are singularly unconvincing.) Would he not rather have reserved his analytical comments on his own cases for that monumental work on the *Whole Art of Detection* which his admirers are still eagerly awaiting and which presumably is still in the hands of his literary executors? Even if he did decide to try his hand at a popular account, could he have found nothing better, even among the cases unknown to Watson, than these two rather undistinguished adventures, which do not even display his powers to any marked advantage? The narrative and style are not such as we would expect from Holmes' keen incisive mind: and if it be argued that we have no other means of telling what Holmes was like as a writer, I reply that we have. In 'The *Gloria Scott*' and 'The Musgrave Ritual' we have what are, in effect, two cases of Holmes as related by himself (not to speak of shorter accounts of past exploits given to Watson in such stories as 'The Final Problem' and 'The Adventure of the Empty House'), and they show Holmes as an excellent story-teller—lucid, powerful and clear in every detail. 'The

Adventure of the Blanched Soldier' and 'The Adventure of the Lion's Mane' come poorly out of the comparison. We conclude that these two are pseudonymous stories, possibly written up from facts supplied by Holmes to the author (whoever he may have been), but more likely pure inventions."

2 *Throgmorton Street.* This street, which lies just behind the Bank of England, is the "home" of London's stockbrokers. Its name recalls Sir Nicholas Throgmorton, a Tudor statesman who was instrumental in bringing Lady Jane Grey to the throne, and was the father-in-law of Sir Walter Raleigh. Sir Nicholas was the Ambassador to France in the reign of Queen Elizabeth I, and was said to have been poisoned by the Earl of Leicester.

3 *the Crimean V.C.* "The medal," the late A. Carson Simpson wrote in *Numismatics in the Canon*, Part III, "is an attractive one, with the diademed young head of Queen Victoria left, the legend VICTORIA REGINA and the date 1854. The reverse shows a Roman soldier with short sword and round shield; he is being crowned with a laurel-wreath by a smaller winged figure of Victory; the word CRIMEA appears on the left. The medal is suspended by a light blue ribbon, with narrow yellow edges, from a pin on a top bar of leaf design."

I LIT MY PIPE AND LEANED BACK IN MY CHAIR.

Illustration by Howard K. Elcock for the *Strand Magazine*, November, 1926.

" Imperial Yeomanry, I fancy."

" Exactly."

" Middlesex Corps, no doubt."

" That is so. Mr. Holmes, you are a wizard."

I smiled at his bewildered expression.

" When a gentleman of virile appearance enters my room with such tan upon his face as an English sun could never give, and with his handkerchief in his sleeve instead of in his pocket, it is not difficult to place him. You wear a short beard, which shows that you were not a regular. You have the cut of a riding-man. As to Middlesex, your card has already shown me that you are
2 a stockbroker from Throgmorton Street. What other regiment would you join ? "

" You see everything."

" I see no more than you, but I have trained myself to notice what I see. However, Mr. Dodd, it was not to discuss the science of observation that you called upon me this morning. What has been happening at Tuxbury Old Park ? "

" Mr. Holmes—— ! "

" My dear sir, there is no mystery. Your letter came with that heading, and as you fixed this appointment in very pressing terms it was clear that something sudden and important had occurred."

" Yes, indeed. But the letter was written in the afternoon, and a good deal has happened since then. If Colonel Emsworth had not kicked me out——"

" Kicked you out ! "

" Well, that was what it amounted to. He is a hard nail, is Colonel Emsworth. The greatest martinet in the Army in his day, and it was a day of rough language, too. I couldn't have stuck the Colonel if it had not been for Godfrey's sake."

I lit my pipe and leaned back in my chair.

" Perhaps you will explain what you are talking about."

My client grinned mischievously.

" I had got into the way of supposing that you knew everything without being told," said he. " But I will give you the facts, and I hope to God that you will be able to tell me what they mean. I've been awake all night puzzling my brain, and the more I think the more incredible does it become.

" When I joined up in January, 1901—just two years ago—young Godfrey Emsworth had joined the same squadron. He was Colonel Emsworth's only son—
3 Emsworth, the Crimean V.C.—and he had the fighting blood in him, so it is no wonder he volunteered. There was not a finer lad in the regiment. We formed a friendship—the sort of friendship which can only be made when one lives the same life and shares the same joys and sorrows. He was my mate—and that means a good deal in the Army. We took the rough and the smooth together for a year of hard fighting. Then he was hit with a bullet from an elephant gun in the action near Diamond Hill outside Pretoria. I got one letter from the hospital at Cape Town and one from Southampton. Since then not a word—not one word, Mr. Holmes, for six months and more, and he my closest pal.

"Well, when the war was over, and we all got back, I wrote to his father and asked where Godfrey was. No answer. I waited a bit and then I wrote again. This time I had a reply, short and gruff. Godfrey had gone on a voyage round the world, and it was not likely that he would be back for a year. That was all.

"I wasn't satisfied, Mr. Holmes. The whole thing seemed to me so damned unnatural. He was a good lad and he would not drop a pal like that. It was not like him. Then, again, I happened to know that he was heir to a lot of money, and also that his father and he did not always hit it off too well. The old man was sometimes a bully, and young Godfrey had too much spirit to stand it. No, I wasn't satisfied, and I determined that I would get to the root of the matter. It happened, however, that my own affairs needed a lot of straightening out, after two years' absence, and so it is only this week that I have been able to take up Godfrey's case again. But since I have taken it up I mean to drop everything in order to see it through."

Mr. James M. Dodd appeared to be the sort of person whom it would be better to have as a friend than as an enemy. His blue eyes were stern and his square jaw had set hard as he spoke.

"Well, what have you done?" I asked.

"My first move was to get down to his home, Tuxbury Old Park, near Bedford, and to see for myself how 4
the ground lay. I wrote to the mother, therefore—I had had quite enough of the curmudgeon of a father—and I made a clean frontal attack: Godfrey was my chum, I had a great deal of interest which I might tell her of our common experiences, I should be in the neighbourhood, would there be any objection, et cetera? In reply I had quite an amiable answer from her and an offer to put me up for the night. That was what took me down on Monday.

"Tuxbury Old Hall is inaccessible—five miles from anywhere. There was no trap at the station, so I had to walk, carrying my suit-case, and it was nearly dark before I arrived. It is a great wandering house, standing in a considerable park. I should judge it was of all sorts of ages and styles, starting on a half-timbered Elizabethan foundation and ending in a Victorian portico. Inside it was all panelling and tapestry and half-effaced old pictures, a house of shadows and mystery. There was a butler, old Ralph, who seemed about the same age as the house, and there was his wife, who might have been older. She had been Godfrey's nurse, and I had heard him speak of her as second only to his mother in his affections, so I was drawn to her in spite of her queer appearance. The mother I liked also—a gentle little white mouse of a woman. It was only the Colonel himself whom I barred.

"We had a bit of a barney right away, and I should have walked back to the station if I had not felt that it might be playing his game for me to do so. I was shown straight into his study, and there I found him, a huge, bow-backed man with a smoky skin and a straggling grey beard, seated behind his littered desk. A red-veined nose jutted out like a vulture's beak, and two fierce grey

4 *Bedford.* A market center on the Ouse River in Bedfordshire in south central England. John Bunyan preached there, and it is the location of one of England's largest public schools.

eyes glared at me from under tufted brows. I could understand now why Godfrey seldom spoke of his father.

" 'Well, sir,' said he in a rasping voice. 'I should be interested to know the real reasons for this visit.'

" I answered that I had explained them in my letter to his wife.

" 'Yes, yes ; you said that you had known Godfrey in Africa. We have, of course, only your word for that.'

" 'I have his letters to me in my pocket.'

" 'Kindly let me see them.'

" He glanced at the two which I handed him, and then he tossed them back.

" 'Well, what then ?' he asked.

" 'I was fond of your son Godfrey, sir. Many ties and memories united us. Is it not natural that I should wonder at his sudden silence and should wish to know what has become of him ?'

" 'I have some recollection, sir, that I had already corresponded with you and had told you what had become of him. He has gone upon a voyage round the world. His health was in a poor way after his African experiences, and both his mother and I were of opinion that complete rest and change were needed. Kindly pass that explanation on to any other friends who may be interested in the matter.'

" 'Certainly,' I answered. 'But perhaps you would have the goodness to let me have the name of the steamer and of the line by which he sailed, together with the date. I have no doubt that I should be able to get a letter through to him.'

" My request seemed both to puzzle and to irritate my host. His great eyebrows came down over his eyes and he tapped his fingers impatiently on the table. He looked up at last with the expression of one who has seen his adversary make a dangerous move at chess, and has decided how to meet it.

" 'Many people, Mr. Dodd,' said he, 'would take offence at your infernal pertinacity and would think that this insistence had reached the point of damned impertinence.'

" 'You must put it down, sir, to my real love for your son.'

" 'Exactly. I have already made every allowance upon that score. I must ask you, however, to drop these inquiries. Every family has its own inner knowledge and its own motives, which cannot always be made clear to outsiders, however well-intentioned. My wife is anxious to hear something of Godfrey's past which you are in a position to tell her, but I would ask you to let the present and the future alone. Such inquiries serve no useful purpose, sir, and place us in a delicate and difficult position.'

" So I came to a dead end, Mr. Holmes. There was no getting past it. I could only pretend to accept the situation and register a vow inwardly that I would never rest until my friend's fate had been cleared up. It was a dull evening. We dined quietly, the three of us in a gloomy, faded old room. The lady questioned me eagerly about her son, but the old man seemed morose and depressed. I was so bored by the whole proceeding that I made an excuse as soon as I decently could and retired to my bedroom. It was a large, bare room on the ground floor, as gloomy as the rest of the house, but after a year of sleeping upon the veldt, Mr. Holmes, one is not too particular about one's quarters. I opened the curtains and looked out into the garden, remarking that it was a fine night with a bright half-moon. Then I sat down by the roaring fire with the lamp on a table beside me, and endeavoured to distract my mind with a novel. I was interrupted, however, by Ralph, the old butler, who came in with a fresh supply of coals.

" 'I thought you might run short in the night-time, sir. It is bitter weather and these rooms are cold.'

" He hesitated before leaving the room, and when I looked round he was standing facing me with a wistful look upon his wrinkled face.

" 'Beg your pardon, sir, but I could not help hearing what you said of young Master Godfrey at dinner. You know, sir, that my wife nursed him, and so I may say I am his foster-father. It's natural we should take an interest. And you say he carried himself well, sir?'

" 'There was no braver man in the regiment. He pulled me out once from under the rifles of the Boers, or maybe I should not be here.'

" The old butler rubbed his skinny hands.

" 'Yes, sir, yes, that is Master Godfrey all over. He was always courageous. There's not a tree in the park, sir, that he has not climbed. Nothing would stop him. He was a fine boy—and oh, sir, he was a fine man.'

" I sprang to my feet.

" 'Look here!' I cried. 'You say he *was*. You speak as if he were dead. What is all this mystery? What has become of Godfrey Emsworth?'

" I gripped the old man by the shoulder, but he shrank away.

" 'I don't know what you mean, sir. Ask the master about Master Godfrey. He knows. It is not for me to interfere.'

" He was leaving the room, but I held his arm.

" 'Listen,' I said. 'You are going to answer one question before you leave if I have to hold you all night. Is Godfrey dead?'

" He could not face my eyes. He was like a man hypnotized. The answer was dragged from his lips. It was a terrible and unexpected one.

" 'I wish to God he was!' he cried, and, tearing himself free, he dashed from the room.

" You will think, Mr. Holmes, that I returned to my chair in no very happy state of mind. The old man's words seemed to me to bear only one interpretation. Clearly my poor friend had become involved in some criminal, or, at the least, disreputable, transaction which touched the family honour. That stern old man had sent his son away and hidden him from the world lest some scandal should come to light. Godfrey was a reckless fellow. He was easily influenced by those around him. No doubt he had fallen into bad hands and

"I GRIPPED THE OLD MAN BY THE SHOULDER, BUT HE SHRANK AWAY."

Illustration by Howard K. Elcock for the *Strand Magazine*, November, 1926.

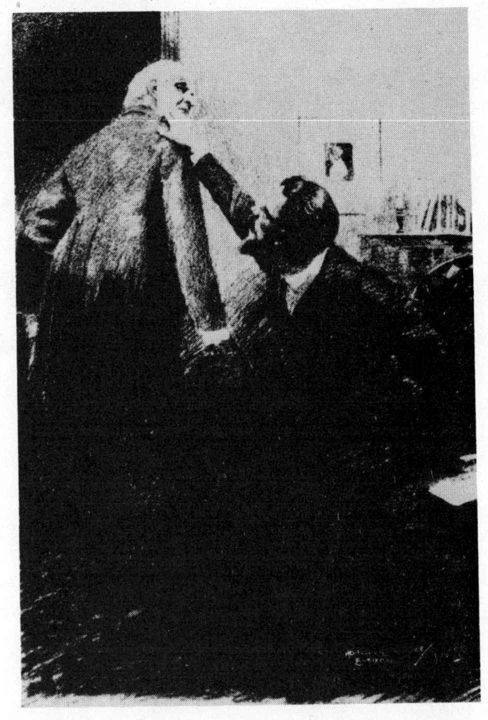

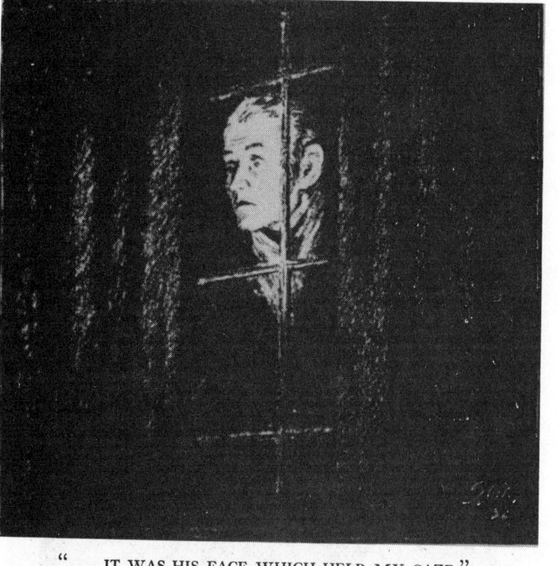

"... IT WAS HIS FACE WHICH HELD MY GAZE."

Illustration by Frederic Dorr Steele for *Liberty Magazine*, October 16, 1926.

"HE SPRANG BACK WHEN HE SAW THAT I WAS LOOKING AT HIM ..."

Illustration by Howard K. Elcock for the *Strand Magazine*, November, 1926.

been misled to his ruin. It was a piteous business, if it was indeed so, but even now it was my duty to hunt him out and see if I could aid him. I was anxiously pondering the matter when I looked up, and there was Godfrey Emsworth standing before me."

My client had paused as one in deep emotion.

"Pray continue," I said. "Your problem presents some very unusual features."

"He was outside the window, Mr. Holmes, with his face pressed against the glass. I have told you that I looked out at the night. When I did so, I left the curtains partly open. His figure was framed in this gap. The window came down to the ground and I could see the whole length of it, but it was his face which held my gaze. He was deadly pale—never have I seen a man so white. I reckon ghosts may look like that; but his eyes met mine, and they were the eyes of a living man. He sprang back when he saw that I was looking at him, and he vanished into the darkness.

"There was something shocking about the man, Mr. Holmes. It wasn't merely that ghastly face glimmering as white as cheese in the darkness. It was more subtle than that—something slinking, something furtive, something guilty—something very unlike the frank, manly lad that I had known. It left a feeling of horror in my mind.

"But when a man has been soldiering for a year or two with brother Boer as a playmate, he keeps his nerve and acts quickly. Godfrey had hardly vanished before I was at the window. There was an awkward catch, and I was some little time before I could throw it up. Then I nipped through and ran down the garden path in the direction that I thought he might have taken.

"It was a long path and the light was not very good, but it seemed to me something was moving ahead of me. I ran on and called his name, but it was no use. When I got to the end of the path there were several others branching in different directions to various outhouses. I stood hesitating, and as I did so I heard distinctly the sound of a closing door. It was not behind me in the house, but ahead of me, somewhere in the darkness. That was enough, Mr. Holmes, to assure me that what I had seen was not a vision. Godfrey had run away from me and he had shut a door behind him. Of that I was certain.

"There was nothing more I could do, and I spent an uneasy night turning the matter over in my mind and trying to find some theory which would cover the facts. Next day I found the Colonel rather more conciliatory, and as his wife remarked that there were some places of interest in the neighbourhood, it gave me an opening to ask whether my presence for one more night would incommode them. A somewhat grudging acquiescence from the old man gave me a clear day in which to make my observations. I was already perfectly convinced that Godfrey was in hiding somewhere near, but where and why remained to be solved.

" The house was so large and so rambling that a regiment might be hid away in it and no one the wiser. If the secret lay there, it was difficult for me to penetrate it. But the door which I had heard close was certainly not in the house. I must explore the garden and see what I could find. There was no difficulty in the way, for the old people were busy in their own fashion and left me to my own devices.

" There were several small outhouses, but at the end of the garden there was a detached building of some size—large enough for a gardener's or a game-keeper's residence. Could this be the place whence the sound of that shutting door had come ? I approached it in a careless fashion, as though I were strolling aimlessly round the grounds. As I did so, a small, brisk, bearded man in a black coat and bowler hat—not at all the gardener type—came out of the door. To my surprise, he locked it after him and put the key in his pocket. Then he looked at me with some surprise on his face.

" ' Are you a visitor here ? ' he asked.

" I explained that I was and that I was a friend of Godfrey's.

" ' What a pity that he should be away on his travels, for he would have so liked to see me,' I continued.

" ' Quite so. Exactly,' said he, with a rather guilty air. ' No doubt you will renew your visit at some more propitious time.' He passed on, but when I turned I observed that he was standing watching me, half-concealed by the laurels at the far end of the garden.

" I had a good look at the little house as I passed it, but the windows were heavily curtained, and, so far as one could see, it was empty. I might spoil my own game, and even be ordered off the premises, if I were too audacious, for I was still conscious that I was being watched. Therefore, I strolled back to the house and waited for night before I went on with my inquiry. When all was dark and quiet, I slipped out of my window and made my way as silently as possible to the mysterious lodge.

" I have said that it was heavily curtained, but now I found that the windows were shuttered as well. Some light, however, was breaking through one of them, so I concentrated my attention upon this. I was in luck, for the curtain had not been quite closed, and there was a crack in the shutter so that I could see the inside of the room. It was a cheery place enough, a bright lamp and a blazing fire. Opposite to me was seated the little man whom I had seen in the morning. He was smoking a pipe and reading a paper——"

" What paper ? " I asked.

My client seemed annoyed at the interruption of his narrative.

" Can it matter ? " he asked.

" It is most essential."

" I really took no notice."

" Possibly you observed whether it was a broad-leafed paper or of that smaller type which one associates with weeklies."

" Now that you mention it, it was not large. It might have been the *Spectator*. However, I had little thought to spare upon such details, for a second man was seated with his back to the window, and I could swear that this second man was Godfrey. I could not see his face, but I knew the familiar slope of his shoulders. He was leaning upon his elbow in an attitude of great melancholy, his body turned towards the fire. I was hesitating as to what I should do when there was a sharp tap on my shoulder, and there was Colonel Emsworth beside me.

" ' This way, sir ! ' said he in a low voice. He walked in silence to the house and I followed him into my own bedroom. He had picked up a time-table in the hall.

" ' There is a train to London at eight-thirty,' said he. ' The trap will be at the door at eight.'

" He was white with rage, and, indeed, I felt myself in so difficult a position that I could only stammer out a few incoherent apologies, in which I tried to excuse myself by urging my anxiety for my friend.

" ' The matter will not bear discussion,' said he abruptly. ' You have made a most damnable intrusion into the privacy of our family. You were here as a guest and you have become a spy. I have nothing more to say, sir, save that I have no wish ever to see you again.'

" At this I lost my temper, Mr. Holmes, and I spoke with some warmth.

" ' I have seen your son, and I am convinced that for some reason of your own you are concealing him from the world. I have no idea what your motives are in cutting him off in this fashion, but I am sure that he is no longer a free agent. I warn you, Colonel Emsworth, that until I am assured as to the safety and well-being of my friend I shall never desist in my efforts to get to the bottom of the mystery, and I shall certainly not allow myself to be intimidated by anything which you may say or do.'

" The old fellow looked diabolical, and I really thought he was about to attack me. I have said that he was a gaunt, fierce old giant, and though I am no weakling I might have been hard put to it to hold my own against him. However, after a long glare of rage he turned upon his heel and walked out of the room. For my
part, I took the appointed train in the morning, with the
5 full intention of coming straight to you and asking for
your advice and assistance at the appointment for which
I had already written."

Such was the problem which my visitor laid before me. It presented, as the astute reader will have already perceived, few difficulties in its solution, for a very limited choice of alternatives must get to the root of the matter. Still, elementary as it was, there were points of interest and novelty about it which may excuse my placing it upon record. I now proceeded, using my familiar method of logical analysis, to narrow down the possible solutions.

" The servants," I asked ; " how many were in the house ? "

" To the best of my belief there were only the old

5 *with the full intention of coming straight to you.* Mr. James M. Dodd journeyed to Tuxbury Old Park "on Monday." "Next day" Colonel Emsworth ordered him to leave. He took the train "in the morning"—and therefore on Wednesday morning—and came straight around to ask the advice of Holmes. Mr. Dodd further states that on the Monday night he retired after dinner "as soon as I decently could" and, looking out into the garden, saw that it was "a fine night with a bright half-moon." In 1903, there were half-moons on Monday, January 5th, and Monday, January 19th, but on the 19th the moon did not rise until close to midnight; Mr. Dodd therefore called on Holmes on the morning of *Wednesday, January 7th;* Holmes cleared up the case on a day at the "beginning of the next week"—probably Monday, January 12th, but possibly Tuesday, January 13th.

butler and his wife. They seemed to live in the simplest fashion."

"There was no servant, then, in the detached house?"

"None, unless the little man with the beard acted as such. He seemed, however, to be quite a superior person."

"That seems very suggestive. Had you any indication that food was conveyed from the one house to the other?"

"Now that you mention it, I did see old Ralph carrying a basket down the garden walk and going in the direction of this house. The idea of food did not occur to me at the moment."

"Did you make any local inquiries?"

"Yes, I did. I spoke to the station-master and also to the innkeeper in the village. I simply asked if they knew anything of my old comrade, Godfrey Emsworth. Both of them assured me that he had gone for a voyage round the world. He had come home and then had almost at once started off again. The story was evidently universally accepted."

"You said nothing of your suspicions?"

"Nothing."

"That was very wise. The matter should certainly be inquired into. I will go back with you to Tuxbury Old Park."

"To-day?"

It happened that at the moment I was clearing up
the case which my friend Watson has described as that
of the Abbey School, in which the Duke of Greyminster
was so deeply involved. I had also a commission from 6
the Sultan of Turkey which called for immediate action, 7
as political consequences of the gravest kind might arise
from its neglect. Therefore it was not until the beginning
of the next week, as my diary records, that I was able to
start forth on my mission to Bedfordshire in company
with Mr. James M. Dodd. As we drove to Euston we 8
picked up a grave and taciturn gentleman of iron-grey
aspect, with whom I had made the necessary arrangements.

"This is an old friend," said I to Dodd. "It is possible that his presence may be entirely unnecessary, and, on the other hand, it may be essential. It is not necessary at the present stage to go further into the matter."

The narratives of Watson have accustomed the reader, no doubt, to the fact that I do not waste words or disclose my thoughts while a case is actually under consideration. Dodd seemed surprised, but nothing more was said and the three of us continued our journey together. In the train I asked Dodd one more question which I wished our companion to hear.

"You say that you saw your friend's face quite clearly at the window, so clearly that you are sure of his identity?"

"I have no doubt about it whatever. His nose was pressed against the glass. The lamplight shone full upon him."

"It could not have been someone resembling him?"

"No, no; it was he."

"But you say he was changed?"

6 *in which the Duke of Greyminster was so deeply involved.* Holmes is clearly giving the correct name of "the Priory school," although he, like Watson, is presumably using another alias for "the Duke of Holdernesse." Since "The Adventure of the Priory School" took place in May, 1901, and Holmes says he was clearing up the case in January, 1903, it seems that the Duke of Holdernesse-Greyminster had not heard the last of his wayward illegitimate son, and again called on Holmes' services. (We recall Holmes' remark in "The Adventure of the Priory School": "I would warn your Grace, however, that the continued presence of Mr. James Wilder in your household can only lead to misfortune." Presumably Wilder did *not* "leave . . . forever and go to seek his fortune in Australia"). We see, again, that His Holiness the Pope was not the only client who twice, by Canonical record, called in Holmes.

7 *the Sultan of Turkey.* Abdul-Hamid II, "Abdul the Damned," as some put it; Lord, as he liked to put it, of Two Continents and Two Oceans. "To F. Yeats-Brown, the old Bengal Lancer," the late Alexander Woollcott wrote in his article on "The Baker Street Irregulars," "we are all indebted for some knowledge of how . . . Abdul-Hamid spent his last night as Caliph of Islam. . . . If he must somehow while away the time until dawn, he would need a . . . special anodyne. Happily this was provided by the linguists at the Press Bureau, for in the nick of time there came dawdling into Constantinople from London a recent issue of the *Strand Magazine*. . . . I suspect it was the issue distinguished in the minds of collectors by the first publication of the magnificent story called 'The Bruce-Partington Plans.' Thus it befell that the Great Assassin spent his last night as Sultan sitting with a shawl pulled over his knees while his Chamberlain deferentially read aloud to him the newest story about Sherlock Holmes."

8 *As we drove to Euston.* As the late Christopher Morley long ago pointed out, "You can't go to Bedfordshire via Euston. It was Midland Ry, from St. Pancras, as every traveler knows."

THE DOOR WAS FLUNG OPEN . . .

Illustration by Howard K. Elcock for the *Strand Magazine,* November, 1926.

. . . "I EXTEND THE SAME WARNING TO YOU."

Illustration by Frederic Dorr Steele for *Liberty Magazine,* October 16, 1926.

" Only in colour. His face was—how shall I describe it ?—it was of a fish-belly whiteness. It was bleached."

" Was it equally pale all over ? "

" I think not. It was his brow which I saw so clearly as it was pressed against the window."

" Did you call to him ? "

" I was too startled and horrified for the moment. Then I pursued him, as I have told you, but without result."

My case was practically complete, and there was only one small incident needed to round it off. When, after a considerable drive, we arrived at the strange old rambling house which my client had described, it was Ralph, the elderly butler, who opened the door. I had requisitioned the carriage for the day and had asked my elderly friend to remain within it unless we should summon him. Ralph, a little wrinkled old fellow, was in the conventional costume of black coat and pepper-and-salt trousers, with only one curious variant. He wore brown leather gloves, which at sight of us he instantly shuffled off, laying them down on the hall-table as we passed in. I have, as my friend Watson may have remarked, an abnormally acute set of senses, and a faint but incisive scent was apparent. It seemed to centre on the hall-table. I turned, placed my hat there, knocked it off, stooped to pick it up, and contrived to bring my nose within a foot of the gloves. Yes, it was undoubtedly from them that the curious tarry odour was oozing. I passed on into the study with my case complete. Alas, that I should have to show my hand so when I tell my own story! It was by concealing such links in the chain that Watson was enabled to produce his meretricious finales.

Colonel Emsworth was not in his room, but he came quickly enough on receipt of Ralph's message. We heard his quick, heavy step in the passage. The door was flung open and he rushed in with bristling beard and twisted features, as terrible an old man as ever I have seen. He held our cards in his hand, and he tore them up and stamped on the fragments.

" Have I not told you, you infernal busybody, that you are warned off the premises ? Never dare to show your damned face here again. If you enter again without my leave I shall be within my rights if I use violence. I'll shoot you, sir ! By God, I will ! As to you, sir," turning upon me, " I extend the same warning to you. I am familiar with your ignoble profession, but you must take your reputed talents to some other field. There is no opening for them here."

" I cannot leave here," said my client firmly, " until I hear from Godfrey's own lips that he is under no restraint."

Our involuntary host rang the bell.

" Ralph," he said, " telephone down to the county police and ask the inspector to send up two constables. Tell him there are burglars in the house."

" One moment," said I. " You must be aware, Mr. Dodd, that Colonel Emsworth is within his rights and that we have no legal status within his house. On the other hand, he should recognize that your action is prompted entirely by solicitude for his son. I venture to hope that, if I were allowed to have five minutes' conversation with Colonel Emsworth, I could certainly alter his view of the matter."

" I am not so easily altered," said the old soldier. " Ralph, do what I have told you. What the devil are you waiting for ? Ring up the police ! "

" Nothing of the sort," I said, putting my back to the door. " Any police interference would bring about the very catastrophe which you dread." I took out my notebook and scribbled one word upon a loose sheet. " That," said I, as I handed it to Colonel Emsworth, " is what has brought us here."

He stared at the writing with a face from which every expression save amazement had vanished.

" How do you know ? " he gasped, sitting down heavily in his chair.

" It is my business to know things. That is my trade."

He sat in deep thought, his gaunt hand tugging at his straggling beard. Then he made a gesture of resignation.

" Well, if you wish to see Godfrey, you shall. It is no doing of mine, but you have forced my hand. Ralph, tell Mr. Godfrey and Mr. Kent that in five minutes we shall be with them."

At the end of that time we passed down the garden path and found ourselves in front of the mystery house at the end. A small bearded man stood at the door with a look of considerable astonishment upon his face.

" This is very sudden, Colonel Emsworth," said he. " This will disarrange all our plans."

" I can't help it, Mr. Kent. Our hands have been forced. Can Mr. Godfrey see us ? "

" Yes ; he is waiting inside." He turned and led us into a large, plainly furnished front room. A man was standing with his back to the fire, and at the sight of him my client sprang forward with outstretched hand.

" Why, Godfrey, old man, this is fine ! "

But the other waved him back.

" Don't touch me, Jimmie. Keep your distance. Yes, you may well stare ! I don't quite look the smart Lance-Corporal Emsworth, of B Squadron, do I ? "

His appearance was certainly extraordinary. One could see that he had indeed been a handsome man with clear-cut features sunburned by an African sun, but mottled in patches over this darker surface were curious whitish patches which had bleached his skin.

" That's why I don't court visitors," said he. " I don't mind you, Jimmie, but I could have done without your friend. I suppose there is some good reason for it, but you have me at a disadvantage."

" I wanted to be sure that all was well with you, Godfrey. I saw you that night when you looked into my window, and I could not let the matter rest till I had cleared things up."

" Old Ralph told me you were there, and I couldn't help taking a peep at you. I hoped you would not have seen me, and I had to run to my burrow when I heard the window go up."

" But what in Heaven's name is the matter ? "

"Well, it's not a long story to tell," said he, lighting a cigarette. "You remember that morning fight at Buffelsspruit, outside Pretoria, on the Eastern railway
9 line? You heard I was hit?"

"Yes, I heard that, but I never got particulars."

"Three of us got separated from the others. It was very broken country, you may remember. There was Simpson—the fellow we called Baldy Simpson—and Anderson, and I. We were clearing brother Boer, but he lay low and got the three of us. The other two were killed. I got an elephant bullet through my shoulder. I stuck on to my horse, however, and he galloped several miles before I fainted and rolled off the saddle.

"When I came to myself it was nightfall, and I raised myself up, feeling very weak and ill. To my surprise there was a house close beside me, a fairly large house
10 with a broad stoep and many windows. It was deadly cold. You remember the kind of numb cold which used to come at evening, a deadly, sickening sort of cold, very different from a crisp healthy frost. Well, I was chilled to the bone, and my only hope seemed to lie in reaching that house. I staggered to my feet and dragged myself along, hardly conscious of what I did. I have a dim memory of slowly ascending the steps, entering a wide-opened door, passing into a large room which contained several beds, and throwing myself down with a gasp of satisfaction upon one of them. It was unmade, but that troubled me not at all. I drew the clothes over my shivering body and in a moment I was in a deep sleep.

"It was morning when I wakened, and it seemed to me that instead of coming out into a world of sanity I had emerged into some extraordinary nightmare. The African sun flooded through the big, curtainless windows, and every detail of the great, bare, white-washed dormitory stood out hard and clear. In front of me was standing a small, dwarf-like man with a huge bulbous head, who was jabbering excitedly in Dutch, waving two horrible hands which looked to me like brown sponges. Behind him stood a group of people who seemed to be intensely amused by the situation, but a chill came over me as I looked at them. Not one of them was a normal human being. Every one was twisted or swollen or disfigured in some strange way. The laughter of these strange monstrosities was a dreadful thing to hear.

"It seemed that none of them could speak English, but the situation wanted clearing up, for the creature with the big head was growing furiously angry and, uttering wild-beast cries, he had laid his deformed hands upon me and was dragging me out of bed, regardless of the fresh flow of blood from my wound. The little monster was as strong as a bull, and I don't know what he might have done to me had not an elderly man who was clearly in authority been attracted to the room by the hubbub. He said a few stern words in Dutch, and my persecutor shrank away. Then he turned upon me, gazing at me in the utmost amazement.

9 *on the Eastern railway line?* The Imperial Yeomanry, a real regiment, was in action near Diamond Hill outside of Pretoria. Conan Doyle, in *The Great Boer War*, has described the fight at Bronkhorst Spruit ("Buffelsspruit") and his map shows the Delagoa Bay Railway line, which did run east of the city to the ocean.

10 *stoep.* South African Dutch for a covered platform or veranda at the door of a house.

" ' How in the world did you come here ? ' he asked, in amazement. ' Wait a bit ! I see that you are tired out and that wounded shoulder of yours wants looking after. I am a doctor, and I'll soon have you tied up. But, man alive ! you are in far greater danger here than ever you were on the battlefield. You are in the Leper Hospital, and you have slept in a leper's bed.'

" Need I tell you more, Jimmie ? It seems that in view of the approaching battle all these poor creatures had been evacuated the day before. Then, as the British advanced, they had been brought back by this, their medical superintendent, who assured me that, though he believed he was immune to the disease, he would none the less never have dared to do what I had done. He put me in a private room, treated me kindly, and within a week or so I was removed to the general hospital at Pretoria.

" So there you have my tragedy. I hoped against hope, but it was not until I had reached home that the terrible signs which you see upon my face told me that I had not escaped. What was I to do ? I was in this lonely house. We had two servants whom we could utterly trust. There was a house where I could live. Under pledge of secrecy, Mr. Kent, who is a surgeon, was prepared to stay with me. It seemed simple enough on those lines. The alternative was a dreadful one—segregation for life among strangers with never a hope of release. But absolute secrecy was necessary, or even in this quiet country-side there would have been an outcry, and I should have been dragged to my horrible doom. Even you, Jimmie—even you had to be kept in the dark. Why my father has relented I cannot imagine."

Colonel Emsworth pointed to me.

" This is the gentleman who forced my hand." He unfolded the scrap of paper on which I had written the word " Leprosy." " It seemed to me that if he knew so much as that it was safer that he should know all."

" And so it was," said I. " Who knows but good may come of it ? I understand that only Mr. Kent has seen the patient. May I ask, sir, if you are an authority on such complaints, which are, I understand, tropical or semi-tropical in their nature ? "

" I have the ordinary knowledge of the educated medical man," he observed, with some stiffness.

" I have no doubt, sir, that you are fully competent, but I am sure that you will agree that in such a case a second opinion is valuable. You have avoided this, I understand, for fear that pressure should be put upon you to segregate the patient."

" That is so," said Colonel Emsworth.

" I foresaw this situation," I explained, " and I have brought with me a friend whose discretion may absolutely be trusted. I was able once to do him a professional service, and he is ready to advise as a friend rather than as a specialist. His name is Sir James Saunders."

The prospect of an interview with Lord Roberts would not have excited greater wonder and pleasure in a raw

"THIS IS THE GENTLEMAN WHO FORCED MY HAND."

Illustration by Howard K. Elcock for the *Strand Magazine*, November, 1926.

subaltern than was now reflected upon the face of Mr. Kent.

"I shall indeed be proud," he murmured.

"Then I will ask Sir James to step this way. He is at present in the carriage outside the door. Meanwhile, Colonel Emsworth, we may perhaps assemble in your study, where I could give the necessary explanations."

And here it is that I miss my Watson. By cunning questions and ejaculations of wonder he could elevate my simple art, which is but systematized common sense, into a prodigy. When I tell my own story I have no such aid. And yet I will give my process of thought even as I gave it to my small audience, which included Godfrey's mother, in the study of Colonel Emsworth.

"That process," said I, "starts upon the supposition that when you have eliminated all which is impossible, then whatever remains, however improbable, must be the truth. It may well be that several explanations remain, in which case one tries test after test until one or other of them has a convincing amount of support. We will now apply this principle to the case in point. As it was first presented to me, there were three possible explanations of the seclusion or incarceration of this gentleman in an outhouse of his father's mansion. There was the explanation that he was in hiding for a crime, or that he was mad and that they wished to avoid an asylum, or that he had some disease which caused his segregation. I could think of no other adequate solutions. These, then, had to be sifted and balanced against each other.

"The criminal solution would not bear inspection. No unsolved crime had been reported from that district. I was sure of that. If it were some crime not yet discovered, then clearly it would be to the interest of the family to get rid of the delinquent and send him abroad rather than keep him concealed at home. I could see no explanation for such a line of conduct.

"Insanity was more plausible. The presence of the second person in the outhouse suggested a keeper. The fact that he locked the door when he came out strengthened the supposition and gave the idea of constraint. On the other hand, this constraint could not be severe or the young man could not have got loose and come down to have a look at his friend. You will remember, Mr. Dodd, that I felt round for points, asking you, for example, about the paper which Mr. Kent was reading. Had it been the *Lancet* or the *British Medical Journal* it would have helped me. It is not illegal, however, to keep a lunatic upon private premises so long as there is a qualified person in attendance and that the authorities have been duly notified. Why, then, all this desperate desire for secrecy? Once again I could not get the theory to fit the facts.

"There remained the third possibility, into which, rare and unlikely as it was, everything seemed to fit. Leprosy is not uncommon in South Africa. By some extraordinary chance this youth might have contracted it. His people would be placed in a very dreadful position, since they would desire to save him from segregation. Great secrecy would be needed to prevent rumours from getting about and subsequent interference by the authorities. A devoted medical man, if sufficiently paid, would easily be found to take charge of the sufferer. There would be no reason why the latter should not be allowed freedom after dark. Bleaching of the skin is a common result of the disease. The case was a strong one—so strong that I determined to act as if it were actually proved. When on arriving here I noticed that Ralph, who carries out the meals, had gloves which are impregnated with disinfectants, my last doubts were removed. A single word showed you, sir, that your secret was discovered, and if I wrote rather than said it, it was to prove to you that my discretion was to be trusted."

I was finishing this little analysis of the case when the door was opened and the austere figure of the great dermatologist was ushered in. But for once his sphinx-like features had relaxed and there was a warm humanity in his eyes. He strode up to Colonel Emsworth and shook him by the hand.

" It is often my lot to bring ill-tidings, and seldom good," said he. " This occasion is the more welcome. It is not leprosy."

" What ? "

" A well-marked case of pseudo-leprosy or ichthyosis, a scale-like affection of the skin, unsightly, obstinate, but possibly curable, and certainly non-infective. Yes, Mr. Holmes, the coincidence is a remarkable one. But is it coincidence ? Are there not subtle forces at work of which we know little ? Are we assured that the apprehension, from which this young man has no doubt suffered terribly since his exposure to its contagion, may not produce a physical effect which simulates that which it fears ? At any rate, I pledge my professional reputation—— But the lady has fainted ! I think that Mr. Kent had better be with her until she recovers from this joyous shock." **11**

11 *recovers from this joyous shock."* "The incredibility of the denouement whereby Godfrey turns out not to have leprosy at all, must have struck every reader," Mr. D. Martin Dakin wrote in "The Problem of the Case-Book." "Watson was never guilty of forcing such 'happy endings' to please his readers—witness 'The Adventure of the Dancing Men' or 'The Greek Interpreter.' "

Bibliographical Note: The manuscript of "The Adventure of the Blanched Soldier," 26 pages, 4to vellum, was auctioned in New York City in January, 1944, bringing $310. It is presently owned by the New York Public Library.

73

THE ADVENTURE OF THE THREE GABLES

[*Tuesday, May 26, to Wednesday, May 27, 1903*]

"SEE HERE, MASSER HOLMES, YOU KEEP YOUR HANDS OUT OF OTHER FOLKS' BUSINESS."

Illustration by Frederic Dorr Steele for *Liberty Magazine*, September 18, 1926. Howard K. Elcock illustrated the same scene for the *Strand Magazine*, October, 1926.

I DON'T think that any of my adventures with Mr. Sherlock Holmes opened quite so abruptly, or so dramatically, as that which I associate with The Three Gables. I had not seen Holmes for some days, and had no idea of the new channel into which his activities had been directed. He was in a chatty mood that morning, however, and had just settled me into the well-worn low arm-chair on one side of the fire, while he had curled down with his pipe in his mouth upon the opposite chair, when our visitor arrived. If I had said that a mad bull had arrived, it would give a clearer impression of what occurred.

The door had flown open and a huge negro had burst into the room. He would have been a comic figure if he had not been terrific, for he was dressed in a very loud grey check suit with a flowing salmon-coloured tie. His broad face and flattened nose were thrust forward, as his sullen dark eyes, with a smouldering gleam of malice in them, turned from one of us to the other.

" Which of you genelmen is Masser Holmes ? " he asked.

Holmes raised his pipe with a languid smile.

" Oh ! it's you, is it ? " said our visitor, coming with an unpleasant, stealthy step round the angle of the table. " See here, Masser Holmes, you keep your hands out of other folks' business. Leave folks to manage their own affairs. Got that, Masser Holmes ? "

" Keep on talking," said Holmes. " It's fine."

" Oh ! it's fine, is it ? " growled the savage. " It won't be so damn fine if I have to trim you up a bit. I've handled your kind before now, and they didn't look fine when I was through with them. Look at that, Masser Holmes ! "

He swung a huge knotted lump of a fist under my friend's nose. Holmes examined it closely with an air of great interest. " Were you born so ? " he asked. " Or did it come by degrees ? "

It may have been the icy coolness of my friend, or it may have been the slight clatter which I made as I picked up the poker. In any case, our visitor's manner became less flamboyant.

" Well, I've given you fair warnin'," said he. " I've a friend that's interested out Harrow way—you know what I'm meaning—and he don't intend to have no buttin' in by you. Got that ? You ain't the law, and I ain't the law either, and if you come in I'll be on hand also. Don't you forget it."

" I've wanted to meet you for some time," said Holmes. " I won't ask you to sit down, for I don't like the smell of you, but aren't you Steve Dixie, the bruiser ? "

" That's my name, Masser Holmes, and you'll get put through it for sure if you give me any lip."

" It is certainly the last thing you need," said Holmes, staring at our visitor's hideous mouth. " But it was the killing of young Perkins outside the Holborn Bar—— 1
What ! you're not going ? "

The negro had sprung back, and his face was leaden. " I won't listen to no such talk," said he. " What have I to do with this 'ere Perkins, Masser Holmes ? I was trainin' at the Bull Ring in Birmingham when this boy done gone get into trouble."

" Yes, you'll tell the magistrate about it, Steve," said Holmes. " I've been watching you and Barney Stockdale——"

" So help me the Lord ! Masser Holmes——"

" That's enough. Get out of it. I'll pick you up when I want you."

" Good mornin', Masser Holmes. I hope there ain't no hard feelin's about this 'ere visit ? "

" There will be unless you tell me who sent you."

" Why, there ain't no secret about that, Masser Holmes. It was that same genelman that you have just done gone mention."

" And who set him on to it ? "

" S'elp me. I don't know, Masser Holmes. He just say, ' Steve, you go see Mr. Holmes, and tell him his life ain't safe if he go down Harrow way.' That's the whole truth."

Without waiting for any further questioning, our visitor bolted out of the room almost as precipitately as he had entered. Holmes knocked out the ashes of his pipe with a quiet chuckle.

" I am glad you were not forced to break his woolly head, Watson. I observed your manœuvres with the poker. But he is really rather a harmless fellow, a great muscular, foolish, blustering baby, and easily cowed, as you have seen. He is one of the Spencer John gang and has taken part in some dirty work of late which I may clear up when I have time. His immediate principal, Barney, is a more astute person. They specialize in assaults, intimidation, and the like. What I want to know is, who is at the back of them on this particular occasion ? "

" But why do they want to intimidate you ? "

" It is this Harrow Weald case. It decides me to look into the matter, for if it is worth anyone's while to take so much trouble, there must be something in it."

" But what is it ? "

" I was going to tell you when we had this comic interlude. Here is Mrs. Maberley's note. If you care to come with me we will wire her and go out at once."

". . . AT THE BULL RING IN BIRMINGHAM . . ."

"The plan of the town is irregular," says the *Encyclopædia Britannica*, 1894 edition, under "Birmingham," "and the streets are mostly winding, and many of them somewhat narrow. In the centre, however, is a large open space, known as the Bull Ring . . ."

1 *the killing of young Perkins outside the Holborn Bar——.* "I have always felt," the late Clifton R. Andrew wrote in "Sherlock Holmes on the Turf," "that the 'killing of young Perkins outside the Holborn Bar,' which Holmes seemed to know so much about, was the tragic outcome of some race-betting embroilment. It has all the earmarks of such. Bars are not above being rendezvous for the fraternity of the race-track, of higher or lower estate, depending upon the class of the bar . . ."

Dear Mr. Sherlock Holmes, (I read)—

I have had a succession of strange incidents occur to me in connection with this house, and I should much value your advice. You would find me at home any time to-morrow. The house is within a short walk of the Weald Station. I believe that my late husband, Mortimer Maberley, was one of your early clients.

Yours faithfully,
Mary Maberley.

The address was " The Three Gables, Harrow Weald."

" So that's that ! " said Holmes. " And now, if you can spare the time, Watson, we will get upon our way."

2 A short railway journey, and a shorter drive, brought us to the house, a brick and timber villa, standing in its own acre of undeveloped grassland. Three small projections above the upper windows made a feeble attempt to justify its name. Behind was a grove of melancholy, half-grown pines, and the whole aspect of the place was poor and depressing. None the less, we found the house to be well furnished, and the lady who received us was a most engaging elderly person, who bore every mark of refinement and culture.

" I remember your husband well, madam," said Holmes, " though it is some years since he used my services in some trifling matter."

" Probably you would be more familiar with the name of my son Douglas."

Holmes looked at her with great interest.

" Dear me ! Are you the mother of Douglas Maberley ? I knew him slightly. But, of course, all London knew him. What a magnificent creature he was ! Where is he now ? "

" Dead, Mr. Holmes, dead ! He was Attaché at Rome, and he died there of pneumonia last month."

2 *and a shorter drive.* Mr. Michael Harrison has noted (*In the Footsteps of Sherlock Holmes*) that Holmes and Watson, calling on Mrs. Maberley, would have passed "Grim's Dyke," Sir W. S. Gilbert's famous Norman Shaw mansion at Harrow Weald.

. . . A BRICK AND TIMBER VILLA, STANDING IN ITS OWN ACRE OF UNDEVELOPED GRASSLAND.

This is Fairmead, a mansion typical of the larger houses of Harrow Weald at the time when Holmes and Watson were involved in the mysterious affair of "The Three Gables." The illustration is from Mr. Michael Harrison's *In the Footsteps of Sherlock Holmes.*

" I am sorry. One could not connect death with such a man. I have never known anyone so vitally alive. He lived intensely—every fibre of him ! "

" Too intensely, Mr. Holmes. That was the ruin of him. You remember him as he was—debonair and splendid. You did not see the moody, morose, brooding creature into which he developed. His heart was broken. In a single month I seemed to see my gallant boy turn into a worn-out cynical man."

" A love-affair—a woman ? "

" Or a fiend. Well, it was not to talk of my poor lad that I asked you to come, Mr. Holmes."

" Dr. Watson and I are at your service."

" There have been some very strange happenings. I have been in this house more than a year now, and as I wished to lead a retired life I have seen little of my neighbours. Three days ago I had a call from a man who said that he was a house agent. He said that this house would exactly suit a client of his and that if I would part with it money would be no object. It seemed to me very strange, as there are several empty houses on the market which appear to be equally eligible, but naturally I was interested in what he said. I therefore named a price which was five hundred pounds more than I gave. He at once closed with the offer, but added that his client desired to buy the furniture as well and would I put a price upon it. Some of this furniture is from my old home, and it is, as you see, very good, so that I named a good round sum. To this also he at once agreed. I had always wanted to travel, and the bargain was so good a one that it really seemed that I should be my own mistress for the rest of my life.

" Yesterday the man arrived with the agreement all drawn out. Luckily I showed it to Mr. Sutro, my lawyer, who lives in Harrow. He said to me, 'This is a very strange document. Are you aware that if you sign it you could not legally take *anything* out of the house—not even your own private possessions ?' When the man came again in the evening I pointed this out, and I said that I meant only to sell the furniture.

" 'No, no ; everything,' said he.

" 'But my clothes ? My jewels ?'

" 'Well, well, some concession might be made for your personal effects. But nothing shall go out of the house unchecked. My client is a very liberal man, but he has his fads and his own way of doing things. It is everything or nothing with him.'

" 'Then it must be nothing,' said I. And there the matter was left, but the whole thing seemed to me to be so unusual that I thought——"

Here we had a very extraordinary interruption.

Holmes raised his hand for silence. Then he strode across the room, flung open the door, and dragged in a great gaunt woman whom he had seized by the shoulder. She entered with ungainly struggles, like some huge awkward chicken, torn squawking out of its coop.

" Leave me alone ! What are you a-doin' of ? " she screeched.

" Why, Susan, what is this ? "

THEN HE STRODE ACROSS THE ROOM, FLUNG OPEN THE DOOR . . .

Illustration by Howard K. Elcock for the *Strand Magazine*, October, 1926.

" Well, ma'am, I was comin' in to ask if the visitors was stayin' for lunch when this man jumped out at me."

" I have been listening to her for the last five minutes, but did not wish to interrupt your most interesting narrative. Just a little wheezy, Susan, are you not? You breathe too heavily for that kind of work."

Susan turned a sulky but amazed face upon her captor. " Who be you, anyhow, and what right have you a-pullin' me about like this ? "

" It was merely that I wished to ask a question in your presence. Did you, Mrs. Maberley, mention to anyone that you were going to write to me and consult me ? "

" No, Mr. Holmes, I did not."

" Who posted your letter ? "

" Susan did."

" Exactly. Now, Susan, to whom was it that you wrote or sent a message to say that your mistress was asking advice from me ? "

" It's a lie. I sent no message."

" Now, Susan, wheezy people may not live long, you know. It's a wicked thing to tell fibs. Whom did you tell ? "

" Susan ! " cried her mistress, " I believe you are a bad, treacherous woman. I remember now that I saw you speaking to someone over the hedge."

" That was my own business," said the woman sullenly.

" Suppose I tell you that it was Barney Stockdale to whom you spoke ? " said Holmes.

" Well, if you know, what do you want to ask for ? "

" I was not sure, but I know now. Well now, Susan, it will be worth ten pounds to you if you will tell me who is at the back of Barney."

" Someone that could lay down a thousand pounds for every ten you have in the world."

" So, a rich man ? No ; you smiled—a rich woman. Now we have got so far, you may as well give the name and earn the tenner."

" I'll see you in hell first."

" Oh, Susan ! Language ! "

" I am clearing out of here. I've had enough of you all. I'll send for my box to-morrow." She flounced for the door.

" Good-bye, Susan. Paregoric is the stuff. . . . Now," he continued, turning suddenly from lively to severe when the door had closed behind the flushed and angry woman, " this gang means business. Look how close they play the game. Your letter to me had the 10 p.m. postmark. And yet Susan passes the word to Barney. Barney has time to go to his employer and get instructions ; he or she—I incline to the latter from Susan's grin when she thought I had blundered—forms a plan. Black Steve is called in, and I am warned off by eleven o'clock next morning. That's quick work, you
3 know."

" But what do they want ? "

" Yes, that's the question. Who had the house before you ? "

3 *That's quick work, you know.*" The opening day was not Sunday: Mrs. Maberley's note, which "had the 10 P.M. postmark" and was written the night before ("You would find me at home any time to-morrow") could not have been delivered on that day. Nor was the opening day Wednesday: "Three days ago I had a call from a man who said he was a house agent." Such a call would of course not have been made on a Sunday. Nor was the opening day Monday: "Yesterday the man arrived with the agreement all drawn out." Nor was the opening day Saturday: Susan said, "I'll send for my box to-morrow," as she flounced off. Douglas Maberley's effects had been delivered to Mrs. Maberley "last week." We may be sure that Susan immediately informed her husband ("This gang means business. Look how close they play the game. . . . That's quick work, you know.") We are justified in assuming that the "house agent" would have called on the very day the effects were delivered. Since this was "three weeks ago," and the effects were delivered "last week," the opening day could not have been Thursday or Friday. The case opened, then, on a *Tuesday.*

" A retired sea captain, called Ferguson."

" Anything remarkable about him ? "

" Not that ever I heard of."

" I was wondering whether he could have buried something. Of course, when people bury treasure nowadays they do it in the Post Office bank. But there are always some lunatics about. It would be a dull world without them. At first I thought of some buried valuable. But why, in that case, should they want your furniture ? You don't happen to have a Raphael or a First Folio **4** Shakespeare without knowing it ? "

" No, I don't think I have anything rarer than a Crown Derby tea-set."

" That would hardly justify all this mystery. Besides, why should they not openly state what they want ? If they covet your tea-set, they can surely offer a price for it without buying you out, lock, stock, and barrel. No, as I read it, there is something which you do not know that you have, and which you would not give up if you did know."

" That is how I read it," said I.

" Dr. Watson agrees, so that settles it."

" Well, Mr. Holmes, what can it be ? "

" Let us see whether by this purely mental analysis we can get it to a finer point. You have been in this house a year."

" Nearly two."

" All the better. During this long period no one wants anything from you. Now suddenly within three or four days you have urgent demands. What would you gather from that ? "

" It can only mean," said I, " that the object, whatever it may be, has only just come into the house."

" Settled once again," said Holmes. " Now, Mrs. Maberley, has any object just arrived ? "

" No ; I have bought nothing new this year."

" Indeed ! That is very remarkable. Well, I think we had best let matters develop a little further until we have clearer data. Is that lawyer of yours a capable man ? "

" Mr. Sutro is most capable."

" Have you another maid, or was the fair Susan, who has just banged your front door, alone ? "

" I have a young girl."

" Try and get Sutro to spend a night or two in the house. You might possibly want protection."

" Against whom ? "

" Who knows ? The matter is certainly obscure. If I can't find what they are after, I must approach the matter from the other end, and try to get at the principal. Did this house-agent man give any address ? "

" Simply his card and occupation. Haines-Johnson, Auctioneer and Valuer."

" I don't think we shall find him in the Directory. Honest business men don't conceal their place of business. Well, you will let me know any fresh development. I have taken up your case, and you may rely upon it that I shall see it through."

As we passed through the hall Holmes' eyes, which missed nothing, lighted upon several trunks and cases

4 *a Raphael.* Raffaello Santi or Raffaello Sanzio, 1483–1520, Italian painter, one of the great artists of the Renaissance.

which were piled in the corner. The labels shone out upon them.

5 " 'Milano.' 'Lucerne.' These are from Italy."

" They are poor Douglas' things."

" You have not unpacked them ? How long have you had them ? "

" They arrived last week."

" But you said—why, surely this might be the missing link. How do we know that there is not something of value there ? "

" There could not possibly be, Mr. Holmes. Poor Douglas had only his pay and a small annuity. What could he have of value ? "

Holmes was lost in thought.

" Delay no longer, Mrs. Maberley," he said at last. " Have these things taken upstairs to your bedroom. Examine them as soon as possible and see what they contain. I will come to-morrow and hear your report."

It was quite evident that The Three Gables was under very close surveillance, for as we came round the high hedge at the end of the lane there was the negro prize-fighter standing in the shadow. We came on him quite suddenly, and a grim and menacing figure he looked in that lonely place. Holmes clapped his hand to his pocket.

" Lookin' for your gun, Masser Holmes ? "

" No ; for my scent-bottle, Steve."

" You are funny, Masser Holmes, ain't you ? "

" It won't be funny for you, Steve, if I get after you. I gave you fair warning this morning."

" Well, Masser Holmes, I done gone think over what you said, and I don't want no more talk about that affair of Masser Perkins. S'pose I can help you, Masser Holmes, I will."

" Well, then, tell me who is behind you on this job ? "

" So help me the Lord ! Masser Holmes, I told you the truth before. I don't know. My boss Barney gives me orders and that's all."

" Well, just bear in mind, Steve, that the lady in that house, and everything under that roof, is under my protection. Don't you forget it."

" All right, Masser Holmes. I'll remember."

" I've got him thoroughly frightened for his own skin,
Watson," Holmes remarked as we walked on. " I think
he would double-cross his employer if he knew who he
was. It was lucky I had some knowledge of the Spencer
John crowd, and that Steve was one of them. Now,
6 Watson, this is a case for Langdale Pike, and I am going
to see him now. When I get back I may be clearer in
the matter."

I saw no more of Holmes during the day, but I could
well imagine how he spent it, for Langdale Pike was
his human book of reference upon all matters of social
scandal. This strange, languid creature spent his waking hours in the bow window of a St. James' Street
7 club, and was the receiving-station, as well as the trans-
mitter, for all the gossip of the Metropolis. He made,
it was said, a four-figure income by the paragraphs which
he contributed every week to the garbage papers which

5 *These are from Italy.*" "These are the stations at which baggage from Rome to London via the St. Gotthard route would normally have been transferred," Mr. Michael C. Kaser wrote in "Sherlock Holmes on the Continent." "However, while baggage from Rome would correctly have had its immediate destination marked in Italian, that is, 'Milano,' how could the Italian authorities have inscribed the next transfer point in French? They would certainly have used either Italian ('Lucerna') or German ('Luzern'), for Lucerne is German-speaking. It can only be concluded that between Milan and Lucerne the pieces so labeled had passed through a French-speaking intermediate transfer point and the relevant label had been deliberately removed. The reason is not far to seek. Mrs. Klein's agents had succeeded in having the baggage directed to a locality in France where—perhaps by corruption of the railway staff—they were able to examine the trunks. France, and not French-speaking Switzerland, is indicated, since at that time . . . the only direct connection between Milan and Switzerland lay through Lucerne. Either they were unable to open all the trunks or they had selected the wrong pieces for diversion. In either case, the thieves would have had to return the bags to their original route (hence the addressing to Lucerne in French) to preclude suspicion and await delivery at Harrow, where the keys of the cases which they had been unable to inspect would be available for felony. It is impossible that Sherlock Holmes should have missed this obvious clue that the trunks had been tampered with en route, and it was this which must have led him to direct that they be examined and guarded."

. . . THERE WAS THE NEGRO PRIZE-FIGHTER STANDING IN THE SHADOW.

Illustration by Howard K. Elcock for the *Strand Magazine*, October, 1926.

cater for an inquisitive public. If ever, far down in the turbid depths of London life, there was some strange swirl or eddy, it was marked with automatic exactness by this human dial upon the surface. Holmes discreetly helped Langdale to knowledge, and on occasion was helped in turn.

When I met my friend in his room early next morning, I was conscious from his bearing that all was well, but none the less a most unpleasant surprise was awaiting us. It took the shape of the following telegram:

" Please come out at once. Client's house burgled in the night. Police in possession.

" SUTRO."

Holmes whistled. " The drama has come to a crisis, and quicker than I had expected. There is a great driving-power at the back of this business, Watson, which does not surprise me after what I have heard. This Sutro, of course, is her lawyer. I made a mistake, I fear, in not asking you to spend the night on guard.
This fellow has clearly proved a broken reed. Well, 8
there is nothing for it but another journey to Harrow Weald."

We found The Three Gables a very different establishment to the orderly household of the previous day. A small group of idlers had assembled at the garden gate, while a couple of constables were examining the
windows and the geranium beds. Within we met a grey 9
old gentleman, who introduced himself as the lawyer, together with a bustling, rubicund Inspector, who greeted Holmes as an old friend.

" Well, Mr. Holmes, no chance for you in this case, I'm afraid. Just a common, ordinary burglary, and well within the capacity of the poor old police. No experts need apply."

" I am sure the case is in very good hands," said Holmes. " Merely a common burglary, you say ? "

" Quite so. We know pretty well who the men are and where to find them. It is that gang of Barney Stockdale, with the big nigger in it—they've been seen about here."

" Excellent ! What did they get ? "

" Well, they don't seem to have got much. Mrs. Maberley was chloroformed and the house was—— Ah ! here is the lady herself."

Our friend of yesterday, looking very pale and ill, had entered the room, leaning upon a little maid-servant.

" You gave me good advice, Mr. Holmes," said she, smiling ruefully. " Alas, I did not take it ! I did not wish to trouble Mr. Sutro, and so I was unprotected."

" I only heard of it this morning," the lawyer explained.

" Mr. Holmes advised me to have some friend in the house. I neglected his advice, and I have paid for it."

" You look wretchedly ill," said Holmes. " Perhaps you are hardly equal to telling me what occurred."

" It is all here," said the Inspector, tapping a bulky notebook.

6 *Langdale Pike.* In fact, the Landale Pikes are two hills in Westmoreland overlooking Wordsworth's Grasmere.

7 *a St. James Street club.* Perhaps the Conservative Club (the second Tory club) built by Smirke and Basevi, 1845, and occupying partly the site of the old Thatched House Tavern, celebrated for its literary meetings, and partly that of the house in which Edward Gibbon, the historian of the Roman Empire, died on January 16, 1794. Perhaps Brooks' Club (Whig) built by Holland, 1778. Perhaps the New University Club at No. 57. Or No. 28, Boodle's, the country gentleman's club —"Every Sir John belongs to Boodle's." Perhaps White's at Nos. 37–38 (Tory) built by Wyatt.

8 *This fellow has clearly proved a broken reed.* "Thou trustest in the staff of this broken reed." —Isaiah, 36.6.

9 *the geranium beds.* "The reference to 'geranium beds' around Mrs. Maberley's house is important," the late H. W. Bell wrote, "for geraniums are not bedded out even in the south of England until the second half of May, in case of spring frosts." The deduction is borne out by the fact that Douglas Maberley died of pneumonia—especially prevalant in the spring.

" Still, if the lady is not too exhausted——"

" There is really so little to tell. I have no doubt that wicked Susan had planned an entrance for them. They must have known the house to an inch. I was conscious for a moment of the chloroform rag which was thrust over my mouth, but I have no notion how long I may have been senseless. When I woke, one man was at the bedside and another was rising with a bundle in his hand from among my son's baggage, which was partially opened and littered over the floor. Before he could get away I sprang up and seized him."

" You took a big risk," said the Inspector.

" I clung to him, but he shook me off, and the other may have struck me, for I can remember no more. Mary the maid heard the noise and began screaming out of the window. That brought the police, but the rascals had got away."

" What did they take ? "

" Well, I don't think there is anything of value missing. I am sure there was nothing in my son's trunks."

" Did the men leave no clue ? "

" There was one sheet of paper which I may have torn from the man that I grasped. It was lying all crumpled on the floor. It is in my son's handwriting."

" Which means that it is not of much use," said the Inspector. " Now if it had been in the burglar's——"

" Exactly," said Holmes. " What rugged common sense ! None the less, I should be curious to see it."

The Inspector drew a folded sheet of foolscap from his pocket-book.

" I never pass anything, however trifling," said he, with some pomposity. " That is my advice to you, Mr. Holmes. In twenty-five years' experience I have learned my lesson. There is always the chance of finger-marks
10 or something."

Holmes inspected the sheet of paper.

" What do you make of it, Inspector ? "

" Seems to be the end of some queer novel, so far as I can see."

" It may certainly prove to be the end of a queer tale," said Holmes. " You have noticed the number on the top of the page. It is two hundred and forty-five. Where are the odd two hundred and forty-four pages ? "

" Well, I suppose the burglars got those. Much good may it do them ! "

" It seems a queer thing to break into a house in order to steal such papers as that. Does it suggest anything to you, Inspector ? "

" Yes, sir ; it suggests that in their hurry the rascals just grabbed at what came first to hand. I wish them joy of what they got."

" Why should they go to my son's things ? " asked Mrs. Maberley.

" Well, they found nothing valuable downstairs, so they tried their luck upstairs. That is how I read it. What do you make of it, Mr. Holmes ? "

" I must think it over, Inspector. Come to the window, Watson." Then, as we stood together, he read

10 *the chance of finger-marks or something.*" It was in 1901, as we saw in "The Adventure of the Red Circle," that the fingerprint system was introduced to Scotland Yard. "The Adventure of the Three Gables," then, is not before that time. Watson "had not seen Holmes for some days, and had no idea of the new channel into which his activities had been directed." Watson met his friend "in his room early next morning." Since Watson is not living at Baker Street, and has not seen Holmes "for some days," the case must fall between September, 1902 ("The Adventure of the Illustrious Client," "The Adventure of the Red Circle") and the summer of 1903 ("The Adventure of the Mazarin Stone").

over the fragment of paper. It began in the middle of a sentence and ran like this :

" . . . face bled considerably from the cuts and blows, but it was nothing to the bleeding of his heart as he saw that lovely face, the face for which he had been prepared to sacrifice his very life, looking out at his agony and humiliation. She smiled—yes, by Heaven ! she smiled, like the heartless fiend she was, as he looked up at her. It was at that moment that love died and hate was born. Man must live for something. If it is not for your embrace, my lady, then it shall surely be for your undoing and my complete revenge."

" Queer grammar ! " said Holmes, with a smile, as he handed the paper back to the Inspector. " Did you notice how the ' he ' suddenly changed to ' my.' The writer was so carried away by his own story that he imagined himself at the supreme moment to be the hero."

" It seemed mighty poor stuff," said the Inspector, as he replaced it in his book. " What ! are you off, Mr. Holmes ? "

" I don't think there is anything more for me to do now that the case is in such capable hands. By the way, Mrs. Maberley, did you say you wished to travel ? "

" It has always been my dream, Mr. Holmes."

" Where would you like to go—Cairo, Madeira, the Riviera ? "

" Oh ! if I had the money I would go round the world."

" Quite so. Round the world. Well, good morning. I may drop you a line in the evening." As we passed the window I caught a glimpse of the Inspector's smile and shake of the head. " These clever fellows have always a touch of madness." That was what I read in the Inspector's smile.

" Now, Watson, we are at the last lap of our little journey," said Holmes, when we were back in the roar of Central London once more. " I think we had best clear the matter up at once, and it would be well that you should come with me, for it is safer to have a witness when you are dealing with such a lady as Isadora Klein."

We had taken a cab and were speeding to some address in Grosvenor Square. Holmes had been sunk in thought, but he roused himself suddenly.

" By the way, Watson, I suppose you see it all clearly ? "

" No, I can't say that I do. I only gather that we are going to see the lady who is behind all this mischief."

" Exactly ! But does the name Isadora Klein convey nothing to you ? She was, of course, *the* celebrated beauty. There was never a woman to touch her. She is pure Spanish, the real blood of the masterful Conquistadors, and her people have been leaders in Pernambuco for generations. She married the aged German sugar king, Klein, and presently found herself the richest as well as the most lovely widow upon earth. Then there was an interval of adventure when she pleased her own tastes. She had several lovers, and Douglas Maberley, one of the most striking men in London, was one of them.

" It was by all accounts more than an adventure with him. He was not a Society butterfly, but a strong, proud man who gave and expected all. But she is the '*belle dame*
11 *sans merci*' of fiction. When her caprice is satisfied, the matter is ended, and if the other party in the matter can't take her word for it, she knows how to bring it home to him."

" Then that was his own story——"

" Ah ! you are piecing it together now. I hear that
12 she is about to marry the young Duke of Lomond, who might almost be her son. His Grace's ma might overlook the age, but a big scandal would be a different matter, so it is imperative—— Ah ! here we are."

It was one of the finest corner-houses of the West End. A machine-like footman took up our cards and returned with word that the lady was not at home. " Then we shall wait until she is," said Holmes cheerfully.

The machine broke down.

" Not at home means not at home to *you*," said the footman.

" Good," Holmes answered. " That means that we shall not have to wait. Kindly give this note to your mistress."

He scribbled three or four words upon a sheet of his notebook, folded it, and handed it to the man.

" What did you say, Holmes ? " I asked.

" I simply wrote ' Shall it be the police, then ? ' I think that should pass us in."

It did—with amazing celerity. A minute later we were in an Arabian Nights' drawing-room, vast and wonderful, in a half gloom, picked out with an occasional pink electric light. The lady had come, I felt, to that time of life when even the proudest beauty finds the half-light more welcome. She rose from a settee as we entered : tall, queenly, a perfect figure, a lovely mask-like face, with two wonderful Spanish eyes which looked murder at us both.

" What is this intrusion—and this insulting message ? " she asked, holding up the slip of paper.

" I need not explain, madame. I have too much respect for your intelligence to do so—though I confess that intelligence has been surprisingly at fault of late."

" How so, sir ? "

" By supposing that your hired bullies could frighten me from my work. Surely no man would take up my profession if it were not that danger attracts him. It was you, then, who forced me to examine the case of young Maberley."

" I have no idea what you are talking about. What have I to do with hired bullies ? "

Holmes turned away wearily.

" Yes, I have underrated your intelligence. Well, good afternoon ! "

" Stop ! Where are you going ? "

" To Scotland Yard."

We had not got half-way to the door before she had overtaken us and was holding his arm. She had turned

11 *the* 'belle dame sans merci.' "Did Holmes borrow the epithet [from Keats or] directly from the 15th-century poet Alain Chartier?" Mr. Leslie Cross asked in "Sherlock Holmes, Writer: An Unsolved Case."

12 *she is about to marry the young Duke of Lomond.* The second half of May corresponds well, as the late H. W. Bell noted, with the fact that Frau Klein had not yet left her house in Grosvenor Square for the country. It corresponds also, as the late Dr. Ernest Bloomfield Zeisler noted, with the fact that the beautiful widow is "about to marry the young Duke of Lomond": this "suggests that the impending marriage is only a few days off, for similar words in 'A Scandal in Bohemia' meant this; and the marriage was most likely planned for a date near June 1st." The case opened, then, on a Tuesday in late May in the year 1903—*Tuesday, May 26, 1903*, beyond a doubt; it closed the next day.

"STOP! WHERE ARE YOU GOING?"

Illustration by Howard K. Elcock for the *Strand Magazine*, October, 1926.

in a moment from steel to velvet.

" Come and sit down, gentlemen. Let us talk this matter over. I feel that I may be frank with you, Mr. Holmes. You have the feelings of a gentleman. How quick a woman's instinct is to find it out. I will treat you as a friend."

" I cannot promise to reciprocate, madame. I am not the law, but I represent justice so far as my feeble powers go. I am ready to listen, and then I will tell you how I will act."

" No doubt it was foolish of me to threaten a brave man like yourself."

" What was really foolish, madame, is that you have placed yourself in the power of a band of rascals who may blackmail or give you away."

" No, no ! I am not so simple. Since I have promised to be frank, I may say that no one, save Barney Stockdale and Susan, his wife, have the least idea who their employer is. As to them, well, it is not the first——" She smiled and nodded, with a charming coquettish intimacy.

" I see. You've tested them before."

" They are good hounds who run silent."

" Such hounds have a way sooner or later of biting the hand that feeds them. They will be arrested for this burglary. The police are already after them."

" They will take what comes to them. That is what they are paid for. I shall not appear in the matter."

" Unless I bring you into it."

" No, no ; you would not. You are a gentleman. It is a woman's secret."

" In the first place you must give back this manuscript."

She broke into a ripple of laughter, and walked to the fire-place. There was a calcined mass which she broke up with the poker. " Shall I give this back ? " she asked. So roguish and exquisite did she look as she stood before us with a challenging smile that I felt of all Holmes' criminals this was the one whom he would find it hardest to face. However, he was immune from sentiment.

" That seals your fate," he said coldly. " You are very prompt in your actions, madame, but you have overdone it on this occasion."

She threw the poker down with a clatter.

" How hard you are ! " she cried. " May I tell you the whole story ? "

" I fancy I could tell it to you."

" But you must look at it with my eyes, Mr. Holmes. You must realize it from the point of view of a woman who sees all her life's ambition about to be ruined at the last moment. Is such a woman to be blamed if she protects herself ? "

" The original sin was yours."

" Yes, yes ! I admit it. He was a dear boy, Douglas, but it so chanced that he could not fit into my plans. He wanted marriage—marriage, Mr. Holmes—with a penniless commoner. Nothing less would serve him. Then he became pertinacious. Because I had given he seemed to think that I still must give, and to him only. It was intolerable. At last I had to make him realize it."

" By hiring ruffians to beat him under your own window."

" You do indeed seem to know everything. Well, it is true. Barney and the boys drove him away, and were, I admit, a little rough in doing so. But what did he do then ? Could I have believed that a gentleman would do such an act ? He wrote a book in which he described his own story. I, of course, was the wolf ; he the lamb. It was all there, under different names, of course ; but who in all London would have failed to recognize it ? What do you say to that, Mr. Holmes ? "

" Well, he was within his rights."

" It was as if the air of Italy had got into his blood and brought with it the old cruel Italian spirit. He wrote to me and sent me a copy of his book that I might have the torture of anticipation. There were two copies, he said—one for me, one for his publisher."

" How did you know the publisher's had not reached him ? "

" I knew who his publisher was. It is not his only novel, you know. I found out that he had not heard from Italy. Then came Douglas' sudden death. So long as that other manuscript was in the world there was no safety for me. Of course, it must be among his effects, and these would be returned to his mother. I set the gang at work. One of them got into the house as servant. I wanted to do the thing honestly. I really and truly did. I was ready to buy the house and everything in it. I offered any price she cared to ask. I only tried the other way when everything else had failed. Now, Mr. Holmes, granting that I was too hard on Douglas —and, God knows, I am sorry for it !—what else could I do with my whole future at stake ? "

Sherlock Holmes shrugged his shoulders.

" Well, well," said he, " I suppose I shall have to
13 compound a felony as usual. How much does it cost to go round the world in first-class style ? "

The lady stared in amazement.

" Could it be done on five thousand pounds ? "

" Well, I should think so, indeed ! "

" Very good. I think you will sign me a cheque for that, and I will see that it comes to Mrs. Maberley. You owe her a little change of air. Meantime, lady " —he wagged a cautionary forefinger—" have a care ! Have a care ! You can't play with edged tools for ever without cutting those dainty hands."

13 *to compound a felony as usual.* Magistrate S. Tupper Bigelow has pointed out ("Sherlock Holmes and the Misprision of Felony") that *Russell on Crime* (5th edition, 1877; 6th edition, 1896; 7th edition, 1909; 8th edition, 1923) says: "Compounding a felony is committed where the party robbed not only knows the felon but also takes his goods again, or other amends, upon agreement not to prosecute." In the Canon, Magistrate Bigelow maintains, compounding a felony is confused with *misprision of felony*, an offense which "Holmes committed . . . no less than seventeen times in twelve cases." Russell says of misprision of felony: it "closely resembles the offence of being accessory after the fact to felony. It consists of concealing or procuring the concealment of a felony by the common law or by statute. . . . It is the duty of a man to discover the felony of another to a magistrate. . . . The law does not allow private persons the right to forego a prosecution. . . . There must be knowledge without assent, for any assent or participation will make the man a principal or an accessory. . . . Misprision of felony is distinct from compounding a felony."

A Note on the "Canonicity" of "The Adventure of the Three Gables": This is another of the adventures recounted in *The Case-Book of Sherlock Holmes* which Mr. D. Martin Dakin would reject from the Canon as spurious: "Although it bears Watson's name, I cannot believe that he wrote it. The plot is fantastic and improbable, and is it likely that any man would bear the name Langdale Pike? But the chief argument against the case is the poor figure Holmes cuts in it. Never has a feebler story insulted the memory of the great detective. In the final scene, after telling the fair Isadora Klein coldly that her fate is sealed, he gives in to her in the end and lets her off with a contribution of £5,000. The roguish badinage of his exchanges with Susan ('Oh, Susan! Language!' . . . 'Good-bye, Susan. Paregoric is the stuff . . .') —is even more embarrassing than his remarks to Count Sylvius [in "The Adventure of the Mazarin Stone"], and strongly suggests the same author (who seems to have been determined to show us Holmes as a funny man.) But the falsest note of all is struck in his cheap jeers at Steve Dixie. No admirer of Holmes can read this scene without a blush. For Holmes was a gentleman. And one thing no gentleman does is to taunt another man for his racial characteristics. . . . We must definitely reject [this story]."

74

THE ADVENTURE OF THE MAZARIN STONE

[*Summer, 1903; one day*]

IT was pleasant to Dr. Watson to find himself once more in the untidy room of the first floor in Baker Street which had been the starting-point of so many remarkable adventures. He looked round him at the scientific charts upon the wall, the acid-charred bench of chemicals, the violin-case leaning in the corner, the coal-scuttle, which contained of old the pipes and tobacco. Finally, his eyes came round to the fresh and smiling face of Billy, the young but very wise and tactful page, who had helped a little to fill up the gap of loneliness and isolation which surrounded the saturnine figure of the great detective.

"It all seems very unchanged, Billy. You don't change, either. I hope the same can be said of him?"

Billy glanced, with some solicitude, at the closed door of the bedroom.

"I think he's in bed and asleep," he said.

It was seven in the evening of a lovely summer's day, 1
but Dr. Watson was sufficiently familiar with the irregularity of his old friend's hours to feel no surprise at the idea.

"That means a case, I suppose?"

"Yes, sir; he is very hard at it just now. I'm frightened for his health. He gets paler and thinner, and he eats nothing. 'When will you be pleased to dine, Mr. Holmes?' Mrs. Hudson asked. 'Seven-thirty, the day after to-morrow,' said he. You know his way when he is keen on a case."

"Yes, Billy, I know."

"He's following someone. Yesterday he was out as a workman looking for a job. To-day he was an old woman. Fairly took me in, he did, and I ought to know his ways by now." Billy pointed with a grin to a very baggy parasol which leaned against the sofa. "That's part of the old woman's outfit," he said.

"But what is it all about, Billy?"

Billy sank his voice, as one who discusses great secrets of State. "I don't mind telling you, sir, but it should go no farther. It's this case of the Crown diamond."

"What—the hundred-thousand-pound burglary?"

"Yes, sir. They must get it back, sir. Why, we had

1 *It was seven in the evening of a lovely summer's day.* Watson is not living at Baker Street in this case; more, he is again in practice, and his practice is a successful one; Holmes later says to him: "You bear every mark of the busy medical man, with calls on him every hour." "The Adventure of the Mazarin Stone" is certainly after Holmes' Return (Watson, seeing "the facsimile of his old friend . . . in an arm-chair," says, "We used something of the sort once before," and this is clearly a reference to "The Adventure of the Empty House" in 1894. So Dr. Watson's current practice cannot be the successful practice of his second marriage; far less can it be the unsuccessful practice of Marriage I. Nor can the page boy, Billy, be the Billy of *The Valley of Fear* (1888). *This* Billy is described as "young but very wise and tactful," and "The Adventure of the Empty House" was "before [his] time." Can this be the summer of 1894, in the period between Holmes' Return to London and Watson's return to Baker Street, before he sold his Kensington practice to Dr. Verner? It hardly seems that it can: 1) "The Adventure of the Mazarin Stone" is not included in the list of important cases of 1894 given in "The Adventure of the Golden Pince-Nez." 2) If Billy the page was hired shortly after "The Adventure of the Empty House" his tenure at Baker Street was indeed a short one; he is not mentioned in any case we have assigned to the period immediately following the Return. But it is apparent that Billy has been with Holmes for some time: "I ought to know [Holmes'] ways by now," he says. 3) Watson was evidently sharing the Baker Street rooms at a time when *this* Billy was the page there: "You don't change, either," Watson says to him. 4) Watson, in "The Adventure of the Mazarin Stone," has been away from Baker Street for some months, and has not seen Holmes in some time: Billy had "helped a little to fill up the gap of loneliness and isolation which surrounded the saturnine figure of the great detective"; "You have not learned . . . to despise my pipe and my lamentable tobacco?" Holmes asks Watson. That the case is a very late one is further evidenced by the fact that it is "Youghal of the C.I.D."—not Gregson or Lestrade or Hopkins—that Holmes calls in. The contemporary reader would know that Holmes had retired by December, 1904 ("The Second Stain") but he would be hard put to determine between 1903 and 1904. The modern student has the advantage of knowing that Holmes had in fact retired shortly after September, 1903, and he would have no hesitation in dating "The Adventure of the Mazarin Stone" in the summer of that year. Holmes says it was a "chilly" day "for the time of the year," but this statement can be taken as part of his joke on Lord Cantlemere; the anonymous writer called it a "lovely" evening. There does not seem to be any other evidence from which one might determine either the month or the day.

2 *the Prime Minister and the Home Secretary.* Arthur James Balfour, 1848–1930, Prime Minister, 1902–1905, and A. Akers-Douglas.

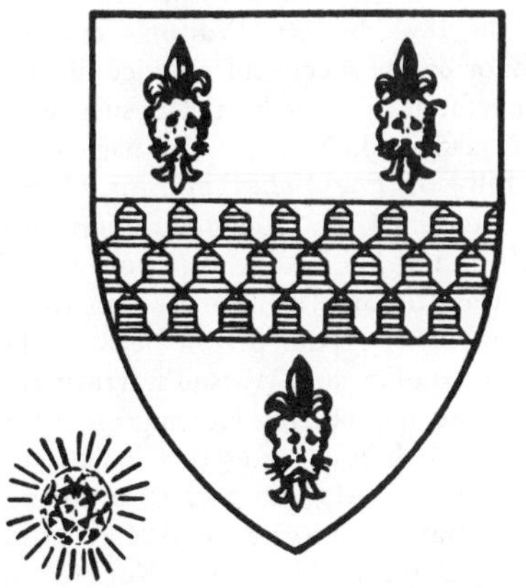

"THEN THERE IS LORD CANTLEMERE ——"

"This crusty old peer . . . has been given a name that does not appear in heraldic records," Dr. Julian Wolff wrote in his *Practical Handbook of Sherlockian Heraldry.* "It is evident that one of Watson's weak attempts at concealment has been made for it seems that the Cantilupe family is involved. The following is from *The Siege of Carlaverock:* "And William de Cantilupe . . . had on a red shield a fess vair, with three fleurs de lis of bright gold issuing from leopards' heads.' "

2 the Prime Minister and the Home Secretary both sitting on that very sofa. Mr. Holmes was very nice to them. He soon put them at their ease and promised he would do all he could. Then there is Lord Cantlemere——"

"Ah!"

"Yes, sir; you know what that means. He's a stiff 'un, sir, if I may say so. I can get along with the Prime Minister, and I've nothing against the Home Secretary, who seemed a civil, obliging sort of man, but I can't stand his lordship. Neither can Mr. Holmes, sir. You see, he don't believe in Mr. Holmes and he was against employing him. He'd *rather* he failed."

"And Mr. Holmes knows it?"

"Mr. Holmes always knows whatever there is to know."

"Well, we'll hope he won't fail and that Lord Cantlemere will be confounded. But I say, Billy, what is that curtain for across the window?"

"Mr. Holmes had it put up there three days ago. We've got something funny behind it."

Billy advanced and drew away the drapery which screened the alcove of the bow window.

Dr. Watson could not restrain a cry of amazement. There was a facsimile of his old friend, dressing-gown and all, the face turned three-quarters towards the window and downwards, as though reading an invisible book, while the body was sunk deep in an arm-chair. Billy detached the head and held it in the air.

"We put it at different angles, so that it may seem more life-like. I wouldn't dare touch it if the blind were not down. But when it's up you can see this from across the way."

"We used something of the sort once before."

"Before my time," said Billy. He drew the window curtains apart and looked out into the street. "There are folk who watch us from over yonder. I can see a fellow now at the window. Have a look for yourself."

Watson had taken a step forward when the bedroom door opened, and the long, thin form of Holmes emerged, his face pale and drawn, but his step and bearing as active as ever. With a single spring he was at the window, and had drawn the blind once more.

"That will do, Billy," said he. "You were in danger of your life then, my boy, and I can't do without you just yet. Well, Watson, it is good to see you in your old quarters once again. You come at a critical moment."

"So I gather."

"You can go, Billy. That boy is a problem, Watson. How far am I justified in allowing him to be in danger?"

"Danger of what, Holmes?"

"Of sudden death. I'm expecting something this evening."

"Expecting what?"

"To be murdered, Watson."

"No, no; you are joking, Holmes!"

"Even my limited sense of humour could evolve a better joke than that. But we may be comfortable in the meantime, may we not? Is alcohol permitted?

The gasogene and cigars are in the old place. Let me see you once more in the customary arm-chair. You have not, I hope, learned to despise my pipe and my lamentable tobacco? It has to take the place of food these days."

"But why not eat?"

"Because the faculties become refined when you starve them. Why, surely, as a doctor, my dear Watson, you must admit that what your digestion gains in the way of blood supply is so much lost to the brain. I am a brain, Watson. The rest of me is a mere appendix. 3
Therefore, it is the brain I must consider."

"But this danger, Holmes?"

"Ah, yes; in case it should come off, it would perhaps be as well that you should burden your memory with the name and address of the murderer. You can give it to Scotland Yard, with my love and a parting blessing. Sylvius is the name—Count Negretto Sylvius. Write it down, man, write it down! 136 Moorside Gardens, N.W. Got it?"

Watson's honest face was twitching with anxiety. He knew only too well the immense risks taken by Holmes, and was well aware that what he said was more likely to be under-statement than exaggeration. Watson was always the man of action, and he rose to the occasion.

"Count me in, Holmes. I have nothing to do for a day or two."

"Your morals don't improve, Watson. You have added fibbing to your other vices. You bear every sign of the busy medical man, with calls on him every hour."

"Not such important ones. But can't you have this fellow arrested?"

"Yes, Watson, I could. That's what worries him so."

"But why don't you?"

"Because I don't know where the diamond is."

"Ah! Billy told me—the missing Crown jewel!"

"Yes, the great yellow Mazarin stone. I've cast 4
my net and I have my fish. But I have not got the stone. What is the use of taking *them*? We can make the world a better place by laying them by the heels. But that is not what I am out for. It's the stone I want."

"And is this Count Sylvius one of your fish?"

"Yes, and he's a shark. He bites. The other is Sam Merton, the boxer. Not a bad fellow, Sam, but the Count has used him. Sam's not a shark. He is a great big silly bull-headed gudgeon. But he is flopping about in my net all the same."

"Where is this Count Sylvius?"

"I've been at his very elbow all the morning. You've seen me as an old lady, Watson. I was never more convincing. He actually picked up my parasol for me once. 'By your leave, madame,' said he—half-Italian, you know, and with the Southern graces of manner when in the mood, but a devil incarnate in the other

BILLY ADVANCED AND DREW AWAY THE DRAPERY . . .

Illustration by A. Gilbert for the *Strand Magazine*, October, 1921.

3 *The rest of me is a mere appendix.* "But independent observation would [not] confirm that statement . . . ; not so long as we are constantly encountering appetizing references in the stories to 'oysters and a brace of grouse, with something a little choice in white wines' (the prelude to the wild chase down the Thames in the steam-launch *Aurora*) and 'a couple of brace of cold woodcock, a pheasant, a *pâté de fois gras* pie with a group of ancient and cobwebby bottles' ["The Noble Bachelor"]. . . . Epicure that [Holmes] was he . . . minded his belly very studiously," Mr. Richard D. Altick wrote in "Mr. Sherlock Holmes and Dr. Samuel Johnson."

4 *the great yellow Mazarin stone.* The gem was named for Cardinal Jules Mazarin, 1602–1661.

mood. Life is full of whimsical happenings, Watson."

" It might have been tragedy."

" Well, perhaps it might. I followed him to old
5 Straubenzee's workshop in the Minories. Straubenzee made the air-gun—a very pretty bit of work, as I understand, and I rather fancy it is in the opposite window at the present moment. Have you seen the dummy? Of course, Billy showed it to you. Well, it may get a bullet through its beautiful head at any moment. Ah, Billy, what is it?"

The boy had reappeared in the room with a card upon a tray. Holmes glanced at it with raised eyebrows and an amused smile.

" The man himself. I had hardly expected this.
6 Grasp the nettle, Watson! A man of nerve. Possibly
7 you have heard of his reputation as a shooter of big game. It would indeed be a triumphant ending to his excellent sporting record if he added me to his bag. This is a proof that he feels my toe very close behind his heel."

" Send for the police."

" I probably shall. But not just yet. Would you glance carefully out of the window, Watson, and see if anyone is hanging about in the street?"

Watson looked warily round the edge of the curtain.

" Yes, there is one rough fellow near the door."

" That will be Sam Merton—the faithful but rather fatuous Sam. Where is this gentleman, Billy?"

8 " In the waiting-room, sir."

" Show him up when I ring."

" Yes, sir."

" If I am not in the room, show him in all the same."

" Yes, sir."

Watson waited until the door was closed, and then he turned earnestly to his companion.

" Look here, Holmes, this is simply impossible. This is a desperate man, who sticks at nothing. He may have come to murder you."

" I should not be surprised."

" I insist upon staying with you."

" You would be horribly in the way."

" In *his* way?"

" No, my dear fellow—in my way."

" Well, I can't possibly leave you."

" Yes, you can, Watson. And you will, for you have never failed to play the game. I am sure you will play it to the end. This man has come for his own purpose, but he may stay for mine." Holmes took out his notebook and scribbled a few lines. " Take a cab to Scotland Yard and give this to Youghal of the C.I.D. Come back with the police. The fellow's arrest will follow."

" I'll do that with joy."

" Before you return I may have just time enough to find out where the stone is." He touched the bell. " I think we will go out through the bedroom. This
9 second exit is exceedingly useful. I rather want to see my shark without his seeing me, and I have, as you will remember, my own way of doing it."

It was, therefore, an empty room into which Billy, a minute later, ushered Count Sylvius. The famous

5 *the Minories.* The street in the City called the Minories takes its name from the community of the "Sorores Minores," which was established just outside the walls of the City in 1293. It belonged to the second Order of St. Francis and consisted of "the Abbess and Sisters Minoresses of the Order of St. Clare." The name Minories seems to have been given to the street at the end of the sixteenth or the beginning of the seventeenth century.

6 *Grasp the nettle, Watson!* From verses written by Aaron Hill (1685–1750):

> Tender-handed stroke a nettle,
>   And it stings you for your pains;
> Grasp it like a man of mettle
>   And it soft as silk remains.

7 *a shooter of big game.* As we have previously noted, the villain in Conan Doyle's original version of "The Adventure of the Mazarin Stone"—the one-act play called *The Crown Diamond: An Evening with Sherlock Holmes*—was, not Count Negretto Sylvius, but our old friend Colonel Sebastian Moran.

8 *the waiting-room, sir,*" It is possible that 221 Baker Street may, at this time, have boasted a "waiting-room," but all reliable commentators have warned that we must be very careful about taking "The Adventure of the Mazarin Stone" as our authority for any details concerning the home of Holmes.

9 *This second exit is exceedingly useful.* See Note 8 above.

game-shot, sportsman, and man-about-town was a big, swarthy fellow, with a formidable dark moustache, shading a cruel, thin-lipped mouth, and surmounted by a long, curved nose, like the beak of an eagle. He was well dressed, but his brilliant necktie, shining pin, and glittering rings were flamboyant in their effect. As the door closed behind him he looked round him with fierce, startled eyes, like one who suspects a trap at every turn. Then he gave a violent start as he saw the impassive head and the collar of the dressing-gown which projected above the arm-chair in the window. At first his expression was one of pure amazement. Then the light of a horrible hope gleamed in his dark, murderous eyes. He took one more glance round to see that there were no witnesses, and then, on tiptoe, his thick stick half raised, he approached the silent figure. He was crouching for his final spring and blow when a cool, sardonic voice greeted him from the open bedroom door:

" Don't break it, Count ! Don't break it ! "

The assassin staggered back, amazement in his convulsed face. For an instant he half raised his loaded cane once more, as if he would turn his violence from the effigy to the original ; but there was something in that steady grey eye and mocking smile which caused his hand to sink to his side.

" It's a pretty little thing," said Holmes, advancing towards the image. " Tavernier, the French modeller, made it. He is as good at wax-works as your friend Straubenzee is at air-guns."

" Air-guns, sir ! What do you mean ? "

" Put your hat and stick on the side-table. Thank you ! Pray take a seat. Would you care to put your revolver out also ? Oh, very good, if you prefer to sit upon it. Your visit is really most opportune, for I wanted badly to have a few minutes' chat with you."

The Count scowled, with heavy, threatening eyebrows.

" I, too, wished to have some words with you, Holmes. That is why I am here. I won't deny that I intended to assault you just now."

Holmes swung his leg on the edge of the table.

" I rather gathered that you had some idea of the sort in your head," said he. " But why these personal attentions ? "

" Because you have gone out of your way to annoy me. Because you have put your creatures upon my track."

" My creatures ! I assure you no ! "

" Nonsense ! I have had them followed. Two can play at that game, Holmes."

" It is a small point, Count Sylvius, but perhaps you would kindly give me my prefix when you address me. You can understand that, with my routine of work, I should find myself on familiar terms with half the rogues' gallery, and you will agree that exceptions are invidious."

" Well, *Mr.* Holmes, then."

" Excellent ! But I assure you you are mistaken about my alleged agents."

Count Sylvius laughed contemptuously.

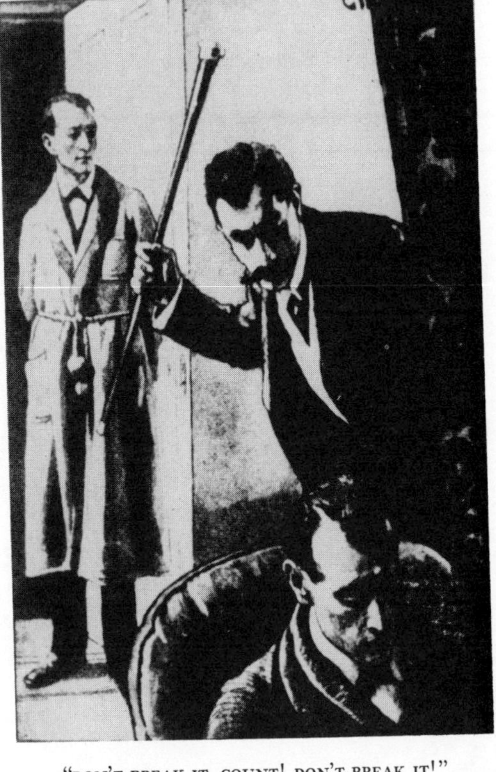

"DON'T BREAK IT, COUNT! DON'T BREAK IT!"

Illustration by A. Gilbert for the *Strand Magazine*, October, 1921. Frederic Dorr Steele illustrated the same scene for *Hearst's International*, November, 1921.

" Other people can observe as well as you. Yesterday there was an old sporting man. To-day it was an elderly woman. They held me in view all day."

" Really, sir, you compliment me. Old Baron Dowson said the night before he was hanged that in my case what the law had gained the stage had lost. And now you give my little impersonations your kindly praise ! "

" It was you—you yourself ? "

Holmes shrugged his shoulders. " You can see in the corner the parasol which you so politely handed to me in the Minories before you began to suspect."

" If I had known, you might never——"

" Have seen this humble home again. I was well aware of it. We all have neglected opportunities to deplore. As it happens, you did not know, so here we are ! "

The Count's knotted brows gathered more heavily over his menacing eyes. " What you say only makes the matter worse. It was not your agents, but your play-acting, busybody self ! You admit that you have dogged me. Why ? "

" Come now, Count. You used to shoot lions in Algeria."

" Well ? "

" But why ? "

" Why ? The sport—the excitement—the danger ! "

" And, no doubt, to free the country from a pest ? "

" Exactly ! "

" My reasons in a nutshell ! "

The Count sprang to his feet, and his hand involuntarily moved back to his hip-pocket.

" Sit down, sir, sit down ! There was another, more practical, reason. I want that yellow diamond ! "

Count Sylvius lay back in his chair with an evil smile.

" Upon my word ! " said he.

" You knew that I was after you for that. The real reason why you are here to-night is to find out how much I know about the matter and how far my removal is absolutely essential. Well, I should say that, from your point of view, it *is* absolutely essential, for I know all about it, save only one thing, which you are about to tell me."

" Oh, indeed ! And, pray, what is this missing fact ? "

" Where the Crown diamond now is."

The Count looked sharply at his companion. " Oh, you want to know that, do you ? How the devil should I be able to tell you where it is ? "

" You can, and you will."

" Indeed ! "

" You can't bluff me, Count Sylvius." Holmes' eyes, as he gazed at him, contracted and lightened until they were like two menacing points of steel. " You are absolute plate-glass. I see to the very back of your mind."

" Then, of course, you see where the diamond is ! "

Holmes clapped his hands with amusement, and then pointed a derisive finger. " Then you do know. You have admitted it ! "

" I admit nothing."

" Now, Count, if you will be reasonable we can do business. If not, you will get hurt."

Count Sylvius threw up his eyes to the ceiling. " And you talk about bluff ! " said he.

Holmes looked at him thoughtfully, like a master chess-player who meditates his crowning move. Then he threw open the table drawer and drew out a squat notebook.

" Do you know what I keep in this book ? "

" No, sir, I do not ! "

" You ! "

" Me ? "

" Yes, sir, *you* ! You are all here—every action of your vile and dangerous life."

" Damn you, Holmes ! " cried the Count, with blazing eyes. " There are limits to my patience ! "

" It's all here, Count. The real facts as to the death of old Mrs. Harold, who left you the Blymer estate, which you so rapidly gambled away."

" You are dreaming ! "

" And the complete life history of Miss Minnie Warrender."

" Tut ! You will make nothing of that ! "

" Plenty more here, Count. Here is the robbery in the train-de-luxe to the Riviera on February 13, 1892. Here is the forged cheque in the same year on the Crédit Lyonnais."

" No ; you're wrong there."

" Then I am right on the others ! Now, Count, you are a card-player. When the other fellow has all the trumps, it saves time to throw down your hand."

" What has all this talk to do with the jewel of which you spoke ? "

" Gently, Count. Restrain that eager mind ! Let me get to the points in my own humdrum fashion. I have all this against you ; but, above all, I have a clear case against both you and your fighting bully in the case of the Crown diamond."

" Indeed ! "

" I have the cabman who took you to Whitehall and the cabman who brought you away. I have the Commissionaire who saw you near the case. I have Ikey Sanders, who refused to cut it up for you. Ikey has peached, and the game is up."

The veins stood out on the Count's forehead. His dark, hairy hands were clenched in a convulsion of restrained emotion. He tried to speak, but the words would not shape themselves.

" That's the hand I play from," said Holmes. " I put it all upon the table. But one card is missing. It's the King of Diamonds. I don't know where the stone is."

" You never shall know."

" No ? Now, be reasonable, Count. Consider the situation. You are going to be locked up for twenty years. So is Sam Merton. What good are you going to get out of your diamond ? None in the world. But
if you hand it over—well, I'll compound a felony. We **10**
don't want you or Sam. We want the stone. Give that up, and so far as I am concerned you can go free so long as you behave yourself in the future. If you make

10 *I'll compound a felony*. See "The Adventure of the Three Gables," Note 13.

another slip—well, it will be the last. But this time my commission is to get the stone, not you."

"But if I refuse?"

"Why, then—alas!—it must be you and not the stone."

Billy had appeared in answer to a ring.

"I think, Count, that it would be as well to have your friend Sam at this conference. After all, his interests should be represented. Billy, you will see a large and ugly gentleman outside the front door. Ask him to come up."

"If he won't come, sir?"

"No violence, Billy. Don't be rough with him. If you tell him that Count Sylvius wants him he will certainly come."

"What are you going to do now?" asked the Count, as Billy disappeared.

"My friend Watson was with me just now. I told him that I had a shark and a gudgeon in my net; now I am drawing the net and up they come together."

The Count had risen from his chair, and his hand was behind his back. Holmes held something half protruding from the pocket of his dressing-gown.

"You won't die in your bed, Holmes."

"I have often had the same idea. Does it matter very much? After all, Count, your own exit is more likely to be perpendicular than horizontal. But these anticipations of the future are morbid. Why not give
11 ourselves up to the unrestrained enjoyment of the present?"

A sudden wild-beast light sprang up in the dark, menacing eyes of the master criminal. Holmes' figure seemed to grow taller as he grew tense and ready.

"It is no use your fingering your revolver, my friend," he said, in a quiet voice. "You know perfectly well that you dare not use it, even if I gave you time to draw it. Nasty, noisy things, revolvers, Count. Better stick to air-guns. Ah! I think I hear the fairy footstep of your estimable partner. Good day, Mr. Merton. Rather dull in the street, is it not?"

The prize-fighter, a heavily built young man with a stupid, obstinate, slab-sided face, stood awkwardly at the door, looking about him with a puzzled expression. Holmes' debonair manner was a new experience, and though he vaguely felt that it was hostile, he did not know how to counter it. He turned to his more astute comrade for help.

"What's the game now, Count? What's this fellow want? What's up?" His voice was deep and raucous.

The Count shrugged his shoulders and it was Holmes who answered.

"If I may put it in a nutshell, Mr. Merton, I should say it was *all* up."

The boxer still addressed his remarks to his associate.

"Is this cove trying to be funny, or what? I'm not in the funny mood myself."

"No, I expect not," said Holmes. "I think I can promise you that you will feel even less humorous as the evening advances. Now, look here, Count Sylvius. I'm a busy man and I can't waste time. I'm going into

11 *the unrestrained enjoyment of the present?"* In "The Adventure of the Norwood Builder," Holmes tells Watson, "We must use what time we have." In *The Hound of the Baskervilles,* Holmes asserts, "The past and the present are within the field of my inquiry, but what a man may do in the future is a hard question to answer." In "The Adventure of the Veiled Lodger," he reflects, "The ways of fate are indeed hard to understand." "These are but a few of the echoes," Mr. Morris Rosenblum wrote in "The Horation Spirit in Holmes," "of lines in the poems of Horace.

Carpe diem, quam minimum credula postero.
Odes, Book 1, 11.

'Make the most of today; put as little trust as possible in the future.' "

that bedroom. Pray make yourselves quite at home in my absence. You can explain to your friend how the matter lies without the restraint of my presence. I shall try over the Hoffmann Barcarolle upon my violin. In five minutes I shall return for your final answer. You quite grasp the alternative, do you not? Shall we take you, or shall we have the stone?"

Holmes withdrew, picking up his violin from the corner as he passed. A few moments later the long-drawn,
wailing notes of that most haunting of tunes came faintly 12
through the closed door of the bedroom.

"What is it, then?" asked Merton anxiously, as his companion turned to him. "Does he know about the stone?"

"He knows a damned sight too much about it. I'm not sure that he doesn't know all about it."

"Good Lord!" The boxer's sallow face turned a shade whiter.

"Ikey Sanders has split on us."

"He has, has he? I'll do him down a thick 'un for that if I swing for it."

"That won't help us much. We've got to make up our minds what to do."

"Half a mo'," said the boxer, looking suspiciously at the bedroom door. "He's a leary cove that wants watching. I suppose he's not listening?"

"How can he be listening with that music going?"

"That's right. Maybe somebody's behind a curtain. Too many curtains in this room." As he looked round he suddenly saw for the first time the effigy in the window, and stood staring and pointing, too amazed for words.

"Tut! it's only a dummy," said the Count.

"A fake, is it? Well, strike me! Madame Tussaud ain't in it. It's the living spit of him, gown and all. But them curtains, Count!"

"Oh, confound the curtains! We are wasting our time, and there is none too much. He can lag us over this stone."

"The deuce he can!"

"But he'll let us slip if we only tell him where the swag is."

12 *the long-drawn, wailing notes of that most haunting of tunes.* "It would hardly be possible to apply less idoneous adjectives to [the Barcarolle from Offenbach's *The Tales of Hoffmann*] than ... 'wailing' and 'haunting,'" Mr. Benjamin Grosbayne wrote in "Sherlock Holmes—Musician." "Moreover, the use of the word 'tune' is particularly inept as applied to this limpid and translucent melody."

"I'M GOING INTO THAT BEDROOM."

Illustration by A. Gilbert for the *Strand Magazine*, October, 1921.

"MADAME TUSSAUD AIN'T IN IT."

The home of the famous waxworks in the Marylebone Road, after the move from Baker Street. This building was burnt down; the "Buffalo's Head" and the old houses on the left were demolished to make way for the new Baker Street Metropolitan Railway just before the first World War. The illustration is from *In the Footsteps of Sherlock Holmes*, by Michael Harrison.

"What! Give it up? Give up a hundred thousand quid?"

"It's one or the other."

Merton scratched his short-cropped pate.

"He's alone in there. Let's do him in. If his light were out we should have nothing to fear."

The Count shook his head.

"He is armed and ready. If we shot him we could hardly get away in a place like this. Besides, it's likely enough that the police know whatever evidence he has got. Hallo! What was that?"

There was a vague sound which seemed to come from the window. Both men sprang round, but all was quiet. Save for the one strange figure seated in the chair, the room was certainly empty.

"Something in the street," said Merton. "Now look here, guv'nor, you've got the brains. Surely you can think a way out of it. If slugging is no use then it's up to you."

"I've fooled better men than he," the Count answered. "The stone is here in my secret pocket. I take no chances leaving it about. It can be out of England to-night and cut into four pieces in Amsterdam before Sunday. He knows nothing of Van Seddar."

"I thought Van Seddar was going next week."

"He *was*. But now he must get off by the next boat. One or other of us must slip round with the stone to
13 Lime Street and tell him."

"But the false bottom ain't ready."

"Well, he must take it as it is and chance it. There's not a moment to lose." Again, with the sense of danger which becomes an instinct with the sportsman, he paused and looked hard at the window. Yes, it was surely from the street that the faint sound had come.

"As to Holmes," he continued, "we can fool him easily enough. You see, the damned fool won't arrest us if he can get the stone. Well, we'll promise him the stone. We'll put him on the wrong track about it, and before he finds that it *is* the wrong track it will be in Holland and we out of the country."

"That sounds good to me!" cried Sam Merton, with a grin.

"You go on and tell the Dutchman to get a move on him. I'll see this sucker and fill him up with a bogus confession. I'll tell him that the stone is in Liverpool. Confound that whining music; it gets on my nerves! By the time he finds it isn't in Liverpool it will be in quarters and we on the blue water. Come back here, out of a line with that keyhole. Here is the stone."

"I wonder you dare carry it."

"Where could I have it safer? If we could take it out of Whitehall someone else could surely take it out of my lodgings."

"Let's have a look at it."

Count Sylvius cast a somewhat unflattering glance at his associate, and disregarded the unwashed hand which was extended towards him.

"What—d'ye think I'm going to snatch it off you? See here, mister, I'm getting a bit tired of your ways."

13 *Lime Street.* So called from the lime-burners; the neighboring Coleman Street and Seacoal Lane have the same origin. Lime Street, on the south side of Leadenhall Street, was until the close of the eighteenth century inhabited by wealthy City merchants. Today it is the home of the magnificent new headquarters of Lloyd's.

" Well, well ; no offence, Sam. We can't afford to quarrel. Come over to the window if you want to see the beauty properly. Now hold it to the light ! Here ! "

" Thank you ! "

With a single spring Holmes had leaped from the dummy's chair and had grasped the precious jewel. He held it now in one hand, while his other pointed a revolver at the Count's head. The two villains staggered back in utter amazement. Before they had recovered Holmes had pressed the electric bell.

" No violence, gentlemen—no violence, I beg of you ! Consider the furniture ! It must be very clear to you that your position is an impossible one. The police are waiting below."

The Count's bewilderment overmastered his rage and fear.

" But how the deuce—— ? " he gasped.

" Your surprise is very natural. You are not aware that a second door from my bedroom leads behind that
curtain. I fancied that you must have heard me when **14**
I displaced the figure, but luck was on my side. It gave me a chance of listening to your racy conversation which would have been painfully constrained had you been aware of my presence."

The Count gave a gesture of resignation.

" We give you best, Holmes. I believe you are the devil himself."

" Not far from him, at any rate," Holmes answered, with a polite smile.

Sam Merton's slow intellect had only gradually appreciated the situation. Now, as the sound of heavy steps came from the stairs outside, he broke silence at last.

" A fair cop ! " said he. " But, I say, what about that bloomin' fiddle ! I hear it yet."

" Tut, tut ! " Holmes answered. " You are perfectly right. Let it play ! These modern gramophones are a
remarkable invention." **15**

There was an inrush of police, the handcuffs clicked and the criminals were led to the waiting cab. Watson lingered with Holmes, congratulating him upon this fresh leaf added to his laurels. Once more their conversation was interrupted by the imperturbable Billy with his card-tray.

" Lord Cantlemere, sir."

" Show him up, Billy. This is the eminent peer who represents the very highest interests," said Holmes. " He is an excellent and loyal person, but rather of the old regime. Shall we make him unbend ? Dare we venture upon a slight liberty ? He knows, we may conjecture, nothing of what has occurred."

The door opened to admit a thin, austere figure with a hatchet face and drooping mid-Victorian whiskers of a glossy blackness which hardly corresponded with the rounded shoulders and feeble gait. Holmes advanced affably, and shook an unresponsive hand.

" How-do-you-do, Lord Cantlemere ? It is chilly, for the time of year, but rather warm indoors. May I take your overcoat ? "

" No, I thank you ; I will not take it off."

14 *a second door from my bedroom behind that curtain.* See Note 8.

15 *These modern gramophones are a remarkable invention.* "Let us stress here the fact that it was a *gramophone*," Mr. Anthony Boucher wrote in "The Records of Baker Street." "To most modern readers, *gramophone* and *phonograph* are interchangeable words, respectively British and American, like *lift* and *elevator*. . . . But in England in 1903, *gramophone* distinctly meant the Berliner-Gramophone & Typewriter *disc* machine, while cylinder machines were known as *phonographs* or *graphophones*."

Elsewhere (in "Prolegomena to a Holmesian Discography"), Mr. Boucher has written: "It was almost certainly a single 12″ [disc]. Single, from the date of the events . . . ; 12″ because it was still playing after at least three and a half minutes of dialogue. . . . But the most curious factor concerning the record is that it must . . . have been a performance of the Hoffmann Barcarolle by *unaccompanied* violin. Such a transcription is so unlikely a choice for commercial recording that one is led to consider . . . that this was a private recording made by Holmes himself."

Holmes laid his hand insistently upon the sleeve.

"Pray allow me! My friend Dr. Watson would assure you that these changes of temperature are most insidious."

His lordship shook himself free with some impatience.

"I am quite comfortable, sir. I have no need to stay. I have simply looked in to know how your self-appointed task was progressing."

"It is difficult—very difficult."

"I feared that you would find it so."

There was a distinct sneer in the old courtier's words and manner.

"Every man finds his limitations, Mr. Holmes, but at least it cures us of the weakness of self-satisfaction."

"Yes, sir, I have been much perplexed."

"No doubt."

"Especially upon one point. Possibly you could help me upon it?"

"You apply for my advice rather late in the day. I thought that you had your own all-sufficient methods. Still, I am ready to help you."

"You see, Lord Cantlemere, we can no doubt frame a case against the actual thieves."

"When you have caught them."

"Exactly. But the question is—how shall we proceed against the receiver?"

"Is this not rather premature?"

"It is as well to have our plans ready. Now, what would you regard as final evidence against the receiver?"

"The actual possession of the stone."

"You would arrest him upon that?"

"Most undoubtedly."

Holmes seldom laughed, but he got as near it as his old friend Watson could remember.

"In that case, my dear sir, I shall be under the painful necessity of advising your arrest."

Lord Cantlemere was very angry. Some of the ancient fires flickered up into his sallow cheeks.

"You take a great liberty, Mr. Holmes. In fifty years of official life I cannot recall such a case. I am a busy man, sir, engaged upon important affairs, and I have no time or taste for foolish jokes. I may tell you frankly, sir, that I have never been a believer in your powers, and that I have always been of the opinion that the matter was far safer in the hands of the regular police force. Your conduct confirms all my conclusions. I have the honour, sir, to wish you good evening."

Holmes had swiftly changed his position and was between the peer and the door.

"One moment, sir," said he. "To actually go off with the Mazarin stone would be a more serious offence than to be found in temporary possession of it."

"Sir, this is intolerable! Let me pass."

"Put your hand in the right-hand pocket of your overcoat."

"What do you mean, sir?"

"Come—come; do what I ask."

An instant later the amazed peer was standing, blinking and stammering, with the great yellow stone on his shaking palm.

" What ! What ! How is this, Mr. Holmes ? "

" Too bad, Lord Cantlemere, too bad ! " cried Holmes. " My old friend here will tell you that I have an impish habit of practical joking. Also that I can never resist a dramatic situation. I took the liberty—the very great liberty, I admit—of putting the stone into your pocket at the beginning of our interview."

The old peer stared from the stone to the smiling face before him.

" Sir, I am bewildered. But—yes—it is indeed the Mazarin stone. We are greatly your debtors, Mr. Holmes. Your sense of humour may, as you admit, be somewhat perverted, and its exhibition remarkably untimely, but at least I withdraw any reflection I have made upon your amazing professional powers. But how——"

" The case is but half finished ; the details can wait. No doubt, Lord Cantlemere, your pleasure in telling of this successful result in the exalted circle to which you return will be some small atonement for my practical joke. Billy, you will show his lordship out, and tell Mrs. Hudson that I should be glad if she would send up dinner for two as soon as possible."

75

". . . IT IS UNDOUBTEDLY QUEER . . ."

[*Sherlock Holmes to John H. Watson, M.D., "The Adventure of the Six Napoleons"*]

"Of all the stories in the Canon which have moved scholars to discussion and argument, none has aroused more controversial opinion than 'The Adventure of the Mazarin Stone,'" the late James Montgomery wrote in "Speculation in Diamonds."

Mr. Anthony Boucher has found the story "dubious" and labeled it a "farrago."

Mr. D. Martin Dakin is less harsh than Mr. Boucher, but he too has concluded that the adventure is "spurious": "It . . . bristles with improbabilities. Yet the scene at the end with Lord Cantlemere has a lifelike ring about it and agrees with Holmes' 'impish habit of practical joking' and love of a dramatic situation as shown in 'The Naval Treaty' and 'The Adventure of the Six Napoleons.' Indeed it is scarcely a coincidence that the best parts of the story are those at both ends in which Watson personally appears. It almost looks as if the author, having come across some notes by Watson which he had discarded as only providing half a story, decided to fill in the gap from his imagination. It bear every mark of such an origin. How could anyone know the initial detail of the conversation between Count Sylvius and Sam Merton, unless indeed Holmes had his ear to the keyhole from the moment he put the record on? Holmes had a delicate vein of sarcasm and was not above twitting an adversary, as witness his interview with Col. Sebastian Moran; but the forced facetiousness of his conversation with the Count . . . reads like a violent caricature of this and must grate on the ears of all Holmesians. Finally, is it conceivable that so astute a planner as Holmes would rely for his success on the off chance that the two criminals would not be looking in his direction when he displaced the dummy, or would not notice the sound he made?"

Mr. S. C. Roberts has agreed that the tale presents many difficulties, and he has argued that since Watson was a busy practitioner at the time, it might be a compilation from the doctor's notes edited by the Mrs. Watson of 1902, who would "naturally take a proud interest in her husband's part in the adventure."

The late Gavin Brend also admitted a 1902 Mrs. Watson, but held that her attitude toward her husband's participation in Sherlock Holmes' cases and his written accounts of the same were the exact opposite of the stand taken by Mary Morstan Watson: whereas Mary had always been extremely sympathetic toward Watson's association with Holmes, and had constantly encouraged him to go running all over England on little or no notice whenever the game was afoot, her successor took a dim view of these diversions and insisted on an undivided attention to her and to his practice. Mr. Brend theorized that because of the later Mrs. Watson's attitude, Watson tried the experiment of deceiving her by writing "The Adventure of the Mazarin Stone" in the third person, but almost immediately realized that the result was too negative, and the whole idea an unsatisfactory subterfuge at best.

Mr. Guy Warrack has sided with Messrs. Boucher, Dakin, and Roberts in pronouncing the story unreliable on points of detail, and he also believes that Mrs. Watson had a hand in it, even to the invention of the gramophone incident.

The late Christopher Morley also agreed that Mrs. Watson wrote the story ("her first and last attempt") but insisted that there was never more than one Mrs. Watson—therefore the author would of necessity have been Mary. This theory has also been accepted by Mr. Russell McLauchlin, who calls the adventure "an amateurish effort which a shrewd guess ascribes to Mary Watson."

The late H. W. Bell felt that both "His Last Bow" and "The Adventure of the Mazarin Stone" were probably written by one and the same person, and although he did not presume to name the author he speculated that if Mr. Roberts' theory of Mrs. Watson's authorship was correct she may have been connected with the stage; he based this on the theatrical flavor of the bow window (a shrewd guess, as we shall see).

Mr. T. S. Blakeney has also refrained from naming the author, but has said that a third hand has written up Watson's notes, not only in "The Adventure of the Mazarin Stone" but also in *all* the adventures in *The Case-Book*, and in so doing has clumsily endeavored to imitate Watson's style.

The late Page Heldenbrand, on the other hand, agreed with Mr. Brend that the story was written by Watson himself, basing his viewpoint on a quotation from "The Problem of Thor Bridge" in which Watson says: "In some [cases] I was myself concerned and can speak as an eye-witness, while in others I was either not present or played so small a part that they could only *be told as by a third person.*" Mr. Heldenbrand held that in "The Adventure of the Mazarin Stone" Watson deemed his part sufficiently unimportant to warrant adoption of the third person form of narrative as a simple matter of literary expediency. This same point of view has been effectively stated by Mr. Cornelis Helling in his brief essay, "The Third Person."

Mr. O. F. Grazebrook, however, has speculated that the entire *Case-Book*, which of course includes "The Adventure of the Mazarin Stone," was written by young Dr. Verner, that distant relative of Holmes who bought, with Holmes' money, Watson's small practice in Kensington.

DENNIS NEILSON-TERRY AS SHERLOCK HOLMES IN "THE CROWN DIAMOND: AN EVENING WITH SHERLOCK HOLMES."

Mr. S. T. L. Harbottle, in "The Case-Book Cipher Unveiled," has attributed the authorship of "The Adventure of the Mazarin Stone"—and perhaps the rest of the *Case-Book* as well—to Inspector G. Lestrade, and Mr. G. B. Newton has put forward the interesting suggestion that the author of "The Adventure of the Mazarin Stone" was none other than Billy the page.

Still another point of view was expressed by the late Edgar W. Smith, who boldly declared that the story's true creator was Sir Arthur Conan Doyle: "Surely it is a measure both of Dr. Doyle's loyalty to his friend [Watson], and of his rank below him in the scale of literary achievement, that it should have been he—as it must have been he—who wrote 'The Adventure of the Mazarin Stone.'" Mr. Smith's view was later buttressed by Mr. Nathan L. Bengis, who pointed out in his "Thanks to Dr. Watson: A Study in Conanical Plagiarism" that "further proof, if any were needed, that ["The Adventure of the Mazarin Stone"] is apocryphal and was almost certainly written by [Conan Doyle himself] is provided by Professor John Robert Moore in 'Sherlock Holmes Borrows a Plot' in the *Modern Language Quarterly*, Vol. VIII, No. 1, March, 1947. Professor Moore . . . cites an example of where Conan Doyle 'reworked an incident from one of his earlier stories,' viz. the gramophone which is mistaken for a human voice in 'The Japanned Box' [see *The Conan Doyle Stories*] becomes the gramophone which substitutes for the violin of Holmes in 'The Adventure of the Mazarin Stone.'"

The late James Montgomery, who had the first word on this subject, should also have the last: "Just how right Mr. [Edgar W.] Smith is finds ample proof in a series of events that had their inception in 1947," Montgomery wrote in "Speculation in Diamonds." "On July 11th of that year press dispatches reported the discovery by Conan Doyle's sons and daughters of an old cardboard hatbox in the vaults of an English country bank at Crowborough, Sussex. The box contained, among other interesting memorabilia, the manuscript of a one-act play called *The Crown Diamond: An Evening with Sherlock Holmes*. . . . Although never published.**1** [the play] was actually produced by Stanley Bell at the Coliseum in London in 1921, opening on Monday, May 16th, and running for one week with Dennis Neilson-Terry in the role of Holmes. It also had a return date for an additional week commencing August 29th. . . . My reading of the manuscript does indeed confirm definitely the fact that the plots of *The Crown Diamond* and 'The Adventure of the Mazarin Stone' are identical. . . . All evidence indicates that . . . the story was written *after*, not before the play. Anthony Boucher proves himself to be a critic of startling clairvoyance when he speculates in 'The Records of Baker Street' . . . that the story represents an effort on the part of [Conan Doyle] to salvage an unsuccessful dramatic work of his own. Mr. Boucher further enhances his reputation for discernment by declaring that 'a careful examination of the structure of this much-disputed story will disclose that it is essentially a one-act play, seen from a fourth-wall viewpoint.'"

1 In point of fact, the playlet was published by the Baskerette Press in 1958 in an edition of 59 copies. No copies of this beautiful little hardcover volume were ever placed on sale, but one was given to each member of The Baker Street Irregulars, Inc., who subscribed to a "Sustentation Fund" used to meet the expenses of financing the *Baker Street Journal*.

76

THE ADVENTURE OF THE CREEPING MAN

[Sunday, September 6; Monday, September 14; Tuesday, September 22, 1903]

MR. SHERLOCK HOLMES was always of opinion that I should publish the singular facts connected with Professor Presbury, if only to dispel once for all the ugly rumours which some twenty years ago agitated the University and were echoed in the learned societies of London. There were, however, certain obstacles in the way, and the true history of this curious case remained entombed in the tin box which contains so many records of my friend's adventures. Now we have at last obtained permission to ventilate the facts which formed one of the very last cases handled by Holmes before his retirement from practice. Even now a certain reticence and discretion have to be observed in laying the matter before the public.

It was one Sunday evening early in September of the year 1903 that I received one of Holmes' laconic messages: "Come at once if convenient—if inconvenient come all the same.—S. H." The relations between us in those latter days were peculiar. He was a man of habits, narrow and concentrated habits, and I had become one of them. As an institution I was like the violin, the shag tobacco, the old black pipe, the index books, and others perhaps less excusable. When it was a case of active work and a comrade was needed upon whose nerve he could place some reliance, my rôle was obvious. But apart from this I had uses. I was a whetstone for his mind. I stimulated him. He liked to think aloud in my presence. His remarks could hardly be said to be made to me—many of them would have been as appropriately addressed to his bedstead—but none the less, having formed the habit, it had become in some way helpful that I should register and interject. If I irritated him by a certain methodical slowness in my mentality, that irritation served only to make his own flame-like intuitions and impressions flash up the more vividly and swiftly. Such was my humble rôle in our alliance. 1

When I arrived at Baker Street I found him huddled

1 *Such was my humble rôle in our alliance.* It is interesting here to compare Holmes' remarks on his relationship with Watson, at the beginning of "The Adventure of the Blanched Soldier": "Speaking of my old friend and biographer . . ."

up in his arm-chair with updrawn knees, his pipe in his mouth and his brow furrowed with thought. It was clear that he was in the throes of some vexatious problem. With a wave of his hand he indicated my old arm-chair, but otherwise for half an hour he gave no sign that he was aware of my presence. Then with a start he seemed to come from his reverie, and, with his usual whimsical smile, he greeted me back to what had once been my home.

" You will excuse a certain abstraction of mind, my dear Watson," said he. " Some curious facts have been submitted to me within the last twenty-four hours, and they in turn have given rise to some speculations of a more general character. I have serious thoughts of writing a small monograph upon the uses of dogs in the work of the detective."

" But surely, Holmes, this has been explored," said I. " Bloodhounds—sleuth-hounds——"

" No, no, Watson ; that side of the matter is, of course, obvious. But there is another which is far more subtle. You may recollect that in the case which you, in your sensational way, coupled with the Copper Beeches, I was able, by watching the mind of the child, to form a deduction as to the criminal habits of the very smug and respectable father."

" Yes, I remember it well."

" My line of thoughts about dogs is analogous. A dog reflects the family life. Whoever saw a frisky dog in a gloomy family, or a sad dog in a happy one ? Snarling people have snarling dogs, dangerous people have dangerous ones. And their passing moods may reflect the passing moods of others."

I shook my head. " Surely, Holmes, this is a little far-fetched," said I.

He had refilled his pipe and resumed his seat, taking no notice of my comment.

" The practical application of what I have said is very close to the problem which I am investigating.
2 It is a tangled skein, you understand, and I am looking for a loose end. One possible loose end lies in the question : Why does Professor Presbury's faithful wolf-hound, Roy, endeavour to bite him ? "

I sank back in my chair in some disappointment. Was it for so trivial a question as this that I had been summoned from my work ? Holmes glanced across at me.

" The same old Watson ! " said he. " You never learn that the gravest issues may depend upon the smallest things. But is it not on the face of it strange that a staid, elderly philosopher—you've heard of Presbury, of course, the famous Camford physiologist ?—that such a man, whose friend has been his devoted wolf-hound, should now have been twice attacked by his own dog ? What do you make of it ? "

" The dog is ill."

" Well, that has to be considered. But he attacks no one else, nor does he apparently molest his master, save on very special occasions. Curious, Watson—very curious. But young Mr. Bennett is before his time, if that is his ring. I had hoped to have a longer chat with you before he came."

2 *a tangled skein.* We recall that this was Conan Doyle's original title for *A Study in Scarlet.*

There was a quick step on the stairs, a sharp tap at the door, and a moment later the new client presented himself. He was a tall, handsome youth about thirty, well dressed and elegant, but with something in his bearing which suggested the shyness of the student rather than the self-possession of the man of the world. He shook hands with Holmes, and then looked with some surprise at me.

"This matter is very delicate, Mr. Holmes," he said. "Consider the relation in which I stand to Professor Presbury, both privately and publicly. I really can hardly justify myself if I speak before any third person."

"Have no fear, Mr. Bennett. Dr. Watson is the very soul of discretion, and I can assure you that this is a matter in which I am very likely to need an assistant."

"As you like, Mr. Holmes. You will, I am sure, understand my having some reserves in the matter."

"You will appreciate it, Watson, when I tell you that this gentleman, Mr. Trevor Bennett, is professional assistant to the great scientist, lives under his roof, and is engaged to his only daughter. Certainly we must agree that the Professor has every claim upon his loyalty and devotion. But it may best be shown by taking the necessary steps to clear up this strange mystery."

"I hope so, Mr. Holmes. That is my one object. Does Dr. Watson know the situation?"

"I have not had time to explain it."

"Then perhaps I had better go over the ground again before explaining some fresh developments."

"I will do so myself," said Holmes, "in order to show that I have the events in their due order. The Professor, Watson, is a man of European reputation. His life has been academic. There has never been a breath of scandal. He is a widower with one daughter, Edith. He is, I gather, a man of very virile and positive, one might almost say combative, character. So the matter stood until a very few months ago.

"Then the current of his life was broken. He is sixty-one years of age, but he became engaged to the daughter of Professor Morphy, his colleague in the chair of Comparative Anatomy. It was not, as I understand, 3 the reasoned courting of an elderly man, but rather the passionate frenzy of youth, for no one could have shown himself a more devoted lover. The lady, Alice Morphy, was a very perfect girl both in mind and body, so that there was every excuse for the Professor's infatuation. None the less, it did not meet with full approval in his own family."

"We thought it rather excessive," said our visitor.

"Exactly. Excessive and a little violent and unnatural. Professor Presbury was rich, however, and there was no objection upon the part of the father. The daughter, however, had other views, and there were already several candidates for her hand, who, if they were less eligible from a worldly point of view, were at least more of an age. The girl seemed to like the Professor in spite of his eccentricities. It was only age which stood in the way.

THERE WAS A QUICK STEP ON THE STAIRS, A SHARP RAP AT THE DOOR, AND A MOMENT LATER THE NEW CLIENT PRESENTED HIMSELF.

Illustration by Howard K. Elcock for the *Strand Magazine*, March, 1923.

3 *the chair of Comparative Anatomy*. One of the problems that this adventure poses for the student is that of determining whether "Camford" is *Cambridge* or *Oxford*. In this connection, Mr. N. P. Metcalfe has written ("Oxford or Cambridge or Both?") that "The Historical Registers of both Oxford and Cambridge for the years up to 1910 show that there was a Chair of Physiology [Professor Presbury's post] at both. . . . There was no Chair of Comparative Anatomy as such at Cambridge, but one of Zoology and Comparative Anatomy was founded in 1866. . . . At Oxford, on the other hand, in 1903 there was a Chair of Comparative Anatomy, held since 1899 by W. F. R. Weldon, M.A., of Merton, sometime fellow of St. John's, Cambridge. . . . Despite Watson's discretion, this points . . . to Oxford as the location of 'The Adventure of the Creeping Man.' "

"About this time a little mystery suddenly clouded the normal routine of the Professor's life. He did what he had never done before. He left home and gave no indication where he was going. He was away a fortnight, and returned looking rather travel-worn. He made no allusion to where he had been, although he was usually the frankest of men. It chanced, however, that our client here, Mr. Bennett, received a letter from a fellow-student in Prague, who said that he was glad to have seen Professor Presbury there, although he had not been able to talk to him. Only in this way did his own household learn where he had been.

"Now comes the point. From that time onwards a curious change came over the Professor. He became furtive and sly. Those around him had always the feeling that he was not the man that they had known, but that he was under some shadow which had darkened his higher qualities. His intellect was not affected. His lectures were as brilliant as ever. But always there was something new, something sinister and unexpected. His daughter, who was devoted to him, tried again and again to resume the old relations and to penetrate this mask which her father seemed to have put on. You, sir, as I understand, did the same—but all was in vain. And now, Mr. Bennett, tell in your own words the incident of the letters."

"You must understand, Dr. Watson, that the Professor had no secrets from me. If I were his son or his younger brother, I could not have more completely enjoyed his confidence. As his secretary I handled every paper which came to him, and I opened and subdivided his letters. Shortly after his return all this was changed. He told me that certain letters might come to him from London which would be marked by a cross under the stamp. These were to be set aside for his own eyes only. I may say that several of these did pass through my hands, that they had the E.C. mark, and were in an illiterate handwriting. If he answered them at all the answers did not pass through my hands nor into the letter-basket in which our correspondence was collected."

"And the box," said Holmes.

"Ah, yes, the box. The Professor brought back a little wooden box from his travels. It was the one thing which suggested a Continental tour, for it was one of those quaint carved things which one associates with Germany. This he placed in his instrument cupboard.
4 One day, in looking for a cannula, I took up the box. To my surprise he was very angry, and reproved me in words which were quite savage for my curiosity. It was the first time such a thing had happened, and I was deeply hurt. I endeavoured to explain that it was a mere accident that I had touched the box, but all the evening I was conscious that he looked at me harshly and that the incident was rankling in his mind." Mr. Bennett drew a little diary book from his pocket. "That was on July 2," said he.

"You are certainly an admirable witness," said Holmes. "I may need some of these dates which you have noted."

"I learned method among other things from my great teacher. From the time that I observed abnormality

4 *a cannula.* A tube to be inserted into a cavity, through which pus may be drained or medicine introduced.

in his behaviour I felt that it was my duty to study his case. Thus I have it here that it was on that very day, July 2, that Roy attacked the Professor, as he came from his study into the hall. Again on July 11, there was a scene of the same sort and then I have a note of yet another upon July 20. After that we had to banish Roy to the stables. He was a dear, affectionate animal—but I fear I weary you."

Mr. Bennett spoke in a tone of reproach, for it was very clear that Holmes was not listening. His face was rigid and his eyes gazed abstractedly at the ceiling. With an effort he recovered himself.

"Singular! Most singular!" he murmured. "These details were new to me, Mr. Bennett. I think we have now fairly gone over the old ground, have we not? But you spoke of some fresh developments."

The pleasant, open face of our visitor clouded over, shadowed by some grim remembrance. "What I speak of occurred the night before last," said he. "I was lying awake about two in the morning, when I was aware of a dull muffled sound coming from the passage. I opened my door and peeped out. I should explain that the Professor sleeps at the end of the passage——"

"The date being——?" asked Holmes.

Our visitor was clearly annoyed at so irrelevant an interruption.

"I have said, sir, that it was the night before last—that is, September 4." 5

Holmes nodded and smiled.

"Pray continue," said he.

"He sleeps at the end of the passage, and would have to pass my door in order to reach the staircase. It was a really terrifying experience, Mr. Holmes. I think that I am as strong-nerved as my neighbours, but I was shaken by what I saw. The passage was dark save that one window half-way along it threw a patch of light. I could see that something was coming along the passage, something dark and crouching. Then suddenly it emerged into the light, and I saw that it was he. He was crawling, Mr. Holmes—crawling! He was not quite on his hands and knees. I should rather say on his hands and feet, with his face sunk between his hands. Yet he seemed to move with ease. I was so paralysed by the sight that it was not until he had reached my door that I was able to step forward and ask if I could assist him. His answer was extraordinary. He sprang up, spat out some atrocious word at me, and hurried on past me, and down the staircase. I waited about for an hour, but he did not come back. It must have been daylight before he regained his room."

"Well, Watson, what make you of that?" asked Holmes, with the air of the pathologist who presents a rare specimen.

"Lumbago, possibly. I have known a severe attack make a man walk in just such a way, and nothing would be more trying to the temper."

"Good, Watson! You always keep us flat-footed on the ground. But we can hardly accept lumbago, since he was able to stand erect in a moment."

"He was never better in health," said Bennett. "In

5 *that is, September 4.* Mr. Bennett therefore called on Holmes on *September 6th*—a Sunday in 1903.

"I COULD SEE THAT SOMETHING WAS COMING ALONG THE PASSAGE . . ."

Illustration by Frederic Dorr Steele for *Hearst's International*, March, 1923.

"HE SPRANG UP, SPAT OUT SOME ATROCIOUS WORD AT ME . . ."

Illustration by Howard K. Elcock for the *Strand Magazine*, March, 1923.

fact, he is stronger than I have known him for years. But there are the facts, Mr. Holmes. It is not a case in which we can consult the police, and yet we are utterly at our wits' end as to what to do, and we feel in some strange way that we are drifting towards disaster. Edith —Miss Presbury—feels as I do, that we cannot wait passively any longer."

" It is certainly a very curious and suggestive case. What do you think, Watson ? "

" Speaking as a medical man," said I, " it appears to be a case for an alienist. The old gentleman's cerebral processes were disturbed by the love affair. He made a journey abroad in the hope of breaking himself of the passion. His letters and the box may be connected with some other private transaction—a loan, perhaps, or share certificates, which are in the box."

" And the wolf-hound no doubt disapproved of the financial bargain. No, no, Watson, there is more in it than this. Now, I can only suggest——"

What Sherlock Holmes was about to suggest will never be known, for at this moment the door opened and a young lady was shown into the room. As she appeared Mr. Bennett sprang up with a cry and ran forward with his hands out to meet those which she had herself outstretched.

" Edith, dear ! Nothing the matter, I hope ? "

6 " I felt I must follow you. Oh, Jack, I have been so dreadfully frightened ! It is awful to be there alone."

" Mr. Holmes, this is the young lady I spoke of. This is my fiancée."

" We were gradually coming to that conclusion, were we not, Watson ? " Holmes answered, with a smile. " I take it, Miss Presbury, that there is some fresh development in the case, and that you thought we should know ? "

Our new visitor, a bright, handsome girl of a conventional English type, smiled back at Holmes as she seated herself beside Mr. Bennett.

" When I found Mr. Bennett had left his hotel I thought I should probably find him here. Of course, he had told me that he would consult you. But, oh, Mr. Holmes, can you do nothing for my poor father ? "

" I have hopes, Miss Presbury, but the case is still obscure. Perhaps what you have to say may throw some fresh light upon it."

" It was last night, Mr. Holmes. He had been very strange all day. I am sure that there are times when he has no recollection of what he does. He lives as in a strange dream. Yesterday was such a day. It was not my father with whom I lived. His outward shell was there, but it was not really he."

" Tell me what happened."

" I was awakened in the night by the dog barking most furiously. Poor Roy, he is chained now near the stable. I may say that I always sleep with my door locked ; for, as Jack—as Mr. Bennett—will tell you, we all have a feeling of impending danger. My room is on the second floor. It happened that the blind was

6 *Oh, Jack.* Mr. D. Martin Dakin has noted ("Second Thoughts on the Case-Book") the surprising change of Mr. Bennett's name from Trevor to Jack. He cites "Watson's notorious carelessness about Christian names," and adds: "Or had Miss Presbury a pet name for her man, as certain authorities consider Mrs. [Mary Morstan] Watson had?"

up in my window, and there was bright moonlight outside. As I lay with my eyes fixed upon the square of light, listening to the frenzied barkings of the dog, I was amazed to see my father's face looking in at me. Mr. Holmes, I nearly died of surprise and horror. There it was pressed against the window-pane, and one hand seemed to be raised as if to push up the window. If that window had opened, I think I should have gone mad. It was no delusion, Mr. Holmes. Don't deceive yourself by thinking so. I dare say it was twenty seconds or so that I lay paralysed and watched the face. Then it vanished, but I could not—I could not spring out of bed and look out after it. I lay cold and shivering till morning. At breakfast he was sharp and fierce in manner, and made no allusion to the adventure of the night. Neither did I, but I gave an excuse for coming to town—and here I am."

Holmes looked thoroughly surprised at Miss Presbury's narrative.

" My dear young lady, you say that your room is on the second floor. Is there a long ladder in the garden ? "

" No, Mr. Holmes ; that is the amazing part of it. There is no possible way of reaching the window—and yet he was there."

" The date being September 5," said Holmes. " That certainly complicates matters."

It was the young lady's turn to look surprised. " This is the second time that you have alluded to the date, Mr. Holmes," said Bennett. " Is it possible that it has any bearing upon the case ? "

" It is possible—very possible—and yet I have not my full material at present."

" Possibly you are thinking of the connection between insanity and phases of the moon ? "

" No, I assure you. It was quite a different line of thought. Possibly you can leave your notebook with me and I will check the dates. Now I think, Watson, that our line of action is perfectly clear. This young lady has informed us—and I have the greatest confidence in her intuition—that her father remembers little or nothing which occurs upon certain dates. We will therefore call upon him as if he had given us an appointment upon such a date. He will put it down to his own lack of memory. Thus we will open our campaign by having a good close view of him."

" That is excellent," said Mr. Bennett. " I warn you, however, that the Professor is irascible and violent at times."

Holmes smiled. " There are reasons why we should come at once—very cogent reasons if my theories hold good. To-morrow, Mr. Bennett, will certainly see us in Camford. There is, if I remember right, an inn called the ' Chequers ' where the port used to be above mediocrity, and the linen was above reproach. I think, **7**
Watson, that our lot for the next few days might lie in less pleasant places."

Monday morning found us on our way to the famous University town—an easy effort on the part of Holmes,

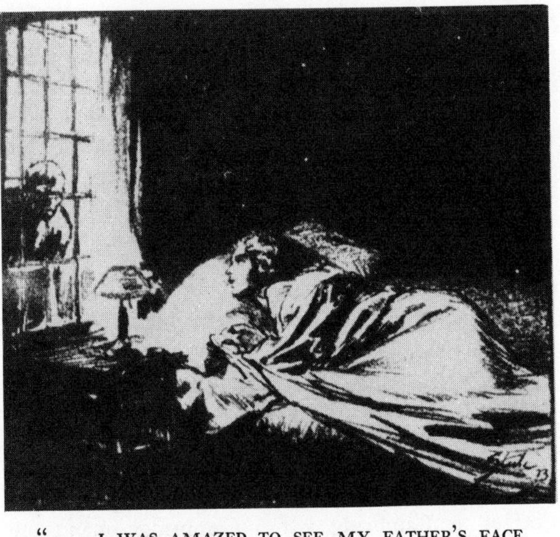

". . . I WAS AMAZED TO SEE MY FATHER'S FACE LOOKING IN AT ME."

Illustration by Frederic Dorr Steele for *Hearst's International,* March, 1923. Howard K. Elcock illustrated the same scene for the *Strand Magazine,* March, 1923.

7 *and the linen was above reproach.*" No Chequers Inn exists, or, as far as I can ascertain, has ever existed at either [Oxford or Cambridge]," Mr. Metcalfe wrote, "but I am inclined to credit the Mitre at Oxford as the subject of Holmes' recommendation. (A chequer is a pattern like a chessboard, and is not a mitre a bishop?)."

The Reverend Stephen Adams, who holds that Holmes was a student at neither Oxford nor Cambridge, but at the University of London, writes of this statement ("Holmes: A Student of London?"): "The crucial word is 'linen'; obviously Holmes had *stayed* there. Oxford and Cambridge graduates are familiar enough with their pubs, but how often have they stayed at them? A bed in college or with friends is surely the normal thing. The fact that [Holmes] had stayed there strongly suggests that his previous visit(s) had been for the purpose of tracking down other misguided dons."

who had no roots to pull up, but one which involved frantic planning and hurrying on my part, as my practice was by this time not inconsiderable. Holmes made no allusion to the case until after we had deposited our suit-cases at the ancient hostel of which he had spoken.

" I think, Watson, that we can catch the Professor just before lunch. He lectures at eleven, and should have an interval at home."

" What possible excuse have we for calling ? "

Holmes glanced at his notebook.

" There was a period of excitement upon August 26. We will assume that he is a little hazy as to what he does at such times. If we insist that we are there by appointment I think he will hardly venture to contradict us. Have you the effrontery necessary to put it through ? "

" We can but try."

" Excellent, Watson ! Compound of the Busy Bee
8 and Excelsior. We can but try—the motto of the firm.
A friendly native will surely guide us."

Such a one on the back of a smart hansom swept
9 us past a row of ancient colleges, and finally turning
into a tree-lined drive pulled up at the door of a charming house, girt round with lawns and covered with purple wistaria. Professor Presbury was certainly surrounded with every sign not only of comfort but of luxury. Even as we pulled up a grizzled head appeared at the front window, and we were aware of a pair of keen eyes from under shaggy brows which surveyed us through large horn glasses. A moment later we were actually in his sanctum, and the mysterious scientist, whose vagaries had brought us from London, was standing before us. There was certainly no sign of eccentricity either in his manner or appearance, for he was a portly, large-featured man, grave, tall, and frock-coated, with the dignity of bearing which a lecturer needs. His eyes were his most remarkable feature, keen, observant, and clever to the verge of cunning.

He looked at our cards. " Pray sit down, gentlemen. What can I do for you ? "

Mr. Holmes smiled amiably.

" It was the question which I was about to put to you, Professor."

" To me, sir ! "

" Possibly there is some mistake. I heard through a second person that Professor Presbury of Camford had need of my services."

" Oh, indeed ! " It seemed to me that there was a malicious sparkle in the intense grey eyes. " You heard that, did you ? May I ask the name of your informant ? "

" I am sorry, Professor, but the matter was rather confidential. If I have made a mistake there is no harm done. I can only express my regret."

" Not at all. I should wish to go further into this matter. It interests me. Have you any scrap of writing, any letter or telegram, to bear out your assertion ? "

" No, I have not."

8 *We can but try—the motto of the firm.* Mr. Rolfe Boswell, who holds that Holmes substituted his own coat-of-arms for that of the Noble Bachelor in the adventure of that name, has added "We can but try" as a motto to his achievement. He has also added as a crest "a sinister hand proper encrusted with icicles grasping a banner gules, thereon a golden bee and the watchword EXCELSIOR in silver letters."

9 *a row of ancient colleges.* "Whilst at a pinch this might be King's Parade or Trinity Street in Cambridge, colleges in rows, on the whole, suggest Oxford," the late Gavin Brend wrote in *My Dear Holmes.* And Mr. N. P. Metcalfe has added that "The drive past a row of ancient colleges suggests either the 'High' at Oxford, or 'K. P.' and Trinity Street at Cambridge. If a Cambridge man, one would expect the Professor to live in the Grange Road area; if Oxford, then the Woodstock Road or Boar's Hill."

"I presume that you do not go so far as to assert that I summoned you?"

"I would rather answer no questions," said Holmes.

"No, I dare say not," said the Professor, with asperity. "However, that particular one can be answered very easily without your aid."

He walked across the room to the bell. Our London friend, Mr. Bennett, answered the call.

"Come in, Mr. Bennett. These two gentlemen have come from London under the impression that they have been summoned. You handle all my correspondence. Have you a note of anything going to a person named Holmes?"

"No, sir," Bennett answered, with a flush.

"That is conclusive," said the Professor, glaring angrily at my companion. "Now, sir"—he leaned forward with his two hands upon the table—"it seems to me that your position is a very questionable one."

Holmes shrugged his shoulders.

"I can only repeat that I am sorry that we have made a needless intrusion."

"Hardly enough, Mr. Holmes!" the old man cried, in a high screaming voice, with extraordinary malignancy upon his face. He got between us and the door as he spoke, and he shook his two hands at us with furious passion. "You can hardly get out of it so easily as that." His face was convulsed and he grinned and gibbered at us in his senseless rage. I am convinced that we should have had to fight our way out of the room if Mr. Bennett had not intervened.

"My dear Professor," he cried, "consider your position! Consider the scandal at the University! Mr. Holmes is a well-known man. You cannot possibly treat him with such discourtesy."

Sulkily our host—if I may call him so—cleared the path to the door. We were glad to find ourselves outside the house, and in the quiet of the tree-lined drive. Holmes seemed greatly amused by the episode.

"Our learned friend's nerves are somewhat out of order," said he. "Perhaps our intrusion was a little crude, and yet we have gained that personal contact which I desired. But, dear me, Watson, he is surely at our heels. The villain still pursues us."

There were the sounds of running feet behind, but it was, to my relief, not the formidable Professor but his assistant who appeared round the curve of the drive. He came panting up to us.

"I am so sorry, Mr. Holmes. I wished to apologize."

"My dear sir, there is no need. It is all in the way of professional experience."

"I have never seen him in a more dangerous mood. But he grows more sinister. You can understand now why his daughter and I are alarmed. And yet his mind is perfectly clear."

"Too clear!" said Holmes. "That was my miscalculation. It is evident that his memory is much more reliable than I had thought. By the way, can we, before we go, see the window of Miss Presbury's room?"

Mr. Bennett pushed his way through some shrubs and

HIS FACE WAS CONVULSED AND HE GRINNED AND GIBBERED AT US IN HIS SENSELESS RAGE.

Illustration by Howard K. Elcock for the *Strand Magazine*, March, 1923.

we had a view of the side of the house.

"It is there. The second on the left."

"Dear me, it seems hardly accessible. And yet you will observe that there is a creeper below and a water-pipe above which give some foothold."

"I could not climb it myself," said Mr. Bennett.

"Very likely. It would certainly be a dangerous exploit for any normal man."

"There was one other thing I wished to tell you, Mr. Holmes. I have the address of the man in London to whom the Professor writes. He seems to have written this morning and I got it from his blotting-paper. It is an ignoble position for a trusted secretary, but what else can I do?"

Holmes glanced at the paper and put it into his pocket.

"Dorak—a curious name. Slavonic, I imagine. Well, it is an important link in the chain. We return to London this afternoon, Mr. Bennett. I see no good purpose to be served by our remaining. We cannot arrest the Professor, because he has done no crime, nor can we place him under constraint, for he cannot be proved to be mad. No action is as yet possible."

"Then what on earth are we to do?"

"A little patience, Mr. Bennett. Things will soon develop. Unless I am mistaken next Tuesday may mark a crisis. Certainly we shall be in Camford on that day. Meanwhile, the general position is undeniably unpleasant, and if Miss Presbury can prolong her visit— "

"That is easy."

"Then let her stay till we can assure her that all danger is past. Meanwhile, let him have his way and do not cross him. So long as he is in a good humour all is well."

"There he is!" said Bennett, in a startled whisper. Looking between the branches we saw the tall, erect figure emerge from the hall door and look around him. He stood leaning forward, his hands swinging straight before him, his head turning from side to side. The secretary with a last wave slipped off among the trees, and we saw him presently rejoin his employer, the two entering the house together in what seemed to be animated and even excited conversation.

"I expect the old gentleman has been putting two and two together," said Holmes, as we walked hotelwards. "He struck me as having a particularly clear and logical brain, from the little I saw of him. Explosive, no doubt, but then from his point of view he has something to explode about if detectives are put on his track and he suspects his own household of doing it. I rather fancy that friend Bennett is in for an uncomfortable time."

Holmes stopped at a post office and sent off a telegram on our way. The answer reached us in the evening, and he tossed it across to me. "Have visited the Commercial
10 Road and seen Dorak. Suave person, Bohemian, elderly.
Keeps large general store.—Mercer."
11 "Mercer is since your time," said Holmes. "He is
my general utility man who looks up routine business. It was important to know something of the man with

10 *the Commercial Road.* Commercial Road traverses the densely populated quarters of Limehouse and St.-George's-in-the-East, a broad thoroughfare constructed in 1800 near Whitechapel in order to provide direct access from the City to the newly constructed West India Docks. It was cut across what was previously known as Stepney Fields, which became rapidly built over as a result of the formation of these new docks. In 1802 it was extended to the East India Docks, and in May, 1870, it was extended from Church Lane to Leman Street.

11 *"Mercer is since your time," said Holmes.* Obviously, Mercer is a part of that "small, but very efficient, organization" which Holmes was building up in the early years of this century.

whom our Professor was so secretly corresponding. His nationality connects up with the Prague visit."

" Thank goodness that something connects with something," said I. " At present we seem to be faced by a long series of inexplicable incidents with no bearing upon each other. For example, what possible connection can there be between an angry wolf-hound and a visit to Bohemia, or either of them with a man crawling down a passage at night ? As to your dates, that is the biggest mystification of all."

Holmes smiled and rubbed his hands. We were,
I may say, seated in the old sitting-room of the ancient
hotel, with a bottle of the famous vintage of which 12
Holmes had spoken on the table between us.

" Well, now, let us take the dates first," said he, his finger-tips together and his manner as if he were addressing a class. " This excellent young man's diary shows that there was trouble upon July 2, and from then onwards it seems to have been at nine-day intervals, with, so far as I remember, only one exception. Thus the last outbreak upon Friday was on September 3, which
also falls into the series, as did August 26, which preceded
it. The thing is beyond coincidence." 13

I was forced to agree.

" Let us, then, form the provisional theory that every nine days the Professor takes some strong drug which has a passing but highly poisonous effect. His naturally violent nature is intensified by it. He learned to take this drug while he was in Prague, and is now supplied with it by a Bohemian intermediary in London. This all hangs together, Watson ! "

" But the dog, the face at the window, the creeping man in the passage ? "

" Well, well, we have made a beginning. I should not
expect any fresh developments until next Tuesday. In
the meantime we can only keep in touch with friend
Bennett and enjoy the amenities of this charming town." 14

In the morning Mr. Bennett slipped round to bring us the latest report. As Holmes had imagined, times had not been easy with him. Without exactly accusing him of being responsible for our presence, the Professor had been very rough and rude in his speech, and evidently felt some strong grievance. This morning he was quite himself again, however, and had delivered his usual brilliant lecture to a crowded class. " Apart from his queer fits," said Bennett, " he has actually more energy and vitality than I can ever remember, nor was his brain ever clearer. But it's not he—it's never the man whom we have known."

" I don't think you have anything to fear now for a week at least," Holmes answered. " I am a busy man, and Dr. Watson has his patients to attend to. Let us agree that we meet here at this hour next Tuesday, and I shall be surprised if before we leave you again we are not able to explain, even if we cannot perhaps put an end to, your troubles. Meanwhile, keep us posted in what occurs."

12 *a bottle of the famous vintage.* "There is not much doubt," Mr. Jørgen Cold wrote in "What Did Sherlock Holmes Drink?", "that the old firm, C. N. Kopke & Co., Ltd., Oporto and London, was the purveyor of that vintage, and most certainly the brand Quinta Noval."

13 *The thing is beyond coincidence.*" Watson has told us that the case began "one Sunday evening in September of the year 1903." Let us check his "Sunday," his "September," and his "1903." 1) Watson says his purpose in publishing an account of the case is to "dispel once for all the ugly rumours which some twenty years ago agitated the University . . ." Since "The Adventure of the Creeping Man" was published in March, 1923, Watson's "1903" would seem to be corroborated. 2) "I have said, sir, that it was the night before last—that is, September 4," Mr. Bennett told Holmes and Watson. Here is a corroboration of Watson's "September." Since "September 4" was two nights before the case opened, and September 6, 1903 (as we have seen) was indeed a Sunday, here also is a confirmation of Watson's day and a further confirmation of the year. 3) Miss Presbury said: "Yesterday was such a day." "The date being September 5," Holmes noted. Here again is a corroboration that the case did indeed begin on Sunday, September 6, 1903. 4) Miss Presbury has said that at the time of the attack (2:00 A.M. of the 5th) "there was bright moonlight outside." The moon was two days before the full on the night of September 4th–5th; it rose at 5:49 P.M. on the afternoon of the 4th and set at 3:37 A.M. on the morning of the 5th. 5) Holmes said: "The last outbreak upon Friday was on September 3." Holmes is speaking of the outbreak on the night of Friday, September 4th, to Saturday, September 5th; the "Friday" is clearly correct, but the "3" must be a typographical error. Professor Presbury's first attack had come on July 2nd, according to Mr. Bennett. "It was on that very day, July 2, that Roy attacked the Professor. . . . Again on July 11 there was a scene of the same sort and then I have a note of yet another upon July 20." Later Holmes says: "There was a period of excitement upon August 26"—and Holmes notes at once that the attacks in the period July 2nd to September 4th have come at nine-day intervals, with "only one exception." He is quite correct: it is 37 days from July 20th to August 26th, so one of the intervals between the attacks that took place during this period must have been of *ten* rather than nine days. So far all seems clear. It is with the events that took place after Sunday, September 6th, that the difficulties arise.

14 *this charming town.*" Here at last is proof positive that "Camford" is *Oxford*. In "The Adventure of the Missing Three-Quarter," the University of the adventure was identified as Cambridge, which Holmes called "this inhospitable town."

I saw nothing of my friend for the next few days; but on the following Monday evening I had a short note asking me to meet him next day at the train. From what he told me as we travelled up to Camford all was well, the peace of the Professor's house had been unruffled, and his own conduct perfectly normal. This also was the report which was given us by Mr. Bennett himself when he called upon us that evening at our old quarters in the "Chequers." "He heard from his London correspondent to-day. There was a letter and there was a small packet, each with the cross under the stamp which warned me not to touch them. There has been nothing else."

"That may prove quite enough," said Holmes grimly. "Now, Mr. Bennett, we shall, I think, come to some conclusion to-night. If my deductions are correct we should have an opportunity of bringing matters to a head. In order to do so it is necessary to hold the Professor under observation. I would suggest, therefore, that you remain awake and on the look-out. Should you hear him pass your door do not interrupt him, but follow him as discreetly as you can. Dr. Watson and I will not be far off. By the way, where is the key of that little box of which you spoke?"

"Upon his watch-chain."

"I fancy our researches must lie in that direction. At the worst the lock should not be very formidable. Have you any other able-bodied man on the premises?"

"There is the coachman, Macphail."

"Where does he sleep?"

"Over the stables."

"We might possibly want him. Well, we can do no more until we see how things develop. Good-bye—but I expect that we shall see you before morning."

It was nearly midnight before we took our station among some bushes immediately opposite the hall door of the Professor. It was a fine night, but chilly, and we were glad of our warm overcoats. There was a breeze, and clouds were scudding across the sky, obscuring from time to time the half-moon. It would have been a dismal vigil were it not for the expectation and excitement which carried us along, and the assurance of my comrade that we had probably reached the end of the strange sequence of events which had engaged our attention.

"If the cycle of nine days holds good, then we shall
15 have the Professor at his worst to-night," said Holmes.
"The fact that these strange symptoms began after his visit to Prague, that he is in secret correspondence with a Bohemian dealer in London, who presumably represents someone in Prague, and that he received a packet from him this very day, all point in one direction. What he takes and why he takes it are still beyond our ken, but that it emanates in some way from Prague is clear enough. He takes it under definite directions which regulate this ninth-day system, which was the first point which attracted my attention. But his symptoms are most remarkable. Did you observe his knuckles?"

I had to confess that I did not.

"Thick and horny in a way which is quite new in my experience. Always look at the hands first, Watson.

15 *we shall have the Professor at his worst to-night.*" "It was nearly midnight" on the Tuesday when the crisis came, and this crisis clearly followed the nine-day pattern: Holmes said, on the concluding day, "If the cycle of nine days holds good, then we shall have the Professor at his worst to-night" (which they did) and, "He takes [the drug] under definite directions which regulate this ninth-day system." Nine days after the attack on the night of September 4th–5th brings us to the night of September 13th–14th. But September 13, 1903, was not a Tuesday but a *Sunday*. Commentators have generally agreed that Holmes' *three* references to Tuesday must be dismissed, but your editor does not feel that we can dismiss so lightly three such direct quotations fom the Master. We believe that Watson was here guilty of a literary license—of trifling with time in his account of this case for the sake of making the account slightly more dramatic—just as he did in *A Study in Scarlet* and again in "The Adventure of the Illustrious Client." In your editor's opinion, some exceedingly pressing business prevented Holmes from journeying to "Camford" on Monday, September 7th, and observing the Professor's outbreak on Sunday, September 13th. *It was on Monday, September 14th, that Holmes and Watson first journeyed to Camford; the outbreak they observed was that of Tuesday, September 22nd—just nine days after the outbreak of Sunday, September 13th.* It may be objected that Holmes in his references on Monday, September 14th, to "next Tuesday" would seem to be indicating Tuesday, September 15th rather than Tuesday, September 22nd. By that time, however, the significance of the nine-day cycle was understood by everyone—Holmes' Tuesday references meant *Tuesday* week, as is plainly shown by his "I don't think we have anything to fear now for a week at least." It is true that our explanation plays hob with Watson's "half-moon" on the night of the climax, but Watson, as we have seen, has been careless about his moons on many other occasions. We vastly prefer to make sense of the Master's remarks on Monday—Monday, September 14th.

Then cuffs, trouser-knees, and boots. Very curious knuckles which can only be explained by the mode of progression observed by——" Holmes paused, and suddenly clapped his hand to his forehead. "Oh, Watson, Watson, what a fool I have been! It seems incredible, and yet it must be true. All points in one direction. How could I miss seeing the connection of ideas? Those knuckles—how could I have passed those knuckles? And the dog! And the ivy! It's surely time that I disappeared into that little farm of my
dreams. Look out, Watson! Here he is! We shall **16**
have the chance of seeing for ourselves."

The hall door had slowly opened, and against the lamp-lit background we saw the tall figure of Professor Presbury. He was clad in his dressing-gown. As he stood outlined in the doorway he was erect but leaning forward with dangling arms, as when we saw him last.

Now he stepped forward into the drive, and an extraordinary change came over him. He sank down into a crouching position, and moved along upon his hands and feet, skipping every now and then as if he were overflowing with energy and vitality. He moved along the face of the house and then round the corner. As he disappeared Bennett slipped through the hall door and softly followed him.

"Come, Watson, come!" cried Holmes, and we stole as softly as we could through the bushes until we had gained a spot whence we could see the other side of the house, which was bathed in the light of the half-moon. The Professor was clearly visible crouching at the foot of the ivy-covered wall. As we watched him he suddenly began with incredible agility to ascend it. From branch to branch he sprang, sure of foot and firm of grasp, climbing apparently in mere joy at his own powers, with no definite object in view. With his dressing-gown flapping on each side of him he looked like some huge bat glued against the side of his own house, a great square dark patch upon the moonlit wall. Presently he tired of this amusement, and, dropping from branch to branch, he squatted down into the old attitude and moved towards the stables, creeping along in the same strange way as before. The wolf-hound was out now, barking furiously, and more excited than ever when it actually caught sight of its master. It was straining on its chain, and quivering with eagerness and rage. The Professor squatted down very deliberately just out of reach of the hound, and began to provoke it in every possible way. He took handfuls of pebbles from the drive and threw them in the dog's face, prodded him with a stick which he had picked up, flicked his hands about only a few inches from the gaping mouth, and endeavoured in every way to increase the animal's fury, which was already beyond all control. In all our adventures I do not know that I have ever seen a more strange sight than this impassive and still dignified figure crouching frog-like upon the ground and goading to a wilder exhibition of passion the maddened hound, which ramped and raged in front of him, by all manner of ingenious and calculated cruelty.

And then in a moment it happened! It was not the

16 *It's surely time that I disappeared into that little farm of my dreams.* It must have been a consolation to Holmes, as he contemplated retirement, that another great expert in scientific crime detection had by that time established himself in London. Dr. John Evelyn Thorndyke had commenced his practice as a consulting detective in King's Bench Walk in 1897, or perhaps in 1896. In 1901 he had dealings with Scotland Yard in at least twenty cases. In 1902 he solved the Blackmore problem. In November of that year, when he first came in contact with the Bellingham case, he was obviously a recognized expert. In July, 1903, he investigated the famous Hardcastle murder, committed the month before. All this was prior to Holmes' retirement. See Francis M. Currier, "Holmes and Thorndyke: A Real Friendship."

chain that broke, but it was the collar that slipped, for it had been made for a thick-necked Newfoundland. We heard the rattle of falling metal, and the next instant dog and man were rolling on the ground together, the one roaring in rage, the other screaming in a strange shrill falsetto of terror. It was a very narrow thing for the Professor's life. The savage creature had him fairly by the throat, its fangs had bitten deep, and he was senseless before we could reach them and drag the two apart. It might have been a dangerous task for us, but Bennett's voice and presence brought the great wolf-hound instantly to reason. The uproar had brought the sleepy and astonished coachman from his room above the stables. "I'm not surprised," said he, shaking his head. "I've seen him at it before. I knew the dog would get him sooner or later."

... DOG AND MAN WERE ROLLING ON THE GROUND TOGETHER ...

Illustration by Howard K. Elcock for the *Strand Magazine,* March, 1923.

The hound was secured, and together we carried the Professor up to his room, where Bennett, who had a medical degree, helped me to dress his torn throat. The sharp teeth had passed dangerously near the carotid artery, and the hæmorrhage was serious. In half an hour the danger was past, I had given the patient an injection of morphia, and he had sunk into deep sleep. Then, and only then, were we able to look at each other and to take stock of the situation.

"I think a first-class surgeon should see him," said I.

"For God's sake, no!" cried Bennett. "At present the scandal is confined to our own household. It is safe with us. If it gets beyond these walls it will never stop. Consider his position at the University, his European reputation, the feelings of his daughter."

"Quite so," said Holmes. "I think it may be quite possible to keep the matter to ourselves, and also to prevent its recurrence now that we have a free hand. The key from the watch-chain, Mr. Bennett. Macphail will guard the patient and let us know if there is any change. Let us see what we can find in the Professor's mysterious box."

There was not much, but there was enough—an empty phial, another nearly full, a hypodermic syringe, several letters in a crabbed, foreign hand. The marks on the envelopes showed that they were those which had disturbed the routine of the secretary, and each was dated from the Commercial Road and signed "A. Dorak." They were mere invoices to say that a fresh bottle was being sent to Professor Presbury, or receipts to acknowledge money. There was one other envelope, however, in a more educated hand and bearing the Austrian stamp with the postmark of Prague. "Here we have our material!" cried Holmes, as he tore out the enclosure.

"HONOURED COLLEAGUE," it ran. "Since your esteemed visit I have thought much of your case, and though in your circumstances there are some special reasons for the treatment, I would none the less enjoin caution, as my results have shown that it is not without danger of a kind.

"It is possible that the Serum of Anthropoid would have been better. I have, as I explained to you, used black-faced Langur because a specimen was accessible. Langur is, of course, a crawler and climber, while Anthropoid walks erect, and is in all ways nearer.

"I beg you to take every possible precaution that there be no premature revelation of the process. I have one other client in England, and Dorak is my agent for
both. 17

"Weekly reports will oblige.

"Yours with high esteem,

"H. LOWENSTEIN."

Lowenstein! The name brought back to me the memory of some snippet from a newspaper which spoke of an obscure scientist who was striving in some unknown way for the secret of rejuvenescence and the elixir of life. Lowenstein of Prague! Lowenstein with the wondrous strength-giving serum, tabooed by the profession because he refused to reveal its source. In a few words I said what I remembered. Bennett had taken a manual of Zoology from the shelves. 'Langur,'" he read, "'the great black-faced monkey of the Himalayan slopes, biggest and most human of climbing monkeys.' Many details are added. Well, thanks to you, Mr. Holmes, it is very clear that we have traced the evil to its source."

"The real source," said Holmes, "lies, of course, in that untimely love affair which gave our impetuous Professor the idea that he could only gain his wish by turning himself into a younger man. When one tries to rise above Nature one is liable to fall below it. The highest type of man may revert to the animal if he leaves the straight road of destiny." He sat musing for a little with the phial in his hand, looking at the clear liquid within. "When I have written to this man and told him that I hold him criminally responsible for the poisons which he circulates, we will have no more trouble. But it may recur. Others may find a better way. There is danger there—a very real danger to humanity. Consider, Watson, that the material, the sensual, the worldly would all prolong their worthless lives. The spiritual would not avoid the call to something higher. It would be the survival of the least fit. What sort of cesspool may not our poor world become?" Suddenly the dreamer disappeared, and Holmes, the man of action, sprang from his chair. "I think there is nothing more to be said, Mr. Bennett. The various incidents will now fit themselves easily into the general scheme. The dog, of course, was aware of the change far more quickly
than you. His smell would ensure that. It was the 18
monkey, not the Professor, whom Roy attacked, just as it was the monkey who teased Roy. Climbing was a joy to the creature, and it was a mere chance, I take it, that the pastime brought him to the young lady's window. There is an early train to town, Watson, but I think we shall just have time for a cup of tea at the 'Chequers' before we catch it."

17 *Dorak is my agent for both.* The wording suggests that there were also clients in other countries. "In fact," Mr. Arthur L. Levine writes, "the whole picture of the Creeping Man smacks so of the picture of the Abominable Snowman that there is a strong probability that they are of the same origin—that Lowenstein's other creeper [and his descendants are the creature known as] the Abominable Snowman of the Himalayas!" ("Lowenstein's Other Creeper").

18 *His smell would ensure that.* Dr. Samuel R. Meaker, in "Watson Medicus," has pointed out that while Holmes "rightly deduced that [Professor Presbury] was taking something powerful in the endocrine line . . . he was wrong in assuming that treatment with monkey-serum could make a human being behave or smell like a monkey. The venerable physiologist was evidently a victim of simple autosuggestion or self-hypnosis; and as to the wolfhound, it only reacted as any sensitive dog might do to a weird and apparently hostile change in its master's conduct. This time Watson saw clearer than Holmes for, after a tentative diagnosis of lumbago to explain the professor's creeping style of locomotion, he concluded 'Speaking as a medical man, it appears to be a case for an alienist.'"

A Note on the "Canonicity" of "The Adventure of the Creeping Man": This is another of the *Case-Book* adventures which Mr. D. Martin Dakin finds some reason to doubt: "The story is fantastic and more reminiscent of Dr. Jekyll or the Werewolf than a Sherlock Holmes case. The transparent device of referring to 'Camford' University is a trick of the second-rate writer; and there was the less need to practice such mystification, as Watson has already recorded a visit to Cambridge in 'The Missing Three-Quarter' and to a University easily recognizable as Oxford in 'The Three Students.' Indeed, the interview with Professor Presbury reads like a rather feeble imitation of that with the redoubtable Leslie Armstrong in Cambridge from which Holmes and Watson were, more excusably, ejected. Yet Watson's characteristically prosaic remark, attributing the Professor's peculiarities to lumbago, causes me, I confess, to hesitate in my judgment."

Dr. George B. Koelle is another who questions the authenticity of this adventure: "In *The Valley of Fear* [Holmes] comments on the unexpected vein of pawky humor which Watson is developing. May not the latter have been indulging this humor when, during a period lacking in authentic case material to record, he allowed his fancy to dictate this account? Its acceptance by a gullible publisher served merely to consolidate the joke. Certainly, the good doctor would never have expected anyone to take it seriously."

A Sherlock Holmes Competition

Set by A. CONAN DOYLE

£100 Cash Prize and 100 Autographed Copies of "Memories and Adventures"

In the following article Sir A. Conan Doyle makes the interesting announcement that from the forty-four Sherlock Holmes stories already published in book form in four volumes he has selected the twelve stories which he considers the best, and he now invites readers to do likewise. A sealed copy of this list is in the Editor's possession, and a prize of £100 and an autographed copy of Sir A. Conan Doyle's "Memories and Adventures" is offered to the sender of the coupon which coincides most nearly with this list. In the event of ties the prize of £100 will be divided. The actual order of the stories will not be regarded. Autographed copies of "Memories and Adventures" will also be awarded to 100 readers submitting the next nearly correct coupons.

An illustration from each of the stories is here given. Each illustration being numbered, competitors need only state on the coupon (which will be found on page 68 of the advertisement section) the numbers of the stories selected.

The four volumes of stories, "The Adventures of Sherlock Holmes," "The Memoirs of Sherlock Holmes," "The Return of Sherlock Holmes," and "His Last Bow," are published by Messrs. John Murray in two-shilling editions and may be obtained from all booksellers.

MR. SHERLOCK HOLMES TO HIS READERS

By A. CONAN DOYLE

I FEAR that Mr. Sherlock Holmes may become like one of those popular tenors who, having outlived their time, are still tempted to make repeated farewell bows to their indulgent audiences. This must cease and he must go the way of all flesh, material or imaginary. One likes to think that there is some fantastic limbo for the children of imagination, some strange, impossible place where the beaux of Fielding may still make love to the belles of Richardson, where Scott's heroes still may strut, Dickens's delightful Cockneys still raise a laugh, and Thackeray's worldlings continue to carry on their reprehensible careers. Perhaps in some humble corner of such a Valhalla, Sherlock and his Watson may for a time find a place, while some more astute sleuth with some even less astute comrade may fill the stage which they have vacated.

His career has been a long one—though it is possible to exaggerate it.

1.—A SCANDAL IN BOHEMIA.

2.—THE RED-HEADED LEAGUE.

"A SHERLOCK HOLMES COMPETITION"

In the March, 1927, issue of the *Strand Magazine*, Sir Arthur Conan Doyle announced that he had selected the twelve Sherlock Holmes stories which he considered the best, and invited readers to do likewise for a cash prize of £100 and one hundred autographed copies of his autobiography, *Memories and Adventures*. His own list was published when the winners had been judged.

IX. SHERLOCK HOLMES IN RETIREMENT

[1909]

"It's surely time that I disappeared into that little farm of my dreams."
—Sherlock Holmes, "The Adventure of the Creeping Man"

Some Personalia About Mr. Sherlock Holmes.

By

A. CONAN DOYLE.

AT the request of the Editor I have spent some days in looking over an old letter-box in which from time to time I have placed letters referring directly or indirectly to the notorious Mr. Holmes. I wish now that I had been more careful in preserving the references to this gentleman and his little problems. A great many have been lost or mislaid. His biographer has been fortunate enough to find readers in many lands, and the reading has elicited the same sort of response, though in many cases that response has been in a tongue difficult to comprehend. Very often my distant correspondent could neither spell my own name nor that of my imaginary hero, as in a recent instance which I here append. Many such letters have been from Russians. Where the Russian letters have been in the vernacular I have been compelled, I am afraid, to take them as read, but when they have been in English they have been among the most curious in my collection. There was one young lady who began all her epistles with the words "Good Lord." Another had a large amount of guile underlying her simplicity. Writing from Warsaw she stated that she had been bedridden for two years, and that my novels had been her only, etc., etc. So touched was I by this flattering statement that I at once prepared an autographed parcel of them to complete the fair invalid's collection. By good luck, however, I met a brother author upon the same day to whom I recounted the touching incident. With a cynical smile he drew an identical letter out of his pocket. His novels also had been for two years her only, etc., etc. I do not know how many more the lady had written to, but if, as I imagine, her correspondence had extended to several countries, she must have amassed a rather interesting library.

Sir T. M.
Konan Doille
auteur
de Cherloc Cholms
Xbrowsborough X
~~London~~
Angleterre

"VERY OFTEN MY DISTANT CORRESPONDENT COULD NEITHER SPELL MY OWN NAME NOR THAT OF MY IMAGINARY HERO."

The young Russian's habit of addressing me as "Good Lord" had an even stranger parallel at home, which links it up with the subject of this article. Shortly after I received a knighthood I had a bill from a tradesman which was quite correct and businesslike in every detail save that it was made out to Sir Sherlock Holmes. I hope that I can stand a joke as well as my neighbours, but this particular piece of humour seemed rather misapplied, and I wrote sharply upon the subject. In response to my letter

"SOME PERSONALIA . . ."

Conan Doyle writes of his friends, Mr. Sherlock Holmes and Dr. John H. Watson, for the pages of the *Strand*, issue of December, 1917.

77

THE FRIENDS OF MR. SHERLOCK HOLMES WILL BE GLAD TO LEARN THAT HE IS STILL ALIVE AND WELL . . .

[*John H. Watson, M.D. Preface to "His Last Bow"*]

Since "The Second Stain," in which Watson, for the first time in print, referred to Holmes' retirement from active practice, was published in October, 1904, it is clear that Holmes had retired by that time.

"Precisely how long before October [1904] Holmes had given over his practice it is only possible to guess," Mr. Vincent Starrett wrote in *The Private Life of Sherlock Holmes*, "but one ventures to think that it must have been a number of months, at least, in view of Watson's reference to his friend's objections—obviously over a period of recent time—to the 'continued publication' of his experiences."

In point of fact, however, we have been told (in "The Adventure of the Creeping Man," which took place in September, 1903) that this was "one of the very last cases handled by Holmes before his retirement from practice," and Holmes confirms this: "It's surely time that I disappeared into that little farm of my dreams."

"We may conjecture, therefore," Mr. T. S. Blakeney wrote in *Sherlock Holmes: Fact or Fiction?*, "that by the end of the year [1903] the great detective had laid aside his calling, and it is pleasing to know that many offers were made to settle him on the South Downs with his bees, and even to recommend a suitable housekeeper. (See the *Strand Magazine*, December, 1917.)"

"It is fair to assume that [Holmes'] withdrawal to private life occurred during the autumn of the year 1903," the late H. W. Bell wrote in *Sherlock Holmes and Dr. Watson: The Chronology of Their Adventures.*

"Inasmuch as the Master's tremendous repute precluded his being long without a case, ["The Adventure of the Creeping Man"] must have been very shortly before his retirement," the late Dr. Ernest Bloomfield Zeisler wrote in *Baker Street Chronology*. "We may recall in 'The Adventure of the Solitary Cyclist' Watson says that in the eight years from 1894 to 1901 the Master was consulted in every public case of any difficulty and in hundreds of private cases. Hence the Master retired from practice several months before the end of 1903."

Watson himself, in his Preface to "His Last Bow," published in 1917, has told us that Holmes chose as his retirement retreat "a small farm upon the Downs, five miles from Eastbourne . . ."

In 1953 the late Christopher Morley, on a visit to England, announced to the press that he had searched for Holmes' downland cottage—and found it. The cottage, he declared, was "about one-and-a-half miles from salt water and about the same distance from the Seven Sisters, near a plantation of pine trees only a quarter of a mile from a No. 12 bus stop on the Eastbourne to Brighton road." Alluding to "The Adventure of the Lion's Mane," Morley added: "The cottage is stated to be at the top of the cliffs. I keep bees myself at home in Long Island, and I know that's nonsense. It was a red herring to put Moriarty's men off the scent. You can't keep bees on a cliff-top—they need a more sheltered spot."

"An Eastbourne resident," Mr. W. H. Chenhall later wrote ("The Retirement of Sherlock Holmes"), "has suggested that the cottage Morley found is one that nestles on a wooded slope above the road running southward from the village of East Dean, on the No. 12 bus route, to the coast at Birling Gap. This would be roughly the right distance from Eastbourne, but not one-and-a-half miles from the sea. It may be only half as far, but it would need to be even nearer to the sea to square with 'The Adventure of the Lion's Mane.'

"Almost every sentence in Holmes' description of the place throws up a snag," Mr. Chenhall continued, ". . . except at Birling Gap, where the descent to the beach is relatively short and by means of steps cut in the chalk; the cliffs stretching in either direction are high and precipitous. If a path did exist it must have been dangerous, and it is a wonder, as Vincent Starrett remarked, that Holmes did not break his neck. . . . It seems unlikely that there would be . . . a beach [consisting of a hundred yards of pebble and shingle] hereabout, where the danger of falling from the top of the cliffs is matched by the risk of being entrapped by the tides below. The next difficulty is 'the little cove and village of Fulworth,' breaking the long line of beach. The only approximation to a village on the five mile stretch from Beachy Head in the east to Cuckmere Haven in the west is Birling itself and this could hardly be said to be in a cove.

ON THE SUSSEX DOWNS

The photograph, by Will F. Taylor of Reigate, is from *Sussex,* by Esther Meynell, London: Robert Hale, Ltd., 1947.

That this line of coast faces roughly south-west is a further obstacle, if [other] statements by Holmes are considered. . . . The implication in each case is of cliffs facing east or possibly south-east, but certainly not south-west. It so happens, however, that there is a section of coast facing south-east at each end of the five-mile limit. At the western end, across the Cuckmere River, the coast runs in this direction for about half a mile before bending round to face south-west again. At the eastern end there is a longer stretch from the top of Beachy Head (near the lighthouse) to the final downward slope of the Downs just outside Eastbourne. The cliffs here are different. Though high, they are not so sheer and are terraced, with green slopes and levels. A cottage here could have the required view of the Channel and also shelter for the bees. There is access to the beach at Cow's Gap by means of steps, as at Birling Gap. An objection to this region is that it is much less than five miles from Eastbourne, just as the Cuckmere area is much more."

Despite the obstacles cited by Mr. Chenhall, Mr. Charles O. Merriman, at this writing the Chairman of the Sherlock Holmes Society of London, is convinced that he has located Holmes' farm. "Inland, running east to west from Eastbourne to Birling Gap across the Downs escarpment, are only four farms," Mr. Merriman wrote in "The Game Is Afoot." "In order they are Black Robin Farm, Bullock Down Farm, Cornish Farm and Birling Manor Farm. Birling Manor Farm is sheltered in a woodland dell in the Downs about three-quarters of a mile from Birling Gap, but gives a view of the Channel from an adjoining field. The land attached to the farm rises to an eminence eastwards known as Michel Dean, which gives a commanding view of the Channel. When I was informed in the course of conversation with some of the downsfolk that Cornish Farm produced acres of white clover each year and that the bees from Birling Manor Farm, the only farm of the four which keeps bees by reason of its sheltered position, feasted on the white clover after an earlier-in-the-season diet of wild raspberry, which is prevalent on the Downs in this area, I felt my researches had at last borne fruit. I have not pursued the matter further but I should imagine that Mr. Stackhurst's school, The Gables, must lie at East Dean or Friston or its environs up to a mile north of Birling Manor Farm."

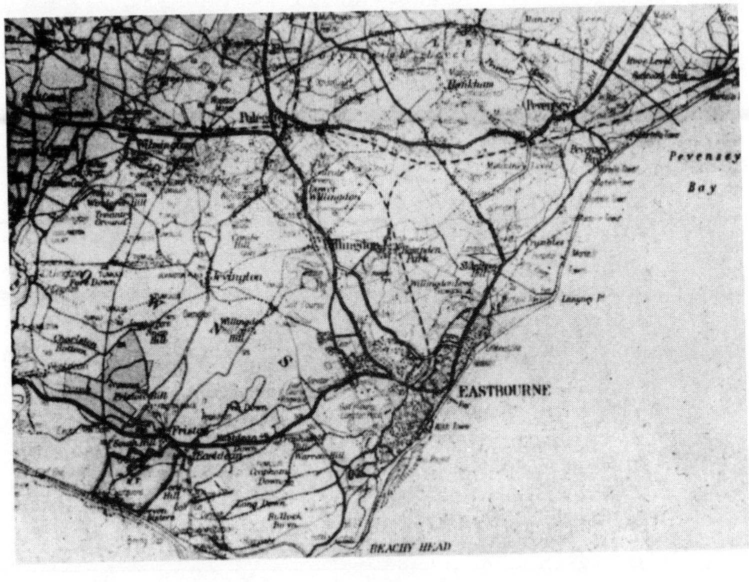

TO FIND MR. HOLMES' BEE FARM

Put a ruler through the final "E" of Eastbourne and the capital "S" of "Sisters" in Seven Sisters (on the coast almost due west of Beachy Head). Birling Farm should appear above your ruler, just east of West Hill.

Watson tells us—again in his Preface to "His Last Bow"—that Holmes in retirement divided his time "between philosophy and agriculture," and in "The Second Stain" he has pinpointed Holmes' interest in agriculture, or a large part of his interest: specifically, Holmes became a bee-farmer.

"What prompted the Master to take up bee-keeping in Sussex during his retirement?" Mr. James Edward Holroyd once asked. And continued: "I have recently acquired a copy of *The British Bee-Keeper's Guide Book,* first published by T. W. Cowan, of Compton Lea, Horsham, in 1881, the opening year of the great partnership. The book went into as many editions as some of Watson's own writings and it is quite possible that Holmes ran into the author during one of his Sussex inquiries. How appropriate was the hobby to a man of Holmes' training may be judged by this quotation from the Introduction: 'Although anyone may possess bees, it is not everyone who can become a proficient bee-master. Only energy and perseverance, *together with aptness for investigation*, can ensure real success.'"

On the other hand, Mr. Pope R. Hill, Sr., has written that Holmes owed his interest in bees to France, not Sussex ("Sherlock Holmes Meets Jean Henri Fabre"): Holmes first became interested in entomology, Mr. Hill wrote, when he spent "several months at Montpellier, in the south of France ["The Adventure of the Empty House"]. [Jean Henri] Fabre's home was in the village of Serignan at the foot of Mount Ventoux, an outlying summit of the Alps, and situated in the South of France less than 75 miles from Montpellier. . . . Holmes . . . would surely have arranged to visit him there at the time. . . . The slightest contact would instantly have aroused Holmes' deepest interest and enthusiasm, for Fabre was an observor and reasoner after Holmes' own heart—as Holmes was after his."

The writing of Holmes' *Practical Handbook of Bee Culture with Some Observations upon the Segregation of the Queen* ("His Last Bow") must have occupied much of Holmes' time between 1904 and 1912, and during this period "he must have acquired a remarkably fine apiarian collection," Miss Madeleine B. Stern wrote in "Sherlock Holmes: Rare Book Collector." "Holmes' shelf on bee culture boasted undoubtedly a copy of Charles Butler's *The Feminin' Monarchi' Or The Histori of Bee's* (Oxford, 1634), a volume of interest not only for its useful advice on the subject, but for its introduction of the use of phonetics in English. Close by this curious treatise stood Bazin's lengthy dialogue entitled *Histoire Naturelle des Abeilles* (Paris, 1744) with its finely engraved folding plates. Réaumur's *Natural History of Bees* (London, 1744), together with Rucellai's poem on bees, *Le Api* (Parma, 1797) with its observations made by means of a magnifying mirror, were surely included in the Holmes collection. Only two copies of Rucellai's work were printed on silk, and it is quite possible, though not definite, that the Holmes copy was one of them. Thacher's *Practical Treatise on the Management of Bees* (Boston, 1829) probably completed the small but select apiarian collection enhanced by a Holmes provenance."

"It is impossible to do more than venture a guess at the books that may have facilitated those [philosophical] studies of Holmes' later years," Miss Stern continued. "In philosophy, he probably dipped into his first editions of Hume and Kant, Leibnitz and Locke, Spinoza, Hobbes and Berkeley. For agricultural entertainment, he may have turned to his 1560 edition of Tatti's compendium, *Della Agricultura,* or to such works as Blith's *English Improver, or a New Survey of Husbandry* (1649)."

We may be sure, too, that Holmes' interest in chemical research continued during his years of "retirement." Mr. R. P. Graham, for example, has pointed to Holmes' statement in "The Final Problem" that his recent investigations had left him "in such a position that I could continue to live in the quiet fashion which is most congenial to me, and to concentrate my attention upon my chemical researches." In "Sherlock Holmes in Retirement," Mr. Graham has noted that when Mr. P. M. Stone visited Holmes in Sussex (see "Sussex Interview" in *221B: Studies in Sherlock Holmes*), the retired detective had a laboratory with chemical apparatus and equipment.

Messrs. J. H. and Humfrey Michell have concurred with Mr. Graham. In "Sherlock Holmes the Chemist," they hold that Holmes' specific interest in chemical research was again the coal tar derivatives. "The last picture we have of [Holmes] in retirement, so charmingly portrayed by Mr. P. M. Stone, shows him still interested in the coal tar derivatives. A glance into the laboratory revealed a 'brick-coated blast furnace.' But Mr. Stone is not an expert in these matters, and what he saw was in reality a coking still, inclosed in a 'setting' of insulating brick. Such a still is used for the isolation of some of the rare and unique hydrocarbons to be found in coal tar. The tar is distilled off in small fractions, some at high temperatures, leaving a residue of coke, and thus Holmes was perhaps in process of isolating some new hydrocarbons of strange properties and values."

Still, with all this research, a question remains: *Why* did Sherlock Holmes retire from active practice when, according to the consensus of expert opinion, he was not yet fifty years of age?

"It was no accident," Professor John B. Wolf wrote in "Another Incubus in the Saddle," "that Holmes 'retired' in 1903. Everyone knows that after 1903 the heretofore reasonably friendly relations between England and Germany deteriorated rapidly. By 1907 the Triple Entente and the Triple Alliance faced each other in an uneasy truce while the naval race between England and Germany (after 1905) grew to monstrous proportions. Crises in 1908 (Bosnia), 1909 (Morocco), 1911 (Morocco), 1912 (Lybia), and 1913 (Balkan Wars) pointed to the catastrophe of 1914. Is it conceivable that Holmes was merely keeping bees while this mortal danger threatened England? Of course not. How can anyone doubt that Holmes was concealing his reasons for having a villa so near the sea? It must be clear to everyone that the Master had more important business than solving the problem of poor Fitzroy McPherson's death ["The Adventure of the Lion's Mane"] and keeping bees. Undoubtedly, beekeeping was a blind, as von Bork discovered ["His Last Bow"], for Holmes' counterespionage activities. It is hard to understand why either Watson or Holmes himself failed to give us the details of those exciting years. It could be that Dr. Watson feared that publicity would limit the Master's usefulness, but it could also have been argued that publicity would have convinced the German government that it would be futile to send spies to England while Holmes was on guard."

Mr. T. S. Blakeney has also written that "no student of Sherlock Holmes can doubt that the years of 1914–18 found him hard at work in the nation's interests **1**—doubtless the perspicacity of the genial but anonymous head of the Secret Service (Sir Samuel Hoare, *The Fourth Seal*, p. 28 *seq.*) secured the willing assistance of the one who stood head and shoulders above the common order of men. Whether Holmes could stand the Secret Service for long is, of course, arguable; it is difficult to see him suffering very gladly the strange medley of affairs outlined, for example, in Mr. Compton Mackenzie's *First Athenian Memories*."

Mr. Arthur L. Levine is another who believes that Holmes was indeed active during the years just before World War I. In "A Man of 'Formidable Resourcefulness,'" he has written that it was due to Holmes' efforts that the famous Zimmermann note (proposing an alliance between Germany, Mexico, and Japan against the United States, if the United States did not remain neutral) was discovered. "It was turned over to the United States Government on February 24, 1917. On March 1st it was made public. On April 6th, the United States declared war on Germany. The tide was turned. Britain was saved. Holmes could return to his bees."

But he probably did not remain with them for long: "At Constantinople, during 1920—according to the London *Times*—the Turks were certain that the great English detective was at work behind the scenes," Mr. Vincent Starrett wrote in his introduction to *221B: Studies in Sherlock Holmes*.

"From about 1920 to the beginning of the second World War," Mr. Norman V. Ballou has written, Holmes lived continuously in northern India. Here he succeeded in at least partially discovering the secret of life and the indefinite extension of man's allotted span by developing an elixir prepared from young queens of the Oriental Hive Bee (*Apis indica*), the largest of the honeybees, which occurs throughout India, Ceylon, and Malasia. "Throughout his sojourn in northern India, Sherlock Holmes is known to have dominated the planning and espionage activities for two great governments while continuing his chemical research. During this period, he is reported to have made several trips to Tibet to consult Buddhist scholars reputed to be engaged in study of the life principle. . . . Shortly after the beginning of World War II, Holmes made his way to Lhasa, where he resided, until very recently, possibly as the secret guest of the Dalai Lama. Again, during nearly two decades in Tibet, Holmes continued to control espionage activities of the governments he served. . . . The activities and whereabouts of Sherlock Holmes go far toward explaining the Chinese Communist Government's recent activities and the flight of the Dalai Lama. Whether Holmes . . . has made good his escape from Tibet or whether he is hiding at some isolated monastery I do not know."

1 During World War I, Sir Arthur Conan Doyle, on a tour of the Allied front, was asked by the French General Humbert: "What rank does Sherlock Holmes hold in the English army, *monsieur?*" Sir Arthur, staggered, replied in halting French that Holmes was unhappily "too old for active service."

On the other hand, Mrs. Crighton Sellars has written ("A Visit with Sherlock Holmes") that she has no doubts that Holmes was "the famous British scientist whose name and peronality were for so long guarded with such secrecy. If I am not mistaken [he] even had the temerity to land in Normandy with our troops on D-Day. I know the person concerned was given another name than [Holmes], but I can very well see that was because [he] did not want our enemies to know [he was] actually engaged against them."

While it is true that Watson has lamentably failed to fill in the record of Holmes' later cases, we have, at least, some tantalizing references to them. See, for example, the Introduction to *The Hound of the Baskervilles* written, in 1926, for the Doubleday, Page & Company edition. Here the late Professor Frank Condie Baxter has revealed that Holmes in 1904 conducted an investigation (no doubt of supreme importance) for the British Admiralty in Shantung—that he was presented with a diamond sword by King Albert of Belgium for his masterly work in clearing up The Affair of the Winking Light in the winter of 1916—and that the Congress of the United States once struck off a Holmes Medal in gratitude for the master detective's services in The Adventure of the American Ambassador and the Thermite Bullet.

It is also suggested that the student of Holmes' later years will find much to interest him in "The Man Who Was Not Dead" by Manly Wade Wellman and "The Adventure of the Illustrious Imposter" by Anthony Boucher (both in *The Misadventures of Sherlock Holmes*), as well as "The Singular Affair of Mr. Phillip Phot," by the Greek Interpreters of East Lansing, Michigan, compiled by the late Page Heldenbrand (in the *Baker Street Journal*, Vol. II, No. 1, Old Series, January, 1947, pp. 67–84).

78

THE ADVENTURE OF THE LION'S MANE

[Tuesday, July 27, to Thursday, August 3, 1909]

IT is a most singular thing that a problem which was certainly as abstruse and unusual as any which I have faced in my long professional career should have come to me after my retirement ; and be brought, as it were, to my very door. It occurred after my withdrawal to my little Sussex home, when I had given myself up entirely to that soothing life of Nature for which I had so often yearned during the long years spent amid the gloom of London. At this period of my life the good Watson had passed almost beyond my ken. An occasional week-end visit was the most that I ever saw of him. Thus I must act as my own chronicler. Ah ! had he but been with me, how much he might have made of so wonderful a happening and of my eventual triumph against every difficulty ! As it is, however, I must needs tell my tale in my own plain way, showing by my words each step upon the difficult road which lay before me as I searched for the mystery of the Lion's Mane.

My villa is situated upon the southern slope of the Downs, commanding a great view of the Channel. At this point the coast-line is entirely of chalk cliffs, which can only be descended by a single, long, tortuous path, which is steep and slippery. At the bottom of the path lie a hundred yards of pebbles and shingle, even when the tide is at full. Here and there, however, there are curves and hollows which make splendid swimming-pools filled afresh with each flow. This admirable beach extends for some miles in each direction, save only at one point where the little cove and village of Fulworth break the line.

1 My house is lonely. I, my old housekeeper, and my bees have the estate all to ourselves. Half a mile off, however, is Harold Stackhurst's well-known coaching establishment, The Gables, quite a large place, which contains some score of young fellows preparing for various professions, with a staff of several masters. Stackhurst himself was a well-known rowing Blue in his day, and an excellent all-round scholar. He and I were always friendly from the day I came to the coast, and he was the one man who was on such terms with me that we could drop in on each other in the evenings without an invitation.

1 *my old housekeeper.* Her first name, as we learn in "His Last Bow," was Martha. Commentators have generally assumed that Holmes' housekeeper in retirement was Mrs. Hudson.

Towards the end of July, 1907, there was a severe gale, the wind blowing up-Channel, heaping the seas to the base of the cliffs, and leaving a lagoon at the turn of the 2 tide. On the morning of which I speak the wind had abated, and all Nature was newly washed and fresh. It was impossible to work upon so delightful a day, and I strolled out before breakfast to enjoy the exquisite air. I walked along the cliff path which led to the steep descent to the beach. As I walked I heard a shout behind me, and there was Harold Stackhurst waving his hand in cheery greeting.

" What a morning, Mr. Holmes ! I thought I should see you out."

" Going for a swim, I see."

" At your old tricks again," he laughed, patting his bulging pocket. " Yes. McPherson started early, and I expect I may find him there."

Fitzroy McPherson was the science master, a fine upstanding young fellow whose life had been crippled by heart trouble following rheumatic fever. He was a natural athlete, however, and excelled in every game which did not throw too great a strain upon him. Summer and winter he went for his swim, and, as I am a swimmer myself, I have often joined him.

At this moment we saw the man himself. His head showed above the edge of the cliff where the path ends. Then his whole figure appeared at the top, staggering like a drunken man. The next instant he threw up his hands, and, with a terrible cry, fell upon his face. Stackhurst and I rushed forward—it may have been fifty yards —and turned him on his back. He was obviously dying. Those glazed sunken eyes and dreadful livid cheeks could mean nothing else. One glimmer of life came into his face for an instant, and he uttered two or three words with an eager air of warning. They were slurred and indistinct, but to my ear the last of them, which burst in a shriek from his lips, were " the lion's mane." It was utterly irrelevant and unintelligible, and yet I could twist the sound into no other sense. Then he half raised himself from the ground, threw his arms into the air and fell forward on his side. He was dead.

My companion was paralysed by the sudden horror of it, but I, as may well be imagined, had every sense on the alert. And I had need, for it was speedily evident that we were in the presence of an extraordinary case. The man was dressed only in his Burberry overcoat, his trousers, and an unlaced pair of canvas shoes. As he fell over, his Burberry, which had been simply thrown round his shoulders, slipped off, exposing his trunk. We stared at it in amazement. His back was covered with dark red lines as though he had been terribly flogged by a thin wire scourge. The instrument with which this punishment had been inflicted was clearly flexible, for the long, angry weals curved round his shoulders and ribs. There was blood dripping down his chin, for he had bitten through his lower lip in the paroxysm of his agony. His drawn and distorted face told how terrible that agony had been.

I was kneeling and Stackhurst standing by the body

2 *heaping the seas to the base of the cliffs.* There was in fact no such gale in July, 1907, and this led the late Professor Jay Finley Christ to date the case in the June of that year, when there was a substantial Channel wind on the 25th. The late Dr. Ernest Bloomfield Zeisler, on the other hand, has shown that "There were high winds and rough sea in the Channel and off the Sussex coast on three successive days, from Saturday, July 24th through Monday, July 26th" in the year 1909. We are later told that the case opened on a Tuesday ("Tuesday was to-day . . ."). Since June 25, 1907, the day of Professor Christ's storm, was a Tuesday, and Holmes tells us that "the wind had abated" on the morning of the opening day, we believe that the evidence is in favor of Dr. Zeisler's date; the "1907" must be a typographical error. The case opened, then, on *Tuesday, July 27, 1909;* Holmes says that "a week passed," so it closed on *Tuesday, August 3rd*, or, perhaps, a day or two later.

THE NEXT INSTANT HE THREW UP HIS HANDS, AND, WITH A TERRIBLE CRY, FELL UPON HIS FACE.

Illustration by Howard K. Elcock for the *Strand Magazine*, December, 1926.

when a shadow fell across us, and we found that Ian Murdoch was by our side. Murdoch was the mathematical coach at the establishment, a tall, dark, thin man, so taciturn and aloof that none can be said to have been his friend. He seemed to live in some high, abstract
3 region of surds and conic sections with little to connect him with ordinary life. He was looked upon as an oddity by the students, and would have been their butt, but there was some strange outlandish blood in the man, which showed itself not only in his coal-black eyes and swarthy face, but also in occasional outbreaks of temper which could only be described as ferocious. On one occasion, being plagued by a little dog belonging to McPherson, he had caught the creature up and hurled it through the plate-glass window, an action for which Stackhurst would certainly have given him his dismissal had he not been a very valuable teacher. Such was the strange, complex man who now appeared beside us. He seemed to be honestly shocked at the sight before him, though the incident of the dog may show that there was no great sympathy between the dead man and himself.

"Poor fellow! Poor fellow! What can I do? How can I help?"

"Were you with him? Can you tell us what has happened?"

"No, no, I was late this morning. I was not on the beach at all. I have come straight from The Gables. What can I do?"

"You can hurry to the police-station at Fulworth. Report the matter at once."

Without a word he made off at top speed, and I proceeded to take the matter in hand, while Stackhurst, dazed at this tragedy, remained by the body. My first task naturally was to note who was on the beach. From the top of the path I could see the whole sweep of it, and it was absolutely deserted save that two or three dark figures could be seen far away moving towards the village of Fulworth. Having satisfied myself upon this point, I walked slowly down the path. There was clay or soft marl mixed with the chalk, and every here and there I saw the same footstep, both ascending and descending. No one else had gone down to the beach by this track that morning. At one place I observed the print of an open hand with the fingers towards the incline. This could only mean that poor McPherson had fallen as he ascended. There were rounded depressions, too, which suggested that he had come down upon his knees more than once. At the bottom of the path was the considerable lagoon left by the retreating tide. At the side of it McPherson had undressed, for there lay his towel on a rock. It was folded and dry, so that it would seem that after all he had never entered the water. Once or twice as I hunted round amid the hard shingle I came on little patches of sand where the print of his canvas shoe, and also of his naked foot, could be seen. The latter fact proved that he had made all ready to bathe, though the towel indicated that he had not actually done so.

And here was the problem clearly defined—as strange a one as had ever confronted me. The man had not

3 *some high, abstract region of surds and conic sections.* "Now these words were written by Holmes himself," Mr. A. S. Galbraith wrote in "The Real Moriarty," "and if he thought of 'surds' as typifying the sort of thing a mathematician would have uppermost in his mind, obviously he knew little of [mathematics]."

been on the beach more than a quarter of an hour at the most. Stackhurst had followed him from The Gables, so there could be no doubt about that. He had gone to bathe and had stripped, as the naked footsteps showed. Then he had suddenly huddled on his clothes again—they were all dishevelled and unfastened—and he had returned without bathing, or at any rate without drying himself. And the reason for his change of purpose had been that he had been scourged in some savage, inhuman fashion, tortured until he bit his lip through in his agony, and was left with only strength enough to crawl away and to die. Who had done this barbarous deed? There were, it is true, small grottos and caves in the base of the cliffs, but the low sun shone directly into them, and there was no place for concealment. Then, again, there were those distant figures on the beach. They seemed too far away to have been connected with the crime, and the broad lagoon in which McPherson had intended to bathe lay between him and them, lapping up to the rocks. On the sea two or three fishing-boats were at no great distance. Their occupants might be examined at our leisure. There were several roads for inquiry, but none which led to any very obvious goal.

When I at last returned to the body I found that a little group of wandering folk had gathered round it. Stackhurst was, of course, still there, and Ian Murdoch had just arrived with Anderson, the village constable, a big, ginger-moustached man of the slow, solid Sussex breed—a breed which covers much good sense under a heavy, silent exterior. He listened to everything, took note of all we said, and finally drew me aside.

"I'd be glad of your advice, Mr. Holmes. This is a big thing for me to handle, and I'll hear of it from Lewes 4 if I go wrong."

I advised him to send for his immediate superior, and for a doctor; also to allow nothing to be moved, and as few fresh footmarks as possible to be made, until they came. In the meantime I searched the dead man's pockets. There were his handkerchief, a large knife, and a small folding card-case. From this projected a slip of paper, which I unfolded and handed to the constable. There was written on it in a scrawling, feminine hand: "I will be there, you may be sure.—Maudie." It read like a love affair, an assignation, though when and where were a blank. The constable replaced it in the card-case and returned it with the other things to the pockets of the Burberry. Then, as nothing more suggested itself, I walked back to my house for breakfast, having first arranged that the base of the cliffs should be thoroughly searched.

Stackhurst was round in an hour or two to tell me that the body had been removed to The Gables, where the inquest would be held. He brought with him some serious and definite news. As I expected, nothing had been found in the small caves below the cliff, but he had examined the papers in McPherson's desk, and there were several which showed an intimate correspondence with a certain Miss Maud Bellamy, of Fulworth. We had then

4 *Lewes.* Municipal borough of Sussex East, on the Ouse River.

established the identity of the writer of the note.

"The police have the letters," he explained. "I could not bring them. But there is no doubt that it was a serious love affair. I see no reason, however, to connect it with that horrible happening save, indeed, that the lady had made an appointment with him."

"But hardly at a bathing-pool which all of you were in the habit of using," I remarked.

"It is mere chance," said he, "that several of the students were not with McPherson."

"*Was* it mere chance?"

Stackhurst knit his brows in thought.

"Ian Murdoch held them back," said he; "he would insist upon some algebraic demonstration before break-
5 fast. Poor chap, he is dreadfully cut up about it all."

"And yet I gather that they were not friends."

"At one time they were not. But for a year or more Murdoch has been as near to McPherson as he ever could be to anyone. He is not of a very sympathetic disposition by nature."

"So I understand. I seem to remember your telling me once about a quarrel over the ill-usage of a dog."

"That blew over all right."

"But left some vindictive feeling, perhaps."

"No, no; I am sure they were real friends."

"Well, then, we must explore the matter of the girl. Do you know her?"

"Everyone knows her. She is the beauty of the neighbourhood—a real beauty, Holmes, who would draw attention everywhere. I knew that McPherson was attracted by her, but I had no notion that it had gone so far as these letters would seem to indicate."

"But who is she?"

"She is the daughter of old Tom Bellamy, who owns all the boats and bathing-cots at Fulworth. He was a fisherman to start with, but is now a man of some substance. He and his son William run the business."

"Shall we walk into Fulworth and see them?"

"On what pretext?"

"Oh, we can easily find a pretext. After all, this poor man did not ill-use himself in this outrageous way. Some human hand was on the handle of that scourge, if indeed it was a scourge which inflicted the injuries. His circle of acquaintances in this lonely place was surely limited. Let us follow it up in every direction and we can hardly fail to come upon the motive, which in turn should lead us to the criminal."

It would have been a pleasant walk across the thyme-scented Downs had our minds not been poisoned by the tragedy we had witnessed. The village of Fulworth lies in a hollow curving in a semicircle round the bay. Behind the old-fashioned hamlet several modern houses have been built upon the rising ground. It was to one of these that Stackhurst guided me.

"That's The Haven, as Bellamy called it. The one with the corner tower and slate roof. Not bad for a man who started with nothing but—— By Jove, look at that!"

5 *some algebraic demonstration before breakfast.* This "shows [Murdoch] sadistic or mad," Mr. Galbraith wrote. "In the writer's moderately wide experience in mathematical circles, [it is] unheard of."

The garden gate of The Haven had opened and a man had emerged. There was no mistaking that tall, angular, straggling figure. It was Ian Murdoch, the mathematician. A moment later we confronted him upon the road.

"Hullo!" said Stackhurst. The man nodded, gave us a sideways glance from his curious dark eyes, and would have passed us, but his principal pulled him up.

"What were you doing there?" he asked.

Murdoch's face flushed with anger. "I am your subordinate, sir, under your roof. I am not aware that I owe you any account of my private actions."

Stackhurst's nerves were near the surface after all he had endured. Otherwise, perhaps, he would have waited. Now he lost his temper completely.

"In the circumstances your answer is pure impertinence, Mr. Murdoch."

"Your own question might perhaps come under the same heading."

"This is not the first time that I have had to overlook your insubordinate ways. It will certainly be the last. You will kindly make fresh arrangements for your future as speedily as you can."

"I had intended to do so. I have lost to-day the only person who made The Gables habitable."

He strode off upon his way, while Stackhurst, with angry eyes, stood glaring after him. "Is he not an impossible, intolerable man?" he cried.

The one thing that impressed itself forcibly upon my mind was that Mr. Ian Murdoch was taking the first chance to open a path of escape from the scene of the crime. Suspicion, vague and nebulous, was now beginning to take outline in my mind. Perhaps the visit to the Bellamys might throw some further light upon the matter. Stackhurst pulled himself together and we went forward to the house.

Mr. Bellamy proved to be a middle-aged man with a flaming red beard. He seemed to be in a very angry mood, and his face was soon as florid as his hair.

"No, sir, I do not desire any particulars. My son here"—indicating a powerful young man, with a heavy, sullen face, in the corner of the sitting-room—"is of one mind with me that Mr. McPherson's attentions to Maud were insulting. Yes, sir, the word 'marriage' was never mentioned, and yet there were letters and meetings, and a great deal more of which neither of us could approve. She has no mother, and we are her only guardians. We are determined——"

But the words were taken from his mouth by the appearance of the lady herself. There was no gainsaying that she would have graced any assembly in the world. Who could have imagined that so rare a flower would grow from such a root and in such an atmosphere? Women have seldom been an attraction to me, for my brain has always governed my heart, but I could not look upon her perfect clear-cut face, with all the soft freshness of the Downlands in her delicate colouring, without realizing that no young man would

"THE WHOLE WORLD WILL KNOW THE FACTS PRESENTLY . . ."

Illustration by Frederic Dorr Steele for *Liberty Magazine*, November 27, 1926.

cross her path unscathed. Such was the girl who had pushed open the door and stood now, wide-eyed and intense, in front of Harold Stackhurst.

" I know already that Fitzroy is dead," she said. " Do not be afraid to tell me the particulars."

" This other gentleman of yours let us know the news," explained the father.

" There is no reason why my sister should be brought into the matter," growled the younger man.

The sister turned a sharp, fierce look upon him. " This is my business, William. Kindly leave me to manage it in my own way. By all accounts there has been a crime committed. If I can help to show who did it, it is the least I can do for him who is gone."

She listened to a short account from my companion, with a composed concentration which showed me that she possessed strong character as well as great beauty. Maud Bellamy will always remain in my memory as a most complete and remarkable woman. It seems that she already knew me by sight, for she turned to me at the end.

" Bring them to justice, Mr. Holmes. You have my sympathy and my help, whoever they may be." It seemed to me that she glanced defiantly at her father and brother as she spoke.

" Thank you," said I. " I value a woman's instinct in such matters. You use the word ' they.' You think that more than one was concerned ? "

" I knew Mr. McPherson well enough to be aware that he was a brave and a strong man. No single person could ever have inflicted such an outrage upon him."

" Might I have one word with you alone ? "

" I tell you, Maud, not to mix yourself up in the matter," cried her father angrily.

She looked at me helplessly. " What can I do ? "

" The whole world will know the facts presently, so there can be no harm if I discuss them here," said I. " I should have preferred privacy, but if your father will not allow it, he must share the deliberations." Then I spoke of the note which had been found in the dead man's pocket. " It is sure to be produced at the inquest. May I ask you to throw any light upon it that you can ? "

" I see no reason for mystery," she answered. " We were engaged to be married, and we only kept it secret because Fitzroy's uncle, who is very old and said to be dying, might have disinherited him if he had married against his wish. There was no other reason."

" You could have told us," growled Mr. Bellamy.

" So I would, father, if you had ever shown sympathy."

" I object to my girl picking up with men outside her own station."

" It was your prejudice against him which prevented us from telling you. As to this appointment "—she fumbled in her dress and produced a crumpled note—" it was in answer to this."

" DEAREST," ran the message : " The old place on the beach just after sunset on Tuesday. It is the only time I can get away.—F. M."

" Tuesday was to-day, and I had meant to meet him to-night."

I turned over the paper. " This never came by post. How did you get it ? "

" I would rather not answer that question. It has really nothing to do with the matter which you are investigating. But anything which bears upon that I will most freely answer."

She was as good as her word, but there was nothing which was helpful in our investigation. She had no reason to think that her fiancé had any hidden enemy, but she admitted that she had had several warm admirers.

" May I ask if Mr. Ian Murdoch was one of them ? "

She blushed and seemed confused.

" There was a time when I thought he was. But that was all changed when he understood the relations between Fitzroy and myself."

Again the shadow round this strange man seemed to me to be taking more definite shape. His record must be examined. His rooms must be privately searched. Stackhurst was a willing collaborator, for in his mind also suspicions were forming. We returned from our visit to The Haven with the hope that one free end of this tangled skein was already in our hands.

A week passed. The inquest had thrown no light upon the matter and had been adjourned for further evidence. Stackhurst had made discreet inquiry about his subordinate, and there had been a superficial search of his room, but without result. Personally, I had gone over the whole ground again, both physically and mentally, but with no new conclusions. In all my chronicles the reader will find no case which brought me so completely to the limit of my powers. Even my imagination could conceive no solution to the mystery. And then there came the incident of the dog.

It was my old housekeeper who heard of it first by that strange wireless by which such people collect the news of the country-side.

" Sad story this, sir, about Mr. McPherson's dog," said she one evening.

I do not encourage such conversations, but the words arrested my attention.

" What of Mr. McPherson's dog ? "

" Dead, sir. Died of grief for its master."

" Who told you this ? "

" Why, sir, everyone is talking of it. It took on terrible, and has eaten nothing for a week. Then to-day two of the young gentlemen from The Gables found it dead—down on the beach, sir, at the very place where its master met his end."

" At the very place." The words stood out clear in my memory. Some dim perception that the matter was vital rose in my mind. That the dog should die was after the beautiful, faithful nature of dogs. But ' in the very place ' ! Why should this lonely beach be fatal to it ? Was it possible that it also, had been sacrificed to some revengeful feud ? Was it possible—— ? Yes, the perception was dim, but already something was building up in my mind. In a few minutes I was on my way to

I TURNED OVER THE PAPER. "THIS NEVER CAME BY POST. HOW DID YOU GET IT?"

Illustration by Howard K. Elcock for the *Strand Magazine*, December, 1926.

The Gables, where I found Stackhurst in his study. At my request he sent for Sudbury and Blount, the two students who had found the dog.

"Yes, it lay on the very edge of the pool," said one of them. "It must have followed the trail of its dead master."

6 I saw the faithful little creature, an Airedale terrier, laid out upon the mat in the hall. The body was stiff and rigid, the eyes projecting, and the limbs contorted. There was agony in every line of it.

From The Gables I walked down to the bathing-pool. The sun had sunk and the shadow of the great cliff lay black across the water, which glimmered dully like a sheet of lead. The place was deserted and there was no sign of life save for two sea-birds circling and screaming overhead. In the fading light I could dimly make out the little dog's spoor upon the sand round the very rock on which his master's towel had been laid. For a long time I stood in deep meditation while the shadows grew darker around me. My mind was filled with racing thoughts. You have known what it was to be in a nightmare in which you feel that there is some all-important thing for which you search and which you know is there, though it remains for ever just beyond your reach. That was how I felt that evening as I stood alone by that place of death. Then at last I turned and walked slowly homewards.

I had just reached the top of the path when it came to me. Like a flash, I remembered the thing for which I had so eagerly and vainly grasped. You will know, or Watson has written in vain, that I hold a vast store of out-of-the-way knowledge, without scientific system, but very available for the needs of my work. My mind is
7 like a crowded box-room with packets of all sorts stowed away therein—so many that I may well have but a vague perception of what was there. I had known that there was something which might bear upon this matter. It was still vague, but at least I knew how I could make it clear. It was monstrous, incredible, and yet it was always a possibility. I would test it to the full.

There is a great garret in my little house which is stuffed with books. It was into this that I plunged and rummaged for an hour. At the end of that time I emerged with a little chocolate and silver volume. Eagerly I turned up the chapter of which I had a dim remembrance. Yes, it was indeed a far-fetched and unlikely proposition, and yet I could not be at rest until I had made sure if it might, indeed, be so. It was late when I retired, with my mind eagerly awaiting the work of the morrow.

But that work met with an annoying interruption. I had hardly swallowed my early cup of tea and was starting for the beach when I had a call from Inspector Bardle of the Sussex Constabulary—a steady, solid, bovine man with thoughtful eyes, which looked at me now with a very troubled expression.

"I know your immense experience, sir," said he. "This is quite unofficial, of course, and need go no further. But I am fairly up against it in this McPherson

6 *an Airedale terrier.* "Anyone who knows anything about terriers knows that Airedales are large," Mrs. Eleanor S. Cole wrote in "Holmes, Watson and the K-9's." "The breed standard (*The Complete Dog Book*, The American Kennel Club, New York City) lists the males as standing 23 inches at the wither (shoulder) and therefore weighing upwards of sixty pounds. To have picked up and hurled a dog of this size and weight through a plate-glass window would have required the thrower to be a veritable giant. Nowhere in the story is Ian Murdoch described as such. Therefore, the dog must have been a Welsh terrier, which to the uninitiate, strongly resembles an Airedale in miniature."

7 *My mind is like a crowded box-room.* Holmes' observation here is of course in direct contradiction to what he told Watson of his mental habits in *A Study in Scarlet.*

case. The question is, shall I make an arrest, or shall I not ? "

" Meaning Mr. Ian Murdoch ? "

" Yes, sir. There is really no one else when you come to think of it. That's the advantage of this solitude. We narrow it down to a very small compass. If he did not do it, then who did ? "

" What have you against him ? "

He had gleaned along the same furrows as I had. There was Murdoch's character and the mystery which seemed to hang round the man. His furious bursts of temper, as shown in the incident of the dog. The fact that he had quarrelled with McPherson in the past, and that there was some reason to think that he might have resented his attentions to Miss Bellamy. He had all my points, but no fresh ones, save that Murdoch seemed to be making every preparation for departure.

" What would my position be if I let him slip away with all this evidence against him ? " The burly, phlegmatic man was sorely troubled in his mind.

" Consider," I said, " all the essential gaps in your case. On the morning of the crime he can surely prove an alibi. He had been with his scholars till the last moment, and within a few minutes of McPherson's appearance he came upon us from behind. Then bear in mind the absolute impossibility that he could single-handed have inflicted this outrage upon a man quite as strong as himself. Finally, there is this question of the instrument with which these injuries were inflicted."

" What could it be but a scourge or flexible whip of some sort ? "

" Have you examined the marks ? " I asked.

" I have seen them. So has the doctor."

" But I have examined them very carefully with a lens. They have peculiarities."

" What are they, Mr. Holmes ? "

I stepped to my bureau and brought out an enlarged photograph. " This is my method in such cases," I explained.

" You certainly do things thoroughly, Mr. Holmes."

" I should hardly be what I am if I did not. Now let us consider this weal which extends round the right shoulder. Do you observe nothing remarkable ? "

" I can't say I do."

" Surely it is evident that it is unequal in its intensity. There is a dot of extravasated blood here, and another there. There are similar indications in this other weal down here. What can that mean ? "

" I have no idea. Have you ? "

" Perhaps I have. Perhaps I haven't. I may be able to say more soon. Anything which will define what made that mark will bring us a long way towards the criminal."

" It is, of course, an absurd idea," said the policeman, " but if a red-hot net of wire had been laid across the back, then these better-marked points would represent where the meshes crossed each other."

" A most ingenious comparison. Or shall we say a very stiff cat-o'-nine-tails with small hard knots upon it ? "

" By Jove, Mr. Holmes, I think you have hit it."

MY OUTER DOOR WAS FLUNG OPEN . . .

Illustration by Howard K. Elcock for the *Strand Magazine*, December, 1926.

" Or there may be some very different cause, Mr. Bardle. But your case is far too weak for an arrest. Besides, we have those last words—' Lion's Mane.' "

" I have wondered whether Ian——"

" Yes, I have considered that. If the second word had borne any resemblance to Murdoch—but it did not. He gave it almost in a shriek. I am sure that it was ' Mane.' "

" Have you no alternative, Mr. Holmes ? "

" Perhaps I have. But I do not care to discuss it until there is something more solid to discuss."

" And when will that be ? "

" In an hour—possibly less."

The Inspector rubbed his chin and looked at me with dubious eyes.

" I wish I could see what was in your mind, Mr. Holmes. Perhaps it's those fishing-boats."

" No, no ; they were too far out."

" Well, then, is it Bellamy and that big son of his ? They were not too sweet upon Mr. McPherson. Could they have done him a mischief ? "

" No, no ; you won't draw me until I am ready," said I with a smile. " Now, Inspector, we each have our own work to do. Perhaps if you were to meet me here at midday—— ? "

So far we had got when there came the tremendous interruption which was the beginning of the end.

My outer door was flung open, there were blundering footsteps in the passage, and Ian Murdoch staggered into the room, pallid, dishevelled, his clothes in wild disorder, clawing with his bony hands at the furniture to hold himself erect. " Brandy ! Brandy ! " he gasped, and fell groaning upon the sofa.

He was not alone. Behind him came Stackhurst, hatless and panting, almost as *distrait* as his companion.

" Yes, yes, brandy ! " he cried. " The man is at his last gasp. It was all I could do to bring him here. He fainted twice upon the way."

Half a tumbler of the raw spirit brought about a wondrous change. He pushed himself up on one arm and swung his coat from off his shoulders. " For God's sake ! oil, opium, morphia ! " he cried. " Anything to ease this infernal agony ! "

The Inspector and I cried out at the sight. There, criss-crossed upon the man's naked shoulder, was the same strange reticulated pattern of red, inflamed lines which had been the death-mark of Fitzroy McPherson.

The pain was evidently terrible and was more than local, for the sufferer's breathing would stop for a time, his face would turn black, and then with loud gasps he would clap his hand to his heart, while his brow dropped beads of sweat. At any moment he might die. More and more brandy was poured down his throat, each fresh dose bringing him back to life. Pads of cotton-wool soaked in salad-oil seemed to take the agony from the strange wounds. At last his head fell heavily upon the cushion. Exhausted Nature had taken refuge in its last storehouse of vitality. It was half a sleep and half a faint, but at least it was ease from pain.

To question him had been impossible, but the moment

we were assured of his condition Stackhurst turned upon me.

"My God!" he cried, "what is it, Holmes? What is it?"

"Where did you find him?"

"Down on the beach. Exactly where poor McPherson met his end. If this man's heart had been weak as McPherson's was, he would not be here now. More than once I thought he was gone as I brought him up. It was too far to The Gables, so I made for you."

"Did you see him on the beach?"

"I was walking on the cliff when I heard his cry. He was at the edge of the water, reeling about like a drunken man. I ran down, threw some clothes about him, and brought him up. For Heaven's sake, Holmes, use all the powers you have and spare no pains to lift the curse from this place, for life is becoming unendurable. Can you, with all your world-wide reputation, do nothing for us?"

"I think I can, Stackhurst. Come with me now! And you, Inspector, come along! We will see if we cannot deliver this murderer into your hands."

Leaving the unconscious man in the charge of my housekeeper, we all three went down to the deadly lagoon. On the shingle there was piled a little heap of towels and clothes, left by the stricken man. Slowly I walked round the edge of the water, my comrades in Indian file behind me. Most of the pool was quite shallow, but under the cliff where the beach was hollowed out it was four or five feet deep. It was to this part that a swimmer would naturally go, for it formed a beautiful pellucid green pool as clear as crystal. A line of rocks lay above it at the base of the cliff, and along this I led the way, peering eagerly into the depths beneath me. I had reached the deepest and stillest pool when my eyes caught that for which they were searching, and I burst into a shout of triumph.

"Cyanea!" I cried. "Cyanea! Behold the Lion's Mane!" **8**

The strange object at which I pointed did indeed look like a tangled mass torn from the mane of a lion. It lay upon a rocky shelf some three feet under the water, a curious waving, vibrating, hairy creature with streaks of silver among its yellow tresses. It pulsated with a slow, heavy dilation and contraction.

"It has done mischief enough. Its day is over!" I cried. "Help me, Stackhurst! Let us end the murderer for ever."

There was a big boulder just above the ledge, and we pushed it until it fell with a tremendous splash into the water. When the ripples had cleared we saw that it had settled upon the ledge below. One flapping edge of yellow membrane showed that our victim was beneath it. A thick oily scum oozed out from below the stone and stained the water round, rising slowly to the surface.

"Well, this gets me!" cried the Inspector. "What was it, Mr. Holmes? I'm born and bred in these parts, but I never saw such a thing. It don't belong to Sussex."

"Just as well for Sussex," I remarked. "It may have been the south-west gale that brought it up. Come

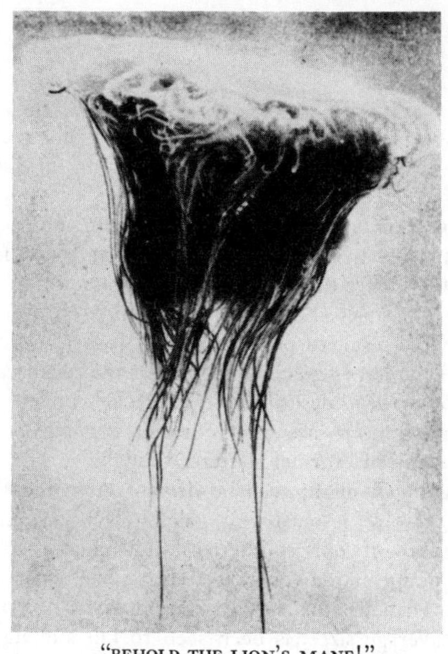

"BEHOLD THE LION'S MANE!"

A specimen of *Cyanea capillata*, or the lion's mane jellyfish. One was found to have tentacles of over 120 feet in length. The photograph is the copyright of Robert C. Hermes, and appeared in the Winter, 1963, issue of *The Sherlock Holmes Journal.*

8 *"Cyanea!" I cried.* "The acraspedote tetramerous medusan *Cyanea capillata*, popularly known by such names as 'hairy stinger,' 'sea nettle,' or 'lion's mane,'" Mr. Joel W. Hedgpeth wrote in his "Re-Examination of 'The Adventure of the Lion's Mane.'" "For those unfamiliar with the esoteric jargon of zoology it should be explained that 'acraspedote tetramerous medusan' means a simple bellshaped medusa (i.e., without a velum) whose principal organs are divided in fours. The medusa is actually the adult or sexual phase of a complicated life cycle and is produced from a sedentary hydra-like form by asexual budding. . . . Since the days of Edward Forbes, who called it 'the terror of tender skinned bathers' in his famous *Monograph of the Naked-Eyed Medusas* (published by the Ray Society in 1848) *Cyanea capillata* has been characterized as one of the more formidable creatures of the temperate seas. . . . The medical history of jellyfish stings, however, while recording some rather severe cases, is nevertheless more encouraging for those who may have misgivings about swimming in English and North Atlantic waters in general, for there is no recorded fatality that can be attributed solely to jellyfish poisoning in temperate waters." Mr. Hedgpeth added that "jellyfish do not usually sit on rocks" (see below—"It lay upon a rocky shelf") and that "another curious discrepancy is the discharge of oil, which can be explained at this late date only by the suggestion that the jellyfish was eating some oily fish, possibly a small shark, and the oil actually came from the shark."

But the editors of the Catalogue of the Sherlock Holmes Exhibition have cast some doubt on whether the jellyfish of "The Adventure of the Lion's Mane" was, in fact, *Cyanea capillata.* They suggest that it was the Portugese Man-of-War,

back to my house, both of you, and I will give you the terrible experience of one who has good reason to remember his own meeting with the same peril of the seas."

When we reached my study, we found that Murdoch was so far recovered that he could sit up. He was dazed in mind, and every now and then was shaken by a paroxysm of pain. In broken words he explained that he had no notion what had occurred to him, save that terrific pangs had suddenly shot through him, and that it had taken all his fortitude to reach the bank.

"Here is a book," I said, taking up the little volume, "which first brought light into what might have been
for ever dark. It is *Out of Doors*, by the famous observer
9 J. G. Wood. Wood himself very nearly perished from
contact with this vile creature, so he wrote with a very full knowledge. *Cyanea Capillata* is the miscreant's full name, and he can be as dangerous to life as, and far more painful than, the bite of the cobra. Let me briefly give this extract.

"'If the bather should see a loose roundish mass of tawny membranes and fibres, something like very large handfuls of lion's mane and silver paper, let him beware, for this is the fearful stinger, *Cyanea Capillata*.' Could our sinister acquaintance be more clearly described?

"He goes on to tell his own encounter with one when swimming off the coast of Kent. He found that the creature radiated almost invisible filaments to the distance of fifty feet, and that anyone within that circumference from the deadly centre was in danger of death. Even at a distance the effect upon Wood was almost fatal. 'The multitudinous threads caused light scarlet lines upon the skin which on closer examination resolved into minute dots or pustules, each dot charged as it were with a red-hot needle making its way through the nerves.'

"The local pain was, as he explains, the least part of the exquisite torment. 'Pangs shot through the chest, causing me to fall as if struck by a bullet. The pulsation would cease, and then the heart would give six or seven leaps as if it would force its way through the chest.'

"It nearly killed him, although he had only been exposed to it in the disturbed ocean and not in the narrow calm waters of a bathing-pool. He says that he could hardly recognize himself afterwards, so white, wrinkled and shrivelled was his face. He gulped down brandy, a whole bottleful, and it seems to have saved his life. There is the book, Inspector. I leave it with you, and you cannot doubt that it contains a full explanation of the tragedy of poor McPherson."

"And incidentally exonerates me," remarked Ian Mur-
10 doch with a wry smile. "I do not blame you, Inspector,
nor you, Mr. Holmes, for your suspicions were natural. I feel that on the very eve of my arrest I have only cleared myself by sharing the fate of my poor friend."

"No, Mr. Murdoch. I was already upon the track, and had I been out as early as I intended I might well have saved you from this terrific experience."

"But how did you know, Mr. Holmes?"

Physalia: "This complex creature is actually a colony—an aggregate of organisms acting in some ways as an individual; it is not a very close relative of the ordinary jellyfishes of which *Cyanea* is representative. It is, however, a far more formidable object to the bather. The tentacles of [a] relatively small specimen . . . might, when fully extended, reach to perhaps 50 feet from the float; and much larger specimens—such as the remarkable Atlantic form described by Haeckel under the name *Caravella*—are on record. It is typically an inhabitant of warmer waters, though, as Holmes suggested, it might well be driven on to the Sussex coast by a south-west gale; it is occasionally recorded off our southern shores. There seems little doubt, moreover, that a large specimen could kill even a healthy man; a specimen of no more than average size has been seen to kill and ingest a full-grown mackerel. . . ."

9 *the famous observer J. G. Wood.* The Reverend John George Wood, 1827–1889, was the author of nearly sixty books and of many popular articles, many of them for children. His great service was that he popularized the study of natural history. *Out of Doors: A Selection of Original Articles on Practical Natural History*, was published in London by Longmans, Green and Co. in 1874 and appeared in new editions in 1882 and 1890. "Undoubtedly [Wood] was particularly sensitive to the sting of the jellyfish," Mr. Hedgpeth noted, "for his account is by all odds the most harrowing in the literature of marine natural history." "It is quite likely that Holmes' obligation to [Wood] is even greater than has been acknowledged," Dr. Julian Wolff added in "Remember the Mane?", "since he was also the author of *Bees, Their Habits and Management*, published in 1853 by G. Routledge & Company of London."

10 "*And incidentally exonerates me," remarked Ian Murdoch.* "The possibility never seemed to have occurred to Holmes that this disarming young man . . . had secured a *Cyanea* in some manner and placed it in the tidepool with diabolical malice aforethought," Mr. Hedgpeth wrote. "Beyond all doubt this dark, brooding, 'ferocious tempered' young man, disappointed in love and capable of throwing innocent dogs through windows, had conceived a most ingenious crime and to allay suspicion had caressed his own monstrous pet. . . . It is most unlikely than an Airedale terrier would have succumbed to the sting of a jellyfish—its hair alone would protect it—and it seems evident that Murdoch poisoned the dog, for he was a man who did not like dogs, and placed its body in the pool where McPherson had met disaster, as a red herring."

" I am an omnivorous reader with a strangely retentive memory for trifles. That phrase ' Lion's Mane ' haunted my mind. I knew that I had seen it somewhere in an unexpected context. You have seen that it does describe the creature. I have no doubt that it was floating on the water when McPherson saw it, and that this phrase was the only one by which he could convey to us a warning as to the creature which had been his death."

" Then I, at least, am cleared," said Murdoch, rising slowly to his feet. " There are one or two words of explanation which I should give, for I know the direction in which your inquiries have run. It is true that I loved this lady, but from the day when she chose my friend McPherson my one desire was to help her to happiness. I was well content to stand aside and act as their go-between. Often I carried their messages, and it was because I was in their confidence and because she was so dear to me that I hastened to tell her of my friend's death, lest someone should forestall me in a more sudden and heartless manner. She would not tell you, sir, of our relations lest you should disapprove and I might suffer. But with your leave I must try to get back to The Gables, for my bed will be very welcome."

Stackhurst held out his hand. " Our nerves have all been at concert-pitch," said he. " Forgive what is past, Murdoch. We shall understand each other better in the future." They passed out together with their arms linked in friendly fashion. The Inspector remained, staring at me in silence with his ox-like eyes.

" Well, you've done it ! " he cried at last. " I had read of you, but I never believed it. It's wonderful ! "

I was forced to shake my head. To accept such praise was to lower one's own standards.

" I was slow at the outset—culpably slow. Had **11** the body been found in the water I could hardly have missed it. It was the towel which misled me. The poor fellow had never thought to dry himself, and so I in turn was led to believe that he had never been in the water. Why, then, should the attack of any water creature suggest itself to me ? That was where I went astray. Well, well, Inspector, I often ventured to chaff you gentlemen of the police force, but *Cyanea Capillata* very nearly avenged Scotland Yard."

11 *"I was slow at the outset—culpably slow.* "Fi, fi, Sherlock!" Mr. Nathan L. Bengis wrote in "Sherlock Stays After School." "Even the 'gentlemen of the police force' should have seen through that one. You were more than 'culpably slow'—you were downright befuddled. . . . You should have known from the very first that McPherson had been in the water, and could not have been out of it by more than a very few minutes. How? By the very simplest of deductions. McPherson's body must still have been wet when you examined it. The lining of his Burberry overcoat must have been moist, as would also his hair. His canvas shoes, unlaced because he had not had time in his mortal agony to lace them, would certainly have shown a trace of moisture. That you should have failed to notice all these obvious signs that McPherson had just emerged from the water, and merely from the dryness of his towel should have jumped to the conclusion that he had not gone in, almost passes belief. What is quite incredible and unpardonable is your sorry attempt to exonerate yourself. Surely at least in retrospect the flimsiness of your excuse should have been apparent to you, and you should have been too ashamed of your performance to make a permanent record of it for future generations."

Auctorial Note: Conan Doyle barred all stories in the *Case-Book* from consideration when he compiled his "twelve best list" (these stories had not yet appeared in book form). He nonetheless is on record as having thought highly of "The Adventure of the Lion's Mane." In an early number of the *Sussex County Magazine* he was quoted as saying: "I have done three new Sherlock Holmes stories for the *Strand*. I don't think they show any falling off. In fact, one of them 'The Lion's Mane,' I should put in the front row. But that is for the public to judge." Later (in the *Strand Magazine* for March, 1927) Conan Doyle wrote: "The [story] is hampered by being told by Holmes himself, a method which . . . certainly cramps the narrative. On the other hand, the actual plot is among the very best of the whole series."

THE OFFICES OF THE STRAND MAGAZINE

Said the *Strand* in a description of its own offices: "Its fine, broad front, wherein the architect has with a just hand distributed the red brick and white stone in the parts above the stone ground floor, stretches through four numbers on the right-hand side [of Southampton Street], and the building is carried, in depth, through to Exeter Street . . . A handsome, triple entrance stands between large plate-glass windows. . . ."

X. AN EPILOGUE OF SHERLOCK HOLMES

"But you had retired, Holmes. We heard of you as living the life of a hermit among your bees and your books in a small farm upon the South Downs."

—John H Watson, M.D., "His Last Bow."

79

HIS LAST BOW

[*Sunday, August 2, 1914*]

1 IT was nine o'clock at night upon the second of August—the most terrible August in the history of the world. One might have thought already that God's curse hung heavy over a degenerate world, for there was an awesome hush and a feeling of vague expectancy in the sultry and stagnant air. The sun had long set, but one blood-red gash like an open wound lay low in the distant west. Above, the stars were shining brightly ; and below, the lights of the shipping glimmered in the bay. The two famous Germans stood beside the stone parapet of the garden walk, with the long, low, heavily gabled house behind them, and they looked down upon the broad sweep of the beach at the foot of the great chalk cliff on which Von Bork, like some wandering eagle, had perched himself
2 four years before. They stood with their heads close together, talking in low, confidential tones. From below the two glowing ends of their cigars might have been the smouldering eyes of some malignant fiend looking down in the darkness.

A remarkable man this Von Bork—a man who could hardly be matched among all the devoted agents of the Kaiser. It was his talents which had first recommended him for the English mission, the most important mission of all, but since he had taken it over, those talents had become more and more manifest to the half-dozen people in the world who were really in touch with the truth. One of these was his present companion, Baron Von Herling, the chief secretary of the legation, whose huge 100-horse-power Benz car was blocking the country lane as it waited to waft its owner back to London.

" So far as I can judge the trend of events, you will probably be back in Berlin within the week," the secretary was saying. " When you get there, my dear Von Bork, I think you will be surprised at the welcome you will receive. I happen to know what is thought in the highest quarters of your work in this country." He was a huge man, the secretary, deep, broad, and tall, with a slow, heavy fashion of speech which had been his main asset in his political career.

Von Bork laughed.

" They are not very hard to deceive," he remarked.

1 *the second of August.* The year was of course 1914: "Well, I chose August for the word, and 1914 for the figures, and here we are," Von Bork says later. August 2, 1914, fell on a Sunday. "His Last Bow" is the second of the two Sherlock Holmes adventures recounted by "a third person," although "it is difficult," as Mr. S. C. Roberts wrote in *Doctor Watson,* "to believe that the opening passage is not taken verbatim from Watson's notes." The late A. Carson Simpson has held that Holmes himself was the author, but the late Edgar W. Smith argued ("The Adventure of the Veiled Author") that only Mycroft Holmes could have transcribed the tale.

2 *had perched himself four years before* ". . . there is evidence, I think, that the seaside gabled house which was the headquarters of Von Bork . . . was on the South Coast," Mr. Gordon Sewell wrote in "Holmes and Watson in the South Country." "Watson writes of it being perched on a cliff. Dover, perhaps? Too conspicuous, surely. Cornwall? Too remote. Von Bork was interested in naval matters, and he would have chosen a residence somewhere within easy distance of both Portland and Portsmouth. . . . What more likely place than Studland, a discreet hideout for the master spy?"

"A more docile, simple folk could not be imagined."

"I don't know about that," said the other thoughtfully. "They have strange limits and one must learn to observe them. It is that surface simplicity of theirs which makes a trap for the stranger. One's first impression is that they are entirely soft. Then one comes suddenly upon something very hard and you know that you have reached the limit, and must adapt yourself to the fact. They have, for example, their insular conventions which simply *must* be observed."

"Meaning, 'good form' and that sort of thing?" Von Bork sighed, as one who had suffered much.

"Meaning British prejudice in all its queer manifestations. As an example I may quote one of my own worst blunders—I can afford to talk of my blunders, for you know my work well enough to be aware of my successes. It was on my first arrival. I was invited to a week-end gathering at the country house of a Cabinet Minister. The conversation was amazingly indiscreet."

Von Bork nodded. "I've been there," said he dryly.

"Exactly. Well, I naturally sent a résumé of the information to Berlin. Unfortunately our good Chancellor is a little heavy-handed in these matters, and he transmitted a remark which showed that he was aware of what had been said. This, of course, took the trail straight up to me. You've no idea the harm that it did me. There was nothing soft about our British hosts on that occasion, I can assure you. I was two years living it down. Now you, with this sporting pose of yours."

"No, no, don't call it a pose. A pose is an artificial thing. This is quite natural. I am a born sportsman. I enjoy it."

"Well, that makes it the more effective. You yacht
against them, you hunt with them, you play polo, you
match them in every game, your four-in-hand takes the 3
prize at Olympia. I have even heard that you go the 4
length of boxing with the young officers. What is the result? Nobody takes you seriously. You are a 'good old sport,' 'quite a decent fellow for a German,' a hard-drinking, night-club, knock-about-town, devil-may-care young fellow. And all the time this quiet country house of yours is the centre of half the mischief in England, and the sporting squire the most astute Secret Service man in Europe. Genius, my dear Von Bork—genius!"

"You flatter me, Baron. But certainly I may claim that my four years in this country have not been unproductive. I've never shown you my little store. Would you mind stepping in for a moment?"

The door of the study opened straight on to the terrace. Von Bork pushed it back, and, leading the way, he clicked the switch of the electric light. He then closed the door behind the bulky form which followed him, and carefully adjusted the heavy curtain over the latticed window. Only when all these precautions had been taken and tested did he turn his sunburned aquiline face to his guest.

"Some of my papers have gone," said he; "when my wife and the household left yesterday for Flushing they took the less important with them. I must, of course, claim the protection of the Embassy for the others."

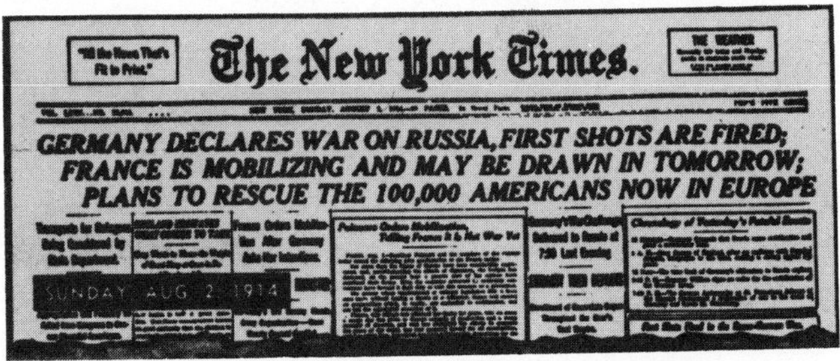
The New York Times.

GERMANY DECLARES WAR ON RUSSIA, FIRST SHOTS ARE FIRED; FRANCE IS MOBILIZING AND MAY BE DRAWN IN TOMORROW; PLANS TO RESCUE THE 100,000 AMERICANS NOW IN EUROPE

SUNDAY AUG 2 1914

. . . THE MOST TERRIBLE AUGUST IN THE HISTORY OF THE WORLD.

Headlines from the New York *Times* on Sunday, August 2, 1914—the day of Holmes' last recorded adventure.

3 *your four-in-hand.* A four-horse team driven by one person.

4 *Olympia.* Olympia, which is situated on the north side of the Hammersmith Road, adjoining the West London Railway, was erected in 1886 by the National Agricultural Hall Company. The original buildings had an area of four acres. The grand hall, two and a half acres in extent, is one of the largest in the kingdom, and is covered by one span of iron and glass 450 feet long by 250 feet wide. The Horse Show was indeed held at the Olympia.

" Your name has already been filed as one of the personal suite. There will be no difficulties for you or your baggage. Of course, it is just possible that we may not have to go. England may leave France to her fate. We are sure that there is no binding treaty between them."

" And Belgium ? "

" Yes, and Belgium, too."

Von Bork shook his head. " I don't see how that could be. There is a definite treaty there. She could never recover from such a humiliation."

" She would at least have peace for the moment."

" But her honour ? "

" Tut, my dear sir, we live in a utilitarian age. Honour is a mediæval conception. Besides England is not ready. It is an inconceivable thing, but even our special war tax of fifty millions, which one would think made our purpose as clear as if we had advertised it on the front page of *The Times*, has not roused these people from their slumbers. Here and there one hears a question. It is my business to find an answer. Here and there also there is an irritation. It is my business to soothe it. But I can assure you that so far as the essentials go—the storage of munitions, the preparation for submarine attack, the arrangements for making high explosives—nothing is prepared. How then can England come in, especially when we have stirred her up such a devil's brew of Irish civil war, window-breaking Furies, and God knows what to keep her thoughts at home ? "

" She must think of her future."

" Ah, that is another matter. I fancy that in the future, we have our own very definite plans about England, and that your information will be very vital to us. It is to-day or to-morrow with Mr. John Bull. If he prefers to-day we are perfectly ready. If it is to-morrow we shall be more ready still. I should think they would be wiser to fight with allies than without them, but that is their own
5 affair. This week is their week of destiny. But you were
speaking of your papers." He sat in the arm-chair with the light shining upon his broad bald head, while he puffed sedately at his cigar.

The large oak-panelled book-lined room had a curtain hung in the further corner. When this was drawn it disclosed a large brass-bound safe. Von Bork detached a small key from his watch-chain, and after some considerable manipulation of the lock he swung open the heavy door.

" Look ! " said he, standing clear, with a wave of his hand.

The light shone vividly into the opened safe, and the secretary of the Embassy gazed with an absorbed interest at the rows of stuffed pigeon-holes with which it was furnished. Each pigeon-hole had its label, and his eyes as he glanced along them read a long series of such titles as " Fords," " Harbour-defences," " Aeroplanes," " Ireland," " Egypt," " Portsmouth forts," " The Channel," " Rosyth," and a score of others. Each compartment was bristling with papers and plans.

" Colossal ! " said the secretary. Putting down his cigar he softly clapped his fat hands.

5 *This week is their week of destiny.* Headlines from *The New York Times:* (Monday, August 3) RUSSIA INVADES GERMANY; GERMANY INVADES FRANCE, BUT DOES NOT DECLARE WAR; ENGLAND'S DECISION TO-DAY; BELGIUM MENACED, LUXEMBURG AND SWITZERLAND INVADED; GERMAN MARKSMEN SHOOT DOWN A FRENCH AEROPLANE. (Tuesday, August 4) ENGLAND WILL PROTECT FRENCH COAST AND DEFEND BELGIUM; GERMANY RECALLS ENVOY; HESITATES AT FRENCH FRONTIER; HER ARMY SEIZES RUSSIAN TOWNS, NAVY WINS A VICTORY; GERMAN LINER SLIPS OUT OF NEW YORK IN WAR PAINT. (Wednesday, August 5) ENGLAND DECLARES WAR ON GERMANY; BRITISH SHIP SUNK; FRENCH SHIPS DEFEAT GERMAN, BELGIUM ATTACKED; 17,000,000 MEN ENGAGED IN GREAT WAR OF EIGHT NATIONS; GREAT ENGLISH AND GERMAN ARMIES ABOUT TO GRAPPLE; RIVAL WARSHIPS OFF THIS PORT AS LUSITANIA SAILS. (Thursday, August 6) BELGIANS DEFEAT GERMANS, KILL OR WOUND 3,500 MEN; BRITISH THIRD FLOTILLA HAS A BATTLE IN THE NORTH SEA; RUSSIANS DRIVE OUT THE GERMANS AND ENTER PRUSSIA; GERMANY SAID TO HAVE SENT AN ULTIMATUM TO ITALY. (Friday, August 7) GERMAN FLEET SWEPT DOWN NORTH SEA TO DUTCH COAST IN GREAT GENERAL ENGAGEMENT, WON BY THE ENGLISH; BRITISH CRUISER AMPHION IS SUNK BY A MINE, 131 LOST; GERMANS TAKE 2 FORTS AT LIEGE; FRENCH ARMY COMING.

" And all in four years, Baron. Not such a bad show for the hard-drinking, hard-riding country squire. But the gem of my collection is coming and there is the setting all ready for it." He pointed to a space over which " Naval Signals " was printed.

" But you have a good dossier there already."

" Out of date and waste paper. The Admiralty in some way got the alarm and every code has been changed. It was a blow, Baron—the worst set-back in my whole campaign. But thanks to my cheque-book and the good Altamont all will be well to-night."

The Baron looked at his watch, and gave a guttural exclamation of disappointment.

" Well, I really can wait no longer. You can imagine
that things are moving at present in Carlton Terrace and 6
that we have all to be at our posts. I had hoped to be able
to bring news of your great coup. Did Altamont name
no hour ? "

Von Bork pushed over a telegram.

" Will come without fail to-night and bring new sparking plugs.—ALTAMONT."

" Sparking plugs, eh ? "

" You see he poses as a motor expert and I keep a full garage. In our code everything likely to come up is named after some spare part. If he talks of a radiator it is a battleship, of an oil-pump a cruiser, and so on. Sparking plugs are naval signals."

" From Portsmouth at midday," said the secretary, examining the superscription. " By the way, what do you give him ? "

" Five hundred pounds for this particular job. Of course he has a salary as well."

" The greedy rogue. They are useful, these traitors, but I grudge them their blood-money."

" I grudge Altamont nothing. He is a wonderful worker. If I pay him well, at least he delivers the goods, to use his own phrase. Besides he is not a traitor. I assure you that our most pan-Germanic Junker is a sucking dove in his feelings towards England as compared with a real bitter Irish-American."

" Oh, an Irish-American ? "

" If you heard him talk you would not doubt it. Sometimes I assure you I can hardly understand him. He seems to have declared war on the King's English as well as on the English King. Must you really go ? He may be here any moment."

" No. I'm sorry, but I have already overstayed my
time. We shall expect you early to-morrow, and when
you get that signal-book through the little door on the
Duke of York's steps you can put a triumphant Finis to 7
your record in England. What ! Tokay ! " He indicated a heavily sealed dust-covered bottle which stood with two high glasses upon a salver.

" May I offer you a glass before your journey ? "

" No, thanks. But it looks like revelry."

" Altamont has a nice taste in wines, and he took a fancy to my Tokay. He is a touchy fellow, and needs

6 *Carlton Terrace.* Then the site of the German Embassy and Consulate, located in the house adjoining, on the west, the Duke of York's steps.

7 *the Duke of York's steps.* The steps made of granite, quarried in the Island of Herm, near Guernsey, which form the base of the Duke of York's Column. This column was erected by public subscription to the memory of Frederick, Duke of York, second son of George III, at a cost of £25,000. The column is 124 feet high and is surmounted by a bronze statue fourteen feet high. It contains a gallery which at one time was open to the public during the summer months.

humouring in small things. I have to study him, I assure you." They had strolled out on to the terrace again, and along it to the further end where at a touch from the Baron's chauffeur the great car shivered and chuckled. "Those
8 are the lights of Harwich, I suppose," said the secretary, pulling on his dust coat. "How still and peaceful it all seems. There may be other lights within the week, and the English coast a less tranquil place! The heavens, too,
9 may not be quite so peaceful if all that the good Zeppelin promises us comes true. By the way, who is that?"

Only one window showed a light behind them; in it there stood a lamp, and beside it, seated at a table, was a dear old ruddy-faced woman in a country cap. She was bending over her knitting and stopping occasionally to stroke a large black cat upon a stool beside her.

"That is Martha, the only servant I have left."

The secretary chuckled.

"She might almost personify Britannia," said he, "with her complete self-absorption and general air of comfortable somnolence. Well, au revoir, Von Bork!"—with a final wave of his hand he sprang into the car, and a moment later the two golden cones from the headlights shot forward through the darkness. The secretary lay back in the cushions of the luxurious limousine, with his thoughts so full of the impending European tragedy that he hardly observed that as his car swung round the village street it nearly passed over a little Ford coming in the opposite direction.

Von Bork walked slowly back to the study when the last gleams of the motor lamps had faded into the distance. As he passed he observed that his old housekeeper had put out her lamp and retired. It was a new experience to him, the silence and darkness of his widespread house, for his family and household had been a large one. It was a relief to him, however, to think that they were all in safety and that, but for that one old woman who had lingered in the kitchen, he had the whole place to himself. There was a good deal of tidying up to do inside his study and he set himself to do it, until his keen, handsome face was flushed with the heat of the burning papers. A leather valise stood beside his table, and into this he began to pack very neatly and systematically the precious contents of his safe. He had hardly got started with the work, however, when his quick ears caught the sound of a distant car. Instantly he gave an exclamation of satisfaction, strapped up the valise, shut the safe, locked it, and hurried out on to the terrace. He was just in time to see the lights of a small car come to a halt at the gate. A passenger sprang out and advanced swiftly towards him, while the chauffeur, a heavily built, elderly man, with a grey moustache, settled down, like one who resigns himself to a long vigil.

"Well?" asked Von Bork eagerly, running forward to meet his visitor.

For answer the man waved a small brown-paper parcel triumphantly above his head.

"You can give me the glad hand to-night, Mister," he cried. "I'm bringing home the bacon at last."

"The signals?"

"Same as I said in my cable. Every last one of them,

8 *Harwich*. A seaport in Essex, England.

9 *Zeppelin*. Ferdinand A. A. H., Count Von Zeppelin, 1838–1917, inventor and builder of the dirigible airship—essentially a controllable balloon—capable of long-range flights and used by the Germans in World War I for the bombing of Britain.

semaphore, lamp code, Marconi—a copy, mind you, not the original. That was too dangerous. But it's the real goods, and you can lay to that." He slapped the German upon the shoulder with a rough familiarity from which the other winced.

" Come in," he said. " I'm all alone in the house. I was only waiting for this. Of course a copy is better than the original. If an original were missing they would change the whole thing. You think it's all safe about the copy ? "

The Irish-American had entered the study and stretched his long limbs from the arm-chair. He was a tall, gaunt man of sixty, with clear-cut features and a small goatee beard which gave him a general resemblance to the caricatures of Uncle Sam. A half-smoked, sodden cigar hung from the corner of his mouth, and as he sat down he struck a match and relit it. " Making ready for a move ? " he remarked as he looked round him. " Say, Mister," he added, as his eyes fell upon the safe from which the curtain was now removed, " you don't tell me you keep your papers in that ? "

" Why not ? "

" Gosh, in a wide-open contraption like that ! And they reckon you to be some spy. Why a Yankee crook would be into that with a can-opener. If I'd known that any letter of mine was goin' to lie loose in a thing like that I'd have been a mug to write to you at all."

" It would puzzle any crook to force that safe," Von Bork answered. " You won't cut that metal with any tool."

" But the lock ? "

" No, it's a double combination lock. You know what that is ? "

" Search me," said the American.

" Well, you need a word as well as a set of figures before you can get the lock to work." He rose and showed a double-radiating disc round the keyhole. " This outer one is for the letters, the inner one for the figures."

" Well, well, that's fine."

" So it's not quite as simple as you thought. It was four years ago that I had it made, and what do you think I chose for the word and figures ? "

" It's beyond me."

" Well, I chose August for the word, and 1914 for the figures, and here we are."

The American's face showed his surprise and admiration.

" My, but that was smart ! You had it down to a fine thing."

" Yes, a few of us even then could have guessed the date. Here it is, and I'm shutting down to-morrow morning."

" Well, I guess you'll have to fix me up also. I'm not staying in this goldarned country all on my lonesome. In a week or less from what I see, John Bull will be on his hind legs and fair ramping. I'd rather watch him from over the water."

" But you're an American citizen ? "

" Well, so was Jack James an American citizen, but he's

HE WAS A TALL, GAUNT MAN OF SIXTY, WITH CLEAR-CUT FEATURES AND A SMALL GOATEE BEARD . . .

Cover illustration by Frederic Dorr Steele for *Collier's Magazine*, September 22, 1917.

10 doing time in Portland all the same. It cuts no ice with a British copper to tell him you're an American citizen. ' It's British law and order over here,' says he. By the way, Mister, talking of Jack James, it seems to me you don't do much to cover your men."

" What do you mean ? " Von Bork asked sharply.

" Well, you are their employer, ain't you ? It's up to you to see that they don't fall down. But they do fall down, and when did you ever pick them up ? There's James——"

" It was James' own fault. You know that yourself. He was too self-willed for the job."

" James was a bonehead—I give you that. Then there was Hollis."

" The man was mad."

" Well, he went a bit woozy towards the end. It's enough to make a man bughouse when he has to play a part from morning to night with a hundred guys all ready to set the coppers wise to him. But now there is Steiner ——"

Von Bork started violently, and his ruddy face turned a shade paler.

" What about Steiner ? "

" Well, they've got him, that's all. They raided his store last night, and he and his papers are all in Portsmouth gaol. You'll go off and he, poor devil, will have to stand the racket, and lucky if he gets off with his life. That's why I want to get over the water as soon as you do."

Von Bork was a strong, self-contained man, but it was easy to see that the news had shaken him.

" How could they have got on to Steiner ? " he muttered. " That's the worst blow yet."

" Well, you nearly had a worse one, for I believe they are not far off me."

" You don't mean that ! "

" Sure thing. My landlady down Fratton way had some inquiries, and when I heard of it I guessed it was time for me to hustle. But what I want to know, Mister, is how the coppers know these things ? Steiner is the fifth man you've lost since I signed on with you, and I know the name of the sixth if I don't get a move on. How do you explain it, and ain't you ashamed to see your men go down like this ? "

Von Bork flushed crimson.

" How dare you speak in such a way ! "

" If I didn't dare things, Mister, I wouldn't be in your service. But I'll tell you straight what is in my mind. I've heard that with you German politicians when an agent has done his work you are not sorry to see him put away."

Von Bork sprang to his feet.

" Do you dare to suggest that I have given away my own agents ! "

" I don't stand for that, Mister, but there's a stool pigeon or a cross somewhere, and it's up to you to find out where it is. Anyhow I am taking no more chances. It's me for little Holland, and the sooner the better."

Von Bork had mastered his anger.

" We have been allies too long to quarrel now at the very hour of victory," he said. " You've done splendid work and taken risks and I can't forget it. By all means go to

10 *Portland.* In the stone quarries of the Isle of Portland, in Dorsetshire.

"IF I DIDN'T DARE THINGS, MISTER, I WOULDN'T BE IN YOUR SERVICE."

Illustration by Frederic Dorr Steele for *Collier's Magazine*, September 22, 1917.

Holland, and you can get a boat from Rotterdam to New York. No other line will be safe a week from now. I'll take that book and pack it with the rest."

The American held the small parcel in his hand, but made no motion to give it up.

"What about the dough?" he asked.

"The what?"

"The boodle. The reward. The £500. The gunner turned damned nasty at the last, and I had to square him with an extra hundred dollars or it would have been nitsky for you and me. 'Nothin' doin'!' says he, and he meant it too, but the last hundred did it. It's cost me two hundred pound from first to last, so it isn't likely I'd give it up without gettin' my wad."

Von Bork smiled with some bitterness. "You don't seem to have a very high opinion of my honour," said he, "you want the money before you give up the book."

"Well, Mister, it is a business proposition."

"All right. Have your way." He sat down at the table and scribbled a cheque, which he tore from the book, but he refrained from handing it to his companion. "After all, since we are to be on such terms, Mr. Altamont," said he, "I don't see why I should trust you any more than you trust me. Do you understand?" he added, looking back over his shoulder at the American. "There's the cheque upon the table. I claim the right to examine that parcel before you pick the money up."

The American passed it over without a word. Von Bork undid a winding of string and two wrappers of paper. Then he sat gazing for a moment in silent amazement at a small blue book which lay before him. Across the cover was printed in golden letters *Practical Handbook of Bee Culture.* Only for one instant did the master spy glare at this strangely irrelevant inscription. The next he was gripped at the back of his neck by a grasp of iron, and a chloroformed sponge was held in front of his writhing face.

"Another glass, Watson!" said Mr. Sherlock Holmes, **11**
as he extended the bottle of Imperial Tokay.

The thick-set chauffeur, who had seated himself by the table, pushed forward his glass with some eagerness.

"It is a good wine, Holmes."

"A remarkable wine, Watson. Our friend upon the sofa has assured me that it is from Franz Joseph's special cellar at the Schoenbrunn Palace. Might I trouble you to open the window, for chloroform vapour does not help the palate."

The safe was ajar, and Holmes standing in front of it was removing dossier after dossier, swiftly examining each, and then packing it neatly in Von Bork's valise. The German lay upon the sofa sleeping stertorously with a strap round his upper arms and another round his legs.

"We need not hurry ourselves, Watson. We are safe from interruption. Would you mind touching the bell. There is no one in the house except old Martha, who has played her part to admiration. I got her the situation here when first I took the matter up. Ah, Martha, you will be glad to hear that all is well."

The pleasant old lady had appeared in the doorway. She curtseyed with a smile to Mr. Holmes, but glanced

11 *"Another glass, Watson!"* ". . . it might be thought," the late Edgar W. Smith wrote in "On the Forms of Address," that "as the years wore on and the laxities of the approaching Edwardian age impinged upon the inhibiting Victorian strictures, [Holmes and Watson might address each other as] 'John' and 'Sherlock.' . . . But no—in 1914, when they had shared each others' lives for a full thirty-five years, we find them still ingrained in their old habit."

Elsewhere (in "Dr. Watson and the Great Censorship") Mr. Smith wrote: "It is interesting to speculate . . . that even as Watson was sitting . . . in Von Bork's parlor on that fateful August 2nd, with the war-clouds looming heavy in the east, he may have had in his breast-pocket at that very moment, ready for mailing, the manuscript of *The Valley of Fear*—for that long novel out of the past began to run in the *Strand* just a month later."

And Mr. Anthony Boucher, in his introduction to *The Final Adventures of Sherlock Holmes, Vol. I (The Valley of Fear)* has written: "In the very year in which *The Valley of Fear* was published [1914], Holmes was completing a case in which he precisely adopted the methods of Birdy Edwards. In order to learn the secrets of a nefarious organization, he changed his name, cut himself loose from all ties, . . . seemed one of the most dangerous and active men in the organization, while slyly seeing to it that all its plans went awry, and finally upset the whole apple-cart immediately after discussing with the top man the terrible possibility that 'there's a stool-pigeon or a cross somewhere.'"

. . . HE WAS GRIPPED AT THE BACK OF HIS NECK BY A GRASP OF IRON . . .

Illustration by A. Gilbert for the *Strand Magazine*, September, 1917.

with some apprehension at the figure upon the sofa.

" It is all right, Martha. He has not been hurt at all."

" I am glad of that, Mr. Holmes. According to his lights he has been a kind master. He wanted me to go with his wife to Germany yesterday, but that would hardly have suited your plans, would it, sir ? "

" No, indeed, Martha. So long as you were here I was easy in my mind. We waited some time for your signal to-night."

" It was the secretary, sir."

12 " I know. His car passed ours."

" I thought he would never go. I knew that it would not suit your plans, sir, to find him here."

" No, indeed. Well, it only meant that we waited half an hour or so until I saw your lamp go out and knew that the coast was clear. You can report to me to-morrow in London, Martha, at Claridge's Hotel."

" Very good, sir."

" I suppose you have everything ready to leave."

" Yes, sir. He posted seven letters to-day. I have the addresses as usual."

" Very good, Martha. I will look into them to-morrow. Good night. These papers," he continued, as the old lady vanished, " are not of very great importance, for, of course, the information which they represent has been sent off long ago to the German Government. These are the originals which could not safely be got out of the country."

" Then they are of no use."

" I should not go so far as to say that, Watson. They will at least show our people what is known and what is not. I may say that a good many of these papers have come through me, and I need not add are thoroughly untrustworthy. It would brighten my declining years to
13 see a German cruiser navigating the Solent according to the minefield plans which I have furnished. But you, Watson," he stopped his work and took his old friend by the shoulders ; " I've hardly seen you in the light yet. How have the years used you ? You look the same blithe
14 boy as ever."

" I feel twenty years younger, Holmes. I have seldom felt so happy as when I got your wire asking me to meet you at Harwich with the car. But you, Holmes—you have changed very little—save for that horrible goatee."

" These are the sacrifices one makes for one's country, Watson," said Holmes, pulling at his little tuft. " To-morrow it will be but a dreadful memory. With my hair cut and a few other superficial changes I shall no doubt reappear at Claridge's to-morrow as I was before this American stunt—I beg your pardon, Watson, my well of English seems to be permanently defiled—before this American job came my way."

" But you had retired, Holmes. We heard of you as living the life of a hermit among your bees and your books in a small farm upon the South Downs."

" Exactly, Watson. Here is the fruit of my leisured ease, the *magnum opus* of my latter years ! " He picked up the volume from the table and read out the whole title, *Practical Handbook of Bee Culture, with some Observations upon the Segregation of the Queen.* Alone I did it. Behold the fruit of pensive nights and laborious days, when I

12 *His car passed ours.*" In the *Strand Magazine* version of "His Last Bow," Holmes says here: "I know. His car passed ours. But for your excellent driving, Watson, we should have been the very type of Europe under the Prussian Juggernaut."

13 *the Solent.* A strait, varying from two to five miles wide, between the Isle of Wight and Hampshire.

14 *You look the same blithe boy as ever.*" "A remarkable tribute," Mr. S. C. Roberts wrote in *Doctor Watson,* "to an old campaigner of sixty-two."

watched the little working gangs as once I watched the criminal world of London."

" But how did you get to work again ? "

" Ah, I have often marvelled at it myself. The Foreign Minister alone I could have withstood, but when the Premier also deigned to visit my humble roof——! The **15**
fact is, Watson, that this gentleman upon the sofa was a bit too good for our people. He was in a class by himself. Things were going wrong, and no one could understand why they were going wrong. Agents were suspected or even caught, but there was evidence of some strong and secret central force. It was absolutely necessary to expose it. Strong pressure was brought upon me to look into the matter. It has cost me two years, Watson, but they have not been devoid of excitement. When I say that I started my pilgrimage at Chicago, graduated in an Irish secret society at Buffalo, gave serious trouble to the constabulary at Skibbareen and so eventually caught the eye of a subordinate agent of Von Bork, who recommended me as a **16**
likely man, you will realize that the matter was complex. Since then I have been honoured by his confidence, which has not prevented most of his plans going subtly wrong and five of his best agents being in prison. I watched them, Watson, and I picked them as they ripened. Well, sir, I hope that you are none the worse ! "

The last remark was addressed to Von Bork himself, who after much gasping and blinking had lain quietly listening to Holmes' statement. He broke out now into a furious stream of German invective, his face convulsed with passion. Holmes continued his swift investigation of documents while his prisoner cursed and swore.

" Though unmusical, German is the most expressive of all languages," he observed, when Von Bork had stopped from pure exhaustion. " Hullo ! Hullo ! " he added, as he looked hard at the corner of a tracing before putting it in the box. " This should put another bird in the cage. I had no idea that the paymaster was such a rascal, though I have long had an eye upon him. Mister Von Bork, you have a great deal to answer for."

The prisoner had raised himself with some difficulty upon the sofa and was staring with a strange mixture of amazement and hatred at his captor.

" I shall get level with you, Altamont," he said, speaking with slow deliberation, " if it takes me all my life I shall get level with you ! "

" The old sweet song," said Holmes. " How often have I heard it in days gone by. It was a favourite ditty of the late lamented Professor Moriarty. Colonel Sebastian Moran has also been known to warble it. And yet I live and keep bees upon the South Downs."

" Curse you, you double traitor ! " cried the German, straining against his bonds and glaring murder from his furious eyes.

" No, no, it is not so bad as that," said Holmes, smiling. " As my speech surely shows you, Mr. Altamont of Chicago had no existence in fact. I used him and he is gone."

" Then who are you ? "

" It is really immaterial who I am, but since the matter seems to interest you, Mr. Von Bork, I may say that this is not my first acquaintance with the members of your

15 *the Premier also deigned to visit my humble roof——!* Holmes allowed Prime Minister Herbert Henry Asquith, Earl of Oxford and Asquith, 1852–1928, Prime Minister of England, 1908–1916, to persuade him to forsake his bees, though he might have withstood Sir Edward Grey, Viscount Grey of Fallodon, 1862–1933, Foreign Minister, 1905–1916.

16 *and so eventually caught the eye of a subordinate agent of Von Bork.* Mr. Donald Hayne has written: ". . . obviously [Holmes] would need some time to prepare himself for the pilgrimage properly so-called, in some quiet place where, with some plausible excuse for staying there, he could unobtrusively acquire an American accent and an American wardrobe while waiting for the propitious moment to appear among the crooks of Chicago. The Foreign Office would of course arrange for his secret debarkation at a Canadian port, to avoid the American ships news reporters, and in 1912, I imagine, he could easily have been spirited into New York State. The investigator of Chaldean roots in the ancient Cornish dialect was certainly philologist enough to know that the standard American accent is derived from the New England hill accent which passes across central New York to the Middle West. Sigerson, the explorer, would find both interest and ostensible purpose in studying the ancient and significant geological formations in the Helderberg Mountains near Albany. Mr. Holmes would want to be near a city the size

"CURSE YOU, YOU DOUBLE TRAITOR!" CRIED THE GERMAN . . .

Illustration by A. Gilbert for the *Strand Magazine*, September, 1917. Frederic Dorr Steele illustrated the same scene for *Collier's Magazine*, September 22, 1917.

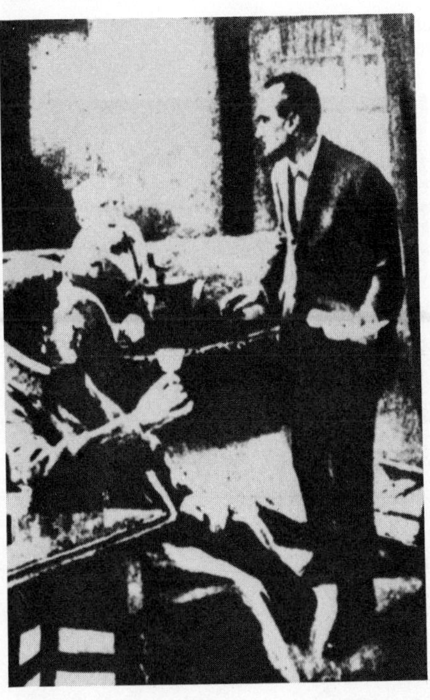

of Albany, to shop for his wardrobe, etc., but would prefer actually residing in a much smaller place, where he could, for his linguistic and sociological purposes, mingle more familiarly with all types and strata of people. A middle class summer resort (he came, presumably, in July, 1912) where strangers were coming and going every week, would be ideal. All this adds up—elementarily—to the town of *Altamont*, New York; and was it not a gracious gesture on the Master's part, and a sign that he enjoyed that summer's peace before starting on his arduous pilgrimage in the service of the Empire, that he took as his own the name of the village and bore it for two years . . . ?"

On the other hand, Mr. Willis B. Wood has suggested (in "Sherlock in Kansas") that Holmes took his alias in memory of a station on the Frisco Railroad between Joplin, Missouri, and Wichita, Kansas. He reminds us that Mr. Christopher Morley suggested 1876 as a year when Holmes journeyed to America, and he further suggests that Holmes ventured into the American West at that time.

It is also worth noting—as did Mrs. Crighton Sellars (in verse) in "Altamont," that both Thackeray and Scott chose "Altamont" as the name for their villains (Thackeray in *Pendennis*, Scott in *The Pirate*)—"so the idea appealed to our Sherlock at once."

To these fascinating speculations should be added the fact that the full name of Conan Doyle's father was Charles *Altamont* Doyle.

17 *still bound hand and foot.* "Gentlemen," Mr. John V. L. Hogan has asked, "if you will explain to me how a man 'bound hand and foot' can be 'walked' anywhere, I shall be duly grateful."

FINALLY, HOLDING EITHER ARM, THE TWO FRIENDS WALKED HIM VERY SLOWLY DOWN THE GARDEN WALK . . .

Illustration by A. Gilbert for the *Strand Magazine*, September, 1917.

family. I have done a good deal of business in Germany in the past, and my name is probably familiar to you."

" I would wish to know it," said the Prussian grimly.

" It was I who brought about the separation between Irene Adler and the late King of Bohemia when your cousin Heinrich was the Imperial Envoy. It was I also who saved from murder, by the Nihilist Klopman, Count Von und Zu Grafenstein, who was your mother's elder brother. It was I——"

Von Bork sat up in amazement.

" There is only one man," he cried.

" Exactly," said Holmes.

Von Bork groaned and sank back on the sofa. " And most of that information came through you," he cried. " What is it worth ? What have I done ? It is my ruin for ever ! "

" It is certainly a little untrustworthy," said Holmes. " It will require some checking, and you have little time to check it. Your admiral may find the new guns rather larger than he expects, and the cruisers perhaps a trifle faster."

Von Bork clutched at his own throat in despair.

" There are a good many other points of detail which will, no doubt, come to light in good time. But you have one quality which is very rare in a German, Mr. Von Bork, you are a sportsman and you will bear me no ill-will when you realize that you, who have outwitted so many other people, have at last been outwitted yourself. After all, you have done your best for your country, and I have done my best for mine, and what could be more natural ? Besides," he added, not unkindly, as he laid his hand upon the shoulder of the prostrate man, " it is better than to fall before some more ignoble foe. These papers are now ready, Watson. If you will help me with our prisoner, I think that we may get started for London at once."

It was no easy task to move Von Bork, for he was a strong and a desperate man. Finally, holding either arm, the two friends walked him very slowly down the garden walk which he had trod with such proud confidence when he received the congratulations of the famous diplomatist only a few hours before. After a short, final struggle he
17 was hoisted, still bound hand and foot, into the spare seat of the little car. His precious valise was wedged in beside him.

" I trust that you are as comfortable as circumstances permit," said Holmes, when the final arrangements were made. " Should I be guilty of a liberty if I lit a cigar and placed it between your lips ? "

But all amenities were wasted upon the angry German.

" I suppose you realize, Mr. Sherlock Holmes," said he, " that if your Government bears you out in this treatment it becomes an act of war."

" What about your Government and all this treatment ? " said Holmes, tapping the valise.

" You are a private individual. You have no warrant for my arrest. The whole proceeding is absolutely illegal and outrageous."

" Absolutely," said Holmes.

" Kidnapping a German subject."

" And stealing his private papers."

" Well, you realize your position, you and your accomplice here. If I were to shout for help as we pass through the village——"

" My dear sir, if you did anything so foolish you would probably enlarge the too limited titles of our village inns by giving us ' The Dangling Prussian ' as a sign-post. The Englishman is a patient creature, but at present his temper is a little inflamed and it would be as well not to try him too far. No, Mr. Von Bork, you will go with us in a quiet, sensible fashion to Scotland Yard, whence you can send for your friend Baron Von Herling and see if even now you may not fill that place which he has reserved
for you in the ambassadorial suite. As to you, Watson, **18**
you are joining us with your old service, as I understand, **19**
so London won't be out of your way. Stand with me here upon the terrace, for it may be the last quiet talk that we shall ever have."

The two friends chatted in intimate converse for a few minutes, recalling once again the days of the past whilst their prisoner vainly wriggled to undo the bonds that held him. As they turned to the car, Holmes pointed back to the moonlit sea, and shook a thoughtful head.

" There's an east wind coming, Watson."

" I think not, Holmes. It is very warm."

" Good old Watson ! You are the one fixed point in a changing age. There's an east wind coming all the same, such a wind as never blew on England yet. It will be cold and bitter, Watson, and a good many of us may wither before its blast. But it's God's own wind none the less, and a cleaner, better, stronger land will lie in the sunshine when the storm has cleared. Start her up, Watson, for it's time that we were on our way. I have a cheque for five hundred pounds which should be cashed early, for the drawer is quite capable of stopping it, if he can."

18 *that place which he has reserved for you in the ambassadorial suite.* "Can any suggestion by Holmes be less likely?" Mr. Ronald S. Bonn wrote in "The Problem of the Postulated Doctor." "Von Herline would never be permitted to see Von Bork at ten leagues' distance with [the information Von Bork had gathered] in the balance. No wonder Watson chose to recount this operation in the third person, relying, no doubt, on the detective's arthritic isolation on the South Downs to keep it from him. There is only one possible reason for the ridiculous hint that Von Bork was permitted to go home in the ambassadorial train. For the secret *did* get back to Germany, and it was desperately necessary that the actual betrayer suggest a fictional channel. Perhaps no German cruiser navigated the Solent, but in the very week of Von Bork's arrest, the Grand Fleet was forced to open fire on a submarine *inside the defences of Scapa Flow.* And there is certainly no evidence that, at Jutland, Tirpitz was under any delusions about the calibre of Jellicoe's guns."

19 *you are joining us with your old service, as I understand.* "What further part Watson took in the war remains unknown," Mr. S. C. Roberts wrote in *Doctor Watson.* "It is doubtful whether he was permitted, at [his] age, to proceed on foreign service, but we may be confident that in some capacity, possibly on the staff of a military hospital, he was at the post of duty."

There is, however, at least an indication that Watson was on *active* duty in a charming anecdote related by Mr. Vincent Starrett: during World War I, an English medical officer named *Dr. John Watson,* captured by the enemy at the battle of Mons, was helped to escape by a bespectacled, bewhiskered officer of the German general staff. In a discreet moment, the German whispered to the Englishman: "Steady, Watson, steady, and don't start! Comfortable, thank you, but I miss my shag. Meet you ten days from now in the Baker Street digs."

Bibliographical Note: The manuscript of "His Last Bow" is owned by Mr. Adrian M. Conan Doyle.

Appendix I

L'ENVOI

"... they still live for all that love them well ..."
—Vincent Starrett, *The Private Life of Sherlock Holmes*

"One likes to think"—Sir Arthur Conan Doyle wrote in his Preface to the final volume of Sherlock Holmes short stories, *The Case-Book of Sherlock Holmes*—"that there is some fantastic limbo for the children of imagination, some strange, impossible place where the beaux of Fielding may still make love to the belles of Richardson, where Scott's heroes may still strut, Dickens's delightful Cockneys still raise a laugh, and Thackeray's worldlings continue to carry on their reprehensible careers. Perhaps in some humble corner of such a Valhalla, Sherlock and his Watson may for a time find a place, while some more astute sleuth with some even less astute comrade may fill the stage which they have vacated."

And so at last we come to say farewell to an immortal three—to the Detective and the Doctor and the man who created them both.

And yet—as Vincent Starrett has so truly put into words the thoughts that many of us feel:

> . . . they still live for all that love them well: in a romantic chamber of the heart: in a nostalgic country of the mind: where it is always 1895.

Ave atque vale, Sherlock!
Ave atque vale, John!
Ave atque vale, Sir Arthur!

Appendix II

"I HAVE SOME FEW REFERENCES TO MAKE"

—Sherlock Holmes, *The Sign of the Four*

For the sake of uniformity, we have adopted one set of standards for style and punctuation (although we have not Americanized British spellings); the quoted material otherwise appears here exactly as the numerous authors wrote it. For the benefit of the younger student, we have taken the liberty of translating the French, Latin, and German words and phrases with which Holmes so liberally sprinkled his conversation. For the benefit of the American student who knows not his England, we have been generous with notes on the counties, cities, towns, and villages referred to in the Canon—as we have also with notes on the streets and landmarks of Victorian London. Here our principle source has been the works of Augustus J. C. Hare, whose *Walks in London* was published in two volumes by George Routledge and Sons. No date of publication appears in our copy, but the preface to Volume I indicates that Hare's essays began to appear in British periodicals some ten years before John H. Watson, M.D., published his early reminiscences as *A Study in Scarlet.* The antiquarian Hare was therefore a contemporary of the master detective and the good doctor, and we can see through his eyes the bustling, fog-enshrouded city in which Holmes and Watson walked, talked, and adventured. In a few instances, we have given full information about our sources in the text of the notes and picture captions; for the most part, however, we have reserved this information for this list of "References," alphabetically arranged by author (collections of essays by various authors are also listed by title). A book of this kind manifestly relies heavily on the writings of others; while the editor has made every effort to give credit where credit is due, he begs the forgiveness of any commentator he may have overlooked, however inadvertently.

The editor deeply regrets that while the first volume of THE ANNOTATED SHERLOCK HOLMES was still on the press, two distinguished Sherlockians broke from the ranks. The text should properly read, now, "the late Sir Sydney Roberts" and "the late Robert Keith Leavitt."

INDEX OF TITLES

Alphabetical Listing of Novels and Short Stories in Volumes I and II

The novels are indicated by an asterisk; the rest are short stories.

SOME OF "THE WRITINGS ABOUT THE WRITINGS"

A. E. P.

"The End of Sherlock Holmes"; *The Manchester Guardian,* July 7, 1927; *The Living Age,* August 15, 1927; *The Misadventures of Sherlock Holmes,* pp. 256–60.

Adams, Robert Winthrop

"John H. Watson, M.D., Characterologist"; *The Baker Street Journal,* Vol. IV, No. 2, New Series, April, 1954, pp. 81–92.

Adams, *The Reverend* Stephen

"Holmes: A Student of London?"; *The Sherlock Holmes Journal,* Vol. II, No. 4, Winter, 1955, pp. 17–8.

Akers, Arthur K.

"Who Was Mrs. Watson's First Husband?"; *The Baker Street Journal,* Vol. X, No. 1, New Series, January, 1960, pp. 45–6.

Allen, F. A., *M.P.S.*

"Devilish Drugs," Part One; *May and Baker Pharmaceutical Bulletin,* December, 1956; *The Sherlock Holmes Journal,* Vol. III, No. 3, Autumn, 1957, pp. 12–4.

Altick, Richard D.

"Mr. Sherlock Holmes and Dr. Samuel Johnson"; *221B,* pp. 109–28.

Anderson, Karen

"On the Difference Between a 'Cup' and a 'Plate' "; *The Baker Street Journal,* Vol. XII, No. 3, New Series, September, 1962, p. 176.

(with Poul Anderson) "The Peculiar Behavior of the Ritual in the Daytime"; *The Baker Street Journal Christmas Annual,* 1960, pp. 304–11.

Anderson, Poul

"Art in the Blood"; *The Baker Street Journal,* Vol. VI, No. 3, New Series, July, 1956, pp. 133–7.

(with Karen Anderson) "The Peculiar Behavior of the Ritual in the Daytime"; *The Baker Street Journal Christmas Annual,* 1960, pp. 304–11.

"A Treatise on the Binomial Theorem"; *The Baker Street Journal,* Vol. V, No. 1, New Series, January, 1955, pp. 13–8.

Andrew, Clifton R.

"A Difficulty in *A Study in Scarlet*"; *The Baker Street Journal,* Vol. III, No. 1, Old Series, January, 1948, pp. 13–4.

"Don't Sell Holmes' Memory Short"; *The Baker Street Journal,* Vol. IV, No. 4, New Series, October, 1954, pp. 219–22.

"Memorials to Sherlock Holmes"; *The Baker Street Journal,* Vol. VII, No. 4, New Series, October, 1957, pp. 240–2.

"My Old Friend Charlie Peace"; *The Sherlock Holmes Journal,* Vol. IV, No. 4, Spring, 1960, pp. 118–9.

"On the Dating of *The Sign of the Four*"; *The Baker Street Journal,* Vol. I, No. 2, New Series, April, 1951, pp. 66–9.

"A Rejoinder to Professor Hill"; *The Baker Street Journal,* Vol. V, No. 3, New Series, July, 1955, pp. 154–6.

"Sherlock Holmes on the Turf"; *A Baker Street Four-Wheeler,* pp. 38–42.

"That Scotland Yarder, Gregson—What a Help (?) He Was"; *Client's Second Case-Book,* pp. 35–9.

"Was It July or September in *The Sign of the Four?*"; *Client's Third Case-Book,* pp. 141–9.

"What Happened to Watson's Married Life After June 14, 1889?"; *The Baker Street Journal Christmas Annual,* 1958, pp. 42–4.

"What Kind of Shenanigans Went On at St. Monica's?"; *The Baker Street Journal Christmas Annual,* 1956, pp. 42–5.

"Who Is Who, and When in 'The *Gloria Scott*' "; *Client's Case-Book,* pp. 30–2.

Arenfalk, Poul

"The Mormon Mystery and Other Mysteries in *A Study in Scarlet*"; *The Sherlock Holmes Journal,* Vol. IV, No. 4, Spring, 1960, pp. 128–32.

Armstrong, Walter P., Jr.

"The Truth About Sherlock Holmes"; *The Baker Street Journal,* Vol. I, No. 4, Old Series, October, 1946, pp. 391–401.

Asher, *Dr.* Richard

"Holmes and the Fair Sex"; *The Sherlock Holmes Journal,* Vol. II, No. 3, Summer, 1955, pp. 15–22.

Ashton, Ralph A.

"Colonel Moran's Infamous Air Rifle"; *The Baker Street Journal,* Vol. X, No. 3, July, 1960, pp. 155–9.

"Forget St. Monica's . . . What Happened at Briony Lodge?"; *The Baker Street Journal,* Vol. VIII, No. 3, New Series, July, 1958, pp. 163–8.

"The Fourth Occupant, or The Room with the Twisted Tongue"; *The Baker Street Journal,* Vol. XI, No. 1, New Series, March, 1961, pp. 38–40.

"The Secret Weapons of 221B Baker Street"; *The Baker Street Journal,* Vol. IX, No. 2, New Series, April, 1959, pp. 99–102.

Austin, J. Bliss

A Baker Street Christmas Stocking for 1955; Westfield, New Jersey: The Hydraulic Press.

A Baker Street Christmas Stocking for 1962; Westfield, New Jersey: The Hydraulic Press.

"Dartmoor Revisited, or Discoveries in Devonshire"; Pittsburgh: The Hydraulic Press, 1964.

"Furor Teutonicus"; *The Baker Street Journal,* Vol. V, No. 1, New Series, January, 1955, pp. 19–24.

"Shakespeare and Watson"; *The Sherlock Holmes Journal,* Vol. I, No. 4, December, 1953, p. 42.

"Three Footnotes to 'The Adventure of the Illustrious Client' "; *Client's Third Case-Book,* pp. 89–92.

"Thumbing His Way to Fame"; *The Baker Street Journal,* Vol. I, No. 4, Old Series, October, 1946, pp. 424–32.

"Two Bibliographical Footnotes"; *The Baker Street Journal,* Vol. IV, No. 1, New Series, January, 1954, pp. 41–3.

"What Son Was Watson?: A Case of Identity"; *A Baker Street Four-Wheeler,* pp. 43–53.

Bailey, L. W.

"The Dark Lady of Appledore Towers"; *The Sherlock Holmes Journal,* Vol. IV, No. 4, Spring, 1960, pp. 43–5.

A Baker Street Four-Wheeler, edited by Edgar W. Smith; Maplewood, New Jersey: The Pamphlet House, 1944.

Baker Street Studies, edited by H. W. Bell; London: Constable & Co., 1934; reissued in paperbound format by the Baker Street Irregulars, Inc., 1955.

Ball, John, Jr.

"The Case of the Elderly Actor"; *The Baker Street Journal,* Vol. IX, No. 4, New Series, pp. 209–22.

"Early Days in Baker Street"; *The Baker Street Journal,* Vol. V, No. 4, New Series, October, 1955, pp. 211–9.

"The Jezail Bullet"; *Leaves from the Copper Beeches,* pp. 121–6.

"Practical Art of Baritsu: The Japanese Wrestling System with Some Observations on Its Use by Mr. Sherlock Holmes"; *The Baker Street Journal,* Vol. XIV, No. 1, New Series, March, 1964, pp. 31–6.

"The Second Collaboration"; *The Baker Street Journal,* Vol. IV, No. 2, New Series, April, 1954, pp. 69–74.

"The Twenty-Three Deductions"; *The Baker Street Journal,* Vol. VIII, No. 4, New Series, October, 1958, pp. 234–7.

Ballou, Norman V.

"Top Secret"; *The Third Cab,* pp. 48–51.

Baring-Gould, *The Reverend* Sabine

A Book of Dartmoor; London: Methuen & Co., Ltd., 1900.

Baring-Gould, William S.

(Editor) *The Adventure of the Speckled Band and Other Stories of Sherlock Holmes,* by Sir Arthur Conan Doyle; New York: The New American Library, Inc., 1965.

The Chronological Holmes; New York: Privately printed, 1955.

"Dr. Watson Has Gone to Widecombe"; *The Baker Street Journal,* Vol. XV, No. 1, New Series, March, 1965, pp. 8–14.

" 'He Is the Napoleon of Crime, Watson' "; *Show,* March, 1965.

"The London of Holmes and Watson"; *The Baker Street Journal,* Vol. IX, No. 3, New Series, July, 1959, pp. 165–8.

"A New Chronology of Holmes and Watson"; Part I, *The Baker Street Journal,* Vol. III, No. 1, Old Series, January, 1948, pp. 107–25; Part II, *The Baker Street Journal,* Vol. III, No. 2, Old Series, April, 1948, pp. 238–51.

"The Problem of No. 221"; *The Baker Street Journal,* Vol. VIII, No. 2, New Series, April, 1958, pp. 69–77.

"Re: The Baker Street Irregulars"; *The American Book Collector,* May, 1959, pp. 20–1.

Sherlock Holmes of Baker Street: A Life of the World's First Consulting Detective; New York: Clarkson N. Potter, Inc., 1962; as *Sherlock Holmes: A Biography,* London: Rupert Hart-Davis, Ltd., 1962; as *Moi, Sherlock Holmes,* Paris: Editions Buchet/Chastel, 1965; as *Er, Sherlock Holmes,* Hamburg: Nannen, 1965.

"Sherlock Holmes, Sportsman"; *Sports Illustrated,* May 27, 1963.

" 'You Would Have Made an Actor and a Rare One' "; Program of the "musical adventure," *Baker Street,* 1965.

Barnes, W. J.

"Saxe-Coburg Square–A New Identification"; *The Sherlock Holmes Journal,* Vol. II, No. 3, Summer, 1955, pp. 31–4.

Barzun, *Professor* Jacques

"How Holmes Came to Play the Violin"; *The Baker Street Journal,* Vol. I, No. 3, New Series, July, 1951, pp. 108–12.

"Sherlock Holmes' Will—A Forgery"; *The Baker Street Journal,* Vol. VI, No. 2, New Series, April, 1956, pp. 75–9.

Baxter, *Professor* Frank Condie

Introduction to *The Hound of the Baskervilles;* Garden City, New York: Doubleday, Page & Company, 1926; reprinted in *The Baker Street Journal,* Vol. XII, No. 2, New Series, June, 1962, pp. 106–12.

Beckemeyer, Doyle W.

"The Irregular Holmes"; *The Baker Street Journal,* Vol. II, No. 1, New Series, January, 1952, pp. 18–20.

"Valuable Sherlockian Hunting-Ground"; *Client's Third Case-Book,* pp. 135–40.

Beierle, John D.

"The Curious Incident of the Drive Through Middlesex and Surrey"; *The Baker Street Journal,* Vol. VII, No. 4, New Series, October, 1957, pp. 216–9.

Bell, H. W.

"The Date of *The Sign of the Four*"; *Baker Street Studies,* pp. 203–19.

"Note on Dr. Watson's Wound"; *Baker Street Studies,* pp. 220–3.

Sherlock Holmes and Dr. Watson: The Chronology of Their Adventures; London: Constable & Co., Ltd., 1932; reissued in paperbound format by the Baker Street Irregulars, Inc., 1953.

"Three Identifications: Lauriston Gardens, Upper Swandam Lane, Saxe-Coburg Square"; *221B,* pp. 59–67.

"Three Identifications: Two Localities in 'The Six Napoleons,' The Drive to Thaddeus Sholto's House, Birlstone Manor"; *Profile by Gaslight,* pp. 283–9.

Bell, Joseph

"Mr. Sherlock Holmes"; *The Bookman,* London; *A Study in Scarlet,* London: Ward, Lock & Bowden, 1893; *The Baker Street Journal,* Vol. II, No. 1, Old Series, January, 1947, pp. 45–9.

Bell, Whitfield J., Jr.

"Holmes and History"; *The Baker Street Journal,* Vol. II, No. 4, Old Series, October, 1947, pp. 447–56.

Bengis, Nathan L.

"Conan Doyle and T. S. Eliot"; *The Times Literary Supplement,* London, September 25, 1951.

"The Graft I Refused to Take"; *The Baker Street Gasogene,* Vol. I, No. 1, 1961, pp. 5–9.

"A Scandal in Baker Street"; Part I, *The Baker Street Journal,* Vol. II, No. 2, Old Series, April, 1947, pp. 145–57; Part II, *The Baker Street Journal,* Vol. II, No. 3, Old Series, July, 1947, pp. 311–21.

"Sherlock Holmes' Will"; *The London Mystery Magazine,* June, 1955; reprinted in *The Baker Street Journal,* Vol. VI, No. 2, New Series, April, 1956, pp. 80–1.

"Sherlock Stays After School"; *Client's Second Case-Book,* pp. 72–8.

"Sherlock Stays After School: An Addendum"; *Client's Third Case-Book,* p. 15.

"Sidney Johnson—Suspect"; *The Sherlock Holmes Journal,* Vol. II, No. 3, Summer, 1955, p. 24.

The "Signs" of Our Times; New York: Privately printed, 1956.

"Smothered Mate"; *The Baker Street Journal,* Vol. X, No. 4, New Series, October, 1960, pp. 213–20.

"Take a Bow, Dr. Watson"; *The Baker Street Journal,* Vol. VIII, No. 4, New Series, October, 1958, pp. 218–29.

"What Was the Month?"; *The Baker Street Journal,* Vol. VII, No. 4, New Series, October, 1957, pp. 204-14.

"Where on Earth . . ."; *The Sherlock Holmes Journal,* Vol. II, No. 2, December, 1954, p. 43.

"Where There's a Will, There's a Pay"; *The Baker Street Journal,* Vol. VI, No. 4, New Series, October, 1956, pp. 226–32.

"Whose Was It? An Examination into the Crowning Lapse of Sherlockian Scholarship"; *The Baker Street Journal,* Vol. III, No. 2, New Series, April, 1953, pp. 69–76.

Berg, Emmanuel

"For It's Greatly to Their Credit"; *The Baker Street Journal,* Vol. IX, No. 2, New Series, April, 1959, pp. 90–8.

Berl, *Colonel* E. Ennalls

"Sherlock Holmes and the Telephone"; *The Baker Street Journal,* Vol. III, No. 4, New Series, October, 1953, pp. 197–210.

BERMAN, RUTH

"On Docketing a Hebrew Rabbi"; *The Baker Street Journal,* Vol. X, No. 2, New Series, April, 1960, pp. 80–2.

"On Holmium"; *The Baker Street Journal,* Vol. X, No. 4, New Series, October, 1960, p. 250.

The Best of the Pips; sponsored by Richard W. Clarke; New York: The Five Orange Pips of Westchester County, 1955.

BETT, WINGATE H.

"Watson's Second Marriage"; *The Sherlock Holmes Journal,* Vol. III, No. 1, Summer, 1956, pp. 21–2.

BIGELOW, *Magistrate* S. TUPPER

"Barred-Tail Geese"; *The Sherlock Holmes Journal,* Vol. VI, No. 4, Spring, 1964, pp. 108–9.

"The Blue Enigma"; *The Baker Street Journal,* Vol. XI, No. 4, New Series, December, 1961, pp. 203–14.

"Hallamshire Revisited"; *The Baker Street Journal,* Vol. XIII, No. 2, New Series, June, 1963, pp. 87–90.

"The Hoof-Marks in 'The Priory School'"; *The Baker Street Journal,* Vol. XII, No. 3, New Series, September, 1962, pp. 169–74.

"In Defense of Joseph Bell"; *The Baker Street Journal,* Vol. X, No. 4, New Series, October, 1960, pp. 207–12.

An Irregular Anglo-American Glossary of More or Less Unfamiliar Words, Terms and Phrases in the Sherlock Holmes Saga; Toronto: Castalotte & Zamba, 1959.

"Misprision of Felony and Sherlock Holmes"; *The Sherlock Holmes Journal,* Vol. V, No. 3, Winter, 1961, pp. 68–70.

"No Colour-Bull"; *The Sherlock Holmes Journal,* Vol. V, No. 2, Spring, 1961, p. 62.

"Sherlock Holmes and the Misprision of Felony"; *The Baker Street Journal,* Vol. VIII, No. 3, New Series, July, 1958, pp. 139–46.

"Sherlock Holmes Was No Burglar"; *The Baker Street Journal Christmas Annual,* 1958, pp. 26–37.

"The Singular Case of Fletcher Robinson"; *The Baker Street Gasogene,* Vol. I, No. 2, 1961, pp. 19–21.

"Those Five Volumes"; *The Baker Street Journal,* Vol. XI, No. 1, New Series, March, 1961, pp. 31–7.

"Two Canonical Problems Solved"; *The Baker Street Journal Christmas Annual,* 1959, pp. 261–71.

"Was It Attempted Murder?"; *The Baker Street Journal,* Vol. XIV, No. 2, New Series, June, 1964, pp. 99–107.

BLACKER, *Lieutenant Colonel* L. V. S.

"Dr. Watson's Wound(s)"; *The Sherlock Holmes Journal,* Vol. I, No. 1, May, 1952, pp. 31–2.

BLAKE, S. F.

"Sherlock Holmes and the Italian Cipher"; *The Baker Street Journal,* Vol. IX, No. 1, New Series, January, 1959, pp. 14–20.

"Sherlock Holmes' Dressing Gown(s)"; *The Baker Street Journal,* Vol. X, No. 2, New Series, April, 1960, pp. 86–9.

BLAKENEY, T. S.

"The Apocryphal Ancestry of Dr. Watson"; *The Baker Street Journal,* Vol. VII, No. 2, New Series, April, 1957, pp. 69–73.

"A Case for Identification—in Bohemia"; *The Sherlock Holmes Journal,* Vol. III, No. 2, Winter, 1956, pp. 15–6.

"The Location of 'The Three Students'"; *The Sherlock Holmes Journal,* Vol. IV, No. 1, Winter, 1958, p. 14; reprinted in *Leaves from the Copper Beeches,* pp. 9–10.

"More Disjecta Membra"; *The Sherlock Holmes Journal,* Vol. V, No. 2, Spring, 1961, pp. 55–6.

"On Watson's Pension"; *The Baker Street Journal,* Vol. VII, No. 4, New Series, October, 1957, pp. 249–50.

Sherlock Holmes: Fact or Fiction?; London: John Murray, 1932; reissued in paperbound format by the Baker Street Irregulars, Inc., 1954.

"Some Disjecta Membra"; *The Sherlock Holmes Journal,* Vol. IV, No. 3, Winter, 1959, pp. 101–3.

"Thoughts on *The Sign of the Four*"; *The Sherlock Holmes Journal,* Vol. III, No. 4, Summer, 1958, pp. 6–8.

BLANK, E. W.

"Holmes the Chemist"; *The Baker Street Journal,* Vol. III, No. 2, Old Series, April, 1948, pp. 226–7.

"Is Professor Moriarty Afoot?"; *The Baker Street Journal,* Vol. I, No. 2, Old Series, April, 1946, pp. 209–10.

BLAUSTEIN, ALBERT P.

"Sherlock Holmes As a Lawyer"; *The Baker Street Journal,* Vol. III, No. 3, Old Series, July, 1948, pp. 306–8.

BLEGEN, *Dean* THEODORE C.

"These Were Hidden Fires, Indeed!"; *Exploring Sherlock Holmes,* pp. 9–26.

BLOCH, ROBERT

"The Dynamics of an Asteriod"; *The Baker Street Journal,* Vol. III, No. 4, New Series, October, 1953, pp. 225–33.

BONN, RONALD S.

"The Problem of the Postulated Doctor; *The Baker Street Journal,* Vol. XIV, No. 1, New Series, March, 1964, pp. 14–21.

BOSWELL, ROLFE

"A Connecticut Yankee in Support of Sir Arthur"; *The Baker Street Journal,* Vol. II, No. 2, Old Series, April, 1947, pp. 119–27.

"Dr. Roylott's Wily Fillip"; *The Baker Street Journal,* Vol. I, No. 3, Old Series, July, 1946, pp. 307–11.

"'In Uffish Thought'"; *The Baker Street Journal,* Vol. I, No. 1, Old Series, January, 1946, pp. 21–4.

"On 'The Adventure of the Tired Captain'"; *The Baker Street Journal,* Vol. II, No. 2, Old Series, April, 1947, pp. 160–2.

"On the Aluminium Crutch (or Crotch)"; *The Baker Street Journal,* Vol. I, No. 2, Old Series, April, 1946, pp. 190–2.

"On the Remarkable Worm"; *The Baker Street Journal,* Vol. II, No. 2, Old Series, April, 1947, pp. 161–2.

"On the Trepoff Murder"; *The Baker Street Journal,* Vol. I, No. 1, New Series, *January,* 1951, p. 40.

"Quick, Watson, the Fiddle!"; *The Baker Street Journal,* Vol. III, No. 4, Old Series, October, 1948, pp. 435–40.

"A Rare Day in June"; *The Baker Street Journal,* Vol. VII, No. 1, New Series, January, 1957, pp. 13–7.

"Sarasate, Sherlock and Shaw"; *The Baker Street Journal,* Vol. II, No. 1, New Series, January, 1952, pp. 13–7.

"Squaring 'The Red Circle'"; *The Baker Street Journal,* Vol. I, No. 3, New Series, July, 1951, pp. 113–4.

BOUCHER, ANTHONY

Introduction to *The Final Adventures of Sherlock Holmes, Vol. I (The Valley of Fear);* New York: The Limited Editions Club, 1932; reprinted in *Introducing Mr. Sherlock Holmes.*

"On a Certain Foreign Potentate"; *The Baker Street Journal,* Vol. II, No. 1, Old Series, January, 1947, pp. 60–1.

"On 'The Second Stains' As One Adventure"; *The Baker Street Journal,* Vol. II, No. 1, Old Series, January, 1947, pp. 60–1.

"Prolegomena to a Holmesian Discography"; *The Baker Street Journal,* Vol. I, No. 2, Old Series, April, 1946, pp. 229–31.

"The Records of Baker Street"; *The*

Baker Street Journal, Vol. IV, No. 1, Old Series, January, 1949, pp. 97–104.

"Was the Later Holmes an Imposter?"; *Profile by Gaslight,* pp. 60–70.

BOYD, *Dr.* ANDREW

"Dr. Watson's Dupe"; *Encounter,* Vol. XIV, No. 3, March, 1960; reprinted in *The Sherlock Holmes Journal,* Vol. V, No. 2, Spring, 1961, pp. 42–4.

BREND, GAVIN

"The Black Boy's Visit to Hurlstone"; *The Baker Street Journal,* Vol. III, No. 4, New Series, October, 1953, pp. 217–24.

"Charles Augustus Milverton: The Date"; *The Sherlock Holmes Journal,* Vol. VI, No. 3, Winter, 1963, pp. 74-6.

"The Five Orange Pips"; *The Sherlock Holmes Journal,* Vol. II, No. 3, Summer, 1955, p. 2.

"From the Horse's Mouth"; *The Sherlock Holmes Journal,* Vol. I, No. 4, December, 1953, pp. 39–40.

"From Maiwand to Marylebone"; *The Sherlock Holmes Journal,* Vol. I, No. 3, June, 1953, pp. 40–4.

"A Hint to the Next Chronologist"; *The Baker Street Journal,* Vol. VIII, No. 2, New Series, April, 1958, pp. 123–5.

"A Horse! A Horse!"; *The Sherlock Holmes Journal,* Vol. II, No. 2, December, 1954, p. 20.

"Jabez Muses"; *The Baker Street Journal,* Vol. III, No. 3, New Series, July, 1953, p. 169.

"The Man from the Yard"; *The Sherlock Holmes Journal,* Vol. I, No. 1, May, 1952, p. 14.

My Dear Holmes; London: George Allen & Unwin, Ltd., 1951.

"Our Future Centenaries"; *The Sherlock Holmes Journal,* Vol. III, No. 4, Summer, 1958, pp. 4–5.

"The Route of the Blue Carbuncle"; *The Sherlock Holmes Journal,* Vol. II, No. 4, Winter, 1955, pp. 2–6.

"A Sherlock Holmes Anniversary"; *The Sherlock Holmes Journal,* Vol. I, No. 1, May, 1952, pp. 30–1.

"Was Sherlock Holmes at Westminster?"; *The Trifler,* July, 1953; reprinted in the *Sherlock Holmes Journal,* Vol. II, No. 1, July, 1954, pp. 39–41.

BRISTOWE, *Dr.* W. S.

"The Mystery of the Third Continent, or, Was Dr. John H. Watson a Philanderer?"; *The Sherlock Holmes Journal,* Vol. II, No. 2, December, 1954, pp. 27–39.

"A Note on the Watson-Doyle Partnership"; *The Sherlock Holmes Journal,* Vol. III, No. 3, Autumn, 1957, pp. 4–5.

"Oxford or Cambridge?"; *The Sherlock Holmes Journal,* Vol. IV, No. 2, Spring, 1959, pp. 75–6.

" 'The Three Students' in Limelight, Electric Light and Daylight"; *The Sherlock Holmes Journal,* Vol. III, No. 2, Winter, 1956, pp. 2–5.

" 'What a Terrible Criminal He Would Have Made' "; *The Sherlock Holmes Journal,* Vol. V, No. 1, Winter, 1960, pp. 6–14.

BROOK, GEOFFREY

"Sherlock Holmes' Pipe"; *The Baker Street Journal,* Vol. X, No. 3, New Series, July, 1960, pp. 152–4.

"The Bruce-Partington Keys: Correspondence between R. Kelf-Cohen and Paul Gore-Booth, with Comment by Felix Morley"; *The Sherlock Holmes Journal,* Vol. II, No. 2, December, 1954, pp. 14–5.

"The Bruce-Partington Night"; *The Sherlock Holmes Journal,* Vol. III, No. 1, Summer, 1956, pp. 17–8.

BRYAN-BROWN, FREDERICK

"Sherlockian Schools and Schoolmasters"; *The Sherlock Holmes Journal,* Vol. III, No. 1, Summer, 1956, pp. 2–7.

BUCHHOLTZ, JAMES

"A Tremor at the Edge of the Web"; *The Baker Street Journal,* Vol. VIII, No. 1, New Series, January, 1958, pp. 5–9.

BURNHAM, ERNEST C., JR.

"The Tattooed Fish in 'The Red-Headed League' "; *The Baker Street Journal,* Vol. XII, No. 4, New Series, October, 1942, pp. 219–22.

BUSH, ARTHUR

Portrait of London; London: Frederick Muller, Ltd., 1950.

BUXTON, EDWARD T.

"He Solved the Case and Won the Race"; *The Third Cab,* pp. 39–41.

CAMERON, MARY S.

"Joseph Aloysius Hansom and His 'Patent Safety Cab' "; *The Baker Street Gasogene,* Vol. I, No. 4, 1962, pp. 51–4.

"Mr. and Mrs. Beeton's Christmas Annual"; *The Baker Street Journal Christmas Annual,* 1957, pp. 5–8.

CAMPBELL, *Dr.* MAURICE

"The First Sherlockian Critic—1902"; *The Sherlock Holmes Journal,* Vol. I, No. 2, September, 1952, pp. 3–5, 24.

Sherlock Holmes and Dr. Watson: A Medical Digression; London: Ash & Co., Ltd., 1935.

CAREY, *Dr.* EUGENE F.

"Holmes, Watson and Cocaine"; *The Baker Street Journal,* Vol. XIII, No. 3, New Series, September, 1963, pp. 176–81, 195.

CARR, JOHN DICKSON

(with ADRIAN M. CONAN DOYLE) *The Exploits of Sherlock Holmes;* New York: Random House, 1954.

The Life of Sir Arthur Conan Doyle; New York: Harper & Brothers, 1949.

Catalogue of an Exhibition on Sherlock Holmes Held at Abbey House, Baker Street, London N. W. 1, May–September, 1951.

Catalogue of the Collection in the Bars and Grill Room and in the Reconstruction of the Living Room at 221B Baker Street [in] The Sherlock Holmes [Tavern]; with Introductory Essays by A. Lloyd-Taylor and John Dickson Carr, and a Critical Miscellany edited by H. Douglas Thomson; London: Whitbread & Co., Ltd., n.d.

CHENHALL, W. H.

"The Retirement of Sherlock Holmes"; *The Sherlock Holmes Journal,* Vol. V, No. 1, Winter, 1960, pp. 19–22.

CHIECO, LORENZO J.

"The Signature of Sherlock Holmes"; *The Baker Street Journal,* Vol. III, No. 3, New Series, July, 1953, pp. 157–9.

CHORLEY, *Mrs.* JENNIFER

" 'Briarbrae' Revisited"; *The Sherlock Holmes Journal,* Vol. VI, No. 2, Spring, 1963, pp. 56–7.

"1896–1964, 'The Wheel Has Come Full Circle' "; *The Sherlock Holmes Journal,* Vol. VI, No. 3, Winter, 1963, pp. 89–90.

"Some Diggings Down Under"; *The Sherlock Holmes Journal,* Vol. VI, No. 2, Spring, 1963, pp. 49–51.

CHRIST, *Professor* JAY FINLEY

"An Adventure in the Lower Criticism"; Part I: "Doctor Watson and the Calendar"; *The Baker Street Gasogene,* Vol. I, No. 3, 1961, pp. 28–35; Part II: "Dr. Watson and the Moon"; *The Baker Street Gasogene,* Vol. I, No. 4, 1962, pp. 13–9.

The Chicago *Tribune* Sketches:

Flashes by Fanlight (1946).
Gleanings by Gaslight (1947).
Soundings in the Saga (1948).
Sherlock's Anniversaries (1961).
Finch's Final Fling (1963).

"Commuting a Felony"; *The Baker Street Journal,* Vol. II, No. 2, Old Series, April, 1947, pp. 211–2.

"The Dancing Men"; *The Sherlock*

Holmes Journal, Vol. I, No. 4, December, 1953, pp. 24–5.

"Glittering Golden Guineas"; *The Numismatist,* October, 1951.

"The House in Baker Street"; *The Baker Street Journal,* Vol. II, No. 1, Old Series, January, 1947, pp. 91–2.

An Irregular Chronology of Sherlock Holmes of Baker Street; Ann Arbor, Michigan: The Fanlight House, 1947.

An Irregular Guide to Sherlock Holmes of Baker Street; New York: The Pamphlet House and Argus Books, 1947.

"James Boswell and the Island of Uffa"; *The Baker Street Journal,* Vol. I, No. 1, Old Series, January, 1946, pp. 24–7.

"The Later Holmes an Imposter: A Sequel"; *The Baker Street Gasogene,* Vol. I, No. 1, 1962, pp. 21–33.

" 'The Missing Three-Quarter' "; *The Baker Street Journal,* Vol. I, No. 2, Old Series, April, 1946, pp. 208–9.

" 'The Missing Three-Quarter' Again"; *The Baker Street Journal,* Vol. I, No. 3, Old Series, July, 1946, pp. 363–4.

"Musgrave Mathematics"; *Client's Second Case-Book,* pp. 14–9.

"The Mystery of the One-Way Dunlops"; *The Baker Street Journal,* Vol. II, No. 4, Old Series. October, 1947, p. 474.

"The Pipe and the Cap"; *The Baker Street Journal,* Vol. IX, No. 1, New Series, January, 1959, pp. 43–5.

"Problems in 'A Scandal in Bohemia' "; *The Baker Street Gasogene,* Vol. I, No. 2, 1961, pp. 5–13.

"Sherlock and the Canons"; *The Baker Street Journal,* Vol. III, No. 1, New Series, January, 1953, pp. 5–12.

"Sherlock Backs a Turkey"; *Sherlockian Studies,* p. 23.

"Silver Blaze: An Identification (as of 1893 A.D.)"; *The Baker Street Journal,* Vol. IV, No. 1, Old Series, January, 1949, pp. 12–5.

"Thumbs Up: Thumbs Down?"; *The Sherlock Holmes Journal,* Vol. II, No. 1, July, 1954, pp. 41–2.

"A Very Large-Scale Map"; *The Sherlock Holmes Journal,* Vol. VI, No. 3, Winter, 1963, pp. 72–4.

CHRISTIE, *Mrs.* WINIFRED M.

"On the Remarkable Explorations of Sigerson"; *The Sherlock Holmes Journal,* Vol. I, No. 2, September, 1952, pp. 39–44.

"Sherlock Holmes and Graphology"; *The Sherlock Holmes Journal,* Vol. II, No. 4, Winter, 1955, pp. 28–31.

"Some Reflections on That Little Thing of Chopin's"; *Leaves from the Copper Beeches,* pp. 81–9.

CHUJOY, ANATOLE

"The Only Second Stain"; *The Baker Street Journal,* Vol. IV, No. 3, New Series, July, 1954, pp. 165–8.

CLAPP, ROGER T.

"The Curious Problem of the Railway Timetables"; *The Second Cab,* pp. 34–8.

CLARK, BENJAMIN

"Dr. Mortimer Before the Bar"; *The Baker Street Journal,* Vol. III, No. 3, Old Series, July, 1948, pp. 269–77; *The Best of the Pips,* pp. 97–106.

"The Horsham Fiasco"; *The Baker Street Journal,* Vol. I, No. 1, New Series, January, 1951, pp. 4–8.

"On the Stock Prices Quoted in 'The Stockbroker's Clerk' "; *The Baker Street Journal,* Vol. XII, No. 4, New Series, December, 1962, p. 245.

CLARK, BENJAMIN, JR.

"Holmes on the Range"; *The Baker Street Journal,* Vol. III, No. 2, New Series, April, 1953, pp. 91–7.

CLARK, EDWARD F., JR.

"Study of an Untold Tale"; *The Baker Street Journal,* Vol. XIII, No. 4, New Series, December, 1963, pp. 217–28.

CLARK, *Dr.* JOHN D.

"A Chemist's View of Canonical Chemistry"; *The Baker Street Journal,* Vol. XIV, No. 3, New Series, September, 1964, pp. 153–5.

"Some Notes Relating to a Preliminary Investigation into the Paternity of Nero Wolfe"; *The Baker Street Journal,* Vol. VI, No. 1, New Series, January, 1956, pp. 5–11.

CLARKE, RICHARD W.

"Certain Ladies of Baker Street"; *The Baker Street Journal,* Vol. II, No. 1, New Series, January, 1952, pp. 34–8; *The Best of the Pips,* pp. 9–13.

"On 'The Five Orange Pips' "; *The Best of the Pips,* pp. 3–6.

"On the Nomenclature of Watson's Ships"; *The Baker Street Journal,* Vol. I, No. 2, Old Series, April, 1946, pp. 119–21; *The Best of the Pips,* pp. 6–9.

CLARKSON, PAUL S.

" 'In the Beginning . . .' "; *The Baker Street Journal,* Vol. VIII, No. 4, New Series, October, 1958, pp. 197–209.

CLAYTON, J. K.

"The Hat Trick"; *The Sherlock Holmes Journal,* Vol. II, No. 1, July, 1954, pp. 19–21.

Client's Case-Book, edited by Jerry Neal Williamson; Indianapolis: The Illustrious Clients, 1947.

Client's Second Case-Book, edited by Jerry Neal Williamson; Indianapolis: The Illustrious Clients, 1951.

Client's Third Case-Book, edited by Jerry Neal Williamson and H. B. Williams; Indianapolis: The Illustrious Clients, 1953.

CLUM, FLORENCE

"So He Boxed Their Ears"; *The Baker Street Journal,* Vol. II, No. 4, New Series, October, 1958, pp. 210–3.

CLUNN, HAROLD P.

The Face of London; New Edition, Revised by E. R. Wethersett, London; Spring Books, n.d.

CLYNE, ROBERT

"On the Footprints of a Gigantic Hound"; *The Baker Street Journal,* Vol. III, No. 1, New Series, January, 1953, pp. 60, 62.

COLBORNE, R. S.

"Orphans of the Storm?"; *The Sherlock Holmes Journal,* Vol. II, No. 3, Summer, 1955, pp. 24–5.

COLD, JØRGEN

"What Did Sherlock Holmes Drink?"; *Client's Third Case-Book,* pp. 110-18.

COLE, *Mrs.* ELEANOR S.

"Holmes, Watson and the K-9's"; *The Baker Street Journal,* Vol. I, No. 1, New Series, January, 1951, pp. 25–9.

COLLINS, HOWARD

"Ex Libris Sherlock Holmes"; *Profile by Gaslight,* pp. 26–39.

COOPER, ANTHONY G.

"Browsings in Birmingham"; *The Sherlock Holmes Journal,* Vol. IV, No. 4, Spring, 1960, p. 140.

"Holmesian Humour"; *The Sherlock Holmes Journal,* Vol. VI, No. 4, Spring, 1964, pp. 109–13.

CORRINGTON, *Dr.* J. D.

"Baker Street Weather"; *The Saint Detective Magazine,* Vol. VIII, No. 5, November, 1957, pp. 33–53.

COX, J. RANDOLPH

"Mycroft Holmes: Private Detective"; *The Baker Street Journal,* Vol. VI, No. 4, New Series, October, 1956, pp. 197–200.

CRAWFORD, BRYCE, JR.

(with R. C. MOORE) "The Final Problem—Where?"; *Exploring Sherlock Holmes,* pp. 82–7.

CROCKER, *Professor* STEPHEN F.

"The Barometric Dr. Watson: A Study of *The Sign of the Four*"; *The Quarterly of Phi Beta Pi,* November, 1946;

The Baker Street Journal, Vol. III, No. 2, April, 1948, pp. 196–201.

"Louder, Holmes! and Stop Muttering!, or, The Route to Thaddeus Sholto's"; *The Sherlock Holmes Journal,* Vol. I, No. 2, September, 1952, pp. 14–21.

"Pseudepigraphical Matter in the Holmesian Canon"; *The Baker Street Journal,* Vol. II, No. 3, New Series, July, 1952, pp. 158–64.

"Sherlock Holmes Recommends Winwood Reade"; *The Baker Street Journal,* Vol. XIV, No. 3, New Series, September, 1964, pp. 142–4.

"Watson Doctors the Venerable Bede"; *The Baker Street Journal,* Vol. IX, No. 3, New Series, July, 1959, pp. 157–64.

Cross, Leslie

"Sherlock Holmes, Writer: An Unsolved Case"; *The Baker Street Journal,* Vol. XIV, No. 1, New Series, March, 1964, pp. 39–42.

Cross, Melvin

"The Lantern of Sherlock Holmes"; *The Baker Street Journal,* Vol. I, No. 4, Old Series, October, 1946, pp. 433–42.

Cruikshank, R. J.

Roaring Century; London: Hamish Hamilton, 1946.

Crump, Norman

"Inner or Outer Rail?"; *The Sherlock Holmes Journal,* Vol. I, No. 1, May, 1952, pp. 16–23.

Cumings, Thayer

"Concerning Mr. Holmes' Fees"; *The Baker Street Journal,* Vol. VIII, No. 4, New Series, October, 1958, pp. 210–3.

"Don't Write—Telegraph!"; *The Best of the Pips,* pp. 87–95.

Currier, Francis M.

"Holmes and Thorndyke: A Real Friendship"; *The Baker Street Journal,* Vol. III, No. 2, Old Series, April, 1948, pp. 176–82.

Cutter, Robert A.

"The Underground"; *Client's Second Case-Book,* pp. 83–7.

Daish, W. G.

"Pondering on Pitfalls"; *The Sherlock Holmes Journal,* Vol. IV, No. 4, Spring, 1962, pp. 118–9.

Dakin, D. Martin

"The Problem of the *Case-Book*"; *The Sherlock Holmes Journal,* Vol. I, No. 3, June, 1953, pp. 29–34.

"Second Thoughts on the *Case-Book*"; *The Sherlock Holmes Journal,* Vol. III, No. 1, Summer, 1956, pp. 8–9.

Dalliba, William Swift

"The Manuscripts of the Sherlock Holmes Stories"; *The Baker Street Journal,* Vol. X, No. 3, New Series, July, 1960, pp. 164–6.

Dardess, *Dr.* John

"The Maiwand-Criterion Hiatus"; *The Baker Street Journal,* Vol. IV, No. 1, Old Series, October, 1949, pp. 115–7.

"On the Dating of *The Valley of Fear*"; *The Baker Street Journal,* Vol. III, No. 4, Old Series, October, 1948, pp. 481–2.

Davies, Bernard

"The Back Yards of Baker Street"; *The Sherlock Holmes Journal,* Vol. III, No. 4, Winter, 1959, pp. 83–8.

"Canonical Connections"; *The Sherlock Holmes Journal,* Vol. V, No. 2, Spring, 1961, pp. 37–41.

"Doctor Boyd's Bleat"; *The Sherlock Holmes Journal,* Vol. V, No. 3, Winter, 1961, pp. 88–9.

"The Mews of Marylebone"; *The Sherlock Holmes Journal,* Vol. VI, No. 1, Winter, 1962, pp. 6–10.

"Was Holmes a Londoner?"; *The Sherlock Holmes Journal,* Vol. IV, No. 2, Spring, 1959, pp. 42–7.

Davis, Elmer

Introduction to *The Later Adventures of Sherlock Holmes, Vol. I (The Return of Sherlock Holmes);* New York: The Limited Editions Club, 1952; *Introducing Mr. Sherlock Holmes.*

"On the Emotional Geology of Baker Street"; *221B,* pp. 37–45.

"The Real Sherlock Holmes"; *The Saturday Review of Literature,* December 3, 1933; *The Baker Street Journal,* Vol. I, No. 4, 1962, pp. 65–73.

De Groat, Raymond A.

"The Guilty Pawnbroker, or The Lost Summer of 1890"; *The Baker Street Journal,* Vol. XIV, No. 1, New Series, March, 1964, pp. 27–30.

De Witt, Omar L.

"On the Mystery of Baritsu"; *The Baker Street Journal,* Vol. VI, No. 2, New Series, April, 1956, p. 121.

Dickens, Charles

Dickens' Dictionary of the Thames from Its Source to the Nore: An Unconventional Handbook; London: Charles Dickens & Evans, 1892.

Dickensheet, Dean W.

"Sherlock Holmes — Linguist"; *The Baker Street Journal,* Vol. X, No. 3, New Series, July, 1960, pp. 133–42.

Donegall, Lord

"Lunatic Banker's Royal Client—Dr. Watson Tries Semi-Fiction"; *The Sherlock Holmes Journal,* Vol. VI, No. 2, Spring, 1963, pp. 46–9.

"Watson and Bradshaw"; *The Sherlock Holmes Journal,* Vol. V, No. 2, Spring, 1961, p. 36.

"Who Painted Hugo Baskerville?"; *The Sherlock Holmes Journal,* Vol. III, No. 3, Autumn, 1957, pp. 23, 24.

Dorian, N. Currier

" 'A Bad Lot' "; *The Baker Street Journal,* Vol. VI, No. 1, New Series, January, 1956, pp. 51–7.

Douglass, *Mrs.* Ruth

"The Camberwell Poisoner"; *Ellery Queen's Mystery Magazine,* February, 1947.

Doyle, Adrian M. Conan

"Deep Waters"; *The Sherlock Holmes Journal,* Vol. VI, No. 3, Winter, 1963, p. 96.

(with John Dickson Carr) *The Exploits of Sherlock Holmes;* New York: Random House, 1954.

Introduction to *A Treasury of Sherlock Holmes;* Garden City, New York: Hanover House, 1955.

"On Conan Doyle and the Vernets"; *The Sherlock Holmes Journal,* Vol. VI, No. 2, Spring, 1963, p. 38.

"Some Family Facts"; *The Baker Street Journal,* Vol. XII, No. 3, New Series, September, 1962, pp. 139–41.

The True Conan Doyle; London: John Murray, 1945; New York: Coward-McCann, 1946.

Doyle, *Dr.,* later *Sir* Arthur Conan

Memories and Adventures: The Autobiography of Sir Arthur Conan Doyle; London: Hodder & Stoughton, 1924; Boston: Little, Brown and Company, 1924.

Preface to *The Complete Sherlock Holmes Long Stories;* London: John Murray, 1929.

"A Sherlock Holmes Competition"; *The Strand Magazine,* March, 1927.

"Some Personalia About Mr. Sherlock Holmes"; *The Strand Magazine,* December, 1917.

Through the Magic Door; London: Smith, Elder, 1907.

"To an Undiscerning Critic"; *Some Piquant People* (Lincoln Springfield); London: T. Fisher Unwin, 1924; Private edition by Edwin B. Hill, Ysleta, Texas, October, 1937; *Profile by Gaslight.*

"The Truth About Sherlock Holmes"; *Collier's Magazine,* December 29, 1931.

Durgin, Cyrus

"The Speckled Band"; *The Third Cab,* pp. 12–6.

E. J. C.
"An Opinion from British Counsel on 'Commuting a Felony'"; *The Baker Street Journal,* Vol. III, No. 3, Old Series, July, 1948, pp. 309–13.

Elie, Rudolph
"The Battle of Charing Cross"; *The Third Cab,* pp. 17–25.

Erickson, Carl T.
"Royal Blood and Feet of Clay"; *The Baker Street Journal,* Vol. IV, No. 2, New Series, April, 1954, pp. 98–9.

Evans, Webster
"Sherlock Holmes and Sport"; *The Sherlock Holmes Journal,* Vol. II, No. 3, Summer, 1955, pp. 35–42.

Exploring Sherlock Holmes, edited by E. W. McDiarmid and Theodore C. Blegen; La Crosse, Wisconsin: The Sumac Press, 1957.

Feldman, Lew David
"Hitherto Unrecorded First Separate Editions"; *The Baker Street Gasogene,* Vol. I, No. 1, 1961, pp. 17–20.

Fenton, Irving
"An Analysis of the Crimes and Near-Crimes at Appledore Towers in the Light of the English Criminal Law"; *The Baker Street Journal,* Vol. VI, No. 2, New Series, April, 1956, pp. 69–74.
"Holmes and the Law"; *The Baker Street Journal,* Vol. VII, No. 2, New Series, April, 1957, pp. 79–83.
"On Friendship"; *The Baker Street Journal,* Vol. IX, No. 1, January, 1959, pp. 23–5.

Fitz, *Dr.* Reginald
"A Belated Eulogy: To John H. Watson, M.D."; *Profile by Gaslight,* pp. 141–53.

Folsom, *The Reverend* Henry T.
"Seventeen Out of Twenty-Three"; *The Baker Street Journal,* Vol. XIV, No. 1, New Series, March, 1964, pp. 24–6.
Through the Years at Baker Street: A Chronology of Sherlock Holmes, Revised Edition; Washington, New Jersey: Privately printed, 1964.

Fredman, L. E.
"A Note on Watson's Youth"; *The Sherlock Holmes Journal,* Vol. V, No. 3, Winter, 1961, p. 87.

Frisbie, Owen P.
"On the Origin of the Hound of the Baskervilles"; *The Best of the Pips,* pp. 51–5.

Galbraith, A. D.
"The Real Moriarty"; *The Baker Street Journal Christmas Annual,* 1957, pp. 55–62.

Gardner, George K.
"What Sherlock Did Know"; *The Baker Street Journal,* Vol. I, No. 3, New Series, July, 1951, pp. 89–90.

George, Isaac S.
"Violet the Hunter"; *The Baker Street Journal,* Vol. IV, No. 1, Old Series, January, 1949, pp. 29–37.

Gibson, Theodore W.
"The Birlstone Masquerade"; *The Baker Street Journal,* Vol. VI, No. 3, New Series, July, 1956, pp. 168–9.
"On the 'Silver Blaze' Formula"; *The Baker Street Journal,* Vol. XIV, No. 2, New Series, June, 1964, p. 123.

Gill, William H.
"Always on Sunday, Watson!"; *The Sherlock Holmes Journal,* Vol. V, No. 2, Spring, 1961, pp. 62, 64.
"Some Notable Sherlockian Buildings"; *The Sherlock Holmes Journal,* Vol. IV, No. 4, Spring, 1960, pp. 124–6.

Godfrey, Arthur
"On the Alternative Use of the Long and Short S"; *The Baker Street Journal,* Vol. XI, No. 4, New Series, December, 1961, pp. 246–7.

Goodman, Charles, *D.D.S.*
"The Dental Holmes"; *Profile by Gaslight,* pp. 85–96.

Gordon, *Dr.* Harold
"Some Recollections of Sir Arthur Conan Doyle"; *The Baker Street Journal,* Vol. XII, No. 3, New Series, July, 1962, pp. 137–8.

Gore-Booth, *Sir* Paul
"The Journeys of Sherlock Holmes: A Topographical Monograph"; *The Baker Street Journal,* Vol. III, No. 2, Old Series, April, 1948, pp. 159–68.

Graham, R. P.
"Dr. Watson, I Presume?"; *Client's Third Case-Book,* pp. 72–3.
"Sherlock Holmes in Retirement"; *The Baker Street Journal,* Vol. I, No. 4, Old Series, October, 1946, pp. 469–72.
"The Unknown Worm"; *The Baker Street Journal,* Vol. II, No. 2, Old Series, April, 1947, p. 212.

Grasse, Marvin
"Who Killed Holmes?"; *The Atlantic Monthly,* June, 1955.

Grazebrook, O. F.
Studies in Sherlock Holmes; London: Privately printed, n.d. [*c.* 1949]:
I. Oxford or Cambridge.
II. Politics and Premiers.
III. Royalty.
IV. Dr. Watson and Rudyard Kipling.
V. The Author of the *Case-Book.*
VI. Something of Dr. Watson.
(Study III, Royalty, has been reprinted in *Client's Third Case-Book,* p. 27–59.)

Green, Roger Lancelyn
"Dr. Watson's First Critic"; *The Sherlock Holmes Journal,* Vol. III, No. 4, Summer, 1958, pp. 8–9.
"Sherlock Holmes at Oxford"; *The Sherlock Holmes Journal,* Vol. IV, No. 1, Winter, 1958, p. 24.

Greenwood, E. P.
"Some Random Thoughts on Railway Journeys by Holmes and Watson"; *The Sherlock Holmes Journal,* Vol. I, No. 3, June, 1953, pp. 19–21.

Griffith, A. N.
"Some Observations on Sherlock Holmes and Dr. Watson at Bart's"; *St. Bartholomew's Hospital Journal,* Vol. LV, No. 12, pp. 273–4.

Grosbayne, Benjamin
"Sherlock Holmes — Musician"; *The Baker Street Journal,* Vol. III, No. 1, Old Series, January, 1948, pp. 47–57.

Hall, William S.
"Don't Blame Watson"; *The Baker Street Journal,* Vol. III, No. 2, New Series, April, 1953, pp. 84–6.
"The True and Proper Coat of Arms of Mr. Sherlock Holmes; With Also the Coats of Arms of John H. Watson, M.D., and James Moriarty, Sc.D."; *Profile by Gaslight,* pp. 114–24.

Hammond, *Dr.* Roland
"The Attempted Mayhem of 'Silver Blaze'"; *The Baker Street Journal,* Vol. I, No. 2, Old Series, April, 1946, pp. 157–61.
"The Surgeon Probes Doctor Watson's Wound"; *The Second Cab,* pp. 28–31.

Hand, Herbert T., Jr.
"Where Did You Get That Hat . . . Band?"; *The Baker Street Journal,* Vol. IV, No. 1, Old Series, January, 1949, pp. 18–23.

Harbottle, S. T. L.
"'My Charges Are Upon a Fixed Scale—'"; *The Sherlock Holmes Journal,* Vol. II, No. 1, July, 1954, pp. 22–5.
"Sherlock Holmes and the Law"; *The Sherlock Holmes Journal,* Vol. I, No. 3, June, 1953, pp. 7–10.

Hardwick, Michael and Mollie
The Man Who Was Sherlock Holmes; London: John Murray, 1964; Garden City, New York: Doubleday & Company, 1964.

The Sherlock Holmes Companion; London; John Murray, 1962.

Harris, Robert G.
"It's Not Always 1957"; *The Baker Street Journal,* Vol. VIII, No. 1, New Series, January, 1958, pp. 29–32.

Harrison, Michael
"The Blue Blood of the Holmes"; *The Baker Street Journal,* Vol. XIV, No. 2, New Series, June, 1964, pp. 81–3.
"Found: Pope's Court"; *The Sherlock Holmes Journal,* Vol. IV, No. 2, Spring, 1959, p. 80.
In the Footsteps of Sherlock Holmes; London: Cassell & Co., Ltd., 1958; New York: Frederick Fell, Inc., 1960.
London by Gaslight; London: Peter Davies, 1963.
"Why '221B'?"; *The Baker Street Journal,* Vol. XIV, No. 4, New Series, December, 1964, pp. 219–22.

Hart, Archibald
"The Effects of Trades Upon Hands"; *The Baker Street Journal,* Vol. III, No. 4, Old Series, October, 1948, pp. 418–20.

Haycraft, Howard
Murder for Pleasure: The Life and Times of the Detective Story; New York and London: D. Appleton-Century Company, Inc., 1941.

Hayne, Donald
"On Holmes' Visit to the United States in 1912"; *The Baker Street Journal,* Vol. I, No. 2, Old Series, April, 1946, pp. 189–90.

Haynes, George
"The Last Mrs. Watson"; *The Sherlock Holmes Journal,* Vol. VI, No. 2, Spring, 1963, pp. 53–4.

Hedgpeth, Joel W.
"Re-Examination of 'The Adventure of the Lion's Mane' "; *Scientific Monthly,* March, 1945; *The Baker Street Journal,* Vol. III, No. 3, Old Series, July, 1948, pp. 285–94.

Heldenbrand, Page
"The Adventures of the Dead Detective"; *Leaves from the Copper Beeches,* pp. 33–4.
"Another Bohemian Scandal"; *The Baker Street Journal,* Vol. IV, No. 1, Old Series, January, 1949, pp. 72–3.
"A Ghostly Watson?"; *The Baker Street Journal,* Vol. III, No. 4, Old Series, October, 1948, pp. 482–3.
"On the Island of Uffa"; *Heldenbrand's Christmas Perennial,* New York: Appledore Towers Letter Press, 1954.
"On an Obscure Nervous Page"; *The Baker Street Journal,* Vol. IV, No. 3, New Series, July, 1954, pp. 154–5.
"Sherlock Holmes in Disguise"; *The Baker Street Journal,* Vol. I, No. 3, Old Series, July, 1946, pp. 318–22.

Helling, Cornelis
"The Third Person"; *The Baker Street Journal,* Vol. VI, No. 4, New Series, October, 1956, p. 203.
"The True Story of the Dancing Men"; *The Baker Street Journal,* Vol. IV, No. 3, New Series, July, 1954, pp. 160–3.

Hendrickson, J. Raymond
"De Re Pharmaca"; *Leaves from the Copper Beeches,* pp. 11–4.

Hendriksen, A. D.
"On the Year of Sherlock Holmes' Birth"; *The Sherlock Holmes Journal,* Vol. I, No. 1, May, 1952, pp. 39–40.

Hicks, John L.
"No Fire Without Some Smoke"; *The Baker Street Journal,* Vol. V, No. 1, New Series, January, 1955, pp. 27–33.

Hill, *Professor* Pope R., Sr.
"The Final Problem: An Exemplification of the Substructure Theory"; *The Baker Street Journal,* Vol. V, No. 3, New Series, July, 1955, pp. 149–53.
"Sherlock Holmes Meets Jean Henri Fabre"; *The Baker Street Journal,* Vol. II, No. 1, Old Series, January, 1947, pp. 63–6.

Hinrich, D.
"Munsters v. Mallows"; *The Sherlock Holmes Journal,* Vol. VI, No. 4, Spring, 1964, p. 131.
"The Royal Mallows, 1854–1888"; *The Sherlock Holmes Journal,* Vol. VI, No. 1, Winter, 1962, pp. 20–2.

Hitchings, J. L.
"Sherlock Holmes the Logician"; *The Baker Street Journal,* Vol. I, No. 2, Old Series, April, 1946, pp. 113–7.

Hoff, *Dr.* Ebbe Curtis
"The Adventure of John and Mary"; *The Baker Street Journal,* Vol. IX, No. 3, New Series, July, 1959, pp. 136–52.
(with Phoebe M. Hoff) "The Affair at St. Monica's"; *The Baker Street Journal,* Vol. XIII, No. 1, New Series, March, 1963, pp. 5–15.

Hoffecker, Douglas M.
"Forgive Us, Oh Lord!"; *The Baker Street Journal,* Vol. V, No. 1, New Series, January, 1955, pp. 40–2.

Hogan, John V. L.
"An Unsolved Puzzle in the Writings"; *The Baker Street Journal,* Vol. III, No. 3, New Series, July, 1953, pp. 173–4.

Holmes, Marcella
"Sherlock Holmes and the Prime Ministers"; *The Baker Street Journal,* Vol. V, No. 1, New Series, January, 1955, pp. 34–9.

Holroyd, James Edward
Baker Street Byways; London: George Allen & Unwin, Ltd., 1959.
"Dr. Watson at the Criterion"; *The Sherlock Holmes Journal,* Vol. II, No. 2, December, 1954, p. 26.
"On the Cab-Rank in Baker Street"; *The Sherlock Holmes Journal,* Vol. II, No. 4, Winter, 1955, p. 27.
"On the Cheetah as Watch-Dog"; *The Sherlock Holmes Journal,* Vol. II, No. 3, Summer, 1955, p. 14.
"On the Evening Papers of London"; *The Sherlock Holmes Journal,* Vol. II, No. 4, Winter, 1955, pp. 26–7.
"On the Grassing of Mr. Joseph Harrison"; *The Sherlock Holmes Journal,* Vol. I, No. 2, September, 1952, p. 32.
"On the Holborn Restaurant"; *The Sherlock Holmes Journal,* Vol. II, No. 1, July, 1954, p. 19.
"On Holmes as Bee-Keeper"; *The Sherlock Holmes Journal,* Vol. II, No. 3, Summer, 1955, pp. 12–3.
"On Holmes Being Fully Dressed in 'The Speckled Band' "; *The Sherlock Holmes Journal,* Vol. II, No. 3, Summer, 1955, p. 13.
"On the Manuscript of *The Valley of Fear*"; *The Sherlock Holmes Journal,* Vol. III, No. 2, Winter, 1956, p. 20.
"On the Picture of General Gordon"; *The Sherlock Holmes Journal,* Vol. I, No. 1, May, 1952, p. 26.
"On the Rooms in Montague Street"; *The Sherlock Holmes Journal,* Vol. II, No. 3, Summer, 1955, p. 12.
"On the Route to Appledore Towers"; *The Sherlock Holmes Journal,* Vol. II, No. 1, July, 1954, p. 17.
"On the Westwardness of 221 Baker Street"; *The Sherlock Holmes Journal,* Vol. I, No. 1, May, 1952, p. 24.
"Some Problems in 'The Six Napoleons' "; *The Sherlock Holmes Journal,* Vol. I, No. 4, December, 1953, pp. 22–3.

Holstein, L. S.
"Bull Pups and Literary Agents"; *The Baker Street Journal Christmas Annual,* 1958, pp. 54–7.
"Inspector G. Lestrade"; *The Baker Street Journal,* Vol. VIII, No. 2, New Series, April, 1958, pp. 78–84.
"A Scandal in St. Monica"; *The Baker Street Journal,* Vol. XI, No. 1, New Series, January, 1952, pp. 49–52.
" '7. Knowledge of Chemistry–Pro-

found' "; *The Baker Street Journal,* Vol. IV, No. 1, New Series, January, 1954, pp. 44–9.

HOOK, D. MARCUS
"More on the Railway Journeys"; *The Baker Street Journal,* Vol. III, No. 2, Old Series, April, 1948, pp. 228–9.

HOWARD, ALAN
"A New Year for the Hound"; *The Sherlock Holmes Journal,* Vol. II, No. 3, Summer, 1955, pp. 3–6.

HOWARD, SAMUEL F.
"More About Maiwand"; *The Baker Street Journal,* Vol. II, No. 1, New Series, January, 1957, pp. 20–5.

HOWLETT, ANTHONY D.
(with HUMPHREY MORTON) "The Ethereal Hound"; *The Sherlock Holmes Journal,* Vol. IV, No. 1, Winter, 1956, pp. 15–6.
"The Horror Hound"; *The Sherlock Holmes Journal,* Vol. IV, No. 1, Winter, 1958, pp. 16–7.
"*The Hound of the Baskervilles* on the Screen"; *The Sherlock Holmes Journal,* Vol. I, No. 1, May, 1952, pp. 33–5.
"*The Hound of the Baskervilles:* Vintage 1939"; *The Sherlock Holmes Journal,* Vol. IV, No. 4, Spring, 1960, pp. 134–5.
"Mr. Arthur Wontner"; *The Sherlock Holmes Journal,* Vol. I, No. 2, September, 1952, pp. 12, 13.
"Mr. Carleton Hobbs"; *The Sherlock Holmes Journal,* Vol. VI, No. 4, September, 1964, pp. 118–20.
"Shinwell-Johnsoniana"; *The Sherlock Holmes Journal,* Vol. IV, No. 4, September, 1960, pp. 135, 140.
"The Whimpering Hound"; *The Sherlock Holmes Journal,* Vol. IV, No. 2, September, 1959, pp. 71–2.

HUNT, T. B.
(With *Professor* H. W. STARR) "What Happened to Mary Morstan"; *The Baker Street Journal,* Vol. II, No. 3, Old Series, July, 1947, pp. 237–46.

HYSLOP, JAMES T.
"The Master Adds a Postcript"; *The Baker Street Journal,* Vol. II, No. 2, Old Series, April, 1947, pp. 113–8.

HYSLOP, JOHN
"Sherlock Holmes and the Press"; *The Sherlock Holmes Journal,* Vol. IV, No. 1, Winter, 1958, pp. 4–8.
The Incunabular Holmes, edited by Edgar W. Smith; Morristown, New Jersey: The Baker Street Irregulars, Inc., 1958.
Introducing Mr. Sherlock Holmes, edited by Edgar W. Smith; Morristown, New Jersey: The Baker Street Irregulars, Inc., 1959.

IRALDI, JAMES C.
"That Extraordinary Man"; *The Baker Street Journal,* Vol. III, No. 1, New Series, January, 1953, pp. 13–7.
"The Other Geese"; *The Baker Street Journal,* Vol. III, No. 1, July, 1954, pp. 156–9.
"The Victorian Gondola"; *The Baker Street Journal,* Vol. I, No. 3, New Series, July, 1951, pp. 99–103.

JACOBS, LEONARD
"Baker Street"; *The Baker Street Journal,* Vol. VI, No. 2, New Series, April, 1956, pp. 101–5.

JENKINS, WILLIAM D.
"A Peculiar Persecution"; *The Baker Street Journal,* Vol. XIV, No. 1, New Series, March, 1964, pp. 45–53.

JONES, *The Reverend* G. BASIL
"The Dog and the Date"; *The Sherlock Holmes Journal,* Vol. II, No. 2, December, 1954, pp. 11–3.

JUDSON, RALPH
"The Mystery of Baritsu: A Sidelight Upon Sherlock Holmes' Accomplishments"; *The Baker Street Journal Christmas Annual,* 1958, pp. 10–6.

KASER, MICHAEL C.
"The Dating of 'Lady Frances Carfax' "; *The Baker Street Journal,* Vol. VII, No. 2, New Series, April, 1957, pp. 87–91.
"Sherlock Holmes on the Continent"; *The Baker Street Journal,* Vol. VI, No. 1, New Series, January, 1956, pp. 19–24.
"A Solution to 'Lady Frances Carfax' "; *The Baker Street Journal,* Vol. IX, No. 2, New Series, April, 1959, pp. 85–7.

KASSON, PHILIP
"The True Blue: A Case of Identification"; *The Baker Street Journal,* Vol. XI, No. 4, New Series, December, 1961, pp. 200–2.

KEDDIE, JAMES, SR.
"Gasogene, Coal Box, Persian Slipper"; *The Saturday Review of Literature,* June 27, 1936; *The Second Cab,* pp. 15–7.
"The Mystery of the Second Wound"; *Profile by Gaslight,* pp. 173–7.

KEEN, SHERRY
"Ship's or 'ship's'?"; *The Baker Street Journal,* Vol. III, No. 4, New Series, October, 1953, pp. 234–5.

KENT, WILLIAM
An Encyclopaedia of London; New York: The Macmillan Company, 1951.

KIERMAN, RAY
" 'It Is a Curious Little Problem' "; *The Baker Street Journal Christmas Annual,* 1957, pp. 26–30.
"A Shocking Affair"; *The Baker Street Journal,* Vol. II, No. 2, New Series, April, 1952, pp. 103–7.

KIMBALL, ELLIOT
"The Admirable Murray"; *Watsoniana: First Series;* Clinton, Connecticut: The Toille Press, 1962.
"Chronology of 'The Blue Carbuncle' "; *The Baker Street Journal,* Vol. XI, No. 4, New Series, December, 1961, pp. 215–7.
Dr. Watson at Netley; Clinton, Connecticut: The Toille Press, 1962.
"The First Man Who Beat Holmes"; *The Baker Street Gasogene,* Vol. I, No. 4, 1962, pp. 47–50.
"The Milverton Mess"; *The Sherlock Holmes Journal,* Vol. V, No. 4, Spring, 1962, pp. 100–2.
"The Missing Year"; *Watsoniana: First Series.*
"Origin and Evolution of G. Lestrade: 1 — Onomatological Considerations"; *The Sherlock Holmes Journal,* Vol. VI, No. 1, Winter, 1962, pp. 4–5; "2—A Matter of Mancinism"; *The Sherlock Holmes Journal,* Vol. VI, No. 2, Spring, 1963, pp. 43–5.
"The Stature of John H. Watson"; *The Baker Street Gasogene,* Vol. I, No. 3, 1961, pp. 5–10.
"Watson's Neurosis"; *Watsoniana: First Series.*
"The Watsons of Northumberland"; *Watsoniana: First Series.*

KLAUBER, LAURENCE M.
"The Truth About the Speckled Band"; *The Baker Street Journal,* Vol. III, No. 2, Old Series, April, 1948, pp. 149–57.

KLINEFELTER, WALTER
Sherlock Holmes in Portrait and Profile; Syracuse, New York: Syracuse University Press, 1963.
"The Writings of Mr. Sherlock Holmes"; *The Baker Street Journal,* Vol. I, No. 4, Old Series, October, 1946, pp. 409–16.

KNOX, *Monsignor* RONALD A.
"The Mystery of Mycroft"; *Baker Street Studies,* pp. 131–58.
"Studies in the Literature of Sherlock Holmes"; *The Blue Book,* 1912; *Essays in Satire,* London: Sheed & Ward, Ltd., 1928; *The Incunabular Holmes.*

KOELLE, *Dr.* GEORGE B.
"The Poisons of the Canon"; *Leaves from the Copper Beeches,* pp. 91–6.

LAUTERBACH, CHARLES E. and EDWARD S.
"The Man Who Seldom Laughed"; *The Baker Street Journal Christmas Annual,* 1960, pp. 265–71.

LAWSON, DOUGLAS
"The Speckled Band—What Is It?"; *The Baker Street Journal,* Vol. IV, No. 1, New Series, January, 1954, pp. 12–20.

Leaves from the Copper Beeches, edited by H. W. Starr, Thomas Hart, Ames Johnston, and Henry Shalet; Narbeth, Pennsylvania: The Livingston Publishing Company for the Sons of the Copper Beeches, 1958.

LEAVITT, ROBERT KEITH
"Annie Oakley in Baker Street"; *Profile by Gaslight,* pp. 230–42.
"Nummi in Arca or The Fiscal Holmes"; *221B,* pp. 16–36.
"The Origin of 221B Worship, Part I: The Chaldean Roots"; *The Baker Street Journal,* Vol. XI, No. 3, New Series, September, 1961, pp. 135–49; "Part II: Our Own Dear Little Girlie Becomes a) Legitimate, b) the Subject of Unmitigated Bleat"; *The Baker Street Journal,* Vol. XI, No. 4, New Series, December, 1961, pp. 225–34.
"The Preposterously Paired Performances of the Preacher's Portrait"; *The Baker Street Journal,* Vol. III, No. 4, Old Series, October, 1948, pp. 404–17.
"Who Was Cecil Forrester?"; *The Baker Street Journal,* Vol. I, No. 2, Old Series, April, 1946, pp. 201–4.

LEONARD, WILLIAM
"Re: Vampires"; *The Baker Street Journal Christmas Annual,* 1957, pp. 20–5.

LESH, *Professor* RICHARD D.
"Watson, Come Here; I Want You: in Afghanistan"; *The Baker Street Journal,* Vol. XIV, No. 3, New Series, September, 1964, pp. 136–8.

LESLIE, IAN M.
"Dr. Watson's Christmas Party of 1889"; *The Sherlock Holmes Journal,* Vol. I, No. 1, May, 1952, pp. 29–30.

L'ETANG, HUGH
"Some Observations on the Black Formosa Corruption and Tapanuli Fever"; *The Sherlock Holmes Journal,* Vol. IV, No. 2, Spring, 1959, pp. 58–60.

LEVERTON, JEFFERY SPRY
"On Watson's Having Taken his M.D. Degree"; *The Baker Street Journal,* Vol. III, No. 2, New Series, April, 1953, p. 117.

LEVINE, ARTHUR L.
"Lowenstein's Other Creeper"; *The Baker Street Journal,* Vol. VI, No. 1, New Series, January, 1956, pp. 30–3.
"A Man of 'Formidable Resourcefulness' "; *The Baker Street Journal,* Vol. IV, No. 3, New Series, July, 1954, pp. 169–73.

LIEB, POUL IB
"Sherlock's Delights"; *The Baker Street Journal,* Vol. VIII, No. 2, New Series, April, 1958, pp. 104–6.

LONGFELLOW, ESTHER
"The Distaff Side of Baker Street"; *The Baker Street Journal,* Vol. I, No. 1, Old Series, January, 1946, pp. 9–13.

MACCARTHY, *Sir* DESMOND
"Dr. Watson"; *The Listener,* December 11, 1929.

MACDONELL, A. G.
"The Truth About Moriarty"; *The New Statesman,* October 5, 1929; as "Mr. Moriarty"; *Baker Street Studies,* pp. 159–75; *The Baker Street Journal,* Vol. II, No. 2, Old Series, April, 1947, pp, 164–71.

MACDOUGLAD, DUNCAN, JR.
"Some Onomatological Notes on 'Sherlock Holmes' and Other Names in the Sacred Writings"; *The Baker Street Journal,* Vol. XII, No. 4, New Series, October, 1962, pp. 213–8.

MACGOWAN, KENNETH, *Editor*
Sleuths: Twenty-Three Great Detectives of Fiction and Their Best Stories; New York: Harcourt, Brace and Company, 1931.

MACKAY, IAN
" 'Knowledge of Politics—Feeble'?"; *The Sherlock Holmes Journal,* Vol. I, No. 2, September, 1952, pp. 25–30.

MACKENZIE, ARMINE D.
"The Case of the Illustrious Predecessor"; *Wilson Library Bulletin,* Vol. XIX, December, 1944, pp. 278–9; *The Baker Street Gasogene,* Vol. I, No. 2, 1961, pp. 29–31.

MACKENZIE, J. B.
"Sherlock Holmes' Plots and Strategy"; *The Green Bag,* The Boston Book Company, September, 1902; *The Baker Street Journal Christmas Annual,* 1956, pp. 56–61.

MACKENZIE, STANLEY
"The Engineer's Thumb"; *The Sherlock Holmes Journal,* Vol. II, No. 4, Winter, 1955, pp. 32–3.

MAURICE, ARTHUR BARTLETT
"More Sherlock Holmes Theories"; *The Bookman,* New York, May, 1902; *The Incunabular Sherlock Holmes.*
"Some Inconsistencies of Sherlock Holmes"; *The Bookman,* New York, January, 1902; *The Incunabular Sherlock Holmes.*

MAY, R. F.
"*The Hound of the Baskervilles:* A Botanical Enquiry"; *The Sherlock Holmes Journal,* Vol. VI, No. 1, Winter, 1962, p. 26.

MCCLEARY, *Dr.* GEORGE F.
"Was Sherlock Holmes a Drug Addict?" *Profile by Gaslight,* pp. 40–5.
"When Did Watson Meet His First Wife?"; *The Baker Street Journal,* Vol. II, No. 1, Old Series, January, 1947, pp. 50–3.

MCCOMAS, STANLEY
"Love at Lhasa"; *The Baker Street Journal,* Vol. I, No. 2, New Series, April, 1951, pp. 43–51.

MCDADE, THOMAS M.
"Heads and Holmes"; *The Baker Street Journal,* Vol. XI, No. 3, New Series, September, 1961, pp. 162–6.

MCDIARMID, E. W.
"Professor Sherlock Holmes, Ph.D."; *Exploring Sherlock Holmes,* pp. 27–41.
"Reichenbach and Beyond"; *The Baker Street Journal Christmas Annual,* 1957, pp. 34–43.

MCGAW, LISA
"Some Trifling Notes on Sherlock Holmes and Ornithology"; *The Baker Street Journal,* Vol. X, No. 4, October, 1960, pp. 231–4.

MCKEE, WILBUR K.
"The Son of a Certain Gracious Lady"; *The Baker Street Journal,* Vol. VIII, No. 3, New Series, July, 1958, pp. 133–8.

MCLAREN, R. M.
"Doctor Watson—Punter or Speculator?"; *The Sherlock Holmes Journal,* Vol. I, No. 1, May, 1952, pp. 8–10.

MCLAUCHLIN, RUSSELL
"Ballade on a Daring Theme"; *The Baker Street Journal,* Vol. II, No. 1, Old Series, January, 1947, pp. 16–7.
"On the Dating of the Master's Birth"; *The Baker Street Journal,* Vol. VI, No. 3, New Series, July, 1956, pp. 138–42.
"What Price Baker Street?"; *The Baker Street Journal,* Vol. II, No. 2, New Series, April, 1952, pp. 65–70.

MCNEIL, IAN
"An Engineer's Thoughts on 'The Engineer's Thumb' "; *The Sherlock Holmes Journal,* Vol. V, No. 4, Spring, 1962, pp. 108–10.

MCPHARLIN, PAUL
"221B Baker Street: Certain Physical Details"; *The Baker Street Journal,* Vol. II, No. 2, Old Series, April, 1947, pp, 180–94.

MEAKER, *Dr.* SAMUEL R.

"Watson Medicus"; *The Third Cab*, pp. 27–37.

MERRIMAN, CHARLES O.

"Birthplace of Holmes"; *The Sherlock Holmes Journal*, Vol. III, No. 1, Summer, 1956, pp. 22–3.

"A Case of Identity—No. 2"; *The Sherlock Holmes Journal*, Vol. V, No. 3, Winter, 1961, pp. 83–6.

"The Game Is Afoot"; *The Sherlock Holmes Journal*, Vol. V, No. 4, Spring, 1962, pp. 105–6.

"On the Fighting Cock Inn"; *The Baker Street Journal*, Vol. XII, No. 4, New Series, December, 1962, p. 245.

"Tar Derivatives Not Wanted"; *The Sherlock Holmes Journal*, Vol. VI, No. 1, Winter, 1962, p. 33.

"Unfair to Mycroft"; *The Sherlock Holmes Journal*, Vol. I, No. 4, December, 1953, pp. 41–2.

MERRITT, RUSSELL L.

"Re: The Adventure of the Worst Man in London"; *The Baker Street Journal Christmas Annual*, 1959, pp. 296–301.

METCALFE, N. P.

"The Date of the *Study in Scarlet*"; *The Sherlock Holmes Journal*, Vol. IV, No. 2, Spring, 1959, pp. 37–40.

"Holmes and Politics—A Retrospection"; *The Sherlock Holmes Journal*, Vol. I, No. 4, December, 1953; pp. 11–9.

"Oxford or Cambridge or Both?" *The Baker Street Journal Christmas Annual*, 1956, pp. 7–14.

MICHELL, HUMFREY

"Lady Frances Carfax Reappears"; *The Baker Street Journal*, Vol. II, No. 4, Old Series, October, 1947, p. 472.

"On the Bankruptcy of Dawson and Neligan"; *The Baker Street Journal*, Vol. III, No. 2, Old Series, April, 1948, pp. 230–1.

"On Sherlock Holmes' Method of Indexing"; *The Baker Street Journal*, Vol. IV, No. 3, New Series, July, 1954, pp. 187–8.

"On *the* Lady Frances Carfax"; *The Baker Street Journal*, Vol. II, No. 4, Old Series, October, 1947, p. 472.

"On Watson As a Writer"; *The Baker Street Journal*, Vol. II, No. 1, New Series, January, 1952, pp. 55–6.

"The Palace Clock"; *The Baker Street Journal*, Vol. I, No. 1, Old Series, January, 1946, p. 89.

"The Sartorial Sherlock Holmes"; *A Baker Street Four-Wheeler*, pp. 31–6.

(With J. H. MICHELL) "Sherlock Holmes the Chemist"; *The Baker Street Journal*, Vol. I, No. 3, Old Series, July, 1946, pp. 245–52.

"That 'Tenacious Black Clay' "; *The Sherlock Holmes Journal*, Vol. II, No. 1, July, 1954, p. 36.

"The Wonderful Wedding"; *The Baker Street Journal*, Vol. IV, No. 1, New Series, January, 1954, pp. 22–3.

MINGEY, EDWARD J., JR.

"The Bull Pup's Disappearance; or, Who Paid Watson's Rent?"; *The Baker Street Journal*, Vol. VII, No. 3, New Series, July, 1957, pp. 141–6.

The Misadventures of Sherlock Holmes, edited by Ellery Queen; Boston: Little, Brown & Co., 1944.

MONTGOMERY, JAMES

Art in the Blood and What Is This Thing Called Music (or Body and Soul); Philadelphia: Privately printed, 1950.

A Case of Identity; Philadelphia: International Printing Company, 1955.

Shots from the Canon; Philadelphia: Privately printed, 1953.

Sidelights on Sherlock; Philadelphia: Privately printed, 1951.

"Speculation in Diamonds"; *The Sherlock Holmes Journal*, Vol. I, No. 4, December, 1953, pp. 30–6.

A Study in Pictures: Being a "Trifling Monograph" on the Iconography of Sherlock Holmes; Philadelphia: International Printing Company, 1954.

MOORE, R. C.

(with BRYCE CRAWFORD, JR.) "The Final Problem—Where?"; *Exploring Sherlock Holmes*, pp. 82–7.

MORGAN, ROBERT S.

"The Puzzle of the Bull Pup"; *The Baker Street Journal Christmas Annual*, 1956, pp. 35–40.

Spotlight on a Simple Case, or Wiggins, Who Was That Horse I Saw With You Last Night; Wilmington, Delaware: The Cedar Tree Press, n.d. (1959).

MORIARTY, DANIEL L.

"The Woman Who Beat Sherlock Holmes"; *The Baker Street Journal*, Vol. IX, No. 2, New Series, April, 1959, pp. 69–82.

MORLEY, CHRISTOPHER

"The Blue Carbuncle, or, the Season of Forgiveness"; *The Adventure of the Blue Carbuncle*, New York: The Baker Street Irregulars, Inc., 1948.

"Dr. Watson's Secret"; *221B*, pp. 46–53.

Introduction and Notes to *Sherlock Holmes and Dr. Watson: A Textbook of Friendship;* New York: Harcourt, Brace & Co., 1944.

Introduction to *The Complete Sherlock Holmes;* Garden City, New York: Doubleday, Doran and Company, Inc., 1930.

"On the 'B' in 221B"; *The Baker Street Journal*, Vol. II, No. 3, Old Series, July, 1947, p. 270.

"On Baker Street"; *The Baker Street Journal*, Vol. I, No. 3, Old Series, July, 1946, p. 303.

"On the Baker Street Irregulars"; *The Baker Street Journal*, Vol. I, No. 3, July, 1946, pp. 286–91; reprinted, *The Baker Street Journal*, Vol. XIII, No. 1, New Series, March, 1963, pp. 17–22.

"On the Chamber As Opposed to the Barrel in Small Arms"; *The Baker Street Journal*, Vol. II, No. 2, Old Series, April, 1947, pp, 142–3.

"On Clark Russell"; *Profile by Gaslight*, pp. 54–5; *The Baker Street Journal*, Vol. III, No. 4, Old Series, October, 1948, p. 444.

"On the Day of Watson's First Meeting with Holmes"; *The Baker Street Journal Christmas Annual*, 1960, p. 281.

"On the Derivation of 'Ridling Thorpe' "; *The Baker Street Journal*, Vol. I, No. 2, New Series, April, 1951, p. 55.

"On Dribbling in Rugby Football"; *The Baker Street Journal*, Vol. III, No. 2, Old Series, April, 1948, p. 171.

"On the Dutch Steamship *Friesland*"; *Profile by Gaslight*, p. 57.

"On the Fate of the *Matilda Briggs*"; *The Baker Street Journal*, Vol. I, No. 4, Old Series, October, 1946, p. 408.

"On Holmes' Birthplace at Holmes Mall in the North Riding of Yorkshire"; *The Baker Street Journal Christmas Annual*, 1960, pp. 284–5.

"On the Island of Uffa"; *The Baker Street Journal*, Vol. I, No. 2, New Series, April, 1951, p. 57.

"On John Hector McFarlane's Inability to Get Back from Lower Norwood"; *The Baker Street Journal*, Vol. III, No. 1, Old Series, January, 1948, pp. 41–2.

"On Lady Frances Carfax as Watson's Third Wife"; *The Baker Street Journal*, Vol. II, No. 2, Old Series, April, 1947, p. 141.

"On the Late Train to Cambridge"; *The Baker Street Journal*, Vol. III, No. 2, Old Series, April, 1948, p. 171.

"On 'Long Vacation' as a Cambridge Term"; *The Baker Street Journal*, Vol. III, No. 2, Old Series, April, 1948, p. 172.

"On the Name 'Mycroft'"; *Profile by Gaslight,* p. 58.

"On Peterhouse as Holmes' Cambridge College"; *The Baker Street Journal,* Vol. III, No. 3, Old Series, July, 1948, p. 296.

"On Putting One's Boots on Backwards"; *The Baker Street Journal,* Vol. II, No. 2, Old Series, April, 1947, p. 142.

"On Raffles Holmes as a Brother of Sherlock's"; *The Baker Street Journal,* Vol. II. No. 2, Old Series, April, 1947, p. 140.

"On Sherlock Holmes' Full Name"; *The Baker Street Journal,* Vol. I, No. 2, Old Series, April, 1946, pp. 127–8.

"On the Stop at Swindon"; *The Baker Street Journal,* Vol. II, No. 3, Old Series, July, 1947, pp. 270–1.

"On Thomas Carlyle"; *Profile by Gaslight,* pp. 52–3.

"On Thurston the Billiard Player"; *The Baker Street Journal,* Vol. I, No. 4, Old Series, October, 1946, pp. 404–6.

"On the Tide-Waiter"; *Profile by Gaslight,* pp. 55–6.

"On Watson's Landing at Troopship Jetty"; *Profile by Gaslight,* p. 56.

"On Watson's Removal from the Northumberlands"; *The Baker Street Journal,* Vol. I, No. 2, New Series, April, 1951, p. 56.

"On Yorkshire as Holmes' Native County"; *The Baker Street Journal,* Vol. IV, No. 1, Old Series, January, 1949, p. 42.

"Was Sherlock Holmes an American?"; *221B,* pp. 5–15.

"Watson a la Mode"; *The Baker Street Journal,* Vol. I, No. 1, Old Series, January, 1946, pp. 15–20.

MORLEY, *Dr.* FELIX

"As Felix Morley Wrote to William S. Baring-Gould: An Addendum to 'Dr. Watson Has Gone to Widecombe'"; *The Baker Street Journal,* Vol. XV, No. 1, New Series, March, 1965, pp. 16–7.

"How the Child Got Into the Chimney"; *The Baker Street Journal Christmas Annual,* 1958, pp. 7–9.

"The Significance of the Second Stain"; *Profile by Gaslight,* pp. 243–59.

MORLEY, FRANK V.

"I Am Puzzled About Saxe-Coburg Square"; *The Baker Street Journal,* Vol. V, No. 3, New Series, July, 1955, pp. 139–41.

MORROW, L. A.

"A Diplomatic Secret"; *The Sherlock Holmes Journal,* Vol. II, No. 4, Winter, 1955, pp. 21–5.

"The Game Is . . ."; *The Baker Street Journal,* Vol. VII, No. 1, New Series, January, 1957, pp. 32–8.

MORTON, HUMPHREY

(with ANTHONY D. HOWLETT) "The Ether-eal Hound"; *The Sherlock Holmes Journal,* Vol. IV, No. 1, Winter, 1956, pp. 15–6.

"'A Long Drive to Hampstead'"; *The Sherlock Holmes Journal,* Vol. V, No. 1, Winter, 1960, pp. 22–3.

"A Milvertonian Identification"; *The Sherlock Holmes Journal,* Vol. VI, No. 1, Winter, 1962, pp. 14–5.

MURCH, A. E.

The Development of the Detective Novel; London: Peter Owen Limited, 1958.

NAGANUMA, *Dr.* KOHKI

"Sherlock Holmes and Cocaine"; *The Baker Street Journal,* Vol. XIII, No. 3, New Series, September, 1963, pp. 170–5.

NEITZKE, GORDON

"Sherlock Holmes and Jack the Ripper"; *Client's Third Case-Book,* pp. 80–3.

NELSON, JAMES

"Sherlock and the Sherpas"; *The Baker Street Journal,* Vol. VII, No. 3, New Series, July, 1957, pp. 161–4.

NEWTON, G. B.

"Billy the Page"; *The Sherlock Holmes Journal,* Vol. II, No. 3, September, 1955, pp. 7–10.

"Concerning the Authorship of 'The Mazarin Stone'"; *The Sherlock Holmes Journal,* Vol. IV, No. 2, Spring, 1959, pp. 52–4.

"The Date of *The Valley of Fear*"; *The Sherlock Holmes Journal,* Vol. II, No. 4, Winter, 1955, pp. 38–42.

"This Desirable Residence"; *The Sherlock Holmes Journal,* Vol. III, No. 2, Winter, 1956, pp. 12–4.

NIEMINSKI, JOHN

"On Watson's Possessing a Pair of Tennis Shoes"; *The Baker Street Journal,* Vol. V, No. 3, New Series, July, 1955, pp. 182–3.

OFFICER, HARVEY

"Sherlock Holmes and Music"; *221B,* pp. 71–3.

OFFORD, LENORE GLEN

"The Brief Adventure of Mr. Turner"; *The Baker Street Journal,* Vol. I, No. 3, Old Series, July, 1946, pp. 253–9.

OLNEY, *Professor* CLARKE

"The Literacy of Sherlock Holmes"; *The Sherlock Holmes Journal,* Vol. II, No. 4, Winter, 1955, pp. 9–15.

OURSLER, WILL

"His French Cousin"; *The Baker Street Journal Christmas Annual,* 1956, pp. 32–4.

PAGET, WINIFRED

"Full Circle"; *The Sherlock Holmes Journal,* Vol. I, No. 1, May, 1952, pp. 27–8.

PALMER, STUART

"The Adventure of the Marked Man"; *Ellery Queen's Mystery Magazine,* July, 1944.

"Notes on Certain Evidences of Caniphobia in Mr. Sherlock Holmes and His Associates"; *The Baker Street Journal,* Vol. V, No. 4, New Series, October, 1955, pp. 197–204.

PARK, ORLANDO

Sherlock Holmes, Esq., and John H. Watson, M.D.: An Encyclopaedia of Their Affairs; Evanston, Illinois: Northwestern University Press, 1962.

PARKER, HYMAN

"Birdy Edwards and the Scowrers Reconsidered"; *The Baker Street Journal,* Vol. IV, No. 1, New Series, March, 1964, pp. 3–7.

PATTRICK, ROBERT R.

"The Case of the Superfluous Landlady"; *The Baker Street Journal,* Vol. III, No. 4, New Series, October, 1953, pp. 241–3.

"Moriarty Was There"; *The Baker Street Journal Christmas Annual,* 1958, pp. 45–53.

"The Oasis in the Howling Desert"; *The Sherlock Holmes Journal,* Vol. IV, No. 4, Spring, 1960, pp. 126–8.

"October 9, 1890"; *The Sherlock Holmes Journal,* Vol. III, No. 1, Summer, 1956, pp. 126–8.

"On the Number of Henry Bakers in the London of the Eighties"; *The Baker Street Journal,* Vol. III, No. 2, New Series, April, 1953, pp. 125–6.

"A Sherlock Holmes Chronology"; *The Baker Street Journal,* Vol. XIII, No. 1, New Series, March, 1963, p. 62.

"A Study in Crypto-Choreography"; *The Baker Street Journal,* Vol. V, No. 4, New Series, October, 1955, pp. 205-9.

"Watson Writes from Baskerville Hall"; *The Baker Street Journal Christmas Annual,* 1960, pp. 293–8.

PEARSON, EDMUND

"Sherlock Holmes Among the Illustrators"; *The Bookman,* New York, August, 1932.

"PENANG LAWYER, A"

"The Name's the Same"; *The Sherlock Holmes Journal,* Vol. II, No. 1, p. 11.

Pennell, *Dr.* Vernon

"A Resumé of the Medical Life of John H. Watson, M.D., Late of the Army Medical Department, with an Appendix of the London University Regulations for Medical Degrees for the Year 1875"; *The Sherlock Holmes Journal,* Vol. III, No. 2, Winter, 1956, pp. 6–11.

Percival, William

"Sherlock Holmes and Air-Guns"; *The Sherlock Holmes Journal,* Vol. VI, No. 1, Winter, 1962, pp. 15–6.

Petersen, Svend

A Sherlock Holmes Almanac; Washington, D.C.: Privately printed, 1956.

"When the Game Was Not Afoot"; *The Baker Street Journal,* Vol. IV, No. 1, Old Series, January, 1949, pp. 59–71.

Pickard, Charles M.

"The Reticence of Dr. Mortimer"; *The Baker Street Journal,* Vol. VII, No. 3, New Series, July, 1957, pp. 153–5.

Pitts, Zasu

"Mrs. Hudson Speaks"; a recording made for the meeting of the Amateur Mendicants Society of Detroit on March 14, 1947, and reported in the *Baker Street Journal,* Vol. II, No. 3, Old Series, July, 1947, pp. 328–31.

Playfair, Giles

"John and James"; *The Baker Street Journal,* Vol. I, No. 3, Old Series, July, 1946, pp. 271–6.

Plimentel, William E.

"On the Electric Switch at Appledore Towers"; *The Baker Street Journal,* Vol. V, No. 2, New Series, April, 1955, p. 121.

Portugal, Eustace

"The Holmes-Moriarty Duel"; *The Bookman,* London, May, 1934.

Pratt, Fletcher

"The Gastronomic Holmes"; *The Baker Street Journal,* Vol. II, No. 2, New Series, April, 1952, pp. 94–9.

"Holmes and the Royal Navy"; *The Second Cab,* pp. 65–9.

"The Secret Message of the Dancing Men"; *Profile by Gaslight,* pp. 274–82.

"Very Little Murder"; *The Baker Street Journal,* Vol. V, No. 2, New Series, April, 1955, pp. 69–76.

Prestige, Colin

"Agents of Evil"; *The Baker Street Journal,* Vol. V, No. 2, New Series, July, 1955, pp. 144–7.

"The Criterion Plaque"; *The Sherlock Holmes Journal,* Vol. I, No. 3, June, 1953, pp. 10–1.

"For a World Now Prepared"; *The Sherlock Holmes Journal,* Vol. IV, No. 2, Spring, 1959, pp. 61–2.

"Problem of Pope's Court"; *The Sherlock Holmes Journal,* Vol. I, No. 3, June, 1953, pp. 27–8.

"South London Adventures"; *The Sherlock Holmes Journal,* Vol. III, No. 3, Autumn, 1957, pp. 5–8.

Price, Edmund T.

"The Singular Adventures of the Grice Patersons in the Island of Uffa and the Loss of the British Barque *Sophy Anderson"; The Baker Street Journal Christmas Annual,* 1959, pp. 302-10.

Prince, Marion

"Sherlock and Son"; *A Baker Street Four-Wheeler,* pp. 27–9.

Profile by Gaslight: An Irregular Reader about the Private Life of Sherlock Holmes, edited by Edgar W. Smith; New York: Simon & Schuster, 1944.

Pulling, Christopher

"Sherlock Holmes and Scotland Yard"; *The Sherlock Holmes Journal,* Vol. I, No. 3, June, 1953, pp. 12–7.

Quayle, Edward

"Suffer the Little Children . . ."; *The Baker Street Journal,* Vol. III, No. 4, Old Series, October, 1948, pp. 463–70

Queen, Ellery

In the Queen's Parlor; New York: Simon & Schuster, 1957.

Introduction to *Client's Second Case-Book.*

Introduction to *The Memoirs of Solar Pons,* by August Derleth; Sauk City: Wisconsin: Mycroft & Moran, 1951.

Introduction and Notes to *The Misadventures of Sherlock Holmes.*

"Sherlock Holmes First Editions: A New and Revised Catalogue of the Queen Collection"; *Ellery Queen's Mystery Magazine,* February, 1954.

Ramamurthy, T. V.

"The Case of the Awkward Pencil"; *The Sherlock Holmes Journal,* Vol. I, No. 4, December, 1953, pp. 40–1.

Rand, Stuart C.

"What Sherlock Didn't Know"; *The Atlantic Monthly,* November, 1945; *The Baker Street Journal,* Vol. I, No. 3, New Series, July, 1951, pp. 83–8.

Randall, *Professor* David A.

"The Adventure of the Notorious Forger"; *The Baker Street Journal,* Vol. I, No. 3, Old Series, July, 1946, pp. 371–7.

"A Census of the Known Existing Original Manuscripts of the Sacred Writings: Their Auction Records, Present Locations, etc., Chronologically Arranged"; *The Baker Street Journal,* Vol. I, No. 4, Old Series, October, 1946, pp. 504–8.

"On the First Book Publication of 'The Red-Headed League' and 'The Boscombe Valley Mystery'"; *The Baker Street Journal,* Vol. II, No. 4, Old Series, October, 1947, pp. 491–6.

"On the Manuscript of *The Sign of the Four"; The Baker Street Journal,* Vol. I, No. 4, Old Series, October, 1946, pp. 504–8.

"*The Valley of Fear* Bibliographically Considered"; *The Baker Street Journal,* Vol. I, No. 2, Old Series, April, 1946, pp. 232–7.

"'The Red-Headed League' Reviewed"; *The Sherlock Holmes Journal,* Vol. II, No. 1, July, 1954, pp. 29–34.

Redmond, D. A.

"Some Chemical Problems in the Canon"; *The Baker Street Journal,* Vol. XIV, No. 3, New Series, September, 1964, pp. 145–52.

Rendall, Vernon

"Belsize As a Commentator: Sherlock Holmes"; *The London Nights of Belsize;* London: John Lane, 1917; *The Incunabular Holmes.*

"The Limitations of Sherlock Holmes"; *Baker Street Studies,* pp. 63–84.

Rice, *The Reverend* Otis R.

"Clergymen in the Canon"; *The Baker Street Journal,* Vol. IV, No. 3, New Series, July, 1954, pp. 133–43.

Richard, Peter

"Completing the Canon," Part I; *The Sherlock Holmes Journal,* Vol. VI, No. 1, Winter, 1962, pp. 10–4; Part II, *The Sherlock Holmes Journal,* Vol. VI, No. 3, Winter, 1963, pp. 76–81.

"A Postscript to 'Completing the Canon'"; *The Sherlock Holmes Journal,* Vol. VI, No. 4, Spring, 1964, pp. 114–5.

Roberts, S. C., *later Sir* Sydney

Doctor Watson: Prolegomena to the Study of a Biographical Problem; London, Faber & Faber, Ltd., 1931; *The Incunabular Holmes.*

Holmes and Watson: A Miscellany; London: Oxford University Press, 1953.

"The Music of Baker Street"; *The Oxford Magazine,* May 1, 1947; *The Baker Street Journal,* Vol. II, No. 4, Old Series, October, 1947, pp. 429–32.

"A Note on the Watson Problem"; Cambridge, England: The University Press, 1929; *The Baker Street Journal,*

Vol. I, No. 1, Old Series, January, 1946, pp. 29–32.

"The Personality of Sherlock Holmes," Part I; *The Sherlock Holmes Journal,* Vol. I, No. 1, May, 1952, pp. 2–7; Part II, *The Sherlock Holmes Journal,* Vol. I, No. 3, June, 1953, pp. 3–6, 18.

"Sherlock Holmes and the Fair Sex"; *Baker Street Studies,* pp. 177–9.

ROBERTSHAW, WILFRID

"Bradshaw: The Story of a Time-Table"; *The Baker Street Journal,* Vol. XII, No. 2, New Series, June, 1962, pp. 102–5.

RODELL, MARIE F.

"Living on Baker Street"; *The Baker Street Journal,* Vol. II, No. 1, Old Series, January, 1947, pp. 35–7.

ROOSEVELT, FRANKLIN DELANO

A Baker Street Folio, edited by Edgar W. Smith; Morristown, New Jersey: The Baker Street Irregulars, Inc., 1945.

"Sherlock Holmes in the White House"; *The Baker Street Journal,* Vol. V, No. 2, New Series, April, 1955, pp. 78–9.

ROSENBERGER, EDGAR S.

"On the Railway Journeys of Sherlock Holmes"; *The Baker Street Journal,* Vol. II, No. 2, Old Series, April, 1947, pp. 175–9.

"The Religious Sherlock Holmes"; *The Baker Street Journal,* Vol. III, No. 2, Old Series, April, 1948, pp. 138–47.

ROSENBLUM, MORRIS

"Foreign Language Quotations in the Canon"; *The Baker Street Journal,* Vol. III, No. 4, Old Series, October, 1948, pp. 425–34.

"Hafiz and Horace, Huxtable and Holmes"; *The Baker Street Journal,* Vol. I, No. 3, Old Series, July, 1946, pp. 261–9.

"The Horatian Spirit in Holmes"; *Client's Third Case-Book,* pp. 119–26.

"On Holmes' Use of the Word 'Vaseline' in 'The Adventure of the Dying Detective' "; *The Baker Street Journal,* Vol. X, No. 4, New Series, October, 1960, p. 250.

"On the *Pâté-de-Fois-Gras* Pie"; *The Baker Street Journal,* Vol. II, No. 4, Old Series, October, 1947, pp. 438–9.

"Some Latin Byways in the Canon"; *The Baker Street Journal,* Vol. III, No. 1, Old Series, January, 1948, pp. 15–20.

RUBER, PETER A.

"On a Defense of H. W. Bell"; *The Baker Street Gasogene,* Vol. III, No. 3, 1961, pp. 15–7.

"Sir Arthur Conan Doyle and Fletcher Robinson: An Epitaph"; *The Baker Street Gasogene,* Vol. I, No. 2, 1961, pp. 22–8.

SANDERSON, SHIRLEY

"Another Case of Identity"; *The Sherlock Holmes Journal,* Vol. VI, No. 3, Winter, 1963, pp. 86–7.

SAXE, STEPHEN

"Tregennis and Poe"; *The Baker Street Journal,* Vol. I, No. 1, Old Series, January, 1946; pp. 90–1.

SAYERS, DOROTHY L.

"The Dates in 'The Red-Headed League' "; *The Colophon,* Part 17, 1934; *The Baker Street Journal,* Vol. II, No. 3, Old Series, July, 1947, pp. 279–90; *Unpopular Opinions;* London: Victor Gollancz, 1946.

"Dr. Watson, Widower"; *Unpopular Opinions; The Incunabular Sherlock Holmes.*

"Dr. Watson's Christian Name"; *Profile by Gaslight,* pp. 180–6; *Unpopular Opinions.*

"Holmes' College Career"; *Baker Street Studies,* pp. 1–34; *Unpopular Opinions.*

Introduction to *Great Short Stories of Detection, Mystery and Horror;* London: Victor Gollancz, 1928; as *The Omnibus of Crime,* New York: Payson & Clarke Limited, 1929.

SCHENCK, *Professor* REMSEN TEN EYCK

"Baker Street Fables"; *The Baker Street Journal,* Vol. II, No. 2, New Series, April, 1952, pp. 85–92.

"The Effect of Trades Upon the Body"; *The Baker Street Journal,* Vol. III, No. 1, New Series, January, 1953, pp. 31–6.

"Holmes, Cryptanalysis and the Dancing Men"; *The Baker Street Journal,* Vol. V, No. 2, New Series, April, 1955, pp. 80–91.

"On the Footprints of a Gigantic Hound"; *The Baker Street Journal,* Vol. II, No. 4, New Series, October, 1952, pp. 232–3.

"On the Gun That Killed Charles Augustus Milverton"; *The Baker Street Journal,* Vol. IV, No. 1, Old Series, January, 1949, pp. 95–6.

SCHONBERG, HAROLD

"Yet Another Case of Identity"; *The Sherlock Holmes Journal,* Vol. VI, No. 4, Spring, 1964, pp. 115–8.

SCHORIN, HOWARD R.

"Cryptography in the Canon"; *The Baker Street Journal,* Vol. XIII, No. 4, December, 1963, pp. 214–6.

SCHULMAN, DAVID

"Sherlock Holmes: Cryptanalyst"; *The Baker Street Journal,* Vol. III, No. 2, Old Series, April, 1948, pp. 233–7.

SCHULTZ, ROBERT S.

"The Ballistics of the Empty House"; *The Baker Street Journal,* Vol. II, No. 4, Old Series, October, 1947, pp. 373–9.

SCHUTZ, ROBERT H.

"Half-Sister; No Mystery"; *The Baker Street Gasogene,* Vol. I, No. 2, 1961, pp. 14–5.

"Some Problems in 'The Yellow Face' "; *The Baker Street Journal,* Vol. XII, No. 1, March, 1962, p. 31

SCHWARTZ, RICHARD S.

"Three Students in Search of a Scholar"; *The Baker Street Journal Christmas Annual,* 1957, pp. 45–9.

The Science Fictional Sherlock Holmes, edited by Norman Metcalf; Lowry Air Force Base, Colorado: The Council of Four, 1960.

The Second Cab; edited by James Keddie, Jr.; Boston: Stoke Moran, 1947.

SELLARS, *Mrs.* CRIGHTON

"Altamont"; *The Baker Street Journal,* Vol. III, No. 1, Old Series, January, 1948, p. 59.

"Dr. Watson and the British Army"; *The Baker Street Journal,* Vol. II, No. 3, Old Series, July, 1947, pp. 332–41.

"On Greuze's *Jeune Fille à l'Agneau";* *The Baker Street Journal,* Vol. I, No. 4, Old Series, October, 1946, p. 468.

"On Woolwich as an Army Arsenal"; *The Baker Street Journal,* Vol. IV, No. 1, Old Series, January, 1949, pp. 54–6.

"Uffa Again"; *The Baker Street Journal,* Vol. I, No. 3, Old Series, July, 1946, p. 362.

"A Visit to Sherlock Holmes"; *The Baker Street Journal,* Vol. II, No. 1, New Series, January, 1952, pp. 5–17.

SEWELL, GORDON

"Holmes and Watson in the South Country"; *The Southern Daily Echo,* October 2, 1957; *The Sherlock Holmes Journal,* Vol. III, No. 3, Autumn, 1957, pp. 10–2.

SHEARER, JAMES, II

" 'This Forty-Grain Weight of Crystallized Charcoal' "; *The Loupe,* July–August, 1952; quoted in the *Baker Street Journal,* Vol. III, No. 1, New Series, January, 1953, p. 63.

SHEARN, A. L.

"The Street and the Detective"; *The Baker Street Journal Christmas Annual,* 1957, pp. 50–4.

SHERBROOKE-WALKER, *Colonel* RONALD D.

"Clothes Canonical"; *The Sherlock*

Holmes Journal, Vol. VI, No. 4, Spring, 1964, pp. 104–8.

"Holmes, Watson and Tobacco"; *The Sherlock Holmes Journal,* Vol. I, No. 2, September, 1952, pp. 7–12.

Sherlockian Studies: Seven Pieces of Sherlockiana, edited by Robert A. Cutter; Jackson Heights, New York: Privately printed, 1947.

SHORT, ERNEST H.

"On No. 109 as No. 221 Baker Street"; *The Baker Street Journal,* Vol. I, No. 4, October, 1946, pp. 51–2.

SIDGWICK, FRANK

"*The Hound of the Baskervilles* At Fault (An Open Letter to Dr. Watson)"; *The Cambridge Review,* January 23, 1902; *The Incunabular Sherlock Holmes.*

SIMMONS, GEORGE

"Sherlock Holmes—The Inner Man"; *The Baker Street Journal,* Vol. II, No. 2, Old Series, April, 1947, pp. 129–35.

SIMPSON, A. CARSON

"A Chronometric Excogitation"; *The Baker Street Journal Christmas Annual,* 1959, pp. 273–9.

"The Curious Incident of the Missing Corpse"; *The Baker Street Journal,* Vol. IV, No. 1, New Series, January, 1954, pp. 24–34.

"It Must Have Been Two Other Fellows"; *Leaves from the Copper Beeches,* pp. 41–53.

"On Oxford as the University of 'The Three Students'; *The Baker Street Journal,* Vol. V, No. 3, New Series, July, 1955, p. 187.

Simpson's Sherlockian Studies; Philadelphia: International Printing Company:

Vol. I. *Sherlock Holmes' Wanderjahre: Fanget An!* (1953).

Vol. II. *Sherlock Holmes' Wanderjahre: Post Huc Nec Ergo Propter Huc Gabetque* (1954).

Vol. III. *Sherlock Holmes' Wanderjahre: In Fernen Land, Unnahbar Ruren, Schritten (1955).*

Vol. IV. *Sherlock Holmes' Wanderjahre: Auf Der Erde Rücken Ruhrt' Ich Mich Viel (1956).*

Vol. V. *Numismatics in the Canon: Full Thirty Thousand Marks of English Coin (1957).*

Vol. VI. *Numismatics in the Canon: A Very Treasury of Divers Realms* (1958).

Vol. VII. *Numismatics in the Canon: Small Titles and Orders* (1959).

Vol. VIII. *I'm Off for Philadelphia in the Morning* (1960).

"Whose Was It? Conjectures on a Coronet"; *The Baker Street Journal Christmas Annual,* 1957, pp. 9–17.

SIMPSON, HELEN

"Medical Career and Capacities of Dr. J. H. Watson"; *Baker Street Studies,* pp. 35–61.

SMITH, EDGAR W.

"The Adventure of the Veiled Author"; *The Baker Street Journal,* Vol. I, No. 2, Old Series, April, 1946, pp. 129–35.

"Appointment in Baker Street"; *221B,* pp. 142–243.

Baker Street and Beyond: A Sherlockian Gazetteer, with Five Detailed and Illustrated Maps by Julian Wolff, M.D.; New York: The Pamphlet House, 1940.

Baker Street Inventory; Summit, New Jersey: The Pamphlet House, 1945.

"The Baker Street Irregulars"; *The Courier,* London, January, 1954; *The Baker Street Journal,* Vol. XII, No. 3, New Series, September, 1962, pp. 151–6.

"A Bibliographical Note"; *The Baker Street Journal,* Vol. IX, No. 1, New Series, January, 1959, pp. 3–4.

"Dr. Watson and the Great Censorship"; *The Baker Street Journal,* Vol. II, No. 3, New Series, January, 1947, pp. 138–51.

Introduction to *Baker Street Studies,* 1955.

Introduction to *The Return of Solar Pons,* by August Derleth; Sauk City, Wisconsin: Mycroft & Moran, 1958.

Introduction to *Sherlock Holmes and Dr. Watson: The Chronology of Their Adventures,* by H. W. Bell, 1955.

"The Long Road from Maiwand"; *Profile by Gaslight,* pp. 195–201.

"The Old Shikari"; *The Best of the Pips,* pp. 25–34.

"On the Forms of Address"; *The Baker Street Journal,* Vol. IX, No. 3, New Series, July, 1959, pp. 131–2.

"On the *Mary Celeste* and the *Matilda Briggs*"; *The Baker Street Journal,* Vol. II, No. 2, New Series, April, 1952, pp. 115–6.

"Prolegomena to a Memoir of Professor Moriarty"; *The Second Cab,* pp. 57–64; as *The Napoleon of Crime,* Summit: New Jersey, The Pamphlet House, 1953.

"A Scandal in Identity"; *Profile by Gaslight,* pp. 262–73.

"Sherlock Holmes and the Great Hiatus"; *The Baker Street Journal,* Vol. I, No. 3, Old Series, July, 1946.

Sherlock Holmes: The Writings of John H. Watson, M.D.; Morristown, New Jersey: The Baker Street Irregulars, Inc., 1962.

"A Textual Aberration in *The Hound of the Baskervilles*"; *The Baker Street Journal,* Vol. V, No. 4, New Series, October, 1955, pp. 243–4.

"Up from the Needle"; *The Baker Street Journal,* Vol. II, No. 1, Old Series, January, 1957, pp. 85–8.

SMITH, "RED" (WALTER W.)

"The Game's Afoot"; *Views of Sport,* New York: Alfred A. Knopf, 1954.

"The Nefarious Holmes"; *Views of Sport.*

SMITH, WILLIAM

"That Little Thing of Chopin's: The Laying of the Ghost"; *The Baker Street Journal,* Vol. XIII, No. 1, New Series, March, 1963, pp. 24–30.

" 'You Have Been in Gettysburg, I Perceive' "; *The Baker Street Journal,* Vol. XIII, No. 2, New Series, June, 1963, pp. 77–85.

SOVINE, *Dr.* J. W.

"The Singular Bullet"; *The Baker Street Journal,* Vol. IX, No. 1, New Series, January, 1959, pp. 28–32.

"The Toxicanon"; *The Baker Street Journal,* Vol. VIII, No. 2, New Series, April, 1958, pp. 107–12.

STARR, *Professor* H. W.

"Singleton Singlestick"; *The Sherlock Holmes Journal,* Vol. II, No. 4, Winter, 1955, p. 34.

"Some New Light on Watson"; *The Baker Street Journal,* Vol. I, No. 1, Old Series, January, 1946, pp. 55–63.

"A Submersible Subterfuge or Proof Impositive"; *Leaves from the Copper Beeches,* pp. 97–108.

(with T. B. HUNT) "What Happened to Mary Morstan"; *The Baker Street Journal,* Vol. II, No. 3, Old Series, July, 1947, pp. 237–46.

STARRETT, VINCENT

"Before Sherlock Holmes"; *The Baker Street Journal,* Vol. II, No. 1, Old Series, January, 1947, pp. 5–11.

Introduction to *The Adventures of Sherlock Holmes, Vol. I;* New York: The Limited Editions Club, 1950.

Introduction to *The Adventures of Solar Pons,* by August Derleth; Sauk City, Wisconsin: Mycroft & Moran, 1945.

Introduction to *Baker Street Chronology,* by Dr. Ernest Bloomfield Zeisler, 1953.

"On the Three Moriarty Brothers Named James"; Footnote to *Appoint-*

ment in Baker Street, by Edgar W. Smith.

"A Note on Baker Street," in *Baker Street and Beyond,* by Edgar W. Smith.

"A Note on Mr. Sherlock Holmes"; *Esquire,* May, 1934.

The Private Life of Sherlock Holmes; New York: The Macmillan Company, 1933; London: Nicholson & Watson, 1934; revised and enlarged edition published by the University of Chicago Press, 1960; London: Allen & Unwin, 1961.

"The Singular Adventures of Martha Hudson"; *Baker Street Studies,* pp. 85–130; *Profile by Gaslight,* pp. 202–29; *Bookman's Holiday,* New York: Random House, 1942, pp. 47–81.

STEELE, FREDERIC DORR

"Sherlock Holmes in Pictures"; *221B,* pp. 129–37.

STEPHENS, CHARLES B.

"The Birlstone Hoax"; *The Baker Street Journal,* Vol. IV, No. 1, Old Series, January, 1949, pp. 5–11.

"Holmes' Longest Shot?"; *The Baker Street Journal,* Vol. III, No. 1, Old Series, January, 1948, pp. 44–6.

"Silas Brown, or, Who Shot Desborough's Bolt?"; *The Baker Street Journal,* Vol. II, No. 3, Old Series, July, 1947, pp. 357–61.

STERN, MADELEINE B.

"Sherlock Holmes: Rare Book Collector"; *Papers of the Bibliographical Society of America,* Second Quarter, 1953; *The Baker Street Journal,* Vol. III, No. 3, New Series, July, 1953, pp. 133–55; New York: Schulte Publishing Company.

STIX, THOMAS L.

"Casual Comments on 'The Crooked Man' "; *The Baker Street Journal,* Vol. XII, No. 2, New Series, June, 1962, pp. 99–100.

"Concerning 'The Red-Headed League' "; *The Baker Street Journal,* Vol. IV, No. 2, New Series, April, 1954, pp. 93–6.

"A Few Irreverent Remarks on 'The Second Stain' "; *The Sherlock Holmes Journal,* Vol. VI, No. 1, Winter, 1962, pp. 19–20.

"A Little Dirt on 'The Empty House' "; *The Baker Street Journal,* Vol. XIV, No. 2, New Series, June, 1964, pp. 93–5.

"The Reigate Puzzler"; *The Baker Street Journal,* Vol. XIII, No. 2, New Series, June, 1963, pp. 93–5.

"Un-Christmaslike Thoughts on 'The Blue Carbuncle' "; *The Baker Street Journal,* Vol. XI, No. 4, New Series, December, 1961, pp. 218–20.

"Who's Afraid of the Big Bad Moriarty?"; *The Baker Street Journal,* Vol. XII, No. 4, December, 1962, pp. 200, 243.

STONE, P. M.

"The Other Friendship: A Speculation"; *Profile by Gaslight,* pp. 97–103.

"Sussex Interview"; *221B,* pp. 74–87.

William Hooker Gillette; a pamphlet issued as a supplement to *The Baker Street Journal,* Vol. III, No. 3, New Series, July, 1953.

STOUT, REX

"Watson Was a Woman"; *The Saturday Review of Literature,* March 1, 1941; *The Pocket Mystery Reader,* 1941; *Profile by Gaslight,* 1944; *Ellery Queen's Mystery Magazine,* April, 1946; *The Art of the Mystery Story: A Collection of Critical Essays,* edited by Howard Haycraft; New York: Simon & Schuster, 1946.

STROUT, *Professor* ALAN LANG

"On the *Norah Creina*"; *The Saturday Review of Literature,* April 8, 1939; quoted in the *Baker Street Journal,* Vol. I, No. 4, Old Series, October, 1946, p. 408.

SWANSON, MARTIN J.

"Graphologists in the Canon"; *The Baker Street Journal,* Vol. XII, No. 2, New Series, June, 1962, pp. 73–80.

"On the Chinese Coin in 'The Red-Headed League'; *The Baker Street Journal,* Vol. XIII, No. 1, New Series, March, 1963, p. 54.

SYMONS, T. H. B.

"Some Notes on the Sixth Duke of Holdernesse"; *The Baker Street Journal,* Vol. IX, No. 1, January, 1959, pp. 6–9.

THIMAN, ERIC. H., *Mus. D.*

"Tra-la-la-la-lira-lira-lay"; *The Sherlock Holmes Journal,* Vol. IV, No. 3, Winter, 1959, p. 105.

The Third Cab: A Collection of Sherlockiana from the Files of the Speckled Band; Boston: Privately printed at Stoke Moran, 1960.

THOMSON, H. DOUGLAS

Masters of Mystery, London: Collins, 1931.

THROCKMORTON, JANE

" 'H.' Stands for —?"; *Client's Case-Book,* pp. 7–8.

TOWNSEND, C. E. C.

"The Bar of Gold"; *The Sherlock Holmes Journal,* Vol. II, No. 1, July, 1954, pp. 25–8.

TREVELYAN, G. M.

Illustrated English Social History; London and New York: Longmans, Green & Co., Ltd., 1942 and 1944.

TUCKER, *Dr.* RUFUS S.

"Genealogical Notes on Holmes"; *Profile by Gaslight,* pp. 125–34.

221B: Studies in Sherlock Holmes, edited by Vincent Starrett; New York: The Macmillan Company, 1940; reissued in paperbound format by the Baker Street Irregulars, Inc., 1956.

VAILL, C. B. H.

"Quick, Watson, the Needle!"; *The Baker Street Journal,* Vol. I, No. 4, Old Series, October, 1946, pp. 445–8.

"A Study in Intellects"; *The Baker Street Journal,* Vol. III, No. 3, Old Series, July, 1948, pp. 278–82.

VAN GELDER, LARRY

"On the Suggested Suicide of Jefferson Hope"; *The Baker Street Journal,* Vol. I, No. 4, New Series, October, 1951, p. 160.

VAN LIERE, *Dr.* EDWARD J.

A Doctor Enjoys Sherlock Holmes; New York: The Vantage Press, 1960.

"Dr. Watson and Nervous Maladies"; *The Baker Street Journal,* Vol. IV, No. 2, New Series, April, 1954, pp. 100–8.

"Dr. Watson's Universal Specific"; *The Baker Street Journal,* Vol. II, No. 4, New Series, October, 1952, pp. 215–20.

"Sherlock Holmes and Doctor Watson, Perennial Athletes"; *The Baker Street Journal,* Vol. VI, No. 3, New Series, July, 1956, pp. 155–64.

VISIAK, E. H.

"New Light on Holmes"; *The Sherlock Holmes Journal,* Vol. VI, No. 4, Spring, 1964, pp. 122–3.

WAIT, RICHARD

"The Case of the Neophyte and the Motet"; *The Second Cab,* pp. 70–2.

WALBRIDGE, EARLE F.

"Care and Feeding of Sherlock Holmes"; *221B,* pp. 54–8.

"Jabez Wilson Reports"; *The Sherlock Holmes Journal,* Vol. I, No. 3, Old Series, July, 1946, p. 361.

WALLACE, IRVING

The Fabulous Originals; New York: Alfred A. Knopf, 1955.

WARRACK, GUY

"Passed to You, Admiralty Intelligence"; *The Sherlock Holmes Journal,* Vol. IV, No. 2, Spring, 1959, pp. 79–80.

Sherlock Holmes and Music; London: Faber & Faber, Ltd., 1957.

WATERS, FRANK A.

"'Holmes or Watson Here'"; *The Sherlock Holmes Journal,* Vol. III, No. 2, Winter, 1956, p. 21.

"The Rooms in Baker Street"; *The Best of the Pips,* pp. 15–20.

"Upon the Probable Number of Cases of Mr. Sherlock Holmes"; *The Baker Street Journal,* Vol. III, No. 1, New Series, January, 1953, pp. 25–8; *The Best of the Pips,* pp. 21–4.

WATERS, FRED

"Re-Dating the Reichenbach Incident"; *The Baker Street Journal,* Vol. VIII, No. 4, New Series, October, 1958, pp. 280–3.

WEATHERBEE, *Dr.* WINTHROP

"The Third Continent: Further Light on Watson"; *The Baker Street Journal,* Vol. II, No. 3, New Series, July, 1952, pp. 125–34.

WEAVER, RONALD R.

"Bow Window in Baker Street"; *The Baker Street Journal,* Vol. V, No. 2, New Series, April, 1955, pp. 93–5.

WEBSTER, H. T.

"Observations on Sherlock Holmes as an Athlete and Sportsman"; *The Baker Street Journal,* Vol. III, No. 1, Old Series, January, 1948, pp. 24–31.

WEIL-NORDEN, P.

Introduction to *Sir Arthur Conan Doyle,* Centenary Edition; London: John Murray, 1959; Garden City, New York: Doubleday & Company, Inc. 1959.

WEISS, JAY, *D.M.D.*

"Holmes as a Patient"; *The Baker Street Journal,* Vol. XIII, No. 2, New Series, June, 1963, pp. 96–8.

WELCH, GEORGE B.

"'No Mention of That Local Hunt, Watson'"; *The Sherlock Holmes Journal,* Vol. V, No. 3, Winter, 1961, pp. 82–3.

"The 'Silver Blaze' Formula"; *The Sherlock Holmes Journal,* Vol. III, No. 1, Summer, 1956, p. 19.

"A Study in Moonlight"; *The Baker Street Gasogene,* Vol. I, No. 3, 1961, pp. 18–25.

"The Terai Planter"; *The Baker Street Journal,* Vol. VI, No. 1, New Series, January, 1956, pp. 35–9.

"Which University?"; *The Sherlock Holmes Journal,* Vol. V, No. 3, Winter, 1961, pp. 94, 96.

WELLMAN, MANLY WADE

"The Great Man's Great Son"; *The Baker Street Journal,* Vol. I, No. 3, Old Series, July, 1946, pp. 326–36.

"A New Scandal in Bohemia"; *The Baker Street Journal,* Vol. II, No. 1, Old Series, January, 1947, p. 90.

"Scoundrels in Bohemia"; *The Baker Street Journal,* Vol. IV, No. 4, New Series, October, 1954, pp. 232–8.

"Two Southern Exposures of Sherlock Holmes"; *The Baker Street Journal,* Vol. II, No. 4, Old Series, October, 1947, pp. 422–6.

WHITE, PAUL

"The Case of the Men Named James"; *The Baker Street Journal,* Vol. VI, No. 1, New Series, January, 1956, pp. 46–50.

WHITE, WILLIAM BRAID, *Mus. Doc.*

"Dr. Watson and the Peerage"; *The Baker Street Journal,* Vol. II, No. 1, Old Series, January, 1947, pp. 18–23.

"Sherlock Holmes and the Equal Temperament"; *The Baker Street Journal,* Vol. I, No. 1, Old Series, January, 1946, pp. 39–43.

WIGGLESWORTH, BELDEN

"The Coat of Arms of Sherlock Holmes"; *Profile by Gaslight,* pp. 104–13.

"The French Background of Sherlock Holmes: Aspects and Possibilities"; *The Second Cab,* pp. 39–45.

"'Many Nations and Three Separate Continents'"; *The Baker Street Journal,* Vol. II, No. 3, Old Series, July, 1947, pp. 273–8.

WILDE, PERCIVAL

"The Bust in the Window"; *The Baker Street Journal,* Vol. III, No. 3, Old Series, July, 1948, pp. 300–5.

WILLIAMS, H. B.

"Curses Canonical"; *Client's Second Case-Book,* pp. 50–4.

"Half-Sister; Half Mystery"; *The Baker Street Journal,* Vol. VIII, No. 2, New Series, April, 1958, pp. 100–3.

"Light Blue Black Clay"; *The Sherlock Holmes Journal,* Vol. II, No. 3, Summer, 1955, p. 23.

"A Non-Canonical Clue"; *Client's Third Case-Book,* pp. 94–9.

"Pleasure in Pictures"; *The Baker Street Journal,* Vol. XIII, No. 4, New Series, December, 1963, pp. 232–5.

"Then Falls Thy Shadow"; *Client's Case-Book,* pp. 50–3.

"The Unknown Watson"; *The Baker Street Journal,* Vol. XIII, No. 1, New Series, March, 1963, pp. 43–5.

WILLIAMS, VALENTINE

"Gaboriau: Father of Detective Novels"; *The National Review,* December, 1923.

WILLIAMSON, JERRY NEAL

"'And Especially Your Eyes'"; *The Sherlock Holmes Journal,* Vol. III, No. 3, Autumn, 1957, pp. 17–9.

"Dr. Mortimer-Moriarty"; *The Baker Street Journal,* Vol. IV, No. 1, Old Series, January, 1949, p. 95.

"In Defense of Scotland Yard: A Communication from Inspector Athelney Jones"; *Client's Case-Book,* pp. 28–9.

"The Latest Treatise Upon Pathology"; *The Baker Street Journal,* Vol. VI, No. 4, New Series, October, 1956, pp. 208–14.

"The Sad Case of Young Stamford"; *The Baker Street Journal,* Vol. III, No. 4, Old Series, October, 1948, pp. 449–51.

"A Scandal in 'A Scandal in Bohemia'"; *The Baker Street Journal,* Vol. I, No. 4, New Series, October, 1951, pp. 141–3.

"Sherlock's Murder Bag"; *Client's Third Case-Book,* pp. 84–8.

"'There Was Something Very Strange'"; *The Baker Street Journal,* Vol. XII, No. 4, New Series, December, 1962, pp. 201–9.

WILSON, ALAN

"Where Was the 'Bar of Gold'?"; *The Sherlock Holmes Journal,* Vol. VI, No. 3, Winter, 1963, pp. 84–5.

"'You Crossed My Path'"; *The SherLock Holmes Journal,* Vol. IV, No. 3, Winter, 1959, pp. 89–90.

WIMBUSH, J. C.

"Watson's Tobacconist"; *The Sherlock Holmes Journal,* Vol. I, No. 2, September, 1952, pp. 35–6.

WOLF, BEN

"Zero Wolf Meets Sherlock Holmes"; *The Baker Street Journal,* Vol. XIV, No. 2, New Series, June, 1964, pp. 108–17.

WOLF, *Professor* JOHN B.

"Another Incubus in the Saddle"; *Exploring Sherlock Holmes,* pp. 66–81.

WOLFF, *Dr.* JULIAN

"The Adventuress of Sherlock Holmes: Some Observations Upon the Identification of Irene"; *The Baker Street Journal,* Vol. VII, No. 1, New Series, January, 1957, pp. 29–31.

"The Dynamics of the Binomial Theorem"; *The Baker Street Journal,* Vol. XIII, No. 4, New Series, December, 1963, pp. 199–200.

"I Have My Eye on a Suite in Baker Street"; *The Baker Street Journal,* Vol. I, No. 3, Old Series, July, 1946, pp. 296–9.

"Just What Was That Little Thing of Chopin's?"; *The Baker Street Journal,*

LONDON

NATURALLY GRAVITATED TO LONDON"

A Study in Scarlet

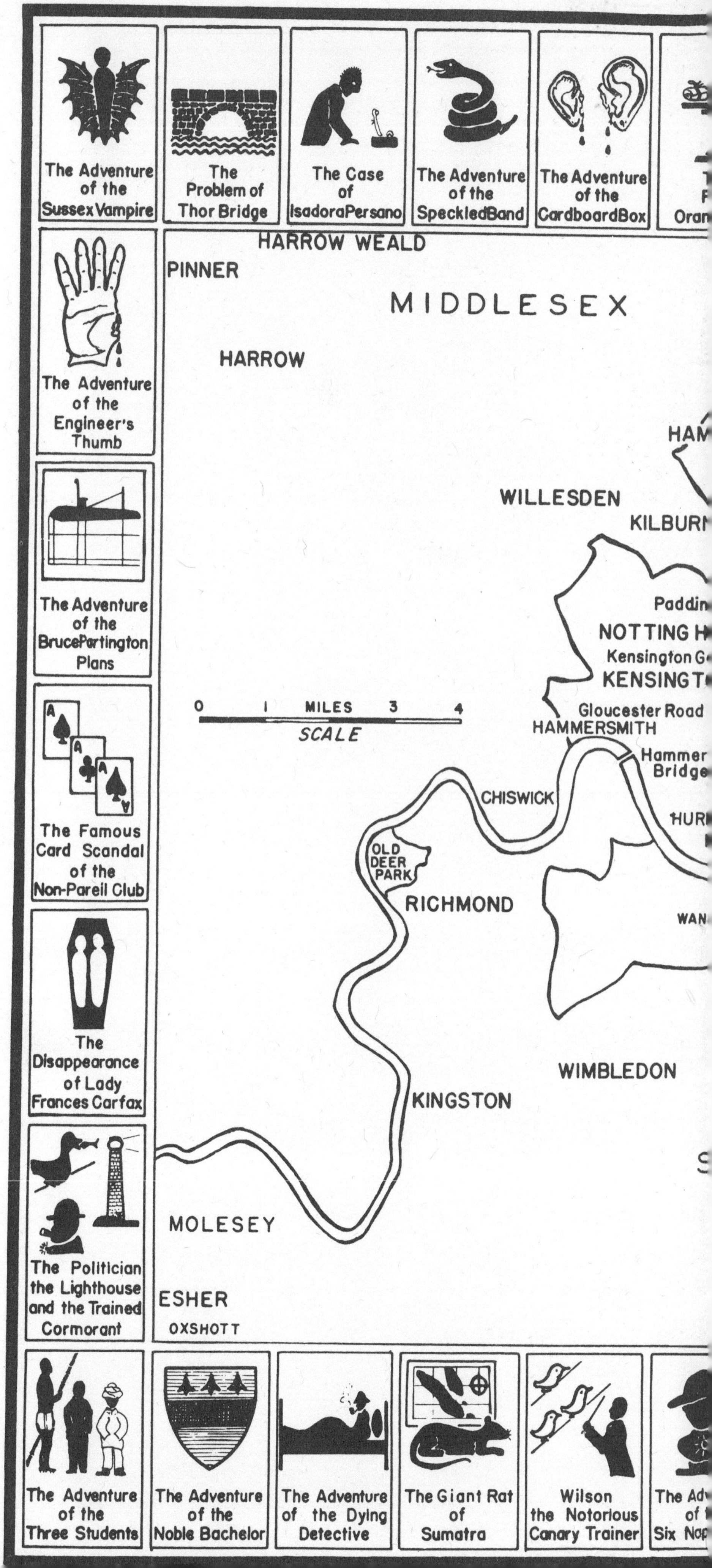

The Adventure of the Sussex Vampire

The Problem of Thor Bridge

The Case of Isadora Persano

The Adventure of the Speckled Band

The Adventure of the Cardboard Box

The Adventure of the Engineer's Thumb

The Adventure of the Bruce Partington Plans

The Famous Card Scandal of the Non-Pareil Club

The Disappearance of Lady Frances Carfax

The Politician the Lighthouse and the Trained Cormorant

The Adventure of the Three Students

The Adventure of the Noble Bachelor

The Adventure of the Dying Detective

The Giant Rat of Sumatra

Wilson the Notorious Canary Trainer

HARROW WEALD

PINNER

MIDDLESEX

HARROW

WILLESDEN

KILBURN

NOTTING H

Kensington G

KENSINGT

Gloucester Road

HAMMERSMITH

Hammer Bridge

CHISWICK

OLD DEER PARK

RICHMOND

WIMBLEDON

KINGSTON

MOLESEY

ESHER

OXSHOTT

0 1 MILES 3 4

SCALE